JOHN COWPER POWYS

A
GLASTONBURY
ROMANCE

MCMXXXII

SIMON AND SCHUSTER
NEW YORK

SECOND PRINTING

20676

CONTENTS

VOLUME ONE

1	*The Will*	1
2	*The River*	50
3	*Stonehenge*	75
4	*Hic Jacet*	97
5	*Whitelake Cottage*	115
6	*The Look of a Saint*	141
7	*Carbonek*	175
8	*Wookey Hole*	211
9	*The Unpardonable Sin*	244
10	*Geard of Glastonbury*	274
11	*Consummation*	301
12	*The Dolorous Blow*	321
13	*King Arthur's Sword*	353
14	*Maundy Thursday*	384
15	*Mark's Court*	418
16	*The Silver Bowl*	474
17	*May Day*	526
18	*Omens and Oracles*	561
19	*The Pageant*	575

VOLUME TWO

20	*Idolatry*	644
21	*Tin*	676
22	*Wind and Rain*	703
23	*The Miracle*	730
24	*"Nature Seems Dead . . ."*	773
25	*Conspiracy*	816
26	*The Christening*	860
27	*The Saxon Arch*	910
28	*The Grail*	944
29	*The Iron Bar*	1032
30	*The Flood*	1114

PRINCIPAL CHARACTERS IN THE ROMANCE

JOHN GEARD, *secretary-valet to the late Canon William Crow; later Mayor of Glastonbury.*

MEGAN, *his wife.*

CORDELIA and CRUMMIE, *their daughters.*

PHILIP CROW, *Glastonbury industrialist.*

TILLY, *his wife.*

JOHN and MARY CROW, *cousins to Philip and to each other.*

ELIZABETH CROW, *daughter of the late Canon Crow; aunt of Philip, John, Mary and*

PERSEPHONE SPEAR, *wife of*

DAVE SPEAR, *half-brother of*

NELL ZOYLAND, *wife of*

WILL ZOYLAND, *bastard son of*

THE MARQUIS OF P., *father of*

LADY RACHEL ZOYLAND.

EDWARD ATHLING, *yeoman farmer and poet.*

EUPHEMIA DREW, *elderly spinster and Mary Crow's employer.*

TOM BARTER, *Philip Crow's manager.*

OWEN EVANS, *Welsh antiquary.*

MAT DEKKER, *Vicar of Glastonbury.*

SAM DEKKER, *his son.*

DOCTOR CHARLES MONTAGU FELL, *a disciple of Epictetus.*

BARBARA, *his sister.*

TITTIE PETHERTON, *a cancer patient.*

RED ROBINSON, *formerly foreman at the Crow Dye-works.*

NANCY ROBINSON, *cousin of Red, Tittie's nurse.*

PENNY PITCHES, *servant at the Dekkers'.*

ABEL TWIG and BARTHOLOMEW JONES *("Number One" and "Number Two"), old cronies.*

ISAAC WEATHERWAX, *gardener at the Dekkers' and Euphemia Drew's.*

LILY *and* LOUIE ROGERS, *sisters; housemaid and cook at Miss Drew's.*

TOSSIE STICKLES, *Elizabeth Crow's servant.*

NANCY STICKLES, *a devoted disciple of Mr. Geard.*

MOTHER LEGGE, *procuress.*

YOUNG TEWSY, *doorkeeper at Mother Legge's "other house."*

BET CHINNOCK, *a madwoman.*

JENNY MORGAN, *Philip Crow's former mistress.*

"MORGAN-NELLY," *their unrecognised little daughter.*

FINN TOLLER, *alias Codfin.*

ELPHIN CANTLE, *a boy-friend of Sam Dekker's.*

PAUL TRENT, *Solicitor, a philosophical anarchist.*

JOHN BEERE, *Solicitor.*

ANGELA BEERE, *his daughter.*

JACKIE JONES
SIS   } *members of "Morgan-Nelly's" robber-band.*
BERT COLE

PLACE: *Glastonbury, England, and its environs.*

TIME: *The present.*

AUTHOR'S NOTE

Not a single scene, or situation, or character, or episode in this book has been drawn in any respect, or in any sense whatsoever, from real life. All are pure invention; and the author is absolutely unacquainted with any living individual or with any existing industry in the Glastonbury of our time. The only two persons, and *they* only misleadingly and remotely, in any way connected with the author's experience, are Canon Crow and the London Architect; and of these the former does not appear till after his death, and the latter only in his buildings, which themselves are entirely imaginary.

TO

MY YOUNGEST SISTER AND OLDEST GOD-DAUGHTER

LUCY AMELIA PENNY

"Bet y march, bet y guythur.
bet y gugaun cletyfrut.
anoeth bid bet y arthur."

"A grave for Mark, a grave for Gwythur,
A grave for Gwgawn of the ruddy Sword,
Not wise (the thought) a grave for Arthur."

BLACK BOOK OF CARMARTHEN
Trans. JOHN RHYS

At the striking of noon on a certain fifth of march, there occurred within a causal radius of Brandon railway-station and yet beyond the deepest pools of emptiness between the uttermost stellar systems one of those infinitesimal ripples in the creative silence of the First Cause which always occur when an exceptional stir of heightened consciousness agitates any living organism in this astronomical universe. Something passed at that moment, a wave, a motion, a vibration, too tenuous to be called magnetic, too subliminal to be called spiritual, between the soul of a particular human being who was emerging from a third-class carriage of the twelve-nineteen train from London and the divine-diabolic soul of the First Cause of all life.

In the soul of the great blazing sun, too, as it poured down its rays upon this man's head, while he settled his black travelling bag comfortably in his left hand and his hazel-stick in his right, there were complicated superhuman vibrations; but these had only the filmiest, faintest, remotest connexion with what the man was feeling. They had more connexion with the feelings of certain primitive tribes of men in the heart of Africa and with the feelings of a few intellectual sages in various places in the world who had enough imagination to recognise the conscious personality of this fiery orb as it flung far and wide its life-giving magnetic forces. Roaring, cresting, heaving, gathering, mounting, advancing, receding, the enormous fire-thoughts of this huge luminary surged resistlessly to and fro, evoking a turbulent aura of psychic activity, corresponding to the physical energy of its colossal chemical body, but affecting this microscopic biped's nerves less than the wind that blew against his face.

Far nearer to the man's conscious and half-conscious feelings, as with his overcoat buttoned under his chin and his fingers tightening upon stick and bag he moved to the station-entrance, were the vast, dreamy life-stirrings of the soul of the earth. Aware in a mysterious manner of every single one of all the conscious-

nesses, human and subhuman, to which she has given birth, the
earth might have touched with a vibrant inspiration this particular child of hers, who at twenty minutes after twelve handed up
his ticket to the station-master and set out along a narrow dusty
March road towards Brandon Heath. That she did not do this was
due to the simple fact that the man instead of calling upon her
for help called habitually upon the soul of his own dead mother.
Jealous and exacting are all the gods, and a divided worship is
abhorrent to them.

John Crow had given a hurried, suspicious sideways glance,
before he left the platform, at the group of fellow-travellers who
were gathered about the heap of luggage flung from the guard's
van. They all, without exception, seemed to his agitated mind to
be attired in funeral garb. He himself had a large band of crape
sewn upon his sleeve and a black tie. "I'm glad I ran in to Monsieur Teste's to buy a black tie," he thought as he met the wind on
the open road. "I never would have thought of it if Lisette hadn't
pushed me to it at the end."

John Crow was a frail, thin, loosely-built man of thirty-five.
He had found himself a penniless orphan at twenty. From that
time onward he had picked up his precarious and somewhat
squalid livelihood in Paris. Traces of these fifteen years of irregular life could be seen writ large on his gaunt features. Something
between the down-drifting weakness of a congenital tramp and
the unbalanced idealism of a Don Quixote hovered about his high
cheek-bones and about the troubled droop of his mouth. One
rather disturbing contradiction existed in his face. There was a
constant twitching of his cheeks beneath his sunken eye-sockets;
and this peculiarity, combined with a furtive, almost foxy, slant
about the contraction of his eyelids, contrasted disconcertingly
with the expression in the eyes themselves. This expression resembled one particular look, as of a sea-creature without a human
soul, that Scopas gives to his creations.

A cold blue sky and a biting east wind were John Crow's companions now as he took the bare grass-edged road towards Brandon Heath. The raw physical discomfort produced by this wind,
and the gathering together of his bodily forces to contend with
it, soon brought down by several pegs the emotional excitement

in which he had left the train. That magnetic ripple in the divine-diabolic soul of the creative energy beyond space and time which had corresponded to, if not directly caused, his agitated state, sank back in reciprocal quiescence; and the physical tenseness and strain which he now experienced were answered in the far-off First Cause by an indrawn passivity as if some portion of that fount of life fell under the constriction of freezing. The soundless roaring of the great solar furnace up there in the vast ether became, too, at that moment worse than merely indifferent to the motions of this infinitesimal creature advancing into the bracken-grown expanses of the historic Heath, like a black ant into a flowerpot. The man's movements now became weary and slow, even though he caught sight of the words "To Northwold" upon a newly whitewashed signpost. Humming and roaring and whirling in its huge confluent maelstroms of fiery gas, the body of that tornado of paternity concealed at that moment a soul that associated John Crow not only with such beings as neglected to invoke its godhead but with such beings as in their malicious rational impiety positively denied it any consciousness. Among all the greater gods around him it was the soul of the earth, however, that remained most jealous and hostile. It must have dimly been aware of the narrow and concentrated feeling, exclusive, misanthropic, which John experienced as he approached the home of his dead mother. And thus as it shot quivering vibrations through the greenish-yellow buds upon the hawthorn bushes, through the tender white blossoms upon the blackthorn, through the folded tremulousness of the fern fronds and the metallic sheen of the celandines, to John Crow it refused to give that exquisite feeling of primordial well-being which it gave to the rest. Why, thinking of his mother, he felt so sad, was a strange fact beyond this man's analysis. How could he know that mingled with their awareness of wet, green mosses, of dry, scaly lichens, of the heady-sweet odours of prickly gorse, of the cool-rooted fragility of lilac-coloured cuckoo flowers, of the sturdy swelling of the woolly calices of early cowslips, of the embryo lives within the miraculous blue shells of hedge-sparrows' eggs, the thoughts of the earth-mother throbbed with a dull, indefinable, unappeasable jealousy of a human mother?

Bending his head a little above his tightly buttoned greatcoat collar, John Crow began to recall now certain actual moments of his recent nights with young Lisette and old Pierre. These moments as he butted his way against this bitter east wind came to him impregnated with the subtle smells of a Latin Quarter street. He saw the neat frippery of Lisette's front room. He saw the grotesque photograph of himself taken by a photographer in a street booth at Saint-Cloud upon her mantelpiece. He saw her absurd muslin curtains, tied with great bows of green ribbon. He saw the big, cracked mirror with the little, carved Cupids at either corner, from one of which the gilt had been chipped, revealing scars of bare wood, black as if they had been burnt in a fire. He saw these things against the far grey horizon, where as a child he had been so often told to look for the great towers of Ely Cathedral, visible across leagues and leagues of level fens. He saw them against old, stunted, lichen-whitened thorn trees. He saw them against the curved, up-pushing, new-born horns of the sap-yellow bracken, protected from the wind by the dead husks of last year's mature ferns, and crouching low, like the heads of innumerable mottled snakes, the better to leap at the throat of life. He saw them against the reddish gnarled trunks of intermittent clumps of Scotch firs and against the scuttling white tails of the rabbits and the hovering wings of solitary kestrel-hawks. And over and over again he said to himself, "Philip will have had all Grandfather's money, of course. Of course Philip will have had all Grandfather's money."

At one point, when he came to a place where Brandon Heath seemed to gather its personality together and to assume a scrutinising, haughty and inquisitive look, as much as to say, "Who, in the devil's name are you, you dog-faced foreigner?" in reply to this look of Brandon Heath John muttered a sulky defiance and ejaculated aloud, as if to let the place know that he was more than a common tramp: "I shall make Philip give me a berth at Glastonbury." He had been on foot now for about an hour, and he had been walking fast too; for the bite of the cold air seemed to give an energy of demonic malice to his defiance of the wind, of the sun, of the hostility of the earth. He had begun to notice too that the heath scenery was transforming itself by degrees into

ordinary farm scenery, when he heard a motor car coming up
fast behind him.

He stepped hastily to the grass by the roadside and without
the least idea as to why he did so stood stock-still and stared at
the approaching machine. "Nothing would induce me to take a
lift," he said to himself. "It must be a good two hours still before the time."

The car, however, lessened its pace the moment he stood still;
and as soon as it reached him stopped dead.

"Canon Crow's funeral, Sir?"

The driver's voice had that peculiar up-drawing, up-tilting,
devil-may-care intonation, no doubt derived from a long line of
Danish ancestors, which renders the Norfolk tongue different
from the speech of every other English county.

John Crow looked up at the speaker. There was something in
the man's tone that gave him a totally unexpected emotion. A
lump of long-frozen tears began to melt in his throat, a frozen
lump twenty years old, composed of all his memories of his childhood; composed of the image of his grandmother, reading to him
in the low-ceilinged, old-pictured, old-brocaded Rectory drawing-
room; composed of the image of his grandfather with his snow-
white hair in short, wavy curls covering his round, brittle-looking
skull, and his voice melodious as a great actor's. Mingled with
these came memories of the taste of a certain species of unusual
pink-coloured strawberries that grew in the walled garden and the
sharp, pure taste of red gooseberries that grew from near the
manure heap there; and surrounding all these as if by an atmosphere of something still more intimately felt, there came over
him, under the impact of that Norfolk utterance, an impression of
acrid smoke, the smoke of burning peat, rising from innumerable
cottage hearths.

"The funeral; Northwold; thank you very much," John Crow
replied in broken phrases; and his own voice was to him as the
voice of one speaking in a dream. As he uttered the words his
eyes glanced in a bewildered daze over the contents of the motor
car. The back seats were all piled up with neat and very new
travelling bags, canvas hold-alls, and bright rugs, from among

which an elderly, gentle, majestic-looking woman smiled at him in an extremely reassuring manner.

"There's room up here then, Mister," went on the driver, after a hurried turn in his seat and a glance backward at the lady amid the pile of bags. "That's to say," he added, with an appeal to a figure at his side, whose presence had hitherto escaped John's notice, "unless you objects to being crowded, Miss."

The pulse of time that followed this remark was one of the most singular in all John Crow's experience. It was not, in fact, like a pulse of time at all. It was like a perfectly calm and perfectly quiet sinking aside, into a region altogether outside the jeopardies and agitations of time. John and the young girl who was seated on the further side of the driver exchanged a long stare.

"You don't mind, Miss, do 'ee?" repeated the man. " 'Tis a long walk for the gentleman; and the Canon would wish all that come to his burying to be treated proper."

The nervous mouth of the young person he thus addressed, which had mechanically opened, showing a row of long, strong, white teeth, shut abruptly, and her eyes, which had become large and round, became little dark-lashed slits in her sallow face. "Of course not," she murmured in a low voice, making herself extremely small and pressing close to the man's elbow.

John Crow walked round the rear of the machine and after a moment's clumsy fumbling at the handle pulled the door open, clambered up, and sat down by the girl's side. "All comfortable?" asked the driver. "Very, thank you!" came so simultaneously from both John and the young girl that it sounded incoherent. The man, however, started the car without further parley.

"Is my nephew expecting you to lunch?" came the pleasant voice of the majestic lady from amid the luggage. "I wonder if you are one of the cousins?" she went on. "There are really a terrible lot of us. And we shall all be here." There was a pause during which the driver remarked that there wouldn't be many of the local people either who'd stay away. "They respect Canon Crow in Northwold more'n anyone would suppose, seeing how little he came out towards the end."

"He speaks as if Grandfather were a snail," thought the young girl.

"My father liked his books better than visiting," the lady continued. "But he used to read beautifully at people's bedsides. I've heard him do that often when I was little. Some clergymen have such poor voices."

"I never heard'n read myself," replied the driver thoughtfully. "Maybe 'twould have been better if I had. My dad brought me up chapel; and chapel I've stayed; though I've often thought 'twere a pity. Chapel be all for salvation but it neglects the King's Majesty. . . ."

"That's where we used to look," broke in John Crow suddenly, addressing the girl as if he had been completely alone with her, "for the towers of Ely!" He pointed with his hand over the wide horizon; and half rising from his seat strained his eyes to catch a glimpse of what he remembered. "Oh, it's too late!" he added, and sank by her side. "These cars go quicker than pony carts. Grandfather used to drive a pony called Judy."

"I'm beginning to think I know who you are," resumed the elderly lady. "Aren't you my nephew John who went to live in France?"

It was the girl who replied for him. "Yes, Aunt Elizabeth, he's Cousin John. I knew him at once. You used to come with us sometimes yourself when John took me down the little river in the old boat. Don't you remember, Aunt Elizabeth? He was with us that day we went to Oxborough Ferry, when Cousin Percy was there. Cousin Percy wouldn't fish with worms! You *must* remember that, Aunt Elizabeth. She kept putting bits of purple loose-strife on her hook." There was a nervous exaltation in the girl's tone that her aunt did not miss.

"I knew Mary at once too," John Crow said, turning round to address their relative, "but you used to be very busy when I stayed at the Rectory so it's no wonder we didn't know each other. *Dear* Aunt Elizabeth!" And with a rather exaggerated foreign gesture he stretched out his arm, and capturing the stout lady's hand lifted it up to his lips. "I came every summer to North-wold, you know," he said, and he remained for a minute leaning sideways and holding the hand he had taken. "And I came when he came," cried Mary with an abrupt and awkward intensity; and she too turned and leaned back and took possession of her aunt's other hand. Thus with their faces so close to each other that the girl's hair brushed his cheek the two cousins, for an appreciable passage of time, clung to the elderly woman as if their mutual contact with her brought them closer.

And thus they entered the outskirts of the village of Northwold. It was Miss Elizabeth Crow who made the motion to release her fingers.

" 'Tis like old times to see ye all back," remarked the driver as his two front-seat passengers resumed their normal position. "It makes anyone wish he were brought up to Church. Us chapel-folk are less liable to be gathered together by funerals. When the Lord divides us, He divides us. But Norfolk gentry, all such as I've seen, and I've seen a deal o'n one way and another, are mighty tender over the family. Me own mother had five of us and I've got more nephies than I knows of, yet devil a one would I want to see coming up me steps. 'Tis as nat'ral to me to turn and run from a blood-relation as it is to some folks to hug 'en to heart."

"I am afraid human nature is much the same all the world over," remarked Miss Elizabeth.

"So 'tis, Madam. So 'tis," said the man, winking at John Crow. "If I were a cousin of the late Canon, not Ameriky itself would keep me from hearing Lawyer Didlington read the old gentleman's will!"

They had reached the middle of the village at this point and the visitor from France laid his hand on the driver's elbow. "You can set me down here," he said.

"No, no," cried Aunt Elizabeth. "I can't allow that. I'll vouch for it that Philip will be glad to welcome you to lunch. He and my niece Tilly went ahead in the first car, leaving us detached females to follow with the luggage."

But the machine had stopped; and John, holding his bag in his hand, was already out in the road.

"There'll be quite enough of us all without me, Aunt," he said.

"Good-bye for a time! As our friend here reminds us, we'll all meet in a few hours, when Lawyer What's-his-name opens Grandfather's will."

But Miss Elizabeth was destined to receive a much severer shock than the escape of her eccentric nephew.

"What are you doing, Mary?" she cried in consternation at the sight of her young niece rapidly following John Crow out of the motor car.

"I'm going to stay with Cousin John," she said. "We'll be at the service. You can tell Philip without fail we'll be at the service."

"But, Mary—you can't do that! What will Tilly say? What will Philip do? Mary—think! We want your help with Persephone and her husband. You know how Philip and Mr. Spear always work each other up. Mary, you really can't do this!"

Mary came close up to the window of the car through which her aunt was protesting. "It's all right, dear," she said. "Tilly will manage. You'll look after Dave Spear yourself and see that he doesn't make Philip *too* angry. You're always doing that sort of thing for all of us. Grandfather's servants are used to entertaining people. *They* won't run away, any more than we shall, before the will is read." The bitter east wind made the girl pull her black woolen scarf tightly round her neck. There was something in the *genius loci* of that Anglo-Danish spot that seemed to evoke all her contrariness. "You're not Euphemia Drew, darling, so don't try to be. It was to get rid of Miss 'Phemia for a bit that I let Philip bring me. *I* know there's nothing for me in Grandfather's will! Be the darling you always are, Aunt, and explain to Philip. I swear I'll bring Cousin John to the service in good time."

In the startled pause that followed the girl's appeal Elizabeth Crow's mind flashed back to those days when she was indeed "busy" as John had said. She had outlived all her generation; and yet she was not even now an old woman. This came from being the youngest by many, many years of William Crow's children. Ah! How her thoughts ran to her dead father. He would have no flesh and blood of his own to keep him company in that crowded graveyard. Mary's parents were gone. Persephone's parents were gone. John had scarcely known *his* parents. And not one of them lay in that place to warm the bones of the old man! Till she herself was brought there he must lie by himself. Their mother had died in a Swiss sanitarium and had been buried out there. Yes, Cousin John was right when he said she had been "busy" in those days. As she stared now at her rebellious niece in a sort of humorous helplessness all that old imbroglio of tragic difficulties patterned itself before her mind's eye. The Crow family always had had a curious vein of gross, drastic common sense; and when her quarrels with her father reached an intolerable point she had simply cut the knot by leaving him alone and going to live with Philip. Thirty years ago she had gone to Philip, when this proud man was a mere boy, beginning his life at Glastonbury. She had achieved this separation with a secretive suddenness that puzzled everyone who knew her; and it flashed upon her mind now that something of this blind animal-like obstinacy had lodged itself in Mary. "Better let her go," she thought. "I don't blame her for being attracted to this trampish fellow. The extreme opposite of Philip he is; and that's enough for Mary. I don't care if she does fall in love with him. Father did his best to shut *me* up and I'm not going to play that game with any other woman."

Mary thought, "Dear old Aunt Elizabeth! She's got that queer wrinkle in her cheeks at this moment which always means she's at war with Philip. She's *glad* I'm going off with John—just glad."

The driver thought, "That young fellow will play upsidaisy with that young lady, soon as they're out of sight! He'll do it, sure enough. Look at's eyes all gimletting through the lass. He'll eat her up, I shouldn't wonder."

John Crow thought, "I'll take her to Harrod's Mill to see those big fish again. Yes, yes, I hugged her at the bottom of the boat on the 'little river' when she was eight and I was ten. Yes, I did! It was a Sunday afternoon I did that. It was drowsy that day; sunny and drowsy. I had rhubarb tart that day with a lot of cream. We went to Harrod's Mill. We left the boat at the dam. We couldn't get it over the dam. There were unripe blackberries round the dam that day." Then all of a sudden a different figure from Mary's rose up in his mind. "I believe it was Tom at the bottom of the boat," he thought, "and not Mary at all!"

Such were the thoughts of four human skulls at that moment; but only to one mood out of all these did the great maternal soul of the Earth respond and that was to a sudden exultant sense of peace and deliciousness in Mary's virginal breasts. Her conscious thoughts were all with Aunt Elizabeth and how that brave woman would deal with Philip's anger; but as she stepped over to John's side and kissed her hand at the departing car something seemed to stir within her like a warm wave that was at once fire, air and water and it shivered up from the centre of her being to the tips of her breasts.

As soon as the car was out of sight John and Mary glanced at each other with unembarrassed satisfaction.

"I was puzzling in my mind ever since you all overtook me how I was going to get you to myself, but now that I've got you," said John, "I don't care what we do or where we go."

"I care very much because I want to escape from everyone but you."

"Well, then! The first thing to think of is to find something to eat. Let's buy some bread and cheese at that Inn over there and see if they'll let us carry away a flask of port wine."

They went into the little hostelry and had no difficulty in obtaining exactly what he had visualised. The Inn lacked a signboard and John asked the girl behind the bar what its name was. "Name?" said the girl with that East Anglian rising inflexion that seemed to mount up to the last word of the sentence as if in a kind of optimistic chant or plain-song. "Dew ye come from far, 'tis Northwold Arms. Dew ye live in these parts, 'tis just the New Inn. The beer be the same dew ye be thirsty. 'Tis Patteson's best ale and brewed in Norwich."

It was at this point that John heard a voice in the interior parlour of this repository of Patteson Ale mentioning his grandfather's name. "They say in Rectory kitchen," said the voice, "that old man Crow have left all his money to that bloke from Glastonbury what preaches in Prayer-meeting." The voice became inaudible then. But presently John caught further words among which "Geard of Glastonbury" came clearly to him.

"May I leave my bag here for an hour or so?" enquired John of the barmaid. As the girl seemed unwilling to do more than murmur some further information about the quality of Norwich ale, he boldly got rid of the shabby, black object he was carrying, hoisting it across the counter with an abrupt swing of his long arm and dropping it shamelessly at the young lady's feet. "It's just possible—that I'll be staying the night here," he threw out, with a catch in his breath from this sudden muscular exertion.

"Single or double?" responded the girl, putting her bare elbows on the counter, staring gravely at Mary, and displaying a much livelier interest in her visitors than she had done before.

The cousins glanced triumphantly at each other. Nothing could have pleased them more at that particular moment than such a question. "Single—at present," he answered, giving the questioner the most foxy and whimsical smile she had ever received.

They were just leaving the place—the flask of wine in John's pocket and the bread and cheese in a neat parcel in Mary's hand —when several labouring men, laughing uproariously, pushed past them towards the bar. Norfolk, here too, showed its independent Danish blood. There was no obsequiousness towards "the gentry," such as would have been apparent in Kent or Surrey. One of the newcomers boldly addressed John.

"Relatives arrived for the funeral, I reckon? 'Tis as we all knew 'twould be. Canon were left lonesome enough when he were alive; but anyone would think the man were a Member o' Parliament now he be dead. Never have I see'd so many folk turn into them gates. Old Ben Pod at the lodge, who counts every wheel that passes—'tis his only joy since he lost the use of his legs— must have broke his 'rithmetic in counting them."

"There won't be so many to count when *we* be put under sod," remarked one of the other men. " 'Tis because there's been Crows in England since King Canute."

"Since when?" cried the other. "There's been Crows in England since earlier than him. He be in History, he be; and this here family goes further back than History. Talking of families," he went on, "I hope your lady won't mind my saying so but it's singular how old customs abide in certain breeds. I don't know how near related to the Canon ye two be; but every man's child

born in this place knows one thing about this family." He lowered his voice as he spoke. "There's not one of ye Crows when 'a
comes to die, that has a son left to bury 'un. They be all sons'
sons that lay 'un in ground. There must be Scripture for't;
though why it should be as 'tis is beyond *my* conjecture. Some
man of old time, amidst 'en, must have done summat turble . . .
eaten his own offspring like enough, in want of kindlier meat
. . . summat o' that . . . and ever since such doings they all
outlive their sons. 'Tis a kind of Divine Dispensation, I reckon."

John and Mary, who had felt it impolite to desert the threshold
where they had been arrested by this discourse, were now enabled
to make their escape. For one second the phrase "Geard of Glastonbury" returned upon John's mind; but it was gone as quickly
as it came.

"To the Mill, to the Mill!" he cried excitedly, and the two
cousins hurried eastward against the sharp wind down the
narrow, straight lane.

Harrod's Mill was approached, by its own drive, through a
couple of open fields. They entered this drive through a gate
leading out of the road to Didlington, just before the bridge over
the River Wissey.

The wind was sharp indeed as they crossed these two big
meadows; but there was a faint fragrance of sap-filled grass in the
air and the sun was hot. Mary's ecstasy of mood increased rather
than diminished as she walked by John's side, following his step
with her step and even picking up a stick from the ground as she
went along. This she did with the conscious desire to have some
sensation of her own exactly parallel to that which her cousin enjoyed as he pressed the end of *his* stick into the ground. Mary felt
that everything she looked at was bathed in a liquid mist and yet
was seen by her for the first time in its real essence. It seemed to
her that the souls of all living things flung forth their inmost
nature that day in a magical rapture. All things seemed anxious
to let all other living things realise how they loved them. As for
herself she felt she could have stroked with her bare fingers
everything she looked at. The very wind, so keen, so bitter, that
now blew in her face and tugged at her clothes; even towards it
she felt a sort of tenderness! She seemed to divine that it felt

itself to be hated by all the human beings it encountered; and she longed to disabuse it of this mistake.

At one moment she caught sight of a patch of small plants in the grass of the field whose leaves seemed to have a glossy texture and a greenish-whitish look that was familiar to her. "Aren't those cowslips over there?" They both hurried to the spot. Yes, they were cowslips; but so early or so stunted were they that the tiny buds were barely yellow. John was immensely relieved that she did not incontinently snatch at these pale, rudimentary, brittle stalks, covered with tiny white hairs, like the forearms of young girls, and hand them to him or keep them in her dress as memorials of this hour. How often in country excursions with his French friends, had he been railed at by them as a prig, a poseur, *un fou Anglais* for his diseased conscience in refusing to pick flowers.

Before reaching Harrod's Mill-pond they came upon an old cow-shed, once black with tar, but now blotched with queer patches of a minutely growing moss, which in some places was green and in others the colour of rusty iron. Against the western side of this shed the grass was twice as tall as in the rest of the field and of a much more vivid green. The cousins surveyed this erection in silence for a moment, he leaning on his hazel-stick which was smooth to his hand, she leaning on the rotten bramble-stick she had picked up which was rough to her hand. Their hesitation was so humorously identical, that when they glanced at each other they smiled broadly, their white strong teeth gleaming in the sun.

"Oh, to the devil with it!" he cried. "It'll get up again as soon as we've got up. It does from under the cows and we're lighter than cows. Come on, Mary—let's have our feast!"

He clutched at her skirt from his seated position and almost pulled her off her balance. She slipped down, however, facing him, her legs drawn up under her, and at once began untying the parcel of bread and cheese, holding it carefully on her lap. High above their heads several larks seemed bursting their little bodies with their shrill canticle. Their song was stoical and continuous, with a kind of harshness in its quivering rapture. "Hark at the larks!" said John to Mary, watching the careful way she was dividing their viands. As a distributor of the bread and cheese both the woman in her and the young girl played their part. She made sandwiches for John and herself as if the two of them had stood back to back measuring their difference in size. He meanwhile pulled out the cork of the flask and held it out to her for her to take the first drink. Preoccupied with the sandwiches, she let him hold it till his weary wrist rested upon her knee. But as soon as she had put it to her lips he jumped to his feet again, murmured some kind of abracadabra and poured out what he told her was a libation to the gods.

When they had finished all there was of both food and drink, he produced a packet of Gold Flake cigarettes, and they smoked for a while, contented and at rest. But the larks had come down. The cold wind rendered their exultation intermittent.

"Those men were perfectly right," said John. "It *has* become almost absurd, the way, from generation to generation of our family the older generation outlives the younger. When you come to think of it it's quite unnatural that four cousins, Philip, you, myself, and Persephone should all be grown-up orphans; and the only child of Grandfather's alive should be Aunt Elizabeth. And I'll tell you another thing that's queer too; not one of our parents is buried in the churchyard! How do you suppose *that* happened, Mary?"

"How do *you* know they're not buried there, Cousin John, when you've lived all your life in France?"

"Oh, I've watched the family, Mary! Don't you make any mistake. I've watched them like a hawk. I know exactly how much money Grandfather's got. I know where every one of the uncles and aunts died and where they were buried. I could write a history of the Crows of Norfolk, I tell you, like Ranke's history of the Popes."

"They've never been very much," murmured Mary dreamily, changing her position and stretching herself out on the grass. "You're sitting on your coat, aren't you?"

"Yeomen, I fancy, for about five hundred years," said John. She lifted up her head to smile at him.

"I've never thought much of yeomen." Her next words came

with a drowsy, luxurious querulousness as she let her head sink down again. "I wish he had been buried yesterday."

They were both silent for a couple of minutes. Then she pushed herself with her hands a little nearer him and took off her hat, flinging it on the grass a few paces off.

"I like your hair, Mary," he said, boldly twisting a wisp of it back from her forehead, round a couple of his fingers. "It's the nicest hair I've ever touched. It's just the right tinge of brown. I say, it's awfully full of electricity!"

"I expect you're a great authority," she said. Her remark was made as if it were simply a grave statement, free from all irony, and she went on in the same tone. "How many girls have you made love to, John, in your whole life?"

As she spoke she propped herself up a little and this time let her shoulders rest against his knees.

"God! My dear," he muttered, "do you think I count them? I'm not Ben Pod."

"I've never been made love to in my life," said Mary. "So I don't know what it's like. Does a girl get as much pleasure out of it as a man, John, do you think?"

"That's the oldest question, Mary, ever asked of any oracle. In fact it was first asked by the gods themselves."

"Tell me about it," said Mary. "I feel just as I did, asking you such questions when we went in the boat."

"They asked the greatest of all soothsayers," John informed her. "The old Teiresias; and do you know what he said? He said that in the act of love it was the woman who enjoyed it most." All the while he was speaking, he was indulging in a delicious feeling of pleasure because she *had* remembered the boat.

"I expect he was right," commented Mary gravely; and then, after a pause, "I think he was right," she concluded.

"The Queen of Heaven must have *known* he was right," said John, "for she was so angry that she turned him into a woman. Does it strike you that was a queer punishment?"

She fixed her brown eyes upon him. "Not at all, Cousin John. It seems a very natural punishment."

From a meadow remote from where they were and at present

concealed by the shed there came to them at that minute the wild familiar cry of the lapwing.

"I've been wanting all the time to ask you, Mary," he recommenced, "whether you remember that day we couldn't get the boat past the dam—the dam between the big river and the little river? You said just now that you'd never been made love to. Why! my dear, I've had a feeling of longing to see you again all my life since that day that I hugged you and so on in the bottom of that boat. Do you remember that too, the way the boat leaked, and how fishy it smelt and the way I held you?" The queer thing was that once more, even as he said these words, the image of the boy Tom Barter rose up.

Mary frowned, struggling desperately to evoke the scene he described. She remembered the day; she remembered the difficulty with the dam; she remembered his pleasure as they leant over the rowlocks to watch the fish; she remembered her grandfather's anger when they came home; she remembered with a peculiar sweet sort of shame having asked him various questions; but the one thing she had completely forgotten was his having hugged her "and so on." A rather sad smile flickered across her face, a smile that she gave way to because her face was invisible to him. "You're sure you remembered right which little girl it was, John," she said, "that you hugged that day?"

Her words arrested his attention. He could not tell whether she was mischievous or grave because he could not see her face. "You mustn't tease me like that, Mary," he said. "You never once teased me in those days and I never once teased you. There's no need for us to be ashamed of being serious now any more than then."

He noticed that one of her hands began to pluck at the grass by her side but she made no reply to his words. "What *do* you remember, Mary," he said, "about that day at the dam?"

The silence that followed his words was like the silence of a field at the bottom of a mountain-valley, when the setting sun touches the flanks of a herd of feeding cattle.

Mary's thoughts were like a rain of bitterness and a dew of sweetness gathered in the hollows of a tree-root. A brimming over from them all would have escaped and vanished if she had tried

to express them in any sort of speech. The shame of those questions she had asked of little Johnny Crow was a sweet shame.
That she had forgotten what he remembered was bitter to her.
Could he be inventing? Could it really have been another little
girl in another boat? How could she have forgotten whatever it
was he did to her? "I must have been an imbecile," she said to
herself. "If he were to hug me now, *and so on*, I should not
forget!"

His voice continued to murmur on over her head; and what
was this? His wrists were under her armpits and his hands covered her breasts. He was holding them very still; but her right
breast was beneath one of his hands and her left breast was beneath the other. That up-flowing wave which she had felt before
seemed now to encounter a down-flowing wave. Every conscious
nerve of her body seemed to be responding to his hands. Her
jacket and her dress intervened, or he would have felt her heart
beating. He probably did feel it beating! Her mind wandered for
a second to the secluded drawing-room of Miss Euphemia Drew
in the Abbey House at Glastonbury. Under the pressure of his
hands she shut her eyes and leaning back in complete relaxation
against his knees she gave herself up to an inner vision of the
Abbey Ruins through those great windows. How often had she
sat there in the late afternoon light in profound unhappiness
watching the rooks gather about the tall elms and the shadow of
the great, mutilated tower arch grow longer and longer upon the
smooth grass! How she had come to hate Glastonbury and hate
the Ruins and above all hate the legend of the Grail! Tom Barter
agreed with her in all this. That had been the secret of her
friendship with Tom. *That* and his having come from Northwold. "Mary—there's a rabbit in the asparagus-bed! *Mary*, the
ducks are in the garden!" Oh, how she hated Miss Drew sometimes—hated her almost as much as the Ruins. And yet how good
the woman had been, putting up with her moods, her sulkiness,
her sheer bad temper, treating her always more like a daughter
than a companion. "I hope he won't kiss me or anything else," she
thought. And then she thought, "I don't want him to take his
hands away. I want him to go on like this, without a change,
forever."

And John thought, "I'm English and she's English and this is England. It's more lovely to feel her little cold breasts under these stiff clothes, on this chilly grass, than all the Paris devices." And without formulating the thought in words he got the impression of the old anonymous ballads writ in northern dialect and full of cold winds and cold sword-points and cold spades and cold rivers; an impression wherein the chilly green grass and the peewits' cries made woman's love into a wild, stoical, romantic thing; and yet a thing calling out for bread and bed and candlelight! "Lisette would not have the faintest shadow of the faintest notion of what I'm now feeling. England! England!" How small, how very small Mary's breasts were! Why, as he held them now they seemed like the cold cups of water-lilies, not like a woman's breasts at all! God! She wasn't a woman, this new-found Love of his. She was an undine out of Harrod's Millpond. Yes, this is what he had been secretly craving; so long! so long! In his foxy shifts, in his wanton driftings, in his stormy reactions against the life of a great city, in his pathetic escapes into those whitewashed villages with their orchards, barley fields, and church steeples, in his crazy, reiterated attempts to do something better than the wretchedest literary hackwork, in it all, through it all, he had been pining for a moment like this. Why, this girl was his very "other self." What luck! What incredible luck! He could *feel* her consciousness as he held her like this, holding her where a woman's identity, her very soul, must surely most of all lie hid! And her inmost consciousness was exactly like his own—he knew it was—exactly like his own. "Oh, I needn't kiss you or anything, Mary," his thoughts ran. "We've met. We're together. We've got each other now. It's all done. Once for all it's all done."

He moved his hands from her breasts and encircled her thin neck with all his fingers. He could feel the luxury of abandonment with which her chin sank on his knuckles and her head fell sideways. She was feeling exactly as he was feeling—only, as was right and proper, the reverse way. Oh, what magical expressions for the only things in love that really counted, were those old ballad phrases. Mary was not pretty. She was not beautiful. She had what the old ballads had. Yes, that was the thing. The best

love was not lust; nor was it passion. Still less was it any *ideal*.
It was pure Romance! But pure Romance was harsh and grim and
stoical and a man must be grim to embrace it. Yes, it went well
with cold March wind and cold rain and long chilly grass.

He released her neck and ran his fingers through her brown
wavy hair. Mary always parted it in the middle and drew it back,
each way. Mary's forehead always seemed fullest just over each
temple where there were little blue veins. Her nose was rather
long and very straight; but it had wide, flexible nostrils, the nostrils of an animal who goes by scent. John's restless fingers now
began feeling over all her features, one by one, as if he had been
a blind old man and she his unseen guide. It gave him a queer
sensation, like touching the exposed belly of some delicate fish or
bird, when he felt the pulses of her eyes beating under her tight-
closed eyelids. He and she were both of them blind now. By God!
And they both of them *felt* blind; and in the blind arms of
chance. When he came to her full lips and her rather large mouth
he hoped in his heart it would come upon her to bite his fingers.
And she *did*. He drew his bitten fingers away and sucked at them
dreamily. He struggled to his feet and catching her under the
shoulder blades lifted her up. The feeling of her body in his
hands excited his senses but he only gave her one savage hug,
pressing her fiercely against him, his long bony hands gripping
the front of her thighs. Then he let her go with an abruptness that
almost flung her on the grass.

"It's time to see the fish if we're not going to miss the funeral,"
he said.

They both picked up their sticks after that and went forward.
John Crow had forgotten how separated from the farm-house
the mill-pond was. He had just begun to feel those fears of dogs
and angry farmers common to all tramps and gipsies. But he was
to be spared any agitation of this kind. The Mill stood by itself;
and the face which it turned to the mill-pond was vacant of
windows. It was a queer blind face, under its heavy East Anglian
tiles. Mary and he soon found themselves leaning over the low
stone parapet and staring into the huge deep pool. . . .

"It's the same!" "I remember!" "I remember!"

Their voices came simultaneously; and for one flash of a frag-

ment of a second something in them held a wind-blown taper to
a scene lost and buried more than twenty years. But from the
depths of John Crow's mind another image suddenly mounted up
and another memory. Tom Barter! Tom Barter! It was more than
once he had come here with Tom, a boy of his own age, the son
of the Squire of Didlington; but the episode came back now with
an overwhelming rush. What a heap of information about fish and
about fishing Tom had known! And he had got the boat up those
shallows and past the dam too . . . got it right into the "big
river," near Didlington bridge! John became very silent now,
staring at the water and thinking of Tom. It seemed very curious,
looking back at that far-off day, that there should ever have been
any boy so strong, so capable, so extraordinarily nice to him as
Tom Barter had been. He and Tom were exactly the same age.
What had become of him?

"On one of those days," he announced now to Mary, "I came
here with Tom Barter. Do you remember Tom, Mary? He was
probably the best friend I shall ever have!"

Their four hands were pressed against the parapet, palms down,
and their two heads were close together. Mary moved one of her
hands a little till it just touched one of his.

"Ye . . . es, I . . . think . . . I do," she replied musingly.
In her heart she said to herself, "I won't tell him now that I know
him quite well and that he's working for Cousin Philip at
Glastonbury."

"Oh, you don't remember him if you don't see him *clearly*!"
cried John emphatically. "Look at that big one, Mary, look at
him rising there! It was that fish that brought him back to my
mind. Directly I saw that big one I thought of Tom. He got the
boat right up the dam that day, Mary, Tom did."

"I . . . don't . . . think . . . *I* was there that day," said Mary
in a low voice. And in her heart she saw two little boys standing
exactly where they two were standing at this minute. Could it
have been Tom, and not her at all, that he had hugged at the
bottom of the boat? Boys no doubt are often shameless on long,
hot afternoons!

"Right over the dam. . . ." went on John Crow. "I can see his face now as he pulled at it. He must have taken off his stockings. The dam was all slippery with moss."

"*Damn the dam!*" cried Mary in her heart. But she said quietly, "I think I remember him in church, John. He used to sit in the front pew. Or if it wasn't your friend it was a great, big, strong-looking boy with curly hair and a freckly face. Yes, I think it *must* have been Tom."

"Tom hadn't freckles," said John Crow with a faint touch of peevishness. There arose in his masculine brain an obscure annoyance with himself for having brought that boy into it at all. His vague thought, thus limned in the darkness, was that certain emotions were best kept separate! But this thought vanished as quickly as it came and both the man and the woman instinctively dropped the subject.

They dropped it without any feeling at all on his part and on hers only a faint obscure sense that she would have to confess sooner or later that this boy was now living at Glastonbury. Then they plunged into the deep pool together now with their eyes, their minds, and their souls.

There are few mill-ponds like Harrod's in all Norfolk and the sensation which these two returning natives got from looking into its depths was unforgettable by both of them. On its outer rim the water was of a pale, neutral colour, a sort of ashen grey, but as the eye moved from circumference to centre it got darker and darker; a faint bluish tinge mingled there with the grey and there appeared a sort of mysterious luminosity as if there had been a subterranean light at the bottom of the pool.

But what a thing it was to see those great fish, one after another, rise up slowly from the unseen depths, mount to the surface as if they were going to breathe the air, and then, with a reversion of their slow ellipse, turn back towards the depths again!

To the girl this sight was purely disinterested—just objectively arresting like a flight of beautiful swallows—but to John, with his boyish memory of fishing-rods and predatory pursuit, there was a spasm of possessiveness in it, intense, disturbing, provocative, erotic. The girl satisfied no sense but that of sight as she watched these mysterious water-denizens, first sub-aqueous clouds, then vague darknesses, then noble fish-shapes, rising up and sinking down as if in the performance of some elaborate court ritual, the rules of which were as strict as in some water palace of the Oceanides! But John's grosser nature was not so easily content. A longing seized him, that seemed to carry with it some primordial phallic tremulousness, to grasp with his hands these slippery creatures, to hold them tight, to feel their fins, their scales, their sliding coolness, their electric livingness.

Making no attempt to analyse why it should have been that the sight of these alien beings, gliding upward, downward, with such intense and yet easy volition, should excite his desire, he moved instinctively behind his companion and slid his arms between her body and the rough fabric of the wall against which they leaned.

"You're like a cormorant," she gasped when she recovered her breath from the disturbance of his protracted embrace.

"Sorry," he muttered. "I couldn't help it. Curse it!" he added. "We've got to go, my dear, and quickly too! So say good-bye trout, or chub, or whatever you are! *I* don't know what you are!"

He caught her hand and pulled her away, as if he feared she might transform herself into one of those cold, slippery fish-shapes, and vanish forever into the bluish-grey twilight. As he led her off, his last glance revealed a gleaming circle of ripples. "There's a rise!" he murmured. "The only one we've seen, but we must hurry! I daren't look at my watch."

The tolling of the bell in the flint tower of the high-roofed Northwold church did indeed begin before they reached the first house of the village. The wind had dropped considerably and the strong sunshine, warming their bodies through all their clothes, combined with the motion of their rapid walk to throw them into a glow of delicious well-being. John felt so well satisfied with what life was offering him that his mind took a leap—unusual for him—into his practical future.

"I'm going to ask Philip to give me a job in Glastonbury," he said.

The girl found a secret vent for the rush of rapturous delight which this news brought to her by clutching the flapping edges of her frayed scarf and pulling them tightly round her neck.

"I'm a companion to an old woman there called 'Phemia Drew," she said eagerly. "Her house is what they call the Abbey House so I can see the Ruins from my bedroom."

"You owe your job to Philip, I suppose?" said John. "I decided before I left the rue Grimoire, that I'd ask him for a job there myself. So my English life will begin side by side with your life."

Her voice was decidedly strained as she asked her next question. "You're not married, are you, John?"

The tolling of the bell in the flint tower fell upon them at that moment like a long, bony arm thrust out of a coffin. He uttered a sardonic chuckle.

"If I *were*, my dear, she'd be a funny kind of Frenchwoman not to have tricked me out better. She *did* buy me this tie——" He pulled out the object referred to and flapped it between his finger and thumb as they hurried down the street. "No, no—I'm not married. And now I've got hold of you I'm not likely to be—" he cast a foxy glance at her out of the corner of his slanted eyelids; a look such as a thievish schoolboy, with a stolen plum in his fingers, might throw upon the owner's daughter—"unless *you* would marry me!"

She gave him a dreamy, abstracted stare in answer, as though she had not heard his last words at all. Then she bit her lip with a little frown and turned away her head. When she looked at him again her face had cleared. "How lucky that Philip got the idea of bringing me here, John. I don't believe you'd have thought of Glastonbury if we hadn't met."

They had now reached the entrance to the churchyard; and they found they had to push their way through a crowd of villagers to get through the narrow gate. They made their way to where two clergymen were standing above a hole in the ground. The white surplices these wore fluttered a little in the wind, displaying at intervals the black trousers underneath. In front of these white figures, on the other side of the hole, all the relations were mutely assembled, the men in a sort of discreet trance, shamefacedly holding their hats, over which their heads were bowed; the women, much more self-possessed, throwing quick little glances here and there and fidgeting with the umbrellas, prayer-books and handkerchiefs which they held in their black-gloved hands. John and Mary advanced instinctively to the side of Miss Elizabeth Crow, who was the only one of the whole company to be showing any deep emotion. She was sobbing bitterly; and she held both hands, bare and empty, pressed against her face.

Quickly enough, however, when Mary reached her side, she realised who it was, and removing her hands from her face, gave her, through her falling tears and the convulsed twitching of her rugged cheeks, a sympathetic and humorous smile. Those were the only tears, that was the only smile, evoked from any human skull at the funeral of William Crow. This stalwart, stout lady, now so sturdily wiping away her tears with the back of one of her plump hands, was indeed, according to that queer destiny which the man in the New Inn had discoursed upon, the only child of the dead man left alive. All the rest of the company were grandchildren; or they were county neighbours. "She treated 'un pretty bad in's lifetime," murmured one of the village onlookers. " 'Tis too late to make a hullabaloo, now the poor man's dead."

The service had begun some while before John and Mary appeared upon the scene; so it was not very long before it was all over and the company trooping back to the Rectory. This was an easy proceeding for the simple reason that at the side of the churchyard opposite to the public entrance there was a private door leading into a portion of the Rectory garden; and not only so, but into that very portion of it, a walled-in courtyard, which surrounded the front entrance to the house.

It was in the large, old-fashioned drawing-room, that room that had made such a deep impression on the mind of the youthful John, that all the relatives were now gathered to hear Lawyer Didlington read the will. It fell to Philip Crow to act the part of host to everybody and also the part of the natural heir to his grandfather; although, as a matter of fact, no one except the lawyer himself had more than the vaguest speculative guess as to what the will was likely to contain. But Philip had so much nervous domination that he was the sort of person who always takes the lead in any group or on any occasion of importance;

nor would an outsider have guessed for a second, watching the man's youthful energy, that in a couple of days from today he would be fifty years old.

The windows opened upon an enormous lawn which itself opened out into a field surrounded by trees. In the middle of the lawn was a great cedar tree. The windows almost reached to the floor of the room; and thus, with the lawn and with the field, entirely secluded from the outer world, the drawing-room itself became the inner sanctuary of "a great good place," a consecrated Arcadia. To the right of anyone standing at these windows and looking out, rose, behind a border of laurel bushes, the high, grey, flint nave of the church. Thus this room possessed that rare delicious quality that certain old chambers come to have that overlook scholastic quadrangles or walled-in college gardens.

It might, however, have appeared to an observer curious in antiquarian lore that compared with similar retreats there was about this scene in spite of the presence of the church something essentially heathen and secular. The disproportioned size of the Rectory and its great lawns compared with both church and village gave an impression of the existence on that spot—at least a *former* existence—of something high-handed and predatory. In other words there was displayed in all this sequestered felicity the same Danish tendency to profane self-assertion that has been noted in the character of the Northwold villagers. "Possess, enjoy, defy" might have been the heraldic motto of both rich and poor in this portion of East Anglia.

While the sexton was lazily and contentedly shovelling into the grave, on the top of the earth-covered coffin, all the good Norfolk clay, so auspicious for the growing of roses, that had been piled up at the foot of the hole—and be it noted that several lob-worms and several lively little red worms, which are so irresistible to Wissey perch, went down into that hole with the clay—there hovered round the body in the coffin a phantasmagoria of dream-like thoughts. These thoughts did not include any distaste for being buried or any physical shrinking, but they included a calm, placid curiosity as to whether this dream-like state was the end of everything, or the beginning of something else. Nerves of enjoyment, nerves of suffering, both were atrophied in this cold, sweet-sickly, stinking corpse; but around and about it, making a diffused "body" for itself out of the ether that penetrated clay and planks and grass-roots and chilly air, all alike, the soul of the dead man was obsessed by confused memories, and deep below these by the vague stirring of an unimpassioned, neutral curiosity.

William Crow was in his ninety-first year but he had never experienced such intense curiosity since his son Philip in *his* twentieth year had run away and married an unknown woman.

Up and down, up and down, these memories kept washing. Backward and forward they washed, they drifted, they eddied. And always, far beneath them, the root of curiosity stirred tremulously, like a lazily swaying seaweed, beneath an ebbing and flowing sea-tide.

The eyelids of the old, dead face under the coffin-lid were tightly closed; and the mouth, that eloquent actor's mouth, was a little open; but what remained totally unchanged was the beautiful, snow-white hair covering the round skull on every side with curls as silky as those of a child.

The memories of this death-cold skull gravitated always towards the image of his long-dead wife. No emotion did they excite, not one tremulous flicker, either of love or hate; only upon each separate memory that calm curiosity turned its neutral gaze.

"A thoroughly mean man . . . that's what you are, William, a thoroughly mean and cruel man! That sad look in your eyes that you always say is sensitiveness is really cruelty! That's what it is. Just cold-blooded malicious cruelty . . . and sensual too, oh, wickedly, wickedly sensual!"

With the absolute calm of a botanist observing a plant did the curiosity in the soul of this corpse listen to this whisper of memory.

And again the voice of the proud lady out of her Swiss grave penetrated the Norfolk clay.

"Elizabeth Devereux to William Crow! I was a fool ever to marry such a person as you, William. Mother always said it was marrying beneath me."

The mouth of the dead face fell open a little further and the terrible, unapproachable silence of decomposition deepened.

"My Philip's son will be like his father," the woman's voice reiterated. "He'll be all me! He'll be a true Philip Devereux. He'll have no touch of the Dane in him."

The confinement of the coffin-boards was nothing to William Crow. The raw clay, rattling noisily down from the sexton's spade, was less than nothing to him. To suffer from anything, to enjoy anything—he had forgotten what those words meant. Enjoyment, suffering? What strange, morbid by-issues of human consciousness were these?

But the voice of the woman began again; and that cold, disinterested curiosity stirred placidly to hear her words.

"Yes! You may look at yourself in the looking-glass as long as you like, William. That sad, weary look under your eyebrows, over your eyelids, is nothing but selfish cruelty . . . such as kills flies and torments people without hitting them! My family has always taken what it wanted. But it never stooped to spiteful tormenting. My father used to say that when Norman families stop ruling England, England will get soft and wordy and mean . . . just like you, William. . . ."

With impervious calm, as he listened to all this, did the soul of that passive corpse wonder vaguely whether this Devereux despotism was, or was not, the true secret of dealing with earth-life below the sun. It wondered too, with the same complacent indifference, whether the humming of these confused memories was going to lapse into what they called "eternal rest" or going to prelude some new and surprising change. Whichever it was, it was equally interesting, now that pleasure and pain were both gone. Annihilation—how strange! A new conscious life—how strange! What indeed the soul of the Rector of Northwold experienced, at that moment of his burial, was more like the Homeric view of death than anything else—only with more indifference to love and fame! Everything human in him was, in fact, subsumed in that primeval urge which originally lost us Paradise. The Reverend William, cold and stiff, cared for nothing except to satisfy his curiosity.

Meanwhile in the great Rectory drawing-room another and a far less disinterested curiosity was mounting up, mounting up to a positive suffering of tantalisation, as Mr. Anthony Didlington—

looking so much like a character of Sir Walter Scott that you
expected him, after every resounding period from his parchment
document, to take a vigorous pinch of snuff—read the late
Canon's will.

John and Mary had ensconced themselves on a small eighteenth-century sofa, that had the air of being the identical sofa
that gave a title to Cowper's poem; and that stood back, behind
the more pretentious pieces of furniture, near the furthest window.

In the most important place in the room sat Tilly Crow, Philip's wife, a small, trim, dark, little woman with a high forehead,
carefully parted hair, black, beady eyes, and under her chin a
colossal wedgewood brooch. Opposite Mrs. Philip, on the further
side of the hearth where a warm fire was burning, sat Elizabeth
Crow in her mother's little green velvet arm-chair which the great
black satin dress of the portly lady filled to overflowing. Her face
was weary and wistful rather than unhappy; but above and beneath her firmly modelled cheeks and rugged cheek-bones those
quaintly indented creases were extremely marked, whose contractions, according to Mary, were an indication that there was
trouble in the wind. Lawyer Didlington with sedate pontifical
gravity sat on a high chair with his back to the largest window.
Not a glance did *he* give at that gracious lawn, across the smooth
surface of which the long afternoon shadows from lime-tree and
cedar-tree were already falling.

Close to the lawyer's table, and taking not much more notice of
the shadows on the lawn than he did, sat at another table, with
writing materials ostentatiously displayed in front of them, Dave
Spear and Persephone Spear. It might have been supposed that
this young couple were desperately transcribing every detail of
the late Rector's will; but this would have been an erroneous sup-
position. The papers which lay before them had been extracted
from a battered leather case which now reposed on the carpet at
their feet. The calculations upon which they were so absorbingly
engaged, and which entailed the passing across the little table of
all manner of pencil scrawls, had not the very remotest connection with what Mr. Didlington was reading with such careful and
explanatory unction; unless indeed all human activities of a revo-

lutionary character are to be regarded as having a relation to the
rights of property.

Persephone Spear and her husband had in fact just come from
a communistic meeting at Leeds and were proceeding to another
one at Norwich before returning to Bristol where they lived. This
matter of consigning Persephone's grandfather to his native Norfolk clay would not have allured them from a mile off if it had
not been for the fact that there was the possibility of a strike just
then at one of Philip's Somersetshire factories. Feeling a family
interest in this event they had naturally got into touch with the
leaders of the strike and were doing their best not only to give the
event a communistic turn but also to use the accident of their relationship with him to win concessions from Philip.

It was a faint amusement to Miss Elizabeth, even in the midst
of her sad thoughts, to observe how curiously unlike each other
these two young revolutionaries were, and yet what a perfect
unanimity existed between them. Spear was a short, humorous,
broad-faced youth, with closely cropped fair hair and small,
merry, blue eyes; while Percy was a tall, lanky maid of a brownish, gipsy-like complexion and with a mop of dusky curls.

Mr. Philip Crow himself had been, until the lawyer actually
commenced reading, moving, like the energetic diplomat he was,
from one to another of all these relatives; and even now, while
everybody else was seated, he stood with alert, polite attention,
leaning against the side of the big window with his back to the
lawn and keeping his eyes fixed upon the old-world physiognomy
of Mr. Anthony Didlington. No one could have denied to Philip
Crow the epithet of handsome. He was indeed the only thoroughly
good-looking one of all the assembled relatives; but his good
looks were attended with so little self-consciousness and were so
completely subordinate to his formidable character that they
played a very minor part in the effect he produced. The man
drove himself—you could see *that* in his hawk's nose, his com-
pressed lips, his narrowed eyelids, his twitching brows—but he
drove others yet more inflexibly, as was apparent from the roving
intensity of his grey eyes, the eyes of a pilot, a harpooner, a big-
game hunter—in a word, of a Norman adventurer who took, kept,

organised, constructed; and who moulded *sans pitié* weaker natures to his far-sighted purpose.

John and Mary were so absorbed in whispering to each other
as first one memory and then another stole into their minds out of
the aura of that old room, some associated with the view outside
the window, some with the furniture, some with the figures of
their grandparents, that they had little attention to spare for any
of the rest of the company. It is true that every now and then
John did cast a swift, foxy glance, past the bowed heads of the
two revolutionaries, at that great parchment document, with its
official red seals, that Mr. Didlington held as reverently as a priest
holds the Gospels at Mass. These hungry, furtive glances were the
tribute he paid to all those excited expectations of incredible
legacies, discussed at so many rue Grimoire suppers with Lisette
and Pierre. But these greedy thoughts came quickly and went
quickly! The seductive softness of Mary's long limbs, as she sat
with crossed legs and clasped hands staring gravely at his face,
made his already achieved good luck more precious than any ecclesiastical bequest.

It really seemed interminable, the list of plots and parcels of
good English ground, inhabited and uninhabited, which, in various portions of Norfolk, William Crow had inherited from his
thrifty yeoman ancestors. Still it went on drawing itself out, this
protracted list; and as yet no hint had appeared as to who was
going to be the gainer by all this accumulation of properties, of
which apparently the dead man had an undisputed right of free
disposal.

The wind had quite dropped now. The shadows on the lawn
were darker and colder. The few yellow dandelions that had escaped the gardener's shears had closed themselves up and looked
—as dandelions do when near sunset—forlorn, impoverished,
empty of all glory. A pallid radiance alternated with velvet-black
shadows upon the trunk of the cedar; and over the daffodils in
the grass and over the hyacinths in the flower-beds a peculiar
chilliness, rising from a large hidden pond beyond the field, and
not yet palpable enough to take the form of vapour, moved
slowly from the edge of the distant shrubbery towards the house.

Philip's thoughts were like far-flung hooks piercing the gills of

some monstrous Fate-Leviathan that he had resolved to harness
to his purpose. He visualised his factory at Wookey Hole. He
visualised those stalactites and stalagmites in the famous caves
there and saw them lit with perpetual electricity. He remembered
how he had stood alone there once by the edge of that subterranean river flowing under the Witch's Rock and how he had felt a
sensation of power down there beyond anything he had ever
known. "These Norwich investments are nothing," he thought,
"these over-taxed properties are nothing. The three big mort-
gages are the thing! Forty thousand they'd sell for. He's left
them to me—I feel it, I sense it, I know it. Besides, he promised
Grandmother. He confessed that to me himself. What a good thing
he died when he did! Never again shall I have to listen to that
voice of his reading Lycidas. Old epicure! I can see him now,
putting cream into his porridge and looking out so voluptuously
across his garden! Living for his sensations! That's what he did,
all his days. Putting cream into his porridge, reading his poetry,
and living for his sensations. What a life for a grown man! The
life of a frog in a lily-pond. Aunt Elizabeth is sorry now he's
dead. But she didn't like it when Johnny Geard became the favourite. She very quickly cleared out. He must have fancied himself
a lot over that. Must have thought he was converting a Methodist
to the true doctrines. Old fantastical-brained, crochetty ass! I
shall rebuild the Wookey Hole plant entirely. That'll take about
ten thousand. *That* will leave thirty thousand to play with. And
by God! I'll play with it. Four thousand would take electricity
beyond the actual known limits of every one of those caves. I'll
do the plant for ten thousand and spend five on the caves. With
five thousand I could electrify the bowels of the Mendips!" What
Philip felt at that second of time when he imagined himself with
all that electric power at his disposal, standing among those prehistoric stalactites, would be hard to put into rational human
speech. The drumming of a meteorite travelling through space
would best express it. "I . . . I . . . I . . . riding on electricity
. . . I . . . I . . . I . . . grasping electricity . . . I . . . I
. . . I . . . alone . . . all-powerful . . . under the Mendips . . . letting loose my will upon Somerset . . . my factories above . . .
my electricity beneath. . . . I . . . I . . . Philip Crow . . .

planting my will upon the future . . . moulding men . . . dominating Nature."

His hard grey eyes began to soften a little and his gaze, leaving Mr. Didlington's face, turned itself towards vacancy.

"I shall have a completely new sort of boat made, to explore that subterranean river," he thought, "flatter than a barge, lighter than a canoe. I'll build an electric engine for it and I'll have myself floated under the Witch's Rock and I'll make them leave me there; and I'll have *that feeling*. . . . I'll make it work too. I'll have water power for my plant run by the buried river in the heart of the Mendips! I'll electrify the caves of the Druids. I'll carry electricity deeper under the earth than anyone's ever done. How slowly this old ass reads!"

But Miss Elizabeth Crow, staring sometimes into the fire and sometimes out of the big window across the lawn, thought to herself, "I should have had an easier life if I'd put up with Johnny Geard and stayed with Father." She remembered how she had first seen this Glastonbury ex-preacher whose mystical ideas got such a fatal hold on William Crow's mind and on William Crow's heart. She had been visiting her mother in Switzerland; and when she came back there he was—the Somersetshire revivalist, installed in Northwold Rectory! "How his black eyes gleamed as he listened to Father's morning prayers! The man *was* fascinating in his own way. I can't blame Father for liking him." She could hear now her father's resonant voice repeating the great poetical chapters in Isaiah. "Comfort ye, comfort ye, my people, saith your God. Speak ye comfortably to Jerusalem and cry unto her, that her warfare is accomplished, that her iniquity is pardoned; for she hath received of the Lord's hands double for all her sin!" And she could hear this charlatan interrupt—an unheard-of thing for a servant to do!—and beg for another chapter of sacred rhetoric.

Tilly Crow's mind was neither conjuring up large legacies nor brooding over ancient grievances. It was occupied entirely with minute problems connected with the larder, the pantry, the kitchen, in her own home at Glastonbury. There was a certain shelf in the pantry that her housemaid always kept too crowded. Tilly Crow could see now a particular stream of light in which the sun motes were wont to flicker when she entered that pantry after breakfast. This light always fell upon a suspended dishcloth, different from the rest, with a little green border, which she kept for drying her best china cups herself when they had visitors. Then her mind left the pantry and made a journey of about a dozen feet to the larder. Here she saw with abominable vividness a bluebottle fly—she maintained a special and constant warfare against these—walking along the edge of a shelf where the butter and cheese were kept. Not being able to endure this image with equanimity she gave a sharp little shake of her head to drive it away and as Mr. Didlington began a long list of freeholds in the parish of Thorpe her adventurous mind took a daring leap to her Glastonbury drawing-room where it concentrated upon the faded pink ottoman wherein she kept her wools. "I must re-line the ottoman," she said to herself. "There's that rent that Elizabeth's cat made. It always bothers me to see it. How sentimental Elizabeth looks, staring out of the window! Oh, I hope the Canon has left her enough money to go and live by herself in some nice seaside place!" At this point in Tilly Crow's thoughts there came an image that she would have been very reluctant to put into words; but as a mere image in the void—brought to her by some housemaid of the air upon a silver tray—she gave herself up to it. This was the image of a solitary cup of tea carried up to her, with her letters, by Emma the cook, during a paradisiac holiday, when Philip—such was Tilly's furthest reach of felicity—had gone to stay for a whole fortnight with Aunt Elizabeth, at that pleasant seaside place!

But what was this? What words of fatal significance had fallen from the lips of Mr. Didlington? By what incantation had this roomful of grown-up people been incontinently jerked upon their feet, protesting, exclaiming, jeering, enquiring, denouncing, arguing; and by no means speaking gently of their Grandfather Crow who, for all that he was one of the chief causes of their being alive upon the earth, seemed to have turned into a deliberate enemy?

"Does it mean that none of us get a penny—not even Philip?" whispered Mary to John.

"Not a penny," the man from Paris answered. "And what's

more, Mary, I'll have to borrow ten shillings from you to get to Glastonbury."

"You'll want more than that," she returned gravely.

"No, I shan't. I'm going to walk. Ten shillings is what I want. Not more, not less. But I want it from you and you'd better give it me now if you've got your purse; for they're terribly excited and it's best to be on the safe side."

Mary fixed a very straight look upon him at this. But seeing that he was perfectly serious she moved back a little towards the window and nodded to him to follow her.

"How much money have you got left?" Mary whispered. He searched his pockets thoroughly and produced three shillings and fourpence. This sum he held out to her in his two hands as if she had demanded it of him. She shook her head. "Put it back," she said. "I'd better get some more for you. You can't walk all that way. I'm sure Aunt Elizabeth ——"

He pulled her nearer to him, interrupting her words. The massive green curtain on the left of the window—for the winter curtains had not been changed yet—hung in bulging folds against his shoulder. Mary long afterward remembered how exactly like a certain Venetian picture she had seen somewhere his refined rogue's face looked against that background. "I'm not going to take a penny from anybody but you!" he whispered fiercely, with a malicious gleam in his eye. "I'll find you out at Glastonbury in a week or so—not longer than two weeks anyway—and *then* we'll see. I may sponge upon you like the devil *then*," he added, giving the girl a quick, searching look. "I *have* sponged on girls before. It's a way of life that seems to suit me!"

Mary showed her strong white teeth in a schoolgirl grin. Turning her back to the room she drew out her purse and took from it three half-crowns, a florin and a sixpence. "Miss Drew," she remarked, "doesn't pay very much. Philip doesn't give tips either. Aunt Elizabeth gave me this for pocket-money."

It would have been clear enough to any close observer that Mary derived an exultant happiness from handing over her pocket-money to John in this childish manner. It would also have been clear that John's feelings were equally those of a romantic lover and a sly, unscrupulous tramp.

"I'll ask Aunt Elizabeth if you can't sleep here tonight," whispered Mary, as they turned away from the darkening window.

He made a wry face at her. "Don't you dare!" he breathed. "I've got more than three shillings without touching your ten and I've left my bag at the Inn. I'll make them give me a room and breakfast for two nights for that—you'll see! I want to go with you to the big river tomorrow. We never went there together."

Mary got red with excitement. "We *did*, John! You've forgotten but I remember. We *did* just once!"

Their dialogue was interrupted by Philip's voice which was not raised, but which was lowered to such a key of indrawn intensity that it compelled attention.

He was now standing with his back to the fire, fronting Mr. Didlington, who, with his fingers inserted between the loose pages of this calamitous will, swayed heavily and limply before him, like an obsequious but surly seneschal whose account has proved faulty.

"The whole of . . . this . . . forty thousand . . . left absolutely to this man . . . and no chance . . . of legal action . . . *that* . . . in short . . . is the situation?"

Mr. Didlington began murmuring something in a husky, injured voice; but it was only the word "legacies" that reached the ears of John and Mary.

"Damn your legacies!" said Philip in the same tone. "Two hundred a year from the Norwich property to my aunt; and a hundred in cash to the servants. That's all of your precious legacies there are. The maddening thing is that it was Tilly and I who introduced this sly dog to Grandfather."

His voice changed a little and he looked towards his wife.

Tilly Crow had drawn up her thin legs in the great arm-chair and, with her hands clasped so violently in her lap that the knuckles showed white, stared at him with frightened eyes.

"Where *is* this thief, Tilly?" he said, in a much gentler voice. "Where *is* this holy rascal who has fooled us all?" The fact that he had displayed self-control enough to speak in a half-humorous tone was in itself sufficient to bring about the recovery of his equanimity. "Why," he finally remarked, looking round with the

air of a monarch addressing his courtiers after the loss of a battle, "why doesn't someone fetch this good, religious man and let
me offer him our united congratulations!"

"The furniture," murmured Tilly. "Did he say the furniture
was to be divided equally? Does that mean, Philip, that we can't
have the silver with your grandmother's crest on it? Ask them,
Philip, ask them now! They *will* give us the silver, won't they?
And the linen? We don't want any more furniture, Philip, but
these girls *must* let me have the linen! Tell them we don't want
any heavy furniture, Philip. Tell them we want the silver and
linen."

Aunt Elizabeth herself rose heavily from her seat now. Her
thoughts had been wandering away to Glastonbury, where thirty
years ago she had been so fond of the youthful Vicar of the place,
who had jilted her to marry a maid-servant. She completely disregarded Tilly and addressed herself to her nephew. "You are
thinking only of your own affairs, Philip," she said sternly. She
looked at him, as she spoke, without a trace of the respectful awe
into which he had bullied the others. "Why don't you and Tilly
congratulate me on my two hundred a year?"

There was a weight of character in Aunt Elizabeth when she
was on her feet and confronting her nephew that enabled her to
reduce his importance and to reduce his loss of forty thousand
pounds! Mary pinched John's arm with delight and whispered to
him something he could not catch. It was from the other young
couple in the room, however, that the next word came.

"Percy and I congratulate you, Aunt," cried Mr. Spear.

"Yes, yes," echoed Persephone, straightening her shoulders and
tossing her head, "and we hope you'll come out of the enemy's
camp now and listen to wisdom."

Miss Crow moved towards them, attracted by something so
kind in their tone that it surprised and disarmed her. "I'm in no
enemy's camp, Percy," she murmured, putting her arm round the
tall girl's waist. "I am an old-fashioned woman, and very fond
of my dear nephew and niece. I know nothing about politics—any
more than Mary does," she added, making an instinctive movement to bring the four young people together. John and Mary
did approach her.

"If there is to be anybody's wisdom thrust upon Aunt Elizabeth," John threw in, "I think *mine* would suit her best."

"What do you mean by that, Mr. Crow?" said young Spear, in an argumentative tone.

"Yes, what do you mean, John?" repeated Persephone. "You don't mean that Dave and I would try and browbeat Aunt Elizabeth, to *force* her to see the light, do you?"

"The light, the light, the light, the light!" cried John suddenly with a convulsed face.

Aunt Elizabeth unconsciously started back a pace or two, dragging Persephone, whose waist she still held, back with her; for there was something about Percy's slender figure that provoked people to touch her and made it difficult to let her go.

But John's face smoothed itself out in a second and the humblest apologies flowed from him. "It's my French mischief coming out, Dave Spear," he said. "It's all acquired cynicism. Really, I love to think that there are people with strong convictions, people who know they are right, like you and Cousin Philip."

Philip's own voice broke into their talk at this moment. It had not failed to strike him that Aunt Elizabeth and the four young cousins, in their obvious indifference to the grotesque event of forty thousand pounds passing from the Crow family to the Geard family, had succeeded in ostracising him in a sort of moral solitude. He and his wife might go on quarrelling with Mr. Didlington over this fiasco. The others were civilised people, prepared to take a mere financial blow with becoming urbanity!

"Don't lump me and Dave Spear together," he interrupted, pushing his way between Aunt Elizabeth and Mary with jocular bluster. "Percy would never cook him another meal if she thought we had anything in common. To my pretty Perse I shall never be anything but a bloated capitalist, shall I?" And he also, just as Aunt Elizabeth had done, put his arm round the tall girl's slender waist.

"Cousin Tilly," cried Dave Spear, with a schoolboy grin on his broad countenance, "come and stop Philip from flirting with my wife!"

But Mrs. Crow, who had just rung the bell and had had a long whispered conversation with the maid who answered it, was herself at that moment upbraiding Mr. Didlington in a plaintive but penetrating voice. "She says that horrible man departed yesterday from Glastonbury. I suppose both of you knew that Grandfather had left him everything." She paused, and then turning to her husband, "Tea's ready in the dining-room, Philip," she said.

The lawyer made his way to the group in the centre of the room and allowed his answer to Tilly's shrewish attack to be a general professional reply to them all.

"It is true," he said, "that Mr. Geard was aware, just as I was aware, of the late Canon's intentions; and as his family live in Glastonbury it was natural and indeed suitable that he should proceed there at once to acquaint them with this very considerable bequest."

"Well, Didlington," returned Philip, looking round at the company, "I hope you will do my wife the pleasure of letting her pour out tea for you? Shall we go into the dining-room? Will you follow Mrs. Crow, Didlington?"

He opened the door and they all trooped out into the passage. Down this they moved, past the broad staircase where the walls were hung with some really valuable oil paintings selected by William Crow's great-uncle. Not far from this staircase was the front door, leading—through a pleasant conservatory—out into the courtyard. It was through this door rather than any other that Mr. Didlington now hastened to pass, picking up his hat from a marble table that offered itself conveniently to his attention.

"Have to get home, Crow. The wife expects me, you know, and it's quite a walk. If I stayed to tea with all you good folk I shouldn't be at Methwold till after dark."

Philip had the wit to see that Tilly's tactless outburst had really upset the worthy man. What wild creatures women are! He followed the lawyer out into the conservatory which was fragrant with heliotrope and lemon verbena. "You must forgive Mrs. Crow, Didlington," he said quietly. And then, as the man only nodded with a faint shrug of his shoulders, "The great point you've made clear," he went on, "is that the family has no case against this fellow? We should have no chance—eh?—not the ghost of a chance—of upsetting this will?"

Mr. Didlington gravely bowed and buttoning his overcoat with his free hand pensively picked a leaf from the lemon verbena with the one that held his stick.

"Not the ghost of a chance, eh?" repeated Philip.

The man straightened and looked him in the face.

"I am acting," he said, "for all parties concerned." He paused, and resumed with real dignity. "My position as executor is a difficult one. Mr. Geard recognises its difficulty. His departure for Glastonbury proves that he does so. I hope that there may arise no occasion for the introduction of further advice and Mr. Geard hopes so too."

"I warrant he does," thought Philip. But he only said: "I confess to be startled, Didlington. You must have expected us to be startled."

The lawyer continued crumpling up between his fingers the lemon verbena leaf. "Mr. Geard has been your grandfather's valet," he said, "his secretary, his confidant, and, I might say, if you'll permit the word, his friend, for the last ten years. No opinion you called in would advise you to contest the will."

Philip Crow bent down and smelt a heliotrope. "Won't you change your mind, Didlington, after all, and let my good wife give you a cup of tea? She was over-excited just now. It was a surprise, you know; and ladies always take things hard. I expect if Mr. Geard wasn't . . . hadn't been . . . well-known to us in Glastonbury as a rather trying local preacher, she wouldn't have felt ——"

The lawyer shook his head. "In case there arose," he said, "in the mind of any of your family, a wish for further advice, I would like to point out that the late Canon's doctor, a good friend of mine, feels as I do, that your grandfather's mind was never clearer than during the time he made this will. No reputable firm would take up this case, Sir, on the grounds of undue influence. Everybody knows—if you'll allow me to be quite frank—that his family left the late Canon very much alone; and it is natural enough that under these circumstances ——"

"Well—well—I'm afraid I must be getting back to my guests," interrupted Philip coldly. "I wish you a pleasant walk home,

Mr. Didlington." He opened the door of the conservatory and bowed the man out.

No sooner had he entered the dining-room than Tilly Crow, peering at him round the great copper urn which stood on the table in front of her, with a little blue flame burning below it, cried out to him in a tearful, plaintive voice. "It was our own doing, Philip. That's what hurts me most. Oh, why, why did we ever let that man go to him?"

"What kind of a man *is* he, this lucky wretch?" Percy Spear enquired, as the head of the family sat down at the end of the table.

"He was an open-air preacher who lived in Glastonbury, Perse," Philip explained. "He was always out of luck and had a wife and two children. He was a nuisance to the whole town; and when your grandfather wanted a lay-reader, or someone who'd combine the duties of a valet and a curate, we packed him off to him. No one would have dreamed of *this* being the result."

"Perhaps he isn't a bad sort of chap after all," remarked Dave Spear. "Did you ever see him, Mary?"

Mary shook her head.

"I suppose," said John in a low voice, as if speaking rather to himself than to anyone in particular, "there is no way he could be persuaded to give up *some* of it?"

Philip gave him a swift glance of infinite disgust. "One doesn't do that sort of thing in England, Mr. Crow," he said, "not, at any rate, people in our position."

"A will is a funny thing," said Dave Spear meditatively. "A dead man arbitrarily gives to some living person the power that he has robbed the community of! The mere existence of a thing like a will is enough to prove the unnaturalness of private property."

Aunt Elizabeth looked anxiously at Philip. "Don't start a discussion of politics now, I beg you, Dave Spear," she said.

"My quarrel with Spear," interjected Philip in a low voice, "is not confined to politics."

"What is it confined to?" cried Persephone sharply. "Don't you begin teasing my Dave," she went on, and as she spoke, she stretched out a long, delicious, young girl's arm across the table and taking Philip's hand in her own gave it a little playful scolding shake.

Philip caught her fingers and held them gravely, while he looked intently into her eyes. John saw the communist's rather rustic countenance wince sharply while this magnetic vibration passed between the cousins.

"What puzzles *me* about all your theories, Mr. Spear," began John, speaking rather rapidly, "is that they contradict the deepest instinct in human nature. *To possess*—doesn't the whole world, for every one of us, turn upon this great pivot? Our philosophy, for instance, what is it but the act by which we possess the Cosmos? Our love? That surely is the quintessence of possession. And isn't this asceticism which you people practice, this giving up of everything except the 'bare essentials' as you call 'em, isn't it a sort of wet blanket thrown upon human nature, a sort of moral rebuke to the natural pleasures?"

"I think you will agree, Mr. Crow ——" began Spear excitedly, but his wife broke in. "Let *me* put it to him, Dave!" she cried. "The point is this, Mr. Crow. We fully agree with you about the importance of a free fling of our whole nature towards happiness. But it's just this that the capitalistic system interferes with! You are confusing two things. You are confusing natural, instinctive happiness and the artificial social pride that we get from private property. Under a just and scientific arrangement of society such as they have achieved in Russia, our human values begin to change. People feel ashamed of having money. It becomes a disgrace, like the reputation of a thief, to have more than the essentials. But everyone has a right to the pleasures that bring happiness. Everyone has a right to ——"

"She means," interrupted her husband, raising his voice to a very vigorous pitch, "she means, Mr. Crow, that everyone who works honestly and doesn't live by exploiting others can have enough to enjoy their life on. The exploiting classes, of course," here he nearly shouted, causing Tilly to give a quick glance at the door, afraid lest the servants should hear him, "must be *starved* out!"

The contrast was so great between the rosy face of this fair-haired youth and the fanaticism of his tone that John stared at him in astonishment. Into the darkening twilight, past all those dim faces sitting round the table, the fierce words "must be starved out" twanged like a bow-string.

Philip Crow from the end of the table cast upon the young revolutionary very much the sort of glance that some Devereux of the Norman Conquest would have cast upon some Saxon Gurth who had dared to challenge him as his horse broke through the brushwood with a raised quarterstaff. "You could starve *me* out, my son, if you won over the army and the air-force, but I assure you you'll have one bloated capitalist you'll never starve out."

"Philip means our friend Mr. Geard, I suppose," murmured Aunt Elizabeth.

"*I mean Nature!*"

Persephone gave vent to a rather uncivil whistle. "Nature?" she mocked. "What *are* you talking about, Philip?"

"Don't you see, my good child," he said quite gently, "that it's always been by the brains and the energy of exceptional individuals, fighting for their own hands, that the world has moved on? What you people are doing now is simply sharing out what has already been won. *We* have the future to think of; or, as I say, Nature has the future to think of."

The blood rushed to the face of Dave Spear and a misty film gathered in front of his eyes, so that what he saw of the room and the people in the room was a swimming blur.

"I can't argue . . . with you . . ." he jerked out as if each word carried with it a streak of his heart's blood, "but I know that . . . if the masses . . . the masses of workers . . . the real workers . . . got . . . got the machinery and the . . . the land and water . . into their hands . . . a new spirit . . . not known before in all the history . . . of . . . of . . . of humanity conscious of its fate . . . would be stronger, greater, more . . . more . . . more god . . . more godlike than anything that your great selfish individuals have . . . have felt."

In his emotion the young man had lurched to his feet, and had seized with his fingers a half-cut loaf of bread which he began squeezing spasmodically. Aunt Elizabeth stretched forth her hand and removed this object; but not before that particular gesture in this darkening room, with the damp, green lawn and the sombre cedar outside, had caught John's attention as something symbolic. Long afterward John remembered that clumsy, bucolic figure leaning forward over the shadowy, unlit table and clutching that bread. With far more force than the slender Percy's eloquence those awkward, blurted words seemed to carry the seal of prophecy upon them. A green-coloured gust of rainy wind came rushing across that spacious garden, came swishing and swirling through the laurel-bushes, came moaning through the cedar-boughs.

"Just touch the bell, would you, Mary, so that they know we want the lamp?" broke in the voice of Tilly Crow.

The coming of the lamp changed the whole mental atmosphere of that group of people. It brought their minds back from the vibrations of the ideal to the agitations of the real. As the round orb of light was placed in the centre of the great table there entered the devastating reminder that forty thousand pounds' worth of power over the lives of men and women had passed from this comfortable room, from this secluded lawn, into some little shabby domicile at Glastonbury.

"How many children has this lucky person got, Philip?" enquired Mary in a low voice.

"Two," was Philip's laconic answer.

"But didn't you say he was a nuisance?" persisted Mary Crow.

"Two great sprawling girls," sneered Philip. "I suppose they'll buy Chalice House; or try and get the Bishop to sell them Abbey House and turn out Euphemia Drew."

"Oh, I hope they will!" cried Mary.

"You hope they will?"

"I'm tired of Abbey House. I'd like the fun of seeing Miss Drew choose new wall-papers."

"I'm afraid you'll never get that pleasure, Mary," said Aunt Elizabeth. " 'Phemia was born in the Abbey House and she'll die in the Abbey House."

"It's all very well for you, Elizabeth," piped up Tilly Crow in a voice like that of a melancholy meadow-pipit, "you've got your two hundred a year."

"Yes, and I'm going to leave you in peace, too, Tilly, and *live*

on my two hundred a year. I shall take one of those little workmen's cottages in Benedict Street that the town-council put up!"

Philip turned upon her with good-humoured bluster. "You'll
take nothing of the sort, Aunt," he cried. "Why, those wretched
socialistic cardboard toys don't even keep the rain out."

"It's simply disgraceful of you, Philip," threw in Persephone,
"the way you do all you can to make the work of that town-
council of yours so difficult."

"By the way," exclaimed Philip suddenly, disregarding her
protest and speaking in a raised and carefully modulated voice,
"where do you intend to sleep tonight, Cousin John?"

"Philip reads all our thoughts, you know," murmured Aunt
Elizabeth. "He thinks you've got an eye to that big sofa in the
drawing-room."

"There won't be any sleeping on sofas in a house where *I* am!"
cried Tilly Crow sharply. Her voice sounded so exactly like the
miserable *tweet-tweet* of a bird soaked in a windy rain that John
felt disarmed and sorry for her.

"Don't be afraid, Philip," he said, "and don't you fret about
the sofa, Cousin Tilly. I've got a room for two nights at the Inn."

Persephone leaned over and whispered something in Philip's
ear. It was impossible for John to hazard the least conjecture as
to what she said; but a minute later Philip addressed him in a
loud if not a very amiable tone.

"I shall be offended, Cousin John, and I'm sure your Cousin
Tilly will be terribly hurt if you don't let us pay for your room
while you're here. How long a holiday have you allowed yourself? How soon are you returning to Paris?"

"I . . . I . . . I haven't—on my soul I haven't thought about
it yet," muttered John Crow. "But thanks very much for the
room at the Inn." His voice suddenly became unnaturally loud.
"Thanks very much, Cousin Philip. I shall be glad to stay two
nights at the Inn at your expense. Shall I tell them to send the
bill to you up here?"

John's tone, when his voice subsided, left everybody a little
uncomfortable.

"Well," Philip said, "well—yes. Yes, of course. Yes, I shall
be here a few days more . . . perhaps. . . ." His voice sank

down at that point in a polite but weary sigh. It was plain to
them all that he felt no very strong attraction to the wanderer
from across the channel. His exact and precise thoughts, in fact,
might be expressed thus: "This fellow never expected any legacy.
He only came to see what he could get out of me. He's on
his beam-ends. He's probably got consumption, diabetes and the
pox. If I give him an inch he'll take an ell. At all costs I mustn't
let him come to Glastonbury."

Miss Elizabeth turned round towards Tilly Crow now, and in
a gentle, unassuming voice asked what time dinner would be.

"I do wish everybody would stop calling it dinner," said Tilly,
peevishly. "It'll be just a cold supper. There is so much over
from lunch. I thought of it just for the family, you know, and I
hoped Mr. Spear would not mind it being cold." She glanced as
she spoke, not at Dave, but at John. And it was John who lifted
up his voice in answer. "Don't think of me, in your hospitality,
Mrs. Crow, I beg. I shall be running up that bill—is it not so,
Philip—that we spoke of at the Inn?"

He rose to his feet as he said this. But Philip rose too. "You
misunderstood me, Mr. Crow," he said sharply. "It was only a
bedroom I was unable to offer you." He paused for a second
while a flicker of unconcealed distaste crossed his features. "But of
course you are jesting. Anyway you're free to enjoy which you
please . . . a hot supper at the Inn or a cold supper with us
here. Well!" he added in a different tone, "I've got some writing
to do; and I think I'll desert you all now and do it in the study."

There was a general movement to leave the table at this point
and under the protection of the confusion John whispered to
Mary, "Look here, I'm not coming up here again. That beggar
hates me *comme le diable*! You come, tomorrow morning, after
breakfast, and call for me at the Inn. Ha? I'll find out if we
can't get a boat on the 'big river'—— Anyway, you tell Aunt
Elizabeth that you're off for the day. How long are you going
to stay here?"

But, woman-like, Mary went straight to the main issue. "What
time shall I call for you, John?"

"Oh, about ten, if that's not too early? That'll give me time
to find out about the boat."

She gave him a peculiar look. It was a steady calm look. Above all it was a stripped look. It held his attention for a second; but he missed everything about it that was important. He missed its touching confidence, its bone-to-bone honesty. He missed its unquestioning, little-girl reliance upon him. He missed its weariness, he missed its singleness of heart.

"You won't change your mind, John, and start off for Glastonbury at dawn?"

It was his turn now to reveal, in an eyelid-flicker of self-abandonment, the animal-primitive basis of his nature. It *had* evidently crossed his mind, in his reaction from the pressure of the family, that it would be nice to escape and be upon the road alone! His face betrayed all this; but the newly born maternal tenderness in her tone expressed itself in such a gleam of humorous indulgence that he was lifted up out of the shame of having been caught in such a treachery, on a delicious wave of sheer repose upon her understanding.

"No, I won't change my mind," he whispered, "but don't let anything they say keep *you* from coming, Mary."

"I think I can get you *a little* more money for—for the road, John," she said hurriedly.

He treated this with the decisive gesture of a strong man showing off before a weak girl. "I'll be *very* angry if you do," he said. "*Nothing* would make me take it! So it's better not to waste breath."

Both dining-room and drawing-room and the hall and the passage outside these rooms were now left to themselves. Silent and alone too the now-darkened conservatory listened to the placid sub-human breathings of heliotrope and lemon verbena, the latter with a faint catch in its drowsy susurration, where one of its twigs was bleeding a little from the impact of the fingers of the indignant Mr. Didlington.

Silent and alone the broad staircase fell into that trance of romantic melancholy which was its invariable mood when the hall lamp was first lit. The oil paintings upon its walls looked out from their gilt frames with that peculiar expression of indrawn expectancy—self-centred and yet patiently waiting—of which human passers-by catch only the psychic echo or shadow or after-taste, for a single flicker of a second, as if they had caught them off-guard.

Of all these rooms the one that now fell into the most intense attitude of strained expectancy was the drawing-room . . . "You ought to have been older than all your brothers, woman, instead of younger." The words emanated from a pale, insubstantial husk upon the air, a husk that resembled the cast-off skin of a snake or the yet more fragile skin of a newt, diaphanous and yet flaccid, a form, a shape, a human transparency, limned upon the darkness above the great chair to the left of the fireplace. The words were almost as faint as the sub-human breathings of the plants in the conservatory. They were like the creakings of chairs after people have left a room for hours. They were like the opening and shutting of a door in an empty house. They were like the groan of a dead branch in an unfrequented shrubbery at the edge of a forsaken garden. They were like the whistle of the wind in a ruined clock-tower, a clock-tower without bell or balustrade, bare to the rainy sky, white with the droppings of jackdaws and starlings, forgetful of its past, without a future save that of anonymous dissolution. They were like words murmured in a ruined court where water from broken cisterns drips disconsolately upon darkening stones, while one shapeless idol talks to another shapeless idol as the night falls. They were like the murmurs of forgotten worm-eaten boards, lying under a dark, swift stream, boards that once were the mossy spokes of some old water-mill and in their day have caught the gleam of many a morning sun but now are hardly noticeable even to swimming water-rats. No sooner were these words uttered, than a simulacrum in human form, seated opposite to the shade of the Rector returned a bitter response.

"A cruel coward is what you are, William Crow, and what you've always been; but if ever, when I am dead, you leave your money to anyone but Philip's son I will punish you with a punishment *worse than God's!*"

While these words were being uttered the thin wraith from whom they came became lividly accentuated in its facial outlines which were of a ghastly pallor and hideously emaciated; but at the close, while she was actually crying out "worse than God's" not a vestige of her lineaments remained visible.

The other wraith too, in the chair opposite, although a faint film of his identity survived hers by two or three seconds, soon likewise faded. The chairs, the pictures, the ornaments on the mantelpiece were already lost in darkness. The fire was now nearly extinct. The only glimmer it was able to throw, in feebler and feebler jets from a little blue flame that kept racing along a charred bit of burnt wood, fell upon a tall, gilded screen painted with mythological figures. These intermittent flickerings soon died down in a dusky red spot that illuminated nothing and itself became dimmer and dimmer.

One of the big windows had been opened by Tilly Crow "to air the room" while they all went to their tea; and through this window the presence of the night flowed in. Sweet-scented, obliterating, equalising, it flowed in, taking the bitterness from defeat, taking the triumph from victory, and diffusing through the air an essence of something inexplicable, something beyond hope and beyond despair, full of pardon and peace.

WHEN MARY ARRIVED AT THE NEW INN, PUNCTUALLY AT TEN o'clock, with their lunch tied up in white paper in a basket, she found John Crow seated on a bench outside the entrance, with two oars and a long boat-hook lying across his knees.

The wind had sheered round to due south and what there was of it was faint-blowing. The sky was covered with an opalescent vapour; the sun was warm; and the wandering odours that were wafted towards the girl from the neighbouring cottages had a sweetness in them beyond the pungency of burning peat; a sweetness that may have come from the new buds in the privet hedges, or from the dug-up earth clods in the little gardens at the back, where the spades and forks of the men still stood fixed in the ground awaiting their return when the day's work was over.

He rose with alacrity to welcome her, the two oars in one hand, the boat-hook in the other. "I've got the key," he announced triumphantly. "It's at the end of Alder Dyke on the big river. They say we'd better go there by Foulden Bridge." He lowered his voice and bent down his head. "Did any of them try to stop you coming? Did Philip say anything?"

She shook her head and stood for a moment without moving, her face averted, looking dreamily down the street. "This will never happen to me again," she thought. "I am in love with him. He is in love with me. I shall never forget this day and I shall never feel just like this ever again, whatever happens." She turned towards John. "I don't care where you take me," her look said, "or what you do with me, as long as we are together!" But her lips said, "Do you mind going in and getting some more of that wine, John? I didn't want to make my basket too heavy, so I left on the table the bottle of milk that Aunt Elizabeth made me take."

He propped up the oars and the boat-hook against the house and went in. Mary moved away, crossed to the other side of the road and bending over a low brick wall stared at a manure-heap in which three black hens were scratching. The manure-heap with the three black fowls became at that second a sort of extension of her own personality. She felt at that moment, as she rested her basket on the top of the wall and heedless of her sleeves stretched her arms along its surface and ran her bare fingers through the cool stone-crop stalks, as if her soul was scarcely attached to her body. Almost without allowing her happy trance to be broken she took down her basket from the wall, recrossed the road and met John at the instant he emerged. "Sorry to have kept you," he chuckled, "but I've made them give me a flask of brandy as well as a flask of port. That's the best of having a greatcoat on, even on a hot day. Its pockets are so useful."

They walked rapidly now side by side past the churchyard and past the gardener's cottage at the drive-gate where Ben Pod had counted the cars. They came to a narrow foot-way that led them across the little river by a bridge that was scarcely more than a plank, and after that across the fields to the big river. Here at Foulden Bridge, which they did not cross, they debouched from the path; and turning to the left, followed   river bank downstream.

They had not spoken a word since leaving the Inn. Mary grew conscious, just before they got to Foulden Bridge, that she had been repeating to herself as she walked along, "That's the best of a greatcoat on a hot day. Its pockets are so useful." What she had been thinking was, how bony and thin was John's hand as it clutched the boat-hook which swung horizontally between them like an antique spear.

John was delving in his memory for something; something important. There had been several patches of yellow marigolds along the path they had followed and these had excited a tantalising feeling in his mind that he could not fathom. Those gleaming yellow flowers kept leading his memory to the verge of something and then deserting him and turning into a blur of blackness! Tom Barter had to do with it; but it was not Barter. This preoccupation with an obscure past, although it made him grave and silent, did not lessen his delight in his companion's presence. They were indeed, both of them, thrillingly happy, these

two flesh-covered skeletons, drifting so lingeringly along the
banks of the Wissey, but John's happiness was much more complicated than Mary's. His return to his native land played a part
in it; the revival of local memories played a still larger part;
and this latter feeling was so intimately associated with Tom
Barter that to oust that sturdy figure from its place was impossible. He kept reverting to the marigolds, especially to their
stalks in muddy water, and he kept thinking too of the stickiness
of certain lumps of flour-dough mixed with cotton-wool and
treacle that Tom and he had used for bait for roach and dace.
Perch, that more rapacious fish, despised these harmless pellets;
and he wondered whether it could be the black stripes of these
deep-water fish and their enormous mouths, or the stickiness of
this bait for the others, or a certain kind of homemade ginger-
beer that their grandfather's cook used to make, and not the
marigolds at all, that had been the tap-root to his rapturous
sensation. It was not that this tantalising sense of being on the
edge of some incredible life-secret interfered with his feeling
for Mary. It was that his possession of Mary had become a calm-
flowing tidal-stream which released and expanded all the antennæ of his nature. These responses leapt up towards the unknown, like those great, slippery fish at Harrod's Mill. Tom
Barter, marigold-stalks, fish-scales, dough-pellets—all these, and
the secret they held, depended, like the long shining river-weeds
upon which his eye now rested, upon the flow of that stream of
contentment which was his possession of Mary.

They were walking now very close to the river bank and it
was not long before they reached Dye's Hole. This spot was really
a series of deep holes in the bed of the Wissey where the stream
made a sweeping curve. Over these dark places in the swirling
water bent the trunks of several massive willow trees and between these trees and the edge of the stream there was a winding
path, too narrow to be trodden by horses and cattle but interspersed with muddy footholds and beaten-down clearings amid
the last year's growths, where it was just possible for two people to stand close together having the willow trunks behind them
and the dark water in front.

John stopped when he reached the largest of these little clear-

ings, and standing on the trodden mud balanced the two oars
and the boat-hook against the branches of an elder bush which
hung over a narrow ditch on the side of their path opposite to
the river. Then he turned round and facing Dye's Hole waited
for the girl to come up. The back of his head touched the vivid
green shoots of a gigantic willow tree whose roots, like great
thirsty serpents, plunged below the flowing water. As soon as
the girl reached him he took her basket from her and laid it down
on the ground, taking care to place it where a fragment of an
old post, of dark, rotting wood pierced by three rusty nails, would
prevent it from toppling over into the ditch. As he placed it
there he chanced to touch, between it and the post, a newly grown
shoot of water mint; and at once a wafture of incredible aromatic
sweetness reached his brain.

They both stood still and gazed round them. "I wonder if
you and I will ever see all this again?" he said.

"It's home to me," she said.

"It's home to both of us," concluded John; and the two of
them as if they were one flesh drank up in great satisfying
draughts the whole essence of that characteristic spot. With the
same unspoken understanding that had brought their thoughts
together before, the girl's hat and the man's cap were now
thrown together on the earth at their feet and they gave themselves up to a protracted love-making. What was remarkable
about this love-making was that during all their embraces, in
which the man held her and caressed her, first with her body
front to front against his, and then with her face turned towards
the river, their male and female sensuality—he "possessing" and
she being "possessed"—was, in its earth-deep difference, of exactly the same magnetic quality. This was not due to his experience or to her inexperience; for, in these matters, Nature, the
great mother of all loves, equalised them completely. It was due
to some abysmal similarity in their nerves which, after making
them fall in love, made them "make love" in exactly the same
manner! There always remained the unfathomable divergence,
in their bodies, in their minds, in their souls, due to their being
male and female; but their similarity of feeling was the exciting

element sounding the depths of ever-new subtleties in this deliciousness of like-in-unlike.

What John and Mary really did was to make love like vicious
children; and this was due to the fact that they were both very
nervous and very excitable but not in the faintest degree tempted
to the usual gestures of excessive human passion. The rationalism
of analytic logic has divided erotic emotion into fixed conventional types, popular opinion offering one set of categories, fashionable psychology offering another. As a matter of fact, each
new encounter of two amorists creates a unique universe. No
existing generalisation, whether of the wise or of the unwise,
covers or ever will cover a tenth part of its thrilling phenomena.
In one respect this love-making by Dye's Hole was the most child-
like that the spot had ever witnessed; in another it was the most
cerebral. The nervous excitement manifested by these two was
so free from traditional sentimentality and normal passion, so
dominated by a certain cold-blooded and elemental lechery, that
something in the fibrous interstices of the old tree against which
they leaned was aroused by it and responded to it.

And so when they forsook that ledge of muddy ground between
the confederate tree and the dark water, it was not only with
relaxed nerves and an absolute sense of mutual understanding,
it was with a dim awareness of some strange virtue having passed
into them. Lingering behind the girl for a moment the man
pressed his forehead against that indented willow trunk and murmured a certain favourite formula of his, relating to his dead
mother. After that, taking up his oars and boat-hook, he followed
the girl along the river bank. It did not take them long now to
reach Alder Dyke.

Alder Dyke! Alder Dyke! It was not marigold stalks nor the
smell of dough. It was alder boughs that brought Tom Barter
and that unknown ecstasy into the arteries of his soul! He made
a fumbling forward movement with his arms as he touched these
alders, as if welcoming a living person, and Mary divined,
merely from the look of his lean vagabond's back, that some new
emotion, entirely unconnected with her, had taken possession of
him. When he dived into the mass of entangled boughs he
plunged his hands into it and only after pressing an armful of

rough twigs against his mouth and cheeks did he turn his head towards her. Any ordinary girl would have been disturbed by the nature of the crazy sound he now made to express his feelings and to summon his mate to enjoy Alder Dyke with him! It was more like the whinnying of a wild horse than anything else and yet it was not as loud as that; nor was it really an animal sound any more than it was a human sound. It was the sort of sound that this thick bed of alders itself might have emitted when tossed and rocked and torn by some fierce buffetting of the March winds. Instead of getting angry with him or thinking to herself "Who is this man I have given myself to?" instead in fact of *thinking* anything at all, Mary simply put down her basket, and ran hastily to his side. Without a word she threw her arms round his neck and pressed her lips against his cold leaf-smelling cheek. An alder twig had chanced to scratch his skin and the girl tasted now the saltish taste of spilt blood. John's cap had been already switched from his head by his dive into the mass of boughs, and Mary instinctively snatched off her own hat. Thus they swayed together for a minute like two wild ponies who in joy bite furiously at each other's necks. Then, using all his strength, though she was nearly as tall as he, he lifted her up and trampling forward like a centaur with a human burden plunged headlong deeper and deeper among those twisted branches.

When he reached the banks of the deep ditch itself he turned towards its mouth, and after an angry and tender struggle to keep the twigs from striking the girl's face, emerged triumphantly at a grassy open space where the Dyke ran into the river. There lay the boat he was looking for, moored by a padlocked chain to a stake in the ground, its rudder embedded in mud, its bottom full of dark rain-water. He put the girl down and the two stood side by side staring into the boat.

"It . . . rather . . . wants . . . bailing," gasped Mary.

John was too much out of breath to make any comment but he glanced at her with a furtive look, half shame, half pride, and his lips twitched into a wry smile.

"I'll look," she cried, jumping into the boat. "You stay where you are for a while, John."

He saw her pass quickly to the stern, stepping from seat to

seat. Then she stooped down and began feeling about in the bottom of the boat. "Here we are!" she cried, holding up a big tin cup. "Now don't you move, John, please, till I've got some of this water out."

He sat still, watching her, hugging his knees and his hands.

"It smells very fishy down here!" she cried. He saw her make a sudden face of disgust and scoop with her hands in the bilge-water under the stern seat. "Ugh! It's the head of an eel." She threw something far into the river, where it sank with a splash.

"I'd sooner be an eel than a worm," he muttered, and the soul within him sensitized by love-making flung forth an obscure prayer across the flowing stream. Over the level Norfolk pastures it went; over the wide fens and the deep dykes, until it came to the sea-banks of the North Sea. Here John's prayer left the earth altogether and shooting outward, beyond the earth's atmosphere, beyond the whole stellar system, just as if it had been an arrow shot from the Bow of Sagittarius the Centaur, reached the heart of his dead mother where she dwelt in the invisible world. "Don't let me ever compete with anyone!" his prayer said. "If I'm a worm and no man, let me enjoy my life as a worm. Let me stop showing off to anyone; even to Mary! Let me live my own life free from the .opinions, good or bad, of all other people! Now that I've found Mary, let me want nothing else!"

He continued to watch his new-found mate bailing out the dark rain-water from the bottom of the boat. "This is our home," he thought. "With the smell of Alder Dyke in our souls we'll defy Glastonbury and Philip together! Our ancestors got their bread from the fens and we'll get our bread from Glastonbury and then come home, home to Alder Dyke! We won't compete with anyone. We'll live our own life free from them all! If we are Alder Dyke eels, let us remain so! If we're worms of Norfolk mud, let us remain so! Eels and worms can suck the breasts of life as well as any of them. What does anything matter as long as Mary's alive and I'm alive; and we're not divided?"

"Are you feeling all right now, John? I'm not going to bail all day, I can tell you!"

The tone of her voice delighted him. It was an earthy tone, like the sound of a horse's hoof on springy turf. He had a peculiar sensation as if he could mount up on that tone of hers as on a flight of mossy stone steps.

Extracting the key from his pocket he now unlocked the boat and they were soon in midstream. "Don't let's row, John," she said. "I'm tired and you've exhausted yourself carrying me. Let's drift with the tide!"

She seated herself in the stern and took possession of the rudder lines. John, holding the oars in the rowlocks at an upraised angle, placed himself opposite to her. Thus she steered the boat and stared gravely forward past his face; while he, balancing the blades of the oars above the water, watched every flicker of her expression, as a look-out man on a ship watches the horizon of all his hopes.

The river weeds, below the tide that bore them on, gleamed emerald green in the warm sunshine. Across and between the weeds darted shoals of glittering dace, their swaying bodies sometimes silver white and sometimes slippery black as they turned and twisted, rose and sank, hovered and flashed by. Beds of golden marigolds reflected their bright cups in the swift water; and here and there, against the brownish clumps of last year's reeds, they caught passing glimpses of pale, delicate-tinged cuckoo flowers. Every now and then they would come upon a group of hornless Norfolk cattle, their brown and white backs, bent heads, and noble udders giving to the whole scene an air of enchanted passivity through which the boat passed forward on its way, as if the quiet pastures and solemn cattle were the dream of some very old god into which the gleaming river and the darting fish entered by a sort of violence, as the dream of a younger and more restless immortal.

"Don't you think, Mary, that there was something rather touching about the way that young Spear hummed and hawed last night, trying to express his ideas?"

"Look out, John! Look out! Push with your left! No, the other one. . . . *Damn!*"

He rose to his feet and shoved the prow of the boat round a muddy promontory. "Can't you do it by steering?"

"No, I can't. Keep your oars down a bit. No! Closer to the water! Give a pull now as I tell you."

He took his seat again and tried to obey her.

"With your left, now!" she cried. "Your left! Your left! Don't you know your left hand from your right?" She loved him for being so clumsy. She loved him for not knowing his left hand from his right. And yet these things irritated her so much that she could have boxed his ears. She would have liked to hit him. She would have liked to throw her arms round his neck and kiss him, after she had hit him!

"Don't you think it *was* rather pathetic, the way he talked? I didn't like him at first. I thought he was a bully. But I came round to him in the end."

"You didn't like Cousin Percy much. I could see *that*!" said Mary.

He was silent for a second, frowning. Then he struck the water with the flat of one of his oars. "Only because she's in love with Philip!" he cried. "That young Spear is what you English call a decent chap and that girl is out for making him a cuckold."

"I think Percy is sweet," said Mary. "She can't help being attractive to men. She's attractive to *you*, my dear, or you wouldn't be so cross with her."

"She's a fatal girl," muttered John Crow.

"What did you call her?"

"*Fatal.* And that's what she is. She's the most dangerous type of all. If *she* goes down to Glastonbury there'll be the devil to pay. I could see Cousin Tilly had her eye on her . . . and Aunt Elizabeth too."

"It's interesting you should concern yourself so much about Dave," said Mary. "I expect he reminds you of that boy Barter," she added.

John gazed at her in astonishment.

"What a little witch you are! God! I must be careful what thoughts cross my mind when I'm with you."

"Now I must tell him," Mary said to herself. "This is the moment to tell him." It was really beginning to amount to something grotesque, this inability of hers to explain that she knew

Tom Barter well and had often been to tea with him in a little tea-shop near the Pilgrims' Inn in the Glastonbury High Street.

She dropped the rudder-lines and clasped her fingers in her lap. "Row now, will you, John? And I'm not going to steer you either. I'm going to have a cigarette."

Her instinct was always to smoke a cigarette at any serious crisis in her life. She lit one now, and out of the midst of a cloud of smoke she made the plunge. "I believe I know your friend Tom Barter," she said. Damn! Why must her voice take that funny tone? "I believe he works in one of Philip's factories. I believe it's your friend; but of course it *may* not be. He's got lodgings next to the Pilgrims' Inn."

Like an experienced fox who hears the dogs in the distance and automatically takes to the hedge, a deep self-preservative instinct in John, a male friend-preservative instinct, made him say hurriedly, "Do you really think it's the same? I don't believe it can be. Tom Barter used to go for endless long walks collecting birds' eggs. Does yours do that? If he doesn't go on long walks alone he's not the same!"

She surrounded her smooth, dark head with smoke that went trailing in spiral wisps down the water-track behind them. "I like Tom very much," she said, scrupulously weighing her words. "There are few people down there that I like better."

They both looked away from each other at the darkly massed woods which terminated the shining meadows on their right.

"It's the aspen poplars that give this scenery its character," he remarked sententiously. "Those rounded masses of foliage, seen across absolutely level fields, and growing in great wild scattered clumps too; they give the whole place a park-like look; and yet it's a neglected, untidy park. Woods on flat ground look much larger and more mysterious than woods on hillsides. Don't you think so?"

He wanted above everything else to keep their conversation away from Tom Barter but the harder he tried to do this the closer to him did the friend of his boyhood come. The darting dace cried out "Tom Barter!" as they flashed through the water. The dazzling sun-gleams upon the surface of the current danced

to a jig of that name. The long swaying weeds laughed languish-
ingly and coquettishly, "Tom, Tom! Come back to us, Tom!"

"Yes, my dear," he continued, "we can't get away from the
fact that we Crows are plain sea-faring Danes, settled for centuries as simple working farmers in the Isle of Ely. We haven't
the goodness of the Saxon, nor the power of the Norman, nor
the imagination of the Celt. We are run-down adventurers; that's
what we are; run-down adventurers; who haven't the gall to steal,
nor the stability to work."

Mary threw her cigarette into the river and resumed her hold
of the rudder lines. "Row a bit, John," she said.

He let his oars sink into the water and commenced pulling
with long furious strokes. He began now to feel a longing to
make love to her again; and in his vicious cold-blooded manner,
like the depravity of a weather-beaten tramp, he began telling
himself stories of exactly *how* he would do this as soon as he
could create the opportunity.

The girl felt at once glad and sorry that she had told him
about Tom Barter. If the sun-sparkles on the water and the shining green weeds were voluble of Tom her girl's heart was heavy
with him.

The whole matter of Barter was a grievous wedge in the sweet
pith of her peace at that moment. She did so love her companion,
as she watched his deep-drawn breathing and noted his pathetic
attempts at feathering with his oars. She loved the way his
knuckles looked as he pulled. She loved the whiteness of his
wrists and even the frayed, travel-stained cuffs of his shirt. She
loved the extraordinary faces he made when the oar got entangled in the weeds! She too began, in her girl's way, but quite
as subnormal a way as his own, to long to be made love to again.
And then at last, so deep was the psychic similarity between
them, they both fell silent; and in their silence, set themselves
to pray to the First Cause that their love might have a happy
future.

They prayed to this unknown Ultimate, out of their hollow
boat, above that gleaming current, so simultaneously and so
intensely, that the magnetism of their prayer shot like a meteorite
out of the earth's planetary atmosphere. Something about its

double origin, and something about the swift and translucent water from which it started on its flight, drove it forward beyond the whole astronomical world, and beyond the darkness enclosing that world, till it reached the primal Cause of all life.

What happens when such a wild-goose, heart-furious arrow of human wanting touches that portion of the First Cause's awareness that encircles the atmospheric circumference of the earth? So many other organisms throughout the stellar constellations and throughout the higher dimensions are unceasingly crying out to this Primordial Power, that it can obviously only offer to the supplications of our planet a limited portion of its magnetic receptivity. And again, as all earth dwellers discover only too quickly, it Itself is divided against Itself in those ultimate regions of primal causation. Its primordial goodness warring forever against its primordial evil holds life up only by vast excess of energy and by oceans of lavish waste. Even though the cry of a particular creature may reach the First Cause, there is always a danger of its being intercepted by the evil will of this vast Janus-faced Force. Down through the abysses of ether, away from the central nucleus of this dualistic Being, descend through the darkness that is beyond the world two parallel streams of magnetic force, one good and one evil; and it is these undulating streams of vibration, resembling infinite spider webs blown about upon an eternal wind, that bring luck or ill luck to the creature praying. The best time for any human being to pray to the First Cause if he wants his prayers to have a prosperous issue is one or other of the Two Twilights; either the twilight preceding the dawn or the twilight following the sunset. Human prayers that are offered up at noon are often intercepted by the Sun—for all creative powers are jealous of one another—and those that are offered up at midnight are liable to be waylaid by the Moon in her seasons or by the spirit of some thwarting planet. It is a natural fact that these Two Twilights are propitious to psychic intercourse with the First Cause while other hours are malignant and baleful. It is also a natural fact, known to very few, that many of the prayers offered to the First Cause by living organisms in their desperation are answered by less powerful but much more pitiful divinities. Priests of our race, wise in the art of prayer, are wont

to advise us to pray to these lesser powers rather than to the
First Cause; and they are wise in this advice. For whereas the evil
in the First Cause is only partially overcome by the good, in
some of these "little gods" there is hardly any evil at all. They
are all compact of magical pity and vibrant tenderness. It happened by ill luck on this particular occasion that the prayer to
their Creator offered up by John Crow and by Mary Crow in
their open boat on the Wissey in Norfolk aroused a response not
in the good will of this ultimate Personality, but in Its evil will.
Neither John nor Mary was aware that if a human being prays
at noonday or at midnight it is better to pray to the Sun or the
Moon rather than to the First Cause. Chance led them to pray
on this occasion almost exactly at twelve o'clock; and although
their prayer reached its destination unintercepted by any other
power, it lost itself, not in the ultimate good, but in the ultimate
evil. . . .

Was it a dim intimation of this that led John to redouble his
furious strokes as he rowed their boat down the Wissey? The
sweat began to pour down his face as he tugged at those long
oars and his mouth, open now and twisted awry, began to resemble the fixed contorted lineaments of an antique tragic mask.

Mary was divided in her mind whether to call to him to stop
or to let him alone until he stopped of his own accord. Assisted
by wind and tide as well as propelled by his desperate efforts,
the boat shot forward now with an incredible speed. The girl
had grown by this time more skilful with the rudder lines. John,
in the tension of his rowing, kept more even time than he had
done before. Thus, though their speed was much greater, they
seemed to avoid the beds of reeds at the river curves, and the
shallows opposite the deeper pools, and the floating masses of cut
weeds that they overtook, with much greater facility, than when
they were casually drifting.

"I'll make him stop in a minute!" she kept saying to herself;
and then something in the very effort they both were making,
he to row and she to steer, something almost religious in their
united tension, compelled her to concentrate upon what she was
doing and to hold her peace. Past deep, muddy estuaries the boat
shot forward, where the marigolds grew so thick as to resemble

heaps of scattered gold, flung out for largesse from some royal
barge, past groups of tall lombardy poplars, their proud tops
bowing gently away from the wind, past long-maned and long-
tailed horses who rushed to look at them as they shot by, their
liquid eyes filled with entranced curiosity, past little farm-
houses with great, sloping red roofs, past massive cattle-sheds
tiled with those large, curved, brick tiles so characteristic of East
Anglia, past sunlit gaps in majestic woods through whose clearings tall, flint church towers could be seen in the far distance,
past huge black windmills, their great arms glittering in the sun
as they turned, grinding white flour for the people of Norfolk,
past all these the boat darted forward, rowed, it seemed, by one
relentless will-power and steered by another. And as he swung
his arms forth and back, repeating his monotonous strokes with
grim pantings and with a glazed, unseeing look in his eyes, it
seemed to John as if merely by making this blind quixotic effort
he was on the way to insure a happy issue for their love.

He had prayed to the First Cause and the superstitious idea took
possession of him that the longer he kept up this struggle the
more likely he was to get a favourable answer.

He was indeed a good deal more exhausted already than his
coxswain had any notion of. If she had not been compelled to
concentrate her attention on rounding the river curves she would
have marked how pale his lips were growing; but she too was
wrought up to a queer hypnosis of blind tension. Every now and
then she would cry out, "Right, John!" or "Left, quick! Left!
I tell you," but apart from these brusque words she remained as
silent as he.

One effect this nervous madness had. It united them as nothing
else could have done. The longer this tension lasted the closer
these two beings drew together. Casual amorists have indeed no
notion of the world-deep sensuality of united physical labour.
More than anything else this can give to a man and a girl a mysterious unity. Nothing in their sweetest and most vicious love-
making had brought these two nearer to becoming one flesh than
did this ecstatic toil.

It may be that a blind instinct had already warned them that
their prayer to the Living God had only stirred up the remorse-

less malice in that Creator-Destroyer's heart. Whether this were so or not, it is certain now that some obscure and lonely fury in them turned upon that tremendous First Cause, and deliberately and recklessly defied it! The two of them were alone on that Norfolk river, a man and a woman, with the same grandmother and the same grandfather, with the same grandparents in a steady line, going back to Agincourt and Crécy, going back to all the yeomen of England, to all the sturdy wenches of England, to all the John Crows and Mary Crows that fill so many church-yards in the Isle of Ely unto this day.

The silver-scaled dace and red-finned roach that their swift movement disturbed seemed actually to pursue this furiously speeding boat. The quivering poplars seemed to bow down their proud tops to watch these two; the cattle lifted their heads to gaze at them as they swept by; beneath air-region after air-region of tremulous lark-music they flashed and glittered for-ward; water-rats fled into their mud-burrows or plopped with a gurgling, sucking sound under the swirling eddies that their boat made; moor-hens flapped across their way with weak, harsh cries; small, greenish-coloured, immature pike, motionless like drowned sticks in the sunny shallows, shot blindly into the middle of the river and were lost in the weeds. The prolonged struggle of these two with the boat and with the water became in a very intimate sense their marriage day upon earth. By his salt-tasting sweat and by her wrought-up passion of guiding, these two "run-down adventurers" plighted their troth for the rest of their days. They plighted it in defiance of the whole universe and of whatever was beyond the universe; and they were aware of no idealisa-tion of each other. They clung to each other with a grim, vicious, indignant resolve to enjoy a sensuality of oneness; a sensuality of unity snatched out of the drifting flood of space and time. It was not directed to anything beyond itself, this desire of theirs. It was innocent of any idea of offspring. It was an absolute, fortified and consecrated by the furious efforts they were making, by the diamond-bright sparkles upon the broken water, by the sullen clicking of the rowlocks.

John had begun to count now. "I'll stop after twenty more strokes," he thought. But when the last of the twenty came, and

he found in the beating pulse of his exhaustion an undreamed-of
nerve of renewal, he did *not* stop. The dazzling spouts of water
drops which followed his oars, each time he drew them from the
water, mingled now with a renewed counting. "Ten . . . eleven
. . . twelve . . . thirteen . . . fourteen . . . fifteen . . ." Those
rhythmic, up-flung splashes of dancing crystal, stirred and subsiding amid the long emerald-green weeds, became the thudding
reverberation of his own unconquerable heartbeats. These again
became triumphant figures of victory, of victory over nature,
over custom, over fate. "Sixteen . . . seventeen . . . eighteen
. . . nine——"

He never reached his second twenty. Disturbed by the appearance of a living javelin of blue fire, flung forth from a muddy
ditch, darting, like a gigantic dragon-fly, down the surface of
the river in front of them and vanishing round a bend of the
bank, Mary gave a startled pull to her left rudder string; and
the prow of the boat, veering in midstream, shot with a queer
sound, like a sound of snarling and sobbing, straight into the
overhung mouth of the weedy estuary, out of which the kingfisher had flown!

John fell forward over his own knees with a groan. His shoulders heaved silently under his heavy sob-drawn breathing. He was
lost to everything except the necessity of finding free and unim-
peded breath.

Mary sat quietly on where she was. "I'll go to him in a minute," she thought. "Better let him get his breath first." She could
not see his face. She could see nothing but his head and his
knees. But she knew, without seeing it, that his face was quite
hideously contorted. She noticed that something wet was falling
down from his face upon the plank under his feet. She peered
forward and stared morbidly into the darkness at his feet. Was
blood dripping from his mouth? "Dear God!" she cried in her
heart, "Have I killed him by my foolishness?" The cry was
followed by such a wave of love for him that she could hardly
bear it and remain passive any longer. She wanted to throw her
arms round him and press his head against her thin chest. This
feeling was followed by another one of an egoistic tightness and
self-pity. "It would be just like my fate," she thought, "just like

the way everything has happened to me all my life, if he has consumption and this has given him a hemorrhage."

She remained rigid, her heart beating, holding herself in by an effort of the will. At last his breath became quieter. For a few seconds after that, his head seemed to sink helplessly down. It looked almost as if it would touch the plank between his knees. The oars, still clutched tight in his hands, stood up at a grotesque angle. "Are you all right, John?" she whispered at last.

He did lift his head at that and smiled at her, drawing a deep sigh. "Ex-hausted," he murmured. "I was a fool to go on so long."

"Lean back a bit in the boat," she said. He tried to obey her and she got up on her feet and crossing over to him took the oars from the rowlocks and laid them side by side. As she did this she thought to herself: "John and I are one now. Nothing in those hateful Ruins will be able to divide us now."

She helped him to lie down on his back in the prow of the boat with his arms extended along its sides and with his head against the acute angle of its wooden bow. "Give me the flask, my sweet!" he murmured.

His overcoat was in the stern and she had to move once more down the whole length of the boat to get it. As he watched her doing this a most delicious languor rippled through him like a warm tide. Something weak and clinging in his nature derived a special satisfaction at that moment from being tended by this girl. "She is what I've waited for all my days."

After he'd drunk the whiskey Mary began to wonder whether she ought to suggest their having their lunch here in this kingfisher ditch. She was secretly very averse to doing so. In her mind's eye, all that morning, she had pictured herself spreading out a Virgilian repast on mossy grass and under great trees for herself and her lover. Anyway it would be much nicer to leave this ill-smelling boat for a time and stretch their legs on the land.

"I'm going to explore the neighbourhood," she said at last, getting up upon the seat where he had been rowing, and seizing a willow branch wherewith to pull the side of the boat nearer the bank. In the glow and relaxation which he enjoyed just then her figure, standing there above him in the flickering shade of the branch she held, gathered to itself that sort of romance which of all things had always stirred him most. Both sun and shadow lay across her brown hair, parted in the middle and drawn back to a rough, simple knot, and upon her plain dress, and upon her sturdy peasant-girl ankles.

"Very good, you beautiful creature!" he murmured. "You might give me a cigarette out of my greatcoat before you go. I'm too comfortable to move."

She jumped down with alacrity, gave him cigarettes and matches, and then stepping lightly for a second on the side of the boat sprang to the bank. "You won't go to sleep and let it drift out, will you? It's fast in the mud; but you don't think I ought to tie it to the tree?"

"You run off and explore, my pretty one!" he said. "I'll deal with the boat." When she was gone he thought to himself, "It's the way she parts her hair and pulls it back and twists it, that I like so well. Who would have guessed that I'd find her like this the first minute I got to my native land?" He frowned a little and then closed his eyes. Though it was warm enough to be May rather than March, it was too early for that confusing murmur of insects which is the usual background for a hot afternoon. When the rustling of her steps died away an incredible silence descended on the place. The newborn reeds were too young to play with the flowing river. The noon had become afternoon. The larks were silent. The fish had ceased to rise. There were no swallows yet and the few spring flies that hovered over that weedy ditch were safe from attack whether from the firmament above or the firmament below. The only sound that reached his ears was the sound of a faint trickle of water which came from some infinitesimal ledge in the bank above his head and fell down drop by drop into the ditch. Not a breath of wind stirred. Not a leaf-bud quivered. Not a grass-blade swayed. There was only that elfin waterfall and, except for that, the very earth herself seemed to have fallen asleep. "This is Norfolk," he said to himself, and in that intense, indrawn silence some old atavistic affiliation with fen-ditches and fen-water and fen-peat tugged at his soul and pulled it earthward. And there came to his nostrils, as he lay with his eyes shut, a far-flung, acrid, aromatic smell. It was not the smell of mud, or leaf-buds, or grass-roots, or cattle-droppings, or ditch-water. It was not the smell of last night's rain, or of the sleeping south wind. It reached him independent of the eel slime that still clung about the bottom of the boat. It was the smell of East Anglia itself. It was the smell to greet which, on uncounted spring mornings, his Isle-of-Ely ancestors had left their beds and opened their back doors! It was the smell that had come wandering over the water-meadows on afternoons like this, to the drowsy heads of innumerable John Crows, resting from their ploughing with their ale mugs in their blistered hands, and their minds running on ewes and lambs and on bawdy Cambridge taverns! A fleeting thought of what lay before him in Glastonbury no sooner touched his mind than he flung it away as Mary had flung the eel's head.

He made a feeble attempt to recall the subtle idea which he had had when he prayed to his mother under the alders, but he could only remember the part about never "competing." "Compete?" he thought vaguely. "What does 'compete' mean?" At that moment there seemed nothing in the world comparable to allowing sleep to steal through and become one with him, just as this tinkling rivulet he listened to lost itself in the body of this ditch. But all the while, though he kept yielding to these invasions of sleep, he could not give himself up to it to the point of losing his consciousness. Every now and then, when his eyelids still unclosed a little, he saw a drooping willow shoot trailing in the ditch beside him. Its extremity seen through the water was different from the upper part of it seen through the air; and as something in him refused to yield to unconsciousness, he came by degrees to identify himself with this trailing shoot. There was a queer imperative upon him not to sink any deeper into sweet oblivion. There was an imperative upon him to remember his vow about "competing." This "never competing" became identified with the slow swirl of the ditch stream as it made tiny ripples round the suspended shoot. He was *allowed*, he dimly felt, to enjoy his paradisiac lassitude, as long as he, this being who was partly John Crow and partly a willow shoot, kept these ripples in mind. All these phenomena made up a complete world, and in this world he was fulfilling all his moral obligations and fulfilling them with a delicious sense of virtue merely by keeping these ripples in mind; and the drip-drop, drip-drop of the tinkling rivulet at his elbow was the voice of the queer imperative which he obeyed.

A moor-hen propelling herself in quaint jerks past this willow shoot towards the river was so startled by confronting the face of a man staring with flickering eyelids down into the water that she rose with a scream and flapped off heavily into the rushes. This aroused John, who in a moment forgot altogether the imperative of the tinkling rivulet; and, clutching the edge of the boat with numb sleep-swollen fingers, raised his neck like a turtle and pricked up his ears to listen for his girl's return.

It was under a great ash tree in the centre of a neighbouring field that they finally had their lunch.

"Why didn't you stand up to Philip more if you disliked him so?" she asked when their meal was over and they were recalling last night's gathering. His face worked expressively before the words came out in answer, a curious pulse appearing in his cheeks at the corner of his nostrils and a certain twitching round his cheek-bones. It was a facial peculiarity not quite the same as that of Miss Elizabeth Crow; and yet it was evidently a family trait. Touching in the women, and no doubt often a signal of danger in the men, this facial sign, like a well-worn coin, must have frequently, in the last three or four hundred years, gone to Norwich for the fair, gone to Cambridge to buy books and silk dresses, appeared in the depths of old-fashioned looking-glasses, above mahogany chests of drawers, before the pushing open of innumerable ivy-shadowed front-bedroom windows to watch visitors come over the home-meadows. It must often have been the last of all their possessions that they were forced to leave behind, when, like William Crow on this beautiful March day, they lay with six feet of East Anglian clay above them!

It appeared now indeed more emphatically than Mary had ever seen it in any of her relative's faces except once when she had asked her grandfather at breakfast, as he dreamily looked out over that smooth secluded lawn, what the word "whore" meant.

"I'll tell you exactly why!" John Crow cried, seizing a clump of soft moss, just beyond where his overcoat extended, with excited fingers. "It's for a reason that I wouldn't tell anyone in the world but you. It's because I've long ago decided always to yield to my cowardice. I was afraid of Philip the moment I saw him. I hated him; but that's another matter. Something in his personality frightens me. I could have struggled against it and made myself say a lot of things. I thought of plenty of them. But it's become a principle with me to yield to my fear of people. I propitiate them, or I'm silent, or I avoid them."

Mary looked at him very earnestly.

"Have you ever loved anyone you were afraid of?"

"You mean a woman?"

She nodded.

"I tell you I've never loved anyone; though of course I've *made* love to endless women. Oh, yes! Yes! It would kill my love to be afraid. Not at once, but by inches and inches. Oh, yes! If I ever got thoroughly afraid of anyone in the end I should stop loving them."

She lowered her eyes and remained silent for a moment. Then she cried with a kind of quivering fierceness, "I won't have you *dare* ever to be afraid of me, *John*!"

He looked at her sharply. There was a note in her voice that he had not heard before. It was the danger-note of the female, beyond reason, *against* reason.

"Why not?" he asked.

She turned away her head and looked across the wide, flat meadow at the Wissey bank, making no reply. A soft gust of south wind stirred the lighter branches of the ash above them. The cold, thin, smooth, grey twigs, with their clean, black buds, moved solemnly up and down like classic dancers.

"Shall I be pleased with Glastonbury?" he asked after a pause.

"I believe you'll feel just as I do, John, about Glastonbury. You'll hate the sentimentality that has been spread over everything there, like scented church-lamp oil! You'll hate the visitors. You'll hate the tradesmen catering for the visitors; you'll hate the sickening superstition of the whole thing."

"I hate it now, quite sufficiently," he interrupted. "Simply because Philip's there. Oh, I wish ——" He became so pensive that she did not like to break into his thought. "I wish, Mary, that you'd leave Glastonbury and try and find something of . . . of the same kind . . . whatever it is . . . that you do . . . somewhere round here."

She smiled a broad, amused smile, showing all her strong white teeth.

"How funny!" she murmured. "Why, my dearest, I can't do anything! You don't seem to realize that I've only been on my own for a couple of years; and before that I did nothing at all but look after Mother."

"Where did you live?"

"In Thorpe, near Norwich. Mother's buried in Thorpe. She couldn't leave me anything because she lived on her pension." Mary's eyes opened very wide as she spoke of her mother. No tears came into them. They just opened very wide, with a curious, self-conscious movement of the facial muscles.

"It was Philip of course who got me the place," she went on. "Miss Drew is some sort of a connection of Tilly's." She leaned forward now, and stretching out her hand caught hold of his foot. "John, my dear John," she said with extreme and childish gravity, "will you really walk all the way to Glastonbury?"

"I shall start very early tomorrow," he replied, "and I expect I'll see you again in ten days. I suppose it will be all right to send you a postcard when I get there? I shall anyway have a penny left to buy that with."

Mary jumped to her feet, and gave her skirts a vigorous shake. His question restored to her with a healthy rush her abrupt woman-of-action quality.

"Yes," she said, "send me a card. Miss Drew, the Abbey House, is the address. You won't forget that? You can think of the Ruins for the Abbey part, and you can think of 'screw' for the rest. 'You,' 'screw,' *Drew*!" and she laughed uneasily.

John slowly pulled up his legs and got upon his feet. The hard, cautious, furtive look of a tramp was upon his face now. "Will . . . you . . . really . . . be able . . . to help me . . . keep body and soul together . . . when I get there?" And then shooting at her a completely impersonal look, as if she were a housemaid hiring him to chop wood, "How often does she pay you?" he asked.

But Mary was totally undisturbed by this revelation of the lower self of her lover. Indeed she looked pleased. "Every month," she replied with shining eyes. "It's my pocket-money, you know."

Her pleasure at the ungentlemanly turn he had given to the conversation brought such a glow to her cheeks and such a smile to her lips that she became for a moment really beautiful. He rushed up to her and caught her in his arms. Long and long did he caress her under that confederate ash tree. "You're a hama-dryad—that's what you are!" he kept repeating. "You're a hamadryad!"

Every girl lives so constantly in the imaginative atmosphere of being made love to that even the most ignorant of them is rarely shocked or surprised. It is the material consequences that they dread, not moral remorse or any idea that they are allowing what is wrong. John's way of love-making might, however, have easily palled on a more passionate nature than Mary's; for he was not only profoundly corrupt but extremely egoistic, touching her and holding her in the manner that most excited his own childishly fantastic imagination and never asking himself whether this was what suited her, nor for one second forgetting himself in any rush of tempestuous tenderness. But Mary, as though she really *were* a hamadryad, who had known the shamelessness of hundreds of whimsical satyrs, treated the whole thing with grave, sweet, indulgent passivity. Something in her kindred nature, some wil-low-rooted, fen-country perversity, seemed to need just this pro-tracted cerebral courtship to stir the essential coldness of her blood and nerves. One quaint feeling often came to her, in the oddest moments of his "sweet usage," namely, that he was one of her old, faded, wooden *dolls*; yes, the most dilapidated and in-jured of all four which used to belong to her, come to life again, but this time full of queer, hardly human exactions that she would willingly prostitute herself for hours and hours to satisfy, so long as she could hear those wooden joints creak and groan in their joy.

They both knew they were safe from interruption. Children of generations of fen-country life, they were well aware how far safer for lovers is the great, wide, flat expanse of grass-meadows, than any thickly grown copse or spinney, where an enemy can easily approach unseen.

Emanations of sympathy were not lacking from the vast, smooth tree, with its upward-clutching branch-ends, though they were of a different kind from those of that aged denizen of Dye's Hole. They both knew well that after the heavy effort of getting the boat back against the current to Alder Dyke, there would be little chance for more than a few kisses before they separated for their unknown future; and this made them loath to cease their play. But the rôle the ash tree served was to bring to them in the midst of their dalliance with incredible vividness the image of their grandfather. Both of them saw clearly in their mind's eye the well-known head of their grandfather, covered with thick curly hair, "as white as wool," with his patient servants sitting in a row on the red-leather dining-room chairs and with his life-weary, King-of-Thule eyes in their hollow eye-sockets, lowered over the page, as with his classic-actor's voice beautifully modulated to the occasion, he intoned one of the poet Cowper's hymns.

The language of trees is even more remote from human intelligence than the language of beasts or of birds. What to these lovers, for instance, would the singular syllables "wuther-quotle-glug" have signified?

"It is extraordinary that we should ever have met!" These words, uttered by John in a moment of relaxed gratefulness, struck the attention of that solitary ash tree in Water-ditch Field with what in trees corresponds to human irony. Five times in its life of a hundred and thirty years had the ash tree of Water-ditch Field heard those words uttered by living organisms. An old horse had uttered them in its own fashion when it rubbed its nose against a young companion's polished flanks. An eccentric fisherman had uttered them addressing an exceptionally large chub which he had caught and killed. A mad clergyman had uttered them about a gipsy girl who did not know of his existence. An old maiden lady had uttered them to the spirit of her only lover, dead fifty years before; and finally, but twelve months ago, William Crow himself had uttered them; uttered them in the grateful, attentive and astonished ears of Mr. Geard of Glastonbury!

All this the ash tree noted; but its vegetative comment thereon

would only have sounded in human ears like the gibberish:
wuther-quotle-glug.

The afternoon had by now advanced far. Long, orange-coloured rays of light fell horizontally across the flat meadow. The
shadow of the ash tree grew dark and cool as a stone-covered
spring. From the ditch where their boat was moored came the sunset melody of a blackbird, full, as that bird's song at that hour
always is, of some withheld secret in nature beyond human sorrow and human joy. Sadly they gathered up the remains of their
feast and retraced their steps to the boat.

Their row back to Alder Dyke against the current was, as they
had anticipated, no light task. Armed with the boat-hook, Mary
at first stood upright in the stern and punted with all her strength
while John stubbornly rowed; but as time went on she became
conscious that they were advancing so slowly that something else
would have to be done.

"Let me sit by your side, John," she said at last, "and both of
us row."

She came over from the prow of the boat and sat down by him,
taking possession of the oar upon his left. In this position, each
pulling at a separate oar, but with elbows and shoulders touching
and their four feet pressing against the same stretcher they
rowed home.

"What is my address, John?" she said, letting the blade of her
oar rest flat upon the water when they reached Alder Dyke.

"Care of Miss Drew, the Abbey House, Glastonbury, Somerset." Thus came his answer quietly and grimly enough; but the
girl had a shrewd and bitter knowledge that, if only their hands
had not at that moment been clutching those heavy oar-handles,
he could easily—when once this simple lesson had been properly
repeated—have let his twitching cheek sink against her small
cold breasts and burst into a fit of convulsive, childish, unreason-
able sobbing.

As HE PLODDED ALONG THE HEDGELESS WHITE ROAD OVER SAL-
isbury Plain John Crow became acquainted with aspects of bodily
and mental suffering till that epoch totally unrevealed to him.
He felt very tired and although he had been lucky, during the
whole of his tramp, with regard to rain, he had been unlucky with
regard to cold. He had indeed endured eight days of exceptionally cold weather and now as he moved forward with the idea of
reaching Stonehenge before dark the thought of having to sleep
again, as he had done ever since he left Didcot, in some sort of
draughty cattle-shed or behind an exposed haystack made him
shiver through every bone of his exhausted body. A warm bed
ran in his mind, a bed like the one to which he had treated himself at Maidenhead, which had one of its brass knobs missing;
and an excellent supper ran in his mind of potatoes and cabbage
such as he had enjoyed in that Maidenhead tavern before sleeping. His overcoat was heavy, his bag was heavy, and what was
worse, one of his heels had got blistered, so that for the last
twelve hours, ever since he had left Andover at dawn, walking
had been a misery to him. He had only eightpence left. This had
to last him till he reached Glastonbury; so bed and supper tonight were quite out of the question. He had got a pot of tea and
a roll and butter at Salisbury and he had still a couple of Social
biscuits and a piece of cheese wrapped up in his pocket. He also
possessed unopened a packet of Navy Cut cigarettes. "I wonder
what these Workhouses are like?" he thought. "I suppose the
officials are bullies; I suppose a person's always in danger of
getting lice. No, I must find a shed or something; but I'm going
to see Stonehenge first."

John Crow had never in his life known a road more bleak and
unfrequented than the one he was now traversing over Salisbury
Plain. He knew that the sun had just sunk below the horizon
though its actual shape was invisible. It had been totally obscured by clouds for an hour at least before it sank; but soon

after its disappearance the north wind which had been his fellow-traveller ever since he left Salisbury dispersed some of these clouds and swept the sky a little clearer. It was clearer, but it was still grey with a greyness that was positively ashen. The difference between the pallor of the road, which was sad with a recognised human sadness and this ashen grey sky overhead was in some way disturbing to his mind. He kept staring at the sky as he dragged his blistered foot forward. Every step he took caused him pain and if the sadness of the road was congenial to this pain, the appearance of the sky was intimately adjusted to it. The north wind which had followed him from Salisbury and had kept on whistling between his cap and his coat collar was not hateful to him. He had almost got attached to its company. Once or twice when he rested, sitting under walls or under hedges, he found himself missing its sullen monotone. Why the juxtaposition of this particular cap and this particular coat collar should cause the wind to hum and drone and sometimes almost to scream in his ear was a puzzle to him. But this north wind travelling with him over Salisbury Plain had many strange peculiarities and although it was surly it did not strike him as in the least malignant. Perhaps since he came from the North, from the rough North Sea region, where this wind had its own habitation, it was busy giving him warnings about Glastonbury. Perhaps it was giving him warnings against believing anything that this ashen sky was putting into his head. What the sky made him think of were fleeing hosts of wounded men with broken spears and torn banners and trails of blood and neighing horses. The sky itself carried no token of such far-off events upon its corpse-cold vastness, but such ruinous disasters seemed to rush along beneath it in their viewless essences, wild-tossed fragments of forgotten flights, catastrophic overthrows, huge migrations of defeated peoples. And upon all these things that sky looked down with a ghastly complicity. Two small motor cars, one dog cart, and a queer-looking lorry with soldiers in it, were the only tangible vehicles that passed him that evening as he went along; but the road seemed full of human memories. There was not a signpost or a milestone on that wayside but had gathered to itself some piteous encounter of heart-struck lovers, some long and woeful farewell, some imperishable remorse! Through ancient and twisted thorn trees, whose faint green buds were growing as indistinct in the after-sunset as specks of green weed on the sides of old ships on a darkened tide, that north wind whistled and shrieked. Once as he rested his bad foot on the fallen stones of a ruined sheepfold and stared across the chalky uplands in front of him he caught sight of an embanked circle of turf with broken-down wooden railings on the top. The look of this object so excited his curiosity that he limped over towards it and wearily climbed its side. It was a circular pond full almost to the brim of bluish-grey water from the middle of whose silent depths rose a few water plants but whose edges were quite clear and transparent. All the light that there was in that fatal-brooding sky seemed concentrated on the surface of this water. "I know what this is," thought John Crow to himself. "This is one of those ponds they call a dew-pond." He advanced cautiously down the slope, leaving his bag on the top of the bank, and supporting himself upon his stick.

Arrived at the edge of the water, he stirred it a little with his stick's end. But in a second he hurriedly drew his stick away. There in that blue-grey, motionless transparency hung suspended a dark object. "A newt!" In his boyhood in Norfolk he had loved these minute saurians more than all living things; and to catch sight of one of these, on this day of all days, filled him with an almost sacred reassurance. "All is going to be all right," he said to himself, "I'm going to get to Glastonbury and to Mary!"

He watched the newt with interest. Disturbed by his stick it had sunk down a short distance below the surface; but there it floated at rest, its four feet stretched out, absolutely immobile. Even as he watched it, it gave the faintest flicker to its tail and with its four feet still immoveably extended it sank slowly out of sight into the depths of the water.

John Crow scrambled up the bank, picked up his bag, and limped back to the road. For the next mile his mood was a good deal happier. He was pleased by the way every milestone he passed recorded the distance to Stonehenge, just as if it were a habitation of living men, instead of what it was.

"Two miles to Stonehenge," said the particular one he now

reached, just as the after-sunset nebulosity began to turn into twilight. He sat on the ground with his back against this milestone. His blistered foot hurt him abominably. "It looks as if I should have to sleep among those Great Stones," he thought. "I shall be at the end of my tether when I get there."

A drowsiness fell upon him now, in spite of the pain in his foot, and his head began to nod over his clasped hands and his tightly hugged knees. Three things, the image of the bed at Maidenhead with one of its brass knobs missing, the image of the Great Stones as he had long ago seen them in pictures, and the image of the newt sinking down into the dew-pond, dominated his mind. He struggled frantically with this obsessing desire to sleep. The wind seemed to have dropped a little. "Perhaps if I see a warm shed," he thought, "I'll leave Stonehenge till tomorrow."

He dragged his body into motion again and limped on. A motor car passed him at top speed, sounding its horn savagely. While it went by his one fear was lest it should stop and offer him a lift. Its vicious look, its ugly noise, its mechanical speed, its villainous stench, the hurried glimpse he got of the smart people in it, all combined to make it seem worse to have any contact with such a thing than to die upon the road.

His foot hurt him most evilly. He knew it was not serious. He had not sprained his ankle or even twisted it. It was only a blister. But the blister throbbed and burned, pulsed and ached as if his heel had been struck with a poisoned arrow.

The grey sky had changed a little in character now. It was dimly interspersed with twinkling points of pale luminosity. Most of these points were so blurred and indistinct that it would have been hard to catch them again at a second glance in the same position in the vast ether. They were like nothing on earth; and to nothing on earth could they be compared. They were the stars, not of the night but of the twilight. The sky around those points of light was neither grey nor black. It was a colour for which there is no name among artists' pigments. But the man limping across Salisbury Plain gave this colour a name. He named it Pain. Where it reached the climax of appropriateness was in the west towards which the road was leading him. Here there was one fragment of sky, exactly where the sun had vanished, that to the neutrality of the rest added an obscure tinge—just the faintest dying tinge—of rusty brown. This low-lying wisp of rusty brown was like the throbbing pulse from the pressure of whose living centre pain spread through the firmament. Walking towards the West Country was like walking towards some mysterious celestial Fount wherein pain was transmuted into an unknown element.

First one leg; then the other leg. He had reached the point now of being conscious of the actual physical automatism of walking. That form of peculiar self-consciousness which as an infant had made the art of walking a triumph of self-assertion now returned upon him to make it a necessity of self-preservation. John Crow felt that he was nearing the end of his power over the very simple achievement of putting one leg in front of the other. He struggled forward for about half a mile. Then he stood still. "I must find a place to lie down in," he thought. "I can't go on." The Maidenhead bed, with the one gilt knob missing, had retreated now beyond the horizon of opportunity. The image of cattle-scented straw floated before him.

A dull, beating thud was proceeding from some portion of his body and travelling away from it into the darkness. He felt like a run-down clock which could not be hindered from a meaningless striking. Whether this thudding came from his heel, his heart, or his head he could not tell. It might, for all he knew, come from that rusty-brown place in the western sky.

"I can't go on," he repeated aloud. And then, quite as naturally as he had before grown conscious, in that infantile fashion, of the triumph of walking, he grew conscious now of the necessity of praying.

And John Crow prayed, calmly, fervently, simply, to the spirit of his mother.

His mother had died when he was six years old and his devotion to her personality had been, ever since that day, not in the least different from the extreme of superstitious idolatry. The childish weakness of his character was just the sort of thing that would endear an only son, as John was, to the protective maternal instinct. The woman had died in a convulsive spasm of tragic tenderness for the child she had to leave; nor is it difficult to conceive how, even on the most material plane, some formidable magnetic vibration, issuing from that grave in the Yaxham churchyard, might linger upon the chemical substratum of the ether, and prove of genuine supernatural value to the child of her womb, when in his weakness he was most in need of her. Thus it happened that when he had finished praying John found he could move forward again, although with very slow steps.

His pace indeed was the pace now of an extremely old man who used his stick as a crutch; and anyone listening to his approach might have taken him for a lame man or a blind man. The heavy tap, tap of his stick upon the road was a sound that travelled further than his footsteps.

At last he came in sight of the faint whiteness of another milestone. This ought to carry the token "One mile to Stonehenge." But this time the roadway opposite the milestone was not empty. Under the nebulousness of that rusty-brown horizon-tinge stood a small dark motor car. It had a red spot at the back but no headlights. It obstructed the road, but it did not impinge upon the scene with the crude violence of the car that had recently passed him by.

As John Crow limped up to it a figure that he had not distinguished from the hedge advanced into the road to intercept him.

"You must let me take you on a bit," said a tall, gaunt, ungainly man wearing a dark bowler hat. "You are too lame to be walking like this. I want to stop presently—a mile from here— but only for a minute or two. I am going to Glastonbury."

A shiver of excitement ran through the worn-out frame of John Crow.

"I was done in, dead beat, at . . . the end . . . of my . . . of my tether," gasped John when he found himself safely inside the little car. And then, as they moved on very slowly, what must this impulsive man do but confess to this stranger how he had just prayed in the middle of the road to the spirit of his mother and how he too was bound for Glastonbury. "There is another explanation, my good friend," said the motorist gravely. "My mind was at the moment absorbed in thoughts of Glastonbury—yours was also—what more natural than that I should ask you to let me take you there?"

John now became aware that although a few faint stars were visible the departing day was still dominant. "It will not be dark for half an hour yet," he thought. "I shall see Stonehenge before night." They were now reaching a little upward slope of the road. The wide Plain stretched around them, cold and mute, and it was as if the daylight had ceased to perish out of the sky, even while the surface of the earth grew dark. The identity of that great space of downland was indrawn upon itself, neither listening nor seeking articulation, lost in an interior world so much vaster and so much more important than the encounters of man with man, whether evoked by prayer or by chance, that such meetings were like the meetings of ants and beetles upon a twilit terrace that had thoughts and memories of its own altogether outside such infinitesimal lives.

To John's surprise, the stranger put on his brake and stopped his car. "Can you see that thorn?" asked the man.

John peered forward through the twilight. Yes, he did clearly see the object indicated. It looked to him like a dead tree. "Is it a dead tree?" he enquired.

But the man went on, "From the foot of that thorn there's a path across the grass leading straight to Stonehenge. You can see Stonehenge from the foot of that thorn."

"Can anyone go there, at this hour? Someone told me in France that it was guarded after sunset by soldiers."

"Are you able to come with me or would you like best to stay here till I come back?" said the man, totally disregarding this remark.

"I must come! Of course I must come with you!" insisted John Crow.

They got out of the little car together. The stranger gave John his arm; and although John would have liked to lean on it a great deal more heavily than he did, it was some support. He hobbled along as best he could, leaning the bulk of his real weight upon his own root-handled hazel-stick, and staring forward at the dead thorn tree with dazed curiosity. Deep in his mind he was thinking to himself, "I'll always pray to her for everything from now on. I'll pray to her that Mary and I can live together in Norfolk!"

When they reached the thorn tree John stopped and drew a deep breath. He pressed heavily now on his companion's wrist and stared across the dark strip of downland turf before him, staggered and thunderstruck. Stonehenge! He had never expected anything like this. He had expected the imposing, but *this* was the overpowering. "This is England," he thought in his heart. "This is my England. This is still alive. This is no dead Ruin like Glastonbury. I am glad I've come to this before I died!" "Will you excuse me, Sir," he said, in a loud, rather rasping voice, the voice he had always assumed when, in the presence of French officials, he wished to assert himself, "will you excuse me if I sit down for a minute?"

"Do you feel queer? Are you ill?"

"I want to look at it from where we are." They sat down on the ground beside the thorn tree; and even as he did so John observed that from one or two dark twigs upon a twisted branch a few leaves were budding. "It's not quite dead," he remarked.

The stranger naturally thought he was speaking of the dark pile in front of them. "You mean its power's not left it?" He paused and then went on in a low voice. "About four thousand years it's been here; but, after all, what's that to some of the antiquities there are in the world? But you're right—it's not quite dead."

"It's very English," said John.

The man turned and gave him a strange, indignant glance. "Is it English then to hide your great secret?" he cried excitedly. "Is it English to keep your secret to the very end?"

"I expect you know much more about it, Sir, than I do," said John humbly, "but I don't feel that those stones have anything hidden. They look to me just what they are, neither more nor less. They look simply like stones, enormous stones, lifted up to be worshipped."

His companion swung round and hugged his shins, resting his chin on the top of his knees and balancing himself on the extreme tips of his haunch-bones. He gave his head an angry toss so that his black bowler fell to the ground and rolled a few inches before lying still.

"Could you worship a stone?"

"I . . . I think . . . I think so. . . ." stammered John, a little disconcerted by the man's intensity. "He must be a nonconformist preacher," he thought.

"Simply *because* it's a stone?" cried the other, and he hugged his ankles so tightly and tilted himself forward so far that John was reminded of a certain goblinish gargoyle that he knew very well, on an out-of-the-way portion of Notre Dame.

"Certainly. *Simply because it's a stone!*"

"And you call that English?" the stranger almost groaned.

"*I* could worship that nearest one," John said, "the one that stands by itself over there."

The man jumped to his feet and, picking up his bowler hat, clamped it upon his head. He was a tall man and he looked preternaturally tall as he stood between John and the stone which John had said he could worship. His profile was like a caricature of a Roman Emperor.

"Do you know what that stone's called?" he cried, "Do you know what it's *called*?" In his excitement he bent down and shook John by his shoulders. John thought to himself, "I wish my stick had a heavier handle. This man is evidently a mad dissenting minister."

"Have all these stones got names?" asked John eagerly, making two desperate attempts to rise to his feet.

The man gave him his hand and John stood up. He surreptitiously substituted the handle of his hazel-stick for its ferrule end and grasped it tightly. "If he becomes dangerous," he thought, "I'll step backward and hit him on the head with all my force." He laughed to himself as he swung his stick in the darkness.

The Great Stone Circle had stirred up in him an excitement the like of which he had never felt in all his life before. The pain of his blistered heel became nothing. He lurched forward, pushed the man aside, and stumbled towards the huge, solitary, unhewn monolith which had attracted his attention. The other strode by his side murmuring indignantly, "It's more than that, it's more than that." When they reached the stone John embraced its rough bulk with his arms, his stick still clutched by the wrong end in his fingers. Three times he pressed his face against it and in his heart he said, "Stone of England, guard Mary Crow and make her happy."

The stranger continued his surly protest. "This stone," he said, "is called the Hêle Stone. It's this stone which stands exactly between the sunrise on a certain day and the Altar Stone inside the Circle—Hêle—you can see what *that* is, can't you? It's Helios, the Sun! You've been playing your little game, Sir, with the Sun Stone."

But John, in that fading twilight, with Stonehenge looming up in front of him, was not to be overawed. He felt too far drunken with the magnetism emanating from these prehistoric monoliths and trilithons. He felt no longer afraid of blaspheming against any God, even against the great Sun Himself!

The two men confronted each other. It was not yet too dark for them to see each other's faces. John leaned on his stick in a normal manner now—the sight of the look of his companion's aquiline nose, combined with his last remark, had reassured him. No religious maniac would have referred to Helios. John continued their disputation, "I believe this stone," he said dogmatically, "is far older than the rest. I believe Stonehenge was built here because of this stone. I think stone-worship is the oldest of all religions and easier to sympathise with than any other religion."

The stranger made no reply and looked round him with the air of one who listens intently.

"Come!" he said peremptorily, taking hold of John by the upper part of his arm. "Let's enter the Circle."

They moved on for a short distance and came upon a large stone lying flat at their feet. The man's fingers clutched John's flesh now with a convulsive clutch.

"You know what *that* is, I suppose?" he said.

John's answer to this was to tear himself loose, go down on his knees, fumble at the stone with his hands, scoop up some seven-days' old rain-water that he came upon in a hollow concavity there and lap it up noisily with his lips. The stranger's tall figure hovered over him like a great, agitated dusky bird. He was wearing a long, old-fashioned overcoat, thin at the waist and very baggy round the legs, and the tails of it kept flapping against his ankles as he went circling about John's crouching figure, gasping forth bewildered protests.

"What are you doing? I've been here more times than I can remember, and I've never dared do that! That water's stagnant. It's worse than stagnant. They've killed thousands and thousands of their enemies here. It's the Slaughtering Stone, I tell you!"

John Crow rose from his feet and drew the back of his hand across his mouth. This childish gesture, visible enough in the twilight, seemed to confound his companion.

"Have you no reverence at all?" he groaned, while the deep-sunken eyes above his Roman nose flashed a disconcerting gleam of anger. John Crow gave vent to a queer animal sound, that was something between a fox-bark and a pig's grunt. Some ancient vein of old Danish profanity seemed to have been aroused in him.

"I've got what I've got, Mister," he said, "but I want to kneel by that Altar Stone in there before it gets too dark." He was already limping forward when the man pulled him back with a jerk.

"How did you know there was an Altar Stone in there?" The words were uttered in such an awed whisper that John gave vent to a gross Isle-of-Ely chuckle.

"Know it? Hee! Hee! Who *doesn't* know it?" Saying this he led the way between two of the perpendicular cyclopean uprights which bore aloft a third, a horizontal one. Vast, shadowy, terrific, this third stone now took the place of the twilight sky. John leaned his back against the left-hand monolith, digging his stick into the ground, and his companion imitated him, standing erect against the right-hand one. Above their heads, concealing the grey mass of the zenith, hung that monolithic roof-tree. The faint stars, as they gazed up at them, past the monstrous obstacle, seemed less obscure than they had been before. To the northward, by the way they had entered, they could dimly see the form of the Hêle Stone. It emerged out of the obscurity like a gigantic, bare-headed man, wrapped in a skin or a blanket.

"I've been told," remarked John, "that the origin of these Stones is entirely unknown."

"Not true," growled the other, in a tone that seemed to say, You are the most irresponsive vandal that has ever entered

Stonehenge and your folly is only equalled by your ignorance. "It is well known," he continued aloud, "that this is the greatest Temple of the Druids."

John's blistered foot caused him at that moment a sharp pang. He lost his self-control and cried aloud in a scandalous voice that rang out far over the silent Plain, "Damn your Druids!" The moment he had uttered the words he knew he had followed the gathering-up and the mounting-up in his nature of an emotion which, unexpressed, would have disgraced him in his own eyes. He moved away towards the centre of the titanic Circle. "He'll bolt now and leave me in the lurch," he thought, "but I can't help it." He stood still and looked eagerly round, observing how two of the largest monoliths had fallen across the ends of a yet larger one but without concealing the centre of it. "If this isn't the Altar Stone, it ought to be," he muttered audibly; and falling down on his knees he tapped his forehead three times against the rough surface of the stone and then continued to hold it there, pressing it against the cold substance with a painful force. This action gave him extraordinary satisfaction. When at last he scrambled to his feet he found his Druidic friend seated on one of the prostrate "foreign stones," surveying him with fearful curiosity.

"You've been here before," he said severely, and heaved a deep sigh, as a man sighs when he finds an intruder at his hearthstone. John came over to him and sat down by his side. "To what kind of stone," he enquired politely, "does that Altar Stone belong?"

The man turned gratefully towards him, free of all suspicion. "The best opinions seem to agree," he said, "that this stone is micaceous sandstone. It no doubt comes from that portion of Wales where the Druids were most powerful; probably from South Wales, like the others; but the others are of a different geological formation."

John Crow felt at that moment as if he were endowed with some magical gift of becoming inhumanly small and weak. And not only small and weak! He felt that he possessed the power of becoming so nearly nothing at all—a speck, an atom, a drifting seed, a sand-grain, a tiny feather, a wisp of thin smoke—that he was completely liberated from the burden of competing with anyone, or disputing with anyone, or assuming any definite mask or any consistent rôle. He seemed to have been given a sort of exultant protean fluidity. He felt an intense desire to make a fool of himself, to act like a clown, a zany, an imbecile. He longed to dance round the grave personage at his side. He longed to go down on all fours before him and scamper in and out of those enormous trilithons like a gambolling animal. He felt as if all his life until this moment he had been concealing his weakness of character, his lack of every kind of principle, his indifference to men's opinions, and a something that was almost subhuman in him. But now beneath these far-off misty stars and under these huge blocks of immemorial stone he felt a wild ecstatic happiness in being exactly as he was.

"Very few people," he remarked to his companion, "could have told me about that Altar Stone being made of micaceous sandstone or about it having come from Wales. I am deeply in your debt, Sir, and I am overjoyed at having met you. My name is John Crow. May I ask what your name is?"

"My name is Evans," said the other, making a dignified inclination of his body towards John. Had he said "My name is Plantagenet," or "My name is Hapsburg," he could not have uttered those syllables with more self-conscious weight. "*Owen* Evans," he added, with a little sigh; and it was as if he desired by this emphasis on Owen to indicate to his interlocutor that it would have been more proper on general grounds if his Christian name had been Caradoc or Roderick or Constantine or even Taliessin. "My home used to be in Wales," he continued, "in South Wales. I was in fact born in Pembrokeshire where that Altar Stone comes from."

"Are you living in Glastonbury now?" John enquired. As soon as he had asked this question he felt he had said something gross, indecent, ill-advised; something lacking in all delicate intuition.

"Staying there . . . for the present," Owen Evans answered, "and what's more," he continued, rising from his seat, "if we want to get there before everyone's in bed we must look sharp."

He seemed to have forgotten—as indeed John himself had almost done—the lameness of his protégé, and he strode off hastily now, past the Hêle Stone, back to the thorn tree, taking for granted that the other was just behind him. But John Crow was not just behind him. He had turned as soon as they were a few paces away from the stones and was now gazing at them with an ecstasy that was like a religious trance. It was an ecstasy that totally abolished Time. Not only was Mr. Owen Evans and his motor car obliterated, but everything, past and future, was obliterated! Mary alone remained. But Mary remained as an essence rather than a person. Mary remained as something that he always carried about with him in the inmost core of his being. She was a dye, a stain, a flavour, an atmosphere. Apart from Mary, Stonehenge and John were all that there was. The enormous body of colossal stones wavered, hovered, swayed and rocked before him; so wrought upon was he, so caught up was he. It rocked like the prow of a vast ship before him. He and It were alone in space. Its dark menacing bulk seemed to grow more and more dominating as he stared at it, but even while it threatened it reassured. And it did not only grow calmer and larger. The taciturn enormity of the uplifted horizontal stones seemed to impose themselves upon his mind with an implication more stupendous than the supporting perpendicular ones. These uplifted stones—these upheld nakednesses—that covered nothing less than the breast of the earth and upon which nothing less than the universal sky rested, seemed to have become, by their very uplifting, more formidable and more sacred than the ones that held them up. They were like cyclopean Sabine women upheld by gigantic ravishers. Both those that upheld and those that were upheld loomed portentous in their passivity, but the passivity of the latter, while more pronounced, was much more imposing. What the instinctive heart of John Crow recognized in this great Body of Stones—both in those bearing-up and in those borne-up—was that they themselves, just as they were, had become, by the mute creative action of four thousand years, authentic Divine Beings. They were so old and great, these Stones, that they assumed godhead by their inherent natural right, gathered godhead up, as a lightning conductor gathers up electricity, and refused to delegate it to any mediator, to any interpreter, to any priest! And what enhanced the primeval grandeur of what John Crow gazed at was the condition of the elements at that hour. Had there been no remnants of twilight left, the darkness and Stonehenge would have completely interpenetrated. Had the stars been bright, their eternal remoteness would have derogated from the mystic enormity of this terrestrial portent. The stars were, however, so blurred and so indistinct, and, atmospherically speaking, so far away, that Stonehenge had no rival. John longed to get some impression of this vast Erection from some subhuman observer, unperverted by historic tradition. What would be the feelings of a sea gull, for example, voyaging thus far inland from Studland or from Lulworth in search of newly turned ploughlands, when it suddenly found itself confronted by this temple of the elements? Would it lodge for a moment on the highest impost of the tallest trilithon? Had any of the Wiltshire shepherds, who lived round about here, ever seen a sea gull actually perched upon the Hêle Stone? What did the foxes make of Stonehenge as they came skulking over the grassy ridges from Normanton Down? Did the sound of their barkings on wild November nights reach the ears of travellers crossing the Plain? Did a power emanating from these stones attract all the adders and grass snakes and blindworms between Amesbury and Warminster, on certain enchanted summer evenings?

Never would Stonehenge look more majestic, more mysterious, than it looked tonight! The wind had almost dropped and yet there was enough left to stir the dead stems of last year's grasses and to make a faint, very faint susurration as it moved among the Stones. The very indistinctness of the dying daylight served also to enhance the impressiveness of the place. Had the night been pitch dark nothing could have been distinguished. On the other hand, had the twilight not advanced so far, the expanding sweep of the surrounding downs would have carried the eye away from the stones themselves and reduced their shadowy immensity. No artificial arrangement of matter, however terrific and unhewn, can compare with the actual hollows and excrescences of the planet itself; but the primeval erection at which John Crow stared now, like the ghost of a neolithic slave at the gods of his masters, was increased in weight and mass by reason of the fact that nothing surrounded it except a vague, neutral, Cimmerian greyness.

"Stonehenge, you great God!" cried John Crow, "I beg you to make Mary a happy girl and I beg you to let me live with her in Norfolk!"

He tore himself away after this and hurried, as fast as he could, towards the thorn tree. The voice of Owen Evans increased his speed as he staggered up the slope. "Mr. Crow! Mr. Crow! Mr. Crow!" came that voice from beyond the tree in a high querulous accent. His blister began to hurt him again. He began again to feel famished and faint. Once more he paused and looked around. The effect at this distance had undergone a change. The stones seemed actually to have melted into one another! It was no longer at a series of stones he was looking, but at one stone. Perhaps indeed just then he was seeing Stonehenge as it would have appeared, not to a wild bird or a fox, but to a flock of sheep travelling from their pastures to the shearing-place.

"Mr. Crow! Mr. Crow!" came the voice of the Welshman; and John felt it incumbent upon him now really to turn his back upon Stonehenge. When he reached the car John Crow was surprised at the urbanity and good-temper of Mr. Owen Evans. He had expected that the man from South Wales, even if he didn't desert him, would reproach him vehemently. Nothing of the sort occurred. John got in and took his seat by the motorist's side, avoiding with some difficulty, for his legs were long and his foot extremely sore, the mechanism that worked the machine.

"Are you going to stay long in Glastonbury?" enquired Mr. Evans. John was perfectly frank with him in answer to this direct question. Indeed, in the entranced and relaxed condition of his nerves, he was more frank than he need have been. He became, in fact, very voluble. He told him everything; only keeping back the existence of Mary and the existence of Tom Barter. By degrees, as he conversed with the man, while their car reached and passed the lighted streets of Warminster, he became conscious that Mr. Evans' questions and answers were composed of two levels of intensity, one below another. The upper, more superficial level, was pedantic and a little patronising, but the lower level struck John's mind as not merely humble and sad but tragically humble and sad. One or two of his remarks were indeed as exciting to John's curiosity as they were stimulating to his sympathy. And another thing he noticed about the conversation of this man in the large bowler hat and the tight black overcoat was that it was always when the conversation returned to Glastonbury that this secondary tone came into his voice.

"We'll get a late supper at Frome," Mr. Evans said at one point; and the idea of this heavenly refreshment spoken of lightly as a "late supper" so preoccupied John's thoughts that by degrees he contented himself with a drowsy attempt to learn the names of the villages through which they passed and dropped all other conversation.

They skirted the wall of Long Leat Park. They passed Upper Whitbourne; they passed Corsley Heath; they passed Lane End and Gradon Farm; and while still the memory of his mother was lulling him with a security beyond description, they entered the main street of Frome. Mr. Evans seemed to know the place well, and having left their car in the yard of one of the smaller inns, the two men walked slowly down the street. Most of the ordinary teashops were shut, but they found at last a little refreshment-place of a more modest kind, where they were given a cordial welcome and a substantial though simple supper in a small private room. During this meal this strangely assorted pair had the first opportunity they had yet enjoyed to study each other's physiognomy under illuminated and relaxed conditions. John found that Mr. Evans had already heard rumours of the strange sequence of events by which the lay-preacher Geard had inherited William Crow's money. Evans himself, he explained, had made the acquaintance of the Geards through the fact of Mrs. Geard being a member of a very ancient South Welsh family called Rhys. The motorist uttered the name Rhys with the most reverential respect. Not that Mrs. Geard's immediate relatives, he made clear to John, were anything but quite simple people, but all the Rhys family were, as an ordinary person would put it, of the blood royal of Wales.

It did not take any great diplomacy on the part of John Crow to lead the conversation up to a point where he learned the not-unexpected fact that the maternal ancestors of Mr. Evans himself belonged to this same ancient House of Rhys. After a little further dalliance round and about the subject of the Geards, John found himself possessed of the further information that Mr. Owen Evans was an admirer of one of Mrs. Geard's daughters, a girl in whom "the very spirit of the old Cymric race" had found a notable habitation. It was in his "first manner," the pontifical one, that Owen Evans described this young lady. The foxy John had begun to wonder indeed whether his whole discovery of these two personalities in his patron were not a crazy fancy of his own, when a chance allusion to the Abbey Ruins brought back in a minute that diffident, hesitant, almost *cowering* tone. It was a queer thing and a thing that John never afterward forgot, as he saw a look of positively tragic suffering cross those strongly marked lineaments, that he himself became extremely uncomfortable when this second tone of his friend's utterances thus predominated. It was exactly as if some bombastic masquerader in theatrical armour had suddenly unclasped his sham gorget and revealed a hairshirt stained with authentic blood. He got the impression, the longer this confidential talk over this felicitous "late supper" lasted, that it was to very few persons, and probably least of all to the maiden with the "very spirit of the old Cymric race," that this singular descendant of the House of Rhys revealed his real nature.

Once more sitting by Mr. Evans in the little motor car and moving swiftly through the darkness, John's attention was distracted now by a certain vivid consciousness of being in a part of England completely new to him and heavy with unique qualities. After walking all day over the chalk uplands of Wiltshire this long, enchanted drive into the western valleys was like plunging into an ever-deepening wave of rich, sepia-brown, century-old leaf-mould. From spinneys and copses and ancestral parks, as they drove between dim, moss-scented banks, a chilly sweetness that seemed wet with the life sap of millions of primrose buds came flowing over him. . . .

As both the men grew more and more dominated, by the motions and stirrings, the silent breathings and floating murmurs, of a spring night in Somersetshire, they seemed to grow steadily more sympathetic to each other.

"Do you believe, Mr. Evans, as so many people do," said John suddenly, "in always struggling to find a meaning to life?" Very slowly and very carefully did the Welshman reply to this.

"It's not . . . it never has been . . . in my . . . in my nature," he murmured, "to . . . to take life . . . in that . . . way
. . . at all. I find meanings everywhere. My . . ." he hesitated
for a long time here, "difficulties," he went on, "are entirely
personal."

John was delighted with this reply. "My difficulties," he said,
"are personal too. I simply cannot understand what people mean
when they talk of life having a purpose. Life to me is simply the
experience of living things; and most things I meet seem to me
to be living things."

In the darkness John felt the car crossing a little bridge.
"Nunney Brook," he heard Mr. Evans murmur. Soon they were
moving along the southern wall of Asham Wood, and then came
East Cranmore and West Cranmore and then a place called
Doulting.

"Look out for Shepton Mallet next," Mr. Evans said. "I'm
afraid all the pubs will be shut, or we'd stop for a drink there to
nerve us up for the last lap of our journey." His words were justified. It was plain that the inn-bars in Shepton Mallet were all
fast closed.

"We must put on speed now," said Mr. Evans, "or everybody
will be fast asleep. They go to bed early in Glastonbury."

John was soon conscious, as they left the last houses of this
little Somersetshire town, solidly built houses under the gas-lamps
at the street corners with old carved lintels and worn buttresses,
that the countryside was again changing its character. A faint
reedy, muddy, watery atmosphere visited his East Anglian nostrils. For a mile or two he was puzzled by these damp waftures
carried upon the cold night air, so different from that leaf-mould
sweetness, that smell of ancient seignorial parklands, through
which they had recently passed. He experienced a pang of sadness which it was easy enough to explain. It was a thousand old
impressions of Isle-of-Ely dykes, called up, out of deep-buried
race memories, by the ditches, or "rhynes," as they call them, of
the Isle-of-Glastonbury.

"I am getting near Mary!" he thought. "She's lying in bed
looking at those Ruins." And then he thought, "Evans is going
to get me a bed somewhere. He knows I've got no money. I'll see

her tomorrow by hook or by crook and then everything will work itself out."

The thoughts of Mr. Evans, as they passed the hamlet of Pilton and crossed the Whitelake River by a small stone bridge, were so absorbing that he instinctively began driving very slowly. Like all thoughts that have tormented a person's mind for many years, these thoughts had bruised and beaten themselves against the mental walls of habit until they had ceased to be thoughts and had become palpable images. The images in Mr. Evans' case were of a very peculiar nature. If they could have been revealed to any average human mind—a mind less vicious and depraved than John's—they would have presented themselves as something so monstrous as to be the creation of an insane person. This they certainly were not, unless all erotic aberrations are insane; and Mr. Evans, apart from these images, was, as John had discovered, a pedantically and even tediously guileless man. They were scenes of sadistic cruelty, these pictures that dwelt in the back chambers of Mr. Evans' mind; and the extraordinary thing about them was that, in spite of their iniquity, which was indeed abominable, they still produced in him—whenever the least glimpse of them took form again—an inebriation of erotic excitement that made his pulses beat, his blood dance, his senses swoon, his knees knock together. The taste of the least of these loathsome scenes was so overpowering to him that it reduced all the rest of life— eating, drinking, working, playing, walking, talking—to tedious occurrences, that had to be got through but that were wanting entirely in the electric quiver of real excitement. What Mr. Evans suffered from was a fever of remorse such as cannot very often have taken possession of human minds in the long course of history. To say that the unhappy man wished that he had never been born would be to put his case mildly. Like Othello he longed to bathe in "steep-down gulfs of liquid fire." No one would ever know—unless Mr. Evans confessed to a priest—how many of these abominations had actually been practised, how many of them described in forbidden books, or how many just simply invented by a perverted imagination. If the victim or victims of Mr. Evans' perversion, supposing they really existed and were not phantoms of his imagination, had suffered cruelly, Mr. Evans himself had suffered, for the last five or six years, a torment to which human history can, we must hope, offer few parallels.

His nature was so riddled and saturated with this appalling habit of mind that it became a mania with him—now that he had rejected all practice of it and all pleasure from all thoughts of it—to blame himself for innumerable forms of suffering in the world, of which he was entirely innocent. He walked about as if the ground under his feet was red-hot iron, so fearful was he of hurting so much as the tiniest beetle or the smallest worm. He used deliberately to walk across heavy grass and heavy under-growth so as to avoid the little half-made paths which always struck his imagination as things that had been hurt. Since a feeling of power, carried to a monstrous intensity, played such a rôle in his vice, it was natural enough that when, aghast at what he had become, he gave the whole thing up, he should labor under the delusion of being a much more powerful force in the world than he really was. Few modern persons, as intelligent as Owen Evans, believed as intensely as he did in the existence of a personal God. Perhaps there is something in the peculiar nature of this vice which especially lends itself to this belief.

Recovering himself from his secret thoughts, as they came nearer and nearer to the end of their journey, Mr. Evans mur-mured to his companion such words as "Havyatt" and "Edgar-ley." He nodded his head, too, towards a great level expanse of low-lying country which extended southward, on their left, as they approached their destination. In connection with these dark fields he uttered the syllables "Kannard Moor" and "Butt Moor." He further indicated that Baltonsborough and Keinton Mande-ville lay on the other side of these wide-stretching water-logged pastures, at which John, in his blunt East Anglian way, declared that in *his* country such places would have had names ending in "ham," not in such finicking sounds as "ville." He told Mr. Evans that Saxmundham was a much more characteristic English name than Keinton Mandeville!

As they approached the outskirts of the place, John became aware of the dim pyramidal form of Glastonbury Tor, towering above the walls and roofs of the town. The moment he caught sight of this great pointed hill, with the massive deserted church tower on its summit, he felt conscious that here was something that suited his nature better than he expected anything to have done in these parts.

Mr. Evans, speaking in his second manner, told him that it was the tower of St. Michael the Archangel. "I am glad," said John, "that St. Michael's tower was the first thing I saw here!" But in his heart he thought, "To the Devil with St. Michael! That tower is nothing but a tall pile of stones. I like that tower—I shall go up to that tower at the first chance!"

But Mr. Evans in his tormented mind cared nothing whether John liked the tower or not. He was crying, like a lost spirit, "O Cross of Christ! O Cross of Christ! O Cross of Christ!"

Thus did these two, the man from Wales and the man from Norfolk, enter the silent streets of the town of Glastonbury.

THE REVEREND MAT DEKKER, VICAR OF GLASTONBURY, WAS working in his garden. He was loosening the earth round his long, straight rows of potatoes, while his son Sam was going backward and forward with an old wheelbarrow to a smouldering rubbish heap under the high wall upon which he deposited the weeds which his father pulled up.

Mat Dekker was a man of sixty. A widower from his only child's birth, twenty-five years ago, his powerfully banked-up affections had long concentrated themselves upon two objects: upon Christ, the Redeemer of his soul, and upon Sam, the son of his loins. It was about ten months this March since the lad had taken his degree at Cambridge; and the first serious misunderstanding between father and son was even now, month by month, gathering weight and momentum. It had to do with the young man's profession, and with the young man's first love-affair. Having brought him up with the constant idea of his taking orders, having seen him graduate with a creditable third-class in the Divinity Tripos, it is not difficult to imagine the crushing blow that fell upon the luckless father, when—the question arising as to what particular theological college he was now to enter —the lad gravely and resolutely declined to carry the thing a step further. And at that point the matter had hung fire for more than half a year. Refusing to give up hope of a change of heart in his son, Mat Dekker had followed the policy of complete inertness. Every opening in life, except unskilled manual labor, requiring the expenditure of some initial sum, the older man, without consciously tyrannising, acted on the assumption that economic pressure, negatively exercised, was the best weapon that age possessed in dealing with the wilfulness of youth.

Apart from religion their tastes were unusually congenial. They both loved gardening, they both loved natural history, they both were proud and shy and anti-social. In their secluded Rectory, surrounded by walls fifteen feet high and faced even across the road by nothing more gregarious than the equally high walls of the Abbey House, they were able to follow their hobbies as botanists, entomologists, geologists, ichthyologists, without cessation or interruption.

Mrs. Dekker had been a French Swiss from the city of Geneva. She had indeed been the pretty housemaid in this very house when Mr. Dekker took it over, and the girl with it, when he entered upon his labours in Glastonbury as a young bachelor priest some thirty years ago. But she had died in childbirth; and since that day there had been no more pretty housemaids; indeed it might be said that there had been no more women of any kind, within the Rectory walls.

For Penny Pitches, their one servant, could only be regarded as a woman under what Sir Thomas Browne would have called, in speaking of other difficult questions, "a wide solution." Penny Pitches had lost her own baby just about the time of Sam's birth; and since that day she had been as good as a mother to Sam. She had suckled him, taught him his letters, taught him his manners—for she was not one to spare the rod—taught him his morality, his mother-wit, his legends and his superstitions. But with these female attributes, Penny Pitches' appearance was more gnomelike than anything else. She was undoubtedly the least human-looking anthropoid mammal in the whole county of Somerset. Penny Pitches was not deformed. She was no humpback. What Nature had done was to make her back so broad and her legs so short that she presented the appearance of a Playing-Card Queen of Spades; a Queen of Spades endowed with the privilege of three dimensions and the power of locomotion, but denied that natural separation of head from shoulders and of bust from hips which is the usual inheritance of female mortality. She was in fact an animated Euclidean Square moving about over the earth. Nature had, however, in order to compensate Penny for these peculiarities, given her a volubility of speech that was womanly and more than womanly. To speak the truth, the tongues of a dozen cantankerous shrews and a dozen loquacious trollops resided in this gnome-like skull.

It was Penny herself who now appeared upon the scene and standing between wheelbarrow and potato row delivered herself of her view of that morning's general outlook. " 'Tis not that I querrel with 'ee for going out to 'lunch,' as they called it. That's as 'ee do please 'eeself about. What I do, and always shall, uphold is that for a person not to know 'inavarst' whether there's to be dinner on table or no dinner on table is a mock to reason."

"Who told you that we were going out today, Penny?" protested Mr. Dekker mildly, leaning upon his fork. He was in his shirtsleeves and his large, rugged cheeks were redder than usual against the clipped grey whiskers that surrounded them. His chin and his upper lip were clean-shaven; and, as if to make up for this, his eyebrows above his formidable grey eyes were so long that they resembled a pair of thatched eaves.

"Wold man Weatherwax," replied the Vicarage servant, "be round to me pantry with sarcy tales enough to turn milk in a pan! He do say that Miss Mary over the way have a cousin come to town what be lodging wi' Mr. Evans, the new Antiquities man who's looking after wold Jones' shop, who's to Hospital again with one of they little cysteses what do trouble he. 'A said 'twere a surprise to 'un—silly wold sinner as 'tis—that Miss Drew allowed of such doings. But I said to 'ee, I said, if Miss Drew thinks enough of Miss Mary's cousin to ask us to meet 'un, though 'a *be* a friend of their new Antiquity man, 'a must be one of they great factory people. Crow ain't no common name. Crow ain't no West-Country name, Crow ain't. And our Miss Mary, as us do know, be related to they rich folks. So I be come straight to 'ee, Master, to reason wi' 'ee as to why, when 'ee be going out for dinner, ye haven't let us so much as hear a word of it."

"I was just this very minute coming to tell you of our invitation, Penny," murmured the clergyman. "It hadn't arrived at breakfast. In fact Weatherwax must have brought it. I suppose there's no excuse for us, eh, Sam?" and he glanced humorously, from above the rim of his spectacles and from beneath his bushy eyebrows, at the lad on the further side of the wheelbarrow.

Young Sam Dekker answered the look with a grin. Then he suddenly got red. "You've not forgotten, Father," he said, "that you promised to have tea at Whitelake Cottage with the Zoylands?"

Before Mr. Dekker could reply to this, Penny Pitches turned

angrily on the lad. "And you're dragging the Master out over they girt marshes, are ye, too, then? It's that little white scut of a Missy Zoyland *ye* be after, Sam Dekker; and don't 'ee forget that I told 'ee of it! Oh, I do know 'ee, I do know 'ee, Sammy, me blessed babe! 'Tis a daffadowndilly day, like this day be, that leads to these unholy doings. On days like this day 'tis hard for young men to bide quiet at home and take their cup of tea with their dad, brought sweet and strong to 'un by such as knows what a minister's table should be. A lot you care, Master Sam, what poisonous foreign sweetmeats your dad'll have to eat, and what devil's dam drinks he'll have to drink, out there over Splott's Moor. It's thik Missy Zoyland ye be after. Look at's cheeks, Master! Look at's hot cheeks!"

"I didn't know Mrs. Zoyland had a daughter, Penny," remarked the Rector gently, looking anywhere except in the direction of his son's confusion.

"I never said she had, Master," averred the woman stoutly, glancing at her embarrassed foster-child with a defiant glare.

"Penny's thinking of that Fair at Hornblotton, Father, when I took Mrs. Zoyland on the merry-go-round with me. You were there yourself. You saw us. I'd be ashamed to say such unkind things of a quiet little lady like that, Penny!"

"I baint said nothing about no quiet lady," protested Mrs. Pitches. "My words be to do wi' a young master, what stands afore us, among these here 'taties."

"Well, Penny," said Mr. Dekker with decision, "I'm afraid it looks, anyhow, as if you'd be a lone woman today. Sam's quite right. I *did* promise the Zoylands to walk over to Whitelake River this afternoon and I did tell Weatherwax that we would come across to lunch. Did Miss Drew send for any brandy as I told her to?"

"Brandy!" cried Penny Pitches in high dudgeon. "Ye'll have plenty of brandy left, ye will, if ye go giving it round to all the old maids in Silver Street!"

"But, my dear Penny," said Mat Dekker, stretching out his long white-shirted arm across the handles of the wheelbarrow and taking the woman caressingly by the shoulder, "Miss Drew sent Weatherwax for that brandy that we might drink it at lunch, we and Mary's new cousin; so I do hope you've not been crotchety and refused it to him."

"Refused it!" The words came like a bullfrog's croak from the geometrical centre of that well-aproned human square that had planted itself before them. "Thik wold Weatherwax be settled in me chair, in me pantry, at me table this blessed minute. *Refused it!* Why, he's been tasting thik brandy for the last hour. He says he be tasting it to see if it be the same as Miss Drew had from 'ee at Christmas. If it *be* the same, he'll take it over, he says, same as she told he to. And I do tell he that if it's not the same there'll be no need to worry about leaving it in bottle; for bottle'll be like thee own stummick, Master, on Sunday morn! Bottle'll be empty and tinklin'!"

"Well! you run off now, Penny, and let Sam and me finish this couple of rows. Tell old Weatherwax it *is* the same. Let Miss Drew have what she wants; and cork up the bottle. I've got to do some work this morning if we're going to Whitelake. Never mind about *those*, Sam! I'll wheel away the rest myself. You go back to the house now with Penny; oh, and if you change the water in the aquarium, do find a bowl of some kind to put that minnow in! It's only been up at the top since yesterday afternoon and I changed the water two days ago." (This expression "up at the top" referred to the habit of minnows when sick or dying of remaining with their heads upslanted at the top of the water breathing heavily.)

Sam Dekker surveyed the retreating form of Penny Pitches. He was of a lankier build than his father; and there was something pathetically animal-like about his shambling limbs. He had a clean-shaved, rather puckered face, with freckles all over it. His nose was long and thin, like the nose of some kind of honey-eating bear; and his small, greenish eyes were surrounded by many wrinkles. His upper lip was long, like his father's, but while Mat Dekker had a massive, square chin to support this peculiarity Sam had a weak, retreating chin. Sam's retreating chin was in many ways the most marked portion of his face, for it was creased with all manner of queer corrugations. He had a nervous trick of opening his mouth a little, drawing in his underjaw, and pulling down the corners of his underlip. The effect of these

movements was to compel the contours of his chin to fuse themselves with the contours of his long neck. Had his face been anything but what it was, this trick of contorting his chin would have
been much more noticeable; but where everything was so much
out of proportion no particular lapse could become prominent.

His greenish eyes almost closed as he stood there in a heavy
daze, while his father, anxious to finish that long piece of weeding, bent again over his work. Sam Dekker was not one for
moralising on the events of his life, nor for analysing his motives.
He took for granted that it was just one more trick of Nature that
his interest in fossils, in birds' eggs, in fishes, should lose its
savour month after month, as he found himself entoiled in the
beauty of Nell Zoyland. He took it for granted that in his weakness he should not dare to mention his entanglement to his father,
that in his weakness he should lie to the old man as to the real
meaning of the long solitary excursions he was always making
these days, past Brindham and Splott's Moor, across Whitelake
River to Queen's Sedgemoor; he took it for granted that he should
be too unpractical and too cowardly to dream of carrying Nell
off or of separating her from the formidable William, or of doing
anything at all to clarify the situation. All he could do was to
go on constantly seeing her, which intensified rather than resolved
the dilemma he was in! He loved his father with the deep passive
animal intensity with which he loved Nell. It was indeed his love
for his father quite as much as his natural timidity that made it
absolutely impossible that he should reveal to the older man the
real tragedy of the situation. This tragedy was that not only did
he love Nell Zoyland, but that Nell loved him, recklessly, shamelessly, and was constantly urging him, cost what it might to both
of them, to carry her off! It had been the deepest and the most
exciting astonishment of his life, the fact that a girl as lovely as
Nell *could* love an ugly, lumpish, uninteresting failure, such as
he felt himself to be; Nell, too, who had so original, so surprisingly good-looking a man as Will Zoyland for her mate! William
was, it is true, a good deal older than Nell; but what a man he
was, with his leonine beard and rolling blue eyes, his enormous
courage, his immense physical strength! Under the low forehead
of Sam Dekker there stirred strange feelings towards this for-

midable rival whose power of character was so little to be trifled
with. Even Sam's father, no negligible personage himself, showed
evident respect for William Zoyland. It was indeed this respect of
Mat Dekker's for the bearded man that had brought about the
excursion this afternoon, an excursion which, though he had himself reminded his father of it, filled Sam's heart with deep
uneasiness.

Now, as he slowly plodded off to refill the aquarium in their
play-room, he cursed Penny Pitches for her uncalled-for outburst.
What had induced the absurd woman to meddle in his affairs?
Never before had she deliberately and wilfully betrayed him to
his father. As a rule in any trifling misunderstanding between
her two men she took the side of her master's son against her
master. The more he thought about it the less he understood it.
Penny, he knew, was anything but puritanical. The indecent jokes
that passed between her and old Weatherwax were the standing
disgrace of Glastonbury Vicarage. "How much does she know?"
he asked himself as he entered the house; and the idea that some
gossiping crony of the old woman had seen his meetings with
Nell on Crannel Moor or in the old barn on Godney Marsh began
to taunt his brain.

Left to himself to finish his weeding, Mat Dekker sternly put
out of his mind the whole matter of Penny's attack upon Sam.
Dekker's nature was a rich, deep, passionate one; but his religion
had assisted him in bringing it under a rare and unusual control.
One of the chief things he had learnt to do was to obliterate every
sexual suspicion. One of Mat's favorite writers was St. Paul; and
he had made a custom of forcing himself *not to think evil*, a
characteristic of that divine Agapé which, according to St. Paul,
held the magic clue to the universe.

But there was a power now shining down upon Mr. Dekker
that cared nothing for St. Paul. The soul of the great burning
sun which illuminated that massive, iron-grey, bent head had
many times ere this been roused to anger against him. Among the
myriads of conscious beings peopling that hemisphere of our
planetary orb who refused in that spring solstice to make the sort
of grateful gesture towards this great Deity which the Powers of
Nature demand of those they favour, this ruddy-faced man in

shirtsleeves bending now over his potato bed seemed to that flaming heart the most obdurate and the most sacrilegious. "Let his
Christ protect him!" thought (if we can call the titanic motions
of super-consciousness in such a Power by the name of
"thought") this great outpourer of life heat. "As for us, we will
let loose his own offspring upon him; and the thing he loves most
in the world we will rouse up against him!"

It must have been about six hours after their talk with Penny
Pitches in the potato garden that Sam Dekker, troubled at heart
by what he considered the gross and inexplicable treachery of his
foster-mother, sat gloomily by himself on the warm steps of the
Abbey House terrace. A little below him, on wooden seats placed
side by side, above a low parapet, sat Miss Euphemia Drew and
her other guests. The more Sam meditated upon that afternoon's
excursion to Whitelake, the more troubled he became. Would his
father detect anything? Would Nell in her agitation as hostess
forget her prudence? Had William Zoyland secretly planned the
whole affair in order to nip in the bud this perilous growth whose
frail seedling-shoot he had already discerned? "I shall get red,"
he thought, "I shall get red as a turkey-cock, just as Penny said.
My hand will shake when she gives me my tea. We shan't dare to
look at each other, or speak to each other. Father's bound to
notice something."

Had Nell Zoyland seen the lad at this moment and watched the
puckering of his freckled forehead and the way, as he rose now
to offer help to Mary, the muscles of his poor chin contracted,
she would have loved him more than ever. Mary's own face, as she
carried a silver tray in one hand and a coffee jug in the other, was
drawn and white. It was all over as far as Miss Drew was concerned! She knew *that* already, though the lady had not spoken
a word to her on the subject. John had behaved with irretrievable
folly at lunch; had talked wildly; had expressed disbelief in the
legend of the Holy Thorn, had announced that it was a pity that
the Danes had been turned back at Havyatt Gap and finally had
declared that the discovery of Joseph of Arimathea's tomb was
the mere mummery of the monks! Yes; it was all over for them
with Miss Drew. She would never ask him again. She would never

let her meet him again. It would be a lucky thing if she didn't pack her off, then and there, merely for having such a cousin!

When Mary, with Sam helping her, for both Miss Drew's cook and housemaid, the sisters Rogers, had begun to wash up, joined the rest of the party on the terrace, John had fallen into a more amiable mood. He still remained irresponsive about the Holy Thorn, but he had evidently taken a fancy to Mr. Dekker, and he was listening now quite humbly while the Vicar narrated to him in a grave and unaffected tone certain historic facts about the Ruins before them.

"Hic jacet sepultus inclitus Rex Arturus in Insula Avallonia," recited Mat Dekker in a deep, quiet voice. "The end of the twelfth century it was," he went on, "when they found the coffin, a great hollowed-out oak trunk, with the bones of the king and queen. Nearly a hundred years later Edward the First buried them before the high altar. The books say that Leland the Antiquary actually saw them as late as the sixteenth century. Since then they have been lost to sight." The Vicar of Glastonbury sighed as he ceased speaking, and at the same moment a light wind from the west, rustling across the masses of ruined masonry caught the topmost twigs of the tall elms on the right of the Tower Arch and made them bow before it.

"When I told my good friend Mr. Evans this morning," began John Crow, "that I had been invited here, it *did* excite him! He quoted what he called a Welsh Triad—something about no one knowing where the grave of Arthur was."

Miss Euphemia Drew folded her cream-coloured cashmere shawl more tightly round her neck, hiding the gold-mounted moonstone brooch that clasped her bodice; and then, turning her chin above the wrinkled fingers she had thus raised to her throat, "Not *know* where it is?" she said sternly. "Fiddle-de-dee! we *all* know where it is! It's under that broken arch."

Mary tried to convey to her cousin by a rapid glance that he must accept the verdict of Miss Drew as to the grave of the great king without further question. But the run-down Danish adventurer refused to be stopped. "My friend Mr. Evans quoted a Latin jingle too. What was it, Sir? I expect you know it. It began with *Hic jacet*, just as yours did."

Mat Dekker smiled sadly. "You mean '*Hic jacet Arturus, rex quondam, rexque futurus*'? Is that what he said? 'King once and king to be,'" he added, with his clerical instinct for making things clear. "Most of our Glastonbury sayings have to do with some sort of '*Hic jacet*,'" he concluded rather wistfully.

"Would you say, Sir," enquired John, "that King Arthur is really the most deeply rooted superstition that this place represents?" The younger Dekker began to feel seriously angry with the East Anglian. It was all very well to display a lack of antiquarian interest. But here, on this terrace, gazing out at Edgar's Chapel, at the great Tower Arch, at St. Mary's Church, at St. Thomas' Chapel, at the rich ruins of the most sacred *ecclesia vetusta* in all Britain, to definitely challenge the whole *genius loci* seemed to Sam's simple mind as much a lapse from Nature's ways as it would have been to allow a minnow to perish for lack of fresh water.

But the elder Dekker seemed totally unconscious of the insult to the spot he loved. "Well, of course to our old-fashioned Protestant ancestors Glastonbury must have reeked with what you call 'superstition.' Three famous Saxon kings are buried here, something like six well-known saints are buried here. All the Holy Grail legends gather to a head here. The Druids played a great part here; and long before the Druids there was a Lake Village" —he gave a grave, characteristically West-country jerk with his head to indicate the northwestern point of the compass—"whose mounds you can still see in the fields. Ancient British *that* probably was; older anyway than History! But I expect the deepest-rooted superstition here, if you could compel Glastonbury Tor to speak, would turn out to be the religion of the people who lived *before* the Ancient Britons; perhaps even before the Neolithic Men. At any rate we have some excuse for being 'superstitious' in these parts. Don't you think so, Miss Drew?"

"I think you are very kind, dear Vicar, to answer Mr. Crow's question at all," said the old lady severely. "For myself I would answer it rather differently. I would assure him that what he calls superstition *we* call the Only True Faith."

This remark produced a complete silence.

"My friend Mr. Evans,"—it was John who broke the spell—

"says that it's neither King Arthur nor Joseph of Arimathea that's the real hidden force still active in Glastonbury."

"What does he say it is?" enquired Mary, hoping against hope that John would, even now, redeem himself.

"He won't say. He gets reserved and touchy. It's my own opinion that it has to do with Merlin. But I expect I'm all wrong. When I mentioned Merlin all he did was to quote a lot of Welsh Triads in Welsh. He's a queer character, my friend Evans, but he interests me very much."

"Will you take some more coffee or some more brandy, Vicar?" interrupted Miss Drew in a tone that seemed to say, "When once I have exposed the unpleasantness of a rude young man there is no need for him to make further efforts to reinstate himself in my favour." And then when the Vicar had shaken his head, "Carry the trays away, child, please; and tell Lily and Rogers that you and I will get our own tea today."

The cook's name was Louie Rogers. She was only a year older than Lily and as a rule Miss Drew called her Louie; but when upset by the spectacle of the world's disorder she always called her Rogers. It had been her mother's as well as her grandmother's custom to call their cooks by their surnames and Miss Drew reverted to it as a sort of invocation of these thin-lipped, tenderly stern women, whose miniatures were on her writing-table. The mere utterance of the word "Rogers" seemed to Miss Drew to bring back decency and respect to human intercourse.

John had not the courage nor the wit to rise from his chair and help his cousin carrying her tray into the house; so it worked out that Sam Dekker once more was her companion. But Sam never addressed a single word to her as he walked by her side. His sole thought was his growing dread of the afternoon's encounter. Mary herself pondered bitterly upon the interior meaning of Miss Drew's little speech about their tea. It meant a kind of emotional unbending, an intimacy, a crisis of sympathetic confidence; but it also meant that under no conceivable circumstances would her employer allow her to go on meeting her cousin. Ladies who live together possess these indirect ways of communicating with each other and by the tone in which Mary replied, "Yes, dear, that will be so nice!" Miss Drew knew that while there would be nothing in the nature of a scene between them, the separation of Mary from John would take more than one evening's dignified protest.

Meanwhile the sun began slanting its rays more and more warmly and mistily upon the group on the terrace. The smooth expanse of grass which separated them from the Ruins bore on its surface now a few dark, fluctuating shadows as the light wind stirred the elm-tree tops. The three hills of the place, Wirral Hill, Chalice Hill and the Tor, were all behind them, and beyond the Ruins and beyond the trees and beyond the vaporous roofs of the town, stretched the wide, low valley where flowed the River Brue, and where that Bridge Perilous was, into which, as Dekker was now telling him, Arthur had thrown his sword. Dim and rich and vague the valley stretched, covered with an undulating veil of blue-purple mist. Orchard upon orchard, pasture upon pasture, it sank away, the lowest pastoral country in the land of England, lower than the level of the sea, heavy with its precious relics as the sea bottom with its drowned ships. As he gazed at all this, feeling more and more friendly to Mr. Dekker and more and more hostile to Miss Drew, John began to say to himself that it was nothing else than this very low-lying character of the country that made it such a fatal receptacle for the superstitions of two thousand years! Into this blue-purple vapour, into the bosom of these fields lower than the sea, floated, drifted upon the wind, all those dangerous enervating myths that had taken the heart out of man's courage and self-reliance upon the earth. The True Faith indeed! Why, the land reeked with the honey lotus of all the superstitions of the world! Here they had come, here they had taken refuge, driven into flight by the great dragon-beaked ships and the long bright spears of his own heathen ancestry! And here, caught by these fatal low-lying flats they had lingered; lingered and clung till they grew rotten and miasmic, full of insidious mind-drugging poison. God! This place must be charged, "thick and slab," with all the sweet-sickly religious lies that had ever medicined the world! Here like green scum over old stagnant water courses, here like green pond weeds upon castle moats, these tender-false mandragoras lulled to sleep the minds of the generations! No wonder Philip, with his accursed machines, found no manhood to resist his despotism in a place like this!

It was at this point in John Crow's contemplations that Mary and Sam came slowly back and reseated themselves by his side. They had exchanged only two sentences on the way back from the house. Mary had asked him whether they could spare Mr. Weatherwax, who worked in both their gardens, for the whole day tomorrow, and Sam had replied that he thought they could, as long as the old man "helped Penny to pump before he came across the road."

John was soon made aware of the miserable depression into which Mary had fallen. Her profile troubled him by its tragic tenseness. He rose abruptly. "Good-bye, Miss Drew," he said, bowing to her from where he stood. "Thank you so much for having asked me here. Good-bye, Sir, I hope you'll let me see you again. Cousin Mary, will you show me that short cut to Wirral Hill?"

He swept her off with him so boldly and decisively, actually taking her by the arm, that Miss Drew was nonplussed. "Don't desert me, Mary!" was all she could cry out after them. They skirted the kitchen garden and reached a little gate in a budding privet-hedge, where old Weatherwax in some wanton mood had planted hyacinths. There was a clump of these heavily fragrant flowers by this gate and a lark high up above them was quivering in the hot sky. Mary put her hand on the latch after giving him minute directions of the way. They could see the whole ridge of Wirral Hill in the distance and the girl knew she ought to leave him at once and return; but it was hard to do so. Mr. Owen Evans was expecting him, he explained, by a lonely tree up there; and as he searched with his eyes the ridge she showed him, he could see clearly a particular tree which stood out in clear relief. He declared he could even see the Welshman's figure propped on the ground against this tree; but the girl contradicted this. "I know that black thing up there well," she said. "I used to take it for a person. It's an old post. I went up there once to make sure."

"What tree is that? Evans said it was a thorn but it doesn't look like a thorn to me."

"It's a sycamore," she answered. "At least I think so. Oh, I don't care what it is!" Her voice trembled. Her lips were quivering.

"What is it, my treasure?"

"*What is it?*" Her tears were swallowed in a sudden gust of anger. She dropped the latch of the little gate and her whole body stiffened. "You know what you've done, I suppose, John, by your silly talk? You've spoilt everything! She'll never ask you again. She'll stop my seeing you again! Oh, how could you do it, *you fool*? How *could* you do it?"

He was so astonished at the flashing eyes and the white face that his eyes and mouth opened with a blank, idiot look. His expression in fact was so exactly like one of those pictures of human beings that school-children draw on their slates, that Mary could not refrain from a faint smile.

"You see, John dear," she said more gently, "it would be very hard for me to get another job. If Miss Drew gave me notice I'd be penniless. I'd have to be a governess or a companion with someone else. *That* would almost certainly mean my leaving Glastonbury. You don't expect to follow me about all over England, do you, while I work in peoples' houses?"

"But I'm going to get work myself, *here*, and soon too," he protested. "Evans knows lots of people. He's going to help me. He's going to take me this very afternoon to see his cousin, Mrs. Geard. Mrs. Geard and Mr. Evans are both Rhyses; if you know what that means! At any rate you know too well who the Geards are."

Mary did smile outright at that. She shook her head. "They call ditches about here by some funny name like that. No! Rhyne, *that's* it, not Rhys. But won't Philip be furious if you go and see those Geards?"

"I don't care a damn about Philip. I hate the fellow! I'll make this Geard chap give me work. He ought to do something for some of us. *Any* decent man would, after collaring all that. And Evans says he's all right."

"But it would hurt Philip terribly, wouldn't it, and Aunt Elizabeth too, if you really did take money from that person? Does your friend know if this Geard man is going to go on living here?"

"Certainly he is! Mrs. Geard—who's a Rhys; and don't you forget *that*, Mary, for God knows all that that means!—has been three times already to look at a place over there"—he swung round on his heel and pointed to a sloping ridge not far from the Tor—"a place they call Chalice House. So they're going to stay here, don't 'ee fear. I tell you, my treasure, you needn't worry. It's going to be all right. We'll go on meeting in that same place in the Ruins where we did that first time. And as soon as I get work we'll be married—and the devil fly away with your old lady!"

Mary seized his wrist with all her fingers and lifted it to her mouth. "I've a great mind to punish you for behaving so badly," she murmured. There was something about the smell of John's bony hand that made her homesick for Norfolk. "It smells like peat," she thought, and she began licking with the tip of her tongue the little hairs which now tickled her lips. This gave her a sharp tingling sensation that ran through her whole frame. In a flash she imagined herself stretched out in bed by John's side. "Oh, my dear, oh, my dear!" she sighed.

"Take care, my treasure; they'll see us," he whispered. "Wait till tomorrow afternoon! About half-past two, eh? When your old lady is asleep? I'll wait for you. So don't you get agitated; even if you can't get away for hours. I'll wait there till they close up the whole place! I'll walk about a bit, you know, and come back. It's dry in that little chapel, even if it's raining outside."

Thus they talked by the gate, unwilling to separate, hugging each other—though they were not actually touching each other now—as tightly as if they were stark naked, but with no wild, irresistible rush of passion. They were Norfolk Crows, Crows from Norwich, from Thorpe, from Yaxham, from Thetford, from East Dereham, from Cringleford, from Methwold. Their love was lust, a healthy, earthy, muddy, weather-washed lust, like the love of water-rats in Alder Dyke or the love of badgers on Brandon Heath. They were shamelessly devoid of any Ideal Love. Born to belong to each other, by the same primordial law that made the Egyptian Ptolemies marry their sisters, they accepted their fatal monogamy as if it were the most casual of sensual attractions.

And in the etheric atmosphere about those two, as they stood there, quivered the immemorial Mystery of Glastonbury. Christians had one name for this Power, the ancient heathen inhabitants of this place had another, and a quite different one. Everyone who came to this spot seemed to draw something from it, attracted by a magnetism too powerful for anyone to resist, but as different people approached it they changed its chemistry, though not its essence, by their own identity, so that upon none of them it had the same psychic effect. This influence was personal and yet impersonal, it was a material centre of force and yet an immaterial fountain of life. It had its own *sui generis* origin in the nature of the Good-Evil First Cause, but it had grown to be more and more an independent entity as the centuries rolled over it. This had doubtless come about by reason of the creative energies pouring into it from the various cults, which, consciously or unconsciously, sucked their life-blood from its wind-blown, gossamer-light vortex. Older than Christianity, older than the Druids, older than the gods of Norsemen or Romans, older than the gods of the neolithic men, this many-named Mystery had been handed down to subsequent generations by three psychic channels; by the channel of popular renown, by the channel of inspired poetry, and by the channel of individual experience.

Names are magical powers. Names can work miracles. But the traditional name of this entity—the Holy Grail—might easily mislead an intelligent historian of our planet. The reality is one thing; the name, with all its strange associations, is only an outward shell of such reality. Apart from the fabulous stories that have become the burden of this wind-blown "Numen" it must be noted that as these two figures—this man and this woman—longed to make love to each other but were withheld by circumstance, their intense desire—all the more electric for being as vicious as it was—was urged by its own intensity (apart altogether from any consciousness in these two as to what was happening) to the very brink of this floating Fount of Life. The strongest of all psychic forces in the world is unsatisfied desire. And the desire of these two at this moment, gathering electric force out of the atomic air and striving blindly towards each

other in despite of the sundering flesh, was so caught up and so
heightened by the frustrated desires of two thousand years, which
in that valley had pulsed and jetted and spouted, that it did
actually draw near to that Secret Thing. Thus the loves of these
two people, both of them hostile to all these miraculous forces,
both of them rooted in fen-mud and vicious heathenism, did, by
reason of the strength of what the old Benedictines would have
called their "brutish and carnal purpose," approach the invisible
rim of that wind-blown mystery. Approach it, but not touch it!
With a heavy heart Mary dragged herself off. Three times she
looked back and waved her hand, watching him make his lingering way towards Wirral Hill. Southwest he went; and, each time
she turned, the afternoon sun seemed more obscuring, more
vaporously concealing, more hopelessly swallowing! He seemed
to disappear into that golden haze like "the knight-at-arms" of
the poet, "alone and palely loitering." But darkly, not "palely,"
did his figure pass away, vanishing amid the yet darker forms
of tree trunks and wall cornices and wooden water butts and
clothes lines and garden pumps; all mingling together in dim,
fantastic, purplish dream stuff; as if the slanting sun-rays had
hollowed out all substance, all solidity, from both them and
him!

As, hot and perspiring, John toiled up that dusty ascent, he
saw the boyish countenance of Tom Barter before him. He was
going to see Tom Barter tomorrow evening. Would he prove a
complete stranger when he was face to face with him? Tomorrow
evening was Saturday. He hoped Mary would be able to reach
that place in the Ruins in good time. Well! if she were late, he
would have to keep Tom waiting. But Tom would not mind. Tom
was always good-natured. Tom never got angry. No, he never
got angry, even when the boat was stranded in the mud, even
when the bait was left behind, even when a float was lost, even
when an oar got adrift, even when you kept him waiting for
hours!

By God! it *was* with Tom, and not with Mary, that he had
played that wicked game, that day, at the bottom of the boat.
How extraordinary that he should have mixed up those two like
that in his mind!

It was a steep and a dusty path he was following up the slope of Wirral Hill. Oh, how he longed for the stormy north wind and the wide fens. His nostalgia for Norfolk became a shrinking back from the strangeness of Glastonbury! He found himself staring at an iron seat which the municipality of the town had placed on a ledge of that long ascent. His sensations were very queer as he stood staring at this iron seat. "When I am having exciting thoughts about making love to Mary," he said to himself, "I feel careless and reckless; but when I think of Tom I have such a sensation of being protected that it makes me frightened of everything! God! I wish Mary and Tom and I were all safe back in that Northwold drawing-room, looking out on that lawn! There's something funny about this place. This place seems to be unreal. I feel exactly as if it were floating on a sea of coloured glass. I feel as if at any moment it might sink and carry me down into God knows what!"

He really did begin, at that moment, to feel physically dizzy. This alarmed him and made him tighten his hold on the handle of his stick and hurry on up the hill. He soon perceived beyond the curve of the incline, lifted above the dust of the pathway in front of him, the gaunt, outstretched branch of the ambiguous tree. And there was the black post; and there, with his back propped against the post and his chin upon his knees, sat Mr. Owen Evans. The sight of Mr. Evans, seated in that manner, brought back, in a flash, to John's mind, the image of Stonehenge. "Ha! those stones are older than Glastonbury!" he muttered to himself. And then feeling his courage and his adventurousness returning to him, "O great Stone Circle," he prayed, "give me my girl into my hands in spite of all these kings and saints and thorn trees!"

WHEN MR. DEKKER AND HIS SON SET OUT TO WALK TO WHITE-
lake River they decided to cross that particular region in the
environs of Glastonbury to which local usage had come to restrict the romantic name of Avalon. Over the uplands known as
Stonedown they directed their way straight to the hamlet of
Wick. At this point Mr. Dekker began to take a little surreptitious
pleasure in their excursion independent of its troublesome and
complicated purpose. He always loved a long walk with Sam
and there was not a field or a lane within several miles of their
home where some rare plant or bird, or, as the Spring advanced,
some butterfly did not arrest their attention.

"I was telling Mr. Crow," said Sam's father, "about this hamlet.
Do you know, it was the one thing I told him that really interested him. A quaint fellow this Crow seems to be."

His last words were spoken in a raised voice for Sam had
moved a little ahead of him and was standing by the side of
an immense oak tree which grew at the edge of the lane. Another
tree of the same species, equally enormous, grew a stone's throw
further on; and these two gigantic living creatures, whose topmost branches were already thickly sprinkled with small, gam-
boge-yellow leaf buds, appeared to be conversing together, in
that golden sun-haze, far up above the rest of the vegetable world
and where none but birds could play the eavesdropper.

The sight of these two titanic trees, trees that might have witnessed at least a fifth portion of the long historic life of Glastonbury, suggested to the mind of the elder Dekker thoughts quite
unconnected with either Vikings or Druids.

"We *must* try again here this summer for those Purple Hair-
streaks, Sam, my boy."

But the lad heard his father's words without his accustomed
sympathy in entomological pursuit. His body was at that moment bowed forward towards the great corrugated trunk, his outstretched arms pressed against it, his fingers extended wide. All
this he was doing in complete unawareness.

Was Sam's gesture, at this moment, destined to prove the existence of an increasing rapprochement in these latter modern days between certain abnormal human beings such as were both Sam and John, and the subhuman organisms in nature? Was it in fact a token, a hint, a prophecy or a catastrophic change imminent in human psychology itself?

Across the soul of that immemorial oak tree, as it flowed upward like an invisible mist from the great roots in the earth to those gamboge-coloured leaf buds, there had passed more wild November rains, more luminous August moons, more desperate March winds whirling and howling over Queen's Sedgemoor and Wick Hollow, than either Sam Dekker or his father had any notion of. Then why to the troubled heart of the younger man, just then, did there not come from the immense repository of this huge tree's vast planetary experience, a kind of healing virtue?

Why did Sam Dekker draw back from that oak tree uncomforted, uncounselled, unsoothed, uninspired? Against that great rough trunk many a gipsy donkey had rubbed its grey haunches and got comfort by it, many a stray heifer had butted with her wanton horns and eased her heart, squirrels had scampered and scratched there, and hung suspended, swaying their tails and scolding, wrens had built their large, green, mossy nests there, chaffinches had scraped and pecked at the lichen for *their* nests, so small, so elegant, in the nearby blackthorn bushes. Past that trunk and its great twin brother further down the lane had ridden men in armour, men in Elizabethan ruffles, men with cavalier ringlets, men in eighteenth-century wigs. Many of these no doubt jumped down from their horses, drawn by an indescribable, magnetic pull, and touched that indented bark with their travel-swollen bare hands. And to many it must have brought luck of some sort, some healing wisdom, some wise decisions, some hints of how to deal with their mates, with their offspring, with the tumult of life!

But nothing of this sort came to Sam Dekker. The son was he of the man who refused to worship the sun! That great reddish orb, now sinking down towards the Bristol Channel, had its own strange superhuman consciousness. And this consciousness, roused to anger against this simple priest, had resolved with a mysterious envenoming tenacity, corrosive and deadly, to separate him from the only earthly thing he loved!

The two men walked on in silence now, Mr. Dekker instinctively understanding that his son was on tenterhooks about this encounter, and beginning himself to feel, in his own sturdy consciousness, certain premonitions of danger on the air.

They passed Wick Hollow. They passed Bushey Combe. As they went on, they were sometimes compelled to stop and stare at the hedges for it was weeks since they had been that way and they were astonished at the extraordinary beauty of the celandines this year. The ground was uneven, broken up into many little depressions and small hillocks, and whether because February had been exceptionally wet, or because the winds had been so steadily blowing from the west, not only were the petals of the celandines more glittering than usual, but their leaves were larger and glossier.

"Celandines were my father's favourite flower," said Mat Dekker as they moved on again after one of these pauses. It always pleased him to think of his father when he was alone with his son and to speak of him to him. It made him feel that the three of them—three generations of Dekkers—were intimately bound together, and bound together too with that fecund Somersetshire soil. His piety in this classical sense was one of the massive single-hearted motives by which he lived.

The landscape around them changed completely now, for they descended from the verdurous island of Avalon down into a confused series of cattle droves which led across the low-lying water-meadows.

Few, even among the dwellers in Glastonbury, could have found their way as these two did over these fields and ditches. When they had passed the outskirts of Brindham Farm and reached the less-frequented marshes of Splott's Moor, it was even more difficult to proceed; for the cattle droves yielded place then to mere foot-tracks from weir to weir and dam to dam. Wider ditches too, interrupted their way, those great ditches of formidable water called rhynes to which Mary Crow had referred in her conversation with John; and the planks across these deep water courses

were, in many places, perilously rotted by rains and floods and
needed to be trodden with extreme wariness by two such heavily
built men. Whitelake River itself was also no contemptible obstacle to surmount, for there were no bridges anywhere near;
but in the end they discovered a willow branch fallen across the
little stream, and managed to make use of this as a bridge. It was
in the overcoming of little chance difficulties like this in exploring the country that Mat Dekker always showed at his best. On
this occasion, with the sun, his heathen enemy, already so near
the horizon he forgot completely the annoying nature of their
excursion and began chuckling and boasting over this or that
achievement of the way, as if they had been crossing the Danube
instead of Whitelake River!

They were now actually upon the marshlands of Queen's Sedgemoor; and here they found themselves without the trace of even
a footpath to follow, and once again the elder Dekker had an
opportunity of displaying to his son his skill as a cross-country
guide.

"Whitelake Cottage is on the bank of this stream, my son," he
said gravely, "and *we* are on the bank of this stream. All we've
got to do is to follow it down."

Sam mechanically obeyed, letting his father move in advance
of him by several paces. In his son's silence the elder man had
reverted to his natural custom of brooding sluggishly upon every
single little natural object they encountered. Nothing was negligible to this despiser of the sun when once he was out-of-doors.
There was no weed that lacked thrilling interest for him. But it
was not a merely scientific interest; still less was it an æsthetic
one. The master-current of the man's passionate West-country
nature found in a thousand queer, little, unattractive objects,
such as mouldering sticks, casual heaps of stones, discoloured
funguses on tree roots, dried-up cattle-droppings, old posts with
rusty nailheads, tree stumps with hollow places full of muddy
rain-water, an expression of itself that wide-stretching horizons
failed to afford.

By approaching their objective this particular afternoon by so
rambling and indirect a road, it was a good deal after half-past

four—the hour when they had been invited—that they reached Whitelake Cottage at last.

In recognition of the abnormally warm day, Nell Zoyland had arranged to give her guests their tea upon a little grassy terrace overlooking the swollen stream. Here then the father and son sat, munching such exquisite thin bread and butter as Mistress Pitches did not often cut for their delectation and trying to conceal both from each other and from their host, the growing measure of their uneasiness. For, truth to tell, the situation was drifting, moment by moment, more and more out of control. Nell Zoyland's cheeks were hot and her breath came quick. Mat Dekker had certainly never seen a girl with more beautiful, more alluring breasts than hers; nor had he ever seen one who dared to wear a bodice so tightly fitting, so mediæval-looking, so unfashionably piquant! These beautiful breasts seemed indeed to dominate the whole occasion. Mat Dekker felt that there was something so unusual about their loveliness that they endowed their owner with a sort of privileged fatality; a fatality that might lead to halcyon happiness; or on the other hand, to tragic devastation and destruction. They seemed meant, Mat Dekker thought as his eyes wistfully followed them, for something beyond the suckling of any human infant. At this point the man's ingrained morality pulled him up short. But he could not resist the feeling that there was something in the loveliness of such breasts that carried a person far from ordinary human life, to those old wild legends of immortal creatures of mist, of dawn, of dew that have troubled good men's minds from the beginning.

"It is only children of the elements," he said to himself, "that such breasts ought to suckle!"

It was at this point in this singular tea-party that William Zoyland began to speak his mind.

Sam Dekker soon ceased to drink any more tea or to eat any more bread and butter. He sat now with his shoulders hunched up and his chin sunk into his neck. His elbows rested heavily upon Nell's wicker-work garden table. His eyes were fixed upon the face of William Zoyland as if upon the face of a well-known animal that had suddenly begun uttering surprising sounds, sounds that belonged to an entirely different type of beast.

Nell, on the contrary, had the aspect of a girl desperate and reckless at the close of a day-long struggle with an equal adversary. She fixed upon her husband's leonine head, as he went on speaking, that careless, contemptuous look, which, of all looks in their harem, men dread the most.

Whitelake Cottage was like a little doll's house by the reedy banks of Whitelake River. It only possessed two rooms downstairs and two upstairs, with a little kitchen at the back, above which, under a sloping roof, which had been attached to the rest of the house at a recent date, was a low-ceilinged attic-study devoted to the use of the master. They evidently had no servants nor was there any sign of a flowerbed, although at the edge of the grassy slope where they all now sat, several wild-flower roots, by the look of the disturbed soil and the appearance of the plants, had been lately put in.

Under that flowing torrent of deep-toned revelations, full of startling import, to which they were perforce listening, Mat Dekker was staring at last year's drooping rushes, brown and crumpled, among which several newly green shoots were sprouting up. The sun was quite below the horizon now; and in the early twilight these green reed shoots threw forth a peculiar coolness of their own, a pure, liquid coolness, after that warm day that was like a calm but tragic Finis to some magical play of a great playwright.

Mat Dekker was gathering up his forces to deal with a situation altogether new in his narrow and single experience, and the effort to cope with this was so great that its effect upon him, as Zoyland went on speaking, began to be the very last anyone would have predicted. He began to grow extremely sleepy. This tendency to grow sleepy at a crisis was indeed an old infirmity in his family. The great-grandfather of his father, James Dekker, had grown sleepy when called upon, with other well-known Somersetshire gentlemen, to rise to the support of William of Orange against the last of the Stuarts.

"It's for the wench to decide for herself," Will Zoyland was saying, as, lying back in his wicker arm-chair with his leather-gaitered legs stretched out in front of him and one hand deep in his corduroy breeches' pocket and the other tugging at his great yellow beard, he rolled his blue eyes from Sam's bowed face to Sam's father's averted face. "I'm a philosopher, Mr. Dekker. I'm not one to let myself suffer, or the girl either, when there's no need for it. But it's too much for her to expect that I'll go on living with her and sleeping in a separate bed. In fact, I refuse to do it! I'm a philosopher, I tell ye; and as such I know that all conventional idealism is puff-ball foolishness. Any girl can love two men if she wants to, just as *we* can love two women. I've no doubt a man like yourself, Mr. Dekker, has frequently loved two women at the same time. It's natural to us. Nell and this silly lad here think they're in love. They've imagined till today, or at any rate Sam has imagined till today, that I was the sort of born cuckold who could be fooled till judgment. Well! I'm not. D'ye hear, Sam, me boy? *I'm not.* I live my own life in my own way and always have. I could live here perfectly well without Nell, though she doesn't think so. She thinks I could live without sleeping with her; but she don't believe I could get my meals for myself or get on without having her to talk to. That's where women are so stupid. They think they're necessary where they're *not* necessary; and they don't know how necessary they are, in another direction! But I'm a philosopher, as I say, Mr. Dekker, my good Sir, and I know very well that my little Nell still loves her old Will (though she doesn't know it herself!) quite as much as she loves this sulky young gentleman here. Now what I say to her, Sir, and to you, my romantic young friend, is simply this. If Nell will stop this foolery of sleeping on the sitting-room sofa, stop, in fact, this foolery of being cross with me and cold to me, I'll be ready—d'ye hear me lad?—I'll be ready to share her with ye. So long as ye don't tumble her 'in me wone bed,' as they say round here, ye can have the lass uphill and down dale—I'm mum. I'm mute. I'm the dumb fish. In fact, to tell ye the truth, Mr. Dekker, I've got ridiculously fond of this great hulking son of yours. I respect the boy. I like talking to the boy. We've had some fine times together, haven't we, Sam? No, no. I agree with that old rogue Voltaire. I'm one who could be quite content to live 'à trois,' as the rascal says. But I'm not one who can live side by side with a girl like Nell and have her cold and cross and savage, like she's been this last month. To

Hell with her cooking! I'm as good a cook as she is; and a better, too. Sam would like her to remain my servant and to become his light o' love. Nell wants to run off with Sam and leave everything. Only when I tell her to stop talking about it and do it, she says Sam hasn't the guts to leave his dad. And then when I laugh at her and tell her to try him and see, she just cries and cries at the thought of how her poor old Will is to get on, all alone, without anyone to get him his meals."

He paused and looked round to make sure that his wife had not slipped away and retreated into the house. No; Nell Zoyland was standing exactly where she had been when he began to speak, her hands pressed against the back of an empty chair. It was then that Will Zoyland's eye, as he looked round, caught sight of a kestrel-hawk hovering in the air above some pollarded willows. He clapped his great hand on his mouth with an inarticulate shishing sound.

"Shish! Shish!" he murmured, glancing at the two Dekkers and then at Nell. He rose to his feet, turned his back upon them all, and stepping lightly on tip-toe, like a gamekeeper in pursuit of a poacher, hurried to the side wall of his house.

Following his motions with his eyes, the elder Dekker remembered now, what everybody in Glastonbury knew, namely that Mr. Zoyland was the bastard son of the Marquis of P., the great Somersetshire landowner. He saw the fellow seize upon his gun, where it lay propped against the wall, and glance quickly upward. Like the dedicated naturalist that he was, Mat Dekker hated to see any bird shot; and even though he had been told that in that low-lying ground, kestrels had grown to be a nuisance, he still would have protested violently.

Without a second's hesitation he lifted up his voice from where he sat and uttered a resounding, "Hoy! a-hoy! hawk-a-hoy!"

The report of the gun followed almost immediately; but, startled by his guest's shout, the bearded bastard of Lord P. missed his bird.

Nell fully expected the roar of a Polyphemus to follow this mischance and a terrible, "Damn your soul, Sir! What do you mean by that?" But neither Mr. Zoyland's voice nor any look in his eyes betrayed a flicker of such emotion.

"Sorry, Sir!" was all he said, as he resumed his seat with his gun across his knees; "I ought to have remembered your penchant for hawks. Sam told me how he used to keep a pair of them when he was at school. I expect it was by taming hawks that he learnt to tame girls. Well, Sam; well, Nell, what are you two romantic children going to decide? Is poor old Will to go on sleeping alone?"

There was something about the man's tone that roused the girl to a level of emotion and a quality of emotion that astonished her lover.

The slow-flowing water beneath them seemed to have taken to itself all the daylight that was left; and between the girl's tense face and its unruffled surface an affinity of whiteness that was almost phosphorescent rose into being, established itself, and became more and more dominant. Had the little house, the pollarded willows, the gun on the bearded man's knees, the twitching chin of Sam, been elements of sound in a momentous orchestra, this whiteness of flowing water and of a woman's face would have been the flute note or the oboe note in the symphonic effect.

Here sat together, on the darkening bank of this steel-white water, three formidable men, any one of whom could have crushed out that frail spark of girlish life as the swish of a horse's tail might crush a currant moth. And yet the tension of that single feminine heart reduced all three of them to the negligibleness of three wooden posts in the palings around an agitated heifer.

And just as such a heifer's up-tossed head and lifted voice might bring some farm girl upon the scene who would pass those paling-posts by as if they did not exist, so the suppressed tempest in Nell Zoyland's nerves brought to her rescue nothing less than the great planet of the evening itself. Whiter than the White-lake stream, whiter even than the girl's face, this celestial luminary, this immortal sign in the heavens "that brings the traveller home by every road," emerged now from the cloudy western lake wherein the sun had vanished.

A long relaxed shiver of nervous relief passed through Nell Zoyland's perfect breasts, and through her ravished but unconceiving womb, and through her thighs and through her trembling knees. Turning her gaze from the evening star she looked, for some reason she could never have explained, *not* into Sam's pathetic bear-eyes that were following her every motion, but into two deep, twilit, granite pools. Into such granite pools—now that his enemy, the Sun, had long since vanished—Mat Dekker's quiet grey eyes, under their bristling eyebrows, had been transformed! The man met the girl's gaze; and the mysterious sweetness of her soul—troubled still but no longer convulsed with anger—rested for a second upon the priest's new strength, as if he and not her lover or her husband were her true friend among those three men.

"Well, you two," repeated Will Zoyland, "aren't you going to answer? I am one for living a civilised life in these things. Could any man make a more liberal offer? If Nell will live again with me, as she did when we were married a couple of years ago, I'll let her see as much of our good Sam as she likes. Will's bed isn't the only place where young blood can cool itself. There's my offer. If you two want to go off together and leave Will to look after himself, *go!* For God's sake, *go!* And good luck to you! I can't hand you the money for expenses, because I haven't got it. She knows—none so well as she!—that I haven't got it. But if you go I won't trouble ye. I won't lift a finger to stay ye. Only I won't take Nell back if she gets sick of it. 'Once gone, always gone' is my motto for runaway little girls.

"Well, Sir,"—and he turned quite definitely to Mr. Dekker now, bowing towards him over his gun—"do you feel like treating these frisky lambs to a trip abroad? Or are you prepared to let 'em kiss and clip under our own roofs?"

Mat Dekker rose slowly to his feet.

"May I be allowed a few words alone with Mrs. Zoyland before we talk any more about this?"

The bearded man looked, for one quarter of a second, a little nonplussed; but he quickly recovered himself and waved his hand towards the house.

"You go in with him, Nell, if you want to! Can you light the sitting-room lamp or do you want me to come and do it? You can? Very well, then! Sam and I will stay out-of-doors. Come and see my otter trap, Sam! It's more likely to catch a water-

rat than an otter in this little puddle; but you never can tell.
Queer if there should be an otter in it tonight—of all nights—
but I don't suppose there is."

The man went so far in his blustering bonhomie as actually
to take Sam by the arm. Sam was so dazed by all these events
that he offered no resistance. His mind seemed to have become
incapable of any thought or any decision. What wavered before
him just then was the gasping mouth of the sick minnow, at the
top of the water in the aquarium, in their play-room. He felt like
that minnow himself!

"You know, Sam, the truth is, since we've broken the ice"—
Zoyland's voice went booming on in the darkness by the lad's
side like a low-toned threshing machine—"our little Nell's not
so much in love with you as she's in love with Love. She's as
romantic as a child of sixteen. In fact mentally, I often think,
she *is* sixteen. That's what it is, Sammy, old friend, mentally sixteen; and with no more idea of the realities of life than a schoolgirl. It's a good thing it was a boy like you who came along.
With anyone else she'd have made herself seriously unhappy; but
with you she's safe. That's what I've said to her from the beginning. 'You'll never make me angry with you over Sam Dekker,'
I've said. 'With that boy you're safe,' I've said. And you *are*
safe, aren't you, Sam?"

He pressed the lad's arm with his free hand as he led him
along the bank of the stream. Sam at least had the wit to notice
that in his other hand he still held his gun. By degrees Sam became conscious too that he did have one clear and strong wish
in his confused brain. He wished that William Zoyland did not
live where it was possible for him to trap otters.

"My father doesn't like the idea of trapping otters," he remarked.

After following a kind of tow-path along the bank they came
to a small river weir. There was a gurgling sound under the
woodwork here, and a low humming and rustling sound; both
sounds were evidently being caused by the position of the dam
at that hour, but it was too dark to distinguish them exactly.

Out of the darkness of that full-brimmed swishing water there
emerged a damp, chilly, but not unpleasant smell, composed of

many separate elements. It was composed of wet moss, of old dead leaves, of yet older dead wood, of long-submerged, slime-coated masonry, of clammy river weeds. The gurgling sound and the rushing sound came forth hollowly together, producing upon the ear a kindred effect to that produced upon the sense of smell by the damp wafture.

The idea of a wild otter caught in a trap by his bearded companion suddenly became unbearable to Sam Dekker. For the first time in his life this much-enduring youth found himself trembling from head to foot with a desire to kill. He imaged to himself the precise nature of the sudden, violent shove which would precipitate this burly offspring of the Marquis of P. into the rushing blackness.

"There *may* be one of them in it, you know. There *may* be one of them in it," William Zoyland kept obstinately repeating. Probably nothing would have happened. Probably some other excuse would have presented itself for refraining from a piece of silly violence that might not even have proved fatal, for it is likely enough that Zoyland was a powerful swimmer. But the excuse he did obey was the hoot of an owl coming from the direction of the cottage, and two or three times repeated. Sam answered the owl's cry, imitating it exactly, and the thing was repeated again and again.

"He wants us back at your house," Sam said. "So we'd better go. That's my father; that's not an owl."

"One minute, then—you go ahead, Sam! I'll be with you in a moment."

But Sam had not waited for this permission from his host and rival. He was already hurrying back with a shambling speed that nearly broke into a run. He felt he was escaping, not from the bearded man but from his own dark impulse. He was surprised to hear strange voices when he neared the house and as he reached it he observed, in the narrow lane behind it, the lights of a motor car. When he entered the little sitting-room, he found it pleasantly illuminated by the large green-shaded lamp to which his host had recently referred; and there were red coals in the grate.

Talking eagerly to his father and Nell, and all of them standing in an animated group in the centre of the room, were Mr.

Philip Crow and Mr. Tom Barter. Sam shook hands awkwardly
and mechanically with the newcomers but all his attention was
concentrated upon Nell. Ever since the moment when some mysterious vibration had passed between the girl and that white
planet in the western sky, Nell's mood had completely changed.
The nervous tension that had been growing week by week ever
since she refused Will Zoyland his nightly embraces, seemed, at
any rate for the present, to have fallen away. In some remote
place in her heart, in some hidden chamber there, not far from
the spot where she had just now been so grievously wounded by
his words, she was, as a matter of fact, experiencing a reaction
in his favour. The realisation that she *could* leave him, if only
Sam would risk all, satisfied her inordinate mania for romance,
while the fact that it was clear that Sam never *would* risk all
helped her reaction towards her husband. Like Helen of Troy,
upon the high tower of the wall, she permitted Aphrodite to be
her guide. And the harlot goddess persuaded her to keep both
her man and her lover!

In Sam's simple brain it had been lodged as a ghastly and
tragic fact that Zoyland's love-making was odious to her. She
had been subtly and gradually impelled to lead him on to this
sinister view. And she had done it half-unconsciously; never exactly lying to him; half-believing the fancy herself, as she yielded
to his pathetic and inexperienced advances. Men, especially young
men, because of something fastidious and idealistic in their own
nature, are always prepared to be touched to the heart by the
idea of a girl's physical loathing for another man. Indeed it is
given to few men, whether old or young, to understand the profound part played by what might be called "the universal prostitute" in every woman's nature. It is indeed always a puzzle to
men, the physical passivity which women have the power of summoning up, to endure the inconvenience of an amorous excitement which they do not share. Few men realize the depth of the
satisfaction to women's nature in the mere possession of the
power to cause such excitement. When a man sees a sensitive
girl with what he considers a thick-skinned, brutal mate, he experiences a twinge—perhaps quite uncalled-for—of the sort of
imaginative pity which is the inverse side of male sadism.

Whatever passivity it was that Nell Zoyland gave herself up to now, it had something about it of that mysterious passivity of fate which the women of antiquity knew. And doubtless this mood had been fortified in this case by the girl's talk with Sam's father. Mat Dekker had risen to the occasion with a weight and an insight that surprised even himself. To beg her to postpone, to delay, to *think*, had been his intention when he spoke to Nell; but below his grave and practical words there had been such a clairvoyant tenderness, such a direct man-to-woman, as well as priest-to-daughter vibration in his tone, that her nervous revolt against her dilemma mounting up to such a pitch of blind anger, and then soothed by the Planet of Love, ebbed altogether under his influence.

"What I really came for," Philip Crow was saying, "was to see whether there was a chance of Mr. Zoyland's helping me out, over at Wookey Hole, as he did last year when I was in difficulties. I know of course"—this was said with a little stiff bow in Nell's direction—"that the remuneration is nothing to him. But the work is interesting—he found it so last Spring—and I'm prepared to pay him a little more this time."

"You mean you want Zoyland to act as official guide in Wookey Hole?" threw in Mat Dekker. "By Heaven, Crow, if Zoyland won't do it for you, I believe my Sam here would be just the person! He's read everything there is to be read on Wookey, and he's better up on neolithic weapons than anyone round here. You'd help Mr. Crow, wouldn't you, Sam, if Zoyland refused?"

Sam, abashed by his father's words, threw a humble glance like that of a bewildered horse in the direction of Nell but uttered no sound at all.

"William *may* be pleased to do it," the girl said hurriedly, speaking to Philip but replying to Sam's look. "But I think Sam would be just as good a guide in those caves—perhaps better. William's inclined to be flippant and off-handed with people when he doesn't like them and there must be lots of very teasing people who come to visit Wookey."

Philip Crow, whose habit was not to beat about the bush, now looked straight at his business companion. He felt no necessity to propitiate, for any direct purpose of his own, any of these people; and that being the case, his narrow, clear-cut, war-axe consciousness simply eliminated them.

"I wish *you* would do it for me, Tom," he said in a hurried, quick voice. "I'd far sooner not trouble Mr. Zoyland; or anyone else for the matter of that"—and he gave a quick, rather derogatory glance at Sam.

"I don't . . . know . . . that I could deal with . . . Wookey Hole, Father," murmured Sam nervously.

What he really felt at that moment was an extreme reluctance to deal with Mr. Philip Crow.

Tom Barter surveyed his employer with complete aplomb. He was a shortish, squarish man of clear complexion and with a round, fair, bullet-shaped head. He was the only person under that green-shaded lamp who seemed entirely at ease and carefree. He had been gazing at Nell Zoyland with a shameless glance of covetous impersonal lechery.

"Can't leave the office, Phil," he said. "You people never know where your own machine is tricky and jumpy. If I left that office, for Wookey Hole, even for a fortnight, 'twould take six weeks to get things straightened out."

Philip Crow made a humorous grimace directed towards Mat Dekker. His gesture said, "You see what a good subordinate I have; and how prettily he plays the rôle I've composed for him."

At that moment Will Zoyland came clattering in, boisterous, burly and jovial, and plumped down his gun against the wall.

"No otter, Sam!" were his first words as he shook hands with his two visitors. "You needn't tell me what you've come for, Crow," was his next remark, "for I see it in your grasping slave-driving eye! You want to kidnap poor Will as your damned showman! That's what he's after, isn't it, Nell! Isn't it, Sam?"

"Well, Zoyland," snapped Philip sharply, evidently disliking intensely the burly giant's familiar tone, "will you come out there for a couple of months? I've got a chap from London, an official antiquary and all that sort of thing, for the summer; but people are beginning to come already and I've got no one there now but just my ordinary workmen to show 'em round."

"Can't answer off the reel like this, Crow. Can't do it!"

He leaned heavily upon a sort of mahogany sideboard that stood against the wall. Three silver salvers, bearing the arms of the Marquis of P., clattered down from their propped-up position; and the whole sideboard groaned under his weight. Philip turned instinctively to Nell. How many times had he not been forced to get what he wanted from a rebellious man by wheedling a practical woman!

"By the way, Mrs. Zoyland," he said, "I hope that wild stepbrother of yours hasn't heard about the trouble that started last week among my people at Wookey. Don't you tell him, if he hasn't! The very last thing I want to see is Dave Spear and his fanatical wife down here at this juncture."

It was a good thing for Philip at that moment that the suspicious and malicious ears of Cousin John didn't catch this speech. John would certainly have translated these words in the very opposite sense from that which they apparently bore. "Write at once," John would have translated them, "to your step-brother, Dave and hold out to him the lure of a possible strike down here, so that he'll bring his wife at once." Nor would John have been greatly mistaken. The truth is that the main motive that brought this Norman conqueror to Whitelake that evening had nothing at all to do with William Zoyland or with Wookey Hole. William was only the official motive. The true dynamo that brought this electrifier of Wookey Hole posthaste to Queen's Sedgemoor was the maddening temptation of Cousin Percy's slender waist.

Astute business man though he was, Philip had, when it came to his passions, a swift-plotting recklessness that stopped at little. Besides, his contempt for the practical ability of Cousin Persephone and, for the matter of that, of the ability of her husband also, was unbounded. No! He'd get Percy down here and give her all the rope she wanted. Let the sweet creature "agitate" as much as she liked. He'd settle the strikers and cuckold the Communist! It was precisely the kind of dangerous human game that suited his Battle-of-Hastings temperament. Did he divine in some sly diplomatic cranny of his secret heart that either Nell Zoyland or William Zoyland would be certain to tell the Spears the very thing he so arrogantly bade them not to tell? He probably did; but as with all daring and successful men the tricks and devices of his subconscious nature were much more formidable than his rational schemes; and so by a sort of automatic protective instinct he kept them subconscious!

Had Nell's wits not been purged of idealistic vapour by the white rays of the great planet she might have missed the singularity of this request. As it was, she was shrewdly struck by it. With quick feminine craft she concealed her surprise. But in her heart she actually formed the words with which she would comment upon this episode to William Zoyland.

"Manufacturers don't as a rule try and stave off the arrival of agitators by appealing to their relatives, do they, Will?" And she could hear the bellowing "Ha! Ha! Ha!" with which William would receive this sally.

"No, I'll be careful, Mr. Crow," she said. "I'll be careful! Not that I often write to poor Dave. We're only half-brothers, you know."

Tom Barter, his eyes fixed on his own old-fashioned gold watch chain from which hung the good upper-middle-class, county-family seal of the Barters of Norfolk, thought to himself, "Think of that funny little Johnny Crow turning up in town! Aye, but I'll be glad to see the little urchin again." And then Tom Barter's mind ceased suddenly to think in definite words. The "little river" and the "big river" at Northwold, the Bridge at Didlington, were more than words. Such memories as they held could not be put even by the practical, cynical, lecherous Tom, into any human sentence. Whitelake Cottage vanished away, as he fumbled with his father's ancestral seal, a tall heron standing on one leg. All these people vanished away. He only felt the presence of little Johnny Crow. He only felt the cold strong wind in the reeds of the Wissey. There was no longer any well-run office, no longer any factory by Wookey Hole. The smell of the bottom of a boat came over him so vividly that if he had not been the practical manager of three factories, he would have walked straight out of that house.

"Tomorrow I shall see little Johnny," he thought. And then he thought, "I'd give a hundred pounds to sleep one night with this girl here!"

Philip himself had now resumed his direct attack upon William Zoyland. Somehow it rather tickled his fancy to be able to say, "My guide at Wookey, related, so everyone maintains, to the Marquis of P."

Meanwhile Nell, seeing him so engaged, had managed to pull Sam out of the open door into the river-scented garden.

"Don't you mind, little Sam," she was saying, "don't you mind the way things are!"

It was fortunate for some of the persons in that small group that the sudden passing of an airplane over Whitelake Cottage completely absorbed the general attention. It was tacitly assumed that it was to watch this illuminated air-equipage that Sam and his hostess had wandered off in the darkness; and soon they were all staring up at it beside the obscure, melancholy shapes of empty chairs, dim tables and shadowy tea-cups upon the chilly lawn.

"Barter! It's the man from Wells!" cried Philip, with nervous, intense interest. "Or it's a plane exactly like his. We ought to have stayed in tonight."

Tom Barter moved in the darkness close to the side of his employer. "All planes look the same, Phil, at night," he said in a low, emphatic tone. He spoke so quietly that no one but Nell, who chanced to be nearest to Mr. Philip, caught these words and this tone.

"He doesn't want Mr. Crow to give away something," the girl thought. "I'll tell William about his hushing him up so. I shouldn't wonder if they aren't buying an airplane."

When the plane had vanished, Philip and Tom Barter moved off towards their car, Zoyland striding alongside of them and the rest following. They soon formed a loquacious group around the car, uttering those spontaneous and lively genialities which among human beings imply instinctive relief at being able to get rid of one another. It was at this moment that Mat Dekker said, "I sometimes have thought of a queer thing, my friends."

Sam, who had been in a sullen daze since the episode of the river bank, pricked up his ears at his father's tone. It was very rare for Mr. Dekker to adopt this sermonising manner. Never was a priest less pontifical than he.

"What, Father?" murmured Sam dutifully, when none of the others took the least notice of this remark.

"I've thought that the conquest of the air," Mat Dekker went on, "is such an enormous event in the history of the human race that it is probably responsible for these reckless and chaotic impulses which we all feel nowadays. What do you people think? I'd go even further," he continued, raising his voice in the darkness, "I'd go so far as to say that all these strange spiritualistic occurrences that we hear so much about are the result of Man's having found out how to fly."

"Tom here would give his head to be an airman," threw out Philip with an explosion of motiveless malignity.

"Get into your seat, Phil, and let's start!" was the quick retort.

Barter's words were simple but his tone was black with indignation. Philip Crow, from the very first time his Norfolk friend had used his Christian name, disliked being called "Phil" by his head-manager. In his displeasure now he was prepared to go on teasing him.

"Barter's the most normal person I've ever met," he said, without moving a step, "but when it becomes a question of flying, he's as jumpy as a girl who hears her lover's name."

"Why don't you go in for flying, Mr. Barter? You could so easily take lessons," said William Zoyland with innocent-wicked mischief.

For a second the reserved Norfolk man was quite silent. Then he burst out.

"Get into the car, Phil, can't you? I'm catching cold!"

But Philip suddenly swung round.

"Can't I take you two home?" he said.

Tom Barter at once echoed this. "Of course we must take them home. There's easy room for three; and I'll sit on my heels."

Philip repeated his invitation. "Please get in, Mr. Dekker; please get in, Sam!"

The husband and wife—his arm had slipped round her waist now, and only peevishly, not with any repulsion, she tossed it from her—joined their persuasions to those of the two motorists. It took quite a little while for these four men to crowd them-

selves in so that Philip, who was driving, could use his brakes.
But they started at last; and the last word was Philip's.

"Think over that offer of mine, Zoyland. And remember I can
give you a few shillings more than I scraped up for you last
year."

Mat Dekker begged the manufacturer to drop them opposite
St. John the Baptist's Church, and it was an incredible relief to
Sam when at last, alone with his father and in complete silence,
he walked up the path to the church porch. To their surprise,
although it was well after eight o'clock, they heard voices in the
nave as soon as they pushed open the door and inhaled the
familiar musty smell. The verger had left a gas-jet burning in
the vestry under the great tower, and the little red light of the
Real Presence was suspended above the altar, but otherwise the
church was completely dark. And yet it was not! The father and
son, with the easy movements of long usage, opened the door
so quietly that they caught the sacrilegious striking of a match
in the western aisle. By the little yellow flame of this match
shaded between human hands, they perceived that two men were
bending over the lidless and empty sarcophagus of Joseph of
Arimathea. One of these men was on his knees, evidently tracing
out, in concentrated absorption and with his index finger, the
famous initials *J. A.* which are so deeply cut upon the northern
end of this huge receptacle. Whether it was a visual illusion due
to the flickering of the match, or whether it really occurred, Mat
Dekker could not be sure, but he fancied he saw this man, the
one whose fingers were fumbling at those formidable initials,
bow down his head as if praying to this empty tomb!

The priest swerved reverently at the sight of this real or imaginary act of devotion and, followed by Sam, moved hurriedly to
the vestry, where with instinctive and discreet disregard of what
he felt to be a legitimate gesture of impulsive piety, he proceeded
to do what he had come to do. This was to rinse out a small glass
chalice and fill it with wine, ready for the morning's consecration. While he did this, Sam sat down on a wooden chair by the
vestment cupboard and stared sombrely up through the vestry
door at the dimly lit receding pillars of the perpendicular nave.
He kept feeling again and again the pressure against him of that

beautiful girlish body. With this feeling there returned too the damp and deathly smell of the river weir and the murderous desire he had had at that spot. He lowered his gaze from the dim vista of high carved arches and with his vision still framed by the vestry door he let it rest upon the red altar light, signifying the living presence of the Body of God. He could hear the trickling of water being poured from one glass into another in the preparation for tomorrow's Mass, and he could catch a little faint squeaky sound, like the voice of a new-born mouse, of a cloth being rubbed against the edges of glass vessels. To what precise point did his father carry his belief in the miracle of Transubstantiation? It went much further anyway than his own vague superstitious uneasiness.

"I feel just like a dog barking at the moon," he thought, "when I see that red light." The pit of his stomach suddenly seemed to sink inward then for he thought to himself, "She *is* going to sleep with him again! I could feel it in the air when we came away." That little, squeaky, rubbing sound behind him seemed to be going on forever. "She's probably taken off all her clothes now," he thought, "and she's holding up her nightgown with her bare arms to slip it over her shoulders. He's got her now; to work his will upon. . . . Oh! Oh! Oh! . . . ." Sam tried to push this image away from him but it persistently returned.

"Father! you *must* stop that rubbing!" he suddenly cried out. "When a thing is clean, it *is* clean. It's no good going on and on like that!"

Mat Dekker stopped what he was doing at once and began putting the sacred vessels away.

"True enough, Sammy," he said with a sigh. "The truth is I was thinking of something else." He closed the cupboard, turned out the gas-jet, and they both emerged into the body of the church. It now became necessary to communicate to the worshippers at St. Joseph's vacant coffin that they were about to lock up the church. They moved to the door and the father held it open while the son crossed the aisle.

Since their appearance on the scene the two intruders had contented themselves with a whispered conversation. They had not dared to strike any more matches.

"Pardon me, gentlemen," said Sam, "my father wants to lock up the church."

The man upon his knees struggled stiffly to his feet, emitting a little groan as his bones creaked. They neither of them spoke a word, but began following their dismisser meekly and humbly to the church door. With a mute bow Mat Dekker indicated to them his gratitude for this obedience and moved aside to let them pass out. It was such a dark night that although he thought he had seen both the men before he could not recall their names. When the key was turned and the empty sarcophagus of the Arimathean was once more left alone with that Presence under the red lamp, the father and son followed the strangers down the flagged path, past the miraculous thorn bush, to the gate into the street. Here there was a suspended gas-globe, and here the strangers turned, revealing the black bowler hat and hooked Roman nose of Mr. Owen Evans, and a broad-shouldered, rather fleshy individual, without any hat, whose grizzled head under that suspended light seemed to Sam the largest human head he had ever seen. It was the head of a hydrocephalic dwarf; but in other respects its owner was not dwarfish. In other respects its owner had the normally plump, rather unpleasantly plump figure of any well-to-do-man, whose back has never been bent nor his muscles hardened by the diurnal heroism of manual labour.

"How do you do, Mr. Dekker? How do you do, Mr. Sam Dekker?" The Welshman threw into these words all the Ciceronian ceremoniousness of what John Crow called his "first manner." "I know you two gentlemen, though you don't know me," Owen Evans went on, "but of course you know my relative, Mr. Geard."

Both father and son looked at "my relative, Mr. Geard," with unashamed curiosity. It gave them both indeed a queer sensation to shake hands with this ambiguous person under the gas-lamp in that silent street; for although Mr. Geard's visits to Glastonbury had been few since he had left his family and gone to Northwold, all the air had been recently vibrant with gossip about him. The money that his employer had left him had been doubled and trebled by such gossip. Wherever, since his return, his bare hydrocephalic head had appeared, the envious feeling and the wondering awe had arisen. "There goes a very rich man!" Mr.

Geard had become in fact a local celebrity, a fairy-story hero; and the rumours about his purchase of Chalice House, one of the famous show-places of the town, had kept alive a romantic interest, which, if the man had left the vicinity, would have soon died down.

"Of course we've heard of Mr. Geard," said the elder Dekker politely, "and we met only today, at Miss Drew's, a very interesting young man, who told us that he was a friend of yours, Mr. Evans."

"I must not keep you, gentlemen, for I know it's late," went on the Roman-faced Welshman, "but I would like to hear which side you'd take in a dispute Mr. Geard and I have been having, under the aegis of St. Joseph."

"I'd like to hear about it very much, Mr. Evans," said Mat Dekker. "Won't you walk a step with us? For I *am* a little afraid that our housekeeper will be getting anxious about us."

"Well . . . perhaps. . . ." murmured the Welshman, hesitating and glancing at his companion, "perhaps my relative, Mr. Geard, is feeling tired."

But they all four set themselves in motion in the direction of the Vicarage; and it was not long before they reached the mediæval front of the Pilgrims' Inn. Although the rest of the street was quiet, there were lights and the sound of raised voices inside the mullioned windows of this old building.

"I was trying," said Mr. Evans, "to convince my relative that the fact that so many visitors come to this spot from all over the world is no proof that it is miraculous; but it *is* a proof that something important can at any moment occur."

"Occur where?" enquired Mr. Dekker.

"*In the mind!*" cried the Welshman, raising his hand to his head and giving his bowler hat such a violent jerk downward that its brim rested on the bridge of his great nose.

Very gravely, as they all four stood still upon the illuminated pavement outside the ancient inn, Mat Dekker extended his hand to this bowler-hatted oracle.

"Good-night, Mr. Evans," he said. "We won't take you further, but it interests me profoundly that you should make that remark, because it's what I've been feeling for several years. I associate it myself, as I told them just now at Whitelake, with the conquest of the air; but as you ——" Mr. Evans did not let him finish the sentence. He had already taken the priest's hand and was shaking it vigorously; but he dropped it now as if it had hurt him.

"The air?" he murmured gloomily. "Did you say the air?"

And pushing back the brim of his hat, as if it had been a visor, he snuffed with angry nostrils at the element referred to.

"No, Mr. Dekker, no! What I was referring to was the mind. When the mind is clean, the change we are looking for will come. It's to clean the mind, Mr. Dekker; to purge it, to wash it, to give it a New Birth, that all these people"—he removed his hat altogether now and waved it, without finishing his sentence, towards the illuminated windows.

"You *do* see a little what I mean?" he added then, addressing the enormous cranium of Mr. Geard.

But the beneficiary of William Crow's fortune was engaged just then in a private quest of his own. He had advanced cautiously towards one of the lighted windows and was peering in. His air was so exactly the air of an inquisitive servant, gazing with aloofness and yet respectful curiosity at a remote revel of his masters that Sam was betrayed into a jest.

"Are they behaving decently or indecently in there, Mr. Geard?"

The Canon's friend swung round upon his heel and surveyed the young man. The lad was astonished at the look of affectionate reproach on his large face. Had Sam been an impertinent young Sadducee addressing an insolent remark to some great Rabbi whose Holy Innocence confounded him, he could hardly have felt more ashamed of himself and more of a flippant fool than he did at that moment. Mr. Geard, however, made no audible reply to these rude words. It was the descendant of the House of Rhys who answered for both of them as they all nodded a final goodnight.

"My relative, Mr. Geard," he said, "intends to bring a great many people to Glastonbury . . . more than have come since . . . since the time of the Druids . . . and we must pray that all who come will be allowed to . . . to wash . . . *their minds clean!*"

These singular words, spoken in Mr. Evans' second manner, kept repeating themselves inside the hollow skulls of all his three listeners, as they walked silently home to their different pillows.

When Mr. Evans took out his latch-key and let himself into his little Antique Shop, he was disturbed by a particular sadistic image that he had not been troubled by since he saw John Crow embrace the Hêle Stone at Stonehenge. This image was concerned with a killing blow delivered by an iron bar. Mechanically he closed the street door; mechanically he lit a candle; mechanically he met the marble gaze of an alabaster bust of Dante; mechanically he ascended the flight of narrow stairs to his bedroom above. Once in his chamber it was with the same automatic movement that he laid the flickering candle down on a rosewood chest of drawers and clicking open the stiff latch of the casement gazed out into the empty street. He saw nothing of the massive chimney across the way. He saw nothing of the carved Gothic doorways. He caught no floating essences of diffused sweetness from the beds of jonquils in the little gardens beyond these houses. The mystical breath of sleep rising from the summit of the Tor and from the pinnacles of Saint John's Church and from the broken cornices of the ruined Abbey arches passed him by untouched. One single image of homicidal violence, at once a torment of remorse and a living temptation, wiped out completely all these impressions.

Had the soul of that planet of love which had done so much that night for Nell Zoyland been made aware of this figure of a lean, hook-nosed man at a window, with a bowler hat upon an unmade bed behind him, what would its attitude to such a one have been?

"He has taken my own violence of ravishment, natural and passionate and sweet," that planet might have thought, "and has turned it into a crime against nature and against life. Never can he be forgiven!"

But long after that star of the west went down behind Brent Knoll, Mr. Evans' tormented murmur floated out over the Glastonbury roofs—"If only I could see it once . . . just once . . .

with my own eyes . . . what Merlin hid . . . what Joseph found
. . . the Cauldron of Yr Echwyd . . . the undying grail . . .
this madness would pass from me . . . but . . . but . . ."

He craned his neck out of the window, pressing the palms of
his hands upon the sill. His pose was grotesque. It was as if he
were about to address a crowd assembled on the opposite roof.

"But," Mr. Evans screamed in his twanging, quivering, twitching nerves; and although no sound but a lamentable sigh passed
his open lips it would have been hard for anyone watching him
not to believe he was shouting, "but . . . but . . . I . . . *don't*
. . . *want* . . . to see it!"

Mr. John Geard lived in a house in Street Road, a road branching westward out of Magdalene Street which itself lies to the west of the Abbey Ruins. In their old sewing-room at the top of their father's ramshackle brick house—a building which seemed completely unaware of the unexpected riches of its owner—there were talking eagerly together, one mid-March day, and with intense absorption in what they were saying, Mr. Geard's two daughters, Cordelia and Crummie. These were "the great sprawling girls" to whom Philip Crow had made such contemptuous reference at the Northwold tea-table.

The sewing-room where they were talking was also Crummie's bedroom, and Crummie, the younger of the two, *was* certainly, at that moment, answering Philip's description. She was lying on her back in the bed, her fair, wavy hair disordered, her violet-coloured eyes full of sleepy petulance, her skirts rumpled, her skin showing white between her drawers and her stockings, her slippered feet kicking peevishly the already crumpled coverlet of the bed.

Cordelia, on the other hand, was in no sort of way fulfilling Philip's unkind picture. A very plain, very dark girl, with nothing lovable in her face except an occasional smile of melancholy amusement and wistful indulgence, and with a thin, awkward, bony figure, Cordelia Geard was an unsympathetic critic of her father, a practical support to her mother, and at once the adviser and the confidante of her lively sister. At the present moment she was sitting bolt upright in front of a little working-table engaged on a piece of embroidery.

"I'm not indiscriminate! How dare you call me indiscriminate, Cordy!"

"Do you want me to count them all for you?"

"I'm talking about, now, now, *now!*" cried Crummie. "There's only Mr. Barter and Red Robinson now. And Red is afraid of me now we are supposed to be rich; so he doesn't count!"

"If by 'now,' you mean *since* we got rich," said Cordelia

gravely, "I believe Mr. Barter would marry you tomorrow if you'd have him."

Crummie toyed coquettishly with her skirt; and then began caressing, with the conscious narcissim of a girl inordinately proud of her legs, the soft flesh above one of her knees. "I'd like to marry Mr. Barter—in a way," she said meditatively.

Cordelia shook her head. "He would never be faithful to you. He's too indiscriminate himself."

"I hate the way you say that—every time," protested Crummie. "I could keep him faithful, you'd see! He's never lived with me. So he doesn't know."

"If he's never lived with you, *you*'ve never lived with him. You'd find it horrid, Crummie, when he went off with other girls!"

"What about you yourself?" retorted Crummie. "You know perfectly well what Mr. Evans said the other night to Mother about your being what he calls 'Cymric.' Cordelia dug her needle into her work and sat up very straight. Her pale cheeks had flushed a little.

"I told you last night, Crummie," she flung out, "I won't hear anything more about Mr. Evans! Mr. Evans is Dad's friend and it's not right to make fun of him."

Crummie removed her soft hand from her satiny flesh and pulled down her skirt with an abrupt jerk. She was a good-natured girl and next to her own rounded limbs she loved Cordy better than anything in the world. But she adored chattering about men; and for Cordelia to rule out of court as a topic for gossip any living man was an annoyance and a vexation.

"You've never stopped me before," said Crummie. "We always discuss Dad's friends. Besides, Owen Evans isn't Dad's friend. He's a cousin of Mother's. He's *our* cousin—so I can say anything about him I like."

Cordelia bit her lip. She felt at that moment that the one thing she could not bear was that her sister should draw her into a discussion of the only man who had ever—in all her virginal life of thirty years—taken any real notice of her. If Crummie loved Cordelia, the elder girl's devotion to Crummie knew no bounds. Megan Geard, their mother, was a reticent woman, even with her children. She was uniformly cold to both and the girls had long ago decided that in her heart she was dissatisfied because neither of them was a boy.

"What . . . I . . . think . . . *is*," went on Crummie, "what . . . I . . . think . . . *is* that Mr. Evans and you——"

"Don't!" cried Cordelia. "I won't have you say it!"

"Well . . . if I mustn't say . . . you know what," went on Crummie obstinately; "at least I can say that I think Dad is fonder of Mr. Evans than Mummy is. I believe Mummy thinks that Mr. Evans is after your——"

This was too much for Cordelia. "If you dare once again," she cried, "to talk about Mr. Evans to me, I'll begin talking about you and young Mr. Dekker!"

It was Crummie's turn to be outraged now. And she was evidently quite as much astonished as she was hurt. She rose up on the bed, propped herself on the palms of her hands, and stared open-mouthed at the dark girl before her, whose uncomely features were at that moment rendered almost beautiful by wrath. "*What?*" Crummie cried. "What *can* you mean, Cordelia? Who told you I ever met Sam Dekker—or had anything to do with him? Except at school-treats of course!—and sometimes when I've taken a few cowslips, in cowslip time, for the church—or gone with Red to a cricket match at Street—or maybe at Michaelmas Fair where everybody meets everybody—and if you *dare* to say I'm sweet on Sam Dekker or have ever spoke to Sam Dekker —except of course as a girl naturally *does* speak to a clergyman's son when she's helping the clergyman to distribute prizes or to carry those texts around that have those big red roses on them—I've only one thing to say of you, Cordelia Geard, and that is—you're telling absolute lies!"

At this point Crummie pulled up her legs under her, with the complete abandonment of a very little girl, bent her head till her wavy hair fell in loose wisps and loops upon her lap, and, covering her face with her hands, burst into passionate sobbing.

If Cordelia had intended to use a formidable weapon, she had never expected that it would prove as deadly a one as this. Her unconscious instinct, as often happens with women who want to hurt each other, had gone to the mark quicker and surer than any reasoned attack could have done. In a flash the elder sister

recognised the truth. She saw to her confusion how possible it is
to live intimately with a person all one's life and at last be absolutely confounded by some revelation as to her secret sexual
life.

So Crummie was in love with young Mr. Dekker; really in
love; just in the same sort of way as she herself was in love with
—but Cordelia pulled her thoughts up with a jerk. *That* was day
dreams and speculations too dear even for herself to dwell upon!
Little Crummie! Why, this was nothing less than tragic. Gossip
had already whispered to the sisters that young Mr. Dekker had
been "keeping company with this Zoyland woman out to Splott's
Moor." And in any case a marriage between the child of Johnny
Geard—even of a rich Mr. Geard—and the son of the Vicar of
St. John's was an unnatural consummation. She laid her embroidery down and went across to her sister's side. "Forgive poor
Cordy!" she murmured self-reproachfully. "Of course I know
that young Dekker is nothing to you. I was just cross, Crummie
darling,"—and she laid her hand caressingly on her sister's
head and bent down to kiss her—"your Cordy was just cross.
But I'm not cross any more, and you mustn't be cross with me!"

Crummie's cheeks were still wet, but her full red lips parted
in a faint smile. "We're a silly pair, Cordy!" she murmured as
they kissed each other, and she threw her arms tenderly round her
sister's neck and drew her close. After a second's tight hug the
younger girl swung her legs off the bed and they sat side by side
upon the ruffled bed-clothes.

"Better tidy yourself up now, Crummie. Sally will be ringing
that bell for tea."

"And Mr. Evans is coming to tea!" laughed the other roguishly.

Cordelia moved now to the table and began folding up her
embroidery.

"I must go down and put on my coral necklace," she said to
herself, "and brush my hair a bit; but what's the use? If he
doesn't like me for myself, he won't care. And if he *does* he won't
care, either!" And then the queer thought came into her head—
"If a man wants to marry a girl, when he likes her *for her mind
alone*, does he get *any* pleasure from kissing her and embracing
her?" So deep did this queer and troubling question sink into

her consciousness that she let her embroidery lie where it fell, unwrapt in its usual piece of blue tissue paper! She herself sank down on her sewing-chair and stared in front of her. She stared at the particular one of the pictures of "The Four Seasons" which represented Autumn. Quite automatically she read: "We *too* have Autumns, when our leaves fall loosely through the misty air, and all our good is bound in sheaves, and we stand reaped and bare." She had read these words in their familiar place on the wall of the sewing-room since she could read at all.

Crummie was now clutching tight in her fingers the midstream of her mass of fragrant hair, pulling it round her white neck and passing the comb, with many little cries at the tangles, through its down-shaken wavy curls. To twist it round her head and stick the hairpins into it was a matter of a second or two. Then she slipped off her dress and bending over the chest of drawers sought leisurely for this and the other garment; weighing, rejecting, appraising, selecting. Hovering there, all in white, with bare arms and bare shoulders, she proceeded to smooth down with indolent outspread fingers the creases of her slip, preparatory to pulling her dress over her head.

Like a patient nun in a courtesan's tiring-room Cordelia watched her, a little twisted smile on her lips. No! Of course Owen Evans couldn't *love* a person like her. But if he really thought she was "Cymric" in her ideas, and liked her for herself enough to marry her, why! she would marry him.

Crummie was sitting on the bed now, changing her stockings, and if she had looked winsome and alluring before, she looked even more so now.

As Cordelia watched the delicate softness of Crummie's limbs during this lengthy ritual, and the whiteness of her flesh thrown into tender shadows by the ruffled hem of her garment, there did come over the plain girl's mind a faint, flickering spasm of revolt. Why should her own poor knees be so bony and rough-textured? Why beneath her bony knees should her legs be like a pair of broom handles? If God had willed everything from the very Beginning of the World, why had He willed that all this exquisite delight in one's own body—Crummie was at the mirror again now, turning this way and that way, as she tried on her new party dress—should be given to one girl, while another girl felt her body to be a troublesome burden to be carried about? Oh, it didn't depend on having men to admire one, or to embrace one. "It is the feeling," thought poor Cordelia, "of being beautiful to one's own self that matters!"

The younger sister was ready now. "Cordy," she cried, reluctantly turning her head from the mirror, "aren't you going to change *anything*?"

But Cordelia, rising to her feet, only gave two contemptuous little pats to her dark hair, only gave a contemptuous shake to her black skirt, only picked off the front of it a few coloured threads left by her embroidery. Instead of glancing at the mirror, she glanced, over her sister's head, at the coloured representation of Spring, the first of those Four Seasons, hanging on the wall. At the bottom of this picture, which had always been the younger's favourite of all four, was a little card, stuck in the edge of the frame, carrying on its surface a childish sketch of a small girl, done in crude pinks and blues, the hair just an enormous smudge of chrome-yellow, which bore the inscription "Crummie by Crummie, Aged Six." "Come on," she said, "let's go down and help Sally."

The presence of Sally in the house—Mrs. Geard would hardly allow her to cross the threshold of her sacred kitchen—was one of the few tokens of domestic grandeur that had appeared in Cardiff Villa, Street Road, since Johnny Geard's accession to wealth.

And Sally—a daughter of Mrs. Jones of the High Street teashop—was anything but a smart or experienced servant. But Cordelia was rather relieved not to be perpetually answering the doorbell; and sometimes, when, in one of her bad moods, she was lying supine on her bed upstairs, she did get a faint, malicious satisfaction in hearing Sally repeat her most difficult lesson— the inhospitable decree, "Not at home."

"Bloody Johnny," as the tavern-cronies in Glastonbury loved to call Mr. Geard because of his preachings in the street and his repeated references to the Blood of Christ, was evidently not intending to use William Crow's money for the embellishing of

Cardiff Villa either with new paint, or furniture, or plate, or servants! Cordelia wondered now, as they entered the kitchen and found Sally Jones staring mute and awestruck before Mrs. Geard's preparations, whether Mr. Evans realized yet how unlikely it was that any large portion of this money would come to her— even if she did marry him. "Never, never, did any man want taking care of more than Mr. Evans does!" she thought. Oddly enough she never thought of her antiquarian suitor as anything but "Mr. Evans." She had reached the point—no very easy point, considering the ponderousness of the Welshman's second manner!—of *calling* him Owen. But she never *thought* of him as Owen . . .

"I really brought Mr. Crow to see you," said Mr. Evans, referring to John Crow, as they all sat around the tea-tray in the front parlour, "because he's in difficulties." At the word "difficulties" Megan Geard's mouth closed tight and she glanced furtively at the preposterously big skull of her reckless husband. She had known too well—and only too recently!—what to be "in difficulties" meant.

But Bloody Johnny seemed to have no such memory. He turned his hydrocephalic head on the pivot of his neck with the slow gravity of the ghost in Punch and Judy and gazed at John across the table. "Your grandfather was a good friend to me," he remarked. "But I served him well. If you'll excuse the word, Mr. Crow, and not think me presumptuous, I believe I can say that I made your grandfather's last years very happy ones."

John reduced his eyes to two narrow slits. Through these apertures he scrutinised Mr. Geard very closely, giving him the appraising glance of a professional beggar, surveying a new countenance at a well-known back door.

"What I don't think is understood by any of your family, Mr. Crow," the ex-preacher went on, "is that I regard your grandfather's bequest in the light of a Divine Responsibility."

At the sound of these surprising words from his host and namesake John Crow's eyes almost closed entirely, while the hereditary twitch in his face became like a tiny jumping-jack under the skin of his lean cheek. "You mean you're going to give the oof back to us, Sir?" he said.

Bloody Johnny was the only person at that table who remained completely at ease under the shock of this rude speech. "Well, Mr. Crow," he remarked serenely, "not exactly give it back to *you*, you know, nor to *any* of you; not, that is, *exactly*, as you might say, *give it back*. But I *do* intend—and my friend Mr. Evans agrees entirely with my intention—to spend your dear grandfather's gift, or at least the bulk of it, on a purpose in no way connected with myself or with my family." Mr. Geard's voice raised itself a little as he uttered these final words and his great head seemed to obey an interior command as it swung resolutely round on its pivot. What it faced now under this interior command, and John Crow seemed to hear an audible creaking of its machinery as it turned, was the extremely agitated countenance of Megan Geard whose mouth, at the words "with my family" had become a thinly outlined half-circle whose drooping horns were surrounded by twitching wrinkles.

"Mr. Evans thinks," went on Bloody Johnny, "that it would be wrong of me not to take my wife and my girls, especially my daughter Cordelia, into my confidence, though, as you know, my treasure,"—here he fixed an unwinking gaze upon his wife's wide-open eyes—"I am not one to reveal my designs till they have matured." The reverberations of these grand words "designs" and "matured" had scarcely died away when Bloody Johnny followed them by a deprecatory murmur, addressed, not to his family but to his God. "I mean," he added, "till they have been blessed from Above."

A lack-lustre film formed over John's eyes, and he said to himself, "If this fellow turns out to be a superstitious fool, instead of a hypocritical knave, I shall get nothing from him. There goes my easy job, up in smoke!"

"My relative, Mr. Geard," said Owen Evans, with a respectful glance at Cordelia, "has come to the conclusion that there are ways of bringing to Glastonbury, by the wise expenditure of a little money, shoals and shoals of pilgrims. They will come from France, from Germany, from Russia. They will flock here in such increasing numbers that Glastonbury will once more rival

Rome and Jerusalem as a centre of mystic influence. It only remains for"—at this point, to Cordelia's complete astonishment,
though she thought, as she had said to Crummie, that she "knew
Mr. Evans through and through," his gaze dropped from her attentive eyes and sank to her clasped hands which rested on the
table, while his voice became broken, spasmodic, intense—"for
some . . . for some . . . for some event to happen . . . and a
new Religion . . . different . . . from any that's ever been . . .
will . . . will . . . will make a crack in the world!" They all
turned their eyes upon his contorted face; all except Crummie
who glanced wonderingly at her sister.

"What do you mean by 'a crack in the world'?" enquired John
Crow, the film of hopelessness passing from his lineaments and
his whole attention aroused.

"A crack in Cause-and-Effect," cried Owen Evans, his voice
rising; "a crack in the Laws of Nature, a crack in Matter! And
Something will break out, through that crack, *that will take away
our torment!*"

The word "torment" was uttered from such twisted lips that
it was as if it really came from a spirit in hell and Cordelia
Geard's heart began to beat. The others, except the profane John,
averted their eyes, as if from some apparition that was as obscene as it was tragic. But as Owen Evans slowly recovered himself, the girl unclasped her hands and very lightly, and with a
gesture that no gentlewoman in the land could have surpassed
for dignity and grace, laid her fingers on the sleeve of his coat.

John, who was intently watching Mr. Evans, could not decide
whether the man even noticed this movement of the devoted girl,
whose fingers were withdrawn as soon as her friend was master
of himself again, but to the sly scrutiny of the "run-down adventurer" the incident was very significant. "He's not out for her
money," he thought, "but he's certainly out of her depth. I *must*
get at the fellow's secret. He's got *some* devilish spike sticking
into his midriff; but *what* it is the Lord only knows!"

As for John Geard, under this explosion from his Welsh ally,
what *he* did was slowly and deliberately to turn, not his head, but
his eyes, in their hollow motionless sockets, completely away from
the agitated man. Mr. Geard had his mouth full of sponge-cake,

of which he was particularly fond, and his voice sounded blurred and thick. "What we ought to have in Glastonbury," he said, "and Midsummer would be a good time for it—is a Religious Fair, or Passion Play, that would attract people. There has not been a Passion Play here for years." He paused and shut his eyes. "Nor a Miracle either," he muttered. "No, not for three hundred years; but the time will come, and the Miracle will come!"

It was at that moment that Crummie, who was much more aware of what Sally was doing than of what any of her father's guests were saying, jumped up from her seat and ran into the kitchen. From the kitchen—for the impulsive girl left the door wide open—everyone could hear her scolding the little maid for inattention. It was clear from the first words that ensued that Crummie found the domestic truant standing in Street Road contemplating the passers-by; but a moment later they heard Crummie's own voice raised in lively salutation. Sally herself came back, shamefacedly enough, into the dining-room and whispered something to Cordelia; but there was such a draught of chilly air entering the room now, that Mr. and Mrs. Geard and their two male guests kept their faces turned and their attention directed towards the two open doors.

"It's young Mr. Dekker," said Cordelia presently, "I know his voice." At the name Dekker there occurred that curious moral stiffening, that gathering together of relaxed social awareness, which always happens in England when an upper middle-class person enters the company of a group of lower middle-class persons. Cordelia had hardly uttered the words, "I know his voice," than Crummie herself came back into the room bringing Sam Dekker with her.

There was a general rising and shuffling and shaking of hands; and in the midst of the confusion, while Sally was pouring lukewarm water upon stale tea-leaves, Cordelia slipped into the kitchen and began to make a fresh pot of tea and to cut fresh bread and butter. Sam Dekker sat down, awkwardly enough, by Crummie's side. Here he was at the end of the table, next Mrs. Geard, but also next the door. He refused to put down his hat and stick and kept protesting that he must not stay and that he had already had tea.

"Oh, Cordy! How nice of you to think of that!" cried the younger sister, when after a few nervous generalities about the balmy mornings and the chilly evenings of this unusual March the ice was broken by the appearance of fresh tea and fresh bread and butter.

Sam *did* now consent to allow Crummie to take his hat and his stick away from him. He had begun to look at John Crow with a stealthy, silent, lowering curiosity, as if John had been a fellow badger in a gathering of foxes.

"May I tell Mr. Dekker," John now found himself saying, "about the grand plot that you two gentlemen are hatching to make this place a sort of English Oberammergau?"

"I could hardly hope," remarked Mr. Geard, with an imperceptible nod of approval towards John, "to convert Mr. Dekker to my immature Design; considering the position held by his father."

"Mr. Geard has the idea," John went on, addressing himself now to Sam Dekker alone, "of holding a sort of Pageant, a sort of Religious Fair at Midsummer. . . . I believe he has the twenty-fourth of June in his mind, . . . in the Tor Fair-field, eh, Sir? His idea is to make this such an event, that people will come to it from France and Germany, as well as from all over England. It will, of course, be entirely friendly to *all* religious bodies. It won't be a church affair. It won't be a nonconformist affair. It'll be . . . I'm right in this, aren't I, Mr. Geard? . . . a Glastonbury Revival, absolutely independent of the churches. I can see you're interested in the idea, Mr. Dekker; and so will everybody be when we've got it advertised a little. Oh, I wish you'd make me your secretary, Sir, or your master of ceremonies—anything of that sort! I know I catch *exactly* what you have in your mind. And it would hush up all gossip too, and look well in the papers, if you had one of us Crows as your chief lieutenant. And incidentally 'twould give me a chance to"—he was going to say "to upset Philip," but as he surveyed Bloody Johnny's face he recognised that malice towards an enemy was completely alien to the man's nature, so he concluded differently—"a chance to marry and settle down. I can see you're surprised, Mr. Dekker, to see me here at all; considering my family's grievance against Mr.

Geard, and our envy and our jealousy of Mr. Geard; but I'm a
black sheep, you know. I don't mind confessing to all you kind
people"—here he raised his voice and glanced at the round, red,
hypnotised face of the maid Sally, who, standing behind Mrs.
Geard's chair, had long since been hanging upon his lips with
as much attention as if he had been the Human Chimpanzee
talking in the Magic Booth at Somerton Circus—"that I came
here hoping that Mr. Geard would let me help him in some way.
I even thought that his employment of me would act as hush-
money to all this gossip . . . a sop to Cerberus, as you might
say . . . but Mr. Geard reads my thoughts . . . you know you
do, Sir! Yes, you really do!"

He stopped now, quite out of breath; and Sam Dekker glowered at him in sulky silence. Sam's attention had been wandering
from the beginning to the end of his discourse. He had been
saying to himself, "I know what it means, seeing Zoyland going
up Wells Road. He's walked in to see Philip! This means that he
is going to Wookey Hole. He wouldn't come to see him otherwise.
He didn't last year; and I fancy he *couldn't* very well . . . not
on a job like that." At this point, hearing the words of John as
if they were perfectly meaningless sounds, his mind ceased to
think in words. He felt himself sleeping with Nell in William's
bed. He felt the pressure of her breasts against his chest. This
voluble fellow opposite him, chattering about a Midsummer
Pageant was of no more significance to him than a quacking duck
in a farm-yard when he was on his way to Queen's Sedgemoor.
In fact as he glared at John, John's nose became the road between the two great oaks and the hamlet of Wick, while John's
forehead became the path over the water-meadows. "I *must* know
the truth, one way or the other," he said to himself. I *must* know
if she's going to be alone out there when he goes to Wookey
Hole."

It was touching to Cordelia to watch the way Crummie was
behaving. She was no longer the wanton, playful, toying girl,
who delighted in tantalising the senses of men. She was a grave
maiden, a tender, drooping-eyed, watchful maiden, who did all
she could, by a thousand little attentions and tactful considerations, to win favour with her absent-minded lord!

"He's a gentleman," Mr. Geard was thinking to himself, "and he's a clever rogue. Of course he's an atheist. He doesn't believe in anything. You can see that with half an eye. But it's the Blessed Lord who's brought him to me. He's the very man for my Design—the very man! A believer would be difficult. A churchman would be impossible. This lad will treat my Design as a masquerade. He'll have no prejudices. He's what I've been looking for ever since I got back from Norfolk. And he is *his* grandchild too—yes, he's perfectly right about the fortune. It'll make a very good impression on all concerned, for me to have one of these Crows as a sort of partner! He'll have a share in spending his grandfather's money. With his help I shall . . . I shall do . . . I shall have . . . I shall be . . . I shall make . . . an absolutely New Thing—sobbing happiness—black earth—rain—dew—peace——"

By this time the towers of his New Jerusalem, thus built to the Glory of the Blood, were rising clear and crystalline to his view, piling themselves up, buttress upon buttress, rampart upon rampart, beyond his wife's windowbox of begonias! Castles of crystal, islands of glass, mirrors and mirages of the invisible, hiding-places of Merlin, horns and urns and wells and cauldrons—hilltops of magic—stones of mystery—all these seemed to Bloody Johnny's brain at that moment no mere fluctuating, undulating mind-pictures, but real things; real as the cracked wood of the old windowbox, real as the indented frown upon Megan's forehead! John Crow could clearly see what an impression his words had made upon his host; but he waited patiently till this fit of absent-mindedness should come to an end.

Crummie had by now reached the point of daring to express, in gentle, hesitating tones, her growing absorption in the study of natural history. She was asking Sam if there were not some easy books that she could buy on such things as aquatic plants, water beetles, pond weeds, and so forth; for these, it seemed, had for many years been Crummie's secret delight; though, for the sake of peace in the family, it had been necessary to conceal her obsession.

"Don't you think, John, it would be wiser," burst out Mrs. Geard at last, finding her opportunity in one of those curious

long silences that seem especially to fall on groups of human
beings of just about the numbers that occupied that room, whereas
fewer people or more people would have been free from that embarrassment, "don't you think, John, it would be wiser to wait
till we moved into Chalice House before employing anyone else?"

"Mother *dear*!" interrupted Cordelia. "Mr. Crow doesn't mean
that he wants to *live* with us! Father will only pay him a small
salary for his help. It'll save Father a great deal. It'll save Father
taking an office."

At the word "office" Megan Geard crumpled up. She sank back
in her chair and gasped. The idea of the golden stream of this
great Northwold legacy being deflected into an "office" seemed
to her almost the worst that could happen. In the moving pictures which she sometimes attended the word "office" was syn-
onymous with dissipation and deception.

Sam Dekker at this moment rose stiffly to his feet. He had
decided upon immediate action. He would go himself that very
second—it could only be about half-past five—and call upon
the Philip Crows. He shook hands hurriedly with his host and
hostess, nodded to John Crow and Mr. Evans, and was escorted
by the silent Crummie to the front door where she reluctantly
handed him his hat and stick. He was so obsessed with what was
in his head to do that he took his things from her with a mere
"thank you," gave her an abstracted nod, and hurried off up the
street. As he approached St. John's Church, on the way to Wells
Road, it occurred to him with extreme vividness that it was likely
enough that Nell had walked into town with her husband from
Queen's Sedgemoor. He had seen William alone, but that meant
little; it was Nell's frequent custom to separate from Zoyland
when they were together in Glastonbury, do her shopping in
peace, and meet him afterward at the Pilgrims' Inn. Sam well
knew this habit of hers and had ere now taken advantage of it,
meeting her in the Ruins, and once, even, but that was a dangerous risk, in a field at the foot of the Tor. His heart beat fiercely
now, therefore, but more from love than from any startled surprise, when he perceived her figure passing under the iron gas-
lamp arch into the churchyard. It had been a grey day; and with
the approach of sunset the air was beginning to grow both chilly

and dark. He took hurried steps in pursuit and reached the
churchyard just in time to see her entering the church porch.

There were several people moving in and out of the church
at that hour. There were still more people passing up and down
in front of the churchyard entrance; and among these latter, as
Sam was about to hurry under the iron arch that held the gas-
lamp, was a figure in working-man's clothes who hesitated not
to stop him and address him. Sam could hardly endure this delay.
The man was polite enough and his general demeanour had the
air of a foreman or a master plumber. But Sam's soul was already inside the church. And what on earth was this pale, intense,
red-haired young artisan talking about? He had caught hold of
Sam by the lappet of his coat. He was agitated about something.
"I beg your pardon," Sam blurted out at last, "but I'm in rather
a hurry. I've got to go, if you don't mind, into the church. I've
got to go!" At that moment such a bitter sneer contracted this
excitable young man's face that Sam did notice it and stopped.
What was the matter with this fellow? Why was he so agitated?

"So you're the gent she can't sigh 'arf enough about," the man
began, in a strong cockney accent. "She sighs you 'ave the *look
of a sighnt*. Well, Crummie, I sighs, the next charnst I gets I'll
tike a good look at 'im. It ain't every die yer sees a bloomin'
sighnt on 'Igh Street. But I'll arst 'im, I sighs, if 'ee won't speak
up for a poor dog like yours 'umbly. A sighnt's word, I'll tell
'im, ought to go pretty far with a gal if he cares to give a bloke
a 'and-up in 'is courtin'."

A light for the first time broke upon Sam's impatient mind.
This must be Red Robinson, the cockney Communist, who was
always plotting troubles and strikes in Philip's factories. Sam
now remembered the fact that Red Robinson's mother, with whom
he lived, was an old charwoman of the most rigid conservative
principles, who worked regularly in the church. Sam knew her
well and had often heard her speak sorrowfully and tragically
of the wicked opinions of her infidel son. The whole episode was
a revelation to him of how poor the Geards had been before
they inherited their legacy. It seemed hard to imagine this well-
to-do workman aspiring to Crummie's hand!

"You've come to see your mother home?" he murmured feebly,

cursing both mother and son, and thinking to himself, "If this chap comes in with me now it'll be the last straw!" And the last straw it was. For Red Robinson, clapping his workman's cap firmly on his head, as if to show that a churchyard was no more sacred than any other yard, resolutely followed as Sam moved away, and as he followed continued to talk of Crummie. Sam's desperation grew worse and worse as they approached the church door. He had never heard a cockney accent carried to such a limit. The truth was that Red's accent was more cockney than any living Londoner's. A deep vein of what might be called "philological malice" in him had come to emphasise this way of speaking as a form of spite against the Glastonbury bourgeoisie.

"She sighs you 'ave the look of a sighnt," Red kept repeating. "She sighs you 'ave haltered 'er whole life. She sighs that since she's known you she's a different gal. So all you've got to do, Mister, is to sigh the word and she'll marry me tomorrow!"

"Well I don't see what I can do for you, Mr. Robinson; but I don't mind speaking to Miss Geard." These words were automatically jerked out of him, like peas shaken out of a bag. But at this moment they passed into the church and Red Robinson and his exaggerated cockney speech became for Sam's mind far less important than the dust now being raised by Red's mother as the old woman swept her brush about between the pews with her long black skirt pinned up above her grey woolen petticoat.

For there before his eyes was Nell Zoyland! The girl was lying back in one of the pews nearest to the font in an attitude not of piety nor of peace, but of apathetic weariness. One of her arms was thrown over the back of the pew. Her face was so shaded by her hat that in the dusk of that interior it was a mere white blur. She did not look unhappy. No one would have taken her for a tragic figure. No one, on the other hand, would have taken her for a care-free visitor to Glastonbury. She might have been a sister of Sam's, some tired daughter of the priest of this very church, resting after a long country walk.

"Are you ready, Mother?" he heard Red Robinson exclaim. "'Urry now, for I wants my tie! Say good-night to Jesus and hunpin yerself quick!"

Sam went straight to the girl's side and greeted her in a whisper. She caught up her hand quick to her throat and gave a little gasping cry. Sam was so excited that he did not modulate his voice as he greeted her while she sprang to her feet and faced him. "Has he gone to see Philip?" he asked eagerly.

Nell Zoyland nodded, clutching three paper parcels which she held, tight against her bosom, and not offering him her hand.

"Is he going to Wookey Hole?"

Again she nodded without a word.

He did lower his voice now to a low whisper that she could hardly catch. But well did she know the drift of that desperate question! Had she gone back to him—*since that night*? Her eyes assumed a strange, weary, indifferent look, in that dim light, and they seemed to leave his face and gaze into the far distance. "Have . . . you . . . gone . . . back . . . to him?" he repeated with almost brutal insistence. For the third time she nodded; and then, moving her feet a little, as if the ground was slippery beneath her, she straightened her body and looked him full in the face; and he thought as she did so that there was a reproachful flash in her eyes.

"Come . . . this way," he said, pulling at her jacket. They moved out of reach of the ears of Red Robinson and his mother; and Sam soon found that he had led her quite unconsciously to the great empty sarcophagus bearing the initials *J. A.* Here they stood side by side, she with her body pressed against the outside edge of the stone, he with his fingers clutching its inside rim.

"How soon is he going to Wookey Hole?"

"In two or three days," she answered, looking at him with an inscrutable expression. "By Saturday," she murmured, "he's certain to be gone." She paused and then added humbly, poking the end of her umbrella into a crevice between two stones, "I can't understand how either of you can put up with such a weak, uncertain creature as I am. I was telling William *that*, just now, all the way from Wick Hollow to Maidencroft Lane. I know I shall bring a curse upon you both! What I deserve is that you both should go off and leave me alone! Oh, Sammy, Sammy, how much nicer men really are, at bottom, than women!"

Sam sighed. "I'd chance all the badness *you* could call up, Nellie," he said, "if only I could get you to myself."

It was her turn to sigh at this. "Why didn't you just carry me off, Sam dearest, that evening on Queen's Sedgemoor? We'd have managed somehow. I'm not a fool; and you've got such strong arms!"

Sam drew a deep breath; so deep that it shook him from head to foot. He felt a leap in the pit of his stomach, as if a fish had risen there. He felt the blood throb above his cheek-bones. "We . . . might . . . still . . . do it, little Nell," he stammered huskily.

"It's too late *now*, my dearest," she said.

"Why is it?" he groaned.

"Because . . . because he's made me give myself to him . . . as I've never done . . . before this."

Sam was silent, pondering in his brain the inscrutable twists and turns of women's hearts. He thought to himself, "What am I to believe? That day we went to Pomparlès Bridge and looked at the dace in those pools, and she told me about Arthur's sword, she made me believe he had ravished her the first day they met; and now she says this! Do women delight to make themselves out victims? She first says this and then that . . . I cannot tell what the truth is!"

"But you still love me, Nell?" he pleaded. "You haven't turned against me? You haven't gone over to him completely?"

"I shall always love you beyond all else in the world," she said. He now led her towards the altar and they seated themselves in the very front pew of all and before their pew was an open space of time-worn floor, carrying several quite illegible and absolutely flat tombstones. Beyond these were the altar rails. But the girl kept her eyes fixed on the ground and ceased not to draw her hand up and down the polished edge of the seat. "But to give myself to you after giving myself to him as I've done since that night has something"—she spoke even more slowly now, but never seemed to hesitate for a word—"something about it that I can't bear." She lifted her eyes from the ground and fixed them shyly and humbly upon Sam's troubled face. "I wouldn't blame any woman," she went on, "who lived with two men, if one was her earthly friend and the other her ideal friend. But you and Will—you mustn't mind my saying it, Sam!—are both earthly friends. It was because of that . . . that I . . . that I made Will sleep alone. I wanted to belong to you altogether."

Sam spoke hurriedly and eagerly. "But I *must* come over and see you when he's away. It'll be madness, Nell, to let such a chance go."

A spasm of anger crossed her face. "Chances, Sam Dekker? You talk of chances? Why didn't you carry me off when you had the 'chance'? No, no! A girl isn't a bottle of wine for a man to lock up in a cupboard, to take a sip from whenever he wants to! Will's a genuine man anyway in these things. *He* doesn't wait for a 'chance.' *He* goes right ahead and takes risks." She stood erect before him, her parcels pressed against her waist, her umbrella clutched crosswise against her bosom.

Her electric flash of anger communicated itself to him in a second and he too got up upon his feet. "If you feel like that," he grumbled sulkily, "perhaps the best thing would be for me to give up altogether going out to see you."

He gave a quick glance round the darkening church. But the stone coffin of Joseph of Arimathea lay undisturbed, a vague blur of insubstantial whiteness in the gathering dusk, and the Robinsons, both mother and son, had disappeared. "I never thought a time would come," he said fiercely, "that we should have a chance like this, only to throw it away! Have you forgotten everything we've done together, and where we've been together? Have you forgotten that reed-hut on Splott's Moor? Have you forgotten Hartlake Railway Bridge? Have you forgotten that withy-bed at Westholme and the Palace Barn at Pilton?"

"I never thought," she said, "that you would ever come to speak of such things in such a tone! I've been a fool to treat you as one of the few men that a girl could trust not to behave like a cad!" This word "cad" she brought out with vibrant relish like a pet dagger from a hidden sheath. She glowed in her indignation to see the twitch of his poor, funny chin as she plunged it in.

"I only spoke of those places to remind you of things," he retorted with flashing eyes. "What you've done in going back to him when you belonged to me was far worse than talking of our little things. It was a kind of . . . a kind of . . . well! I won't

say *that* to you. But you know what I mean! You've never put him
out of your heart—never!"

"How *can* you say that to me after everything?" she interjected.

"Because that's what you're like! Because when you went back
to him you were acting *like a whore*." (I've done it now, he
thought. I've dropped the last straw on the heap by calling her
that!) "Where does he want you to meet him? Can't I take you
anywhere?" he said in a toneless mechanical voice. He took her
hand. He repeated this hopeless formula. His lips seemed to have
gone dry. He dropped her limp fingers, but she held him back for
a second by the look on her face.

"You've . . . made . . . me . . . very . . . happy . . .
Sam," she whispered, while her eyes brimmed with tears. Sam
ought to have had the wit to realise at this moment that had he
swallowed his pride and changed his tone all would have been
well. Apparently a man *can* call his love a whore and be forgiven! But he was at once too aggrieved and too simple-minded to
take advantage of the tears that were now pouring down her face.

"Good-bye," he repeated doggedly; "good-bye, Nell."

A little later that evening, Red Robinson sat talking to his
mother and Sally Jones in Mrs. Robinson's kitchen in an alley in
Bove Town, a district of Glastonbury situated south of Old Wells
Road and Edmund Hill Lane. Red was questioning Sally about
the tea-party at the Geards', while his mother, in a clean dress, a
clean lace collar, a clean blue apron, was preparing supper.
"Why do you torment poor Sal so grievous, sonny?" protested
the old lady. "You'll be the death of me with your hinsurrec-
tions. List to a hold 'ooman, Sal, and leave not the paths of God's
'oly Word. Lot of good me son's 'Party' will be to 'im, with 'is
Rooshian Spies when 'is ole Mother be dead and gone! And this
Crummie Geard 'ee pines for! Your mother and me, Sal, have
known Crummie Geard, and Bloody Johnny 'er dad too, since she
were a tot in harms. Could Crummie dish up a nice tighsty dish
'o liver and 'am and fried tighties such as ye'll tighst in a minute? Not on your little loife!"

"But, Mother," protested Red Robinson, "Crummie's dad is a

rich man now. Since I 'eard of that I ain't gone near 'er. I 'as me
own pride, Mother; and dahn't yer forget it!"

"Pride be 'anged!" cried the old woman, banging his supper-
plate down in front of him and pouring water into the empty
frying-pan, "you and 'er were keeping company; or I dunno
what helse it were!"

"Well, anyway," went on Red, hungrily beginning to eat his
supper, "whether I get Crummie or not, Crummie's promised to
'arst 'er dad—and she can twist the old boy round her little
finger—to hinvest 'is cash in 'elping us bankrupt this Crow concern. She says he told the Almighty 'Imself at family prayers that
Crow was 'eading for ruin. He 'ates Crow, 'ee *must* 'ate Crow,
because of his filling the town with factories; whereas Bloody
Johnny wants to preach to the visitors; and visitors don't like
factories. With a little of Geard's cash to back us up we'll mike
the brute 'owl and maybe get the Town to tike over his concern.
That's the idea anyway they've got at 'eadquarters."

"But didn't you hear what I said?" put in Sally Jones. "Don't
I keep telling you he's going to employ Crow's cousin? Crow's
cousin be a tidy lad and a nice-spoken gentleman too; and old
man Geard be goin' to hire he to bring a girt Fair into Tor Field
with a grand Roman Circus and a Golden-Jerusalem Theayter and
a 'normous Guy Fawkes Pope, and more o' they gipoos and For-
tune-Tellers than have been seen since the King cut off Abbot
Whiting's head!" Sally's cheeks flamed and her eyes glittered as
she described these wonders.

Red Robinson spat into the stove. "Don't yer make no mistake,
Baby Sal," he said; "there won't be no Fair in Glastonbury in
our time except the regular Autumn one."

"Did Mr. Geard really talk like that?" enquired Mrs. Robinson, as she removed her son's plate and substituted another with
a plump piece of pudding thereon. "There's no telling what a man
will do, who's been poor, when he grows rich. Common folk like
that ain't no notion how to spend money. It tikes the real gentry
to spend money as it ought to be spended."

"You shut yer hold mouth, Mother!" cried Red with a chuckle.
It was the cause of endless pleasantries between these two that the

revolutionary ideas of the man were countered by the inflexible
Toryism of the woman.

"Don't you go on, then, putting these crazy notions into Sal's
mind. Don't you 'eed 'im, Sally, me gurl. Red's not been as I've
'a been, 'ousekeeper to the Bishop of Bath and Wells what was a
Lord—rest his sweet soul!—in's own right, seeing 'ee was uncle-
born to the Marquis of P."

"Is it really true, Mrs. Robinson," asked Sally timidly, "that
Mr. Zoyland, out to Queen's Sedgemoor, be thik Markises wicked
by-blow?" The two women, the old one and the young one,
pulled their kitchen chairs closer to each other; while an identical
expression of complacent awe animated their faces.

"That's what I've 'a 'eered from folks what do know, Sal. 'Tis
true I've never arst Mr. Zoyland 'isself. 'Tis a thing a gent like
that—as I knows from my hexperience with 'is Lordship—be apt
to be ticklish about. Not that in 'igh society, Sal, them by-blows
be rare. They be common as hidiots be with us. There haint no
great family, from on 'igh down, what 'asn't got 'en, Sal. 'Tis
nature with they to have 'en."

By this time, in surprisingly few gulps, Red Robinson had dis-
patched his pudding. He now pushed back his plate and rising to
his feet proceeded to light his pipe. That done, he took down his
woolen scarf from one nail and his cap from another. "Don't yer
sit up for me, Mother," he said. " 'Tis quarterly meeting tonight;
and the Comrades from Wells and Wookey will be there and
high'm the one delegated for the chief haddress."

"I'll stay and help Mrs. Robinson wash up," said Sally
brightly. She made no move, however, to rise from her chair. She
was clearly anxious to satisfy at one and the same time her natural kindness of heart and her longing to hear more about the
Marquis of P.'s by-blow.

Red was on the point of laying his hand on the door-handle
when the door itself opened from without. It opened with the
peculiar impetus that inrushing children give, and no fewer than
four lively youngsters precipitated themselves into the room.
Sally did not rise from her chair now; for the leader of this little
gang was her brother Jackie. Jackie was accompanied by Nelly
Morgan, a wild, dishevelled little girl of eight. Sis was ten, as old

as Jackie himself, and an incorruptible devotee of Jackie's; but being a heavily built and heavily witted child and burdened, furthermore, by the care of her brother Bert, an infant of five, who in placidity and appearance resembled a giant mushroom, Sis was outplayed, outrun, outdared, outjumped, outclimbed, outfought, outpassioned by Nelly Morgan, in spite of her advantage over Nelly of two whole years. Nelly's mother was a charwoman and was always at work; which gave the little girl an independence from parental control envied by all the rest. Jackie had Sally to order him about, in addition to their mother; and the little Coles, although orphans, had a very active and formidable grandmother. Nelly Morgan had no one; for her charwoman-mother, although an incredibly good worker during the day, had the peculiarity, indeed the unusual gift, of being able to drink gin with no bodily ill-effect every night until she was completely fuddled. Every day she would rise again by five o'clock; get her own and Nelly's breakfast, and go off cheerfully to her laborious work. She never uttered an unkind word to Nelly; far less ever struck her. But on the other hand she was wont to fall into a sentimental trance, as soon as she had washed up after supper, from which she never emerged again that evening. During this trance she would shed silent tears, sigh repeatedly, and talk in mumbling tones of Nelly's dead father; but Nelly herself became to her mother at these times as if she were totally invisible, inaudible, and non-existent. For a little girl of eight to become non-existent to her only relation every single day of her life at seven o'clock was an experience likely to have a noticeable effect; and Nelly's nature got steadily more and more self-absorbed and more and more eccentric. Though still only eight, the child had the intelligence of a girl of eleven; and on the few occasions when even the bold Jackie showed the white feather, Nelly—lieutenant of this robber band—played the devil with all strategy and all prudence.

Bert Cole—that titanic mushroom—was at once awed and entranced by Nelly, who, in Sis's occasional absences, dragged him, pushed him, carried him, transported him, upon undertakings of fearful excitement. Bert never cried, never laughed, never smiled, and very rarely uttered a word; but, although the youngest of the robber band, he could not be called the least inter-

ested, for of all the people in Glastonbury, including even Mr.
Wollop, the draper, who had been three times Mayor, none—I
say none—contemplated the Dream of Life with a more concentrated gusto. A little bewildered, but not, even then, profoundly
disturbed, when Nelly Morgan insisted on carrying his enormous
weight upon her slim back, Bert Cole surveyed the panorama of
existence with an unpossessive, grave-eyed relish that would have
put Diogenes himself to shame.

The inrush of this hurly-burly of excited children delayed for
a moment Red Robinson's departure. Sis and Nelly were both
favourites of his; and there was a general hullabaloo in that
peaceful kitchen while he " 'unted," as he said, " 'igh and low"
for a bag of sweets he had secreted somewhere. Mrs. Robinson
had even to move to another place her pile of mending from the
stately black-oak hall-chair, which came from the Bishop's Palace
and which served her as a work-table. She had to disarrange, too,
her reproduction of Constable's "Hay-Wagon"—another relic of
the Bishop's Palace—which was balanced on the top of her
dresser. All was joyous confusion; with Bert, like some ideal
prize boy, surveying life from Sally's knees, his plump legs
hanging down, his plump fists clutching together some bits of
blue glass he had picked up, and his grave eyes taking in the
Platonic Essence of the whole unique scene.

As for Jackie, a slender, fragile-looking but passionately intense little boy, with chestnut-brown hair and hazel eyes, he had
begun a dramatic story to his sister Sal, the points of which he
had continually to emphasise, when Sally's attention wandered,
by tugging at the locket round her neck. Long experience had
taught him that the threat of a broken locket was the most atten-
tion-provoking of all gestures on the part of a younger brother.
"I seed she over Tor and over Wirral. I seed she again over
Chalice and over Stonedown. 'Twere a girt big 'un she were; and
'un flew low, like 'twere goin' to turn topsy. 'Twere the biggest
flyer ever made, out of Ameriky; and Nelly says she knows for
sure 'tis Mr. Tom Barter what be steerin' of 'er. 'Tis Mr. Crow's
airplane, Nelly says, and Mr. Barter be pilot on she."

"Didn't I tell you, Mother?" broke in Red Robinson, who had
been listening intently to all this. "*That's* what he's doing with

the money he takes out of the labouring man's sweat! You're main right, Nelly, you're main right! Barter *is* the pilot. And *that* means that he's letting the office down. And *that* means that the whole business will be a washout. I'll tell 'em at the Quarterly tonight what you've seen, Jackie. You wait, Mr. Crow! You wait! You'll find Red Robinson isn't a fellow to spit upon, little though you *may* think of his dependableness!" This word referred to a personal quarrel which Red had had, just a year before, with Philip Crow. Philip had dismissed him without proper warning and when angrily challenged by the man had coldly told him that he did not find him "dependable." The truth is that Red Robinson —although politically a Communist—was temperamentally a Jacobin. A rankling personal hatred of Philip Crow had grown by degrees to be the dominant passion of his life, stronger even than his devotion to Crummie Geard. That "not dependable" had become a kind of vicious quartering on the great, heraldic blazon of Mr. Robinson's revolutionary faith.

Automatically replacing his mother's basket of mending for the church upon the stately hall-chair, which bore upon its back the episcopal arms of Bath and Wells—God knows how the ex-housekeeper had got hold of it!—Red Robinson picked up for the second time his cap and scarf and let himself out into the little dark street. On his way to the small upper room in Old Jones' Antiquity Shop, which had for years been the Comrades' meeting-place, Robinson found it necessary to pass quite close to a low stone wall, over which—at a single field's distance—he could not escape from seeing in the starlight the richly carved ruin of that oldest and most sacred building in Glastonbury, the Church of St. Mary, usually known as Saint Joseph's Chapel. On this spot stood the original Wattle Church built by Joseph of Arimathea. Here was the stone church erected much later by Saint David of Wales; and here too was discovered, in comparatively modern times, the carefully preserved Well, into which a blood-red stream of magical water once trickled down from the very slope of Chalice Hill. It was to the monkish guardians of this mystical spot, doubtless carrying in its enchanted soil, fed by the bones of untold centuries, the psychic chemistry of religious cults far older than Christianity, far older than the Druids, that King

Ina's charter was given, the charter which still exists, an actual piece of material parchment, inscribed by an unknown human hand in the year seven hundred and twenty-five. One of the most familiar of the constellations—was it Cassiopeia?—Red Robinson was weak on the subject of the stars—hung suspended just above this famous fragment of antiquity. Red surveyed this stellar sign with approbation. It was useful; it afforded light—though in a primitive form and not very freely—to the delegate who was to address the Comrades that evening. *There was no nonsense about it.* Those twinkling celestial orbs might have been electric bulbs, inaugurated by some disillusioned Lenin of the Ether. Thus did Red Robinson set the seal of his revolutionary approval upon the stellar system. But the shadowy Norman arches of St. Mary's Chapel, as he surveyed them now, filled him with anger and contempt. He went so far as to spit over the low wall in the direction of that Bastille of Superstition. That his spittle only fell on the back of a small snail that was travelling across a dockleaf by the light of those same stars was an incident of small importance. He had expressed his disgust with Saint Joseph, Saint David, Saint Patrick, Saint Dunstan, Saint Indractus, Saint Gildas, Saint Benignus. He had expressed his disapproval of King Edgar the Peace-Maker, of two King Edmunds, and of more Abbots than he could possibly name! As to King Arthur—but he swallowed his wrath now and moved on.

He was soon entering the little shop of Old Jones. Old Jones was still in hospital. The little cyst, referred to by Penny Pitches, had been successfully cut out of Old Jones' withered frame; but the shock of the operation delayed his recovery. Mr. Evans was still, therefore, playing the rôle of his representative. It was in a bare room, filled with school-forms, and a little school-platform—for it served on Sunday as a meeting-place for a handful of Plymouth Brethren—that the quarterly gathering of Comrades was held. This room was on the third floor and was just above the bedroom occupied by Mr. Evans.

The Welshman was now seated at his open window finishing for exactly the twenty-fifth time, the "Morte d'Arthur" of Sir Thomas Malory. The indescribable sadness of those final pages was wrapping him round in a delicate melancholy, when he became aware of the bustle and the clatter of the meeting above his head. He tried to render himself oblivious to these intrusive sounds. He even placed his pair of guttering candles upon the broad window-sill and the book between them. But to no avail! The voices of the Comrades, the scraping of their feet, the vigorous clapping of their hands, entered his window, descended his chimney, and came down through the cracks between the creaking boards of his ceiling. The voice of Red Robinson raised in indignant denunciation, lowered in Machiavellian persuasion, clear and incisive in practical suggestion, presently drove the sorrowful piety of the repentant Lancelot completely off the field.

The unfortunate thing was—but such was Mr. Evans' psychic constitution—that he no sooner lost his sacred and sweet melancholy under this downpour of communistic reasoning than his old fatal temptation began to trouble his mind. It attacked him vaguely, mistily, atmospherically, with a sort of deadly diffused sweetness of indescribable poison. And what was the worst thing about the way it attacked him was the fact that it made the project of being married to Cordelia Geard an expectation of such withering *dullness* that it made him groan to think of it. And yet he did genuinely love Cordelia. Not with any kind of physical love. That was impossible. But with a feeling of pity that shook the foundations of his nature. He had never pitied anyone as he had come to pity Cordelia. His pity for her had grown step by step with his admiration for her mental and spiritual qualities. Why then this intolerable sense of dullness—oh, much worse than dullness!—this sense that the very leap of life in his deepest fibres would perish of sapless sterility if he were to live forever by her side, day and night, night and day by her side! How *could* he have permitted this corrosive poison so to soak, with its fatal fungus-juice, every nerve of his being? Struggling with this vague temptation now, he began to dally with the ghastly idea that apart from *some* element of sadistic feeling it would be impossible for him not to shrink away with infinite loathing from any physical contact with Cordelia. He had thought at first, on finding how fond he was getting of Cordelia, that here—in this one single point—he had the advantage over normally amorous people. Since with him the natural urge towards feminine beauty *as* feminine beauty was less than nothing, surely he might be permitted to indulge his pity—this pity, that was the magnetism of his love—to the limit, without fear of feeling repulsion? If, without the sadistic shiver, if, without this infernal Nightshade juice, all flesh was literally grass, why couldn't he "make hay" in human pastures from which normal people would shrink in sick aversion? But the ghastly doubt began assailing him now; suppose he had so drained away every drop of magnetic attraction to natural human flesh that the daily presence of another person would strew his life with the dust of the ultimate boredom to such a degree that everything he felt, everything he saw, everything he tasted, everything he heard, would exude a withering dry-rot?

He began inadvertently to listen to what Red Robinson was saying in the room above. He had been hearing him, it seemed, for hours; but he began to *listen* to him now. He blew out one of his candles and moved the other one, and the volume of Malory with it, back into the room. Sitting at his table, with the candle and book in front of him, he set himself to listen attentively. But it was hard to listen attentively. Oh, it all seemed so unimportant —this problem of what became of mankind in general—compared with what he was feeling in his own solitary being! Well! Anyway that perilous quiver upon the air was drifting away now! What brought it at some moments so much more strongly than at others? Were there really powers of good and evil moving about in the ether and touching us all *at their own* will, not at ours, and at the strangest moments? He closed the book and pushed the candle further from him. Through the open window came the sound of a single, old, cracked bell. He couldn't imagine where that bell hung. In some little neighbouring nonconformist chapel, he supposed!

Still the voice of Red Robinson went on, arguing and proving and denouncing and cajoling and persuading; and it was a curious thing that in his public oratory the man largely succeeded in dropping his cockney accent. "Incorrigible heretic! Curse him with bell, book, and candle!" thought Mr. Evans. The Welshman's triadic mind dived like a plummet, then, to the sea-bottom of loathing from which he was always trying to escape. How queer that that fainting sweetness, that quivering, shivering, swooning

sweetness, that was all about him in the air now, making everything *not touched by itself* an ash-bin of intolerable dullness,
should be the thing that led him on and on and on till he incurred
this undying Horror!

Owen Evans leaped up upon his feet as if Something far worse
than any conceivable hell-torture had come into his head. He
stood still for a second and then swung round and faced the
window. And by slow degrees it came over him that what he was
really seeking from Cordelia was punishment. If he punished
himself enough, might not the Horror be disarmed, be repelled?
"Christ!" he murmured, staring out at the darkened windows on
the opposite side of the street, "if it is *like that* to live with her,
why should not that be my punishment? Why should not that
save me?" This sudden unmasking of a secret motive in his own
action which had hitherto been concealed from him gave Owen
Evans such a consoling sensation after his recent self-torture that
he lit his second candle again and sitting down once more at his
table re-opened Malory. He was careful to open the book this
time not at the end, but at the beginning; and he turned over the
pages till he came to a particular passage about Merlin which
always stirred him profoundly. Everything that he could discover
about Merlin sank into Mr. Evans' mind and took a permanent
place there. Scraps and morsels and fragments, mythical, historical, natural, supernatural, as long as they had some bearing,
however remote, upon the life of Merlin, filtered down into Mr.
Evans' soul. He had already begun to write a life of Merlin more
comprehensive than any in existence. In fact Mr. Evans' "Life
of Merlin" was to include all that has been written of that greatest of enchanters in Welsh, in English, in French, and in Old
French. As all Merlin's disciples well know, there is a mysterious
word used in one of the Grail Books about his final disappearance. This is the word "Esplumeoir." It is inevitable from the
context to interpret this as some "Great Good Place," some mystic Fourth Dimension, or Nirvanic apotheosis, into which the
magician deliberately sank, or rose; thus committing a sort of
inspired suicide, a mysterious dying in order to live more fully.
As he sought for one of his favourite passages—for "Esplumeoir"
does not appear in Malory—he kept murmuring that particular

invocation under his breath, pondering intently on the occult escape offered by this runic clue from all the pain of the world, an escape so strangely handed down from far-off centuries in these thaumaturgic syllables.

While Mr. Evans was thus occupied, Red Robinson in the room above where the Comrades were assembled to hear his speech was thinking to himself that he must conceal one little fact about his grand message to them and the scheme he intended to lay before them. This was the fact that it was really none other than Persephone Spear, who, through her husband's mouth, had first broached the idea of starting a Municipal Factory in Glastonbury. It needed the wit of a woman to think of such a simple thing. But Red Robinson, like many another masculine politician, was re-solved to take all the credit to himself of this flash of feminine inspiration! It was not long before the cockney's penetrating voice began to make itself again audible to the ears of Mr. Evans, lifted up to a yet shriller pitch as Red approached his main argument.

As a propagandist Mr. Robinson always aimed at a disciplined art that resembled that of a Catholic peasant-priest carefully trained in a Seminary; but it often happened that his art broke down. "We have several Comrades," Mr. Evans heard him ex-claim now, "who are on the Glastonbury Town Council. I appeal to these Comrades; I beg these Comrades, to use every means at their disposal to familiarize their colleagues with the prin-ciples of municipal ownership. These factories depend upon natural resources. The Wookey Hole one depends on the sub-terranean River Axe which flows from beneath the Mendips. The Glastonbury one depends on the waters of the River Brue. Does this man Crow, does this selfish, luxurious rich man, cause these rivers to flow, or create the rains and the springs that fill these rivers? We are all Comrades here; and I may talk freely here. I have come to learn that this religious fanatic we are accustomed to hear called by the name of Bloody Johnny"—here there was a terrific stamping of feet and loud hilarious laughter above Mr. Evans' head!—"is intending to use his legacy of ill-gotten bour-geois money, of which all the Comrades here have heard, to bring crowds of visitors to the town. You know, Comrades, how such bourgeois visitors dislike everything industrial. But their dislike is not shared by the man I refer to. Now this is what I propose to you, Comrades; I propose that some one among us should be delegated to approach this man Geard, who is evidently prepared to throw his money away, and try and persuade him to lend the Town Council, of which he is now a member, funds large enough to buy out this devil Crow! I propose that this delegate from the Party persuade Geard to buy for himself the factories, if he cannot induce the town to purchase them. Anything is better than leaving them in the hands of such a devilish enemy of the working-man as we know this Crow to be. And they'll go for a song, I tell you, Comrades. They'll go for a song; because a really big strike will throw the concern into bankruptcy.

"Don't interrupt me, Comrades from Wells! This is only half my plan. As you all know this is the year for the election of our Mayor. Geard is a fool. But he is a well-meaning fool. He is sympathetic to our cause. He is almost one of us. He is furthermore the sort of man that could be persuaded into anything! I have myself the entrée into his house . . . I needn't say any more at this moment . . . and if this Quarterly Meeting of the Comrades of Wells and Glastonbury delegated me to approach him as their representative, I believe there would be a good chance of persuading him. We would have to make his name prominent— that's what all bourgeois philanthropists want—to be talked of, to be heard of! The Comrades on the Town Council would then propose him for Mayor—to succeed that prize ass, Wollop. Nothing would please him better than to be proposed for Mayor. With Geard as Mayor, and the Party behind the Mayor, we might municipalise the water, the gas, the electricity and finally these factories! This, Comrades, is simply common sense. Some Comrades here may object that this is a wild-goose scheme; that in proposing it to them I am departing from practical politics. Let such Comrades bethink themselves a little! Here is this sum of money, inherited by this incredible fool who wants to spend it on being talked about. Why should not we elect him Mayor when the elections come on? No Party but our Party would bother with such a catspaw. But that's just why we *must* win in the end. *Because we despise no means!*

The Conservatives of course will oppose him. But the Liberals and Labour men will support us if we take a strong lead. That's the great thing; to take a strong, clear lead! Half the Town Council are sick to death of Wollop. He's been Mayor of Glastonbury so long that everyone wants a change. The drinking men would all vote for Bloody Johnny, just for the sport of it and to stir things up. All the Nonconformists would vote for him. Crow hates the mere thought of the fellow. Crow will get angry and say wild things and make some howling blunder; and then the Town Council, with our Party in the background, will have Glastonbury in their ——"

It was clear to Mr. Evans, who had begun at last to grow seriously interested in this discourse when he realized how closely it concerned "his relative, Mr. Geard" that the meeting had called the speaker to order and shouted him down. Some other voice was speaking now in cold, low, sarcastic tones. Evans caught the words "personal ambition," "fancy scheme," "fairy-tale poppycock," "wasting the Party's funds," "Menshevik-claptrap." He even imagined he heard the name of "Crummie" coupled with a very gross epithet. The Quarterly Meeting evidently regarded itself as free from eavesdroppers and was permitting its speakers untrammelled licence. After a while Red Robinson's voice was audible again. Evans had met him once at the Geards' and was sure he was not mistaken as to his identity.

This time it was clear that the cockney orator was trying to carry the day by an emotional appeal. "We shall never have such a chance again, Comrades," he was saying. "Geard is a fool but Geard has a good heart. By electing Geard as Mayor we shall be electing ourselves into the power behind the throne. And what *could* we not achieve then? Away with all these mediæval superstitions! Away with all these pious Pilgrimages! Glastonbury is only one town among other towns. There's nothing wonderful about Glastonbury but the health and freedom and happiness of its men, its women, its children! While this fellow Crow exploits the natural resources to his own profit, and while our bourgeois tradesmen exploit all this mediæval superstition to *their* profit, what becomes of the real men and women, able-bodied Somersetshire men and comely Somersetshire women? They can't afford meat or butter! They can't afford fresh eggs! Their children are underfed. Look at them, Comrades! Look at the children in Beckery and Bove Town. Look at the children in Benignus Alley! and Paradise! There you have the whole issue! On the one hand Crow and Wollop exploiting the people's bodies; on the other these pious mountebanks exploiting their souls! And all these fine bourgeois gentry, Lawyer Beere, Doctor Fell, Parson Dekker and so on; and old Wollop the worst of all; what are they doing? They are burning toy candles to the 'oly Grail! Yes, they are burning incense while women and children haven't enough to eat! I tell you, Comrades, Geard is our man. I've talked to him already . . . I have already . . . I needn't go into that . . . though the Comrade from Wells did use insulting language I scorn to answer him. . . . I have already a certain influence over Geard through his favorite daughter. . . . I've already made Geard see the light upon many economic points . . . I have already made Geard open his mind to many bourgeois tricks. Geard has had the working-class mentality opened up to him. It is the Comrade from Wells, not I, who has departed from the Party's principles in his abuse of me and Geard. The time has come for real action. The election of the Mayor comes on in a few weeks. We can't elect one of ourselves Mayor. The Comrade from Wells knows that perfectly well. But we *could* elect Geard; and then work the Council *through* Geard. My plan is *not* a wild-goose plan; it's a carefully thought-out scheme based upon *psychology*. That is the reason, no doubt, why the Comrade from Wells found it so hard to understand!"

Mr. Evans heard uproarious laughter and applause as the speaker ceased. It was evident that that final hit at the opposition was very popular with the Comrades. He himself sneezed violently at this point and the sound must have ascended to the room above, raising the disturbing question as to their conclave having been overheard. After a profound silence he heard the sound of steps descending the stairs and there were whispers outside his door. In order to make clear to the whisperers that he knew what they were up to, Mr. Evans began clattering with his fire-irons among the cold ashes of his grate. No sooner had he done this than the steps receded up the stairs again. All subsequent discussions in the room above were henceforth quite inaudible and it was not long before the Quarterly Meeting broke up.

When Mr. Evans was at length in bed, with the little table and one of his two candles convenient to his hand, he proceeded, while he smoked his final cigarette, to take stock of what he had overheard. "I shall tell Cordelia all they are plotting," he said to himself. "But I don't see why they shouldn't elect my relative Mayor. I think he would make a very good Mayor." And before the Welshman's mind, as he squeezed out the fiery embers of his cigarette on a broken china saucer that he had brought up from the shop below, there floated an exciting dream of a communistic Glastonbury, presided over by his relative Geard; a Glastonbury in which he himself would play a sort of court-magician part and with Cordelia—that free spirit of the Cymric race—inaugurating the laws and regulations! As he finally turned over to the wall and shut his eyes, he felt happier, thinking of this, than he had felt for many a long week. "If these working-men decide upon this," he thought, "I suppose it'll really happen. I wonder whether it's the Town Council, or the Church, or the Government that gives a person leave to excavate?" He saw himself possessed of John Crow's hazel-stick with its queer root-handle. He remembered how John had assured him that with such a stick a person could find anything buried in the earth.

"*Hic jacet Arturus . . . Hic jacet . . . Arturus . . . Hic jacet . . . hic . . .*"

TWO OR THREE DAYS AFTER THE QUARTERLY MEETING ABOVE Old Jones' shop, the Bove Town robber band, that is to say Captain Jackie and his infantile followers, were deploying, if such a word may be used for the movements of so diminutive a troop, in loose marching order up the narrow Godney Road. They had left all the decent houses far behind when they debouched from the Wells Road. They had long ago passed the drive-gates of The Elms where Philip Crow lived. They were now on the edge of what was called Common Moor and were not far from Backwear Farm which is the site of the British Lake Village. The road they followed did not carry much traffic along its hard, tarred surface; but the weather was so warm that the robber band was exhausted. The air would have been dusty if the road had not been so polished and so hard, but wherever the brown earth showed between the clumps of rough grass by the roadside it was dry and sapless and unsympathetic and depressing. The day was one of those early Spring days that for some mysterious reason, very hard to analyse, are felt to be ill-omened and unpleasant. Something was certainly wrong with this day! All animal nerves felt it. All human nerves felt it. All living things were irritable, restless, disturbed; sick without being sick; sad without being sad; annoyed without any apparent cause for annoyance!

Sis was already carrying Bert on her back. "Plo-chuck . . . plo-chuck . . ." went her sturdy legs, under the weight of the complacent and impervious infant. Nelly and Jackie were a little in advance; but even *they* were walking in single file, silent and grim. Nothing but the indomitable will of Captain Jackie could have kept this exhausted cortège on the move; or brought it so far afield on that nervous, touchy, irritable March afternoon.

At last they came to a standstill by a low, ancient, broken iron railing which separated an object from the Godney Road. This object could hardly be called a house. It was a tiny, little, stucco building of two storeys, each with two windows, one looking towards the road and one looking away from the road. The stucco was of a whitish-yellowish colour and was peeling off. It was stained here and there, too, with stains of a rusty brown. Only an expert in the decline of material substance under weather invasions could have interpreted these stains. They were not lichen. They were not moss. They looked like rusty blood; but they could not have really been blood; for no one would have thrown blood against the wall of a house eight or nine feet from the ground? Weather stains they obviously were, of chemical origin; but this did not lessen the strangeness of the fact that these rusty stains upon this stucco house had seen fit to assume the surprising shape of a map of North and South America.

On the left-hand side of this tiny house was an open shed, one portion of which served as the roosting-place for half a dozen white fowls who were now wandering in the adjoining field.

At the back of the house was one of those large dykes or rhynes on the edge of which grew three pollarded willows; and between this little stream and the back door of the one single ground-floor room there was a small vegetable garden, the leafy promise of which was a good deal further advanced above the loamy clay than in either of the grand bourgeois gardens tended by Mr. Weatherwax.

Seated in his shed, sharpening a faggot of sticks for the support of his young peas, crouched the owner of Backwear Hut, a very old man called Abel Twig.

No sooner did Jackie catch sight of Mr. Twig than he caused his lieutenant Nelly to proclaim a halt.

It was not difficult to obtain obedience to this command, so exhausted was the main body of the Alley Gang; and Bert, slipping like a sack of flour from the back of Sis, was soon propped up against the iron railings, through which his round eyes stared in wonder at the map of North and South America.

The small hands of Jackie, Nelly and Sis clung in a row to the topmost railing of Mr. Twig's sole line of defense while the hatless heads of Jackie, Nelly, and Sis looked down in unabashed curiosity upon the interior of Mr. Twig's shed.

"Hullo!" cried Jackie in a shrill voice. "Hullo, Number One!"

In every town of the size of Glastonbury there are produced

by great creative Nature certain laughing-stocks, or butts of derision, for the amusement of the rabble. Old Jones of the Antiquity Shop—now in the local hospital—and Old Twig, now before us in his shed, were the butts of Glastonbury. They were bosom cronies, these two old men, and not a child in the poorer district but had not at one time or other followed these queer ones down the street mocking and shouting. They were always called Number One and Number Two; and so widely spread were these nicknames that in some of the bewildered heads of the contemporaries of Young Bert the two great excretory functions of our poor animal organism, so prominent in children's lives, were confusedly associated with these venerable old persons.

"Hullo, Number One!" repeated Jackie.

"Number Two be in Orspital!" echoed Nelly.

"Bert wants a glass o' water, Bert do," added Sis in a less combative voice.

"What did I tell 'ee, eh? What did I tell 'ee, ye young scamooches? I told 'ee yesternight I'd set Bumboggle at ye if ye came again. Hi there! Good dog! Hi there! Hi there, Bumboggle! Hi! Bumboggle! Ye girt sleepy beast! Come and eat up these three impidents!"

Captain Jackie did not budge. Lieutenant Nelly did not flinch. It is impossible, however, to conceal the fact that after this alarming invocation there were only five little hands clutching the railings. Sis, concerned for Bert, had thrown one arm round her small brother's neck. Bert himself, however, to the honour of the Alley Gang, replied to the challenge in a momentous sentence.

"I baint afeard o' no fancy dogs, I baint."

"Bert wants a glass o' water, Number One, Bert do!" repeated Sis in a singsong monotone.

"Oh, he does, does he?" growled Old Twig. "I'll water him. I'll firk him! I'll ferret him! Oh, he does, does he?"

Talking to himself all the time in the manner of a ferocious ogre, Old Twig got up and retired into that square object which went by the name of Backwear Hut. He returned almost immediately with a tin cup, full of water, which he handed to Bert between the railings, not relinquishing it himself, but tilting it up, while the child drank long and deep. No sooner had the old man returned to his shed and his task of whittling his pea-sticks than Nelly lifted up her high-pitched voice.

"Tell us some more about they funny men what lived in Lake Village in your grand-dad's time."

Muttering and chuckling the old man moved up to the railings and leaning over tried to lift Bert across. But Bert, far too heavy for him, was already pushing himself under the lowest bar. The three older children were now scrambling over the top of the railings; and in about three minutes after their first "Hullo" they were all seated at Old Twig's feet in the front of his shed listening spellbound to what he was saying.

" 'Twould be in me wone field," he began, "this here Lake Village if all had their rights. Grand-dad sold 'un to Lawyer Beere's father and Lawyer Beere's father sold 'un to Mr. Crow up at Elms, and Mr. Crow, they say, is goin' to turn sheep out and make it a visitors' field. He've a-brought one party here already this season and so have Mr. Barter. Other folks say he be going to turn this wold field into one of they landings for airboats. If this be true 'twill be terrible disturbing for them old ghosties in Lake Village."

"Have you ever seed one of they funny men's ghosties, Mr. Twig?" enquired Sis.

"Don't interrupt, Sis!" cried Nelly. "Number One ain't begun his story yet! His story ain't about Mr. Crow."

"It ain't about any of the like of us," echoed Captain Jackie, taking the cue from his lieutenant. " 'Tis about they old men theyselves."

"Be I telling this 'ere tale or be ye telling this 'ere tale?" said Abel Twig. It dawned upon him rather sadly that his listeners envisaged the ancient heroes of Lake Village as so many feeble replicas of Number One.

"Bert be a good boy, Bert be!" ejaculated irrelevantly the owner of that name.

"When I tell this 'ere tale to Bumboggle," said Mr. Twig, "Bumboggle do prick his girt ears and say nothink."

There was a complete silence among the Alley Gang at this, and Old Twig went on.

" 'Twas years and years afore King Arthur that they Ancient

British funny men lived in Lake Village. Them funny men were terrible feared of beasties in they days, beasties as big as my house."

"Your house baint as big as my mummie's be," interrupted Jackie.

"Number One's house be a very *nice* house," threw in Sis, evidently feeling for a second as if Mr. Twig were a larger edition of Bert.

"Were it afore your grand-dad sold thik field that they Ancient Britons lived in they reed-houses?"

Nelly looked with astonishment at her gallant captain when he made this unintelligent remark. She began to recognise, as many romantic young women have been forced to do before, that high military achievement is compatible with very crude historical perspective.

But Mr. Twig was rather pleased than otherwise at this reference to his grandfather's hasty disposal of landed property.

"'Twere a *little* while afore poor old Grand-dad's days," he said, "that they Ancient British lived."

"Bert's got pins and needles," said Sis. "He be waggling wi' his foot."

"Sit ride-a-cock on Number One's knee!" rejoined Old Twig, placing the little boy upon one of his thin legs.

Seated solemn and erect, without moving an eyelid, Bert contemplated the countenance of his host while Sis began rubbing the child's instep.

A faint smile flickered over the little boy's face.

"Bert be pee-ing his trowsies," cried Sis with concern.

"No, I baint," retorted the infant indignantly.

"Why did yer look like that then?" argued his sister.

The child got very red and said nothing.

"You be," the girl reiterated.

"I baint," shrilled the youngster. And driven by the injustice of the world to break his own rule of politeness—"He be like Guy Fawkes!" he brought out, while the corners of his mouth went down.

It was an unusual event for Bert to smile; it was no less than a historic event for him to show signs of tears. Sis lifted him from the old man's knee, took him upon her own little lap and hugged him against her sturdy frame.

"There was one of they funny men in them times," went on the old man hurriedly, "who killed a girt beastie wi' a flint arrow. Thik beastie was called Giant What's-his-name on account of his name bein' so hard to say; but when the funny man killed it he took off all its skin and made a fire and his sister, who was his wife too, cooked thik girt beastie."

Bert lifted up his head at this exciting point.

"Sis be Bert's wife," he remarked with intense gravity.

Sis slapped him sharply and turned reproachfully to Mr. Twig.

"Those times baint our times," she protested.

"I wish I lived in those times!" cried Nelly with flashing eyes. "I'd have helped Jackie to shoot thik girt beast. I'd have carried a bundle of they flinties!"

"My grand-dad's field what he sold to wold Lawyer Beere baint the only field he had. Yon field, over thik dyke, were his'n, and it be mine today."

Into this chorus of boastings it was natural enough that Captain Jackie should fling his contribution.

"When Mr. Barter do fly from this here Lake Village 'twon't be with any ghosty, 'twill be wi' I!"

The whole robber band regarded their leader with wondering awe.

"I'll be there to wave to 'ee!" cried Nelly. "And I'll throw summat at 'ee, maybe, for luck!"

"Will you fly above your mother's chimney, Jackie?" enquired Sis.

"Sis be Bert's airship," remarked the wide-eyed infant, glancing obstinately at his sister in full expectation of being slapped again.

But it was old Twig, not Sis, who broke up this happy colloquy. He suddenly clapped his hand to his head and beat on his hard skull.

"Oh, the duck-a-duck!" he cried. "In sense! Out foolishness!" And still beating his old pate he set himself to run with shambling gait into Backwear Hut and up the single flight of stairs.

"Be off! Be off! B'off! Quick! Quick! If ye love Old Twig the price of a bright penny, be off! Out of here! Afore they come!"

These remarks were addressed to the robber band from the upper window of Backwear Hut, out of which the old man's withered neck and grizzled head protruded.

It was clear that Captain Jackie was seized with panic—the bravest are subject to such emotions once or twice in their lives—for forgetting entirely about his little army he scrambled at top speed over the railings and bolted up the road in the opposite direction from the town. It was then that the heart of the band's fiery lieutenant was torn in two; for while both fear and love urged her to follow Jackie, an impulse in her girl's breast stronger than fear and love constrained her to help Sis get Bert out of the shed and over the railings. *Then*, however, she waited not a second, but followed her lord on flying feet!

Poor Sis! The stolid little lass suffered a most evil moment, as under the eyes of the frantic old man leaning out of the window she tried in vain to get the panic-stricken Bert to mount upon her back. Desperately she propped him up upon the lowest bar of the railings and, turning round, clutched wildly at his legs. Each time she seized his legs he toppled back against the railings. In vain she lost her temper. In vain she slapped him. The panic of Jackie and Nelly, the old man's frightened voice out of the window, her own unusual agitation, quite broke down the philosophy of Bert. The little boy, for the first time since he was two years old, burst into a howl of desolate crying.

Two events now occurred simultaneously, while Sis, on her knees by the blubbering child, soothed him with words and caresses. The old man withdrew from the window, stumbled downstairs and rushed into the road. At the same moment two extremely neat young ladies, both in elegant black, one with a blue ribbon round her neck, and the other with a pink ribbon, advancing side by side from the direction of the town, arrived at Mr. Twig's gate.

They surveyed the sobbing Bert, who was making up for the rarity of his departure from philosophic calm by his difficulty in regaining it, with aloof distaste. This was the sort of thing that both Louie and Lily Rogers—for such they were—had become handmaidens to escape. The mere sight of Sis and Bert brought back vividly to their minds their own early experiences. They edged away from the little girl and the little boy and one of them began fumbling rather nervously with the dilapidated latch of the still more dilapidated gate. This gate had not, as a matter of fact, been opened for years—perhaps not since the death of Mr. Twig's grand-dad—and it became apparent to Louie, for in Miss Drew's absence no human creature addressed her or thought of her as "Rogers," that whatever entrance or exit Uncle Abel may have possessed this rusty gate was not it.

Meanwhile Uncle Abel himself, full of the most obsequious apologies, had appeared upon the scene and was now hovering like the bewildered physician at Dunsinane, between the mental trouble of one claimant on his attention and the physical impasse of the other.

" 'Tis here, my dears! 'Tis here I steps over," he cried, waving to his dainty nieces to follow him and hurrying along the edge of his domain till he reached a place where the top rail was nonexistent. "Here's the place, my precious ducks, 'tis only to lift your pretty skirts a trifle so's not to get rust on 'en. 'Tis here, 'tis here, my sweethearts! Up she goes, and over the hurdle! Here! 'Tis here I goes in and out!"

But the two elegant creatures—for they were really goodhearted girls—had both of them by this time drifted up to where Sis knelt by the prostrate Bert. The philosopher's sobs were over, but his deep shame remained; and this emotion, as often happens with wise men who have been unwise, displayed itself in irrational anger towards his nearest and dearest. Bert, lying on his face in the grass, kicked obstreperously every time Sis touched him. Matters were further complicated at this moment by the return of Jackie and Nelly. Nelly in a moment jerked Bert upon his feet; and once in a perpendicular position the child's interest in the surprising scene around him made him forget his disgrace.

"Who *are* these children, Uncle?" enquired Louie of Mr. Twig.

"Hadn't you better be taking that little boy home to his mother, child?" said Lily to Sis.

" 'Tis Grannie," replied Sis. "Mother be dead and buried."

Abel Twig was now scrutinising with sly interest a paper bag carried by Lily. The girls were accustomed to bring him some casual token of Mr. Weatherwax's activity and it presented itself very strongly to his mind that here was a providential chance of getting rid of the children.

So he spoke up. "They be *good* children, they be, my rosebuds. 'Twere the sight of such *good* children, walking quietly along road, while their decent mothers cleaned house, that made Uncle Abel call 'em in. But now be time for ye all"—he turned to Sis as being the one among the group who was most grown-up—"to begin traipsin' home-along."

He gave Lily, who carried the paper bag, a little twitch of the sleeve and pulled her a few steps aside.

"Have 'ee brought some o' they sweet apples what old Weatherwax do keep so long in hayloft?" he whispered craftily. "If 'ee have brought they, I be terrible thirsty for 'en. Me stummick be watering to get me teeth into 'en—them nice little firm sweet fruities. Poor old Uncle have a girt fancy to taste, now and quick, what his pretty nieces have brought to he in thik little bag."

"Of course, Uncle Abel," said Lily sweetly. "You shall have them at once. There! I haven't had my kiss yet," and she touched his bristly cheeks with her lips. "Of course they are all for you! Eat them, keep them, cook them —— They're yours entirely! Louie and I brought them for you with our love."

She gladly enough handed the paper bag over to him and smoothed out with her cream-coloured, neatly gloved fingers the ruffled front of her black dress.

Once in possession of this great bag of Hesperidean fruit the astute owner of Backwear Hut felt himself to be master of the situation. He took out five beautiful apples, one by one, and began munching with hurried bites, though not without difficulty, for his teeth were few, the first of these. The other four with a cunning leer he handed over to Captain Jackie.

"These apples," he said, "what these young ladies have brought be the cause why them funny men, what I tell 'ee of, called our town Avallonia which be ancient British for orchard." Here the wily old man addressed himself to Lieutenant Nelly. "Ye be a robber band, ye be, same as they fierce invaders what plundered poor old King Avallach. These apples be rich plunder. Robber bands do march, robber bands do, slow and quiet, carrying their plunder, till they be round thik corner of road; then they do eat what they've taken from frightened natives!"

He had said quite enough. Without a second's hesitation, in the most resolute order and in profound silence, the four children went off hand in hand along the footpath by the roadside in the direction of home.

Louie and Lily, now safely inside the railings, watched with wonder the surprising exhibition of discipline in this well-executed retreat. When the four were near the twist of the road which would take them out of sight, they saw Jackie turn and give one hurried glance round. He then began running. He was followed by Nelly first, then by Sis who carried Bert like a bundle of something precious and heavy, hugged against her body.

As if ashamed of their prolonged observation of this ragamuffin crew, Louie and Lily now devoted themselves to being as ladylike and patronising as they could to their eccentric uncle. They were, however, so attached to the old man that it was not long before they were unburdening their bosoms of a thousand intimate troubles, triumphs and grievances. It appeared they were due in an hour's time to take tea with Emma, the confidential servant of Tilly Crow; and much that they had to relate had to do with the Philip Crow establishment.

Uncle Abel on his part had a good deal to say about the recent experiences of his ancient crony and ally, Old Jones, in his ward in the hospital. To anything concerning the hospital both the girls lent a curious ear, Louie being especially interested in the culinary economies, which were notoriously generous in this institution, while Lily kept enquiring about the bed-covers, the linen-chests, the nurses' caps, the doctors' white coats, the slippery floors; and whether it was from Miss Bibby Fell's daffodil-beds, or Mrs. Crow's conservatory, or Mayor Wollop's greenhouse, that the best gifts of flowers were received.

"Emma says that poor Mrs. Crow is very concerned about all this flying," observed Louie.

"Yes," threw in Lily, who being the younger was more romantic than the buxom cook and if possible more ladylike, "yes,

Emma says that the mistress cries her poor self to sleep night after night thinking of all the money they're spending."

"But they be rich, baint they?" commented Number One, thinking to himself, "I be a wonderful comfortable man—I be! I baint one for envying they rich." And full of complacency the old man surveyed the tops of the budding willow trees, the brown and white back of the cow Betsy and these two gracious visitors seated side by side on his kitchen chairs.

"Emma says," went on Louie, whose character it was to give the practical details of life their due proportion, leaving to the more pensive and more romantic Lily the psychological aura of the events under discussion, "that Mr. Crow made certain he was going to have all Canon Crow's money; and that he's been spending more than he could afford on Wookey Hole alone."

"He likes electrifying things," murmured Lily dreamily. "They tell about the Wookey Hole witch up in Wells. Do you remember, Louie, what that woman said when we were out there on choir-treat day, how that she'd once been down there, where those stalagmites and stalactites grow, and that she ran out in hysterics, thinking she saw the witch?"

"It's this flying he's started on now," went on Louie, holding the topic resolutely down to facts, "that's the main trouble. Of course on the top of his well-known electric schemes it *does* mean a very considerable expenditure."

As she uttered this judicial remark Louie crossed her knees, as if her neat shoes were resting upon an embroidered footstool instead of upon Number One's brick floor, and folding her gloved hands over her knees she began rubbing her right hand very slowly over her left hand.

It must have been with this precise gesture, with these exact words, and with this identical intonation combined with a frowning glance given to some remote object—in the present case, alas! to nothing more dignified than Number One's swill-pail, turned upside down—that Miss Euphemia Drew had received the town gossip about Philip Crow's financial state.

"Who was that wild-looking child you had here just now, Uncle?" enquired Louie, dropping her Miss Drew airs.

"Eh? Who? Which on 'em do you mean?" muttered the old

man with startled embarrassment. He had been secretly hoping that no more would be said about his previous visitors.

"The thin little girl, with great black eyes, and her hair all uncombed, and her clothes so dirty."

"As far as I knows that be Nelly," replied Abel Twig.

"But Nelly what, Uncle?" insisted Louie. "She must have a surname."

"I talked to my friend Jones in hospital about Nelly," confessed the old man reluctantly. "I told him all about she, and how she went round with Jackie Jones and Sis Cole; and he did say that her mother's name was Morgan. So I suppose—though, mind ye, I baint sure—that *her* name be similarwise." He was silent and then muttered under his breath, "Morgan, Nelly Morgan, Eleanor Morgan," as if he were wondering how to give to these syllables some special rhythmic secret. At the name "Morgan" he was surprised to notice the two sisters exchanging a swift, significant glance. Louie actually nodded at Lily, as who should say, "You see! That's just what would happen, that *that* child, of all children, should be picked up by Uncle!"

Full of greater fear than ever, after he had caught this interchange of glances, that by continuing the topic he should bring harm in some way upon his little friend, Number One hurriedly went on.

"I expect Nelly's name isn't Morgan at all. No . . . no. When I come to think of it, Number—I mean my friend Jones—was sure it wasn't! Jackie calls she Nelly. Sis calls she Nelly. There be many well-thought-on women in the world what have only one name." Number One racked his brains to think of some of these famous monosyllabic females. At last his face lit up. He recalled his grand-dad's Lake Village. "The Lady of the Lake," he cried triumphantly, "had only——" He stopped in dismay; for there came into his head a conversation with old Mr. Merry, the Curator of the Glastonbury Museum, from whom he had sought to get information about his grandfather's historic field. This authority had told him that the real Lady of the Lake was none other than Morgan Le Fay, the very ambiguous sister of King Arthur!

"It's Nelly Morgan that was here with Jackie Jones and Sis Cole," said Louie with decision. "You've let your kind heart run away with you again, Uncle. It's lucky no one but Lily and me knows about this. But we've told you now and you *do* know, so you can act according."

"What be talking about, me pretty?" stammered Uncle Abel.

Lily meanwhile had assumed a sad, poetic expression. "What *he* feels, 'tis strange to think," she interrupted dreamily, "as he lies pondering on a poor betrayed girl, and on a little child who belongs to him and yet doesn't belong to him."

"Stuff and nonsense!" cried Louie. "All *he* thinks about is electricity and flying machines and asking Mayor Wollop to drop in to dinner. He doesn't think of anyone's feelings."

"Will it be best to tell Emma about that child being with Jackie and Sis; and about her having been in Uncle's house?" Lily put into this question as much dramatic gravity as if she were taking a personal part in some great *cause célèbre*.

Louie knitted her brows in solemn consideration.

"It will be wisest," she replied, in the very manner of Euphemia Drew, "to leave what we say till we see how things arrange themselves. I would not like to upset Emma; and it might make it harder for Emma too, if she knew what Mrs. Crow *didn't* know."

Number One could stand all this no longer. His awe of his nieces broke down completely under the pressure of his mental bewilderment. He rose up from his chair. "What the holy terror," he cried, "are you gals gabbling about?"

Lily's expression was a masterpiece of refined protest, sentimental relish for the whole situation, and an irresistible desire to be the one permitted to tell him all.

But she was not that one; for that one was Louie.

"Don't get agitated, you poor darling, and do please sit down. It's all very dreadful"—the intonation of Miss Drew was mingled here with a vague mimicry of certain lady-visitors—"but we must be as collected and sensible as we can. The truth is that Emma has found out a very unhappy story. It appears"—here Louie took breath and fidgetted in a modest manner with her ribbon—"that Mr. Crow misconducted himself some eight years ago with Jenny Morgan. Jenny seems to have forgotten herself completely and the result was that she had a baby."

The style in which Louie delivered herself of this grand climax was, it is needless to point out, entirely her own. No one but Louie would have used that derogatory and indeed disagreeable word "misconducted." No one but Louie would have used the expression "forgot herself" for the normal lapse from the virginal state.

"Jenny has taken to drink," Louie went on, "since then, but she works for the child. She couldn't bring herself to dispose of the child. She used to hear such terrible things of those institutions. Emma thinks he sends her a little money every second Wednesday. Emma knows he always goes to the Post Office on that day. That's what Emma *thinks*, mind you,—that he sends her a little regularly. Emma doesn't know for certain whether he does or not, but she is *almost* sure he does."

Number One's countenance had begun to beam with relief and satisfaction. He had feared he knew not what; and now to learn that all this agitation was only about Nelly's illegitimacy completely reassured him.

"Nelly Morgan," he repeated cheerfully. And then, thinking of the Curator's words, "Morgan Nelly," he added.

"Mr. Crow isn't altogether a wicked man," threw in Lily. "He is a strange man though. I believe he lives a wild life unknown to the world." Her voice sank and ceased. She looked away into the distance, far away beyond the pollarded willows. A skilful observer might have read in her face that she felt that shame and even desertion would not have been without their own melancholy compensations if it had been her lot, in place of Jenny Morgan, to "forget herself" with so Byronic a seducer as Philip Crow.

Number One, who had quite recovered his spirits since he had learned that his elegant nieces had nothing against Jackie's lieutenant except her birth, suggested now that before they left Backwear Hut they should see his "garden."

In pursuance of this design he led the way through his back door, past the post to which Betsy was tethered, till he reached a little square plot surrounded by a low, whitewashed fence. Here were several rows of young peas and scarlet-runners and one row of freshly sprouting celery. But at the corner of the garden—a reserved space of about a square yard—waved in the warm air a fragrant patch of pheasant-eyed narcissus. Number One clicked open a little toy gate into his garden and stepping carefully over the young vegetables picked with reckless impetuosity at least half of these lotus-scented flowers. These he divided into two bouquets of exactly the same size; and when, after a few affectionate good-byes—for Louie and Lily felt very protective to their only male relation—the girls went off, up Godney Road to where it joined Wells Road, these white flowers, pinned on their black dresses and matching most felicitously their black and white Easter hats, gave them a really charming appearance.

It must have been about an hour later that the discreet Emma was serving tea in her immaculate kitchen to these pretty wearers of Abel Twig's nosegays. Emma was also dressed in black but over her dress she wore a spotless white apron and upon her head, the most carefully brushed and tidied head in Glastonbury, she wore an old-fashioned cap trimmed with handmade lace.

Emma, unlike her visitors, had never made any attempt to copy her mistress' manners or speech. Emma's manners were dignified, but they were those of one, who as she always expressed it, "knew her place," and her speech was as local as a Mendip quarry. She was the kind of servant who in place of losing herself in her employer's fortunes or way of life made of those things the background for her own resolute character. The character of Emma was not eccentric like that of Penny Pitches. Emma detested eccentricity. She was no worshipper of the aristocracy either, like Red Robinson's mother. What she really was was a strict Professional; and her Profession was that of the Perfect Servant. In Tilly Crow she had found what she considered to be the Perfect Mistress. Mrs. Philip's deplorable limitations, obvious to all the rest of the world, were not limitations at all to Emma. They were virtues high and rare; and for the sake of these virtues she was as devoted to this neurotic and shrewish recluse as any old-fashioned lawyer's clerk was ever devoted to a narrow-minded, pettifogging scrivener.

In this great turbulent universe, wherein ships at sea, certain farms on land, certain soldiers' camps, certain outposts of civilisation, conducted under scrupulous authority, become oases of order in the midst of chaos, the miniature polity entitled The

Elms, ruled over by Emma and Tilly Crow, was in its own way
almost without rival. The kitchen tea-party which was now proceeding would have been as much disturbed by the presence of
any of the "gentry" who were contemporaneously taking tea in
Tilly's drawing-room as any of Tilly's guests would have been
had Emma, in place of answering the bell, sat down on the sofa
beside her mistress. But the domestic ritual in the drawing-room
under the rule of Mrs. Philip was no less punctilious than the
ritual in Mrs. Philip's kitchen under the rule of Emma; and between these two women, on this nice professional point, there was
a uniformity of opinion too deep to be expressed in words.
Their mutual ideal was, as a matter of fact, as different from the
aristocratic way of taking things as it was different from the proletarian way, or from the easy-going, lower-middle-class way of
Mr. and Mrs. Geard. It was upper-middle-class. And not for
nothing does one note that it has been from houses conducted
under the Emmas and the Tillys of life that such characteristically
English characters as Charles Darwin and Horatio Nelson have
projected their world-shaping opinions and their heroic deeds.
Indeed it might with justice be said that two oases of perfect
order and peace, and two alone, existed in Glastonbury at that
epoch—the draper's shop of Mr. Wollop, the Mayor, and the
home of Tilly Crow! Outside these harbours of tenoned and mor-
tised security everything ebbed and flowed. These were, so to
speak, the Parmenidean rafts of stillness in the Heraclitean flux
of Glastonbury life.

The lights had been lit in both drawing-room and kitchen before the visitors departed. In other houses they would not have
been lit! In other houses people would have been too absorbed
in talk, too enamoured of the twilight, to have sent for lamps and
candles, or thought of closing shutters, drawing curtains, pulling
down blinds! This closing out of the twilight was indeed a characteristic Norfolk habit. The great green curtains in Northwold
Rectory were always drawn close, had been drawn close for years,
when twilight began. So no doubt had the old Vikings, when they
landed at Wick, gathered round their bivouac fires and turned
their backs to the ghostly Druidic light lingering in the west!
This closing of the shutters at The Elms was in fact a Norse cus-

tom. All the West-Country servants hated it, except Emma, whose own people in their high Mendip farms, had practised the same habit.

Tilly Crow's guests were William Zoyland, who tonight was to be transported to Wookey Hole in Mr. Barter's airplane, and Dave and Persephone Spear, who had arrived that morning from Bristol and had taken lodgings in High Street.

William Zoyland rather enjoyed the thought of a couple of months' showmanship in Wookey Hole. A descendant of a long line of attendants upon kings, there was nothing unpleasant or undignified to Will in the office of lord chamberlain to a subterranean river. Yet another cause of the delicious feeling of well-being that flowed through him at this moment was the frank and shameless delight he took in the society of the dark-haired girl now occupied in amusing their hostess. The man he was talking to was Nell's half-brother; so he had every justification in treating the husband as cavalierly and the wife as gallantly as he pleased. There was indeed something piquant about keeping up a conservative argument with a passionate enemy of society while at the same time he played the courtier with his opponent's lady. The more deeply he got entangled in argument with Dave the more frankly unashamed were the glances of admiration which he bestowed upon Persephone. He experienced at this moment a feeling as if, with that firelight warming his great limbs and the boyish hips of this curly-haired girl warming his proud soul, there was nothing in heaven or hell he wouldn't enjoy facing! If this cropped skull and patient eyes opposite him were to condemn him to the guillotine at dawn as a cumberer of the earth—he'd still be happy. If this enchanting girl would slip into his bedroom tonight, undress before his eyes, and be off before he touched her—he'd still be happy. If he knew he were to be compelled that very evening to eat a basketful of otter's dung while Sam Dekker embraced Nell before his eyes and they both mocked at him—he'd still be happy.

"There's something almost awful," he said to himself, using those exact words, "about my power of enjoyment. I believe I could enjoy smelling a bunch of violets if I were on the rack." He began lazily throwing into his retorts to Dave's careful logic a little spice of this savage aplomb; and as his roving blue eyes caught the fact that the treacherous girl was listening, and even encouraging him, they commenced to darken in the candlelight with feline zest. But the sense of having carried the proletarian gonfalon into the very heart of the enemy's camp was inspiring Dave Spear that evening beyond his wont, and it was not long before both of the women, as well as the life-loving adventurer, were gazing at him in reluctant respect. It was when he dropped his logic and became oracular that this crop-headed, prosaic young man swept the field.

"Nature is on our side," he was saying, "and the dark, blind, non-moral creative tidal wave. The inarticulate masses of man-kind are only beginning to wake up. The millions of the Orient are only beginning to wake up. We use reason and we are pre-pared to use force without a shred of compunction. But in reality we are only the 'mediums' of destiny. Communism is the destined *next phase* of evolutionary, planetary life. Nothing can stop it. That is why the stupidest, the silliest, the clumsiest among us has something that you vainglorious individualists completely lack. We are the still, small voice of the next phase. We may be un-imaginative, undistinguished, lacking in all sense of humour. We may even be inhuman. We can afford to be what no one else can afford to be; for the simple reason that we are the solidifying of the *intention of evolution*."

While this argument was going on in the most perfect of upper-middle-class drawing-rooms, in the equally perfect kitchen a somewhat similar discussion was proceeding. Destiny found its voice here, however, in the dreamy, sentimental utterances of Lily Rogers. Louie and Emma both strongly upheld the view that the longer the existence of Nelly Morgan was kept secret from Mrs. Crow the better it would be for all. Lily, on the other hand, advanced the startling and disturbing doctrine that "since things which are hid are fated to become known, and things which are dark are fated to be made clear"—this was the girl's own phrase-ology—"it would be kinder to make Mrs. Crow acquainted with the sad truth." This "kindness" presented itself to the temporis-ing, Mendip-bred mind of Emma Sly as plain cruelty, and a con-troversy began between them that almost spoilt the taste of

Emma's famous pear-ginger jam in the connoisseur-mouth of Louie. Thus, in both drawing-room and kitchen of The Elms there gathered on the horizon certain clouds of danger to the master of the house. In the one case, these vanguards of evil omen were held off by Lord P.'s bastard; in the other case, by the daughter of Amos Sly, Lord P.'s shepherd, but in neither case, for all the closing of shutters against the blue twilight, were the clouds altogether dispelled. They did not advance; but night fell leaving them undispersed.

Perhaps the two persons in all Glastonbury who caught most fully the essence of this cool blue twilight, falling at the end of so unnaturally warm a day, were Mat Dekker and Miss Elizabeth Crow. The Vicar, upon whose conscience it was to enter every house in the town, had invaded the domain of Doctor Sodbury, the parson of St. Benignus. Miss Elizabeth had already done what she said she would do at the reading of the will in Northwold Rectory. She had taken one of the smallest of all the Town Council's workmen's houses—a tiny little place with a tinier little garden with the word "Rosemary" inscribed on the top of the wooden gate. Here she lived with a little maid of eighteen, called Tossie Stickles, the plumpest as well as the most good-tempered young woman who ever put on an apron. She paid Tossie five shillings a week, and every penny of this Tossie put into the savings bank, "to bide there till she were bedded or buried."

Miss Elizabeth had seen Mat Dekker's tall figure passing down the street and had sent Tossie to call him in to partake of an early tea. No one but Mat Dekker himself knew the effort that it cost him to accept this thoughtful invitation. He particularly wanted to finish his visiting in Benedict Street in one afternoon and Penny expected him back to his own high tea—for they dined early—at half-past six. He was counting on an afternoon quite free from visiting on the morrow, for a treasured walk with Sam over to Butleigh Wood, beyond the village of Street, which was a favorite objective of his; and this summons from Rosemary meant not only the spoiling of his appetite for his evening's meal, which he enjoyed more than any other, but made it likely enough that in place of this excursion he would have to return tomorrow to this row of little houses. Once launched, however, in a deep colloquy with his old friend he began to feel that neither of these sacrifices was wasted. Miss Crow was the only woman he could confide in, in all Glastonbury, on the point where he most wanted feminine advice, and he found himself, as he sat opposite her in the bow-window side by side with boxes of yellow pansies, talking more freely to her than he had done to anyone for years.

Not only did Miss Elizabeth forbid Tossie to touch the window-blinds, but she even opened one of the windows when she saw her friend arrested by the beauty of the evening. Thus together they sipped their tea, inhaled the fragrance of the yellow pansies and were soothed by the mystical blueness in the air.

"It's exactly the colour those early Venetians always used," said Miss Crow, "for the Madonna's dress. I shouldn't be surprised if it had some peculiar effect on human nerves, this particular blue."

"I've seen it in many places, Betty," said Mat Dekker, "but never as deep a shade as here in Glastonbury. It's nice to think we live in a place that's famous for its twilights."

Miss Elizabeth adored to be called "Betty," and here, sitting opposite her in her bow-window, was the only person she would have allowed to do it.

"By the way, what's this I hear about Philip turning away some of his hands and threatening to close up one of his mills? Why can't he come to terms with his men? All the old wives I've been talking to in Benedict Street say that their husbands don't want to strike and it's only this Barter fellow who's making the trouble. What's up with Philip, Bett? Is he getting under this fellow's thumb?"

Miss Elizabeth tossed up her head. Every woman, old and young alike, has certain gestures, whether of anger or surprise or sadness or detachment, that only one or two persons in the world are permitted to see, and this smile of hers now with her head held high up and a little back, and her eyes half closed, was one of Miss Crow's gestures that no one in the world, except her mother and Mat Dekker, had *ever* seen.

"It's no good coming to me again to interfere between Philip and his hands," she said. "You remember how angry he got when I did it before and how it hurt the men rather than helped them? My advice to both sides would always be—come to terms."

"Do you think Philip realises what a lot of feeling there is in the town against him?" went on Mat. "They told me today that there's a movement going on to elect a new Mayor; and, of all people in the world, do you know who it's to be?" Miss Elizabeth shook her head. "Your father's Mr. Geard!"

"No, no—Mat! You're fooling."

"Yes, I say yes . . . *Mr. Geard!*"

"Impossible, Mat Dekker!"

"Ask any of your neighbors and you'll soon see!"

"Does Philip know this? Does Mayor Wollop know this?"

"I can't tell what Philip knows. Old Wollop certainly knows for he told me himself."

She made an impatient movement with her hands. "I'm tired of town politics," she said.

Mat's face assumed the rather sulky expression that is natural to a man when his interlocutor changes the conversation. But it was then that she soothed this sulkiness away by beginning to talk of Sam.

"Has he been over there lately?" she asked.

"Not since the woman began living with her husband again," said Mat Dekker; "but now they tell me Zoyland's going to leave her alone out there while he's at Wookey Hole." He sighed deeply. "I like the girl, Betty," he added gravely.

Miss Elizabeth smiled. "I have seen *that* for a long time," she said. "But you wouldn't like her so well if she made him carry her off."

He frowned and sighed deeply again. "No, I suppose not," he said, "though one feels ashamed sometimes at interfering with a real love-affair. I'm a believer in love, Bett, my dear. All passion, I know, is *not* love, and lechery, of course, is lechery. But all the same there *is* such a thing as love and I have a fixed and rooted notion that when a man and woman really love each other it becomes, Bett, my dear ——" He lowered his voice.

"What does it become, Mat?" she asked, moving his cup a little further from the edge of the tray and brushing off with

her fingertips a few crumbs which were adhering to its beautiful
pattern of inlaid mother-of-pearl.

"It becomes a transaction . . . a transaction . . ." He broke
off with a shrug.

"What kind of a transaction?" she enquired in a calm, controlled voice.

"I only meant," he said, "that just as what I call the Mass is
an act that belongs to more than one plane of existence, so any
great love between two people may have an importance beyond
the world we know."

Miss Crow's hands began nervously fidgetting among the objects on the tray. Her portly figure had erected itself very straight
as she sat in her chair, but it seemed as if her fingers found it
difficult to be as reserved and as dignified as their mistress.

"I cannot imagine what Sam is feeling or thinking these days,"
Mat Dekker went on. "His mind is working it all out in its own
way, I think, but I am quite in the dark how he's working it
out."

Miss Elizabeth looked her friend straight in his troubled eyes.
"You've changed yourself, Mat," she said, "over all this. You
seem prepared to let them go off. Surely it would mean disaster
to you if they did?"

He rubbed his great, ruddy face with both his bony hands, as
if to rub off the sticky remnants of a discarded mask.

"I thought it was just a wanton child's caprice, her taking
up with him," he said, letting his hands drop down heavily on
the table. "But I soon found, when I talked to her, that it was
much more than that."

Elizabeth shot a quick, sharp glance at him. "You've not
gone and fallen in love with that woman yourself, Mat, have
you?"

He rose from his chair noisily, making the contents of the tray
rattle. "Shut up, do, Bett!" he groaned. "I'm worried by all this.
It's too serious to jest about. But I must be off now. You know
what our Penny is!"

He went over to get his hat and stick from her little parlour
sofa. She opened the door for him and held out her hand. "I

wasn't jesting, Mat," she said. "I believe you *are* a little bit in love with that girl."

An electric shock of fury made his big frame tremble from head to foot. "I won't . . . allow . . . anyone . . . to talk to me like that!" The words burst from him before he had the remotest idea that he was going to be seized by this rush of blind anger. He experienced a little difficulty in the gathering dusk over the latch of the small gate.

Miss Crow was soon standing by his side. "I didn't mean to tease you, Mat. I ought to have known better," she whispered.

He bowed his head so that she could see only his rough eyebrows sticking out beneath the frontal corrugations, like those of a Neanderthal skull, of his heavy forehead. He regained his composure by staring at a minute ant that was making a dead moth move as if it were alive upon the ground under the gate. He swallowed his saliva in a fierce gulp and raised his head with a jerk. "We are a pair of old fools, Elizabeth," he said, "and that's the long and short of it. You're much too good to me, and don't you ever think I don't know it! Well! Take care of yourself and don't 'ee carry that heavy coal-scuttle any more. Tossie's got twice the strength you've got. I suppose you carry your own water upstairs too?"

"Not always, Mat dear; not often! Good night and God bless you." And she turned and re-entered her door.

While Mat Dekker, the father, was parting from Elizabeth Crow to return to the kingdom ruled over by Penny Pitches, Sam Dekker, the son, was unwillingly tearing himself away from the lodgings of John Crow, Elizabeth's erratic nephew.

It was John, now the salaried secretary of Mr. Geard, who had made the advances. It was part of his new job to make advances in every direction. John had already "approached" nearly a third of the educated citizens of Glastonbury and it had become time to approach the younger Dekker. He had given Sam tea in his new room, and Sam too, like his father, had cursed himself for eating so much bread and butter while the despotic Penny waited for him in the offing. And he had cast a complete glamour over Sam. Sam, unlike his father in this, had no living soul to whom he could tell his troubles. His heavy, brooding nature had been gathering emotional, volcanic lava for three days, and this night—the night of Zoyland's airtrip to Wookey Hole—his whole being was seething and fermenting with contending passions. While the father sat in Miss Crow's bow-window on Benedict Street, the son stood at John's casement-window at the back of Northload Street. The window looked across a level meadow and across Dye House Lane to the fields lying north of the district called "Paradise," and from it could be seen not only the Polden Hills but, rising up against the horizon, beyond the Bridgewater fens, the far-off blue ridge of the Quantocks. The heavy, powerful youth and the lean, emaciated man were standing side by side looking out upon this scene. A cheerful fire was burning in John's little grate and something about his shelves, his chairs, his books, his pots and pans, his gas-stove, his couch-bed with cushions on it, his few cheap prints, his yet cheaper rug, his shining fender, bore witness to the hand and brain of Mary; while the fact that he was there at all, with everything so comfortable round him, bore witness to the liberality of Bloody Johnny.

"I'm not saying I've ever practised or ever *could* practise what I'm talking about," Sam was asseverating in an excited voice. "All I'm saying is that there's no life that frees anyone so completely from unhappiness as does the mystic life. If you give up *possession*, if you give up trying to possess what attracts you, a lovely, thrilling happiness flows through you and you feel you're in touch with the secret of everything. There are only two mortal sins in the world; one of these is to be cruel and the other is *to possess*, and they are both destructive of happiness."

"I agree with you! I agree with you!" cried John. "The only thing is that the opposite of what you say is true too. No, no! There's a great deal in your Christian method, there's *everything* in your Christian method; but it must be applied for heathen ends! That's the great doctrine of the Tao, which no one understands—except me!" A positively diabolic light gleamed in John's glaucous eyes and his sinuous, feeble form seemed actually to curve in tiny ripples of magnetic coils, like the coils of smoke which followed his cigarette.

"You're too subtle for me," growled Sam, extending his grey-stockinged legs and looking down at his enormous dirty boots and at the bright rug, chosen so carefully by Mary at Mayor Wollop's shop.

"I'm only subtle because I'm simple," replied the other. "Listen, Dekker," he went on, "you mustn't think I'm meddling with your private affairs if I give you a piece of advice."

A spasm of annoyance crossed Sam's face and the muscles of his chin contracted. For a second of time the two men regarded each other, like animals of a different species, who have met by accident in a forest glade. The twitch in John's left cheek made its silent signal to Sam's wrinkled chin very much as the quiver of a rat's whiskers might answer the sniff of a badger's snout.

"Lord-a-lord!" ejaculated Sam, beginning to stride up and down his host's room with his hands in his pocket. "So it's come to it, then? Come to what I always feared—that everybody in Glastonbury would know about my troubles. Lord! how I do loathe and hate the human race! That's the 'advice' I'd like you to give me, Crow. I'd like you to say 'escape from it all, Sam, you blundering dizzard, escape from it all and try and imitate those old mediæval saints!' "

John Crow looked away. It was one of his peculiarities to be able to stare into people's eyes with a shameless, unsympathetic scrutiny; but Sam's emotion gave him a peculiar feeling of shame. To look at Sam's agitated face any longer at that moment seemed like eavesdropping at a confessional-box. So he glanced at the now faintly observable ridge of the Poldens and thought to himself, "There's something in spiritual excitement that makes me uncomfortable. I must have the heart of a stone!"

"My advice would be, Dekker," he said, in an obstinate low voice, still staring out of the window, "my advice would be to do what hares do when they catch sight of something dangerous—that's to say, *freeze*. You know that word? Turn, pro tem., into the inanimate . . . turn into a stump, a post, a clod of clay. Then, after a while, when things have worked themselves out, you can scamper back to your feeding-place!"

He got up from his chair-arm and stood hovering at the window. As Sam paused in his sentry's march and threw a glance at him out of his screwed-up bear-eyes, his figure at the window seemed made of something less solid than flesh and blood, seemed as if it would need very little to turn it into one of those drifting vapours that floated over the ditches.

"It's like this, Crow," he began; but he felt so much as if that trampish figure at the window, even as he addressed it, might decompose, dissolve, disintegrate, that he couldn't go on. The chemistry of human bodies, even apart from their shape, is an extraverted manifestation of the souls that animate them, and doubtless in all Glastonbury there couldn't have been found souls more different than John's and Sam's.

When he began saying—"It's like this, Crow," Sam could feel his own lanky, lumbering frame gather itself together, to express his new-grown purpose. But to set the seal of his solemn intention upon this feeble and fluid apparition at the window was as hard as if he were to shoot an arrow into a bundle of feathers or write a "credo" upon flowing water! Nevertheless he made one more attempt. "It's like this, Crow. For me the whole thing is dualism. It's a perpetual war between good and evil. Whichever side you take you get inspiration from outside the visible world. But inspiration from the outside evil means in the long run anguish and insanity, while inspiration from the outside good means an ecstasy that grows and grows! To possess is evil. The whole idea of private property is evil. It comes from the devil. What made those mediæval saints so happy was that they always said to themselves 'Let the beautiful girl go free!'"

"What's that? What's that your saints say?"

It was as if a mild mist-phantom had been transformed into a mocking goblin. Crow slid back into the room, lurched towards the fire, crouched down on a stool by the grate, and leaning forward towards it, as he crouched, struck a match for his cigarette against the bars.

Sam watched him gloomily. The man seemed to be worshipping fire. Sam took his great fist from the mantelpiece and stepped back a pace or two. Damn the fellow! That it had been such a hot, dusty sort of nondescript, unpleasant day made the fact of there being a fire at all in that room a grotesque thing. The chap had seemed to be melting into the twilight outside the window; and now he seemed to be on the point of diving into the flame!

He raised his hand to his chin. "He said she said I had the look of a saint," he thought to himself. And then there came over him the realisation that tonight Zoyland was really off—piloted by Barter or some London crony of Barter's—to Wookey Hole. Everybody in Glastonbury knew it! Everybody in Glastonbury knew that Nell was all alone on Queen's Sedgemoor. "I could bear it," he thought, "if she'd never leant against me with her breasts. Who could bear that and not want to 'possess'; and not *have* to 'possess'?"

The wild idea came surging into his head that he would wait till his father and Penny were asleep; and then let himself out of the house, and hurry over there; even if it were the middle of the night, even if he didn't get there till dawn!

"Well, Crow, I've got to be off," he said. "I'm late as it is. Thanks awfully for the tea. God knows how I'll be able to drink any more. We'll go on with this another time."

The demon by the fire leapt to its feet and became once more the drooping, feeble, nervous beneficiary of the bounty of Mr. Geard.

"Good-bye," he said, "and don't forget to tell your father that I want to see him about the Midsummer Fair. The only person who won't like our Fair will be my precious cousin. And I can promise him we're going to give him a reason for not liking it. We're going to 'larn' him, as we say in Norfolk, to turn Glastonbury into a factory-town! We're going to shake up his capitalistic complacency—you'll see! Well, good-bye, Dekker, and don't forget to 'freeze' like a hare and let chance and destiny fight it out for themselves!"

While father and son were slowly gravitating back to Silver Street, snug in the Vicarage kitchen sat Penny Pitches and Mr. Weatherwax. If Penny was all body, and a very square body too, Weatherwax was all face. He was like one of those absurd political caricatures that represent some familiar physiognomy enlarged to monstrous size and unnaturally balanced upon a manikin's frame. The face of Isaac Weatherwax was a large, flat, sunburnt expanse, like an ancient map of some "Terra Incog-

nita." Arranged at traditional distances in this expanse were
eyes and nose and mouth. There were also various excrescences
of a less usual kind, "mountains," one might say, in this sun-
scorched moon, to which Mr. Weatherwax was wont sometimes to
refer, as "these here bugg-uncles what do grow out of me cheeks."

All the preparations for the Vicarage high tea were awaiting
the return of the old and the young master; but meanwhile the
two ancient gossips, as if a Square were entertaining a Circle,
were enjoying themselves well enough, independent of the
tea-pot. Mr. Weatherwax was tasting in advance a bottle of
cognac, so that whenever the Abbey House sideboard should be
debtor again to the Vicarage cellar, there should be no abrupt
or disconcerting change in the nature of the loan!

"So us be going to have a new Mayor, come election-day,
among they councilmen," remarked Mr. Weatherwax dreamily,
"all of we work-folks be requested by some as we do know to
nudge they councilmen and stir 'em up. 'Tis said by some as we
do know that Mr. Wollop and Mr. Crow be out to turn our
quiet town into a girt city Borough by increasing the population.
But whatever they says, my gal, I holds by authority. I holds
by Mr. Crow. 'Tis said this here Geard, a man no different from
I, a man what can pray high and drink deep like any common
man, will be for letting visitors in and keeping hindustry out;
but I holds with Mr. Crow and his hindustries. Do 'ee want to
know, my gal, why I holds wi' he?"

"Will 'ee have a taste of me 'gorlas,' Isaac?" interrupted
Penny. " 'Tis better than usual today."

Mr. Weatherwax permitted a faint sign of affirmation to flicker
across his political gravity while Penny rose from her chair.
She proceeded to make some rapid changes in the relative position of pots and the lids of pots upon her great stove while her
visitor finished the brandy. This flat expanse of rusty iron surface with its many round-lidded apertures, was Penny's Colosseum of Encounters with Brute Matter. It was an older stove
than that used by Emma Sly up at The Elms and it was handled
in a more primitive manner. The Elm's stove was always kept
well blacked. Like Louie's stove at The Abbey House it possessed
polished knobs and shining ornamentations, whereas the Vicarage

stove might have been the stove of a tribe of gipsies. All sorts
of things would be spilt on it. Penny didn't care. Penny was as
sylvan in her ways as if she had been the Salvage Man of *The
Faery Queen* fresh from some primordial Arcadia.

At the back of her stove there rested a large simmering cauldron
that she used for making a particular kind of broth. This cauldron
was literally never empty. It was like the cauldron of "the Head
of Hades" in the poetry of Taliessin. Penny had a name of her
own for this perennial brew of hers. She called it "gorlas."
Whether this extraordinary word had come down to her in
some very old Glastonbury tradition and was really a corrup-
tion of the word "gorlasser," which seems to have meant a dark-
blue, livid color, and was used to describe a mysterious "corpse-
God" or "Rex Semi-mortuus" in the old Cymric mythology, is
a question that Penny, less lucky in her introductions to learned
men than Abel Twig, had never had a chance of referring to the
Curator of the Museum.

"Do 'ee know, Penny," said Mr. Weatherwax, as he partook of
his friend's brew, "what be the pivot of life upon earth?"

Penny smiled the smile of all women at all philosophy, but
she shook her head obediently.

"Well, me good soul," Mr. Weatherwax continued, "I be the
one what be tellin' thee what thik thing be. Thik thing be Authority. When I sees true livin' Authority I knows vegetables
grow, and hens lay, and cattle breed, and poor folk be fed and
clothed." His voice sank into a low, confidential whisper—"There
be only one true, livin' Authority in our town and that Authority
be Mr. Crow. If so be as your silly women and your fly-by-night
preachers do turn our town from serving Mr. Crow to serving
idols, then I says, 'Look well to it! The end of all things be at
hand.'" His voice ceased. He lifted up the bowl of gorlas to
his capacious mouth and leered tipsily over its brim.

"Folks be queerer than ye wold bachelors do mindy," retorted
Penny enigmatically. "Folks 'ud rayther brew their own broth
theyselves than be fed wi' all the Milk o' Paradise."

When Sam returned to his father's house it had grown quite
dark. He heard old Weatherwax muttering tipsily as he shuffled

down the back drive, and he himself, to avoid the gardener, moved on to the front-drive gate. He felt so disturbed in his thoughts that when he laid his hand on the handle of the great iron gate it came over him that it was almost impossible to face his father. Heavily and slowly he drifted on a little way further up the road. He soon came to the end of Silver Street, and wavering there a moment finally turned to his right and followed the outside eastern wall of the Abbey grounds down the ancient road leading to the Tor that bears the historic, but confused, name of Chilkwell Street. When he reached the turning into Bere Lane he saw before him the vast Gothic shape rising rich and dim in the darkness, of the greatest Abbey Barn in England. This edifice is still used as an ordinary farm barn, but Sam knew every lineament of its façade so well that through the darkness, as he now approached it, the four mystic creatures of the Evangelists that protect its ramparts seemed to murmur at him and signal to him. Sam scowled gloomily back at these Apocalyptic Beings. They had watched so many huge wagonloads of hay, of straw, of oats, of wheat, of barley, so many litters of pigs, so many cartloads of turnips and mangels, being carried under that Gothic archway, that they seemed to call upon Sam also to bring them something, to bring them anything! But Sam had only one offering in his heart just then, and that offering he felt he could not offer! Sullenly and heavily he dragged himself a little further along Chilkwell Street, till on his left hand he saw the stone walls of Chalice House—at that time completely unoccupied—and on his right the lighted windows of St. Michael's Inn. Both these buildings were still many hundreds of yards away and the paved footpath he was following was raised about six feet above the level of the road. There were a few small stone houses here abutting upon this footpath and, behind these, several small garden-paths. These paths, ascending between low mossy walls, led up to the lower slopes of Chalice Hill. Sam was unfamiliar with that far-rumoured version of the Grail story which places the enchanted Castle of Carbonek, where the Mystery was guarded, upon the summit of Chalice Hill; and he now turned his abstracted gaze, as one by one these dark ascents between the shadowy lines of masonry came into his scope, upon the Hill's higher reaches as if it had been any ordinary upland. At the base of one of these ascents, however, he was suddenly arrested by the sight of a dusky figure leaning against a low wall. The manner in which the outlines of the figure resolved themselves into what surrounded it, into the soil, into the stones, into the stone-crop, into the darkness, enabled Sam, though he had the eye neither of a Rembrandt nor a Hardy, to recognize it for that of a woman. His poor head was so full of one particular woman that it was natural enough that his first thought was: "*She* has come to *me!*" But he soon realised that the figure was that of a lean, ungainly person, as totally unlike his Nell as a raven is unlike a dove. It then came vaguely over him that he had seen this person before and not very long ago either. Who the devil did she make him think of? He stared sullenly and gloomily at this solitary, motionless form till at last it began to strike his mind that whoever it was it was someone who had no wish to be watched. Then he knew in a flash who it was. It was Cordelia Geard! Simultaneously with this knowledge it came over him that Cordelia had been seated by the side of that queer-looking devil from Old Jones' shop when he met her in that funny Geard room. So that was it! She was waiting for that fellow now. They were keeping company; and he'd left her for a minute for some reason; probably to relieve nature. They were no doubt prowling round the environs of Chalice House. Her father had very likely been buying up these little cottages. The shock of seeing Cordelia when he so little expected it pulled his wits together with a jerk.

"God! how selfish of me to keep old Dad waiting for so long! I must get back at once!"

He disappeared, and Cordelia, who had been watching him from above, far more intently and nervously than he had been watching her, breathed a sigh of relief.

She was alone again. "Shall I go on?" she thought, "or go back? Crummie wants me. Mother wants me. Dad will be fussing about me. If Mr. Evans comes and I'm out, he'll think my feelings were hurt by the way he acted this morning. Oh, let them all want me! I've been considerate to everybody too long. I've thought of everybody except myself too long." She looked round, pondering.

"No, no, I don't care if they *do* want me!" and she turned resolutely to the dark hillside above her. "I don't care if they *do* have to wait for me! I don't care if I never see any of them again; if I never go back, down there, *ever* again!"

She began rapidly ascending the hill. The air seemed to grow fresher as she advanced. What a dusty, colourless, neutral day it had been! But the blue twilight had been strange! And what queer vapours, though there was nothing damp in the air, had kept gathering, separating, rolling away, in confused retreat, over the banks of the Brue and over the gardens of Street Road. It had been partly the strange twilight that had lured her forth—that and this new restlessness in her blood. . . .

This slope of Chalice Hill had been one of her favorite resorts. When her "bad" moods were upon her she always went off alone to one or other of such places. "It's one of my resorts," she would have said, if Crummie had questioned her.

In every little town in England there are probably several eccentric women who habitually break loose from their family and realise their inmost selves by excursions to certain particular spots. Such people often end by becoming half-crazy. Sometimes they end by committing suicide; but it is without question that in the interim between their slavery to their family and this madness or this suicide, as they visit these favorite resorts and carry there their inhuman, *contra-human* thoughts, they experience raptures of a dark, strange quality such as so-called "contented" people may go through a whole life and never know! What a destiny these lonely resorts of these lonely people come to know! There can hardly be a village in England or a small town in England—the great cities of course drown all such things by the washing of their huge tides of humanity—where there are not certain isolated spots loaded with the wild thoughts of these solitary ones. They have a fate like Io, the heifer-maid, these women, driven mad by the gadfly of Hera! Every one of them is a prophetess, a companion of Prometheus! Every one of them has been spiritually ravished by the great unmerciful Father of all Lies! How those lonely spots must be impregnated with these women's rebellious imaginations! How they must carry these strange, rapturous thought-children, watered by floods and deluges of releasing, melting, dissolving obliterating tears, and leave them there to be nourished by the Mother of us all!

The lonely meadows and orchards of this particular hillside and especially certain bare patches of common land, without hedge, or railing, or furrow, or crop, or bush, or tree, had long rendered Chalice Hill one of Cordelia's favorite refuges. These had been her escape years before her father inherited the Rector of Northwold's money. Of late, since the local chatter about their buying Chalice House, she had rather tended to avoid the place and to select others. Tonight, however, she felt that nothing but Chalice Hill would ease her mind. She had fancied that she knew the spot so well that she would attain with ease a certain bare expanse of grass that she held in her thoughts; but she had not allowed, as we seldom do allow, for the psychic pressure of the darkness itself, like a living entity surrounding her. This invasion of the bewildered senses of a day-dweller by the enfolding presence of night is a unique phenomenon in human experience. However frequently it may have been felt it always returns with a shock of disturbing surprise. The darkness becomes a polymorphous amorist, irresistible, not to be stayed! We beat it back with blinded sight, paralysed touch, confused hearing. But there is nothing of us that it does not invade! When it is a woman who is in its grasp it seems to arouse something in the feminine nature corresponding to itself, so that the recessive mystery of darkness in the woman—that underground tide of the old ancestral chaos that ebbs and flows at the bottom of her being—rushes forth to meet this primal sister, this twin daughter of the Aboriginal Abyss, whose incestuous embrace is all about her! Cordelia seemed unable to escape from the apple orchards on Chalice Hill. She was perfectly familiar with these in the daylight and had often lightly and quickly clambered over the low walls that surround them; but tonight they seemed to extend like an enchanted forest. Insula Avallonia! She was certainly wrestling with a soil and with the growths of a soil that were more soaked in legends than any other hillside in Wessex. Legends seemed to thicken around her as she struggled blindly on between these budding apple trees. The fresh spring grass at the feet of these trees seemed in that darkness to be growing

out of an earth that yielded to each step she took, an earth that
was porous with mystery, an earth that was descending into
supernatural dimensions where it had its unrealisable roots. How
soft to her touch, as she stretched out her arms and her bare
hands, were the branches and the trunks of these apple trees!
Would she never escape into the high bare uplands? These apple
trunks that she encountered seemed to grow thicker around her
as she struggled up the grassy slope. They seemed to respond to
her groping hands with a magnetic effluence of dark, rich, inscrutable vitality. They were like a sisterhood of invisible beings
about her, full of sympathy with her feeling, impeding her
progress with their mute conspiracy of understanding. Her brain
was whirling with wild imaginings. Tears were now pouring
down her cheeks; not unhappy tears, but sweet, relieving, aban-
doning, delicious tears. She wanted to free herself from these
sister-arms, but the darkness itself was weakening her resistance
to them with its own sister-passion, a passion older than the
world. The master thought that drove her on was the thought of
the unhappiness of her lover. "What is it? What is it?" her
brain kept repeating. "He is unhappy; and I know not what it
is! I thought I knew him through and through—but oh, I know
not what it is!"

Cordelia had almost reached the point of feeling as if she *had*
become enchanted, or, in a more realistic sense, as if she had
gone crazy and were going round and round in a circle instead
of ascending, when she suddenly found herself on the top of the
hill and in open ground. Not only was she now in a bare field,
but she knew exactly where she was. She was near the place
where a footpath over the other side of Chalice Hill led to the
lane where the two giant oaks grew. Mr. Evans had talked to
her many times about these oaks. He of course associated them
with the Druids. But Cordelia had heard quite a different story
from her father's new secretary who had informed her that they
had been planted to mark the spot where the Vikings had landed!

Mr. Geard's daughter now became aware that some large and
mysterious release had come to her vexed spirit.

There came a change in the weather too as she made her way
across Stonedown and approached the hamlet of Wick. She felt

it at once as she swung along, walking so fast and free, sometimes with her hands tightly clenched, and sometimes with her
fingers so loosely extended that they trailed amid the chilly
umbrageousness on both sides of the little lane. Cold gusts of
wind she felt rising. She felt them blowing, not regularly, but
intermittently. They blew over Wick Hollow, over Bulwarks
Lane, over Maidencroft Lane, and whenever they reached her
body they swirled round it as if they would have washed her, or
laved her or exorcised her! Intermittent and erratic as they were
and though they veered a little according to the lay of the land,
they came on the whole from the northwest. From the Bristol
Channel they came, and from further away than that. They came
from Mr. Evans' native country, from the native country of her
own ancestors; they came—like those strange stones at Stonehenge—from South Wales.

Cordelia reached the nearest of her great oaks—whether Viking
or Druid—in what seemed to her so short a time that she felt
as if she had been spirited there in the teeth of these western
gusts. She came upon the oaks from the top of the eastern hedge-
bank, for she had come, on her wild approach, recklessly across
the country. Here on the top of this hedge-bank she rested, clutching a sweet-scented hazel-branch with one hand and a bitter-
scented elder-branch with the other. The wind rose about her as
she stood there, in wilder and wilder gusts. And then Cordelia,
gazing directly into the wide-flung branches of the biggest of
the two giant trees, was aware of something else upon the wind.
Those enormous branches seemed to have begun an orchestral
monotone, composed of the notes of many instruments gathered
up into one. It was a cumulative and rustling sigh that came to
the woman's ears, as if a group of sorrowful Titans had lifted up
their united voices in one lamentable dirge over the downfall
of their race. It kept beginning afresh, this solemn moan upon
the air—a moan which always mounted to a certain pitch and
then sank down. Sometimes, such were the vagaries of the wind,
before this portentous requiem started afresh, there was a singular
humming and droning in those huge branches, as if the tree
wished to utter a private secret of its own to Cordelia's ears,
before it recommenced its official chant. Yes! the peculiarity of

this humming sound was that it shivered and shook with a special intonation for the woman standing upon the bank! And Cordelia knew well what that message was. The great tree was telling the hillside that there was rain upon the wind; but it was telling Cordelia something else! Then all was absolutely still; and in that stillness, a stillness like the terrible stillness of uttermost strain in travail, there came the first cry of birth, the fall of a single drop of rain. That first drop was followed by another and that again by another. Cordelia did not hear them in the same place. One drop would fall upon the roadway beneath her; one upon a dead burdock leaf; one upon a faded hart's tongue fern of last year's growth. Then the sound of the falling drops would be drowned in a reawakening of that orchestral dirge. Then the wind would die down over all the upland, and once more an absolute stillness would descend; and in the stillness again—only now in an increased number—the big raindrops would splash to earth, one falling upon a dead leaf, one upon a naked stone, one upon a knot of close-grown twigs, one upon Cordelia's bare forehead. Her feeling at that moment was that some deep psychic chain had been broken in her inmost being.

Hola—Hola! She could not restrain herself from giving vent to a wild cry of exultant delight as the first bursting deluge followed these premonitory drops. She waited for a minute or two with upturned head and closed eyes, letting the water stream upon her face. Then, slithering down the wet bank she reached the lane; and without a glance in the direction of the oaks, which were now totally invisible, she began, with head bowed down and fingers tightening upon her jacket collar, to make her way back to the town. Only once, on her way back, did she pause and glance upward at the down-pouring blackness. This was when she distinctly heard the drumming of an airplane somewhere above her head. "That's Philip Crow," she thought to herself, "travelling like the devil through the black rain! He's off to Wookey Hole."

THE MAYOR OF GLASTONBURY HAD FINISHED HIS BREAKFAST
and was reading the Western Gazette. Mr. Timothy Wollop was
an honest man. He had never deliberately cheated a fellow-
creature of a farthing. He was a self-controlled man. He had
never, since the death of his father, Mr. Constantine Wollop, lost
his temper with any living soul. To his father, now in his grave
in the cemetery on the Wells Road, Mr. Wollop *had* been irritable
on several occasions. But old Constantine's ways towards the
end had been past all bearing. A saint would have cursed the
old wretch. A philosopher would have done worse. An ordinary
man would have murdered him. But Timothy had only been just
perceptibly cross! Mr. Wollop had neither wife nor children.
His servants were kept at such a respectful distance that they
may be said to have been non-existent. They were the hands that
kept his house clean and warm and that brought him his moderate
meals at reasonable hours. Had they been the Ravens that fed
Elisha, or the invisible attendants who waited upon the Prince
in the fairy story, they could not have been more de-humanised.
Mr. Timothy Wollop lived to himself. To say that because he
was lonely he was unhappy would have been to utter the extreme
opposite of the truth. Mr. Wollop was one of the happiest men
in Somersetshire. He neither smoked, nor drank, nor whored.
He never gave way, even in the solitary watches of the night, to
the feverish pricks of sensual desire. As soon as his head touched
the pillow he fell asleep. Of what did Mayor Wollop dream? He
never dreamed; or, if he did, he forgot his dream so completely
on awakening, that for a man to say, "I dreamed like Mayor
Wollop," would be tantamount to saying "My sleep was dreamless." Of what did Mayor Wollop think as he walked from his
house in Wells Road to his shop in High Street? *He thought of
what he saw.* In truth it may be said that with the exception of
Bert Cole no one in Glastonbury regarded the Panorama of
Things and Persons with more absorbing interest than did its
Mayor. Not a stick or a stone, not a bit of orange-peel in any gut-

ter, not a sparrow upon any roof, not a crack in any window, not any aspect of the weather, wet or fine, not any old face or any new face, not any familiar suit of clothes or any unexpected suit of clothes, not any dog, or cat, or canary, or pigeon, or horse, or bicycle or motor car, not any new leaf on an old branch, not any old leaf on a new roof—but Timothy Wollop noted it, liked to see it there, and thought about its being there.

The Mayor was one of those rare beings who really *like* the world we all have been born into. More than that; oh, much more than that! The Mayor was obsessed with a trance-like absorption of interest, by the appearance of our world *exactly as it appeared*. What worries some, disconcerts others, agitates others, saddens others, torments others, makes others feel responsibility, sympathy, shame, remorse, had no effect upon the duck's back of Mr. Wollop beyond the peaceful titillation of surface-interest. Below *appearances* Mr. Wollop never went. Below the *surfaces* of appearances he never went! If the unbearable crotchets of his father had been confined to the old man's thoughts, Mr. Wollop would never have been ruffled. People's thoughts were non-existent to the Mayor of Glastonbury; and if there is a level of possibility more non-existent than non-existence itself, such a level was filled (for him) by people's instincts, feelings, impulses, aspirations, intuitions. The servants in his house, as far as any interior personality was concerned, might have been labelled A. B. C. and the assistants in his shop, in the same sense, might have been named D. E. F. When B. (shall we say?), a female servant in a fit of hysterics, put on her cap back to front, Mr. Wollop was as interested as when on his walk to his shop he mildly observed that a well-known tabby-cat's ear had been bitten off. When E. (shall we say?), a male shop-assistant, appeared one morning tricked up for a funeral, Mr. Wollop enjoyed the same quiet stir as when on his walk down High Street he noticed that a black frost had killed all the petunias in old Mrs. Cole's window-box. Mr. Wollop had once overheard one of his younger shop-assistants—a young man in whose sleek black hair he had come to take a quiet interest, wondering what hair-wash the lad patronised—refer to something called "Neetchky." From the context Mr. Wollop gathered that "Neetchky" could hardly be the name of a hair-wash. It seemed rather to be some pious formula used by the young man, by which he threw off responsibility for having got some young woman into trouble. At that point Mr. Wollop's interest ceased, just as it had ceased when the question arose as to *how* the tabby-cat had lost its ear. Mr. Wollop had no quarrel with young men who had formulas for dodging responsibility, as long as they did their work in the shop. What he *was* conscious of was a certain puzzled contempt for anyone whose selfishness was so weak and shaky that it required a pious formula! Mr. Wollop needed no formula, pious or otherwise. The appearance of things was the nature of things; and all things, as they presented themselves to his attention, in his house, in the street, and in his shop, fed his mind with slow, agreeable, unruffled ponderings. Mr. Wollop was not greedy at his meals, though he frequently thought of his meals; and, as I have hinted, he was totally devoid of specialised sensuality. No man, no woman, no child could ever have said, if they spoke the truth, that they had caught the Mayor of Glastonbury fixing upon them a lecherous eye. The truth seems to be that the Mayor was exactly like young Bert Cole. Bert and Mayor Wollop diffused the projection of their amorous propensities over the whole surface of their world; and their world was *what they saw.*

Little did the more intelligent inhabitants of Glastonbury realise what a happy life was lived by their Mayor. Mat Dekker pitied him for never taking any exercise (beyond his daily walks to and from the shop) and for not smoking a pipe. The young men in his employment pitied him profoundly, when they thought of him at all, for having no lady to flirt with by day and no lady to sleep with by night. Philip Crow pitied him for having no spirit, no initiative, no adventurousness, no River Axe and no airplane. Mrs. Philip Crow pitied him for having no Emma. Emma herself had announced once to Lily Rogers that of all the houses in Glastonbury that poor lonely Mr. Wollop's "was the unhome-liest she'd ever set eyes on, outside the workhouse."

In his dealings with his fellow-citizens upon the town council the Mayor held his own very well. He did this by the enormous advantage he possessed over people who believed in the reality

of thoughts and feelings. Sometimes when a thief or a liar came
into conflict with him the offender was bewildered by the Mayor's
penetration. In reality it was not penetration. It was common
sense. But it was common sense of such prodigious proportions
as utterly to confound the victim of its shrewd judgment. Mr.
Wollop had only twice, in his life of sixty years, "taken," as they
say, "to his bed." On these occasions he had been pitied by every
gossip in the place. "Thik poor old gentleman, wi' his silver
whiskies and his girt stummick, 'a has no soul to care for 'en,
whether 'a lives or dies!" The Vicar of Glastonbury had arrived,
on one of these occasions, when the patient had a dangerous
attack of pneumonia, to pay an official call upon the Mayor. It
was Mat Dekker's notion that the hour had come for the man
to think of his immortal soul. In place of such thoughts he
found Mr. Wollop's placid countenance, his great silver whiskers
extended on either side of the pillow, irradiated with absorbed
interest in the movements of three wasps upon the ceiling.
"They keep going round and round," he told the Vicar; and the
visitor was sadly aware that when he finally uttered the words,
"In the name of the Father, of the Son, and of the Holy Ghost,"
the sick man was still rapt in interest in those three soulless
insects.

For two whole days after the rainstorm that Cordelia had
watched beginning, by the great oaks of Wick, the rain had
fallen almost incessantly. Towards the close of the third day it
began to show signs of clearing off; and about four o'clock, although it was getting so near tea-time, quite a number of people
drifted into the draper's shop. Wollop's was well known all
over that part of Somersetshire; and the business did not depend
upon local patronage; but since the great, quiet, cavernous place
had plenty of seats, both against its broad counters and otherwise, there were often quite a number of ladies, who knew one
another well, chatting together there with their parcels in their
hands. Since the old shop did not depend altogether on local
trade, activity at Wollop's had the power of languishing without
serious loss to its owner. But these idle hours hung heavily on
the heads of many of the assistants. The older ones suffered the
most. The younger assistants had so many thoughts of love,

thoughts hidden away in that non-existing world which Mr. Wollop disregarded, and so much to tell each other about these thoughts, that they did not mind these interims of ebb-tides among the customers. The older assistants—and some of them had acquired a peculiar look, that Mary Crow told John Crow was the Wollop "grievance-look"—not having love-affairs to share, were wont to have the meanest, bitterest, most indurated quarrels among themselves that existed in all Glastonbury. Mr. Wollop being occupied with the apparitional world was certainly not oblivious of these seething recriminations, for Mary's "grievance-look" was quite apparent; but he must have accepted it as a mysterious ultimate, just as he accepted the fact that Tor Hill was opposite Chalice Hill, and regarded its cause as belonging to that world of non-existent essences which a sensible man ruled out of court. On this particular afternoon Mr. Wollop was seated serenely (as he always was) on a polished swivel-chair in a small iron cage. He had bought this cage from a bankrupt bank in Taunton, bought it at an auction for next to nothing. No living person except the Mayor and Bert Cole would have been as much interested in a man-cage as in a bird-cage. But Mr. Wollop, casting his Bert-like eye round the auction-room, had been agreeably struck by this object, and had promptly bought it. That he bought it for no sinister purpose was soon obvious; for the person he put into it was himself. The Mayor's shop-assistants, especially the youger ones, seemed to have the privilege of wandering all over the place; but once in his cage for the day, the Mayor himself never came out except at such times as nature compelled him to do so. His lunch was brought to him in the cage.

Close to the great man's retreat, a day or two after Cordelia's visit to Chalice Hill, while in his contentment Mr. Wollop was murmuring over his accounts like an amiable sea-elephant, there sat on a stool at one of the counters none other than Mary Crow. She had come to buy a tablecloth for John's room in Northload Street. As the young man who waited upon her was the young man who took hair-wash for his appearance and "Neetchky" for his conscience, it may be believed that the buying of this simple thing was a slow business. The young man and Mary Crow differed in every point of taste and choice where tablecloths were concerned.

"Have you heard the news, Miss Mary?" These words came from the cage. The Mayor was addressing his customer.

"How do you do, Mr. Wollop! I hope you've been well lately?"

"Some folks in this town, Miss Mary," the man in the cage went on, "are so solicitous for my health that they've decided on my retirement from public life."

"Pardon me—no! Oh no! I don't like *that* at all." This was addressed to the young man, who promptly went off, whistling. "Pardon me, Mr. Wollop, did you say your retirement? I don't quite understand."

"These folks want for me to stop being Mayor," explained the caged man. "They want for me to turn into a Hex-Mayor."

"Why I thought you were Mayor for life, Mr. Wollop," cried Mary sympathetically.

He shook his head; and then in a lowered voice, bending down towards her so that his forehead touched the bars of his cage— "It's that Mr. Geard who's to be the Mayor instead of me, so that I can keep my good 'ealth hunimpeded."

Mary had no need to pretend her astonishment at this. She was genuinely amazed. "I can't believe it, Mr. Wollop. Surely it isn't true! The councilmen elect the Mayor, don't they? They'd never, *never* elect Mr. Geard instead of you!"

"That's what they're going to do. I can see it as plain as a map, Miss Mary."

"But it's a shame! It's a scandalous shame! Why everybody in Wessex knows the Mayor of Glastonbury. Why! Weren't you Chairman of that grand Public Meeting when the Bishop bought the Ruins for the Church?"

"It's what they're going to do, Miss Mary."

"But Cousin Philip is on the council, isn't he?"

"Only as one among the rest, Miss Mary. And though I don't want—" he lowered his voice to a penetrating whisper—"though I don't want to be a Halarmist, what with 'is trouble with 'is workmen and one thing and the other, I'm afraid Mr. Crow is not altogether the Hinfluence in the Borough that he once was."

"But . . . Mr. Wollop——" she stopped in sudden consternation, remembering John's close association with Mr. Wollop's rival. "But, Mr. Wollop, my cousin, John Crow, would have told me about this if there'd been anything in it. He's working for Mr. Geard now over this tiresome Midsummer Fair they're getting up, and he's never told me a word."

The Mayor of Glastonbury permitted a broad smile to flicker across his face. He pulled back his head from the bars and stretched out his cramped legs as far as they would go. "People don't tell people everything, Miss Mary, even when they *are* engaged to be married."

The word "married" came as a second authentic shock to the sympathetic young lady. She had never guessed that the gossip about her and John had gone so far as to reach the ears of the Mayor. Obstinately she returned to the main issue of the discussion. "They would *never* do it! They would never *dare* to do it!"

"The Liberal and the Labour councilmen, Miss Mary, if they vote with these Bolsheviki, 'ave the majority, and if the majority says so, so it has to be."

The sleek-haired young man now returned with a great pile of tablecloths over his arm. Mary impulsively got up and approaching the cage thrust her arm through the little aperture in front of it. "I can only tell you, Mr. Wollop," she said, "that whatever John thinks, or is bound now to say he thinks, I shall always think of you as the Mayor of Glastonbury!"

The white whiskers bowed low over the outstretched hand. For a second Mary had the wild fancy that he was going to kiss it; but instead of that he shook it vigorously. "I expect I'll see you next week, Miss Mary," he said, "at Mrs. Philip's tea-party. Look after Miss Crow well, Booty!"

This remark from his employer had become really necessary; for on her return to her seat at the counter Mary found such an array of highly coloured tablecloths, all after the taste of Mr. Booty and none after her own, that her difficulty recommenced with accumulated weight. She bought something at last, however; and nodding to the Mayor walked away with her parcel down the central aisle of the shop. The "Wollop grievance-look" had left most of the faces she passed, for the clock was moving round towards closing time, but the smell of the place, that peculiar smell of rent fabric, especially of rent-linen fabric, sank like a thin, delicate dust into her nostrils, into her throat, into her consciousness.

"I'm glad I don't work here yet," she thought, "but if Miss Drew turns me out, when I'm married to John, I swear I'll ask the old chap to let me come to him. I could sell tablecloths, anyway, better than that conceited boy." Once on the pavement she hesitated as to whether she had time to take John's tablecloth to his rooms in Northload Street before returning to tea with Miss Drew. Pondering on this point she remained in front of Wollop's shop staring into the window. It happened that the light fell in such a way upon the window-glass as to throw back a reflexion of her face. Mary was startled at its pallor and its haggardness. How many weeks had she been looking like that?

"Girls ought not to have anything to do when they're in love," she thought. "They ought to be let off everything!"

She turned away now from her reflexion in the shop window. "I'll just leave this parcel with the landlady," she said to herself. John was not expecting to see her today at all. She assumed he was spending all his time today with Mr. Geard. "No; I won't go up those stairs," she thought. "I'll leave this with the woman." She hurried down the street, turned to the right by St. John's Church, followed the railings of the cattle-market, turned to the left down George Street, and finally arrived at the door of number fifteen, Northload. She could not find the landlady. Always present when she would have given anything for the woman not to be there, today when she wanted her she was nowhere to be seen. Nor were there any neighbours around. Over the whole of number fifteen hung a sinister and unnatural silence. The street door was wide open, and just inside it was the landlady's door; but all was silent, forbidding, desolate. Three times she rang the bell. Not a sound! She went back upon the doorstep and rang the outside bell. Not a sound!

"Well, I'll just run up and leave it outside," she said to herself and began ascending the stairs. What was her astonishment when she heard voices up there while she paused to take breath on the first landing. At the top of the second flight she could catch actual words. She stopped there hesitating. Yes! He had someone

in there with him; and she knew who it was too! It was Tom
Barter. She stood for a second, resting herself, with her parcel
propped upon the balustrade. She did not pause there to listen;
she paused because she felt unable to enter and equally unable
to go away. It was one of the most wretched moments of her
life in these last agitating weeks.

"I'm going to make a little money," she heard Barter say,
"and then I'm going to clear out of this blasted hole. That was
what Mary and I used to do all the time when we were so thick.
We used to curse these bloody superstitions! It's all a fake. It's
only to draw visitors. Your precious boss, Geard, is the greatest
humbug of all. But of course you know that! You're out for
making a little money, just as I am; and then, Holy Moses!
you'll do a bunk just as I shall!" There was a sound of shuffled
chairs and the clatter of china. Mary Crow became suddenly conscious that her attitude to Glastonbury had changed of late. It
was Tom Barter she hated now, not Glastonbury.

John's voice uttered the next words, and they did not improve
matters. "Where on earth has she put my whiskey?" she heard
him cry. "Oh, I wish to God women wouldn't always tidy things
up!"

Then came Barter's voice again. As far as she could catch his
words he seemed to be criticising John's biscuits: those Huntley
and Palmer biscuits that she had bought with such care a week
ago! "It's just as if it were a rough-and-tumble undergraduate's
room in Oxford," she thought. Yes, Tom was criticising her biscuits. He was strewing her rug with them too, no doubt, and
trampling them into it! They had now apparently found the
whiskey and were hunting for glasses. Then ensued more clatter
and more half-humorous and half-peevish groans. Then when
they had seated themselves again, still worse ensued.

"Don't be later than nine, Tom, will you?" she heard John
say. "And I'll get another bottle of this when the pub's open
again. If they're funny, where you live, about your coming in
late, you can sleep here with me. I've got a double bed."

She was unable to catch Tom's reply to this, but presently her
whole frame stiffened and a cold shiver ran through her.

"I suppose Mary's often told you what friends we were," she heard Tom Barter say.

John's voice was a little indistinct. "Something of the sort," she thought she heard him murmur.

"I ought perhaps to tell you that I got so fond of her," went on Tom Barter, "that I once even spoke about our being married. I suppose she never told you *that*, did she?"

"No," John's voice replied. And oh how she dreaded the tone he was using now! It was not a frank, single-hearted, trusting lover's tone. "No," said John, "she never told me you'd spoken of that."

"It came to nothing, of course," said the other, "and I changed my mind about it before you came along. . . . Are *you* going to marry her?"

At this point Mary let the parcel containing the tablecloth slip down to the floor between her body and the balustrade. She thrust her fingers into her ears and ran hurriedly down the stairs. Down both flights of stairs she ran, and it was not till she was out of the house that she realised that she'd dropped her parcel. Her misery of mind rose up now out of all proportion to its cause.

She had come to feel towards that room of John's a peculiarly tender feeling, the feeling that a woman naturally gets towards her first real possession. To find that that room, which had been of late the centre of all her thoughts by day and by night, was being turned into a ramshackle bachelors' rendezvous was an outrage to something so deep in her that her emotion about it puzzled herself. She felt as if she were an outsider—a light-of-love—whose visits to number fifteen were devoid of all lasting significance. And Tom's tone about Glastonbury—how she disliked it! Those many secret meetings with John she had had in St. Mary's ruined Chapel had recently, by a natural process of association, begun to convert her to the ancient place. And this room—her room with John, their ménage together—to have it henceforth associated with Barter's rough cynicism and supercilious brutality was the last straw. For herself she cared nothing about his thinking of her as a girl he had decided against marrying. It was only John's hurt vanity she was nervous about. She herself was only too thankful he *had* decided against her! Besides—*always was she Mary Crow*. Her personal pride was far too deep to be affected by the opinion of her held by any man. No, it was none of these things that rankled now in her heart and made her face so white and tense as she hurried back to the Abbey House. It was something much deeper, something that she had secretly been dreading ever since those two sacred Northwold days. It was in fact a dark, bitter, suspicious, corrosive and yet intangible jealousy of Tom Barter. She knew—none better than she—what a deep vein there was of erotic attraction to men in John's nature. She knew—and she had good cause to know—how little of the normal, passionate lover there was about him. She and he were bound together by imponderable cravings, by inexplicable, magnetic lusts, which were as sterile as they were intense and unsatisfied. Had he already possessed her as men possess women, what would she have to fear, what to be jealous of, in his love for Tom? She would belong to him as Tom never *could* belong to him. It was because she knew that she might never be possessed in that sense, even though they were married by the most apostolical of priestly hands, that she felt the ghastly fingers of cold fear fumbling at her vitals. Not a single tear trickled down her cheek as she walked resolutely home. Home she walked with steady lips and a swift, quiet tread. Home to Miss Euphemia Drew!

When Miss Drew, a quarter of an hour later, asked her, "Was it not a nice, warm day for March," she found she could not remember one single moment when she had been conscious of warmth or of the absence of warmth. That, however, did not prevent her giving the old lady a lively and picturesque account of her visit to Wollop's.

"What did you go in to buy, my pretty?"

"I went in to buy some hairpins, dear."

Miss Drew took up a little piece of one of Louie's most successful tea-cakes and nibbled at it elegantly with her false teeth. There was a physical stir at the bottom of Miss Drew's stomach as she delicately lifted up her tea-cup, her little finger fastidiously extended, to wash down—for otherwise she would have had difficulty in swallowing—this honey-sweet fragment. Well did she

know that Mary was lying when she spoke of hairpins. And
Mary, sitting opposite her, every now and then taking a whiff of
eau-de-cologne from a little green-edged handkerchief, made for
her by Miss Drew, knew that she knew that she had lied. Miss
Drew's inmost feelings at the moment when Lily answered the
bell and went away, in dreamy sadness, to bring more hot water,
might have been described in the following manner: "She is buying things for that male brute to furnish some slum-room in the
town. She's either married him already or she's going to live with
him *as if* they were married. It's almost more than I can bear, but
I must be strong! If I lose her—but I can't think of it, consider
it, imagine it—for a minute! I don't know why God has laid this
upon me. But I've come to *depend* on her; and if ——" Miss
Drew, even to herself, was forced to cover up the passion of her
love for her companion by the use of the vague word "depend."
As a matter of fact, she loved Mary with a love like that which
John would have had to content himself with if he had been forbidden by some inexplicable mandate to make love to her. Every
movement of Mary's was delicious to Miss Drew. Every word she
uttered entranced the poor lady. Every garment she wore was as
sacred to her as the paten that held the bread at Holy Com-
munion.

Lily was longer than usual fetching the hot water, and when
she finally came in it was with a much quicker movement and a
less dreamy gesture than usual that she laid down the little silver
jug, a jug whose lid had been soldered once under the régime of
Miss Drew's grandmother, and once more under the régime of
Miss Drew's mother, beside the silver tea-pot.

"Please, Miss, Louie wants to know if you'd mind if we ran
out for a minute to King Edgar's Lawn to see Mr. Crow's airplane. It's passing now, Weatherwax says, and Louie's never seen
it close by."

"Certainly; of course; run off; both of you!" replied Miss
Drew; and she turned to her companion with the same look of
benevolent superiority to the tastes of the lower classes that her
grandmother displayed when *her* servants ran out to see the first
bicycle and which her mother displayed when *her* servants ran
out to see the first motor car. "King Edgar's Lawn" was a popu-

lar name that had locally arisen when a famous modern antiquary—guided, he himself declared, by supernatural agency—
had traced the foundations of that great monarch's chapel.

"Let's go out, child, and see this wonder ourselves!" said Miss
Drew, after filling the tea-pot from the silver jug.

The two ladies left the room together, picked up their cloaks
in the hall, descended the terrace-steps, stepped carefully across
a thin strip of crocuses and a sunken wall, and joined their
maids and old Weatherwax on the smooth-cut expanse of velvety
grass beyond which rose the ruins of the Tower Arch. It certainly
was a startling sight to see the airplane, like a colossal dragon-
fly, cross the empty air-spaces above these historic Ruins.

Mr. Weatherwax, however, gave the thing the most brief and
cursory glance. "Me broad-beans be going to make a fine show
this year. Have 'ee been round to see 'em, Miss?"

Euphemia Drew took her arm away from the wrist of Mary
and turned her eyes from the calm expanse of the sky to the
lesser but by no means negligible expanse of the countenance of
Isaac Weatherwax. "Are they as high as our good friends' across
the road, Isaac?"

This remark somewhat nonplussed the gardener. Between the
two gardens which he presided over he liked to keep up a pretended rivalry. He was "Weatherwax" to the Vicar, and "Isaac"
to Miss Drew; and between "Isaac" and "Weatherwax" there was
a lively competition. "Well, Miss," he confessed, after a disdain-
ful glance upward at the stupendous humming of the flying-ma-
chine, "Well, Miss, 'tis true they broad-beans across the way
may be a miserable couple o' inches *taller* than ours. 'Tis when
us considers the 'ealth and 'spansion o' the plants that ours do
take the prize. They be vigorous growers, they beans of ours, and
them tall ones can't hold a candle to 'en."

Mary was thinking to herself, "Tom must have left John
directly after I ran away, or he couldn't be piloting this thing
now!"

The afternoon was slowly turning into evening. A delicate
golden glow filled the western and the southern quarters of the
firmament. In the midst of this glow a number of rose-coloured
clouds, floating filaments of vapour, air, feathery wefts, undu-

lated, fluctuated, thickened, dissolved, as the chance-strewn cata-
falque of that particular day's obsequies limned itself in space.

Totally disregarding Tom Barter, who was gravely piloting
the machine in the control of which his whole being seemed satisfied, Philip Crow was looking down intently at the moving panorama below them. How unfamiliar those ancient Ruins looked
as he saw them now gliding away beneath him—aye! and how
unimportant, how negligible! Surely it was the round earth itself
that was moving; not the shining, steely projectile in which he
was being hurtled through the sky! He snatched a second to stare
straight down at St. Michael's Tower on the top of the Tor as they
shot drumming and droning over it. Philip's thoughts were disturbed at the moment. Three separate dangerous blows had been
struck of late at him and his factories. Red Robinson's machinations had consummated in a formidable movement among the
town-councillors to make Geard Mayor. Dave Spear had got
twice as long a list of the factory-hands ready to strike than had
been expected by either party. And now this crazy ne'er-do-well
cousin of his, John Crow, had opened an office near the station
and was feverishly advertising some sort of religious hocus-pocus!
This last blow struck him the hardest; though it would have been
hard to explain exactly why. Perhaps he himself could not have
explained why. One thing was clear, all his own activity, all his
own effort, all his own prestige were connected with turning Glastonbury from an idle show-place into a prosperous industrial
centre. On this particular point he was at one with Red Robinson
just as he was at one with Tom Barter. To beat down this pious
Glastonbury legend, this piece of monkish mummery, to beat it
down and trample it into dust. He longed to do this beyond everything in the world except electrifying the entrails of the Mendips; and he would do it too! He would do it alone if the labour
element—short-sighted as it always was in regard to their true
interests—betrayed him for this sneak-thief, this crafty hypocrite
Geard!

He hoped at this moment that Barter would be minded to
extend his circular hovering for hours so as to give him a long
hawk's flight over this idyllic Somersetshire. He would conquer
it, this effeminate flower-garden of pretty-pretty superstitions and

mediæval abracadabra! He would plant factory upon factory in it, dynamo upon dynamo! He would have mines beneath it, railways across it, airlines above it!

If Barter had not been a novice at flying and consequently afraid to remove his attention for a moment from his task, he might have divined his passenger's mental state and humoured him by staying up longer. But Philip was in no mood openly to confess such feelings. He had told his subordinate laconically enough to take him to Wookey Hole; and to Wookey Hole Barter must take him! There was a good field for landing on the Mendips side of the Hole, away from the direction of Wells; but he decided to make a small détour first. Philip recognised the general lie of the land tonight and its natural landmarks more quickly than most passengers would have done in one of their first ascents. So might some hawk-eye among his Norman ancestors have surveyed the landscape from the high keep of some newly built castle and known it hill by hill, stream by stream, valley by valley, forest by forest, for what it was.

As he looked down upon the earth, that clear March evening, and watched the chess-board fields pass in procession beneath him, and watched the trees fall into strange patterns and watched the villages, some red, some brown, some grey, according as brick or stone or slate predominated, approach or recede, as the plane sank or rose, Philip's spirit felt as if it had wings of its own that were carrying it over this conquered land independent of Barter's piloting. They passed over Havyatt, where the monks on one occasion persuaded the Danes to draw back and refrain from plundering the Abbey; they passed over West Pennard, and over Pylle and Evercreech; they passed over Batcombe and over Wanstraw and over Postlebury Wood; and it was not till they reached Marston Bigot where they could see to the eastward the lividgrey waters of the Somersetshire Frome that Barter swung the plane round and headed west again. Due west, they flew now, over the stone roofs of Shepton Mallet, straight to the city of Wells. When they were above Wells and they could look down on the Cathedral directly beneath them, they turned northwest; and soon, without trouble or mishap, they descended in the precise place they had aimed for, between Wookey Hole and Ebbor Rocks.

The impressions which rioted in Philip's brain as he clambered out of his seat, and stretched his legs upon solid earth in that darkening meadow, resembled the release of a charge of electricity. How small and unimportant Wells Cathedral had looked from up there in the air! It was of the planetary earth, a sensitised round orb circling through space, not of any calm earth-mother, lying back upon her secret life, that his mind was full. It had all passed only too quickly! It seemed only just a minute ago that he had scrambled into his seat on the back of this shining torpedo with dragon-fly wings. But what thoughts, what sensations! His brain whirled with the vision of an earth-life dominated absolutely by Science, of a human race that had shaken off its fearful childhood and looked at things with a clear, unfilmed, unperverted eye. He said to himself, as he walked out of the field with Barter—for they were intending to stay the night at Wookey Hole—that this conquest of air had reduced those Glastonbury Ruins to nothing. And how utterly unimportant and irrelevant all this disputing about capital and labour and private property! Science must soon, he thought, give into the hands of every individual so much power—power of creation, power of destruction—that this dogmatic doctrine about common ownership will cease to have any meaning.

"Don't wait supper for me," he said to his companion as they closed the gate leading into the highway. He and Barter had their own particular bedrooms, in a little wayside inn called the Zoyland Arms, close to the entrance to Wookey Hole Cave. The factory there held no accommodation for travellers, for though its wheels were turned by the River Axe as it emerged from its underground caverns, it was not much more than a series of large workshops. The working-people came on foot or by lorry from the Wells suburbs which were only a couple of miles away and people who wished to remain overnight were at the mercy of the landlord of the inn. The two men were expected that evening to supper, and Will Zoyland was already seated at the parlour-table, with an uncorked bottle of wine at his side, enjoying his soup, when they entered the place.

Philip was still in an unusual state of excitement as he ran upstairs to his little room, where the gas had already been lit.

His window looked out on the white road, and opposite it in the darkening hedge there was a small ash tree, whose black, sticky buds had already burst here and there into the blurred shapes of embryo leaves, shadowy and indistinct against the livid western sky. A strange exultation still throbbed in his pulses as he found himself alone in this small chamber looking out on the silent road and on that tree. He felt in no hurry to join the others. Let Zoyland entertain Barter as he pleased till he chose to go down! He was their employer. He would dine when he felt inclined. He pushed his way past the heavy, cheap dressing-table with its great, ugly looking-glass and jerked aside the sham-lace curtains that obstructed his view. He made an effort to open the window at the top. In the flare of the gas-lamp suspended from the ceiling he saw a couple of dead flies on the narrow ledge where the window-latch was. Something about these flies, combined with the lace curtains and with the fact that he found difficulty in opening the window, brought his spirits down to earth. When he did jerk the window open, one of the dead flies followed it, but the other one remained upside-down, its legs stiff, its small cuirassed head inert, its body drained of all life-juices, husk-like and hollow. He flicked the dead fly with his finger-nail out of the window, and resting his elbows on the woodwork leaned far out. A faint odour of funguses came to him, mingled with that peculiar smell of road-dust that bears upon it the first weight of the falling night. A rustling sound followed by a series of sleepy, peevish clucks and then by more rustling indicated the presence of roosting fowls. The little ash tree against the dying fragments of steely whiteness in the sky stretched out its branches; stretched them out with that particular upward clutch of the twig ends that characterises its tribe.

Philip's face at that moment would have presented a mask of stony human fanaticism to the senses of that little tree if they could have pierced the dark. From this air-flight, one of the first he had ever taken, he had gathered a momentum that no dead fly, however discouraging, could retard. He used it now to shoot his mind, like a rock-shattering projectile, into those remote caves of Wookey Hole out of which rolled the subterranean river that turned the wheels of his factory. A grim smile crossed his mouth when he recalled how contemptible, how unimportant, the massed towers and buttresses of Wells Cathedral had appeared as he flew above them! His thoughts clanked harshly along the up-curving branch in front of him, like a proud brigade of arrogant tin soldiers. A cold fury of destruction possessed him when he thought of Glastonbury. Arthur and the Holy Grail, Abbey Ruins and Saint Joseph—he was the man to blow them all sky-high! Communism? A thing of mere distribution of spoils! What did a meticulous economy of that kind matter? On, on, on! —destroying the past, creating the future—on, on! The hard light of his electric bulbs on the stalactites in Wookey Hole could not have glittered more fiercely, the steel surface of his new plane could not have shone more coldly than the narrowed eye-slits of Philip Crow as he drew his head back, under the hanging gas-globe, and walked over to the wash-basin.

Damn! Another dead fly in his soap-dish! He tossed out the soap and carried the dish to the window and shook it there with a vindictive sweep of his arm. He felt as if his glittering onrush through the world, engine after engine after engine, and himself yanking them forward with an iron heart, was outraged by the mere existence in the world of dead flies. That fellow, John— damn him, oh damn him!—was a dead fly come to life. Geard was another. Those ridiculous Dekkers were others too. Tilly, in his own house, with her black beady eyes, was yet another! All were buzzing flies, whose existence stung him in life and dispirited him in death. What was that line, in some old poet, that he had had to learn by heart at school and that he'd never forgotten? "Heads without name, no more rememberèd than summer-flies!" "Heads without name." *His* head had a name. Devereux—that was a name for a man to face life with!

He hurriedly washed his hands and face; plastered down his iron-grey hair over his narrow skull, grinned like a wolf at himself in the ugly looking-glass and ran downstairs. An unexpected shock was awaiting him as he entered the little parlour full of small supper-tables. There were Zoyland and Barter, laughing together, already warmed by Zoyland's wine; but there at another table—and they rose at once to greet him—were Dave and Percy Spear! They must have been agitating all day and collecting

names in his Wookey Hole plant. But he could not restrain his
pleasure in seeing them there. How perfect she looked in this dim
inn-parlour light! He thought Dave looked a trifle embarrassed
—and no wonder, the revolutionary rogue!—as they shook hands;
but she—she was *his*; her eyes told him she was his! He knew
it in the marrow of his bones as she leant towards him, giving
him—not only her ungloved hand, but everything! Yes; she was
like that long swaying ash-tree branch, just budding, in the night
out there. He hurriedly crossed over to his own place, jested
coldly about Zoyland having opened the bottle, murmured something sarcastically to Barter about "propitiating his Bolsheviki
relatives" and carried his chair to the Spears' table.

"Have you brought your stiletto for the wicked Capitalist?"
cried Will Zoyland.

"Aye, what's that, Will?" threw in Dave.

"I asked Percy if she'd got her dagger hidden away in her
underlinen to give Crow his quietus," repeated Lord P.'s bastard,
winking at Barter.

Barter's face at that moment was indeed one in which could
be read "strange matters." The wine had heated him; otherwise
he would have found the whole situation bristling with discomfort. His cautious upper-middle-class respectability had already
been outraged to its foundations by Zoyland's noisy camaraderie.
Zoyland and his brother-in-law's wife had by this time exchanged
not a few strokes of reckless roguery. "Better join my first lot of
sight-seers tomorrow, Percy," he had said, "and I'll show you
the stalactite mentioned by Clement of Alexandria. I only show
it to pretty young women like you, and among *them* only to the
naughty ones! I shan't show it to Dave. It would corrupt his
pure mind! Ha! Ha! Ha! Ha!" Persephone had retorted in kind;
and thick and fast had their rough pleasantries been bandied
about. Barter's lecherousness had for years been roused to a
fever of aggravation by Percy Spear. He had seen more of her
in their Norfolk childhood than he had seen of any of her
cousins and he had used her young figure on many a sex-starved
occasion for the satisfaction of his amorous thoughts. But Percy
had never let him touch her. She disliked him mentally and she
loathed him physically. But she was ready enough to chaff him;

and when she did this she always bewildered him by her clever modernity.

Barter had felt a horrible sense of social inferiority just now as he had sat sullenly drinking William Zoyland's wine. His family was in reality quite as "good" as that of the Crows; but he totally lacked the suppleness of the Crow mind. He was in fact socially old-fashioned; and to be old-fashioned at this date meant being made a fool of by clever women. It was still more uncomfortable for him when Philip appeared and began his dinner at the Spears' table. Zoyland had called for a second bottle and had begun to grow slightly tipsy; and with his tipsiness extremely confidential. Even so, he didn't treat Barter—at least so Barter thought—like a real equal. He confided in him blindly, grossly, callously; a good deal as a gentleman would confide in a faithful servant of whose discretion he was sure but towards whose personal reactions to what he confessed he felt complete indifference. Tom Barter had not one single relative of any kind living. He had never been to the university. His diploma of social position went back to an earlier date; for he had been to Sherborne School. He had entered an office at nineteen and since then had lived for two things, lechery and money. He had seen to it that these two things did not clash by habitually taking his pleasures cheaply. This he did by eschewing harlots and mistresses and by enjoying constantly new adventures with flirtatious middle-class girls. With shopgirls, business-girls, waitresses, barmaids, Barter always won favour, partly by reason of his being a gentleman, partly by his shameless advances, but most of all by a certain direct, unassumed, cynical but very honest interest in all their professional problems. They felt at home with him. They trusted him. And except for depriving them of pretensions to "purity," he really *was* to be trusted!

"She's alone there; and of course he *may* have gone over. He may be over there now, as I clink this glass! But I don't think so. A person has instincts in these things, don't you agree, Barter? Instincts. You know what I mean, Barter? But perhaps you don't! Perhaps you despise instincts! You rather look like someone who despises instincts. What would you do, Barter, if you were married and your wife fell in love with a young chap of her own age? Eh? What would you do? Would you let him pull your nose and say nothing? Have you ever had your nose pulled, Barter? I mean really and truly pulled? Would you let him do it? Tweak your nose, and give it a good pull?"

Tom Barter's fingers itched to give his aristocratic friend what at school was called a bloody nose. Short of hitting him, how- ever (and what chance would he have in fisticuffs with such a fellow?), he could not just then think of any method of putting him to rout.

"That's my way, Barter, and so now you know it. It mayn't be a good way; but it's my way and when it comes to women it's no good unless you're playing your own hand. They don't give a fig for book-learning, Barter. Perhaps you've never seen thro' their pinnies far enough to know that? But that's the truth. Not a fig! What women like is bed-rock-bottom—every time! You can't go wrong with them—from Queen Gargamelle to Maid Marian—if you talk facts and think smut. You seem to me a downright man-to-woman kind of chap, Barter, so I expect you've found that out for yourself. But perhaps not. Perhaps you're puritanical and have never meddled with the hussies. I don't think so, though—you look to me as if you knew a hawk from a hernshaw!"

Tom Barter could only drink more and more wine, as he did his best to carry off this uncomfortable situation. In his heart he longed to be back at number fifteen, Northload Street, drinking whiskey with John. How different John was from this bearded ruffian! If hatred had the power to kill, Lord P.'s bastard would certainly not have played guide again to any more stalactite caves! "Not one of these people cares a fig what becomes of poor Tom," Barter thought, as he grew more and more sulkily mono- syllabic, under Zoyland's heavy joking. "At this moment, as I sit here, not one single human being is giving me a thought. None of the wenches I make love to in Glastonbury care a tinker's dam for me really! Mary used to think of me sometimes; a little; just a little; but God! now John's appeared, I am out of it there, too. Crummie turned on me like a spitfire pussy-cat the last time I saw her. Who *have* I got in the whole bloody world? Nemo, nihil, none! Not a living soul!" And then his mind went back to the

Northwold River and the talk he had had with John about those childish times. John *was* something. He was the Past and that was something. "I like old John," he said to himself. "By God I believe when I'm fooling with old John I don't feel as if I were quite alone. 'Twas a queer idea of his though—what he hinted at this afternoon—that I should get a job under Geard, when they make him Mayor, and give Philip the go-by! I must talk to John a bit more about that. There'd be nothing permanent in that though. But, by Jiminy, it would be almost worth it, just to watch Philip's face when I told him!"

"Why do you say 'yes' like that, Barter? You think I'm drunk. You're not listening! I asked you whether you thought I was a fellow who could be cuckolded with impunity. And you said 'yes.' "

"I meant 'impunity' *for a time*, Will; while you led the person on; and let them make a fool of themselves."

A dangerous gleam shot forth between the candles from Zoyland's drunken Teutonic eyes. It annoyed him to be called "Will" by Barter, just as it annoyed Philip to be called "Phil." "Fool be damned! You don't know what I'm talking about, Barter. When I give up my girl to her lover I'm not revenging myself on anyone; I'm . . . I'm . . . I'm acting altogether outside the wretched herd of common human animals! I'm . . . I'm . . . *I'm acting like a god*, little man!" His drunken voice was so loud that Dave and Percy and Philip ceased talking among themselves and stared at him. Philip got up and came towards him, followed after an interval by the husband and wife.

"Don't you start bullying our friend Tom, Zoyland," said Philip coldly, fixing a Norseman's eye upon the gigantic toper.

"Oh, you shut up!" growled the other. "For a very little I'd chuck both of ye into the bally road!"

Philip shrugged his shoulders and turned to Spear. "Dave," he said, while Barter got up sulkily from his seat and went over to Persephone, who stood regarding the whole group with dreamy amusement, "do you mind, Dave, if I took Cousin Percy out for a stroll down this 'road' he talks about?"

The girl gave a start and glanced quickly at her husband. A look, quick as lightning, from her dark, languorous eyelids, said,

"May I go with him? I'd rather *like* to go with him, Dave. But I won't if you don't want me to!" While a look, a little slower to come, replied from Dave's ruddy face, "Go, by all means, if you want to, my dear; why not?"

"Hullo, Dave, are *you* going to lecture me, too?" drawled Zoyland, as if he had noticed the presence of his brother-in-law for the first time. "*Tu Brute*, Dave! Then Big Willy must really behave himself and be polite to these solemn money-grubbers."

"Dave will amuse you, William, while Philip and I get a breath of air," said the girl cajolingly. "And mind I'll speak to Nell about you, if you drink any more tonight! I'll be seeing her at Tilly's party, if not before."

Dave obediently sat down by the man with the great beard. He looked, as he did so, just as if he had been some sagacious young clerk-in-holy-orders taking his seat at the dais by the side of an angry Charlemagne.

"I like you, Dave Spear," said the Bastard, "your bloody Communism is all poppycock, but I'm damned if you're not more of a man than any of us here; and you can tell Nell I said so." He stretched out his hand as he spoke, and laid it on Dave's knee, while an effusion of melting German-student sentimentality made his blue eyes moist.

"I think I'll adjourn, if you people don't mind," said Tom Barter, addressing the whole company and making a little nod with his head as he leaned his hand against the back of a chair. "Philip can bear witness," he glanced furtively at his employer, "that I've got a lot to do at the office tomorrow; so I think bed is the place for me. Good-night, Mrs. Spear, you'll excuse me, won't you?" He had isolated himself completely from the rest of them by this time; not exactly by what he said but by the way he looked at them. He might have been a Frenchman in that group, instead of the descendant of a family of Methwold squires who were landowners when the Crows were just Isle-of-Ely farmers.

Some visitor from Venus or Mars, interested in human social differences, would have been puzzled to know what the real psychic cause was of Barter's repeated humiliations. How could such an one know that the sole and simple cause of it was the manner in which, when a boy, he had been bullied at Sherborne

School? But this *was* the cause and none other. Barter had been so humiliated at Sherborne, at Gladman's House there, that in his heart he felt himself to be inferior to every educated man he met. And this feeling in his own mind every educated man he met, without knowing why, was compelled by some invisible urge to take advantage of! "Bullied at Sherborne—always bullied" might have been a truth-speaking Wessex proverb. It was only at rare moments, when he lost his temper, that he dared to look Philip straight in the face; and yet, curiously enough, Philip came much nearer being afraid of Barter than of anyone else in Glastonbury. It was that Sherborne bullying, those memories of what went on at Gladman's House, that made a neurotic catchpole of this sturdy descendant of Norfolk fox-hunters.

Philip ran immediately upstairs to his small bedroom. Here he snatched a rough overcoat from a nail and an old sporting cap of the same faded cloth. This latter he instinctively—as if bound for some dark adventure—pulled low down over his narrow forehead. The ugly looking-glass by the window made him think of dead flies. His angry contempt for Barter, "going to bed like that because he'd been insulted by a hulking zany," made him think of "heads without name, no more remembered"—and with this on the mute lips of his mind he turned the gasjet low and hurried down again. Here, in the porch of the little inn, he found Persephone, wrapped, she too, in a long cloth coat, and wearing over her fuzzy, dusky hair a boyish cap. They went out together in silence. In silence he led her up the road, round a turn to the right, till they came to a closed gate in the hedge. This he opened for her, lifting it bodily off its latch and replacing it by the same main force when she had stepped through. He now led her, still in a sort of guilty silence, up a narrow winding hill-path on each side of which grew large, indistinct trees, their roots in the sloping bank. At this point Philip produced an electric flashlight from his overcoat pocket and held it so as to illuminate their way.

Persephone became aware now of the sound of water, down somewhere in the darkness to their right, and it was not long before he made her stop and look between the tree trunks, upon whose rough surface he threw the light of his flashlight. There she saw a single bright lamp burning, throwing morbid shadows upon an expanse of grass. By this radiance a little lawn with chairs and tables set out became apparent, all these things motionless and deserted, looking ghostly, and even ghastly there. "I keep it lit," whispered Philip in her ear. There was no obvious need for him to whisper. It was hard to raise his voice just then. "It's my electric plant. That's where we serve tea to visitors. I expect you've been there yourself, only you came in a different way."

They went on again, the path they followed growing steadily narrower and steeper. They walked closely side by side and presently Philip without a word possessed himself of her hand. At last she saw before her the upward rise of a precipitous rock, covered with moss and last year's ferns, and right before them, at the base of the rock, a little square doorway. Philip took from his waistcoat pocket a large key, like the key to a drive gate, and using his flashlight turned it in the lock and pushed the door open. When once they were both inside he locked the gate again, put the key in his pocket and drew a deep breath. "Perse, Perse," he whispered, and hugging the girl fiercely to his heart kissed her with a long clinging kiss full on the mouth. She hung limp and yielding in his arms. His kiss was of the kind that needs no response, that could be aware of no response except a desperate resistance. But there was no flicker of resistance in Persephone's yielded mouth and abandoned body. She yielded to him utterly, as dark water yields to the plunge of a diver. When he let her go she appeared so drugged by his embrace that for a second she swayed and staggered. But he caught her, with a strong clutch round the waist, and holding her so led her forward. Up and up they climbed, and then, after stopping to breathe at ease for a moment on a little level platform, down, and again down they went. This was repeated, in spiral curves of progression, several times. The girl seemed still too dazed to realise the curious character of the path he led her by, and though he often flashed his light to the right and the left neither of them breathed a syllable.

They were isolated from human interference as completely as if they had descended into some cavern at the bottom of the sea. There was only that one entrance to Wookey Hole Caves, at least only one known to modern man, and the key to that one entrance lay in Philip's pocket. It was his money that had opened these caves. It was his money that would presently electrify these caves. He was like a solitary magician, whose secret kingdom hidden in the bowels of the earth and guarded by invisible demons, was as impenetrable to invasion as the private thoughts in his own mind were impenetrable. Philip had never, in all his conscious days, known a moment to compare with this moment. He had got her! The rapacity of his desire to possess her wholly, to ravish, not only her body, but her inmost soul, compelled him now to exercise an adamantine restraint upon his passion. He suddenly became a Fabius Cunctator of erotic strategy. A cold and calculating calm rose up from the crater of his desire, as if a volcano had engendered a shaft of ice. He supported her now down a long, narrow, winding flight of rough steps and not until they reached the bottom of these steps did he utter a word. Once at the bottom, however, and on the edge of a limestone platform leading into a vast cathedral-like cavern, he raised aloft his flashlight and directed it against the amazing walls that surrounded them.

These were walls composed of enormous stalactites hanging from the roof and of equally monstrous stalagmites rising up from the floor. These strange things—objects for which, since so few of mortal men ever beheld them, there are in our language no adequate descriptive words—showed themselves to be, under the beam of light which he threw upon them, of the most staggering variety of iridescent colours. A livid greenishness and a livid bluishness were what predominated; and next to these a ghastly kind of phosphorescent orange. But it was *the shape* of these stalactites and stalagmites that was so overpowering to the imagination. They were all of them phallic. Not one single excrescence in that huge cavern that was not wrought, for the imagination of men and women, into some variety of phallic form. They were like the phalluses of hordes of cyclops and of herds of behemoths. It was as if the Witch of Wookey—the mere idea of whose legendary personality, described to that friend of Louie and Lily Rogers, had made the woman fall into hysterics—had hung these trophies, as memorials of her monstrous encounters, upon the walls of her obscene cave.

Philip found it possible to lift up his voice now; but it was still an effort for him to speak above a whisper and he yielded to this weakness without shame. "See those two, over there, Perse?" he said, holding out his flashlight with one hand and pointing his other towards what he wanted his companion to see. What he pointed at were two of these barbarous shapes that had advanced, one from below and one from above, in slow accretions, until they were within an ace of each other, their extreme points, in fact, almost touching.

"How long did they take?" whispered Persephone.

"To grow, you mean?" he whispered back. "I forget exactly. About an inch in a thousand years. Those two things would only have been separated from each other by about two inches when Christ was crucified!"

"Stop! Is that water?" she cried suddenly, breaking the spell in her excitement. Her cry was caught up by a singular echo that did not confine itself to a single note but repeated her last four syllables.

"Is that water?" reverberated the echo. "Is that water?"

"It's uncanny!" she cried, catching hold of his arm.

"Uncanny!" repeated the echo.

The girl still clung tight to his arm, but child-like she wanted to show off her courage. "Who are you?" she shouted at the top of her voice.

"Who are you?" returned the echo.

"Are you a devil?" cried Persephone Spear.

"—you a devil?" threw back the echo.

Philip interrupted this dialogue by directing his flashlight towards the water. It was of an indescribable tint, this water. It might indeed have been the Styx, that mysterious river by which the gods swore their only inviolable oath.

"Is it the Axe?" she asked.

"A tributary from it, I think," he said. "One day I'm going to make it carry me to the Axe!"

The girl yielded to a delicious shiver. "Down there, do you— oh, there's a boat, Philip! There's a boat!"

"Yes, that's *my boat*," said Philip Crow in a tone wherein Jason might have said, "my Argo."

"Let's go down to that water," she said. "Can we do that?"

Since this was precisely what he had long since decided upon,

he promptly acceded to the girl's request. They walked with
careful steps down to the very edge of this prehistoric estuary.
He was trembling too much with the near approach of the consummation of his desire to have time for such imaginations; and
she was too excited by the sight of the boat down there; otherwise
they might have wondered what strange shapes of what neolithic cavemen, long before the epoch of Abel Twig's Lake
Dwellers, had bent down to drink, or to wash the blood from
their hands, in that Stygian flood. "In the bowels of the Mendips,"
his wild feelings ran, "*my* girl . . . *my* pleasure . . . I, I, I,
. . . taking *my* pleasure . . . conquering this land underneath
the earth . . . as I conquer it in the air . . . I, I, I, stamping *my*
will on life . . . on woman . . . on . . . on . . . on the
Future!"

"Can't we get *into* the boat, Philip?" she whispered. Her subdued voice made his pulses beat. Had her girl's instinct already
divined his proud intention?

He made no reply, but seizing the rope which moored the boat
to an iron stake at their feet pulled it to land. At the bottom of
the boat were lying a pair of oars. He helped her to get in and to
sit down on one side of the two small benches. Hauling the rope
after him he sat down himself on the other bench and gathered
up the oars from where they lay. He handed the flashlight into
her keeping. She put up her free hand and touched his shoulder
as he began to row, taking long, hard strokes.

"You are Charon!" she whispered into the back of his Bayeux
Tapestry skull.

He panted in quick little gasps as he rowed. The light from the
flashlight which she held fell upon the water and upon the black
stones of the shore and upon frieze after frieze of gigantic phalluses, rising up and hanging down between what represented the
surface of the earth, but was really "full fathom-five" beneath
earth, and what represented the sky, but was really the cellar-roof
of the Witch of Wookey Hole. It suddenly occurred to Philip's
mind as he rowed—what if their little flashlight went out? He
let his oars rest on the surface of the livid water, where strange
terrific shadows kept moving, shadows that might well have been
the upheaving forms of monstrous, antediluvian creatures—ich-

thyosauri perhaps—that had escaped the doom, down here below
the Mendips, of the evolutionary process of a hundred thousand
years. With feverish fingers he searched his pockets. Thanks be!
In both his coat *and* his overcoat reposed boxes of good Swan
Vesta matches. So *that* was as it should be. He knew the place
well enough to be perfectly safe, with all those miniature torches
in his possession!

"Why don't you go on, Philip? You make me nervous. What
are you looking for? Cigarettes?"

"You shall have your cigarette presently, my girl," he thought.
But aloud he cried, "Careful, Perse! Careful! Hold it a bit
higher!"

Their craft grounded now upon a broad, low slab of prehistoric
limestone. Above it a great, slippery, precipitous wall ascended to
the roof. Here there was a very strangely shaped formation of
petrification such as would have required the grossest of modern
minds to endow with a human image; although Dante might not
have hesitated tò find words for it. "They call *that*," he said, pointing at this curious stalagmitic conformation as he helped her
from the boat, "they call *that*, the Witch of Wookey Hole. They
say a monk from Glastonbury turned her into—I say! What's
the matter, child? What is it? Oh, for God's sake, what is it,
Perse?"

The girl had fallen into a hunched-up crouching position upon
the slippery limestone slab by the water's edge and had covered
her head with both her hands. He was convinced she was weeping
by the movement of her shoulders, though she did not utter a
sound. There was not in all Philip Crow's profoundest being one
least little grain, one tiniest atom, of what Mr. Evans suffered
from. With all his maniacal lust for power, his was probably the
least cruel human soul within a radius of twenty miles from that
singular spot. That his high-spirited Percy—his secretest, most
private "possession"—should suddenly be seized with an excess
of trouble to which he lacked the clue, shook the foundations of
his pride. There was something nobly courteous, nobly tender, in
the timorous gesture with which, having tossed the oars back in
the boat and pulled its prow up the shelving rock, he bent down
and folded his long fingers round that head in the boy's cap.

What was his astonishment and relief when, under this grave caress, the extraordinary girl rose to her knees before him. Persephone Spear *was shaking with laughter*! She had not been weeping at all. For a second he thought she was hysterical; but when, through the contortions of her childish paroxysm, she put out her tongue at him, he was assured. So disturbed had he been, however, that for a minute or two all the erotic feelings in him became as petrified as that stone image of the Witch that stood over against him. The girl could see he was disturbed and the sight of his gravity increased her mirth. She dropped the flashlight upon the ledge of rock and clutching at her sides she swayed to and fro in a breath-taking laughing-fit. Every time she came near to stopping, something about her lover's face would send her off again. It almost seemed as if the pent-up little-girl gaiety of her whole mature life had broken loose by the waters of this miniature Styx!

Philip simply could not understand this exhibition of schoolgirlishness at this particular moment and in this particular place. But he was too relieved that it was not any emotional reaction or any distress in her, to feel angry with her as she struggled to regain her composure. He felt a slight sensation of being made a fool of, but not to any embarrassing extent. How could he know that the deepest rift between his cousin and her husband had been that during the whole three years of their marriage Dave Spear had never once shown one single flicker of humour. And here, in her seducer of this mad night under the roots of the Mendips, she had suddenly recognized the same lack! It was the contemplation of Philip's portentously grave face—grave with the gravest of all emotions in the world!—that, combined with the strangeness of her surroundings, had brought on that fit of laughing. She had laughed exactly as a child laughs in church; simply because she knew it would be outrageous, unseemly, inartistic, and even a little monstrous to get a laughing-fit at such a moment! Of course, the fact that Persephone *could* laugh like that, under the circumstances, was a revelation of her character. It showed the detachment of her soul from her senses. It showed that, at the core of her being, there was a profane mocking demon, that scrutinised derisively, in cold blood, every situation in which she found herself. But Percy's burst of laughter only shamelessly expressed what many and quite normal women have often felt; namely the grotesque gravity of masculine lust. It is possible that Aphrodite herself was called "laughter-loving" by her lover Ares when he was furiously angry with her. In any case, it was queer enough to hear such a ringing peal of shameless girlish mischief rising up from the plutonian edge of that ghastly water.

What gave the whole scene, too, an element of fantastic *bizarrerie* was the fact that the fallen flashlight illuminated at this moment only the girl's legs, leaving the rest of her figure in dark shadow.

Philip held out his hands to her at last; and she became quiet and quite calm when he lifted her up upon her feet. He allowed their flashlight to remain on the ground. He pulled her back a little way, where the rock was smoother, under the dark wall of the cavern. "Do you see where the water disappears, Perse?" he said, making her sit down by him. Their backs were now resting against the side of the cavern; and from this position they could follow the long beam of the prostrate flashlight which now illuminated for them a strange phenomenon. Not more than a dozen yards from where they crouched, the water flowed under a low, flat bridge of solid stone. There was only about three feet of hollow space between the outflowing water and the massive rock that hung above it.

"One day, Perse, I'll have a barge made, flat enough to carry me under that rock, and back again. No one can tell what I may not find if I follow that water!"

She threw her arms round his neck and gave him a quick, passionate kiss. "I'll go with you, Phil, if you do!"

The horizontal beam projected by their fallen light was wide enough, before it reached this vanishing-point of the illuminated water, to throw into evidence a strip of soft greyish sand a little distance off. As a contrast to the weird colours thrown out by the copper, iron, lead, and manganese in the walls of the cave, this strip of grey sand assumed an appearance of Cimmerian neutrality.

Persephone followed Philip's glance at this unusual lovers' bed and showed no surprise and no reluctance when he took her by the hand to lead her there. "Kiss me, kiss me, Philip!" she cried, when they reached the place. "Kiss me and love me before you take me!"

The man's feudal-baron's senses were as quickly stirred as they were quickly chilled. Her wistful gallantry roused a profound response in him. They were of one blood, after all! It was Devereux mating with Devereux in the bowels of that prehistoric sanctuary. She laughed once again before they rose from their Stygian bed.

"Give the adulteress a cigarette!" she cried at last. "Did you know? Did you guess, Philip, that he had let me stay a virgin? You didn't? And all the time we were coming down that path I thought you did. Give the adulteress a cigarette!" she repeated with a happy sigh.

The level beam of flashlight fell upon the hem of her dress and upon her feet, while the rest of her remained in shadow. Her slender ankles, resting motionless there side by side, suddenly struck Philip's mind with a sense of extreme human pathos. They looked like a doll's ankles; and they hit his fancy as being so quaintly irresponsible, so oddly detached! They had to carry all this burden of a girl's turbulent heart, her blunders, her errors, her triumphs, through the long track of her days; and what had *they* done? He opened one of his precious boxes of Swan Vestas, casting, as he did so, a fellow-bandit's leer in the direction of the flashlight. "You've served me well, old boy," his look said, "but I'm glad I'm not *quite* dependent on you!" He lit her cigarette and then lit one of his own. The tortoise-shell case that had held them took on in his eyes at that moment the welcome reassurance of a familiar possession in a strange surrounding. For a few minutes they smoked side by side in a delicious languor of contentment and peace. Certainly, if the girl had held up a lighted match to his face at that moment she would have seen upon it what William Blake says women love best of all to see.

Philip's fierce predatoriness had melted into the sweet security of possession; while Percy's proud wilfulness had melted into the delicious passivity of being possessed. No thought of their treachery, no thought of Dave or of Tilly came to disturb their peace. The satisfied physical desire of each of them had transformed itself into an indescribable tenderness for the bodily presence of the other one. It was as if their two souls—like the souls of a pair of triumphant chemists brooding above the successfully mingled elements in a passive crucible—awaited the creative act of the occult life-force. Their bodies felt as though they were still linked together in an indescribable sweetness of identity, while their minds felt a profound reluctance to allowing any hasty movement of thought to tilt the brimming cup of their bodies' satisfaction and spill the precious ichor. So strong was the bent bow of their proud contentment that in the twanging of its string it shot their spasm of gratitude straight to the heart of the Cause of Life. And unlike the prayer of John and Mary from the surface of the sun-lit Wissey, this singular cry from the banks of the Styx reached the good in the nature of the Eternal Being and dodged the evil. By pure chance—as in the other case—did this occur; but in its occurrence it brought a backwash of profane delight down there to that strip of grey sand such as that ancient spot, in all its prehistoric longevity, had never known before. The luck which that spasm of gratitude from these two cousins stole from the double-natured Cause of Life continued to soothe their nerves even after they had risen from their Cimmerian bed and re-crossed their Styx.

The girl's cynical detachment neutralized this luck in the end; but all the long journey back it remained with them. It remained with them even when they had finally parted at their adjoining doors on the little upper landing of the Zoyland Arms, he to re-enter his solitary room of the dead flies, she to clamber across the sleeping, or apparently sleeping, body of her husband and to stretch herself out and make herself as imperceptible as she could close up against the thin, hard, wooden partition that now separated her from the owner of Wookey Hole.

Mr. Owen Evans, SEATED BY THE GAS-STOVE AT THE BACK OF Old Jones' shop, was enjoying a late breakfast. It was the day following the one wherein Philip Crow conducted Persephone to his subterranean kingdom. Mr. Evans' breakfast differed a great deal from the breakfast partaken by Mayor Wollop on the preceding morning. It lacked the Mayor's invisible attendants. It lacked the Mayor's Dundee Marmalade. It lacked the Mayor's Western Gazette. In place of this latter purveyor of topical items, Mr. Evans' bodily refreshment—consisting of a pot of tea and three stale rolls—was heightened by the presence of an old edition of the *Inferno* in the original Italian, open at the page that describes the blasphemous obstinacy of the heathen giant, Capaneus.

"As I was *then*," howled this unconscionable rebel against the Emperor of the Universe, "such am I *still!*"

Mr. Evans found no difficulty in translating this passage, even though the lettering of the old book was such a stumbling-block to modern eyes; and in his troubled response to its terrible import he placed no less than half of all the butter he possessed upon the piece of roll-crust which he now proceeded to munch in absent-minded voracity.

He was disturbed by a heavy knock upon Number Two's shop-door. He cursed audibly and glanced angrily at one particular clock, among all the old ticking timepieces, which he had grown accustomed to consulting. He consulted this one not because it kept better time, but because he pitied its woebegone face. He cherished the fancy—in his confused South Wales mind—that he might restore the prestige of this silly old clock among its grander companions if he made this little diurnal preference. But the clock only confirmed the knock. The knock and the clock said the same thing. "Reading done . . . business begun," said the clock and the knock.

Mr. Evans angrily opened the shop-door. This proceeding took more time than one would have supposed the stock-in-trade of Number Two justified. Never were there so many or such rusty bolts! But the Welshman got them all drawn at last; and red in the face and panting hard he opened the barricaded door. Into the shop stepped Sam Dekker. Sam's face, to anyone who saw it less frequently than his father and Penny Pitches, would have displayed a startling change. It had changed from the face of a lad to the face of a man. Sam had come to know something of the terms upon which the happiness of being alive has been offered us.

"How do you do, Mr. Evans," he said. "Oh, you are having your coffee! I'm awfully sorry I've disturbed you."

He made no motion however to go away; but proceeded to remove his coat and hat, and lay them both, together with his stick, upon one of Number Two's best specimens of the art of eighteenth-century chair-making. Then he sat down; and Mr. Evans, bringing up his own chair from the rear of the shop, sat down too.

"I've come to ask you rather a funny question, Sir," the visitor began, "but if you knew how few people in Glastonbury have books, or care anything for books, you'd understand my coming to you. By the way, do you people—does Old Jones, I mean—*sell* books as well as antiques? Has he got any old books here? Any old . . . you know? . . . any old *theological* books?"

The Welshman's face assumed a very odd expression. "Yes!" he said with a sort of resigned hesitation. "Oh, yes! There *are* quite a lot here. I've been going through them. They're down in the basement. It was chiefly because of them that I consented to undertake this shop. Oh, yes! There are quite a lot of interesting books down there, Mr. Dekker. But I don't know ——"

There was a moment's silence during which the shrill cockney voice of Mrs. Robinson addressing herself to Grandmother Cole, as the ladies moved slowly downtown on their way to St. John's Church, entered through the closed door.

"If 'twere only a rat what gnawed 'en 'twill be a heasy bit o' 'emming; but if what 'ee seed to-die be goin' to be worse tomorrow, *then* 'tis more nor rats! Then 'tis moth. And if 'tis moth, 'twill be 'ell's own job. If 'tis moth, I'd sigh 'No, Mr. Vicar! Not hon your little life will I hundertake sech a 'eart-breakin' job!' "

Sam couldn't restrain a faint grin at this overheard revelation of a labour-revolt in the ecclesiastical sphere; but Mr. Evans lacked all sense of humour in such matters. The man's hooked nose, sardonic eyebrows and long upper lip looked as impenetrable to High Street back-chat as the bust of Dante itself which he was now regarding with a secretive eye. The charwoman and the sewing-woman of St. John's Church passed on down the street; and Sam became as grave as the Welshman.

"I may as well be quite open with you, Sir," Sam said. "For more than a year now my father has been hoping that I'd accept his offer to send me to a theological college. I've refused to go; and I *never* shall go. But I ought to . . . I want to . . . read a little more. When I was at Corpus ——"

Mr. Evans interrupted him. "Corpus!" he cried, leaping to his feet, "do you mean Corpus Cambridge? I was at Oxford myself, but you Corpus people at Cambridge have got a library . . . I say you've got a library . . . that would madden Paracelsus himself. There are folios and quartos there that are ——" He lowered his voice and lifting the second finger of his left hand tapped with it the bony knuckle of the first finger of his right hand. "There are Welsh manuscripts there, my good Sir, that are priceless. They are prejudiced against me there; but that's nothing. I'm nothing. But if they'd let me have those manuscripts and take hem to South Wales with me and compare them with—Why! my good man!—They are prejudiced against me there; but that's nothing. What am I? Nothing. Nothing at all! But they've got a number of Bardic Triads there . . . in an underground chamber . . . a Welsh bedmaker told me all about it . . . that give incredible details of Merlin's life! Think of your being at Corpus! They are prejudiced against me there . . . a trifle . . . a little . . . They mean well . . . but of course! . . . but that's nothing . . . for what am I? Obviously nothing!"

Sam Dekker watched Mr. Evans' back as he moved about in that stuffy little shop, looking for something. A cold watery sun filtered into the shop through the street-window. This window was full of an extraordinary assortment of ill-chosen objects. One could hardly have called them objects of art. They were more like a Noah's Ark or a raft of candidates for Limbo. There was a cracked Chinese vase decorated by a series of she-dragons each of whom was apparently giving birth to, or being suckled by a double-tailed goldfish. Next to this vase there was a pepper-box of unnatural proportions on the top of which, where it was perforated for shaking, gaped the head of a preposterous Punchinello. A rusty faucet, of ornamental brass, serviceable now for no conceivable purpose, was propped up against the pepper-box. At the base of the vase reposed a white-feathered shuttlecock with a vermilion centre; while between the pepper-box and the window-frame was a small croquet-mallet of a kind that had become quite extinct. Resting on the handle of this croquet-mallet was a large Pacific Ocean shell, on the back of which some meticulous Miss Drew of a hundred years ago had painted a sad little landscape wherein a diminutive goatherd and a gigantic goat contemplated a sinking ship from a green island. Leaning against the rim of this painted shell was a big, old-fashioned shaving-cup, upon the side of which was sketched a distant view of a castle on the Rhine, seen between two nameless trees and above the back of an overloaded mule.

The watery sun which struggled into Old Jones' shop, through what portion of the window was not obscured by these objects, enabled Sam to watch every movement of Mr. Evans.

The man was standing on tiptoe against a shelf and struggling to open a little china pot which stood there without removing a marble paperweight which rested on its lid.

Sam got hesitatingly up from his seat; but remained with his hand on its arm. There was something distressing, teasing to the nerves, something that set one's teeth on edge, about Mr. Evans' effort to get his fingers into this little oblong pot.

"Ah!" he ejaculated at last, "I feel it now. Ah!"

Sam had never seen the human form stretched to such tension as was the form of Mr. Evans with his fingers in that small receptacle. He couldn't help looking at the man's bare heels, both of which were protruding now, as his feet rose out of his slippers, through large round holes in his knitted socks. His feet came back into their shoes as he uttered this exclaimation, and he himself turned with a tiny key in his hand.

"Come," he said. "Come . . . come . . . come!"

He led the way to the back of the shop where on the opposite

side to the narrow staircase going up was a still narrower staircase going down. At the top of this he paused; and taking a
candlestick from a little bracket began fumbling awkwardly with
a matchbox.

His helpless struggles with all these inanimate objects had now
got on Sam's nerves to such a pitch that he rushed forward to
assist him. Between them the tiny key fell upon the floor. Sam
picked it up and handed it to him. A faint stream of sunlight from
the window, full of little wavering motes, fell upon Mr. Evans'
countenance, as, with the key clutched in the palm of his hand, he
at last managed to light the candle. Sam was shocked by the nervous trouble upon the man's face. Was it due only to the obduracy
of all these little teasing inanimates, vexing like demons the
movements of a philosopher? Or was his request for these books
the most ill-advised demand with which he could have come
upon him?

Once more he had an opportunity of studying Mr. Evans' back
as he followed him down that dark little staircase. The lifted
candle the man carried caused that hooked nose of his, as he
turned to warn Sam of a particular step, to become like the nose
of an extremely old miser visiting his hoard of ducats and guil-
ders. The one eye too, which was all Sam could see in that shadowy profile, as he went down after him, was like the eye of a demented goshawk.

They reached the cellar at last. It was small enough. It was
tidier than the shop above. It was a little low room lined with tall
book-shelves. Sam saw at once that most of the books were of no
interest to him. They were almost all of them ancient magazines
bound in leather covers and interspersed with tattered school edi-
tions of the classics. One shelf, however, had glass over it; and
it was to a key-hole in this glass door that Mr. Evans applied his
little key.

What was the matter now with the man? His legs were shaking. His knees were knocking together! His fingers must have been
shaking too; for the candle grease began dripping over the front
of the glass case as he tried to open it with his key.

Sam stepped forward and made as if he would take the candle
from him. His gesture was a very natural one under the circum-

stances. Why then did the Welshman turn upon him a look of contorted fury? But the latter got the glass doors open finally; and Sam, peering over his shoulder, surveyed the exposed books. They were indeed "theological" works! Sam had never seen so many parchment-covered and vellum-covered and leather-covered folios. He read the names. There were Bonaventura, and Duns Scotus, and Thomas Aquinas, and Albertus Magnus, and Avicenna, and Bernard, and Jerome, and Anselm.

Sam could not restrain a weary, disappointed groan. What good were these to him? He was no scholar. What he wanted was something—well! He really didn't know exactly what he *had* wanted; for in the world of theological books Sam had the simple imagination of a student of minnows and butterflies.

But he saw Mr. Evans' hand now hurriedly withdrawn from the shelf with a beautifully bound book clutched in his fingers. There was a big gap where he had just removed this work and another book, that had been standing erect by the one he had taken, toppled sideways now across this gap, and lay there diagonally, resting against some thick mediæval tome with an obscure Latin title. Towards this book Sam's attention was at once attracted, for it was different in appearance from the rest. His sharp, observant bear's eyes caught its title in a second. It was called "The Unpardonable Sin."

Mr. Evans now turned upon him hurriedly.

"Here's the one for *your* purposes," he said, emphasising the "your." "They didn't teach you at Corpus to read Church-Latin I'm afraid," he went on. "But this is the 'Confessions' in English . . . the best modern edition . . . it's worth twenty pounds . . . I don't know how Jones ever picked it up."

He was beginning to close the glass doors again when Sam made a motion towards the book fallen across the gap. Mr. Evans jerked his arm away but in such a manner as to make it appear that he did so by accident. He *might* have done it by accident; for here he was, fumbling as helplessly as ever, with his precious key!

Sam had grown really impatient by this time—Saint Augustine's "Confessions"! Why his father had got that book on a shelf that Sam had known from his childhood, side by side, not with "The Unpardonable Sin," but with Bewick's "Birds." Whatever it had been that he had in his mind when he came here this morning it certainly had not been Saint Augustine. No! It had been just a vague craving to make one more attempt to find some possible attitude, less sceptical than the one he had grown to adopt, towards his father's creed.

He felt indignant with Mr. Evans for rousing his hopes like that and then presenting him with undecipherable parchment-folios and with "The Unpardonable Sin."

But he hadn't lived cheek by jowl with a priest of God for nothing. He had wit enough to know now why Mr. Evans' knees had knocked together! Either that book was some monstrous Aphrodisiac of Obscenities or it was some pseudo-Biblical fantasy that had turned, or was in process of turning, this poor lonely devil's head. But what was the astonishing fellow doing now? Mr. Evans had put down his candle upon the floor and was on his knees by a carved chest, on the top of which was something tied up in brown paper. The man was cursing under his breath as he tugged at a knot in the string of this large flat parcel.

Sam received the impression that he was under the guidance of a non-human puppet, for whom the least attempt to cope with the obstinacy of matter was an impossible task.

But Mr. Evans summoned him now to his side. He had completely recovered his equilibrium. He was once again the long-winded antiquary.

"Merlinus Ambrosianus," Sam proceeded to spell out from the cover of the large volume now presented to his view.

"Is this your own make-up?" he asked, using a word that his foster-mother Penny might have used.

"You mean my own composition?" said Mr. Evans, turning to his interlocutor the bland, bewildered, blinking face of a harmless Dominie Sampson.

"Oh, no! My *Vita Merlini*, when it is finished—I have only just begun my collection of notes—will include elaborate details of the Magician's life that this blundering idiot here does not seem even aware exist. Oh, no! This is a reprint of an eighteenth-century compendium of excerpts from the Bodleian. It has certain documents that they won't let you take out of the Bodleian. For instance, it has the famous Pontyprid version of the disappearance of Merlin; proving conclusively that the Turning Castle called Carbonek was not at Bardsey, but here at Glastonbury; probably on what you people call Chalice Hill; but it is not an important book. I would never have purchased it if those Oxford fools—they are worse at Oxford than at Cambridge—hadn't got suspicious of me. I don't know why it is, Mr. Dekker"—he now scrambled to his feet, and Sam was relieved to see that he relinquished all attempt to tie up those strings again—"but I seem to excite suspicion when I go about. It's something to do with my appearance. I don't inspire confidence."

He stretched himself up to his full height as he spoke. He had re-possessed himself of the candle and also of the volume of Saint Augustine, worth twenty pounds. He now rose and fell in his loose slippers as if performing some species of gymnastic exercise.

"Have *you* any idea why it is? Is it my nose, do you think?"

He lifted his hand, apparently quite forgetting that it held the candle, towards this feature of his face; and as he did so he smiled at Sam with such an ingenious, Don Quixote kind of smile, that Sam felt singularly disarmed.

But Mr. Evans shook his head whimsically and hugging the big volume of Saint Augustine and carrying his candle, he led the way up the stairs, back into the shop.

"Well, I must be off, I suppose," murmured Sam vaguely. "I certainly can't afford twenty pounds." After a pause he added rather sadly: "I can't afford twenty shillings."

"I'll *lend* you the book," cried Mr. Evans. "You'll never find another edition as pleasant to read; and if you haven't read it lately you'll get a lot out of it. It's an interesting book; only rather morbid. But you are morbid yourself, just as I am! I should think it would rather suit you."

Sam remained, for what seemed to him an interminable time, staring at the back of the Punchinello pepper-box in the window.

Mr. Evans was engaged in one of his perennial struggles with the inanimate. He was wrapping up the Saint Augustine in cardboard boards, making as he did so such facial contortions as would have been extravagant in a wrestling bout.

When the Welshman at last handed him the parcel, Sam remarked nervously, "Are you very busy this morning, Mr. Evans?"

Number Two's representative looked at him in surprise.

"Not especially," he said.

"I only asked you," wavered Sam, laying his fingers on the shop-door handle, "because my father wanted me to go to the station to see your friend Crow, who's sending round all these queer announcements. He's sent you a lot, no doubt."

Mr. Evans nodded. "You want me to go with you?" he asked.

"I thought it would be nice," returned Sam.

"All right. Why not?" said Mr. Evans. "I've got nothing to do but lock the door! People don't often drop in in the mornings."

When the two men reached the little office, down by the station, they found John preparing to sally forth on a private expedition of his own. It was difficult to catch his explanation of the purport of this expedition, because the wooden shanty he occupied was invaded at that moment by a violent outpouring of steam from the engine of a luggage-train that had stopped close behind it.

Geard's office having been the temporary office of a coal company and consequently situated in the goods-yard of the Great Western station, it had been to the accompaniment of the day-long shunting of trucks and puffing of engines that John Crow had composed his extravagant advertisement of their Midsummer Pageant.

As the three men stood together now at the door of the little office, Sam was unable to avoid a sidelong glance at the majestic proportions and almost personal dignity of the great green engine towering above them. The vast Creature carried its name in clear gold letters upon its belly. It was called "Sedgemoor." It may well be imagined how the appearance of this particular word, in so unexpected a place, gave to all these polished pistons and cog wheels a symbolic significance to the enamoured heart of Sam!

Just for the sake of that word "Sedgemoor" there floated—like the "disarrayed" Loveliness that so tantalised Spenser's stern Sir Guyon—the white limbs and the tender bosom of Nell, in and out of the iron entrails of this majestic monster.

"I've got to go to Tor Field," John Crow was saying, "before

I can get on with my next set of circulars. I *must* see the lie of the
land. Why don't you two come with me? At any rate as far as the
Vicarage? I don't want to drag you any further; but it'll be easier
to talk if we get away from here."

Sam and Mr. Evans both signified their willingness to accompany him.

"I really came," said Sam, with a disarming candour, "as my
father's plenipotentiary. He's read your first batch of circulars
and he's anxious to know more about the whole business. You
mustn't think it's just impertinent interfering; but my father
could really be an immense help to you if he got interested and
liked your ideas—as I'm sure he would!"

"Well, I'll tell you how far we've got," said John, "and then
you'll have something definite to tell your father. I ought to have
called on him about it long ago and asked his advice, before it
got as far as it has. Mr. Geard wanted me to. But these last days
have slipped by with such speed that I don't seem to have had
time for anything.

"What we propose," he went on, as they all three walked
slowly up Benedict Street, "is to have a mixed entertainment.
Part of it will be just an ordinary Fair, like what you have here,
at Michaelmas, only more lively, I hope! Part of it, though, will
be quite different from that. We propose to have"—he peered
craftily and furtively into the faces of his companions—"a Glastonbury Passion Play."

John had a suspicion in his Isle-of-Ely mind that the words
"Passion Play" would excite annoyance in both these men. He
forgot the indelible egoism of human beings! Because his own
head was just then so full of this scheme of Geard's, it seemed to
him that the mere mention of it would arrest lively attention, and
evoke either hostility or sympathy. He was not prepared for
casual indifference. But casual indifference, tempered by politeness, was precisely what his grand news received.

Sam's brain was full of Nell and of his struggle with his own
passion.

Mr. Evan's head was full of the sinister thoughts which his
visit to that bookshelf had stirred up.

Thus John's mentioning the historic Passion of Jesus passed as lightly over both their heads as if he had been referring to a famine in China.

Twice on their walk through the town, from Benedict Street to Chilkwell Street, Mr. Evans was on the point of leaving them and going back to his shop. When they passed the Vicarage gate in Silver Street, Sam was on the verge of bidding them good-bye.

It was one of those occasions when a casual group of people seems held together by some invisible bond, contrary to the individual desire of every person composing the group. The dreamy passivity of both Mr. Evans and Sam was partly due to the fact that their own fate seemed to them to be hanging in the balance. Sam retained an obstinate clutch upon the edition of Saint Augustine which he had borrowed. This he could sweep into the master-current of his feelings more easily than any vague purpose of John Crow's in Tor Field.

Mr. Evans was able to get rid of every embodiment of his dark temptation, except one single passage in "The Unpardonable Sin," which some supernaturally crafty devil might have composed especially to devastate and overwhelm him. Certain images called up by this particular passage were so seductive that his knees grew weak as he thought of them. The worst of these images had to do with a killing blow delivered by an iron bar.

The three men had reached the Abbey Barn at the corner of Bere Lane when things came to the worst with Mr. Evans.

The wild and desperate thought seized him . . . as it had done only once before since he came to Glastonbury . . . "Why not fling away every scruple?"

His mind seemed at that second absolutely balanced on a taut and twanging wire between two terrible eternities, an eternity of wilful horror, and an eternity of bleached, arid futility, devoid of all life-sap. He could feel the path to the horror, shivering with deadly phosphorescent sweetness. He could feel the path to the renunciation filling his nostrils with acrid dust, parching his naked feet, withering every human sensation till it was hollow as the shard of a dead beetle! The nature of his temptation was such that it had nothing to redeem it. Such abominable wickedness came straight out of the evil in the heart of the First Cause, travelled through the interlunar spaces, and entered the particular nerve in the erotic organism of Mr. Evans which was predestined to respond to it.

The unhappy man now surveyed with a sick eye those symbols of the Evangelists which endow this ancient barn with such a majestic consecration. He felt a sudden loathing for the human spirit, so hampered by matter as to be driven to shifts like this— to the ransacking of the kingdoms of terrestrial life for their clue to the beyond-life.

Drifting forward up Chilkwell Street went the three men; and it was between the Barn and St. Michael's Inn that the bloody sweat of Mr. Evans' mental struggle poured down till he felt actually faint.

"If I yield," he said to himself, "what then?"

Oh, with what blasting clearness he saw that terrible alternative! He saw himself obsessed again with the old bite, the old itch, the old sting, the old insatiable torture of desire ——

"The thing has no end," he thought. "The other way leads to places where you can rest. *This* goes on . . . and on . . . and on . . . without an end. The struggle to renounce it is pain. Each day new pain. The pain of unspeakable dreariness. But if I don't struggle against it, it is worse than that. These men don't know whom they are walking with. They don't know! Oh, why should there be such a thing in the world as *this*?"

His mind recoiled from an attempt to envisage the nature of what it was that had first engendered the poison-seed which had attracted to itself so much kindred evil from the heart of the universe.

"If I yield to it—if I yield to it ——" he kept repeating; while the image that worked the madness in him slid again into the fibres of his being and nestled, nestled there, like a soft-winged bird. And his imagination, as they drew near St. Michael's Inn, settled itself like a dung-wasp upon the nature of his conscious life if he *did* yield to it. He saw his soul in the form of an unspeakable worm, writhing in pursuit of new, and ever new mental victims, drinking new, and ever new innocent blood. *And he saw the face of this worm.* And it happened to him now that he obtained what is given to few to obtain, an actual certain knowledge of what thoughts they were, if they could be called thoughts, that would come to stir in the darkness under the mask of that face that was no face!

Absolutely alone except for its consciousness of a certain little, round, red eye—the eye of the Evil in the double-natured First Cause—fixed upon it with a bottomless enjoyment of its suffering, the worst of the thoughts of this creature would be the intolerable effort required of it if it were to struggle to escape its doom. It would know that it *could* escape if it struggled. But the effort would be worse than what it suffered. And it would know its doom. It would see Remorse slowly changing its nature and becoming Something Else in the process of self-torture. It would know that its doom was no crashing annihilation, but a death as slow as the disintegration of certain mineral deposits which under chemical pressure gradually lose their identity and are converted into amorphous dust.

They were now passing the entrance to St. Michael's Inn, a simple little tavern, frequented chiefly by the poorer class, and possessed of only two storeys.

As Mr. Evans cast his eye upon the windows of the upper storey he saw the muslin curtains of one of them pulled aside. They were not pulled far . . . only a little way . . . and the hand that pulled them remained clutching them tightly, as if in fear of being interfered with. Between these curtains Mr. Evans saw a face looking out at him, apparently the face of a woman. The head of this apparition shocked Mr. Evans and indeed caused him to feel queasy in the pit of his stomach; for it was totally bald. An ordinary observer would have regarded this face as that of an idiot; but Mr. Evans knew better. It was the face of a remorseful sadist. Yes! it was a face of unspeakable cruelty, but the nature of its cruelty had changed. The mind behind that face was still occupied with devices for causing suffering; but the object of these devices was no longer—by the blessed interposition of chance—external to the woman herself.

He imagined her, or rather he saw her, for the woman looked at him and he looked at the woman, slowly torturing herself to death; and this by a process that Mr. Evans completely understood. It was a process of pleasure-killing. He knew the part played in this process by everything in the woman's room. He saw

her refusing to pick up crumbs from the floor, although to remove crumbs from the floor was a pleasure to her. He saw her
draw the muslin curtains across the window when it rained—and
he knew she liked rain—and drawing them back when the sun
shone; and he knew she loathed the sun. He could see the chair
she longed to sit upon and never allowed herself to sit upon. He
could hear the ticking of the clock which she wound up so carefully every night; although it was the ticking of this clock more
than anything else that she found intolerable.

Mr. Evans was well aware of the efforts that the people of the
house must be making all the while to persuade the woman to
cease this maniacal self-punishment, this slow murdering of all
the little diurnal sensations of pleasure. But these efforts were
doubtless of no avail. Oh, no! They were wrong to call her an
idiot. Mr. Evans knew all about her. He knew how she poured
water out of her washing-jug over the red coals in her grate the
minute she caught herself getting any pleasure from the warmth.

He knew—but he had already lingered ridiculously long behind
John and Sam. He must catch them up.

They arrived now at an old rickety gate on their right which
led direct into Tor Field where at Michaelmas for a thousand
years, the great Glastonbury Fair had been held; although of
recent years it had been moved to a meadow on the further side
of the town.

Sam opened the gate and they all three entered the field. When
Sam turned to his companions, after lifting the gate back into
place, he was met by a somewhat bewildered, vaguely appealing
stare from both of them. It was entirely instinctive, this movement
of theirs. It must have been a deep unconscious impulse. Just in
this manner, on countless forgotten pilgrimages, men must have
turned to some fate-appointed leader, drawn by what Mr. Weatherwax would have called "nat'rel authority."

It was as if they both secretly in their hearts expected Sam to
say: "Follow me up the hill."

Sam, however, said nothing of the sort. He laid down his parcel
on the grass and began searching about at the side of an ancient
fallen tree for a certain kind of moss that he knew grew here, of
a rather uncommon variety.

John and Mr. Evans both turned their eyes to St. Michael's Tower. The Tower upon Glastonbury Tor varies in appearance as much as any hill-erection in Wessex. This is due to the extraordinary variety of atmospheric changes which the climate of that district evokes.

On this particular day the weather conditions had assumed a cloud-pattern, an air-pressure, a perspective of light and shadow, such as dwellers in Glastonbury recognized as more natural and normal than any other. Over the surface of the sky extended a feathery white film of vapour. The effect of this filmy screen upon the sun was to make it seem as if it shone through a roof of water. As a matter of fact, this vaporous film reduced the sun-rays to so mild a diffusion that they ceased to be rays. The sun's orb, thus shorn of its outpouring of radiance, came to resemble the disk of the moon. The great Luminary was so reduced by this film of clouds that, like Agamemnon in the toils of Clytemnestra, it could hardly be said to shine at all. It peered helplessly forth over the green meadows of Avalon; so that stubborn Christian spirits, such as Mat Dekker, had the satisfaction of being able to confront the great Light-Lord, and stare him full in the face without blinking.

The result of this veiling of the sun was that only a watery suffusion of liquid luminousness flowed over every object that emerged into prominence at all, over every object that had any form or any outline.

All were equally blurred and softened. Thus it came about that a moon-like circle of pallid whiteness looked forth upon a world from which every harsh projection, whether of stone, or wood, or metal, or horn, or scale, or feather, or bone, or rock, had been obliterated; a world of flowing curves and sliding shadows, a world of fluctuating shapes and melting contours.

What this veiling of the sun further did was to heighten the effect of colour. Colour as a phenomenon in the world became doubly important. Every shade, every richness, every variety of colour, lent itself to this colour-invasion of the kingdom of form.

Thus as these three men stood together at the foot of Glastonbury Tor the grass of the hillside seemed of an incredibly rich depth. It was like a mounting wave of palpable greenness into which, if you began to walk, your feet would sink down.

"My idea is," said John at length, when Sam had risen up from his search for mosses on the underside of the prostrate tree, "my idea is to have the regular Fair down here, on this level ground. But the Miracle Play, or whatever you like to call it, I want to have on the slope of the hill, with that Tower as my background. Do you catch my idea?"

"Let's sit down a second," said Sam, taking his seat on the fallen tree.

"What I want to do," said John, looking around him, "is to try and realise this place with a crowd of people moving about, and booths and tents and bands and so on. I can't imagine it! But, after all, when you cross any ordinary fair-field at *this* time of the year, it's impossible to see it as it is when it's crowded with people."

He seated himself by Sam's side as he spoke and Mr. Evans sat down, too. The position of the three men when thus seated was as follows: John was nearest the Tor; that is to say, southward of the others; Mr. Evans was nearest Chalice Hill; that is to say, northward of the others; while Sam had the middle place, opposite that spot in the horizon where the gap called Havyatt breaks the ancient line of trenches, thrown up to repel the Danes.

Mr. Evans sat starkly upright on their log. His black overcoat hung about his thin knees like a priest's cassock. His black bowler hat was pulled so low down over his forehead as to resemble the hat of a Jewish comedian on a music-hall stage. He leaned forward on a nondescript cane, picked up anywhere, but he bent his head over his folded hands as if he had been a chieftain out of Ossian's poetry, brooding over some irrevocable doom.

Sam wore a very rough, thick, Norfolk jacket. His knickerbockers were stained, worn threadbare, very faded, his woolen stockings were slipping down, and as they slipped they no longer concealed his heavy woolen drawers. Sam's cap had been pushed back off his forehead, and his wrinkled, animal physiognomy scowled forth in a puzzled and nonplussed protest at a world that contained both good and evil to a degree beyond the fathoming of his simple spirit.

As for John, he had bought by Mary's advice an overcoat at Wollop's which was really a bargain. Not that this new overcoat destroyed his trampish appearance, but it made him look more like a thief or a rogue or even a furtive-eyed cardsharper than he had done when tidied up for his English adventure by his French grisette. Mary's attempts to give him a gentlemanly air had only given him a shabby-genteel air; an air that was very disconcerting to the girl, and for which she could not quite account.

John looked, in fact, exactly like the tricky showman he was, calculating the possibilities of his Midsummer Circus. The overcoat which Mary had chosen for him hung on his lean figure like a garment he had stolen. It was as if some well-dressed man, passing down a road, had tossed that coat over the wooden cross-beam of a dilapidated scarecrow. He sat sideways, in a hunched-up posture, prodding the earth with his hazel-stick and looking first at one of his companions and then at the other. Every now and then, however, he glanced stealthily at St. Michael's Tower on the top of the Tor, as if that were a Fourth Person in this colloquy, whose temper, just as incalculable as that of the other two, had to be kept an eye upon, lest it should make trouble.

It was after one of these surreptitious glances that he suddenly broke out—"You see that ledge over there? That's where I'm going to have my Crucifixion."

The terrible word came with a shock to the ears of the other two men.

"Will it be allowed?" asked Mr. Evans.

"How do you mean, 'allowed,' " said John.

"By the police, Mr. Evans means," said Sam, "and by public opinion. You must remember, Crow, this is a Protestant country. You seem to have forgotten how they killed Abbot Whiting on this very hill."

"I really meant by the Glastonbury people themselves," explained Mr. Evans. "But it's true they let that devilish king kill their Abbot here."

"He was a Welshman like you," said John.

Mr. Evans surprised them by the depth of the sigh he gave at this point.

"What a sigh was there!" quoted John. "The heart is sorely charged."

Mr. Evans sighed again.

"Whose is not?" he muttered.

Sam was now lost in heavy ponderings, as he stared at the brown-paper parcel containing Saint Augustine which he had tossed down on the grass when he began searching for that specimen of moss.

His was not a nature to be carried away by any sudden idea. The feelings that had been fomenting within him of late had only been stirred up. They had not been created by his passion for Nell. But the girl's having gone back to Zoyland's bed had been a shock to his deepest pride; and by his new gesture of complete renunciation he was, in some subtle way, recovering his threatened life-illusion.

As for Mr. Evans a most singular idea had just entered that Roman skull under the Jewish-comedian black hat. Why should he himself not play the part of the Crucified in the blasphemous mummery of this mountebank?

In the agitation of this thought Mr. Evans actually took off his bowler hat and standing up on his feet stretched out his arms in the manner of a crucified person. That one of his hands held his hat while he did this was nothing to him. He was startled by the magnetic wave of emotion that poured through him as he made this sudden gesture.

Sam did not notice what he was doing. John thought he had got cramped and was stretching himself.

Mr. Evans let his arms drop and addressed John in an eager voice.

"I'll go over to your terrace, Crow," he said, "and play the Crucified for you; so that you can see how it looks."

John was delighted with this offer.

"Isn't that splendid!" he cried in a high-pitched tone. "Bravo! That's the *very* idea! How decent of you, Evans! What a good thought!"

Sam regarded this transaction with a very uneasy eye. If he found it hard to say the Creed with the simplicity of his father, anything that smacked of blasphemy brought an evil taste into his mouth.

Mr. Evans walked up the hill till he reached the grassy terrace. This time he put down both his hat and his cane. He also buttoned up tightly his long black overcoat. In this guise he raised himself to his full height, flung back his head and stretched out his arms.

John leapt to his feet in an ecstasy.

"Wonderful! It's wonderful!" he cried. He came hurrying up to Mr. Evans.

"Seriously, Sir," he blurted out, "you'll *have* to play Christ in my Pageant. You will! You will! You're not exactly the *type* . . . but that doesn't matter a bit. Oh, you will! You will! Why, you'll beat that Oberammergau person hollow."

Mr. Evans picked up his hat and nondescript cane and advanced hurriedly to meet John. In his secret heart he was astonished and even puzzled by the feelings that again poured through him as he made the terrible symbolic gesture.

"I . . . don't . . . mind," he panted in a hoarse voice. "Only you'll have to make it as real as you can."

John regarded his friend through shrewd, screwed-up, meditative eyelids.

"Oh, we'll make it real enough," he said. But he was too occupied with an imaginative picture of that future scene to care very much what he was promising Mr. Evans.

"Come on up to the top of the hill, you two, won't you?" he pleaded now.

"Can I leave this book here?" said Sam, looking first at Saint Augustine and then at Mr. Evans.

The Welshman surveyed the parcel which he had done up so carefully. He evidently remembered that it was worth twenty pounds.

"I'll carry it," he said. "Boys might come. You never know."

The fear of "boys" was one of Mr. Evans' peculiarities. In fact he was nervously scared of all children.

But Sam tucked the big parcel under his own arm.

"It's not heavy," he said.

It must have been about thirty minutes after twelve when they all reached the top of the Tor. They surveyed the great entrance to the hollow tower and John tapped with his stick at the boardings with which it had been closed up.

"Mayor Wollop had *that* done," he remarked savagely. "Old Sheperd found a boy and girl making love inside; and that was enough for our precious procurator. Boarded up it must be; so that the king should not have to fight his enemies with bastards!"

"Let's sit down for a minute," said Sam.

They all obeyed him, sitting side by side on the grass, with their backs leaning against the western flank of the cold, slate-coloured base of the tower. Before them to the westward stretched the green water meadows, among which, a mile or so out of town, could be detected the wide Lake Village Fen and even the little shanty of Abel Twig; while to the southwest, beyond the fens, rose the blue-grey ridge of the low Polden hills. All these were softly suffused by the cloud-latticed vapour-filmed sun; a sun which, though riding at high noon, lacked the potency to dominate what it bathed with that glamorous and watery light.

Here under St. Michael's Tower sat these three figures, the lean shabby-genteel John, the hulking weather-bleached Sam, the black-coated Mr. Evans—all atheists towards the life-giving Sun-God, and all expanding now, in their thoughts, their feelings, their secretest hopes, because of the victory of vapour over light and of dampness over heat!

A landscape of green and grey, a landscape with all hard outlines obliterated, was what just suited these three fantastical human beings. A common relaxation, a common inertia, a common languor descended upon them as they sat there, gazing down on that pastoral scene.

And as they sat there they each thought of a particular girl. They thought of these three feminine identities so intently that by the automatic preoccupation of their feelings the souls of all three girls were drawn towards them; three wraithlike eidola! Ah! How little do the feminine creatures of the human race realise what long journeys they are compelled to take . . . what long, rapid journeys . . . swifter than light . . . under the compulsive magic of their men's imaginations!

To the supernatural eyes of that veiled sun as he dreamed his indescribable planetary thoughts, vaguely hostile and vaguely menacing, one of these feminine forms came naked to the waist—that was Nell; one came naked from the thighs downward—that was Mary; and one came garmented like a nun, from head to foot in black—and that was Cordelia!

Together these three men represented—in Remorse, in Renunciation, in Roguery—everything that separates our race from nature. Their three intelligences floated there, on that hilltop, above their clothed and crouching skeletons, like wild demented birds that had escaped from all normal restraint.

Any student of ancient mythology might well have fancied that Gwyn-ap-Nud, with a host of his elementals, finding these three detached intelligences—Remorse, Renunciation, Roguery—separated from natural human life—had cast his immemorial spell over them; that oldest of supernatural spells against which St. Michael's aid had been so often implored in vain.

"What slaves we all are," remarked Mr. Evans suddenly, "to traditional ideas! People say we ought to be always admiring Nature. God help me! There are endless occasions when I loathe Nature. I think the truth is that God is outside Nature . . . altogether outside . . . creator of it . . . but often loathing it as much as I do! I feel sometimes that Matter is entirely evil . . . and that to cleanse our minds we must destroy its power . . . destroy . . . its power."

He repeated these last words in his most serious tone; that tone which John had noticed when they first met; that tone in which each word seemed torn out of him like the deep-burrowing dock root.

Sam's hulking form swayed like a gnarled thorn bush in a high wind.

"I protest against what you've just said, Evans, with every instinct I have! That's the essence of the Incarnation . . . that's the . . ."

He had become so excited that without knowing what he did he was plucking great handfuls of the turf-grass from between his huge thick-soled boots.

"That's what they really killed the Abbot for," he went on, "because he wouldn't let anything come between him and It. It's the whole secret. It's where the most commonplace Christians can refute the greatest sages. Matter must be redeemed; and only Christ can redeem it. *Christ*, I say; not Jesus. *Verbum caro factum est.* Your making Matter evil undoes the whole thing. It's the Incarnation that transforms Nature. It has been done once. Nothing can reverse it. Something has come into it from outside; from that Outside you talk about. But It's *in it* now! You can't get rid of it. The simplest person has an instinct about this, wiser than the greatest philosophers. Something has taken up Matter into Itself. Two and two can now make five! It's the Thing Outside breaking into our closed circle. And every atom of Matter feels it. Matter is no longer separate from Spirit. It has become the living flesh of Spirit. *Verbum caro factum est!*"

Sam stopped. He gazed with confused surprise at the little weeds he had grubbed up in his agitation. He began planting them again in the hole he had made. He squeezed them into the yielding sod. He pressed them down with his strong thumbs; while his retreating chin, with all its quivering muscles, seemed to echo his discourse, in a mute ripple of the Matter whose redemption he had been defending.

John regarded him with intense curiosity, as if he had been Balaam's ass suddenly endowed with the gift of speech. "I suppose," John said, "you would call the Mass this kind of miracle?"

Sam's reply to this was a vague groan.

"Maybe you're right," he muttered. "Maybe you're right."

"I suppose," said John to Sam, "*you* don't want to come to our rehearsals of the Miracle Play? The chap I'd meant for the central figure will be glad enough to give it up to Evans. Shall I make the lad who is doing St. Peter, hand that part over to *you*?"

Sam felt at that moment as if he were a child whose secretest and most private game, a game he'd never revealed to a living soul, had become the sport of a noisy dormitory of jeering boys. He lowered his freckled face and drew down the corners of his mouth. Three times he swallowed his saliva; and then he said with a forced unnatural chuckle, "I'll pay the entrance-fee and come and see your Circus, Crow. But nothing you could give me, *nothing*; not all the fortune of your Rector of Northwold, would make me take part in it."

"Oh, don't say that, Dekker! What makes you say that?"

"We'll . . . call . . . it . . . shyness . . . Crow," said Sam slowly, but in a tone that was decisive.

"Well, gentlemen," said Mr. Evans rising to his feet, "I'm afraid I must get back to my shop! There's always a chance of visitors after lunch and it's half-past one already."

"Don't you have lunch yourself, then?" enquired John. "I was just going to suggest that we all have lunch together at that little tea-shop in George Street ——"

Mr. Evans pondered. He felt very hungry and there was nothing in his larder except half a roll and a small piece of butter.

Sam had felt so restless that morning that he had told his father not to expect him back to their mid-day dinner. If he hadn't found Mr. Evans in his shop he would have probably gone off on a long solitary walk—perhaps in the direction of Queen's Sedgemoor and perhaps not.

He got up slowly upon his feet, as also did John. They were all three erect now under the tower of St. Michael; that same tower against which the murderous Tudor's executioners had leaned as they prepared for butchering Abbot Whiting.

Sam spoke up boldly.

"You two have given me so much to . . . to think about . . . that I . . . that I shall . . . have to walk off . . . my excitement. I wonder . . ." he hesitated for a second with bowed head and working chin. Then his words came out with a rush. ". . . I wonder if you'd mind leaving this book at the Vicarage as you go by?"

There was no difficulty thrown in Sam's way by either Mr. Evans or John, and he strode off alone down St. Michael's Hill. In order to leave them abruptly while it was easy for him to do so, he descended the Tor by its eastern slope. He had indeed stated no less than the exact truth when he said he wanted to walk off his excitement.

His gaze swept the countryside as he climbed down into the valley. He glanced at Pennard Hill and Folly Wood and at the fields and hedges round Stony Stratton. He glanced at the low-lying downs near Chesterblade; and thought to himself—"That's the source of the Alham; and where the Alham runs into the Brue is only a mile south of Hornblotton."

Thus was the little river Alham compelled to be the bearer of a lover's memory. For it was at Hornblotton that Sam had ridden with Nell when at that circus, so fatally remembered by Penny Pitches, he had taken her on the roundabout.

When he reached the valley he struck across country heedless as to lanes or paths. His instinct for geography was only second to that of his father; and it was easy for him by following the meadows beyond the town-reservoir, between Norwood Farm and Havyatt, to reach the village of West Pennard without touching any road. Here he turned due north; and still crossing every hedge and ditch with the same animal-like straightness of direction, he made his way over Hearty Moor, across the tracks of the Burnham and Evercreech railroad, till he came to Whitelake River at Whitelake Bridge.

This he reached when the watch in his pocket pointed at seventeen minutes past three. He had no idea what the time was. In fact he did not give the matter a thought. His thoughts followed one another like horses round a treadmill. Anyone reading his thoughts, and contemplating the motion of the hands of his watch in his pocket might have been tempted to an extremely deterministic view of life. The mainspring in the one case was made of metal, and the other case made of the brutish sting of desire; but there was in both cases the same monotonous revolution around predetermined figures of demarcation.

The filmy screen that hid the sun had grown thicker since high noon. The surface of the small river reflected now what appeared to be a very cloudy sky and the willows and alders were not mirrored there at all. Staring at the water, he tried to summon back every link in the dragging chain that had pulled him to this place. He meditated on the curious difference which exists—when you consider the life of a river—between the outlines of reflections in its flow and the outlines of shadows.

He sat down on a willow stump and stared at the river as intently as if it held a secret for him that at all costs must be drawn forth. At what point, since he stood by Mr. Evans' side in that queer basement of Old Jones' shop, had the determination

seized upon him to come out here? Was it when he was looking
at that surprising volume . . . he could envisage its dirty-whitish
modern binding now . . . that fell across the gap in the shelf
left by the extraction of St. Augustine? Was it when he was
looking for that "fairy-cup" moss by the log on which the three
of them had sat down? Was it at the very moment when he had
that sudden inspiration about the secret of Christianity and the
redemption of Matter?

The willow stump on which he sat now had one living sprout;
and from this sprout a little cluster of emerald-green buds had
burst forth. These buds now became a portion of what he was
feeling and thinking. One conclusion certainly had formulated
itself in his slowly moving mind, during that ascent of the Tor;
the conclusion, namely, that it was unnecessary to trouble himself one way or the other about his father's Creed; since the
essence of the thing lay in the conduct of life rather than in any
intellectual doctrine.

"She said you had the look of a saint." What a funny remark
that was of Red Robinson's; and how hard to associate it with
any impression he had ever received from Crummie Geard! Well,
the look of a saint or the look of a satyr, he knew what he could
not help doing now! For good or for evil he must see Nell
Zoyland that day.

He got up from the willow stump, crossed the bridge, and
began tramping westward, along the opposite bank, which, at
that portion of the river's progress, resembled a natural tow-path.

When John and his Welsh companion came out of their tea-
shop on George Street, they encountered Tom Barter. John had
taken the opportunity of carrying further his sudden inspiration
as to using "my good friend Evans" as the central figure of his
profane Passion Play. The idea of this appealed to a vein of
sheer devilry in his impulsive nature. The less there appeared
of the Christ-like in the degenerate Roman physiognomy of his
Celtic ally the better pleased and the more tickled did this nerve
of roguery in him become!

Having agreed to the wild scheme in his "second manner,"
the Welshman was now prepared, it seemed, to throw into the

notion all the ponderous, pedantic weight of his "first manner"; and the more he talked about it with John the fuller of dramatic possibilities did the plan seem for John's lively imagination.

But Mr. Evans went off to his shop now; and the two old friends, of the far-off Northwold days, were left together in that drowsy Glastonbury street. It came back to John, as he drifted by his friend's side towards the office of Philip's factory, how full of this man's personality every glittering, rippling reach of that "big river" had been. It came back to him how he had thought of Tom as he stood with Mary at the mill-pond looking at those great salmon-trout. It came to him how he had recalled, without realising the full import of it, their vicious play that hot Sunday afternoon at the bottom of the boat! Vicious with every sort of East-Anglian sensuality had they both been; and John was surprised at himself, glancing furtively at Tom's stolid profile, to find what an intense thrill it still gave him, what a delicious, voluptuous sensation, to feel himself weak and soft, where Tom was strong and hard!

Their way took them—John knew he ought to return to *his* office but he simply could not tear himself away from his friend —past some of the worst of the Glastonbury slums. These were altogether minor slums compared with those of any big city; but such as they were they were not a pretty sight. Here in these back alleys lived the failures in the merciless struggle of life. At this present moment many of the people who lived in these houses were men and women who would have found employment if Philip Crow's factories had been working full-time.

The sight of the two leisurely men, both of them absolutely sure of two more pleasant meals that day, and of good clean sheets and a quiet bedroom to sleep in, when that day was over, strolling past, did not enhance the peace of mind of such dwellers in "loop'd and windowed raggedness" as chanced to watch them go by.

They had scarcely got past this quarter when they were hailed from behind; and on turning round found Dave Spear hurrying after them. Dave's cheeks were less rosy than usual and there was a dangerous glint in his eye.

"Do you mind if I walk with you a step or two?" he gasped, panting a little, like a dog that has been overtaxed.

"I'm always glad to see you, Spear," said John. "You know Mr. Barter, of course?"

"Why I troubled you, Crow," said Dave, when he had nodded gravely at Tom Barter, and they had moved on together, "was that I've just been reading some of your circulars. They're very good, man. They're topnotch in their way, let me tell you! And I'm a connoisseur, being a Communist, of the art of propaganda."

"I'm glad you like 'em," said John, mightily pleased at this unexpected praise from so experienced an expert.

"But what I want you to do, what *we* want you to do"—it was not clear to John whether this "we" referred to Persephone or to the Bristol headquarters—"is to mention in your circulars that in addition to her *other* interests, your town here is going to try the experiment of running a municipal factory. You might mention it as an important experiment in the economic life of the town and suggest that visitors come to see it."

John's eyes gleamed with malicious delight at hearing these words.

"Certainly, certainly, certainly!" he cried eagerly. "I'll have what you say printed in my new set that I'm getting out next week."

"Would it be a philistine thing, Mr. Spear," put in Tom Barter in a casual and supercilious tone, "if I enquired *where* this municipal factory of yours *is*?"

"We'll have it in working order by the time Mr. Geard's visitors are really here. You'll know where it is *then*, Mr. Barter."

John looked a little glum at this remark.

"At first we *did* think of June the first," he said, "but we decided that it would be better to have more time to prepare. I'm in favour . . . for reasons of my own . . . of St. John's Day."

They came in sight of the factory where Barter's office was. There was a wooden gate leading to a narrow lane between high walls here, which was the access to his labours usually employed by this Norfolk manager of a Somerset mill.

The others leaned over this gate with him for a moment out of politeness; for he didn't wish them to come any further. There was a very wretched house adjoining this gate, an old house, probably built during the Wars of the Roses, for its stone buttresses and lintels still carried deeply cut Gothic foliations, and its crumbling walls were thick as those of a castle. But its rafters were rotting, its thatch dilapidated and full of holes, its broken panes stuffed with rags, and so many bricks were missing from the top of its chimney that one interior side, covered with black soot, was open to the air.

Out of the interior of this house there emerged at equal intervals a low moaning sound, a sound that had something in it that was peculiarly disconcerting.

"Hear that?" said Barter in a flat, toneless voice.

"Is anything wrong?" said John.

"Oh, no . . . all is in order," said Dave Spear. "I heard this noise the other night, Mr. Barter, when I was calling on the people round here. All is quite regular. No one is being tortured. Oh no! nothing is wrong. It's only an old woman who can't afford any comfort, dying of cancer. I can even tell you, gentlemen, her name. Her name is Tittie Petherton. She is not entirely unhappy, in spite of that sound; for her only fear is to die in the hospital. She'd be in the hospital now if the Vicar didn't pay someone to look after her. I've been in there. I've seen her. And though she can't help making that noise her mind is reasonably satisfied. She has no fear of death. All she fears is the hospital. Our good cousin Philip would have sent her there, too, if the Vicar hadn't come to her rescue. Oh, no, gentlemen, all is quite in order."

"Aren't you making rather too much of one sad case, Spear?" said Barter.

Dave Spear gripped the gate with both his hands and began to shake it. This proceeding arrested the full attention of John who was one who always took note of such manifestations of sudden feeling.

"Besides, my good Sir," Barter went on, "your Communistic State wouldn't prevent people from getting cancer."

A curious thing occurred then; . . . or at least to the insatiable nervous attention of John it was curious . . . for it was as if this short, broad-shouldered, sturdy, little man, without any overcoat, and in a neat, navy-blue suit of serge, spoke in a voice like the voice of a terrible prophet. John, for his part, never forgot that moment. He was himself standing close to his friend Barter. He even had his arm over Barter's shoulder and the smell of Barter's leather coat was in his nostrils. But what he kept his eyes upon, as he stood like that, was a broken corbel that must once have supported some kind of stone shaft, belonging perhaps to a vanished archway between this ruined house and another house. This disfigured fragment of stone came to resemble, as John gazed at it, a face whose eyes were at the end of its snout.

"Maybe it *was* a face once," he thought, "a gargoyle-face, deliberately carved by some mad workman in those old days to ease his mind of some frightful thing."

Every time that the moaning sound from the interior of the house came again, an invisible hand upon his twitching cheek seemed to turn his face towards the petrified snout, endowed with eyes.

"Come now, Spear, *that* really is going a bit too far!" were the words that lay, like a tedious meaningless scripture, upon the counter, so to speak, of Tom Barter's practical mouth. But he could not utter them in a convincing tone.

"Come now, Spear!" he began again. And then he flung out "Going a bit too far!" And then his voice could be heard in a sort of stage aside—"Now, Spear, *that* really *is* ——."

"The pleasure we get from chaos," Spear was saying, "is not a patch upon the pleasure we get in reducing chaos to order. Life will never be really pruned and clipped and trimmed, whatever we do to it. It will always brim over and escape us. The Communistic State is the only way that's ever been found for using *force* on the side of the weak. The whole system of human life depends on two things; on work and on pain. Communism takes our power of work and our power of bearing pain and, puts these two, like the immortal horses of Achilles, into the harness of the State. Politics are intolerable to all sensitive people. But why are they so? Because they don't touch the real quick, the real nerve, the real ganglia, of the situation! The situation is not political. It's economic. It isn't want of a Napoleon. It's want of a world-machine, run by impersonal force, on behalf of the Weak. When I say 'weak' I mean the poor and the children of the poor. Money is strength, power, comfort, leisure, thought, philosophy, art, health, liberty, freedom, faith, hope, peace, rest. Money is sleep. Money is love. Money is ease from pain. Those who deny this are lower than men or higher than men. They are rogues or madmen. They are liars or madmen. They are fools or madmen. Money is the blood of life. Life is created out of work and pain. Life is defended by force. The Communist State is the *organised force* of humanity. Evolution has been fumbling, groping, staggering, through blood, through tears, through torture, to this organising of human force to human ends. Evolution has created money and it has created the Communistic State to monopolise money. Money—the engine of life—is an engine of death when it is in the hands of individuals. Put it in the hands of the Communist State and whatever blunders are committed the whole situation is transformed! The individual has no more right to own money than he has to own earth, air, water, fire. We are all a herd of gibbering monkeys in a madhouse of inherited superstitions; and the maddest and wickedest of all these superstitions is the idea that private people have a right to be rich! *No one* has a right to be rich. It is crime to be rich. It is a perversion, an obscenity, a monstrosity. It is an offence against nature, against intelligence, against good taste. To be rich is to be a moral leper. To be rich is to be on the side of Cancer!"

"—a bit too far, Spear!" came the voice of Barter, like the sound of a rain-gutter dripping on a tin roof.

"I wish Mary could have heard that," thought John; and he found himself taking his arm from his friend's shoulder and feeling a certain nausea from the smell of the leather jacket.

His nerves were so much on edge at that moment, that, as Barter quietly unlatched the gate and let himself through, he burst out as if they had been alone:

"Don't forget, Tom, that, if you get fed up with Philip, Geard would willingly take you over. You've only to say the word! Only to say it, Tom!"

THE TWILIGHT OF THAT DAY HAD TURNED INTO DARKNESS BEFORE Tom Barter returned to his lodgings in High Street to wash his hands preparatory to his going out to supper. Tom very rarely had a chance to enjoy any tea. His diurnal relaxation was his mid-day dinner at the Pilgrims', which he relished with the appetite of a fox-hunter. The waitresses there, with every one of whom, especially with a girl called Clarissa Smith, he had a separate and complete understanding, rivalled each other in catering to his taste. Tom's taste was all for freshly cooked meats and substantial puddings. Any petticoat fluttering about these solid viands was sauce enough for him; and when he blew off the froth from the top of his pewter flagon of brown Taunton ale and followed with his eyes these buxom attendants, passing in and out of the old red-baize swing-door into the mediæval kitchen, a massive sensual satisfaction, worthy of any of those tall Vikings who grounded their keels at Wick, filled the veins of this short, broad-shouldered man.

Tom was no adventurer like his tyrant vagabond-friend John. He was no devil-may-care swashbuckler like my lord's bastard. He would have made a first-rate sergeant-major of a regiment, a first-rate boatswain of a ship. Something . . . a certain pride, a certain fling, a certain chivalrous magnanimity . . . had been knocked out of him forever by those bullies in Gladman's House at Sherborne. They had found Tom Barter a frank gentleman—they had left him a secretive cad. It was only with John, whose friendship antedated those Sherborne days, that this reserved man let himself go; only with John and with any petticoat of the lower classes!

How often had he stared into the bottom of his pewter-pot, where a little brown liquid made a fairy moat around the bubbles of white froth! "I have not got a soul in the world that really cares," he would think then, "except John; and he's nothing much to rely on!" and then he would sigh, put his finger and thumb into his waistcoat pocket, where he kept his silver, and

place a sixpence beside his plate. Aye! but how he did sympathise with these working-girls: Oh, what kind, sweet creatures!
Oh, what pretty ways of making a man feel that he was a man!

As he entered his comfortless room at the top of a saddler's
shop, and poured out the water from the bare white jug and
selected the thin little bit of Pear's soap, which he had been
using for a fortnight, rather than the big new square yellow
piece, with such hard edges, that his landlady had put there this
morning, it came over him that he really was leading rather a
desolate sort of life. "But if I can get Tossie Stickles to undress
for me somewhere or other, or even to let me play with her in
one of those spinneys beyond Bushey Combe, it'll make up for
a lot! It's certain that if I were married and had a nice fireside
and my books and a garden, I couldn't enjoy myself with these
girls any more. And they are so sweet and unexacting! Oh,
they're so different from these finicking bitches who think themselves ladies!"

He ran down the stairs and out into the street. The remainder
of the hours from now on, till he was asleep in his chilly room
above the saddler's, seemed invariably to fall below the average
of normal human experience. The day did not become actually
miserable, but it was far from gathering any glow or lustre as
it waned. It was just a day dying out; of no more interest, of
no more importance, than a bonfire of cabbage stalks, over
which someone has thrown a bucket of water.

The bruise in his nature never hurt him except when confronted by a man or by a woman of his own class. It was this
bruise which Mary, all unwitting, must have struck again and
again. It was because of this bruise that he had never dared,
in the whole course of their platonic friendship, to attempt to
make love to Mary or even to kiss her. "Will you marry me?"
he had blurted out one day, on the side of Tor Hill, and Mary
—reacting from her morbid slavery to Miss Drew—had murmured a reluctant "Yes, if you want me to, Tom!"

Once in the street today, Barter made his way, as usual, not
to the cheerful tea-shop in George Street, where John and Evans
had had lunch, nor to the one presided over by Sally's mother
in High Street, but to a common little restaurant called the

Abbey Café where a waitress whose name was Joan brought him a plate of fish and potato chips. This overworked attendant resembled that Joan in the song, "While greasy Joan doth keel the pot," and no other educated man in Somersetshire would have flirted with her as Barter did. But it was but a poor pleasure he got from this—indeed, night after night he would swallow his ill-chosen supper and answer the wench in sulky monosyllables while he stayed on and on; merely putting off the moment when he had to face the sight of his cold bed, his portmanteau on the floor, and the picture of Tel-El-Kebir over his fireless grate. Tonight, he managed, by his extraordinary power of sympathy with the economic side of a waitress' life, to put off his moment of rising from that hard seat at that dirty tablecloth till nearly nine o'clock.

Again in the lighted street, he was seized with a sudden loathing for that wretched bedroom of his, and something like a spasm of bitter distaste for his whole life in Glastonbury.

"I'll go and see Mary," he thought. And then he thought, "What's the use?" But when he came opposite the darkened windows of the saddler's and heard, through the open side door, the sound of his landlady's voice scolding her husband, his feet began automatically taking him to the Abbey House.

When Lily Rogers opened the door to his ring, she smiled more pleasantly upon him than she would have done upon any other surprise-visitor at that late hour. Barter had long been the chief favorite, out of all the gentlemen in Glastonbury, with Miss Drew's servants, just as he was a great *persona grata* with Miss Drew herself.

"We've got company in the drawing-room," Lily said. "Mr. Dekker has brought that man Geard here, to see Miss Drew. She never would have seen him if the Vicar hadn't told her it was her duty. They're all in there now! Would you prefer that I called Miss Crow out, Sir, and brought the lamp into the dining-room?"

Barter nodded; but seemed in no hurry to dismiss Lily, who, in the dim hall-light and in her black dress and white apron, looked a sweet picture of domestic security.

"How's Louie?" he asked. "Have you been up to The Elms

lately?" he asked. "You two had such pretty hats on last Sunday," he said. "One day I must take you up in the air with me," he said. "Would Louie be frightened?" he asked.

It was with a rosy spot in each of her soft cheeks that the girl finally escaped, and with the utmost discretion ushered Mary into the dining-room, lit the candles there, and closed the door softly upon them. Once back in the kitchen with Louie, she burst out:

"It's that nice-looking Mr. Barter, I declare, that Miss Mary ought to marry! What's the use of her keeping company and acting soft with a queer one like that Mr. Crow? Mr. Barter is a real gentleman, he is. She's gone to him now—don't make such a noise, Lou! Maybe if you stopped gollumping round on those creaky shoes we could hear them talk in there."

The sisters Rogers advanced into the passage and stood listening. Not otherwise might a pair of white doves, perched upon a roof, have watched their young lady's casement close tight behind an adventurous gallant. Lily had forgotten, in her appreciation of the sly Barter, to fetch the lamp she had referred to, so it was by no brighter light than that of two tall silver candles standing between several vases of daffodils, that the two natives of Norfolk exchanged their confidences over the dying fire. Barter sat in the faded leather arm-chair of Miss Drew's father, while Mary crouched on the rug at his feet.

The girl was sadder than usual that night. She spread out her strong hands over the fading coals and lifted her chin towards the figure of the man in the arm-chair. The flickering glow irradiated her dusky hair, touched the sad circles under her grey eyes, fell upon her parted lips and made her white teeth shine.

"No, she isn't as pretty as she was," thought Barter and a shameless comparison between what it would be like to have Mary "between him and the wall" and Lily Rogers, passed through his mind.

"My goodness!" he thought. "But I suppose Lily would be like a cold flower-stalk; whereas this girl ——"

"I've come to think I'm one of the biggest fools in town," he remarked.

"Why, Tom?" she murmured wearily.

"I was an ass not to rush you off, Mary, and get married before old John turned up! You'd have had your friend Tom, wouldn't you, you lovely creature?"

"What's wrong with you, Tom?" she asked abruptly. He looked at her sharply.

"Nothing," he said, "what are you talking about? Nothing's wrong with me."

"When I think of your life sometimes," she said, "between the office and that awful room of yours, I can hardly bear it." This she said gravely and intensely, looking in his face; and every syllable of it was true; for this man had become like a brother and more than a brother to her; and yet, as she looked at him now, in that familiar, grey office suit, actually wearing a purple tie she had chosen for him at Wollop's, when John was no more than a name, she could have found in her heart to wish that she had never seen him; never known that such a person as Tom Barter was in the world. It was an odd feeling to look up at him now, sitting there so easy and natural in old Mr. Drew's leather chair, and say to herself—"There's the man who couldn't bring himself to marry me!"

He had been, all along, a fatal apparition in her life. Yes, he was an unconscious nemesis; although their relations had been so innocent.

She remembered an occasion at Thorpe, near Norwich, when, sitting with her mother by the river bank watching a barge go by, the older woman had suddenly said, "You're a deep nature, Mary. Your danger won't come from any little ripples on the tide of your life. It will come from large things bearing down— like that barge."

This man sitting there opposite her now was just like that barge on their native river, which her mother had noticed, coming so strongly and massively forward with the tide.

"It's no good hiding it from each other, Tom," she began now, "we old friends had better be frank with each other. Neither of us are happy in our life. You're sick to death of running Philip's business for him and flying his plane for him. You long to be on your own; to whistle Philip and his affairs down the wind and be your own master. I'm bored to death by Miss Drew and everything in this house. Sometimes I think of leaving John and all the rest of them here, and of getting a place somewhere else. Glastonbury doesn't suit me any better than it suits you; though I *have*, I confess, come to like these ruins a *little* better than we did at the beginning. Do you remember how we hated it all, Tom?"

Her eyes shone so strangely now as she looked up at him, that the wild idea came into Barter's head that if he pressed her in one grand *coup* she might even, out of pique for John's neglect, throw John over and allow herself to be carried off by him, carried back to Norfolk perhaps, if he dared to chance it!

"No," she went on, "no, old friend. You and I are both pretty miserable, this fine Spring! Come, confess to me, Tom, wasn't it because you were feeling lonely that you came to me tonight? I'm feeling lonely myself, to tell you the truth, and it does me good to see your solid, old Norfolk face in this weird place. What would we not give, Tom, you and I, for a breath of real east wind, coming up sharp and salt from the North Sea?"

His face had something about it at this moment so like the face of a reticent school-boy who wants to cry but is ashamed to cry, that, moved by an impulse that surprised herself, she scrambled to her feet and coming up to him sat down on the arm of his leather chair, placing her hand lightly on his shoulder to balance herself, and smiling sadly down upon him.

"A breath from the East Coast is what *we* want, Tom, old friend! Am I not right? This holy earth with its hundreds of saints and its scores of kings is a bit sickly to us sometimes, isn't it? That arch-conjurer Geard has got such a hold on John, that he doesn't seem to feel the oppression, does he? He's got John as fast as he got our grandfather. He's in there now—Lily told you, I expect? Even Miss Drew treats him with—with —— But I don't like him. There's something about him that makes me feel shivery and funny—as if he were a great toad. Poor old Tom. This isn't a very nice world, is it?"

She did a thing then that astonished herself as much as it astonished the object of her gesture—she lightly touched the man's forehead with the tips of her firm fingers, pushing back his stubbly hair. He made a sort of fumbling movement to take possession of this friendly hand; but the girl slipped quickly then off his chair's arm, and went over to the mantelpiece against which she leaned her elbow.

"John is fonder of you in one way than he'll ever be of me—even if we *were* married," she said gravely.

Barter thought he had never seen grey eyes look so large and dark and appealing as hers looked now.

"She's getting at me, to make it up between *them*," he thought; and the idea that all this kindness in her tone was just to cajole him, made something grow rough as a peat-brick beneath his ribs.

"What the deuce are you talking about, Mary?" he said sulkily, rubbing his face with both his hands as an angry, independent, proud boy might do, who had been kissed by a woman who was attempting to play the mother over him.

"You're not such a fool," she said, "as not to know that he's desperately fond of you?"

"Oh, old John's all right," he muttered awkwardly, thinking in his mind, "This is the worst of these clever women. They're always probing people with what they call psychological questions. I'll never come and see her again! I'll take Tossie Stickles out to Bushey Combe tomorrow night. It's no use! I ought to have known it was no use coming to her. She only wants to play some game with me to get at John—John'll be helpless in her hands if she *does* get hold of him."

Her next question made him jerk up his back very straight in the leather chair and draw his eyebrows together till they made a continuous line across his brow.

"What made you think you liked me enough to want to marry me, Tom?"

He looked first to the right of her dark-flashing eyes and white cheeks and then to the left. His expression at that moment so exactly resembled that of a great Newfoundland dog, whom she had troubled with her gaze, that she smiled at him with renewed sweetness.

"You're a dear, Tom; do you know it?" she said, taking her elbow off the chimney-piece. "I like you a lot better than you ever liked me. I could have made you happy, Tom, if I'd married you; a good deal happier, I'm afraid, than I'll ever make *him*. And yet, my dear, I'd see you dead in your coffin . . . if . . . if . . . if I could pluck out of you . . . whatever it is"—her heavy, lower lip began trembling a little—"whatever it is that John likes in you so much more than ——"

She bit her lip and lifting her head back, stretched out her arms, clenching her hands.

"Oh, dear, it's a business, isn't it, old Tom, this affair of being alive?"

She let her arms drop to her sides with a sigh that heaved through her whole body. Tom Barter rose slowly to his feet. He felt now that he had wronged her with his vulgar suspicions. After all, she was laying bare her heart to him. She was a good, honest Norfolk girl. Perhaps what she said *was* true. Perhaps she *could* have made him happy.

He moved up close to her. She could see by his eyes that he was going to touch her.

"No, no! No, no!" she murmured. "You and I are too old for *that*, Tom. Listen, my dear! Why don't you do what John is always talking to me about? Why don't you chuck Philip and work with John for a bit? That man wants you; you know he does. He'd jump out of his skin to have you with him!"

They stared at each other with a long, puzzled stare, after these words had left her lips. Both of them, with an unconscious movement, glanced towards the door. Mary had not had the least idea that she was going to suggest what she had just suggested. It was as if the presence of Mr. Geard under the same roof had confused her wits.

"No! Of course you can't leave Philip," she said hurriedly. "It's your work; I know—and there's your plane too. I can't think what made me say that, just then —— It was only . . . it was only . . . Oh, I feel that both you and I, Tom, want something to change . . . something to go to smash in our life; so that we can start again. Isn't that true? But, you needn't speak. I know too well it's true!"

They looked at each other then with another of their long, heavy-eyed, puzzled, unyielding. East-Anglian looks, those old heathen, sullen looks, full of the obduracy of rooted poplars in driving sleet.

They each needed something from the other—something which, in all the world, that other alone could give—but between them there seemed to emerge, emanating like a monstrous offspring from their sterile psychic embraces, a huge, dark *obstacle*, not to be overstepped.

Mary had come out of that room, where the presence of Mr. Geard was so odious to her, and where the whole aura reeked of these Glastonbury morbidities; she had come out with a reckless urge of forlorn hope to get some help from Tom.

He had come from his wretched vigil in that café, at a desperate run and with a blind leap, like a frantic prisoner catching at one chance in a thousand, to get he knew not what from this Norfolk girl. But, their mutual plunge ended here . . . they both knew it . . . ended here with this long, sullen, helpless look . . . ended here with the same baffled frustration with which their friendship had always ended, when it tried to break away from the impeding limits set by the fatality of their own characters!

"Can I get out of here?" he said, when his eyes had drawn up the great empty plummet-net he had let down from the unanswering depths of her eyes, "Out of this place, without meeting anyone?"

She gave a quick sigh as if aroused by his words from a trance that was obscurely baffling into a reality that was labour and struggle.

"Of course, Tom," she said. "Come this way! I'll let you out through the back."

She blew out the two candles on the table and with his nostrils full of the sour taste of carbonic-acid gas he followed her to the door. There was one moment, as she touched the door-handle by the dying flicker of the fire, that he felt a longing . . . not sensual nor passionate, but simply sad and love-starved . . . to clasp her well-known form in his arms. But he did not dare. The moment perished forever in the white smoke of those two tall candles, and he followed her on tip-toe through the dim-lighted hall. He was not unaware of the irony of his passing now, with only a silent nod and a casual glance, those two pretty figures seated at the kitchen-table enjoying their supper. Purged he surely was, at that moment, of his wonted lechery!

Mary opened the door into the garden and shivering a little, for she had forgotten to put on any wrap, led him, across the daffodil-bed and the fading crocuses, to the edge of King Edgar's Lawn.

Here she gave him her hand and let him squeeze it in his strong air-pilot's fingers, till it tingled and smarted.

"You know that place in the wall," she called out softly after him, "where it's easy to climb?"

He made no answer. He only turned and lifted his hand to his head, saluting her thus as he would have saluted some superior officer if he had been . . . what would have suited him so well to be! . . . the careful sergeant-major of a garrison of besieged soldiers.

She watched his short sturdy figure, after that, as it vanished with never another look round.

A tide of inexpressible sadness flowed through her heart. Tom was gone; and she had got scant comfort from him—and Tom was gone; back to his wretched quarters in High Street! Or would his lonely, unsatisfied mood put into his stubborn head to drift on, past his own door, to that cheerful Northload room, which was her own prepared bridal-chamber?

She glanced up at the great broken tower-columns of the vanished nave of the Abbey Church. Would other girls, all the way down the centuries, she thought, look up at those two stupendous pillars and fill the space between them, in their sad imagination, with the high carved arch full of wafted incense and choir-echoes and deep-voiced prayers? What had she hoped to get from Tom, or he from her? Neither of them had seemed to know! It had all ended anyway, just as so many of their old encounters had done, in a sense of weary frustration.

Ruins! Ruins! It was not only in ancient stone that baffled human hopes held up their broken outlines, their sad skeleton-patterns, as resting places for the birds of the night! She was on the point of turning, of retracing her steps across the dark flower-beds where fading crocuses and new-sprouting tulips drank in, in silent long-breath'd draughts, the secret influences of the darkness, when she was suddenly caught up, completely caught up, out of herself, as she never in her life had been before by any natural power.

There, very low down in the western sky, about a couple of yards, according to human measurement, above the bounding wall of the enclosure, was the coracle-like crystal shell of the crescent moon in her first quarter.

There was nothing to which it could be compared! Unique, in all the universe of matter, if only by reason of the associations hung about it of twenty-five thousand years of human yearning, it floated there before her, daughter and darling of the dark terrestrial orb, elf-waif of the infinite night! What hands, what arms, had stretched forth to it, out of their human misery—brown arms, white arms, black arms—what heart-cries, "I want! I want! I want!" had been tossed up towards it, from groaning hairy chests and soft-swelling tender breasts and the troubled nerves of bewildered children! And ever, and especially, had it been the comforter and the accomplice, and the confederate of women, gathering their life-streams towards itself, guarding their mystic chastity, nourishing their withdrawals, their reticences, their furtive retreats and denials, companioning them when all else failed!

It would draw the vast, bottomless salt tides towards it—this slender night-waif, this leaf of tender sorrow, this filmy weft of hope against hope—ere it had rounded to its full! Shoals of glittering fins would follow its pathway across the Atlantic . . . on far-off untraversed moorlands its reflection would turn the ripples to silver. In pools where even the wild geese in their equinoctial migrations, never disturbed the silence, its frail image would rock among the reeds. On no different, on no changed a shape from this, upon which she now gazed and trembled, the great magicians of antiquity had stared and muttered; their predictions confounded, their inspirations perverted, their wits turned! Here floated the virgin-mistress of the tragic madness of maids, the patroness of all defiers of man's laws! Here was the girl-child from the dim shores of ancient anarchy, at whose bright and horned head the kings and the priests of man-made tradition have always shivered and quaked in their sacred sandals! She has

been the tutelary mistress of all sterile passions, of all wild re-
volts against "the Mothers," that have led the virgins of prophecy
to shatter this world's laws. That shapeless conch of dangerous
whiteness, tossing herself, through the scudding drifts of ship-
swallowing seas, rocking like a sea-mew in the rigging of doomed
ships, gleaming in the cold dews of uncounted dawns upon
blood-stained Golgothas and lost battlefields, and now shining
down, calm and lovely, upon hillside fairy-rings and upon
smooth, wide-stretching, glittering sands, has always been the
forlorn hope of the impossible; has always been the immortal
challenge to What Is, from the wavering margins of What
Might Be!

The popular opinion that the moon is a planetary fragment,
broken off from the earth or from the sun, is probably a gross
and clumsily conceived error! Much more likely is it that she
is the last-remaining fragment of some earlier stellar system, a
system of material forms and shapes now altogether lost, but in
its origin nearer to the beginning of things in the ambiguous
imaginings of the Primal Cause.

Surely, not only in the Religions of *this* planet has she played
a dominant and inextinguishable rôle. But she has always been
on the side of the weak and the sick against the strong and the
well-constituted! With her silvery horns of Mystery gathered in
the folds of that blue robe or bearing up those divine feet of the
Maid-Mother of the Crucified she has challenged the whole
authoritative reign of Cause-and-Effect itself. And it was this
whiteness beyond all whiteness; it was this whiteness, like the
wet curves of unimaginable sea-shells and like the spray about
the prows of fairy ships, that now came with its magical touch
to bring healing to Mary Crow.

The girl stood transfixed on the chilly edge of that bed of
cold, pale-leafed immature tulips. She stared and stared at the
celestial visitant, as if she had never before seen the moon,
under any sky.

"What does it make me feel?" she thought. "Is there something
about it that every woman who has ever lived in Glastonbury
must feel? Something that the Lake Village women felt? Something that immured, mediæval nuns were comforted by?"

Her body as well as her spirit fell now into a wordless prayer to that white, floating, immortal creature. "Bury, oh, bury your strange secret in my breast!" the girl's heart cried out. "Bury it deep, deep in my womb, so that henceforth to the end of my days, something cold and free and uncaught may make me strong!"

As soon as Mat Dekker and Mr. Geard were out of the house, the former explained to the latter that he had an important visit to make that night before he retired, "to a woman dying of cancer near the Crow factory."

Mr. Geard seemed, in spite of this information, very reluctant to part from the Vicar of Glastonbury. He proposed to Mr. Dekker that they should stroll up Chilkwell Street together and take a glance in the darkness at Chalice House. "I'd like to know what you think, Vicar," he said, in his thick, unctuous voice, "about my scheme for altering the old place. If I don't buy it it may fall into the hands of the Papists again. And yet they're asking a fancy price. Just come and take a look, won't you, Sir?"

Mat Dekker permitted himself to be led past the Tithe Barn and up Chilkwell Street.

"What I had in my mind," said Mr. Geard, in a self-satisfied voice, when they had skirted the high blank wall of Chalice House and had reached the particular garden hedge beyond which lay the Sacred Fount, "was to build a wall here that would be worthy of *the Blood*." He uttered this last word in a casual, matter-of-fact way, as if he had said, "worthy of the view" or "worthy of our age," and a certain flavor of unctuous gusto in his tone was especially repellent to Mat Dekker.

"With an entrance, I suppose?" said this latter.

But it now transpired that Mr. Geard had not considered an entrance. What he had been thinking about was guarding, protecting, defending, consecrating "the Blood," as he called this chalybeate spring. He had been so preoccupied in keeping sacrilege out, that he had not considered how to bring devotion in.

Mat Dekker as a professional priest naturally had his flock in mind. "You won't charge any entrance-fee, I hope?" he went on. "Since the place has been empty the caretaker has been taking tips; but I don't like that at all. Everybody ought to be free to drink of this water!"

Mr. Geard approached the thick hedge; and ascending the little bank below it plunged his arms and his face into the early spring freshness—the hedge exhaled a delicate fragrance as he touched it; a fragrance that flowed out into the darkness on all sides.

"No—no," said Bloody Johnny, stepping back into the road, "I'll have a Saxon arch and a heavy door with a bell inside—a loud bell—with a rope hanging down."

"Why a Saxon arch?" remarked Mr. Dekker. "I don't think there *were* any Saxon arches—wasn't it the Normans who——"

"Brought the Devil with 'em," cried Mr. Geard, "and the Devil's gentlemen! No, no. There's going to be one Saxon arch at any rate in Glastonbury. Our oldest charter is a Saxon Charter. Our oldest real Abbots are Saxon Abbots. Our oldest real kings are Saxon kings. If King Arthur comes back—as my wife's cousin says he will—he'll have to ring my Saxon bell in my Saxon wall. My own folk haven't one drop—not one drop—of gentlemen's blood. I'm going to give back Chalice Well to the People, Mr. Dekker!"

The man's hoarse voice had risen to that rich, rolling tone of rhetorical unction that the Glastonbury street corners had come to know so well before he went away to Norfolk.

"Give back Chalice Well to the People," sounded over and over again in Mr. Dekker's ears, as the two men retraced their steps. Outside the Vicarage gate they stopped to say good-night to each other. They instinctively turned round, as they did so, to catch a glimpse of the tall elms growing in the Abbey enclosure between the boundary wall and those foundations of the Chapel of King Edgar that had been discovered by supernatural aid.

The new moon had long ago gone down but the sky was clear; and over their heads stretched the long, faint, whitish track of the Milky Way.

Geard snuffed the night air like a great sick ox, that had been kept too long in its winter-stall. As Mat Dekker looked at him now he got an impression of a reserve of power—of some kind of power—that was actually startling.

"This Religious Fair of mine," said Mr. Geard, "will be some-

thing quite different from the Oberammergau Passion Play. Mr.
John Crow, who, by the way, is a most intelligent young man,"
(Mat Dekker smiled in the darkness at this) "with a good deal
more religion than he thinks he has—has received so many re-
plies from all over the world, that I really think this occasion
is going to be quite an important one in the history of our
country."

"That's just what I wanted to know, Sir," said Mat Dekker—
"only I mustn't keep you now; and my son, if he has come in,
will wonder where I am, but I did want to know what your real
inmost purpose was. Of course, if you don't care to speak of
such things, I would not press you; but I'd be happier if I knew
what was really in your mind. But won't you come in for a minute, Mr. Geard? Please do! We can talk quietly in my little
museum—if my son *is* at home, I know he'll be delighted to see
you; for he has heard so much about you. Indeed, he told me
he had been to tea with you. Your second daughter . . . she *is*
your second, isn't she? . . . has been a great help to us, quite
often, in so many ways. Do come in, Mr. Geard. I've got to go
out later to see that woman with cancer; but I told her nurse not
to come for me till late, so that she would know if the poor thing
was going to get any sleep tonight. Please come in now anyway."

The ex-preacher of the gospel hesitated for a moment.

"I don't want to intrude," he murmured; but Mat Dekker swept
this aside.

"It *is* really important, Sir," he said emphatically, taking the
other by the arm, "that I should hear everything about your
scheme. I may be of use to you; more use to you than you
realise."

Bloody Johnny permitted himself to be persuaded; and soon
found himself seated in a comfortable wicker chair by a warm
fire in what the father and son called their "museum." The door
of this chamber having been left ajar, the legatee of Canon
Crow was enabled to listen to a rather singular conversation in
the kitchen-passage.

"Master Sam ain't come in," he heard the voice of Penny
Pitches saying, "and Weatherwax were in kitchen just now with
a tale of having talked wi' gamekeeper's young man from West

Pennard, come in for pheasant-feed, or summat o' that, and
Weatherwax said 'a told 'un that 'a seed our Sam walking across
Hearty Moor like as the Deil were arter he. 'Twas Tommy Blake,
the young man were, what used to live down Bere Lane, so he
know'd our Sam as 'twere his own kin; and ye do know, thee
wone self, Master, what be beyond Hearty! Whitelake River be
beyond Hearty; where thik Missy Zoyland do live. And so, I
reckon our Sam be gone to see she; gone to see she while she's
old man be out to Wookey Hole."

"He may have been walking in that direction, Penny, without
going to that house."

Mr. Geard uncrossed his legs and purposely made his chair
creak by shifting his position in it. One of the grand secrets of
the man's magnetic power was that he forced himself to see nothing, to hear nothing, to think nothing of other people's affairs.

"Direction be shot!" cried the old woman. "Young men will
do it, an' they come to 't! Direction, say ye? He'll direction her,
and direct her too; don't 'ee make no mistake, Master."

"Well, I hope she'll give him a good supper anyway, Penny,"
threw out Mat Dekker, with a forced smile.

"Don't lock the front door, Penny, when you go to bed," he
went on, "and will you bring me some brandy into the museum,
the very best, you know, one of those bottles you hid from
Weatherwax last Christmas?"

He returned to his guest and sat down opposite him. He too
had a very creaky wicker chair; and for a little time, while Penny
waited on them, in sulky silence, there was nothing audible in
that ramshackle room but the creaking of those two chairs under
their heavy bodies.

Mat Dekker's mind was away at Whitelake Cottage. A spasm
of unreasoning anger against his son kept surging up in the
depths of his being and a wild imaginary dialogue between himself and Nell Zoyland began incoherently to shape itself on the
tongue of his hidden soul—"She turned to me," he kept thinking, "she turned to me in her trouble. She looked at me more
than at either of them. She would do exactly what I told her.
She said as much as that with her eyes." The dangerous hidden
waters in this man's rock-rooted Quantock nature began now to

toss and foam and churn, as he thought of Sam and his sweet adulteress.

Mat Dekker repeated to himself now what his old flame, Elizabeth Crow, had said, as he looked at Mr. Geard's greenish-black trousers—"I believe you are in love with that girl yourself." A dusky flush of anger came into his ruddy cheeks as he recalled this. But if it was all nonsense, why did the thought "Sam will probably sleep with her tonight" cause him such singular perturbation? Not because of any moral distress about Sam behaving badly. Mat had absolutely nothing in him of the congenital Puritan; and his long association with birds and beasts and reptiles had given him a very natural and earthy attitude towards erotic emotion—nor had he any particular concern about William Zoyland's feelings! He had always regarded Lord P.'s bastard as something of a ruffian and a bully. Secretly in his heart he was rather proud of Sam for having been able to steal away a girl's heart from a handsome rogue like that.

It may be well imagined that with all these stirrings and upheavings going on in his mind it was very hard for Mat to give any concentrated attention to Mr. Geard and what the bar-rooms of the town called Bloody Johnny's Midsummer Kick-up.

Mr. Geard was not one to miss the preoccupation of his host; but such was his nature that it caused him no particular annoyance. He enjoyed the Vicar's brandy; and kept re-filling his glass and sipping its contents with a quiet relish, while he talked on and on, apparently quite as much for his own edification as for that of his abstracted hearer. His eyes, as he talked, kept wandering about the room, which was more like the play-room of a whole family of young naturalists than a theologian's study, though on one side of the apartment there was a large gloomy bookcase full of standard Anglican works.

What arrested Mr. Geard's attention most was an enormous aquarium standing on a bench in the middle of the room. There was a lamp, not far from this object, on a table littered with magazines, and the light from this, falling on one side of the aquarium, made an illuminated segment of bright water through which some very energetic and very large minnows kept darting and hovering. These lively fish, circumscribed in a luminous void, associated themselves very vividly with what Bloody Johnny was feeling as he rambled on. "Someone must make the start," he was saying, "and why should not I? Life advances by leaps and bounds, and so does Religion. There's no doubt that this is the moment for something drastic . . . for something"—he hesitated for a word, while a soft-mottled loach, lifting its white belly from the gravel at the bottom of the aquarium, pressed an open mouth against the illuminated glass side of the vessel and fixed upon this singular Prophet a cold fish-eye—"for something . . . *miraculous.* There are only about half a dozen reservoirs of world-magic on the whole surface of the globe—Jerusalem . . . Rome . . . Mecca . . . Lhassa—and of these Glastonbury has the largest residue of unused power. Generations of mankind, æons of past races, have—by their concentrated will—made Glastonbury miraculous. But since the time of that incredible fool, Henry the Eighth, the magic of Glastonbury has been unused."

Bloody Johnny permitted his host to re-fill his glass. The bottle was two-thirds empty already. Here was an unexpected rival for poor Mr. Weatherwax! The lower the liquor sank in the bottle, the less water did the visitor mix with it. And the more he drank the more metaphysical he became. Mat Dekker kept replenishing his own pipe from an earthenware jar of Craven Mixture which stood between the lamp and the aquarium. There were no other sources of light in this study-museum beyond the fire and this one lamp, and the two men's massive physiognomies were lit up by this two-fold radiation in a manner that would have delighted any connoisseur in the mystery of lines and contours, of plane surfaces and carved-out hollows. Bloody Johnny did not, apparently, make use of tobacco in any form. This was one of those Nonconformist traits in his curious character that a little disconcerted his host. The brandy-drinking, however, carried to such a surprising length, and producing no sign of tipsiness, was a considerable comfort to the priest's Quantock-bred mind. If only the fellow had smoked too! But with these queer chaps one couldn't have everything. If the man had neither smoked *nor* drank the priest-naturalist would have experienced a positive *physical* distaste for this alien presence in his museum. He would have

snuffed the air suspiciously, like a hound who smells a weasel
in place of a fox.

"Why shouldn't the Lord have chosen me," Mr. Geard was
now saying, as he leaned forward in his wicker chair, hugging
his legs and wagging his hydrocephalic head, "to bring back an
Age of Faith to our Western World? The way I am doing it
will seem heresy to some, blasphemy to others, pure hocus-pocus
to most. But that's exactly, my dear, what all new out-spurts of
the Real Presence have seemed. Do 'ee think anyone can put a
stopper on me?"

Mat Dekker had never, since Sam's mother's death, been called
"my dear" by any living soul; but it was such a quaint word
for the man to use just then, at such a moment, this word
"stopper," that he looked at him with something like real respect.
The chap *could not* be a humbug! No humbug would say "put a
stopper on me."

Mat Dekker now began scrutinising his guest's great bowed
head as Bloody Johnny grew somnolent, and the way his huge,
plump, clenched fist lay on the rough little garden-table by the
edge of his bottle and glass. "There's the head of a heretic," he
thought. "No doubt the great Marcion, with his skull full of
spiritual errors, had a head like that. *But it's all wrong!* Christ
has chosen to reveal Himself through the traditions of His
Church, and in no other way. When the Church's authority is
undermined life falls back into chaos . . . into the blind grop-
ings of Matter or at least of Nature."

"The Lord . . . has . . . filled me . . ." rumbled Bloody
Johnny again in his hoarse voice, "with the power of His spirit,
my dear, and nothing can stop me from doing His will! I feel
His will pouring through me, my dear, by night and by day.
Let the glory go to whom He pleases! I am but a reed, a miserable pipe, a wretched conduit, a contemptible sluice. But never
mind what I am! Through me, at this moment of time, the
Eternal is breaking through. Yes, dear, *dear* Sir, for I admire 'ee
and respect 'ee, it's breaking through! I'm going to make Glastonbury the centre of the Religion of all the West. I feel it in
me, this power; I feel it, dear, *dear* Mr. Dekker, and nothing
can stop me, *nothing!*" He lifted his heavy fist and emptied the

remainder of the bottle into his glass, and tossed it, this time
without one drop of water, down his capacious throat. After
this, the man's chin sank down again upon his chest and his host
had time to abandon himself in peace once more to his troubled
thoughts.

Mat Dekker, noticing at last that his guest's eyes had actually
closed, brought out his great old-fashioned watch with its blue
enamelled back and looked at it with puckered brows. A deep
sigh came from his heart as he replaced this timepiece, for he
had seen the little hand approaching eleven and the big hand
approaching ten. Ten minutes to eleven—and Sam not back. He
must be staying with her, sleeping with her. His hands, old
clumsy Sam's rough hands, the hands that had hammered together the little garden-table on which that empty bottle rested,
must be now caressing her naked satiny limbs. Mat Dekker's
face positively contorted itself with suffering as this image or
rather as this imaginative projection of his own feelings into
those of his son's, went on dominating his senses. . . . Suddenly
there was a loud ring at the front-door bell. Mat Dekker started
up upon his feet. John Geard jerked up his head, and pushing
away the empty bottle with the back of his knuckles, gathered himself together to face whatever new incursion into the museum
this sound portended. The clatter of Penny Pitches' heavy shoes
came echoing down the passage.

"Is it your son?" broke in Mr. Geard, but the priest shook his
head.

"He'd never ring," he murmured. "The door's always———"

His voice was lost in the noisy opening of the front door
while an alarming colloquy, overheard by both of the men, began to take place on the doorstep. "She can't abide the pain one
hour longer, and Doctor said she couldn't 'ave no more morphia
till he comes tomorrow. I've run near all the way, for I can't
bear leaving the pore thing like as she is. She be crazy with pain,
and that's the truth."

Mat Dekker was out into the hall now; and Mr. Geard, his
deserted chair creaking like an anxious goblin, was in the museum
doorway. "This is Nurse Robinson. She is a niece of our Mrs.
Robinson whom I expect you know. *Nancy*, I call her," said Mr.

Dekker; and, as Penny Pitches retreated down the passage to her own domain, the nurse and Mr. Geard shook hands. The new-comer was certainly more like a "Nancy" than like a nurse. A red-faced lusty creature she appeared, when she threw back her hood, but her face betrayed a natural agitation at this moment that was more humane than it was professional. "But this is out-rageous!" cried Mr. Dekker; and by the light of the hall-lamp, hanging from the ceiling, Geard could see a vein in the priest's forehead swell and swell, till it resembled a little thin snake beneath his skin. "This is unbearable! Have you called the doctor up? Have you talked to him?"

Nurse Robinson nodded. " 'Ee says 'tis the law," she responded. " 'Ee says Hi've 'a given 'er already more'n the law allows. 'Ee says if the chemist gave me more for 'er till hate tomorrow, I should be 'eld responsible if anythink 'appened."

"You must excuse me, Mr. Geard," cried Mat Dekker, snatch-ing his coat and hat from a peg. "I'll come straight with you to the doctor's, Nancy, and stir him up. I'll take the responsibility myself. It's outrageous. It's intolerable. *Penny!*" The square servant advanced down the passage at her master's summons. "Don't go to bed till Mr. Sam comes in, Penny, and keep some-thing hot for his supper. He may have been walking miles and miles."

"*We* do know where he have been walking!" grumbled Penny. "*I'll* stay up for he, right and certain, Master, and when he comes in, it'll go hard but I'll give he a piece of me mind, gal-lumping over they girt moors, to the disturbance of our decent house—and all because of a whey-faced missy what's another man's wife!"

"Hush! Hush, Penny!" commanded her master, nodding to-wards Mr. Geard to indicate that they were not alone. "Help the gentleman into his coat, Penny, can't you? Our way lies in the same direction, doesn't it, Sir?" he went on. "Ready, Nurse? You've got your breath again? That poor woman . . . left alone in positive torture . . . Perhaps you'd prefer to walk more slowly, Mr. Geard? But Nurse and I *must* hurry on!"

Bloody Johnny proved himself able to walk quite as fast as his companions, though it is true he covered the ground in rather an eccentric manner. He walked with a sort of dot-and-go-one step, and in addition to this mode of progression he also had a kind of sailor's lurch, as if he had just landed from a rolling deck. "What doctor are you going to disturb?" he enquired breathlessly when they reached the town.

"Doctor Fell, Sir, Doctor Fell," replied the nurse. "Doctor Fell be a kind-'earted man, but he lives with 'is old sister Miss Bibby who be reglar devil. And if we ring at Doctor's door it won't be the doctor we'll see. We'll see old Bibby for sure and Bibby'll knock our 'eads off waking of 'er up."

"I'll have the doctor out of bed," muttered Mr. Dekker grimly, "if once you get them to open the door for us, Nurse."

But at this point Mr. Geard laid his hand on the Vicar's arm. "Let me go with Miss Robinson and sit up with this woman," he said. "You can telephone to my family when you return home, so that they won't be alarmed. I can sleep wherever I am. It's a trick I possess."

Mat Dekker showed some impatience at this. "It isn't a question of sitting up with her, Mr. Geard. It's a question of stopping the torture she's enduring. It's a question of giving *her* sleep! Morphia alone can do that."

"Christ alone can do that!" cried Bloody Johnny in a voice that sounded like the voice of an angry boatswain, so resonantly did it reverberate through the empty street! "Pardon me, Sir," he went on. "Pardon me, Miss Robinson. When I said just now that I would sit up with this woman, I meant of course that in the Power of the Blood I would send *her* to sleep. Please take me there quickly, Nurse! There is no reason why we should trouble Mr. Dekker any more tonight. Only don't forget, Mister, to telephone to Mrs. Geard."

Nurse Robinson looked from one to the other. They were all three now standing outside Saint John's Churchyard, in the obscurity of which the Holy Thorn was just visible and the vast bulk of the shadowy tower. But Mat Dekker's face was clouded with indecision. He kept turning his head, first to the right and then to the left under the pressure of Mr. Geard's words, exactly as a large dog might have done under a human eye. He seemed unwilling to look at Mr. Geard. He struck the pavement with the end of his stick once or twice, muttering, "Well, I don't know, on my soul, I really don't know." Then, with a deeply drawn breath and a queer, little, fluttering movement of one of his big hands, "Come," he said, "and see what you can do. But for God's sake let's be quick! She may be crazy with the pain."

Walking fast up George Street they were soon at Tittie Petherton's ruined Gothic cottage. Nurse Robinson opened the door and went in first. A small oil-lamp was burning on the kitchen-table and a black, sooty kettle simmered feebly upon a coal-stove whose fire had almost gone out. Nurse Robinson had begun to turn up the wick of the little lamp when they were startled by a moan of anguish more horribly acute than Mat Dekker had ever heard in his life. He had heard Tittie's groans before, under her abominable affliction . . . but never a sound quite like that. The blood rushed to his face. "*Damn* these doctors!" he cried. Nurse Robinson glanced at Mr. Geard to see what effect this horrible sound had upon him. She was astonished to see his face twisted in a spasm of physical pain. She was so startled by the twisted mouth of Mr. Geard that she found herself expecting to hear from it the same cry of torment as that which they had just heard from the room above. But the spasm was over in a second of time and she turned to the door which concealed the steps that led to her patient's bedroom. Up these steps she now climbed, followed first by Mat Dekker and then by Mr. Geard. There was a second little oil-lamp, identical with the one downstairs, upon a table by the bedside, above which the massive eaves of the roof sloped down.

A gaunt woman, propped upon pillows, who had pulled herself up so desperately to a sitting posture that the bed-clothes were clinging in a disordered mass about her knees, was leaning forward with a terribly fixed stare. She began at once an incoherent and piteous pleading. "Have you the stuff? Have you brought the stuff? Oh, for Jesus' sake, give me the stuff! Is it there? Have you got it?" At this point she gasped and struggled for breath, clutching at her body with her fingers. Then she began again. "Give me the stuff, Nurse, give it to me quickly! If I don't have it, this minute, I shall curse Them Above. Oh, the stuff! the stuff! I want nothing but the stuff!"

Mat Dekker was aware of a sleepy twittering above the gutter-pipe outside the window. "Sparrows," he said to himself, "but too early for nesting . . . a little too early; but they must be thinking of it . . . they must be pairing." The oil-lamp reeked vilely, and from the tortured woman's bed there emanated a sweetish-sour and very sickly smell, which made Mat Dekker shudder as he stood there mute and helpless. It was as if, beyond and behind the living-room, some unspeakable Entity of Pain writhed in the darkness, and it was from the substance of this thing and not from any human flesh and blood that this abominable smell issued forth.

Nurse Robinson approached the bed. "Lie down now, Mrs. Petherton. It'll be better if you lie down. There! Let me turn your pillows." The woman opened her mouth and drew in her lips. Her expression was that of a despairing animal who would blindly bite at the whole world. But she allowed herself in her weakness to be laid flat upon the pillow by the strong hands of the nurse.

Then Mat Dekker approached the bed and folding his great knuckles together and bowing his grey head began praying: "In the name of the Father and of the Son and of the Holy Ghost, give unto this woman, thy poor stricken servant, O God, strength to endure the grievous sufferings which Thou in Thy wisdom hast been pleased ——" He got no further, for the woman's eyes, which she had momentarily closed, opened again and a look of renewed torment, combined with wild hatred for the priest, came into her face. Nor was this all. Unable in any other way to express the abyss of her defiance she made the motion of spitting at the worthy man. Her wretched drop of ejected saliva did no more than drip down the wrinkles of her own cheek. But Dekker caught her intention and it froze his heart.

It was at this moment that Mr. Geard came forward. Unobserved by his companions he had removed his coat and waistcoat, and now showed himself in his purple braces and grey shirt. He did not even look at the woman's face. To the astonishment of the others he stretched himself out flat by her side upon the bed, using the little table as a support for one of his great elbows. Mat Dekker could not help noticing that the bulge of his stomach had burst the top button of his trousers. But from this position he rolled his eyes towards the nurse. "Put summat under me head, will 'ee, kindly," he muttered, relapsing into the broadest Somerset. The nurse promptly obeyed him, snatching a faded cushion from a chair on the further side of the attic. "Take thik lamp away, one o' ye, if ye doänt mind. No! No! Put the little bugger on floor, Missus, where't woänt shine in our pore eyes." Again the astonished nurse obeyed this singular authority, placing the lamp in the centre of the floor, and turning the wick down as low as she dared. "Now, Tittie, old gurl, thee and me be 'a goin' to have some blessed sleep. I be drowsy as a spent bullick, I be. Night to ye both; night to ye all. Tittie and me be all right. Us 'ull be safe and sound till mornin'. And then maybe ye'll bring up a cup o' tea for we to bless the Lord in!"

With the lamp placed where it was, it had become impossible now for either Mr. Dekker or Miss Robinson to see anything but two blurred human faces, laid side by side. "Are we really to leave you like this, Mr. Geard?" enquired Mat Dekker. Not a sound, not a movement came from the bed. The priest picked up Mr. Geard's overcoat and his other clothes from where the man had let them fall on the floor. These objects he carefully stretched out over Bloody Johnny's prostrate form. "Come, Nancy," he muttered. "For God's sake let's do exactly what he says. I really think that, by the mercy of God, he's done what I couldn't do; and perhaps"—here he sighed deeply—"what no doctor could do. Come, Nancy! Better leave them just as they are." He led the way down the narrow stairs, and Nurse Robinson followed after him. The nurse looked at a dilapidated arm-chair covered with a big red shawl full of holes which stood by one of the Gothic windows. Mat Dekker lifted up the sooty kettle and peeped into the stove. "Wait a second, Nancy," he said. He opened the back door of the wretched room, from the rafters and walls of which the damp of centuries seemed to emanate. A draught of chilly midnight air entered and made the little lamp flicker and the shadow of Nurse Robinson move portentously across the yellowish strips of torn wallpaper that hung from the opposite wall.

He returned in a minute, carrying a bundle of small pieces of wood pressed against his black waistcoat. These he piled up by the side of the stove, and then threw into the aperture the most auspicious-looking of the pieces. "Well! I'll be getting home, Nance," he said. "You'll be all right, won't 'ee?" He moved up to a small cupboard and shamelessly opened it. "Yes, you've got some tea and some biscuits, I see. Have you got anything to read?" He looked round, but could see nothing except Tittie Petherton's great family Bible. Being the man he was, this particular work seemed in some way inadequate for a night-long vigil. He searched his great overcoat pockets and giving a grunt of satisfaction extracted from one of them a small copy of White's *Selborne*. This he presented to the watcher with many nods and smiles. " 'Twill help 'ee awake or send 'ee to sleep, Nance, just as 'ee do have a mind!" Like Geard of Glastonbury, Mr. Dekker was always ready to revert at a pinch to the West-Country turns of speech. In sheer physical relief at escaping from the strain of Tittie Petherton's suffering the good man now rubbed his big hands together and chuckled benevolently. For the last quarter of an hour he had forgotten Whitelake Cottage! Thus, in the huge compensatory ebb and flow of great creative Nature, one tension of human feeling has the power of ejecting, or completely cancelling, another strain of feeling. For the emotional tension of a frustrated passion there is no better cure than to spend an hour or two in the presence of terrible bodily anguish. Mat Dekker was not an idealist, but he was a man of a proud and stormy heart, and what he had seen tonight had had the famous Aristotelian effect upon him. As he walked rapidly home, however, down George Street and High Street and Silver Street, this catharsis relaxed its calming force. By the time he reached the gate of his Vicarage, poor Tittie and her heretical hypnotist were forgotten. He found his heart beating, his pulses throbbing, to the old fatal tune. Had Sam come back?

He strode up the winding driveway and burst into the hall of his house. "Penny!" he shouted. "Penny!" The old servant came grumbling and blinking out of her kitchen where she had been asleep in her chair. "Has Sam come home?" he enquired sternly.

"Not that I knows, Master," the woman answered; "not unless he crept upstairs on his stockinged feet."

Mat Dekker ran upstairs just as he was, too perturbed in

mind to take off either his hat or his coat. He flung open the door
of Sam's bedroom. Empty it was with that indescribable look of
desolation that bedrooms of the absent and of the dead so quickly
assume; and Sam's father stood for a second on the dimly lit
landing, chewing the bitter cud of remediless loss. Then he went
slowly to his own bedroom; and having telephoned to the Geards'
house to tell them what had become of their man, he undressed
and sought his pillow.

But the priest's rest that night was feverish and disturbed.
Nor was its Vicar the only troubled sleeper in Glastonbury. Under
many of her roofs, from the brick tilings of the Town Council's
houses in Benedict Street, to the slate roofs of the tradesmen's
villas in Wells Street, outraged and wounded hearts kept human
souls awake.

Perhaps in one house alone there was absolute peace, in one
house alone a "deep and liquid rest, forgetful of all ill," and that
was the house in which Bloody Johnny and Tittie Petherton slept
on the same bed.

W HEN SAM DEKKER REACHED WHITELAKE COTTAGE THAT DAY
it was nearly four o'clock. He had remained standing motionless once or twice during his rapid walk; standing in that fixed
position and in that same abstracted trance into which it is recorded that the philosophic Socrates fell at certain crises in his
life; and he had no idea how long these moments of abstraction
had lasted. Once at the place, however, he knocked resolutely at
the door. There was a sound inside which made him think that
the young mistress of the house was upstairs, cleaning the floor;
and when the girl came running down to let him in, this suppo-
sition proved the correct one, for she was garbed in a long,
green linen over-all, covering the whole of her dress.

"Sam . . . oh, Sam!" She was in his arms in a moment; and
for a brief space of time their simple, unadulterated craving for
each other's presence, satisfied now so deeply, drowned every
other consideration. "Sit down, Sam; oh my dear, oh my dear!"
And she pulled, with violent tugs, at her linen over-all till she
had got it over her head. She tossed the thing down on the sofa
first; and then, to make room for them to sit side by side on that
piece of furniture, she quickly folded up the garment and flung
it across the back of a chair.

They sat side by side, now, his hand clasping hers; too happy,
simply to be together, to do anything but drink up each other's
identity. "I thought this morning," she murmured, "Sam *may*
come today! But I never thought you really would."

"Oh, Nelly, my little, little Nelly!" He lifted up his hands
and pushing back her hair from her forehead drew her face
towards him. The girl's lips parted under his passionate kiss;
and when he let her go her head dropped forward like a flower
whose stem has been broken. Not a flicker, not a ripple of
shame, not a shadow of the least awareness of any change in
his recent mood swept across his consciousness when he kissed
Nell Zoyland like that!

It must be remembered that Sam's idea of what it meant to

struggle to live "the life of a saint" was a very different thing
from any notion that his father would have entertained, had
Mat Dekker aimed at such a state! Not that it would be any easier
to be a saint in Sam's way than to be a saint in his father's way.
In some respects it would be more difficult. For one thing it
would require a casuistry more sharp-edged, more flexible, more
searching and yet not less exacting! Sam's whole attitude towards
his feelings as he sat on Nell's sofa turned on the point—though
he did not analyse it—as to whether this ecstasy he got from the
girl was just sensuality or something quite different from sensuality. Without analysing his feelings, he knew in his heart that
it *was* very different; and this knowledge, penetrating his whole
being, saved him from any pricks of conscience. In his unanalyti-
cal way, Sam was not so blinded by passion, as he breathed in
and breathed out the paradisiac air of her presence, as not to be
vaguely conscious of a delicious surprise. It was a surprise to
him to find that he was not torn by any moral conflict. He had
pushed back the thought of such a conflict to the furthest margin
of his mind. But somewhere in his spirit he had been expecting it;
and now it had not come! There was no conflict. His thrilling
happiness with Nell, since the girl was as she was, brought him
nothing but a great flooding wave of absolute peace. The trouble
between them had risen from Nell's nature then, not from his?
It was the woman, not the man, whose conscience had been torn?
Well! if Nell felt no shame now; if Nell felt no division in her
heart, all was well. The personality of Will Zoyland on the moral
horizon of Sam's life was no more to him than the willows and
poplars of Queen's Sedgemoor on its physical horizon.

As for the girl herself, her recent decision in Zoyland's favour
and her return to his bed had been all along of a very special and
peculiar nature. The girl's real unconscious motive in this action
—an action whose immediate repercussion upon herself had produced that terrible turmoil of mal-ease which had seized upon
her in Saint John's Church—had been revenge upon Sam for not
taking a bold, drastic and final step in their relations, in other
words, for not carrying her off!

It is women's fatal susceptibility to passionate touch that
hypnotises them into by far the greater number of their disasters;

for under this touch-hypnosis the present transforms itself into the eternal, and their grand sex-defence, their consciousness of continuity, their awareness of the future as an integral portion of the present, is shattered and broken up. The ideal love-affairs for women are when it is easy for them, after these momentary plunges into the eternal, to fall back again upon their realistic sense of continuity; whereas the ideal love-affairs for men are when their feeling for novelty and for adventure is perpetually being re-aroused by the bewildering variability of women's moods.

"I've been thinking of you all the while, Sam," she said now, as Sam leant over her, clutching one of her hands with both his, and pressing it deeply into the fold of her lap. "The other day— was it the day before yesterday?—Yes! I think so . . . but I seem to have lost all sense of time . . . I started re-planting some wild-flowers, out there on the bank . . . meadow orchises they were . . . and suddenly I couldn't bear it, not seeing you, and I came running in and fell on the sofa and cried and cried. It was this very sofa," she went on in a changed voice and with what was evidently a swift, sudden vision of the vagaries of time, "where we're now sitting. Oh, my dear, oh, my dear, I never thought it would all come true!"

She cried from pure happiness now, letting the tears fall upon the back of his fingers as he pressed her clenched hand deep into her lap; and she got a wild, exultant pleasure from the very shamelessness of her tears, not attempting to stay them, but letting them roll down her cheeks even while she lifted up her bowed head and looked at him.

"Have you been cooking properly for yourself, Nell?" Sam suddenly enquired. The question mightily amused her; and she laughed out loud as she wiped away her tears.

"Why yes, Sam . . . yes, I have," she answered, "only I don't quite know what you mean by 'properly.' I've got a large bit of cold boiled bacon. That's the only meat I've been having just now . . . but I've been making myself some cheese omelets and . . . oh, I don't know! Why are you so inquisitive?"

Sam didn't smile. With some reason he felt he had got upon shaky ground. That bacon had been, no doubt, provided to suit the taste of the master of the house! "I went this morning," he said, "with John Crow and that man Evans, who's at Old Jones' shop, to the top of the Tor. Crow's working for Geard; you know that? They're going to have some sort of a Passion Play on Midsummer's Day. Crow asked this fellow Evans to act as the Christ in it. He's been sending off their circulars far and wide . . . even abroad, so he says. I am sure I can't imagine what Father will make of it all."

"Geard's working against Philip and his factories, isn't he?" she responded. "Do you know, Sam, I'm sure there's something between Philip and my sister-in-law, Percy. My brother sees nothing. He'll never see anything, till it's all too late!"

Sam pondered; but not on the misdoings of Percy Spear. "I like what I've seen of your brother, Nell," he said. "But he doesn't really think there's a chance of England becoming communistic in our lifetime, does he?"

The girl gave a little sigh. "Oh, I don't know, my dear! I've never thought much about it . . . one way or the other. I suppose he does. But I oughtn't to speak for Dave. I'm afraid he doesn't find me clever enough to talk to, about things like that. Sam, have *you* heard any gossip in town about Philip and Persephone?"

Sam smiled grimly. "I've heard gossip in town about Mrs. Zoyland and Sam Dekker," he said.

Her eyelashes flickered under his word and she turned her head; but a second later she tore her hands from his grasp and flung them round his neck. "Love me, love me, Sam!" she whispered. They forgot everything then in a much more passionate kiss than their first one.

When they drew apart at last, Sam could not help murmuring a very naïve question. "How on earth was it that you ever came to care for me, Nell? Except one poor little town-girl at Cambridge, that I ought never to have meddled with, no woman has ever bothered herself about me. You're far too beautiful for a clown like me, Nell. You ought to be the pet of the greatest prince on the earth!"

The oldest of all feminine smiles crossed her face. Towards her lover's high-pitched worship a woman can grow as tenderly humorous as the slyest cynic in the world. His infatuated rapture in her beauty becomes as nothing, in comparison with the desperate sweetness of her surrender to him. There are levels of feminine emotion in the state of love entirely and forever unknown to men. Man's imaginative recognition of feminine charm, man's greedy lust, man's pride in possession, man's tremulous sense of the pathos of femininity, man's awe in the presence of an abysmal mystery—all these feelings exist in a curious detachment in his consciousness. They are all separate from the blind subcurrent that sweeps the two together. But with women, when they are really giving themselves up without reserve, a deep underflow of abandonment is reached, where such detachment from Nature ceases completely. At such times the woman does not feel herself to be beautiful or desirable. She does not feel her lover to be handsome or strong or clever or brave. She might be the most abject of the daughters of her race. He might be the least admirable of the sons of his race. His body, his face, might be disfigured, deformed, dirty, derelict; his personality might be contemptible. She has reached a level of emotion where everything about him is accepted and taken for granted; and not only so, but actually seen for what it is, without a flicker of idealism. She has reached a level where in sublime, unconscious humility she takes as her possessor this image, this simulacrum, this poor figure of earth; and as she does so, she accepts in exactly the same way her own most grievous limitations, discounting ironically and tenderly, with an understanding that is deeper than cynicism itself, all his erotic amorous illusions.

There is thus, in a woman's love, when it has sunk to this level, *no illusion left*. He is what he is and she may be what she may be! Infirm, cowardly, conceited, stupid, he is her man. She has given herself to him as a free gift. He is her possessor. She belongs now, not to herself, but to him. The danger implicit in this absoluteness of a woman's love, when she really gives herself up, is that a man should get a glimpse of its sublime realism. Architect of illusion as he is, it is only in the full volume and top crest of his love that a man can bear an inkling of how realistically his woman regards him below the surface of her flattery. His love for her will probably weaken before hers does for him. And this will happen just because his love depends on an exaggerated admiration of her, which, if he is not something of a Don Quixote, will pass away by degrees. The tragic danger of the "absoluteness" of her love will arrive when he has really got tired of her and has come to regard her as a stranger to his mind and a burden upon his spirit. At this point his vanity will soon teach him, and her "crossness" and "sensitiveness" will soon teach him, that she is completely free from every illusion about his personality. And then another element will enter. The slow cooling of his love for her will rouse in the woman a blind anger; an anger directed, not so much against the poor, weak man himself, as against *all men*, and incidentally against all the laws of Nature; and yielding to this anger she will not care how much she hurts his feelings. Let him suffer a little *on the surface*—which is all he understands!—while she is suffering such tortures in the depths! In this mood how can she resist taking advantage of her knowledge of his character? How can she help prodding and stinging him where she knows it will hurt the most?

What in any woman renders a union lasting is the power of letting her man see that *she likes him extremely* in addition to loving him. What in any man renders a union lasting is this element of the rational-irrational "Don Quixote" in his mind and soul. And wherein consists this Don Quixote element? It consists in an act of the *imaginative will*; an act of the man's soul that is actually creative; an act by means of which he sets up his particular Dulcinea del Toboso in an indestructible and imperishable niche. The act of the imaginative will to which I refer gives a man, in fact, the power to treat his woman, in her lifetime, *as if she were dead* . . . which is the rarest essence of human relationship and the supreme triumph over matter of the human spirit.

It was when Sam looked at her after he had said, "You ought to be the pet of the greatest prince upon earth," that Nell Zoyland knew that if she could belong to him, and to him alone, they two would be constantly and permanently happy. For the girl saw in his look at that moment that deep, obstinate, half-mad *creative* look, the look of the artist, of the saint; the look of Something which the ebb and the flow of her woman's moods would have no power to change; and which nothing in life could change; for it sprang from that Don Quixote element in a man's spirit which transcends the astronomical universe.

The girl became very silent and quiet after she had caught that look on Sam's face. Her realistic woman's mind was now running, like a little ash-coloured mouse, from plank to plank of the drifting barge of their imbroglio, hunting for the least cranny or crack or hole, by which they could slip overboard and change their destiny. Sam naturally mistook her rapid concentrated thinking for the descent of sadness upon her; and to change her mood he asked her what she thought of Tom Barter. He had arrived at this gentleman, as a topic of harmless conversation, by recalling how the man had been present with Philip on the last occasion when he himself was in this room. It seemed a whole year ago, tonight, that feverish encounter, and he had no wish to dwell on it now. But Mr. Barter of the Crow Dye Mills would serve as well as anything else to distract a sad mistress! She awoke from her abstracted train of thought with a start; but could not help smiling at his question. "He thinks I'm only interested, like all women," she said to herself, "in personal matters."

"I heard Dave talk about him the other day," she remarked, while Sam rose to his feet and stood with his hands in his pockets gazing at her in a peaceful ecstasy. "He said the Corporation of Glastonbury was going to start a factory of their own . . . a factory belonging to the working-people of the town . . . to everybody in fact, but of course the poor people are the majority. He says this man Geard is going to be the new Mayor and going to see this through. He says Geard's going to get Mr. Barter to leave Philip, and be the manager of this new concern. He says their Midsummer Pageant will be the opening day of it; and that it'll be a real communistic experiment. He says John Crow has made this man Geard quite enthusiastic about it; and you know how rich *he* is!"

Her words ran on with a lively fluency, but to both of them at that moment they were like the sound of the ripples of the river of fate, on whose calm tide they were being irrevocably carried forward. Behind her words she was thinking to herself,

"It's nearly half-past five. It'll soon be dark. I must be alone to think what I'm going to do. I would . . . like . . . to give . . . him . . . a surprise . . . a sort of . . . celebration . . . of this day." And behind listening to her words—which, to confess the truth, interested him very little—Sam was thinking—"I'm the luckiest man in all Somersetshire. How beautiful she is, that exquisite Being over there . . . and she's my girl! Yes, you old Sam, you've got a real girl of your very own and one that's worthy to be the pet of princes!"

Slowly, then, she too got up upon her feet. "Sam, darling," she said. "I want to be alone for a little, to collect my thoughts and get things straight. I'm going to get you a nice tea, too, a real high tea, such as I know Penny gets for you and your father. Where did you have your lunch, Sam?"

He stared at her. "Lunch?" he murmured. "They went . . . they said . . . I told them . . . yes," he said, "I believe I *could* eat something presently. Do you want me to go out for a little while, Nell? Is that what you mean?"

As soon as she found that he had caught the drift of her wishes, though still in complete darkness as to her mood, she became calm, competent, radiant. "Run off then, my dear," she said, opening the door for him, "and give me an hour, will you? Have you got your watch?" She gave him a quick, unimpassioned, practical kiss as he went out; but the minute she had shut the door on him she fell on her knees in front of the fire and clasped her hands together in an ecstasy of gratitude to the gods.

Nell now realized, for the first time, how completely her heart belonged to Sam; and with this knowledge all outside things became comparatively unimportant. The portentous figure of her husband loomed, indeed, like a distant mountain range upon the background of her thoughts; but the present hour seemed to be hers with such an absolute benediction, that no fears, no doubts, about the future could assail or spoil it. Yes, she would give herself to Sam; now that at last he had come to her. All the moments that she had endured alone, since Zoyland had gone to Wookey, gathered now, like an airy squadron of strong-winged birds, to push her forward to this consummation. To let this chance go by untaken would be to betray, through weakness and feebleness, the very stride of fate itself.

The first thing she did was to look at the clock to see exactly how much time she had at her disposal. "He'll be away just as long as I said," she thought. "Poor old Sam, what a shame to send him off!" Then she retreated into her kitchen and hurriedly filled her kettle with fresh water for their tea, transferring what water there was already in the kettle into an enamelled saucepan for the boiling of their eggs. She glanced then at the fire in her sitting-room to make sure that her lover had not spoiled the glowing redness of it by his absent-minded putting on of more wood. "I'll make the toast the last thing!" she thought, and returning again into her kitchen she cut up half a loaf into neat slices of bread. She then set to work with rapid, deft fingers to lay the table. This proceeding, swift though it was, gave her as deep a satisfaction as Sam's father was wont to derive from his preparations for the Sacrament. She did not precisely think, as she put a teaspoon in each of their two saucers and an egg-spoon by each of their two egg-cups, how over all this darkening quarter of the planet, female forms of the same love-demented race were doing just this same thing at this same moment. But she was fully aware of a delicious atmosphere of romantic sensuality in what she did. Their more dangerous passion hovered like an invisible incense round the sugar-bowl, the slop-basin, the milk-jug, and round all these little silver spoons, some with the great Zoyland Falcon and some with her own Spear crest upon them! She proceeded then to set light in her parlour to candles, bringing a veritable illumination of them from every other part of the house to throw lustre upon her love-feast.

The expression on her face when all this had been done and when she had finally placed two chairs opposite each other, on either side of the little card-table covered with a white cloth, was of the kind that only one of the great early masters could have done justice to. Its dominant note was an earthy, irrational, *almost stupid* complacency; a complacency that doubtless derived, in a long atavistic retrogression, from æons of passive, brooding female contemplation of the imperishable elements of continuity in the turbid torrent of life! Leaning for a while against the

back of the chair she intended for Sam, she allowed herself to
fall into the waking trance of a very young girl. Zoyland had
destroyed her physical virginity; but he had not touched—no,
not so much as ruffled—that virginal dream-state in a young girl's
consciousness wherein she awaits her first lover; and the bloom
of which she keeps, like a handful of soft, white swan's-down, or
dandelion-seed, to lull the sleep of Eros when he really does at
last come to her and pitch his tent.

The clock on her mantelpiece now struck the half-hour from
when she had sent Sam away; and she had other things to do.
Leaving the table she stared long and long at the sofa where
they had been sitting together. This sofa had no back. It was, in
fact, a large-sized, single-bed couch, standing against the wall of
the room. With shining eyes she ran upstairs and came down
with a great armful of fresh bed-clothes, snatched from her linen-
chest. These she stretched out carefully upon the couch, tucking
them in between it and the wall. With the gleam in the eyes and
the quiver on the lips of one mischievous young girl making
sport of another, she brought down, after a second run upstairs,
a single pillow and a single pillow-case. When all was ready and
she had made the bed she cast the same stupidly happy stare
upon this achievement. The next thing she did was to give an
anxious glance at the clock and then run upstairs for her final
act of preparation. It was almost dark outside the window now;
and she had carried downstairs every available candlestick. But
her personal preparations were of such classic simplicity that
they could be done perfectly well in this grey, perishing light.
She kept both the door at the top of her stairs and the door at
the bottom wide open, so that up there in her bedroom the dying
light of the natural day and the ritualistic light of her Fête
d'Amour mingled together with that peculiar and mysterious
charm which candlelight and daylight assume when they are
associated with each other at either of the two twilights.

Once more she ran downstairs, and filling a small hot-water
can from her enamelled saucepan, which had by this time begun
to steam a little, she hurried back to her twilit chamber, poured
out the water into her basin and stripping herself with eager
fingers of every shred of clothing set to work to sponge her bare,

soft skin from head to foot. She felt, as she did this, as if her flesh and blood were something entirely apart from the deep consciousness wherewith she loved her lover. It was as if her body— after the tea-table and the bed—were a sort of final and triumphant offering, the last and the dearest thing she could give to him, so that he might take his full pleasure on that sacred night! Violently she rubbed herself after this, all over, with her bath-towel, till her limbs glowed warm and sweet; and then pulling on stockings, slippers, and a night-dress she had never worn before, she threw over herself a long, warm, dark-blue dressing-gown. Snatching up her brush and comb she now descended to her illuminated sitting-room, where, by an old-fashioned mirror, she combed out her hair, and then fastened it back, much more carefully than she had ever done in her life before. She removed carefully the strands of her hair adhering to the comb; and as she threw them into the fire she remembered what an old nurse of her mother's had once told her—not her childhood's nurse, but a very old woman who used to stay with the Spears when she was a little girl—that if a girl's hair makes a sound as it burns— a sound that the girl herself can hear—she will lose her maidenhood within the year. "Mine's gone already," she thought, "but *not really*!"

She was ready for him now; and behold! as she looked at the clock the hour she had given him was all but five minutes used up! She looked anxiously at her bright array of burning candles. Then she looked at herself, in her blue dressing-gown, in the mirror. For a passing second she got a real thrill of pleasure from the shining eyes and bright cheeks which she saw reflected; but a sudden memory of one evening when she had been waiting for Zoyland swept over her and she turned hastily away.

Meanwhile Sam had been walking slowly through the twilight in the same direction as that from which he had come. He was conscious of a vague feeling of fertility in the damp spring air and of the hidden stirrings of vegetable juices in roots and stalks as his feet sank in the soft turf of the river-bank, where thick swaths of last year's grass, lying along the ground and trodden by the feet of cattle, were interspersed with patches of young spring shoots and with the immature foliage of yarrow and bed straw. He felt, as he walked along, that life was at once far more exciting and far more dangerous than he had ever suspected. The freedom of conscience with which he had twice kissed Nell this afternoon, giving full rein to his feelings, was not threatened, even now, by any moral scruple. His heavy, sluggish nature, once roused to the magic of sex, had so little that was vicious in it—in the sense of being isolated and detached from tenderness and pity—that it brought with it no sense of guilt. It justified itself; and he felt pure and simple exultation in it. The strange thing was—and as the twilight darkened about him this was what he found hard to understand in himself—that the renunciation of all "possessiveness," which was his new ideal, did not debar him from snatching at this chance-given moment of love. The real reason was that Sam's devotion to Nell—as his unique true-love—was so unqualified and heart-whole, that his feeling, at this heaven-sent moment, did not carry with it that sense of "taking" which he had set himself to renounce. To love Nell, now that he felt she really loved him, seemed to him quite as much a giving as a taking. What did a little trouble him, as he burst through the river-mists and dug his heels and his stick into that magnetic springtime soil, was the quivering exultation of his own mood. Life seemed to him, just then, almost too exciting, almost too charged with electric dangers and raptures. Sam was no coward, but he was essentially a slow-moving, slow-witted, timid animal. The even tenor of his ways, until Nell appeared, had been so unruffled and so solidly earthy, that he felt scared at this new riot in his nerves, at this new quicksilver, running like an unknown "perilous stuff" through every vein! As he strode blindly on in the grey dampness he actually dared to articulate that word "saint" that was carried in the remotest portion of his consciousness. "I will be a lover *and* a saint!" his heart cried.

He never afterward forgot that hour's walk by the side of Whitelake stream. Carried along upon the cresting wave of his delicious adventure what Sam resembled most nearly was a boy who has "run away to sea"; and who suddenly finds himself in the midst of an overwhelming predicament; a predicament which realizes at the same time all his desire to be "heroic," and all his craving for romance. At the bottom of his nature Sam had no small modicum of phlegmatic common sense; and in the very whirl and splash of the adventure to which he was responding, he retained a certain background of bewildered surprise that it should be himself—the timid, plodding, unenterprising self he knew so well—that had been given such a disturbing privilege! Compared with what Nell was feeling at this moment of time, Sam's emotions were pathetically youthful. The Don Quixote in him had been stirred. But that was really the only thing in him upon which the girl could lean. For the rest he was in a mood of such turbulent bewilderment that the occasion with all it brought was only half-real to him. In most love-affairs between men and women this element of "reality" is unequally distributed; but in this case it was especially so; for whereas every aspect of what was happening was vividly clear to Nell, to Sam it was all wrapped in a vague mist. Not exactly in an idealistic mist, however; for the sly Quantock fox in him kept up all the time a sniffing scrutiny of what was going on! Nell's whole being, on the contrary, was melted into "realism," on this momentous night. Everything was twice as real to her as usually was the case; and things were always real enough. While Sam kept thinking to himself—"What a puzzling confusion life is! Here am I, longing to be a saint and yet with a chance of spending the night with the sweetest girl in Somersetshire!"—Nell thought simply and solely, "I want to give everything I've got to Sam. He has come to me at last. He has come to me at last!"

When Sam paused at last, close by Whitelake Bridge, and lit a match to look at his watch, he saw that he had already allowed forty minutes to pass since he had left the house. This vexed him; for he could hardly traverse in twenty minutes fields that had taken him forty minutes to cross. His chin began to work as he put his watch away and he cursed himself for his absent-minded blundering. The moment he swung round, however, he noticed a faint, dim, filmy light in the western sky. He knew at once what *that* sign hung in the heavens was—the young moon! The mist from the river, and the still more insidious vapours wafted across Queen's Sedgemoor, so obscured this fragmentary luminary that it was no bright object that he stared at. He was standing almost due east of Whitelake Cottage now; so that

this dim white blur in the darkness hung directly over the dwelling of his Love. To his excited feelings at that moment that
phantasmal object seemed much more than a natural phenomenon.
Eagerly he grasped with one of his hands a tuft of willow
sprigs growing out of the head of an old bowed pollard, whose
roots were in the wet earth at his feet, and leaning forward
raised his stick exultantly in the air. The dark earth beneath him
seemed to him then like a vast, wild-maned horse, upon whose
broad back he was being borne through space! A poignant smell
of musk rose up from where his heavy boots pressed against that
huge living creature. Young plants of common water mint must
have been growing there to cause this scent; but its aromatic
sweetness added yet another element to his enchantment.

From that fragment of white mystery there slid across land and
water into the soul of Sam Dekker a thin, long-rippling confederate stream of sweet disturbance. Where John Crow would
have subtly reasoned upon the mythical significance of this frail
vessel of "furious fancies," Sam just gave himself up to its
palpable power. He became a wave in the Bristol Channel, a
bracken-frond in the Quantock hills, a crystal in a Mendip stone
wall, a black-striped perch in the Brue under Pomparlès Bridge.
Sam and that old bent pollard, whose youthful sprouts he was
clutching with such blind intensity, gave themselves up together
so completely to the power of that obscured moon that an identical
magnetism poured through the man's flesh and blood and shivered through the vegetable fibres of the tree. Yes! Sam felt as
if he were a reckless rider, awkward and stiff, in his new release,
but mounted on the dark equine back and behind the streaming
mane of the revolving earth; and carried wildly through the wet
mists towards his desire. He little knew what superhuman Naturalists were watching him then, as interested in his present antics
(and not less sympathetic) as he himself had so often been over
the aquarium in his father's museum. That shapeless white blur,
that still delayed to sink below the reedy horizon in the Sedgemoor vapours, was to these watchers like the candle which Sam
would hold sometimes above some favourite finned pet! In a universe so thrilling and so aching with teeming consciousness, the
man and the bowed pollard tree strained and yearned together

towards that misty image in the west. Cold against his clenched fingers were those smooth twigs. Cold against his mouth was the river's breathing. Wild and yet faint in his ears were the gurgling sobs of the water as it rippled in the darkness around hidden roots and around the hollow stalks of last year's reeds.

He boldly broke up his trance now, tearing at it as if he were some prehistoric dinosaur, rending its way through a matted entanglement of monstrous moonlit vegetation. Clenching his stick by its centre and closing his fists, he now set himself, in an obstinate jog-trot, to re-cross those long meadow-reaches in less than half the time he had taken to cross them. It was thus only about a quarter of an hour later than the hour his Love had given him when he arrived panting at the door of Whitelake Cottage and gave a series of quick low knocks. She didn't let him wait out there for one second. She had been sitting on that couch she had turned into his bed, listening and listening! It was not *her* destiny to see the moon that night. When Sam, all blinking and panting, threw down his hat and stick on an empty chair and hugged her to his heart he thought to himself—"If life goes on like this, my heart will burst from too much joy." But he need not have been afraid! The great suction-process of cosmogonic matter—always waiting to drain up in its huge, blind, clay belly, these rapturous overtones of its foster-children—was soon at work, sucking up the spilt drops of his happiness.

They sat down to their incredible meal. Wise had Nell been to restrict their portion that night to the simplest elements! Tea, eggs, butter, bread, honey, and black-currant jam. The taste of each of these things—and Sam swallowed them all in rapid, boyish gulps of heavenly greediness—carried nothing but the very poetry of mortal sustenance into their amorous blood. She kept pulling the loose front of her blue dressing-gown tightly round her classical breasts; so that Sam remained, all through this delicious meal, in complete ignorance of the fact that she had stripped herself naked for him save for her flimsy night-gown.

As to the difference between the sensations of Sam and Nell, as they ate their meal in the midst of this blaze of candlelight and with their bed prepared, the situation was reversed from what it was under former conditions. It was Nell who had become the

self-conscious, detached one, savouring every morsel that both she
and her lover put into their mouths and lingering out their tea-
drinking when their hunger was satisfied. Sam on the other hand,
with beating heart, could not keep out of his mind the thought
that when their meal was over he would be allowed to embrace
her. He had noticed on his entrance the changed aspect of the
couch and though with a lover's tact he had avoided any reference to this transformation, it was evident to him that the girl
was tacitly assuming he was going to stay the night; and this was
a fact in itself enough to stir his senses. Thus, though he ate
his food hungrily and with an eager, nervous greed, he found
himself far too excited to enjoy with the whole-hearted contentment
which the girl experienced the progress of their perfect meal.
The Theban prophet may have been right when he said that in
the act of love the woman feels a greater thrill than the man;
but he would have been wrong if he had said this about the *expectation* of such a consummation. A girl's physical love, except at the moment of actual contact, is much more diffused than
a man's. While they were enjoying their tea, therefore, Nell
kept saying to herself—"This is my Sam! My Sam has come at
last! My Sam belongs to me and I to him! There is no girl in
the whole world happier than I. He has come to me at last with
a free heart! He loves only me and I love only him! How beautifully those candles shine! What a good thing Sam likes black-
currant jam. Always, henceforth, when I see black-currant jam,
I shall think of him. How glad I am I've put on my blue dressing-gown."

But Sam's felicity was all this while a little marred by the
impetuous craving of his tingling senses. "Will she let me embrace her to the uttermost presently? How soon shall I dare to
embrace her? Will she sleep with me all the night on this bed
she has made up? Or is it *only for me*; and will she insist on
going upstairs in the night and leaving me here alone?" He
finally got so impatient that he could not wait to give her time
to finish her second cigarette. He rose up and came round the
table and snatched it from her hand. He threw it into the fire.
He lifted her up to her feet. He blew out the brightly burning

candles on the chimney-piece even while he still clutched her wrist!

This was the moment, as she felt herself pulled across the room by her wrist, that she knew her first real spasm of *fear of her man*; that delicious fear which is an element in every authentic encounter between the sexes. For all William Zoyland's amorous brutality, though Nell had felt embarrassment and even physical distress when he was embracing her, she had never felt this indescribably delicious quiver of fear. The awkwardness, the material shock of ravishment under Zoyland's violence, had been mitigated by a certain passive inertia, as of the original resistance of matter itself to the stir of blind creation. But now as she felt her blue dressing-gown torn from her body and saw the impersonal glint in Sam's bear-like eyes, she knew a fear much deeper than the mere fear of a girl in the hands of a ravisher. She knew the fear of seeing her Sam, her own well-known Sam, transformed into something unknown and sweetly dreadful! This fear, however, only lasted till he had carried her to that carefully made bed. Then with incredible rapidity it entirely vanished! The cause of its vanishing—though she analysed it not—was that there had been aroused in her, at last and for the first time, the strongest, the most poignant, the most transporting sensation which exists in the world—the sensation of a feminine body abandoned to the man she loves! To the man; not to the man's *body*. For the curious thing is that while at this supreme moment she for him had become absolutely impersonal—a woman's flesh in empty space—he remained for her the *actual, personal, conscious man she loved*. The extremity of her sensation—that sensation which Teiresias (to his own disaster!) had placed above the man's—implied a vivid consciousness that she, Nell, was being possessed by him, Sam.

But with him it was altogether different. His authentic love for her, his pity, his tenderness, his feeling for her beauty, had simply opened wide the gates of ecstasy. Through these gates there rushed now a rapture of bodiless, mindless, delirious sensation. This sensation, dominating now the whole field of his conscious and unconscious being, was much blinder, simpler, less complicated than anything which she felt. Both their sensations centred in *her* body, not in his. His body was merely the engine of the well-known personality that was now enjoying her. His body might have been ugly, coarse, deformed, grotesque. It might have been made of wood, of iron, of stone, of cement, of peat, of clay. It was her man's dear body; and that was enough! If it had been the body of a leper, it would have been the same. But with him, once again, it was otherwise. His consciousness, even at the beginning of his delight, could only have expressed its rapture by the concept—"She is too sweet." Then there came a further point in his ecstasy when he could not have even articulated as much as that; when he could perhaps have said no more to describe what he felt than some perfectly incoherent gibberish, some subhuman gibberish that would be identical with what a bird, a beast, a reptile, would utter, or try to utter, as it plunged into that sweet oblivion.

In spite of the unnumbered occasions of erotic satisfaction—paroxysms of normal and of abnormal claspings—which are forever reaching their consummation on all sides of us in the great swirling life-tide, it is surprising how few encounters between amorists, whether human or subhuman, attain to the sublime and absolute ecstasy which was reached tonight by these two. Much more is needed for this than mere physical attraction, or mere mental reciprocity—or even both of these things together! It would almost seem as if every one of us hides in the secret recesses of his being a potentiality for this supreme rapture—but a potentiality that can only be roused by one particular person. It may be an illusion, this feeling that lovers so often have, that they have found the one solitary "alter-ego" in the universe whose identity supplements their own, but it is certainly not an illusion, but a tragic fact, that many human beings—and not by any means sex-starved persons either—go down to their graves without ever having known this indescribable transport. Sam and Nell certainly knew it to the full this night of the New Moon! They took such spacious draughts of it; they plunged into it so desperately, so utterly, that in the mingling of their identities there seemed no portion of either of them—body, soul or spirit— *left over*, that was not merged and lost in the other.

What Lord P.'s bastard would have seen if he had flung open

that door upon them—a man and a girl struggling to return to a primal platonic unity that some terrestrial curse had interrupted—would have been a poor, false, meagre, crude parody of what their submerged consciousnesses were feeling. It was not in any bodily form that reality presented itself to those two at that moment. Their ecstasy itself was the reality, the truth, the essence of what occurred between them! Yes; the "entelecheia," so to speak, of their desperate claspings upon that couch, was not in the idea of their bodies; was not in the form of their bodies. Such aspects of this event in time and space would have been false if taken as the real reality of that moment. The "reality" of that moment—of that infinite series of moments—was what they felt; and what they felt was beyond all human symbolism. What they felt was more rapturous than a rain of blinding, dazzling meteors falling through eternity. It was an iridescent cloudburst, rushing down from unknown translunar regions, and meeting a toppling tower of deep-sea waters, flung up from the abyss!

Nell was a natural, simple girl; and as far as her intellect went, a commonplace girl. Sam was a natural, simple man; and as far as his intellect went, a commonplace man. But compared with the projection of delirious ecstasy which their encounter that night lodged in the atmosphere around Whitelake Cottage the neurotic intensity of the attraction between John and Mary Crow—baffled, tantalised, provoked, throbbing with unrealised and perhaps unrealisable cravings for a consummation that mocked them with its nearness only to withdraw from them again—was something as sad as it was sterile.

It was the girl who, when night fell, slipped from his arms and blew out the spluttering wicks of the two dying candles and balanced the fire-guard against the bars of the grate. He hardly awakened when she returned, so drowsy was he. It was not only the happiness of love that made sleep cover him with such swan's-down feathers; it was the excitement of the last two weeks, weeks that had been full of a mental agitation entirely new to his earth-bound nature. Into this heavenly forgetfulness Nell too was soon sucked down as she nestled close against him; and had Lord P.'s bastard rapped loudly at the door which divided these lovers from that hushed spring night, it would have

been long seconds of time before their two souls, so deeply involved, yes! involved down into the very profoundest subcon-
sciousness of each of them, had risen up to deal with this fatal
intrusion! But no knock at that locked door, no tap at that darkened window, disturbed the peace of those two sleepers. Like
poor Tittie Petherton, sleeping now with an expression of felicity
such as she had not worn since her disease first attacked her, they
slept the sleep of such as are "free among the dead." The sleep of
consummated love has indeed nothing in the world comparable
to it except the sleep of mother and child.

As these two slept, the shapeless moon sank down over the rim
of the Polden Hills. As these two slept, little gusts of midnight
air, less noticeable than any wind but breaking the absolute stillness, stirred the pale, green leaf-buds above many a half-finished
hedge-sparrow's nest between Queen's Sedgemoor and the Lake
Village flats. Here and there, unknown to Sam Dekker or any
other naturalist, a few among such nests held one or two cold
untimely eggs, over whose brittle blue-tinted rondure moved in
stealthy motion these light-borne air-stirrings pursuing their
mysterious journeys from one dark horizon to another. Drooping
over the rich, black earth in Mr. Weatherwax's two walled gardens hung motionless the heads of the honey-sweet jonquils and
the faint-breath'd narcissi, too heavily asleep in that primordial
sleep of green-calyxed vegetation, deeper and older than the sleep
of birds or beasts or men, to respond, even by the shiver of the
least petal among them, to these light motions of the midnight
air. The sensitised earth-nerves of that portion of the maternal
planet upon which these beings lived responded, as she swung
forward on her orbit, to the sleep of her numerous offspring by
a drowsy deliciousness of her own in the arms of the night, enclosing them all in those interstellar spaces and comforting them
all with a peace greater than their peace.

Iɴ ᴛʜᴇ Gʀᴇᴇɴ Pʜᴇᴀsᴀɴᴛ Iɴɴ ᴀᴛ Tᴀᴜɴᴛᴏɴ, ᴀ ʟɪᴛᴛʟᴇ ᴏᴜᴛ-ᴏꜰ-ᴛʜᴇ-
way tavern in a back street of that ancient town on one of the
chilliest mornings of this eventful March, Persephone Spear sat
on the bed where she and Philip had been spending the night.
She sat there in her white slip, her straight Artemis shoulders
bare, pulling on her black stockings. Philip had just gone to the
end of the passage to take a bath and the girl could detect now
amid the other early morning sounds in that small hostelry—such
as the bootblack replacing the commercial travellers' boots at
their several doors, such as the house-girl bringing cans of shav-
ing-water to their doors and giving bold, shameless knocks, such
as the barking of dogs in the cobbled yard, the trampling of an
old horse in its stable, the scrubbing of a motor car in an open
garage by a whistling boy, the sound of the rush of water from
the bath-faucet. The girl's whole nature felt as if it were drawing
itself together into a little round ball, tying itself up into a little
tight knot, and making itself as small and hard and *unattractive*
as it could possibly make itself. She treated her slim boyish legs
very roughly as she pulled on her stockings. She thought, "Oh, if
I can only get my stockings and skirt on before he comes back he
won't touch me any more!" With vicious jerks she *did* get her
stockings on; and then, heedless of the dust on the carpet, she
stepped into her skirt, allowing it to trail upon the floor. The
pattern upon the carpet consisted of big, bunchy roses, each rose
encased in a square frame of dull, brown lines. The disgust she
felt at seeing her nice grey skirt in contact with this horrible
carpet made her prick her fingers as she pinned its black band
with a big safety pin. "My waist has never looked so small!" she
thought, and indeed the use of the safety pin had come about because, after the excitement of her experience in Wookey Hole, the
band of her skirt had become too wide. Hurriedly she rushed to
the chair where her grey jacket was lying and pressed one arm—
and then another—breathlessly and violently into its reassuring
tailor-made protection.

Artemis-like, she had found that by far the worst part of her affair with Philip—and it had been just the same with Dave—was the fact that she had to undress and be made love to without the defence of her sweet-smelling Harris-tweed jacket and skirt. "I like driving through the lanes," she thought, "by Philip's side, while he gets fonder and fonder of me, but can't touch me! I like his kissing me and hugging me so hard the moment he gets me alone when the long drive has excited him to such a pitch. I like the way his cheeks smell of the wind and of the fresh dust of the road. I like the dinners we have together in these places with the shy young waitresses at table and the impudent hussies in the bar and the yard-boys touching their cropped foreheads and sneaking a look at my ankles and staring so respectfully at Phil! It's these nights that are so awful. Oh, *why* are men made as they are? Why *are* they made as they are? What's the matter with me that I shrink from these nights with Philip so . . . and yet enjoy the days with him? Do other women feel what I feel? Is there some deep, secret conspiracy among us to be silent about this loathing of skin to skin, this disgust of the way they are when they have their will of us? Am I betraying some tragic silence that Nature from the beginning has imposed in dark whispers upon her daughters? Is the pain of ravishment only one of the inevitable sufferings of girls . . . laid upon us since the dawn of time? Is this shrinking, this loathing, something that every girl feels?" She took up the comb to comb out her short, clipped curls. "Damn!" she muttered aloud. Her anger rose up suddenly against all the intolerable things a person had to put up with. Her anger rose against the washing-stand—with the two white basins side by side and the soap-dish into which she had put a piece of lavender soap which Philip had now carried off to the bathroom.

"I wonder," she thought, "whether those double-dyed asses of Glastonbury aldermen, now that they've elected Geard, will do what I suggested to Dave and try and start a real communistic factory . . . something on a much bigger scale than this silly souvenir business?" She stood in the middle of the room holding the comb in her hands. Impelled by a lurid fascination, she moved to the door and opened it gently . . . gently . . . biting her lower lip as she turned the handle. She was met by that combination of curious stuffy smells which a bedroom passage in a small inn always exhales. The passage was full, too, of that particular morning light that seems to have nothing to do with the sun at all, that seems to come from some reservoir of pallid, terrestrial illumination that is neither natural nor artificial, but is a light especially dedicated to inn-passages when only the Boots and the oldest of the house-maids are stirring, and a smell of cigar-smoke and stale cheese pervades the staircase. She continued to hold the door ajar, as she leaned forward listening, her unwashed eyelids still heavy with sleep and her chestnut curls all tumbled and rumpled.

There was the sound of Philip's splashing! It came from behind that door, with a white marble plate upon it carrying the word "Bath." Persephone listened to it with petrified attention. "Do all girls," she thought, "feel these queer sensations of lurid attraction and nervous disgust towards men? How much more conscious a girl is than a man of the relations between men and women! I *know* that at this moment Phil is enjoying his bath, its precise depth, its exact heat, the fact that he brought his big sponge, just as a child might enjoy these things! He's forgotten altogether about my jumping out of bed and staying so long at the window in the middle of the night. He's practically forgotten that I exist!"

She was not far wrong. Extended at full length in the bath, luxuriating in its hot water—for there was no bathroom at The Elms—Philip's thoughts might be expressed as follows: "Warm . . . nice . . . soap . . . nice . . . stain on wall shaped like Barter's profile . . . start digging at Wookey . . . Except for old Merry, not a soul knows . . . a lot of tin in Wookey . . . diabolus metallorum . . . plumbum candidum . . . Hermes . . . stream-tin . . . alluvial deposit . . . tourmaline . . . spar . . . quartz . . . stannic oxide . . . cassiterite . . . stannic chloride . . . purple precipitate . . . purple of Cassius . . . . . . tin salt . . . tin crystal . . . tin-ash." He began to derive extraordinary satisfactory from taking up his great sponge, filling it with water and squeezing it over his knees with both hands. The sponge became the hill above Wookey where he intended to mine for tin and his knees became jagged fragments of this precious alluvial deposit and the water on either side of his thighs

was the subterranean river. "Let Geard have his Pageant," he
thought. "Let him dig for Merlin's tomb! I'm going to dig for tin
. . . diabolus metallorum . . . I'll turn this town into something different from a humbugging show-place! I'll sell my dyes
and I'll sell my tin to all the dealers in Europe . . . What a
good thing I'm not responsible for Perse! Let Monsieur Agitator
support my sweet Coz, while I enjoy her at my leisure!"

He began to squeeze his sponge with still fiercer pressure and
still deeper satisfaction. He found that there was a little window-
pane opposite him where the coloured glass had been replaced by
ordinary glass and out of this window he could see quite a long
way over the roofs of Taunton. He even fancied he could see the
ridge of the Polden Hills between two chimneys. He propped
himself up in the bath on the palms of his hands. But the ridge
vanished then, and in its place rose one of the great Taunton
Church Towers celebrated all over Somersetshire and only rivalled by St. John's at Glastonbury. The sight of this religious
edifice, so tall and massive, disturbed the current of his thoughts.
He sank back in the bath. Once more that little far-off line between the chimneys re-appeared. Automatically he began squeezing his big sponge again, but the water was getting cold and the
sight of that tower had broken up his complacency.

"What did she do that for?" he asked himself, thinking, with
a frown, of the incident in the night when the girl had jumped
out of bed and stayed so long at the window. "I don't believe
she'll bear me a child," he said to himself. "There's something
about her —— No! she's not the maternal type, my sweet Perse,
there's no getting over that!" He gave himself up then, as he got
out of the bath and began hurriedly drying, to his own peculiar
and favourite voluptuous thoughts. Every man has his own set of
voluptuous images with which his mind tends to dally at such a
moment when his body is glowing and refreshed. Philip's thoughts
had to do with Persephone's bare shoulders as they looked—not
in her night-gown, for she dreamed like a boy at night and though
this would have pleased John it did not suit Philip, but in her slip.
It was therefore no little blow to him—for he had anticipated quite
the contrary—when, on his entering their room with a quick,

sharp knock, he found her fully dressed and seated again by that accursed window.

That moment was indeed a fatal and memorable moment in the history of their relations. It was as if in the process of *his* bath and of *her* combing her hair a deadly gulf had yawned between them. She was seated on the arm of a chair and leaning against the window-sill. Her pose was withdrawn, chaste, reserved, remote, her face cold and pale, her eyelids half closed. She was intently surveying the head of the old carriage horse whose hoofs trampling on its stable floor had drummed a bitter tune into her mind at certain intervals during that night. The old horse was peering out of a small square window and the lad who had been cleaning the motor car was stroking its neck. He was still whistling the same tune, and as Philip paused at their window to follow the girl's gaze he started singing. "I've made up my mind to sail away . . . sail away . . . sail away . . . In the Colonies I mean to try . . . mean to try . . ." The lad sang in a silly drawling voice. "He's heard that tune on a roundabout," remarked Percy, drawing in her head and evading the arm with which Philip attempted to capture her. "I used to hear it when I first came to Somerset."

They stood side by side for a moment without touching, watching some pigeons that were fluttering about on the stable roof. Philip felt obscurely angry with these sleek birds whose wings gleamed like the metallic shimmerings in Wookey Hole. Their chucklings and croonings made an orchestral accompaniment to the lad's voice. Persephone said to herself: "Damn! Damn! Damn! How can I get out of having to submit to this sort of thing with him again?" As she turned back into the room their eyes met and both of them knew without the passage of a word between them that a barrier had sprung up which it would be very hard to destroy.

"Well! Well!" he now remarked with forced jocularity, "if you're satisfied with your concert, run down, while I dress, and see how long we've got to wait for breakfast! I'm due at the office by nine this morning. There's a lawyer from Yeovil coming in, by the early train, to see me."

She looked at him coldly and quizzically. "What trouble are

you in now, Phil? Have you been found out at last?" She spoke at random, but when she had spoken she wished that she hadn't said just that.

Philip's swarthy cheeks had darkened, and she saw that this "lawyer from Yeovil" *was* coming on some unpleasant errand. As a matter of fact Philip had summoned him because of a paragraph in the Western Gazette that looked extremely like a covert reference to Jenny Morgan and her child Nelly. "Good Lord, Perse!" he cried, pushing her to the door. "Don't begin inventing reasons for *my* legal interviews. Why, I've got a whole series of lawyers coming to the office this week. Today's is the most harmless of 'em!"

The day that had begun for Philip and Persephone with the croonings of these pigeons and the sing-song tune of "I've made up my mind to sail away," waxed unusually hot for the last fortnight of March when it reached its noon hour.

Sam and his father, having had occasion to visit a house in Hill Head, which is a street leading to the foot of Wirral Hill, happened to be making a short cut home to their early dinner across the grassy expanse of the Abbey Ruins. They had carefully avoided the dangerous topic hitherto that day, being occupied with an attempt to bribe, threaten, cajole, persuade, or terrify, one of their recalcitrant choir-boys into giving up his habit of waylaying the girls of Hill Head as they passed a piece of common land out there on their way home from school. There were several ancient thorn bushes growing on this patch of Waste Land, some of them the merest stumps, which Mr. Evans, in his daily ramblings about the place, had already decided were far older than the more famous one in St. John's churchyard. Indeed, in the heat of his frenzies and his fancies, Mr. Evans had got so far as to persuade himself that this particular tract of land —which certainly wears even at our epoch a somewhat forlorn look—was the actual site of that Terre Gastée, of the mediæval romances, which became withered and blighted after the Dolorous Blow delivered by the unlucky Balin upon King Pelleas, the Guardian of the Grail.

Young Chinnock's "Dolorous Blows"—aimed from the shelter

of these desolate thorn stumps—were directed not against any man, king or otherwise, but against anonymous and youthful femininity, and took the form of rudely flung sticks and stones, and still more rudely flung taunts of a kind more grossly obscene than even these sturdy wenches were accustomed to. The mildest of these taunts of which Chinnock was accused was the repetition of the phrase—shouted in the ears of several grown-up young women as well as children: "*I'd like to*, Dolly!" "*I'd like to*, Lettie!" "*I'd like to*, Rosie!" accompanied, on each occasion, by the flinging of some kind of natural missile. It was in a visit from old Mr. Sheperd, the aged Glastonbury policeman, that Mat Dekker was informed that his sweetest-voiced choir-boy was in serious danger of arrest, and in his anxiety to suppress this outburst of barbarity, while he saved the boy from jail, he had begged Sam, whose power over boys—though he did not like them—was always great, to accompany him on this disturbing errand.

In nothing does the grotesque injustice and thoughtless self-righteousness of human beings show itself more blindly than in these matters of sex-abuse. The two Dekkers were certainly justified in their invasion of the retreat of this perverse thrower of sticks and stones in the Terre Gastée of Hill Head Road. But when their own dialogue touched the dangerous topic of Nell Zoyland there was just the same "*I'd like to*, Nell!" at the back of their rugged skulls. And between this "*I'd like to*, Nell!" felt by these two grown men and the "*I'd like to*, Rosie!" shouted by Tom Chinnock, there could have been very little difference in the eyes of that Christ worshipped by Sam who uttered those searching words: "Whoever looketh at . . . to lust after . . . *hath* committed . . . already . . . in his heart." It was as they were passing the north doorway of St. Mary's ruined church that this dialogue began to take its dangerous "*I'd like to*" form. Confronting this old edifice of the end of the twelfth century the two men paused, their eyes attracted automatically by the lavish blaze of sunshine which fell from that cloudless noon sky upon this richly carved entrance. An arcade or frieze of interlacing arches cut in bold relief, alternately round and pointed as the curves intersect, and decorated with Norman zig-zag ornament, is broken, in the centre of the doorway, by a pyramidal cornice of delicate moulding, which covers, like a high peaked helmet, the interior arch-mouldings. These are in four concentric rings, containing numberless medallions of deeply cut carvings, telling the story of the Nativity and of the Massacre of the Innocents. Only trained experts in such matters can today interpret this dim, confused, obscure entanglement of animals, leaves, flowers, angels and impassioned human figures. Neither of the Dekkers was an expert of this kind, and to their simple naturalist eyes it was comfort enough to contemplate in that rich confusion of organic shapes a general impression of earth-life that resembled some sumptuous entanglement of moss and rubble and lichen, amid the twisted roots of old forest trees.

It would have been better for Mat Dekker, at that moment, if he had been endowed with a little of the analytic irresponsibility which John Crow possessed. He would have known better, then, what was going on in his deep, heavy, massive nature. He would have known better, then, why it was that he burst out upon his only-begotten son, as he did, in such a spasm of blundered, ill-chosen words! Gazing through that richly storied arch into the body of the Virgin's Chapel and out through a south window into the sunlit branches beyond, Sam listened to his father with lowering astonishment, his chin working frantically, and his little green eyes full of queer lights. In the roaring, raving, towering, cresting, cascading whirl of its huge centrifugal flames the superhuman consciousness of that noon-day sun recognised, amid the billions upon billions of other organisms that floated through its non-human awareness, his brief-lived biped enemy—the stalwart priest of Christ. The sun's awareness of any particular living creature may be for good and may be for evil, but towards these two men, each of whom, deep in his heart, was crying out—just like poor Tom—"*I'd like to*, Nell!" it was certainly for evil.

The sun indeed blazed down in unusual strength for a Glastonbury March day. It turned all this mass of complicated stone imagery into something as radiant as it was obscure, into something resembling the checquered patterns of dead leaves and dead twigs, mingled with little mosses and funguses, that are suddenly revealed in a forest opening, and yet into something so hot and dry and dusty that it suggested the carved stonework in classical southern countries, across which lizards slide and above which the air seems to droop and gasp and pant. That unique stonework doorway under which for at least seven hundred years human skeletons, clothed in flesh, had been passing, was on this March day a proof of what far-removed opposites in Nature the mind of man can reduce to an imaginative unity. While the hot and dusty texture of these deep mouldings suggested that languorous feeling of burning noons under copper skies when the hot bosom of the air lies sweltering and swooning upon the slabs of shadowless stone thresholds, and where upon the marble brims of dried-up fountains the coiled snake scarce seems even to breathe in its glittering sleep, the actual shapes and forms of this limestone imagery were born of dripping forest boughs and dark rainy moorlands and the wind-swept ramparts of Gothic castles.

As Sam gazed now at these four concentric rings of convoluted sculpture, listening to his father's troubled voice, he could not be called conscious that these sun-warmed intricacies of obscure carving represented the birth of his Man-God . . . that magical Event which could thus bring together the tents of the South and the chilly ramparts of the North . . . but a feeling did come over him that he was staring into the very roots of the earth, where the creatures that he so loved were engendered by the mingling of primordial heat and cold.

"We *have* to renounce," the priest was saying with a dangerous quiver of his long, clean-shaven upper lip, "and she is the test given unto you now, my son, as to whether you *can* renounce." His words burst out in a jerky, violent, spasmodic manner, for the force behind them was nothing less than that "*I'd like to! I'd like to!*" which, in Tom Chinnock's case, had been accompanied by sticks and stones. He was secretly proud that this child of his sturdy Quantock loins had made the son of the great Marquis of P. a shamefaced wittol. In those imaginative senses below the senses which create that terrible glamour-world of thrilling illusion wherein all exquisite temptations lie, Mat Dekker had derived a wild and savage joy from the thought that *his* son had lain in bed by the side of those unequalled breasts.

The conventional phrases, "desire of the flesh" . . . "sins of the flesh" . . . "lusts of the flesh" are totally at variance with the real phenomena of erotic temptation. In real temptation the "flesh" does not enter at all. There is the generative nerve where like a twisted serpent the scales of the embryo Lust-Dragon simmer and ferment, and there is the brain nerve towards which that quivering forked tongue sends out its cry of confederacy! The repercussions of both these things are mental, spiritual, ethereal, astral, immaterial, psychic and as utterly removed from the "flesh" as they are from "matter." It is a thing of *nerves*, this "brutish sting," this erotic obsession, of nerves and of the psyche, the soul, the self! The flesh is pathetically, beautifully, grotesquely *innocent*. It is in the nerves that all lecheries, all lusts, all passions lie . . . in the nerves and the imagination. It is the erotic nerve, the tightly coiled snake with the flickering tongue, always waiting to leap, that creates that under-sea of fluctuating images, wherein Matter and Flesh have been reduced to tenuous and filmy wraiths, but from which the "nerve perilous" can feed with its vibrant tantalisations the excited soul! All good springs from the nerves and from the mind. All evil springs from the nerves and from the mind. Innocent, neutral, harmless, beautiful, neither good nor evil, is the mortal flesh of men and of beasts and of the grasses of the field!

"She is the test for you, my son," went on Mat Dekker while his erotic nerve kept repeating: *"I'd like to, I'd like to!"* like a rat gnawing in a hollow wall, "she is the test for you. You have done what you wanted to do. But it must go on no longer. Any man can give way to physical temptation once. Where a man shows his mettle is where he refuses to *go on* yielding." As he spoke Mat Dekker took off his hat and wiped his forehead. This gave his superhuman enemy, the sun, his supreme opportunity, and he poured down his burning noon rays upon that bare grey head with redoubled concentration. "Not to go on with a fleshly sin," continued Mat Dekker, "is the great victory of the spirit over the body. None of us can help yielding *once*. It . . . is . . . too . . . sweet. But after the excess of the first plunge a man with any character must pull himself together and climb back into the trench of the faithful."

"Don't, Dad!" muttered Sam sulkily. "I've got to think. You only worry me, talking like that."

They moved away together now out of the Abbey Grounds; and by a short cut, permitted only to residents of the town, passed into Silver Street. Sam surprised his parent by his imperviousness to a new appeal. "Sorry, Father," he muttered presently, "I was thinking of something else . . . I didn't hear what you said!"

As the two Dekkers were turning into Silver Street, John Crow, playing truant from his little office by the station, was dawdling in front of the old men's almshouses and staring up at the bell-cot of St. Margaret's thirteenth-century chapel.

It was part of John's deep "selfishness," of this egoism which he deliberately and shamelessly cultivated, that he always preferred to allow his imagination to be stirred by little out-of-the-way buildings of this kind rather than by more famous ancient erections. The aura of "visitors" gathered for him round any notable show-spot, and was enough to turn him against it. But a fragment of old wall, a broken piece of old coping, or, much more, a building like this that had retained its own humble, patient identity throughout so many generations, always held his imagination in a dream-heavy trance of curious felicity. As he now surveyed this old bell-cot of St. Margaret's Chapel, out of whose stones grew intermittent stone-crop and green moss, the thought of how long this little tower, with its two bells and its statue of the saint, had been mingled with the thoughts of the generations of life-broken, life-weary, life-sated, life-hungry old men, going in and out of these men's almshouses, gave the selfish John a thrilling rapture of delight. Like a lovely wine, light and dreamy, made out of old, old mosses softer than sleep, this incorrigible and mischievous wanderer drank deep of these ancient men's long secular lives under St. Margaret's bell tower. He had drifted now to where Street Road branched off to the west, and instead of walking on to Hill Head and crossing that strip of waste land which was the arena of Tom Chinnock's erotic activities he turned down Street Road. He had in his mind a little dairy-shop, not far from Cardiff Villa where the new Mayor lived. This meant a furtive and foxy shuffle, for the misanthropic John, along *the other side of the road*. It might indeed be said that the whole of John Crow's life was a sequence of "other sides"—

"other sides" of roads, "other sides" of thoughts, "other sides" of ideas, religions, labours, activities, in the whole great, dusty, bustling panorama of life. It was the same thing, even when he held Mary in his arms, for he liked better to hold her as if he had caught her escaping from him, than as if she had rushed to meet him with outstretched arms.

He pretended to be extremely interested in the small suburban gardens on his right as he advanced hurriedly and surreptitiously along the path. He was seized, however, with such a strong feeling of being waved at and called to and summoned to stop from the single upper window, the window of Crummie's bedroom, visible between the tall bushes, that he raised one quick nervous glance at that dark aperture. But though his fancy filled that small space with the heads of the whole Geard family he knew in his mind that no one was there and he hurried on, trailing the point of his stick along the hedges, the gates, the railings, the walls of "the other side" of Street Road. At last he came to the little isolated dairy-shop. It stood close to the road, this little shop, and occupied the whole ground floor of a small square Jacobean house that made an odd contrast to the Victorian tradesmen's villas that formed its neighbourhood.

The hot sun beat down on the front of this little establishment where the ground before the open door had been strewn with gravel. There were two wooden benches on either side of the entrance, and inside there were several little wooden tables. The spot had an old-fashioned, mellow look, and yet the fact that milk in place of beer was the beverage sold gave a peculiar character to the whole place which it would have been hard to define. John had discovered this innocent refuge several weeks ago and it had grown to be a favourite retreat of his, though so far he had not revealed its whereabouts to Mary. The blending of Jacobean brickwork with warm dusty sunshine and both of these with large, cool, white receptacles full of milk, made of Othery's Creamery in Street Road and oasis of senuous, West-Country peace for such as did not require the more biblical stimulant of alcohol to bathe them in enchantment. John walked in and ordered a pint of milk and a couple of cheese sandwiches. These he carried himself to a place at the back of the room, from whose cool, dark shelter he could see the hot sunshine outside, not so much lying upon, as absorbing into itself, the gravel, the wooden benches, the strip of road-dust. John had not settled himself for very long enjoying the look of that shimmering picture framed so caressingly in the doorway, a picture whose only background was a tiny space of misty blue between two ramshackle sheds across the road, when he became aware of a stockily built young man with an open countenance correcting a piece of manuscript.

The fingers which held this person's pencil were those of a manual labourer, but the face that alternately bent down and rose to stare into vacancy was that of a refined scholar. Panic seized the misanthropic John and he thought to himself: "All is lost . . . all is spoilt." He began gobbling his sandwich and gulping his milk. "I'll clear out of here before he speaks. He's sure to speak if I stay. He's a born hailer of strangers!" But the fair young man, who must have been about ten years younger than John, showed no sign of speaking. He continued to stare alternately at his manuscript and at space. John's mind worked in a most characteristic manner now. "My good meal has been spoilt, my good moment has been ruined. But in for a penny in for a pound. I may as well take the plunge."

"Are you a visitor to Glastonbury, Sir?" he asked in a friendly tone. The young man did not seem surprised at being addressed, nor did he seem to take it in ill part. He laid his glass of milk on the top of his manuscript to prevent the wind from ruffling it and pulled his chair a little nearer John's table.

"In a way I am, and in a way I'm not. I'm Edward Athling, from Middlezoy. I live at Haw Bottom Old Farm out there. But perhaps *you* are a stranger? It's nice on a day like this in Glastonbury, isn't it?"

John, in his easily acquired manner of Pageant Advertiser, began at once talking about the new Mayor and his scheme of a Passion Play. Edward Athling listened with extreme interest.

"I believe I could help you over this if you'll let me," he said. "I helped Mr. King with that Sherborne Pageant, in which the Headmaster played Saint Aldhelm."

"We're negotiating," said John, "with two people from the Abbey Theatre in Dublin to come and do the directing for us.

What we *are* in want of—though most of the affair will be just pantomime and dumb show—is a little fragment of libretto. Is that a poem you're writing, Sir, may I ask? It looks like poetry from here."

But the young man waved aside the topic of his immediate occupation. "I'd like uncommonly well," he said, "to try my hand at that bit of libretto for you. Is it about Arthur you'll want it?"

So differently do events work out from what we anticipate that the evasive John, who had locked up his office and was looking forward to a couple of hours of solitary mystic-sensuous enjoyment, now found himself confronted by a regular circus master's dilemma—fear of losing a unique talent and fear of fatally committing himself to the untried!

Ned Athling must have read his thoughts. "I know the kind of poetry you want," he said eagerly. "It must be easy to recite; it must be a bit rhetorical; it must be grandiose; but it must have a touch, a flavour, somewhere about it, of genuine magic."

John experienced a shock of an extremely unpleasant kind when he heard these words. Deep in his sidelong, shifty, dodging, sheering-off nature there was lodged an invincible distaste for all artistic theories. He could recognise genius *in the raw*; but a certain particular expository tone made him feel as if his stomach was full of grey ashes.

Ned Athling scrutinised this lean, uncomfortable person who was now occupied in making little bread pellets of the crumbs of his meal. With every trace of absent-mindedness gone, the young man had the wit to see that his last remark had made the Mayor's secretary wince. He got up boldly therefore and brought both his manuscript and his chair over to John's table.

"I'm going to take the liberty of reading to you the poem I've just written. Its landscape is an imaginary one, like that of Kubla Khan. I've called it 'Merlin, the Enchanter.'"

"One minute, if you don't mind!" cried John, getting up himself and hurrying to the counter. Here he scrupulously and meticulously paid for his milk and cheese, prolonging this transaction all he could, and commenting in the ears of young Pet Othery —a dreamy maid with a Pansy novelette always on her lap—on the unseasonableness of the day's heat. John rushed to pay his bill at this moment because of the mingling in him of an unalloyed impulse to escape from this lad and an invincible dislike of hurting anyone's feelings. It was his private doctrine, based on constant experience, that if you could postpone a disagreeable event even by three minutes, the chances were in favour of something intervening that might save you from it altogether!

Pet Othery, however, as she laid her novelette down on the counter, between a great bowl of milk and a smaller bowl of Devonshire cream, closing a pair of scissors within it, and even her thimble and thread, so that her place should not be lost, began to address John in an excited whisper. "Don't 'ee know, Mister, who that gentleman be who's talkin' to 'ee? 'Tis Mr. Athling from Middlezoy, who everybody says be keeping company with Lady Rachel, the Marquis's only girl. Her father won't have none of 'im, so they say, though the Athlings *be* a good Somerset family; but Lady Rachel, from all accounts, do bide by her own choice and small blame to her, *I* say!" Having uttered her grand piece of communication Miss Othery picked up her novelette again and spread it out luxuriously upon her lap. Her place now proved to have been kept, not only by thimble and thread and scissors, but also by a bit of chocolate, done up in silver paper, which she now proceeded to enjoy. The idea that Mr. Crow might prefer *her* conversation to that of Lady Rachel's young man never for a single second entered her romantic head. Ever afterwards indeed Pet Othery associated this particular volume, which was called "Lizzie Upton's Temptation," with this encounter between the Mayor's secretary and Lady Rachel's lover.

John was compelled therefore to return to his little, round, china-topped table, upon which, heedless of spilt milk, Edward Athling had spread out his poem. The Middlezoy poet read his lines in a low chanting sing-song that mounted up to a quite stirring climax at the end.

Pet Othery lifted her rounded chin from her sewing and from her story, and regarded him with eyes of soft and melting tenderness. The sunlight flooded the gravel outside the open door with such a warm dusty glow that it gave to the interior of this little shop a dim cloistral coolness that lent itself well to this occasion.

"This wind has blown the sun out of his place!
I look towards the West and lo! a vast,
Lost-battle-broken bastion covers up
The natural sky; to what rain-ramparted
Region of huge disaster, do these hills,
Toppling above each other, ridge on ridge,
With trees that in the night are heaped like moss,
With trees that darken into tapestries
Of vaporous moss, with roads that travelling
Thro' terraces of twilight lose themselves
In green-black tumuli of mystery,
In piled-up mounds of moss and mystery,
Lead my soul thro' the silence? Not a stone
But talks in muffled tongue to other stones.
There's not a wild, wet-beaked, night-flying bird
That does not scream upon this tossing wind
To other, darker birds, my cry, my cry,
Of rumours and of runes and reckonings,
Of rain-whirled storm-wrack rolls of malediction!
And I the Enchanter, riding on these hills,
And on the stags that trample on these hills,
And on this twilight and on these heaped mounds
Of mystery and on these wild birds' wings,
Death-runes, death-rumours, ruins and rains of death
Am now myself this wind, this wind, this wind,
This wind, that's blown the sun out of his place!"

John Crow's countenance would have been worthy of the stage as it changed from nervous boredom to startled surprise and from surprise to imaginative arrest and from imaginative arrest to a rush of excited resolution. But it was characteristic of him to jump at once—without any intervening steps—to the main issue. "Come on, Mr. Athling, come on, Sir!" he cried, rising to his feet, and, clutching at the poet's modest bill, which was inscribed on a slip of paper with the words "Othery's Dairy" printed on the top of it, he rushed over to the young lady. Unfortunately for this impulsive motion of premature hospitality John's pockets contained no more than a penny half-penny, whereas Athling's debt to the shop was fourpence.

But the farmer-poet produced sixpence, and ignorant of the fact that he was tipping the daughter of the house he left the change, in addition to John's penny half-penny, upon the counter.

"Have you time to come to the Mayor's house?" said John

eagerly. "It's quite close. I was going to watch the boys playing rounders on Wirral Hill for a bit, and then go back to the office, but I know Mr. Geard will jump at your help if he hears that poem. It's exactly the sort of thing we want! It's almost as if you were thinking of us when you wrote it. You must come to our first rehearsals. Those Dublin people won't be able to come till we've got pretty far advanced and there are . . . I don't know quite how to put it . . . several ways of taking the Grail-Cult . . . which . . . which . . . the Mayor and I . . . don't want to appear at all! There are . . . a few things too . . . that I am very keen to get put in . . . and if you ——"

Never has any cardsharper, never has any pickpocket, never has any scallywag of a circus camp-follower, leered as craftily as John did then, into the open countenance of Edward Athling. The young man himself was struck by the look, and he had penetration enough to detect the fact that this excess of exaggerated cunning was really as transparent as the lying of a child.

"I feel," Athling said to John, as they approached Cardiff Villa, "as if I were the Player King being taught my sprinkling of miching mallecho."

"This Pageant," said John with a quick sidelong glance to see how the youth would take it, "is going to upset a great many people."

"Of course," said Athling, "any original work of art is upsetting to the mob."

John held his peace at this point. It was not his custom to weigh a person's character by anything that he said, least of all by any of these rather sententious remarks that Mr. Athling seemed to have a tendency to utter. John had his own secret and peculiar method of sounding a stranger's intellectual and emotional nature. It was a kind of etheric, psychic embrace, but not necessarily of an amorous character. The truth is that for John the soul of every person he met was something that he was doomed to explore. His own soul was like a vaporous serpent, and it rushed forth from the envelope of his body and wound itself round this other, licking this other's eye-sockets with its forked tongue, peering into its heart and into its brain, and pressing a cold snake-head against its feverish nerves.

The result of the coiling of John's soul round the soul of Athling as he walked by his side along this hot dusty path, towards
Cardiff Villa, was that he realised that nothing could conceivably
ever make Athling understand the mystical ecstasy of destruction
and the deep metaphysical malice with which he longed to under-
mine the Grail Legend. The whole tone of the lad when he said
that original art was upsetting to the mob was distasteful to John.
John's instincts were profoundly anti-æsthetic. When he enjoyed
anything it was by direct contact, as if the thing were a physical
sensation, and the laws, principles, rules, methods, purposes, intentions, and above all the *opinions* that led up to this especial
thing, seemed to him nothing but exhausting and tedious pedantry, devoid of all value.

They came now to Cardiff Villa, and John, opening the iron
gate with a click, led Edward Athling up the little path between
the privet bushes to the front entrance. Sally Jones, who had been
watching their approach through the kitchen door, which opened
straight upon the street, hurried through the hallway in a fever
of excitement to let them in. She too, like Pet Othery, knew Ned
Athling, as a local celebrity, and like all the Glastonbury girls
had been thrilled by the rumours connecting him with Lady Rachel
Zoyland, the daughter of the Marquis of P.

The master of Cardiff Villa gave his visitors a very cordial
welcome when he found them in his dining-room, and John lost
no time in making his captured poet recite the lines about Merlin.
The Mayor listened with his big head sunk on his chest and his
eyes closed; but when Athling had finished it was clear that something in the verses had touched a kindred chord in him, for he
clapped his plump hands together and uttered several times a
sound which it is impossible to represent in print otherwise than
by the syllables "urr-rorr . . . urr-rorr . . . urr-rorr!" This
sound was eminently satisfactory to John, and apparently not less
so to the author, for the latter plunged at once into an impassioned
description as to what he would do if they gave him a free hand
with the libretto.

One of the most practical results that followed from this introduction of young Athling to Mr. Geard—and John was not one

to suffer from jealousy—was the fact that a few days later the whole place was placarded with posters announcing a public meeting in the Abbot's Tribunal to consider "a new scheme for increasing the prestige of our ancient Town." This public meeting was announced for eight o'clock on the first of the month, and as a result of this choice of a date the word circulated among the frivolous that the Mayor-elect was to address his fellow-citizens adorned with a fool's cap. It was characteristic of the man that in order to gather together his ideas for this momentous oration— the first that it was his destiny to deliver to the general public since those early street-corner harangues—he should make a private visit on the morning of April Fool's Day to the recesses of Wookey Hole.

Intentionally or not Mr. Geard paid his sixpence at the gate of Wookey Hole at such an early hour that the person who received it was not Will Zoyland but Mr. Lamb, the landlord of the Zoyland Arms, an individual who, though he had heard of the new Mayor of Glastonbury, had never set eyes on him, and had not, therefore, the least idea that he was admitting to his subterranean domain Philip's grand antagonist. Bloody Johnny had never, as it happened, visited the cavernous shrine of the Witch of Wookey since Philip had electrified the famous caves and it was an exciting experience for him to wander down that illuminated pathway, watching the amazing metallic colours which these brilliant globes of light drew forth from the stalactites. He had the whole place to himself, a thing that Zoyland, when he was at the gate, always tried to avoid, being afraid of people losing themselves, and also afraid of the intrusion of tin-mining agents from alien firms; but Mr. Lamb, naturally a very easy-going person, was not one to have his wits about him at nine in the morning. What he ought to have done was to make this early visitor sit down in the little shanty at the entrance and wait till more strangers arrived, before turning on the lights, but Mr. Geard got the full benefit, as he often did in the general drift of things, of this example of human negligence.

He descended slowly between the rows of stalactites till he came to the level floor in the biggest of the caverns where ran that tributary of the subterranean River Axe. Here he saw Philip's boat, pulled up on a shelving bank of sand and left exactly as it was when Persephone had stepped out of it. After a moment's hesitation, for he was no oarsman, Mr. Geard entered this boat, and with a good many blunderings and splashings, contrived at last to row himself to the strip of shingle beneath that huge array of phallic symbols over which the formidable stone image of the Witch of Wookey held her obscene vigil of immeasurable æons. Here Bloody Johnny awkwardly disembarked, feeling, though he knew nothing of Dante, very much what that mediæval Harrower of Hell felt, when he, still a man of flesh-and-blood, moved among the infernal wraiths. He advanced under the precipitous wall of the vast cavern, his feet sinking, as he walked, in the loose shingle of that Acherontic shore. Here he seated himself on a strip of dry sand and leaned his back against the wall of stone. He could not help wondering to himself what it would feel like if these electric lights were suddenly to be extinguished!

Staring into the face of that stone image, in that place lighted up by the science of his enemy, Mr. Geard found it easy enough to restore to Wookey Hole the thick, long darkness into which it had fallen after the last human tribe deserted it. It was out of the midst of this long darkness rather than in the new electric light that his nature now expanded. His large hands lay palms down, and with the fingers spread out, like two great, white starfish, on the shingle at both sides of him. No sign of life was there, no grass-blade, no insect, no bird. He was alone with the metallic elements out of which all organic entities are formed.

Mr. Geard was not good at concentrated thinking. His deepest thoughts always came to him, as the author of *Faust* declared *his* did, crying, like happy children, "Here we are!" and the result of this was that a brief half an hour spent in composing his speech for that night exhausted him far more than the most protracted physical exertion would have done. He found himself caught and, as it were, pilloried, in the repetition of certain particular phrases. This happened to him every time he deserted his vague, rich, semi-erotic feelings and tried to condense his scheme into a rational statement, and it became really troublesome when, with his eyes tightly closed, he set himself to call up that audience of people and to imagine their response to what he said. The thought of the audience and of this accursed appeal to reason seemed to throw a thin dust of unpalatable sand over his whole life-purpose.

He continued to sit in the same position, with his fingers outstretched on that subterranean shingle, and his eyes closed; but the rational effort his mind had begun to make brought about him all the unpleasant aspects of his normal life. A certain little piece of lead-piping scrawled with a mark that always looked to him like a crocodile's snout, and which he invariably caught sight of from the window of the water-closet on the landing of Cardiff Villa, now presented itself before his closed eyes as he began to phrase his speech. A certain stair-rod that had got hopelessly loose and that caused a peculiar rumpling of the stair-carpet obtruded itself before his vision. A certain indescribable familiarity which hung about the old doormat at Cardiff Villa and the scraper—as if these things had been placed at his gate by the Evil One himself, especially to keep down the tempo of his mystical thoughts—came stealing over his mind. The painted metal cover of a certain matchbox which was kept on the dining-room mantelpiece and which always seemed to evoke the sterile aridity of hours of flat, spiritless repletion hove also in sight. Certain physical aspects of his wife and his elder daughter, certain tones of their voices, when they were least sympathetic to him, rushed pell-mell into his head. The gigantic phlegm of Mr. Geard and his massive, lumbering, lubberly passivity seemed to bring it about that these trifles adhered thus viciously to his memory, like burrs and prickles to the fur of some great drowsy beast. With what repulsive clearness too, as he went on struggling to formulate his ideas, a certain glittering and yet curiously insipid light appeared before his fast-shut eyes, the "two o'clock" and "three o'clock" light, falling on the galvanised-iron roof of the unused toolshed in his neglected garden!

Teased to the top of his bent by what he had evoked in his dangerous gesture of damming up the sluices of his feelings by the machinery of reason, Bloody Johnny had recourse now to the grand human panacea for all mental aggravations. He did what he ought to have done at once, before he started worrying his mind about his speech at all; he allowed his chin to sink down upon his burly chest and subsided into a deep and dreamless sleep. Down upon the bowed head of Geard of Glastonbury fell Philip's electric light. Over his head the Stone Witch stared at her morgue of petrified indecencies. Beneath his feet rolled the swift, silent, metal-gleaming current of that water of Lethe. Noon came upon those Somersetshire spring-meadows above his sleeping-place, with their cuckoo flowers and marsh marigolds, and gave place to an afternoon of rain-threatening cloud-racks that gathered heavily upon the western horizon. But still Mr. Geard slept. Several times he changed his position without awakening, and at last his head and his shoulders actually slid down to the stalagmite base of the Stone Witch, and instinctively sought there a smooth concavity against which to lie at rest.

The long cloudy afternoon of April Fool's day ebbed slowly away. Those cloud-racks, gathering above the distant Welsh mountains, grew more and more ominous. Long swaying arms, outstretched hooked fingers, hooded shoulders, nodding plumes, far-streaming tattered banners, huge-tilted swords and monstrous axes, towered there over the Western Channel and neither advanced nor dispersed! In this portentous hovering and lingering they resembled those spirits of the departed in the ancient British Isles, of which Plutarch makes mention, quoting from the traveller Demetrius: "Demetrius further said, that of the islands around Britain many were uninhabited. . . . He went to the island which lay nearest to those uninhabited and found it occupied by few inhabitants . . . who were, however, sacrosant and inviolable in the eyes of the Britons. Soon after his arrival a great disturbance of the atmosphere took place, accompanied by many portents, by the winds bursting forth into hurricanes and by fiery bolts falling. When it was over, the islanders said that some one of the mighty had passed away . . . moreover there is there, they said, an island in which Cronos is imprisoned, with Briareus keeping guard over him as he sleeps, for, as they put it, sleep is the bond forged for Cronos. They add that around him are many deities, his henchmen and attendants."

And when that threatened and menaced day drew to a close at last, if Will Zoyland before turning off the electric light had decided to take a stroll down these passages and had got as far as the edge of the subterranean water he would have been astonished to see a second figure, "couchant, in-bend, sable," lying beside that stalagmitish sorceress.

There was quite a large audience collected together that night to hear the first public speech of the new Mayor. The Abbot's Tribunal did not offer very extensive accommodation nor a very liberal number of seats for those who *did* get in, but, as the entertainment was given gratis, the late-comers to the meeting had no cause for grievance if they found themselves somewhat uncomfortably crowded.

The only representative from The Elms was the redoubtable Emma Sly who came, in a very literal sense, to "spy out the land," for it may well be believed what a shrewd account, and a more succinct one than any other Glastonbury hand-maid could have given, the mistress of The Elms looked forward to receiving while she ordered Philip's dinner on the following day.

Miss Drew, too, refrained from attending "this silly speechifying"; but the Misses Rogers came from the Abbey House just as Penny Pitches, escorted by Isaac Weatherwax, came from the Vicarage.

Both the Dekkers were there, as were also Dr. Fell and his formidable sister, Miss Bibby.

Old Lawyer Beere turned up, rather to John Crow's surprise, bringing with him his daughter Angela, who had never looked paler, colder, more unapproachable, and more completely bored than she looked as she took her seat between her father and Mr. Stilly, the cashier of the bank.

Miss Elizabeth Crow arrived in very good time, escorted, in true old-fashioned style, by her plump maid, Tossie Stickles, who, once in the hall, separated herself from her mistress and became all eyes to get a glimpse of her gentleman-admirer, the nympholeptish Mr. Barter. In this hope, however, the girl was disappointed, for Barter was not present.

Megan Geard was in the front of the hall, taciturn and indifferent, wearing a velvet gown cut and flounced according to the fashion of at least a decade ago, and treating the whole occasion with a withdrawn disdain more worthy of the house of Rhys than of the position of Mayoress. Crummie, in a dress of bewitching simplicity, was turning her beautiful chin all the time to steal hurried and furtive glimpses of Sam Dekker, whose own attention was focussed upon the entrance-door, for he was at once hoping and dreading that Zoyland might have taken it into his impulsive head to bring Nell into town for this one occasion!

Among the humbler members of the crowd there were present Mrs. Robinson and Mrs. Cole, Sally Jones and her brother Jackie. Jenny Morgan, the once lovely Glastonbury charwoman, had come too, bringing Number One's little friend "Morgan Nelly" with her, but from the manner in which this woman's large tragic eyes kept closing and her sad underlip kept drooping and her shoulder kept leaning against the wall by one of the windows, it looked as if the Mayor's speech would have to be very lively indeed to keep her from falling asleep.

The old cronies, Number One and Number Two, were seated, in anticipatory bliss, side by side. Red Robinson sat at the back of the room, in what he felt to be the precise strategic position for the art of heckling, but he never once looked at Crummie. If he looked at any girl at all, all that evening, it was at the Geard servant, Sally, but even these glances were quickly exhausted. Red's head was so full of politics that he had scant energy left to include love.

Mr. Evans and Cordelia sat at the edge of one of the aisles in the centre of the room. Mr. Evans seemed to be as much withdrawn into his thoughts as Mrs. Geard was withdrawn into the pride of her South Wales blood, for it was only once or twice that he glanced at the platform, although he was seated so near it.

John and Mary, the former arrayed—as the insignia of a Master of Ceremonies—in a neat dinner-jacket, borrowed for the occasion from Tom Barter but which was at once much too short and much too loose for him, were seated in the front row, which was occupied, otherwise, by old Mr. and Mrs. Stilly, the parents of the cashier, by the Reverend Dr. Sodbury, the Rector of St. Benignus, and by Mr. Wollop, the ex-Mayor. It cannot be said that Mr. Wollop looked *quite* as happy seated in the front row of his rival's audience as he looked in his cage, but he looked, all the same, about twice as happy as anyone else in the Tribunal.

Dave Spear and Persephone sat just behind the ex-Mayor; and

it gradually became a cause of much suppressed giggling and tittering at the back of the room to notice the manner in which the worthy obese man kept twisting his head round to talk to the beautiful Percy, whose brown boy-curls and white shoulders— for though Dave was in plain ordinary clothes, Percy, for some caprice of her own, appeared in evening dress—seemed of great interest to him.

Towards the roofs of Glastonbury, towards the Gothic roof of the Abbot's Tribunal, advanced that black cloud-rack from the western sea, but although every now and then there was a deep, rolling peal of thunder, not one single drop of rain fell. These heavy jagged clouds, this first of April night, were like the evil clouds spoken of in the Scriptures, for they were "clouds without water."

But the big church-clock in St. John's Tower struck eight, which was the hour of the meeting, and there was no sign of the Mayor, nor of any move to supply his place if he did not come. There were three Aldermen in the little waiting-room at the back of the platform, and these worthy men were now beginning to perspire with perturbation. On the empty platform were five empty chairs, one for the Mayor, one for old Mr. Bishop, the Town Clerk, and the others for these anxious and nervous officials who were now growing distressingly conscious of their boots and trousers and socks and were continually retiring to the little lavatory in the rear of their room. There were quite a number of young people at the back of the hall, some seated, some standing, some moving restlessly about, and every now and then there would arise from this turbulent element various cries and laughter and even clappings and hissings, as this or that crude jest was bandied about in connection with the absence of the Mayor.

St. John's clock now chimed the news laconically and briefly that it was a quarter past eight. The unruly element in that tightly packed little hall began to grow seriously troublesome. The jokes grew grosser and broader. "Mayor be drunk!" cried one. "Better send they Aldermen to look for he in Michael's Inn!" cried another. "Mayor be making April Fools of us poor dogs, now 'ee be so rich and so set up!" growled a third. "Mayor be enjoyin isself wi' wold Mother Legge in Paradise!" declared one lad, bolder than the rest. "Shush! Shush!" cried several voices.

Meanwhile Abel Twig and his crony Bart Jones were whispering together in high excitement. "Them Posters said 'twas for Glast'n 'ee were holdin' meetin'. Seems to I 'twere for to see how much foolin' Glast'n folk could stand, afore us cast he down, back where he were afore us lifted he up." Thus spoke Old Jones in the ear of his friend, but Number One was kinder in his interpretation. "Maybe Mayor have been taken wi' the dizzies, like what woming do suffer from, when 'tis near their time. 'Tis a hard thing for even a Preacher like he to stand up afore such a proud assembling!"

Penny Pitches who had taken her seat without shame by the side of Mr. Weatherwax now addressed a personal appeal to that potentate. " 'Twould be a moment for thee to strike up wi' one o' thee pretty songs, Isaac," she declared stoutly. "Thik Bloody Johnny baint the only one what can lift up voice."

"Chut, chut, woman!" murmured the gardener reproachfully. "This be a time for Authority to speak. The man *I* be wantin' to hear from, be Mr. Philip Crow. He'd be the gent to send all these gabbling geese to the right-about."

A long rolling thunder-clap responded to the gardener's words from those slowly gathering clouds above the Tribunal. "Hark to't!" cried Penny Pitches, "he'll have to come quick or he'll be drenched to the skin!"

The sympathetic Sally Jones, seriously concerned about the fate of her master, murmured anxiously in Jackie's ear: "I can't keep me eyes from Missuses' back, I can't. She must be shiverin' and shakin' inside, poor dear! 'Tis turble 'sponsive to be sittin' up so straight and Master not here."

"You don't think, Sal, do 'ee," whispered the excited Jackie, "that the thunder have hit 'im in the eyeball like it used to hit they bad girt men in Bible?"

St. John's deep-voiced clock now chimed the half hour and its sound died away in the midst of a thick, deep, reverberating peal of sullen thunder.

"Why isn't there any lightning, Father?" said Angela Beere to Lawyer Beere. "I haven't seen one single flash all the evening."

The girl let her eyes rest, as she spoke, upon the beautiful nape of Persephone's neck. Those brown boyish curls were beginning to touch a vein of perilous susceptibility in that reserved nature.

It is, in fact, at moments of this kind, when a company of fellow-townspeople are gathered in close proximity, with nothing to do but to stare at one another, that all sorts of unexpected relationships leap up into being.

"We needn't have hurried through our dinner after all, it seems," was her father's characteristic reply to this question about the lightning.

"Not a drop of rain, Sam," said the Vicar of Glastonbury to his son.

"I'm glad of it," murmured Sam, thinking to himself that his Nell might, even yet, be on her way to the Tribunal.

It was at that moment that old Mr. Sheperd, the Glastonbury policeman, moved up to the back of the Town Clerk's chair. "Hadn't 'ee better begin, Sir?" he said earnestly. "Maybe his Worship ain't coming, and these young rogues will be getting out of hand soon."

The Town Clerk nodded wearily, got up with difficulty from his creaking chair, for he was past eighty, and made his way down the hall. He paused for a minute by the side of John Crow, with whom he held a brief consultation, watched with intense curiosity by everybody in the place. Then he entered the room at the back of the platform. Here he found the three Aldermen, who advanced to greet him in trepidation and consternation. "Come on, gentlemen," he said, in the tone of an aged warrior, who has weathered crises far worse than this trifling one in the course of his long life. "On to the stage with ye! I'll open the meeting and call on the Mayor's secretary." Herding the three nervous magnates in front of him, like three reluctant and sulky bullocks, the gallant Mr. Bishop scrambled up the platform steps after them and took his seat in the Mayor's chair.

The four men were greeted with uproarious applause, and the clapping and shouting continued for at least three solid minutes. "Three cheers for Mr. Bishop!" shouted one young scaramouch who had perched himself upon the high sill of one of the great mullioned windows. The Town Clerk rose to his feet and advanced to the square table in the centre of the platform. Here he raised his hand for silence. The general relief at the presence of some-one was so great that he was responded to by an impressive and startling hush.

"Ladies and gentlemen," Mr. Bishop began, "we have come here to listen to our distinguished fellow-citizen, the newly elected Mayor of Glastonbury, Mr. John Geard."

" 'Ear, 'ear!" came the magnanimous and comfortable voice of Mr. Wollop from his place in the front row.

"But since," Mr. Bishop went on, "the inclement weather, or some other cause at present unknown, has prevented our much-regretted Mayor from being present at this meeting which he himself called together, it behoves me, as his humble official sub-ordinate, to call upon his secretary, my young friend, Mr. John Crow, to tell us, or read to us, if possible, in the Mayor's own words, a resoomy"—this was the only long word in the Town Clerk's repertoire of public speaking that he pronounced incor-rectly—"a resoomy of our distinguished friend's inspiring ideas with regard to the future of our beloved town. I therefore call upon Mr. Crow to ——"

There arose at that instant such a curious hubbub at the back of the room that the three Aldermen leaned forward from the edge of their chairs and craned their necks to see round the speaker's back and under the speaker's armpits what it was that caused the disturbance. When the worthy men *did* realise what was the cause of the confusion, they gazed at one another and at the back of Mr. Bishop in sheer dumbfounded stupor. The people in the front of the audience began themselves turning round now, and some among them when they realised what was occurring began to raise that hoarse, grating susurration which indicates, to any experienced speaker, the complete impossibility of receiving a quiet hearing.

"I therefore call upon Mr. Crow," went on the old Town Clerk, "to ——" John Crow, who was on his feet now and facing the back of the room, realised in a flash the bitter humour—as far as he was concerned—of what had occurred, but his first feeling was one of indescribable relief. He felt like a hunted fox, with all the pack at his heels, who unexpectedly finds a hole—and a

hole with a second exit! When Mr. Bishop told him he would have
to speak he had had a spasm of sick terror and had come near to
flatly refusing. Then he had thought: "After all, why not? Geard
will probably come in while I'm getting up steam. And there's
nothing really to funk in these people!"

But now it wasn't Geard who had come, but Philip!

"I therefore call upon Mr. Crow ——" the Town Clerk had
said, and some anonymous voice, in the crowd at the rear of the
hall, had cried out "*He's here!* Mr. Crow be here!" and everyone
who turned round saw Philip standing there, in the leather jacket
of a flyer, motionless and with a grim smile on his face. "He's
here, Sir; Mr. Crow is here, Sir!" shouted a second voice.

Philip's contemptuous smile changed its nature in a moment.
He threw down his leather cap, and stepped rapidly down the
centre aisle towards the platform.

The three Aldermen, hypnotised by their inherited West-
Country respect for the richest man of their town, rose from their
chairs to welcome him. Mr. Bishop, who still stood by the speaker's table, murmured rather feebly: "I am sure that everyone here
will be glad to learn if Mr. . . . if Mr. *Philip* Crow has any
opinions which he would care ——" But here his voice was
drowned in a resounding and quite unpremeditated salvo of
clapping.

Every audience, however hurriedly collected, quickly takes to
itself a queer identity of its own and becomes a living organism
whose reactions are as spontaneous and incalculable as those of
a single human being. There had naturally arisen a certain obscure
feeling against the newly elected Mayor for his non-appearance, a
feeling that they had been fooled and cheated. This was combined with a hardly conscious sense that Geard, as a man risen
from the ranks, demanded less consideration at their hands than
the well-known manufacturer. Philip's unpopularity, too, was
much more serious with the poorest and least educated in the
town, an element that was hardly represented in the Tribunal
tonight.

Thus when, encouraged by the applause with which he was
greeted, Philip mounted the platform and advanced to the table,
while Mr. Bishop and the three Aldermen sat down, there was

given to him—in one of those psychological up-burstings of feeling to which the crowd-organism is subject—a terrific ovation, by
far the most spontaneous he had ever received in Glastonbury. It
may well be believed that it was the conservative Mr. Weatherwax
—excited beyond all measure by the actual appearance of that
"authority" he so greatly admired—who now lifted up his manly
voice and shouted loudly: "Three cheers for Mr. Crow!"

The uproar that followed was deafening. When silence was at
last obtained, Philip leaned forward across the table and made
one of the cleverest political speeches of his life. When it was
over, and Mr. Bishop rose to make a few polite comments, John
whispered to Mary: "What a fellow he is! I hate him, but I can't
help being . . . in some odd way . . . you know? . . . our old
Norfolk blood . . . able to . . . assert itself still . . . and
make . . . these fools . . . sit up a bit!"

Philip's hard, cold, clear voice was indeed ringing in the ears
of everyone present. "And so," his final words had run, "the best
way to make our town the sort of place we would all be proud of
living in is to make it independent of these precious visitors from
Europe and America. A living wage for every man who wants
to do a good honest day's work is what *I* am aiming at. Not old
fairy stories but new factories is what *I* want to see; not fake-
miracles but solid hard work; not fancy toys and mystical gibberish but smoking chimneys and well-filled larders! Let these
visitors, when they come to Glastonbury, find in place of vague
chatter about Chalice Hill a prosperous, independent community;
a community that does not need to beg or dance or 'sing,' as the
old song says, 'for its supper'; a community that can afford to
hire its theatrical performances; a community that is too busy
and too well-employed to have its head turned by crazy preachers
and self-appointed Popes!"

It is not contrary to the weakness of human nature to enjoy the
spectacle of a crafty blow aimed at an absent adversary, but if it
had not been for his audience's obscure sense that their dignity
had been outraged by Mr. Geard's non-appearance, Philip's malicious words would not have had the effect they had. He was
vociferously applauded as he sat down, and when, after Mr.
Bishop's diplomatic closing of the meeting and after everyone

had risen up to sing the first verse of "God save the King," there was a general feeling in that audience's mind, intensified rather than diminished by the distant thunder—still unaccompanied by a single drop of rain—that a leader who allowed himself to be betrayed into deserting his post at so crucial a crisis had received no less than his due from this hawk-faced despot in a leather jacket, who advocated *laborem et panem*, rather than any kind of *circenses*, as his panacea for the ills of their town.

Thus in the criss-cross currents of this eventful April Fool's Day, dominated by "clouds without water," Bloody Johnny and his ambiguous Grail received a Dolorous Blow from which it appeared possible that neither of them might recover. In that sequence of spiral recurrences—in which past events are eternally returning, but with momentous difference—the same psychological situation had been produced as when in those long-vanished mysterious days the wistful and audacious Balin wounded the Guardian of the Grail in both his thighs with the terrible Spear of Longinus.

Every person, as that motley audience left the Abbot's Tribunal, was conscious that something deep had been stirred up, ready to respond to Geard of Glastonbury's communication, and that this Something had been suppressed by the malice of superficial human nature, played upon by a practised hand. There was a feeling among them all as they went off as if they had stretched out their arms to grasp a Golden Bough and had been rewarded for their pains with a handful of dust.

It was with a queer, vague, irritated sense of uncomfortable remorse that they went home, with the murmur of that strange spring thunder in their ears that brought neither rain nor lightning. And as the night fell on the roofs of Glastonbury it was as if She Herself, the historic matrix of all these happenings, had been thwarted and fooled at the critical moment of her mystic response.

The generative nerve of Her body had descended into Her womb, but all to no purpose! Cold and hard and pragmatic, the words of the Norfolk iconoclast had cut off the consummation of Her desire. From the forlorn thorn stumps of Tom Chinnock's Terre Gastée at the foot of Wirral Hill the effects of this Dolorous

Blow seemed likely to spread over the whole psychic landscape. Let Her labor and let Her eat, but let the Stone of Merlin remain a stone, and the Fountain of Blood remain a chalybeate spring!

When Mrs. Geard and her daughters reached Cardiff Villa that night they found the master of the house seated alone by the fire in the dining-room, with a glass of gin and water by his side. Above him on the mantelpiece lay, in its accustomed place, the little ornamental matchbox. From the water-closet window on the landing above he had heard the familiar lead-piping give itself to the night once more, with its wonted word—"the unessential shall swallow up the essential!" The well-worn doormat and the rusty scraper outside his door emanated the same spiritless and domesticated monotony. As all these things had looked before he went to Northwold, so they looked now, when, after extricating himself with characteristic phlegm and obstinate patience from a darkened Wookey Hole, he had come straight home to his empty house.

THE FIRST HESITATING SPROUTINGS OF CHILLY, DUMB, WHITISH-green vegetation had forced their way into the clear air and established themselves above ground. The mysteriously released saps and life-essences, faint, mute and fitful, had now risen high enough to fill the cold stiff stalks and fling a new smoothness and a new resilience into their upward-striving curves.

The early, perilously sweet blooms, such as those greenish-yellow calyxes of the first daffodils, catching the spouts and jets of the chilly sunshine from between the wind-tossed clouds, and bowing their wet petals to the brown earth under the heavy showers of rain, had given place to the far sturdier, if less poignant, growths of the later spring season. Tulips were now out by the edge of most of the Glastonbury lawns and the heavy waxen towers of the garden hyacinths—purple and pink and white and blue—had already passed their apogee of inebriating sweetness and were sinking down day by day into their rich death. The more innocent and more childlike scent of lilacs too was already on the air; and the renewal of the earth had even advanced far enough for the great drooping sprays of the laburnum trees in Mr. Weatherwax's two old gardens to be bursting out into delicate buds. Peonies also—those unrestricting, unwithholding orbs of lavish wholesomeness—were now to be seen in many warm parterres; while across the old masonry of the smaller gardens where bright-cheeked girls flitting in and out of their houses into the sunshine, like moving flowers themselves in their fresh Easter frocks, kept laughing and challenging one another as they heard that familiar sound, came on the southwest wind the mocking cry of the cuckoo.

Three weeks had slipped by since Sam Dekker had lain with Nell Zoyland upon that carefully prepared couch by the White-lake waters—three fecund weeks; and hours sweet as honey, and hours bitter as coloquintida, had slid down the same fatal slope into everlasting oblivion.

Glastonbury had the air, in that halcyon weather, of being

some ancient mediæval city, enclosed in paradisiac green
pastures; a city that Fra Angelico might have painted, giving it
a foreground of watercresses and long-legged herons.

April was now more than a fortnight old and a late Easter
was approaching. On the morning of Maundy Thursday, after a
windless night when the moon, already nearly full, had flooded
the hazel copses and the withy beds with such liquid radiance
that every brittle primrose stalk and every sap-heavy bluebell
stalk had cast its own particular shadow on wet clay or cold
stone, Cordelia Geard, dressed herself like a blue hyacinth and
with her plain face quite illuminated by the regenerative stirrings
on all sides of her, opened the street door of Old Jones' shop in
the High Street and plunged boldly into its cluttered and century-
mellowed obscurity.

The sun was warm upon the High Street pavement outside;
but a kind of misty eidolon of the sun—a sort of secondary sun,
more golden, just because it was more dimmed, than the first—
poured its rich glow, crowded thick with gleaming air-motes,
upon all the entanglement of bric-à-brac within the shop walls.
This secondary sun, more golden than the first, as if Number
Two's shop had been a forest glade in some fairyland where roots
were old chairs and where branches were old copper candlesticks,
fell in long streaming rays from above the dragon vase and the
Pierrot-lidded pepper-pot and the red-feathered shuttlecock and
the unfashionable croquet-mallet and the shaving-mug with the
Rhine castle upon it and made a thick, dim, rusty glory, full of
portentous curves and colours and contours, of the piled-up furniture and twisted brasses of that dim place. It was an arcana of
the crazy imaginations of old anonymous craftsmen, this shop of
Number Two. Old Bartholomew Jones was not a modern virtuoso
or a sophisticated connoisseur. He was a Glastonbury character.
But something deeply instinctive in the man had led him for
years and years—for something like half a century in fact—to
collect his objects with a personal predilection all his own, a
predilection which, while neither very learned nor very æsthetic,
had a certain pathos of choice peculiar to itself. The shop was
in fact a limbo of the characteristic symbols of the life of former
times.

Glastonbury here, layer by layer through the centuries, was revealed in certain significant petrifactions, certain frozen gestures of the flowing spirit of life, as it was caught up, waylaid, turned into silk, satin, brass, iron, wood, leather, silver, china, linen, pictured books, printed books, play utensils, kitchen utensils, timepieces, wine decanters, toys, traps, walking-sticks and weapons.

It was not an Aladdin's cave for children; and indeed about many of the objects, warming-pans and bird-cages and fire-dogs and so forth, there was something that suggested besotted and miserly old age rather than youth. But it was a treasure-trove for the type of imagination that loves to brood, a little sardonically and unfastidiously perhaps, upon the wayward whims and caprices of the human spirit.

Mr. Evans had even discovered—for Number Two's system of collecting curiosities was evidently rather philosophic than artistic—certain quaint objects, much more recent than the numerous antimacassars and artificial fruits under glass which he had selected, objects that the owner apparently thought significant of the age of his own early youth, such as rusty bicycle handles and tricycle wheels and parlour games like Lotto and Spelicans.

The thick, golden light seemed to reach the eyes through some indescribably rich medium, like old sherry wine, which hung above all this chaos. And it was as if it had gathered to itself some magical potency that particular morning.

Cordelia Geard, for all her new blue dress and over-ladylike hat, could not resist a queer sensation as she looked round the place as if she had entered a magician's cave, and had exposed herself to some unknown possibility of bodily transmutation. She felt as though Number Two's shop, in the same way as it could make mid-Victorian parlour games look like Roman antiquities, could transform a girl of the second decade of the twentieth century into some platonic symbol of erotic expectation. It had been the southwestern wind and the lilac-scented air that had brought her into her fiancé's domain; but she had not suspected that this leaping up of life outside would be answered reciprocally among the littered simulacra inside! But as she stood waiting now, seeing no one and afraid of lifting her voice, she felt as if she were greeted in that sun-illumined space by a chorus of muted whispers. The carved knobs of an early-Victorian bed murmured extraordinary things to her. A blue vase with big white basketwork handles became still more voluble.

The girl in blue fixed a frowning glance upon this latter object. "He must be upstairs making his bed," she thought. "I would dearly like to make his bed for him!"

And then, gathering up all her forces into one terrific resolve, "I'll *make* him love me like other men love their women," she said to herself. "I'll *make* him love me like Crummie makes Red and Mr. Barter love her. Women *can* do these things! Women can make themselves like tinder to a match, like filings to a magnet, like straw to a spark!"

Cordelia's dark eyes began to gather a strange, excited light as her heart went on telling her heart what she would do to rouse the desire of Mr. Evans on this Maundy Thursday morning. She set herself to listen intently; and she thought she *did* hear sounds; but oddly enough these faint sounds that she heard seemed to come from under her feet rather than from above her head and they resembled the scraping of a nervous heel against a bare board rather than the rustling of sheets on a bed.

Cordelia had never heard Mr. Evans refer to the chamber below stairs where reposed that curious volume—now separated from the Saint Augustine, its aforetime companion—that was such a danger to the Welshman's peace of mind; but she began to experience a vague sense of feminine uneasiness, totally without any rational cause, about her friend.

"He *ought* to be in the shop by this time," she thought. "It must be nearly ten o'clock."

The sudden opening of the street door made her swing round. It made her heart give a wild jump. The figure who entered was Red Robinson.

The man gave Cordelia a nervous nod; but he neither took off his cap, nor offered her his hand, nor even closed the shop door. "I'm looking for his Worship," he said, with a sneer upon the syllables "Worship." " 'E's not at 'ome. 'E's not at Town-'All. 'E's not at 'is Hoffice. Where *his* 'is Worship? *That's* what I want to know. I've got somethink himportant to harx 'im."

"Can I give my father any message, Red?" asked Cordelia. "He'll no doubt be home for dinner . . . our mid-day dinner, you know, Red."

The man hesitated.

"Well! You might tell him that I'll say nothing more to that Morgan woman; since that his 'is Worship's pleasure. Nothing more to 'er, tell 'im; and hall shall be has 'e wishes!"

Cordelia bowed gravely. "Surely, Red, surely! Yes, I'll certainly tell Father that. You'll say no more to the Morgan woman according as my father wishes."

Red nodded, took out his pipe and lit it in the doorway, and then cleared off.

When Cordelia turned round after his departure, there was Mr. Evans standing before her. Mr. Evans looked at her in astonishment; as well he might. She was not only prettier than he had ever seen her; she was much better dressed. Cordelia had in fact gone with Crummie to Wollop's three days before—a thing which she had done only two or three times in their life—and had delighted her good-natured sister by the unusual interest she had shown in the new Easter display. The ex-Mayor himself had come out of his self-appointed cage to wait upon the supposedly rich daughters of his ambiguous successor; and both girls had done all they could to soothe what they felt must be his deeply wounded feelings.

Crummie had positively forced Cordelia to buy a really becoming costume, and since their father had given the girls a hint that he wished them "to deck themselves out well and do credit to their mother," this costume, including a specially graceful and very ladylike hat, now showed Cordelia, as the golden-moted rays surrounded her figure, to an advantage that surprised and bewildered Mr. Evans.

The beautiful April weather—for seldom had Glastonbury known the approach of a more auspicious Easter—had quickened the blood and heightened the colour of Mr. Geard's eldest child. Ever since she had put on this dark-blue, charmingly cut dress, and this neat, grey coat with a gentian-blue lining, the girl had felt as if she were a different person. A faint sense of spiritual shame at her own unexpected pleasure in these new clothes height-

ened the charm of her manner as she now talked to her fiancé;
gave her, in fact, an air of virginal shyness and timorous self-
consciousness which Mr. Evans had never seen in her before.

The boniness of her rather haggard face, the height of her
rather sullen forehead, the forward-drooping tilt of her awkward
shoulders—all these things seemed mitigated to a point where
they almost became the interesting characteristics of a woman of
original distinction.

For some reason—better understood doubtless by the Nietzschean young man, who was Mr. Wollop's buyer, than by Mr.
Evans or the young lady herself—the coat-lining, and the blue
dress with its thin braid of Brussels lace, when she threw the coat
open, made the skin that covered the girl's collarbones seem as
satiny and white as the sweet flesh of any much more favoured
daughter of Eve.

Whether from pure shyness or whether some subtle feminine
instinct warned her to be careful at this important crisis in her
life, Cordelia refused to do more than throw her cloak back as
she took the seat in the rear of the shop offered her by her lover.
Mr. Evans hovered over her there and exchanged casual unimportant remarks with her about he scarcely knew what, while
his burning eyes, flashing forth from beneath his bushy eyebrows,
devoured this little expanse of feminine whiteness. Something
like a fresh-water stream of quite new feelings towards this quiet
girl surged through the man's poisoned and brackish senses. With
an interior movement of his will—and the dire necessity of his
distorted nature had endowed Mr. Evans' will with engines of
iron—he now closed down a formidable mental portcullis upon
his dark congenital perversity. Not a trickle, not a drop, from
that deadly sluice must be allowed to poison this new feeling.

For he recognised in a flash that if he could, at that very moment hustle his guest off to his unmade bed upstairs, it would not
be a penance at all but a spontaneous pleasure to embrace her
there. This was the first time in Mr. Evans' life that such a normal and natural impulse had ever come upon him. And it remained. Yes! It remained at the background of all the torrent of
words which he now poured out, in spasmodic spurts of volcanic
agitation, at the back of that sun-illumined shop.

"I've been going on reading Dante, Cordy,—how sweet you *do* look today!—and I tell you, my dear, he's the only one of the great poets who really, to my thinking, understands life. Life's a war-to-the-death, Cordelia,—that's the truth, my precious!—between the Spirits of Good and Evil. These Spirits are everywhere. They are encountering each other in every crevice of consciousness and on every plane of Being. Life springs from their conflict. Life *is* their conflict. If the Spirit of Good conquered entirely— as one day I hope it will—the whole teeming ocean of life would dry up. There would be no more life!"

Cordelia watched him carry off his breakfast things—for he had evidently risen hurriedly, for some purpose, from his tea and rolls—and lay them in a row on a little shelf above his gas-stove. A dedicated stream of sunlight, thick and mellow like sunlight in a monk's cell, kept turning his Roman profile, with its great hooked nose and long upper lip into a dusky bronze image that flickered vaguely before her, first on one hand, then on the other, as she listened and pondered in a passive trance of content.

"This is happiness," she thought to herself. "This is what Crummie must often have known." And a great wave of pity ransacked her heart on behalf of all the old maids in Glastonbury who had *no man*; no hulking, blundering Incompetent, fumbling helplessly with truculent inanimates! Oh, how easily she could have done what he was even now so gropingly trying to do! And how near she had come herself never to have had one of these creatures who could talk so excitingly and—*crash* went one of Mr. Evans' plates upon the floor!—could find the task of clearing a table so pathetically difficult.

He came back to her side now, lugging a great carved arm-chair after him, and upon this throne-like object he compelled her to sit, while he himself took possession of the small, upright Sheraton chair which she vacated.

"What none of you people in Glastonbury seem to understand," Mr. Evans went on now, "is that this place is charged and soaked with a desperate invisible struggle."

"Isn't there the same confusion," Cordelia dared to remark in a low voice, "in ourselves?"

"Certainly there is!" Mr. Evans cried, leaning forward over the girl's blue skirt and pressing the palm of his left hand upon the arm-knob of her antique throne.

"There's the whole pit of Hell in ourselves, fire, smoke, sulphur, pitch, stench, burning! Some souls have a firm floor, Cordelia, that anyone can stamp on and it makes no difference. But other souls have trapdoors in their floors leading down to . . . to . . . to places unthinkable!"

The girl's mouth was a little open and the black pupils of her eyes had grown round and large. She was sitting up very straight in that antique chair with her gloved hands—he hadn't thought of asking her to take her gloves off and she had hesitated to do so lest it should seem a too familiar gesture—holding tight to the wooden arms; but there was a space of several inches, between her hand and his fierce grip upon the arm-knob.

"I'm an unhappy man, Cordelia," he whispered hoarsely.

Her eyelids contracted. A faint return of the exultant strength which had seized her that night on Chalice Hill shivered up through her rigid body. Now was the moment to let him know how he could depend on her—how she was ready to sacrifice everything for him! But fear and shyness made her numb, mute, helpless.

"Unhappy," he repeated in an almost inaudible voice.

Her bloodless lips moved. She formed the words, "I'm so sorry," but whether they reached him or not she could not tell.

"I've felt things, I've done things," he burst out, "in my life, which have put me . . ."—he drew his hand away from the arm of her big chair and leaned back, making the inlaid woodwork of the delicate piece of carpentry he sat on creak ominously—"put me *outside the pale*!"

Then thrusting his hands deep in his pockets he gave vent to two unpleasant emissions of sound which he meant to be a cynical laugh.

"Canst thou not minister to a mind diseased, Cordelia?"

The girl responded—it was a sign of more devotion than he realised—by slipping off her new jacket and struggling to pull off her new gloves.

"I am sorry . . . *Owen*," she murmured.

The way she said "Owen" tickled the fancy of Mr. Evans and he smiled at her grimly.

"I know you are, my dear," he said. "I would have told you about this weeks ago, if I could. There's no earthly reason why I shouldn't tell you everything . . . except . . . that *I can't*."

"I am sorry . . . Owen," she repeated, folding back with frowning intensity the second of the two gloves and finally pulling it off and laying it on the chair by her side.

"Why I should have ever been born like I am," said Mr. Evans, "is what I can't understand. But that's what the worst men who've ever lived might have said."

He got up from his seat and began walking up and down the small space at the end of the shop. Every time he swung round he looked at the handle of the door leading to the room below. How often had he struggled against the irresistible temptation to turn that handle and steal a few feverish moments of reading from *that book*!

"Cordelia, do you think there are forms of evil so horrible that nothing can wash them out?"

The girl was sitting sideways now in her dusky gilded throne. A long quivering stream of reddish sunlight fell full upon her profile and gave to all its eccentricities an emphasis that was startling.

"Wash . . . them . . . out?" she repeated stupidly.

"I mean, do you think there are certain things anyone can do . . . cruel, abominable things . . . which bring in their train undying remorse? Listen, Cordelia! Do you think when Christ sweated that bloody sweat it talks about, He felt the weight of things like that? Not what He'd done himself, of course; but what, before He died, He had to take on Himself? Shall I tell you something, Cordy? I *can* tell you *that* much anyway . . . John Crow has asked me to play the Christ in your father's Pageant; and I said I would, if he'd let me be really tied to a Cross. You can see why I said that, Cordelia, can't you. It'll be hard to bear"; he emitted those same unpleasant guttural sounds again that he evidently supposed resembled a brutal guffaw, "it'll probably be more painful than I've any idea of; but I thought

I'd realise in that way how He really did take such things on Him."

"It has been terrible for you, Owen, all this that you have gone through," she said. "But I can't believe that there are any things so awful that Christ cannot pardon them."

He stopped in his walk and faced her, his hands still deep in his pockets.

"People . . . don't . . . seem . . . to realise," he said, "what Evil is. They don't . . . seem . . . to realise how far it goes down! It has holes . . . that go down . . . beyond the mind . . . beyond the reason . . . beyond all we can think of! Something comes up from these holes that gives you power when you're in certain . . . in certain moods . . . and it's then that you feel things . . . and . . . Do Things"—his voice rose here to such a pitch that the girl started up and made a movement of her hand towards him—"which nothing in Nature can forgive!"

He moved backward away from her now with a lurching motion until his shoulder struck against a tall walnut-wood bureau. The shock of this seemed to calm him a little.

"Of course," he murmured, turning his back to her and passing his fingers up and down along the bureau's edge, "Christ is outside Nature; and *that's* my chance! He's outside, isn't He, Cordelia . . . outside altogether?"

Cordelia did somehow find the courage now to move up close to him and lay a nervous hand on the sleeve of his coat. He started at her touch and the expression of his face frightened her; but he must have pressed at once in the dark machinery of his mind one of those iron engines of his morbidly active will and it was with quite a courtly gesture that he raised her hands to his lips.

"You're sweeter to me than I deserve, my dear," he said gently. "I wish indeed, for your sake, I were a very different person."

"I am quite happy with you as you are, Owen," whispered Cordelia with a beating heart. "Oh, why," she cried in all her nerves, "oh, why doesn't he take me in his arms?"

While these events were occurring in Number Two's shop, Number Two himself, namely Mr. Bartholomew Jones, already a little recovered from the extraction of what Penny Pitches called a "sisty" in his lower regions, was out of the hospital for a morning's drive. One of the doctors had offered to take the old man with him on a trip to Godney; but had dropped him instead for an hour's visit to the house of his aged crony, Abel Twig. Here at the door of the latter's woodshed, the two old gentlemen were exchanging comments upon life, just as they had been accustomed to do for the last fifty years.

"Me grand-daughter Sally do din me ears with talk about our new Mayor. The gal gives herself as much airs as if she were a she-mayor; and yet 'tis only because of her being their maid-of-all! 'Tis wondrous, Abel, how they pettykits do take on about Public Doings. In them old days, brother, 'twas upon pasties and apple turnovers and sech-like that their mindies rinned."

"Fill up thee pipe, Bart; fill up thee pipe and think no more o' such pitiful goings-on," said Mr. Twig firmly. " 'Tis thoughts such as these thoughts what bring poor buggers like we into hospitals and infirmaries. When sun do shine and birds do zing, 'tis best to stretch out legs, brother, and hummy and drummy!"

"But 'tisn't only of thik new Mayor that my grand-darter talks to I of; 'tis of sad, wicked, fleshly doings what would bring some girt folks into trouble if all were known."

The two old heads moved closer to one another now and the two old caked and crusted briar pipes were tapped simultaneously on Abel Twig's wood-chopping stump.

"Be they the fleshly doings of they that be Mayors, or of they that *baint* Mayors?" enquired Number One evasively.

" 'Tis Sally Jones what sez so, Aby, not us, thee knows," murmured Number Two, casting a wary eye up the road and down the road, "but she tells I that thik little gal what plays with our Jackie be an Illegit of Mr. Crow up to Elms. She do say there were hintings and blinkings in the Gazette, about thik little job. 'Twere in last Wednesday's number or thereabouts, she said, and she herself reckons 'twas Red Robinson what put 'un there."

Two matches were simultaneously held to two charred and blackened orifices; and two thick clouds of blue smoke erupted from beneath a bird-like nose and a dog-like nose.

"Our Midsummer Day Fair, partner, be making this Nation ring and ting, so I hears," said Abel Twig.

"So it be, brother, so it be," said the other. "For me wone part, I've never been one for they roundabouts and they May-pole junketings and they Aunt Sally throws and they spotted men and pink-headed women. I were born over-modest, the Head-Doctor at hospital told Nurse Robinson, which were a way of saying that me stummick be easy turned. Thik Head-Doctor be all for they spick and span inventions, 'sknow, and I do seem to be an old-fangled man what were better in grave."

"Don't 'ee say such words, brother Bart," protested Mr. Twig hurriedly, "don't 'ee say 'em! Ye'll be stretching thee's legs in me woodshed, this pretty Spring-time, come seven years away, when Head-Doctor be turned to midden-dust."

"But 'tisn't only of cock-shys and merry-go-rounds and fat men and cannibals that Mayor Geard be thinking!" went on the other; "Thik young John Crow, what he brought over from France, be teaching all the lads and gals of our town to act in a Play what'll show God the Father, God the Son, and God the Holy Ghost, walking and talking like common men! 'Tis bloody Blasphemy most folk says. Others say 'tis True Religion brought back to earth! I do shiver and shake sometimes o' nights in hospital, Aby, when I do think of what be in the air, and what be in the future, for this wold town, and for me and thee's wold bones."

"Ye've allus been a nervous man of your heart, Bart," said Abel Twig consolingly, laying his scrawny fist upon the neat Sunday trousers of his friend, from which emanated the extremely musty smell of a ready-made man's counter, of the days of Mr. Wollop's father, "but there be nothing in thik Midsummer Fair to worry we."

Number Two shook his head. He assumed the haughty and melancholy air of a famous pathological case, about whose bed's head the greatest doctors in Europe had disputed for years in vain.

"I be afeared of what the future will bring to our wold town, Aby," he said. "There do come to I, of nights, the shaky-shivers, as ye might say, when, as I lies awake in thik girt white ward, where thro' they cold windies be blowin' every draught of

Heaven; and I do hear they ghosties come out of they Ruings, brother, and go whush, whush, whush over all the roofs, and I feel, for sure, that some girt change be coming over this town."

"Thee's talk be silly talk, brother," said Mr. Twig. "What do 'ee mean by a girt change?"

"I do mean what the planks and the stones of this town do feel in their wet innards, when night be over they, and all be sleeping! I do mean the shivery-shaky of they wold posties and windies and chimbleys and rafties, when dark be on 'un. Say what ye will, brother Aby, say what ye will, 'tis the nature of stones and timber to know when changes be coming upon the earth. 'Tis the same with they dumb beasties afore a storm. Thee knows, for thee be a farmer, how it be with they slugs and snails when rain be coming. And yet mortal man, brother, sees naught of it! 'Tis hid from 'un; and 'tis hid from his women too;— tho' sometimes 'tis true that one o' they will talk terrible wise, if so be as a man had the patience to listen."

Abel Twig shifted his position a little to ease himself from the hardness of the wood-bench he sat upon, for being a man of singularly lean flanks his bones were unprotected.

"Have 'ee ever knowed a day, brother Bart, when these here prophesyings of rafties and chimbleys and wold church-roofs, what 'ee do hear in hospital, have brought summat to pass that a man could name, summat that newspapers and history books could mention, summat that girt noblemen like our Lord P. could lozey and dozey over, as they sips their cellar wine after their black-cock pasties?"

Number Two contorted his countenance into a hideous caricature of humanity, in the sheer effort of ransacking his memory. Then the outlines of his face relaxed and a tremulous smile curled his lip.

"So I do, Aby; so I do," he murmured complacently. "I recollect clear as daylight now, when there was three bad harvests in session; yes! and whole factories closed down. They were Hyde's Dye-Works then, what now be Crow's, and many sons of bitches were nigh to starving in they days; and vittles was so scarce that even the rich tradesmen could scarce afford sauce to their meat; and these terrible starving times was prophysied, just as I be telling ye now—by creakings and groanings in the wold stones o' they Ruings! Something be coming upon our town, Aby, sure as my pore side be suffering from Head-Doctor's whimsies. 'Tis coming, brother, don't yer make no mistake! 'Tis coming; and all these changes of Mayors, and proclaimings of Fairs, be the outward signs, as Catechism do say, of some Holy Terror. It may be Pestilence and it may be Famine, Aby. I'm not saying it *will* be shortage of bread and the burying of human skeletons; but I'm not saying it *won't* be they things. But something it will be; for the moanings and groanings in they Ruings be getting worse and worse. They keeps a person awake, brother. Not but what I sleeps well in hospital when I *do* sleep. . . . Don't 'ee let on nothing of *that* to Head-Doctor, Aby, . . . but 'tis when I *don't* sleep that they prophesyings do bring death and judgement to me wold ears."

The relaxed warmth of the April weather that had brought Cordelia into Number Two's shop and had brought Number Two himself into Mr. Twig's woodshed, was not devoid of its effect upon the susceptible temperament of John Crow, as he sat in his noisy little office, down by the whistling and creaking luggage trains, composing more and ever more daring advertisements in regard to his Midsummer Pageant. He had been working in this hot, dusty, little room since half-past eight that morning; and it was now five minutes after eleven.

He looked round; he flung open the door of the little office; he snuffed the air. The air tasted so delicious that he did not hesitate for a second. If his thoughts had assembled themselves in words, which they did *not* do on this occasion, the words would have been "Green . . . sky . . . air . . . cool . . . mud . . . grass . . . willows . . . water . . . green . . . air . . . space . . . mud."

He snatched up his plain straw hat surrounded by a black ribbon. He snatched up his hazel-stick with its queer-shaped root-handle. The handle of this stick of John's resembled the horn of a rhinoceros; and John, with his ineradicable superstition, had already endowed it with as much identity, and perhaps a little more, as any young girl pours out from her own soul upon her sawdust-filled doll.

Armed with his stick and wearing the same clothes that he had worn at his grandfather's funeral with the band of crêpe round the arm that his French friend had sewn on some seven weeks ago, he now set out, at a pace as rapid as its direction was motiveless, towards the southwest. He soon found himself following the road which led to the village of Street. The road John followed now may have been as old as the days of the Saxon King Ina, whose charter to the Benedictines of Glastonbury is still extant; but the chances are that in those early times all cautious travellers leaving Glastonbury for the south followed the Roman Road, the remains of which lie less than a stone's throw away from the one upon the surface of which John's stick was now so sharply and so motivelessly tapping.

But whether he followed a Roman or a Saxon road it is certain that before he arrived at the village of Street John found himself crossing the River Brue at Pomparlès Bridge. Mentioned in a Court Roll of the second decade of the fifteenth century as Pons Periculosus, it was from this spot or near this spot, Pons Perilis, Pontparlous, Pontperlus, Pomparlès, that the mysterious personage known as King Arthur threw away his sword Excalibur.

John leaned against the parapet and surveyed the trickling water of the Brue. There was much mud there, and several extraneous objects carrying little association with Excalibur, rested half-buried in this mud, while a pathetically small stream of tawny-coloured water struggled with weakened impetus to deliver itself of such degrading obstacles. John's eyes, roaming in search of anything that might recover the ambiguous romance that hung about the spot, fell eventually upon a dead cat whose distended belly, almost devoid of fur, presented itself, together with two paws and a shapeless head that was one desperate grin of despair, to the mockery of the sunshine.

Still suffering from a violent reaction against all his mystical praise of Glastonbury, and suffering also from a too vivid memory of a dangerous quarrel he had had with Mary the last time they were together, this encounter with the distorted face and up-blown belly of this poor corpse caused him a diabolical twinge of mental and even physical misery. A strange vibration of malignant revolt against the whole panorama of earth-life took possession of him. What he felt was this—"I would be content to endure a good deal if I could convey to the conscious intelligence of any sort of Deity my contempt for the terms upon which our life has been offered to us."

John's scepticism as to the dogmas of pseudo-scientific materialism was abysmal but he had gone so far in his rôle as a circus-manager retailing all the Glastonbury myths with a twist of his own, that his mood now was one virulent atheistical fury. He pressed his lean stomach against the parapet in a bitter sympathy with that hairless belly in the mud; and he replied to the despairing grin of that scarcely recognisable head with a grin of his own that was not less unredeemed.

Thus across the Bridge Perilous of the old romances a stare of desperation out of Somersetshire mud met a stare of malice out of a Norfolk skull. In the super-consciousness of the blazing sun, now almost at its zenith for that day, the whirling and thundering, the crackling and growling and blasting and exploding of that orbit-revolving body of flame was accompanied by no consciousness of the existence of John Crow. And with the Earth it was the same! Below the mud of the Brue there was a bed of clay; below the clay, the original granite of the planet's skeleton; below the granite an ocean of liquid rock upon which the granite floated; below this again, black gulfs of hollow emptiness full of smouldering gases, and down below these—as the plummet of John's mind dived and sank—this "down" became an "up," and the liquid rock-basis of the "antipodes" of Glastonbury, like the root-sea of Dante's Purgatorial Mount, fumed and seethed and bubbled.

But neither in her granite bones, nor in her fiery entrails; neither in her soft, wet, rank vegetation, nor in her burning sands; neither inwards nor outwards, from centre to circumference, as her diffused super-consciousness accompanied the pulses of her material envelope, and followed the wind of her material revolution, did the mind of the Earth grow aware of the existence of John Crow. Nor finally was there potency enough in the cold fury of the man's mephistophelian malice, as he answered the mindless despair in that decomposed cat-head in the filthy Brue-mud, to draw the least, remotest flicker of awareness from the double-natured, ultimate First Cause of the world!

On this particular noon-day not one of these great Elemental Powers became aware, for the flicker of a single second, of the existence by Pomparlès Bridge, between the town of Glastonbury and the village of Street, of the entity known as John Crow. But the Great Powers among the natural forces possessed of consciousness no more exhaust or fulfil the innumerable categories of the supernatural than the Great Powers among the nations of the earth exhaust or fulfil the categories of humanity. There are countless supernumerary beings—all sons and daughters of the First Cause—whose meddlings and interferences with the affairs of earth have not received the philosophical attention they deserve.

It must have been by some mental movement of which he was totally unconscious that John Crow, in his present sullen and cynical mood, brought down upon his head a supernatural visitation from one of these lesser potencies in the midst of that warm noon-day sunshine. Yes, it must have been by some unconscious mental gesture; or else it was brought upon him by the whole trend of his activities for the last month!

There undoubtedly appear in every generation certain portentous human beings to whose personalities some mysterious destiny gives abnormal power, abnormal capacity for emotion and finally an abnormal closeness to the secret processes of nature. Such an one must that personage have been whose ghostly figure, gathering to itself so many kinds of occult significance, so many kinds of vital life-sap, as the centuries rise up and fall away about it, passes still, among such as have the least interest in such things, by the familiar name of King Arthur.

In all the old books about these matters it is recorded that from some bridge across the Brue at this spot—some Bridge Perilous corresponding to the Castle Perilous where Merlin concealed that heathen prototype, whatever it may have been, of the Grail, this Arthur of the histories threw away his sword. This particular action of this singular Person must have been one that was accompanied by some intense convulsion of human feeling in his own mind parallel with the shock in Cæsar's mind when he crossed the Rubicon, in Alexander's mind when he slew his friend Clytus, in Our Lord's mind when He was in the Garden of Gethsemane. It is doubtless these violent storms of intense feeling in great magnetic human personalities that are responsible for many of the supernatural occurrences vouched for by history and so crudely questioned by scoffing historians.

Pomparlès Bridge, although on the road to Street, is much nearer the town on its north than the village on its south, and it is probable that most of the refuse, such as old cans, old pieces of rusty iron, drowned cats and dogs, human abortions, vegetable garbage, tramps' discarded boots, heads and entrails of fishes, brick-shards, empty tobacco tins, broken bottles, and so forth, which are to be seen sticking in the Brue-mud, comes from Glastonbury rather than from its smaller neighbor.

An overgrown river-path, on the stream's northern bank, that once may have been a tow-path but now was only used by casual pedestrians, followed the river northeast where it flowed between Cradle Bridge Farm and Beckery Mill, across Glastonbury Heath, under Cold Harbour Bridge, by Pool Reed Farm, till it reached the village of Meare. The same path, on the Brue's north bank, followed the river southeast as it flowed under Cow Bridge and across South Moor, Kennard Moor, Butt Moor, then a mile below Baltonsborough, till it reached the villages of West Lydford and East Lydford.

Out of the midst of a dazed condition of his senses, John stared down at the abominable despair in the hollow eye-sockets of that decomposed cat-head. A whitish-yellowish cabbage stalk lay buried in the mud near it; vegetable decomposition and animal decomposition taking place side by side. The man's senses were so drugged by the sunshine that his mind, as happens to anyone awakening from real sleep, narrowed its awareness to one single groove. This groove was the suffering that the dead cat must have undergone to stamp such a ghastliness of despair upon its physiognomy.

In all normal suffering there are certain natural laws such as mitigate what the entity in question is enduring. When these laws are broken an element enters that is monstrous, bestial, obscene. John began to feel that what the First Cause had chosen to inflict upon this cat belonged to this No-Man's-Land of outrage; and an anger rose up within him against whatever Power it was that was responsible for the creation of such sensitive nerves in such a torturing world, an anger that was like a saraband of raving fury.

He felt that the cat-head was exactly sharing his feelings. Its swollen hairless belly . . . its paws that resembled the claws of a bird . . . the snarling ecstasy of its curse . . . something at once bestial and eternal in the protest against the First Cause which it lifted up from the Brue-mud . . . all these things made John aware that if, like the Pistoian in the Inferno he should "make the fig" at the Emperor of the Universe, this cat-head would be wholly with him.

It was while the bow-string of his malediction was still quivering that John was struck, there, leaning as he was against the sun-warmed parapet, by a sudden rending and blinding shock. He had been thinking about King Arthur a good deal in the course of his recent advertising but only in a childish and very ignorant way. He had never read the romances. But at this second, in the blaze of Something that afterward seemed to him to resemble what he had heard of the so-called Cosmic Rays, he distinctly saw . . . literally shearing the sun-lit air with a whiteness like milk, like snow, like birch-bark, like maiden's flesh, like chalk, like paper, like a dead fish's eye, like Italian marble, . . . an object, *resembling a sword*, falling into the mud of the river! When it struck the mud it disappeared. Nor was there any trace . . . when John looked later . . . to show where it had disappeared.

Under the stress of the shock, at the moment, John lurched sideways, scraping his hands and knees against the stonework of the parapet. He would certainly have fallen on his side if he had not been clutching tightly the root-handle of his hazel-stick, with which, automatically stabbing the surface of the road as he stumbled, he just saved himself. What he saw at that moment certainly flashed into his brain, in one blinding, deadly shock, as being a supernatural event. Something it was that quivered and gleamed, as it whirled past him, and vanished in the mud of the

Brue! To the end of his life he was obstinate in maintaining that he really saw what he felt he saw with his bodily eyes.

When Mary asked him, for he told only Mary and Mr. Evans of this event, how it was that he knew it was Arthur's sword, he could only say that the same shock that staggered his bodily senses like a bolt of noon-day lightning, staggered his mental consciousness with a rending and crashing certainty.

He whose life was now occupied with turning the whole Glastonbury Legend into a mockery and a popular farce had no reason to offer now as to how he knew what this thing was. But that it was a definite and perhaps a dangerous sign from the supernatural and that it was directed towards himself alone, he never had any doubt. That of all the persons he knew, he never told anyone about it save those two, was itself significant. His choice of Mr. Evans as his confidant was not surprising; for the fact that it was with Mr. Evans that he had visited Stonehenge gave to the quaint figure of the pedantic Welshman a certain disarming glamour.

"What was it like, John?" Mary kept asking him when, for the fiftieth time, he described the occurrence; but all he could tell her was that what he saw was milk-white and that it had a dusky handle. That the handle was dark instead of bright and glittering was certainly a peculiarity of the appearance that did not fit in with the atmosphere of the old stories. All the authorities who spoke of that sword indicated that its handle was shining gold. But then these *famosi fabulatores* were poetical romancers; and it was possible that a real weapon with something queer and dark about its handle was thrown into the Brue at this spot by the person who subsequently became known as Arthur, quite independently of what the romancers said.

The object which John saw thrown into the Brue from Pomparlès Bridge was undoubtedly thrown from some point in space that lay behind his back; but it was from the appearance of the thing itself that he staggered away and came near falling; not from any consciousness of a supernatural presence behind him. The first thing he did, when he saved himself from falling by stabbing at the ground with his stick and leaning upon it till he got his balance, was to clamber through some railings by the roadside, climb down the road-bank and standing on the northern tow-path of the Brue, search the river with an intense, disturbed, bewildered curiosity. But nothing could he see except the accustomed rubbish! From this position he could not even see the face of the dead cat. There was one large shiny-leaved marigold growing down there; but its round golden flowers were all gone. They must have been picked long ago by someone or other. He grasped his stock tightly by its curiously moulded handle, that handle which had grown into its shape by the mysterious chances of underground life, and set out with rapid steps northeast following the course of the Brue in the direction of Meare.

Preoccupied with what had happened to him, he rejected totally as he walked along such explanations of this startling occurrence as would have dispensed with the supernatural. The first and the easiest of these explanations was that he had been the solitary witness of the descent of a meteorite or thunderbolt. Another was that his protracted mental playing with all these legends had resulted in some sort of nervous hallucination. But without laying any stress upon Arthur or his Sword, John felt that *something* had touched him from beyond the limits of the known.

As his footpath along the bank wound its way through the low water-meadows, with the red-tiled roof of the workmen's houses of Northover on its right, John's mind began to be invaded by doubts and worries about his whole life. It was as if he had been living for the last five weeks in an enchanted dream. The heady opiate fumes of the Glastonbury legends, even while he misused them and abused them with deliberate irony, had obsessed him to such a point that in all the other affairs of his life he had just drifted. It was this mood of drifting that had been the cause of one sharp quarrel after another that he had had with Mary.

"I'll tell Mary everything at our tea, today," he said to himself, as he stiffened his back and ran the end of his stick up and down through his fingers, to make sure it was clean, "I'll tell her that it won't make any real difference our having to wait to be married till after Midsummer. The truth is we *must* wait till then. Surely Mary will *see* we must! But oh, dear! Girls are so funny in these things."

He set himself to walk faster now, following the Brue across

water-meadows that not many centuries ago must have been submerged every spring—and are still submerged in floodtime—by
brackish waters from the Bristol Channel. He had crossed the
Somerset-and-Dorset railway track and had found himself approaching Lake Village Field, when he came suddenly upon a
group of children who apparently were engaged in some extremely violent quarrel. One of these children, a passionate, dark
little girl, with bare head and dirty clothes, was balancing herself
on a small landing-stage which jutted out into the river, while,
on the muddy bank beneath this wooden erection, three other
children—a boy, a girl and a much smaller child—were shouting
insults at her, and even throwing various missiles, such as dried
horses' droppings and handfuls of loose earth, picked up from
the shelving bank, which, if they missed her thin little legs, hit
very often, as John could see as he drew near, her faded and
ragged skirt.

The children on the bank had their backs turned to him and
the little girl, though her face was directed towards him seemed
too intent in defying her enemies to take any notice of his approach. Thus John, leaning on his stick and taking breath—for
he had been walking fast—had time to listen for a minute or two
very closely to what was going on before his presence made any
difference at all.

"Thee baint got no proper father, thee baint!" cried the virtuous Jackie, throwing the muddy root of a last year's bulrush at
his former lieutenant. "This here robbers' band, of which I be
chief, don't want any gals in it what have no proper fathers!"

"What about thee own father, Jackie?" retorted the flushed outlaw from her point of vantage on the shaky wooden promontory.
"What about having a father what went to prison all along of his
making a nuisince of 'isself?"

The sedate Sis joined in at this point. "Thee's mother never
had no weddin' ring, and thee's father have never said, 'I thee
wed.'"

"*You* can't say nothin', Sis," flung back Nelly Morgan fiercely,
"when you and Bert have got neither the one nor 'tother . . .
only Grandmother Cole with a girt wart on her nose! Why, Bert,
I be 'shamed of 'ee. Oh, yer little fat scrub, what do 'ee mean by

throwing mud at me who's carried 'ee so often on me back? What do 'ee mean by't, yer little staring owl? Yes! You may well run to Sis to save 'ee, yer little cry-baby! 'Tis to thee I be talkin, you Baby Bunting! Aren't 'ee 'shamed of yerself?"

Bert did indeed show signs of discomfort when this fusillade of fiery words, from so high above his head, came rattling down like grape-shot upon him. His philosophic gusto at the contemplation of the Visible World had evidently not yet allowed, in its cosmic repertoire, for female wrath when directed quite so bitterly at himself. Like many another male philosopher he now hid both his astonishment and his chagrin in the nearest folds of a kindlier feminine lap. And from this refuge, it must alas! be confessed, there shortly arose the sound of sobs.

But while the mischievous Jackie hunted about for a lump of horses' dung that would be a better missile than any he had yet found, the sedate Sis, over the head of the weeping Bert, flung out the most dangerous and deadly word yet uttered. "Thee's mother be a whore, Nelly Morgan, and thee can't deny it! Thee's mother let Mr. Crow do it. Yes, she did! She did let Mr. Crow do it, and all the town knows how thee be a Bastie!"

"Oh, you great coward!" cried the little Valkyrie from her plank above their heads. She was addressing Jackie now, who had just missed hitting one of her thin shoulders with his fragment of weather-dried manure. "Oh, you great, lumping, common coward! Ye be a pretty robber captain, ye be, to join three to one, and against a girl too! I'll tell yer Sister Sally on ye. That's who I'll tell! And she'll larn 'ee to throw shit at anyone, she will, and quickly too! Jackie Jones did run away, run away, from Number One's dog"—in her genius for invective Nelly was inspired to utter this biting reproach in the form of an impersonal chant—"run away, run away, when there weren't no dog at all!" The infuriated child, as she chanted her war-song, pointed her fingers at her former leader with such wild and witchlike ferocity that her words sounded to John's ears like an incantation. He began to feel almost sorry for this young Boadicea's three enemies, all of whom were now apparently heading for something like complete collapse.

Jackie was indeed spluttering with indignant denials and had grown red in the face, as, with his hands on the edge of her platform, he proceeded to try to shake her down. The daughter of Philip Crow finished *his* discomfiture, in a very summary manner! With the electric rapidity of a born dancer she advanced one of her little untidy feet and trod viciously upon the boy's exposed knuckles. Jackie, tumbling on the grass and licking his injured hand, howled now like the Homeric Ares wounded by Diomed. Bert's sobs and Jackie's howls were at once punctuated by a quick interchange of feminine artillery between Nelly and Sis.

"I'll tell your mother on 'ee, ye nasty, ugly, dirty little bitch!" cried the protective maternal heart of the sturdy sister. It was at this point that Nelly began consciously to be aware of John's presence and she glanced at him almost coquettishly, while she proceeded to chant triumphantly, shooting out her tongue, between the strophe and anti-strophe of her triumph-song, at the fallen Jackie,

> "Sissie Jones at Sunday School,
> Answered Teacher like a Fool;
> Teacher said, 'you little silly,
> Shut your mouth and dilly dilly!'"

As she uttered this dithyramb over her defeated rival, the exultant little girl began to dance up and down upon the shaky plank. It was at this moment that John came forward. He came forward with the same sort of blush upon his twitching cheek that Dante displayed when Virgil caught him taking a wicked pleasure in an obscene and venomous quarrel. But he held out his arms to lift Nelly the Conqueror down from her perch, with a surprised sense that if these children's accusations were true, he and she were blood-relations, both of them drawing their devilish Norman spirit from William Crow's wife, the proud Devereux woman.

Certainly it was with the very gesture of a Devereux now that Philip's little daughter—"Morgan Nelly" as Number One called her—offered her hand, as soon as John placed her on her feet, to help the fallen Jackie to arise. It was a whole psychological drama—a drama beyond the reach of any living European pen—when Jackie's blubbered features came in view, the knuckles of his wounded hand pressed into his mouth and his little black eyes darting furtively backward and forward between John's face and Nelly's.

"Stop that, can't you?—you great baby—stop that now!" Thus did Sis, with an accompanying violent shake, vent her indignation with her successful rival upon the nearest and dearest object of her maternal affection. Bert received this shaking with his accustomed phlegm, and his sobs instantaneously ceased. His round eyes fell upon John's figure and as they surveyed that object the old insatiable gusto came back into them. Exactly as it would have been with poor ex-Mayor Wollop, what interested Bert most about this new human apparition was that it had put its cap upon its head back to front! This accident had no doubt resulted from the shock of the sword-incident at Pomparlès Bridge, but John was now fortunately saved from looking ridiculous when he got into the streets again.

"Bert be telling 'ee, Mister," said Sis eagerly, for the situation was one that exactly lent itself to her protective-corrective passion, "that thee's cap be put on back-to-front. You mid 'scuse Bert for mentioning it, Mister, but Bert be one, Bert be, for noticing things what's topsy-turvy. He do notice when Nell or me have left our ribands at whoäm or haven't got no safety pins. He do notice when his Grandma have forgot her false teeth, or when she's put she's best blue cap on when her wanted her common purple. He do notice his Teacher, Mister, so close and thorough that her do punish he for 't, like as if he'd misbehaved on school-room floor. 'Tis 'markable what Bert do notice when people——" Her proud volubility was suddenly broken off by Morgan Nelly, who, while Sis was talking to John, had been whispering to Jackie. She addressed herself sternly to Sis now.

"Jackie says that tomorrow *I* be going to be the Captain of this Robber Band, and he be going to be my Court-Martial. Jackie says that you've got to be lower nor a Private, and Bert's got to be the Band's Pack-Horse."

Sis glanced quickly at John's face as she heard this summary bulletin from the conqueror's tent. Seeing him smile a little, she planted her sturdy ankles firmly in the grass and bending down, as if they had been playing at daisy-chains rather than at bandits, she picked several of those whitish cuckoo flowers that John had already noticed and with a certain brusque sagacity, acting as she must have acted a thousand times with Jackie and Bert, handed this little nosegay, along with a spray of hedge parsley, for like all neophyte housekeepers she felt that blossoms without leaves— the leaves of cuckoo flowers being very inadequate from this particular point of view—were in some way wanting, to this stranger whose cap, caught so deplorably awry, was now pulled down, as it should be, over his amused and submissive eyebrows.

"Well! Good luck to you all, and many thanks!" cried John, making a feeble effort, almost worthy of Mr. Evans himself, to stick this collection of sap-wet stalks into his buttonhole, "I've got to get back to work. How is it you're not at school?"

It was Jackie who replied to this, taking his wounded knuckles out of his mouth, "Mr. Dekker came yesterday when Teacher were cross, and he said she ought to have more holiday; and she said she'd like to go to Yeovil where her sweetheart be and Mr. Dekker told she to shut up school till after Easter Monday and she did get red as fire when he said that and when Mr. Dekker were gone she made faces behind her hands and then she cried behind her hands; but I did see what she were doing *I* did."

"And our Bert saw Teacher cry too," threw in Sis, at this juncture, anxious that the Cole family should have its equal share of drama.

"See Teacher cry, *I* did!" echoed Bert himself.

The faint uprising of a remote sympathy with this unknown woman weeping for joy that she could go to Yeovil on Maundy Thursday instead of Good Friday, gave place now in John's mind to a curious sensation that he had experienced only once or twice before in his life. He saw this little group of children, outlined against that ricketty landing-stage—which must have been built in the days when there were still barges on the Brue— under a sudden illuminated aura. He saw them as a recurrence, a recurrence of a human group of vividly living bodies and minds, with cuckoo flowers and hedge-parsley and dock leaves and river-mud gathered about their forms, as if arranged there by a celebrated artist. The badness of the children, the sweetness and charm of the children, with these spring growths all about them and a solitary invisible lark quivering in the blue, seemed to carry his perturbed spirit beyond some psychic threshold, where the whole pell-mell of the mad torrent of existence took on a different appearance. "Good-bye and good luck!" he called out to them as he went off.

He had hardly time, however, to reach a spot at the curve of the river that was near to his friend Barter's airplane landing-place—and there, across a field or two, he could see the motion-less air-vessel—when he heard a panting breath behind him and the sound of little running feet. He swung round and found Morgan Nelly at his side. The child was too breathless to speak at first, but she caught the flap of his overcoat with her hand and kept pace with him as he walked slowly on. "Going my way, Nelly?" he said. He had heard them call her "Nelly" in their quarrel; but the syllables "Morgan" had escaped him.

"They tease I terrible, Mister, in school-yard," announced the new captain of the robber band. "They call I 'Bastie, Bastie.' They did run after I in dinner-hour yesterday, till I bit Amy Brown's wrist so she bled awful bad."

"They mustn't tease you, Nelly, and you mustn't bite people's hands," murmured John helplessly, thinking to himself that if, when Bloody Johnny got on his nerves, he could bite him, "so he bled awful bad," it would be an immense clearing of the air.

"Red Robinson made me mother go up Wells Road one time and ring at The Elms' front door. He told she to 'Harx' for the bleeding son of a bitch and make 'im cough up. 'Harx'—that's the way he talks, Mister! 'Tis London language they tell I, though me mother says 'tisn't as King George do speak. Do *you* think King George do say 'Harx' instead of 'arst,' Mister?"

"Did your mother go?" enquired the inquisitive John, post-poning the problem of King's English till he had learned more of this rich piece of scandal.

"Yes, she went, and I went with her," explained Morgan Nelly eagerly, "and Emma Sly—that's one of the servants at The Elms —gave Mother port wine and plum cake, and she gave me lime-juice and Selective biscuits, and I did select they kind what has sugar on 'em and 'H. P.' in pink stripes. Emma told me and mother what 'H. P.' stands for. She said her Dad who be shepherd for Lord P. up Mendip way did think thik 'P' stood for his mas-

ter's wone self. But Emma told me and Mother what folks as
knows knows what it really be. Do *you* know what it really be,
Mister? Sis Cole doesn't know, 'cos I baint 'a told she, and I
baint a-going to tell she, nor Bert either, what 'H. P.' stand for.
You wouldn't, would you, Mister? Ignorant, common, ordinary
kids, like what they be!"

"Did your mother ask to see Mr. Crow?" enquired the insatiable John.

"She did say summat about it," replied Morgan Nelly, "but
she never called 'un no names, as 'bleeding son of a bitch' and
such like; and she just sat down again, by kitchen-fire and went
on drinking thik wine and eating thik cake, when Emma Sly said
her master had company that evening."

"I'll talk to a cousin of mine who's in town over the holiday,"
pronounced John, thinking in his mind of Dave Spear. "He knows
this chap Robinson well, and I'll tell him to make the fellow
stop worrying your mother. Did she say anything to this servant
about 'coughing up' and so forth?"

"Mother were so thick with Emma Sly when we camed away,"
replied Morgan Nelly, "that she hadn't the tongue—oh, there's
Betsy got loose and Number One running after she!"

The diplomatic John cast his eyes over Lake Village Field
towards Backwear Hut and there, sure enough, was the distracted
figure of Abel Twig, looking, for all the world, like the old man
in Mother Goose who had lost his crooked sixpence. Mr. Twig
was frantically limping after the mischievous animal, who was
tossing up her heels and leaping into the air as she evaded him,
in a manner more worthy of a frolicsome heifer than a calm,
mature giver of sacred milk.

"He aint got no girt dog, really and truly," Morgan Nelly informed her new friend. "Sis thinks he have, and Bert do dream
he have. But he hasn't, has he, Mister?"

All the way back to his little office John's thoughts kept hovering around that startling episode of the milk-white sword with
the dark handle. "I don't care what they do; I don't care what
signs and omens they fling down; I don't care how much I in-
furiate them. They stopped those old Danes at Havyatt, but by
God! they shan't stop me! I'm going to blow this whole unhealthy

business sky-high. And I'm going to do it through this Pageant of Geard's!"

In the depths of John's consciousness something very lonely and very cold began to congeal itself into a little, hard, round stone. "I am myself," he thought, "I am myself alone." His mood, as he advanced down that narrow little cobble-stone road called Dyehouse Lane, towards the station, became, for some reason more and more anti-social and more and more inhuman. Miss Drew would have said he showed himself to himself at that moment, as the lecherous, cold-blooded, slippery, heartless, treacherous reptile that he was! "Mary belongs to me," he thought. "I'm the only man who'll ever suit her. She couldn't let Tom touch her finger! *I know her.* And the feeling I get from making love to her is far beyond anything I could ever get from any other human being. But I won't let Mary think she can rule my whole life. I'm not one to stand that kind of thing. The truth is that though I like making love to her, in my own way, I'm not at all sure that I *would* like sleeping with her every night! She's an absolute necessity to me. I know *that.* But there's something about giving up my liberty in that room that worries me. And Tom too—I like to have Tom all to myself! What I really am is a hard, round stone defying the whole universe. And I *can* defy it, and get what I want out of it too! It's a lovely feeling to feel absolutely alone, watching everything from outside, uncommitted to anything. Why should I accept the common view that you have to 'love' other people? Mary belongs to me; but sometimes I wonder whether I 'love' even Mary. I certainly don't 'love' myself! I'm a hard, round, glass ball, that is a mirror of everything, but that has a secret landscape of its own in the centre of it. O great Stones of Stonehenge, you are the only gods for me!"

He caught sight of a little round, light-coloured pebble at that moment half-embedded in the rough cement wall of an old shed that abutted upon the narrow footpath of Dyehouse Lane. He stopped and ran the tips of his fingers over this little object. It had once evidently been a unit, a portion, of some anonymous heap of pebbles taken from a sea-bank, to be used, as it was used here—for there were others like it embedded not far off—with mortar and gravel in building inexpensive walls. It was, however, very unusual to find such pebbles used in this way in Glastonbury, and this was the first in the town that John had set eyes upon. The afternoon sun shone bright and warm upon the shed wall, as John touched this small, round stone, and in a yard behind the building some unseen tame pigeons began making a low, sweet, unctuous cooing full of sensual contentment. But the touch of the pebble carried John's mind far away from this peaceful spot. A dark, wild, atavistic sea-spirit stirred within him, a spirit that reinforced and nourished afresh all the pride of his inmost being. "This morbid religion of renouncement, of penance, of occult purgations and transformations"—so his reckless thoughts ran on—"I'll never yield to this betrayal of life! If I *am* weak and nervous and timid, I'll win by cunning. And I won't compete either! I'll steer my life in a region of values totally unknown to any of them! I won't fight them *on their terms*. But I'll conquer them all the same! I'll become air, water, fire. I'll flow through their souls. I'll flow into their inmost being. I'll possess them without being possessed *by* them!" He scrutinised the pebble still more closely. It was not exactly round; it was hard to tell its precise shape, because it was so firmly embedded in the mortar. It was of a dull pinkish colour. Where did it come from? From Chesil Beach? John had never seen either of the two coastlines nearest to Glastonbury, but he knew vaguely that the southern coast was steep and rocky, while the shores of the Bristol Channel were flat expanses of tidal mud. That was all he knew. But never mind where it came from! As he stared at this hard opaque object an indescribable rush of nervous maliciousness and vehement destructiveness coursed through his veins. Oh, it would please him, oh, it would satisfy him, if a great wild salt wave coming out of the dark heathen sea, were to sweep over this whole morbid place and wash the earth clean of all these phantasms!

He had now reached the railroad crossing, but he found the gates closed. An interminable luggage train had to jerk, and thud, and rattle, and groan itself by, before those gates would open. He allowed his eyes to wander with a sudden penetrating attention—an almost savage attention—over each one of these lumbering goods trucks as they clattered and clanged past him.

"Real!" he muttered viciously. "That's what you think you are!
—Real and true . . . the only undoubted fact. *A luggage train*,
taking Philip's dyes down to Exeter. In old days it would have
been a Roman convoy taking tin to the coast from the Mendips.
I expect that damned Sword was really made of tin . . . tin
swords! Tin shields! Tin souls!" Clutching one of the bars of
the railroad gate and shaking it, he now relinquished all restraint
and burst into a childish doggerel:—"In my Midsummer Pageant
I'll mock the Grail; mock the Grail; mock the Grail; in my Midsummer Pageant I'll mock the Grail; for Arthur's sword is tin!"
When the train had passed at last and the gates were opened he
walked very slowly over the dusty, sunny tracks, thinking, thinking, thinking. John's character had altered considerably, and he
had begun to realise it himself during these weeks of working
with Mr. Geard. A certain chaotic tendency to drift in him—the
drifting of the congenital tramp and the recklessness of the anti-
social adventurer—had tightened and hardened into a kind of
psychic intensity of revolt, of revolt against all the gregarious
traditions of the human crowd. "There must be destruction," he
said to himself, as he entered the Great Western station-yard, "before any fresh wind from the gods can put new life into a place
like this!" So he said to himself in the fierce strength which the
pebble from Chesil Beach had poured into his heart; but when
he put his hand on the handle of his little office door there came
filtering up to the surface of his mind the old chilly sediment of
sceptical contempt. "Let these things of gilded vapour," he
thought, "these things of tinsel and tin have their day! Let the
savage opposites of them have their day too. They are all dreams,
all dreams within dreams, and the underlying reality beneath
them is something completely different from them all."

THE PROCESSES OF ALL CREATIVE FORCE ARE COMPLICATED, tortuous and arbitrary. They are also infinitely various. The simple notion of one single vital urge displaying itself in spontaneous generation from inorganic matter and then thrusting forth, in its chemical transmutations, all the astounding forms of evolutionary life, does not cover one-half of the dark continents of real creation. None knoweth the beginning of things; but under the anarchy of present existence are galaxies of warring minds; and the immense future depends upon the wills of multitudinous hosts of minds. But not, alas! upon well-meaning, tender, indulgent, generous, forgiving, considerate, man-loving minds! The mind of the First Cause was twofold, self-contradictory, divided against itself. The multifarious minds that stir up the chemistry of matter today are all descended from the First Cause and share its dualistic nature, its mingling of abominable cruelty with magnanimous consideration. Many of these minds have far more simple goodness in them, more simple pity, more simple tenderness, than the double-edged mind of the First Cause; but none are reliable, none can be trusted. While none of them are entirely evil, none are entirely good. There is no creative energy divorced from some level either high or low of what we call consciousness; and there is no consciousness, whether of demiurge, demon, angel, elf, elemental, planetary spirit, demigod, wraith, phantasm, sun, moon, earth, or star, which is not composed of both good and evil.

It was about seven o'clock in the evening of this same Maundy Thursday, when John had the vision—if such it were—of Arthur's sword at Pomparlès Bridge, that a company of cheerful human beings were gathered together, snug and warm, full of chittering gossip, full of lively hummings and buzzings of released roguery, in the kitchen and scullery and museum of Glastonbury Vicarage. Mat Dekker's high-church doctrines had always been of a nature to admit large, generous, and even eccentric undertakings; and on this eve of the anniversary of his Man-God's cruel death he had seen fit to give to the inner circle of his parishioners what he was pleased to denominate as the choir-supper. This name was absurdly inappropriate; for most of the best actual singers in St. John's Church were uninvited to this homely and secular feast. They were uninvited because they would have refused to come. They were of the type of Anglican piety that regards fasting rather than feasting as appropriate to the eve of the Crucifixion. Mat Dekker, although fully as Catholic in his dogmas as his most austere parishioner, had the natural easy-going earthiness of an old-fashioned French curé. There was something in the deepest part of his spirit that the word "homely" could alone describe. He loved little, ordinary, negligible things: little, ordinary events, little, casual objects in Nature. This choir-supper on the eve of Good Friday would not interfere with the humble devotion with which he would labour, patiently and solemnly, through the long invocations and supplications of the morrow's services; but there was something about it that peculiarly satisfied Mat Dekker's whole personality. He took a profound, but perhaps quite uncon-scious delight in the various degrees of glowing idiosyncrasy which illuminated the physiognomies of his guests. It was indeed a scene worthy of Teniers or Jan Steen or Breughel, this choir-supper at Glastonbury Vicarage. The centre of it was the kitchen, where Penny Pitches, standing at her famous and ancient stove, played the part of the arch-sorceress of the occasion. On an old nursery chair, with a low wicker seat, was seated, next to the stove, the portly form of Mr. Weatherwax. The forehead of Mr. Weatherwax shone with amiability and heat. He had found a corner of the great stove—which was really like a world in itself —where he could deposit his glass of brandy. His enormous face at this low level—and exposed to periodic emissions of extreme heat from the oven—looked larger than human there. He looked like a colossal gnome or goblin present at the cooking of an ogre's meal. Indeed when Penny placed a special morsel from some dainty dish upon a plate on his lap he looked, it must be confessed, like the ogre himself. Moving about with the dishes in support of Penny was quite a phalanx of serving-maids, all of them with their Sunday clothes on, but covered up in big loose overalls. Sally Jones was here and Tossie Stickles. Lily and Louie

Rogers were here. Even the redoubtable Emma Sly, as an especial
honour to Mr. Dekker, who was her favourite official in the town,
was among these amateur and yet these professional ministrants.

Let no humorous adept in the whimsicalities of human manners
think that there were any fewer exquisite morsels of class distinction, of character distinction, of distinction in social prestige, in
this group of Glastonbury servants, than there would be when
Tilly Crow, up at The Elms, gave her next grand tea-party to
their mistresses. Emma, of course, was the *grande dame* of the
occasion. Lily and Louie did their utmost to monopolise her attention; but this, by reason of Emma's long training in the diplomacy of parties, proved quite an impossible task. The little
elderly woman was the only one of the servants there whose dress
would have been appropriate if they had all been suddenly summoned to carry tea-trays into the drawing-room. And yet it was
not her ordinary service-dress. Its quietness and modesty retained
somewhere about it—perhaps in a tiny piece of dark-blue ribbon
round Emma's neck—the impression that it was put on to do
especial honour to somebody or something outside the routine of
her diurnal labours. That touch of blue round Emma's neck was
a delicate intimation that the great professional was an amateur
that night. It had doubtless been put on partly in honour of tomorrow's being Good Friday and partly in honour of Mat Dekker's
being Emma's Vicar. The roguish blue eyes of Sally Jones were
always flinging furtive glances of mischievous girlish understanding into the soft, dark-brown, lethargic eyes, constantly growing
misty with tender, self-conscious sentiment when her friend teased
her about Mr. Barter, of Tossie Stickles. Tossie was undoubtedly
the favourite amateur waitress, on this occasion, with the lively
crowd of guests assembled round the big trestle-tables set up in
the museum. Her plump figure, irradiated by her love for her
gentleman-seducer, threw about her, wherever she went, a warm,
amorous cloud of magnetic attraction; while her ready jests, as
she carried the rabbit pasties and the pigeon pies and the great
bowls of Irish stew—which were Penny's particular achievement
and which filled the museum with a fragrant onion-heavy steam—
from one to the other of the men and women seated round the
table, were continually starting fresh guffaws of laughter and

causing various old gossips to nudge each other and wink as she pushed her way among them.

The candles on the chimney-piece, as well as on the table, threw over all these faces a soft yellow glow that seemed to draw out something peculiarly individual from their folds and creases and wrinkles and heavy meaningless surfaces of flesh, all of which in daylight might have been inexpressive and insignificant. Every now and then Mat Dekker's eyes wandered to the old-fashioned pictures of his father and mother on the mantelpiece and to the faded, wistful picture of Sam's mother. These faces did not seem as alien to the scene that was going on as one would have suspected. But then all these Vicarage guests, however ugly and deformed, possessed a certain winnowed quality of sensitiveness which had come to them through their ancestors—common or gentle—down the long centuries of Glastonbury's life. Nowhere else indeed in the town that night—certainly not at the Pilgrims' Inn and not even in St. Michael's Inn—was there assembled such a characteristic group of Glastonbury people.

This accounted for the fact that towards the roof of Mat Dekker's house, through the hushed envelope of the earth's moonlit atmosphere, all manner of subhuman and superhuman influences were directed. Cold, mute, silent in the moonlight rose the Tower Arch of the ruined Abbey. From the fluted columns, from the foliated capitals, from the broken stone bases in the hushed grass, indestructible emanations of the wild liturgical calls of the old tune—"Save us from Eternal Death! Save us from Eternal Death!"—that these carved stones had known, vibrated forth over the smooth lawns, over the treetops, and then, floating away upon the moonlight, were attracted, as if by a lodestone composed of living souls, down into that hot, noisy, steamy, candlelighted room. "Save us from Eternal Death! Save us from Eternal Death!" This chant was wailed faintly above them all in that place, drifting through the high trees of King Edgar's lawn, from those myriads of dead, mediæval throats! And mingled with this faint wailing, of which it was unlikely enough that any one among these revellers would catch the least echo, came a vast shadowy Image. Between the moonlight and the Vicarage roof it came, the Image of the Man-God of the West, the Image of the Being whose death by torture was to be celebrated that next day. It was as if this Image, with those unspeakable eye-sockets wherein quivered the death-cries of all the victims of the cruelty of Man and the cruelty of Life and the cruelty of the First Cause, had been itself created by the unpardonable suffering of all sentient nerves from the zenith to the nadir of the physical universe. It brought with it through that moonlit night, as it floated over the treetops, a terrible smell of pain; a smell that was sweet as burning sticks of cinnamon, a smell that was bitter as burning branches of laurel, a smell as of a sponge soaked in the hyssop of a dead sea of anguish! But as none in that room noticed that cry above the roof—"Save us from Eternal Death!"—none noticed that floating Image, none smelt that indescribable smell. In fact, the good, humble natu-ralist-priest, who was the entertainer of this noisy gathering and who, in the absence, for the next ten or eleven hours, of his enemy the sun-god, was so sturdily radiating around him his high-spirits that everyone was conscious of some especial reassurance, decided now, while Emma—for that was *her* task—was carrying round numerous little cups of coffee to the more epicurean of the guests, that it would be a good thing to have a little music.

His first thought was of Tossie Stickles who possessed a man-dolin upon which she often played various little tunes. Tossie had been so gay and lively during the first part of the evening that it was a shock to the good host when he learned from Sally Jones, whose blue eyes as she came to confess it were themselves blubbered with crying, that Tossie had been "taken funny-like," and been carried upstairs "to rest."

Mr. Dekker's ruddy countenance lost its complacency and an extremely anxious frown gathered about his eyes. Tossie Stickles would never be "taken funny" at choir-supper if there weren't something seriously amiss. "That girl's in trouble," he said to himself, "as sure as I'm a priest.

"Listen, Sally," he said gravely, "tell Tossie from me, when you're alone with her, that I'm not angry with her and I'll talk to her before she goes." He still kept the young woman by his side with a penetrating stare from beneath his bushy eyebrows; but though he had spoken to her in a low whisper their colloquy had not passed unobserved. Several of the older women had stopped sipping their coffee and were watching them intently. "Run off to her now, Sal; there's a good girl; and stay with her, will you? And pack all the others out of the room, won't you?"

But as soon as the girl had left the room he shut his eyes tight and rubbed his face with the palms of his hands, uttering a faint husky sound, that was not exactly a groan, but which was near a groan. When he took his fingers away he sighed heavily, drawing up this long breath from the depths of his broad chest, as if it had been a bucket of water out of a garden well.

Sam Dekker, who had been all this while silently and gravely carving a large joint of hot bacon—fragrant slices of which he placed upon the edges of various people's plates, already well-filled, while Crummie, seated beside him, added to the same plates certain quotas of pickled walnuts and roast chestnuts—was the only person at the long table who received the real significance of this deep sigh of his father's. He caught his father's eye as soon as he could. "Aren't we going to have any music, Father?" he said. Mat Dekker regarded his son tenderly from the end of the table and with an affectionate narrowing of his great eyebrows answered that he had just sent their mandolin-player on a mission that he feared would prevent her from performing. "But if you think it would be all right, Sam, my boy, we could get old Weatherwax in from the kitchen to sing us one of his catches. I suppose it would be no use trying to persuade Miss Geard"—he smiled at Crummie as he spoke—"to help us out with a song or anything?"

This word from the head of the table attracted the general attention to poor Crummie—who had already taken a certain risk of publicity by assenting to Sam's courteous request that she should sit by his side—and now she could not stop herself from blushing scarlet. It was one of the most charming signs of Crummie's essential innocence, amid all her flirtations, that when she was embarrassed she got as red as a little girl of ten.

"I'm afraid I couldn't possibly—Mr. Dekker; oh, no, I couldn't possibly," Crummie murmured. "There! a few more pickles for this one, Lily. Who is it? Oh, Jackie Cole! Yes, I'm sure Jackie likes pickles"; and the girl did her best to distract the public attention away from herself.

"Perhaps you wouldn't mind, Louie," said Mat Dekker, "asking Weatherwax to come in and give us a song. He'll do it if a pretty girl like you asks him." This remark was greeted with guffaws of laughter from many in the company; for the goatish disposition of the Vicarage gardener had become a popular byword. The silence following Louie's exit was now interrupted by the opening of the kitchen door at the end of the passage. From that portion of the room came a hubbub of voices, Penny's witchlike tones rising above the rest and mounting up in shrill spirals of sound above the murmuring growls of Mr. Weatherwax. The old rogue hesitated not to precede Louie into the museum—Louie following after him with an expression of self-conscious pride, as if he'd been a puppet whose strings she was pulling from behind.

Sam, who had cut by now the last slice of bacon that anyone could possibly call for, turned to Crummie and whispered in the girl's ear, "Isn't that just like my father? He knows perfectly well that the old villain will shock half the people here and yet he persists in lugging him out from where he's as happy as a cricket, and where Penny's there to look after him."

Crummie expressed the complete identity of her opinions with those just expressed. Her eyes lingered for a moment, clinging timidly to Sam's, like a goldfinch to a thistle-head, and then, dropping her soft eyelashes till they nearly rested upon her cheek, she looked down at her hands which were clasped very tight upon her lap. She began wondering if there would be any possible chance that he might offer to take her home that night. None of her family was here. She prayed to God that there might be thunder and lightning, so that it would seem a monstrous thing for her to have to go alone! How lucky that Sally Jones lived in the opposite direction and that there was indeed no one here who came from her end of the town! "If he only thinks of it, or if his father thinks of it I believe he will!" But she had no sooner begun to imagine what it would be like walking in the darkness at Sam's side or clinging to his arm amid terrific claps of thunder, than she was seized with a fit of shivering; not violent shivering but a constant recurrence of that sensation of cold shivering which is described as "a goose walking over your grave." Crummie became afraid lest Sam would notice that this queer irresistible shudder kept running through her body. To herself it seemed so terribly apparent that she was intensely grateful to old Weatherwax for not waiting to be seated but commencing his ditty from the middle of the floor between the fireplace and the table. There was a really intense stillness round that candle-lit disordered table covered with half-empty cups and wine glasses and with orange skins and nut shells as the great perspiring countenance of the satyrish gardener composed itself into what he felt to be his singing expression. Mr. Weatherwax's singing expression was as a matter of fact little short of maudlin. What might be called a radiant imbecility beamed from that great face, the eyes of which were tightly closed.

In the silence that awaited his first note, Sam Dekker, whose ears were as sharp as the ears of a fox, caught distinctly the sound, from some room on the landing above, of a low-pitched miserable weeping. Sam had been all that evening aware of many things that had been unnoticed even by his father. He alone among them all had not been oblivious of that insubstantial shadow forming in the moonlight, melting away in the moonlight, and then reshaping itself there; swaying and hovering above the Glastonbury roofs, in vaporous convulsed movements, as if the atmosphere of that night contained an element that could gather itself up, condense itself, solidify itself, and take the form of the beams of a vast cross upon which that shadowy figure was hung. But Sam's consciousness of this vaporous shadow, twisting and turning in pain up there, now began to be blent and confused in his mind with a definite human suffering that was going on, below the roof of the Vicarage but above the ceiling of the museum. Old Weatherwax's rumbling bass voice singing the following stave seemed to his ears to be a fit symbol of the world's attitude to both these griefs.

"The Brewer, the Malster, the Miller and I
    Had a heifer, had a filly, had a Ding-Dong;
  When Daffadowndillies look up at the sky;
    Pass along boys! Pass along!

"The Brewer, the Malster, the Miller and I
    Lost a heifer, lost a filly, lost a Ding-Dong;
When oak-leaves do fall and when swallows do fly;
    Pass along boys! Pass along!

"The Brewer, the Malster, the Miller and me
    Found a heifer, found a filly, found a Ding-Dong;
They weren't the same pretties, but what's that to we?
    Pass along boys! Pass along!

"The Brewer, the Malster, the Miller and I
    Left a heifer, left a filly, left a Ding-Dong;
Down in a grassy green grave for to lie;
    Pass along boys! Pass along!"

Many of the older men present seemed to know this ditty well.
They must have often heard the old man humming it in the bar
of St. Michael's Inn. Several voices therefore joined in that rather
brutal chorus of "Pass along, boys! Pass along!"

Mat Dekker, who himself was so congenitally ignorant of music
that he could not distinguish "God Save the King" from "The
British Grenadiers," kept swaying his rugged grey head from
side to side, not retaining any sort of time, but with a general
idea of helping matters forward by this token. Crummie kept a
sly, sideways watch upon Sam's face; and when she saw that
he had begun to work the muscles of his chin up and down, and
to lower his head over his plate and over the mutilated joint of
bacon in front of him, she too allowed her expression to assume
an air of weary melancholy; and instead of looking at old
Weatherwax she looked with tender sympathy at the pathetically
wagging head of the master of the house at the end of the table.
The close of the gardener's song was greeted with resounding
applause. "Hen-cor! Hen-cor!" screamed Mrs. Robinson in a
shrill voice. "Give us another, Mister!" cried the Nietzschean
young man from Wollop's. Old Weatherwax cleared his throat,
passed his hand over his brow, straddled his gaitered legs more
widely, planted his leather boots more firmly, turned his head to
wink at the square form of Penny Pitches which was now block-
ing up the door into the passage, shut his eyes tightly once more,
lifted his chin a little, and began:—

"With backside and so 'gainst they bars, Peggee,
  With backside and so 'gainst they bars,
With a flagon o' Zomerset ale in me hand,
  There baint none as merry as we in the land,
    Beneath they twinklin' stars, Peggee,
    Beneath they twinklin' stars.
Hips and haws; and up and down dale!
And the Devil may fill the wold 'ooman's pail!

"With a doxy like thee on me knees, Peggee,
  With a doxy like thee on me knees
And his Lordship's plumpest bird i' me pot,
  And a Sedgemoor-peat-fire to baste 'un hot,
There be luck in the barrel's lees, Peggee,
  There be luck in the barrel's lees.
Hips and haws, and up and down dale!
And the Devil may fill the wold 'ooman's pail!"

Like the crafty comedian that he was, Isaac Weatherwax paused at the end of this second verse in order to enjoy to the full the exquisite savour of rich response to which he knew himself entitled.

It was at this point that Sam, under cover of the beating of heels on the ground, the knocking of knife-handles on the table, the clapping of hands, the well-satisfied chuckles, the boisterous "bravos" and "hear-hears," got up from Crummie's side and began making his way to his father's end of the table. Crummie followed him with a gaze of intense concern; but she discreetly kept her place, and indeed moved up a little closer to Grandmother Cole, whose seat was on the further edge of Sam's empty place. She saw him ask some question of his father and caught a surprised look on the older man's face. This look was followed, however, by a grave nod, as if he said—"Do what you please, but I cannot see any good that can come of it!"

Sam paused at the top of the stairs to ascertain from which of the rooms that sound of crying proceeded—had his father let them take the girl into his mother's room, the one he always kept unused?—and, as he stood there listening, he became conscious once more, as he had been intermittently conscious all that night, of that vast, outraged shadow, hovering there in the moonlight above the roofs of the town. He also became conscious —as if it were the executioners themselves, at that official assassi-

nation, bawling out some bawdy ditty from the Suburra of Rome—
of the thick-throated gardener's finale:—

> "There be Gammer Death at the sill, Peggee!
>   There be Gammer Death at the sill!
> And the Lord, his wone self, be a-hanging for we;
>   And Leviathan be coming up out of the sea;
> And Behemoth over the hill, Peggee,
>   And Behemoth over the hill!
> Hips and haws, and up and down dale;
>   But the Devil may have we for wold 'ooman's pail!"

No, it was not from his mother's room; it was from the spare-
room that the sound was coming. It was not the sound of crying now, either; it was the sound of several voices, some of them
raised quite high. He strode down the passage, knocked sharply
at the spare-door and entered without awaiting a reply.

Tossie Stickles was lying on the great four-poster bed under
the curtained canopy. She had not disturbed the embroidered
counterpane. She had not disturbed the carefully folded ends
of the curtains whose fringes, matching the valances that touched
the floor, lay at the outer edges of the two pillows. This bed had
come from their ancestral home in the Quantocks. William of
Orange had been one of those who had slept under that canopy.
Perhaps that wise and indulgent ruler had been, in his hour,
as careful as Tossie herself not to disturb those elegantly folded
fringes.

"Mr. Dekker said as ye was all to clear out and leave I with
'er and none body else!" was what Sam heard Sally Jones saying
as he opened the door. Sally's blue eyes were flashing with indignation on behalf of her friend; but standing immovably before
her, not budging an inch, was—or *had* been until Sam entered—
the slender and virginal figure of Lily Rogers. Lily's melancholy
gusto for romantic situations, her almost maniacal penchant for
seduced maidens, as long as their seducers belonged to the class
known as gentlefolk, were emotions that had been satisfied this
evening as they had never been satisfied in all Lily's conscious
life. The fact that the general gossip of the town pointed its finger
at Mr. Barter as the Villain in the case was a coincidence that

heightened Lily's excitement to fever-pitch. She herself had been kissed more than once by the dissolute East Anglian; and it had been much more the propinquity of Louie—who *also* liked him —than any ice-cold resistance in herself that had kept her relations with this gentleman at such a discreet point.

Sam was not by any means a virtuoso in the delicate entanglements of female quarrels, so that all he did at this moment was to continue holding the door wide open as if he took for granted that Lily would retire. But Lily—who had known "young Master Sam" a good many years and was several years older than he was—showed no sign of retiring. "Penny thought I'd better come up to see ——" she began. But Sam cut her short. "My father told me to amuse these young ladies till he could leave the table," he said. "I wish you'd tell Penny, Lily, not to forget those boxes of sweets that I bought for dessert. Please run down now and tell her—there's a good girl!"

Lily cast a final gloating look at the youthful sufferer stretched out on William the Third's bed, a look that was replied to by a glare of fury from the blubbered face and brown eyes of Tossie. She then gave her graceful head a delicate little toss and went off. Sam came straight over and sat down on the edge of the bed, motioning to Sally to subside into a stately Louis Quatorze chair, whose gilded arms and embroidered roses had hitherto kept this slum-born niece of Number Two at a respectful distance. "Don't 'ee cry about it, little girl," he said tenderly, laying his hand on one of the plump knees of the prostrate victim of East Anglian incontinence. "Dad'll be up to see you soon. Won't he, Sally? And as long as I've known Dad's ways, and that's as long as I've known the difference between girls and boys, I've never known him not to make everything easy for anyone who's in your trouble."

"I be 'shamed to look 'ee in the face, Mr. Dekker, and that's the truth and Sal do know it. I never thought 'twould come out about me at choir-supper, making a reproach to all present and the singing and speeching scarce begun and all. I never thought 'twould be like it be or I never would ——" And the corners of Tossie's mouth dropped into the threat of another burst of crying.

" 'Twere Lily what upset she, Master Sam," threw in Sally spitefully. "Her had stopped yallering and were nigh sweet-asleep, when Penny and Lily came in. Emma Sly sent 'em all away, and told I to go and tell the Master; but Lily Rogers, she come back again, soon as Emma's back were turned; and 'twas more than Toss could bide, being as she be, to see thik white-faced ninny starin' at she out of her girt owl-eyes."

"Don't you cry, kid," said Sam, quietly patting the plump hands which were now folded in the very style of one of Greuze's ambiguous Innocents, "don't cry, there's a brave girl! Dad'll do everything for you. And what's more he'll not let Miss Fell or Miss Drew or Lily Rogers, or anyone else, say one single nasty thing about you."

"Toss do say what worries she worst nor anythink, be lest your Dad want she to tell on the gent she's kept company with. Be I right, Tossie; or baint I right?"

Tossie snatched her hands away from under Sam's and covered her face. "I won't tell a thing . . . not if I goes to prison for it! I won't! I won't! I won't!" The girl flung out these words so passionately that both Sam and Sally looked nervously at the door.

"That's all right, little one," said the former soothingly. "Dad doesn't believe in telling tales."

"He ain't so rich as they all say he be! He baint looked after at all. He baint got no girl to be nice to he, 'cept me—and now he'll have no one, he'll have no one . . . never no more . . . when I be in workhouse!" The bitter crying that had disturbed Sam's peace in the room below began again now, under those white, short, plump fingers.

"Listen, Tossie Stickles, listen to what I say," quoth Sam sternly. "Take your hands from your face and stop that now! Do you hear? Stop that now, and listen to me!"

Sally Jones was so astonished at this unexpected tone of severity that she found the courage to lay her sticky fingers on the gilded arms of her Louis Quatorze chair as she leaned forward. Tossie permitted Sam to remove her hands from her face and swallowed down her sobs.

"That's right," he said. "Now listen. No one's going to put

you in the workhouse. No one's going to separate you from your friend. Dad's not one for forcing people to marry each other when they don't want to, though! You must get that clearly into your head. He'll ask Miss Crow to keep you just as you are; and you can go to the hospital here when your time comes; and then we'll see what's to be done."

"I don't want to go to no horse-pital!" wailed Tossie, beginning to cry again.

"Well! You don't *have* to . . . *yet* . . . child," Sam responded with something like a faint smile. "You're going to be all right, anyhow. No one's going to say a word; and you must go on being a good, hard-working girl at Miss Crow's, like you've always been."

"What will I tell Auntie, out to Sherborne?" murmured the figure on the big bed.

"She needn't tell her auntie nothink, Sir, need she?" threw in the considerate Sally.

But the problem of "Auntie, out to Sherborne" was at that moment a little too complicated for Sam's wits. "Plenty of time, Tossie, plenty of time for all such matters," was all he could say. "And now I must go down; and Sally shall stay with you. You feel much better now, don't you?" He rose to his feet and turned to the girl in the gilded chair. "You can lock the door if you like, Sally, and not open it till my father comes up. Good-bye, Tossie. Everything's going to be all right."

It was nine o'clock when Sam went back to the museum and he found the company grown much more lively than it was when he left the scene. The extreme heat of the room, the guttering of so many candles, the mingling of so many steamy and unctuous smells, the loud boisterousness of the voices, all combined to make him feel a little sick in his stomach. Instead of returning, therefore, to Crummie's side, he went straight up to his father. "I hate to desert you, Dad," he whispered, "but I must get out for a breath of air. I left Sally to look after Tossie and told her to lock the door till you came. They've been bullying her already. It's that chap Barter, I suppose. But it's only beginning— I don't know! She's a nice little thing, but very simple—*terribly* simple. But he's a fairly decent chap. He won't marry her, of course; but he'll fork up. He won't run away."

"You do look white, me boy," responded Mat Dekker with much concern. "Here—drink a drop of this! Emma rescued it for me from old Weatherwax. This beer and this port together are enough to upset anyone. This is my father's stuff." And he handed his son a wine glass of richly fragrant, neat brandy.

Sam drank off about half of what his father had offered him. "Finish it yourself, Dad," he murmured affectionately. "It'll be our loving cup. I'll go out for a bit now. I'll be all right. Louie and Lily are going to stay to help Penny, aren't they? Yes, I thought so. Well, I'll be back when the decks are clear, Dad. Don't worry." He left the room without a thought of Crummie. In his haste to escape he did not give her so much as a nod.

The girl watched him through the half-open door putting on his overcoat. Her soft cheeks were tightly drawn, her white teeth were biting her underlip; her large eyes were wild and dry and miserable. This was the end of her chance that he might take her home! Where was he going? On what errand had his father sent him? She had watched their conversation just now and had not missed their affectionate look when they pledged each other in the same cup. Probably Mat Dekker had sent him to fetch the doctor to see Tossie Stickles! Crummie had heard of Tossie's fainting-fit. Indeed she had listened on all sides to many unsympathetic explanations of that event. And where was their own Sally? She must be upstairs with the sick girl. Oh, what a difficult world it was! What a world of harsh, stabbing, scraping, jarring events; when everything *could* be so lovely!

When Sam opened the front door without a thought of his supper companion and walked quickly down the moonlit drive, not a breath of air was stirring. Delicate fragrances rose and sank around him as if they had been aroused and as if they had been suppressed by their own mysterious volition. There were two big lilac bushes and several clumps of white peonies on the edge of the dew-wet grass; and near the drive gate was an ancient red-blossoming hawthorn tree. There must have been scents from all these upon the air; but what Sam felt in his troubled fancy was that the tormented body of his Redeemer Himself, bathed, in its nakedness and its blood, by the waves of the cool moonlight, was diffusing this almost mortal sweetness through the atmosphere of the night. Once out in the road this fancy of his took to itself a more intimate aspect. He began to feel as if this tremendous shadow over Glastonbury of the martyred God-Man were calling upon him to fulfil some purpose, to make some decision. He crossed the road to the base of that high wall of the Abbey Grounds over which hung the tall elm trees that from his earliest childhood had been associated with certain turning-points of his life. He turned to the left now and walking sometimes in the roadway, and sometimes on the uneven grass under the wall, he followed the outskirts of Miss Drew's garden until he reached the entrance to Abbey House. In his mind he thought now: "I'll go as far as Tithe Barn and then swing round to the right, where there are those open fields on the east side of Bere Lane." But just at this point he heard several footsteps and voices behind him and he lessened his pace to let these unknown persons pass.

While so large a group of the respectable proletariat of Glastonbury was listening to the rumbling bass tones of Isaac Weatherwax, John Crow was making love to Mary Crow in his snug room in Northload Street.

Panting hard and fast, in an interval of his absorbed and vicious love-making, while the girl, with dishevelled hair and rumpled garments, leaned back with closed eyes in his leather arm-chair, John Crow opened the window and gazed out over the water-meadows. How he did drink up those damp odours of watermint and watercress, of reed beds and mossy hatches, of dew-soaked grasses and river mud! The moonlight was flooding everything that night; but it seemed to irradiate with some especial kind of benediction those vast level fields, where the ancient Lake Village had been, and which John had crossed that very morning with little Nelly Morgan at his heels. By leaning far out of his window he could just make out a little red light to the north of the Lake Village Field which may well have shone from the upper window of Backwear Hut where at this very second Abel Twig, seated on his iron bed, was pulling off his trousers. Whether it came from Abel's bedroom or not, there was something in the

sight of that little red light, shining across the dew-soaked, moonlit expanse of fields and ditches, that thrilled John with a keen
ecstasy. He turned to give a swift glance at the girl behind him,
and the look of her figure as she rested there, her dark eyelashes
lying softly on her white cheeks, her long legs outstretched from
beneath her disarranged and disordered clothes, her slender arms
raised up and her sturdy, competent fingers clasped behind her
dusky head, increased his sensation of predatory rapture. "I
won't compete with anyone," he thought. "I won't fight these
monkish phantasms with material weapons. I'll pillage the place
with my wits. I'll snatch the beauty of their pastures from them,
while I lay bare their hocus-pocus. My girl is enough for me!
Her body is more delicious than all their fancies. I'll drain up
the magic of this spring night, and of every night, as it sinks
down on these pollards and poplars and reedy ditches; but I'll
fight these dead saints with a devilish cunning beyond anything
they've ever encountered! I'll ransack the beauty of their moons
and their marshes. I'll drink it up! I'll drain it to the dregs; I'll
penetrate all their secrets too! I'll twist like a serpent into their
deepest souls! I'll *become what they are*; and then I'll betray
them! And all the while I'll make love to Mary. Mary belongs to
me. She belongs to me as much as my hazel-stick belongs to me.
Oh, how sweet she looks over there at this moment. Those enchanting knees are my girl's. Those maddeningly sweet ankles are my
girl's ankles. That white neck is my girl's neck. From head to
foot my girl belongs to me. I've eaten her up tonight! I've eaten
her up just as I've drunk up this moonlight floating over Lake
Village Field."

As he gazed at Mary, what John noticed now was that one of
the ribbons that held up her slip across her shoulders was hanging loose and exposed. This minute and trifling disorder about the
girl's person was more provocative to his senses than any drastic
disarray could have been. It seemed pathetic that a little thing
such as this, so natural to her, and which she had refastened so
many times with her needle on its return from the laundress
should be so disturbing to him and should excite in him such a
triumph of possession. He pressed the palms of his hands against
the windowsill and breathed intoxicating draughts of what seemed

to him like melted moonlight. "I have possessed her," he thought, "far more completely by making love to her like I have than I ever could by going to the normal extreme. It is her soul I have taken. Yes! her nerves, her veins, her fibres. I have possessed her so completely that henceforth she will be compelled to dwell within my soul. Wherever I go *she* will go! Whatever I hate, she will hate. O great Stones of Stonehenge, let me keep her, let me hold her, let me possess her, for years and years and years as I do at this moment, for this is the secret of life!"

The natural reaction from this ecstasy of his came only too quickly. At an attempt he made to renew his love-making Mary grew touchy and even cold. They drew away from each other and some bitter words passed between them.

John said to himself in his heart:—"This is your girl, this girl will *always* be your girl. What is the use of quarrelling with her?" But although his deeper nature knew that he was making a fool of himself, knew that he would regret it afterward, his superficial nerves seemed to take delight in contending with her and he now proceeded to carry on this tiresome dispute, in a peevish, querulous, grievanced, complaining whine. "You know perfectly well, Mary, that you've been sulky for the last three weeks because I've been forced to put off our marriage."

She really did flash out at him now with a more dangerous glint in her grey eyes than he had ever seen. "You won't . . . find . . . me . . . 'sulky,'" she hissed out between her strong, large, white teeth, "ever again . . . on . . . *that* . . . point . . . my . . . friend!"

"You needn't take me up like that," he went on more querulously than ever—although in the lower levels of his nature something kept crying out to him—"Stop that, you fool! Stop that now!"—"It's just like a woman to go and bring up a thing like that and get furious about it! You know perfectly well that what I say is true. Why can't you be generous and considerate to a person, when he's worried like I am now with all I've got to think of?"

"No," she said in a low, hard, cold voice. "I'm an idiot to beg a man to marry me, when he doesn't think enough of our love to stop from calling me sulky when I'm sad at our being separated so long."

"Mary, you are too absurd! And you *know* you're being unfair. I'm not accusing you. You take the words out of my mouth. I'm only saying that something's changed in you lately; so that you don't trust me like you used to. Tom was telling me only yesterday what . . . what you said about old Geard's having got me under his ——"

"Stop there!" the girl cried, snatching her arm from the mantelpiece and clenching both her hands. "Stop just there! And don't bring *other* people into this! Oh, I thought . . . I thought . . . oh, I *never* thought," here her voice did really begin to break, "that we'd be bringing *him* into our quarrels with each other!"

"I'm not bringing Tom in," he cried, "and, if I *were*, Tom's a friend of us both, isn't he? But of course that's what you women always do. You can never remain content till a man hasn't a friend left that he can talk to!"

Mary gave him a terrible glance at that, a glance that was as piercing as if she'd thrown a sharp knife at him. She then swung across to the olive-coloured couch and sat down there, desperately and wearily, resting her chin on the palms of her hands and her elbows on her knees.

John got up from the arm of the leather arm-chair and walking in silence to the window closed it with a bang. He tapped a vicious tattoo with his knuckles upon the very sill that he had gripped so tightly, in a rapture of exultation, so short a time before.

Little did John guess how far from the echoes of their angry quarrel her thoughts had wandered, behind those staring grey eyes, behind that forehead where the dark hair was generally parted so evenly, but where tonight a loose tress of it hung so disorderly. John did at any rate make a *kind* of movement, however, towards relieving the tension, for he walked across the room to where he had pushed their unwashed tea-pot in a hurry among the glasses on the shelf and taking it up in his hand asked her if she wouldn't help him to wash up before she had to go.

"Why, what on earth's the time?" she asked with a start.

"Oh, about a quarter ——" he began. "Who's that?" he cried, for heavy and rapid steps were now heard ascending the stairs.

He had barely time to put down the tea-pot and she barely time to rise from the couch and smooth back the errant lock from off her forehead when, with a couple of loud, easy knocks, such as those that a young collegian might give at a colleague's door on any familiar academic staircase, Tom Barter burst into the room.

"Hull . . . *lo!*" His tone expressed genuine surprise, not unmingled with a certain dismay at finding his two friends together on Maundy Thursday evening. "Well! Isn't this splendid, you two!" He growled out these words with a certain aplomb as he pulled off his overcoat and cloth cap; but when he added, "By God! I never guessed I'd kill two such birds with one stone!" as he accepted a cigarette from Mary's case—for he did not shake hands with either of them—there was an unmistakable ring of the hollow, propitiatory bonhommie of the manager of a factory about the sound of his words. Mary herself hurried to the fire and threw on some more coals. John, having made the visitor sit down in the leather arm-chair, began clattering with the tumblers on the shelf so that he could reach a bottle placed behind them, and finally, putting three glasses on the tea-table as well as this bottle, cried out in an excited, high-pitched voice, "Let's all have a loving-cup. That's the thing! Let's all have a loving-cup! Eh, Cousin? Isn't *that* an inspiration?"

Mary shot a quick glance at him. He'd never called her "cousin" since that first day when they met at their grandfather's funeral. Was it a token of rejection? Were they to be only *cousins* henceforward?

But John seemed to be seized with an almost unnatural excitement. He filled up two of the glasses with whiskey and cold water but into the third, in place of the water, he poured milk from the milk-jug on the table. "Here are three human beings," he cried wildly, while Barter watched him with a phlegmatic but indulgent smile, and then turned to Mary with a lift of one of his eyebrows, as much as to say: "We know him, don't we? He's not as crazy as anyone would suppose!"

"Here are," John cried out, "three human beings; what they call in France, a situation *à trois!* Two of us, in this *à trois*, must, the French think, by a law of Nature, be plotting against the third. They need not *consciously* be doing this, you understand.

They can't help doing it! So now you see—Cousin Mary—so now you see—my dear Tom—why I've filled up one of these glasses with milk. The one with milk is the weak one. The one with milk is the one that the other two—unconsciously, you understand, always unconsciously,—are plotting against. I hope, by the way, that neither of you loathes milk with whiskey: I rather like it myself. *There* are the three glasses . . . I'll shuffle them a bit . . . like this. . . . *Now* do you two, keeping your eyes tight shut, choose a glass . . . and I'll take the one that's left over."

Such was the hypnotism of John's mood, or such was the affectionate indulgence towards him of his friend and his girl, that they obeyed him literally. They both ran their fingers blindly along the edge of the table till they encountered the glasses; then blindly chose one and held the choice high up in the air. "You see! You see!" John cried triumphantly. They certainly *did* see, when they opened their eyes, that the glass left upon the table was the one with milk in it; but they were both so convinced that John had arranged this result that all the portentousness was taken out of it. John swallowed his whiskey and milk in two or three gulps and put down the empty glass. "Come," he said, "if I'm the weak, idiotic fool that you two are plotting against, let me at least enjoy the voluptuousness of it!" And he poured himself out an excessively stiff glass and tossed it off with the same impetuosity.

It soon came to pass that Mary and he were sitting side by side on the olive-green couch, while their guest, with his grey office trousers and striped blue socks very much in evidence, was stretched out in the leather chair.

"I say! But you keep this place pretty hot," said Mr. Barter brusquely.

"Open the window, John, will you?" said Mary. "It's your coming in from outside, Tom; but it *has* got rather warm." There was an awkward pause while John went to the window.

"It's *too* warm . . . *I* think . . . to have a fire at all today," said Mr. Barter. "I haven't got one at the office; and I've never *had* one all this winter in my lodging. . . . Oh, yes, I did once and that was when I had a visitor!" As he said this he smiled significantly at John to indicate that this visitor was none other than Mary. Mary knew from the back of Mr. Barter's head that he and John were exchanging a long look as the latter returned from opening the window.

"They have talked about me," she thought. "They are always talking about me."

She and her lover were now seated again side by side on the couch.

"Your lamp is smoking," said Tom Barter.

"Let it smoke," murmured John.

But Barter rose from the armchair, went up to the red-shaded lamp, turned it low, and blowing violently down its funnel extinguished it altogether. "You're too fond of *red*, you two," he blurted out rudely. "This room, as I've told John before, is like a damned Chelsea studio."

"You're fairly bullying us tonight, Tom; aren't you?" said Mary.

"He wants to show that our room is as much his as it is ours," said John. "And so it is, old chap! And so it is! What's ours is our old Tom's, isn't it, Mary?"

"I'm not . . . quite . . . so . . . sure . . . that . . . Tom . . . wants it to be like that," said Mary slowly as she got up from the couch and went to fetch a third candle. There were two burning on the mantelpiece already. She lighted this third one and laid it on the crumb-strewn table. "Three persons," she thought, "and three candle-flames."

There was a long pause; for the same thought had entered all their three heads simultaneously, the awkward, ticklish, embarrassing thought about Barter's leaving Philip. Barter said to himself, "Shall I tell them that I've signed up today with Geard? They both hate Philip; but, after all, they are his cousins; and I'm playing him a dirty trick." Without putting his feelings into definite expression his treachery to Philip remained in his nerves as an unpleasant taste. What Barter craved for at that minute was some humorously cynical talk to encourage him in his betrayal of his employer or at least condone it.

John said to himself, "When is he going to confess he's come over to Geard? It was a bit funny his doing that at Geard's word when he wouldn't do it at mine. Did old Geard bribe him a lot higher than he told me he was going to? Aye! But I'd like to see Philip's face when he hears about it. I'd like to see his face!"

But Mary thought:—"I hope old Tom hasn't decided to leave Philip. I don't believe this municipal factory will last. I'm afraid it's only a fad of Geard's, and Geard cannot be Mayor forever. Besides, it will mean that John and Tom will be closer than ever; and my life will never be happy till I've got John to myself."

Their three pairs of eyes were turned simultaneously to the fire now, where at last there had appeared a solitary tongue of orange-coloured flame dancing up and down on the top of the black coals. And there fell upon them all, at that moment, that mysterious, paralysing quiescence, full of inertia and a strange numbness, which sometimes seizes a group of human conscious-nesses when conversation flags. It is an inertia made *cubic*, so to speak, by being shared. It was, at that second of time, as if the souls of these three East Anglians had suddenly clung together and plunged down the great backward slide of biological evolu-tion. They had become one vegetative soul, these three conscious-nesses, weary of their troublesome misunderstandings.

John was the first to shake himself clear of this inertia. He moved to the window and laid his hand on the sill. "Did you hear that?" he said. "That was a bird's cry from the banks of the Brue. I've never heard that cry before. Listen!" John leaned for-ward as he spoke and stared out through the oblong window-space, on each side of which Mary's rose-coloured curtains—looking as if the mist had dimmed them—wavered slightly in the night air. But the bird cry, if it were a bird cry, was not repeated.

"It must have been a spirit," said Mary.

"The spirit of one of those old Lake Village men," said John, "come to warn us three heathens not to fuss ourselves about tomorrow!"

"Tomorrow?" questioned Barter, pulling in his legs and yawn-ing, "why tomorrow?"

"Have you forgotten tomorrow's Good Friday, Tom?" said Mary; "and that reminds me," the girl went on, jumping up from the couch, "that it's fully time I was getting back! Eu-phemia's been expecting me already for an hour and more. I told her I might be out for dinner; but if I don't get back soon, it'll be her bedtime, poor dear."

The two men exchanged glances. Their look said, as plain as any masculine look could say anything, "When she's gone we'll have some more whiskey, and a real good talk about this affair of leaving the dye-works."

But Mary said, "Which of you is going to take me home?"

They both rose to their feet. All three were standing now in the centre of the room. The twitch in John's cheek became very active as they stood there. Barter said to himself, "I believe there was something funny about that onion soup I had tonight."

Mary said to herself, "Heavens! I hope I'm not going to develop influenza or anything. I feel a bit shivery."

What had happened was this: that with their rising to their feet, the sensation of oneness which their staring together into the fire had generated fell to pieces. They were like children who had erected a house of play-bricks into the hollow space of which their minds had retreated. They were like birds in a nest, warm and snug against each other, their individualities overlapping and interpenetrating, feathers and beaks all confused, till suddenly the nest was torn down and they were astray and agog and accurst, some on the boughs and some on the ground. Any small group of human beings gathered close together acquires a certain warmth of protectiveness against the Outside, against all those unknown angers of which the outside world is full. A curious psychic entity—like a great, fluffy, feathery hen-breast—is evoked at such times, under which these separate beings crouch, into which they merge, beneath which they are fused. Every human creature is a terror to every other human creature. Human minds are like unknown planets, encountering and colliding. Every one of them contains jagged precipices, splintered rock-peaks, ghastly crevasses, smouldering volcanoes, scorched and scorching deserts, blistering sands, evil dungeons from behind whose barred windows mad and terrible faces peer out. Every pair of human eyes is a custom-house gate into a completely foreign port; a port whose palaces and slums, whose insane asylums and hospitals, whose market-places and sacred shrines, represent the terrifying and the menacing as well as the promising and the

pleasure-giving! But when once any small group of persons has
been together for any reasonable length of time the official
warders of these custom-house gates are withdrawn. Each individual in such a group feels he can wander freely through the
purlieus of these other enclosed fortresses! He does not necessarily move a step. The point is that the gates into the unknown
streets no longer bristle with bayonets, are no longer thronged
with "dreadful faces" and "fiery arms."

What happened, therefore, when John and Barter and Mary
stood up, knowing that they were now going to separate, or at
least going to leave the psychic shelter of that room, was that
they each fell back upon the isolated worries of their individual
lives.

Thus it was that Tom Barter began to recognise that he was
suffering from indigestion because of the onion soup of that
miserable eating-house. Thus it was that John Crow remembered
the annoying fact that he had been constipated of late, and should
have, that very evening, to do something drastic about it. Thus
it was that Mary, as both the men helped her into her cloak,
thought to herself, "I believe I *have* caught a chill from that
open window." Unable to shake off their selfish preoccupations,
they all three went out into Northload Street in a fretful, troubled
mood.

"Hullo! Who's that?" murmured Barter as they caught sight
of the figure of Sam Dekker advancing along in front of them
under the wall of King Edgar's lawn. They soon realised who it
was, for Sam, hearing their footsteps, swung round and awaited
their approach.

Sam had never got on very well with Mary; though the subtle
causes of the coldness between them would offer psychological
material enough to fill a volume. Perhaps the basic cause was
that Sam's erotic nature was—like his father's—as simple and
primitive as a cave-man's, while Mary had enough of the contorted perversity of the Crow temperament to arm herself with
invisible spear and shield at his mere approach. Thus as they
encountered in the moonlight on this eve of Good Friday, the
Mary who shook hands with him was, for Sam, a hard, reserved,
contemptuous, designing woman, a woman whose aim, if he had

been driven to speak out all he felt, was to inherit old Miss Drew's money and carry on meanwhile, without being found out, a furtive intrigue, devoid of all noble feelings, with her cousin John! And if the Mary who gave a limp, unsympathetic, gloved hand to Sam was a cold-blooded adventuress, the Sam who gave a perfunctory squeeze to Mary's fingers, as he blinked suspiciously with his little bear-eyes at her two companions, was a lazy self-indulgent crank who spent his do-nothing leisure in an attempt to corrupt that silly little fool, Nell Zoyland.

Thus, on the eve of the Crucifixion of the Redeemer of all flesh, did the two noblest hearts in Glastonbury weigh, judge, condemn, and execute each other! They dropped the silent Mary at the drive gate of Abbey House. "Good-night, John!" was all she was allowed to say to the man whose body she would have liked to cling to, with frantic unappeasable desire, all night long.

"Listen, you two!" cried John, when the girl's figure was lost behind the big laurel bushes, each leaf of which shone like a goblin's shield in the moonlight, "I've never been up to the top of Wirral Hill on a moonlit night. Tomorrow's a holiday. Barter's office will be closed tomorow and so will mine. Let's climb up there together, eh? It'll be exciting on such a night as this!" His eagerness was so intense, and the appeal in his voice so much stronger than any word he used, that the two men consented without demur. They all walked on, still in the middle of the road, while the noise of their footsteps as they walked was mathematically increased by the substitution of Sam's heavy boots for Mary's light ones. They passed the Tithe Barn, where the mystic symbols of the four Evangelists seemed supernaturally large in the moonlight; they turned down Bere Lane and skirted the eastern side of the Abbey Grounds; they turned southwest, not far from the little Catholic chapel; they took a short, back-yard cut to gain time; and in less than twenty minutes from the moment John had suggested it they were halfway up Wirral Hill.

"That dead tree by that post, up there," panted John, "is the queerest dead tree I've ever seen! Evans swore it was a thorn . . . in fact a descendant of the original thorn . . . but Mary maintains it's a sycamore. When I saw it the other day with

Evans I examined it pretty closely and came to the conclusion that it was some tree completely unknown to me."

"I've been puzzled myself," began Sam, "about that dead tree up here. Father said, what Evans said, that it was the Saint's Thorn. But, as you say, it's clearly *not* a thorn, whatever else it may be. I'm sometimes inclined to think ———" He was interrupted by the raised voices of some other people who were climbing Wirral Hill that eve of the Crucifixion. Two of these were apparently extremely aged men who had only that moment just stopped to address some remark to a grotesque female figure who was seated on one of the municipal iron seats that adorn the slopes of Wirral. Sam, who knew every soul in the town, became instantaneously aware of the identity of each one of this little group of night-wanderers. He realised in a flash that one of the old men must have overtaken the other in this ascent, and that neither of them had any connection with the female they were now so earnestly addressing. Sam, in fact, was sure he knew, what it would have been difficult for either John or Barter to know, that each one of these three wanderers had reached this spot independently of the other two. But they formed, as the new-arrivals slowly approached them, a singular and even a monumental group. Had Mr. Evans been present he would have been reminded of one of those eternal vignettes in his favourite poet's Purgatorio; for the hill was steep at this point; its ascent took the breath of the three men and dulled their apprehension, while the flooding moonlight, giving to all objects both near and far a certain unearthly grandioseness, rendered their visual powers dreamlike and distorted. When they reached the iron seat they also stopped and stood, all three, side by side with the two old men, surveying the solitary female who remained calmly seated in front of all the five of them.

With the same speed with which it had turned upon its axis, millions of years before the event occurred which gave to the immemorial Grail of Glastonbury its new and Christian significance, the old earth turned now, carrying with it Wirral Hill, like the hump of a great sacred dromedary, and upon Wirral Hill these five male bipeds, each with his staff of office decently concealed, each with a wooden walking-stick, cut from the vegetable world, as an additional masculine prerogative, each with his orderly and rationally working skull full of one single thought. This thought might have been summed up in the words which the oldest, and certainly the poorest, of all the five, now addressed to the woman on the seat.

"What be thee doing out o' bed, Mad Bet? 'Tain't Zummertime, 'ee seely wold 'ooman; 'tis cuckoo-time, 's know! Bed be the plëace for crazy folks. Wurral Hill, of a shiny night, baint a plëace for thee. Wurral Hill be a plëace for quiet bachelor men, not for a crazy wold 'ooman like thee!" The speaker was a tall grey-haired man dressed in clothes that looked as if they did not belong to him.

"He's a good one, he is, to talk to the likes of she," expostulated the tall man's recent companion, edging himself as close as he dared to the newcomers, with evident grateful relief at their appearance upon the scene.

"Why, Mr. Jones," cried Sam, for the tall man's companion turned out to be none other than Number Two himself, "what are you doing out of Hospital? Have they finished your cure? Are you taking a walk?"

Number Two glanced uneasily at Mr. Barter, whom he recognised with infallible instinct as the official one, the unbending one, the pillar of society, in this little group.

"I be going back . . . I be going back . . . I be going back," he mumbled. "Doorman be a friend of mine. I be going back."

"What brought you out so far?" enquired Sam.

"Can't sleep o' nights, Mr. Dekker, and that's the truth. If 'tisn't one thing, 'tis another. 'Twere they winds and rains 'afore, and now 't be this shining moon. I've never knowed such carryings-on as come to me in thik horse-spital. As I were telling Mr. Twig, only this morning, there's something going to happen in this here town 'afore long, or my name's not Bartholomew Jones! What with ghosties coming out of they Ruings on rainy nights, and spirits coming out of they Ruings on shiny nights, that horse-spital aint a place for a quiet tradesman like I be."

"You oughtn't to have climbed up a steep place like this, Mr. Jones," expostulated Sam.

Number Two came close up to him and whispered in his ear.

"*He* helped me. I dursn't have done it alone. I knew *he* when 'a were a self-respectin' tradesman his own self. Don't 'ee go spreading no tales, Mr. Dekker, about me and him. 'Tisn't right I know for he to help a decent person; but I dursn't have come so far, with my poor 'innards and all, if I hadn't met he. Don't 'ee worrit about me, Mr. Dekker. He'll take me back where I came, for a copper or two. He'll take me back for less than a sixpence and nothing said!"

"Where does he sleep nowadays?" asked Sam.

"He? Young Tewsy? Why, Mother Legge, what bought Miss Kitty Camel's wold house, lets he sleep next door. He do open next door for she when couples come for a short-time bed or summat ungodly like that, and she gives he a bite, along o' her girt tabby-cat, what she calls Pretty Maid, though it be as ugly as an abortion. You do know Mother Legge, down in Paradise, Mr. Dekker? Her be a real bad 'un, her be; but what decent-living party, I'd like to know, would let a scarecrow like Young Tewsy into 'is cellar?"

While Sam was whispering to Number Two a very different conversation was going on between Mr. Barter and Young Tewsy. Young Tewsy was a man of incredible age. Number Two was correct in his statement that he remembered him as a respectable Glastonbury tradesman. He had been, as a matter of fact, a well-established chemist in the days of Mr. Wollop's father. Mr. Wollop's father was another of these "respectable" tradesmen who were always on the verge of coming to grief; but old Wollop had his redoubtable son to keep things going, whereas Tewsy, who had lost his offspring, just as he had apparently lost even his Christian name, came to disaster by frequenting, day in and day out, the "Paradise" of *that* epoch of Glastonbury's history. Young Tewsy's face was more lank and lean than the face of Don Quixote. It was the face of a walking skeleton. And yet it was —strange to say—engraved by no savage lines of revolt. Whether if a human being lives cheek by jowl with utter desperation for half a century he acquires a kind of abnormal resignation resembling that of maggots in carrion no outsider can possibly tell. Probably Young Tewsy would carry the secret of his real attitude to the world hidden behind his cadaverous countenance to the

end of his days. But the attitude that he *presented* to the world
was a perpetual grin. This grin of Young Tewsy's may have been
the grin of the clown of the Pit . . . always beaten, always tram-
pled on, always derided. On the other hand it may have been the
grin of the death-skull itself, revealed during Young Tewsy's
lifetime, by reason of the extreme cadaverousness of his face.
But, whatever it was, it was with this eternal grin, that now, in
the bright moonlight upon Wirral Hill, the aged protégé of
Mother Legge turned his face to the dry and cautious questionings
of Tom Barter.

There was more in this brief dialogue than the rest of that
group could possibly guess, for, as a matter of fact, it had been
in Mother Legge's most expensive bedroom that Mr. Barter had
come of late to meet Tossie Stickles; and it was a striking evidence of the old gaol-bird's diplomatic self-control that never
for one eyelid's flicker of his corpse-like face in that bright moonlight did he betray a recognition of which both of them must
have been perfectly aware. Young Tewsy had many a time presented the same inscrutable grin in the presence of the great
Philip himself, when he begged of the manufacturer at the street-
corner; though Philip, less master of his facial muscles than his
manager, had been unable, on several occasions, to refrain from
a swift, recognisant glance, before he produced his sixpence. For
Mr. Crow of The Elms had also found, in his day and hour, a
convenient use for Mother Legge's best bedroom. Young Tewsy
with his death-skull grin must, in fact, have been known to the
tutelary spirits of Glastonbury as a sort of Psychopompus, or
inverted Charon, of Limbo. For both Morgan Nelly, and the
little nameless embryo now forming in the womb of Tossie, owed
their start, in the long human march, to the door-opening and
lamp-bearing service of this once "respectable" tradesman of
South High Street.

"Did you find her like this?" said Tom Barter to Young
Tewsy as they all stood helplessly and rather foolishly before
this disconcerting representative of the sex that had conceived
them.

"Sure and I did, Mister," replied the grinning old man, "that
is *this gentleman* and me did, what I've 'a 'elped up this 'ere

'eavy 'ill. What be doin' of, out of yer bed, ye seely wold bitch, at this time of the bloody night?"

In these words of the old man were hopelessly confused the North London accent of his childhood and the broad Somerset of his youth and later life.

"I've never been up here in full Moon before," said John, addressing Mad Bet.

" *'Tisn't* full tonight," said Mad Bet.

"I meant practically full," said John. "Haven't you noticed, lady, how the moon *looks* full for almost four days if the sky is free of clouds?"

"I be mighty fond of thik moon," said the woman, "when it's new."

"I agree with you; I certainly agree with you, lady," asseverated John eagerly. "It's when it's neither round like it is tonight, nor new like you describe, but all funny and shapeless, that it's not nearly so nice."

"It don't melt a person's sorrows away till it be big and round," said the woman.

"Do you suppose people in all ages have climbed up Wirral Hill in moonlight like this?" enquired John.

"Shouldn't wonder, young man, shouldn't wonder," replied Mad Bet. "You and me be come and that be summat, baint it? And these other folks be come, baint they? But *some* folks do come in they's bodies but leave they's souls down in street. Don't 'ee be like one o' they, young man, don't 'ee be like one o' they!"

"I certainly will not, lady," announced John in the most emphatic tone of malicious finality.

"Come on, you two," said Barter addressing his friends. "Let's go on now! I want to get to the top of the hill. I want to look at that tree you were talking about."

"But what about this woman?" said Sam.

"Dekker thinks an unknown woman is more interesting than an unknown tree," remarked John.

"Be it the Tree of Life, you gents are seeking?" threw in Mad Bet.

"Precisely, lady," said John. "That's just it! Don't you want to come on, too, up to the top, with us?"

"Don't be a fool, Crow," whispered Mr. Barter. "Can't you see she's mad?"

"Mad . . . mad . . . mad," murmured Young Tewsy with his everlasting grin.

"This is Mr. Jones of the old Curiosity Shop," said Sam, addressing his two friends, in reply to a glance from Number Two which seemed to say—"These gentlemen don't seem to be very alert to the situation"—"the shop that your Welshman is looking after, Crow. He's got to go back to the hospital, Barter."

"It be the Tree of Life what be up there," reiterated the woman.

"For a silver sixpence I'd take 'er 'ome myself," interjected Young Tewsy, "if you gents 'ud see the Old Party back to 'orsepital."

"Come on, come on," grumbled Barter. "These people can take care of themselves."

"Somebody must see this woman home," said Sam.

"She'd like to come to the top of the hill with us," said John. "Wouldn't you, lady? She's only resting . . . halfway up. . . . Why *should* she have to go home on such a night as this? Why should anybody have to go home?"

"Mad . . . mad . . . mad," murmured Young Tewsy dreamily, contemplating with a lack-lustre eye the revelation of the woman's bald head, as her black-beaded, black-feathered hat slipped awry.

"Me niece Sally what works for our new Mayor," threw in Number Two, "do say that there'll be no peace in Glastonbury till either Geard or Crow be on top; and me wone thought be that they ghosties from they Ruings, what do worrit I in horsespital, be comed out o' grave to see which o' they two 'twill be."

"For God's sake, come on!" expostulated Mr. Barter.

"Shall I dance for 'ee, me pretty gents all?" cried Mad Bet, rising unexpectedly from the iron seat and catching hold of the heavy flannel skirt which she wore and exposing her wrinkled woolen stockings. "Here we go round the Mulberry Bush!" chanted the old woman, skipping up and down with an expression of childish gravity, while the loose, beaded tassels hanging from her hat bobbed this way and that over her ghastly white skull.

"It's like seeing moonlight on a gibbet," thought John. "Well, lady?" he said aloud, "Are you coming up hill with us or going down hill with these men?"

But Mad Bet waved away the arm which John had half-consciously stretched out towards her. "In and out the window," she now piped in a shrill scream, tossing up her withered shanks and wagging her bald head from which the hat soon fell to the ground, "in and out the window . . . as you have done before!"

Young Tewsy limped forward now and picked up the woman's hat from the grass. The effect of the moonlight, the presence of three gentlemen and one tradesman, thus transformed perforce into an embarrassed audience, seemed to go to the head of this Psychopompus of unwanted infants from Limbo, for, waving Mad Bet's hat in the air, he began to hop up and down on one foot.

"Over the garden-wall," chanted Young Tewsy as he hopped up and down, "I've let the baby fall, and missus came out and gave me a clout, and asked me what the row's about . . . over the garden-wall!"

"If you chaps won't come on with me," cried Barter, really quite angry now, "I'll go on alone. These people are all right. These people can take care of themselves. We can't take all Glastonbury home."

"You go on with him, Crow," said Sam. "And don't forget to tell me what tree you think it is, up there. My father *will* hold to it, through thick and thin, that it's a Levantine thorn tree!"

"And leave you here till we come back?" said John.

"No, no. I'm going to take this woman with me. She lives at St. Michael's Inn. It's on my way to the Vicarage."

"I be going with my sweetheart," cried Mad Bet, suddenly clutching hold of John's arm. "I be going with my dearie to eat o' the Tree of Life!" There was an awkward pause.

"Well, I'm off, anyway," said Barter, "I'm tired of this," and he strode away up the hill without looking back, his shadow accompanying him. His outward shadow! There was, however, as Barter ascended the final slope of Wirral Hill, an interior shadow that also accompanied him. "I am like Judas, though Philip is certainly not like Christ," he said to himself.

John's countenance in the moonlight must have expressed anything but pleasure at the woman's grip on his arm, though, to do him justice, he made no effort to free himself. He even placed his other arm around Mad Bet's shoulder. But either because her woman's instinct had survived her insanity and she caught this look upon his face, or because, as Mr. Evans would explain, she was bent upon forcing herself to do the one thing she didn't want to do, she now flung herself loose from John, pushing him violently away from her with the enigmatic words, "Spit it out, spit it out, or it'll grow into a Death-Tree!" And then crying out, just as King Lear did on the cliffs of Dover when he was crowned with fumitory—"If you get me you'll get me by running!" she started off rushing wildly down the hill.

Sam flung a hurried farewell to the others and set off after her, leaving Young Tewsy, who had now sat down by Number Two's side, so tickled by this spectacle that for a minute or two his death's-head countenance became positively grave. Sam had no difficulty in overtaking Mad Bet and she behaved with exemplary quietness all the way to her home. She was indeed so lost in some particular thought that she allowed Sam to take her not only into the inn but up the stairs to her own chamber above the signboard. Here he left her seated on her bed in a kind of dream, a dream so deep that when he bade her good-night, the only thing she said to him was, " 'Tis so, 'tis so," repeated incessantly till he went away. After he had left her and was walking towards the Vicarage his own thoughts began voyaging over strange seas.

He said to himself, "It must be near midnight now," and the impression came upon him that the actual identity of Christ—like a vast, shadowy, tortured ghost hovering over the moonlit town—was summoning him to make some final inward decision. It would have been impossible for him to put into words what this decision was that he felt he was being inevitably, irretrievably led to make. But it was a decision which, if he made it before midnight, that is to say, before the first minute struck of the day when Christ died, he would never be able to retract.

Mr. Geard woke up before dawn on Easter morning. The outer levels of his consciousness were at once assailed by two annoyances proceeding from opposite directions.

The first of these annoyances was connected with Mr. Barter. The teasing memory of Mr. Barter's face, the rankling impression of the man's materialism, the extravagant salary he had been compelled to offer him, the unpleasantness—as if he had touched some sticky and poisonous plant,—left in his mind by the fellow's hatred of Philip; all this became something that descended on him like a leaden weight the moment he opened his eyes.

The second vexation that rose up in his mind assumed the shape of a letter, with a peer's coronet on it, which he had received by yesterday's afternoon post. This letter was from the Marquis of P. asking him whether he couldn't manage to "run over"—the great nobleman expressed himself very casually—and "have a bite with me incog." at Mark Moor Court, this very Easter Sunday.

Mark Moor Court was a small but very ancient farmhouse, which this owner of half the Mendips kept as a private pleasure-house of escape; allowing few of his own family and absolutely none of the conventional county people to cross its historic threshold.

Save for the crypt beneath Saint Mary's ruined chapel in Glastonbury and the foundations of the Roman Road between Glastonbury and Street, there was not a fragment of masonry in all Somersetshire older than this little solitary grey farm standing, like Mariana's moated grange, upon a sort of fortified island in the vast expanse of water-meadows that followed the movement of the Brue, as that river flowed northwest towards the sea-flats of Burnham.

Mark Moor Court could be easily reached from Glastonbury. It was exactly seven miles away, beyond Meare Heath, beyond Westhay Level, and beyond the Burnham and Evercreech branch of the Somerset and Dorset Railway. Save for the river and the railway, the only connection between Glastonbury and Mark Moor was this one winding, grass-grown road, a road that no modern traffic ever disturbed; for although it was just possible for initiates in the rhynes and hatches and weirs of these queer flats to reach by its means a path to Highbridge and thence to Burnham, this particular road lost itself completely in the desolate marshes of Mark Moor.

The old farm-house called Mark Court, or Mark Moor Court, was, according to a local tradition unbroken for a thousand years, the site of a terrible final encounter between Mark, King of Cornwal, and the Magician Merlin. This particular tradition declares that Merlin—long after he had disappeared with the original heathen Grail into the recesses of Chalice Hill or into the sea-inlets of the Isle of Bardsey—returned once, and once only, to meddle with normal human affairs. This was when he visited King Mark at Mark Moor Court and punished him there for all his misdeeds by reducing him, in the wide low chamber that runs beneath the heavy stone roof, to a pinch of thin grey dust. With this dust . . . so the legend ran . . . Merlin, standing at one of the narrow windows between two stone buttresses, and sprinkling it upon the air, fed the eastward-flying herons that came—as indeed they still come—hunting for fish in the ditches of Mark Moor, from their nests in the beech-groves at the foot of Brent Knoll.

The grass-grown road, disused for so long between Glastonbury and Mark Moor, must have witnessed many a strange mediæval pilgrimage; and, in its long history, worse things than that; for it was along the embankments of this road that the Norse Vikings, following the spring floods up the estuaries of the sea, were wont to push the beaks of their pirate ships as they sought for plunder and rape in the fields of the unknown.

The hurried, informal invitation to lunch this Easter Sunday at Mark Moor Court was only one of a series of such invitations that Bloody Johnny had recently received from the Marquis of P. He owed these remarkable summonses to the fact that in his boyhood he had been a servant at the great Elizabethan House in his native Montacute.

At this house Henry Zoyland, tenth Marquis of P., had frequently been a guest; and the striking originality—and, it must also be confessed, the curious physical magnetism—of the young servant had made an indelible impression upon the peer's mind.

The Marquis had been reminded of this early infatuation by reading in the Western Gazette of Mr. Geard's unexpected fortune; and as he was attached to Glastonbury, and more than attached to his lonely shooting-lodge amid the dykes of Mark Moor, he had become still further interested in his former friend's career, when he heard rumours of his having been elected Mayor.

Mr. Geard now set himself to call upon those deeper levels of his consciousness that would be undisturbed by these various vexations, whether material or immaterial, that were now besieging so viciously his awakened soul.

He turned on his back and stretched out his arm, extending it beneath his sleeping lady's head; while in immediate response to this affectionate movement, the woman, without awakening, nestled down confidingly upon his shoulder. With his free hand he jerked up the bed-clothes till they were tight under both their chins; and from this snug security he watched, in motionless contemplation, the gradual processes of the dawn.

The familiar feeling, unlike all other possible sensations, of his wife's grey head resting on his shoulder was soon further accentuated by the woman's turning towards him still more closely in her sleep so that their bodies came into contact below the sheet that covered them. By giving her shoulder a few little shakes with his left hand Bloody Johnny now changed the rhythm of her breathing to an easy and silent respiration. His power over his own sensations when once he was really aroused was so dominant that although they had slept together for forty years he still was able by saying to himself "this is my woman" to evoke feelings not only of tenderness towards the grey-haired figure he thus held, but even—strange though it may sound—of actual amorousness.

If Mr. Wollop—the ex-Mayor of Glastonbury—was the most childlike of all the dwellers in the town in his simple zest for the visible world, Mr. Geard—the present Mayor—was possessed of a bottomless richness of sensuality that put to shame every frequenter, high and low, who made use of the services of Mother

Legge and the attendance of Young Tewsy, in that quarter of the town known as Paradise.

Bloody Johnny's rival, Philip Crow, was undeniably fond of his wife Tilly, a woman at least ten years younger than Megan Geard; but never for one second, for fifteen long years, had Philip experienced a single erotic thrill from contact with her.

As the light grew stronger it became obvious to Mr. Geard that this Easter morning was destined to prove cloudy and windy, if not stormy; but this did not prevent him from discovering somehow a scent of primroses upon the air or even from hearing —and it was almost as if his will-power was so great that he called up this long-tailed grey bird from the orchards beyond the Brue—the cry of the cuckoo upon the blowing gusts.

When he had made up his mind that the sun, although quite concealed by wildly driven clouds, must have arisen beyond the Tor and beyond Havyatt Gap, Bloody Johnny gently lifted his still unconscious lady from his shoulder and proceeded cautiously and silently to get out of bed. Retiring on tiptoe to his dressing-room which adjoined their bedroom he shut himself in with his cold bath and his shaving materials.

Emerging thence in about half an hour he presented to the eye of all observers a figure that might with equal congruity have been described as an undertaker, a head-waiter or a congregational minister. His big white face, which, unlike the countenance of Mr. Weatherwax, looked smaller, if anything, than it really was owing to the unnatural size of the back of his great head, showed whiter than ever in the greyness of this Easter morning by reason of the diabolic intensity of his dark eyes.

The pupils of Mr. Geard's eyes, like those of the author of "Faust," had the power of dilating until they left only a very narrow margin of white. But this white rim, just because it was so reduced, gleamed with an incredible lustre as he rolled his eyes—for this was a trick of his; and a trick shared by many prince-prelates of the Roman Catholic Church—without moving his head.

He now went downstairs, every stair creaking under his heavy weight, and shuffled, in his soft carpet-slippers, into the kitchen. No sign of Sally Jones at present! Well! he could find what he wanted on Easter morning without any help from any Sally. He did in fact lay his hand upon an uncut loaf of bread. This he conveyed into the dining-room, where the family had all their meals, and placing it on the table, now covered with a tablecloth such as one sees in the illustrations of Dickens, he opened the mahogany sideboard and lifted out therefrom a decanter of port wine. Finding no wine glass—indeed no glass of any description —upon the sideboard, Bloody Johnny uttered a growling expletive that sounded like a single syllable much more condemned in polite society than the word "damn" and retired into the pantry; from which retreat he presently emerged with a large tumbler.

He now stood for a moment in puzzled hesitation. What he muttered under his breath at that second was—"The East . . . the East . . . the East!"

Carrying loaf and decanter and tumbler pressed, all together, against his stomach, he now sought the small postern of his suburban villa and drawing a couple of rusty bolts opened it wide.

The East welcomed Mr. Geard with a rush of extremely chilly air; but undeterred by this reception, after listening intently to make sure that Cordelia and Crummie were as fast asleep as their mother, he sank down on his knees in the presence of a little square patch of grass, a few privet bushes, and a tiny round bed with three dead hyacinths in it, and in this position began, with a sort of ravenous greed, tearing open the loaf and gobbling great lumps of crumb from the centre of it. These mouthfuls he washed down with repeated gulps of port wine. As he ate and drank, with the cold wind blowing against his white face, his diabolically dark eyes kept roving about that small garden. So queer a figure must he have presented, and with so formidable a stare must he have raked that small enclosure, that a couple of wagtails who were looking for worms in the grass instead of flying off hopped towards him in hypnotised amazement, while a female chaffinch that had alighted for a second on one of the privet bushes left the bush and joined the two wagtails upon the patch of grass.

The more greedily Mr. Geard ate the flesh of his Master and

drank His blood, the nearer and nearer hopped these three birds. What other smaller dwellers upon this clouded earth, such as worms and snails and slugs and beetles and wood lice and shrew mice joined with these feathered creatures to make up the congregation at this heretical Easter Mass, neither the celebrant himself nor anyone else will ever know.

"Christ is risen! Christ is risen!" muttered Bloody Johnny, with his mouth full of the inside of his loaf. "Christ our Passover," he went on, "is sacrificed for us; let us therefore keep the Feast!"

As he uttered these words he tossed off his third tumbler of port wine; and then, emptying the remainder of the decanter upon the gravel outside the threshold where he knelt, he struggled up, heavily and awkwardly, upon his feet and closed the garden door.

He was only just in time; for the voice of Cordelia was heard from the top of the stairs near his own bedroom;—"Is that you, Dad?"

"Come down, Cordy . . . come down, my pet!" cried Mr. Geard in reply. But without waiting for her appearance he hurriedly conveyed the mutilated loaf and the other things into the kitchen and deposited them on the dresser.

He was just emerging from the kitchen when Cordelia came running downstairs. She was in her dressing-gown and was clearly only just awake.

Mr. Geard, his eyes blazing from out of their deep sockets in his white face, hugged her to his heart.

"Christ is risen!" he mumbled rapturously as he kissed her again and again; surrounding her as he did so with an aura of port wine that was like a purple mist.

"Dear old Dad! Dear old Dad!" was all she could find breath to say.

"Crummie awake?" he asked as soon as he let her go.

"Not yet," she replied, smiling into his burning eyes, "I've come down to get her tray ready; and then I'll wake her and we'll have our cup of tea before she gets up. She wants me to come to the early service at St. John's with her."

"Early service? Crummie?" murmured Mr. Geard in astonishment.

"She's taken a fancy to the Church, Dad, ever since you came back from Northwold. Oh, dear! I doubt if either of your daughters will ever get married! You and Mother aren't any good at matchmaking, Dad."

"Well . . . well . . . well," muttered Mr. Geard with a heavy sigh.

But as Cordy guessed shrewdly enough it was not the virginity of his children that was worrying him. Her surmise was justified by his next word.

"Well . . . well . . . you'll have the Wine and the Bread . . . you'll have Christ's Blood and His Body. They'll give it to you of course in those silly little biscuits that don't look like bread at all . . . but it'll be the Master's Body . . . and that's the chief thing."

He stopped and sighed heavily again.

"Oh, Cordy, my child, my child!" he groaned, while a film like that which would cover the eyes of a dog that saw its master being executed crossed the irises of his dark eyes, "there aren't many Christians who feel Him beside them and yet He's nearer us now than we are to each other!"

"Yes, Dad dear," murmured Cordie.

She always felt extremely embarrassed when her father spoke in this way. The peculiar weight and mass of the man's mystical realism confused and disturbed her. Her own vein of "spirituality," or whatever it was, was invariably associated with aspects of life that were imaginative or at least intellectual.

Mr. Geard's gross and staggering actuality in these things not only disconcerted her, but, to confess the truth, a little disgusted her. It was certainly not in these mystical moods of his that she felt most drawn to her father. *That* happened when she heard him issuing tactical instructions, like some great strategic general, to John Crow; or when she heard him disputing with Owen Evans on some debatable point of Glastonbury mythology.

Mr. Geard followed her into the kitchen now and sitting down upon one of the extremely hard chairs there—Cordy's mother was not one for pampering a wench like Sally Jones—he continued to

embarrass her, while she lit the fire in the stove and began preparing the thin bread and butter, by talking about Christ.

"He is with us, of course, all the time," Bloody Johnny said,—
while the physical accident that this singular evangelist was interrupted now and again by a hiccough increased his daughter's
distaste—"but today He is with us more powerfully . . . much
more powerfully . . . than any other day in the year."

"More powerfully, Dad? I don't quite understand," protested
Cordelia, as having poured quite a lot of water out of the kettle,
in order to accelerate its boiling, she began spreading the butter
upon an oblong, square-edged "tin-loaf," of a different appearance altogether from the one which the master of the house had
just ravaged.

As he watched her quick, competent movements, Mr. Geard
thought to himself—"Mahomet easily converted *his wife* to his
prophesying. Did he have just this same trouble as I have with
a daughter?"

Somehow the cutting of that practical tin-loaf, with its sharp
edges and uninteresting crust, brought down the ecstasy of
Bloody Johnny more effectively than almost anything else could
have done.

The Mayor of Glastonbury felt at that moment as if he were
disturbing the work, not of a mere daughter, but of all the competent executives in the world.

"I mean by more powerful, Cordy," he went on, the film over
his eyes growing thicker and thicker as the kettle began to simmer, "that He has more direct power over *matter* today than on
ordinary days. He's always ready to work miracles if you call on
Him strongly enough; but today, when He broke loose, He can
change everything if you only make a sign."

Getting up from his seat and moving across the room, to his
daughter's dismay, Mr. Geard opened the kitchen door and looked
out to the westward. As he turned his face towards this quarter
where, beyond the terrace of tradesmen's houses, a milk-cart was
standing in front of Othery's Dairy, he could see high up in the
air a great flock of starlings, tossed up and down in disordered,
broken masses, and darkly outlined against the driving grey
clouds.

"Do shut the door, Dad!" cried Cordelia crossly, "and either come in, or go out!"

Mr. Geard came in and closed the door with extreme gentleness. He did not say to himself—"How careless of me not to think of the poor girl being in her dressing-gown!" He said to himself—"She must have an instinct that that fellow Evans told me he was engaged for dinner today . . . or at any rate couldn't come. Poor little girl! It's a shame! The only man she's ever had . . . a madman like that . . . with God knows what on his conscience . . . possibly a murder."

But the tea was made now, the bread and butter cut and the tray ready to be carried upstairs.

"I've put out four cups," said Cordelia; "for I thought I'd get Crummie up and we'd come into Mother's room. Mother loves a cup of tea in bed and never lets herself have one!"

It must be confessed that neither of the girls expressed any great disappointment when they heard of the absence of their father from today's mid-day meal. Cordelia still entertained a hope that Owen Evans was coming. Crummie knew that Red Robinson was *not* coming; but that, on the contrary, Mr. Barter, who had spoken to her on the street yesterday, had said he might call in the early afternoon.

Since Mr. Geard had spoken severely to Mr. Robinson on the subject of his officious activity with regard to "the Morgan woman," there had been a definite estrangement between Red and Crummie which Crummie's mood, when she met him after the choir-supper, had not helped to remove.

No, the girls were not sorry to hear of their father's visit to Lord P. His presence was always a restraint on these occasions and not infrequently a positive embarrassment; so that in their hearts both daughters felt a thrill of gratitude to the Marquis for his eccentric partiality. It was always a puzzle to both of them what the secret was of their father's success when he went out into the great world; and this particular interest in his personality, displayed by Lord P., was a complete mystery to them.

"He said in his letter that there was no one with him at Mark Moor but Rachel," announced Mr. Geard.

The three women's faces lit up at this piece of news. Hitherto they had displayed only the faintest interest in his excursion. But the mention of Rachel brought down on Mr. Geard's head a volley of questions. How old was she? Why was she at Mark Moor? Was it true that she was very fragile and almost an invalid? Wasn't Mark Moor Court a rough-and-tumble kind of place for a delicately nurtured young girl to stay in? Did Lord P. bring any servants with him? What did Lady Rachel do with her time when her father was out shooting?

Chuckling over these questions as he lurched heavily out of the room and down the stairs, Mr. Geard was soon making his way, with an old faded semi-ecclesiastical ulster, that had once belonged to Canon Crow, thrown over his black clothes, towards the Pilgrims' Inn.

"I'll go leisurely," he thought to himself. "Lord P. won't be at church anyway . . . that's certain, but if he can't see me till noon, I'll look about a bit, over there."

Mr. Geard was indeed successful beyond his own private expectations, which were a good deal less optimistic than he had allowed his family to suspect, in his quest for a quiet steed that day. His ostler-friend supplied him with an old roan mare, who had been a famous hunter in her time and was still a very handsome creature.

"Wouldn't trust her," avowed the man, winking, "with anyone but your Worship. But us do all know what a firm hand you has with the females, old *and* young, and Daisy-Queen's got the int-lect of a bitch dawg."

With his canonical ulster buttoned tight under his chin and a heavy riding-crop, lent him by his ex-convertite, clutched in his ungloved fingers, Bloody Johnny mounted upon Daisy-Queen took the road for Mark Moor Court. The wind came from the southeast and he was riding almost due northwest. Directly in front of him, about ten miles away, he could see the strangely shaped protuberance of Brent Knoll, drowsing there in the midst of the level fens like a great sleepy amphibian, whose sea-skin was too tough and slippery to feel the rush of the wind, that was now careering like a host of demons over the reedy expanse.

The only drawback to Mr. Geard's immense feeling of liberation was the flapping of his ulster, which the wind, blowing violently behind his back, kept lifting up and whirling about his ears. But he rode on at a steady pace, every now and then rubbing the thick handle of his crop against his horse's neck, as he leaned forward in the saddle, and murmuring her name with chuckling endearments—such as "That's the time o'day, Daisy-Queen! Best lass in the stables thee be, Daisy-Queen! Clean straw and a peck of oats, Daisy, when old John and thee gets safe to King Mark's lodge!"

The mad rush of the southeast wind, whistling past the rider's head, lifting the mare's mane and tail and causing her to turn her ears now and again, as if she were listening to invisible and ghostly hoofbeats behind her, gave to the green spring landscape across which they trotted—horse and man, in this turmoil of the elements, grown as close as if they had been one creature—a curiously phantasmal appearance.

The groups of poplars bowing themselves westward were so blown down by the wind that the normal fluttering of their thin-stalked leaves was taken up and absorbed in one long, wild straining, as if each leaf were trying to escape from the burden of clinging any more to its parent twig and as if the whole soul of the tree were trying to escape from its rooted posture and float away, over the dykes and ditches, till it lost itself in the Bristol Channel.

The green, thickly grown tops of the pollards, as they too were blown westward, became the wild heads of armies of girl-witches, while great beds of reeds where the young shoots were mingled with tall dead stalks and brown feathery husks, set up, as the wind swept through them, an accumulated shivering cry, a cry like the cry of the Cranes of Ibycus, that ran from weir to weir, from gate to gate, from dyke to dyke, and kept gathering strength as it ran.

It was hard to restrain Daisy-Queen from breaking into a gallop as this shrieking demon drove them faster and faster towards Mark Moor. But the man and the horse had now become, for Bloody Johnny, in spite of his weight, had the true instincts of a rider, enough of one solid unit on the crest of this raving wind-wave to enable the man's desire not to shorten the ride by any such speed to be strong enough to rule the occasion.

Thus it was nearly eleven o'clock . . . about the time when the "five-minutes bell" in the towers of all the Somerset churches from the Quantocks to the Mendips was calling the loiterers in porch and purlieu to enter the building and take their places, when John Geard rode into the long avenue of sycamores that led up the steep slope to the eastern entrance of Mark Court.

The old trees were groaning in the great wind as he rode up this slope; and in several places Daisy-Queen had to veer aside to avoid fallen branches. The greenness of these broken boughs, as Geard pulled up to walk his mare past them, had a lividness in the grey light that struck him as startling and unusual. It was extraordinary how that grey light between these massive trunks responded to the wind. It seemed *itself* to be in the process of flying through the air, along with ragged-winged rooks and hoarsely crying jackdaws!

Before he caught sight of the grey walls of Mark Court itself, hidden round the third curve of the leafy ascent, he heard a series of shrill discordant screams from somewhere in front of him, the crying, as he well knew from his old experiences at Montacute, of peacocks wildly excited by the wind.

"Queer that he should keep *them* out here," he thought to himself. They swung round a bend of the drive now, the mare panting a little from the steepness of the way and from the weight of the man on her back. Then, all suddenly, she plunged and swerved to the right of the path.

There was a high, dark bank just here, out of which the polished roots of some tall white-trunked beeches stretched forth, patched with clumps of emerald-green moss. It was perhaps well that Daisy-Queen was somewhat spent. It certainly was well that her hasty shying brought her bolt up against the clay slope of this steep bank.

Twisting his body round to see what had frightened the mare, Mr. Geard became conscious of the slight figure of a bare-headed young girl watching him with excited brown eyes and a faint smile of nervous concern. As soon as he got his horse under control again and was safely back on the level path quite close to where she stood, he took off his battered felt hat with a sweeping bow. The girl was the sort of figure that a visitor might expect to come upon in a glade at Fontainebleau or Blois or Chantilly.

Mr. Geard had never been out of his native land, but it was with the sort of historic glamour that these names summon up that he at once surrounded this frail apparition.

"Lady Rachel?" he murmured, bending low down over Daisy-Queen's neck and whispering the words.

The girl smiled up at him, stretched out her arm and touched his fingers. Then she began caressing the roan mare and muttering hurried endearments to her.

"What a lovely horse!" she said, looking up again into the face above her.

There must have been some truth in what his friend the ostler had remarked about Bloody Johnny's power over females of all kinds, for the reassurance that this slim little creature—she was really eighteen, but she looked no more than fifteen—received from the steady gleam of his dark eyes, was so deep that they became friends at once.

"She came from the Glastonbury stables," explained Mr. Geard. Obeying some occult instinct in his unconscious nature he continued to address the girl in tones so low as to be practically whispers.

The wind was blowing her clothes, her hair, her scarf, as it whirled, rustling and eddying between the tree-rooted banks of that green glade.

"Let me take you up," he now found himself saying, raising his voice a little against the swishing and soughing of the wind around them.

"Hold her still and I'll come!" she said; and thrusting herself between Daisy-Queen's rump and the high mossy bank she made use of a beech-tree root as one step and the man's foot in his stirrup as another and in a second was mounted behind him, perched sideways in the rear of his saddle, her thin arms round his waist and her fingers clutching tight to the flaps of Canon Crow's old ulster.

Daisy-Queen, feeling this new burden on her back, leaped forward with a wild bound; but the path being steep just there, it did not require any great display of horsemanship on Bloody

Johnny's part to bring the mare again under control. They trotted forward now comfortably enough under the swaying archway of the tossing and creaking branches.

It was a wild-blown arcade of newly budded leaves through which they burst, the smooth beech trunks rising up like pillars at each side of them and the fallen twigs and broken branches trodden in the mud below them by Daisy-Queen's hooves.

In Bloody Johnny's nostrils was the sweet spring sap of the torn foliage above and beneath them and the fainter sweetness, but not less spring-like and youthful, of the young girl's chestnut-coloured curls, that were now blowing loose and free, after her struggle to attain her seat.

They were soon in full sight of the grey stone roof and grey buttressed walls of the Cornish King's hunting lodge. The place resembled one of those Gothic turrets, with low-flanking heavy masonry, that one sees in roughly engraved vignettes of German fairy tales. Its small, compact size rather increased than diminished the Nordic massiveness of its time-battered cornices, its moss-grown ledges with grey carved balustrades, its narrow, foliated window-arches, its lichen-covered battlements. The emerald-green grass blades that were sprouting freshly between the time-worn stones and the torn twigs with soft young leaves upon them that the wind was tossing against the masonry enhanced, like new-plucked petals against an aged skin, the hoary antiquity of this strange building.

The moment they reached the entrance, the young girl slipped lightly from Daisy-Queen's flanks and running up the steps opened the massive door. This she held open, clinging to the iron handle in the wind and calling loudly to someone within, while Mr. Geard slowly got down from his saddle and moved to the mare's head.

Two servants came hurrying out at her call, a nervous little old man with a straggly white beard and a sturdy, soldier-like, middle-aged man with a rugged, solemn face and grave eyes. The ex-soldier took Daisy-Queen's bridle from Mr. Geard's hand, touched his hat politely to Mr. Geard, and led the mare round the corner of the building, while the old man entered into a hurried, low-toned colloquy with Lady Rachel.

Bloody Johnny struck his crumpled black trousers several times with his riding-crop, gazed round him with calm interest, and then removing his hat and wiping his forehead with the back of his hand, came slowly up the time-indented steps.

When they were all three inside the hallway where burned a large open fire and where the visitor became aware of all manner of trophies of hunting and of fishing hung about rough, smoke-begrimed walls, the old man assisted Bloody Johnny to remove his ulster, gave a glance at his feet as if he expected to have to pull off heavy boots as well, and pushed up a great carved chair to the side of the hearth.

"Do you smoke, Mr. Geard?" enquired Lady Rachel, bringing him a box of cigarettes and holding it out to him with one hand while she gathered up her disordered curls with the other. She came close up to the arm of his chair pressing her young body against the side of it with something of the wild-animal's coaxing movement in her gesture and smiled down into his face, as he leaned his big head back, against the escutcheon of the family carved in smoke-darkened oak, and stretched out his feet towards the blaze.

One of Mr. Geard's deepest characteristics, a characteristic wherein his long line of Saxon ancestors, preserving their obstinate identity under centuries of Norman tyranny, had provided the basis, and his own singular psychic aplomb the magnetic poise, was his power of relaxing his whole being and enjoying his physical sensations without the least self-consciousness or embarrassment in anyone's presence. This characteristic, this complete absence of nervous self-consciousness, always had a reassuring effect upon women, children and animals, as it doubtless would have had upon savages.

It was this deep secret of physical ease, this curious freedom from bodily self-consciousness, that gave Mr. Geard his advantage with the real aristocracy, who strongly resemble women and savages in their contempt for corporeal uneasiness.

Thus as Rachel Zoyland—whose ancestors in the male line had fought under Charlemagne and in the female line had been Varangian henchmen of Byzantine Emperors—bent over the figure of Bloody Johnny, resting after his ride in that heraldic

chair, she felt completely untroubled by his crumpled black
trousers, by his absurd tie, that looked like the tie of an undertaker, by his grey flannel shirt, the cuffs of which protruded so
far beyond the sleeves of his coat, and by his rumpled woollen
socks fallen so low over his boots that the skin of his ankles was
clearly visible.

She turned now and spoke to the old servant who was still
hovering about the hall.

"Tell Mrs. Bellamy she can begin dishing up, John," she said.
"Father's only gone down to the end of the South Drive, to see if
Mr. Geard was coming *that* way. He'll be in any minute now."

When the old man had vanished she finished adjusting her hair
at a tall gilt-framed mirror between a stuffed fox's head and a
stuffed pike.

"We had a bet which way you'd come, Mr. Geard," she said
after a pause, seating herself on a footstool close to the fire, and
rubbing the palms of her hands slowly up and down over the
surface of her brown stockings which were in danger of being
scorched.

She became thoughtful then as if a very serious and risky idea
had come into her head.

Geard watched her silent profile with the firelight playing upon
it and he thought to himself—"It would be a wicked thing if these
enchanting looks of girls . . . these grave looks when their
thoughts are lost in the life-stream . . . should just pass away
and be forgotten forever!" He turned his consciousness inward
and sent it rattling down like a bucket . . . down and down and
down . . . into the black, smooth, slippery well of his deeper
soul.

But Lady Rachel was not thinking any vague, inarticulate
thoughts. She was thinking hard and desperately about a most
concrete and practical question. *Should she confide in this man?*
She knew her father had an unbounded respect for him. But after
all—to speak of such a sacred thing . . . her whole inner life
. . . the consecration of all her days . . . to a complete stranger
. . . five minutes after she had met him—was it possible to do
such a thing as that? Wouldn't it be like one of those reckless
girls in Russian stories who pour out their burning heart-secrets

at a touch, at a sign, at a glance? No; not altogether. There was a difference. The difference consisted in Mr. Geard! A young girl is like a horse or a dog. She judges by a man's eye. Mr. Geard's eye inspired confidence. Rachel, staring gravely and dreamily into Mr. Geard's eye, as she turned from the fire, felt she could trust him with her secret life, as she could not have trusted anyone of those she had known from childhood. But if she were going to say the word, she must say it at once! Her father would be in any second now. Old Bellamy would be in, telling her lunch was ready.

Hark? Was that a door opening? No; only the wind in the chimney. Oh, it would be too late in one minute now. Perhaps her whole future . . . yes! and Ned's whole future depended on her being brave now. It was like putting her horse to a fence! He *looked* trustworthy. If not for her own sake, for Ned's sake, then, she must do it now . . . Ned . . . Ned . . . Ned . . .

She leapt to her feet and came up to Mr. Geard's side. She was closer to him now even than she had been before. Her hands were clasped behind her back. Her little-girl breasts tightened and shivered. She pressed herself against the edge of his chair.

"Mr. Geard!"

"Yes, Lady Rachel."

"When my father talks about me to you, about my drinking the waters at Bath or Glastonbury, and about Mr. Edward Athling— he's my friend, you know, and my father doesn't approve of him for me—will you promise to take my side, Mr. Geard? Quick! He'll be back in a second. Will you promise to take my side?"

Bloody Johnny found his cold plump fingers clutched fiercely by two hot, feverish, little hands. He turned his dark eyes towards her, without moving his head. It was exactly as if the eyes of an Aztec idol had followed the gestures of a worshipper.

"All right, child," said Mr. Geard, "I'll take your side; as long as ——"

A door at the end of the hall opened and old Mr. Bellamy came shakily in.

The girl was standing upright in a second and as proud as a young Artemis.

"Is my father back?" she flung out.

"Yes, my lady, he's gone upstairs to wash his hands. Luncheon is served, my lady. His lordship said not to wait for him."

They had hardly sat down at the table, and Mr. Geard had barely tasted his soup, when the master of the house came hurrying round the table. He shook hands warmly with Mr. Geard and would not allow him to rise from his seat, pressing his hand on his shoulder to prevent such a movement; although to confess the truth, the phlegmatic Mayor of Glastonbury had shown no very energetic sign of getting up.

The meal did not last long and when it was over Lord P. sent his daughter away. "Don't be cross, child," he said. "I want to talk blood and iron with our good friend."

The girl rose obediently; throwing, however, a quick sideways glance at Mr. Geard from beneath her long eyelashes. The Marquis got up from the table, led her to the door, opened it and dismissed her with a kiss. Seated again at the table he poured out more wine for both of them, cleared his throat with the impressiveness of an ambassador and began to speak frankly.

The Marquis of P. had a high, thin retreating forehead, an enormous nose, not bridged in the Roman way like the nose of Mr. Evans and not thinly curved like a hawk as was the nose of Philip Crow. It was a very massive, bony nose; but it had nostrils that quivered with nervous excitement when the rest of the face was quite calm; nostrils like those of an old war-horse. On his short upper lip Lord P. wore a clipped, grey, military mustache, and on his chin a pointed, grey beard.

"What I really wanted to see you about, Geard," he said, "was simply this. Rachel, as you know, has no mother. My eldest boy is in the Embassy at Budapest, the other one at Prague. My son William, whom I'd like to legitimise if I dared—for he's been more to me than both the others put together—is working for this man Crow at Wookey Hole; acting showman, so he tells me, for the British Public there. Anyway his wife, from what I hear, is a flighty little bitch and no possible help. Well! The point is this. My little Rachel has fallen in love with a young farmer, over at Middlezoy, called Ned Athling. Athling's a good old Saxon name, none better I believe and the boy's people are well-to-do yeomen. But, apart from everything else, my girl's only eighteen; too young for marriage, too young for anything serious or permanent. The women-folk of my family have heard of this lad and they're all up in arms—jumpy in fact, jumpy and vicious. They want me to pack the kid off to the Continent with some terrible old dragon. . . . Then another thing, Geard . . . The child's health's not good . . . not enough red corpuscles in her blood or something . . . and the doctors say she ought to take the waters at Bath, or some damned place. I'm no doctor, Johnny, my friend, and I'm no psychologist; but I do know *this*, that to tear her away, bag and baggage from any glimpse of this Athling boy would be just to finish her off. My sister Lady Bessie lives at Bath and wants to have her there. But Bess is a positively ferocious old maid. She'd kill the child's heart in a month! I can see it like a map.

"Now what I was wondering was this. Isn't there anyone I could send her to in Glastonbury? Those Chalice Hill waters of yours have enough iron in 'em to put red corpuscles into a hundred anæmic little gals. For God's sake, tell me, Johnny. You're Mayor of the confounded place! Who could I send the kid to, in your town? Who would look after her and feed her properly and see she didn't get into trouble? Mind you, it's a bit of a delicate situation and wants rather nice handling . . . I want her to go on seeing this young chap; not often, you know, but once in a while. I don't want her to get into her little head that I'm acting the enraged papa and trying to separate 'em! What I'd like, of course, would be for her to get a glimpse of those people of his, out at Middlezoy, *and have her own reaction*—as I'm pretty sure she would; for she's a regular little Zoyland—against the whole tribe of 'em.

"That's my line, you see, Geard; not to bully her, not to play the tyrannical parent; but, if possible, by giving this Athling boy full rope, to let him hang himself with her! These are not the days for acting the feudal baron. These are days when young people *do what they like*. My own feeling is that if my women-folk had not started worrying her about it and insulting young Athling, it would never have got as far as it has. What I was wondering, Johnny, was this . . . whether . . . perhaps . . . you could see your way . . . to take her into your own house . . . for a time? You've got an official position in the place. My savage sister in

Bath couldn't say you were an irresponsible person to put a young girl with.

" 'My niece is staying with the Mayor of Glastonbury and taking the waters there,' I can hear the old spitfire retailing it to her cronies. 'My brother's put his foot down at last on this Bohemian life of hers at Mark Court.' Well, my boy, what do you say to all this? We could tell the dear ladies that the child was helping you with your Pageant . . . the rag-doll factory and so on . . . eh?"

Bloody Johnny's face had been a scroll of flickering enigmas while this surprising discourse flowed from his entertainer's lips. He had had time to imagine with intense vividness the stir that it would make in his quiet ménage, this sudden introduction of Lady Rachel under his roof. He *was* more than a little tempted to cry out an immediate assent to Lord P.'s complimentary suggestion. How thrilled his faithful Megan would be! How she would murmur about the antiquity of the Rhys family and their connection with the old Welsh princes! Why, before he knew it, the good lady would be discovering some remote cousinship between herself and their noble guest.

But it would never do! He saw awkwardness, difficulties, complications at every turn ——

"No, no," he said emphatically, looking straight into the peer's little, piercing, sky-blue eyes. "No, no, Lord P., I cannot take Lady Rachel into my house. Nor do I wish even to talk about it. I beg you to let it rest at that. It would never, never do! But"— and he laid his hand on his host's wrist who had impatiently pushed back his chair and was apparently about to rise—"I can tell you someone who would be the very person to send your child to and leave her with; someone about whom you'd have no reason to worry at all."

"I've no intention of thrusting my daughter on *any* of you good Glastonbury people!" replied the Marquis in a huff. "I would never have talked to you about this at all if I hadn't supposed ——"

"Enough, my Lord," interjected Mr. Geard sternly. "I assure you I am serving you well in this. Let me at least talk to the person I have in mind. I believe she would be overjoyed to take

Lady Rachel. And I swear to you, she and she only, in all our town, would serve your purpose as I understand it."

"Hum . . . hum . . . hum," mumbled the Marquis, allowing himself to melt a little; but still taking a high and mighty tone. "And who is this very kind and condescending lady, if I may take the liberty of asking?"

"It was Miss Elizabeth Crow, Lord P., that I had in mind. She's an aunt of the manufacturer; but she takes after her mother, the wife of my old Norfolk friend, a woman who was a Devereux, a woman who was, Sir, entirely and utterly, if I may say so, a lady in your most intimate Zoyland sense of that word. She is in fact . . . I whisper this in your ears, Lord P. . . . the only real lady, in *your* sense of the word, in all Glastonbury. Your sister, Lady Bessie Zoyland, could not take exception to her. Miss Elizabeth talks and feels and acts like a Devereux. You yourself would feel it in a second."

The Marquis smiled grimly.

"But it seems to me, my good Johnny, that you missed the whole drift of my long oration. The point is that I *don't want* a Devereux for my daughter. Your Miss Crow would be just the same as if I sent her to Bessie, in Bath! The child would run away, I tell you. She'd run away; and elope with her Middlezoy farmer!"

Mr. Geard held his own, obstinately and calmly.

"Well, my Lord, we don't know yet that Miss Crow would be willing to take your daughter. This I *do* know; that if she is, she would fill the bill ex—actly. I *did* get all you implied in what you said just now . . . *everything* . . . and I swear to you that in no single point could you do better than Miss Elizabeth. She is—if you'll allow me to say so—a lady after your own heart, Lord P."

The Marquis pulled up his chair to the table again and re-filled his own and his guest's wine glass. His fierce, little, blue eyes kept wandering uneasily about the room as if he expected at any moment to learn that Mr. Edward Athling of Middlezoy was waiting to see him.

"Well, Johnny, you go ahead and test your woman out. You know exactly what I want from her. I don't want Rachel *separated* from Athling. But I don't want her affair with him *encouraged*. What I really want is for Rachel herself to get fed up with the boy! If your Miss Crow can catch the nuance of all that, she certainly is, as you say, a woman after my own heart."

The Mayor of Glastonbury had won his little game of chess only just in time; for at this moment the door opened and old Bellamy came shuffling in to announce that "Mr. William" had driven over from Wells and was waiting in the Hall.

"Is Lady Rachel with him?"

"Yes, your Lordship."

"Tell him we'll be down at once."

It was some three hours later that Mr. Geard and Will Zoyland, together with Lady Rachel and her father, were drinking tea by the library fire.

The library at Mark's Court was a room very seldom used. Indeed Lord P.'s orders to have the fire lit there this Sunday afternoon were received with sheer indignation by Mr. and Mrs. Bellamy. If the persecuted Sergeant Blimp—who pined for London as a tropical animal pines in a Nordic zoo—had not offered to light the fire himself, it may well be that his lordship's commands would have led to a mutiny in the kitchen. The walls of this room were brown with old folios. There were no modern books in these shelves at all. Folios and quartos of every shade of brown and yellow and dirty-white, but principally brown, combined in some of the upper shelves with a few duodecimos, bound in the same manner, presented to Mr. Geard's eye and mind a most curious and almost dreamlike impression.

The presence of these books had a peculiar effect upon him as he sat sipping his tea and listening to these three Zoylands talking of their family affairs. He became suddenly conscious, with a grim exaltation, of the long history of the human race. And he felt as if every movement in that history had been a thing of books and would always be a thing of books! He thought of the great books that have moulded history—books like Plato, Rousseau, Marx—and there came over him an overpowering sense of the dramatic pliancy, suggestibility, malleability, of the masses of human beings.

The three Zoyland heads fell, as he looked at them, and looked past them at those huge shadowy brown shelves, into a symbolic group of human countenances. The high thin brow, big nose and pointed beard of the Marquis, the roving blue eyes and great yellow beard of Will Zoyland, the white face, clustering brown curls and long black eyelashes of the young girl, became to him an allegorical picture, rich with Rembrandt-like chiaroscuro, of the three ages of the journeying human psyche.

Their three extended shadows—with a huge toadlike image of watchful detachment, hovering above them, that was himself— became to him the dreamlike epitome of what those silent, brown-backed creators had projected, had manifested in palpable form, from their teeming Limbo of bodiless archetypes.

It was beginning to become for Bloody Johnny, as he drank cup after cup of strong tea and withdrew more and more into his secret thoughts, one of the great ocean-wave crests of his conscious life. Something seemed pouring through him, a strange, unconquerable magnetic force, pouring through him out of that piled-up mystery of printed matter. He seemed to visualise humanity as a great, turbid stream of tumultuous waters, from the surface of which multitudinous faces, upheaved shoulders, outflung arms, all vaporous and dim, were tossed forth continually.

And he was standing there with wide-straddled legs and deep-planted feet, armed with a colossal spade. And with this spade he was digging the actual river-bed—the *new* river-bed—along which this wild, half-elemental, half-human flood was destined to pour!

And there flowed into Mr. Geard's soul, as he gazed at the brown books above the silver candlesticks and above those three Zoyland heads, a feeling of almost unbounded power. He felt as though he possessed, in that invisible, ethereal Being at his side, a fountain of occult force upon which he could draw without stint. He felt that his own personal will—the will of John Geard —was "free" beyond all limitation, beyond all credibility, beyond all expectation. And it was "free" because he had faith in its freedom.

It was extremely distasteful to Mr. Geard when these three Zoylands began to grow aware that they had been neglecting their guest. Lady Rachel was the first to grow conscious of this and she plunged at once into the most dangerous of all common topics just then; the character of Mr. Philip Crow.

"How do you get on with your boss, Will?" the girl asked during a pause in their talk with a gleam of roguery in her soft, gipsy-like eyes.

"*You* won't like it very much, if I tell you everything I think of Philip Crow," growled the Bastard in his deep base voice, addressing Mr. Geard point-blank.

"Why should *I* mind?" murmured Mr. Geard casually. But he began frowning and turning away his smouldering black eyes rather awkwardly from the careless blue ones of his adversary.

Like all possessors of magical power, Mr. Geard was liable to be thwarted, baffled, frustrated, nonplussed, by the simplest defiance; whereas with complicated and subtle antagonisms he would be all alert. The shameless candour and rough dog-and-gun manners of Will Zoyland had always rather worried Mr. Geard; not exactly frightened him, but confused and discomfited him.

The Bastard now laughed loudly till his great yellow beard wagged.

"Why should *you* mind? Lordy! Lordy! but that's funny! It's as though I were watching two great hound-dogs fighting like mad and when I kicked one of 'em with my foot it tried to make out that it was only playing. Why should *you* mind? Oh, my dear Sir, only because all the county knows that you and Philip Crow are like a bull and a bull-dog!"

"Which is which?" enquired Lady Rachel. "I mean which is the bull and which is the dog?"

Bloody Johnny turned an almost reproachful look towards the girl; as if she had betrayed him by joining in her half-brother's buffoonery.

But Zoyland had worse bolts than that in his arsenal and he was in a mood to use them all. He turned to the Marquis now.

"I think you're a fool, Father," he said, "if you let our business-like Mayor here entangle you in his grand row with Crow. No, no! hear me out, Father; hear me out! I know very well what old friends you and Mr. Geard are. That's not the point. The point's hard, bed-rock *business*. The point's politics, Father, local politics; of which, if I may say so, you know very little!"

"William's not being offensive to you, Geard, I hope?" broke in the Marquis. "If you *are*, William, I won't have it! I won't have these modern manners at my tea-table. Do you hear, boy?"

"I don't think William meant to be rude to Mr. Geard, Father. I think it was a sort of challenge to him, like those of old days. Wasn't it, William? You feel you are bound to be faithful to Mr. Crow; isn't it that, William?"

All three men stared at the young girl. They stared at her with the puckered foreheads of grown people irritated by a child's simplicity and with the screwed-up eyelids of men wondering what a woman was going to say next.

Rachel had managed somehow, in a manner at once feminine and childish, to take the wind out of all their sails. Mr. Geard looked at her with deep reproach.

The Marquis thought in his heart: "Sensible infant! She won't let Will bully Johnny. But Johnny's getting touchy. By God, he is! That's where *hoi polloi* comes out! Doesn't know how to deal with a blunt rascal like our William! Damned if his eyes haven't already got that shifty, resentful, mean look you see in any low-class person when you've kicked his shin or hustled him a bit! Gad! I'd have thought old Johnny was above getting that look!"

"It seems to me that I'm doing Mr. Geard a good turn," went on Will Zoyland obstinately, "by telling you what I think about his quarrel with Crow straight to his face rather than waiting till he's gone and can't defend himself. Anyway, I'm one, as you know, Father, for throwing down all the cards."

The Marquis stroked his little pointed beard pensively. The yellow-haired ruffian was evidently a pet of his and held a rôle in his house, whenever he turned up, parallel to that of the ancient court-jester; only the Zoyland Bastard was more realistic.

"No doubt you've agreed to let him have your name for his Midsummer Fair! No doubt you've agreed to take an interest in his communistic factory! But has it occurred to either of you, either to you, Mr. Mayor, or to you, Father, what this struggle really implies?"

The Marquis looked sharply at Bloody Johnny who was now rapidly recovering his usual *sang-froid*.

"Do you want me to shut this lad's mouth, your Worship?" he

said with a chuckle, "or shall we follow the fashion of the hour and give youth its free fling?"

"By all means . . . its fling," replied the Mayor of Glastonbury gravely. "Go ahead, Mr. Zoyland! I like your frankness. I'll repay it, never fear, when you've had your say . . . in the same coin, if I can."

"Bravo, Geard, bravo!" cried my Lord, his little sharp eyes glancing with relish from one to the other. He began indeed to assume the expression of a virtuoso at a bear-baiting or a cock-fight.

Lady Rachel, who knew her father pretty well, began to feel sorry for her rider upon the roan mare. "He has no idea how wicked and wilful Father can be!" she thought.

"Our wily Mayor here has doubtless already committed you, Father—and you too, Rachel, I'll be bound!—to his precious midsummer antics and to his communistic experiment. All I want to point out, both to him and to you, is simply this." As he spoke the great yellow-bearded swashbuckler shifted his position in his hard-backed library chair and flung one leather-gaitered leg over its arm. "Simply this—that you're both on the losing side! Inevitably, by a law of nature impossible to evade, Philip Crow is going to win. No Midsummer Fairs, no rush of tourists to Glastonbury from overseas, no municipal factories filled with souvenirs, no bribing of dirty cads like Barter, can prevent Philip Crow from winning. You'll only make an ass of yourself before the whole County, Father, if you go into this; just as you will, of *yourself*—if I may say so—Mr. Geard!

"It won't do. You're heading for disaster. This strike that's beginning now, engineered by that little fool of a brother-in-law of mine, will be utterly broken in a month or two. The labouring men of Glastonbury aren't idiots. They'll see, quickly enough, on which side of the bread their butter is.

"Crow has the brains. Crow has the cash. Crow has the banks behind him and the great upper middle class behind him. He has, above everything else, the economic traditions of England behind him. You can't beat Crow, my good Mr. Geard. Hire all the play-actors you please; you can't beat him."

He jerked his leg back, from across his chair arm, and stretched it straight out by the side of the other, thrusting his hands deep into his pockets.

"I'll tell you a secret, Father; a secret of high politics; and you can make all the use of it you please, my good Mr. Geard! Philip Crow doesn't want Glastonbury flooded with visitors from overseas. That's not his taste and I don't blame him. All this demi-semi-religious hocus-pocus doesn't in the end do any good to a town. What does good to a town is to have *plenty of work*— real work, not this sycophantic, parasitic sponging on visitors, not all this poppycock about the Holy Grail. I tell you I can see the whole thing as clearly as if I were a bloody oracle. You can smile as much as you like, Father; what I'm saying is the truth. This strike in Crow's factories will only hurt the people. Dave Spear's a young idealistic fool—a mere bookish doctrinaire. So are you too, my good Mr. Geard, if you'll let me say so, with your Midsummer Fairs. What you've managed to do is simply this. You've divided the place into two camps. On your side are all the faddists and the cranks and the soft heads. On Crow's side is hard common sense. And let me tell you that in our old England, even yet, it'll be common sense that'll win!"

He stopped breathlessly and pouring out all the milk that was left in the milk-jug into the unused slop-basin swallowed it in a couple of gulps.

The Marquis of P. exchanged glances with his daughter. The Mayor of Glastonbury clasped his plump hands on the edge of the table and leant forward as if to speak. Then he changed his mind, unclasped his fingers, and sank back in his chair.

Lady Rachel said: "This new factory of Mr. Geard's is going to manufacture little figures. They are going to be figures of people like Arthur and Merlin. I'd sooner put my faith in these little figures, Will, than in all your common sense!"

William Zoyland emitted a merry laugh.

"Merlin forsooth!" he cried. "Well, Rachel, I suppose this *is* the right place for bringing Merlin in; but I've never yet heard of the Mayor of any modern town who would pin his faith upon Merlin!"

A long silence fell upon this group of four persons; a silence that was only broken by the crying of the wind in the great chimney above their heads. Then the Marquis said:—

"It's all very well for a healthy materialist like you, Will, to scoff at our old superstitions. I've noticed, however, that neither you nor anyone else I've talked to, who've come to this house, will ever agree to sleep the night in King Mark's Gallery.here."

"Do you mean the big room, Lord P.," enquired Mr. Geard, "that they say extends along the whole top floor of Mark's Court?" He paused for a minute—"I've often heard of this big room," he went on, "but I've never met anyone who's seen it."

Will Zoyland got up upon his feet, with a movement that shook the tea-table, and made the cups and saucers rattle.

"I tell you what, you Mayor of Glastonbury," he muttered in a queer husky voice, "if you'd sleep a whole night in that room up there, I'd—I'd—well! I'd say there was something, *some* bloody spunk at any rate, in this precious Pageant of yours!"

"William!" protested the Marquis, "you're going a bit too far, my boy."

Rachel's face had gone white and her eyes had grown large and very dark.

"You ought to be ashamed of yourself, Will!" she murmured in a tone that was scarcely audible.

But Mr. Geard's aplomb and self-possession had completely come back to him. He looked quietly at his host.

"I don't want to intrude," he said slowly, "or to outstay my welcome; but if there were . . . any way . . . of getting . . . a message to my family . . . I'd be . . . honoured . . . I say honoured . . . to sleep tonight . . . in the room you're . . . talking about."

"Don't let him, Father! Oh, you *mustn't* let him!" cried Lady Rachel with passionate intensity.

Bloody Johnny stretched out one of his plump hands and touched the young girl's knee.

"Listen, child," he said solemnly.

Rachel, still very white, looked him in the face.

"I swear to you, Lady Rachel," said the Mayor of Glastonbury slowly, "that I shall be all right up there."

He was the first, of the two of them, to remove his eyes. As soon as he had done so the girl drew a long breath and smiled, and a rush of blood, flooding her cheeks and even her soft, thin neck with a lovely rose tint, suffused her pale skin. Mr. Geard's own gaze encountered now the bold, restless, unsympathetic stare of Will Zoyland.

The Marquis of P., who, after his fashion, was no mean discerner of spirits, thought to himself, "Hurrah for old Johnny! I'm damned if he hasn't picked himself up. There's nothing of the bounder about him now. He's standing up to Will now."

"I don't . . . mean . . . to say," pronounced Mr. Geard emphatically, "that there are not terrors which are beyond my powers to overcome or to exorcise. I'll confess at once, Mr. Zoyland, that if there are bugs and fleas and spiders and dust up there, I here and now retract my pledge. But if your people, my Lord," and he turned to the Marquis, "have cleaned up that room fairly lately, and if you can get your Sergeant to carry up some kind of a bed there, I'd love to spend the night under your roof . . . only someone must tell my family."

The Marquis gave an imperceptible shrug of his shoulders, as much as to say, "I'm beginning to wish I were alone here with my daughter; as I intended to be!" but he rose stiffly to his feet, went to the mantelpiece and rang the bell.

Sergeant Blimp must have been driven out of the warmth of the kitchen by the spiteful hatred of the old couple; for he answered his master's ring almost as quickly as if he had been standing on the threshold like an old-fashioned man-at-arms. The way he now presented himself within the restricted radiance of the candlelight, and stood erect and silent there, suggested to Bloody Johnny's mind the idea that he carried a hauberk or at least an arquebus.

"Blimp," said the Marquis laconically. "I want you to go up to King Mark's chamber and see if the Bellamys have been dusting it and scrubbing it lately."

"Yes, my Lord. Certainly, my Lord," murmured the Sergeant.

"Run off then! . . . King Mark's chamber," repeated the Marquis peevishly.

But Sergeant Blimp showed no sign of stirring.

"Off with you, man! Are ye deaf?" cried my Lord crossly.

"It's . . . it's . . . it's," stammered the powerful-looking henchman.

"It's *what*?" enquired his master grimly. "Speak up, you fool! Don't stand staring like that, you idiot!"

"It's . . . a long story, your Lordship!" stammered the troubled servant.

"A long story!" cried Lord P., bursting into an unpleasant, sneering laugh. "What on earth are you muttering about? Do what I tell you."

"Your Lordship's orders were," burst out the man, with a rush of hasty words, "that I should have the whole place thoroughly cleaned, this time; afore you and my Lady Rachel came down. Mr. and Mrs. Bellamy wouldn't have a hand in it. They said they'd clean Lady Rachel's room, they said, but nothing more. So I had the remover's van men come in and do it . . . the same as brought down your Lordship's last load from London . . . and . . . and . . . to be frank with your Lordship, I haven't been up there since! The men said as how they had cleaned up wonderful clean; and 'twere a good tidy job, they said; and so, seeing as Mr. and Mrs. Bellamy were not ——"

The Marquis of P. jumped incontinently to his feet. Mr. Geard at first fancied he was going to strike the luckless Sergeant. When this did not occur he expected him to burst into a torrent of abuse and order him up to King Mark's chamber on pain of instant dismissal. But neither did this happen.

To Mr. Geard's complete astonishment, though not, it seemed, to the astonishment of his son and daughter, the Marquis took not the slightest notice of poor Blimp but walked hurriedly to the door, opened it, went out, and closed it behind him.

The man turned shamefacedly to Lady Rachel.

"I dursn't go up there, your Ladyship. I dursn't do it! I've served his Lordship for ten years, come good, come ill; and I've always done his bidding, and more than his bidding. But go into that room I dursn't . . . not to save my neck from the rope."

"It's all right, Blimp," said Lady Rachel kindly. "Father won't really mind. Don't you worry! He knows what he's got in anyone as devoted as you are. It'll be perfectly all right. You'd better take away the tray now that you are here."

"Well," began Will Zoyland, as soon as the man had departed with the tea-things. "I expect I'd better be seeing that Father doesn't come to any harm up there."

He rose from his seat like a great sulky tom-cat, yawning ostentatiously, stretching himself and running his fingers through his yellow beard; and then he strolled heavily and leisurely to the door.

"This all comes of your confounded Pageant, Mr. Mayor," he rapped out harshly as he left the room.

Left to themselves the young girl got up too, and came over to Mr. Geard's side. There was no room for her to sit on the arm of his chair; but she leaned against it, bending over him and pressing near to him. This tendency of Lady Rachel's to nestle up very close to anyone she trusted, to touch them with her warm body, to yield herself to them, was it a sign that the child in her was not yet absorbed or subsumed in the young woman? Or was it simply an indication that no cruel life-experience had as yet warned her against following a natural, almost universal girlish impulse? Possibly the true explanation of her instinctive desire to let Mr. Geard touch her would have been found to have had more to do with him than with her! It is indeed undeniable that had the Mayor of Glastonbury been free to do exactly what he *liked* he would have now pulled her down upon his knees; but he was not at all a man to follow any erotic feeling the moment it appeared, and in place of doing this he contented himself with taking her hand.

The girl's feelings were far too vague and floating and ephemeral for her to understand why it was that this taking of her hand at this moment gave her something of a cold chill and partook of the nature of a rebuff.

But although Mr. Geard kept an iron lid firmly screwed down upon his erotic feelings, some inner disturbance, evoking a tantalisingly vivid sensation of what he *might* have felt had he not screwed down this iron lid, must have communicated itself to the girl whose hand he held.

"Did you take my side as you promised to?" she murmured tenderly.

He pressed her fingers.

"Not much need, little lady," he said. "Your father has no intention of handing you over to that woman in Bath. I suggested that you should stop with Miss Crow in Glastonbury . . . Miss Elizabeth Crow . . . and I think I'll be able to arrange that for you. It's a little house in Benedict Street. You and she will be great friends."

Lady Rachel disengaged her hand.

"I thought *you* would have me . . . in *your* house . . . Mr. Geard!" she cried indignantly. "Didn't Father ask you about that?"

But Bloody Johnny was spared the embarrassment of explaining to her how little he desired to stir up the muddy waters of snobbishness in his sober dwelling, by the entrance of the Marquis and Will Zoyland.

"Well, Geard," said my Lord, "it's all arranged. Will has helped me with the bed; and he's told Mrs. Bellamy to do the rest. Poor Blimp is as terrified of ghosts as *you* seem to be of bugs and spiders! But I assure you the place is as clean as our hall. It's cold though. It's cold as the North Pole. I've told her to light a good fire for you. But it's clean. Those furniture chaps of Blimp's must have had step-ladders up there. It's like a church."

"I've got my Ford here," added Will Zoyland, "and I can easily go back to Wookey round by Glastonbury. No, I can't, Father! I tell you I can't!"—The Marquis had begun to press him to stay the night—"Easter Monday's a great day for trippers; one of the greatest; and I've really *got* to be on the job."

Some four or five hours later, after a pleasant supper over the open fire in the great hall, Lord P. and his daughter escorted the Mayor of Glastonbury up to the chamber of phantoms. They mounted an ancient staircase beyond the landing where the Marquis' bedroom was, and where the old couple, as well as the Sergeant, had their sleeping quarters. Here there was another small landing, from which a door opened upon the steps leading to a high turret-chamber of which Lady Rachel had taken possession.

"Let's show the Mayor my room, Father," cried Rachel eagerly.

The Marquis led the way. He carried in his hand a flat silver candlestick, from which the yellow candle-flames suddenly grown large and smoky, streamed backward, as the wind, whistling through the arrow-slits of the tower, blew about them as they went slowly up.

A fire was burning in Rachel's chamber and Bloody Johnny, when he caught the glowing essence of this enchanting room, felt a sudden clutch in the pit of his stomach while an outrageous and wild thought seized upon his mind.

Mr. Geard noticed on one side of this vaulted chamber, a subsidiary archway containing a small heavily bolted door.

Lady Rachel intercepted his glance.

"Let's take him over the Bridge of Sighs!" she whispered excitedly to her father.

The Marquis swung round on his heel and glowered for a moment with a cold glint of something worse than animosity at Mr. Geard. Lord P. possessed a peculiarity, inherited from his ancestors, of being subject at times to a savage anti-social spasm, a spasm of dangerous repugnance, dividing him and his, as if by a wedge of boreal ice from the particular specimens of humanity he encountered. This characteristic was one which almost all the intimates of Lord P.—unless they had blood in their veins recognised by himself as equal with his own—sooner or later came into collision with.

It is a sentimental mistake to assume that the real aristocracy is free from snobbishness. It is free from that perturbation of spirit in the presence of social ritual which is an accompaniment of snobbishness in ordinary people; but if any psychologist plays with the illusion that such great gentlemen are simple, natural, and naïve, in their absence of pride, he is making a profound mistake.

The historic House of Zoyland, descended from Charlemagne on the one hand, and from Rollo the Varangian on the other, had certain peculiarities that separated them altogether from the humbler gentlefolk of England. They had qualities that were unique to themselves and will die with them. One of these was this ice-cold, blindly pitiless frenzy of scorn for normal flesh-and-blood when they grew aware of it in a certain condition of their nerves.

This was the first and last occasion, however, in the life of the Marquis of P. when this projectile of frozen scorn for his interlocutor produced absolutely no effect on the person at whom it was directed.

Mr. Geard was in touch with a Presence that had defeated the Principalities and Powers of this proud planet centuries before the Norsemen came to Byzantium or Roland's horn was heard at Fontarabia!

Thus it was with a slightly weary indulgence, too patient and unperturbed to be even ironical, that Bloody Johnny returned, stare for stare, the withering *œilliade* of his noble host.

Lady Rachel, however, quite oblivious of this psychic episode, had begun to unbolt with girlish impetuosity the great iron bars that secured this archway-door. She pulled it open, inwards into the room, when she had drawn its final bolt; and Mr. Geard, whose eyes, leaving those of the devil-ridden nobleman, had wandered over this warm, virginal, mediæval room, and now met hers as she held fast to the thing's iron-wrought handle and kept the door ajar, smiled at her in unembarrassed response. From the girl's face his eyes now wandered again round the various objects in this remote little turret-chamber. There was a queer silence among the three of them while he did this; the reddened smoke from the fireplace, and the long yellow flame from the candle which the Marquis held, moving fitfully to and fro, as the wind rushing in from the stone archway she had uncovered, went eddying querulously round the walls.

Bloody Johnny noticed that the girl's bed—situated in an archway opposite to the one where she was now standing—was covered with a dark green coverlet, upon the centre of which the Zoyland arms, a falcon clutching a bare sword, was worked in dusky crimson. A small shelf of books—they all seemed to be unbound French books whose paper backs looked singularly out of keeping with the rest of that interior—hung at the bed's head, while over the wall space of the corresponding archway opposite the hearth was suspended a strip of faded tapestry, the figures upon which it was impossible to decipher in that flickering light, as the wind, stealing behind it, made it swell and bulge like a heavy sail and then again subside into the level darkness of its obscurity.

But the silence in that room became itself a tapestry of obscure figures that lifted and sank, sank and lifted, each one of those three minds offering its own secret pattern to the occult weaving of that pregnant moment.

The girl alone, woman-like, was aware of the flowingness of time. For the others time was static. For Geard it was a static Eternal, with that wind-shaken piece of old tapestry sinking down with all three of them into other dimensions. For Lord P. it was a static Superficial, with the tension stretched taut, like the leash of a straining dog.

But to the girl, as she held ajar that heavy oaken door, keeping the wild wind out and yet not keeping it quite out, there came just then an exultant feeling of lovely, continuous flowingness. "How strong and mysterious men are," she thought to herself. "But oh, I'm glad I'm not a man. Ned isn't a man either. And what a good thing he isn't. Ned's only a boy. He couldn't manage these strong mysterious men like I can."

It was the Marquis who made the gesture that broke the spell; but even he did not speak in order to do it. He made a sign to his daughter to go ahead and he made a sign to Geard to follow her. He himself followed with his hand over the candle-flame; and indeed it was necessary for him to give the door a vicious kick with his foot to close it before he could cross the covered stone-way after them, and enter King Mark's death-chamber. This they entered by a similar door to the one he had closed and he managed to get the candle safe into the great empty place without letting the wind annihilate its tender flame.

Once inside King Mark's room and the little door shut behind him, Lord P. laid the candle down on a vast piece of furniture that looked like a long refectory table in a monastery in South Russia, and, returning to the door through which they had come, closed it with unnecessary violence.

The young girl ran forward now to the hearth-fire which was burning very badly. Huge clouds of smoke kept issuing from it; clouds that rolled across the room and mounted up among the high rafters. Mr. Geard watched her intently for a second as she bent down to select a few more inflammable billets of wood to throw in, on the top of the ones that were smouldering so slowly and unsatisfactorily there. With the smoke rising up in wisps and

eddies around her, her figure took on an almost unearthly waver-
ingness; as if she had been a sylph of the elements, a Being that
was taking refuge from the wind-demon outside, in the arms of
the fire-demon inside.

He then glanced at the couch that Will Zoyland had carried up
for him. It was just a boy-scout camp-bed; but they had covered
it with a vast, ancient coverlet, like the one that covered Lady
Rachel's bed, only this was of a dark purplish colour; and while
it had upon it, in faded embroidery, the falcon clutching the
sword, an ugly rent in it had rendered the bird headless.

Mr. Geard moved slowly to the fireplace; but he began to cough
as the smoke got into his throat.

"There!" cried the girl with a deep breath, prodding the
smouldering logs with a thick iron rod, hooked at the end, which
looked as if it had served for this purpose in days when iron had
only just begun to be used. She let this Homeric utensil fall with
a clatter on the stone coping of the hearth.

"If the smoke makes you cough when you're in bed," she said,
while a darting red flame lit up her face, "you can lug your
couch under the window and leave the window open. That's what
I do when *my* fire smokes. These old chimneys always smoke
when they're first lit." She paused and a spasm of intense concern
puckered her brow.

"You don't suppose there were any swallows' nests in the chimney, do you?" she asked.

Her mouth remained open after the words left and her eyes
grew round.

The Marquis, who had been fumbling at the latches of one of
the windows, got it open now, and as he got it open the wind came
in with such a wild rush that he jumped back in dismay. Lady
Rachel observed this occurrence with childish interest; and in
her fit of momentary nervousness, being wrought up by her
anxiety over the possibility of nests in the chimney, she forgot her
good breeding and laughed aloud. Her laughter must have been
the final issue of a long series of suppressed days; for it burst out
through the smoke with the quivering ring of something
hysterical.

Through the brain of Mr. Geard there rushed like a frantic

swallow, beating its wings to escape, the word "Nimeue"; and with this word, the original of the name Vivian, a spasm of mingled emotions, sweet and troubling.

But the Marquis was really annoyed now. That there should have arisen all this unusual fuss over his old friend Johnny Geard of Montacute was in itself not a little inappropriate. But, after all, he himself had been responsible for it. But the Bastard's words, though rejected at the time, had already begun to work on the subtle old statesman's mind; and he felt as if there was something in the air in King Mark's chamber that night which was unsuitable, incongruous, and out of control. That hysterical note in his daughter's laugh, when the inrush of wind made him leap back, "taunted" his mind, as they say in Somerset. He bit his underlip as he pushed the casement to again with both his hands and clicked the two iron latches.

"Women and ——" he muttered under his breath impatiently. He meant to say "women and conjurers," but instead of "conjurers," the lips within the lips, which people use when they are obsessed in this curious way, uttered the words—"Caer Sidi"; words which an eccentric Oxford scholar, when drunk enough to talk freely to him, had once repeated in his ears with tipsy reiteration.

The Mayor of Glastonbury had himself drawn back from that childish laughing-fit; and coughing quite uncomfortably now from the acrid smoke he had swallowed, sat himself down on his scout bed. But this bed began so to creak and groan under his weight that he turned to his host and said peevishly, "Mr. Zoyland's not been setting a booby-trap for me, I hope?"

"You've not won your bet yet, Geard," returned the Marquis laconically. "You understand, I suppose, quite clearly," he went on, taking his daughter by the arm and leading her to a different door from the one they had entered by, "that no one has managed to sleep in this room? Some mediæval clerk, called Blehis or Bleheris, wrote his histories here, they tell me; but he wouldn't sleep up here."

But Mr. Geard, rising from his creaking bed, dismissed with a wave of his plump hand this nervousness of Messire Bleheris.

Placidly he bowed good-night to them both, and was apparently only anxious to get rid of them.

The Marquis, however, with his daughter clinging to his arm, her white face and dark eyes looking wild and scared in the candlelight, was seized with the devil's own malice.

"I met a crazy Oxford scholar, Geard," he said, "not so long ago; who told me that he'd sooner commit murder than sleep in this old place. He said that Merlin ——"

"Stop, Father; stop! How can you be so cruel?" cried Lady Rachel, actually clapping her free hand over the man's sneering mouth.

"Hee! Hee! Hee!" chuckled my Lord. "You won't have won your bet with Will, your Worship, till Bellamy lets you out in the morning! I'm to lock you in, Geard, I hope you understand? And of course the turret-room will be bolted. They say that a man, in the time of Edward the Fourth, spent the whole night out there, on the Bridge of Sighs; and another fellow, only a hundred years ago, was found ——" but the girl pulled him hastily and indignantly through the door.

"Good-night, Mr. Geard!" she called out, while the huge mass of oaken boards, bound with hand-wrought iron, groaned as it closed.

Bloody Johnny heard the faint metallic clang, muffled and muted, of the bolts being thrust into place. Then there ensued a tremendous silence. He sat down again on his creaking scout bed and surveyed King Mark's chamber. The tall candle, burning steadily and brightly now on the refectory table, and the red flames that were coming from a pile of wood on the hearth, served to illumine the vast, shadowy expanse. The place was like the interior of an early Norman church and it seemed to the Mayor of Glastonbury that upon many of the enormous rafters above his head there were obscure patches and blotches of what must once have been painted scrolls. He walked to one of the arched windows and gazed out into the night. It was too dark to see more than the faintest outlines of the trees beneath him, but at one spot in the sky the wild-tossed racks of swift-blown clouds had thinned a little, revealing a dim moon that looked sick and giddy; as if she also, even she, were being blown, like a great pale leaf, before this devilish wind.

The chamber was certainly clean. The Marquis had not deceived him on *that* point at any rate. He hesitated a minute or two; and then, quietly and deliberately, took off his coat, waistcoat, shirt and trousers. He experienced, as he always did, a vague, humorous distaste for his plump, unathletic body, as he looked down upon his ungainly legs, encased in grotesque woolen drawers, and upon his protruding belly, like the paunch of a figure upon a beer mug, in its soft, tight-fitting vest.

He walked to the refectory table and took up the candle, placing it on the floor by his bedside. He went across to the chair where he had laid his clothes and took from his coat pocket a box of matches which he placed on the floor by the side of the candle. Then, with heavy deliberation he got down upon his knees by the side of that ridiculous little couch, draped in its ragged armorial coverlet, and shutting his eyes tight and letting his clasped hands rest on his stomach, which at that moment resembled the belly of a wooden Punchinello, he proceeded to murmur his usual evening prayer.

This was a singular one, in that it was addressed to the air on the other side of his bed.

"Master be with me," prayed Bloody Johnny, "Master be with me! Give me strength to change the whole course of human history upon earth! Give me strength to make Glastonbury the centre of a completely new life! Master be with me! Be with me now and forever, by thy most precious Blood!"

The image he evoked in his imagination did not resemble in the least degree the tortured Figure of Pain worshipped by Sam Dekker, and it did not fade away till he got himself slowly into bed. He did this most carefully and gingerly and though the little couch shivered and creaked lamentably under his weight, it did not let him down. His feet, however, protruded under the coverlet, like the feet of a corpse under a purple pall, almost six inches beyond the end of the bed. He then bent down, picked up the candle, blew it out, and replaced it upon the floor.

He lay flat now upon the bed . . . on his broad back . . . his massive skull on the soft white pillow. With his hands he pulled up the heraldic coverlet, till it was thickly disposed beneath his chin. He tucked its heavy folds tight about his shoulders, being totally unable to cope with the smooth compactness in which Mrs. Bellamy had so trimly turned back the sheet over the stiff blankets.

His eyes watched the flickering firelight as it touched with warm, rosy reflections the huge dark rafters and the curved oaken supports of the baronial roof.

A pleasant aromatic smell . . . the smell of pine wood . . . began now to comfort his senses. The smoke was no longer bitter. It had become fragrant . . . soothing as incense but more wholesome and natural, almost forest-like.

"Master be with me!" his lips repeated; "be with me now and forever; by thy most precious Blood!"

Mr. Geard's nature was about ten times as *thick* as most men's. With the seven or eight under layers of this nature he was entirely absorbed, by day and by night, in his contact with Christ, which resembled, though it was not identical with, the physical embrace of an erotic obsession.

Thus it was only now . . . when things had at last subsided and he was left alone . . . that the two or three *upper* layers of his thick, phlegmatic nature became really conscious of the difference between going to bed in the chamber where Merlin turned King Mark into dust and going to bed with his faithful Megan. He recalled Lord P.'s malicious "Hee! Hee! Hee!" as he dragged his daughter off and the wild, frightened look—both for him and for the imaginary nests in the chimney—with which Rachel had been pulled through the doorway.

It was not with a very deep layer of his being, perhaps not even with the deepest of the two or three uppermost ones, that he meditated for a while upon the virginal provocativeness of that soft, slim, girlish body, that he had so nearly pulled down upon his knees just now. These sensual thoughts were entirely unresisted by Mr. Geard. It was a peculiarity of Bloody Johnny's "thick" nature, that his religious, and what many people might have called his "spiritual" feelings, had absolutely no connection with morality. But although not resisted but rather, on the contrary, *encouraged* by his conscious will, these amorous stirrings within him were so weak and so languid, as very soon to subside into a delicious drowsiness.

The Mayor of Glastonbury's drowsiness, however, soon ceased to be delicious. No sooner had it become an actual sleep, although a very light sleep, than a fantastic philological problem tormented the dreaming man.

Was it "Nineue," or "Nimeue," that Owen Evans had told him was the original version of the popular "Vivian"? These three words, "Nineue," "Nimeue" and "Vivian," became for him now three flying herons with outstretched legs. Bloody Johnny's own heart, escaped somehow from his body, was the sick, giddy moon that he had caught a glimpse of; and it was this accurst philological problem—*which* heron was Merlin's paramour—that made this moon-heart of his, as the wild wind tossed it about, so sick, so yellow, so dizzy.

He suddenly awoke into full consciousness with a violent start. He had heard a voice . . . Oh, it was unmistakably real! It wasn't in his dream at all! . . . which cried out from beside the hearth, "Nineue! Nineue!" He listened now, fully awake and with a heart that was most assuredly safe back where it belonged, for it was pounding like a clock with broken machinery.

How the wind was howling! Never had he heard such a wind! It was a sheer, simple, childish terror that Mark Moor Court was going to be blown down that night, which was making his heart beat in this way. Mr. Geard kept telling himself just this. "It's the wind," he repeated firmly and emphatically. "It's the wind that's making my heart beat!"

He craned his neck round, staring at the fire that was now very large and very red. The voice he had heard was that of a man, and it had come from somewhere behind the masonry of the wall, just to the right of that burning blaze. And then, without any ambiguity *this* time, he heard an unmistakable sound clear and distinct, in some room just below his floor. He moved his head back upon his pillow. The sound ceased at once. Again he stretched out his head, like the head of a saurian, over the side of the bed. The sound once more became audible. It was an unmistakable sound; but it was anything but a romantic sound. It was in fact the sound of a man making water.

Mr. Geard could not be mistaken. The man was making water into a metallic chamber-pot; and as he made it he broke wind several times. The Mayor of Glastonbury continued to crane his neck over the side of his bed. He now became aware of a crack, just in that place, between the bare, dark, oak planks of the floor. A faint, a very faint light was observable through this slit in the floor. He continued to listen with his whole soul. Never had he listened so intently to any sound in his life. He heard the man replace the chamber-pot . . . it must have been made of tin or perhaps of iron . . . and then there were steps and gaspings and creakings and low grumbling groans. Soon he heard another sound, similar to the first and yet dissimiliar. A second human being was making water. This time the flow was noisier, quicker, sooner over. "It's a woman," thought Bloody Johnny.

He tried to make his awkward position, as he hung over the crack in the floor, a more comfortable one. He extended his arm until his fingers touched the floor. Yes! this gave a necessary support to his outstretched head.

There were more shufflings and groanings, more creakings and obscure murmurs, then dead silence. He waited, still stretched out over the crack. He thought to himself, "A man makes water. A woman makes water. These sounds are being heard all over Somersetshire tonight, in thousands and thousands of bedrooms. Other unpleasant sounds are being heard too. The sounds of the teeth of incredibly ravenous rats inside hundreds of slaughter-houses. I wonder," so the thoughts of the Mayor ran on, "I wonder if there are any ears subtle enough to hear the worms at work in the churchyards? A man making water. A woman making water. Every sound a vibration. Every vibration a radiation, a detonation. Every sound travelling from the earth outward into space. Will the sound of Mr. and Mrs. Bellamy making water in their room at Mark Court go on voyaging through space until it reaches the Milky Way? And not stop even then? No! No! Why should it stop then? Nothing once started can ever stop! It can come back perhaps, if space is round, but that's the best it can do. Here we go round Tom Tiddler's ground! The everlasting pissing of Mr. and Mrs. Bellamy."

But the silence was broken again now; broken just as the

Mayor of Glastonbury was going to withdraw his outstretched head. There was a sound of expectoration; and this sound was a good deal more disagreeable to the ears of Mr. Geard than the other had been. And then he heard with appalling distinctness the voice of the old woman saying to the old man, "Spit on the brown paper, John. Spit on the brown paper I did lay out for 'ee!"

Bloody Johnny drew back his head and once more pulled the purple coverlet tightly round his chin. "Nineue" he murmured aloud, trying to recall what it had been in the intonation of that voice from behind the fireplace that had given his heart such a shock. Had he dreamed of his heart being sick and yellow, like the driven moon, *before* he heard that voice crying out? Yes he had. He most assuredly had. And he had been dreaming of the name "Nineue" before he heard it cried. And he had thought of the word "Nineue" . . . it had come suddenly into his head in place of something else . . . *before* he dreamed of it. Or had he dreamed of it and thought of it too *after* he had heard that voice?

"Damn!" said Bloody Johnny to himself, "It must have been that old pantaloon, down there, talking to his wife; and in my dream I made it out to be a voice."

He had reached this point in his cogitations when he suddenly found himself sitting straight up in the creaking little bed in a grievous fit of pure fear. He knew that voice was going to be lifted up again. He knew it was. Nothing could stop it from being lifted up again. In just one second he would be hearing it again. It would be crying "Nineue" just as it had done before. "If it does," he thought, "I shall run out on that bridge. I shall knock at that girl's door. She couldn't not let me in. She *couldn't* not!"

But he clenched his hands together stubbornly and stared at the red fire, resolute, in his massive way, to beat down this fear, to beat it down and hold it down, so that it should not grow into panic; so that it should not *get into his legs*. So far it was only in his heart and in his throat. But he could feel it descending. It ran down a funnel . . . the fear-funnel it was that it ran down . . . inside his ribs . . . no, between his spine and his stomach. Tightly, tightly, he clasped his hands together staring at the fire.

He thought of various quiet, sturdy people in his life. He thought of Megan sleeping in their familiar room.

And then, in a flash, he thought of Canon Crow. The Canon had been accustomed to read Rabelais to him sometimes of a night, when the servants were in bed. The Canon had laughed at him at such times and called him "Friar John des Entommeures," "Friar John of the Funnels." He was all one great Funnel now . . . waiting till the repetition of that voice pumped fear into him . . . out of him . . . through him . . . pumped . . . *pumped*. . . . But all might yet be well if this fear didn't get into his legs!

Now came a second of time when he actually *wanted* the voice to come again. "When it's come, it's come," he thought. "It's past then . . . come and gone." But it was his own mouth that now opened like a crack in thick ice. It was his own voice that resounded wildly through King Mark's chamber, till the rafters rang again; "Nineue! Nineue!"

He did feel a certain relief when he had uttered this rending and tearing scream. He found he had sufficient self-control now to ask himself what it had been in the intonation of that voice that had made his heart so sick. The horror he had felt was not precisely fear. What it really was was *pity*. It was pity carried to such a point by the intonation of that reiterated "Nineue! Nineue!" that it became worse than fear. The relief he experienced when—impelled by a nervous force he was unable to resist—he had himself cried out that name was like the relief which some spectator at the Colosseum might have felt, when unable to endure what he saw, he had jumped down into the arena and was fighting there tooth and nail among the murderers and the murdered.

He now found himself mumbling forth a sort of personal appeal to the Being who had cried "Nineue! Nineue!"

"Why don't you come forth? Why don't you show yourself? Yes, yes, why don't you come forth now, close up to my bed, near me, near me, so that I can touch you, see you, feel you?"

He uttered these words in a low tone, swaying and shivering there in the reddish fire-gleams. If any human eye had been watching him he would have resembled a picture that one could imagine being painted by Rembrandt if Rembrandt had gone mad.

The fire-gleams flickered upon the tight woolen vest that covered the exposed half of his protuberant belly. They flickered upon his great white face. They flickered upon the headless falcon embroidered on the torn rug about his legs. They flickered on his stockinged feet, which stuck out grotesquely beyond the end of his diminutive bed.

"Why don't you let me see you?" he whined again in a voice that was almost wheedling; and he began suddenly nodding his great head in a manner that suggested the impulse of a powerful dog anxious to propitiate a yet more powerful dog by an obsequious fawning and wagging of its great tail.

"Let me see you! Yes, yes; let me touch you with my hands!"

It was as if he were addressing a Being whose presence he felt much more certainly, much more closely than he felt the pressure of that heraldic rug at which he now began twitching; pinching it with his fingers and thumbs, much as a dying man plays with the bedclothes that cover his nakedness. What he felt in all his pulses was that if this desperate lover of Nineue . . . this great and lost magician . . . were to come forth now from behind that reddened smoke and approach his bed his heart would have become calm as a saint's.

It was the tone of that cry. He could not bear it. If he heard it again his heart would crack. Pity carried to that point was intolerable. . . . He ceased his picking at the rug. He bent his great head as a wrestler or a boxer might have done. And he took hold of his heavy, phlegmatic soul in the iron pincers of his massive will and he pressed it down, like a bar of molten metal into those lower levels of his thick nature where he held fast hold of his Christ.

And then Mr. Geard gathered himself together. There were physical movements in his body of which he was quite unconscious. His thick shoulders under his woolen vest heaved and shuddered. His exposed belly went in and out, sinking and expanding; while the stature of his torso from hips to crown palpably distended. Three times he struggled to utter words; but in vain. He attempted it the fourth time; but in vain. Then . . .

the fifth time, of his Atlantean heaving . . . words came; words mingled with bloody spume came; forcing themselves out of his mouth they came; with a wrench as if they brought his entrails with them.

"Christ have mercy upon you!" gasped Mr. Geard. The words were no sooner out of his mouth than a relaxed shivering fit seized upon him and his head fell forward. His whole body drooped forward, bending at the waist, the arms limp. Had there been anyone to see his face at that moment it would have appeared like the face of a corpse before its fallen chin has been caught up and bandaged.

Perfectly still he remained, his eyelids drooping, his whole frame limp. He was like a person who has been shaken by the convulsions of some terrible fit, till, in the ensuing stillness, his spirit seems to have gone out of him.

He remained, for what seemed to his own dazed consciousness like several hours, in this position. Then, very slowly the life-energy returned to him. All his dread was over now and a great peacefulness descended upon him. Leisurely and comfortably and with an exquisite feeling of sensual contentment he stretched himself out once more in his little bed and pulled the purple coverlet over his shoulders.

He began to feel very sleepy and with his sleepiness there fell upon him a delicious sense of inscrutable, unutterable achievement. But the Mayor of Glastonbury was not allowed just yet to enjoy his hard-earned repose.

There came a very definite sound to his ears at the end of the room, at that place in the wall of King Mark's chamber where was the door leading out upon the Bridge of Sighs. It was the sound of that little door opening inward upon its rusty hinges. With a drowsy and a rather irritable movement he heaved himself up again in his bed.

And the door was closed carefully and gently, there before him; and a slender black figure, holding a flat candlestick in its hand, advanced with bare feet across the floor towards his bed.

Rachel Zoyland did not utter a word till she reached his bedside. Then in a voice that trembled on the edge of a child's passionate crying-fit she said brokenly:

"I heard . . . I heard . . . I was listening . . . I couldn't sleep . . . I heard. . . ."

The long black cloak she was wearing fell open displaying her white night-gown.

He stretched out his arm. Not for the first time in his life Bloody Johnny became uncomfortably aware of the grotesqueness of his physical appearance. He took hold of her hand and tried to make her sit down at the foot of his bed, but she remained standing there in her naked feet, her long straight night-gown showing white as her cloak swung open. Her brown hair fell in tumbled curls over one of her small bare shoulders. Her childish mouth, twitching in the light of the candle which she clutched, could not utter a word. The candle was so shaken by the way she was trembling that its grease began to drip upon the emblazoned coverlet.

"I heard . . . I heard you call . . . and I had to come," she whispered.

Bloody Johnny, blinking with his sleepy eyelids because of the flame of the candle, made a humorous grimace and pointed to the floor at her feet.

"The Bellamys are just below," he whispered hoarsely. "For God's sake don't get me into trouble with the household! If *you* heard me shout, I'm afraid *they* must; and they may be rushing in now any second!"

He uttered these words in so whimsical a manner and smiled at her so naturally and so quietly that the girl swallowed her approaching sobs in a gallant gulp.

"Put down the candle, Lady Rachel," he said gravely, sinking back on his pillow; "you're spilling the grease on your father's rug."

She obeyed him with docility now and sat down on the flimsy couch, which promptly gave vent to an ominous creak.

But he stretched out his arm, in its tight woolen sleeve, and took her hand.

"It'll stand your weight," he said, "if it's stood all my antics."

"Don't make me go to Miss Crow," she whispered. "Let me come and live with you!"

He looked at her through his half-shut eyelids, while the sylla-

bles "Nineue" floated dreamily through his soothed consciousness. It was indeed the first time in Bloody Johnny's life that the
indescribable magic of a young girl's identity dominated his
mind. It floated forth from everything about her, from the soft
brown curls resting on her exposed shoulder, where her cloak
had slipped, from the fragrant warmth of her light limbs, from
the cold virginal curves of her mouth, from the tiny rondures,
like water-lilies under her night-gown, of her girl's breasts, from
the softness about her childish figure that made it different from
what a boy's would have been, and beyond and above all these
from a flower-like sweetness which emanated rather from her soul
than from her body, troubling the senses of Mr. Geard with an
awakened consciousness of the loveliness which all the young
leaves and shoots and petals out there in that spring wind must
have possessed this Easter night.

It would have been erroneous to say that Mr. Geard experienced any poignant temptation. The appalling struggle he had
just been through had left his vital energies at their lowest possible ebb. It would have been possible for the girl to have slid
much closer to him than she was, sitting there like a little marble
figure at the foot of his couch, and still he would have suffered
no carnal stir.

Calmly he allowed himself to drink up her delicate beauty; to
drink it up out of the midst of that vast, shadowy chamber; as if
he were drinking it from a great basin of cold black basalt.

"Let me come and live with you, Mr. Geard! Please, please let
me!" she pleaded in a passionate whisper.

He smiled a little; he sighed a little; he pressed her cold fingers tightly; but he gave his big head as it rested on the pillow
an imperceptible shake.

"Don't 'ee say it, girlie," he murmured. "Don't 'ee say it, my
pretty! I dursn't let 'ee. No, no, no; I dursn't let 'ee. But 'ee
shall often come to see I; sure 'ee shall; and see me good Mr.
Barter, and tell he all about they pretty, pretty images."

The tears came into her eyes again and her mouth began
twitching, just as it had done when she first appeared.

"Tell 'ee what, wenchie," continued Mr. Geard, deliberately
reverting to his old Montacute Town's End speech, "tell 'ee what.

Us 'ull ask that fine lad o' your'n, from Middlezoy, to sup wi' the Missus and me; and ye shall come and meet 'un. Ye'll like *that*, girlie, eh? Ye'll like *that*, won't ye?"

He felt, rather than saw, the hot young blood rush into her cheeks.

"Well, well," he murmured. "We mustn't tease a good, kind, little girl, what's come across the cold stones in her bare feet to save an old man from they ghosties. No, no, we mustn't tease her; but, say what you will, Missy, you'll be monstrous pleased with my Miss Crow. And remember this, Rachel, if it hadn't been that there *was* a person like Miss Crow in our town I could never have pressed your father to let you come to us."

"I wish she was at the Devil!" cried the angry child with a flash of fierce Varangian fury.

"Come, come," he retorted, "for all you know she may be at the Devil; and it'll be the Devil's own kettle of fish when Rachel Zoyland comes to Glastonbury!"

But the girl suddenly stiffened all over.

It was now nearly two o'clock, when the resistant power, not only of young descendants of Charlemagne but of birds and fishes and plants and beasts is at its faintest, the hour when the very seaweeds in the deep salt tides shrink inward upon themselves, when the sap is weak in the forest mosses, when the pine needles in the frozen hills carry their burden of snow most feebly, when the fern fronds on a thousand wide-stretched moors are numb and cold and indrawn.

The girl's nerves were thoroughly jangled. She had been suppressing a fit of bitter crying all that night. This final resistance to her will, this denial of her intense wish, coming at the moment when she had been so brave, coming from the person she had rushed to rescue from God knows what, was for her the breaking-point. Ned Athling, for that moment, passed altogether out of her mind's foreground. She only wanted one thing just then; to live under this man's roof in Glastonbury; and the man himself, lying there so drowsily before her, was calmly denying her this. This, then, was what a girl got for getting out of her warm bed, for crossing the windy flagstones of the Bridge of Sighs, for daring to face the ghost of the Enchanter. This is what she got—

an easy, unctuous, humorous, grown-up denial of her natural reward! The indignant Zoyland blood froze in her veins. She slid
down from the couch and lay stretched out, face downward, on
the floor.

"Oh—oh—oh!" She uttered this "Oh" as if it were a thin,
little jet of saliva, spat out from under the darting tongue of
a small deadly snake.

Mr. Geard stretched out his head from the side of his bed,
like a monster lizard from a primeval mud-ledge, and squinnied
askance at that motionless heap of white and black, lying on the
floor. Then he leaned over and pulled the candle away from beside the edge of her night-gown.

"Oh—oh—oh!" Her prostrate body separated that candle-flame
now from the crevice between the oaken boards through which
he had seen the light in the room below and heard those peculiar
sounds.

In the deep shadow between the girl's back and the edge of
the couch, where the folds of the coverlet rested on the floor, he
saw this thin aperture; and he saw that there *was* a light in the
room below. Mr. Geard did not delay. The last thing he desired,
at that crucial moment, was an inrush into King Mark's chamber
of Mr. and Mrs. Bellamy! He determined to prevent such a
contingency by a decisive move. He got quickly out of bed. The
heap of black and white fabrics upon the floor neither stirred
nor uttered a moan.

He went hurriedly across the floor to the chair where he had
flung his clothes. He pulled on his trousers, buttoning them
tightly round his waist without bothering about his braces. He
put his coat on over his woolen vest. Then he returned to his
bed and snatching up the velvet coverlet stooped down and
wrapped it about the figure on the floor.

Rachel's thin arms resisted him.

"I hate you!"

Mr. Geard prayed in his deep heart.

"Christ, don't let her scream! Christ, don't let her scream!"

He rolled her up in the great heraldic coverlet. The wings of
the headless falcon were round her waist. Thus bundled up he
lifted her in his arms like an infant. A fold of the rug hung over

her face. Kneeling down on one knee and supporting her upon the other—"So, you *have* got what you wanted!" something cynically whispered in his ears—he picked up her silver candle-stick and then rising to his feet, carried both candle and girl resolutely to the door. Out upon the Bridge of Sighs he carried them, that flaring candle-flame and that pride-broken maid; and he felt upon his forehead the air that comes before the air of dawn and is chilliest of all earthly airs. He felt it under his sleeves and between his coat and his vest. He felt it in the marrow of his bones.

"Holy Christ, don't let her scream!" he prayed.

And then it suddenly occurred to him that the girl couldn't possibly have heard *his* scream . . . couldn't possibly have heard a sound carried from his chamber to hers . . . with this stone causeway dividing them. Puzzled by this thought and losing now in this pre-dawn air, so full of a particular sort of dew-heavy fatality, the sharper edges of his anxiety, he made the excuse to himself of re-settling the folds of the rug about her throat and propped her body, all bundled up, all mute and unstruggling, against one of the stone parapets of the bridge.

Far away in the west he could see the large, low-hanging, shapeless moon; no longer sick-looking and yellowish, but steely cold and bright, and sailing scornful and proud in a blue-black gulf that held not a single star. For less than half a second Mr. Geard's warm, thick, Christ-supported nature felt the ice-cold paw upon its throat of the unappeased Cerberus of life-devouring annihilation.

Holding tightly to his living bundle and unconsciously giving it little taps with the rim of the flat candlestick whose flame was being blown sideways so gustily that it was almost extinct, Mr. Geard stared into the cold blue-black emptiness that surrounded that distorted moon. He projected his human consciousness as if it had been a stone slung from a catapult,—such stones no doubt *had* been flung in the days of Bleheris from this very parapet— till it reached the side of that radiant abortion. From that van-tage-ground in space he projected it again till it reached the unthinkable circumference of the astronomical universe. From this dizzy point he surveyed the whole sidereal world . . . the whole inconceivable ensemble of etheric and stellar and telluric Matter. Contemplating this ghastly and mind-bewildering Enormity, Mr. Geard, tapping the dark bundle he held with the now quite extinct candle, thought to himself, "My mind has something in it, some background, some basis of secret truth, that is completely outside the visible world, outside the whole staggering vision of Matter! Without the existence of this something else I could not envisage this immense universe at all. Without this deeper thing there would be no universe!"

His thought at that point suddenly became something that was quite different from thought. He felt as people feel when in the midst of a vivid dream they get the sensation that, if they pleased, they could wake themselves up! This bundle he held, those beech-tree tops down there, that huge stone buttress descending into the moonlit shadows, this sharp-smelling blown-out candle—why, they were all half-insubstantial, half-unreal! But the Christ by his side was wholly real. The Christ within him and about him belonged to a reality that at any minute could reduce all this to a pinch of dust, of thin dust, to feed the *Herons of Eternity*!

He was startled out of his trance by nothing less than an audible murmur from the bundle he carried.

"Please take me in, Mr. Geard," sighed this muffled sound. "I am good now."

He raised her incontinently from the perilous edge of that high parapet and bore her over the bridge to the door in the archway. This door he found ajar. It was easy for him to swing it open with his foot and carry her forward. Down one step they went, down another step, then they emerged into her own warm firelit room.

So brightly was her fire burning—she must have fed it with fresh fuel before she left the turret—that the sheets of her bed, rolled up as when she had tossed them back, gleamed white as swans' down in the rosy glow. He carried her across the floor and laid her gently upon these disordered sheets. With fingers tender as a woman's he pulled away the coverlet from her face. There were her big, amused eyes; there were her brown curls; there was her tremulous mouth, the lips divided in a reassuring smile!

"Sorry I was cross," she whispered. "I'll go to your Miss

Crow's, and you shall ask Ned and me to supper. Did you see the ghost of Merlin, Mr. Geard?"

"How long have you been a good girl like this, Lady Rachel?" he asked.

"Since the moment you picked me up off the floor," she answered. "I thought to myself, it's worth getting into a rage to be carried to bed by the Mayor of Glastonbury; and so I stayed still. I liked your carrying me, Mr. Geard. I felt like a doll."

"You'll keep your promise, Rachel, and help Mr. Barter with those little images?"

She made an effort to get her arms free of the purple coverlet; but he laid his hand on its surface and stopped her.

"Good-night," he said. "I'll find my way back. It's moonlight now."

"I believe you *will* make Glastonbury all you want it to be!" she cried with shining eyes.

Her face looked so fragile emerging quaintly from the folds of the rug and resting on the white sheet, that, hardly realising what he was doing, he bent down and kissed her cold cheek.

"Good-night, Lady Rachel," he repeated.

Back once again in King Mark's vast dusky chamber, Mr. Geard set himself seriously to think of his grand design. The girl's words, "You *will* make Glastonbury all you want it to be," had started a train of cogitation that it was hard to bring to a pause. To confess the truth, too, he felt a little chilly now in his flimsy bed without that noble covering! But his mind went back to that vast array of ancient folios in the room where Will Zoyland had challenged him.

"What those old Scholastics aimed at," he thought, "I shall fulfil. All their fine-spun logic is dipped in Christ's Blood; and I shall make of that Blood a living Fountain on Chalice Hill, to which all the nations of the earth shall come for healing!"

He tried to warm himself by rolling the bed-clothes tightly around his body, very much as he had rolled the purple coverlet around . . . *Nineue*. There it was! The two Beings, the old Magician's paramour, and this sweet young creatuure who so believed in the power of poor Johnny Geard, had at last merged in each other. Well! That was how it *should* be. There was destiny in it. He had been well-advised to ride over to Mark Moor Court on the day of Christ's Resurrection. The old magic monger had vanished with his heathen Grail—so Mr. Evans said—in the heart of Chalice Hill. Well! He, Bloody Johnny, the new miracle-worker, would show the world, before *he* vanished, that the real Grail still existed in Glastonbury.

Wrapped up, like a great fat chrysalis, in his bed-clothes, with his big white face turned to the dying fire, Mr. Geard now awaited the first approaches of dawn. His long vigil that night seemed to have left his brain preternaturally clear. He began to review in calm retrospect the illumination he had received that night as he clutched his living bundle on the edge of those moonlit gulfs of space.

"I know now," he thought, "what the Grail is. It is something that has been dropped upon our planet, dropped within the earthly atmosphere that surrounds Glastonbury, dropped from Somewhere Else . . .

"I don't know," he went on thinking, "of what substance this thing is made; or whether it was flung into our material dimension purposely, or by accident, or by . . . It is evidently possessed of radiations that can affect both our souls and . . . Everyone who believes in it increases its power. *That*, at least, is clear—wherever it came from!"

He stared up at the dark, massive rafters, catching desperately at a thought which tantalised him and evaded him.

"Sometimes in dreams," he thought, "some little inanimate thing becomes terrible to us . . . becomes tremendous and terrible . . . producing ghastly shiverings and cold sweats . . . I once woke up," he thought, "crying out 'the Twig! the Twig!' and it *was* a little twig, from off some bush, that I had seen . . . just a little tiny twig! I think it was of a dark brown colour . . . sometimes the colour in these things is very important! . . . it was bent . . . yes! I'm sure of *that* . . . it was a little, dark-brown twig and bent at one end."

He once more felt that he was on the very brink of catching hold of some tremendously important clue.

"Little inanimate things," he thought, "can become great symbols, and symbols are—No!" he thought, "bugger me black!

That's not what I mean at all! I mean something much deeper, much more living than symbols. Bugger me black! What *do* I mean? Certain material objects can become charged with super-natural power. *That's* what I mean. They can get filled with a kind of electricity that's more than electricity, with a kind of magnetism that's more than magnetism! And this is especially the case when . . . when . . . when . . ."

He heard a half-extinguished brand, in the centre of the dying fire, fall heavily among the red ashes; and for the tick of a second his heart began to beat again, wildly, helplessly, violently, just as it had done when he heard . . . or dreamed he heard . . . that terrible voice.

"This is especially the case when a number of people, century after century, has believed. . . . Thought is a real thing ———"

Here Mr. Geard's own process of thought—as he tugged at his pillow to prop up his head a little—was interrupted by a prick-ing of his conscience. His effort to get the pillow into a com-fortable position conveyed his mind, over the seven miles of moonlit water-meadows, to his sleeping wife. He remembered how the grey head of the descendant of the House of Rhys always lay on her own pillow, at her own side of the bed, leaving *his* all smooth and undisturbed and never removing it. He remem-bered how astonished he had been to learn from Crummie—who loved to play the rôle of sentimental ambassador between her mother and father—that all the time he was away in Norfolk with Canon Crow, Megan Geard had left his pillow untouched in its place. . . .

But he made an effort of his will and dismissed Megan com-pletely from his mind, as completely as if they had never lived together. In these deep interior inhumanities, Mr. Geard was shameless. This devotee of Christ frequently took up his con-science by the heels and hung it clear outside the remotest house-walls of his consciousness. He now worked the interior cogs and pistons of his mind till, like a great gaping engine, with grap-pling-irons held outward, towards those dusky rafters above him, his consciousness adjusted itself to catch a clue that kept teasing and tantalising him.

"Thought is a real thing," he said to himself. "It is a live thing. It creates; it destroys; it begets; it projects its living off-spring. Like certain forms of physical pain thoughts can take or-ganic shapes. They can live and grow and generate, independ-ently of the person in whose being they originated.

"For a thousand years the Grail has been attracting thought to itself, because of the magnetism of Christ's Blood. The Grail is now an organic nucleus of creation and destruction. Christ's Blood cries aloud from it by day and by night. Yes, yes," so his thoughts ran on, "yes, and bugger me black!"—This was a queer original oath peculiar to Mr. Geard—"I know now what the Grail is. It is the desire of the generations mingling like water with the Blood of Christ, and caught in a fragment of Substance that is beyond Matter! It is a little nucleus of Eternity, dropped somehow from the outer spaces upon one particular spot!"

Here Mr. Geard stretched out his head, like a mud-turtle, and peered down at the crack in the floor, through which he had heard the old couple in the room below relieving Nature.

"I hope," said Mr. Geard to himself, "that that extremely nervous Sergeant didn't forget to give my pretty Daisy-Queen a good feed of oats!"

"I WANT A CHILD FROM YOU, DO YOU HEAR? WHAT'S THE matter with you? I want a child, I tell you!"

It was these words of Will Zoyland—flung out angrily at her as he jumped in his car to drive to Mark Court early on Sunday afternoon—that kept ringing in the ears of Nell as she moved about Whitelake Cottage, cleaning and tidying things up, on Easter Monday.

"What made him think of *that* just now?" she said to herself. "He can't read a person's thoughts. He *can't* know about it . . . how could he? Oh no, no, no!" The truth was that the girl was pretty sure . . . although not absolutely sure . . . that Sam's child had already begun its obscure, embryonic life within her.

She had begged him to come out to see her today, knowing that the popular holiday would keep Will safe at Wookey Hole. She had been longing with a great longing to tell Sam what she hoped for. But now she was teased by this tormenting question—should she tell him what Will had said? And should she raise the agitating point whether or no it was best to pretend to Will that this child, if it *did* really come, was his child?

Oh, if only Sam could gather up the spirit and resolution to carry her off, to find work to do, so that he could support her, her and their child, somewhere, anywhere, so it were far from Glastonbury!

Let Will do what he liked *then*; divorce her; refuse to divorce her! What did she care, as long as Sam and she were together?

She had been living in one long delicious trance since that night. Sam had come out only once to see her since; and on that occasion had seemed absorbed in his own thoughts; but he had been gentle and sweet to her and she had felt so happy, pressing him against her, holding him, hugging him, tight and fast, with this thrilling chance of all chances between them, that she had not inquisitioned him or persecuted him with her problem. But this angry challenge of Will's flung out at her after she had managed to evade any serious love-making, had broken up her radiant dream.

Troubled and anxious and full of nameless fears she went about her work this morning. She had risen early, after waking before dawn, from a disturbed sleep—a sleep in which she dreamed that it really was Will's child and not Sam's at all that had just begun its mysterious life-processes within her—and her mental agitation had been increased rather than diminished by the nature of the day as it grew light.

It was absolutely still after the wind of the previous twenty-four hours; but it was grey and damp, clouds in the sky, heavy mists clinging to the meadows. It looked as if it were going to prove a very gloomy, if not a disastrously wet Bank Holiday.

Nell was startled at the havoc the great wind had done among her wild plants, so carefully tended. Her little grass lawn, sloping down to the river bank, was strewn with twigs and leaves from trees quite far away; and some brick tiles, too, had been blown from the roof. The dead stillness of the air after such a wind-hurricane was itself disturbing.

The day was one of those days when human beings who have anything on their minds, anything on their consciences, cannot refrain from a certain listening. It was a day when guilty people could hear their hearts beating, hear their clocks ticking, hear the faint dripping into sink or barrel of the least drop of water from tap or pipe.

Nell washed up her breakfast things more rapidly than usual. She made her bed and tidied her bedroom quicker than she was wont to do. She dusted her parlour. She went down on her knees and washed with soap and water the chequered linoleum on her kitchen floor. All the time she was doing these things she would glance at the window to see if Sam's figure were approaching and then draw her eyes hurriedly away from the menacing inertness of the weather outside.

But below her trouble over Will's fierce words . . . so fatally well-timed . . . and below the preoccupation of her work and her longing for her lover to come . . . there kept drumming and humming in her deeper ears a low refrain of exultation. "It's begun! It's begun! To me myself, and not another, it has happened! My true love's child inside me . . . safe inside me . . . and going to grow and grow and grow!"

She sat down on the sofa-couch and picked up a booklet, bound in paper, that lay there. It was a Marxian pamphlet left by her brother Dave.

Stubbornly she tried to concentrate her thoughts upon the formidable argument this little work unfolded. "Children," she read, "are wards of the State, even in their mother's womb. Motherhood is an occupation as dangerous, as necessary, as important to society, as to be a peasant, a factory-worker, a miner. Religious marriage is a bourgeois superstition, grossly intermingled with the historic iniquity of private property. No human creature has a right to claim possession of the person of another. Children are the creation of Nature, but their well-being is the responsibility of the State. When the life of the fœtus is ——"

As Nell read these words a sudden panic seized her. Something leapt up from these compact, official, emphatic sentences that was much more formidable than their obvious meaning. Sitting there in her bright, crocus-yellow spring dress, covered with a loose, light-green over-all, she suddenly began to shiver from head to foot. Her teeth began to chatter; and she threw up her hands and pressed them against her ears, as if she heard the marching feet of an army of executioners. She had not really understood at all the impact of what she read but something about the tone of it—its air of irreversible and doom-like finality —filled her with a blind terror.

Her teeth chattered so loudly that she clapped her hands to her mouth. Her shiverings made the skirt of the crocus-yellow gown stir faintly, like the underwing of the moth that boys call Yellow Underwing, when the wind catches it. She got a vision of herself as being caught in a long fatal process of Nature from which there was no outlet, no possible escape. She felt the intimate quality of her own private personality now; she felt the Nell she had lived with all her grown-up life, the Nell with the soft hair, the passionate mouth, the full breasts, the Nell with the mania for planting wild flowers in a flower garden, the Nell who loved scrubbing but hated cooking, the Nell who used to endure a husband and now idolised a lover, the Nell who loathed reading and liked using her needle, the Nell who preferred dreaming by open windows to talking by glowing hearths, the Nell who always found oranges so sweet and marmalade so bitter, and it seemed to her now, as she began crumpling in her fingers this odious pamphlet written by men who knew nothing about women, that this Nell who was so dear to her, whose every expression in the mirror she knew so well, this Nell whose teeth she cleaned, whose hair she brushed, whose little ways were *her* ways, was no longer hers, no longer her private possession. This soft body, every part of which held secret nerves of its own, was now bought and sold. Yes, yes, it was handed over, bound and fettered, to a long inescapable doom that had been prepared, millions of years ago—not for the Nell she knew—but for Females in General; a doom that must needs lead her on, deeper and deeper, into the raw, heavy, monstrous, impersonal mire of brutal creation!

She crumpled the unlucky pamphlet into a tight ball of paper and tossed it into the fire. She felt better after she had done this: but she still felt as if it were more than she could bear to hear any man, even Sam, laying down rules for human life. Blind, and dumb, and inarticulate, she felt something surging up within her, that, if she only could express it, would blow all the institutions in the world sky-high. "My womb has conceived," was the burden of what she ached to cry aloud, "and I tell you this is something that has broken all your laws. It's a miracle; do you hear me? A miracle has happened. And I'm the one—not any of you mutterers and starers and examiners and inspectors—I'm the one to tell the world what is the secret of life!"

She went into the kitchen and snatched up an orange from a bowl on her dresser. Into the top of this orange she thrust her forefinger till she had made a deep round hole. Into the hole in the orange she now pushed one, two, three small lumps of sugar; and then clutching the sticky, fragrant, yellow skin tightly in her fingers, she pressed her mouth to the hole and sucked furiously, keeping her teeth sufficiently closed so as to push back the half-melted sugar but drawing up the sweet juice into her mouth. She placed herself in front of the fire and stared down into the red coals squeezing, sucking, swallowing.

She found the warmth of the fire comforting as it reached her legs and her skin; and when the moment came for her to tear open the orange and bury her face in its sugary interior, tearing the sticky pulp from the bitter rind with her teeth, she found that her whole mood had completely changed.

She threw the orange skin into the flames then and gathering her over-all tightly about her she moved still closer to the bars, letting the warmth extend to as much of her person as she possibly could, and snuffing up with luxurious satisfaction the smell of the burning orange skin. She began to grow impatient for Sam now. She thought of how she would kiss him when he held her in his arms. "I'll kiss his eyes," she thought. "It's nice when he shuts his eyes." And then she thought, "I love him when he works his chin up and down, when he gets worried by anything."

But Sam did not come. It was half-past one now; and she said to herself, "I ought to get myself something to eat but I shan't do it."

She put more coals on the fire and went to the couch and lay down upon it. She could see a fragment of the garden out of the window; and how dark it was, and how frighteningly hushed and still!

She had an abscess in her gum above one of her back teeth; and this began to hurt her a good deal. The orange-sucking must have started it. She searched for it with her tongue. She suddenly began to feel more occupied with this trifling annoyance than with Sam or her child or Zoyland or the strange nature of the weather outside. She shut her eyes. At last as she pressed her tongue against her aching gum a drowsiness stole over her that almost took her consciousness away. The hurting in her mouth became a thing entirely distinct from her personality; and when her drifting thoughts reverted to the embryo life within her, *that* also seemed something quite outside of her and independent of her.

And then before she realised what had happened Sam had come. Before she was fully awake he had given her a fierce, violent hug, too hard and breathless to be called tender, too brief to be called passionate; and there they were, sitting on the couch side by side, staring wildly, confusedly, and helplessly at each other.

She had told him already about the child.

"Are you absolutely sure?" he had murmured.

And she had nodded emphatically.

Something in his manner had driven her to go on talking about it in a way she had never intended to do. It was a remoteness in him different from anything she had ever known! It was as if he had been clothed from head to foot in invisible chain armour; and not only so, but had had his vizor down, through which his little, bewildered, bear-eyes gazed out at her, puzzled, ambiguous, and with an obstinate film over them.

Everything was so wretchedly different from what she had expected! Her thoughts as to what he would do had been very vague. But she had in her dreamy way, been feeding herself with the fantastic hope that he would cry out to her at once—"Come then, my true love! Nothing henceforth shall part us!"

But he had done nothing of the kind. And in place of anything like that from him, she had found herself explaining hurriedly that Will Zoyland would naturally think, if she acted with any kind of discretion in so delicate a matter, that the child was his.

"*Would* he?" Sam had asked; as if, even then, his mind was not really grasping the significance of what she was saying. It must have been at that point that the "all-is-equal" wave of drowsy indifference that had swept over her before he came, once more had exercised its fatal numbing power; for she had seemed paralysed, as people are in dreams, and unable to break through the mysterious barrier between them.

She had found herself taking an almost apologetic tone about her condition; as if her lover had a right to be angry with her for it! She had found herself explaining that even if Will Zoyland were not absolutely convinced, the existence of a doubt in his mind would not make him act violently or abruptly, if she did not leave his bed till everything was further advanced.

It was then that Sam had said: "You are sure it *is* ours?"

The brutality of this question had brought tears to her eyes; but she had only looked reproachfully at him and had murmured —"Of course it's ours, you silly!"

But the revolting idea *had* crossed her mind, as he put that pointblank question —— "Suppose I didn't know myself which of them it was?"

The relief that she did know—and as far as *that* went—knew beyond all question that it was Sam's, held now, for her dazed intelligence, such a comfort, after that diabolically horrid idea, that she threw still further emphasis into her plausible argument that everything would go on quite naturally and as if it were her husband's.

"But suppose it's like me when it's born?" Sam had scrupled not to interject with an almost comic solemnity.

"Oh, it's not born yet, you wretch!" she had replied in quite a flighty tone.

And there had been an interchange of tender, half-humorous speculation between them, after that, as to whether this unknown offspring of theirs would be a boy or a girl; and Sam had said he hoped it would be a girl; and she had said—her mind all the time thinking, "How different this is from what I thought it would be!"—that if he *really* wanted it to be a girl she would *make* it a girl, by thinking of nothing else all the time!

And then the trouble between them began. Sam started it by talking on and on to her about some startling experience he had recently had . . . something to do with a mad woman and the old-curiosity-shop man on Maundy Thursday, when he was climbing Wirral Hill with John Crow and Tom Barter; but he was so clumsy at expressing himself, and she was so slow in catching the drift of his thought, that they irritated each other, in the way simple-minded people so easily do, by their mutual misunderstanding long before he even reached the real danger-point of what he was trying to tell her.

"It's something that's been coming over me for some time, Nell," he said, with his hand tightening so fast upon hers, in his anxiety to make himself clear, that he hurt her fingers. "It's not religion in my father's sense; for I don't believe . . . in anything . . . at all."

"I like your father, very, very much," Nell threw in.

"No, no," he went on, "it's not religion in *his* sense, because I don't believe in one single one of all those things."

He knew he was expressing himself lamely and badly, in fact childishly; but all he could do was to go on hurting her soft, formless, school-girl fingers in his muscular grip.

Her own mind was so benumbed, that the discourse between them, as the dark, hushed afternoon of Easter Monday wore on, would have seemed to any eavesdropper as incoherent as the talk of a couple of inmates in that State Asylum so much dreaded by Mad Bet.

"It's not that I'm considering Christ simply as an ordinary man," affirmed Sam in a high-pitched dialectical tone. "I'm considering him as a God. But I'm considering Him as a God among Other Gods. I'm considering Him as a God who is *against* the cruelty of the great Creator-God. What has given me such an extraordinary feeling of happiness these last days is the idea that ever since Christ was tortured to death by the Romans to please the Jews there has been a secret company of disciples who have believed in His methods of fighting the cruel Creator-God . . . these methods of His . . . simple and yet very hard to catch the drift of . . . till you get . . . a sudden illumination . . . like Saint Paul . . . only mine came to me on Silver Street, at the bottom of the drive, where you can see the elms over the wall . . ."

"Let go my hand, you're hurting me." Up went her fingers to her sulky red mouth when he released her. He had certainly left them bloodless.

She began to feel hungry. "I wish," she thought, "I could just run into the kitchen and put the kettle on without hurting his feelings. How queer men are. He has already completely forgotten that I've made him a father."

"I don't believe in the Church, Nell," Sam went on, "like Father does. I don't believe in the Creed at all. But I believe in the Mass; what in *our* Church we call the Sacrament; I believe as it says in Latin, *Verbum caro factum est,* the Word was made Flesh."

"I think I'll put the kettle on," she murmured, without realising the irony of these last words so apparently unrelated in his mind to the "word-made-flesh" in herself! She had grown so hungry and had come to long so desperately for a cup of tea that when he came to utter the word "Creed" it was on the tip of her tongue to give vent to a quivering, long-drawn-out scream, so that the great Latin syllables fell on deaf ears.

Sam the naturalist had certainly been overlaid by Sam the theologian; but there was a sturdy animal instinct in him that now broke through the spiritual chain-armour that he was wearing like a tight-fitting aura or like an etheric body. It broke through this aura with such a leap that the girl was frightened.

"I'll put it on for you!" he cried suddenly getting up with a bound from her side. He rushed into the kitchen, and she heard him empty and fill the kettle; and then she heard him clattering with the iron cover of the stove as he pushed it aside with the short poker she kept for that purpose and settled the kettle in its place.

"He hasn't even looked to see how the fire is," she thought. With a weary sigh she got up and followed him.

She caught him staring out of the kitchen window as she entered, an ecstatical stare, like the stare of a village boy watching the circus clown.

"What is it?" she asked, putting her arm on his shoulder. She wanted him to fondle her and tell her how wonderful she'd been to make him a father. Instead of this he drew away from her touch.

"Oh, you *will* understand, Nell darling," he said, "when I've told you everything, why I can't be like I was before?" He turned his broad back upon her and walked out of the kitchen. He made blindly for the couch where they had been sitting when she murmured about the kettle. And she followed him submissively to that familiar couch.

She made a motion as though to sit on his knee, but he warded her off, clutching her wrist with a rough violence and pulling her down by his side.

"That's what I really came to see you about, Nell; to be absolutely frank with you; as we always are with each other, aren't we?"

She thought bitterly to herself that if she had been less frank with him this afternoon, never said a single syllable about her condition, he would not have acted the least differently from the way he was acting now!

A faint shivering, like the shivering that had seized her when she read her brother's pamphlet, came over her now. Was Sam—her dear Sam—going to join that great staring army of men, men, men, men with hairy wrists and hairy chests, men with hard sharp knees, men with brains like printing presses, between whom she had to run the gauntlet . . . and to take her place . . . and her child had to take its place . . . in a regimented State, ordered, not by Nature, but by tyrannical Science?

What was it that Sam was saying now?

"—and so, though of course I shall always love you, and you will always be my true love, and we'll be seeing each other just as much as we do now, I've come to the conclusion that it's wrong for me to make love to you any more. The pleasure I get from that kind of thing is so intense for me—it may not be so with other people but it is so with me—that it kills this new feeling."

Not a tear came to her eyes. They did not open, or shut, or twitch, or blink, or quiver. Her hands remained lying quietly on her lap just as they had been when he first let them go. She did not clasp them now, nor did she fumble with the loose folds of the green apron which covered her crocus-yellow gown.

She forced herself to look into the eyes of this speaking man, into the eyes of this man-mask, whose chin as he uttered his unkind words imitated the familiar contractions of her dear Sam's chin.

Her simplicity of nature was such that the blow itself brought her one recompense. She was not tormented by doubt. Her Sam had changed into someone else. Her Sam had changed into a Being who called himself the lover of a God called Christ and who henceforth would think it wrong to love Nell Zoyland. Nell made absolutely nothing of what he said about loving her still, though it would be wrong to "make love" to her. Such was her character, such was her conception of love, that to "make love" meant simply to love, and not to "make love" meant simply not to love.

"I don't . . . quite . . . understand . . . Sam dear."

He put his arm about her and pressed her to him and they stayed like that for a while in sorrowful silence, while outside their walls nothing stirred except the flowing of the river that was like a channel without a bottom, so darkly it poured its flood, as if the sombreness of the low grey skies and their forlorn 'depths, had been transferred to it to augment its desolation.

"Sam dearest, did you like me the first time you saw me?"

This innocent question which had passed between them, question and answer, so often already, had become like a familiar nosegay by this time which was handed from one to another, to smell at and pass back again, when it was not the moment for more ardent caresses.

Now, when caresses were to be altogether renounced this invisible nosegay gathered to itself a poignant significance.

There were actually tears in Sam's eyes as he lifted her hand to his lips and swore that he had liked her *before* he saw her; that he had dreamed of her, from Penny Pitches' description, when he had first heard her name!

She made a little movement at this, cuddling up yet closer to him so that the warmth of her body flowed into his. Her green pinafore was open at the sides and as she leant against him he could see—oh, and feel too!—the rounded tightness of her yellow bodice as a deep-drawn sigh expanded her lovely breasts.

It was only by forcing himself to think of that tortured Shadow hovering above his father's roof; it was only by forcing himself to visualise the actual prints of the nails in that Shadow's hands; that he had the strength to stiffen himself and not to yield, that he had the strength to hold that clinging sweetness away from him. But so piteously was his whole nature stirred that big tears now rolled slowly down his cheeks; several of them actually reaching his twitching chin. They were tears of miserable pity for himself and for her; and for more than themselves. In the pressure of that dark hour there weighed upon him the whole burden of the round world's tragic grief as it swung on its axis. The loneliness of the cold-gurgling stream outside, with that sorrowful sky reflected in it, the silence of that little house enclosing them amid the larger silence of the wide moors; all these things flowed into Sam's heart till it felt as if it must break. To have been given such quivering sweetness, and to have to push it away with his own hand! He had known that it would be hard; but this was worse than he had imagined. The feeling that their passionate mixing together had created a new life—a life that was the knot of their intertwining—made it seem as if an outrage was being done to them both, a rending, tearing, remorseless outrage, that must make a red wound in Time itself, that slippery-smooth Time, that long black snake, that was gliding away under their feet! She kept making little heart-breaking movements to cling closer to him; and he had to put all his will into the arm that held her back, to keep it stiff, to make it like a sword between them.

"I thought you'd be pleased when you knew I was going to have a child."

"I *am* pleased, Nell. Your child will be the only child I shall ever have now. And I'm glad it's yours! Zoyland may be generous . . . I mean later on . . . when things are different."

"I can't believe it . . . Sam . . . when I look at you sitting so close to me . . . that you have stopped loving me . . . just when I'm sure about our child."

Sam was the extreme opposite of a moral casuist. It would have been better for Nell if his conscience had been more sensitive and his passion less strong. It was the strength of his passion for her that made the issue between her and Christ so deadly clear to him.

In these subtle human relations Sam had the blunt obtuseness of a beast, a beast with far less conscience than a faithful dog. He was indeed a forest bear at this moment, a bear that was rejecting a treasure-trove of wild-honey for the sake of a garden-hive that he had found.

Nell was just then too stunned to feel anything but this fatal change in him; but later—when she had time to think—she found herself amazed at the unscrupulousness with which he was prepared to allow her to deceive Zoyland about the child. Whatever it was that had touched him with its terrible spell it had left him as non-moral as a savage. There was nothing human left in him to which a girl could appeal.

In his mind at that moment there seemed to be only two alternatives; possessing Nell, or being possessed by Christ. A month-old conception, a year-old love, what were these beside the ecstasy, the blind exultation of sharing the sufferings of a God?

"Sam . . . Sam . . . Love me again! Love me again!"

He made a funny little gurgling sound in his throat and looked away from her; looked towards the window. At that moment there were steps on the brick path outside and a sharp knock at the door.

They both leapt to their feet; and Nell, after a moment's hesitation and a quick glance round the room, went to the door and opened it.

There stood Persephone Spear!

The tall, equivocal girl entered furtively and quietly, closing the door behind her. Her appearance altered everything in a moment. It caused to surge up in both Nell and Sam that curious blind irritation, unique in life, that the invasion of an outsider evokes in the souls of two people who are in the throes of some nervous dispute.

Persephone wore her usual rough ulster-cape and below this a grey jersey and black skirt. On her head was a tight-fitting, dark woolen cap. She was certainly in an agitated mood and in a dogmatic, tyrannical one. She moved uneasily about the little room, disregarding Nell's entreaties to sit down. She went up to the tiny cottage piano which the Marquis of P. had given the Zoylands on their marriage and ran her fingers over its wistful untuned keys. "What's this?" she said, picking up the loose cover of the pamphlet that Nell had burned. "Did Dave leave it?" Then she came and stood in front of them, staring out of the window. "What's it going to do?" she asked, frowning. "It's the worst day we've had since I've been down here. It's a terrible day." There was a tone in her voice that reduced the weather to a troublesome appendage to human life, to a tiresome dog that was behaving badly. Then she left the window and crossed over to the fire. "Why don't you burn more wood, Nell?" she said. "It gives out much more heat than this wretched coal." Then again, before Nell had time to reply, she was pulling out a book from Will Zoyland's bookshelf. "Does your William read 'Arabia Deserta'? No! I can see he doesn't. It's not cut." She turned the pages irritably. "You know what Doughty would call a little creature like you, Nell, in this Bedouin tent. He'd call you a 'Bint.' That's a good word, isn't it? To describe a sweet

little girl like you!" She returned Doughty to the shelf with a
violent shove and hurried again to the window. "It looks as if
it wanted to rain black rain today. I've never seen anything so
miserable—except my life."

She put into these final words so much bitterness that Nell
was startled out of her irritation and out of her own grief.

"What is it, Percy dear? Are things going wrong? Won't you
take off your ulster?"

Sam got up and made several clumsy attempts to help the
restless intruder out of her cape. When it was off and she stood
before them slim and erect in her jersey and skirt she had a
warm, youthful-bodied look like a young skater with tingling
veins and bright colour, that completely contradicted her
pessimism.

"You look awfully well, Percy," said Nell. "It isn't your
health that's wrong, anyway."

"You're quite out of it, my dear," returned the other. "I've
been feeling dizzy and funny all day. It's this black devilry in
the air, I expect, that won't come down. I'd like to *tell* this day
how I detest it!"

Her childish way of talking about the weather had something
that was vaguely reassuring both to Nell and Sam. They had
both been feeling an element of fatality in the atmosphere outside; and Percy's petulant detachment of herself from the elements and her concentration upon her personal quarrel with life
brought back that sense that the world was malleable and that
anything was possible which they had both lost.

"You two look as if I'd interrupted a lovers' quarrel!" cried
the girl suddenly, with a forced laugh, throwing back her beautiful head.

Persephone herself had had two fierce quarrels that Easter;
one with her husband and one with Philip; and her present
mood was a furious revolt against all men, combined with a melting tenderness for all women. With a sudden impulse she now
went across to Nell's little piano and after aimlessly playing
for a few moments plunged into the notes of a wistful song. This
after a moment she began to sing as well as to play. Her voice
was surprisingly moving as she sang the words:

"Woman's grief for a woman's breast—
The winds howl fierce over Dunkery Beacon!
The heart beats faint in its sad unrest
And the knees weaken.

"Woman's hair for a woman's tying—
The waves break wild upon Lulworth Cove!
Cover your face and quit your crying
And quell your love.

"Woman's womb by Lodmoor water—
The frost bites bitter on White Nose head!
Best for the child, whether son or daughter,
It lay dead.

"Woman's tears for a woman's drying—
The long night lingers on Salisbury Plain!
Love can't reach you where you'll be lying
Nor any pain.

"Woman's bones for a woman's tending—
The wet dawn gathers on Wirral Hill!
No more saving and no more spending,
She lies still.

"Woman's dust for a woman's wonder—
The cold stars shine on the Mendip snows!
A grassy mound—but who lies under
No man knows."

The song ended; but its spell was not broken for a couple of long minutes.

"Is that an old song?" Sam asked.

"Not at all! Don't you realise we've got a Wessex poet of our own? Haven't you heard of young Edward Athling of Middlezoy? There's been enough talk going around about him and Lady Rachel to make him famous if his poetry hasn't done it."

Sam glanced at the clock on the chimney-piece. It was already nearly four. "I'll have to leave them and start walking back," he said to himself. "I *must* be at that woman's house by half-past five."

He rose heavily to his feet. The movement he made roused

Nell from the woeful passivity into which she had been thrown by the song.

"You're not going away, Sam?" she cried piteously. "You *can't* be going away—and you and I not having had hardly a word yet together!"

Persephone rose to her feet, too, at this juncture. She was as tall as Sam as she stood up in front of him; for his slouching form was bent a little forward and his long arms were hanging loosely down, like those of a gorilla.

She placed one of her own arms protectively round Nell's neck, caressing the girl's chin.

"I suppose," she said slowly, staring defiantly at Sam, "I suppose . . . you've landed her . . . now . . . with a child?"

"I didn't tell her, Sam, I didn't!" protested Nell.

"She doesn't know," he cried in a harsh, loud voice. "You know you don't know *for certain*, Nell! It's far too soon. It's only ——" But he finished his sentence by repeating his first words. "It's much too soon to be so sure!"

"You've hurt her feelings abominably anyway," said Persephone curtly.

"It's always . . . better . . ." said Sam calmly, accepting the girl's resentful stare with an impassive front, "for people who love each other like Nell and me, to settle our difficulties alone." He paused and there was something approaching a humorous glint in his little eyes. "Perhaps . . . you would not mind . . . going . . . into the garden or into the . . . kitchen for a minute or two!"

Persephone jerked herself away and retreated across the room towards the staircase.

"Well, go on, Sam Dekker," she cried sarcastically. "You've only got a 'bint' to deal with. Go on *explaining*—without the faintest notion of what Nell's thinking and feeling." She turned at the staircase foot and flung her final bolt with uncalled-for vehemence. "The fact remains that you found one of the happiest girls in Somerset; and you've made her one of the unhappiest!"

The surly native of Glastonbury, converted into such a singular kind of a saint, with an exercise of self-control that made his jerking lower jaw positively subhuman, answered her quietly.

"Oh, come now, if you think so little of men, aren't you rather exaggerating my importance?"

"Well, I hope you'll never *have* a child!" She gave a little cynical laugh that yet had a hysterical note in it. "I hope Nell will have *seven* beautiful girls by Will Zoyland; and not one of them will ever let any man come near them!"

"Percy!" gasped Nell in consternation, but noticing how white Percy looked as she came forward now towards them her tone changed to one of concern. "Percy, you're ill! What's the matter?"

Percy held out her hand to Sam. "I apologise, Sam. Don't take anything I say today seriously. The truth is I've had my own troubles and it's rather upset me. I daresay . . . you are . . . all right."

She sank down on the nearest chair. "Have you any whiskey, Nell?"

Nell made a sign to Sam to get the drink. When he handed her the whiskey his face expressed genuine concern and this Persephone did not miss.

"Oh, I'm all right," she gasped, choking a little and spilling the drink on her grey jersey. Then she handed him the glass and tilting back her chair stretched out her long arms in a gesture of utter weariness, her fingers clenched.

"Damn it! I'm sorry, you two," she murmured, letting her arms sink down again. She jerked her chair back now into its natural position and covering her mouth with her hand yawned extravagantly. Then she rose to her feet. "I don't know what's the matter with me today," she said. "No, no, I don't want to sit down, Nell. I've been sitting down too much today. Look here, you two, wouldn't you like to ride into Glastonbury? I'll bring you back here . . . one of you . . . both of you . . . just as you want. But it would be a change to get our tea in town. Come on! I'll treat you! Let's go to the Pilgrims' and have an amusing time."

Sam indicated his promise to be at Tittie Petherton's that afternoon at half-past five. "Crummie Geard has been looking after the woman today while the nurse takes a holiday," he explained. "Ever since the Geards have shown an interest in her she's been better. She gets up now and comes down, though of course she can't ever get well, and she still suffers a lot. Mr. Geard can always spirit her pain away; but it's a conjuring-trick and I *don't like* the man."

Sam began walking up and down the room, a puzzled frown on his face. The two girls watched him. A quick, feminine glance passed between them; a glance as old as the camel's hair tents of "Arabia Deserta"; a glance that said—"See how these masculine Prophets of the Lord refuse credit to each other!"

"I can't understand it," Sam went on, mumbling his words as if speaking to himself. "The man talks in an almost jocular fashion of the Blood of Christ. But he does drive Tittie Petherton's pain away. I've seen it! I've seen the woman fall asleep. But there's something evil about him to me. Father doesn't feel like that. Father gave him the Sacrament once. Father rather likes him and is glad for him to visit Tittie. But I'm not so sure! Sometimes I feel as if, when he sends her pain away, he were doing it by the power of the Devil—only," here Sam smiled a rather boyish smile, "only I don't believe in the Devil!"

The two girls had drifted across to the couch now, and were sitting there side by side, Percy's arm about Nell's waist.

"I could help you with that sick woman just as well as Crummie Geard," was Nell's comment upon his discourse.

"I've promised to take Tittie over to her aunt's, old Mrs. Legge," Sam said.

"*That* woman!" cried Percy. She looked at Nell. "Do *you* know what Mrs. Legge is?"

"Look here, you two," said Sam disregarding her question, "why don't you two come with me to Mrs. Legge's? It's in the slums, you know, but there'll be tea of some sort."

"Oh, I don't want to go at all!" Nell faltered. "I'd much sooner be left alone here."

"I know you would," said Persephone, "and cry your eyes out too. I know *that*! But the point is that's the worst thing you could do. I know I can't persuade you; but perhaps if you get it into your head that if you did it would certainly spoil Sam's evening ——"

Half an hour later and they were all three speeding towards Glastonbury; Persephone driving her car at a reckless pace; Nell watching Sam's countenance with intense, puzzled scrutiny; and

Sam himself anxiously pulling out his watch every minute or two and exclaiming—"I don't want to hurry you . . . but if you *could* pass that thing we should be ——"

Persephone kept persuading Nell that their accompanying him to Mother Legge's respectable but comprehensive party would make no difference to the lady who was giving it. "If she expects him and Miss Geard," she said, "I don't suppose she'll mind our coming."

Nell was more diffident. "You go with Sam, Percy, and I'll go and see Dave. He's still in the same rooms, isn't he, where you were before? I don't really see how we can invade this woman's place . . . so many of us . . . and without a word of invitation."

Percy burst into a wild fit of laughing when she heard this. They were standing on the cobblestones now outside Mrs. Petherton's dilapidated Gothic house; and the tall girl bent herself down over the wooden railings, where John Crow had first broached to Barter the idea of betraying Philip and coming over to Geard. She gave herself up to such a violent laughing-fit in this dingy ramshackle spot of pigsties and puddles, that tears ran down her convulsed cheeks.

"Well! I'll go into the house now," said Sam. "Of course she may be too ill to come out. I expect you two had better wait here till I bring her out. I was going to take her round in a taxi; and even now that may be the best. But I'll go in and see."

He had no sooner disappeared than a taxi drew up beside their car. There was a huddled figure inside this conveyance; but the driver got out, touched his cap and asked them if this was the house where Mr. Dekker was.

"'Ad a call to come 'ere straight from St. Michael's Inn, ladies," he declared with some embarrassment. Then he hurriedly went back to his cab, peered through its closed window for a second, and returned to their side.

"Is he drunk, do you think?" whispered Nell to her companion.

"I be in awkward case, ladies," the man mumbled. "There be a 'ooman come wi' I, 'gainst all sense. She be wambly in she's poor head. She were in bar wi' I because 'twere holiday, and she likes to bide wi' I on holiday, and have a bite o' summat. But she heard me boss say to I—'Solly Lew,' says me boss, 'here be a order from Vicarage. 'Tis to pick up Mr. Sam Dekker at Tittie Petherton's and take three o' they out to Mrs. Legge's, to Paradise.' And's soon as this poor crazy 'ooman heard the name Mr. Dekker what must the glimsey body do but climb into taxi; and nought that I could do could get she out! And now I be terrible worried what Mr. Dekker will say to I when I tell he there be a crazy 'ooman in taxi."

Both the ladies glanced nervously at the taxi window. Yes, Solly Lew had spoken no less than the truth! There, just inside, her face actually touching the glass of the window, and her eight bony knuckles pressed against the bottom of the window-frame, was the wild, staring countenance of Mad Bet.

She wore a grander hat than usual, all decorated with artificial forget-me-nots, in honor of Easter Monday; but as she stretched her thin neck forward to stare at the two ladies this appendage tilted a little sideways, betraying to their astonished eyes the fact that her skull was as smooth and white as an uncracked egg.

The girls had moved towards the window of the taxi—Nell with her trembling hand on Percy's wrist—for Mad Bet was now making obscure signs to them both, while Solly Lew was gazing in melancholy interest at Mrs. Spear's car, when three figures came round the corner from the old house. Crummie was supporting the invalid woman on the left while Sam held her up on the right.

The girls hurried to meet them; as did also the agitated taxi-driver. A look of aggrieved bewilderment crossed Sam's face when he learned of this new complication. It had been an effort to deal with Tittie but this was really too much! However, evidently there was nothing for it but to take Mad Bet along. To thwart her now seemed worse than any agitation later on.

"But surely," protested Nell, "we can't, we *can't* all intrude upon Mrs. Legge! It's too much to expect that anyone could welcome so many complete strangers."

Percy intervened again. "You simply don't know Glastonbury, Nell," she whispered eagerly into Nell's ears while Sam was helping the sick woman into the Ford. "Mother Legge's Easter Monday parties are as fixed a custom as the Lord Mayor's show! The fact that she has a house next door full of bedrooms, with Young Tewsy as door-opener, doesn't prevent her from entertaining all the world in her *own* house. It certainly . . ."

She was interrupted by Sam, who came hurriedly across the dark cobblestones from the Ford to the taxi, anxious to make a start. "I've got the woman into your car, Mrs. Spear," he said. "She's in great pain and I doubt if she ought to go."

No sooner, however, had he opened the taxi door than Mad Bet came scrambling out of it.

"Where be the other gentleman?" she cried wildly, seizing Sam by the arm. "Where be me sly heart, me high heart, me pretty laddie, me pecking sparrow, me proper dilly-darling? Where be the other gentleman? Thee knows who I do mean, Mr. Sam? The one who did dancy and prancy wi' Bessie when moon were full? The one who wanted to hurt poor Bessie under thik Tree of Life, on Wirral Hill?"

"You mean Mr. John Crow, Bet?" replied Sam with the grave, punctilious consideration of the faithful naturalist, whose specimens must be treated with respect under all conditions. "Well, jump in here, with me and Mrs. Zoyland and perhaps we'll find Mr. Crow at Mrs. Legge's party."

The two conveyances at last were really in motion; Persephone Spear driving Crummie and Mrs. Petherton in her Ford while Solly Lew took Sam and Nell, along with Mad Bet, in his taxi.

In many quarters of Glastonbury, as six o'clock of this holiday Monday drew near, there were searchings of heart as to who should go, and who should not go, to this famous party in Paradise. It was indeed the fantastic opinion of Mr. Evans that there was a non-moral tradition about this part of Somerset that went back to very old days. He declared that this Easter Monday party was the last surviving relic of some ancient Druidic custom of Religious Prostitution; that there was even something of the kind in the Arthurian days; that the Grail itself was always guarded by virgins who were no virgins; and that Arthur's sister, the famous Morgan Le Fay, was not much better in her time than old Mrs. Legge today.

Mother Legge never *invited* anyone. Her personal relatives in the town, of whom there were many and who were mostly poorer as well as more respectable than she was, flocked naturally there *en masse*. It thrilled them to observe the manners of the gentry who came and the dresses of the ladies, and though Mother Legge was notoriously stingy over the food, she was fairly liberal—perhaps on general professional grounds—over the drink!

Red Robinson together with his pious mother, the ex-episcopal servant, were among those whose minds were focussed on Paradise that afternoon. Red was too poor to go to Weymouth or to Weston-super-Mare for the day as so many of the working men did, for the municipal factory, where he was now employed, was not yet able to compete with the Crow Dye-Works in the amount paid their workers. As soon as she had cleared away their midday meal Mrs. Robinson began talking about Mrs. Legge's party. Not being Glastonbury people, both she and her son were thoroughly puzzled, in fact completely nonplussed, in presence of this social phenomenon. This queer mingling of rich and poor, of respectable and disreputable, at a party given by a person who was—as Percy had told Nell—not very different from a "Madame," was an inexplicable thing to this family from London.

Nor had Mrs. Robinson—so she now explained at some length —"ever met the like of it" in her refined experiences at the great moated palace at Wells.

"Naught 'ud mike me go to see such fantastical doings," Mrs. Robinson announced. "When high've rested meself a bit, high'll take a stroll down 'igh Street; and maybe drop in and 'ave a cup 'o tie with Mrs. Cole. If it weren't such an 'ellish-looking die high'd sit on one of them 'igh hiron seats on Wirral and watch the sights. This 'ere new Mayor ought to 'ave a band playing on Wirral 'ill, same as they does at 'abitable towns; towns that 'ave theayters and Pictures and 'ave some loife in 'em!"

"Well, Mother, I reckon I'll be getting a move on," said Red Robinson. "I don't sigh as high'll go to this here fandangle in Paradise any more than you. Reckon high'll 'ave tie out somewheres if you're 'aving it with Granny Cole."

He got up, took his cap and coat—for the afternoon looked decidedly menacing—nodded to his mother and shogged off.

He made his way to a portion of the town that was on the outskirts of Paradise; and moving rapidly and cautiously down a narrow street into a grim-looking dwelling he paid a visit, not altogether an unexpected visit either, to "that Morgan woman," as the Western Gazette always called her, about whose existence he had been trying to worry Philip Crow.

Red Robinson certainly was, at heart, more of a Jacobin than a Communist. That is to say, his revolutionary feelings did not run in a calm, implacable, patient, scientific groove, but were feverishly eager to hurt and cause suffering to the enemies of the people, whether it benefited the cause or not!

Red Robinson's hatred of Philip Crow was indeed rapidly growing to the dimensions of a monomania. It was gall and wormwood to him to be rebuked by the new Mayor and have these secret activities of his exposed and sidetracked. He did not like, he did not understand, Mr. Geard—and it was only the sheer pressure of economic necessity that drove him to accept a job in this municipal work-shop. It was hateful to find Barter once more his boss. He detested the artistic and mythological aspects of the work he had to do. He distrusted the success of the scheme. Deep in his heart he pined for a job that had no idealistic non-sense about it. What brought him to pay these increasing visits to Mrs. Morgan was an emotion that was on the road to become an urge beyond his control.

He was trying to persuade the mother of little Nelly—who was still in her way a beautiful woman—to give herself up to his lust. "Lust" was the true word for it, for Red Robinson's heart had been monopolised by Crummie; and Crummie since his mis-understanding with her father had grown shy of him.

But it was a velvety lust, an orchid-spotted lust, a dark, de-licious, quivering, maddening lust, which surprised the man him-self by its intensity. In his heart he had said—"To hell with them all! As long as I stick to Blackie"—for such was Red's playful and tender nickname for his would-be doxy—"I'll have one day my chance of bringing the bewger down!" But the maniacal and obsessional element in his design soon began to run away with the practical element. Day and night he told himself stories of what it would be like when he persuaded Jenny Morgan to give herself up to him; and these stories were not of a kind that corre-sponded to any tenderness for the woman. Unfortunately "the

Morgan woman" unless she was drunk loathed Red Robinson.
And when she was drunk she melted into tearful sentiment over
the memory of her dead husband. There was not a chance—
drunk or sober—that the Morgan woman would allow Red to enjoy her in her own little flat. His only chance was to take her
out somewhere. And it was with the idea of taking her out to that
house next door to Mother Legge's, rumours of which had excited
his cockney lasciviousness, that Red was visiting her today.

He was nervous of the adventure; and it was because he
vaguely felt that the general stir of the Easter Monday party
would make it natural for him to be taking the woman to that
locality, that he chose this afternoon for his attempt.

On reaching her flat Red found that Nelly's mother was only
in the early stage of her habitual intoxication. Chance was in his
favour so far, anyway! Red was in a feverish state of anticipation.
The idea of satisfying his lust upon the body of Philip Crow's
mistress roused something in him the intensity of which carried
him beyond his control and altogether out of his normal depths.
Red indeed had brooded so long upon his hatred for Philip and
had nourished so passionately the thought of hurting him through
his child's mother, that the idea of enjoying the woman herself—
even if she *were* tipsy—made him feel literally sick with excitement. His half-engagement to Crummie Geard, now broken off,
he hardly knew why, had tantalised his senses while it kept him
comparatively chaste. It was an added spice to his purpose this
afternoon that he would be—so in his fury he pretended—revenging himself upon Crummie as well as upon Philip if he could
only satisfy his tormented desire with this once-handsome drink-
confused creature.

The steady aggravation of his hatred for Philip had indeed so
mingled with his lust for Philip's girl that they formed together
a completely new passion for which there is at present no name.
As he shaved in the morning, as he went to the little wooden
privy in his mother's back-garden, as he paused in his work at
the municipal factory, he would mutter to himself half-aloud—
"I 'ate 'im! I 'ate 'im! I'll 'ave 'er! I'll 'ave 'er!"

There can be no doubt that when in his cockney fashion, he
used the word " 'ate" instead of "hate," this curious difference

between two monosyllabic sounds was not without its own faint psychic repercussion upon his nervous organism. Between the human feeling expressed by the word "hate" and the feeling expressed by the same word without the aspirate there may be little difference; and yet there probably *was* some infinitesimal difference, which a new science—halfway between philology and psychology—may one day elucidate. Some would say that when Red muttered to himself, as he washed, as he shaved, as he excreted, as he worked, as he walked, as he lay down, as he rose up, "I 'ate 'im, I 'ate 'im!" what he really focussed in his mind was the emotional state—symbolised as a sensation in his lower jaw—indicated by the dictionary word "hate"; but it seems as if this were too simple and easy a solution of the problem.

However this may be, it can be imagined how the man's heart beat as he stood at last, after a prolonged struggle with the girl—Morgan Nelly's mother was now only about thirty—at the entrance to the house next door to Mrs. Legge's!

The woman was of a much darker complexion and much more foreign appearance than her daughter. Her face was colourless and so ravaged by hard work and drink that it had the particular kind of haggardness in the day which moonlight sometimes produces on human faces. The remains of her beauty were like a shattered arch whose sculptured figures have been defaced by wind and sand. Grey eyes, so large as to give at moments almost a grotesque effect, looked forth from her face contemplating the world with melancholy vacancy. Red derived a curious satisfaction from his endearing nickname for her, which he only dared to use to her face when she was in that early favourable stage of inebriation in which he had succeeded in catching her this afternoon. Even then he did not pronounce the word as he was wont to do in his lascivious dreams of possessing her when he would cry out, "Yes, Blackie! Yes, Blackie! Yes, Blackie!" over and over again. He now rapped timidly at the knocker of the door in front of him; for there was no bell.

"High know what's what, Blackie! You 'old your noise!"

This courtly quietus was delivered at this point because Blackie—even in her tipsy confusion—began to realise, when she saw herself being stared at by several passers-by, that Mr.

Robinson, in his ignorance of local customs, had chosen a most unsuitable hour for their "short time" in this place of resort. After a most uncomfortable period of waiting, the door at last opened a little way; and there stood Young Tewsy in the narrow aperture! The old man let them in without a word, following his habitual manner—that is 'to say using a sort of soft rapidity and opening the door only just wide enough for them to come in and closing it the very second they were inside.

But once in the hallway where there was nothing to calm Red Robinson's nervousness but a small battered bust of an expressionless human head, standing on a rickety table and bearing the word "Peel" upon its pedestal, Young Tewsy became disconcertingly voluble. He began, in fact, explaining, in a hurried apologetic whisper, "that, since it was Missuses party today, the rooms was all being cleaned, and none was to be 'ad; no, not if Lord P. his own self wanted to take one!"

Blackie stared at Young Tewsy in a bewildered daze; while Red, feeling as he looked at the bust of "Peel" that he would like to spit upon it, experienced such a craving for a *room*, that any room, large, small, cold, warm, carpeted, uncarpeted seemed a dispensation of providence beyond all mortal hope.

Had the half-tipsy Mrs. Morgan been interested in that delicate nerve-region of the human mind, where philology and psychology merge their margins, it would have been fascinating to her to note the minute ways in which the North London bourgeois cockney of Young Tewsy whose bringing up had been in the metropolis differed from the East London proletarian cockney of Red Robinson; but in place of any such observations, all that this sad, old-young woman of thirty felt, as she listened to the prolonged whispering that now went on between these two men in that gloomy and dingy hallway, was a wave of infinite, unspeakable life-weariness. Morgan Nelly's mother, as her dark eyes turned from the bust of Peel to the patched trousers of Young Tewsy, felt indeed just then a very clear and very definite desire to be dead. When a woman was once safely dead there would be no longer any need for bargainings about a room, in which she might be legally and uninterruptedly subjected to indecent usage.

Blackie had at this juncture, however, one great advantage

over both these gentlemen from London. She was Glastonbury-born. Too drunk at first for it to occur to her to make use of this advantage she suddenly began to feel, as she became simultaneously more sober and more disgusted, that nothing would induce her, *nothing*, to spend "a short time" in that house alone with Mr. Robinson. But how to escape? For it was becoming clear that Young Tewsy, softened by the transference of half a crown from the pocket of Red's holiday trousers to that of his own workhouse trousers, was yielding a little. An inspiration seized her. She turned boldly to Young Tewsy and demanded to be taken at once into the presence of his mistress!

Red's eyes opened wide. Young Tewsy's eyes, on the contrary, screwed themselves up into little points of confused amusement. He hesitated for a moment, looking from one to the other.

"The gentleman must wait, then," he mumbled. " 'Ee must wait just where 'ee his, till I brings yer back 'ere."

Mr. Robinson's imagination instantaneously pictured a warm, brightly lit bedroom, free from the intrusion of British Statesmen, and blessed, so to speak, especially for his delectation, by the high priestess of lascivious delights.

"High'll wait with pleasure," he cried eagerly, thinking to himself, "She can't charge more than five shillings." "You go with 'im, sweet'eart," he said, "honely don't be long!"

There was evidently an entrance from the one house to the other, for Young Tewsy now proceeded to escort the lady up the unpromising flight of stairs which loomed dismally in front of them.

Red Robinson set himself to wait.

He waited excitedly for ten minutes, hopefully for ten minutes, patiently for a quarter of an hour. Then he began to experience extreme dismay. He cautiously ascended the dismal stairs to the first landing.

Here he found an uncurtained window, looking out, across the slums of Glastonbury, towards the eastern horizon. It was an extremely gloomy evening; but the background of the view now angrily stared at by Mr. Robinson was filled by the massive and noble up-rising of St. John's Tower. And Red Robinson set himself to curse this tower. He cursed the men who made it, who prayed under it, who rang the bells. He cursed the imaginary God it rose up there, so massive and so square, to greet in those gloomy menacing heavens. He cursed its rich architecture and the richer Abbots who designed it. He cursed its buttresses, its crochets, its arches, its pinnacles, its finicals!

Could the ghost of a mediæval builder, with a wicked eye for wild grotesques, have stripped Mr. Robinson then and there of his cockney clothes he would have found him in a state of furious phallic excitement. His frustrated enjoyment of Blackie ran and seethed and fermented through every vein. The image of his grand enemy, Philip Crow, mocked him from St. John's Tower. The feelings that found their human expression in the monosyllable " 'ate" frothed and foamed like an acid poured out upon the stonework of St. John's Tower. "St. John the Baptist!" he thought. " 'Ow I 'ate them! I 'ate them all like 'ell!"

The peculiar mingling of his hate for Philip and his insatiable lust for Philip's girl stiffened and tightened as he stood at that dingy window till they became a demonic entity. No gargoyle on any gothic tower, certainly not on the tower he was gazing at, equalled in contorted malice, intertwisted with the fury of lust, this psychic demon concealed under the neat holiday clothes of Mr. Robinson. He felt as if the passion that filled him might at any moment rend his clothes, crack open his brittle body, and shoot forth over the roofs of Paradise towards that hateful tower! He swept all Glastonbury, all its past, all its future, into the four-square erection that was thickening and darkening there before him against the sombre east.

He imagined himself as the leader of a wild mob of men occupied in destroying with hammers and mallets every old building in the " 'ateful" place.

Then he would blot it out! He would plough up the ground where it had been, and sprinkle it with ashes. He remembered from early lessons in his London board-school that something of this kind used to be done to offensive cities. And this is what *he* would do! Raze it flat. Plough up its earth. Sprinkle it with ashes. Those old peoples knew a thing or two; *they* did!

When he had reduced the place to a heap of ploughed-up earth, when he had sprinkled that earth with ashes—with ashes from all the filthy buckets in his mother's alley—then he would enjoy Blackie in the best room of the Pilgrims' Inn. Then he would cry "Yes, Blackie!" and Blackie would cry, "I loves yer better than 'im, yer 'andsome hangry man!"

Mr. Robinson must have remained for at least twenty minutes at this window, on the first landing of Mother Legge's "next door."

His imaginative orgy was interrupted by the voice of Young Tewsy from the hall below.

"Mister! Be 'ee here, Mister? Where be 'ee, Mister?"

In his surprise at finding no man where he had left a very impatient man, in that house of "rooms" for the delights of men, Young Tewsy forgot his manners—that is to say he forgot his North London accent—and relapsed into his acquired Somerset-shire, the language of his long residence in Glastonbury.

"Dang yer! Where be 'ee hiding then? This baint a railway station!"

Red Robinson came hastily downstairs.

"Thee's 'ooman be biding along wi' Missus for thik party, Mister," said Young Tewsy. Thus speaking he moved to the door leading into the street and held it ajar, glancing furtively out to make sure there was no one at the next entrance.

It became evident to Mr. Robinson that he was being politely but firmly ushered forth into a "roomless" world.

" 'Asn't she arst for me? Hain't *high* hinvited, yer blimey hold idiot!"

"I was to tell 'ee, Sir," said Young Tewsy with dignity and reserve, but with a glittering eye, "that they ladies will send for 'ee when they do want 'ee!"

Thus speaking he continued to hold the door open, opening it just wide enough for the passage of a single gentleman whose shoulders were not very broad.

"Give me back that 'alf crown then, you old blighter, and don't you dare to snigger at people who mean no 'arm . . . or one of these 'ere days somebody'll knock your grinning phiz into bloody beeswax!"

Mr. Robinson's anger was like water beginning to drip from a paper bag. It began with trickling drops—"give me back that

half a crown"—it went on with a squirted thin jet of wrath—
"snigger at people who mean no 'arm"—and then the paper bag
burst outright.

Young Tewsy threw the door open wide. This was the only
reprisal that he indulged in, though it was more of a retort than
Mr. Robinson realised; for in all his experience as a Cyprian
doorkeeper, Young Tewsy had only once before done this; and
that was when he ushered out Mr. Wollop's father, that disreputable old haberdasher.

"Out with you, Sir," said Young Tewsy laconically. "Out with
you!"

There was nothing else indeed that Mr. Robinson could do but
go out. But as he went out he gave the ex-inmate of Wells Workhouse one glance of so much fury that the old man jerked himself backward as if he had received a villainous blow.

Red Robinson walked down the street without looking back.
"High'll make you pay for this! High'll make you pay for this,
my fine bitch!"

But the unfortunate man had now to decide where he would
get his tea and how he would spend his evening. He decided to
go and see if Sally Jones was at home. Mrs. Jones, he knew,
admired him; and there was a pallid pleasure in certain innocent liberties that Sally sometimes permitted. He had received
the sort of affront that makes a person's own society for the next
few hours extremely distasteful and so he hurriedly directed his
steps towards the Jones ménage, much as a badly bitten tom-cat
returns sulkily to the familiar wainscot of his habitual mouse-
hunting.

But he found no one at home except Jackie Jones, who had
already had his tea and was gravely studying his geography book
at the kitchen table.

"What be a estuary, Red?" enquired Jackie after Robinson had
waited there for an hour, hoping against hope for the return
of the widow and her daughter.

"Hestuary?" the man repeated. "Hestuary did you say?" He
went to the door, opened it and looked out. "Hestuary," he announced to the empty alley, "I hain't got no one!"

Mrs. Legge's hospitality was both large and varied. Tittie Petherton who was in considerable pain, but not so acute as to make it necessary that she should leave the assembly, sat in an arm-chair by the fire with one of Mrs. Legge's best rugs over her knees. Here she struggled to suppress her groans and enjoy this memorable occasion.

Mad Bet was behaving with wonderful self-restraint, due entirely to the presence of John Crow, who not only talked to her a good deal; but talked to her more than to anyone else in the room.

After the departure of Mr. Robinson from "me little place next door," which was Mrs. Legge's polite name for her Temple of Venus, Young Tewsy locked and bolted this dubious annex and returned to the main dwelling to help wait on his mistresses' guests. All the rooms on the ground floor of this house—the biggest as well as the oldest in Paradise—were crowded with people; and it would have been a significant discrimination among the old residents of Glastonbury to note just who *were* the persons who came.

Mother Legge was, as has been remarked, liberal in drinks but stingy in food. Even the drinks, however, were limited to whiskey and gin and to a concoction of the lady's own which she called Bridgewater Punch; among the ingredients of which the particular kind of fiery rum used by sailors was most in evidence.

Sam Dekker, actuated by what in his single-hearted simplicity, he regarded as the proper attitude for a neophyte in sanctity, did his utmost to interest Nell Zoyland and Crummie Geard in each other's personalities. This would have been more difficult—for Nell's mind was still stunned by the change in him and still preoccupied by the certainty that she *was*, whatever anyone said about it, really with child—if Crummie hadn't been such an exceptionally good-hearted girl. Crummie caught the secret of her rival's sadness with a psychic penetration almost worthy of her father and "laid herself out" to be sweet to her. And when Crummie did this there were few women—as there were certainly no men—who could resist her coaxing ways.

Thus Sam's simple mind was eminently gratified, as if he had achieved this consummation by something akin to a miracle, when he saw the two girls seated at last side by side munching Osborne biscuits and sipping with wry faces the famous Bridgewater Punch, as if they were old friends.

Mother Legge herself, too portly to do much service with her great silver trays, soon settled herself comfortably in an arm-chair, opposite poor Tittie, from which position of sovereignty she received such obeisance as her dignity, and, it must be confessed, too, her Rabelaisian tongue spontaneously exacted.

She was a vast, dusky, double-chinned mountain of a woman, with astute, little grey eyes; eyes that seemed rather to aim at *not* seeing what she wanted to avoid, than at seeing what she wanted to see. Attracted by both John Crow and Mr. Evans, it was Mother Legge's desire to have both these men at her side. Being the hostess, however, and both these men being occupied with a lady, Mr. Evans with Cordelia and John with Mad Bet, it was some time before Mother Legge obtained her wish. But she got it at last and she got it finally so completely that John was caught on a big footstool between her right elbow and the fire, while Mr. Evans was pilloried on a high-backed chair on her left hand with his profile to the fire.

A fire—and you may be sure that this old sorceress knew this well—is a sure magnet for the magnetism of excitable men, and a sure sedative for the nerves of cantankerous men; and now, with the fire as a second or super-female to give her aid, Mother Legge had her own way with her favourite guests.

All the lights, in the reception room of this huge Priestess of Immorality, hung from the ceiling in the shape of two colossal, cut-glass candelabra, burning gas within enormous figured globes from beneath which hung the heaviest festoons of prismatic pendants that John had ever seen. Squinnying cautiously round the room at those moments when his portentous capturer—who resembled a gigantic Gargamelle seeking information from Ponoc-rates—was engaged with Mr. Evans, John took occasion to observe that there was nothing in this high-ceilinged chamber which jarred upon his nature except the physical contortions of the poor woman opposite him as her pain, intensified by her inability to move from where she had been placed, grew upon her. These twitchings under that rug, these spasms across that emaciated face, he *did* find it hard to bear, though no one else except Crummie, who now and then got up and went across to her, seemed conscious of her sufferings.

Sam had left the apartment now, feeling it incumbent upon him to be where he least liked to be, namely among the *petit-bourgeois* of the gathering, who were consuming tea and bread and jam at the tables with tablecloths, in the other two rooms. The sight of Sam's self-conscious unselfishness would have fretted John's heathen mind as much as the tablecloths would have done and the homely tea-drinkers. Here in this great chamber, so brilliantly lit by the flashing candelabra every person and every object seemed to fall into a delicious harmony.

He had drunk enough Bridgewater Punch already to be feeling exceptionally serene and as he watched Nell Zoyland and Crummie, Percy and Blackie, Mr. Wollop and Cordelia, Dave Spear—who to Percy's astonishment had just drifted in—talking to Mad Bet, and Tom Barter who was now lost in a deep colloquy with a pretty waitress from the Pilgrims', the whole scene swam and shimmered before him in an incredible luxury of significance. People and objects as John now looked at them seemed transferred from the confused dynamic scramble of life into something just beneath life; something that was there all the time, but that needed a few glasses of Bridgewater Punch to enable it to steal silently forth and show itself as the eternal essence.

This old house of Mrs. Legge's had belonged in former times, before Paradise was overbuilt, to a famous West-Country family called Camel. Certain portions of it were older still and associated with that Richard Atwelle who is buried in St. John's Church and of whom it is said: "This Atwelle did much cost in this chirch and gave fair Housing that he had builded in the Towne onto it." What the grave shades of these old Camels and still older Atwelles would have felt if they could have seen the present company, who can tell? It did not even occur to John Crow, as he hugged his knees on that footstool by the fire or sipped his punch from a glass placed in the polished fender at his side, to wonder what the future denizens of this spacious room, Comrades perhaps of the Glastonbury Commune, would feel if they could look back upon the existing scene!

On John's left, behind his hostess and Mr. Evans, were two high windows, covered now by heavy black curtains that fell from great wooden curtain-rods painted red.

Similar curtains hung over the doorway; but these were now partly drawn.

All round the walls were rough, crudely painted oil pictures of the ancient Recorders of Glastonbury, an office which eventually gave place to that of Mayor. These old worthies now looked down upon this motley assembly with that ineffable complacence which the passing of time combined with crude and faded oil-pigments alone can give.

But their presence gave a touch that was required; as did also the mouldering dark-brown wallpaper, a relic from the days of the Camels; and the black frames out of which these burgesses stared; and the big bare mahogany table in the centre of the room.

As John glanced dreamily into their faces they seemed to look back upon him with a look that said—"When a Glastonbury Recorder dies he passes into a land where men of solid worth are permitted to despise the vulgar, without qualm of conscience or rebuke of priest!"

Thus did old Peter King, whose uncle was John Locke, the philosopher, thus did Fortescue Tuberville, thus did Edward Phellips, Davidge Gould, Henry Bosanquet, Edmund Griffiths and William Dickinson, look down upon John Crow; and it seemed to John as if there were some residual secret of human experience that this particular group of human beings, these living, and those dead, could reveal, if only with one mysteriously wide mouth, like the mouth of some great, wise, pontifical salmon from the River Severn—a veritable Recorder among fishes—they could utter the word! It would, John felt, be a word that allowed for human imperfection, proceeded from human imperfection; yes, and even *exacted* human imperfection. It would be a clue that exacted meanness, weakness, pettiness, ordinariness, conceit, vanity, complacency, commonplaceness, mediocrity, conventionality, smugness, hypocrisy; before the full significance of human life could emerge.

John wondered to himself for a moment to whom in all this

gathering of people he could speak about this inspiration of his —this revelation as to the value of inconsistency, complacency, weakness, silliness, conceit—which he now derived from the contemplation of Mother Legge's guests, both living and dead; and he decided that the only one who would understand him would be Mad Bet.

"I must go over to her in a minute," he thought. "She won't be able to stand Cousin Dave's discourses much longer. How her eyes do stare at me! I must go over and tell her what I've just thought before I forget it. Damn! It's going . . . it's gone! What *was* it? Could it have been that laziness, self-satisfaction, self-deception,—stupidity even—are *necessary* if life is to be grasped in its essence? That sounds quite silly. How her eyes do stare at me!"

He turned his own eyes appealingly to those old Recorders, each one of whom had been collected for Mrs. Legge with patient labour by Number Two. "Recorders of Glastonbury!" he thought. "Is it my destiny to learn the secret of the mystic value of the commonplace from you? No—it can't have been *just* that. It *was* damned near it, though."

His erratic mind now found itself dallying with the monstrous thought of what it would be like to embrace a woman as old and hideous as Mad Bet! He felt a certain surprise because this thought—so queerly were his nerves adjusted—did not cause him any terrible shrinking. Was that because he was congenitally more attracted to men than women? "Is the way I make love to Mary," he thought, "a sign that I am all the time half-thinking of her as a boy?"

"Evans!" he suddenly said aloud, addressing his friend and jerking his stool forward a little so as to see that grotesque Roman profile of the Welshman. "Evans! Do you think it would be possible to make love to a woman who was—I beg your pardon Mrs. Legge, I interrupted you, I'm afraid."

Mrs. Legge stretched out a small plump hand and with a gesture as royal as Queen Victoria herself patted John's shoulder. "Aye, what's that, young man?" she chuckled amiably in her thick throat.

"I was asking Mr. Evans," reiterated John shamelessly,

"whether he thought it was possible to make love to a person who was perfectly hideous."

"You don't mean *here*?" purred the preposterous lady, tapping her bosom, which resembled Glastonbury Tor, except that in place of the tower, it held aloft a big golden brooch, with the tips of her fingers. "You mustn't encourage my astrologer to make fun of his old woman in her own house."

Mr. Evans' countenance as he now turned it towards John showed no distaste at being called Mrs. Legge's astrologer. It was animated by a rush of all the learned and recondite folklore that John's question summed up.

"There is a profound esoteric doctrine, Crow," he said solemnly, "in what you've just remarked. Our old Cymric poetry is full of references to it. Ceridwen herself, the Welsh Demeter, appeared frequently in an unpleasing shape; and in the History of the Grail it is recorded again and again that the Grail-Messenger was of striking ugliness. Ugliness seems indeed to have been one of the most common disguises of that Feminine Principle in Nature which ——"

"But Evans, Evans!" interrupted John, "Wasn't it a Phorkyad that Goethe in Faust makes Mephistopheles ——"

"Chut! Chut! Man-alive!" cried Mother Legge. "Don't 'ee invocate Mr. Orphanage in me Best Parlour. Such devils, as he be, *may* be ones for liking we when us be frights; but *I* baint asking for their hot hugs yet awhile! What do *you* think of these naughty lads' chatter, Tittie, me poor child?" And she leaned forward out of her big chair raising her voice.

"I can't hear . . . hear . . . you . . . very well, Auntie. Me pains be bad."

"These gentlemen say that there be men what 'ud cosset we," shouted Mother Legge, "when us hadn't a tooth left in our head!"

"You were allus one for your bit o' mischie, Aunt," replied the sick woman with a great effort, fumbling at the rug over her knees with her bony hand, "but 'twould be different if . . . 'twould be different if ——" Her voice died away in a moan of pain. The pain took various shapes in Tittie Petherton's consciousness according to its intensity. What it resembled now was a round black iron ball of a rusty blood-colour, covered with spikes. Tittie herself was hugging this ball to her bosom. When she pressed it, the hurt from those iron spikes was intolerable, but she couldn't see its bloodiness any more, which was the thing that turned her stomach most.

"He says no one is going to be allowed to have anythink to theyselves. Be that true, my precious marrow?"

Mad Bet's shrill voice from her seat by the mahogany table rang through the room. She had stretched out her long arm and was pointing to John. There was a general hush.

"It *is* true," pronounced Dave Spear in a firm resolute voice.

"Let my True-Love speak," cried Mad Bet again. "If He says it's true I'll believe you. But if He says it's a lie, I'll never be lieve you!"

What made John answer this interrogation as to whether, in a hundred years—for so he worded the question to himself—Glas tonbury would be communistic, exactly as he did, was due purely and solely to his idea that it would please Mad Bet! He suspected that Mad Bet must be naturally so hostile to the existing system of society that it would give her immense satisfaction to think of any drastic change.

He also—such was his ridiculously weak nature—disliked the idea, after this formidable silence, of hurting the feelings of Dave Spear who took this matter of Communism in such dead earnest.

Thus he lifted up his head, unclosed his eyes, met the intense stare of the madwoman, who was waiting for his response as though it were the verdict of Heaven, and cried out in a queer, husky voice as if he really *had* been seized with the spirit of prophecy—*"Mr. Spear is right!"*

He had no sooner uttered these words, than above the clamour of loosened tongues from all quarters of the room, there came the unmistakable sound of rain, striking heavily against the windows.

Mother Legge struggled to her feet in a moment.

"Tewsy! Tewsy!" she called out in her most deep-throated tones.

The door-opener of "my other house" came hurrying in from where he was superintending the tea-drinkers.

"Run upstairs and shut the window of the Nursery, Tewsy! I left it wide open."

Mr. Evans and John and Barter and Dave, along with Nell and Percy, were the only persons present who heard the word "Nursery" with surprise. Everyone else knew that it was Mrs. Legge's humour to call her own private little sitting-room upstairs by this familiar name.

The big lady herself now walked to the black curtains and pulled them aside. She pulled also aside a pair of gigantic muslin curtains, yellowish from age, which had been there as long as she had, which had, indeed, been her very first purchase after she leased the house from old Miss Kitty Camel; for, said she, "I can't abide Over-lookers!"

Then she looked forth into the night. Many heads were turned towards her as she stood there, with her broad black back to them all; and there came into the mind of John, who kept his eye on her as he went across to Mad Bet, a queer feeling as if this whole great room, under those glittering suspended lights, were a real nursery and he and all the rest of the company frightened children at a disturbed party, with Something more menacing than ordinary rain beating out there at the window!

The old lady came back into the room.

"Well, it's been coming all day," she said, "and now it's come. It's a good thing it's waited till now, for the holiday."

John thought to himself, "How often must those words, *for the holiday*, have been uttered in Glastonbury houses by comfortable people gathered in snug interiors; people whose whole life was one long 'holiday'!"

She had come back to her "children" now, that old black-backed Mother Goose, and her soothing words "for the holiday," went about the room, like an eiderdown coverlet endowed with soft wings, whispering to everybody—"Your frightened soul can tuck itself in bed again, little one. Mother has sent away that Something, so much more terrifying than the rain, that was coming after you!"

The fantastic notion now entered John's shameless head that this rich old Procuress, who had arranged so long for the unlawful pleasures of Glastonbury, had in very truth been a kind of mystical Mother—like one of the Mothers in Faust—in driving away fear. There were other "queer sons of chaos" than "Mr. Orphanage"; and no escape from cosmic isolation was more complete than that to which Young Tewsy held the candle!

Mother Legge went out now, doubtless to reassure her guests in the other rooms; and to the accompaniment of what was now torrents of lashing rain the general conversation went on.

The men of the party—and even some of the women—began drinking again now. Young Tewsy brought in a colossal Silver Bowl and placed it on the mahogany table. This turned out to be a much stronger concoction of Bridgewater Punch than the previous jugs had contained.

A very curious incident occurred at this point of the evening's happenings. At the departure of Mrs. Legge followed by the appearance of this great Silver Bowl a general movement had occurred among the guests. Some of the people in the room left it, others entered it, and many changed their seats, their companions, their mood. Mr. Evans for instance vacated his chair by the old lady's now empty seat and moved hurriedly into the group gathered about the table. As he came forward he passed the pretty waitress towards whom Tom Barter was carefully steering his way holding the first tumbler that anyone had dared to dip into that Silver Bowl.

Against this tumbler Mr. Evans, pushing frantically forward, clumsily, but as it appeared accidentally, propelled himself, knocking it out of Barter's fingers. Other hands which, following Barter's example, were now ladling liquor out of the Silver Bowl, paused in their pleasant task when Barter's glass fell, while their owners looked about to see whose drink had been spilt.

Mr. Evans, however, hurried quickly to the Silver Bowl, snatched a mug from the table, scooped up some punch with a sweep of his long arm, and rushing to Cordelia's side pressed it upon her.

"Quick," he cried, panting and agitated, "drink quick!"

But Cordelia, vexed by her friend's impetuosity, instead of doing what he told her handed the mug to Nell, to whom she was talking; and Nell, still too preoccupied with her private thoughts to be alert to what was going on, lifted it heedlessly to her lips.

Thus, among all that company, Nell Zoyland was the first to drink from Mother Legge's Silver Bowl.

When Mr. Evans perceived that his rude if not violent haste had been in vain, he left Cordelia as brusquely as he had approached her, and returning to where Barter's glass had been broken, began patiently to help that gentleman in collecting the scattered fragments and placing them on the table.

"I'll finish it—now I've begun," he cried to Barter, from his stooping position upon the floor, "You go and get Miss ——" he paused from ignorance of the waitress' name—"another one. I'm sorry I did it."

Barter gave the Welshman's bent back one of his most vindictive scowls. But he went off to do what the man had bidden him. Blackie, who had been observing this scene from the beginning with her wide grey eyes, now turned to Persephone Spear who alone among these people had been talking to her. "Be that Mrs. Zoyland from out Sedgemoor way?" she murmured softly.

Percy smiled, lifting her dark eyebrows. "Yes, that's Nell. She's my husband's sister."

"She was the first to drink," rejoined the other, still in a timid whisper.

"Well?" said Percy still smiling. "Why not?"

"It's the Camel bowl," murmured Morgan Nelly's mother. "Mrs. Legge bought it from old Miss Kitty. It's from the Abbot's Kitchen they do tell. 'Twas what they old Popish Monks did drink from, afore King Harry's time."

"How did Miss Camel get it?" enquired Percy, relieved to see that her husband was deep in conversation with John Crow, while Mad Bet, from her seat at the table which she seemed afraid of leaving, watched the latter's face with doglike attention.

"Her were descended from they wold Papists," whispered Blackie. "There be wondrous witchcraft in thik Silver Bowl. I do know, for I've done charwork in this here house since I were a young maid."

Cordelia meanwhile had left Nell's side and had taken her seat by Mr. Wollop whose experiences as a youth in dealing with his disreputable parent had made him careful to avoid the contents of the Silver Bowl.

"The rain is spitting in the fire," said the ex-Mayor.

"I thought I heard a funny noise just now," said Cordelia.

"Is your Dad here tonight?" said Mr. Wollop.

Cordelia glanced anxiously at the sick woman by the fire, at whose knees Crummie was now standing, bending over her.

"Not yet," she answered, "but I hope he'll come in soon. Mrs. Petherton's getting worse."

"I've a'heard about how he can cure folk by laying of his hands on 'em, your Dad." Mr. Wollop sighed lightly. "Never cured no one in all me life," he went on, "so I reckon I weren't the Mayor he be. But I took a interest in the people of this town, rich and poor alike . . . no distinction! . . . and they knowed it too."

"I'm *sure* they knew it, Mr. Wollop," said Cordelia kindly, soothing the fallen official, as she might have soothed a deposed king.

Mr. Wollop looked extremely gratified. "They knew it, me dear. They knew it," he muttered, stretching out his arm for an anchovy-paste sandwich, snapping a neat bite out of it with his white false teeth, and then holding it in his finger and thumb like the picture of the Hatter in *Alice*.

"Oh, me God take pity on me! Oh, me God take pity on me!"

Tittie Petherton, with Crummie by her side, was twisting and moaning in a manner that was distressing to see and hear.

"Haven't no one got any o' they pellets handy," whispered Mr. Wollop, "what has mercy and pity in 'un?" He looked closely at the scene by the fire. "Sister's skirt was never bought at me shop," he remarked gravely.

"Crummie told me she's given her already every one of the morphia tablets Nurse left," said Cordelia. "Oh, I wish Father would come!"

"I wish he would come too," echoed Mr. Wollop. " 'Twould be a wondrous sight, with this rain spitting down chimney, to see your Dad stop this poor woman's groans."

Cordelia had an intelligence that was accustomed to wander more than most minds, among the mysteries of life; but she never included her father among these mysteries. For some reason she took her father for granted on the lowest possible level. It seemed, in some way, quite an ordinary thing when her father stopped Mrs. Petherton's cancer from hurting; though if Mr. Evans had done it it would have seemed wonderful.

Barter and the waitress were all this time growing steadily more affectionate and confidential. He had got her to himself at a little table now at the side of the room opposite the windows under the portrait of the seventeenth-century Recorder who was the nephew of John Locke. To this table he kept bringing fresh supplies of Bridgewater Punch and the flushed cheeks and sparkling eyes of Clarissa Smith were an evidence of his success. He had already ascertained the exact amount of her salary, of the income of her father, a taxi-driver in Dorchester, of the expense she had been betrayed into this Easter "over at Wollop's" in the little matter of underclothes and stockings, and even of what she had had to pay for her shoes last Christmas.

He had now reached the stage—his second stage in the process of seduction—of telling her fortune by the lines in her warm palm. It was becoming clear that poor Tossie Stickles, now under ecclesiastical and domestic protection, need not have worried about her gentleman's lack of feminine support. With Tossie rendered *hors-de-combat* it had become the turn of Clarissa. A new girl was a new world to Mr. Barter and his sluggish East Anglian senses stirred in their fen-peat depths, like great crocodiles heaving up out of sun-baked mud, to meet this new world.

The fact that novelty was so irresistible to him in these matters was a proof of something essentially stupid in his nature. It is one of the psychological mistakes that the world makes, to assume that a man whose inclination drives him on to attempt seduction after seduction is a man of more ardent erotic passion than the more constant lover. The very reverse is the case.

The most absorbing and distracting, the most delicately satisfying, of all lovers for a girl, are neither the thick-witted novelty-hunters, nor the sour puritans. They are the vicious monogamists! Such indeed are the triumphant Accomplices of Life; and when you see the pleasures of unsated and natural lust carried on between two elderly people—as, owing to Bloody Johnny's occult wisdom, they were carried on between Mr. and Mrs. Geard—you see a checkmating of Thanatos by Eros such as makes Mr.

Barter's brutal approaches and Miss Clarissa's silly yieldings as commonplace as they are uneventful.

"You should hear what the girls down at our place do say about what you rich gentlemen do in this house," giggled Clarissa.

"I must say I think you Glastonbury young ladies haven't much to learn," responded Mr. Barter, whose experience had taught him the exactly correct tone to take.

"They do say that this house be called Camelot," said the girl, drawing back her hand from across the table but grudging in her heart that the conversation—even though she had led it astray herself—should have wandered from her good heart line and promising fate line.

"I didn't know that," said Mr. Barter. "There! Finish up your glass and I'll get you some more. No, I didn't know that. I come from London, you know."

For two reasons did he tell this lie; first because he knew that the word London always had a glamour for provincial young ladies, but secondly because the deepest thing in his nature being his feeling for Norfolk he never referred to it, with any of his light-of-loves, any more than he referred to his passion for airplanes.

If Barter had put the imagination into his love-making that he put into these two integral passions the gross stimulus of novelty would have been less important to him.

"I suppose," said Clarissa Smith sententiously, dropping her Dorset accent to impress her educated admirer, "that in the Dark Ages you gentlemen did what you liked with us poor girls."

"I hate the name Camelot," said Mr. Barter; and for a second, even in the salt-tide of his rising lechery, he longed to pour out his feelings to Mary Crow. How that rain beat on the windows! It must be a wild night outside.

Clarissa didn't like the change in his voice or the change—momentary though it was—in the expression of his face. She toyed with the sham pearls that adorned her plump white neck and her melting brown eyes wandered to the moaning figure by the fire. "They oughtn't to bring sick people to parties," she thought.

"I suppose in them days," she remarked, the Dorchester accent slipping back, "Camelot was a place where a quiet girl dursn't show her face."

"Have you lived here long?" Persephone Spear was saying just then to Blackie Morgan.

"Born here, Mrs. Spear, and me mother before me. Father came from Wales."

"How soon do a mother's thoughts begin to influence her child?" thought Nell Zoyland as she listened with sweet attention to what Mr. Evans was now saying to Cordelia.

Cordelia thought she had never met such a nice, unassuming lady as Mrs. Zoyland. It flattered her profoundly to watch the tender interest with which, considering how little she knew either of them, she was now listening to Owen's words.

Mr. Evans himself had almost forgiven her for being the first to drink from the Silver Bowl!

"What is going to happen to me? Oh, what is going to happen to me and Sam's child?" Nell thought. "Oh, I wish it wouldn't rain so hard. It gets on my nerves the way it sounds. I must ask Percy soon what we'd better do if it goes on like this. But I mustn't fuss and get silly! From now on, till Sam's child is born, I must be calm and sensible about everything. I wonder why Sam doesn't come and talk to me."

The noise of the rain seemed now to be steadily increasing in that room of glittering lights and black curtains. Nor was it only Nell Zoyland who felt aware of it as something coming upon them all from outside—from *far* outside—coming over the wide-drenched moors, over the hissing muddy ditches, over the sobbing reeds, over the salt-marshes; coming from somewhere unearthly, somewhere beyond the natural!

There was a curious instinctive movement in that big room as if all those who were present were seeking to get reassurance from one another and to gather closer together. There was more drinking too. Cups and glasses were dipped again and again in the great Silver Bowl; and the voices rose and rose, as that little group of human consciousnesses—arguing, reproaching, challenging, jesting, sneering, accusing—sought in some subconscious way to outbrave a Presence which they all felt pressing in upon them from that unearthly "outside." Mr. Evans had moved away

now from Cordelia and Nell. A strange restlessness had come
upon him. He began walking up and down beneath the pictures
of the Recorders.

"To let it all go," he thought, "to go home now through the
rain and go down those stairs and read that book! Yes, yes, yes,
yes, to read that passage, *that* page, which I've avoided since I
first found it . . . to look at *that* picture . . . to tell myself that
story . . . to remember . . ."

He stood still, his eyes on the crossed legs of one of the complacent Recorders. And it was allowed to him as he stared at
those silver-buckled shoes, so crudely painted, to travel with the
speed of lightning along the road that he would have to follow
if he did begin all that again. He *became* the terrible craving, he
became the thing he was doing, he *became* the itch, the bite, the
sting, the torment, the horror, he *became* the loathing that refused to stop doing what it loathed to do. He *became* the shapeless mouth that——

Human thoughts, those mysterious projections from the creative
nuclei of living organisms, have a way of radiating from the brain
that gives them birth. Such emanations, composed of ethereal
vibrations, take invisible shapes and forms as they float forth.
Thus to any supermaterial eye, endowed with psychic perception,
the atmosphere of Mrs. Legge's front parlour that night must
have been a strange scene. The secret thoughts of her guests rose
and floated, hovered and wavered, formed and re-formed, under
those glittering candelabra, making as it were a second party, a
gathering of thought-shapes, that would remain when all these
people had left the room. All thought-eidola are not of the same
consistency or of the same endurance. It is the amount of life-
energy thrown into them that makes the difference. Some are
barely out of the body before they fade away. Others—and this is
the cause of many ghostly phenomena—survive long after the
organism that projected them is buried in the earth.

All the while Tom Barter was progressing so prosperously
with his seduction of the brown-eyed, white-throated Clarissa,
the remorseful thought of himself as the traitor to his late employer took the shape of a shadowy creature bent double under

a swollen load, from beneath which its lamentable eyes strained upward, tugging at the strings that held them in their sockets.

Meanwhile Persephone Spear was projecting from her graceful body, whose provocative outward form was at this moment interesting but not exciting the senses of Mr. Wollop as he sat placid and content at the mahogany table, a very queer homuncula of desperation.

"I hate all men," she had kept thinking to herself, "all, all, all! I have found that out *now*! I thought it was because Dave was just Dave that I drew back from him. I thought that if I let Philip take me some new feeling would be born in me. But it *hasn't* been born. In Wookey Hole it was exciting. Just the shock of it. Just the pain of it. But I hate the way men are *made*! I knew it when I first saw Dave naked and now—since yesterday at that inn in Taunton; which was worse, far worse, when Philip —— Oh, what shall I do? Where shall I go? Why was I born in this world at all? I want to love, I want to love, but there's no one!"

The moans of Tittie Petherton as she hugged to her tortured entrails those iron spikes of that round globe of pain which was all that *she* could think of—though a hideous reproduction of that engine hung in the air above her for eyes that could see it —had now become so dominant in that room that conversation began to lapse.

"Can't anything be done to ease her?" said John to Dave Spear.

"I'll go and fetch Dekker," replied the practical Communist. "He brought her here. He'd better take her home."

With these words the fair young man hurried away. "Dekker!" John could hear him calling. "Dekker! Dekker!"

John turned to Cordelia. "Have you *ever* heard such rain?" he said. "I'm afraid the Mayor won't come at all on such a night. I think one or other of us ought to call a taxi and take that woman straight to the hospital."

Cordelia looked at him contemptuously. She often felt as if her father had never shown his inherent stupidity more clearly than in his choice of this grotesque individual with a St. Vitus dance in his cheek and the look of a deboshed actor. "I don't believe he ever has a bath either," she said to herself.

There came over Cordelia at that moment a blind physical wave of hatred for John Crow.

"I don't like the way he smells," she thought.

Nothing would have amused John himself more than this particular reaction of Cordelia's. To most human persons a physical repulsion on the part of another to so intimate a thing as *the smell of their skin* would have been an insult never forgiven. But the consciousness of John Crow was so loosely attached to his bodily frame that he would have been capable of meekly retiring from Cordelia's bed—had she been his mistress—and sprinkling himself with Attar of Roses, if it pleased her, without bearing her the least grudge.

"I like my cousin Dave, don't you?" was all he said now. "He's the only really unselfish person I've ever met. And yet, I suppose, if it brought his Communistic State a year nearer, he'd have us all shot tonight without the flicker of an eyelid."

A terrible moan from the woman by the fire interrupted them and they both caught a tearful, helpless appeal in Crummie's eyes as she turned from her patient.

"The hospital ——" began John; but Cordelia cut him short.

"She won't go," she said. "They tried it once. They'd have to make her unconscious first."

"I understand exactly what she feels," said John. "I'd much sooner plague everyone with my death-cries—God! I'd *like* to plague 'em with 'em—than go to any of those places. Hospitals, prisons, workhouses—*Mon Dieu!* They make me shudder."

Cordelia thought to herself, "That's *just* what a jail-bird like you *would* think. You ought to leave Father's service and be employed by Mrs. Legge along with Young Tewsy!"

John went over to Tittie's side. "Christ! My dear, can't we do anything to stop this?" he whispered to Crummie.

Mad Bet had been watching every movement of John's all the evening from her seat at the table. Mr. Wollop was addressing a few friendly words to her now; but she seemed unable to hear him. She now cried out to John so loudly that everyone stopped talking.

"Why don't 'ee pray to thik Tree o' Life, my king, what us two do know of? If you'd 'a thought 'o praying before, Mr. Geard mid come before!"

In a moment of respite from her pain, and arrested by the silence and by the madwoman's voice, Tittie herself spoke now. "It's began to rain," she said in a dull flat voice.

John stared into the fire across Tittie's fidgetty knees. "Bet's right," he thought. "It's absurd that in all this company not a soul has thought of praying. Young Dekker, who is out for living a saintly life, doesn't believe in anything to pray to. God! What we want here is someone to really *pray*, then perhaps old Geard will hurry up and come."

And with his face still towards the fire John dropped down surreptitiously upon one knee. "In Glastonbury," he thought, "it would seem popery or paganism to be caught really kneeling if you aren't in church."

And John secretly prayed in his heart that Mr. Geard might appear during the next five minutes. He prayed to his dead parent, exactly as he had done on his terrible walk to Stonehenge, when Mr. Evans had been sent to his rescue.

Mrs. Legge, accompanied by Sam Dekker and Dave Spear and several other people, now came into the room; but the general attention was distracted from their entrance by Mad Bet who suddenly rose to her feet.

John noticed that Mr. Evans was standing against the wall under one of the Recorders. John had just time to think to himself, after his fashion, "Evans looks as if he were standing against a hedge," when Mad Bet stretched out both her arms towards Mr. Evans and uttered a piercing cry.

Evans himself swung round, his teeth chattering.

"What has he done to that thing? Oh, what has he done to it?" screamed Mad Bet. "Stop him! Stop him! It's too much! Stop him, you people! He's doing it again! Stop him! Can't you stop him?"

The woman's hands were pointing, and her eyes were fixed, at a spot about a yard above Mr. Evans' head.

The shock of her words brought Mr. Evans back to his normal frame of mind. He came hurriedly towards the excited woman,

mumbling as he did so something in Welsh. He did not stop till
he was close up to her, where she had been pulled down to her
seat by Cordelia and Mr. Wollop.

He came up to her like a penitential monk approaching his
superior for punishment.

The madwoman shrunk away from him at first, trying to free
her arms from those of Cordelia, who was holding her tight, as if
afraid she would do something violent.

But Mr. Evans, who kept on mumbling in Welsh, set her free
from Cordelia's hold, and as soon as she felt herself free she
stopped shrinking away from him.

"It's not . . . it's not," whispered Mr. Evans to Mad Bet, so
that no one heard him but Mr. Wollop and Cordelia. "It's my
devil who does it . . . but I'm going to drive him out . . . on
Midsummer Day . . . you shall see . . . you shall be there
. . . you shall see him driven out . . . he will never . . ."

Once more he began mumbling something hurriedly in Welsh.

Then Mad Bet did a very queer thing. She snatched off her
black hat from her bald head and stretching out her arms seized
Mr. Evans round the neck and drew his head down towards her
own. No one but Cordelia and Mr. Wollop saw what happened;
but Mr. Wollop's eyes opened as wide as Bert Cole's would have
done when he beheld Mr. Evans' great Roman nose pressing
against that horrible white rondure and his twisted mouth kissing it.

"The Grail Messenger!" thought Mr. Evans as he straightened
his back and helped Mad Bet to straighten her hat and replace it
on her head.

"Tewsy!" It was the voice of Mother Legge who had hardly
entered the room than she was once more standing at the window.
"Tewsy! Go to the front door, there's someone coming."

There had been a general movement meanwhile towards the
group that surrounded Mad Bet. Something in the human mind
leaps up with rapturous release when some outrageous event is
occurring. Most men live but a half-life, dull, tame, monotonous.
The occurrence of something that is outrageously startling, upsetting to all proprieties, to all conventions, stirs such people
with a primordial satisfaction. The submerged Cro-Magnon in

them, or at least the submerged Neolithic man, swims up in them like a rising diver from the bottom of the atavistic sea and they rush forward, or steal forward, towards the spot where the forbidden thing is occurring.

Once more as John watched the broad back of his hostess standing at the window, while with her plump hands, each of which had a wedding ring upon it, she held the black and white curtains apart, he got the feeling that she was protecting a nursery of naughty children from some monstrous invasion . . . from some unearthly "questing Beast" whose featureless face made of decomposing stuff of darkness was even now pressing against the window.

"It is a wet night," remarked Mr. Wollop to Cordelia; but Cordelia was desperately trying to remember what it was when she was alone on Chalice Hill before the rain caught her by the giant oaks, that had made her feel so strong to deal with Mr. Evans. But as she watched him now seated at the mahogany table with an immobile face, like the very face upon that biblical "Penny" that made Christ utter the words—"Render unto Caesar"—she began to question whether it were in her power to help him. "He has got something serious on his conscience," she thought, "or he has got some mania that I can't understand. Why did he do that to Betsy just now? It was horrible to see him."

"Yes," she responded aloud to Mr. Wollop's mild remark, "but it's because people aren't talking so loud that we hear it now. Everyone seems whispering as if something were going to happen. I hope that miserable woman isn't going to die."

"She's kicked off her nice rug," remarked the ex-Mayor reproachfully.

"Yes," Dave Spear replied to a question of Barter who had just appeared at the mahogany table to re-fill Clarissa's glass from Miss Camel's Silver Bowl, "Yes, my wife and I have received word from Bristol that we'd better stay till June at any rate if we can't get them to strike till then."

Mr. Barter felt one of the most grievous pangs of self-reproach that he had ever known when he heard this calm declaration. What a Judas to Philip he had been! Oh, he should never have

let these contemptible Somersetshire workmen gct so out of
hand! What *would* he do without him? And what was *he* doing?
Making toys! While a real industry like those Dye-Works was
being threatened. Aye! He would like to be flying through this
wild rain *now*, with his fingers on the control, heading for Glastonbury from Wookey, through the liquid darkness. Bah! What
jumpy idiots these Glastonbury fools were. What the devil ——

"I can't bear it! Oh, my God!" Tittie's voice was hardly the
voice of a human being. The iron ball with spikes had changed
its shape . . .

Young Tewsy's voice rang out so quickly after the woman's
cry as to seem a portion of the same litany of chaos.

"His Worship, the Mayor, Madame!"

Mr. Geard did not stop to take off his dripping overcoat. He
pushed Mrs. Legge aside as if she had been a feather's weight.
Everyone stared at him now as shamelessly as did his predecessor
in office. The very Recorders on the wall seemed staring at him.

And well they might be!

The heavily built man in his dripping clothes was now pushing
his way through them, bent double, and with his hands pressed
against his great belly. "Oh, my God! Oh, my God!" he was
groaning out, as he stumbled forward.

The man's whole body seemed undergoing some sort of convulsion. Blindly he stumbled against the mahogany table. The
Silver Bowl seemed to catch his attention. He caught it up as he
passed. Mr. Barter, who had just dipped Clarissa's glass in it,
drew back hurriedly, spilling the liquour he held.

"Let this cup ——" howled Mr. Geard in a tone that made
even Mr. Wollop shiver, for it seemed more like the bark of a
great Sedgemoor fox than the voice of a man; and even as he
cried he flung the thing with all his force upon the ground, flung
it just at Crummie's feet, who was running, laughing and weeping, in wild hysterics towards him. When he reached Tittie, whose
voice had now sunk again into moans, he snatched her up in his
arms, as a fireman in a whirl of flame might seize a burning
woman, sank down in the chair with her on his lap, and began,
in his own natural voice, that familiar refrain which had won

him his nickname. "Blood of Christ deliver us! Blood of Christ save us! Blood of Christ have mercy upon us!"

His voice got lower and lower as he went on. Then it fell into complete silence. Still he continued hugging the figure in his arms and slowly rocking himself and her, backward and forward, backward and forward. There was such a dead silence in the room all this while, that the voices in the other rooms became like the intrusion of revellers at an execution or at a childbirth.

Then there came a grotesque and even rather an unpleasant sound. It was the stertorous breathing of the sleeping woman.

Iᴛ ᴡᴀs ᴛʜᴇ Fɪʀsᴛ ᴏf Mᴀʏ, ᴀɴᴅ ᴛʜʀᴏᴜɢʜ ᴛʜᴇ ᴏᴘᴇɴ ᴋɪᴛᴄʜᴇɴ window of Elizabeth Crow's little house on Benedict Street floated delicious sun-warmed airs. The house looked to the north, across the outskirts of Paradise. There was a small oblong patch of ground, outside, with a rough wooden fence round it, identical with all the other back-gardens of that street; and as in the case of most of the others this patch of earth was devoted rather to vegetables than to flowers. Beyond the garden was a triangular field where one of Miss Crow's neighbours kept a couple of cows; but beyond this, except for the roofs of a few scattered Paradise hovels, the water-meadows stretched clear away towards the site of the Lake Village, and Philip's landing field, and Number One's Backwear Hut. On the stove in this kitchen stood a sauce-pan of boiling potatoes and a large black pot full of some sort of savoury stew. In the centre of the kitchen was a bare deal table, the well-scrubbed top of which had as- sumed, so soft and friendly did it look, the whiteness of a pail of rich cream. On this table was a huge glass bowl filled with an immense, tightly packed mass of bluebells. The gorgeous blue- ness, a deep Prussian blue mingled with blotches of purplish colour, rose up like a thickly packed cloud of almost opaque es- sence out of this bowl of heavy-drooping blooms and expanded and expanded till its richness of tint attracted towards it and seemed utterly to absorb all other coloured things in the room. It dominated the gleam of the shining pots and pans of that small kitchen as completely as its fragrance overpowered the smell of the cooking. An empty basket with a few torn blossoms, a few long, pallid leaf-spears, and a few sap-oozing stalks, stood on the dresser, indicating that the flowers had been brought here that very morning. They had indeed been picked by Jackie and his little band in Wick Wood, and one could see that they were at their very height of blooming and would not last much longer. The children had found two or three early pink campions on the way to Wick Wood, in the leafy banks of Maidencroft Lane, and these were now protruding, like carmine flags in a purple sea, from the midst of the rest. These bluebells must have been the direct descendants of flowers that had been the background of many a Druidic May Day ritual round those great oaks. They brought with them in their oozy stalks and in their drooping heads the feeling of a thousand springs of English history. They brought too the sense of masses of hazel-branches darkly clustering around these blue spaces in the deep wood and hiding the fluttering chaffinches and blackcaps whose songs issued forth from their entanglement.

Nor had this great bunch lost that imprint of children's fingers that country people recognize so quickly—the stalks plucked off so short under the flower-heads and the blossoms pressed so tightly together! In addition to these flowers there were two girls in Miss Crow's kitchen.

The May-Day feeling in the air, the warm sunshine, the presence of such a quantity of flowers at their full height of blossom, gave to the high spirits of the girls, as they chatted volubly together, that delicious quality of young feminine life which is so fleeting and so easily destroyed. The presence of a man destroys it in a second, introducing a different element altogether. Totally unconscious of what is happening to their young bodies and souls, girls, when they are thus alone together, give themselves up to all manner of little gestures, movements, abandonments, which not only the presence of a man but the presence of an older woman would drive away. Certain filmy and delicate essences in young girls' beings come to the surface only when they are alone like this with one another. When any of them is alone by herself it is different again; for then her own thoughts are apt to play the part of intruders and cause these fragile petals of her identity to draw in and close up.

The two girls I am now speaking of were seated at the table on straw-bottomed chairs. They were Sally Jones and Tossie Stickles, the plump form of the latter enveloped in a capacious white apron, while the former wore a gay spring hat and a bright scarf round her warm young neck. The girls were sipping hot cocoa from big steaming cups, and as they chatted across the mass of bluebells the clock in St. Benignus' Church struck the hour of noon.

"Did her ladyship open the letter her own self?" enquired Sally.

" 'Twere 'dressed to her for I read the words meself as I came along. It said 'The Lady Rachel Zoyland, care of John Geard Esquire, Glastonbury, Somerset.' It didn't say our street and it didn't say our number. It said 'Esquire.' Be our Mayor really a Esquire, Tossie, do 'ee reckon, now he be a worshipful?"

"Read it? I should say her *didn't* read it," cried Tossie. "Not with Missus watching she and smiling kind-a patronizing all the while. No, Sally Jones, no, you Simple-Sal! Her took she's letter up to bedroom, same as you nor me might have done and she slammed her door and locked it too—bless her pretty heart! She be a one, she be a one, Sal, and no mistake about it."

"Have you ——" whispered Sally gravely, leaning forward, till the broad brim of her straw hat overshadowed the table.

Tossie put down her cup and nodded emphatically, her eyes gleaming. "Told she yesterday," she replied. "She were helping I in kitchen and she talked so natural-like that I just up and told her. I didn't mention no names, you understand, but I told her he weren't no marrying man nor never would be. I told her he were a gentleman; and you should have seen the face she made at that!"

"There have been a kind of a trouble, Toss, down our way," threw in Sally. "I allus knew'd 'twould never last between Red and Miss Crummie. I telled 'ee so, didn't I, time and again? Red be a working-man, though 'tis true he baint a common man. But Miss Crummie be quite different. She isn't a lady. We know *that*! But she's different from Red."

"They weren't engaged, were they?" said Tossie.

"Oh, no, it hadn't come to that yet," admitted Sal. "For me own part I think Miss Crummie was so haughty and offish with the pore man that he just up and quit."

Tossie opened her eyes wide. She felt it a little hard to visualise this haughty, obstreperous Crummie!

Both girls lifted their cups to their lips and took a deep drink. They each searched their minds for something startling to say.

Their encounter seemed an important occasion in their lives; and they were very unwilling to let it slide by unenjoyed to the full.

"Mr. Philip and Mrs. Philip be coming to tea this afternoon," announced Tossie.

"Mercy on us!" cried Sally, "and what if this letter to her Ladyship be to say that Mr. Athling be coming to see she?"

Tossie had now the opportunity she had been waiting for. She had not seemed to impress her friend sufficiently with the fact of her intimacy with Lady Rachel. It was not very surprising that she should have confessed her troubles to Rachel. But surely it must startle Sal if she revealed that Lady Rachel had mentioned Mr. Athling to *her*.

She finished her cocoa gravely, rose from her chair, prodded the potatoes with a fork, stirred the stew, and then leaning across the table smelt at the bluebells. Straightening herself up she next glanced at the door. Then she looked out of the window. Still upon her feet she stared significantly at Sally. Her expression said: "These are no light matters."

A thrush was singing in a laburnum bush at the end of the little garden. A faint scent of trodden grass from where the two cows were feeding floated in upon the warm air along with that rich song. Both the girls felt a penetrating thrill of happiness. It was May Day; and the spirit of Romance was abroad upon the air.

"He do write poetry," said Tossie in a low, awed voice. "There be too much talk in this wold town about she and him. People be awful careless the way they talk."

"Master said to Missus this morning," remarked Sally, "that he be a true-blood Saxon."

"Meaning he over to Middlezoy?" asked Tossie, sliding down upon her chair. How teasing it was when a person didn't give a person the credit for things! Why didn't Sally, instead of telling her what Mr. Geard had said to Mrs. Geard, cry out, "Oh, Tossie Stickles, how wonderful it is that Lady Rachel talks to 'ee so nice and natural!"

"Master said to Missus," continued Sally, "that Athling be the oldest name round here. He said Zoyland were nothing to it."

"His folks be plain farmer folks," protested Tossie. Then taking advantage of Sally's cup being at her lips, "He do write poetry about she."

"Did she tell you *that*?" cried Sally, really astonished at last. Tossie was abashed. The truth was that it was she herself, and not Lady Rachel, who had referred to Mr. Athling. "A little bird told I," she murmured evasively.

"Be Mr. Philip *really* coming to tea?" said Sally, beginning to feel—as she listened to that thrush—that there were too many little birds in Benedict Street. One wanted more solid facts. "It's not often, so people do say, that they Elms folk go out together."

"There was extra orders gived for they little rock cakes, to Baker, this morning," said Tossie firmly.

It was Sally's turn now to bend forward and inhale the heavy bluebell fragrance. She tilted back the big straw brim of her hat with her fingers as she did so.

"Be 'ee going to hospital when your time comes?" she murmured between her sniffs at the flowers.

"Maybe," said Tossie.

"Do they let 'ee see Mr. Barter these days?" her friend went on.

Tossie's cheeks got red. "What do I want with seeing a bloke that can keep company with they baggages at Pilgrims'."

"Lily Rogers told old Mrs. Robinson," remarked Sally, "that 'Rissa Smith were angling for Mr. Barter to marry she."

Tossie's reply to this was more expressive than polite. She put out her tongue at her friend.

"Master were all worked up this morning," said Sally, content to change the conversation now that she had made mention of Clarissa. "Mr. Philip wrote to he a turble stiff letter about his Midsummer Circus. He said he'd get the Police to stop it."

"Baint our Mayor above all they Police and suchlike?" pondered Tossie Stickles in a wistful tone. A little bell above the dresser began to tinkle.

"Missus wants summat," said the girl getting up from her chair.

Lady Rachel did not breathe a word to Miss Crow about the

contents of the letter she had received till the two ladies were
weeding side by side in the little back-garden.

"I've heard from Ned," she said quietly then, looking across
the sweet-pea sticks at her hostess.

"Yes, Rachel," replied Miss Crow.

"He's coming to tea this afternoon," said the young girl, "if
you'll let him."

"Why, my dear, that's as nice as it can be! You know I've
only seen him that once, when the Mayor asked us to meet him."

"He doesn't expect to find anybody else here," said Rachel.

"Only my nephew and Tilly," said Miss Crow, planting her
fork in the ground and resting her hand, in her rough gardening
gloves, upon its handle. The thrush had flown off into the next
little garden, but from there its voice was still audible. The
warm air smelt of the disturbed earth-mould, but it smelt too of
a more subtle odour than that—it smelt of an odour that came voyaging across the water-meadows from spinneys and copses and
withy beds and high uplands and deep lanes and sequestered
gulleys and hidden combes and narrow hazel-paths and mossy
openings in old woods—the odour of Somersetshire itself! It is
only certain days, days under unique conditions of the wind and
the weather, that call out from the soil of a particular district
that district's own native, peculiar smell. And this May Day was
precisely such an especial day. Had any traveller come back to
Glastonbury on this day he would have been aware in a second
that it was one of those days when the spirit of that portion of
the earth distils itself in a rare unique essence. And of what is
this voyaging mystery composed? Chiefly of the smell of primroses! Different from all other essences in the world the smell
of primroses has a sweetness that is faint and tremulous, and yet
possesses a sort of tragic intensity. There exists in this flower,
its soft petals, its cool, crinkled leaves, its pinkish stalk that
breaks at a touch, something which seems able to pour its whole
self into the scent it flings on the air. Other flowers have petals
that are fragrant. The primrose has something more than that.
The primrose throws its very life into this essence of itself which
travels upon the air. But the odour which floated now over that
little garden of Benedict Street and hovered about Miss Crow as

she looked at the proud timidity in those grey eyes that faced her
so steadily, at that light-poised figure gripping so tightly the long
hoe she had been using, had yet another pervading element in it
—*the scent of moss.* Not a patch of earth in any of those spinneys, and copses, and withy beds, that edged those water-
meadows, not a plank, not a post, in the sluices and weirs and
gates of those wide moors, but had its own growth, somewhere
about it, of moss "softer than sleep." More delicately, more in-
tricately fashioned than any grasses of the field, more subtle in
texture than any seaweed of the sea, more thickly woven, and
with a sort of intimate passionate patience, by the creative spirit
within it, than any forest leaves or any lichen upon any tree
trunk, this sacred moss of Somersetshire would remain as a perfectly satisfying symbol of life if all other vegetation were destroyed out of that country. There is a religious reticence in the
nature of moss. It vaunts itself not; it proclaims not its beauty;
its infinite variety of minute shapes is not apprehended until you
survey it with concentrated care. With its peculiar velvety green,
a greenness that seems to spring up like a dark froth from the
living skin pores of the earth-mother, this primeval growth covers with its shadowy texture every rock and stone and fragment
of masonry, every tree root and hovel roof and ancient boarding,
over which the rain can sweep or the dew can fall. The magical
softness of its presence gathers about the margins of every human
dream that draws its background from life in the West Country.
The memories of youth are full of it; the memories of old people
who have gone to and fro in West-Country villages wear it like
a dim, dark garment against the cold of the grave; and when
the thoughts of the bedridden turn with piteous craving to the
life outside their walls, it is upon deep, rain-soaked, wet moss,
sprinkled with red toadstools or with brown leaves or with drifting gossamer seed, that they most covetously brood!

"You know what to expect from my nephew, Rachel, because
you've seen him already," went on Miss Crow. "If he doesn't
treat our young poet with proper respect, you and I will squash
him. He's not hard to put down, as you've seen, when a woman
stands up to him."

Rachel shifted her hoe from one hand to the other and lifting

her young head, inhaled the moss-primrose odour upon those floating airs. She listened to the exultant trillings of the thrush from
the unseen bushes in the neighbouring garden.

"You are very kind to me, Miss Crow," she said.

"Oh, and I've asked the Vicar," added Miss Elizabeth apologetically. "But there's not a boy under heaven however sensitive
who could mind him. He's as easy to manage as that queer, surly
son of his you didn't like—is difficult. But even poor old Sam
is nice when you approach him in the right way."

"Your nephew won't abuse Mr. Geard, will he?" said Lady
Rachel. "Ned will be rude to him if he does. Ned likes Mr. Geard
as much as I do."

"Oh, you and I will see to that, child," laughed Miss Crow.
"We'll be three to one; for Tilly doesn't count. The Mayor will
be well championed, whatever Philip says!"

A couple of hours later and the little drawing-room facing
Benedict Street was full of a lively party drinking tea and eating
rock cakes. So strong, although so tactfully diffused, was Elizabeth Crow's protective aura, that not only were troublesome
topics warded off, but the demonic influences from the great
Powers of earth and air were prevented from touching her little
group. Miss Elizabeth Crow not only pulled green-fringed muslin curtains across the little window, but she managed somehow
to place her own substantial frame between her old friend and
his flaming enemy, so that the Vicar—who was often obscurely
worried and fretted in full sunlight—felt unusually happy that
afternoon. There was a subtle reason for his happiness, too, in
a motion of his consciousness of which he was thoroughly
ashamed although its baseness, as he knew, had the grand excuse
of so many base human feelings! Try as he might to take a
larger, more generous, less professional view of the case, he had
not been able to resist a spasm of ignoble jealous relief when
he divined, as he soon did, for he and his son were in close accord, that some new twist in the latter's eccentric mind was
keeping him apart from Nell Zoyland.

Ned Athling was certainly not the sort of youth that any ordinary girl would have fallen in love with. He was short and very
fair, so fair indeed that his eyebrows and eyelashes seemed al-

most non-existent. He was much more ruggedly built than Dave Spear, another fair Saxon, and his hands, tanned and hardened by farm-work, were as large as they were powerful. A cloud of nervous timidity seemed to hover over him like smoke over burning weeds and he had a trick of casting down his full-lidded, eyebrowless eyes when anyone addressed him and staring intently at some spot, that conveniently besought attention, in the fabric of his trousers.

The May Day sunlight, modified by the green-edged muslin curtains, filtered agreeably into the little room. There was something piquant in the way Miss Crow had arranged her old pieces of furniture in this little working-man's parlour. The eighteenth-century chairs and tables, the seventeenth-century prints, mostly of sea-faring worthies and of old maps of the West Indies inherited from a Crow who had been a Norwich merchant in Cromwell's time, gave the room a rich and intricate look. This was increased by a vast amount of old china of which Miss Crow was particularly fond and the bulk of which had come to her from a Devereux aunt, a venerable maiden lady who had lived for half a century in the same small house, at Cromer in Norfolk.

There were primroses and cowslips and even bluebells about the room, all with much more greenery among them than was possessed by Jackie's bunch in the kitchen. The muslin curtains waved gently in the air that blew in from the street, where the very dust—recently allayed by a blue-painted water-cart inscribed "Town Council"—carried into the house a curious smell that resembled rain and yet was different from rain.

Miss Elizabeth, Tilly Crow and Lady Rachel had all chosen, by that human instinct which follows the weather almost as closely as do the hedge-weeds, especially airy and light-coloured dresses. Philip himself had put on a new fawn-tinted tie which looked well upon his heather-mottled suit, while Edward Athling had a newly budded meadow-orchid in his buttonhole, the first specimen of this flower that any of the rest of them were likely to see for several weeks yet.

There was a liberal supply of thin bread and butter, and Tossie had cut it so carefully that even the lady who had Emma for a servant looked at these two great Dresden platefuls with arrested attention. But the rock cakes were the most daring innovation, most Glastonbury hostesses priding themselves upon not having to go outside their own kitchens for the replenishing of their tea-tables. This bold departure from the norm proved, however, a great success.

"No," Tilly was saying to an enquiry from Mr. Dekker about the rhubarb in her garden. "I cannot say that I like the look of it this year as much as I did last year. It is redder than last year of course. I admit that. But my cook always prefers the stalks that have green streaks mixed with the red. She says they are more succulent."

"They are not so sweet, Madam; they are not so sweet," affirmed Mat Dekker.

"But my cook has her own way of handling rhubarb," reiterated Tilly, her black eyes shining. In her mind she resolved to have a whole morning, presently, entirely devoted to making rhubarb jam. The question was what sort of brandy to use for the fastening up of the jam-pots. As she watched Mr. Dekker's watch-chain and wondered how soon a crumb of rock cake would dislodge itself from between one of its links and one of the good man's waistcoat buttons—Tilly longed to brush him then and there—she recalled how she used to stand for hours in the kitchen watching her grandmother tie up jam-pots. The smell of brandy always made her think of a certain blue apron she had liked wearing in those days, not because it made her look pretty, but because it made her look grown-up and competent. "Always use the best, Dearie," the old woman had been wont to say to her hypnotised companion. And little Tilly had vowed to herself that whatever might be her future destiny she would never use, like her slipshod mother did, in the making up of jam-pots, anything but the best brandy. And this vow Tilly had rigorously kept ever since.

"No, it wasn't exactly yellow from where I saw it."

Philip had been talking dogmatically about yesterday's weather and the timid poet had been aroused to assert himself when he heard Philip who had gone to Bath in his airplane—driven now by a pilot from London—praising the sky for its yellowness. "It was green when I saw it," he cried eagerly. "And that's by far the most beautiful kind of sky. I call it the fields of the sky."

Philip stared at the lad. He was in the middle of telling them all about his flight to Bath. The colour of the sky was of minor importance.

"What you say, young man, interests me very much," said Mr. Dekker. "Most of us don't give enough attention to these things. When I kept a diary at college ——"

"Talking of diaries," interrupted Tilly, "I wish all of you men would begin ordering diaries at Wollop's! That impertinent young man there—you know the one I mean, Aunt?— won't keep diaries. He says there's no demand for them."

Aunt Elizabeth burst into a peal of delicious silvery laughter. She did not often laugh. But when she did her laughter was like the clearest of rippling streams.

"Why are you so amused, Aunt?" enquired Tilly; but in no vexed or aggrieved voice. Now that Aunt Elizabeth had a house of her own she felt very friendly to her.

"Do you keep a diary, Tilly?" asked Miss Elizabeth.

"Oh, dear no! What do you suppose? It's for my cook. You don't know my cook, Lady Rachel. Her name is Emma."

"You don't mean to say that Emma keeps a diary?" threw in Mr. Dekker with a chuckle.

"Tilly!" The way Philip uttered these two syllables was a masterpiece in rich psychological nuances. In the first place his tone protected his wife from Aunt Elizabeth and from all these strangers. In the second place his tone warned his wife that there were proper limits to this fashion of hers of giving herself away. In the third place his tone expressed an indulgent appreciation, a tender recognition, that Tilly *was* Tilly, and that she was the kind of thing in a person's life that he himself was glad to possess; though it might seem strange, and even absurd, to others!

"No, no," said Tilly quietly, quite unperturbed at being laughed at by Emma's favourite clergyman, "she doesn't want them for *that*. She wants them to keep accounts in. The ordinary tradesmen's books don't suit Emma. She has her own ways of keeping accounts."

"My new pilot's name is Tankerville," said Philip suddenly, seeing in his mind that bird's-eye view of his Dye-Works which had made it impossible for him to be sure whether the sky was green or yellow.

In the general silence that followed this irrelevant observation Lady Rachel remarked that her father would never have a servant whose name was more than one syllable. But Philip's mind had wandered far away from Bob Tankerville. He was saying to himself, "I shan't replace Barter for a while. I shall wait a bit. Those office-lads seem able to scramble on somehow. Yes, I shall wait a little, and get a tight hand on all the reins myself. What I've got to do now is to give Geard more rope—give him all the rope he wants—while I egg him on by talk of the Law. He'll hang himself—if he has rope enough!"

"Seen any otters down your way at Middlezoy this year?" said Mr. Dekker to Ned Athling, whose shyness was so intense in this pause of the conversation he had commenced licking his lips with his tongue just as dogs do when they feel embarrassed. He now glanced quickly and nervously at Lady Rachel.

"No," he replied with a blush. "I mean," he went on, "that I wouldn't say if I had." Everyone looked at him and his colour deepened.

"Oh, I won't tell Will, Ned!" cried Rachel, reading his thoughts.

"I wasn't . . . I wasn't only thinking of *him*," he blurted out; and then, with a gallant effort to give the conversation a new turn, "I was telling the Mayor that he ought to hire a real pantomime clown for his show, and have some mummers like they did in the old days."

"He wants to keep it all for the local talent, doesn't he?" said Rachel.

"Those professionals are the best though," went on Athling, while Tilly fixed a nervous eye upon her husband. "To have a real professional, of the sort Dan Leno was, bred up in the theatre or the circus, and to let him play his part like one of those old mummers or mountebanks . . . don't you think," he spoke hesitatingly, diffidently, brokenly, "don't you think . . . there would be something . . . in that kind of thing? I haven't got

it quite clear . . . but I seem to see in my mind a sort of Passion
Play—with—" he spoke more eagerly and rapidly now, as he
warmed to the subject, "with a real pantomime clown of the
Leno tradition—improvising wild Rabelaisian 'gags' . . . like
the Fool in Lear . . . while Our Lord is before Caiaphas or before Pilate . . . don't you think there's something in that? The
Mayor caught my idea, I think—though whether——"

Philip restrained himself with creditable self-control under
this imaginative tirade. He thought in his heart—"This is the
only kind of thing our young England is interested in, and it's
absolutely futile. It's not only futile, it's destructive. A Dan
Leno introduced into a Mystery Play of the Crucifixion—that is
exactly the sort of thing that *would* appeal to this new generation! They are never happy until they've given everything—even
Religion—an uncomfortable, ironic, disillusioned twist."

Lady Rachel had been watching her friend with a mixture of
pride and bewilderment. Her nature was too direct to be altogether satisfied by something as bizarre as a modern clown at
the Crucifixion, but she liked to see Mr. Crow nonplussed and
Mr. Dekker confused. Their hostess had to come to the rescue of
her nephew.

"You've put off your spring cleaning, Tilly, I hear?" she said.

Mrs. Philip Crow fidgetted in her seat and looked reproachfully at her aunt. To interpolate a matter of such primary importance as spring cleaning into this bagatelle about clowns and
crucifixions seemed to her mind a sort of wilful outrage to the
bed-rock of human seriousness.

"Of course not," Tilly rapped out, "but Philip *may* have to
take a holiday when this troublesome strike and this tiresome
pageant are settled, and Emma and I have been thinking that the
carpets in the front-rooms had better wait until——"

Lady Rachel gave her a quick glance of appreciation. Why,
this little lady, with the beady black eyes, really *was* like a child
who had got a doll's house to play with! "I wonder," she thought,
"what she'd make of the way the Bellamys manage these things
at Mark's Court?"

Ned Athling had begun to grow very restless. He tried not to
stare reproachfully at Lady Rachel. Miss Crow's enamelled tray,

with its bowl of primroses so carefully interspersed with their heavy green leaves, was the ritual centre of this group of people. The Vicar's gold watch-chain, Philip's fawn-coloured tie, and the gay dresses of the three ladies would have lacked their mirror of platonic essences had the tray been carried off. Athling tried to concentrate his attention upon this tray.

"I sometimes think," said Mr. Dekker, "that we don't realise half enough the influence we all have upon the personality of our town. Don't you feel, Elizabeth, that Glastonbury has a most definite personality of its own?"

Ned's timid eyes under their pale eyebrows gleamed at the clergyman's words but he felt shy of asserting himself again.

"I know a place that's got twice as much of what you call personality than this town has," remarked Philip.

"Tell us!" cried Rachel. "Tell us, Mr. Crow!"

"Wookey Hole!" he announced emphatically, crossing his legs in their neat heather-tinted trousers and surveying with satisfaction his unwrinkled brown socks. "Wookey Hole has more real character in its prehistoric stalactites than all your Ruins."

In the silence that followed this remark Miss Crow, who was shepherding her little party with as much care as Emma's father in the Mendips ever guided his flock down to the washing-pool, took the opportunity of handing to Rachel and Ned a veritable May-Day nosegay. She noticed Philip turn to the Vicar and ask *him* for sympathy about Wookey Hole. She noticed that her new cat, a big stray tabby that Tossie had christened Tiger, had come in, as Tossie went out, and had jumped upon Tilly's lap. Tilly was now absorbed in this cat. She had been watching it ever since it entered, hoping against hope that she would be the preferred one in winning its favour, and now this had happened she was in bliss. So Miss Crow turned to the lovers.

"I want you to take Lady Rachel to Chalice Hill, this afternoon, Mr. Athling," she said. "There was an antiquary down here yesterday—not the one who found the Edgar Chapel by the help of that spirit, but quite a different one—and he unearthed a stone up there, somewhere to the west of the hill, so they tell me, and near Bulwarks Lane, which has completely puzzled him. You might tell me what *your* opinion of that stone is, Mr. Athling. At any rate, I'd like you to see it before you begin your long drive home. And I want you to have a bite of supper with us, too, before you start."

Rachel's cheeks flamed with pleasure at this, and Mr. Athling met his hostess' eyes without blinking and smiled with childish gratitude.

It was a shame that Tossie had left the room too soon to hear this. As it was, it had been with a deep sigh for the presence of her friend that she had returned to the kitchen without the tray. She could hardly bear to look at the bluebells on the table now, so greatly did she long to tell their absent donor all about what was going on in the drawing-room.

"You don't mind my speaking freely to you, Dekker, do you?" Philip was now saying. "But it really won't do; it simply *won't do* for you to mix yourself up, and your position and everything, with this man Geard. The man's a rascal. That's the long and short of it. He's an extremely cunning rogue and an arrant charlatan. He'd like to play the part of a sort of Abbot in this town. This Pageant of his, or pious circus, or whatever it may be, is getting to be a nuisance. *You* were saying, weren't you, Aunt Elizabeth, that you've been worried by these endless notices from that little fool, John? Geard must learn that in these days to be Mayor of a town like ours means nothing at all. This, and that money he got from my grandfather, seem to have turned his head. He's begun to encroach on *your* domain, Dekker—hasn't he?—with all these rehearsals that I hear are going on."

Lady Rachel glanced quickly at her young farmer, but it was impossible to stop him.

"I like Mr. Geard," he said, with a rush of hot blood to his face. "I think he's done a great deal for Glastonbury. I think this Pageant will bring a lot of people here." He stopped abruptly and glanced apologetically at his hostess. "From abroad," he added, "Germans especially."

Philip glanced at Tilly, but she was oblivious to everything except the cat on her lap. He then sought to exchange with Mat Dekker the particular look with which older people condone the impetuosity of youth.

"The most important thing for any town nowadays," he said

calmly, looking not at Athling but at his aunt, "is to give the populace constant employment. That is not done by Pageants. Is it, Aunt Elizabeth?"

"What about the municipal factory, Sir?" threw in young Athling.

"May I ask if you have seen that concern?" said Philip.

"Seen it? No . . . Yes . . . I mean I've been to their new shop in George Street and bought some . . . some little things."

"May we hear what things, Mr. Athling?"

"Charming things!" broke in Rachel. "I've got lots of them in my room upstairs."

"I'm glad you've found something, Lady Rachel, among their toys, that thrills you so much, but I'm afraid Mr. Dekker will agree with me that the men employed in making those toys are being rapidly unfitted for any properly paid job. They hardly give 'em enough to live upon. I expect you did not know that, Mr. Athling."

"They're going to let me design some figures for them, Mr. Crow," said Rachel irrelevantly.

"Who is?" enquired Philip.

"Mr. Barter," the girl answered.

"*Barter!*" Philip brought out these two syllables as if he had been King James referring to Guy Fawkes. "I suppose you've heard, Dekker, the inside story of that man's leaving me? It had to do with——" He stopped abruptly remembering that the victim in the story had just been handing him those rock cakes he had enjoyed so much. "Well, at all events," he went on, lowering his voice a little, out of respect to Lady Rachel if not to Tossie, "Barter, as we know him, isn't exactly the sort of person that any concern would be proud of. I've never heard, either, that he knows very much about the manufacturing of toys. You can't do these things in that sort of slipshod, amateur, arts-and-crafts way."

"Why do you say 'arts-and-crafts' so disparagingly, Sir?" threw in Edward Athling.

Elizabeth intervened. "I can explain *that*," she said. "When Philip was at Cambridge there was a lot of æsthetic tittle-tattle going on about that sort of thing. It's all very old-fashioned! You two children are too young to understand the point."

"I can understand that Mr. Crow, being a manufacturer of machine-made articles, naturally has a dislike of hand-made things," said Edward Athling, getting very red.

"Just as a farmer," remarked Philip sternly, "naturally has a dislike of townspeople getting high wages."

"What about this strike in the Dye-Works then? Isn't that for better wages?" The young man had scarcely uttered these impetuous words than he gave a curious kind of laugh and stretched out his hand to Philip, touching his sleeve. "Sorry, Sir," he said. "That was an impertinent thing to say. I'm enough of a farmer to hate the way we ignoramuses rush into arguments. No doubt there's a lot to be said for your ideas of industry as something that gives the people steady employment, rather than just a dramatic adventure for the moment."

"But the municipal factory is sure to last, isn't it?" insisted Rachel, noticing how stiff Philip was in the way he received Ned's gesture and feeling angry with Ned for making it.

Philip shrugged his shoulders in silence. "What I feel in all this," said Mat Dekker, "is that Glastonbury needs both its scientific manufacturer and its dramatic Mayor." Mat Dekker was so happy at this moment, being at once pampered by his ancient love and jealously pleased that his son was separated from Zoyland's wife, that he uttered this peaceful remark with a certain careless unction, without thinking very much what he was saying.

Lady Rachel looked at him with flashing eyes. That smug antithesis—"its scientific manufacturer and dramatic Mayor"—filled her with contempt.

Simple earthy natures like Mat Dekker, especially when they have, by luck, found themselves in a social position which cannot easily be menaced, frequently allow themselves to be dominated by their physical moods. When Mr. Dekker on this occasion threw out that smug remark about "scientific manufacturers and dramatic Mayors" it was in reality no more than if he had said—"It is May Day. I enjoy rock cakes. I am glad that my unaccountable desire for Nell Zoyland has been quieted by Sam's separation from her. I like being petted once more by

dear old Elizabeth. It's nice here, now that she has shut the
sun out." Nothing that was being talked about just then touched
—for Mat Dekker—the real essential things in life. He did not,
in his heart of hearts, think that it mattered very greatly to Glastonbury, or to any immortal soul in Glastonbury, whether it were
Mr. Crow or Mr. Geard who was cock of the dung-hill! And since
this was the case, it was easy for him, treating Philip as he
would have treated a greedy minnow in his aquarium, to give the
man a soothing sop with the surface of his mind, and push the
whole thing away from him as unimportant. But how was Lady
Rachel, trembling with eager excitement in the presence of her
first love and full of the intense partisanship of youth, to be tol-
erant of a hard-working priest's mental indolence? All that
afternoon, as she had surveyed this big red-faced personage
drinking so much tea and letting himself be waited upon by a
gentle, elderly lady, she had suspected him of being a repulsive
time-server and now she knew him for just that.

But Miss Elizabeth Crow was not one to be baffled by any
clash of temperament among her guests or by anything as negligible as a flash of anger on the part of the excitable little
daughter of Lord P. By the time her elder guests had departed
she had beguiled them all into good temper. Indeed, both the
young people were found making Tilly laugh with girlish delight
by their antics with Tiger in the sunny doorway, when Elizabeth
had finished saying good-bye to her other guests.

When Rachel and Ned Athling had reached the top of Chalice
Hill they spent a happy quarter of an hour hunting about for
that stone of which they had been told. At last, not greatly worried because they had not yet found it, they sat down together
on a fallen log with the greenest of new-grown ferns and bracken
at their feet and a sweet-smelling gorse bush behind them.

"Do you believe it was really here," said Rachel, "that Merlin
disappeared with the Grail?"

Ned did not reply for a second or two. Then he burst out irrelevantly—"You're like an Exmoor pony, Rachel, that's what
you're like."

"He wasn't a Christian,—was he, Ned? Merlin I mean. What
was the Grail to *him*? That's what I can't imagine."

"Rachel!"

"Yes, Ned."

"Did you have a fear when you were little that you'd never meet anyone as exciting as the people in books?"

"Oh, Ned, how curious! How like we are! That's just what I always felt." She picked a cowslip within reach of her arm and gave it to him. He smelt at it and held it tight between his finger and thumb, waiting to hide it away in his pocket as soon as her attention wandered.

"May I ask you something, Ned?" was her next speech.

"If it's not about poetry, Rachel. Since I've known you I've been changing my ideas about what poetry is and it's got all confused."

"No, it's nothing about poetry, it's ——"

"Well, what is it, Rachel?"

"It's about people, one's own people. Don't you sometimes feel as if you were a changeling? Don't you sometimes feel that when your own people are talking and telling you this and that —quite ordinary things—that you're all the time living in a different world? I don't mean exactly a different *place*. The same place, only seen in quite a different way?"

"It's in that different way I've seen everything, Rachel, since I've known you. My horses, my cattle, my sheep, aren't the same creatures that they used to be. Of course those fields, down our way at Middlezoy, *look* the same as they always did but they look *more* the same, if you know what I mean. I mean I never knew before how different they are from all other fields and how much like themselves!"

"Could you ever endure to live anywhere else, Ned, than at Middlezoy?"

"I used to think I couldn't; but *now*—" he paused and plucked at the fern-like leaves of an incipient yarrow, "I believe I could live almost anywhere if I were absolutely sure of one thing."

She refrained from pressing him as to what that "one thing" was.

"I suppose you've sunk your soul into those fields at Middlezoy!"

"Well, even if I *have*, I could pull my soul out again, couldn't I, like anyone might pull out a deep thorn?"

"I didn't want you to say you could. I wanted you to say you couldn't."

The log they were seated upon was not large enough for any space to exist between them. At those moments in the conversation when one or other of them would naturally have indicated a psychic misunderstanding by a physical withdrawal, all they could do was to move their knees or their feet a trifle further away from those of the other. The girl shifted her legs a little now and in this slight movement the profile of her cheek was turned. Ned snatched the opportunity and slipped the cowslip into his waistcoat pocket.

The magic of that moment, the scent of the primroses and the damp moss, the tremulous ecstasy of the birds and insects, the unusual greenness that washed up against their feet like a wave of the primal sap of creation, covered them now as a couple of early violets might be covered, by lush transparent overgrowths that guard and enhance their poignant breath.

"If you and I were ever, by any chance, to marry, Ned, should we live at Middlezoy?"

"*Would* you marry me, Rachel?"

"I *might*, Ned. But you mustn't take this as a promise! Besides, what am I saying? I am acting as forwardly as Juliet did! But we must see each other a lot more, lots and lots more, before we can know for certain that we dare do it."

Edward Athling sighed deeply, a profound sadness took the place of the excitement he had just felt. The way she'd spoken—though anything but frivolous—had not been exactly the kind of ambrosial food that a lover demands.

"Don't get glum, Ned. Let's pretend! *Would* we live at Middlezoy?"

"What do you mean?" he asked. "With my parents?"

She didn't like to tell him—for fear of hurting his feelings—that that had *not* been her dream. Her dream included a thatched cottage at Middlezoy down close by one of those great rhynes where the otters were found.

But she now plunged boldly on—"With them for a while,

Ned, perhaps, till we had money enough to have a farm of our own."

A farm of their own! This phrase of hers was so delicious, so filled with a floating incense of enchantment, that for a second he dallied with it as if it were serious.

But it was *not* serious; none of it was serious! He had against him before he could marry the daughter of the great Wessex nobleman such a solid weight of conventional obstacles that it seemed madness to think about it. Noblemen's daughters *had* married commoners before now, but not often—and as far as all accounts went—never a Zoyland! He wasn't an adventurer, he wasn't a rascally pilgarlic like one of those lean rogues lambasted in Rabelais who set their scurvy wits to deface, deflower, debauch and abduct, some sweet-blooded noble wench of an ancient breed.

"It would only be for a time," she began again, "that I'd have to live with your people. We should soon be able to find a place, somewhere *near* Middlezoy anyhow, with a few acres that would suit us."

"Oh, please stop, Rachel! Please stop!" His voice was really tormented and the girl looked at him in astonishment. "You simply *don't know* what you're talking about," he went on irritably. "It's impossible to imagine—for one second—your living with my parents; impossible, I tell you; impossible!"

"I don't understand you," she said. "Oh, well! Anyhow we haven't to consider it just yet. We'll have many a lovely time together, Ned—before we *have* to consider it. So don't look so sad!" But she herself sighed long and deep, as she looked across at Glastonbury Tor.

Ned moved now. He had been vaguely conscious for several minutes that every time he leaned back his shoulders encountered the prickles of the gorse bush under which lay their log. It occurred to him that his companion, whose clothes were thinner than his, might be suffering from these gorse prickles. He twisted his head round, yes! they must be pricking her shoulders! He jumped up and pulled her to her feet with him.

"Too near the gorse," he murmured. He had only grasped her arm, but his touch sent an electric vibration through her, a quivering like that which sometimes seizes upon one single tree-twig when everything else is still.

"I wonder how long it's been lying there," she said. "It's very old."

Both the young people gazed down at their recent seat. The log was certainly very old. Neither of them could tell what sort of a tree it had once been, or even if it had once grown near where it lay. It was covered with dark moss and grey lichen, and at one end of it was a cluster of little yellowish toadstools.

"It may have been here hundreds of years," she whispered. A rush of thoughts, vague and indistinct, but full of a curious pleasure, floated through her mind. How many people, old and young, must have passed this way and glanced at that old log—long before she was born! A sense of the wistful and terrible beauty of life took possession of her—especially of life lived long and quietly in one place.

"I'd like to grow slowly old, day by day, very gradually, older and older," she said.

Ned looked at her with his forehead gathered in great puckers. She looked incredibly childish in her long straight dress and black straw hat.

"I suppose you never know what you mightn't find buried on this hill," he said. "I am glad the Mayor's going to buy the house where the red spring is and build an arch. He talked a lot to me, when you were gone last time, about an arch. He's got into his head that a Saxon arch would be the thing, but someone, the Vicar I think, had told him there weren't such things as Saxon arches."

"I hate that Vicar," said the girl fiercely.

"Oh, come now, Rachel! He's not a bad old codger. He told me, as we were going out of the house, that he collected butterflies."

"Just what he *would* do!" cried Lady Rachel. "Think of killing a thing like that!" And she pointed to a somnolent Meadow Brown that was fluttering over the green bracken.

"I used to collect butterflies when I was young," said Athling gravely.

"All the more shame to you!" She longed to scold him, to

agitate him, to make him feel troubled in his mind. Not necessarily about butterflies—about anything! The sun, slanting now from the west, was drawing out every kind of fragrance from that hill-slope, but the wandering airs that stirred the curls under her hat were full of the scent of primroses and moss. Bees kept flying by them; and every now and then a great blue-bottle fly drummed past their ears, with that peculiar come-and-gone quiver of tiny wings that holds a whole summer in its sound.

"I sometimes feel," he said, with an evident struggle in his mind to tell her something that was hard to express, "that it's a weakness of mine to go on writing poetry about what I enjoy and what is so easy to describe. New forms are coming into art, drawn from inventions and machinery,—well! you know more about that than I do, having been to Paris and so on—and drawn too, anyone can see, from the life of people in masses, working people in masses; and I sometimes feel as if there were something babyish in going on with the old country themes, with the old love and death themes, when the other arts are following the new way."

He had given her her opportunity! With burning cheeks and gesticulating hands, she freely attacked him now, all the stirrings of her love transferred to her argument.

"It's pure snobbishness, what you're talking about," she cried. "You say to yourself, 'I must be modern,' when you ought only to say, 'I want to find out how to express what I feel.'"

He looked at her gravely. "But isn't it important to keep in touch with the World-Spirit? I feel somehow, Rachel, as if all these Grail stories, all this mediæval mysticism, had grown tiresome and antiquated."

"You'd better ask Philip Crow to give you a ride in his airplane!" Her voice was quivering. Had she come down here from listening to all this talk in London only to find her Ned repeating it?

"You'd better go over to Wookey Hole and see the remarkable electricity they've installed there. And if you're interested in machines there are some fine up-to-date ones in Crow's Dye-Works! You'd better go to Philip Crow and tell him how impressed you are by his great industrial undertaking!"

"What has made you so angry with me, Lady Rachel? What have I done? It was since I've known you that I've grown dissatisfied with my poetry, so full of all the old tags; it's since I've known you that I've wanted to make it more original, more subtle, more in line with our times!"

Her face was a picture to see, as she struggled with her contending feelings.

"I don't want you to alter at all; not in anything!" she cried.

"I wish you hadn't made me talk about my poetry," he said. "I had a feeling it would annoy you."

"It hasn't *annoyed* me! Only standing on this hill where Merlin was and everything—I feel as if you were taking the wrong turn. You spoke up so splendidly for Mr. Geard just now in that house and now you seem to be taking the other side."

"What's poetry got to do with taking sides? Poetry is an art."

"Oh, don't use that word, Ned! If you'd heard what I've heard—the talk—the affectations—the boredom——"

"But isn't it an art?"

Her reply was almost screamed at him.

"No! It *isn't*! It's Poetry. Poetry's something entirely different. Oh, I *know* I'm right, Ned! If you go and get hold of this horrible modern idea that poetry is an art, I don't know what——" She stopped and clasped her hands behind her back.

"Well, anyway, Lady Rachel," he said, "it has nothing to do with this Glastonbury quarrel between Geard and Crow."

"It *has*. It has everything to do with it! Can't you feel, Ned, as we stand here that this place is magical? What's Poetry if it isn't something that has to fight for the unseen against the seen, for the dead against the living, for the mysterious against the obvious? Poetry always takes sides. It's the only Lost Cause we've got left! It fights for the . . . for the . . . for the Impossible!"

Young Athling answered in a mumbling, muttering voice. He stooped down and picking up a bent stick that lay on the grass, flicked his boots with it. "It was meeting you that started me thinking of these things; and now you go and ride over me. I tell you, Lady Rachel——"

"Don't be silly. Call me Rachel!"

"I tell you," he went on, "I want my poetry to be a new, living, original thing. I *want* it to deal with machinery and inventions! It's all very well"—he kept flicking his ankles harder and harder with the stick he had picked up—"to go on writing about Middlezoy hedges and ditches and Sedgemoor tombstones, but I want my writing to flow forward, where life is flowing."

The girl's face grew stern and very sad. Not realising what he was doing to her, young Athling had outraged something in her that was almost as deep as her love for him, that was indeed mingled with her love for him, and was one of the causes of it.

"Ned, listen to me," she said. "I've heard all about this quarrel between Mr. Geard and Mr. Crow. It's been mounting up and mounting up till it's become, like the Montagus and Capulets, something you can't escape from. If you and I are to go on seeing each other we must agree about this. It's . . . it's dangerous not to agree about it." She uttered these last words in a low solemn tone.

Ned Athling looked at her in bewildered astonishment. To his mind it was simply unbelievable that she should take seriously— even to the point of quarreling with him—these ridiculous local politics of Glastonbury. He did not realise how deep in her inherited Zoyland blood the passion for causes and statecraft and for all the transactions in what is called History went. He suddenly felt that it was incumbent upon him, at all costs, to change their topic of discourse. She herself had called it "dangerous" and it evidently *was* dangerous. He looked down at their log. It was not only invaded by the gorse prickles, but it was now covered by the shadow of the gorse bush.

"Do you say I could lift that log," he said, "or do you say I couldn't?"

"I say you *mustn't*, because it's been there so long, Ned, and has all those funguses on it!" But she now gave him the first smile he had had since they got up from their seat on that log. He threw away the stick he had picked up and his cap after it. He bent down and handled the log, tugging at it first in one direction and then in the other. It only moved a few inches. It was deeply buried in the grass and hundreds of infinitesimal weeds grew at its sides. He knelt down, the better to get purchase, and tugged at it. It moved a few inches and then fell back into its bed of a hundred years.

"You can't, Ned! It's silly to try to do something that you can't do. Let the old thing alone, please, Ned . . . please . . . I ask you to!"

But he did not heed her. He now straddled across the log and, bending low down, his feet planted deep upon the grass, he folded his hands under one end of the thing, slipping his fingers carefully through the weeds so as not to disturb the toadstools, scratching his knuckles on various little roots, but at last getting a really strong hold upon it.

The girl was watching him now with rivetted attention. Her hands hanging loose at her sides, began plucking nervously at her belt, and with one of her feet she tapped at the ground. Athling possessed the muscles of a farm-labourer. All his life, since he had revolted at leaving home and had only gone to a dame's school in a neighbouring village, he had done heavy manual labour; but he now tugged and strained at this wayward enterprise to no avail. All he could do was just to tilt up the end of the log about half an inch. But he had not *yet* made full use of his shoulders or of the muscles of his flanks. Drawing a deep breath and balancing his feet firmly on each side of the log he grappled with it again. It began to move. It moved. No! Settling itself down again with a weight of gravitation that seemed abnormal, and as it were intentional, the log slipped from his hands and subsiding into its former position lay there inert, motionless, triumphant. *He had failed.*

"Don't 'ee mind, Ned." cried the girl, coming towards him and touching his shoulder with her bare hand. That touch was, as it were, the sweet accolade of the defeated! It was the first time in their experience of each other that she had made such a gesture, and at a good moment did she make it now.

"Avanti!" she said, "we must hunt for that stone! Soon we shall be late for Miss Crow's supper."

Not a word did he speak as he walked by her side across the hill. Humiliation gnawed at his midriff like a rat at a thick sweet-smelling board in an old barn.

She was nice about it. She had said, "Don't 'ee mind, Ned"—

and had touched him with her hand; but it was not her *pity*
he wanted; he wanted her admiration; he wanted her respect;
he wanted her hero-worship.

"It'll be a shame to keep Tossie waiting," she said suddenly.
"But listen; if we didn't bother about the stone any more we
could go round by the Two Oaks. There'll be plenty of time, if
we go back by Bove Town and straight down High Street. Oh,
let's do that, Ned."

At this point, while several invisible blackbirds were answering one another from the purple distance, Lady Rachel offered
the boy her hand.

"Let's run down," she whispered.

Athling proved to be more skilful in guiding a girl past
mole-hills and rabbit-holes, as they stumbled down that uneven
slope, than he had been at lifting logs for her sake. Their speed
gathered and gathered till they were racing with dangerous rapidity through bracken and bent, past thorn bushes and gorse
thickets, over elm stumps, under red-barked Scotch firs, by little
clumps of elder, mingled with holly. He guided her so well that
they reached the bottom without mishap.

"Let's go to the Oaks before we hit the road," she whispered,
slipping her warm ungloved hand out of his and shaking the
seeds and straws from her skirt.

He would have gone further than to the Oaks "before they
hit the road" if it meant the prolonging of their day. That holding her hand had given him such oblivious satisfaction that all
he wanted now was to remain at her side and forget both grass-
grown logs and Ambrosianus Merlinus.

"Oh, there are *people* there!" cried Rachel, "what a pity!
Well, we'll go straight to the road now and get home. We should
probably have made ourselves late if we'd gone down there."

The "people" Lady Rachel had seen were, as a matter of fact,
none other than Sam and Nell.

Will Zoyland had been warned of a crowd of sightseers expected at Wookey on this May Day, though it was no official
holiday, so he had written to Nell putting off a visit home which
he had proposed to make. Nell had promptly communicated
with Sam and they had arranged a meeting at this spot. Nell

had only just this moment arrived. Had Athling and Rachel scrambled down the hill five minutes sooner they would have found only Sam there.

"Dear Sam, oh, my dear Sam," the girl was saying now. "I *had* to see you again because I must have given you a wrong impression when I came over yesterday. I didn't mean to worry you, Sam, or cling to you when you don't want me, but when you've given a person a wrong impression you feel you have to do something. I couldn't sleep last night with thinking what I'd said. It was wrong of me to get so angry and to say all those wild things. I didn't *really* mean what I said, you know, Sam. A person can say things like that without really meaning them."

Sam took her hand and lifting it to his mouth, kissed it long and hungrily. He had made a rule for himself that he mustn't kiss her on the lips. "I was thinking about you all last night, Nell," he said, "I couldn't sleep till dawn. There's a great deal I want to tell you about."

"Were you really thinking of me, Sam? Oh, Sam," and a look of wild hope came into her eyes, "were you thinking that perhaps ——"

"Let's find some place to sit down," he said. "There's a cowshed back there, half full of hay. I noticed it as I came along. Let's go and sit in there for a bit. I mustn't smoke there—that's the only thing—but that doesn't matter."

The look of hope that had come into Nell's face vanished. There was nothing in his tone to suggest any change of purpose. But she let him lead her along the lane. He led her in the opposite direction from that Wick Wood where Jackie and his band had picked the bluebells and into which she had herself gazed this afternoon as she skirted it in her walk to this spot.

He led her to a gap in the hedge through which it was possible to reach a large field that was lying fallow. Across this field he led her, their shadows making long monumental outlines that were scarcely human as the rays of the sinking sun fell on their backs. These two vast shadows moved in front and Nell and Sam followed behind. It was a silent procession in that isolated field full of so much old corn stubble and so many small green weeds; for the two inhuman shadows spoke not nor made any sign and the two solid figures behind them were also silent. The shadows were, however, luckier than the figures, for they had the power of overlapping with each other and merging and mixing with each other, so that they frequently lost themselves in each other. This desirable power was denied the human figures who now followed after them, silent, solemn and tragic,— two Solids following two Shadows across the dead stubble and the green weeds.

Nell felt a spasm of bitter sadness as she watched these elongated shadows intermingling in front of them and then separating again and growing distinct. All over this part of the country, she thought, there are shadows accompanying people, some of them in front, some of them behind. And their appearance is the same whatever is going on in the hearts of the figures that throw them. People going to be executed, people going to deathbeds, people going to bury their dead—their shadows look the same. Shadows, thought Nell, have no hearts. Shadows are like men who have decided to follow Christ and to leave their loves and their loves' children!

He led her into that cowshed which he knew of. Yes! it was, as he had said, half full of last year's hay. He made her sit down on a heap of loose hay with her back to more hay tied in bundles, and he himself sat down by her side. They remained silent for a minute or two, and then, with an instinct to put off their serious talk, he began telling her of various occurrences in town. He told her that there were rumours that Philip Crow was trying to obtain some legal injunction to stop Mr. Geard's Midsummer Pageant. He told her that there had been a fierce quarrel at the new Municipal Factory between Mr. Barter and some of the Communists, led by Red Robinson.

Nell's heart sank lower and lower as she listened to him. "How can he? Oh, how *can* he?" she thought. "He isn't a cruel man—he isn't doing it to hurt me. How *can* he take me into this place and then talk like this?"

The field they had crossed, with the wide horizon behind it, and with Brent Knoll rising in the distance out of the northwest, was framed in the oblong doorway of the shed. The framing turned the scene they now looked upon into a curious "work of

art," isolating it from the rest of Nature, and giving it a symbolic significance. The sun was now almost gone. It had become
a red, globular excrescence on the horizon. It resembled a Glastonbury Tor from which St. Michael's Tower had been cut by
some celestial sword-stroke, soaking the hill with blood redder
than human blood. Slowly this bleeding convexity sank down
over the edge of the horizon. Apparently it sank into Bridgewater Bay, into the Bristol Channel, into that South Wales from
which came Mr. Evans, Mrs. Geard, and the "foreign" stones of
Stonehenge; but at any rate it no longer occupied the central
position in that arbitrary picture produced by the door-frame of
the cowshed. Brent Knoll, however, still remained—remained
till the twilight mists arose out of the watery flats of Weston-
super-mare and hid it, and the horizon with it, from the eyes of
Nell and Sam.

"Sam, I *must* talk to you about it; I must; I have to. Sam,
you can't really mean to go on with your life in Glastonbury as
if we had never met—as if we didn't belong to each other—as if
we hadn't got . . . now . . . a new life . . . to think about, to
consider, to ——"

"Dearest, listen—listen to me!" he interrupted. "I've been
thinking all the time . . . all last night I was thinking . . . till
I couldn't think any more . . . of some way . . . of something
I could do . . . of something we both could do. I know I can't
make you feel, as I feel it, this—this struggle of mine . . . but
I've come to see . . . in the last few days . . . that I've shirked
something . . . in us . . . in our feeling for each other . . . in
the child."

It was already too obscure in that shed, as they faced a long
jagged blood-line in the west fading slowly out, the last of the
May-Day journey-prints of the sun, for him to see the faint
flickering up of a tantalised hope that these words of his summoned into her face.

"I must confess to you something, Nell, though it's to my
shame. Penny Pitches, our servant, my old nurse and foster-
mother, followed me up to my bedroom last night and talked
about you."

He had the wit to feel that Nell winced at this and he hurriedly added—"You mustn't mind, dearest. I'm only telling you this because I want you to know the very worst of me. It's a penance to *me* to speak of it. But I can't bear ———"

"Sam!" She was sitting very straight up now by his side. He could not see her face but he felt the indignant tension of her nerves. "Sam, it's like this. I can put up with what you do to me, and make me bear, when you do it from your own self. But to have to listen—no! you *must* hear me out!—to have to listen to what other women think, of the way you're treating me, it's too much!"

"Little Nell"—he spoke with a vibrancy in his voice that was new to her in him and that awed her a little—"I've come to see that there *is* something queer about me . . . that I didn't realise. I've come to see that I *have* thought only of my own feelings and *have* been stupid and blind to yours. I've come to see that in the whole thing there's been a lack in me . . . I don't know how to say it . . . a lack of power to see things, as they appear—as they *are*—to others . . . to you. As I lay thinking about it all last night—after Penny had gone away—I felt as if I could see myself as I never have done before. My cowardice . . . my weakness . . . seemed to—I don't know how to put it!—seemed to take an actual shape in the darkness! I shall never forget it. The darkness glittered all about me. It was phosphorescent. Spurts and splashes of light, shootings and jettings of light and there I was in the middle of it . . . like a great black slug. It wasn't a nightmare, for I was absolutely wide-awake; I wasn't even sleepy. But I suddenly knew, when I felt myself to be that black slug, that I was grosser than other human beings. I knew that I had a dead nerve . . . an atrophied nerve . . . in me . . . where certain feelings ought to be."

He stretched himself out by her side and shifted into a more comfortable position. He mechanically took a packet of cigarettes from his pocket, fumbled with them, remembered that he mustn't smoke, and put them back again.

"I mean by a dead nerve that there are feelings in human beings which save them from acting in a certain way and from doing certain things . . . and that this nerve has never been touched in me. I knew when I became that slug in the middle of those phosphorescent lights that in the way I'd acted to you I'd behaved blindly, monstrously—without using that nerve!"

He could not have realised how intently her eyes were fixed on him. He could not have realised how her mouth was drawn down and hanging open; how her lower lip was pulled awry, just as if it were imitating in unconscious sympathy the way his own face worked!

But he went on as if she had been some exterior conscience that he was talking to, some conscience to whom he had to confess everything, everything! "It gave me a sudden shock of fear, of ghastly fear, when I realised that I lacked that human nerve which everyone else has. I was afraid of myself, Nell. It was as if I had put my hand to my back and suddenly found that I was growing a tail! It was as if I had looked into the looking-glass, and seen, not my own face, but the face of a beast. I felt alone and set apart, as if I were a pariah, a leper, a half-man."

"Oh, Sam, my dear love, my poor, sweet Sam, come back to me and let me love you again!"

Any onlooker at this scene catching the emotion in her voice would have supposed that he would turn to her now and press her to his heart. He did not do anything of the kind—he went on talking, but he laid his hand on her wrist as it rested in the hay and gripped it tight.

"I loathed myself when I saw how blind I'd been about it all . . . about you and about our child . . . and everything. I tried to think out what *kind* of a lack it is in me that makes me so that I can't go straight off with you and leave Glastonbury. For I can't do it, my sweet! I thought of doing it last night just before dawn, hours after Penny had gone away. I thought of making Father give me money, and taking the train with you to London. I imagined us getting into the train. I could even see how that little shanty would look, as the train pulled out, where John Crow works! But when I thought of it I knew—all in a moment—that I couldn't do it. I grew cold and paralysed, like in dreams, when I took the first step . . . but I want to tell you this, Nell,"—his voice dropped to a solemn whisper—"when I thought of us getting into the train *I thought of us as three.* So you see, though I haven't got that 'nerve' I've got something. Oh,

Nell, I've been so unhappy these last days! I don't know why
I tell you. What's the use of telling you—you who have to bear
it all? But I've been more unhappy than I thought I *could* be.
I've been torn in two between you and Christ and it's made me
very unhappy. I knew I'd have to bear a lot for Him, if I let
Him take me, but I never thought it would be anything like this."

"My poor, sweet Sam, come back to me!" the girl whispered,
cuddling close up to him in the hay and clinging to his elbow.

"I can't, Nell," he groaned, "I can't. Christ has got me by
the throat, by the hair of my head. If you made me come to you
tonight He would pull me back to Him. I can't escape from
Him! He's going to hold me tighter and tighter all my life."
Sam shuddered as he uttered these words. With the warmth of
her body against his as they lay side by side in the soft hay, his
nature was so stirred within him that a blasphemous fury seized
him with the Being who was causing him and his love so much
suffering.

"No! He's got me, my darling, my sweet, my only love. He's
got me and there's no help for it."

"Sam, stop! I can't *let* you talk like this! It's the Devil you're
talking about, not Christ! Christ would never want to separate
people who love each other as we do."

Sam tore himself from her embrace and scrambled up upon
his feet. She saw him outlined dark against the doorway. His figure seemed to contort and to twist, as with frightened eyes she
stared at him. "Never want to separate us! You don't know Him,
Nell. He's a lover, I tell you—a lover . . . a lover!" He almost
shouted these words at her as she lay there on the ground. Then
he swung round and stood in the doorway.

The evening of this perfect May Day was of a loveliness comparable with the hours that had preceded it. In certain subtle respects it was even more beautiful, just as in certain ways sleep
is more beautiful than waking and death than life. But into the
loveliness of this evening Sam Dekker poured the bitterness of
his heart. He beat his hands on his head and then stretched out
his arms with his fists clenched.

"A lover . . . that's what you are, . . . a lover . . . a cruel
lover!" Nell was not a particularly nervous girl. She took Sam's

excitement for a sort of religious madness—as it very likely may have been—but she felt vibrant concern for him. In fact, she forgot for the moment the brutality of his desertion of her in her anxiety for him. He could not have selected a better psychological trick in order to make his treatment of her tolerable, and it may well be—such is the labyrinthine subtlety of the human mind—that mingled with the genuine anguish of his frustrated passion there was a thin thread of awareness in him that to simulate more than he actually felt was the best way of distracting her from her own suffering.

Beyond the dark figure of her equivocal lover, leaning sullenly now against one of the doorposts of their shed, she caught sight of the evening star. This luminous planet hung low above the place where the sun had sunk; and as when her love was first menaced by Zoyland's outburst, on the evening when father and son had come to Whitelake, this planet had cast its spell upon her, so now once more this great Being, the one which, after the Sun and the Moon, holds the highest place among the heavenly bodies, dominated her troubled consciousness and held her attention; until she was aware of a sort of comfort coming from its beauty as it floated there in that greenish-coloured ocean of space. But although she knew it not, and in all likelihood, the great planet knew it not, there flowed forth from that swimmer in that far-off greenish sea a magical influence which soothed the girl as soon as it touched her, and brought her a faint return of hope. After the Sun and the Moon, but a long way before the other lords of the sky, whether planets or constellations, this great luminary, either as Evening Star or as Morning Star, has gathered to itself the worship of the generations. Feeling its power upon her now, though not knowing what it was she was feeling, Nell got up from her hay couch, brushed her clothes mechanically and came over to where Sam was. There they stood together staring at the dying glow in that greenish sky and at the increasing size and brilliance of that solitary star.

She put her hand on his shoulder and he let it remain there. The evening itself gathered them into its own universal and primordial sadness—the sadness of all lost chances and lost causes since history began. Under the power of that moment, of the slow dying of that unequalled day, these two and their child within her did indeed become a conscious three as he had imagined. But the third was more than a child. The liquid immensity of that hushed twilight enlarged that little embryonic identity into something over-shadowing and mysterious, something that became the premonitory presence of that unknown future which was before them both. On its soft muffled wings this embodiment of their fate flew across their vision, its silent flight pressing down still more, like the fall of a handful of feathers from the brooding breast of the night itself, the lowered pulse of the earth's huge swing into darkness.

There came over Nell's mind the slow, faint intimation that it would be useless to struggle any more to bind Sam to her side. As she leaned against his shoulder now in her tragic acquiescence she felt that this was the moment in her life when she must gather her forces together and accept her destiny, struggle no more against it but adjust herself to it as best she might. Always would she love this strange man by her side, so much older in his troubled thoughts than he was in inexperienced years. But her love must accept the hint of this largely expanded, fragrant twilight, darkening slowly, tenderly, solemnly befoie her eyes, smelling vaguely of primroses and moss.

"Sam!" she whispered softly.

He turned his discomforted face towards her, and she seemed in that obscure light to detect upon it a pitiful appeal to her that she should have mercy upon him and not drive him to desperation; not compel him to struggle to do what it was beyond his nature to do.

"Sam," she repeated. "You shall do exactly what you want. Oh, my darling, oh, my poor Sam! It's more than I can bear to see you so troubled. Our love has been very sweet to me,"—her voice trembled a little but it did not break—"but it must accept what has come to it; and so it *shall* be. You have changed my life. In my heart I shall be always yours and never anyone else's."

He made no answer but she heard him swallow down a queer sort of half-animal sob.

MAT DEKKER WAS RIGHT WHEN HE SAID THAT A TOWN WHICH has had so long an historic continuity as Glastonbury acquires a personality of its own. And just as in human organisms there are slowly developed changes, sometimes maladies, sometimes regenerations, which take place under the surface and then at a crisis burst out into prominence, so does it happen with any community as old and intricate as this one. Individual agencies help to bring about these upheavals, but the preparation for them is a long, silent, hidden growth, subject quite as much to the influence of non-human forces as to the will of humanity.

Old Dr. Fell and his sister Barbara were to dine at Abbey House one day early in June—to be exact on June the Second— and when this day came there was the usual fuss and stir all over the rambling, untidy dwelling where for some fifty years the brother and sister had lived at the corner of Northload Street and Manor House Road. Though the Fells had lived here so long it was notorious that their successive batches of maids only stayed with them for very limited periods, such was the cantankerous and testy disposition of Miss Barbara Fell. Thus when any day arrived for a real dining out, and this came only some half a dozen times a year, the Doctor's best dress-tie and Miss Barbara's best piece of black lace, and sometimes even her tiger-claw brooch set in opals, were apt to be in the wrong drawer or in the wrong chest of drawers. Dr. Fell took the precaution on this occasion of being dressed a complete hour before it was necessary. He had learned by bitter experience that it was advisable that the dressing difficulties of the two of them should not occur simultaneously! Dr. Fell in this crafty manner took upon himself to outwit the malevolence of Hobbididance, the Demon of curst households. And so now he sat in his receiving room awaiting the forward-glide of events and reading the Enchiridion of Epictetus. Dr. Fell was not unaware that he lived in a town which had a very ancient Christian Church. He had indeed only to ascend the eastern slope of Wirral Hill to discover, set up by the Town Council, when Wollop's predecessor was Mayor, a handsomely inscribed marble slab upon which was recorded the fact that, thirty-one years after the Death of our Saviour, Joseph of Arimathea brought His Blood to this spot. Dr. Fell was also in a position to discover in the guide-books the fact that not only was the church in his town the oldest church, Orbis Terrarum, in the whole earth, but that this fact had been sustained against rival churches at the Council of Pisa in 1409, at the Council of Constance in 1417, at the Council of Siena in 1424, and at the Council of Basle in 1434, establishing beyond refutation that Glastonbury possessed a church that had been founded *statim post passionem Christi*—"immediately after the Passion of Christ." Nevertheless although he denied not that he lived in a town where perhaps an altar still existed that had been used in the original wattle-edifice, built by one who had touched the flesh of the Man-God, Dr. Fell was not a Christian. He was, on the contrary, a Stoic, and when he was not reading for the thousandth time the sturdy *logoi* of the stoical slave, he was reading for the hundredth time the wistful meditations of the stoical Emperor.

"Manny! Manny!" It was Barbara's voice ringing through the house. *He* was Manny. His name was really Charles Montagu. Manny had been a nursery nickname, and since it reduced his dignity more completely than anything else his sister was never tired of using it. He wearily got up and opened the door. "Tell Rosie I want her, Manny!" He made three or four steps to the stairs that went down to the basement where the kitchen was and opened the door. "Rosie!" he called. "Yes, Doctor!" "Your mistress wants you."

Back he came to his study, and again sat down. This time he closed the Enchiridion and flung it on his desk. Once more in that warm dusty June sunshine his head sank down over his knees; and he thought how his sister had managed to spoil the whole of his life. He thought to himself—"What on earth have I lived for all these years? I've not really enjoyed myself, I suppose, on an average, for more than a single hour every day. An hour a day! I wonder how much more than that most people in Glastonbury get, when you add up their pleasant moments?

I can't believe I'd hold back from those morphia tablets for an hour a day! No! It's the hope that keeps me going on, just going on; for that's all it is. It's the hope." By what he always thought of in his mind as "the hope" the Doctor meant nothing less than the death of his sister Barbara.

"Manny! Manny!" Out of his chair he sprang again and out of his study he flew. Once in the passage he waited for a second, praying that she was only having a row with Rosie, and that this calling for him was a strategic move in a feminine battle. "Manny!"

"Yes, Barbara?"

"Oh, don't say 'yes' in *that* tone"—she was leaning over the bannisters—"Come up, quick! Come here, come *here*! You must hook me up. Rosie is too helpless for anything!"

Dr. Fell sighed heavily and began mounting the stairs. Weariness and a great disgust for life weighed upon him. He followed Barbara into her bedroom, even to cross the threshold of which was a purgatorial punishment to him; and as he hooked her up his loathing for her was so intense that the idea of murder came into his mind.

Euphemia Drew's dining-room had all the windows open; but so still was the atmosphere that the six steady flames above the silver candlesticks—for though the western sun came slanting in from between the columns of the Tower Arch she had made Lily light up the table—preserved their small, blue-burning centres of life undisturbed.

"How nice your candles look!" cried old Lawyer Beere, who with his daughter Angela and Mr. Thomas Barter made up the roll of the guests. The old man's grizzled head, flaccid cheeks, and thin, spectacled nose bent again over his plate of clear soup, on the surface of which floated minute wafers of white paste.

But Angela, a grave, fair girl, of about twenty-seven summers —an old man's child—improved upon her father's observation. "Candlelight by daylight always makes me think of Rome," she remarked.

"So unnatural, the girl means," said Barbara Fell, "but you always did have a taste for the artificial, Euphemia."

Lily Rogers, removing Miss Bibby's soup plate at that moment, was so arrested by this indictment against her mistress that she touched the lady's brimming wine glass, and a tiny trickle of claret ran down upon the cloth. "Salt does it! Don't fret, girl," cried Miss Fell, covering the red stain with the minute crystals. Lily was not one to fret at such a misfortune while Mr. Barter was looking at her. She plunged, on the contrary, into a prolonged and pensive reverie. But Charles Montagu glanced in surprise at his sister. Why was she so considerate to Lily and so harsh with Rosie?

Was he wrong in disliking that thin, angular, grey face with such heart-burning detestation? She was always amiable to Tom Barter. If Rosie were Lily and *he* were Barter, would peace, love and harmony reign at Old Town Lodge?

Tom Barter spoke up now. He was impatient to throw all his weight upon the side of the Pageant before these formidable women began condemning it. "I've got a personal favour," he said, "to beg of you three ladies," and he made a gallant little bow in the direction of Angela whom he had only met once or twice before, and of whose cold, chaste, direct glances he was somewhat afraid. "I want you all to make sure you get good seats at the Pageant by buying your tickets early. There are a lot of foreigners coming—several whole parties of them from Germany—and it won't look nice if the front rows are vacant. The Mayor has been saving the front rows for the leading ladies of the town. He has not let his agent sell one ticket for those."

At this reference to the Mayor's "agent," Mary, who was sitting next to old Mr. Beere, hesitated not to lift up her voice. "It isn't whether you approve," she said eagerly and with a heightened colour, "or disapprove, of the thing as a whole. It's simply whether you would care to be entirely absent from something that's likely to be . . . quite an historical event in the life of . . . of everybody here."

Euphemia glanced quickly at her, as she accepted a gold-bordered plate from the dreamy Lily. "Only too historical," she thought, "in *your* life, my unhappy darling." But she said to Miss Fell—"I think perhaps Mary is right, Barbara. We all owe a duty to Glastonbury, and whatever we may *personally* think of our new Mayor and his methods, we must admit that the man has the place very much at heart."

"There won't be anything Romish about it, will there?" said Miss Fell.

"*I* can answer for that," cried Barter hastily. "Oh, no! Our fear at first was that, in his Evangelical simplicity, Mr. Geard might be laughed at by some of our cleverer church people. But the Vicar has been talking to him and has made him see ——" He stopped abruptly, anxious not to overdo his argument and also, it must be confessed, a little puzzled how to round off this imaginary conversation.

The sun was sinking now and through the open windows floating lightly and gently across the Ruins, came the fragrance of many hayfields. Uncut as yet, the grass had become tall and feathery, and mingled with its vague aroma was a foretaste of something far more intimately sweet, the first breath of budding honeysuckle and dog-roses. Angela Beere—beneath that calm white bosom in the low-cut light-blue frock, under that quiet forehead with the fair hair parted so smoothly—was thinking just then very strange thoughts. She had recently met Persephone, for the first time after a long interval, and the attraction of that equivocal creature had grown upon her night by night, since she had talked with her, into something like a feverish obsession. It had been difficult for her to behave adequately, even politely, in Persephone's presence, so troubling had the girl's personality been. She had wanted to run away from her; she had wanted to toss herself tempestuously, distractedly, into her new friend's arms! "Did she like me," she was thinking now, "did I look well? What did she mean by talking to me as she did, if she didn't want me for a friend? When she said that about life being so difficult, and the love of men being so gross and brutal, and it being so hard to find a person you could love whole-heartedly, did I make her understand how I sympathised?"

"There's going to be a bad strike in this town," announced Mr. Barter, "if those Crow people aren't careful. You'd better give your cousin a hint, Mary. He wouldn't take *my* advice." He paused and looked at old Mr. Beere, anxious to make the lawyer

believe that it was over a pure point of industrial politics that
he had quarrelled with his late employer.

Mr. Beere, however, as he ate his cutlets at once greedily and
daintily with his old wrinkled face close to his plate, was thinking to himself—"It's astonishing how Crow could put up with
this fellow so long. He's an interloper. He's an intriguer. He's
thoroughly shifty. I hope he doesn't take a fancy to Angela. No
doubt he was feathering his nest in some scurvy way when Crow
kicked him out."

"Who's this Capporelli they're talking so much about in the
Gazette?" enquired Miss Euphemia Drew.

Since no one else seemed inclined to reply Mary began explaining to her friend how the person in question was one of
the famous old French clowns of thirty years ago. "He's retired
for a long time," she said. "But he comes back occasionally for
things of this sort. He's had an unhappy life. His wife ran away
with a Chinaman. Cousin John told Geard about him. He took
me to see him at one of the rehearsals. He's acting Dagonet in
their play."

"Acting *who*, my dear?" enquired Miss Bibby.

"Dagonet, Miss Fell, King Arthur's Fool."

Barbara turned to Mr. Barter. "I thought you said that this
performance was an Evangelical affair, something like Pilgrim's
Progress?"

Old Mr. Beere lifted up his head. "I expect 'tis pretty well
what the boys and girls like best," he said. "A little incense and
a lot of kissing."

"It cannot of course be true, Mr. Barter," threw in Miss Drew,
"what dear old Wollop told me yesterday, when I talked to him
at that cage he's always shut up in?"

"It's true, Madam," threw in Mr. Beere with a humorous grimace. "You can count on it's being true if Wollop said it."

But Miss Drew shook her head. "What he said was that the
part of our Saviour was going to be played by that shabby
Welshman who's looking after old Jones' shop."

"Mr. Evans *is* a queer bird to look at," said Tom Barter
gravely, catching the eye of Lily as he spoke, and giving her
one of those lightning-quick recognisant glances of his that girls

always understood and responded to, "but he was at Jesus, Oxford, he tells me. He certainly knows more about the history of this place than anyone else."

"But to act the part of Our Lord ——" reiterated Miss Drew. "It has always struck me as strange that anyone could do it, even in those old Miracle Plays; but now—and with this French clown you talk of ——"

But Mr. Barter's mind had already wandered some distance from Paul Capporelli. He answered vaguely that he felt sure Miss Drew would find nothing objectionable in the Pageant. He thought to himself, "I've been a fool to tie myself up with that designing little bitch at the Pilgrims'. I must edge out of that. I must give her the go-by. She's begun to rate her bloody virtue a trifle too high. I wonder if Lily would —— But of course there's her sister! *That's* what has always stopped me. But by God she's a beautiful girl—yes! and a sensible girl too." And the incorrigible imagination of Mr. Barter began calling up such enticing and seductive images that when the real Lily, in her puritanical black dress and apron, came in again, the sight of her gave him quite a shock. She had re-assumed her normal attire with a too-bewildering rapidity!

The dinner drew to its end at last. Lily was now taking the cheese-plates away and placing before the guests Miss Drew's best set of Dresden fruit-plates. The Meissen coffee-cups too were brought in and a silver pot that had belonged to her grandmother. She had even instructed Mary to buy a box of cigarettes for the close of the meal and Mary—knowing the taste of her friend Tom—had bought some first-rate Virginian ones. The conversation began to revolve round the enigmatic figure of the new Mayor.

"Young Robert Stilly at the Bank," said Lawyer Beere, "tells me the fellow's spent thousands on this affair. I should think his family must be feeling it."

Mr. Barter hastened to bring forward an aspect of Mr. Geard that had nothing to do with the expenditure of money. His reward for leaving Philip bit at his conscience like a maggot at a rosy-cheeked apple. "He talks of Our Lord," he remarked, "as if He were standing close beside him."

"The man's always smelt of drink when *I've* been close behind him," said Barbara Fell.

"Rogers tells me," said Miss Drew, "that he's been seen making faces at that poor slobbering boy who always stands on the pavement outside the Pilgrims'."

"I don't think," threw in Barter, "that Louie got that story quite right. The version I've heard"—and he glanced at Mary, for his informant had been none other than John—"is that he made that boy understand him by signs, and that he always stops when he passes him and that——"

Mary interrupted. "I believe he's got some weird nervous sympathy . . . mind you I don't like him . . . there's something unpleasant about him . . . something frightening . . . but from all I hear he has some nervous peculiarity which makes him *imitate* every infirmity he meets. That must have been what Louie meant. He must act idiotically whenever he talks to that idiot."

"All I can say is," said Miss Bibby, "it's an outrage for a town like ours to have a Mayor who's not responsible for his actions."

"He's a better doctor than I am in such cases," muttered her brother crustily.

"Hear how you talk, Manny!" the lady cried. "Anyone would think you were one of his converts. *I've* heard he drinks at the pubs with the worst characters in the town. And they say that last bank holiday he got so drunk at the Legge woman's party that he took that sick niece of hers—Manny goes to see her—she's got some frightful disease—on his knees."

"I'd be ashamed to talk like that, Barbara!"

Everyone looked at Dr. Fell. He had spoken in a low voice, but with bitter distinctness.

Miss Drew intervened. "We're all of us talking scandal, I'm afraid," she said. "You're right to rebuke us, Doctor. What do *you* think about it, Mr. Beere?"

Mr. Beere looked up from his grapes. "Stilly thinks the fellow's mad," he said. "He's been spending money like water this last couple of months."

Charles Montagu Fell thought to himself—"If it wasn't for my Mary here, and some of those young girls who come to my

Clinic, I swear I'd take those tablets and end it." He finished his coffee in a gulp and there came over him, as he put the empty cup down, a sensation that he had been suffering from several times lately, a sensation as if his life were merely running on by the mechanism wound up within it, while its heart, its soul, its meaning had fled somewhere else and he had only to cry out in a loud voice: "But it's all husks and hollowness! But it's all worm-rot and dust!" and it would crumble to pieces. . . . The conversation drifted on now to an uneventful exchange of local gossip.

While Miss Drew's dinner-party ebbed thus to its lame and impotent conclusion, Mr. Philip Crow emerged from the drive gate of The Elms to inspect the appearance of the weather.

Once out in that lovely June evening—it was now only a few minutes after eight—he strolled into the town. In the open space outside St. John's he encountered Mr. Stilly, the cashier of the Glastonbury bank. Mr. Stilly had himself come out after an early supper—he was a hard-working man of forty who supported a pair of aged parents—to take the air, walk the streets a little, and see what was toward. Mr. Stilly had thin, reddish hair, a still thinner, reddish mustache, and a drooping, melancholic face. But he was not really a melancholy man. Mr. Stilly accepted the pin-pricks of chance and the joltings of time and tide with patient equanimity. He concealed a passion for taking photographs beneath his unruffled demeanour and he was also extremely fond of using a fret-saw. He adored his parents, who were both exacting and tyrannical; and, one of the greatest pleasures of his life was when at this time of the year he went down to the brooks so that the old people might have water-cress to their tea. Mr. Stilly had unbounded respect for Philip Crow. When he found himself tonight overtaken by this gentleman his tendency was at once without question to nod to him politely and sheer off. It was with surprise—and even with some misgiving—that Mr. Stilly heard Mr. Crow express a wish that he would accompany him to Tor Field to have a glance at what might be going on out there, on this fine night of the second of June. Mr. Stilly, conscious that he had left his "only father and his only mother," as he was accustomed facetiously to call them, playing at dominoes, acceded to the manufacturer's suggestion.

The two men walked rapidly down Chilkwell Street, past the Vicarage Gate, past Miss Drew's gate, past the Tithe Barn, from which the symbolic creatures of Matthew, Mark, Luke and John regarded them without an eyelid's flicker, past St. Michael's Inn, where Mad Bet made silent faces at them, past Chalice Well where the red water gurgled at them in disregarded neglect, till they came to Tor Field. The gate was open and they went in. It was just like the field of any ordinary Fair, this place tonight, with sail-cloth barriers pegged firmly into the earth and a confusion of lively voices reaching them through the warm twilight. They skirted the barrier and standing behind a crowd of casual intruders, whom the Players had no authority to exclude, they surveyed, with the distasting wonder of grown-up people in the presence of childish nonsense, the bewildering chaos of the unusual scene.

Mr. Stilly opened his mouth twice to utter some suitable comment before he had the courage to speak. Then he said: "It makes one think of what one reads about America."

"What do you mean?" asked Philip. This natural but not very kind question disturbed the play of Mr. Stilly's already agitated intelligence.

"They perform . . . performances . . . a good deal . . . don't they . . . in the . . . open air?" muttered the cashier of the bank.

"Do they?" said the other, laconically. "I was never there."

Mr. Stilly murmured something about Indians and sank into nervous silence. To be standing at this hour with the owner of the Glastonbury Dye-Works and in the presence of such an unusual scene was too much for him. He hoped that his parents had not yet noticed the length of his absence.

It was apparent that it would not be for lack of varied and fantastic costumes or of contradictory and vehement directions, or of excitable crowds of emotional young people, that the Geard Pageant would fail, if it *did* fail. Philip glared at it all with a cold, pinched disdain from beneath his cloth cap. There shot forth into the hurly-burly of that motley assembly, from this man's concentrated detachment, radiated waves of accumulated contempt. His angry thoughts pursued one another through his brain like marching soldiers. They came and went; they wheeled and counter-wheeled; they obeyed the commands of Philip's will in much better order than these excitable lads and lasses were obeying their distracted Professionals from Dublin. "Humanity!" he thought. "As they were two, three, four thousand years ago, so today! To mould them, to drill them, to dominate them—it's all too sickeningly easy." And he thought: "How much more worthy a resistance is offered to me by the deep, dark, interior rocks of the Mendips! How much better to struggle with machinery against the inertness of blind matter than to try to make anything of such insects! It won't be necessary to plot and scheme to defeat Geard. All I shall have to do will be to hold off my hands. This crazy confusion, these bewildered people; these bare legs and riotous dancing, why! it's a Bacchanalian orgy. He'll make the town a laughing-stock. The thing he's stirring up here—any fool can see it—is pure religious madness under the mask of theatricals. The man's a lunatic. This sort of thing never has been, and never will be, tolerated in England."

"I'm afraid I've got to go now, Mr. Crow. I didn't expect to stay out so long. My . . . my people will be wondering where . . . where I am." It had taken Mr. Stilly a long time to make up his mind to utter this daring ultimatum. His voice when he did utter it was like the voice of an unhappy school-boy murmuring something about cricket or football to a preoccupied headmaster absorbed in a nice point of Thucydidean grammar.

"Eh? What did you say? Oh, all right," returned Philip. "Wait one minute, Stilly, and I'll walk back with you."

They left the field, passing on their way out that fallen trunk on the mossy sides of which Sam Dekker had searched for rare toadstools on the day when Mr. Evans first thought of taking the part of Christ in the pageant.

Meanwhile this same Sam, struggling pitifully with his love for Nell, had entered his favourite shrine in Glastonbury. This was a little chapel dedicated to St. Patrick lying behind the Women's Almshouse near the entrance to the Ruins, a chapel which still

possessed an original stone altar left undisturbed by the Protestant Reformation and carried upon its wall the heraldic arms
of St. Joseph, a green cross between two golden cruets.

Never had those Arimathean arms, never had that stone altar,
beheld a worshipper such as poor Sam showed himself that
night.

He was on his knees at the altar. He was alone in the little
chapel. Lower and lower he bowed his head, clenching his fingers
as he bent forward.

But it was not in the attitude of prayer that his hands hung
by his side. They swung there savagely in the manner of a prize-
fighter's fists and, as they swung, the backs of his knuckles kept
striking against the front of the stone altar.

There was something about his posture as he knelt—swaying
his whole body backward and forward—that was pitiably grotesque. An imaginative observer might have received the impression that an animal was praying.

Was there any portion of Sam's nature that exulted in the
atrocious task that he had laid upon himself—the task of doing
not his will but what he conceived to be the will of a tragic
superhuman Being?

Yes, the soul itself, in this grotesque swaying body with
clenched fists, exulted in what it was doing! Sam's soul seemed
to be able to gather to itself a peculiar consciousness quite apart
from the rest of Sam's sensibility. His soul seemed to be holding
his body and his will in a tight leash, as a man might hold a
wild-eyed bull, by a ring through its nose.

His soul seemed to be saying to his natural senses and his
natural will: "You must go through this because Christ went
through it! I care not how you suffer; so long as you go on,
day by day, doing His will and not your own!"

And all the while Sam suffered there, swaying in his anguish
like a great bleeding animal held by a steel ring through his
nose, the Man-God that he invoked was struggling in vain to
reach the consciousness of this mad perverter of His secret. In
vain! In vain! Against the power-lust in the soul of a man, when
it has once tasted the wild delight of taking up its own body
and its own will and its own nervous sensibility and forcing them

to *act against the grain*, there is only one Deity that can prevail; and that Deity is not Christ. How could Christ as He swept now like a cloud of weed-smoke under the door of St. Patrick's chapel, relax the tension of this soul, that pulled and jerked so remorselessly at the nose of a praying earth-beast?

But Christ was not, on that vaporous Glastonbury afternoon, oblivious of His poor, besotted servant Sam. Although He tried in vain to change by invisible reasoning the incorrigible obstinacy of Sam's perverted *mind*, upon external events He *could* exercise a certain degree of control.

He now put it into the head of young Elphin Cantle, with whom Sam used sometimes to go for walks, to come surreptitiously into the church. Elphin, like many other boys of the town, had a passionate love of Sam. Mother Legge, when in her cups, had recently said to Young Tewsy that Sam Dekker had become a seducer of boys. Nothing could have been more pathetically unjust! Sam did not in his secret heart, care at all for boys. His walks with the oddest, queerest, and most unhandsome among them—and Elphin was certainly one of these—were part of his general scheme of life. He knew that there were lots of boys in Glastonbury who, hating cricket and football and not caring for girls, were profoundly lonely and unhappy. To these boys he gave a good deal of his attention, which they repaid tenfold, as far as emotional response was concerned; but Sam knew nothing of the strength of the feelings he excited.

When Elphin peeped into St. Patrick's chapel he was thrilled but not surprised to find Sam there. He had looked in before, under similar occasions; but had never dared to approach the object of his passionate adoration. Today, however, pushed forward by the invisible pressure of a Hand upon his shoulder, the thin-legged, pale-faced boy moved shyly up to his idol's side. As he approached, he fancied he caught the sound of a huskily drawn sob in the man's throat. This sound hurt him to the quick. Well did Elphin Cantle know what it was to go into solitary places and utter sounds like that!

The boy went close up to him and still pushed forward by the invisible Hand, whispered his name, doing as he whispered it, what Russian serfs in former times did to their masters, that is to say, kissing him lightly on the shoulder. Anyone but a born naturalist like Sam would have started violently and even uttered a cry; but long training in the woods and fields had given Sam under any nervous shock—and indeed in all these things his nerves were like tough wood—the poise of a Red Indian.

"Oh, it's you, Elf, is it?" was all he said. And he began rising stiffly to his feet, unceremoniously wiping his eyes with the back of one of his relaxed fists.

Elphin Cantle said not a word.

"Had your tea yet?" enquired Sam, stretching himself and looking round for his cap and stick.

Elphin shook his head.

"Come on then. Let's see what Penny has got for us today!"

MIDSUMMER DAY DAWNED LONG BEFORE MOST OF THE PER-
formers destined to take their share in Mr. Geard's religious
circus had awakened from sleep. Mary Crow, however, who was
to take no part in it save as a spectator, was awake soon after
the first glimmer of dawn.

To watch the processes of dawn from a window that faces
west is in a sense like the contemplation of various excited expressions crossing a human countenance when the cause of such
feelings is absent. The girl propped herself up in bed, reached
for her dressing-gown which was at her bed's foot, wound it like
a shawl round her neck, and watched the slow, stealthy expanding of the grey light. She remembered having heard John
once defend the Biblical account of the creation, when Tom
Barter criticised it as separating the creation of the sun from
the creation of light. John had maintained that light was an
entity quite independent of its immediate origin. Certainly it did
look to Mary now as if light were an entity free of all connection
with the sun.

She could see the great ruined Tower Arch of the Abbey
Church as she lay there, and she could see the tops of the elm
trees beyond it, very ghostly and phantom-like, their greenness
only half-born. The arch, it seemed, assimilated itself to this
dawn-light far less easily than the treetops. It isolated itself in
some way from this process of dawn and emphasised its own
curves and mouldings and masonry, in resistance, as it were, to
these atmospheric effects. But the foliage of the treetops was
part of it. The foliage of the treetops, as Mary watched it now,
seemed to contain within itself the infinite sadness of this grey,
half-born, Cimmerian light that was now slowly invading the
world and establishing itself in the cold aisles and in the blank
corridors of darkness. Filmy wisps of grey mist hung about
these treetops, mist that was liker to dewdrops than raindrops
and yet did not really suggest water-drops at all. Nor did it
suggest clouds! They were things by themselves, *sui generis,* those

dawn-mists, and they seemed to have as remote a connection with
water in any localised form, as the dim light, in which they
dropped and wavered and rose and sank, had with the invisible
sun. "Yes," thought Mary, "something in the foliage of those
trees flows forth to greet this sad light, that does not seem like
sunlight, just as something in me flows out to greet it."

Will it be fine today? That was the next thought that Mary
had. She had been to the Northload Street room for a few
minutes yesterday evening and had found John and Tom together. They were drinking whiskey and the former was in a
state of complete exhaustion. John had told her that the Mayor
was resolved to carry the affair through, wet or fine, but that
he had somehow convinced himself—"You know the way he
talks to his God, as if He were standing by his side?"—that it
would not be "allowed" to rain on this day of "Glaston Re-
surgens." Mary felt full of doubt and anxiety. All manner of
troubling thoughts assailed her. Suppose the whole thing were a
monstrous failure? Suppose the performers got panic-stricken
and that French clown lost his head in some wild antic or im-
provisation quite out of keeping with the rest? She had seen
a fragment of the Passion Play rehearsed and she felt totally
unable to conceive how Mr. Evans could even carry his part
off, far less be successful in it. Rumours had been running wildly
through the town for the last week about the police from
Taunton interfering and arresting the principal players, and the
last thing Mary had heard before she went to bed last night was
news brought into the kitchen by Weatherwax that the expected
strike in the Dye-Works had come and that the Glastonbury factory had locked out all its hands that morning. So far, the gardener's story said, the trouble had not extended to the Crow plant
at Wookey, but *that* also, so Weatherwax declared, might have a
lockout tomorrow. Even the Wookey hands had demanded, and
apparently had been given, a holiday today, so that as Mary lay
propped up on her pillows, waiting for the first yellow beams
to strike the great broken arch in front of her, she seemed to
catch trouble on the air, coming from every side. Barter had told
her that the town was already filled to overflowing with visitors.
Parties of Germans, Dutchmen, Scandinavians—even a few

French people—had filled the streets yesterday. She herself had
been startled by the crowds as she went to Northload Street.

Mary was of a realistic and practical turn of mind, but her
nerves felt thoroughly shaky now. In this cool dawn-air, alone
with rooks, elm-tree tops, ruins and wood-pigeons, a thousand
alarms and terrors visited her. She imagined all those factory-
hands—the strikers from the Glastonbury works, the holiday-
makers from Wookey—joining in a great mob and invading the
field. She imagined a wild tumult taking place in the midst of
the performance, wherein John would be arrested by the police,
handcuffed, and carried off in a motor car to Taunton. The
pageant itself, she had learned, was not to begin till two in
the afternoon, but since a portion of the field had been handed
over to the ordinary booth-holders, toy-and-sweet vendors, trinket
sellers, fruit-and-nut dealers, and so forth—whirligigs and roundabouts alone being excluded—and since gipsy caravans too were
to be allowed in by the Mayor's especial indulgence, there would
be festivities going on in Tor Field long before that hour and
plenty of opportunities for such a mixed public to work themselves up into a riotous state of mind before the official pro-
gramme began.

It was with a shock of real amazement, as something that
seemed more blood-red than sunlight hit the left-hand column
of the great broken arch, that the girl lifted her head now. She
let her twisted dressing-gown fall loose about her shoulders and
propped herself still higher in the bed, with the palms of her
hands pressed against the mattress, for she became aware that
the sight of this unnatural light—in reality it was a wine-coloured
red, touched with a quite indescribable nuance of purple—was
giving her a spasm of irrational happiness. She leaned forward,
allowing her dislodged dressing-gown to slide down upon the
pillows behind her and quite disregarding the fact that a cool
sunrise wind was blowing against her flimsily clad figure. Her
soul had come back with a violent spasm, like a rush of blood
to her head, and her whole nature seemed to pour itself out
towards the reddish light on that tall column. Her pulse of
happiness was intense. What she experienced was like a quivering
love-ecstasy that had no human object. She could actually feel

the small round breasts under her night-gown shiver and distend. Her head instinctively fell back a little, while her chin was lifted up. Her lips parted, and a smile that was a smile of indescribable peace flickered over her face. She would have served at that moment as a model for some primitive Flemish artist **painting** a passionately concentrated vision of the rape of Danaë.

Whatever it was that stirred her so, the effect of it soon passed; but Mary told no one, not even John, of the experience she had had on the dawn of the Baptist's day. The invisible Watchers however of human life in Glastonbury noted well this event. "She has been allowed to see It," they said to one another. "Will she be the only one among all these people?"

When two o'clock struck in the belfries and towers of the town there was an expectant stir amid the great company of spectators in the wide sloping field at the foot of the Tor. A surprising number of seats and wooden benches had been procured for the Mayor's great occasion, and upon these seats sat a vast crowd of people, all of them roused at that moment to a pitch of excitement such as had not been experienced in that place since the day when the last Abbot of Glastonbury had met his doom. Like the famous Homeric wind sweeping over a cornfield, this cumulative wave of crowd-hypnosis shivered through these assembled people, straightening their shoulders, lifting their heads, turning their faces towards the grassy terrace on the slope above them. Had Philip Crow's airplane been flying low down then, over this tightly packed crowd who had seats to sit upon and over the equally large crowd at the back of them and at their flanks who had no seats except the grass, it would have been of fascinating interest to note the varieties of human types gathered so close together. Many of those without seats lay sideways on the sward, or sat crouched and hugging their knees, while behind them all, drifting about or standing still, as their vagrant mood dictated, were large stray groups of what might be termed casual transients. Gipsies from the caravans ranged in rows along the hedge, nut-vendors, pedlars with their trays, hawkers with packs strapped to their backs, beggars, tramps, groups of astonished and cautious shepherds from the high Mendips, stray factory-hands from Wookey and Street and the city of Wells, all these, mingled with a number of strikers from the Dye-Works of the town itself, kept circulating and surging, advancing and retreating, jostling, edging, dodging, hovering, spying, mocking, criticising, deriding, applauding, just as the wind of accident and the beckoning of caprice carried them here or there.

The two front rows of seats had been reserved for local magnates, and in spite of all the suspicion, jealousy, distrust, that was about, these seats had very few empty spaces. Miss Elizabeth Crow was there with Lady Rachel. Mrs. Philip Crow ought to have been there, for although Philip had taken the opportunity of flying to Wookey Hole, his wife, under the influence of Emma who was here with Louie and Lily, had decided not to miss what she now spoke of as "something to rest a person's mind." But Tilly's dislike of publicity was so great that she had refused this place of honour and had had to be ensconced in the fourth row. On the other side of Lady Rachel, however, there was an empty chair, for the girl had done all she could to persuade her father to come and there was still a good chance that he might. Ned Athling, who had written a considerable portion of the words of the whole performance, was one of the principal play-actors. Miss Bibby Fell was duly seated by Dr. Fell's side and next to her were Lawyer Beere and Angela, and beyond them Miss Drew and Mary. By Mary's side John had found a place for a foreign priest. In the central portion of the second row of seats, behind these personages, were the Vicar and his son, for though Sam had steadily refused to have anything to do with the performance and was now reduced to agitated burnings of heart by the presence of Nell, he had been unwilling to refuse his father when Mat had made an especial appeal to him not to desert him on this occasion. Next to Mat and Sam sat Mr. Wollop and in company with Mr. Wollop almost the whole staff of Wollop's shop. Being a bachelor, and also having an equal and unfailing interest in all mundane spectacles, Mr. Wollop had felt it incumbent upon him to be found on this occasion "holding up," as he called it, "his proper end."

It was a sign of something really grandly democratic in the

soul of Glastonbury's leading tradesman that there never entered his head for a single second a doubt about the staff of Wollop's —all its "young ladies" and all its "young gentlemen"—being worthy of the second row of the select seats. It *had*, however, several times already entered the head of the Nietzschean young man—whose name was Booty—that he was in a place of embarrassing honour, since just in front of him was the vacant chair reserved for the Marquis and to his right, for he was at the end of the row of his fellows, sat Mr. Stilly of the bank.

In the third row of seats, but some distance from Sam, indeed just behind Mr. Stilly's aged parents, were none others than Will Zoyland and Nell. Nell had her brother Dave on her right, and beyond Dave sat the Vicar of St. Benignus, the eloquent Dr. Sodbury, whose ministrations were so pleasing to Megan Geard. Persephone Spear had been enrolled rather late in the proceedings among the players, but though so late a comer, she had been given a rôle second to none, having been called upon to play the part of the Virgin Mother.

It was only in the fourth row, just behind Will and Nell Zoyland that seats had been reserved for the family of the Mayor. Here Mrs. Geard sat, between Cordelia and Mr. Bishop, the Town Clerk, for Crummie was to take the important rôle of the Lady of Shalott in the Arthurian part of the Pageant. Next to the Town Clerk sat Mrs. Philip, and by Mrs. Philip's side was the Curator of the Glastonbury Museum.

The fifth row of these reserved seats had been dedicated—Mr. Tom Barter had been careful to see to this—to the servants of the leading families of the town and all their especial friends and relations. In this row, therefore, there sat a most motley collection of persons, sweet-natured young girls, hypercritical spinsters, nervous old men, complacent old women, and a great many very riotous children. Here were Emma Sly, Louie and Lily Rogers, Sally Jones and her friend Tossie Stickles—this latter, because of her delicate state of health, armed with her mistress's oldest and largest scent-bottle—Miss Bibby's latest two servants, Rose Nicker and Edith Bates, both of whom had twice over "given notice," those formidable connoisseurs of mortal life, Mr. Weatherwax and Penny Pitches, those garrulous supporters of the dignity of the church, Mrs. Robinson and Grandmother Cole, together with the whole robber band from the alley, Jackie, Nelly Morgan, Sis and Bert—the last-named being planted by a devilish trick of chance just behind the curator of the museum whose devotion to fossils was only rivalled by his maniacal hatred of children.

At the extreme end of the sixth row, flanked by a voluble contingent of Germans from Bremen and Lübeck, sat Mother Legge with her faithful bodyguard, Young Tewsy, by her side, the old lady in her best black silk and the old man in a suit of cast-off broadcloth, hired from the laundryman, and formerly belonging to a Baptist minister. On the other side of Mrs. Legge sat Blackie Morgan, between whom and the old procuress a curious and quite unprofessional friendship had sprung up.

Mr. Geard had surprised both John and Barter by insisting on remaining completely independent of the whole thing—independent of the actors, independent of the spectators—and the only indication he had given to his family of his present whereabouts was a word he had casually dropped after their early dinner about seeing how the performance looked from the top of the Tor!

The number of foreigners who were present surpassed even John's expectation and they constantly increased. Crowds of them kept entering the field long after the performance had commenced. Every train that arrived brought more of them. They were French, German, Spanish, Bohemian, Dutch, Danish, Scandinavian and Russian. There were even two oriental, long-haired monks from a monastery in the Caucasus. John Crow imagined these two men setting out on this westward instead of eastward pilgrimage at the very first hearing of its possibility, when two and a half months ago he had sent his announcements across Europe.

The only person among all this immense crowd who had bothered about trying to get into personal relations with the organisers of the event was a mysterious-looking priest from Constantinople who called himself Father Paleologue. It was this man to whom John—when he found that he could speak English—had given a place by Mary's side, in the front seats. At the opposite end of the sixth row from where Mrs. Legge and Blackie were seated were Old Jones and Abel Twig. The Ward Matron who had brought them—a handsome buxom woman always spoken of as Aunt Laura—was doing her best to amuse the two old men. In this task she was not assisted very much by her neighbour on the other side, who was an exceedingly caustic French journalist famous for his biting wit. This man, who had come to Glastonbury solely to report on the doings of Paul Capporelli, was alternately scribbling in a notebook what presumedly were light touches of local colour, suitable as a background for the great clown, and stretching his neck to catch more of the profile of Lady Rachel. Every now and then he would turn a ferocious stare upon Abel Twig, who was seated between Aunt Laura and Old Jones. There was something about Number One's physiognomy, not to speak of his Sedgemoor dialect, which this critical Parisian found peculiarly irritating. He was trying to catch stray sentences—characteristic of English phlegm and English snobbishness—from the "aristocracy" in the front rows, among whom rumour had informed him was sitting the daughter of Lord P., who represented one of the oldest Marquisates in the Kingdom, but Number One's expressions of wonder as to what had become of "thik big flock of good South-Downs what old man Chinnock used to turn into this here field," were spoken so loudly that it was hard to hear anything else.

If the critic from Paris had desired to put down in his little book a really significant trait of the English character, he would have noted how respectfully and tactfully the brigade of Taunton constables called in by Philip kept themselves in the background. It was natural enough perhaps that the police-sergeant responsible for this large body of tactful officers had chosen to confine their activity that afternoon to the outskirts of the crowd in the Tor Field, but such strategy unfortunately played into the hands of the really formidable trouble-makers. These were the revolutionary leaders of the strikers at the Dye-Works. Led by Red Robinson, who since his rebuff on Easter Monday, had deserted the primrose-path for blood-and-iron politics, the Dye-Works strikers with as many adherents as they could collect from the Wookey and Wells workshops were even now at this very moment parading the streets with revolutionary banners. By means of a real inspiration of the genius of " 'ate," Red had made a bid for the Nonconformist element among the populace of Glastonbury and side by side with his political insignia he had caused to be displayed at the head of his rapidly growing procession inscriptions denouncing the Mayor's Pageant. "Down with Mediævalism," these crafty scrolls read. "Down with Superstition," "No Lourdes, no Lisieux Here," "Down with Religious Mummery."

Thus while Philip's police force was protecting the morals of Glastonbury from the dangerous pieties of its Mayor, these street-rioters were lumping both capitalist and pietist together as joint-enemies of the people. Up and down the streets tossed and swayed these varied and singular ensigns, gathering numbers as they went and collecting in their train all the roughest elements of the town. At last the cry arose—inspired by the Æolus-breath of Red's genius for action—"To the field!" and the whole turbulent tide of people, the actual strikers far outnumbered by the less orderly elements, began pouring down Chilkwell Street towards the scene of the performance. It soon began to spread, as Lily would put it, "like wildfire," or as Penny would put it, "like Satan's own stink," through the poorer portions of the place that "The Town was up."

Like an animal organism that has taken an emetic, Glastonbury now disembogued from the obscurest recesses of its complex being all manner of queer chemical substances. Such substances, though they were living creatures, needed a shock like this cry, "The Town is up," to fling them forth from their profound hiding-places. Most of the destitute people and drunken people and half-witted people who now poured forth from the most unexpected quarters were indigenous to the place. Thus for the first time since the Battle of Sedgemoor when that strange cry went about the streets just as it was doing now—"The Town is up"— the real People of Glastonbury emerged and asserted itself. The last time it had asserted itself was on behalf of that sweet, honeysuckle bastard, Monmouth, for it was the "great gentlemen," like Lord P.'s ancestor and Mat Dekker's ancestor, who had brought Dutch William in, not the people. And before that, for

it had allowed the Abbot to persecute heretics and it had allowed the King to murder the Abbot without interfering, it had
responded to the cry "The Town is up" when Jack Cade revolted
against every privilege under the sun. It had rioted in honour of
Mother Shipton, Jane Shore, Lambert Simnel, John Wycliffe, John
Wesley, Lord George Gordon, and had even received and concealed from royal vengeance the crafty Welshman Owen Glen-
dower. In fact the ingrown, inbred, integrated People of
Glastonbury had raised their famous cry "The Town is up!" on
behalf of every scandal that had worried the well-constituted
authorities since under the crazy Arviragus they had defied the
gods for the sake of the blood of a mad demigod, and on behalf of the abductor Modred had waylaid the lovely queen of
Rex Arturus himself.

These were the people who poured forth now on this historic
Midsummer Day from Paradise and Bove Town and Butts Close
and Manor House Road to join with the strikers from Philip's
Dye-Works and with the holiday-makers from Wookey Hole. So
fantastical did some of this queer crowd look, who thus enlisted
themselves under the banner of Red Robinson's " 'ate," that the
German and French and Scandinavian visitors—not to speak of
the monks from the monastery in the Caucasus and the super-
sophisticated Father Paleologue—would almost have been pardoned for taking them as lineal descendants of the dwellers in
Abel Twig's Lake Village.

Unfortunately for Red's purpose his impatience for action got
himself and his strikers much too quickly upon the scene. His
strikers were orderly and respectable Wessex workmen, not easy
to excite to acts of violence. Thus although before they reached
the entrance they were shrewdly hustled by the strategic Red,
over several gaps in the hedge, into the field and thus were enabled to approach the western flank of the crowd of spectators
from an unexpected and unconventional quarter, things did not
work out as he had hoped. If this heterogeneous mob of invaders
had come *en masse*, in one grand rush, there is no doubt they
would have stampeded the players and ended Mr. Geard's
Pageant. But Red's " 'ate"—directed equally against Mayor and
Manufacturer—had, as Number Two would have put it, "stam-

peded its wone self" and ruined all his skilful strategy. He ought
to have waited in Chilkwell Street, opposite St. Michael's Inn—
and what a sight for Mad Bet that would have been!—until his
ragged camp-followers, descendants of the heroic populace who
fought with scythes and bill-hooks against a trained army and
a great general, had all reached the spot. It was the lack of
these irresponsible pilgarlics that spoilt Red's plan, for his
orderly strikers soon found themselves faced by the first five
rows of seats occupied by the gentry of the town, and even the
"Down with Mummery" banners paused and wavered, if they
were not actually lowered, before the indignant glances and the
cries of "Order! Order!" that now arose from these seats. To the
crowd that were following these patient factory-hands such
glances would have meant little. But many of these hands had
come to labour in Philip's Dye-Works from Bath and Yeovil and
Taunton and Shepton Mallet, and they lacked the recklessness of
the true Glastonbury tradition.

There might, however, have been trouble, even then, if Philip's
police had appeared on the scene, but fortunately these officers
had chosen to remain in that portion of the field devoted to the
gipsy caravans, for it was there that the hobbledehoys and riotous
young apprentices of the town who regarded this occasion as their
grand opportunity for causing annoyance, were shouting, singing, skylarking, making a resounding hullabaloo, and trying to
draw the attention of the vast audience to themselves. The moment was a crucial one, for the brightly attired groups of the
first part of the Pageant were already hovering about the two
mediæval pavilions on the ledge of the hillside that served for
a platform, and Red, well-nigh desperate now and ready to risk
anything, was calling upon his banner-holders to ascend the
slope and invade this natural stage.

A spirited verbal altercation now began between Miss Drew,
who happened to be nearest to the banner which carried the word
"Mummery" and the young striker who held one of its poles.
In her excitement, for Mary could do nothing to calm her, and
Father Paleologue only laughed, the old lady rose to her feet
and bandied recriminations with the young striker, who to tell
the truth was more sulky and irritable than violent or rude.

There was an extremely large and very decorative canvas pavilion at each end of the grassy stage where the Pageant was
now beginning and from these the players emerged and into
these they retreated as occasion demanded. These huge tents had
been copied from old books of chivalry; from the tops of them
floated many bright-coloured streamers and the fluttering canvas
that composed them was painted with heraldic symbols. It was
from the interior of the western one of these two pavilions that
John Crow watched in consternation the march of these hostile
banners. He despatched a messenger for Tom Barter who was in
the other tent and when Tom arrived, crossing the grassy stage
with a great deal of haste and not a little awkwardness, the only
thing he could suggest was that they should get the police away
from the caravans as speedily as possible.

"But why haven't they come already?" demanded John.

"They don't realise what's up," cried Tom. "How should they?
They think it's a deputation to the Mayor or something! They're
strangers. They don't know the town. They think it's part of the
affair . . . those flags and so on! They think it's part of *our*
performance!"

The two men went to the western entrance of the great heraldic
tent and held open the sail-cloth hangings and stared helplessly
at the disturbance. They could hear contentious voices from the
invaded front rows! They could see figures on their feet among
them. John, concerned for Mary, caught sight of the unmistakable figure of Miss Drew brandishing her parasol. "But good
God, old man," cried Barter, "look at them coming across the
field! They're *pouring* through the hedge! We're being hustled
by the populace. There's no doubt about it! Philip's been rousing the mob to break things up, since his police are no good."

"What are you all doing?" John cried now, turning fiercely
round on the actors with whom the tent was crowded. It was
the moment for the opening dumb show of the Pageant, which
consisted of a concourse of people in mediæval dress gathered
to watch the Coronation of Arthur and Gwenevere. The part of
Gwenevere was taken by the tallest young lady in Wollop's, but
for the rôle of Arthur, Ned Athling had brought from his own
village his father's foreman, a majestic-looking middle-aged in-

dividual, bearded and broad-shouldered, but whose red-stock-
inged knees at that crisis were knocking together with panic.
The thrones of the king and queen were now standing near them,
inside the tent, a couple of Mat Dekker's choir-lads, in crimson
doublet and hose, waiting the word to drag them out. From the
eastern pavilion the knights and ladies of Camelot—Sunday
School children from St. John's and St. Benignus'—were already,
in the absence of anyone to stop them, gliding nervously forth
and presenting themselves before the audience. It was then that
the absence of the thrones—delayed by the consternation of the
officials in the western tent—proved bewildering to these be-
dizened youngsters.

John's fury, directing itself blindly towards the Middlezoy
King Arthur and towards the equally frightened pages who were
to drag out the thrones, was now confronted by the soft protests of the prostrate Crummie, who, lying upon a lathe-and-
plaster stretcher, roughly bulwarked to represent a barge, was
attended by two lusty youths from the Congregational Chapel
who were to carry her in, at the critical moment of the coronation, and lay her at the feet of the king and queen. Across the
body of Crummie, who was wrapped in a dark blanket over which
her long fair hair fell in dishevelled allurement, a mitred bishop,
Bob Carter, from the Godney grocery, who was clinging frantically to the crown of Britain, which an agitated page, Ted
Sparks from the bakery at Meare, was trying to take away from
him, burst now into angry abuse of Lancelot du Lac. This melancholy Mirror of Courtesy was Billy Pratt of the St. John's
Bell-Ringers, and Billy had infuriated Bob by insisting that it
was his right to stand at the head of Crummie when the moment
came for them all to emerge into public view, whereas Bishop
Bob declared that Lancelot's place was near the queen. It was
out of the midst of this noisy wrangle of Church and State over
the beautiful corpse that the soft voice of the Lady of Shalott
herself arose, enquiring of John what for mercy's sake was the
matter, and why the performance didn't commence. "It's so stuffy
in here," murmured the love-slain damsel.

"There's the devil to pay out here, Miss Geard," cried John,
in a state bordering on complete nervous collapse. "There's a

mob pouring across the field from the town with flags and sticks and God knows what, and they're now collecting in front of the audience. They're pointing at us too and I believe"—he cast a glance through the tent-hangings—"Christ! They are! They're coming up the hill, and all the front-row people are on their feet and the foreigners are beginning to make a row."

John's account of things, however, was a little exaggerated. Only one flag-carrier—the young Communist who had been threatened by Miss Drew's parasol—had begun to ascend the hill, but he had paused when he saw that no one was following him. It was true that the foreign element in the audience—especially the Swedes and Norwegians—were shouting protests in strange tongues, but although matters were critical nothing had yet occurred that was irretrievable.

"Are those Taunton police quiet still?" murmured the caressing voice of the Lady of Shalott.

"Quiet?" cried John, rushing once more to the opening of the tent. When he came back to her side—for this fair creature under the dark blanket seemed just then all the human wisdom he could cling to—he informed her that a body of policemen were even now hastening round between the rear of the audience and the hedge, with an evident intention of cutting off the strikers' retreat.

"Stop them!" commanded Crummie, lifting up her lovely bare shoulders from the black cushions on which they were resting. "Father said that *under no conditions* were those Taunton police to interfere!"

"Tom!" cried poor John, in complete distraction, "Miss Geard says the police must be stopped!"

Barter approached, fixing upon the Lady of Shalott's shoulders an eye of covetous lechery.

"Are you a friend of mine, Mr. Barter?" said the girl. Into these words Crummie threw all that world of erotic appeal of which she was the perfect mistress. Paralysed by her passion for Sam this appeal had been storing up for the last two or three months like a precious wine "cooled a long age in the deep-delvèd earth," but at this delicate crisis, when the whole success of her father's Pageant was at stake, it poured forth from her voice, her hair, her shoulders, her bosom, like undulant music.

"Yours to command, Miss Geard," said Tom Barter, gloating over her with a drugged, fatuous smile. "She's the most beautiful thing I've ever seen in my whole life," he thought.

"Run down the field, then, Mr. Barter, for mercy's sake, and stop those policemen! Talk to their sergeant, if he's there. Talk to any of them. Tell them these people are friends of the Mayor, and that it's all right."

Barter didn't hesitate for a second. His face changed, however. Action always steadied him. "I'm off!" he cried and disappeared from the tent.

John and the Bishop and Lancelot du Lac and a group of pretty pages with bare legs and tumbled curls watched the process of events from the tent entrance. Edward Athling from the other tent had already saved the situation as far as the Pageant was concerned, for he had himself carried out upon the grassy stage the Arthurian flag, "the Dragon of the great Pendragonship," towards which, as he planted it in the earth, a group of his companions lifted their glittering sword-points in a reverential salute. Then leaving the flag there, midway between the two tents, he had withdrawn his followers from view. Thus from the emblazoned folds of the royal standard of Romanized Britain, the golden Dragon looked forth towards the black heraldic Lions upon one tent and the Sacred Symbols of Saint Joseph upon the other. The spectators had now something to hold their attention.

John suddenly resolved that they should have something else, and he gave a signal to the pages, who were scraping at the golden thrones with their nails to see how deep the gilding went, to carry them out and place them on the left of the Dragon Ensign. Meanwhile he watched with trembling interest Barter's encounter with the Taunton police. He could see his friend talking eagerly and earnestly to the sergeant in command, but he could also see the straggling procession of nondescripts from the town pouring constantly over the hedge and towards their leader's banners that now seemed to be remaining stationary side by side with the no longer protesting occupants of the front seats.

"Begin! Begin!" vociferated some Frenchman from Avignon. "The Play!" shouted some Spanish students from Salamanca. "Hush! Hush!" retorted a German contingent from Weimar, to whose more patient minds, schooled in Faustian mysteries, those two golden thrones with the sunny hillside as a background, held a symbolic if not metaphysical signification.

The situation was still very tense, as John well knew, much more tense than any of these excitable masqueraders in the tent realised. One of the younger mistresses in the Church School—the one who had gone to Yeovil to see her lover on Maundy Thursday—now appeared in much perturbation to say that there was a quarrel going on in the other pavilion between Mr. Athling and the professional directors from Dublin. These people, it transpired, a man and a woman, were great admirers of Monsieur Capporelli and they were indignant now because the famous clown, who had been sitting patiently in a corner of the tent smoking cigarettes for the last hour, was being kept waiting so long for his pantomimic performance. Made up as Dagonet, in a disguisement learnedly and exquisitely copied from museum specimens of mediæval costume, Paul Capporelli was now engaged in a lively conversation with Persephone Spear, by whose personality, in her blue robe and red bodice, as the Virgin Mother, he had clearly been fascinated. But the Dubliners were full of annoyance over this protracted conversation between their precious Fool and this very local Madonna.

The conversation between Barter and the Taunton police force had ended in the latter taking their stand all along the hedge to prevent any more of the mob from entering from that unauthorised direction. But there were enough now of the irresponsible element, crowding up behind the assembled strikers, to make things look very threatening. These newcomers were by no means of the sort to be stopped by the waving of Miss Drew's green parasol, and between them and Mother Legge, who was sitting at the end of the sixth row, there had already begun a volley of scurrilous badinage that showed every sign of starting a really unpleasant contretemps. Things indeed had reached that stage—it was already nearly three o'clock and there was nothing to see on the stage but two gilded thrones and the great Pendragon flag—when the smallest spark, like the accident of Mother Legge and her Rabelaisian tongue being on the extreme west of the audience, might have led to a general pandemonium, out of which, with all these foreigners already getting nervous and irritable, it would have been impossible to get back to any sort of order. Such a spark seemed now to have been really struck, not by Mother Legge, but by the arrival upon the scene of the Marquis of P.

It was the manner of this nobleman's approach that started the trouble. Completely unaware of the arrival of the real People of Glastonbury upon the field, my Lord had taken it into his head to have himself driven by Sergeant Blimp in a light dog-cart, over from Mark Court. Taking for granted that his daughter was keeping a seat for him—as indeed she had written to say she would do—Lord P. told Blimp to drive him straight round the field—they entered it from a gate at the town-end— till he reached the front row of seats and there drop him. "You can go," he had said, "to the Pilgrims' then, Blimp, and put up. I'll walk round there later."

Now Sergeant Blimp, although he would have submitted to torture rather than have slept in Merlin's room, had no fear of a mob. So when it became obvious that there *was* a mob—and a rather dangerous-looking one, between them and their objective— the Sergeant cracked his whip and trotted his tall black horse all the more resolutely. Then the disturbance which had been on the edge of breaking out for so long really did seem inevitable. Hundreds of angry voices were raised; people who were further off pushed others who were nearer, right into the path of the dog-cart; sticks were brandished, and if stones were not thrown it was rather due to the fact that there were none in that grassy field than to any want of a will to throw them! Lord P., though courted by the Wessex bourgeoisie, was—for certain particular reasons—detested by its proletariat; and his appearance at this juncture gave this latter a chance that was not likely to be repeated. In all human communities—indeed in all human groups—there are strange atavistic forces that are held in chains deep down under the surface. Like the imprisoned Titans, these Enceladuses and Sisyphuses and Briareuses, dwell in the nether depths of human nature ready to break forth in blind scoriac fury under a given touch. In these violent upheavals of class against class there is something far deeper than principle or opinion at stake. Skin against skin . . . blood against blood . . . nerves against nerves . . . rise up from incalculable depths.

Lord P. himself was not less than astounded at the intensity of the feeling that his figure in that dog-cart by the side of his placid servant excited in this mob. It was as if everything in these people's lives that they had suffered from . . . indifference . . . neglect . . . contempt . . . cold malignant distaste . . . fastidious disgust . . . everything that had weighed on them, day by day, in a tacit conspiracy to press them down and keep them down, suddenly incarnated itself in that grizzled man with the small pointed grey beard and big wrinkled nose. Lord P. was absolutely startled, and, though by no means a coward, he was even a little frightened, by the looks he caught on some of the women's faces in that surging mass of people.

While his black horse plunged and reared in its harness, while men tugged at its bridle and tried to pull the reins out of Blimp's hands, while there was danger not only of the shafts of the cart being broken but of the whole equipage being upset, he caught on the face of one woman from Paradise—she was a remote cousin, by the way, of Abel Twig—a look of such insane ferocity, free from every other feeling, that a spasm of sheer panic seized upon him. It was one of those moments that are apt to occur in the most carefully regulated communities. My Lord was no longer under the protection of an invisible network of magnetic wires. He was a man, and a man acquainted with fear. But what had frightened him was not the violence of other men. What had frightened him was a glance into a black crater. For that black crater possessed eyes, and the Marquis of P., clinging to his swaying and heaving dog-cart, had looked into those eyes.

People rarely receive these revelations of the underside of life unaccompanied by some funny little triviality which, like a mime or a mommet, goes ever afterward hand in hand with that chimera. The trivial thing on this occasion was some black horse-hairs which lay smeared in a little patch against one of the green shafts now in such eminent danger of being broken. Black horse-hairs, wet with sweat and sticking to painted wood, were henceforth always associated in his mind with this deadly popular fury surging up out of the cracks and crevices of Tor Field.

It was impossible for the Taunton police to remain long in ignorance of the nature of this howling and struggling group of persons who were apparently hustling two men in a painted cart and trying to pull them out; but for the next three or four minutes their official attention was so completely occupied in holding back the crowd which kept pouring down the lane from entering the field that they could not cope with this new trouble. "Even a Zomerset orficer," as one of them said to Lord P. on a subsequent occasion, "couldn't be in two carners of the same girt field at the same time."

It was, however, much easier for Mr. Geard, who *was*, quite simply, as he had told his family he would be, surveying matters from the top of the Tor, to get the full significance of the danger to Lord P. than it was for Taunton policemen. *They* were forced to look up, being fully occupied. He was in a position to look down, having nothing to do. There would certainly have been a rush from the bourgeois portion of the native audience to rescue the hustled nobleman; in fact, his own son, Will Zoyland, would have been at his side in a couple of minutes; if it had not been for two things: first, that there was a rise in the ground to the west of that audience, which prevented them from seeing what was transpiring over there, and secondly that the long-expected Pageant now commenced in real earnest, absorbing everyone's attention.

A couple of hundred lads and lasses gorgeously attired in mediæval costume marched forth now from the two heraldic pavilions and grouped themselves round the Dragon Flag and round the two golden thrones. The body of the dead Elaine was carried in—never in her life had Crummie looked so lovely— and the Archbishop of Canterbury accompanied by a Knight carrying the crown of Britain on a green cushion, stood at the feet of the dead. Lancelot du Lac leaned against the side of

Queen Gwenevere's throne, while, for those initiated in such matters, the forms of Sir Percival, Sir Galahad, and Sir Gawain, clearly distinguishable from one another by the devices on their shields, could be made out conversing together at the back of Arthur's throne. To the west of the Queen's throne and at a little distance from the rest—as if retaining their own mythical independence—stood Tristram and Iseult, while, in a position of ferocious skulking, spying, and murderously tracking down was King Mark of Cornwall.

In regard to the choice of characters for this first part of the Pageant there had been no difficulty save for one curious exception. This exception was Merlin. John had been very anxious to have a Merlin and so had Edward Athling. Mr. Geard, however, had steadily and—to the mind of the whole company, obstinately—refused to allow Merlin to be represented at all. "But we're going to represent Christ, Daddy," Crummie had pleaded. "You don't mean to say that Merlin's more sacred than Christ." Mr. Geard had smiled and shook his head. "Christ was buried in Jerusalem," was his curious answer; by which John understood him to mean that while for the world at large Christ was by far the more sacred, here, in Glastonbury, where he disappeared from view, Merlin must always be the "numen" or the "Tremendum Mysterium" that can be second to none.

Mr. Geard had reached the top of the hill by a circuitous route long before the Pageant was due to begin. The performance was divided—and the Dubliners had displayed their nicest virtuosity in the way this had been done—into three parts. All three parts had a lot of dumb show, a limited amount of dialogue and a great many choral songs. But the point in which the high technical skill of the Dubliners was most revealed was in the manner in which the Pageant was fused and blended with the Passion Play, the two together forming a trilogy to which a strange and original unity had been given by the rôle played by Arthur's Fool. The Dubliners, with Irish audacity, had given Capporelli the leading rôle in all three parts, and by an artful reversal of chronology in the interests of symbolism, the thing began with the latest epoch of time and worked back to the earliest. Thus the opening dealt with the Arthurian Cycle, the interlude with the Passion of Christ, and the conclusion with the ancient Cymric Mythology, Capporelli being Dagonet in the first, Momus, a comic Roman soldier in the second, and none other than the bard Taliessin in the third.

In the intervals of their violent quarrels with Athling the Dubliners had worked very enthusiastically with him over these mystical effects. Athling had indulged himself with a passionate wistfulness in the kind of poetry he had made up his mind to forsake, but the new note, the modern note that was so obnoxious to Lady Rachel, had forced its way in, and had given a bizarre and even an uncomfortable twist to many scenes of this strange Pageant. This was especially the case with the scenes in which Capporelli entered, and the great clown consenting to use several poignant and mocking apothegms composed by the Middlezoy poet had added to them certain curious touches of his own. There was such a distance between the grassy ledge where the performance took place and the front row of seats that the voices of individual players were liable to be blown away upon the wind. This was, however, compensated for by a printed libretto which the audience could read while they enjoyed the dancing, the studied gestures, the symbolic ritual, of the trilogy.

Mr. Geard had many deep and strange feelings as he watched the gathering crowd from the top of the Tor. He had found quite a large group of noisy lads up there when he reached the top, but, knowing the Mayor by sight, they had hurriedly shogged off, running down the hill at top speed to join in the sport of baiting the policemen where the booths and caravans stood in a line under the hedge and where ginger-pop was to be sold. All except one. This was the small offspring of Solly Lew, the taxi-driver, a grave little boy called Steve, who had manifested for Mr. Geard the moment he appeared the peculiar fascination that a child will sometimes display for a formidable middle-aged man. Mr. Geard, finding himself alone with this child on the summit of the great haunted hill, the hill of Gwynap-Nud, the Welsh Fairy-Demon, the hill where Abbot Whiting had been so bloodily murdered, called Steve to his side and made him sit down with him under the tower.

It was indeed upon a remarkable scene that Mr. Geard and

his small companion looked down now as they surveyed the verdurous undulations of those island-valleys—Ynys Witrin, Ynys Avallach, Insula Avallonia the land of Modred, Melwas, Meleagnant, Mellygraunce, Aestiva Regio, Insula Pomorum, Gwlad yr Hav, Insula Vitrea, Isle de Voirre, yr Echwyd, Glast, Glastenic, Glastonia, Glaston—over which the intense sky, that Midsummer Day, seemed actually to be bowing down, bowing and bending and battening upon those lovely green undulations, as if the greatest and most powerful of all created Beings was taking His pleasure with the sweet grass-scented earth.

The crowds of people seated on the chairs and benches in the centre of the bottom of the field resembled a magician's carpet that Mr. Geard by his incantations from up there under St. Michael's Tower had caused to be laid down. He himself now, like a modern Gwyn-ap-Nud, surveyed his astonishing evocation with a silent gratitude, with an up-welling feeling of fulfilment, deep as that fount of red water whose flowing he could detect at the foot of the opposite hill. The hats and garments and parasols of the feminine element in his audience—for they were all dressed for summer weather that day—caused the great expectant crowd to resemble, spread out upon the grass, that many-coloured coat which the original nomadic Joseph had received of his father Jacob. Westward of the crowd Mr. Geard could see the roofs of Glastonbury, looking, with all their bright red tiles, as if a great wave of spray from the chalybeate fountain had washed over them. Rising from among these red-tiled roofs he could see the massive tower of St. John's and the lesser tower of St. Benignus'. These two towers from any distance were, with the one under which he sat, the characteristic land-marks of the place, for the Abbey Ruins, although to a careful scrutiny they were just distinguishable among the trees, were unable to stand out in clear relief.

Mr. Geard now cast his eyes upon a long, low tent, one of the biggest tents that he himself had ever seen, which he had caused to be set up under the hedge, to the northwest of where the audience was seated, and on the opposite side of the entrance from where stood the line of caravans. Inside this big tent, which was really five or six tents thrown into one, Mr.

Geard had prepared a substantial tea—and not only a tea. He had used as his caterer the landlord of a Glastonbury Inn that overlooked the cattle-market and had many historic associations, and this man had brought over from his cellar an enormous amount of liquour of every kind. This man, whose name was Dickery Cantle, had the peculiarity of being the weakest and most helpless human creature that Mr. Geard had ever seen. The Cantles had handed down this inn from father to son for no less than four generations. Rumour says that the recruiters for Monmouth's rebellion used to meet here, and that John Locke, uncle of the first Recorder of Glastonbury, used to sit, of a summer evening, on the wooden bench outside, drinking gin and cider, while he meditated upon the pragmatic limitations of the human spirit.

Dickery Cantle would never have suceeded in avoiding ruin if it had not been that his stomach was so weak that the least touch of alcohol made him vomit. His wife was not a woman of much more energy than her husband and it was notorious in the town that while their cellar was celebrated for the rare and high quality of its wines their personal table often lacked meat and they could not afford to buy new shoes for their only child, Elphin. Mr. Geard would never have undertaken to provide such extensive preparations for his audience if he had not been struck one day by the wasted consumptive look of Elphin Cantle. This chance encounter, when he was drinking in their bar, had remained in his mind. "I'll give those Cantles some business," he had told Megan; and this big tent was the result.

But the eyes of Mr. Geard now turned westward, and in turning in that direction they caught sight of the mob surrounding the green-wheeled dog-cart; a scene that was visible to him from the Tor's summit, although quite invisible to the spectators of the Pageant.

"They be pulling they chaps out of thik cart, Mister," Steve Lew remarked; and Mr. Geard very quickly realised to whom the green dog-cart and the big black horse must belong. Seldom has an elderly man raced down a hill more quickly than Bloody Johnny ran now. "He was only just in time," Steve said to

Elphin Cantle afterwards as he was helping him open bottles and hand round beer-mugs. "Yon Mayor be a good 'un for a fast sprint, looksee, spite o' his girt belly! 'Twas all I could do to keep pace wi' he!"

It is always difficult to disentangle the element of pure chance from the other forces that bring about any startling event, from the pressure, for instance, of that mysterious undertide that we call Destiny, or from the creative energy spontaneously generated, from the central point of its absolute freedom, in the will of a living organism. What happened now seemed to submerge Mr. Geard's personal prestige among that crowd, his official position as Mayor of the Town, as well as the extraordinary magnetic power that always burned at any dangerous crisis in his unholy eyes. Certainly his advance towards the swaying dog-cart and the plunging horse, when once he approached the scene, was not an easy one. One ruffian from the slums of Street, down by the banks of the Brue, struck him in the face with a stick leaving a bleeding mark across his white, moist, flabby cheek. A woman from Butts Close—she was a sister of Tom Barter's landlady, but a more reckless sort of character—dragged at his clothes and tore his waistcoat open, so that the grey flannel shirt (that he never would let Megan send to the wash more than once a fortnight and that he insisted on wearing summer and winter alike) hung out almost indecently over the front part of his trousers. It must be remembered that between this surging mob around Lord P. and the original crowd of invaders of the field, who had now subsided into quiescence about their banners, there was a protuberant rib of the hillside which prevented both the Dye-Works strikers and the seated audience from seeing what was going on. Red Robinson, whose seething and fermenting " 'ate" had, it almost seemed, been paralysed by the mere waving of Miss Drew's green parasol, was now drifting with baffled fury from one to another of the banner-bearers, cajoling, commanding, imploring, entreating them, like a distracted leader in a lost battle, to rush forward and invade the grassy eminence where the coronation of King Arthur was now triumphantly proceeding, teasing him, mocking him, a veritable charade of Tantalus, with its glittering and fantastical fooling.

Lord P.'s fate depended, therefore, as in most physical struggles between bewildered human antagonists, upon the configuration of the ground. If Mr. Geard had not been playing, quite unconsciously, the primeval rôle of Gwyn-ap-Nud, the old Welsh Prince of Darkness, and enjoying the spectacle he had wrought from the summit of Tor, Lord P. would certainly have come to grief and there would have doubtless appeared some modern Judge Jeffreys holding grim inquisition into a popular uprising. As it was, Mr. Geard's desperate struggle to reach the besieged dog-cart created such a hurly-burly of shouts and counter-shouts, of imprecations and protestations, that the Taunton police guarding the hedge caught the clamour on the wind and came rushing across the grassy hillocks to intervene.

It was the sight of these officers' helmets above the heads of the rioters that, when he recalled his sensations later, remained with Mr. Geard as the most sinister of his impressions. His other impressions, the dazzling sunshine, the blue sky, the trodden grass, the stink of human sweat and foul garments, the taste of his own blood from his bleeding cheek, the sight of the green wheels tipped up on one side and spinning round, the hoofs of the black horse pawing the air, the unmoved countenance of Sergeant Blimp, the panic in the eyes of the Marquis, the confusion of human arms and legs and contorted faces through which he struggled and sweated and fought and tore his way, left upon his mind rather a sense of exhilaration than anything else. Mr. Geard was one of those men whose physical phlegm is so thick and deep that it requires a series of material shocks to rouse the full awareness in them of the taste and tang of life. Something in him—some savage atavistic reversion to his heathen ancestors—had tasted blood in this tossing *mêlée* of sweating, dragging, resisting human bodies. The moments when infuriated women—their bodies forced into contact with his body by pressure from behind—clung to his plump figure, tearing, scratching, clinging, striking, shrieking, were moments of a wild physical exultation. Mr. Geard panted like a dog. The spittle from his thick sensual lips mingling with the blood from his hurt cheek trickled down his chin. With heaving chest, straining limbs, and bare head—for he had now lost his hat—he struggled blindly

forward, those spinning green wheels, those almost vertical green
shafts, the scared eyes of the Marquis, drawing him forward, like
the jutting out of a wharf with a swinging lamp in a turbulent
sea. His big mouth was wide open now as he fought his way on,
the black fire in his eyes burned with a terrible glee, his pantings became like the pantings of that beast called the Questing
Beast in the legends. Guttural noises, different from mere human
breathings, rose from his tormented lungs.

The curious thing was, however, that Mr. Geard's mind had
never been calmer or clearer in its working than at that moment. "This is Life!" he thought to himself; and something like
a sobbed-out chuckle rose up from the pit of his labouring belly.
His old refrain—"Blood of Christ—Blood of Christ—Blood of
Christ"—drummed in his throat and blent itself with his bestial
groanings and with his Hengist-and-Horsa chucklings. As he beat
his way on, reeling, staggering, stumbling, his queer battle-
frenzy increased rather than diminished. "This is Life!" he said
to himself, with exactly the same clear awareness of the enjoyment he was getting, as if he had been a sturdy swimmer in
huge wave-bursts of tossing surf. And there gradually arose in
his consciousness a very queer notion, the feeling, namely, that
what he was doing now was not rescuing a frightened aristocrat
from a mob, but rescuing the Blood of Christ from loss, from
destruction, from annihilation. The fancy lodged itself in his
brain—quite cool and clear above his pantings—that if he could
only touch one of those upheaved green shafts with his hand, if
he could only get his fingers on the bridle of that rearing black
horse, he would prevent the Blood of Christ from sinking into
the deep earth and being lost forever! "Yes, yes, yes," he
thought, "I'll build a Saxon arch about the Chalice Well—a
round Saxon arch!" And then it was that he caught sight of
the helmets of Philip Crow's policemen.

The sight of these officials completely broke up his mood. It
was a policeman's hand—not his hand—that dragged down
those green shafts. It was a policeman's arm—not his arm—that
brought to earth the rearing front hoofs of the black horse. It
was between a couple of Philip's policemen, too, that Lady
Rachel's father was now standing, angrily stroking his beard

and gazing round vindictively in order to point out to the officials
the worst offenders and ring-leaders of the crowd. Not as yet had
the officers of the law laid hands upon anyone, but it was clear
to the exhausted and disconcerted Mayor that this was what
they were now thinking of doing. Many of the crowd were evidently of the same opinion, for they were beginning to sneak
off with extraordinary celerity, each of the retreating ones assuming an absent-minded air with regard to immediate phenomena and an intensely interested air with regard to pressing
events which demanded their presence upon the far horizon.

Mr. Geard, disappointed though he was, and with no fire left
in his eyes, now pulled himself together. He tucked his shirt
back into its proper place. He took out his handkerchief and
wiped the blood from his cheek. He buttoned his coat tightly
under his chin. Then he advanced, although with tottering steps
and heaving lungs, and presented himself before Lord P. His
Lordship welcomed him warmly. Luckily he took it at once for
granted that it was by his anxiety for the safety of the patron
of his Pageant that he had caused these officials—like the war-
riors of Cadmus—to spring out of the earth. "Well, Mr. Mayor,"
he began, "this is indeed ——" Philip's policemen, hearing the
word "Mayor" and seeing Lord P. shake hands so warmly with
this perspiring, panting, hatless member of the crowd, became
convinced that they were in the presence of another distinguished
victim of this breaking of His Majesty's peace.

Mr. Geard's brain now moved very actively as he shook hands
with Sergeant Blimp, a thing which he did quite as warmly as
the Sergeant's master had done with himself. He spoke in an
authoritative voice, conveying the impression to both the nobleman and the policemen that he was accustomed to order officials
about. "One or two of you take his Lordship to his seat. It's the
front row. Lady Rachel is keeping it for him. The performance
has begun."

"Won't you yourself ——" began Lord P.

"No," said Mr. Geard abruptly; and he surprised the owner
of the dog-cart by clambering up into the high seat along with
Blimp who was already once more in possession of horse and

reins. "I presume he's going to put up at the Pilgrims', eh?" he said.

"You're not deserting your own show, Geard?"

"Seen enough of it for a while," replied Mr. Geard. "I may come back before it's finished though. I want to hear how you've enjoyed it."

Blimp's hands were on the reins to pull the vehicle round.

"You won't mind if I use your cart for a minute before he takes it back to town?"

"Not at all, Geard, not at all," Lord P. rejoined, "as long as you don't ask *me* to get up again!" He uttered these last words with a grimace that was clearly intended to make a jest of his recent attack of nerves. Not a soul had seen the fear in his eyes except Mr. Geard and possibly Sergeant Blimp, but it was characteristic of the man to make a point of honour of this humorous confession.

"Yes, the front row, officer," the Mayor added, in answer to one of the policemen. "Lady Rachel is keeping a seat for him." He laid his bare hand on Blimp's neatly gloved one. "Wait a little," he murmured. "I want him to get well ahead."

"Right you are, your Worship," said the sergeant.

"You two had a near shave," said Mr. Geard.

"Tut, tut! 'Twere nothing to the dust I've seen kicked up in *my* time," replied the sergeant. "His Lordship ain't as young a man as he was ten years ago."

"A mob's a nasty thing," said Mr. Geard, giving the man such an understanding glance that Blimp answered with a wink.

"His nerves ain't what they were," he said. The Mayor looked round. It was extraordinary how quickly the crowd had scattered.

"I don't want any arrests made, nor does Lord P.," he remarked emphatically to a policeman who was holding their horse's head. The animal was still trembling a little.

The man touched his helmet. "As your Worship wishes."

"Drive after your master, Sergeant," Mr. Geard directed, "but not fast. I want to see him safely in his seat."

The policeman let go of the bridle and the green-wheeled dog-cart set off at a walking pace towards the scene of the Pageant. They soon reached a spot from which it was possible to get a clear view of both audience and performers. "Pull her up a second, Sergeant." The man obeyed, and they waited till they could observe the figure of Lord P., with the two policemen close behind him, threading their way through the crowd of strikers. When they had disappeared, "Drive over to that tent if you don't mind," commanded the Mayor.

Arrived at the entrance to his huge refreshment pavilion, Mr. Geard told Steve Lew, who had now resumed his fascinated attendance, to run in and ask Mr. Cantle to come out. It was now the destiny of Sergeant Blimp to set eyes on the feeblest, weakest, most worried and most bewildered caterer he had ever seen, or ever desired to see. "I'm going to send you some guests of my own straight away, Dickery," said the Mayor. "Treat 'em well. Don't let 'em get drunk. And turn 'em out without fail before five o'clock. All out before five o'clock!"

Dickery Cantle, whose eyes were a pale, light, moist blue, and whose beard was straggly and thin and like bleached tow, was so surprised at the sight of the green cart and black horse that he could only open his mouth and blink.

"Is Elphin inside?" enquired Mr. Geard. Steve Lew heard this, if Elphin's parent didn't, and the young Cantle with his thin legs in black Sunday stockings soon made his appearance. "Tell your mother and her people that I'm going to send her some guests for refreshments in a minute. Tell her 'beer and wine and sandwiches' and tell her all out before five, will you, Elphin? All out by five! I don't want 'em to clash with the other people."

Elphin Cantle's blue eyes—not pale blue like his father's, who was now muttering something quite incoherent about "brands" and "vintages"—but deep blue like the broad sky above them, gleamed with intelligent understanding. "Am I to tell Mother any . . . any sum . . . that your Worship wants . . . would wish . . . her . . . to——" he began.

"Tell her—'all that's reasonable,'" pronounced Mr. Geard emphatically.

Elphin's blue eyes deepened in colour till they grew nearly black. Then brushing some dust from his legs, thin as matches, —those poor emaciated legs that were the *fons et origo* of this big tent—he lifted up his face. "Mother will understand. Mother thanks you from her heart, your Worship! Come, Father!" he added.

Dickery Cantle followed Elphin into the tent, as did also Steve Lew, bestowing on the Mayor before he departed a final glance of fanatical devotion.

The green-wheeled dog-cart drove off now. It encircled the seated audience from whose throats excited and vociferous applause was now arising as the King and Queen with their great golden crowns upon their heads rose from their thrones and moved to the side of the Lady of Shalott.

The movement of the Dye-Works factory-hands, with their protestant allies and their secular banners, had not been missed by Mr. Geard. All the way down that hillside—as he was racing to the rescue of the Marquis—he was thinking desperately how to cope with this menacing invasion. He could catch, as Blimp trotted his horse along the edge of the vast concourse of people, the constant murmurs of "Order! Order! Hush! Hush!" addressed to these men, who continued to talk loudly among themselves, even though the poles of their banners were now planted in the earth. When they came level with the row of seats at the end of which sat Mother Legge, Mr. Geard called upon Blimp to pull up. Here they waited, watching for the close of the scene on the grassy stage above. It was near the end. After a second or two of waiting, it ended, and the play-actors, well contented with the ovations they had just received, marched off to their respective pavilions.

A general buzz of excited talk ran through the whole mass of people. The dog-cart had drawn up close to where Mrs. Legge and Blackie Morgan were sitting. Between their horse's head and the ends of the first five rows of seats was the back of a banner, the poles of which rested on the grass, carrying the words, "Down with Mummery!" These words Mr. Geard now contemplated, as he acknowledged the salutations of the people near enough to recognise him. Mother Legge herself made an airy gesture with her black-gloved hand, that was almost as if she kissed the tips of her fingers to the Mayor of Glastonbury, and many of the seated crowd looked towards him and nodded towards him as they continued their boisterous clapping, as if directing their applause to the organiser of the performance as much as to the players.

The crowd of Dye-Works strikers was obviously ill at ease at this juncture. The big audience behind them had time now to concentrate their attention on these men, whose banners, "Down with Religion!" "Down with Capital!" "Down with Mummery!" flapped beside them in the warm summer wind. Several of Philip's policemen were now standing about, surveying these revolutionary scrolls with humorous detachment, but Mr. Geard observed one of these officers edge himself in front of the knees of the people in the second row, till he came behind Lord P., into whose ear he whispered something, something that made the Marquis turn round and glance at the strikers.

The applause had been prolonged by the foreigners long after it had ceased among the native-born, but it died down now and a general murmur of conversation all over the big audience took its place in the midst of which some very curious and surprising preparations were going on on the stage in front of them all. A big wooden cross was brought out, from which were hanging thick ropes, like those used on shipboard, twisted loosely round its cross-beams, and this object was laid on the ground, where the thrones of Arthur and Gwenevere had formerly been, beside a capacious hole that had been dug to receive it. Across the faces of the audience was blown at intervals the warm sun-sweet smell of trodden grass and mingled with this the pungent smell of nicotine from the short clay pipes which many of the strikers— quiet, patient family-men—had lit to cheer their suspense.

It was at this moment that the voice of Red Robinson was heard in shrill penetrating tones. Red got hold of a chair and had jumped up upon it. From this elevation he began to scream forth a hurried torrent of abuse, raising his hands high into the air and making them tremble there, using in fact that particular gesture which has become almost a convention with street-orators, but which still retains a power that has its own peculiar quality.

Mr. Geard saw two or three policemen pushing their way towards this shouting man. "Give him five minutes, officers, if you please!" This command from the green dog-cart was flung out in those stentorian tones which used to be the delight of the slums in Bloody Johnny's revivalistic meetings.

The officers stopped, turned, and remained motionless, glancing alternatively at Lord P., seated by his daughter's side, and at the bare-headed Mayor in Lord P.'s cart.

"You Wessex people who 'ave come 'ere to 'ear this folly, listen to me! And you, foreign people, who have come from hover the seas to see this folly, listen to me! And you, Glastonbury comrades, who know what this folly is, listen to me! High 'ave only one thing to say this harfternoon! The capitalistic system of society is doomed. In a 'undred years from now, private property in Glastonbury will be hun-known! This 'ere new Mayor of hours is no better than the light one and has for Crow hup there with 'is blasted airpline ——" He jumped down hurriedly from his chair and took refuge within the close-packed ranks of his friends, for the enraged figure of Lord P. standing erect now and calling furiously upon the policemen to stop him had counteracted the command from the green cart and the officers had moved towards him. It was then that Dave Spear jumped up from *his* seat and lifted up his voice.

"This man," shouted Spear, "may have been too angry to choose his words as he ought. But what he says is true! Humanity will soon ——" At the scholarly intonation of the young philosopher all the Germans in the audience—who were the ones who knew English best—leaned forward, listening gravely and intently. Indeed they cried out in guttural protest against some nasal French voices lifted up in derision of Spear's words, and for a moment it looked as if the old hostility between Gothic blood and Mediterranean blood would burst out that day in Urbs Vitrea under Gwyn-ap-Nud's mischievous rogueries! The particular tone Spear plunged into at once, so earnest and so academic, and his introduction of the word "humanity," beguiled the Russians who were present—all except the monks from the Caucasus who took him for a devilish heretic—and brought them over to his side. The Spanish contingent, which was unusually large, agreed on the contrary very strongly with the French and joined the French in calling angrily upon the young man to sit down.

But Dave Spear, in spite of cries of "Order!", "Silence!", "Turn him out!" refused to sit down. "Humanity will soon," he shouted, "be no longer Germans, Englishmen, Frenchmen, Russians! We shall all be men and women—working for ourselves —not for the rich—in one great community of Comrades!" The clamour round him got now so confused that it became impossible to out-shout it, and after calmly surveying the whole crowd with his eyes and watching them as if he were a shepherd counting his sheep, Dave Spear sat down.

The group of strikers from the Crow Works were now thrown into a most awkward and uncomfortable position. The bulk of them had no sympathy with the communistic opinions of their leaders. They were unable to enjoy "thik open air theayter" as they regarded it, because of their near neighbourhood to the gentry. At the same time, being honest Somerset workingmen, they were reluctant to desert their flags. One of the most dignified among them, a certain Josh Witcombe from Queen's Camel, articulated the thoughts of the majority among them when he said to himself—"What in the name of crikey be I doing here? A danged fool I be, when I might be digging taties, in me bit o' garden, this fine holiday! This ere Crow be a bloody blighter. There ain't two opinions about that, but what be all this high-falutin' palaver got to do wi' I? Crikey! I wish I were sittin' peaceful-like in me back-garden, watching me sweet peas how girt they be grown! This here Glaston will never be a place for quiet folk to enjoy theyselves in, till both this blighter Crow and this blighter Geard be drove out o' town."

Mr. Geard was not oblivious of the growing discomfort of this body of worthy men. Left to themselves now by both agitators and police they were being subjected to the animosity of an increasing number of the audience, who had come to regard their presence at the field at all as a lugubrious spoil-sport. Mr. Geard now made Blimp drive my Lord's cart forward, about twice its own length, till it was in the very centre of this sulky and disconcerted crowd. Then he stood up in the cart with his hand on the sergeant's shoulder. "Gentlemen," he began.

All eyes were turned towards him. He managed to temper his voice so that it was only audible to the men he was addressing.

It was an immense relief to him to observe that Elphin Cantle
had joined his young adherent Steve Lew, and that both the boys
were standing now close up to one of the green wheels of his
cart. "Gentlemen," he repeated. "I'm sorry that you should have
come out today only to find things unsatisfactory. I am the
Mayor of this town and I wish all Glastonbury people to enjoy
themselves today. I have told Mr. Cantle down there in that
tent,"—he waved one of his plump hands in the direction of the
hedge—"that I wish him to give all you men of the Crow Dye-
Works something to eat and drink at my expense. Elphin Cantle
I see is here. He'll show you where to go. Take them with you,
Elphin!" Then, as an after thought, he added, " 'Twill be a
shame on ye all, and a disgrace to your Mayor, if the good liquour
that's in yon tent be taken back to cellar!"

There was a moment's hesitation, and then Mr. Burt of Stoke-
sub-Ham spoke up. "Three cheers for the Mayor of Glastonbury!" he cried. At once another voice in the crowd was raised,
but it was impossible for Mr. Geard to identify him—"Three
cheers for Bloody Johnny!" The cheers were somewhat nervously and somewhat shamefacedly given, and the big audience
of seated people extending now as far down almost as the hedge
craned their necks to see what new thing now was toward.

Suddenly Mat Dekker rose from where he sat by his son's
side. "Three cheers for the Mayor of Glastonbury who has given
us this——" His voice was drowned in a terrific volley of
applause.

In every great audience there is a certain accumulation of
magnetic emotion which seems to store itself up, as if in great
invisible tanks, above the people's heads. Mat Dekker's words
had turned the tap of these psychic reservoirs. The crowd lost
its head altogether in its excitement. It had been stirred already
by the romance of the Arthurian scene and by the rich, poignant
fooling, in amazing dumb-show, of the inspired French clown.
Dave Spear's revolutionary speech had increased this tension,
and it now broke loose in a whirlwind of excitement. Women
waved their handkerchiefs and kissed their hands; men jumped
upon their chairs and shouted; children yelled and screamed.
The vague rumours that had hovered about the figure of Mr.

Geard helped to intensify this demonstration. Those in the front
seats who had heard his speech to the striking dye workers and
had been hopelessly shocked were swept along on the current.
Lady Rachel clapped long and desperately, her cheeks white
with excitement, her eyes flashing with girlish ecstasy. The Marquis wore the expression of a far-sighted statesman who has had
recourse to some irresponsible prophet. Old Mother Legge's
spacious and maternal bosom—the bosom of an immoral earth-
mother—was heaving with unsuppressed sobs. Mrs. Geard too
was crying uncontrollably. But Cordelia sat straight up in her
chair. Her eyes were fixed in miserable fascination upon that
great wooden cross lying upon the grass. When the noise died
down a little, Mr. Geard got up upon his feet for the second
time that day in Lord P.'s high dog-cart.

"What will he say?" thought Lady Rachel. "What the deuce
will old Johnny do now?" thought the Marquis. "I would not be
in Geard's shoes for something," whispered Mat Dekker to Sam.

Mr. Geard cleared his throat. Then he bent down over his
impassive driver upon whose shoulder he was pressing heavily.
"The moment I sit down, you drive off, Sergeant," he whispered, "and make her go too!" Then rising to his full height and
throwing back his head he lifted his free arm high into the air.
And there fell upon that enormous mass of people one of those
tremendous and awe-inspiring silences that seem as if they were
supported, like dim catafalques of expectation, by unseen spiritual hands. "Not unto us," he shouted in slow reverberating
tones, "not unto us be the Glory for this great Day but unto . . .
unto—" he was enough of a Cagliostro, enough of the charlatan
they accused him of being, deliberately to pretend to hesitate at
this point. It was a subtle oratorical trick and was not defrauded
of its effect—"unto . . . unto the Christ of Glastonbury!" He
sank back in his seat by the side of Sergeant Blimp, who, since
there was no question of encountering Merlin's ghost was as cool
as he would have been at a Royal garden-party. In a second the
green-painted wheels were revolving at a dizzy pace and the
dog-cart was whirling off westwards, over the grassy slopes of
the great field, as if it had entered a desperate race with some
fairy chariot of Gwyn-ap-Nud.

"I hope Blimp will breathe her a bit before the end of the field," whispered the Marquis to his daughter.

"Hush, Father!" rejoined the girl. "Do be quiet. The Passion Play is beginning."

The girl was right. Not oblivious of the dramatic effect of allowing their sacred interlude to follow quickly on the heels of Geard's last words John Crow had taken upon himself—oblivious as to whether the Dubliners or Ned Athling or Paul Capporelli were ready—to give the sign to begin. And the beginning of their elaborately rehearsed "Mystery" was really a very impressive spectacle.

The Dye-Works strikers, however, saw nothing of it. Turning their backs to it altogether and this time followed instead of led, by the banner denouncing "Mummery," they made their way hurriedly down the hill towards the big refreshment tent. Elphin and Steve—this latter delighted to play so prominent a part in the affairs of Mr. Geard—ran on in front of them to warn the Cantles of their arrival.

It was at this point that all eyes were concentrated upon the stage. And there entered upon it first a legion of Roman soldiers marching behind their centurion, then—issuing forth from the other pavilion—the chief priests and rulers of the Jewish people, and finally, approaching by himself, attended only by Momus, the comic Roman soldier who served as his bodyguard, the Procurator of Jerusalem, Pontius Pilate. The part of Pontius Pilate was played by the assistant schoolmaster in St. Benignus' church-school, a man who had been chosen for this part by the eloquent Dr. Sodbury largely on account of his imposing countenance, a countenance which in its juristic dignity might certainly have belonged to the supercilious Procurator of Judea. The Roman legionaries grouped themselves around Pilate who now, accompanied by his bodyguard Momus, ascended the wooden rostrum or judgment-seat.

"It's like a magnified Punch-and-Judy show," whispered Will Zoyland to Nell; nor were the Bastard's words without point, for in their mutual elevation above the soldiers, and above the group of Jewish Elders who stood apart from the soldiers, the

figures of Pilate and Momus appeared to be isolated in a grotesque Punchinello-like proscenium.

Nell made no reply. She was wondering what Sam was feeling
at this moment while Momus-Capporelli was out-jesting Pontius
Pilate in that ridiculous puppet-box, and players and audience
alike were awaiting breathlessly the appearance of the condemned God-Man. If she had known what Sam was feeling her
heart would have been less heavy than it was. For such was
the contradictoriness of human emotion that the soldiers' Roman
swords and the elders' turbans made the whole thing so fantastic and unreal to him that in his bitter coldness and deep
melancholy his heart turned wistfully to Nell and her child.
His father sitting by his side felt the same sort of distaste; only
with him it was more positive. Both these big, bare-headed men
—for though the sun was smiting them with that mid-afternoon
heat which seems hotter than noon, they held their hats in their
hands—had something in them that felt deep aversion for this
Passion Play. Mat hated it as a silly, frivolous blasphemy. Sam
hated it as a lifeless and ghastly parody upon the death of his
God.

The two Dekkers had less aesthetic feeling in them for performances of this sort than Mr. Whitcombe of Queen's Camel
or Mrs. Legge of Camelot! Such passionate naturalists were they
that a profound *realism*, earthy, simple, almost barbarous, reduced any theatrical show to something flimsy and childish. They
neither of them could go one psychic inch in sympathy for such
things. What to the father seemed gross profanity, to the son
seemed pure unqualified trifling. They neither of them could
catch any stage-illusion in the whole thing. What they now beheld was simply "old Sodbury's schoolmaster dressed up as a
Roman Governor, and that wretched skipping Frenchman, bowing and scraping at his side, and making sacrilegious jokes."

And when escorted by more Roman soldiers and with his
hands tied behind him and an enormous crown of thorns upon
his head, Mr. Evans was led slowly across the grass between the
long-robed Jews and the heathen legionaries, Sam turned round
to his father with the words—"This is awful, isn't it, Dad? It's

worse than I expected. How can they all sit quiet and put up with such disgusting tomfoolery?"

But his father was watching a butterfly. "I believe that's a Clifton Blue," he whispered. "Do look at that little fellow, son; there! over by that thistle!"

But the effect of the appearance of this Evans-Christ upon Sam's mind was to assail with one swift, terrible doubt the ascetic ideal of his whole present life and give him a craving for Nell that made his bones melt within him. That she should be sitting near him, now, within a few yards of him, so that by moving his head he could catch a glimpse of her, gave him a feeling of her identity that was as sharp as he had ever known. A new sensation began to lift up its rattlesnake head within him, a torture that he had hitherto been spared, by reason of his dull imagination and that "dead nerve" within him. But they were upon him now, those devil's pincers! They had got him now, by the umbilical cord in the pit of his stomach! Oh, to think that Will Zoyland could hear that voice day by day, and could see her as he had *never* seen her! For what was one blind, rapturous night of passion compared with what *he* had? "I have never," Sam thought as he watched the Christ-Evans standing before Pilate, *"seen her bare shoulders."*

It often happens that when real love touches with its quivering dart the covetousness of desire, some aspect of a girl's body, not usually associated with amorous dalliance at all, hits her lover's consciousness with a pathos that is well-nigh intolerable. Thus although he had given her a child, there came over him, as the Trial of Christ began before his eyes, a craving that made him heartsick just once to touch her bare shoulders, just to trace with his fingertips the line of her bare spine. Though he had lain with her he had never thought of doing just that. Why hadn't he? Oh, why hadn't he?

The scene that meant so little to the two Dekkers and so little to the two Zoylands appeared to be of absorbing interest to Father Paleologue. Mary was thrilled at his quick, intense, piercing comments. Every movement that Mr. Evans made roused his keenest attention. Every word he caught—though he could catch but few—from Christ or Pilate or Momus or the Chief Priest, became a text for a rapid volley of hurried criticisms. Even Miss Drew grew calm under the compelling intellectual charm of the Byzantine priest and began to feel that there could not be anything very blasphemous going on.

"Has he yet said, 'What *is* Truth?' " enquired Mary with shining eyes. She felt infinitely relieved at the triumphant success that John's labours seemed to be winning. She put everything down to John. Athling, the Dublin people, Capporelli, were completely discounted in her mind. *They* might have invented a few details, a few fancies; it was John's imagination that gave the whole thing that strange and curious unity which Father Paleologue was now talking about to Miss Drew.

"No, lady, not yet," answered Father Paleologue, "but they soon will be. There! Didn't you catch *that*?"

And there came to her ears upon the warm June air, scented with honeysuckle, as the girl intently listened, those words that seem to come from some mysterious level of life where the laws of cause-and-effect have no place—*"To this end was I born, and for this cause came I into the world, that I should bear witness unto the truth. Every one that is of the truth heareth my voice."*

"It's extraordinary," whispered Father Paleologue, passionately, while a light gust of wind lifted Pilate's famous retort and carried it over the hill, "how that man acts! He *can't* be a local shop-man. I've seen every Passion Play in Europe worth seeing for the last twenty years. Oberammergau of course isn't the only one. And I tell you I've never seen anything so convincing as this man. And he's *modern* too. He's got that queer modern touch that's so hard to define. He's a strong, *ugly* Christ too; and that's a vast improvement. Do you remember Rembrandt's Christ in 'The Healing of the Sick?' I forget where it is. Rembrandt's idea of Him was just like this. And it's Biblical too!" And the Byzantine father quoted in an intense whisper in Mary's ears, "He hath no comeliness . . . that men should desire Him."

Athling and the two Dubliners, working together, had managed this world-historical scene in such a way as to mingle Our Lord's trial before Pilate with His trial before the High Priest, and by dispensing with the Scourging and with the Stations of the Cross had made the Crucifixion to follow immediately upon this synthesised condemnation.

"What is that funny man doing, Robert, in the Judge's pulpit?" enquired Mr. Stilly's father of Mr. Stilly. Mr. Stilly hurriedly consulted the printed booklet which John had caused to be placed upon all the seats.

"It says he's Momus, Dad—'a Roman Soldier attending on the Procurator,' who plays a part like that of the Fool in Shakespear's 'Lear.'"

Mr. Stilly's mother now lifted up her high-pitched, querulous voice, the voice of a woman who "didn't like servants messing about in her kitchen." "But isn't this the simple Gospel story, Robert? We don't read of Momus, do we? Or is he in the Apocrypha?"

"*Maria!* how *can* you be so stupid!" whispered Mr. Stilly's father. "There's no New Testament Apocrypha." Mr. Stilly vaguely recalled having once, in Old Jones' shop, been shown something extremely like a New Testament Apocrypha, but out of piety he kept this recollection sealed up in his heart.

"He's talking now, Robert. He's saying such funny things . . . only I can't hear them quite," said old Mrs. Stilly.

Momus-Capporelli had scampered off now from the Procurator's side and was passing from group to group of the Roman soldiers, among whom he was venting monstrous Aristophanic jests. Some of these jests were improvised in a fantastical mixture of French argot and what might be called dog-English and they were accompanied by gestures of a kind more appropriate to the sawdust floor of a Montparnasse dancing-hall than to the greensward of Glastonbury Tor.

Lily Rogers began to give expression to her discomfort under the tension of this tragical-comical fooling. "I wish those soldiers would arrest that fellow," she murmured in the ear of her sister. "Our Glastonbury policeman would have arrested him before this, only the poor man be so deaf."

"These Taunton officers have no more gumption than a lot of cassowaries," replied Louie.

But the wise Emma Sly put forward a different point of view, worthy of the daughter of a Mendip shepherd. "That's the devil in disguise," she explained. "He's telling all those Romans that if they don't crucify the Good Lord quick they won't be able to crucify Him at all."

"This isn't like what Master tells we to say in Creed," remarked Penny Pitches to Mr. Weatherwax, "when it says 'suffered under Pontius Pilate.' If there'd been a Zany like this on Green-Hill-Far-Away Master'd have spoken of it, wouldn't 'un, in the thirty years I've looked after he?"

" 'Twere long agone," remarked the wise gardener. "Maybe Bible itself have forgotten how 'twere. Them hefty lads be Romans, 'sknow, and Romans be heathens, and they heathens baint as reverend as your master, my good gurl. But *'tis* queer, honey, and it do make a man's stomach queasy to see such things. 'Tis like Saturday afternoon in private bar and yet 'tis like Good Friday in Church. It makes a person feel sort o' wobbly in his innards."

The opinion of the Marquis of P. upon the spectacle he was regarding was little different from that of the old gardener and the old servant. "I can't stand much more of this chap Momus," whispered his Lordship to Lady Rachel. "I want to give the little brute a good caning and kick him out! What on earth possessed Geard to allow such a hodge-podge as this?"

"It's my young scaramouch nephew John, Lord P.," said Miss Elizabeth Crow with an indulgent smile, "who is responsible for all this. Rachel knows more about it than I do, but it's the new idea, I believe—isn't it, Rachel?—to bring in, what do you call it? a sort of classical chorus . . . only satirical of course instead of serious."

"I don't . . . know . . . quite . . . what I feel, Miss Crow," whispered Rachel nervously. "I hope . . . it *was* your nephew . . . but I'm afraid . . . there are . . . others——" In her heart, for she was torn between her romantic idealising of Ned Athling and her dislike of his new methods, she heartily wished that Paul Capporelli had been left in Paris!

"Isn't that young man who's jumping about and playing the giddy goat, Tewsy," Mrs. Legge was now remarking to her aged henchman, "the same one that made fun of poor King Mark just now when he was following his lawful wife?"

"And at Lancelot too, Missus! 'A cocked some fine snooks at Lancelot when 'a seen 'un try to cuddle up 'gainst Queen Gwenderver's sweet shanks!"

"Hush Tewsy! Even though it *be* the same, as I think it *be*, haven't they what pulls the strings the right to choose the poppets? Old folk like you and me, Tewsy, don't have no idea what young folks have in their heads these days. Why I heard Mr. Tom Barter tell as how there weren't a wench in Wollop's—and that's who Queen Gwendy was—who wouldn't slip off her skirt if a fellow went the right way about it. 'Twill be bad for *our* trade, Tewsy, if this gets worse. Who'll give half a sovereign for a private room when every room can tell the same tale? That's what I say about such performances as this. 'Tis spoiling the trade, Tewsy; 'tis spoiling the trade."

"You're one for keeping up the family, Mother, ain't you?" whispered Blackie wearily.

"Why sure I be, kid, sure I be!" cried the old lady with a wicked leer. "When all be for all without paying a penny what's to keep the market going?"

Blackie Morgan held her peace. Her enormous grey eyes fixed themselves upon the ubiquitous Momus and upon the thorn-crowned figure, to whose side the clown had now skipped, and the abysmal disillusionment of her gaze seemed to reduce the solid bulk of Glastonbury Tor to insubstantial vapour.

"Why is Pontius Pilate lolling like that now against the side of his ricketty platform?" enquired Tilly Crow of the curator of the museum.

"I hadn't noticed . . . there's so much going on at the same time . . . I was watching that funny soldier wagging his head at Christ . . . but yes, Pilate *is* lolling as you say. Oh, I see what he's doing, Mrs. Crow. He's reading! That's a roll of parchment he's got in his hands. Eh? What's that? He's soliloquising now, I think."

"Could you hear what he said?" asked Tilly anxiously, just as she would have asked Emma if she could hear what the groceryman was saying at the kitchen door.

"Something about Epicurus," replied the curator in a complacent voice, keeping a shrewd eye upon the libretto in his hand. "That roll he's reading is the Logoi of Epicurus, Mrs. Crow."

Tilly was silent. She made a mental note that she would enquire of Emma, later on, what sort of a mariner Epicurus was, that his log-book must needs be dragged in at the Trial of Jesus.

A beautiful Greek slave now appeared upon the scene carrying a silver ewer full of water. "There it is!" cried Mother Legge. "There's Miss Kitty's punch bowl! Now I know what Mr. Crow borrowed it for. Don't 'ee drop it now, you long-haired baggage! Don't 'ee get thinking so much about your bare legs that you go and drop me silver bowl!"

Sis Cole, who had been till now wrapped in a cloud of beatified wonder at all she saw, spoke up when she observed this glittering silver object being carried so carefully towards the pensive Procurator. "Be he feeling sick, Jackie, that King with a coronet on, and all they gold jingle-jangles? Be she bringing he a basin to be sick in?"

Jackie was as proud of his knowledge of the history of the world as the curator had been, as he now replied in his shrill voice just behind that gentleman's back—" 'Tis Pontius Pilate a-washing of his hands! There's a picture in school that they must have took it from. Only 'tis a man in picture, not a gal, what holds the soap and water for'n."

"Be it Pear's soap, Jackie? I don't see thik soap, Jackie."

"I wants to pee!" interposed Bert at this grave juncture.

The curator's head twisted round, and a look of fury was launched at the shameless infant. Tilly turned too. "Take him into the field, girl. Take him into the field at once," she said sternly.

Sis looked helplessly round. There was a deep hush over that whole vast audience while the Procurator of Judea dipped his fingers in Mother Legge's silver bowl. "You've gone and done it," murmured Sis after an awkward pause, but she was too honest a little girl to scold the child when from her heart she thanked all the Powers that it was no longer incumbent upon her to obey this great lady who sat so close to them.

The Curator ostentatiously lit an Egyptian cigarette. "They

oughtn't bring children to a thing that lasts so long," remarked
Tilly. "They can't contain themselves like older people," and
the good lady gave Sis, behind the curator's indignant back, a
reassuring feminine nod. This nod—the symbol of that secret
freemasonry of unfastidious realism that binds all women together—comforted Sis amazingly.

Bert continued his rapturous envisaging of the visible world.
The stiff back and protuberant skull of the learned man in front
of him was as much a portion of the great general Pageant as
was the dragging of our Saviour—for Athling and the Dubliners had altered the details of chronology without the least
scruple—before Caiaphas the High Priest. The laws of perspective as well as the facts of chronology had been interfered
with by these daring stage-directors until the Passion Play on
the terrace of Gwyn-ap-Nud's Hill looked as if it had been designed from various primitive pictures and from pieces of very
old tapestry.

It need hardly be said that there was reached through Mr.
Wollop's round little pig's eyes no dissimilar vision of ecstasy.
All that there was in sight was wonderfully comforting and
thrilling to him. The persons in front of him, the deep blue of
the sky, the green grass, a tiny little red spider that was now
crawling across his own plump hand, were of equal interest to
him with Peter denying his Master. For, as in certain primitive
pictures, where a great number of memorable scenes are enacted
close together, these scenes in the Pageant followed each other
in such quick succession and in such close proximity that they
produced, or almost produced, a pictorial unity.

Thus, in immediate juxtaposition with Pilate's prolonged
soliloquy and also with the pantomimic fooling of Capporelli,
as the clown moved from group to group, Christ was led before
Caiaphas and Peter denied Christ. The part of the cock was
introduced. This was a too dangerous experiment even for the
two Dubliners. They maintained that there was such a deep and
primordial poetry about the crowing of cocks, drenched in the
dews of ten thousand tragic dawns of human suffering, full of
such equivocal, treacherous, and yet Homeric braggadoccio,
carrying memories of women in travail, of dying soldiers, of

millions of tortured, imprisoned and executed victims of Society, memories of insomnia, memories of madness, memories of love— that it would be vulgar, sacrilegious, a blasphemy against the dignity of the human spirit, impious, gross, offensive, ridiculous to introduce a pantomimic cock upon the stage. Besides—the two Dubliners had argued—no human eye ever actually sees the cock that makes its eyelids open. The crowing of the cock brings with it the passionate revolt of all the desperate lovers who like Romeo and Juliet would fain, if they could, hold back the coming of the dawn! It has become—so the Dubliners pro- tested—one of the eternal symbols of the human race, recognized from Ultima Thule to Thibet, from Greenland to the Cape of Good Hope; and to introduce a *visual mockery* of such a thing in any performance would not be merely Aristophanic. It would be diabolic.

But the young poet from Middlezoy countered these arguments by saying that it was the Betrayal of the Christ by Peter that was the outrage upon the primordial mystery of the Cock's Crow, and that by representing the Cock in visual form, this Betrayal was pilloried as it deserved; and that so, and only so, was its full tragical sordidness, baseness, weakness, cowardice, emphasised and felt, as it was meet it should be.

Grandmother Cole it was, who, sitting next to Mrs. Robinson, had a sagacious word to say upon this matter. When she saw appearing suddenly, as if out of the side of the hill, perched upon the steps of Pilate's wooden rostrum, an admirably de- signed and powerfully conventionalized Cock, the old vestment- cleaner remarked to the ex-servant of the Bishop's Palace— "Thik red-combed bird be come to put all chicken-hearted men to shame. Me old man used allus to say to I when 'a did hear thik noisy bird—'Ye wiming-folk be all broody hens. It takes a man- bird to call up the bleeding sun!' But I did tell he 'twere all a vaunt and a vanity, for though cock might crow ever so, the sun only rose when it chose to rise of its wone self."

But the only remark that Red's mother made when she heard this and beheld the feathered apparition, was as follows: " 'Tisn't only to-die that little Ben 'Awker 'as crowed. High've 'a 'eared 'im in our street long afore they pliced all them feathers on 'is pore little 'ead!"

Grandmother Cole expressed astonishment. As a Somerset-born woman, a native of Gwlad yr Hav, she had much more power of accepting illusion than this daughter of the East End. That feathered object, four feet high, with a huge red comb, was to her as real as the tower on the top of the Tor. It disturbed her mind to think of it as concealing little Ben Hawker of her friend's alley. "Be thik bird little Ben then?" she murmured. "What things be coming on the world when little Ben whose birth I do mind, and 'a cost his mother a sore time, should be a-crowing like a cock and making thik bearded man holler and run!"

Saint Peter's remorse of mind did indeed seem so extreme that it almost looked as if he were going to seek refuge from his shame in the arms of Lady Rachel, so far down the hill was he now flying! The Dubliners had told him to run towards the audience and utter his tragic soliloquy so that every word could be heard. Ned Athling had composed one of his best poetical rhapsodies for this Rock of the Apostolic Church, but he had not expected the ringing tones with which—only a few paces from the astonished Lord P.—St. Peter howled out his lines. But Father Paleologue, Mary was relieved to note, seemed well pleased by this episode.

"It's as it used to be in the old Miracle Plays," he whispered, leaning forward with flashing eyes. "I wouldn't have missed this for the Patriarchate! And look at Christ watching him over His shoulder! There's been genius in the invention of this! I wish my Greeks could see it."

The retreat of the errant Saint when he realised how far he had run was even a greater masterpiece of shame. His back, as he slunk off to one of the Arthurian pavilions, was the back of all the deniers of their love since the world began.

"And it's only Billy Bates, the Pilgrims' boot-black!" thought Mary; and she began to tell herself that this triumph of her John was worth all her sacrifices.

And now, according to this strange and primitive Gothic picture that Mr. Geard had caused to be painted upon the slopes of Turris Vitrea like a veritable enchantment of his favourite Mer-

lin, the moment came for the binding of Mr. Evans upon that
great cross of wood. It had been the fidgetty persistence of the
man himself that had got them at last—or rather got Mr. Johnson of the Great Western station timber-yard—to make that cross
out of oak. Nothing but oak, and oak too from one of the spinneys of Wick Wood, would satisfy this lover of the Druids.

"Don't 'ee look, girlie! Don't 'ee look!" whispered Sally Jones
to Tossie Stickles. " 'Twill upset 'ee to see they cruel soldiers
torment thik poor man."

"But 'tis only Mr. Evans," protested the imperturbable Tossie.
"And they be only tying of he. They baint nailing of he, nor
nothing!"

"Don't 'ee look, girlie!" repeated her friend. "Just shut your
eyes tight and I'll report to 'ee how things be with the man, and
how he do bear up under being crucified."

"They're lifting of him now! Oh, looksee! looksee! They're
hauling of him up!"

"Shut your eyes, Toss! Mercy on us, shut your eyes!"

But it was the sympathetic Sally, and not the prospective girl-
mother, who was now the one to shut her eyes. "You tell I, then,
how he be bearing it," she murmured now.

" 'Tis nothing to see, Sal, 'tis nothing to take on about so!
'Twere much worse when I did see a sheep killed, in old man
Chinnock's shed, in this same very field."

"It says 'un . . . were . . . like a sheep . . . it says 'un were
. . . and dumb like a sheep in slaughter!" The tender-hearted
Sally was crying now, but Tossie, keeping the palms of her hands
pressed against her bowels of compassion, continued to stare at
the motionless Figure suspended on the cross.

It was left to the acute Mr. Weatherwax to remark to Penny
Pitches that there were no Thieves by the Lord's side. "This be a
poor Crucifixion," he grumbled. "This be a stingy Crucifixion
when they've only got one cross to set up!"

"Thee be worse nor Pontius Pilate, Isaac," replied Penny. "It
be the same to the good Lord whether he be hung in company
or hung single; and since it be for we sinners anyway ——"

"Old 'ooman, old 'ooman," whispered Mr. Weatherwax, "thee
don't really think, do 'ee, that the murdering of one honest man

could save such beggars and bitches as we be? I baint what you might call a infidel, but there don't seem no justice nor right to my mind in me and you being let off because of people persecuting one good man—like thik poor man over there! Anyway, 'tis not by tormenting folk that good parsnips be growed and good 'taties be dug. What us wants in this here town be more men with Authority, not more o' these here play-actors."

Father Paleologue kept drawing deep breaths of satisfaction all this time. He was interested to observe that the two bearded monks from the Caucasus seemed profoundly impressed. The younger of the two—so he whispered in Mary's ears, but she was too much afraid of staring to corroborate his words—was weeping openly and passionately. How deeply this Byzantine scholar thanked his stars that good luck had thrown one of John's proclamations into his path! He would never forget this stupendous spectacle. Mr. Evans' figure, as it hung there between the two heraldic pavilions—they had carried away Arthur's Dragon Flag—had a dim grandeur that was really startling. The man looked majestic, a real murdered Man-God, hanging there between earth and heaven; and the intense greenness of the hill behind him with that erect, immobile tower, and the gleam of the Roman swords, and the richness of the Hebraic garments, and all this huge gathering of the people, hushed, awestruck, solemnised, gave to that single Figure, suspended against the grassy steep, a magnitude of importance that was overpowering.

"What are those old men counting up their money for?"

"Mother, Mother!" whispered Mr. Stilly reproachfully, for it was one of his parents who uttered these words, "that's the thirty pieces of silver."

"It's easy for you, Robert, of course," retorted the old lady testily. "Your father and I haven't had your privileges at the bank, but to me it looks more like round bits of wood covered with gilt tinsel."

It was not given to Mr. Stilly's parents—much as they loved a quiet game of dominoes—to catch the horrible pathos of the way Judas was now behaving.

Perhaps in that whole vast assembly only Father Paleologue

and one other realised the full poignancy of the acting of Judas.
That "other" was Morgan Nelly. The little girl uttered no word.
She allowed Jackie to explain to Sis that it was Judas who was
being repulsed by those old men with the money-bags and that
he was now going out to hang himself. Jackie explained that
these old men were now saying—"What is that to us? See thou
to that!" and that Judas was now going to hunt for a good place
to "see to it" from. But Morgan Nelly's heart leapt up in sympathy as she followed the figure of Judas wandering among
some small thorn bushes and a patch of stunted hollies, looking
in vain for what he wanted. In the end he disappeared behind
the western pavilion, and long before he had disappeared the
main interest of the Pageant had shifted from him altogether;
but the little girl's heart was still with him. She knew who it was.
While the public knew him as a crazy and good-for-nothing elder
brother of the Nietzschean young man at Wollop's, Nelly Morgan knew him as "old Mr. Booty" who used to read Grimm's
fairy tales on the cricket-field when his side was in.

The Madonna now, all dressed in dusky blood-colour save for
her sky-blue robe, was clinging to the foot of the Cross, while
near her the Roman soldiers were throwing dice and playing
cards in stiff circles upon the green grass. Momus, perched upon
the steps of the empty judgment-seat, was idly tossing up a toy-
balloon into the air and catching it as it came down; and to give
the scene its true character, as some old Flemish painter would
have visualised it, as a tragedy, namely, that drew its poignance
from the pell-mell of that human life which was so indifferent
to its superhuman anguish, either the Dubliners or Athling had
brought it about that Pilate and Caiaphas should be playing
chess together at a little round table in front of that western
pavilion behind which Judas had withdrawn to hang himself.

Persephone's grief at the foot of the cross that bore Mr. Evans
was the finest piece of acting in the whole Pageant. Its emotion
was so sincere that it swept the whole picture together as nothing
else could have done. The girl's monumental gestures were like
those of some classic representation of her own namesake, the
great Goddess of the Dead. Her sublime suffering gave a strange
unity to all the minor groups and personages, their businesses,

their occupations, their pastimes. She seemed to gather the diurnal preoccupations of the whole race together and with passionate solicitude to offer it up, like a cup of hyssop, to the lips of the dying. The other Marys, Mary the sister of Lazarus and Mary Magdalene, came now to Our Lady's side, however, and with their approach an unhappy crisis in the directing of the performance came to the surface.

Ned Athling, anxious to try every sort of new experiment, wanted to introduce a tragic dance at this point by the two Marys round the prostrate figure of Christ's Mother. This, in view of their Catholic up-bringing in Ireland, was too much for the Dubliners. They refused to countenance it. Athling, however —and this had happened in other cases as well—insisted on going on with it, with the result that the two girls who were playing the two Marys, Bessie and Lizzie Marsh from Bove Town, were completely confused, and as they bent together over the prostrate form of the Virgin, they made several sinuous movements with their flexible hips and several swaying movements with their bare arms, while at the same time they lifted up their voices and chanted the ballad-like refrain that Athling had written for them.

The nervous blundering of these young and pretty girls was not at all distasteful to the bulk of the foreigners, to some of whom it appeared as the final touch of modern art, to others as a naïve example of English barbarism; but to the feelings of Mary Crow, who recognised at once that someone had made a mistake, it was a harrowing spectacle. She turned hurriedly to catch the eye of Father Paleologue, but he smiled back at her reassuringly, however, and when she murmured her fears, "Oh, of course one can see that!" he whispered. "But chance has favoured these people at every turn, and though to many these dancing gestures—there! they are doing it again!—must seem ridiculous enough and even outrageous, still you must remember that the Magdalene must in her time have danced for her patrons. Why should she not now, poor girl—like the Jongleur of Paris before the altar—dance for the Crucified?"

"But, Father," she protested, "the other Mary . . . the type of contemplation . . . surely——"

"Yes, yes, lady," he conceded. "It's a mistake. It's the only bad mistake they've made. But those little girls are sweet creatures and——"

"Father, I believe you're laughing at us all the time!"

Father Paleologue became in a moment intensely grave. "If I did *that*, dear daughter," he said earnestly, "I'd deserve to be unfrocked. I'd deserve to be cut in pieces like your last Abbot. I'd deserve anyhow——" and he gave her an irresistibly winning smile that broke through the mask of his stiff archaic face as though a lamp had been lit within his soul—"not to have had the exquisite pleasure I've had today."

"Thank God they're going—those girls!" cried Miss Drew in a shrill voice. "And they're dancing away, hand in hand, now, as if it were a may-pole they were leaving, not their dying Saviour." Her words reached the ears of the Marquis of P. who turned and gave her a gracious little bow. It was the first time he had recognised Miss Drew today, but these caustic sentiments of hers met with his entire approval.

"Are those baggages," remarked Miss Barbara Fell, "who have just gone dancing off into that tent, supposed to be camp-followers to those soldiers gambling there?"

Fell returned no answer.

"I asked you, Manny, if those girls——" and she repeated her whole remark.

"One of them is a Saint still invoked in Glastonbury, sister" —the doctor's voice was strained to the breaking-point and in his heart he was saying to himself, "I can't bear it . . . I can't bear it . . . I can't bear it"—"and the other is that Mary, the sister of Lazarus, who was such an especial friend of Jesus. I don't know why they swayed about like that. Perhaps they were so unhappy that they took to drink!"

"What's the matter, Angela," asked Mr. Beere crossly. "You can't sit still a moment. We can't go before the end. I suppose it's getting on for the end now." These extraordinary words that could scarcely have been uttered on the continent of Europe were luckily heard by no one except Angela and to her they were no more than the portentous yawn from the old gentleman that followed them. They were no more than the buzzing of a blue-bottle fly that at that moment flew past her ears. Her face was white and her whole body was trembling with excitement. The soul within her yearned to that beautiful form that now with uplifted arms was embracing the feet of the suspended Figure.

There was another person in that big audience who was as agitated as Angela Beere and that was the Vicar of Glastonbury. Indignation had coloured Mat Dekker's face a dusky red and his heavy brows were knotted over his bushy eyebrows. The whole business filled him with sick aversion. Why, oh why had he ever allowed such a thing as this to take place in his loved town? For all his High Church practices Mat Dekker at heart was as simple an Evangelical as John Bunyan or John Wesley. He regarded this whole performance as a monstrous and ghastly parody of an historic Event that had changed the life of the cosmos. "I can't stick it out, son, I can't stick it out!" he groaned.

Sam laid his large hand on his father's knee. "It's the end now, Dad, I think. Those fellows, lugging that step-ladder, are going to take Him down. Ned Athling is with them himself. He's supposed to be Joseph of Arimathea."

"Damn Ned Athling!"

It was at that moment that the Christ-Evans uttered the only words he had spoken since he had been lifted up. He cried suddenly in a great voice that rang out across Tor Field and across the gipsy caravans, and across Chilkwell Street, till it reached the blood-red fountain in Chalice Hill: *"Eloi, Eloi, Lama, Sabachthani!"*

The two Dekkers rose simultaneously to their feet. "That man . . . that Evans . . . wasn't playing *then* . . . Look, me boy, his head's really hanging down now. I must see to this!"

"Go slow, Dad! He *may* be all right. It may only be his damned acting. Don't make a fool of yourself, Dad! No! It's no joke. They are running out of the tents! They're breaking up. Something *is* wrong. He *is* ill. He's hurt. He's fainted!" They pushed their way together between the rows of seats and began running towards the stage. They were not the first to do this, however. A good distance in front of them Cordelia Geard was rushing wildly towards that great cross of oak-wood. Their movement was a signal for a general uprising. Many others—among them Dr. Fell—were running now up the slope, towards the terrace, where Mr. Evans hung by his armpits. Meanwhile it was the ironical duty of the pretended Saint Joseph to act in real genuine earnest in this unrehearsed Descent from the Cross.

Inside the western pavilion there was now a scene of the utmost confusion. The two Marys, little Bessie and Lizzie, had been both sobbing hysterically in shame over their fiasco. John Crow had been vainly trying to comfort them. "Us have spoilt the Pageant!" Bessie was moaning. "Oh, why did 'ee let we do it?"

"Us'll never be able to look anyone in the face again!" Lizzie was wailing. "I wish I were dead! I wish I were dead!"

But the little maids' distress was now broken into by a wild uproar. "Evans have fainted! Evans have burst a blood-vessel! There be blood pouring out of Evans' mouth!" Both John and Barter—careless now about appearing before the audience in their ordinary clothes—rushed out of the tent and ran to the scene of the trouble. The Roman soldiers had already left their dice and their cards and were engaged in helping the Jewish elders lift the cross bodily out of the ground and lower it down upon the grass. There were so many powerful young farmhands among them that this was not a difficult undertaking.

Capporelli had come up meanwhile and was gesticulating violently, talking so rapidly in French that everyone near him only stared. Some of the Roman soldiers—rough lads from the Sedgemoor farms—nudged each other and made fun of him. "Play over. Play quite done," they cried to him in pidgin English as if he were a Chinaman.

Cordelia had become cold and calm. She was giving rapid, incisive directions to the lads who were lowering the cross. Ned Athling, in a bewildered trance, perched upon the upper steps of his step-ladder, was contemplating the surging movements which looked for a time like a dangerous panic, that were now rocking the excited audience. He tried to make out the figure of Lady Rachel, but the crowd was too dense.

Barter was one of the few who kept his head at this juncture. "Did you say that those Dublin people had got a megaphone somewhere?" he asked.

John looked at him quickly. "To quiet the audience, you mean?"

"Of course. We can't let 'em break up without a word."

"Let's go and see."

They crossed over to the eastern tent and there, sure enough, after a word with the Dubliners, whom they found on their knees hurriedly flinging all their private belongings into two black handbags, like passengers in a sinking ship, the megaphone was produced.

"What shall we say? Will *you* do it?" Barter found himself yelling these words into John's ears as they carried their megaphone past the outskirts of the crowd that was now surging and shouting about the prostrate cross and above the unconscious form of Mr. Evans. It must have been that vision of the Dubliners packing their black bags that compelled him to yell like that when John could have perfectly well have heard a whisper!

And what unconscious force was it that made the two friends —like two field-marshals whose army is defeated and in full flight—carry the megaphone back to their own eastern tent instead of using it at once where they had found it? The power of habit with these two men had been more quickly established than one would have believed possible! John and Barter must have hurried with their megaphone to the spot where they were *used* to giving their orders, as instinctively as a dog carries a bone to his kennel. Probably in a boat of starving derelicts who have just killed and torn to pieces one of their companions each man would be driven to convey his portion of the cannibal feast to his own bench, by the side of his own row-lock. At the door of their own tent they encountered Crummie freshly emerged from the ladies' tiring-room and as trim and lovely as ever in an ordinary summer frock.

"Oh, I'm so glad you've got *that* thing!" she cried. "I was just going to ask you if there wasn't something of that sort to quiet them. I suppose if he's only fainted you'll go on with the Pageant?"

John looked at Barter and Barter looked at John. What a girl this was! "I . . . we . . . they——" began Barter. "We thought we'd let it end here," said John.

Crummie surveyed the two disconcerted representatives of her father with a puzzled frown. She then turned her eyes upon the audience. Yes! they were all on their feet and most of them pushing and struggling to extricate themselves from the chairs and benches. Soon they would be scattered in all directions. Many were already rushing wildly up the hill towards the pavilions. The girl smiled sweetly. "Better do it now if you're going to do it," she said. "Tell them that the Mayor bids them good-bye and thanks them for coming."

John lifted the megaphone to his mouth. "Do I just shout it out?" he asked her nervously.

Mr. Geard's daughter looked round. The Middlezoy foreman, still dressed up as King Arthur, was standing nearby, quietly lighting his pipe. She called the man by name and he slouched up to them. "Take this," said Crummie. "Run over to Pilate's what-do-you-call-it, will you? Shout out to them that the Mayor bids them good-bye, and tell them to go home quietly, and that Mr. Evans has only fainted!"

King Arthur lost no time in obeying to the letter this clear command of the resuscitated Lady of Shalott. He ascended the wooden rostrum and standing erect there—a majestic and imposing figure—he bellowed forth in a terrific voice—"Ladies and Gentlemen; attention all, please!" His words were audible all over the field. Even the gipsies in their caravans heard them. The Dye-Works strikers came pouring out of Dickery Cantle's tent, well refreshed with meat and wine. Everybody stood still and listened. It was as if the real Rex Arturus himself had suddenly reappeared to restore peace upon earth and fulfill his magician's prophecy.

"What a girl!" whispered Barter to John as they followed Crummie with their eyes as she stood behind the rostrum, prompting the Middlezoy foreman.

"But Evans may be dead," murmured John.

"Not he," returned the other. "But even if he is ——"

"The Mayor wishes to assure ye all that the gentleman be only fainted. The Mayor thinks best for Pageant to end here and now. The Mayor thanks ye all for coming, especially those of ye what come from far. The Mayor hopes ye'll all come to

Glastonbury again. The Mayor ———" There was a pause at this point while King Arthur bent his head to catch his prompter's words. Then raising the megaphone again—"The Mayor gives ye all the Blessing of the Living Christ!" The foreman came carefully down the creaking wooden steps with the megaphone under his arm.

Crummie was watching with delight the surprising effect of these words from the slope of the hill. It was as if, in the very midst of some wild panic under the urge of an earthquake or a volcano, every person had been struck mute and immobile, exactly where they were.

Even John and Barter were silent for a moment staring down at that petrified mass of people. John had time to observe that when the crowd began to move again it was in quite a different manner. There was no longer a tendency to rush up the hill in a dense mob. Everyone seemed to become a separate individual again. The crowd-hypnosis had been entirely dispelled by this invocation of the Redeemer of the Individual.

"What a pity," thought Ned Athling, as he came out of his trance and scrambled down his step-ladder, tripping awkwardly over his Arimathean robes, "What a pity that they never heard my verses about the Heathen Grail!"

Meanwhile a burly Taunton policeman, under Cordelia's direction, was pouring brandy down Mr. Evans' throat. Other policemen were pushing the crowd back, so that the prostrate man might have more air and space round him. Megan Geard, supported by Mr. Bishop, the town clerk, and by Bob Sheperd, the old Glastonbury policeman, was now standing near-by, out of breath and very much concerned.

"He'll come round now, Marm. Don't 'ee take on. He'll come round now. Miss Cordy'll bring 'un to's senses, quick enough, you'll see, Marm!" Thus did old Bob comfort his Worship's lady while the equally infirm town clerk made feeble efforts to get down on his knees by the side of the ghastly figure on the ground. But the aged public servant was so "fat and scant of breath" that this gesture remained unfulfilled.

"Oh, Mother, Mother, what shall we do, what shall we do?" moaned Cordelia, losing her nerve at the familiar sound of her

mother's panting breath. "I've poured a lot of this stuff down
his throat but he doesn't ——"

"Doctor be here! Doctor be come!" This welcome cry arose
among a group of Roman soldiers, the smell of whose bare legs,
hot and grass-stained, had become a part of that day that lodged
itself in Cordelia's memory. The Taunton policemen now cleared
a path for Dr. Fell.

"His heart's beating, Doctor!" cried Cordelia. "I've got my
hand on it. It's beating funnily, but it's beating still."

The doctor placed his hat on the grass and knelt down over the
prostrate man who lay with his mouth grimly open. There was
a great streak of blood on his chest and another on his shirt and
his lips were caked with blood. "He's burst a blood-vessel . . .
of some kind," murmured Dr. Fell. "The question is *what* kind.
Did he faint away as soon as he had shouted those words?"

It was to Persephone, who had been sitting all this while upon
the fallen cross as it lay on the ground, that the doctor addressed
this remark. She leaned forward to answer him, re-arranging as
she did so the folds of her sky-blue robe. "Yes, Doctor," she
said in a low, rather guttural voice. "It was the strain of that
shout. But I think he was uncomfortable before. I think he was
in distress before. I believe he was in considerable *pain*, for quite
a long time before!" There was a queer hysterical ring in the
girl's voice as her words mounted up. When she came to the
word "pain" she shouted it with a vibration of anger.

The doctor mechanically wiped off some blood from Mr.
Evans' bare chest with the tips of his fingers. "We'll have to get
him to the hospital," he said, "and, what's more, get him there
as quickly as we can!" He rose on one knee still keeping the tips
of his fingers on the unconscious man's chest. "Who's got a car
on the field?" he said.

Persephone rose to her feet and came forward, catching up
her trailing blue garment round one bare arm, and hitching another fold of it into her belt as she moved. "My car is just over
that ridge, Doctor," she said. "It's by itself there, and there are
no others nearer than the road. If you don't mind my being *like
this*," and she spread out her long bare arms and gave a toss to
her head from which her curls hung in a loose mass, "I'll drive

him there in a jiffy! Only he must be carried to my car. I can't get it over that bank!"

Dr. Fell stood up. "Will *you* carry him, officers?" he said, addressing the nearest policemen.

Three of the men in uniform stepped forward and under the doctor's directions lifted up the unconscious Mr. Evans.

Cordelia turned to Persephone. The last time she had spoken to this girl was in the reception room of Mother Legge and as their eyes met now they both recalled this encounter. It was Cordelia *then* who had been dressed in blue! "Thank you, thank you, Mrs. Spear," she murmured with intense emphasis. "You may be saving his life by this."

The three policemen with Cordelia walking behind them carried their burden where Persephone led. She and Dr. Fell moved on fast in front, talking earnestly. The doctor was explaining to Persephone, in as unprofessional language as he could, just what he feared, just what he hoped, as to the injured man's chances.

"You'd better go home, Mother!" cried Cordelia stopping for a moment to turn her troubled face to Mrs. Geard.

"But you're coming back, aren't you, darling?" cried the descendant of the House of Rhys, extricating her arm from that of old Bob Sheperd. "They'll never have room for *you* in her little car!"

Cordelia waved her hand impatiently at her mother, as much as to say—"You look after yourself, dear!"—but she turned then, and running after the slowly moving bearers joined the melancholy cortège without another word.

Megan Geard sighed deeply. "I wish the Mayor were here," she remarked to the old Glastonbury policeman.

Bob Sheperd cordially endorsed her wish. "If his Worship had been here that poor man would never have died," he said.

Megan Geard gave a start and a sudden shiver ran through her. "You don't think he *is* dead, Mr. Sheperd, do you?" she groaned.

The old policeman wagged his head. "I've 'a seen many a corpse in me time, Marm, and not a one o' them but had blood o' just that colour, dry-like and sticky-like, on they's poor lips."

When they reached the little car it became only too plain that if one of the policemen sat by Persephone's side to help carry him in when they got to the hospital there was only just room for Dr. Fell and his unconscious patient.

"Take care! Go gently! Oh, go gently!" Cordelia cried, clutching the sun-warmed door-frame of the machine as it swung open, while they were lifting Mr. Evans in.

But an intruder now appeared upon the scene whose strange appearance startled and shocked the girl even in her desperate concern. It was none other than Mad Bet, who had persuaded her good friend Solly Lew to conduct her to this particular spot, from which she could observe and not be observed. The kind-hearted taxi-driver had remained here with the woman for quite a long while. Then, watching with the eye of a hungry man the rush of the Dye-Works people into Dickery Cantle's tent, he had gone off, "to get a bite of summat for five minutes." The mad-woman had left her hat, trimmed with forget-me-nots, under the hornbeam bush where she had been sitting, and her egg-white cranium was a disturbing object even to Dr. Fell who had known her from his youth up.

To the Taunton policemen, as panting and perspiring, they withdrew from the car's door, this new apparition was still more startling. They thought for a moment that she was one of the players and that this shocking baldness was a mask.

"Only to touch the hem of his garment! Only to touch his coaties or trowsies!" gabbled Mad Bet, pushing Cordelia out of her way and struggling to stretch her arm into the car. "He told I, at Mother Legge's," the woman went on, "to come Midsummer Day, and see he cast out his Devil and I've seed he do it! I've seed that girt Devil flyin' over Tor-top with wings of dragon! He be Jesus, his wone self now, the poor man be. Don't 'ee drop 'un in grave, Doctor! Don't 'ee let them put stones on his poor bleeding heart. Where be going to lay him then, gents, where be? Where be? Mad Bet'll come and watch over he. Night and day she will, till he rolls they stones away!"

"Don't do *that*!" cried Dr. Fell sharply, when one of the Taunton policemen began unceremoniously pulling the woman back. "Let her just touch him once. There! There! That's enough now. Look . . . here's a friend of yours coming!"

The doctor's words were justified, for hatless as herself and very much the worse for drink, Solly Lew could be observed staggering up the hill and frantically waving his arms. "He thinks the police are taking her," remarked the doctor laconically, clambering in beside the unconscious man, who was lying limp and heavy across the seat.

Mad Bet caught the word "police" and the word "take"; but her whole soul was so stirred by what she had seen that no fear for her own skin could touch her. She had been allowed to do what she had set her heart on doing, and she drew back now quite quietly and stood immobile, looking like a ghastly waxwork at Madame Tussaud's.

Dr. Fell's attention, the moment he had settled himself on the edge of the seat, against the patient's bare rope-bruised ankles, was attracted by the sight of a little bird deliberately alighting upon the topmost twig of the stunted hornbeam. "It's a Lesser Whitethroat," he thought to himself.

Cordelia's distracted face was thrust into the window of the car. "He won't die, Doctor, will he?" He could do nothing but shake his head and murmur, "Careful now, careful now!" as the unhappy girl snatched at one of the injured man's hands and, careless of who saw her, pressed upon it a feverish kiss. "He won't die, Doctor, will he? He won't die, Doctor? I couldn't ——" But Persephone had already got her machine in motion.

"He's in good hands, Miss, in very good hands," murmured one of the Taunton policemen who had been left behind, as they watched the car descend the rough cattle-track that led round the eastern side of the Tor.

"That clever actress be a first-class driver, Miss," remarked the other man, "and everybody knows Dr. Fell. I've 'a seed 'un meself many a time, in Tarnton 'Firmary, when he were younger than he be now. There aint such a man as old Fell, no! not this side o' Bristol."

The policemen were so terrifying to Solly Lew that he had not dared to advance. Mad Bet, however, walked slowly towards him, keeping her eyes on the disappearing car.

As Persephone drove into town with her heavy load that eventful afternoon her nature was undergoing the strangest upheaval. Since her quarrel with Philip she had spoken to him only once. There had been indeed nothing to be said between them. She had "turned," as people say, "against him." His particular kind of passion had come to be revolting to her. Her deep riddle now was how she had ever been attracted to him, or let him touch her at all! In her husband's case she had only arrived at a point of departure towards which she had been steadily moving for months. With him she had no overt rupture, but for the last week or two she had ceased to share his bed. But the sight of this man Evans hanging on that cross had hit something in her that went very deep. A nerve, perhaps it was, rather than anything else, in her weary heart; but it was a dark, strange pull, a rending tug at this queer nerve, an inexplicable feeling, and one to which she yielded now in an abandoned mood of delicious languor. This sudden, melting tender sensation—utterly unexpected and mysterious to herself—did not seem to affect her recognition of Mr. Evans as a queer, impossible person. He might be the most ridiculous person in the world; he might be a madman. It remained that something wild, dark, desperate, in the man, as he hung there, something in his sombre contorted face, with his great Roman nose and massive forehead, something in his lean, extended arms, something in his exposed shoulder-blades, something even in the black hairs on his chest, now caked with crimson blood, had touched a nerve in her being, an organic nerve, that went down to the dark deep knot of erotic mystery in the centre of her woman's nature. She had divined in a way no other soul had done—certainly not Cordelia— the vein of thrilling exultation in Mr. Evans' mood, that had supported him in that atrocious endurance.

There always was in Cordelia's attitude to Mr. Evans—there had been from the start—something at once "old-maidish" and maternal, something of the passion which frustrated, love-starved women feel for cats and dogs and parrots—especially the cantankerous and eccentric among such creatures. To Cordelia this whole business of the Pageant had been a vexation and an annoyance. She regarded it as a mere characteristic whimsy of her father, while Mr. Evans' mania for playing the Crucified she

looked upon as an arbitrary madness, a sort of wilful mental indulgence, that she had feared all the time might lead to disaster.

Persephone, on the other hand, had so many neurotic manias
in herself that she responded like touchwood to the quiver of Mr.
Evans' perverted heroism. As she had embraced that wooden beam
beneath his feet she had felt, vibrating through its dense oaken
veins the wild triumph of his tense tormented nerves, the savage
rapture of his self-immolation. And she had fancied too, in a
passionate delusion that had sent an electric wave of reckless
confederacy through her woman's flesh, that Mr. Evans was not
indifferent to her presence there, was not unaware of the reciprocity of her mood. A strange Virgin-Mother had she been to a singular Saviour of a wounded world! Pressing her flat boy's breasts
against that oaken post and straining upward towards her imaginary God-Man and Divine Son, she had allowed herself to yield
to the uttermost to this new unexpected tenderness for a man she
knew nothing of!

Such and not otherwise had been the feelings of Persephone
Spear as she had lifted up her voice and wailed aloud—"My Son
and my God! My God and my Son!"—as the Middlezoy young
man had instructed her. Little had Ned Athling known, little had
those Dubliners known, the wild maenad-like feelings that their
gothic dumb-show had evoked in this morbid girl! Had she been
aware, as she crouched and moaned at the feet of her madman, of
the psychic waves of swooning adoration, flung towards her figure, from the white-cheeked girl seated there by the yawning Mr.
Beere? Not consciously aware, of a surety; but such waves of
electric passion seldom, like lightning-bolts, lose themselves in
the unrestoring earth. Some tremour, some vibrant residue, however faint, reaches, as a rule, the object towards which such feelings are directed, and it may well have been that this shivering,
yearning idolatry for her—reckless as some young nun's worship
of the real blue-robed Maid of Heaven—had quickened the pulse-
beats of her own passion, as she poured forth her spirit in this
strange new tenderness, never felt before.

Such were the feelings of Persephone. But the girl was wrong,
wrong as so many other worshippers of gods and men and beasts
and demons are wrong. Mr. Evans was totally and entirely un-

conscious of her presence at the foot of his cross. That oaken beam that had carried the trembling of his emotion to her, and had made it shiver through every channel of her frame till it reached the centre of her organic life, had, for some occult reason, absorbed and not transferred the emotion which she felt. All that wild, dark, lovely sense of being isolated with this hook-nosed, contorted-mouthed victim of his own strange mania, isolated with him on an austere promontory of confederate fate, was in reality a groundless illusion. In this particular case—quite otherwise than in Angela's—there had been a break of contact. Perhaps a girl's nerves respond to the nerves of another girl and send out magnetic currents that can be caught from far off; whereas something in the masculine constitution, something dense, thick, opaque, obtuse, *stupid*, has the power of rejecting such contacts. Or it may be that the erotic emotions, when they brim over from the masculine spirit, extricate themselves, as women's feelings never do, from the bitter-sweet honeycomb of Nature, and shoot off, up, out, and away, into dimensions of non-natural existence, where the nerve-rays of women cannot follow.

Those queer analytic elementals, those inquisitive naturalists that very old places, full of contorted human history, attract by a species of spontaneous selection, must have derived a malignant pleasure from the words they heard spoken by Monsieur Capporelli when both the protagonists of the Passion had disappeared with Dr. Fell. In true French style, reducing every mortal human feeling to a rigid pattern of logical amorousness, the famous clown had uttered to Ned Athling words full of an ironic and blasphemous amusement when the unconscious King of the Jews and his blue-robed Mother had vanished together to the hospital. A touch of jealousy may have mingled, too, with his sly tone, for Capporelli had been really and truly caught by Percy's slender hips and her graceless tomboy humour. "An engaging situation," the clown had remarked, as he was changing his clothes in the gentlemen's portion of the eastward-facing pavilion, "and a very piquant one, for those two, it's been, we may be sure, ever since they hoisted him up."

The Middlezoy poet turned upon the laughing brown eyes of

the speaker a pair of blue-grey eyes more chilly-cold than the wettest sea-fog that comes up out of Bridgewater Bay. "Do you think so?" he remarked. "It was lucky she had her car so near."

Capporelli fixed a sentimental and whimsical eye upon the spot where he had been so happy with Percy. "Who knows?" he sighed. "You people are all so peculiar and so—inhuman that it is difficult to say!"

The elementals of Glastonbury—those naturalists that had hovered over the vaporous humours of three thousand years of criss-cross human tangles—must have howled with laughter when they heard this clever Frenchman "explain," in accents dry and logical, the relations between Mr. Owen Evans and Mrs. Persephone Spear.

Mr. Evans had, as a matter of fact, been caught up into a region of feeling utterly beyond the comprehension of any Latin or any Teutonic mind. This had gone on since he stood before Pilate until the moment when he shouted *"Eloi, Eloi!"* It was not, as St. Paul has put it so well—he the one among them all who would really have understood Mr. Evans—it was not with flesh and blood that he was contending, but with mysterious powers of evil upon levels revealed to few. No equivocal perversity gratified by divining the feelings of Persephone entered for a second into the terrible visions with which, as he hung between heaven and earth, his mind was bruised and broken. The perverse girl had detected, as Cordelia never could have done, the *quality* of Mr. Evans' feelings, but what she had no idea of was the tragic lengths to which he had carried them. The physical pain he suffered before he shouted that *"Eloi! Eloi!"* was more acute than he had ever dreamed of undergoing. Both Athling and the Dubliners were to blame, and indeed still more so was John, for not insisting on Dr. Fell—they could have had confidence in him— being present at one of their rehearsals. Evans had suffered, but not acutely suffered, at these rehearsals, and what he had endured he had kept to himself, for *it was what he wanted.* It was the prolongation of the scene—drawn out so foolishly by that luckless Dance of Death of the two Marys—that had brought about his collapse, and it was the strain on his arms, bound too tightly by those ropes, and the tension of the muscles of his shoulders, stretched between the cross-bars, that had caused him such anguish. But not since the bloody King put the last Abbot of Glastonbury to death had such physical pain been experienced by anyone upon the slopes of Gwyn-ap-Nud's hill. But it would be a mistake to say that the spirit of Mr. Evans yielded, or weakened, or regretted his undertaking. Right up to the end, till by straining his torso to the breaking-point he lost consciousness, he not only endured this anguish but he exulted in enduring it. His exultation kept mounting and mounting—extreme pain and ecstatic triumph embracing each other in dark mystic copulation.

Mr. Evans became indeed Three Persons as he hung on his self-imposed cross. One person was his body, another was his soul. He felt his soul—or rather his soul felt itself—to be entirely outside of his body. This phenomenon was to him, as he hung alone there, looking down on that vast crowd, as much of a definite, concrete experience as the pain itself. The pain became a Third Person, and the soul of Mr. Evans kept urging on the pain. He felt as if that crowd beneath him was the whole human race and that by the transaction that was now proceeding between these Three Persons, thus suspended in the air above them, this crowd, an immense animal passivity, was in some way re-created, purged, cleansed, transformed. His body, as the pain increased— as his soul deliberately caused the pain to increase—began to overbrim the confines of its human shape. His body projected itself under the pain in great waves of filmy chemical substance. It flung forth this filmy substance in streams, in torrents, in a mighty, rushing rain! And then there arrived a moment when Mr. Evans knew that his body was the whole hill, the whole field, nay! the whole wide-stretching landscape. Into this landscape, into this earth-bulk that was his body, his soul kept driving the pain, compelling it to bury itself deeper and deeper into this living mass. This continued till his body became more than the mere immediate landscape. It became the whole round earth, swinging on its orbit through space. And above this earth-body hung the master-spirit of Mr. Evans still driving the pain on. He was the Zeus and Prometheus and the Vulture—all three linked indestructibly together! And all the while a triumphant ecstasy poured down from him like a bloody sweat.

Nor must it be supposed that Mr. Evans' rational mind—that portion of his consciousness that indulged its activity apart from pain or pleasure—was paralysed all this while. Those two manners, which John Crow had noted as long ago as their encounter at Stonehenge as peculiar to the man, were not superficial. They represented the workings of his deepest nature. His pedantry as people called it, was as much heightened by his present suffering as was his imagination. As other men visualise their past lives at the moment of drowning, so Mr. Evans, in the midst of his anguish,—even while he identified the substance of his flesh with the whole round earth from which it was projected—was intensely aware of the peculiar history of the spot beneath him. The pain he endured turned his pedantic acquisitiveness into a living medium, acutely sensitive, quiveringly receptive, through which the whole history of Glastonbury began to pour.

Glastonbury seemed to have waited for the sacrifice of Mr. Evans to exhale upon the air its darkest and most terrible secrets. That no one heard these secrets, except the man himself who was the medium for them, mattered nothing to these singular revenants. They found Mr. Evans' anguished entity suspended above the soil of that historic spot and they seized upon it, just as a horde of wild and gusty winds, blown here, blown there, might seize upon an Æolian harp hung aloft in a lonely place. Thus it came about that another Pageant,—much more grim and much less romantic than the one that had been played that day—passed through Mr. Evans' brain. Kings and Prelates, Saints and Sodomites, Madmen and Monks, Whores and Nuns, People Executed and People Imprisoned, together with a woeful procession of common, nameless People upon whose toil and hunger others lived, streamed in a wild torrent of heads and faces and arms and limbs through the tormented consciousness of Mr. Evans. And the crowd was not only human! *There* lay one of the worst horrors of it. Mingled with the human torrent were other living things, animals, birds, and even fish. All the *eyes* that in the long history of this place had looked in vain into those of the killer— all these tormented *eyes* gathered now about Mr. Evans! And it was all connected with his deadly, his irremediable vice. The figures that flooded his brain were all torturers or victims, every one of them; and as the thing grew and grew upon him, as he hung there, all the victims flowed into one and became one, and all the torturers flowed into one and became one. Then it came about that between Mr. Evans as the torturer and this one victim, who yet was all victims, a dialogue arose; so that from their divided localities in space they addressed each other, and from their horrible association in time they answered each other.

"Forgiveness for *you*," cried this voice, rising from all the victims of Glastonbury since the tribes of men had first come there, "can never, never be. For you did this thing, and went on doing it, *knowing what it meant!* Others tortured me from brutality, from insensitiveness, from stupidity. You and those who were like you did it, *knowing what it meant.* It was *that* knowledge, knowing what I felt, and yet not stopping, that has made forgiveness impossible."

The terror of the voice made Mr. Evans feel like a thing that twisted on the floor of the Pit and yet out of the smoke of his torment he uttered a reply. "In Eternity we are as one!" he cried hoarsely. There was a silence for a moment or—so it seemed to him, as he hung there—for a thousand years.

Then the voice was lifted up again. "Never can we be as one! I have looked into your eyes and you did not stop. Each moment you went on made the difference greater. It can never be crossed now. It is a gulf in eternity now. You could not hear me if I did forgive you."

And once more as he heaved himself to and fro he replied to the voice. "Christ can forgive me. Christ holds eternity in His hand." And again there was a silence of a thousand years. "I *am* Christ!" cried the voice, in a tone that made the flesh wrinkle like blown sand upon Mr. Evans' bones. "Every victim, whether you've done it for your science or your ambition or your religion or your lust; whether it be a beaten prisoner, a trapped beast, a dog strapped down for vivisection, a racked heretic, a burnt Negro, a tortured child, *is I*; yes, is I myself! And you are right when you say that I hold Eternity in my hand! These voices come, these voices that are *my* voice! Can you gather them up, these victims of yours, these tortured, hunted, trapped victims, by their thousands upon thousands? Can you gather them up where you have crucified them? Can you cause the earth to yield again to you their black blood? Can you cause the air to return to you their pitiful cries? I have heard the voices of men—yes! and of wise men too—how they have said, 'All is equal, all is permitted.' It is I and none other—I, the Christ—who speak thus to you from Eternity, and I say unto you 'All is *not* equal! All is *not* permitted!' "

Even yet, even after hearing these things—such power hath the spirit of a mortal creature to fight for its life—Mr. Evans was still able to reply to the voice. "I could not answer you," he murmured hoarsely, "if I were not answering you from the Cross."

"You forget what you have done," went on the voice, and it was like the voice of the wind over the sea. "You forget! You forget!"

Mr. Evans' tone had a terrible veracity now. "Is it *you* who say that to *me*?" he cried out. "No! No! Christ or Devil, you are wrong there! Never have you let me forget, never for one moment!" And it was then that the voice became a vast anonymous voice, gathered up, it seemed, from so much suffering in the world as to be rendered almost inarticulate! It came to Mr. Evans' ears out of the gills of fishes, out of the gullets of beasts, out of the shards of insects, out of the throats of birds, out of the wounded coils of slowworms, out of prisons, out of hospitals, out of madhouses and domestic torture-rooms, and as it rose and sank, as it sank and rose, it accused Man—man the cruel, man the blood-fiend, man the voluptuous tormentor, man the rejoicer in pain, man the inventor of pain, man the pain-begetter, the pain-eater, the pain-drinker, the pain-devil! And from the abysses of Mr. Evans' consciousness leaped up into the day, like an eel, out of fathomless mud, a question for the crucified Man-God. "So evil, so cruel, so base, O Lord, are the generations of men, why dost Thou seek to redeem them with Thy suffering? Why dost Thou not cause a flood to arise—as at the beginning—and drown forever their itching, biting, stinging, scorpion-lusts in smooth, deep fathoms of oblivious water?"

And the voice replied to him again and it was now so low and yet so searching that it was like a wind stirring the horns of snails and touching the hairs in the throats of night-jars, and moving the antennae of butterflies, and lifting the gold-dust from the cracks of puff-balls, and blowing the grey dust from the droppings of weasels, and rippling the brown rain-fall in the cups of fungi, and fretting the light scurf on the brittle skulls of the newborn, and the rheum-drops on the eyelids of extreme age, and the sweat-drops on the forehead of death. And the voice whispered—"For those that are forgiven there shall be a new heaven and a new earth!" And Mr. Evans groaned forth his retort to this: "But what of those that *cannot* be forgiven? Is that new heaven and that new earth built upon the Golgotha of the Second Death?" The voice at this became so low that the ears of the man, clairaudient as he was through his suffering, could not distinguish words.

"It is God and He is lying to me," thought Mr. Evans. "He is lying to me. People lie to the condemned for whom there is no hope."

And Mr. Evans hanging there in his great anguish hardened his heart against the voice. "We are alone," his soul whispered to his body and to the pain that he was inflicting on his body. "They have left us quite alone."

And it was then that he lost consciousness. This was what only one person afterwards would believe when he told them about it, namely, that he had no recollection of shouting with a great shout that *"Eloi! Eloi!"* which brought the blood from his mouth.

Cordelia would not believe it, nor would Persephone, nor would John, nor would Mr. Barter, nor would Aunt Laura, the matron of the ward where he "came presently"—as the ironic human phrase runs—"to himself." The only person who believed it was Mr. Geard; and the extraordinary thing was, when, a couple of weeks after, the Mayor of Glastonbury was visiting him in the hospital, and he was telling him about this, such must have been the heat of the day, or the distressing sights in that particular ward, that Mr. Geard, after accepting his account without question, fainted dead away!

It was now already two whole months since the Pageant; and the ebbings and flowings of Glastonbury lives were proceeding under a scorching mid-August sun.

It was a Saturday afternoon; and resting against the warm bank of a high hawthorn hedge, John and Mary Crow were watching the tall pale-gold stalks of a ripe cornfield over against Bulwark's Lane leading to Bushey Combe.

The girl wore a cream-coloured frock covered with little light-green spots, like the spots upon the inside wings of the butterfly called a Green-veined White. She had on black stockings and very thin shoes, and as she lay between the golden wheat-stalks and the tall hedge-grasses, she allowed one of her outstretched hands to caress the cloudy pink blossoms of a tuft of fumitory. Her white straw hat lay on the ground beside her feet, upside down, and into the place where her head would naturally have been, John was now with meticulous care constructing an imaginary thrushes' nest out of twisted blades of grass and bits of rubble.

Her face was averted from his as she lay on her side but, as they both rested on their elbows, John would vary his preoccupation with her up-turned hat by allowing his long nervous fingers alternately to rumple up and restraighten that green-spotted frock, so warm, as was the form beneath it, in the glowing afternoon sun.

The girl's whole being responded to these satyrish caresses with a luxurious and delicious contentment of mind and body, such as she had not known for many a long month.

She had been married now to John for exactly two days and she had at last persuaded—or believed she had persuaded—Miss Drew to allow her to live with him in that Northload room, while she continued to spend the bulk of each day in her old employment as that lady's companion. They had not yet had their first night together; but ever since they had been married, secretly but not surreptitiously, by Mat Dekker in St. John's Church, the

unbedded bride had been transferring her clothes and other
private belongings to this happy retreat, the first ménage that
she could call her own! Whether it would be tonight that the
grand move would be made or tomorrow, Sunday night, she was
not quite sure. She had extracted a sort of reluctant half-promise
from Miss Drew that it should be tonight; but on that issue she
was prepared to be flexible, if, when it came to the point, it *had*
to be tomorrow instead!

John also was happier than he had been for months; probably
as happy as he had ever been since that day on the Northwold
"big river." This girl by his side seemed on that warm August
afternoon to satisfy his whole nature in a way that he had more
than once doubted it ever *could* be satisfied.

What a delicious mystery—frond-leaf beneath frond-leaf, shell-
whorl beneath shell-whorl, calyx beneath calyx—the identity of
a girl was! It seemed to John, as he followed with his electric
fingers the delicate curves of this body lying by his side and as
he threw out one trifling remark after another, just to hear her
voice, just to note what such a being would say, or wouldn't say,
that the renunciation of *all this* made by Sam Dekker was a monstrous outrage upon life.

"I'll set Mary at him!" he thought to himself, and then he
thought, "No! he won't listen to *any* girl. I must fight it out with
him myself. It's mad what he's doing. The fellow's worse than
a murderer. He's got the uttermost mystery of mysteries under
his fingertips, and instead of worshipping it he's starving it
to death!"

He had a delicious opportunity for enjoying Mary at this
moment with his most intense idolatry and concentrated fetish-
worship; for her back being turned to him, she could not distract
him by any look.

Both her words and her silences, as he caressed them now,
along with the rest, seemed to have about them the very lines and
curves of this form that he found so intensely appealing. "What
is it," he thought to himself, as he contemplated her long slim
legs in their black stockings, "what is it about a girl's shape that
excites a person so?"

The girl seemed in such a dreamy and passive state just then that she appeared ready to yield to the least pressure of the hands that caressed her. John took advantage of this to make her lie prone on her face, where she seemed perfectly content to stay quite motionless inhaling the sun-warm aromatic smells of those infinitesimal plants such as tiny yellow pansies, that seem to love wheatfields better than any other place, and idly pushing at the brim of her grass-filled hat with the tips of her shoes.

He began strewing her prone limbs now with little bits of grass taken from the bird's nest he had made. Holding these grasses in the air above her, he let them fall down in showers; and it pleased him to watch which of them would find rest upon her, and which would drift aside into the hedge-weeds, caught by some scarce-perceptible breath of the soft southerly wind. "What *is* it about the way they are made?" he asked himself again; and it seemed to him that the most exquisite thrill came to him—the thrill that was at once most satyrish and most infinitely tender—from the feeling of the piquancy of such desirable limbs being inseparably united *to a conscious mind*—a mind that bore about with it, wherever it went, this sweet provocative burden. "But it's only," he thought to himself as he stopped strewing her with grass and began smoothing down that cream-coloured frock, "because it's Mary! If this were another girl, instead of what I feel I should feel either savage lust or furious disgust. God! I would not stay here a second with another girl—except of course Lisette; but that's different. I'd hate for another girl to think to herself, 'I've got him! He likes me!' I'd hate for another girl to have *that* kind of triumph."

The maliciousness he now began to feel towards this imaginary other one drew to itself all that natural loathing of the opposite sex felt in certain moods by both men and women; but such was John's nature that he could take this repulsion, this sex-loathing, which is a far more powerful and deep-rooted feeling than any mere sex-hatred, and bury it in the ground; bury it as a dog might bury a piece of offal, knowing that if his maliciousness or his roguery required it, he could dig it up.

The chances are that for pure unmitigated lechery John Crow ranked highest among the whole population of Glastonbury. Others might have far more powerful erotic sensations; but for pure delight derived from lust, John would, with one exception, have carried away the palm. This exception was Angela Beere, the chaste-looking, unapproachable daughter of old Lawyer Beere. Angela lived for nothing else but for erotic dreaming— her mind by night and day was a temple full of "chain-swung censers" to the Cyprian; and in this temple was a sacred niche that was occupied by many different figures, but by only one figure at a time. At present the niche was occupied by the figure of Persephone; and it was before the figure of Persephone that Angela prostrated herself exactly in the same way that John prostrated himself before Mary. Between the pleasure that Angela was enjoying, at this very minute of time, as she sat at her easel—for she dabbled in water colours—sketching among the Abbey Ruins, by calling up Persephone's form, and the pleasure that John derived from the actual presence of Mary's there was no difference at all.

Above every community, above every town, there are invisible Powers hovering, as interested in the minnows, male and female, swimming about in that particular human aquarium, as Mat Dekker was in his fish.

It is only a very few human beings, however, in each community, who are able to slip out of their skins and share this super-mundane observation of themselves. For the most part the inhabitants of a given locality—or aquarium—just go blindly on, unconsciously swimming about, following their affairs, obeying their necessities, pursuing the smaller fry, making their weed-nests or their mud-nurseries. Nor have we any right to assume—rather the contrary—that the few persons, who *have* this power of slipping out of their skins and joining those super-mundane naturalists, are nobler, or even wiser, than the rest. Very often they are the extreme weaklings—dwelling on the verge of nervous idiocy.

In Glastonbury at this particular epoch, John Crow, Persephone Spear, and that emaciated son of Dickery Cantle, whose wasted legs so troubled Mr. Geard, were probably the only ones who could attain this detached view. And certainly it would be absurd to maintain that any of these was nobler, or wiser, or nearer the secret of life than Mr. Geard for instance, or than

Miss Elizabeth Crow, neither of whom ever *looked down,* so to speak, from above the surface of the aquarium. At this particular moment of the fifteenth of August, that is to say at nine minutes and forty seconds past three o'clock, had any of these super-mundane naturalists been studying the physical and psychic movements of the Glastonbury aquarium, they would certainly have come to the conclusion that John Crow, contemplating the real figure of Mary toying with the little wild pansies, and Angela Beere contemplating the imaginary figure of Persephone, first in one aspect and then in another, as she sketched the famous ruin usually known as St. Joseph's Chapel, were the two water-creatures whose amorous excitement was most intense. And quite apart from super-mundane observers it is likely enough that the most desirable of all electric vibrations is just this very sort of erotic desire, neither altogether gratified nor altogether denied.

A small red poppy, such as linger on after their season, with so many other cornfield plants, was dying in front of him and a great black slug was drawing its slime over the pink pea-like petals of a little rest-harrow. But the curious shrivelled blackness of the dying poppy, with a strange *wet* look upon it, as if it wept in its death, or as if it poured forth the most hidden store of all its hoarded nepenthe, for nothing but the voyaging south wind, that needed no anodyne nor any healing, to take and carry away, did not lessen John's emotion.

Into the poppied juices of black death's own veins that perfect sweetness by his side had crept, cozening him, cajoling him, anointing him, with an ointment that was like a Lethe within Lethe, an oblivion within oblivion.

The girl's yieldingness and sweetness as she lay there, bathed in that golden sunshine and in those flickering shadows, seemed to extend itself, like an element of eternal kindness and reassurance, to everything in life.

The little rest-harrow seemed indeed to be holding its breath till the black slug passed on its way; but its leaves were sturdy. The slug had eaten only one pea-shaped petal. And lo! in a moment the small strong plant could breathe again! A scarf of rainbow-glittering slime it would wear till night-fall, but even if

no dews washed it down there would probably be rain in a day
or two and naught left of that trail. What a thing that he had
found a creature so sweet, so divinely chiselled by the great
Pygmalion of the universe! There had been a long epoch in his
life, all those years in France—though Lisette had been generous
and tender—when he would have mocked at the idea of finding
such absolute content, such fathomless peace of mind, in idolis-
ing a girl's body.

It had nothing to do with Glastonbury; that was certain! No,
it was in Norfolk they had met, and to Norfolk they would return one day.

Propping himself up upon his left arm and looking across the
girl's body, he could see the mouth of a big rabbit-hole; and
beyond that, lying close under the hedge, an old disused plough.
Upon one of the handles of this plough, which stretched up towards the sky, some child or some tramp had tied a fragment of
red flannel, such as might once have been an old woman's petticoat. The sight of this object sent quivering through John's mind
a sudden piercing sense of the tragic pell-mell of human life
upon the earth. That bit of red petticoat tied to the plough
seemed to become a symbol—like a gallant flag held up by the
old battered sun-warmed earth—that there yet remained, in spite
of everything, a hope, a chance, faint, so faint! but still a chance,
that all the hideous miseries beneath the sun might have, down
deep underneath them, some issue, some flickering outlet, some
remedial hope.

"If there is," thought John, "it's through women that it comes
to us now." It seemed to him at that moment as if upon the kindness of women, upon the yieldingness and patience of women,
and upon a certain reassurance—the mere absence from their
nature of the horns of the male beast—that their presence gives,
as of the anonymous weeds and hedge-rubble under his fingers,
all hope for better things depended. "They are all profoundly
immoral," he thought. "This accursed Glastonbury saint-myth
that has gone, like bad wine—like wine made of the poison-
berries of that Levantine thorn tree in the churchyard—into so
many heads in this degenerate town, has never really appealed

to women—they have always seen through it—they have always known it for what it is."

John, now finding the hand that clutched at the weeds growing paralysed and numb from supporting him so long as he thus leaned upon it, moved his position and sat up straight, hugging his knees with his wrists.

"As long as I don't move or speak," thought the prostrate girl to herself, "he will go on loving me!" And it indeed seemed as if Mary was not mistaken in this, for it was as if all that earth-born, sun-warmed bread of life, rising from the tops of its millions of golden stalks, had entered into John's being, giving to the thrill-ing happiness with which he enjoyed her—all untouched as she was—an infinity of protraction. The hum of insects, the shiver-ing music of the larks, as if their very heart-strings were voluble within those little up-borne handfuls of feathers, the distant bark-ing of sheep-dogs, the monotonous refrain of some invisible chiff-chaff in a hedge elm a hundred yards away, the sight of a mountainous ridge, slope upon slope, peak upon peak, of huge white clouds on the southern horizon, and, above all, that de-licious appearance known as heat waves which he could see hovering beyond the plough handles, like floating nets, he thought, with which the elementals of the air fish for the amorous dreams of plants and mosses and lichen and stones, as the sun draws them forth—all these things partook of the sweetness of the girl he loved and became part of that sweetness.

"How lucky I am," thought John, "to have had the wit to es-cape all the traps that the Evil Spirit sets for nervous, excitable, hypnotised men and women. If I were Sam Dekker, I should be saying to myself 'what ought I to be doing *now*? What's my *next* labour and burden, O Lord of Miseries and Sorrows?' If I were poor old Tom I should be rushing madly from wench to wench, trying to forget that I hadn't money enough to live in Norfolk or buy an airplane! If I were Philip I'd be working ten solid hours a day, building up my business. If I were Evans—but it's beyond me to know what goes on behind those Silurian eye-brows. But—O you wheat-stalks and little bindweeds!—I'd like to leave some dint, some signal, some impress upon this very exact spot; so that in future times, when some miserable Philip or Sam or Tom comes groaning along this hedge looking for a branch on that chiff-chaff tree to hang himself on, he may suddenly step into what these air beggars call a pocket of incredible happiness; and think to himself 'God! I'll trick the Devil yet.' "

The moment finally came when John decided that he would arouse his prostrate companion. This was a new delight; for, as he knew by experience, a girl is never so provocative as when she wakes up from a long trance of passivity during which her whole being has been charged to overflowing by the electricity of desire.

He jumped quickly to his feet. "Up with you, my treasure," he cried. "I'm getting restless." Nothing, not a shade, not a flicker, not a glow, not a breath, did he miss of the girl's identity, as he helped her to get upon her feet. Her benumbed, half-unconscious shyness—for she swayed like a drugged creature when first she found herself erect—the way her cheeks smelt of sunshine and moss, the way her lips tasted of the stalks of grass, the way she glanced, with an indrawn "chut-chut" of tongue and teeth, at the untidy state of her dress, the way she half-yawned and half-smiled, all these things doubled the enchantment with which he now embraced her, turning her this way and that, as he pretended to brush the hedge-rubble from her clothes.

The very fact that she was such a grave, self-contained and dignified girl made all her little feminine peculiarities much sweeter to him. Mary indeed had got in John what women so rarely get, a lover who was as conscious *as another girl would have been*, only actively instead of passively so, of the thousand and one little infinitesimal flickerings of physical feeling which create the aura in which the mind functions.

"John!"

"Yes, Mary?"

"I believe it would have been easier, after all, if we'd done the natural and obvious thing and gone straight to the room after we were married."

"Now don't fuss over that, any more," he retorted, picking up her hat for her. "It was to please *her* we did as we did. It was *her* idea. She begged you to wait till Sunday and we promised we would. Nobody knows we're married but her and Tom and Dekker."

"Perhaps . . . I'll have . . . to wait . . . till Sunday," said Mary.

John looked so aghast at this that she kissed him of her own accord.

"Well . . . I'll do my best. But how shall I let you know whether to come and meet me at the gate or not?" she continued rather wistfully. "She may make such a scene, when it comes to the point, that I'll *have* to put it off till tomorrow."

"Oh, I'll come at nine, my treasure, and hang about there for half an hour, for an hour if you like! And then, if you're not out before St. John's strikes ten, I'll know you can't do it. But you *will* do it—if the woman hasn't fallen into a fit or anything—you will, won't you?"

"I *will*," said Mary solemnly; and she felt if she were making a vow before that whole, sacred, golden cornfield.

"We ought to have done it as I wanted," he grumbled now, picking up his stick and his own hat. "We ought to have done it directly after the Pageant."

"Now stop!" the girl cried with a flushed cheek. "I absolutely refuse to go over all that again. You know perfectly well why I wouldn't do it then. You know how mixed up everything was and how—but, oh, my dear, don't let's quarrel over that old story now! I'm too happy today. It's all been too lovely today. Don't let's go and spoil it now, just at the end. My dearest, my dearest, don't 'ee bring up those old grievances now, please, don't 'ee!" And she slipped her hand into his with a gesture of intense pleading.

John shrugged his lean shoulders with a gesture learnt in France; but he obeyed her and let the dangerous topic drop.

Hand in hand they soon recovered their equanimity as they moved along the hedge towards the gate leading into Bulwark's Lane.

John never took Mary's hand without a dim, delicious feeling that he was holding her—as he never yet *had* held her—undressed and lying by his side.

"Well," he thought, "tonight . . . tonight!" and then as he lifted up the heavy gate to close it, when they were safe in the lane, and took a final glance at that shimmering corn, "I must never forget this afternoon; never, never!" Slowly, lingeringly, they drifted down the uneven decline, following the windings of that narrow lane, and he held her fingers tighter and tighter in his clasp. Why, oh, why, had he not kept her there in the corn-field till it was too late for her to go back to the Abbey House; till there was nothing to be done but just let Miss Drew go, and lock themselves into their Northload room for the night!

But it was wiser, always wiser, to accept the appointed end of happy hours! His incorrigible mind set itself wondering now whether this might not be the real solution of the problem of evil, of pain, of deprivation and frustration in the world. Suppose things were so made that there was nothing in life that need interrupt an eternity of August afternoons like this one? Would that not take away from *this* afternoon its perfect thrill, its wonderful essence, its strange and abiding entelechy?

Though he hadn't thought of such matters *up there*, wasn't it the awareness, at the back of his mind, of his noisy shanty in the Great Western yard, of old Tom's cynical troubles, of Miss Drew's tragic passion, of Geard's mania about Chalice Well, of Philip's scornful hostility, of the difficulty of propitiating their landlady, of the way Mad Bet was forever waylaying him, yes! and of the sights and sounds, so many of them disagreeable, that crowded in on his days, as he went back and forth between Northload Street and the railway station, which, like the solid masonry of the bulk of St. John's Tower, making its rich turrets and pinnacles so much the lovelier, had given the final magic touch to those golden wheat-stalks and those black stockings?

John dug his root-handled hazel-stick viciously into the dry cart-ruts as this thought came to him.

"My sweet!" he cried aloud.

"What is it, John?"

"Do you suppose all our happiness depends on contrast?"

"You mean our having to come down here; and my having to go back for dinner?"

"That *kind* of thing . . . yes!"

"Better walk alone now," she said, drawing her hand away and moving it quickly to her hat and then to her waistband. "I know what you mean, John, and I've thought of that too—but some-

times I get a feeling that there's a world, just inside or just outside *this* world, where these opposites that are so hard to understand, lose their difference altogether."

"But that means death, doesn't it?"

She turned her heads towards him and he was astonished at
the softness, the bloom, the glow that suffused her face at that
moment.

"Not . . . necessarily . . . not always," she said slowly; and
then, before turning her head away, she smiled one of those
deep, mysterious, feminine smiles, that only the greatest poets
and artists, such as Dante, Leonardo, Blake, have dared to note,
depict and comment on, in their troubled search for the absolute.

St. John's clock struck six as they reached the centre of the
town. "Too late for tea, John," she said. And then she added,
"We'll have *our* tea at midnight and all to ourselves. But, oh,
goodness! I do feel so frightened all of a sudden."

"What's the matter, sweetheart?"

"Oh, I don't know! John, I'm afraid, she'll be *terribly* upset.
You won't be angry if I don't come, and you've waited and
waited?"

"Of course not," he replied hurriedly. "By God, it'll only be
what I deserve if I *have* to come back alone. Besides, it's only
putting it off till tomorrow!"

The girl stared in front of her, fixing her eyes on that well-
preserved Gothic building that is usually called the Abbot's
Tribunal. Something had profoundly disturbed her.

"Tomorrow . . . tomorrow," she murmured vaguely.

"What is it, my sweet? What is it, Mary?"

She gave a quick sigh and a shake of her head.

"Oh, nothing . . . I expect I'm just nervous. But when you've
looked forward to a thing for a *very* long time and it's just ——"
She bit her lower lip; she pushed back the hair beneath her hat
with the unconscious gesture of a woman facing the worst tidily
"Well, my dear," she said resolutely, fighting down a craving
to burst into tears and to cry frantically: "Let's go to the room
now, straight away, quick—to the room—now!" "Well, my dear,
I suppose we'd better part here. I'll just have a comfortable time
to see her for a moment or two before we dress for dinner."

"Will you come over . . . to the room . . . in your—dress?" John asked, feeling as if he were a tramp making a rendezvous with a princess.

"Of course; I've got my warm cloak, haven't I? I'll bring my little black bag."

John looked at her with astonishment. That she should be able—this delicate exquisite provoker of feelings such as could ascend the steps of the ultimate Heaven—to manage such a drastic undertaking as to have a scene with Miss Drew and leave the house with a black bag, seemed to him wonderful. That she was ready to do it, that she was fond of him enough to do it, amazed him. He had never been a man who attracted women, and he exaggerated their coldness towards him. Indeed in regard to the love of women he had a physical humility that was almost a mania. One of the strongest holds that Mary had over him was the simple fact that she, a sweet-looking, intellectual girl, *could* be in love with him at all! Secretly John regarded himself as the most unlovable human creature then living in Glastonbury.

As he continued to hold the hand which she had given him and to stare at her like a person in a trance, Mary had herself to make the move she dreaded.

"Good-bye . . . till tonight!" she said and tore her hand away. But she was back again before John had left the spot. It was a crowded piece of pavement where they had stopped in front of the mullioned windows of the old Tribunal, and John, following the cream-coloured frock with his eyes, had stepped into the gutter so as not to be jostled.

Here they met as she pushed her way back against the current of the crowd.

"If I don't come tonight, I'll come tomorrow morning. You won't go out till I come, will you?"

"I should say not!"

And she had flown for the second time.

She still had that queer disturbed feeling, as coming down Silver Street, she passed the high Vicarage wall. "It looks like a monastery!" she thought. She was anything but reassured when she caught sight of Sam Dekker at the Vicarage gate, talking to Crummie Geard. Crummie had recently taken to helping old

Mrs. Robinson arrange the flowers for the church altar, and she had come—quite naturally that Saturday night—to fetch a bunch of white geraniums from the Vicarage garden.

Sam raised his hat as Mary passed and Crummie nodded; but the impression left by this encounter was an unpleasant one.

"She holds those white flowers like a nun," Mary thought. "And she used to be such a lovely, merry creature. I believe that man is putting horrible ideas into her head! He's got a sort of furtive inquisitor's look. He'll be making that pretty little thing enter some terrible Order. How she *is* listening to him, drinking in every word! He's worse than a priest—that young man. And what a shifty sensual look he's got. He gave me a look as much as to say: 'Go on and take your pleasure! Go on and break Miss Drew's heart! A time will soon come when you too will come here for white geraniums!'"

As Mary hurriedly slipt off her cream-coloured frock—and she felt a desire to crumple that dress between her hands and press it to her face instead of folding it up so carefully—and began taking down her hair, she became conscious that her panic just now went deeper than the struggle with poor Miss Drew and deeper even than the difference between the Tribunal and that golden field. She paused in her task, with her bare arms lifted to her head at the mirror, and stared into her own grey eyes. Mary was as little conceited of her looks (nor, to confess the truth, were they of any startling quality) as her lover-cousin, for he could hardly be called a husband yet, with those bridal sheets still cold, was conceited of his.

Into her grey eyes she looked therefore, as a spirit might look that would fain give pleasure to the man she loved by giving him her body. "The *next* time," she thought, "I look in the glass will be in our room!" She took the comb now and began combing out her hair, holding her head so far back that she made her long tresses hang straight as seaweed, clinging to a smooth-oval-shaped stone. And she really did forget her anxiety now and Miss Drew and everything; for the electricity in her hair, as she pulled the comb through it, gave her such a delicate, amorous shiver that it made her feel as if butterfly wings were caressing her nipples under her soft shift.

And she thought: "What *will* it be like tonight? Shall I feel awkward and ashamed? Will I be able to sleep?"

There came a puckered wrinkle to her forehead now, as she put the comb down and began plaiting her smoothed-out locks. John was funny. John's manias and fastidiousnesses, where girls were concerned, seemed to be endless. "I'll be a fool, an idiotic fool, if I let him see me undressed too soon. I'd better put out the lights while I'm slipping on my nightgown."

Her mind pondered on gravely and intently, thinking to herself, "Well—there you are again, you curious creature!" It was indeed a fierce mania of Mary's to stare into her own eyes at the looking-glass. She did it as a rule more angrily than with any other feeling; and, when she did it, she always thought of the self that looked back at her there as something quite different from the self she was conscious of really being. Her real self didn't seem to have eyes at all; didn't, in some mysterious way, seem to need eyes or nose, or mouth! Her real self seemed compounded out of pure ether and totally independent of bodily form.

"I've felt this unsafe feeling somewhere else," she now told her staring grey eyes; "and I know where it was too! It was the night when I undressed after being in the boat with John, on the Wissey; the night when I was in the room next to Dave and Persephone, and when John was at that inn."

What Mary could not know was that the original cause of this feeling was that the desperate prayer which they had sent up from the boat that day had only reached the malice in the First Cause instead of its beneficence. She tried angrily now to shake off the feeling.

"If I *do* make Miss Drew let me go tonight," she thought, "I'll have it out with you, looking so wild and troubled!" And then, not thinking of herself as beautiful, she set herself to think of the best method of procedure when the great moment came. No young lady from Wollop's, led by Young Tewsy into "my other house," could have meditated more carefully on the diplomacy of provocation. But this grave, true-hearted girl, before she had finished arranging her hair as she wished it to be, *had* smiled once at her own image. It was a flurried, faint, flickering smile, like a watery sun on vaporous ice; but, when she came to kneel before her chest of drawers to take out her best white evening dress—that she had not put on since the night when Tom Barter came—she suddenly fell to laughing aloud. The memory had come into her head of those everlasting Elizabethan bawdy jests about the taking of maidenheads. "I don't fancy I'll be much changed in *that respect*," she thought to herself, as she unfolded her big crimson sash.

But she had no sooner placed dress and sash side by side upon the bed and had begun to wonder what stockings to select, when there came a faint, hesitating knock at the door.

It turned out to be Lily; and Lily with tears running down her cheeks.

"What is it? What's the matter?" she cried. "Come in, Lily! Come in and tell me what it is."

She pulled the girl in and closed the door. "There! There!" she murmured soothingly. "Don't you cry! You'll spoil your nice, clean apron. Look! Here's a new handkerchief; and I'll *give* it to you, Lily, to *keep*. It's real Norwich linen."

"Louie was . . . I thought . . . Mr. Weatherwax said . . ."

"Now stop, Lily! There's a good girl. Stop and tell me about it quietly."

" 'Twas to do with . . . 'twas because of . . . 'twere about Mr. Barter, Miss Mary."

Mary was a kind-hearted, generous girl and not devoid of her own queer slant of Norfolk humour; but her attitude to Lily did unconsciously change a little at the introduction of Mr. Barter's name.

"Well, Lily, what was it?"

"Thank you . . . ever . . . so much . . . Miss . . . for this love . . . lovely handkerchief! I shall keep it as . . . as a keepsake, Miss."

"But what is it, Lily? What's upset you so?"

"Mr. Weatherwax said he'd tell Mistress that he'd seen Mr. Barter talking to me in Ruins a week agone come Sunday. He've a bad tongue, that old man has; and Louie thought if I told *you*,

Miss, what tales he's going about telling of me, maybe Mistress would . . . I mean maybe Mistress wouldn't ——"

"But *did* Mr. Barter talk to you last Sunday, Lily?"

"Not *talk*—of course, Miss Mary"—and Lily, folding up the handkerchief into little squares, uplifted a face as innocent of all guile as a wrongfully accused heroine in a story by the author of *The Channings*—"not talk, of course, Miss—Mr. Barter happened to pass by when I was reading under the wall at Ruins' End and naturally, being the gentleman he is ——"

Mary found her good-temper coming back to her with a rush. The image of the sedate Lily with her book, the expression, "Ruins' End," the casual Barter taking a blameless stroll in the Abbey grounds—in the presence of these things it was impossible to nourish grievances. Besides, Lily could take care of herself. Lily was no little goose like Tossie Stickles.

"Tom, Tom," she thought, "you'd better take care. If I know anything of our Lily you'll meet your match if you don't look out!"

"I understand, Lily. . . . It's all right. Miss Drew knows how careful you always are of the credit of her house. If I were you I would only laugh when old Weatherwax teases you. Answer him back! Pay him off in his own coin. Above all, don't make him angry."

Mary paused for a moment, and then, while she moved to her chest of drawers to finish her dressing, the thought of Crummie and the white geraniums made her burst out scandalously to Lily who was fumbling with the red sash on the bed: "We girls can only be young once, Lily," she surprised herself by saying. "But we must keep our wits about us, for men are ticklish creatures."

It may be believed how wide Lily's eyes opened when she heard these words. "Mr. Barter has always behaved very proper, Miss," she stammered, "and I'm sure, Miss, you know that I ——"

"That's enough, now, Lily," said Mary firmly, pushing the astonished maid gently towards the door. "Go and see if Miss Drew wants any help; and if she's gone down, tell her I won't be a minute. By the way, Lily, it may interest you to know that I was married the day before yesterday!"

Lily's face expressed unalloyed dramatic interest; but, a second later, bewildered consternation.

"She thinks it's to Tom," passed through Mary's mind. "Yes," she went on, "to my cousin, Mr. John Crow, who did so much in the Pageant."

Lily sighed a deep sigh of relief. "Are you going to . . . to leave us . . . Miss . . . I mean Mam?"

"We'll see what your mistress says about *that*," replied Mrs. John Crow with a brazen chuckle. "I've got two homes now, Lily—one here and one—not here. Now run off, please, there's a good girl! Oh, and you can tell Louie to send in some of those tartlets she made yesterday. I know there's rice pudding; but if she wants to give me a treat——"

"May I tell——" murmured Lily from the doorway.

"Of course, of course! Only say it's a great secret—especially from Mr. Weatherwax!"

It was only eight by the French clock on the mantelpiece when dinner was over and Miss Drew and her rebellious companion were seated opposite each other, with the Dresden coffee-cups between them. Not a sip of her coffee, however, had Miss Drew taken. Her face was tense and white, her nostrils twitching, her fingers fretting with her white shawl, her shoes tapping the ground, her back straight.

"—like an elopement; that's what it is . . . stealing off at night to a man's room . . . no! it's worse than that . . . it's like *an assignation*!"

"It's my husband's room," maintained the girl firmly; and she said to herself: "I believe she's going to let me go."

Miss Drew visibly shuddered.

"Mary!" she said.

"Yes, dear?"

"Go to the dining-room sideboard, please, and get me half a wine glass of Mr. Dekker's brandy!"

The girl made haste to obey her and was glad to find that the room was already nearly dark and that Lily had taken away both rice pudding and tartlets.

Miss Drew drank the brandy in two quick gulps.

"Is he coming for you tonight?"

The girl nodded.

"I won't have him cross my threshold! I've told you that already."

"He's not coming in. I'm to meet him at the gate."

The woman rose from her seat and, moving to the chimney-piece, drew her shawl tight round her shoulders.

There were no flower-pots in the grate tonight. Its cold polished black cavity looked back at her like the ribs of death.

"This moment had to come," she said in a low voice, speaking more to herself than to the girl. "It had to come; and now it's come."

"But I'll be over every day, dear," whispered Mary, wishing bitterly that she had never let John come for her tonight. "It's worse than I expected," she thought.

"You don't know," said Miss Drew, "you simply don't know what you're to me."

"Dear . . . my dear!" murmured Mary, rising, she also, from her seat, and making a little wavering, fluctuating movement towards her friend.

But Miss Drew continued: "No, you don't know, you never have known! This man . . . this 'husband' as you call him, this cunning scamp . . . has less feeling in his whole body than I've got in my little finger!"

She must have caught, just then, an involuntary glance of Mary's towards the door. The younger woman was indeed afraid that Lily might suddenly appear to carry off the coffee.

But to Mary's amazement Miss Drew now rushed to the door and locked it! Such a thing as locking the drawing-room door of the Abbey House to prevent interruption from the servants was as much of a tragic and historic event—if the real proportion of things be considered—as the eviction of the royal spy, before Sedgemoor, from the bar-room of Dickery Cantle's great-great-great-grandfather.

When Miss Drew came back from crossing the room the two women confronted each other between the fragile coffee-table and the fireless grate. The elder wore her usual black silk garment with the heavy brooch securing the old lace frill on her withered neck. Opposed to her gaunt figure, Mary's form, in her low-cut white dress and big crimson sash, looked very young and soft and girlish.

"I'd like you . . . I'd like you not to . . ."

Miss Drew was evidently struggling to say something that tore at her vitals.

"I'd like ——" she gasped again.

"What is it, oh, what *is* it?" stammered Mary, awed, a little scared and completely bewildered.

"I'd like you not to go to him tonight. I'd like you to stay with me tonight . . . our last night . . . as you are!"

"Of course, my dear, if you feel it like that ——"

"I mean . . . not leave me at all . . . just this once . . . I mean . . . let me hold you . . . all night . . . close to me ——"

Mary's face must have expressed such trouble, such pity, such confused agitation, that the old woman changed her tone to a quieter one. "It would be nothing to you . . . to watch . . . to be there . . . to be near me . . . just this once . . . and then" —she swallowed a rasping, dry sob—"tomorrow . . . you shall go."

"Dear! I must think. He'll be at the gate in a few minutes; I must—I don't know *what* to say. For him to go back alone— through the streets—to that room—oh, I don't know what to do!"

She flung herself down on a chair, her red sash trailing to the carpet, lying on the carpet, like a great stream of blood from a stab in her side.

Miss Drew leaned one of her long, tight-sleeved arms upon the mantelpiece and watched her.

The void of her longing for her, of her losing her, throbbed within her like a hollow cave, round the walls of which a bitter stifling smoke was whirling, seeking an exit.

The French clock on the mantelpiece ticked on remorselessly: *tick-tock, tock-tick, tick-tock*, as if there were behind its hidden wheels, some demon of the inanimate, that was taking vengeance for all the hammerings and tinkerings it had had at the hands of its man-creators.

Mary glanced hopelessly, helplessly, at the clock. She remembered how it had ticked, just like this, the night she had felt so

sad with Tom before the Pageant. Her thoughts kept taking first
one road of trouble and then another. "It isn't fair!" her heart
cried. "I belong to John. It isn't fair!" And then a vast pity for
this unloved, childless old woman surged up within her. "After
all," she said to herself, "it's only for one short night; and how
could I be happy, over there, thinking that I'd denied her such
a little thing?"

"Let me think," she whispered, giving Miss Drew a faint smile
and a reassuring nod. "Sit down, dear—don't stand like that!
You make me nervous. I only want to think . . . just to think
. . . a little more."

But Miss Drew did not show any inclination to sit down. She
kept her eyes fixed upon the girl in the chair, as if that red sash
were a death warrant. And something from her Isle-of-Ely ancestors now rose up in Mary's nature; something sturdy, earth-
rooted and with a smack of indulgent humour in it, like the taste
of peat-smoke.

"The poor heart!" she said to herself. "John and I can surely
wait for twenty-four hours. If *I* can—God knows!—*he* can."

To her consternation Miss Drew now rushed forward and with
a heart-rending groan flung herself on her knees at the girl's feet.
"I'm not a bad woman! I'm not a bad woman!" she sobbed out;
and then to Mary's dismay she began pressing the red sash
against her lips. "I'm not . . . I'm not a bad woman!" she
groaned again, uplifting to the girl a face contorted with shame
and passion.

"Miss Drew! *dear* Miss Drew! Get up, for Christ's sake. It's
not right for you—it's not right for either of us! Oh, *what* shall
I do? What shall I——"

But the other had buried her face in the girl's lap and with
her arms outstretched was clutching at the sash where it was
wound about the young woman's waist. She was murmuring all
sorts of wild things now to which the girl could only helplessly
listen, looking distractedly at the clock, which went on with its
infernal ticking in exactly the same tone as if its mistress had
been pouring out tea for Matthew Dekker.

"Oh, I love you so! Oh, I would give up my life for you! I
can't bear it any more—it's lasted too long. But you will? My

child, my little one, my only one, you will? You *will* be with me, watch with me, let me hold you, just this one single night? I'm not a bad woman! *Say* I'm not, child! It's . . . it's . . . *it's this Love* that's burning my life up!"

The clock selected this particular moment to begin striking nine, the hour when John was to be at the gate! She had done nothing towards putting her day-dress and her night-dress into that black bag she had told him about. The intrusion of Lily at that juncture had left her barely time to get dressed at all.

She had to struggle now with a definite anger against this frantic creature; but her sturdy East-Anglian nature stood her in good stead and she fought that feeling down. She saw in her mind's eye the drooping forehead, the lowered eyelids of the nun-like Crummie. She saw Sam Dekker's white geraniums; and she murmured to herself again: "The poor heart! The poor heart!"

"Get up, dear! Get up!" she now cried aloud in a voice not untender but resolute and emphatic. As she spoke, she herself struggled out of the chair. Standing erect now she felt in more control of the situation; and she took hold of Miss Drew's hands and managed to drag her up from her knees. She was startled as she did this by the burning feverishness in the woman's fingers. But when she got her safe on her feet the agitated lady fell into a fit of violent shivering as if, in the fever of her emotion, she had been plunged into ice-cold water.

But she resumed her old place by the empty grate; though Mary could see the thin black arm that she extended along the mantelpiece was trembling so much that it made a couple of ornaments that stood there jingle and tinkle against each other.

Miss Drew glanced sideways now at the ticking clock, as if she could have struck out its life with one blow and left it pointing at ten minutes past nine in an eternal paralysis!

"Well," she whispered huskily, "why don't you go up and pack your things, if . . . that man . . . is waiting for you?"

Mary walked slowly to the window. She was once more in an anguish of indecision. The tragedy of passion often consists in the depths of harsh unlovableness into which it throws its victims. Miss Drew, by the tone in which she said, "Go up . . . that man is waiting," had done her utmost to destroy the very pity upon which her fate depended. The "poor heart," as her red-sashed companion had called her in her thoughts, was indeed in a tragic impasse.

"Well . . . have you decided against me . . . against the one thing I've ever begged . . . on my knees . . . of a living soul?"

Her words seemed to come, not from her own mouth, but from some other Miss Drew,—a towering image of devastated frustration—that hung and wavered in the air between them.

But Mary continued obstinately staring out of the window into the round half-circle of trimly weeded gravel, surrounded by thick laurel bushes from which a winding driveway led to the gate. The window was open at the top; but not content with this, she presently pulled aside the muslin curtains and opened it at the bottom. She now stood there motionless, listening intently, while the warm August air stirred her gown and, entering the room, made the candles flicker.

Several little brown moths took the opportunity of flying in past her white figure. Some rushed to perish at the candles on the table, while others beat themselves against the lamp till they fell upon the floor. Neither Miss Drew nor her companion had any margin of consciousness left for these little suicides of blind desire. Miss Drew's thoughts flickered much more wildly than the softly fluttering curtains or the lightly stirred folds of her companion's frock.

They were a strange jumble, these thoughts; a jumble of old, conservative prejudices and passionately covetous longings; longings rendered intensely concrete and circumscribed by reason of their long suppression.

"Mamma . . . Mamma . . . never sit on sofas . . . weakness to sit on sofas . . . hold your back straight now . . . straight Euphemia . . . Betty Newton in hay-loft . . . kissing . . . Mamma . . . angry like God . . . God sees all . . . he will hold her all night . . . a sneak . . . a tramp . . . a trickster . . . a thief . . . friend of Geard . . . Geard meddling with Chalice Well . . . Geard letting loose all the devils . . . burning . . . burning . . . Betty Newton . . . Mamma . . . bed all day . . . bread and water . . . too long, too long, too long

. . . sweet . . . so very sweet . . . and for him, all for a dirty trickster . . . no one knows how sweet but me . . . too old now . . . old . . . old . . . never sit on sofas . . . weakness . . . hold your back straight, Euphemia . . . a dirty adventurer must have her . . . hard she is . . . hard to me . . . soft as clay to him . . . *it burns* . . . it would be only once . . . peace, rest . . . lovely, heavenly peace! . . . her red sash . . . *it burns* . . . Lily and Rogers in bed . . . never knocked . . . never rang . . . everything changed since that man became Mayor . . . Chalice Well . . . blood . . . her sash . . . red blood . . . *it burns* . . . never for me . . . after this . . . never for me . . . she'll be gone soon . . . listening for him out there . . . gone . . . gone . . . a maid no more . . . *it burns* . . . Lily and Rogers in bed . . . two pillows . . . slept watching . . . watching slept . . . mamma . . . grand-mamma . . . crying all night . . . never came . . . never heard . . . it burns and burns and burns."

"I couldn't be happy in our room tonight," thought Mary. "And after all—no! I'll do it. The poor woman! It's better than giving her white geraniums to hold in her hand."

She shut the window with a violent jerk of her strong bare arms. She turned and came slowly, gravely, gently, towards the figure by the mantelpiece. She came close up to Miss Drew and threw her arms round her as she would have thrown them around a wounded animal.

"I'll stay," she whispered softly to her, "I'll stay, dear!"

The rush of wild excitement, relief, passion, shame, the motion of racing blood from heart to nerves, brain, throat, were too much for the wrought-up feelings of the woman.

Her head sank down, like the head of a reed in the water when a sluice is opened, and upon Mary's shoulders her tears fell now without stint, while a queer whimpering, like the crying of a child whose mother has suddenly appeared among a crowd of strangers, showed signs of changing into hysterical laughter.

"Come and lie down, dear . . . There! I'm not going to leave you . . . not for one moment . . . my poor, poor darling! Come and lie down . . . only just a minute."

Thus murmuring, Mary half-dragged, half-supported her till

she got her safe upon the sofa . . . upon that very sofa where "Mamma" had so often told the little Euphemia that it was "weakness" to recline. Then the girl's practical mind began to work fast. "I *must*," she thought, "run out and tell John. I'd better go and get hold of Lily. Oh, mercy! Her eyes are shutting! I hope she's not going to faint."

Thrusting a pillow under Miss Drew's head, Mary ran to the door, unlocked it and hurried down the passage. She had shut the door carefully behind her; but even so, she did not want the lady to hear her shouting for help.

"Lily!" she called gently.

There was no answer; but she thought she detected the sound of hurried movements and disturbed voices in the far distance.

"Lily! Louie! Where are you?"

Then she heard the unmistakable sound of a man's voice—the voice of Mr. Weatherwax. She opened the kitchen door. "Come here, Lily, come quick, please; I want you! Miss Drew's ill!"

There was bread and cheese upon the kitchen table and also— Mary noted it with a house-wife's indignation, even at that crisis! —the brandy decanter from the dining-room sideboard.

The scullery door opened—just wide enough to allow the entrance of a very slim virgin—and Lily, hurriedly pinning on her white cap, slipped into the kitchen, with eyes very wide and even her pretty mouth a little open.

"Oh, Lily, Miss Drew's unwell—I've made her lie down on the sofa; and I think ——"

"La, Miss!—I mean Mam—does Mistress want the brandy? Mr. Weatherwax just dropped in to ask how we was off for vegetables, and Louie thought ——"

"Listen, Lily. We must try and help Miss Drew upstairs, and get her into bed. I shall sleep with her tonight; so you can take my pillow and things into her room. One minute, Lily! Just go and tell Mr. Weatherwax not to go for a moment. If she's too heavy for us, he could carry her up."

"Yes, Mam; yes, Mrs. Crow."

Mary hurried back into the drawing-room.

To her astonishment Miss Drew was standing by the mantelpiece again, but her whole manner was changed from what it had been. She was self-possessed now and very quiet.

"Come here, child," she said.

Mary went up to her and she took the girl's head gravely between her hands and kissed her forehead.

"I've changed my mind," she whispered, very dignified and commanding. "I wish you to go after all. Run out now quickly and tell that man to wait for you; and then come back and pack your things. And I shan't expect you back till Monday morning. I *wish* it, Mary! You must do what I tell you. I shall be absolutely all right. I shall get up early and go to St. John's."

The curious thing about this long, hurried speech was that Miss Drew never raised her voice above a whisper. Mary stared at her. The sight of their two untasted coffee-cups brought back so vividly the painful scene she had gone through that night, that this change in her employer's tone seemed dreamlike and unnatural.

But, before she had time to reply, Lily came quickly in without even a pretence at a knock.

"Lily," said Miss Drew calmly, raising her voice now, so that it sounded quite as usual, "you know, of course, that Miss Mary is married?"

"Yes'm, Miss Mary told me, Mum."

"But she's going to be with us, as before, I'm glad to hear," Miss Drew went on, making several little movements with her hands among the objects on the coffee-tray—"that is, during the day-time. But I've told her we'll be able to manage without her tomorrow; for we mustn't be selfish, must we, Lily?"

"Yes'm . . . no Mum."

But the lady of the Abbey House now turned to the extremely embarrassed Mrs. John Crow.

"Run out, dear, and tell your—good man, that we're all helping you to pack and that you won't keep him long."

Dominated by the authority in her tone and spared any protest by the presence of Lily, Mary had nothing for it but to obey her to the letter. She went to the door, which Lily gravely opened for her, and slipped out into the hall.

She did not soon forget her queer sensation—as if she had

been turned into a bit of seaweed on the top of a great cresting wave of compulsion—as she looked hurriedly round for some-thing to throw round her. There was a big, eighteenth-century mirror hanging in the hall; and in a flash of queer detachment as one of her hands mechanically went up to her hair, she thought to herself, "Women must have wrapped things around their white shoulders like this, while arrows were flying, guns firing, torches waving, men shouting, for hundreds and hundreds of years!" She opened the front door and descended the stone steps. Then, with the cloak she'd picked up clutched tight round her— more as a protection from the night, from obscure invasions of her nakedness, than for warmth in that summer air—she ran rapidly down the drive. Yes! There he was.

"No . . . no! Not now, John!" she panted breathlessly, as he hugged her against him, almost lifting her off the ground in his thankfulness to have got her again. "There . . . there! Let me go, John!"—and when she was free—"I must go back now for my things . . . I only came . . . to tell you I was—" she could hardly get the words out in her agitation—"to tell you I was coming. You wait here, John ———"

She was off up the drive again, and out of his sight, almost before his unspeakable relief had found time to flow to his con-fused brain from the arms which had held her.

He could not remain still. Every pulse in his body was beating and his heart was as voluble as the French clock, still ticking behind Miss Drew, as she talked quietly to Lily. He set himself to pace up and down the road like a sentinel guarding some royal palace.

There were all sorts of vague delicious scents upon the soft air that rustled through the laurel bushes, stirred the wall-flowers in the crannies of the grey wall, went sighing off like the breath of an invisible spirit over the tops of the trees. But from some remote cowshed somewhere out towards Havyatt Gap, on the road to West Pennard, he could hear the pitiful cry of a beast in pain.

As this cry went on, tossed forth upon the summer night with woeful persistence, John stood and listened nervously, leaning upon his hazel-root stick.

"Damn!" he thought, "and it must be a pain like that, that

this woman's enduring now, only in the heart . . . in the heart . . . at my carrying off Mary! What a thing—that not one perfect day can be enjoyed by anyone without hearing something groan or moan! What would young Dekker be doing in my case? Well—it's clear what he'd be doing, by what he's done over Mrs. Zoyland! Cleared out of it . . . hands off . . . and spends his time between Paradise and Bove Town, comforting the sick."

He resumed his sentry's march, but his mind was beating now against the blood-stained wedge of the world's pain, and he could not give up himself with absolute assent to his good hour.

He prodded the crumbling stonework of the wall with the end of his stick in angry pity: pity for Miss Drew, pity for that suffering beast on the West Pennard Road, pity for the whole array of anguished nerves upon which the great, blunt thumb of evil was strumming its nightly gamut amid these sweet summer scents.

Once more he listened intently. How hard not to listen! What was the trouble with that beast over there? What were they doing to it? What were he and Mary doing to Miss Drew? If only he knew that there were a God, who *for one second* had an ear open, what things he would pour into that gaping, hairy, stupid orifice. In the old days their gods made them sacrifice their enemies to propitiate the great pain-engine.

"I'll put into old Geard's head," he thought, "to burn an image of God, like a great Guy Fawkes, when he has his Festival of Christ's Blood."

He resumed his sentry's march. The suffering beast was silent now. He prayed that Miss Drew also was either rocking herself to sleep in a fit of hysterics or hardening her heart in pain-killing hate.

"But if everyone waited," he said to himself, "to snatch their hour, till not a cry, a groan, a moan, could be heard in the whole world, who would *ever* be happy?" There! Wasn't *that* the opening of the front door? No! 'Twas one of those inexplicable noises that are liable to occur in all silent places, as though some ambushed eavesdropper struck something with his foot.

"What an awful mood Tom was in when I saw him yesterday! He doesn't seem to like it very much our being married. Perhaps I oughtn't to have asked him to the church. She said not to! Girls are wise in these things . . . wise . . . *There!* That surely *was* the door? Yes, there are her steps! Oh, the darling! Oh, the heavenly darling!" He snatched the bag from her hands and laid it on the ground, flinging his hazel-stick after it. His whispers of rapture as he welcomed her, touching her, here, there, with his hands, as if to make sure that it was she and none else, drifted off among the other faint sounds of the night and went on their airy voyage eastward. The wind came from the west; so that, long after no human ear could have heard them, those sounds— or those vibrations that would have been sounds to more sensitive ears than man's—went journeying due east. Over the roofs of West Pennard and East Pennard they went; over Ditcheat and Milton Clevedon; over Cogley Wood and King's Wood Warren; over Monkton Deverill and Danes' Bottom; till they left the West-Country altogether; and were resolved into thin air somewhere beyond Stonehenge.

But Mary soon made him pick up her bag and his stick and set off down Silver Street.

"I was within an ace—an ace I tell you—of not coming to-night! In fact I'd told her I *wouldn't* come; and it was quite decided; when, all suddenly, she changed her mind and became absolutely generous. She just *made* me come, John, just *made* me!"

"Poor old thing!" he interjected at this point. And then he caught himself up. "Damn it, my sweet, how self-complacent a person gets, *in a second,* when luck turns—but I can't help it; I've got you! I've got you! I've got you!"

Mary smiled to herself in the warm velvety darkness that hung, like a great priestly alb, around the masonry of St. John's Tower; for she said in her heart: "How different women are from men! I suppose we all accept from our earliest childhood, this tragic division between the happy and the unhappy. Men seem to *discover* it, like a new light on things; and at once want to do something, or at least to make some grand *sign* of doing something!" But she forgot Miss Drew herself when they reached that door in the lamp-lit silence of Northload Street. John produced his latch-key.

"Think if I'd forgotten it!" he whispered. "Think if we'd had

to ring and bring that woman down!" And she remembered, as
they ascended the two flights of stairs to their top floor, glancing
with an almost guilty nervousness at the various doors they
passed, how miserable she had been so many times, on these
stairs. She recalled the day when she had bought the tablecloth
at Wollop's and had found Tom there and came away without
even knocking. As she followed John now with her hand on the
gas-lit bannisters and watched the ends of his grey flannel trousers clinging about his down-trodden heels, she wondered to
herself why it was that he loved her now so much more than
during those wretched months before the Pageant. Was it Tom's
fault in those days? or Geard's? or just the agitation of the
Pageant?

"I don't understand him," she said to herself, as they reached
their own landing, "but I belong to him, I belong to him! He
loves me more today than he's loved me since the boat on the
Wissey."

Her feelings were a thrilling mixture of contradictions when
they stood in the room at last—alone together—and with the
night before them. But they were all happy sensations; though
so opposite! It was a delicious sense of a furtive, guilty assignation she had, as she heard him lock the door behind her. But it
was also a heavenly sense, as she looked around her, of being in
a room she had made according to her own taste; for in Thorpe,
at Norwich, it had just been "Mary's bedroom," something she
had accepted exactly as she had grown up in it; and of course,
at Miss Drew's, everything belonged to the house.

She felt also—and this was totally unexpected—a hot wave of
shyness mounting up through her as she hesitated for a second
to throw off her cloak. She pressed her knuckles quickly to her
face, before she looked round, and prayed he wouldn't notice
how burning her cheeks were! But he was snatching off her cloak
now; and now he was standing back, for a minute, to gaze at her
with adoration in her low white dress and bare arms and
shoulders.

"What a . . . lovely . . . sash!" he whispered solemnly; and
he seemed to be drinking her up with his eyes, just as if he were
kneeling at her feet and she were the very cup at the altar. And

then his hands, his lips, his very soul, were pressed rapturously against her shoulders, her throat, her shy cold breasts.

The touch of her body began very soon to change this worship of her beauty into a more intense but less sacramental desire. His fingers began feverishly plucking at the fastenings of her bodice. But Mary remembered her carefully thought-out erotic diplomacy and she slipped away from him.

"No . . . no . . . no, John, I'm going to undress behind our screen. That's what I bought it for, at Wollop's! It's my dressing-room behind there—as well as my kitchen! You go and get quite ready for bed . . . give me my bag, though, my night-gown's in there . . . yes! get into bed as quick as you like, and I'll turn out the gas!"

When John recalled every conscious moment of all this night, after she had left him on Monday, the thing that remained in his mind as most entrancing was the marbly smoothness of her body when he held her at last. Being as queer as he had always been in his amorous peculiarities, and being as frantically fastidious as he was vicious, this smoothness of Mary's flesh was a new experience to him. He hadn't exactly expected her to be as scaly as a gryphon, or even as bony as old Tom was, but this heavenly smoothness was something quite unlooked for!

And she was so docile, too; that was another surprise to him; for he had expected, from what he had read in books, that she would be capricious, nervous, agitated, difficult.

Yes, Mary was indeed "docile." John was right in that! She too had her surprises that night; and the greatest of all these was the sense of absolute naturalness and freedom from embarrassment.

When she had felt that first rush of blood to her cheeks she had thought to herself: "Mercy! I'm not going to be silly in that way, am I?" But when once she had turned out that gas-flame . . . why! it was all as easy and nice as it had been in the wheatfield. It was nicer, in fact; for in place of the great Mother's confederacy with her daughter's psychic ravishing, as she lay on that sun-warmed bank, here, in this Northload bed, with the water-meadow scents coming in through the window almost as if they came from her own Norfolk fens, there was about her an older, deeper, darker protection than even of the earth; here there was about her the protection of the ancient night itself, oldest of all the gods, older than all the Thrones, Dominations, Principalities, and Powers that brood over Glastonbury, older than any Holy Grail. And Mary thought to herself: "Because I have found my love and because I have come to belong to my love, I will bear now, without making a fuss, whatever chance may give me to bear! I will think of what I feel now—pure gratitude; and I'll be sweeter to Miss Drew than anyone in all her days has been!"

And John thought to himself: "I wish I could get old Tom's troubles out of my mind! I wish I'd stirred up the Mayor a bit more to make things easier for Tom at the factory. I wish I hadn't asked him to come to the church. I wish I'd seen more of him lately! I've just dropped old Tom, I've just forgot him, neglected him, let him slide out of my mind!"

And as John lay there, discovering in the smoothness of Mary's limbs something that was as surprising to him as if he'd found a white seaweed or a blue wood-anemone, his shame about neglecting Tom became like a bruise, a definite bruise in some back-ledge of his consciousness. "*I must accept it,*" he said to himself; and he began to think, as he slowly sank to sleep— the girl was asleep at least an hour before he was—that the only morality he possessed was a feeling of shame whenever he allowed himself to cry out, "I am miserable . . . I am un- happy . . . I am wretched." Not to pity himself whatever hap- pened and not to be miserable whatever happened: such was John's morality. To allow himself to go to sleep feeling dis- tressed about Tom would have been a lapse from his interior code of honour.

As he heard St. John's clock strike two he gathered himself together within himself in a curious habit-gesture of the will. This gesture he always thought of in a particular way, using a special image for it. The image he used for it was a certain kind of black travelling trunk studded with brass nails.

Such a trunk he had once seen on a barge on the Seine. A man—a young working-man—was sitting upon it; and it was from this lad's expression that John had derived this particular symbol of refusing, whatever happened, to be unhappy, which constituted in his own mind the only morality. At the first temptation to such weakness, as at this very moment, when he was tempted to stay awake worrying about old Tom, he would make this habitual gesture of the will and visualise the black trunk with brass knobs!

It was a further proof of how women receive the tragedies of others with a more vegetable-like acceptance than men, that while Mary went to sleep at half-past one full of a delicious sense of fulfilment, John found it very difficult, in spite of his black trunk with brass nails, to get the troubles of Tom Barter out of his mind.

No doubt a large part of this difference between them lay in the fact that Mary was much less nervous about sleeping with John than John was about sleeping with Mary!

Being one layer or one skin, so to say, nearer Nature than he, her love for him saturated her deeper identity more completely than his for her; so that the contact of strange flesh—strange at least under these new conditions—was much less of a nervous shock to her, for all her greater receptivity, than it was to him. His deeper soul had not really yet *accepted* this new experience, so that while *her* love made it possible for her to fall into a childlike sleep of absolute peace and security, John stayed awake for some while longer, worrying about Tom, and when he did sleep it was a sleep less deep than hers.

But before the church clock had struck another hour, both of the cousins were fast wrapt in unconsciousness in that little Northload room; and the wandering mists from the water-meadows of the Isle of Glass, floating in and out of their open window, renewed their strength as they slept; for these airs carried with them a far-off dim remembrance of the vaporous summer mists that at this very moment were rising from Dye's Hole and from Oxborough Ferry and from that great pool at Harrod's Mill where the personality of Tom Barter had first risen up between them.

IT WAS NOW MID-SEPTEMBER. THE HARVEST—A PARTICULARLY good one that year—had been gathered in, and the apples in those immemorial orchards of Insula Pomorum, those deep-grassed, grey-green orchards with their twisted trunks under which the cuckoo flowers are so dewy-fresh in the spring and the wasps so drunken-sleepy in the autumn, were beginning to grow yellow and red.

The elderly curator of the little Glastonbury museum was walking up and down between the famous Ancient British boat, over which he had kept guard for forty years, and the almost equally famous Lake Village pottery, much of which, during his long indefatigable régime, he had dug up with his own hands. That old canoe-boat had still a serviceable air. It looked as if it would almost have served the owner of Wookey Hole himself, to push his daring explorations beyond that Stone Witch, up his subterranean river; and the pottery too looked as if it could still hold the milk and honey of Avalon.

But Mr. Merry felt worried at that moment. It was Wednesday—early-closing day in the town—and he had been promised by Mr. Crow that if he could get down to the starting-field by two o'clock he should be taken for his first air-ride.

Bob Tankerville, the pilot, was going to fly to a certain factory town in France that day, one of a series of such expeditions that Philip had been making of late, but today, the master himself being unable to go, he had offered Mr. Merry this unique chance.

"Tankerville can do my business," he had said. "All he wants is someone to grumble to."

But it was now a quarter to one and there was no sign of an expected visitor for whom he had been waiting since twelve o'clock.

"It'll be a rush to get my dinner," thought Mr. Merry, as he stroked with his old fingers the edge of the ancient canoe. Being a bachelor, and very rigid in his habits, Mr. Merry made much of his dinner hour at the Pilgrims'. Since the Pageant, he had enjoyed these meals with especial zest, because his *bête noire*, Barter, whose flirtations with the waitresses were a source of perpetual irritation to him, had, since he left the dye works for the municipal factory, ceased to appear.

A rush! If there was one thing in life that Mr. Merry could not abide it was what he called "one of those damned rushes when you don't know what you're eating." And here he was, heading steadily, moment by moment, towards a rush. Partly by disposition, for he was one of those slowly moving persons who savour intensely their own physical functioning as they go to and fro over the earth, and partly from the habit of his profession, which dealt in huge tracts of time, the curator had come to resemble the biblical Creator; for to his erudite and historic mind, "a thousand years were as one day."

He had been pestered now for nearly a fortnight by letters from the foreman of the municipal factory—an individual who signed himself "Radley Robinson"—for permission to talk to him on what the applicant called "affairs of importance."

Did the passionate Red, whose baptismal name was Radley, feel any sense of a psychic-philological shock when he murmured to himself, pen in hand, "haffairs of himportance" and then wrote down the un-aspirated words?

Since the Pageant and since the unsatisfactory compromise—from *his* point of view—that had ended the dye-works strike, Mr. Robinson had been hardening his heart and concentrating his energies. Deep in his soul shone still the illuminating lamp of " 'ate"; but to his Jacobin destructiveness he had had the wit to add a great deal of indomitable cockney patience; and on the strength of this he had been promoted to the position of second-in-command under Barter. He had set himself to propitiate Barter with a ferocity of sly, satiric unction, that made that shrewd East-Anglian positively sick with aversion. But there was nothing else to be done! The manufacturing of souvenirs flourished well under Red's astuteness. He alone seemed able to keep the hot-heads and cranks, of which the works were full, in any sort of order.

Above all, the Mayor, doubtless at his daughter's instigation, was evidently anxious to soothe the man's wounded feelings by giving him material advancement.

Anyone watching old Mr. Merry at this minute, rubbing with a privileged forefinger this precious aquatic relic, under the very nose of his own proclamation against such doings, would have supposed that he was wondering what actual prehistoric human rump once squatted in this frail skiff; but not at all. He was thinking to himself "If he doesn't come soon, I'll have to let the pudding go."

But suddenly the door opened and there, quite unmistakably, was the pestering man.

Red looked like what is called a ticklish customer. He looked like a person capable of employment by Scotland Yard. But he also—with his neat foreman's suit and new cloth cap—looked a little like a master-plumber. He didn't look the kind of person, anyway, that Mr. Merry, from forty years' experience, felt he could dismiss with a well-worn jest about its being "early-closing."

The curator sighed deeply as he requested his visitor to take a chair and learned that his name was Robinson.

"He's a pesterer," he thought, "but he isn't an arch-pesterer. I *may* have time for pudding."

He was right. Mr. Robinson plunged into business without any beating about the bush.

"What would *you* call this, Sir?" he enquired promptly, taking a stone from his pocket and handing it to the curator.

Mr. Merry took the object in his hand. It resembled a thunderbolt. It also resembled a lump of clay. The old gentleman's face became very animated.

"So *you've* found a bit, have you? Mr.—Robinson—ah! I thought—someone would—would find another—before long."

He jerked out these detached syllables as if he were accepting the object in question for his museum. He *did* lick his finger now and rub violently one corner of it.

"Yes; you've found another, Mr. Robinson. That's the seventh!"

Mr. Robinson, who had a friend among the apothecaries, now uttered a mysterious chemical formula. And then, immediately afterwards, looking Mr. Merry cheerfully in the face, pronounced the single syllable—"*tin*."

"It's the helement, hain't hit, Sir, what the Romans used to trade in; them that wore the himperial purple?"

"I've known this was coming for twenty years," thought the distracted curator, his face changing from animation to profound dismay.

He looked sharply at his interrogator. How much did this fellow know? He wasn't a chemist. He wasn't an antiquary. *Could* he be palmed off with a learned lie, or *couldn't* he? But Mr. Merry as a result of his scrutiny decided that lies were useless. "It's begun!" he said to himself. "It's begun! This fellow will take it to Crow; sure as I'm a dizzard. The beauty of Wookey Hole is departed! Crow will start quarrying the moment he sees this. The wonder is that he has missed it himself; he's always going down there—with his electricity. This is the end; the end of all those lovely stalactite caves that Clement of Alexandria talks about!"

"I can see, Sir," said Mr. Robinson rising to his feet, "that my hinformant was right; and that it *his* the helement after which the Corinthians——"

"Not Corinthians, my good man; *Carthaginians!*" cried the curator, "and what you've got there isn't an element you must understand. It's a chemical deposit, precipitated from the subterranean river down there and brought up from some deep mineral pocket in the Mendips."

"O lordy! lordy! lordy!" he thought to himself, "why can't I hold my silly old tongue?"

"It's the hold Roman metal, henny-'ow," said Mr. Robinson with emphatic assurance. "I thought it was myself; but I thought I'd just run in to-die and arst so as to mike sure. I'm not cryzy about telling people what hisn't their business any more nor you be, as I plinely see! But in dies like these dies, it's best to be sife!"

Mr. Robinson buttoned his coat complacently over the inner pocket containing the specimen he had brought.

"A *mineral* the harticle is then, Sir; a nice little mineral! And this sime mineral is what the himperial Romans used? I thought so. I thought there weren't no mistike; but I said to myself, 'tis best to get the word of sich has knows!"

He put on his cap, adjusted it carefully, though with a touch of rakishness, gave a contemptuous glance at the Lake Village pottery—as much as to say: "No himperial metal in your die!" and then, as he said afterwards to his mother, "took me bleedin' 'ook, leaving the old gent, and small blime to 'im, not knowing 'is 'ead from 'is tile."

The next person Red Robinson went to see was a small chemist in High Street of the name of Harry Stickles, a remote relative of Tossie's. He got into the shop just before it closed; and when the last shutter was put up, Mr. Stickles took him out into his little back garden; where they sat down, in that drowsy autumn noonday on a bench beneath the wall. Opposite them was a pear tree and under the pear tree a big yellow cat. Several brooms and mops were propped up against the wall and a broken earthenware bowl lay at their feet.

" 'Ad yer dinner, 'Arry?" said Red.

"What do you suppose, you bloody Londoner? I dines at twelve sharp, I'd have you to know, and what's more I've got as tidy a little missus as any tradesman in town, and don't you forget it,—when it comes to the cookery department——"

Red looked at the yellow cat.

"Where is your lidy now, then, 'Arry? Washin' the soup-lidles?"

Mr. Stickles made a gesture with his thumb and a slight motion with one of his eyebrows. This signified that the mistress of the house was upstairs just above their heads, and that if they were to talk blood and iron business it would be wise to lower their voices.

"You've 'it the mark, 'Arry; you've 'it it strite this time! 'Tis that nice, little metal what mide them hemperors so rich. You've got it. You've got it! The honely question now his, 'ow much will you be 'ighbel to soak 'im for."

Red took off his cap and laid it down at his feet, upside down. The joy of his " 'ate," and the thought of "soaking" his enemy had caused drops of sweat to moisten the front of this object; and upon this 'ate-sweat a blue-bottle fly began to feed with such intense avidity that one might have thought there was a nourishing potency in Mr. Robinson's wrath.

Harry Stickles did not reply for a while. Both men now took out their pipes and contented themselves with contemplating the yellow cat, as their smoke ascended in filmy-blue curves into the misty air. The cat stretched out its front paws and yawned voluptuously, displaying a throat as pink as a wild rose. Then Mr. Stickles said, in a carefully modulated voice, so that his wife, even if she was listening at the window above, could hardly have caught his words:

"The number of sixpences I've a-spent overlooking for this here thing in Wookey would keep me in tobacco for a year. But there's a big lot of it down there—a big lot! It only wants digging for. There be tons and tons, I shouldn't wonder."

Mr. Stickles was a short man, even a dwarfish one, with long muscular arms and a face like a mad baby. His face was a soft, round, roguish face, with pleasant dimples; but into it, as if in some fantastic experimentation, had been thrust a pair of eyes that glittered with insane avarice. The truth was that long before Philip had begun charging sixpences for the privilege of visiting Wookey Hole, Mr. Stickles had been wont to spend Sunday after Sunday among those stalactites.

"Don't yer let 'im horf under a 'undred thousand!" said Red Robinson cheerfully.

"Lucky if I get a hundred quid out of him," whispered the other; "but he can't have found it or 'twould have been in the paper."

"Piper be 'anged!" whispered Red ferociously. "What price *'im* putting 'is gines and 'is tikings in the piper! What *eel* do to-die, we pore dawgs will know tomorrow, and that's hall there's to it!"

Mr. Stickles contemplated his yellow cat with intense and concentrated attention. Suddenly he slapped his hands on his knees.

"I'd catch him just about right—after he's had his lunch and all—if I were to go round and see him *now*—straight off the blooming reel!"

Red Robinson squirmed and fidgetted on hearing his friend's

bold utterance. In the secret malice of his heart he had seen *himself* as the one, dedicated by a just providence, to dangle the metal of Carthage and Rome before the eyes of the greedy manufacturer.

"He's been flying all hover Europe; so 'is pilot's landlidy in Butts' Alley told Sally Jones . . . stealin' secrets from they foreign dye-works; so 'tisn't likely he'll be in The Helms to-die."

Mr. Stickles was however already upon his feet, while his yellow cat, as if to give oracular encouragement to his daring master, left the pear tree and rubbed himself against his legs.

"Maybe 'twould be better if someone helse, someone that 'adn't no hinterest in the money, someone who were a good friend o' both parties, some quiet honlooker, you might say, willin' to serve hall and sundry, were to go and talk to 'im, rather than he who's the principal hagent!"

"Meaning?" whispered the gnome-like discoverer of tin, with a leer. "Meaning?"

But Robinson had drawn back in some disquietude; for the dwarfish chemist had suddenly thrust his face very close to *his* face, and was displaying, between his thin lips, the flickering point of a red tongue.

"Well—why not?" said the cautious foreman of the municipal factory. "Why shouldn't you ring 'is bell henny-'ow, and tell the servant you kime? No 'arm in that! Henny gent may ring henny other gent's front door-bell and arst to see 'is collection of bricky-backs. No 'arm in *that!*"

But Mr. Stickles did not feel the same inspiration, or the same sympathy, in his friend's voice that he had felt in the yellow cat's uplifted tail.

"I'm off," he said abruptly. "I don't suppose you want to wait here all the afternoon, till I come back, eh?" he added.

"Oh, you'll come back, quicker nor *that!*" cried the other. "*Eel* not be for arstin' yer to stay and drink fizz with 'im, all the afternoon, hunder 'is shady helms."

No sooner were both men gone than the head of a pretty, fair-haired young woman appeared at the window.

"Goin' to see Mr. Crow, are ye?" she murmured to herself.

"Going to surprise your little Nancy with a hundred pounds—
I *don't* think!"

And then, kneeling on the floor with her elbows on the
window-sill, Nancy Stickles caught sight of young Mrs. Glover
and her baby reclining in a wicker chair by the edge of her
tiny lawn, while Mr. Glover—the ironmonger—with a large
pair of garden scissors was trimming the straggling border of a
bed of London Pride.

At once the girl's thoughts ceased to be malicious, or vindictive, or even self-pitiful! She thrust her fingers into her apron
pocket and extracted a little, sticky paper bag. Out of this she
took a lemon-drop and put it into her mouth.

"He'll be twelve months old, next Thursday, Billy Glover
will! It's nice for Betsy Jane the way Mr. Glover do stay at
home on closing-days and tidy up garden."

It was as if some great consolatory spirit in things, perfectly
indifferent to the blood-and-iron activities of her mate and her
mate's ally, now began to pour out upon this head at the window,
lemon-drop and all, everything that it had to bestow.

A wood pigeon's voice became audible in the small lime trees
at the bottom of Mr. Glover's garden; and in spite of the noise
of the traffic in the street in front, it was possible to catch the
pleasant sound of a lawn-mower in the garden beyond Mr. Glover's. That mysterious relaxing of everything hard, everything
tense and strung-up, that comes with autumn was all around
Nancy as she looked out, breathing a vague cider-sweet smell
of apples. If moss and primroses were the dominant spring scent
in Glastonbury, apples were the autumn one.

This particular day was indeed as characteristic of autumn
in Somerset as any day could be. A blue haze was over everything, so thick and intense, that it was as if the blueness in the
sky had fallen upon the earth, leaving only a vague grey hollowness in the upper air. This blue haze invaded everything. It
crept through gaps in hedges; it floated over old crumbling
walls; it slipped into open stickhouses and haysheds. And though
it was blue in colour, it smelled strongly of brown mud and of
yellow apples. This blue mist, reeking of cider-juice and ditches,
seems to possess a peculiar somnolent power. Travellers from

the north, or from the east, coming into Glastonbury by train through Wareham, may be sitting erect and alert as they pass Stalbridge and Templecombe but they will find it difficult to keep their eyes on the landscape when the train has carried them beyond Evercreech and they come into the purlieus of Avalon.

Sleep seems to emanate from this district like a thin, penetrating anæsthetic, possessed of a definite healing power, and it is a sleep full of dreams; not of the gross, violent, repulsive dreams of the night, but of lovely, floating, evasive day-dreams, lighter, more voluptuous, nearer the heart's desire, than the raw, crude, violent visions of the bed.

Nancy Stickles felt a wave of delicious languor steal over her as she contemplated the Glover family enjoying themselves on their little lawn and as she watched the blue mists floating over the old walls and lying in hollows between the narrow alleys, and hovering in pigsty doors, and privy doors and fowl-run doors, and flowing like the vaporous essence of some great blue apple of the orchards of space over everything she could see. She felt quite friendly to her husband. He never struck her. He never abused her. He always gave her exactly the same sum of money every Saturday, whatever receipts the shop brought in. He didn't drink. He praised her cooking. But on the other hand—oh, how happy she always was when he was well out of the way and she was left alone!

There must have been something in Nancy of the unconquerable zest for life that the gods had given to old Mother Legge who was her great-aunt. She was an extraordinarily pretty girl; and she had so fair and clear a complexion and such a rounded figure that people turned to look at her as she went by. But Nancy had no self-pity. It never occurred to her that she had been wronged by God or by humanity because her father died in the workhouse and her mother in the county asylum; or because she had been cajoled by the accident of propinquity into marrying the poorest and most miserly of all Glastonbury's tradesmen.

She did not like it very much when Red Robinson, her husband's friend, showed a tendency to take liberties with her; but she managed to rebuff him without "making trouble," and as

soon as he was out of sight she had the power of casting him
from her thoughts. Nancy Stickles was perhaps more perfectly
adjusted to the ways of Nature, and to the terms upon which
we all live upon this earth, than any other conscious person in
Glastonbury except Mr. Wollop and Bert Cole. But Nancy had
a double advantage over both these adherents of the visible
world in the fact that she included many undertones and overtones of a psychological character completely out of reach of
Bert and the ex-Mayor.

She shared with her great-aunt a certain Rabelaisian habit of
mind, or at least a habit of mind that liked life none the worse
because of its animal basis.

At this moment, for example, when it became clear that Billy
Glover had "forgot where he was" and was being carried kicking
and screaming into the house, Nancy Stickles felt no repugnance.
If she'd been called upon at this moment to give Billy Glover
a bath she would have gone into Billy's room without the flicker
of a sigh, and been soon looking out of Billy's window, just as she
was now looking out of Harry's!

When not in acute physical pain, or in the presence of acute
physical pain, Nancy Stickles enjoyed every moment of life.
She liked to touch life, hear life, smell life, taste life, see life;
but she went far beyond Mr. Wollop and Bert, as she did indeed beyond everybody in Glastonbury, except its present Mayor,
in the enjoyment of religion. To Nancy Stickles, God was a dignified, well-meaning, but rather helpless Person, like Parson
Dekker; Christ was a lovable, but rather disturbing Person, like
Sam Dekker; the Holy Spirit was, quite simply and quite reverently, a very large and very voluble Wood Pigeon; but all
these Entities moved to and fro in an inner, behind-stage Glastonbury; a Glastonbury with greener fields, a redder Chalice
Well, yellower apples and even bluer mists, than the one Nancy
knew best, but one—all the same—that she felt frequently conscious of, and towards which her deepest feminine soul expanded
in delicious waves of admiration, hope and love.

It was not every woman in Glastonbury for instance, who,
running down now to answer a light ring at the closed chemist's
door, and finding her husband's relative Tossie, obviously pretty

far advanced in her pregnancy, standing in the doorway, would have greeted her with the lively hug and kiss of Nancy's welcome.

Tossie, however, showed no sign of being surprised at these manifestations. Everyone knew that Nancy "were one for kissing and cuddling," and the younger damsel behaved now with a grave, indulgent toleration, and an air that seemed to say, "We women have a right to be made a fuss of by you girls, but if you'd had *our* experience of life you would be less excited."

The two of them moved together into the back garden and sat down on the bench under the wall, lately occupied by Harry and Red. The yellow cat was no longer in sight and the young mistress of the house very soon carried off the unsightly scrubbing mops. She even picked up the fragments of the earthenware bowl and carried them in. Tossie, sitting with folded hands, took no notice of these movements.

"I shan't be going to hospital till after Christmas," she remarked. "Maybe not till the New Year."

"Will ye be staying where ye be till your time be come?"

"That's what Missus do say; but her'll have to get a girl to help soon in house, me being liable to be taken wi' dizzies."

"Do it feel pretty lonesome-like when you do have they dizzies?"

"Not particular," replied the other carelessly.

As a matter of fact, up to this day, and indeed up to the day of her delivery, Tossie never had a flicker of either dizziness or faintness.

"Who be Miss Crow going to have into house to help 'ee?"

Tossie proceeded to add to her air of a mother of the generations the air of a bestower of sinecures.

"She have asked I if I know'd of a friend of me own maybe; and I told she, I'll go round, I said, and see Harry's wife, Nancy; but of course, I said, being well-to-do people, as you might say, and high-class tradesmen, it's doubtful if Nancy would come."

"I *might* come—afternoons and evenings," said Nancy pensively.

She was thinking to herself—and yet not *thinking*—for it was a less definite process than that—*feeling* rather, with every ounce of her flesh, every nerve of her body, every pulse-beat of her blood, that it would be extraordinarily pleasant to walk over to Benedict Street every afternoon and have tea with Tossie instead of at home. "Harry rather *likes* getting his own tea," she said to herself.

"Could 'ee cook dinner and help I washing up?" cried Tossie eagerly. "They'd be having nothing to speak of for lunch. Goodness, Nance! but I'd dearly love for 'ee to come. 'Twould drive all they faintings away to have thee there wi' I!"

Nancy pondered. "I expect," she said, "Harry would be pleased for me to go. He's been making terrible little in shop this last year, owing to competition."

"Does Harry let 'ee *see* what he do make," asked the sagacious Tossie, "or does he take it out of till and tell 'ee any tale 'a likes?"

"Men prefers to manage their own business, as a general rule," replied Nancy cautiously; and then to change the subject, she asked Tossie about Lady Rachel.

Tossie became, in a second, extremely secretive and extremely consequential.

"She's unhappy. Anyone can see that. But she doesn't tell things to everyone. She only tells things to folks as she do know very well . . . folks in house."

"Does Mr. Athling come over regular to see her?"

The importance printed on Tossie's countenance as she prepared to reply to this question delighted Nancy. All this was part of those undertones of life that she enjoyed quite as much as the littered surface.

"People can meet people, when they wants to—especially if them be Ladies of Title—without coming to house, can't they?"

Nancy's eyes sparkled with glee. The idea of being initiated into fashionable intrigue thrilled her.

"Maybe you'd like to walk up wi' I now, and see Miss Crow?" said Tossie casually.

She spoke with the airy negligence of one royal ambassador throwing out a bait to another royal ambassador. Nancy got up from the bench, went to the window of the back room, the chemical dispensing-room, and looked into the house. It was only five minutes to three by the clock in that small back room. The litter in that room, its hand-to-mouth look—not like a real chemist's shop at all; like an extremely humble apothecary's place, where there might be a barber's chair!—made her feel more than ever sure that Harry would agree to her going.

"Yes, if you have rested long enough, Toss, and are sure the walk won't tire you, I'd love to go with you now. I'm not a bit afraid of Miss Crow. She talked to me once on the cricket-field for a long time. I like her. She's nice."

On their way the two young women caught sight of John Crow, hurrying along on the other side of the street.

"Is that there Mr. Crow still working for the Mayor, Toss?" enquired Nancy.

"Sure he is; and what is more he's married his cousin who do live with old Miss Drew out to Abbey House. Missus went to call on 'em one day last week in Mrs. Boul's house in North-load. They ain't only got one room; they ain't; and 'tis all crowded with curtings and cushings and such like oddments. 'Tain't like a real room, Missus did say; 'tis like a Stoodio in Chelsea-town."

"Did she tell *you* that, Toss?"

"Me and Lady Rachel," replied Tossie.

"Be Mr. Crow working for the Mayor still, Toss?"

"Some say he be, and some say he baint. *Some* say he be a Roosian Spy. But anyway he be Philip Crow's cousin, though they aren't on speaking terms."

"What's this I hear, Toss, about the Mayor digging great pits in Chalice Hill for to find Jesus Christ's Supper Cup?"

"That's just ignorant talk," explained Tossie from her superior level. "Mr. Geard baint digging pits; he be setting up foundations. He be going to build a girt arch, so they do tell at our place, and make thik red spring run under 'un."

"There be a wonderful lot of they foreigners come to Glaston since Pageant-day."

"Stop a minute, Nance, while I gets me breath. When you be as I be you won't skip as you walks."

Nancy obeyed and they paused by the wall of St. Benignus'.

"Sally Jones told I," whispered Tossie, in a tone as pregnant as her own form, "that she heard the Mayor tell his lady there'd be a girt miracle when thik red water do run under his new arch. Sal said he looked like a prophet when he spoke of it. She said he told his wife about some Welshmen of ancient days, with a name what begun with a 'T' like me own name, what writ about this here miracle afore King Arthur's time."

Nancy contemplated the tower of St. Benignus' Church round which several black swifts were cutting the misty air, as they swayed and circled. Her eyes had an entranced faraway look in them.

"These be wondrous exciting times we do live in, Toss. I've always had a mind that I'd live to see a miracle since I were confirmed in cathedral."

As Nancy uttered these words she laid her hand upon the wall of St. Benignus' graveyard, and gently stroked its green cushion of thick moss.

"Think, Toss, what it would be like," she went on in a low, awed voice, "if there *were* a real miracle in Glastonbury!"

Tossie Stickles felt she was deriving more comfort from the gentle pressure of that old wall against her fecund frame than from any conceivable departure from the normal system of things.

"I don't lay no stock on miracles," she said. "I reckon 'tis because I've got so much on me mind."

Tossie Stickles was not the only person in the town that fine afternoon whose mind was preoccupied. Philip Crow, after an interview with Harry the chemist, looked at the clock in his study. Only half-past three! He'd got rid of that greedy dwarf in double-quick time. What a funny-looking man—his face so round and smooth and his eyes so hungry for bank-notes! He hurried out of the study, where he had been showing Mr. Stickles his own specimens of Wookey Hole tin, and went down the passage. The drawing-room door was open. He looked in. How nice those phloxes smelt! How well Tilly arranged flowers in a room —so different from those untidy wildflower bunches, that Aunt Elizabeth always left about! Dear old Tilly! He closed the door, thinking to himself: "It must be very unpleasant in those countries where the rooms have no doors to shut!"

He stood for a second in the hall, listening. The rich, misty autumn sunlight poured through the lozenge-shaped panes of mid-Victorian coloured glass, inset above the front door, fell upon the hall table, throwing a rosy light upon the tray of calling cards that stood there, upon the top of which Emma, true daughter of Sly the shepherd, had placed the virgin card of Lady Rachel Zoyland, fell upon the stuffed pike, brought, like the famous picture of the poet Cowper's mother, "out of Norfolk," and fell finally upon a leather-bound Bradshaw with a brass paperweight laid upon it.

No! There wasn't a sound in the house. It must be the servants' day out; and Emma must be "lying down," upstairs. His eyes fell by chance—perhaps because it was so rosy from that coloured glass above the door—upon the Bradshaw, and upon that little brassy Lion of Saint Mark which kept it in its place. He sighed—a quick, little, deep-drawn sigh. Persephone had brought him that absurd little brass object from Venice. What a strange girl! What on earth had he done to offend her, to make her so cold to him? He had been tender, considerate, tactful. He had been everything they liked! He couldn't help making love to her when they slept in those places—Taunton, Bath, Exeter, Bristol. What else did she expect? Did she think men and women could lie quietly side by side, like two girls? That was precisely —as far as he could make out—what she did think. Why on earth, else, had she turned against him? Well! *Let her go.* Alone! That was his manifest destiny; to wrestle with this chaotic world alone; without the warm comfort of a girl's faithful sweetness. For the flicker of a second as he stared at that rosy gleam, and the slanting, dust-mote sunglide that led down to it, he thought that it would be nice, *as he got older*, if Tilly would consent to adopt his little Morgan daughter. But her mother would never give her up; and Tilly would never consent. Besides —what a handle to his enemies!

He took down his grey felt hat and chose a stick from half a dozen that stood there, huddling, as if for protection, in their painted stand round Tilly's big umbrella. He never bothered much about sticks. Who was it he'd come across in the last week who made such a fuss of his stick? Oh, that scallywag John!

He'd met the scamp only the other day, at Aunt Elizabeth's and, do what he could, he couldn't keep his temper with the fellow.

Well! He must hurry up now and get to the office. But he wished that rosy light on that brass thing hadn't made him think of that sweet waist and those boy's hips! He opened the door and walked with his quick short steps down the drive and into the Wells Road. It didn't take him long—he had often timed it exactly, not more than a quarter of an hour—to get to his office.

"No! It would never have done to fly to the Continent today!" he thought, as he was greeted by a chorus of anxious appeals from his young men and saw the applicants for his attention waiting in his ante-room and the pile of letters, come by the second post, on his desk.

He settled himself in his swivel-chair in front of the big, familiar blotting-pad, covered with neat calculations. He gave one quick glance out of the window at the well-known factory chimney. "Ha!" he said to himself, "There'll be some more of *you*, my fine boys, spouting your smoke, before Philip Crow is done for!"

It took him three-quarters of an hour to dictate his most important answers, and then another twenty minutes to deal with his two most important visitors. Then there came a call for him to go to the telephone.

"That'll be the chap I want," he thought. "That'll be my good Will!"

Will Zoyland indeed it was; and so pressing and crucial was the Bastard's communication, that there was a violent running to and fro in the office of the Crow Dye Works.

"No tea at home today," thought Philip, as he hurriedly set about despatching the rest of that day's business. He dismissed all his local suppliants now, telling them to come again tomorrow; and he gave just ten minutes apiece to a man from London and a man from Birmingham.

"A busy cove, our gentleman seems to be," said the London man to the Birmingham man as they went off together. "When does your train go? The five o'clock to Bristol? I'm going to take the Somerset and Dorset to Wareham and catch the old six-thirty to town."

"This little hole's going to look up, I shouldn't wonder," said the Birmingham man presently when they were halfway down Benedict Street. "It's a nice little place."

"So long as this freak Mayor they've elected," assented the other, "doesn't ruin things with his damned Socialism! They tell *me* that the bloke's starting a regular commune down here. They'll be hoisting the red flag next. But they've got a tough customer to deal with, that's evident, in our friend Crow."

Philip himself, later that afternoon, was walking rapidly, from where he had left Zoyland, to the exit out of Wookey Hole Wood. "I'll start contracting at once over that tin," he thought. "I'll not draw in one bit with the new Dye Works business. I'll play 'em off against each other! If the tin *does* come out in good quantities, I'll begin that piece of road too, straight away. If the Romans had a road there, I can have a road there. The good Will got pretty excited? How his beard wagged."

Philip's mind now ceased to adumbrate forth even the most blurred sentences. It ceased to evoke even those mysterious shorthand hieroglyphs, half-word, half-picture, that we so often use. In the orbic emanation from his body, projected like a moving nimbus round his figure as he moved, enormous images built themselves up, and then annihilating themselves as if by the mandate of some interior stage-manager, built themselves up anew, in other, stranger shapes.

His energy as he walked along with those quick, short, commander-of-men steps that were so characteristic of him seemed to be simply limitless! He felt it pouring through him, like some as yet unnamed magnetic fluid. He felt as if he were tapping some immense reservoir of power, stored up in those caverns he was leaving—power that had accumulated there for centuries and centuries, like the metallic deposit he would soon quarry out—and in the strength of which nothing could balk him, nothing could frustrate him. The curious thing was that as he gave himself up to this intoxicating feeling he felt an excitement that was actually phallic. Nor was there anything unnatural in this.

Both the two great forces pouring forth from the double-natured First Cause possess the energy of sex. One is creative, the other destructive; one is good, the other evil; one loves, the other hates. But through both of them pours forth the magnetic energy that moves and disturbs the lethargy of Matter. Both of them have abysmal levels in their being that transcend all that we at present know of the duality of life and death.

There is no *ultimate* mystery! Such a phrase is meaningless, because the reality of Being is forever changing under the primal and arbitrary will of the First Cause. The mystery of mysteries is Personality, a living Person; and there is *that* in Personality which is indetermined, unaccountable, changing at every second! The Hindu philosophies that dream of the One, the Eternal, as an Ultimate behind the arbitrariness of Personal Will are deluded. They are in reality—although they talk of "Spirit"—under the bondage of the idea of the body and under the bondage of the idea of physical matter as an "ultimate."

Apart from Personality, apart from Personal Will, there is no such "ultimate" as Matter, there is no such "ultimate" as Spirit. Beyond Life and beyond Death there is Personality, dominating both Life and Death to its own arbitrary and wilful purposes.

What mortals call Sex is only a manifestation in human life, and in animal and vegetable life, of a certain spasm, a certain delicious shudder, a certain orgasm of a purely psychic nature, which belongs to the Personality of the First Cause.

There are human minds—and they find it easy to hypnotise the shallowly clever—who apply to the primordial mysteries of life and sex certain erudite names, and by this naming, and by the noting of certain sequences, they think things are explained. Nothing is explained. The only causal energy in Nature is the energy of the double-natured First Cause and of the innumerable lesser personalities whose existence is revealed in the unrolling of Time. And the ecstatic quiver of that great cosmic ripple we call Sex runs through the whole universe and functions in every organism independent of external objects of desire!

Parthenogenesis, as Christian clairvoyance has long ago defined it, is a symbol of what the soul constantly achieves. So are the Dragon's Teeth sown by Cadmus; and the pebbles cast behind them by Deucalion and Pyrrha.

The composers of fiction aim at an æsthetic verisimilitude which seldom corresponds to the much more eccentric and chaotic dispositions of Nature. Only rarely are such writers so torn and rent by the Demon within them that they can add their own touch to the wave-crests of *real actuality* as these foam up, bringing wreckage and sea-tangle and living and dead ocean monsters and bloody spume and bottom silt into the rainbow spray!

They intersperse their "comic" and their "tragic" in a manner quite different—so hard is it to throw off the clinging conventions of human tradition!—from the ghastly monotonies and sublime surprises that Nature delights in.

All thoughts, all conscious feelings belonging to living organisms, in a particular spot upon the earth's rondure, mount up and radiate outward from such a spot, overtaking in their ascent the sound-eidola and the sight-eidola which accompany them!

Philip was now pausing for a minute on the path that led to the little gate out of the wood. His hands were deep in his trouser pockets. He wore no hat. He carried no stick. His suit was the same suit of rough heather-coloured tweed that he had worn in the Spring at his aunt's tea-party. What he could see of the sky above the trees was cloudy. The white mist rising from the Wookey Hole river that issued from the side of the wet green precipice below him soon lost itself in that peculiar Somersetshire blueness which is neither air nor vapour, water nor cloud, but a phenomenon, an entity, unique to itself.

With this atmospheric blueness there came to his nostrils a sweet, pungent, rather morbid odour, an odour which Philip would have simply called "the smell of Autumn"; but which was really composed of the dying of many large sycamore leaves, the emanations from certain rain-sodden, yellow toadstools, the faint fragrance of bowed-down ferns, the wholesome but very musky scent of herb Robert growing amid faded, tangled masses of dog's mercury and enchanter's nightshade.

Philip stared at the ground in front of him in a species of trance. There were a few dark-green shiny leaves of heart's tongue ferns hanging over a muddy ledge just there, and near them the smooth round roots of a beech tree covered with a black, oozy moisture. Cupped within the folds of the beech roots that were nearest the trunk were infinitesimal pools of ink-black rain water, the presence of which reduced the duskiness of the vegetable ooze that trickled near-by, to an indescribable green-black. Across the roots of this tree lay several small, rotten twigs, some of which were covered with a soft, brilliantly green moss out of which protruded those minute fungoid growths which children call fairy-cups.

What Philip would have simply called a "feeling of Autumn" manifested itself also in the clamorous cawing of the rooks above the taller trees and in an obscure smell of damp leaf mould that came drifting by, like a tremulous and voluptuous breath out of the very mouth of Death itself.

When he jumped into his car to drive back to Glastonbury he found that by making this effort to explain things to Will Zoyland, who had a mind which was about as capable of grasping such matters as Cœur de Lion's would have been, he had not only cleared up a great deal in his own head but had made several drastic decisions with regard to immediate action.

Zoyland's careless "desperateness" had not been without its effect upon him, childish though the fellow's notions of business were, and as he swept through the narrow lanes to hit the main road without the necessity of going through Wells, he kept thinking, under the damp, overclouded sky where not a star was visible, that a really important crisis *had* at last arrived in his carefully-laid schemes.

"I'll begin mining at once," he thought, "and I'll fly to Taunton tomorrow and see those road-contractors. Better get well ahead before the frosts begin in earnest. But the weather will stay open till Christmas! It always does in these muggy regions —so different from Norfolk!"

He drove faster and faster through the damp, chilly night, and the earth-scents that rose round him from the deep ditches and the wide fields became so much nourishment to his dominant thoughts. He did not articulate his feelings about life. He was no philosopher. But there came over him just then, like a de-

licious plunge into ice-cold water, a sense of his absolute loneliness in the world.

As he turned those leafy corners and allowed the low-hanging
foliage to brush against his machine, he felt an exultant pride
in being thus alone and fighting for his own hand against the
whole system of things! Like many another competent statesman, both before and after Signor Machiavelli, the obtuse narrowness of Philip's atheism, dogmatic with the dogmatism of
instinct rather than of reason, discounted all possibility of supernatural aid in this crisis of his affairs. He did feel a certain
outward-rushing urge, surging up from deep within him; but
how was he—with his innate incredulity—to know that this was
the umbilical nerve within him vibrating in response to the nerves
of the Great Mother?

He did feel a faint, strange, far-off intimation of some fount
of energy, kindred to *his* energy, outside the dense, damp, autumnal darkness that flowed around him; but how was he to
know that this was the eternal movement and counter-movement,
in its abysmal pools of being, of the First Cause of all life? He
was not even quite oblivious of an obscure something, hostile to
him, unappeasably inimical to all his schemes, struggling un-
weariedly against him in the world. But how was he, with his
small, narrow Bayeux Tapestry skull, to know that this something was the undying Personality of Christ?

When he reached the main road he began to drive faster still.

"This Glastonbury mediævalism," he thought, "won't stand up
long against the crowds of modern workmen I'll bring into the
place. My trouble will always be the same—strikes engineered
by these damned Communists."

Tilly had gone to bed when he got home and so had Emma.
He had not slept in the same room with his wife for years; and
things were always arranged for him so that he found whiskey
and biscuits and butter and cheese left out for him on a black
tray on the green tablecloth on the dining-room table; and his
bed nicely turned down and a hot-water bottle, usually quite
cold when he arrived, but giving a friendly look to the bed
where the clothes were uplifted into a little hill near the foot.

All these small things, the particular look of that black tray against the green tablecloth, the particular appearance of the napkin that Emma always placed over the butter and cheese, the welcoming friendliness of that stone hot-water bottle—Philip was old-fashioned in certain matters—gave him a delicious sense of being humoured and considered, not only by one, but by two competent housewives. He found tonight, so careful had Emma been to tuck his towel tightly around the metal hot-water jug in his china basin, that the water was still hot; and as he washed his hands he thought to himself:

"My life is exactly as I like it to be. This year is going to be the crisis of my life."

No knee did Philip Crow, Esquire, of The Elms, Glastonbury, Somerset, bend to any supernatural power, as he clicked off his electric globe, climbed into bed, and stretched his feet downward, delighted to find there was still warmth in the stone bottle.

"There's an autumn feeling in the air tonight," he thought. "It was chilly in those lanes."

But he did a thing then which proved how excited he was after his resolute conversation with Zoyland. He pressed his knuckles against his closed eyeballs. When he had been quite a little boy—after his Devereux grandmother had repeated over his pillow in her stern and yet doting voice:

"Angels one and two and three guard thy counterpane for thee;
  While above thy sleeping head be the wings of Michael
          spread!"——

he had been accustomed to do this; finding that the kaleidoscope of astonishing colours which this pressure made to pass before his vision was curiously soothing to his young mind in the black darkness.

And now as he removed his knuckles he beheld the Glastonbury which his present plans would create. He beheld his heavy lorries tearing along a broad road from Wookey to the outskirts of Lake Village Field. He beheld his good concrete road cutting diagonally over the meadows from this point to the centre of Street. He beheld his great new bridge (making the old Pomparlès one—the Bridge Perilous of the Legends—look insignificant and negligible) by which his motor-trucks would cross the Brue. He beheld three tall new factory-chimneys rising up from his dye works in the town. He saw the rows and rows and rows of workpeople's cottages—not silly, fancy ones, but solid serviceable ones—to which labouring men from Bristol and Cardiff, and even further afield, would be attracted. He saw the sign "To Let!" set up over their precious, socialistic toy-factory, which he would not even bother to purchase from them!

"And I alone shall have done all this," he said to himself.

One quaint and surprising peculiarity Philip had. He always slept—except in the very warmest summer nights—with his window shut. This was a peculiarity that, without his being aware of it, he shared with most of his factory-hands. But it was no doubt one of his old-fashioned early-Victorian habits. Grandmother Devereux used, for instance, always to say, "Beware, children, of the night air!" Thus, as he now turned over upon his left side to compose himself to sleep, the smell in his nostrils had very little of that autumn feeling that had made his stone bottle so welcome. It was a composite smell, a smell composed partly of his quilted eiderdown, partly of the paint of his hot-water jug, partly of his cake of recently used brown Windsor soap, and partly of a large cedar press in which Tilly and Emma kept his winter clothes.

Small physical movements, nay! the scarcely conscious physical positions of human bodies in sleep have at many great crises of history tilted ponderous scales. Had Constantine, for instance, slept on his right, in place of his left side, before his decisive battle, had Cæsar slept on his right side instead of his left before they called him to the senate-house, had Boadicea slept on her back before fighting the Romans, or Cleopatra on her face before sending Antony to fight them, great issues might have fallen out in a changed manner and the upshot of vast events been different.

Philip Crow on this occasion turned over on his left side to sleep. Now when he had slept with his cousin Percy he had always had the girl on his left side and therefore it was natural enough that when the ferment of his schemes had died down and he tried to sleep, instead of sleep coming upon him, love came upon him and began to tantalise him and to torment him.

There is doubtless in certain old, indurated families a deep ineradicable strain of what might be called centripetal eroticism. A tendency to inbreeding is not always a sign of degeneracy in a race. It is often an instinct of ethos-preservation, suspicious of the menace of mixed bloods. Doubtless something of the inordinate individuality of the Crows was due to a constant intermarriage between cousins among them, doubling and redoubling the peculiarities of their "Gens."

It was Persephone's long slender waist and narrow boyish hips that tormented Philip now. He had often in his life fancied to himself that he was chaster than most men, because of the cold, critical eye with which he was able to regard women. His only passionate love-affair before he met his cousin again, after a long separation, had been with a boy at school, whose figure, girlish for that of a youth, was almost identical with Percy's.

The natural softness, sweetness, submissiveness of normal girls had always been repulsive to him. To quicken his pulse at all there had to be something wilful, evasive, difficult, withdrawn; and since all these qualities were of the very essence of his cousin's nature she had attracted him fatally, the first second she reappeared. She was still in Glastonbury. He knew *that*, though he had not seen her for weeks and weeks, and had not spoken to her for a couple of months. She had apparently left Dave. At any rate, he had returned to Bristol without her after the strike ended. The gossip of the town—reported to Tilly by Emma and retailed by Tilly to him over some subsequent teatable—declared that she had become the inseparable companion of Angela Beere.

Philip knew Angela well, of course, as her father, by no means an incompetent lawyer although a besotted glutton, had often done work for him; but her Madonna-like coldness—she certainly was "withdrawn" enough—had somehow repelled him. That a passionate friendship should have come to exist between such a silent, cold-blooded creature and the lively Percy struck him as weird, incongruous, incredible. But then—as he knew well enough—it was the incredible that was always happening in these things.

After the Pageant, when the fellow was well enough to leave the hospital, Tilly had reported the most fantastical tales of "something going on" between that crazy Welshman and Persephone. This he had never believed; but he had thought he understood the cause of the report, knowing only too well his cousin's passion for the bizarre and the exotic.

Philip stretched out his right arm now as he lay on his left side and seized in the dark the cold rosewood bedpost at his pillow's head. Out of the dream-dimension which surrounds our visible world the wraith of his Devereux grandmother struggled frantically to give him a warning. To be able to see his small, neat, well-moulded head—for these insubstantial tenants of the etheric envelope of our material plane find physical darkness no hindrance—lying on the pillow and not to be able to attract his attention was an atrocious tantalisation to this proud spirit from beyond our palpable dream-world.

The occasion was indeed only too characteristic of what the First Cause, in its malicious moods, delights to evoke; for while Philip, in a spasm of savage yearning for the slender waist of his cousin, gripped angrily that smooth bar of wood, the wraith of the only woman who had ever passionately loved him wrestled frantically with the laws of the universe to give him a sign, a token, a warning, that he was putting, not a blind hand upon a bedpost, but a blind foot upon a road that led to desperation and madness.

"Perse! Perse! Oh, Perse, where are you? Come back to me, Perse!"

But Persephone, in a little cheap bedroom she had taken at Dickery Cantle's dilapidated place, was even then, with her flushed cheek resting on her thin arm and her dusky boyish curls making a nimbus of darkness within the darkness, dreaming peacefully of Angela's devotion as they wandered together beneath the ruined carvings, so delicately foliated, so tenderly moulded by long-buried fingers, in Saint Mary's Chapel!

Into that narrow Bayeux Tapestry skull, while:—"Stop thinking that! Stop thinking that!" cries the old ghost-wraith more and more desperately, come scattered memories now of little inn-rooms in Taunton, in Exeter, in Bath, in Bristol, in Dorchester, in Tewkesbury; a curtain from that room, a flapping blind from this, a bedpost from that, a coloured print from this, a cock-crow full of a thousand misty Wessex dawns, a dog's barking, the rattle of early milk-cans—and mingled with all these things those slender hips and the waist like that torso— what the devil was it called?—that she had brought back to show him when she went to Italy!

To lie awake wanting, wanting, and with so little hope; to turn over on the *right* now ("But it's too late now, Philip my grand-son; you should have done that at once!"), to turn on your back now, kicking the stone bottle viciously aside; and stretch-ing out so stiff and so straight, till the soles of your feet press against the woodwork; to snuff up nothing but the smell of brown Windsor soap, and eider-down coverlet, and a faint odour of dog's dung from your muddy boots, in place of that mad-dening fragrance that always made you think of the sun-baked apricots in Canon Crow's walled-garden, the sweetness of those bare sun-burnt shoulders, was all this the result of that "autumn feeling" which you had encountered as you went to your interview with Zoyland at Wookey Hole?

"I could bear it," he thought; "I could bear it if only her hips weren't *just* like they are . . . yes! yes! . . . and if only her curls didn't curl so tight against the back of her neck! It's those curls and those hips *together* that torment me so!"

He went to sleep at last, just about three o'clock; and while Emma was dreaming that she was helping old Sly on the Men-dips to shear a great black-faced ewe, with a face like the face of her mistress, and while Tilly was dreaming that the new silk lining of her ottoman had *dyed itself*—without the help of her husband's dye works— into an incredible shell-pink, the master of The Elms dreamed that the Mayor of Glastonbury brought him a vast basin made of glittering *tin* and held it before him and cried "Vomit!" and he dreamed that although he retched and retched he could not bring up anything except a little white saliva! But behold! Mr. Geard himself spat into that huge caul-dron; and it came to pass that out of the mingling of their spittle there was created in the centre of that glittering vessel of shining tin, a little homuncula . . . a little dazzling girl-child

. . . and Philip found himself hoping frantically that the face of this homuncula would be Percy's face. But when the dazzlingness of the little creature lessened or when his eyes could bear its brightness better, the features disclosed to him were such as he had never before seen. But Mr. Geard lifted up the cauldron to the full stretch of his arms and cried out with a thundering cry:—*"Who is the Tin-Merchant now?"* and then as Philip looked up at the vessel in the man's hands, behold! the bottom of it became ruddy as blood, and even as he gazed, drops of blood fell from it upon the ground and the ground was dyed purple; and he murmured in his dream:—"The lost dye! The lost purple dye!" and he fell on his knees beneath the vessel and he made his hands into a cup and he thought in his heart: "When he has gone I shall take this to my dye works . . . and it will go over all the world; and it will be called the Glastonbury Purple!"

It was with his head full of the image of this dye that he finally sank into a dreamless sleep; and when he awoke, long after the birds of his garden had greeted the dawn, of all his dreaming it was only the dye he remembered. Geard, the shining vessel, the girl-child with the unknown features—all these he had completely forgotten.

And the slim waist of Persephone Spear had also receded into the far background of his mind.

W E WILL HAVE A GRAND OPENING, CROW," SAID MR. GEARD
to his faithful John as they sat talking after supper in the old
faded parlour of the Geard house. Not a thing had been done to
improve this grotesque room since those times when, as Philip
had assured the assembled family after his grandfather's will
had been read, Geard had been "a nuisance to everyone, with
his two sprawling daughters, his preaching and his poverty."

It was the first of October and a spell of wild stormy weather
had set in. As John sat on the sofa by Mrs. Geard's side—for
both the girls were out that evening—and watched his employer
rubbing his big white hands and nodding his big white face over
a warm fire of mixed coal and wood, the rain was streaming
down the panes, and every now and then the two gas-flames hanging from the ceiling were caught in a draught of wind (for Mrs.
Geard cared more for air than for the protection of curtains),
and were blown sideways, in spite of their glass globes, in
sinister tongues of blue flame, producing a startling flickering
effect all over the room.

"We'll have more than that, Sir," responded John, "if you and
I are still alive."

Round that faded old room, in that faded old *petit bourgeois*
house, the October wind seemed to howl as if it had been sent
from Stonehenge to hunt for Mr. Geard and was rejoicing at
having found him.

"Hunt out this False Druid," the gods of that Altar Stone
must have said, "and put our Terror into him!"

There came into Mrs. Geard's thin, long face, with its mobile
eyebrows and queer, troubled, flickering smile, a very curious
expression as she looked up from her knitting. A Rhys of Pembrokeshire, as she was, there was something in a night like
this that appealed to a deep-buried instinct in her, and in some
odd way she relished the spectacle of all her old domestic objects cowering under the storm.

Funny old things they were—Mrs. Geard's possessions—the

woollen antimacassars, the sickly yellow pears and blue grapes under a big glass covering, with red plush round its base, the staring picture of her father, the Plymouth Brother, with whiskers like a sailor and a mouth like a letter-box closed for Sunday; the old, worn, ash-coloured carpet, the black bear rug with broad red-flannel edgings and more mouse-grey skin than black hairs left to view, and all the ancient, stained, blotched, greasy cushions that always were to be, and never *had* been, re-covered; and the rickety little tables with glaring tablecloths, and so many brackets with green and red tassels hanging from photograph frames, containing groups of Geards and Rhyses, the former a good deal less pompous-looking but hardly less stiff and uncomfortable in their photographer's parlours—all these things made up a sort of dusty, cushiony ensemble, like the huge nest of some kind of stuffed bird, now extinct.

And Mrs. Geard derived such a queer, sensual pleasure, as she listened to the wind howling round this room, just as if its ceiling were the roof of the whole house, and its walls the walls of the whole house! She had the feeling that this whole warm, cushiony, greasy, human-smelling place were being carried along through vast spaces of rainy night-air. She put down her knitting, left John's side, bade him "please remain seated, Mr. Crow!" and going to the window opened it yet a little more at the top, so that the gas-flames grew still more agitated and the red curtains bulged into still fuller convexities.

"Always the one for fresh air is my good wife," said Bloody Johnny contentedly, as he watched this move of his lady's, and then returned with a zest to his conversation with John.

But Mrs. Geard, as she took up her knitting again,—thick, grey socks for her man's winter-wear—felt a further increase of voluptuous satisfaction as the draught from the window fumbled about with its blind gusty fingers through that comfortable room. Perhaps her princely South-Wales ancestors had felt something of the same feeling when the arras bulged out from their chilly walls and the smoke blew into the hall from their blackened fireplaces.

In good spirits that night was the Mayoress of Glastonbury, for her eldest daughter had told her, when she and Crummie

were putting on their waterproofs and galoshes to go out to
Lawyer Beere's party, that Mr. Evans had asked to have their
banns read out next Sunday at St. Benignus' Church.

So the flickering smile on the woman's face kept returning,
as she knitted, and her eyebrows kept wrinkling up and wrinkling
down, as they did when she was listening to Dr. Sodbury's sermons. If at this moment, in her high spirits, she had done *exactly*
what she would have liked to do, she would have put on her old,
weather-worn cloak, covered her head in her black shawl, snuffed
up the whole cosy essence of this adored parlour of hers with
one rapturous sniff, and set out to "call for" her two children,
doing it just as if she had been a nurse, come to take her little
charges home from a children's dance.

Then as they took off their wet things in the hall she would
have whispered to Cordelia, "I'll give you my wedding umbrella
when you're married, Cordy!" Nor was Mrs. Geard's wedding
umbrella a gift to be despised, for it possessed a handle of
solid gold carved in the most majestic proportions.

"You're sure, Sir, that that London architect understood your
design?" the crafty John was now remarking. "Some of these
local people laugh at the idea of a Saxon arch associated with
a Byzantine dome."

"Ain't Saint Sophia's got a dome?" said Mr. Geard. "Ain't
there domes in Russia? And ain't I seen a Saxon arch with me
own eyes in a wall at Sherborne? 'Tis true it were walled-up,
that good Saxon arch, but an architect from a place like London
can un-wall 'un, can't he? I mean, see what 'twould be, if the
stones were took out and make one similar to 'un?"

One quaint and very characteristic peculiarity now manifested by the Mayor of Glastonbury was a strong tendency, since
his accession to wealth and power, deliberately to revert to his
old South-Somerset dialect, which was a mingling of the purer
Somerset speech with a tincture of Dorset.

"Somewhere around Christmas would you have it, Mr. Geard,
your grand opening celebration?"

Bloody Johnny smiled.

"Maybe then, and maybe *not* then," he answered laconically.

"It all depends, Crow, and you know it do, on how things work out."

"As I've said before," remarked John, "you won't get a real rush of people from the Continent till you've had a Miracle performed by this chalybeate spring of yours."

Mr. Geard threw upon the fire another piece of wood. Most people in Glastonbury kept a wood-box by the side of their coal-scuttle. And then he amused his secretary, but did not at all surprise him, for John was getting used to the man's little ways, by a sly wink. "They shall have their Miracle all right, Crow; they shall have their Miracle!" he chuckled.

"The man's a prize charlatan," thought John, "and yet he isn't! God knows *what* he is!" But aloud he said, "Well, Sir, supposing it gets into all the English papers, and supposing the Berlin, Paris, Vienna, Warsaw, Brussels, Rome, Madrid, Copenhagen papers report it, and supposing a regular Lourdes and Lisieux kind of a rush begins, how do you propose to stop the Anglicans, or the Roman Catholics, from exploiting such an event?"

"Ah, my boy," grumbled Bloody Johnny, "you've hit our trouble in *those* words of yours, pretty closely, but I have me Blessed Lord at hand, and He's already begun taking up that matter with me." The man rubbed his shins meditatively and leaning forward in his low arm-chair, pulled with both hands the shiny black material of one of his trousers close round his leg. This action seemed to give him some kind of spiritual comfort and he continued to enjoy the warmth, gazing into the fire with a curious film over his black eyes, the sort of film that might have covered the ophidian stare of the world-snake, at the bottom of the Northern Sea.

John Crow crossed one of his own scarecrow legs over the other and watched him, listening to the clicking of his companion's knitting needles and to the moaning of the wind in the chimney.

"The moment has come," murmured Mr. Geard, thinking aloud, "for a fresh shoot to appear from the Glastonbury Thorn."

"Why don't you keep a cat?" burst out John irrelevantly, turning to the lady at his side.

But it was from her husband that the answer came.

"All flesh is a conductor of force, didn't 'ee know that, lad? And when thoughts are being born they must be fed. *He* here," —and the extraordinary man actually made a jerk with his great thumb towards the space in the centre of this snug, cushiony, be-tasseled, be-rugged, be-fringed, be-carpeted interior—"*He* here wants all the force there is about, if I'm to keep Him close!"

John bit his underlip and looked down at those mouse-grey hairless islands in the black bear rug. He thought to himself: "Damn the fellow! He's nothing but a gross, overfed Cagliostro! What the devil am I doing in this muggy hole, selling my soul and swallowing all this tosh?"

"So our Mayoress isn't allowed to keep even a cat?" he brought out in a tone that did not conceal his feelings.

There was rather an uncomfortable silence for a while after that, broken only by the queer *plop* . . . *plop* . . . *plop* which the curtains made, as they bulged out and then went limp again, answering the gusts. But John thought of his nights with Mary in their Northload room. "It's worth it!" he said to himself. "I never knew a girl *could* be so sweet."

"You'll be more indulgent, laddie, when you've seen a little more of me," said Mr. Geard suddenly, sinking back in his armchair and clasping his plump fingers together over his heavy gold watch-chain. "If you'd been a young Arab in the tent of Mahomet you'd have heard the Prophet break wind once and again!"

"*John!*" cried Megan Geard, letting her knitting sink upon her lap.

"It's all right, apple of me eye! The old man were only talking." And he cast upon her a glance of such radiant affection, the heavy films vanishing from his black eyes, that John's emotions were once more swung in the opposite direction.

"I believe you've got in your head, Sir," he couldn't help blurting out, "a whole new religion—but what I can't see is, how you're going to graft it upon the old one. These curst Anglicans are bound to give your Miracle their own twist. They'll say it's a proof that Rome hasn't a monopoly, and so on. They'll say it's the Grail of Arthur come back. They'll say ——"

"Let 'em," cried Bloody Johnny, in a hoarse, thick voice. "Let 'em say all they like and the Papists too. I've got a little something in store for 'em, lad—a little surprise—that even *you*, sly as you be, you rogue, haven't guessed yet!"

The ball of grey wool now rolled off Mrs. Geard's lap and John Crow got up to fetch it for her. He was still standing up holding the ball in his hands and trying to wind the loose thread when above the noise of wind and rain came the sound of the front door opening, and the excited voices of the girls come back. Both their parents rose to their feet and John, handing the woollen ball to Mrs. Geard, hurried out to help them take off their cloaks. He caught sight of Cordelia's rain-drenched profile as she struggled to shut the front door against the storm.

"She isn't a bad-looking girl after all," he thought. "It must be the party!"

Crummie meanwhile had taken a seat on the only hall-chair, a miserably battered upright wicker chair, bought at a sale by her mother before she was born. John bent upon one knee to help her get off her galoshes. Aye! how the rain ran down in little pools from her drenched clothes. Both the parents had appeared now and her father was tugging awkwardly at Crummie's mackintosh, while Mrs. Geard helped Cordelia to push the bolts to of the closed door. Then she also turned to Crummie. "How nice you do look, child, if I say it myself."

"She always *was* the prettiest little wench in town, wasn't she, my chuck?" and Mr. Geard kissed the girl's wet cheeks.

John hurried to Cordelia and held *her* dripping cloak while she slipped out of it. "You come out, like a Naked Nannie from its calyx!" he whispered. And then, as he held the drenched cloak in his hands, not knowing where to put it, "What's that you were saying to Cordy, Mr. Crow?" threw in her mother.

"Only telling her how well her evening dress suits her, Missus! And so it does; don't you think so, Sir?" and he hung the cloak up on the only peg that was not overcrowded.

"No! Not there!" cried Cordelia sharply. "You're putting it over Mother's."

It was the first remark either of the girls had yet made, but it let loose a flood of chatter from Crummie as they all went into the parlour. "Angela looked sweet, Dad. You'd have *loved* her. She had on that white dress I told you about. Mr. Wollop himself ordered it from London. She had one, little, single moss-rose pinned on the front. She looked bewitching, and she was more animated too than I've ever seen her. Oh, and you *should* have seen Mrs. Spear! She had an old-gold dress on. How she's been keeping it I don't know, in that awful room she's got at Cantle's. It looks out on the yard! She took me up once, when we met down there. It's the worst place for a girl like ——" She caught her breath, remembering John's relationship to this present cynosure of delicate scandal. Mrs. Geard broke in at this point as they all stood round the fire; Crummie with her frock folded up above her petticoat crouching on the bear-rug, with her white arms spread out to the blaze.

"May I tell Mr. Crow—for he's such a friend of the family now, and knows us *all* so well—what you told me when you started out tonight, Cordy dear?"

Cordelia's whole body stiffened. Her dislike of John had by no means modified with closer knowledge. The more she knew, the more she disliked! She turned towards him now a pair of the coldest, haughtiest eyes that had ever challenged him.

"It's nothing. Mother makes much too much of it. Besides, you probably know it already, being such a friend of Owen's. It's only that our banns are to be given out next Sunday."

John made a funny little bow. "I'm sure," he said, "I congratulate you—I mean I'm sure I congratulate Mr. Evans."

"You ought to give my daughter a kiss, lad," chuckled Mr. Geard, and he drew Cordy's proud head down with both his hands and kissed her himself on the forehead.

"He'd better kiss Crummie," the tall girl murmured spitefully. "Perhaps it'll bring *her* the same good luck—if it *is* good luck."

Her voice had died away to so faint a tone as she breathed these last words that only her father caught them.

"Hush, child!" he whispered, patting her bare shoulders with his plump hand. "You'll feel quite differently bye and bye."

Mrs. Geard, with a delicacy worthy of the House of Rhys, avoided her daughter's eye as her husband spoke, while Crummie, with the laudable desire of drawing the general attention away from her angry, confused sister, glanced roguishly at John.

"Aren't I going to have that kiss?" she laughed.

John had expected this, and he had made up his mind exactly what he would do. He sprung forward, caught Crummie's fair head in both his bony hands exactly as her father had held Cordy's and gave it a gentle shaking, ending up with the lightest possible brushing of his lips amid her wavy hair.

"You tease! You tease! You tease!" he cried, as he shook her.

Between Crummie and John quite a piquant understanding had arisen. The pretty girl, in her silent, tantalised passion for Sam Dekker, had dropped all association with her other men friends. Red she never spoke to now, and in avoiding Red—for they worked in the same place—she found it easy to avoid Barter. To John, in a sense, she found herself positively clinging, and as Mary seemed, just at present, far too happy to be jealous, and as it was a situation that lent itself perfectly to John's artful nature, Crummie's spirits had revived a little during the last month or two; a little, not very much. Not very much! How often to her hot, tear-soaked pillow had the wretched girl moaned out the madness of her relentless love! What was the use of having a father who could exorcise devils, who could give sleep to the tormented, if he could not heal his own child's wounded heart?

At the very moment when John was tickling his lips with Crummie's shining tresses, the queer object of the girl's unfortunate craving was having a prolonged and distressing argument with his father on the subject of Nell.

"I tell you it only torments the woman the way you treat her! Better never see her at all than sneak off over there every day he's away!" The museum actually echoed to the indignant tone of the Vicar, and the lid of his tobacco-jar that stood adjacent to the aquarium tinkled ominously against the glass.

"But she's gone seven months with our child, Father. And since the end of August he's been at Wookey nearly all the time."

"But Mrs. Pippard's with her, boy! You found Mrs. Pippard for her yourself. She's fond of her, isn't she?"

"But, Father, when a woman's going to have a child she's nervous and sensitive anyway, and when it's your own child she's going to have ——"

The Vicar's rugged face had become very red and his formidable little eyes—like Sam's, only much greyer—had ceased to be grey and had become a curious blue colour under his bushy eyebrows.

He rose from his chair and stood with his broad shoulders to the mantelpiece, angrily jerking up the tails of his long black coat and holding his hands beneath them while he warmed his back at the fire.

"It's all wrong," he shouted. "The whole thing's outrageous! If you'd had the spunk of half a man in you you'd have made him divorce her; you'd have ——"

He suddenly remembered that divorce was one of the things against which the party in the Church to which he belonged was especially opposed.

"Well, anyway," he added. "You'd have done one thing or the other; not gone about dickering and havering and dodging in the way you have."

Sam was silent for a second or two. His face did not show the faintest trace of any resentment against his father. Then he suddenly said, "Would you like her to leave Zoyland, Father? Would you like her to come and live with us here?"

His father's mouth opened with astonishment and he stared blankly.

"And be divorced, you mean? And you marry her, you mean?"

"No, no! Just live here with us. I'm not going to marry her nor any other woman—just live with us here, I mean."

"As your mistress, after the child is born?"

"Father!"

"Well, isn't that what you mean? But perhaps you don't want to wait till the child is born. Perhaps you'd like to sleep with her, as she is, under my roof!"

If Sam had been endowed with a little more penetration he

would have understood better what a surge of suppressed feeling underlay his father's outburst.

As it was he could only sigh helplessly and cast his eyes upon the aquarium. Often and often had the sight of those fish, disturbed by the lamplight and behaving in a manner contrary to their ordinary routine, distracted his mind from weightier troubles. He got up now and placed over them the kitchen dishcloth, which, in the agitation of that night, both he and his father had forgotten.

"I suppose she'll be going into the hospital," he said, as he sat down again, "in another month."

His father let his coat-tails drop and began striding up and down the room. "I can't understand that fellow Zoyland," he flung out, "any better than I can understand you. That sweet little woman between you two rogues! Yes! That's the word for it,— between you *two rogues*!"

He glared at Sam out of eye-sockets that seemed like two deep, livid-blue holes in a rock of red clay.

Sam surveyed him helplessly, not shrinking from his gaze, but looking at him as he would have looked at Wirral Hill if it had suddenly become a volcano. His father's wrath was beginning to affect him like a wild dream out of which he felt he ought to be able to force himself to awake.

"What would you wish me to do, Father; if I did exactly what would please you?"

"*Please* me, does he say?" roared the exasperated man. "I tell you I *hate* the whole affair; and I've a mind to—a mind to— wash my hands of it!" It was on his tongue to say—"my hands of you!" but he corrected himself in time.

"But what would you *tell* me to do, Father, if I did exactly what you told me?"

This point-blank question did quiet the angry man a little. He put his hands into his trouser-pockets, and walked with a somewhat less assured stride. Sam had nonplussed him a bit by this question. It was much easier to storm and rage at his son than to give him intelligent advice. But he satisfied both his anger and his conscience when he finally came out with his reply.

"I think, if you haven't the guts to act like a man in the matter, you ought to leave this girl alone." This was probably the wickedest thing Mat Dekker had ever done in his life—the utterance of this opinion.

Sam's strange fixed idea of sharing in Christ's sacrifice might quite conceivably have put it into his head that it was his duty to do exactly as his father bade him, in which case Nell would have had the experience of losing her headstrong lover at the precise moment when the sort of companionship he felt *allowed* to give her was exactly the comfort which she craved most to receive, which was indeed all she *could* receive. But Sam was not yet a complete maniac; nor had his father's constant harping upon this string of "being a man" and "having guts," failed altogether to arouse a natural reaction. He rose firmly to his feet. "Well, Father," he said, "if *that's* all the help you can give me, I think we'd better bring the conversation to a close." He paused for a moment, and then, ashamed of the abruptness of his tone, he added more gently, "You've always been good to me, Father. This is the first time in my life that I've—troubled you like this. I daresay we'll both of us see things more . . . calmly . . . more . . . more quietly . . . later . . . on." He took a few steps towards the door and then stopped and turned. It had always been their custom, a custom rather unusual among sons and fathers in Glastonbury, and perhaps one that was an emotional legacy left to the atmosphere of that house by Sam's Swiss mother, to kiss each other good-night. On this occasion it needed one of the greatest spiritual efforts he had ever undertaken when Sam forced himself to go up to his father and make the motion of offering to kiss him.

A red-faced, righteously indignant, dignified and outraged man is not an easy objective for such an advance as Sam now made. But the power of habit is great, and Mat Dekker, after all, loved nobody in the world—certainly not this girl whose troubling beauty had so upset him—as much as he loved his son. So now, though in deep and gloomy gravity, he did bend his head and allow his rough, bristly cheek—for he was a man who needed shaving twice a day—to touch, for the tenth part of a second, Sam's up-raised and twitching chin.

"Good-night, Father."

"Good-night, my boy."

Sam's betaking himself to his bedroom that night coincided, after about five minutes leeway, with the departure to bed of another Glastonbury bachelor, namely, Mr. Thomas Barter. The steps up which this gentleman slowly and wearily climbed were much less pleasant to ascend than those dusted and polished by Penny Pitches. Mr. Barter was no longer in his High Street room. Since his salary at the Municipal, as it was called, was based on the success of the venture under his management and as his task in organising it was a Herculean one, he found himself for the moment with a very meagre income. He had been forced to economise if he were to be able to continue his daily table d'hôtes at the Pilgrims', and *not* to continue these meant the last straw of misery. His adventure with Lily had turned out anything but a success. This dreamy, romantic maiden had unexpectedly proven herself a past mistress in the art of giving nothing for nothing! As much kissing as he liked, where the auspicious Ruins—an entrance-fee every time, for Lily refused to steal into the grounds over the Abbey-House wall!—hid such chaste delinquencies; but beyond kissing, absolutely not one single stolen sweet. Thus, for the last month, for he had long ago quarrelled with the mercenary Clarissa, Mr. Barter had been compelled to be chaste. His sole pleasure during this epoch had been the tender but rather anxious one of snatching difficult assignations with Tossie Stickles.

In default of all other feminine society, for Mary seemed, since her marriage, deliberately to avoid seeing him alone, Mr. Barter clung quite pathetically to his interviews with his "ruined" Toss. *Her* sweetness to him knew no bounds. With her, if they could only manage to escape observation, everything was permitted; nothing was forbidden; and all was for pure love. He got fonder and fonder of Tossie. Her ways, in her state of pregnancy, astonished him by their sweetness and quaintness. He even became interested—and this for the first time in his masterful career—in his future progeny. Many were the whimsical colloquies, interspersed with bursts of impious merriment, that they had together over this serious event. The girl had recently got into her head, so big had her belly grown and so violent were the movements within her, that they were destined to be the parents of twins; and even this prospect, conceivably one of humorous horror to an unscrupulous Don Juan, appeared to be by no means distasteful to Mr. Barter. But dear to him as were these happy encounters, they had become so infrequent of late as the girl's time drew nearer, that they no longer served to remove the gloom which kept gathering deeper and deeper upon him.

Tonight, as he mounted those disgusting stairs in George Street, after a long wretched evening spent in his miserable little restaurant, he really felt as if he were approaching the end of his tether. When he had turned on the gas-jet—the burner had not even got a globe—he sat down on his chilly bed and surveyed his washing-basin and heavy white jug with a nauseated resentment that could see nothing in front of him but a leaden urinal-wall of blank despair.

"God!" he thought, "this won't do. I'll go cracked if this goes on. I must get hold of a new girl." But the worst of it was whenever he tried to think of a new girl, and he knew quite a lot of them—Wollop's alone had at least half a dozen and only one of these was impossible—he always thought of Toss. What *was* it about Toss that caught him so? It must be the way she laughed. She laughed with such rich merriment. She went off at anything he'd say or do and nothing could stop her. He'd never known a girl before who laughed with such a bubbling chuckle and then such ringing peals. And she used to laugh like that when he was making love to her. God! she would laugh sometimes when really—a girl ought to be grave. But he didn't care. He liked her to laugh. Her laugh was like all the curves of her plump body. Well! Well! She won't laugh, poor little thing, when her time comes. But perhaps she will. Perhaps her child will be born in one prolonged, rich peal of laughter. Her child? Her twins! A boy and a girl. A Toss and a Tom. Yes, her laugh was like her arms between her shoulders and elbows—the inside of them, when she bent them. Her laugh was like those rings above her knees, made by those ridiculous garters.

A new girl? Damn them all! Thin, sour, puritanical, avaricious, cold-blooded hussies!

He turned his miserable gaze upon his one wretched pillow, dirty from his head, for he had grown remiss in having his bath since the weather got so chilly and "the woman down there" made such a fuss about hot water. He unlaced his boots. His socks were a sight! "I must do something about all this," he thought. "I can't go on like this." He took down his pyjamas from a hook behind the door and surveyed the cold thin cotton sheets and the frayed edge of the cheap blanket. "I'm damned if I'll take off my vest and drawers," he thought, "just for tonight!" This "just for tonight" had been repeated ever since the middle of September. Mr. Barter, the sturdy fen-man, was certainly becoming degenerate.

He turned off the light and got into bed. "I can't go on like this," he repeated. And he set himself to do what he disliked extremely to do—to consider his financial position. He had saved up, since his parents died, leaving him nothing, exactly a thousand pounds. He remembered the day when, in his balance-book received from Mr. Robert Stilly, he had first beheld the figures of that sum. It was just before John came. It was when he was going about with Mary. To have saved a thousand pounds, all earned by yourself, when you were only thirty-five—that was something as things went in England nowadays! No! He could not, he must not, break into that thousand. But what could he do if he didn't break into it? Until the factory was really on a production basis he had to get on as best he could. His dinners at the Pilgrims' always cost him five shillings—that is, if he had two bottles of ale. And he must have ale. Ale to his meat. Ale to his pudding. It might not be a gentleman's taste, but it was *his* taste. He had been a fool to leave Philip. But there it was! How was he to know then, what he knew now, that he'd have this brute Robinson to work with?

He tried to imagine himself back again with Philip, but somehow, miserable though he was, those galling, rankling insults— no! they were worse than his present nervousness with Robinson. At any rate he could heartily *despise* Robinson—even while he recognised the man's infernal industry. And he couldn't despise

Philip! He hated them both, but it was better to live with what you loathed and despised, than with what you loathed and admired! God! how it was raining tonight and how the wind howled! He remembered the look of the old chimney-stack on this wretched house, as he came just now along those few yards of streaming pavement. It looked damnably shaky as the rain beat against it. He wouldn't wonder if one of these nights it didn't come down. And what room would it hit? *His* of course; *his* room. What a nice death *that* would be. Crushed under that filthy ceiling, covered with bricks, cement and wet mortar. Who would have my thousand then? One of those fourth-removed Warwickshire cousins? "I must certainly make my will," thought Mr. Barter. "And I'll leave every penny of that thousand to Toss. God! these ricketty old houses, how they do shake in a storm."

He began to hope that Tossie wasn't frightened by this high wind in her room at the back of that Benedict house. "I suppose if she got scared," he said to himself, "she'd call out and Miss Crow would go to her." And Barter's mind went through the process—it took less than half a second—of summoning up the image of Miss Elizabeth and giving this image his hearty commendation. He did not articulate this in the sort of words he would have *spoken*—such as, "Miss Crow's a decent sort," or "Miss Crow's the only lady in the whole blooming family except Mary," but it was as if towards the portly figure of Miss Crow he gave a sort of mental nod as a man entering the Salon Carré in the Louvre might give a nod towards the Mona Lisa, as much as to say, "So *you* are there still."

His reflections were interrupted by an unusual noise and his heart gave a most unpleasant jump. Some door on the landing below—the house was let in single and double rooms—had been flung open and a voice was shrieking—"Call the doctor, someone! Who's there? Someone *must* go for a doctor at once!"

Mr. Barter was for a moment tempted to pull that cotton sheet and the two thin blankets tightly over his head. "If a person's fast asleep," he thought, "they can't disturb a person."

"Mrs. Smith! Betsy Burt!" screamed the voice on the landing below.

"It is extraordinary how fast I sleep—I was deep asleep then

and never heard a sound." These were the words that passed
through Barter's head as his excuse on the following morning.
But the curious thing was that even while he was completing
this rigmarole he was already out of bed, striking matches,
lighting the gas, and pulling on his trousers. Mr. Barter's arms
and legs, it appeared, were more benevolent than his thoughts.
Not only did he pull on his trousers but he hurriedly began putting on his boots. That done, he went to his door and threw it
open. "One minute, down there!" he cried. "One minute, and I'll
go." He flung on his waistcoat, coat and overcoat, snatched up
his cap, shut his door and ran downstairs.

It appeared that the child of a solitary and rather unpleasant
woman who lived in the room parallel to his own on the floor
below had been taken with some kind of fit. It was a little boy
of six and the child was now, as Barter pushed Mrs. Carey and
Betsy Burt aside, lying on the bed with a ghastly white face and
his eyes tight shut.

"'Tis convulsions, Mr. Barter," said Betsy Burt, when he
pushed his way in.

"'Tis 'pocalypse, Mister," cried old Mrs. Carey, "for I do know
how it takes 'em. 'Twere 'pocalypse that thee own blood-brother
died of, Miss Burt; so you oughtn't to be the one to talk of
convulsions. But I do know! I've a seed un and handled un in
many a corpsy, and they was all took just as this child be. He's
gone already—looks so to I. First they gets red and then they
gets turble white. 'Pocalypse takes them i' the heart, 's know,
and that's what do make their colour fly!"

The woman whose screams in the middle of that night had
brought nobody out of bed but Mr. Barter and these two crones,
was kneeling on the floor frantically chafing the hands of her
child.

"I'll bring the doctor here in five minutes," Barter said, touching her on the shoulder, but the woman did not turn round;
did not, as a matter of fact, take any notice at all.

"She were whöam late last night, Mister," said old Mrs.
Carey, tugging at his coat as he hurried out. "Don't tell doctor
I said it! Don't bring no inquest tales on I!" she called after
him, as he went downstairs.

It didn't take him long, for he ran fast all the way, butting against the deluging rain like a Norfolk gamekeeper, to reach Dr. Fell's house at the corner of Northload Street. Luckily— though it was long past twelve—the doctor was still "reading" the "Enchiridion" in his study. In other words, his favourite book was open on his knees and his broad low forehead, with the grizzled hair sticking out of it like the bristles of an aged hog, was nodding above the book. He opened the street-door himself and let Mr. Barter in.

He agreed to go at once, but when they opened the door again to make a start the rain was so terrific that he begged his summoner to wait till he got back. "Then I can send anything by you, Barter, that they may want. Besides, no use your getting wetter than you are. It can't go on like this. I know the house. There's whiskey on my table, man, and a glass somewhere. Take a good pull. It'll do 'ee good."

It was an incredible comfort to Mr. Barter to pour himself out a half-and-half tumbler of whiskey and water, and to draw in his chair close to the red coals. He made towards his friend, the doctor, the same sort of mental nod of inarticulate approval that he had made towards Miss Crow. A warm glow of the first unadulterated pleasure he had had since he last saw Miss Stickles, ran through his veins as he gulped down the good drink and dried his wet boots at the fire. "I believe I'll give up my dinners at the Pilgrims'," he thought, "and buy whiskey with that money! Drink's better than the best cooking, when a man's got the doldrums."

Half an hour passed. Barter went to the doctor's table and poured himself out half a glass more, which he now proceeded to sip, without putting in any water. He moved to the doctor's big leather chair and placed his glass upon the floor. A delicious drowsiness began to flow through him like a ripple of warm etherealised honey.

In an hour the doctor entered. "He'll be all right—the little lad," he said cheerfully. "It was that kind of mock-epilepsy that children sometimes get. He's asleep now, and so I hope is the mother. There's no hurry for you to go, my boy. Wait till the rain's subsided. Let's make a night of it. I've got plenty more of this stuff. It's good, isn't it? . . . That woman will kill that child with her drunken ways, unless I get the Society to take him away from her," he went on when they had settled down. "Do you know that I know at this moment one, two—*five* mothers that are killing their children in this town?"

"Well, they'll be out of it when they're dead," said Thomas Barter.

"And do you realise, my good friend, that Tittie Petherton's cancer is following a track that won't kill her for months and months—maybe not for six months! I made sure it would finish her off in a week or two, when I examined her in August, but not at all!"

"Well! in a year, anyway, she will be dead and all that pain wiped out."

"Wiped out, Barter? What are you talking about? Are you such a happy man as really to believe that in the whole sweep and surge and swing of things pain like that is *wiped out*? I read a Russian book once, Barter, by that man whose name begins with D, and a character there says he believes in God but rejects God's World. Now I feel just the opposite! I think the whole of God's World is infinitely to be pitied—tortured and torturers alike—but I think that God Himself, the great Living God, responsible for it all, the powerful Creator who deliberately gave such reptiles, such sharks, such hyænas, such jackals as we are, this accursed gift of Free Will, ought to have *such a Cancer* ——" The quiet doctor actually jerked himself forward to the edge of his arm-chair, till, with only the tip of his buttocks—where his erect and angry tail would have been switching if he had possessed one—resting upon its very verge, he drew with his forefinger a crucial outline upon the air—"such a Cancer," he cried, "as would keep him Alive and Howling for a Million Years!"

"I went through Paradise yesterday," remarked Barter. "The poverty's pretty bad down there still, in spite of all this new work that Crow's been giving people."

The doctor, who had now relapsed panting into the depths of his chair, took up the subject with a groan. "I should think it *was* pretty bad! It's few of the natives who get this work. He's brought in a lot of new men from Bristol and Bath, a stronger, better-fed type, and more docile too! There'll be another riot before our folk expect it, and a much more serious one than that little affair at the Pageant, when they mobbed Lord P."

"What do you think, Doctor, will really come of all these diggings and buildings out at that well? Do you think Geard will get a steady crowd down here every year—or only just on the day he opens the thing? John was telling me it would be opened between Christmas and the first of January."

"My good friend," said Charles Montagu Fell, pointing at Barter with the stem of his cherry-wood pipe, "what people forget is *this*! In all these improvements, whether Geard brings them in or Crow, the real pain of mind and body goes on where people haven't the heart or the health to get the benefit of such things. That's the point that's always forgotten. I'm a doctor, and a doctor's profession's naturally with the unfit rather than the fit. And I tell you the tragedy of life is in the rubbish heap. People talk of the sufferings of the strong, and how you ought to help the strong rather than the weak, as if the weak were a type of animal that didn't feel. I tell you suffering is like a fungus that the strong can carry about with them, and still bustle and strut, whereas with the weak the fungus is too heavy. They can't hold it up. It pulls 'em down. But it don't numb their feeling! They're nothing else but feeling—feeling and fungus!"

"But aren't the poor *used to it*?" protested the man from Norfolk.

Dr. Fell sank back in his chair and pushed his fingers through the stubbly grey hairs that stuck out from his low forehead.

"He's one of the ugliest chaps I've ever seen," thought Barter, "but he has good ideas and good drink."

"No, Barter, no, no! that's another pretty, comforting, easy lie! The human consciousness is not confined to what you can see of the body, or of the habits of the body. We all carry about with us something distinct from the body, the thing that says, 'I am I.' This something, this soul, never gets *used* to any human situation! It finds itself 'landed' or it finds itself riding the waves. It's never *used* to anything."

At this point in the conversation both the men started up straight in their chairs and glanced at each other.

"Someone's moving about, up there," said Mr. Barter grimly.

Dr. Fell's countenance expressed savage loathing. He listened intently. Then he gave a sigh of relief. "It's the rats, Barter. It must be the rats. They become lively in the Autumn."

"I hope so," remarked the other.

They both listened again. No! that was the sound—to the doctor's ears quite unmistakable—of heavy woollen slippers, a little too large for the feet that wore them, stumping, *plockety-plock . . . plockety-plock,* along the landing above.

"It's her!" whispered the doctor. "My God! It's Bibby!"

They listened again and once more there was silence. Everything in the house was as still as the centre of a wood covered with new-fallen snow. And then the sound began again—*plockety-plock . . . plockety-plock . . .* above their heads.

Mr. Barter was not easily disturbed, but he was shocked to see a man he liked as he liked the doctor, give way to his nerves as he did now.

Charles Montagu Fell leapt to his feet and began hitting that low forehead of his with his two fists, hitting it quite hard and repeating as he did so, over and over again, an expressive if not ancient English word of one syllable, which the propriety of learned taste has excluded from the Oxford Dictionary.

"Sorry, Barter," he murmured, with a shame-faced grimace, when this manifestation was over, "but you've never known what it is to live with someone who . . . with someone who . . . gets on your nerves to such a pitch." He came up close to his friend now and laying a finger on the man's sleeve, whispered in his ear: "You don't know what the word loathing means, do you, Barter? Loathing . . . loathing . . . loathing! It's much worse than hatred. I can tell you *that,* anyway!"

Once more they drew apart and stood listening. And once more those flopping steps inside those loose, soft slippers became audible.

Mr. Barter was of an unimaginative disposition, but even he became aware of something rather horrible in the sound of those steps, combined with its effect upon the nerves of his friend.

"I don't like going off," he said, looking round uneasily, "and leaving you like this."

"Oh, she'll quiet down as soon as we open the door," returned the doctor. "You note how she does. It's really rather funny; but the joke, as Heine said of something else, is somewhat stale."

He moved to the door as he spoke and opened it, making a sign to the other man to listen. It was exactly as he had said. The steps in the loose slippers retreated, with that peculiarly unpleasant sound, a little accelerated, as they caught the vibration of the closing of a door.

"Gone to earth," said the doctor grossly, and he proceeded to open the street door. They stood together on the doorstep. The rain had ceased, and there was upon the night a faint taste, like a thin, diffused chemical salt, of that early hour of the morning.

Suddenly there was uplifted into the silence of the sleeping town a premature cock-crow. At once, though it was really just as dark, both of the men seemed to *feel* the approaching dawn, feel it like the smell of some kind of sea-breath brought up on the winding tidal ditches, from Bridgewater Bay. The absolute stillness of the wet pavements and clammy cobblestones and slippery roofs and drenched eaves had a curious effect upon the two men. They both had the same feeling although neither told the other. They both felt as if Glastonbury, at least, in her sleep, were an actual, living Creature!

Barter turned round before he descended the dripping steps to the silent pavement and shook hands with his friend. Very tightly did he grasp the man's fingers.

"Finish the bottle before you go up!" he said, and the words seemed to fall upon the wet nakedness of Glastonbury like a rattle of shot from a boy's catapult.

"One of these days I'll *murder* her," returned Charles Montagu. "Would you come to the Taunton Jail to see me, Barter?"

"Shut up, you fool, and finish that bottle!" But when he glanced back, before he went down Northload Street towards High Street, he saw that the doctor was standing there still, watching him go. "Maybe I ought to have stayed all night with him," he thought. He waited for a minute watching his figure at that door and wishing it would go into the house. Something seemed to be holding Thomas Barter back on that spot, and not allowing him to depart and forget Dr. Fell. No situation between human beings is more curious than when, after a separation, two people look back at each other. It is especially curious when, as now, they both seem unable to stop looking at each other, clinging to each other with their eyes! Barter had the feeling that it was not he who was going off—but his friend. He felt as if the doctor were standing on the deck of a liner, and as if he had just one more chance of running down the gangway. But no! The bridge was up now, and a widening gap of wickedly dark water was separating its hull from the wharf!

He waved his hand. He could not resist the impulse to do this. It was indeed the merest chance that he resisted the urge to run back. But the figure on the steps turned now without making any sign and went into the house and the door was shut.

Mr. Barter proceeded slowly down Northload Street. He walked a little faster when he reached the centre of the town, directing his steps towards his George Street room, but, for all the good whiskey he had drunk, his thoughts were heavy, cold and stiff, like a load of staring-eyed dead fish on a blood-stained wheelbarrow. He met no one—not even the old Glastonbury policeman, not even a prowling cat. All the shops had their shutters fast closed. All the houses had their blinds down. He cast an indifferent lack-lustre eye upon these houses as he went along. Here was one a little bigger than the others and even more obstinately closed up. There were iron railings with spikes upon them in front of it and along these railings rows and rows of minute raindrops hung. The whole place was so silent, under the chilly darkness before dawn, so motionless and sepulchral, that these little quivering rain-drops catching specks of faint light from a pallid street-lamp seemed more alive than such water-drops usually are. Barter, however, cast an unseeing, unappreciative eye upon them. It would be hard to say what natural object at that moment—short of a falling meteorite—would have arrested his attention. Probably even his foreman at the Municipal, an artist in his showing off before Sally Jones, had more of what is called æsthetic appreciation than Mr. Barter. But he *did* observe one object with a faint interest in connection with this particular house, as he moved along by these pallid raindrops, and that was a massive gilded plate, which was also illuminated by the neighbouring lamp, and upon which he read the words "John Beere, Solicitor." He had often been nudged by a loquacious waitress in the Pilgrims' dining-room—this was in Clarissa's day—and told to observe the passionate gluttony of this shortsighted old gentleman. "I'll buy whiskey in future," he thought, "and keep the bottle at the restaurant. That girl would look after it for me. The woman at home would drink it."

His mind called up the alternatives, and he tried to weigh them against each other. The cosiness, the good cooking, the ale, on the one hand, but with hostile wenches, set on to bait him by Clarissa; and on the other, a filthy, dreary little chop house, with wretched cooking, but with a buxom, nice girl, to bring him his bottle, carefully guarded by herself, and with hot water and lemon gratis if he wanted them!

The importance of this dilemma had brought his steps to a momentary stand in front of Lawyer Beere's house, and before going on he glanced up at its mellow Queen Anne façade. There was a night-light, at any rate, some extremely faint lamp-light, burning behind the closed blinds of one of the upper rooms.

"That awful Angela!" he said to himself with a little shudder, as he went on down the street. To a nympholept, of Barter's pragmatic complex, the mere fact of a feminine creature being unresponsive to his advances relegated her to a worse than undesirable category.

Angela Beere, as a matter of fact,—for Barter was right about it being her room—always put out her light when she went to bed, but today, because of the terrific storm of rain that had descended upon the close of her party, she had pressed her friend Persephone to stay the night with her and not to attempt to return to Dickery Cantle's unappealing place, and to this proposal Percy had consented, making the stipulation, however— for she never slept in total darkness—that there should be at least a night-light in the room. At the very moment Mr. Barter was going by, the younger of the two girls, excited and restless, was whispering to the other.

"I can't read *enough* of those books about it," Angela was saying. "He's got the most thrilling ones—every one that's been written, I should think!" She was referring to the heathen Grail of the old Celtic mythology and to her new friend, Mr. Evans.

There was something weird about this whispered conversation in those last hours of that night, before the faint, cold dawn-breath—more like a sigh of something dying than a cry of something newly born—crept over the wet hills, stole along the tow-paths, touched the gateposts and the dams and the stone bridges and the floating weeds in the ditches with its silent approach. Both the girls were sensitised and spiritualised to an unusual pitch of feeling, but nothing could have been more different than the way they felt.

"I love to hear you, Angela! Go on, go on! Tell me more!" Thus did Percy reply; thus did Percy encourage her, but in her heart she drew away. Why was it that nothing seemed to satisfy her, to hold her, to cast a spell upon her that could last? A curious and subtle weariness weighed upon her now. There seemed something mysteriously sad about everything in life, as she saw things now, in the deep silence, only broken by this feverish voice at her ear.

Had Mr. Evans been permitted—like Iachimo in Shakespear's play—to pass a vigil in that chamber, his Druidic imagination would certainly have been stirred to the depths by the sight of those two lovely heads under the faint illumination of that flickering night-light in its small crimson glass. How white was the complexion of the younger! How gipsy-brown that of the other! Persephone's dusky curls lay against her pillow like autumn leaves upon snow, and her face had a far-away, weary look, as if the enchantment she sought were not here . . . not anywhere in this rain-drenched, silent town . . . not anywhere in all this Gwlad-yr-Hav of Somerset . . . perhaps not anywhere in all the round earth! The soft hair of the other head, on the contrary, under that dim light, looked like a heap of scattered autumn crocuses, but her cold eyes and her smooth white cheeks were alive with feverish excitement as she narrated, in her passionate, furtive whispers, the story of the Cauldron of Ceridwen.

"*That* Cauldron was the real Grail, you know, and it was *that*

that made Taliessin young!" Then, without a second's pause, catching her breath in a particular way she had, she plunged into the tale of Math, Son of Mathonwy, which Mr. Evans had shown her in the Mabinogion. "Arianrod—which means Silver Circle—laid a destiny upon her son Llew," she whispered, "that he shall never have a wife of the race that now inhabits this earth. 'Well,' said Math, 'we will seek, thou and I, by charms and illusion, to form a wife for him out of flowers.' So they took the blossoms of the oak, and the blossoms of the broom, and the blossoms of the meadow-sweet, and produced from them a maid, and they baptised her and gave her the name of Blodenwedd."

As she told this story to Percy, Percy could not help feeling, as she looked at the transparency of this white face by her side, that the girl herself might well have been named Blodenwedd!

Lovely were they both, as they lay there in that glimmering light, but whereas Angela seemed to draw to herself from out of the storm-cleansed darkness everything that was pallid and phantasmal in the rain-soaked meadows, in the dripping hazel-spinneys, in the cold, moss-covered hill slopes, Persephone seemed, as she lay listening to her friend, as if she were an incarnation of all the magic of the brown rain-pools and the smooth-washed beech boughs and the drenched, carved eaves of fragrant woodwork, and the wet reed roofs of the dyke-hovels down there in the marshes of the Brue.

"I believe I know who *you* are in these Grail stories!" Angela was now whispering. "You are Lorie de la Roche Florie, the mistress of Gawain!"

"I've not found him yet, anyway," smiled the other.

"He says," whispered Angela, "Mr. Evans says, that Mayor Geard is really in league with the old magical Powers, and that the new inscription they've found on Chalice Hill has to do with Merlin, and not with Saint Joseph at all!"

The girl's Madonna-like face had a flaming spot on both her cheeks and her breath came in quick gasps as these hurried syllables left her lips.

But Percy listened languidly. Her lonely, unsettled, restless soul had not yet found what she craved. "Perhaps," she was thinking now, "what I want is not in this world at all!" Something in her anyway—probably her sceptical Norfolk blood—felt profoundly suspicious of all this chatter about the old gods. She liked flirting—if her ambiguous relations with the Welshman could be called by that name—with Mr. Evans, but his Cymric mythology left her absolutely cold. She fancied she had made the discovery of late that there was a certain type of nature that could not enjoy life in a frankly amorous, or honestly vicious way, but must be always complicating the issue by bringing into it all sorts of half-mystical, half-religious notions.

While the fair girl continued her esoteric whisperings with burning cheeks and eyes growing brighter and brighter, Percy was thinking to herself, "If Dave would do nothing but talk about Communism in his curious way I could live with him forever. If Philip would go on driving me in his car *sans cesse*, I could live with *him*! And it's going to be just the same with you, my angel, only the other way round! I like your being fond of me but your ideas wear me out. What a wild, excited way she's whispering now! God bless me! Owen Evans hasn't discovered any new sins that aren't practised every day among people who've never heard of his Guardians of the Grail or his Daughters of King Avallach!"

She knew that the dim light from their little night-light fell upon her face, and she knew that the other's spasmodic outburst of hot, quick, excited words would cease in a second and the girl's feelings be cruelly wounded if she realised the effect she was having. So, born actress as she was, Percy assumed an expression of exhausted but responsive intentness. But her soul wandered far away.

Ned Athling, who had come to know her quite well during their rehearsals together, had introduced her recently to Lady Rachel, and Rachel's passionate love of old ballad-poetry and her hatred of everything modern, had amused her not a little. The image of Rachel hovered now very clearly before her mind. Mr. Evans' pupil in mysticism would have been staggered and her heart stabbed had she been able to read her friend's thoughts.

Taliessin and Aneurin, Bendigeitvran, or Bran the Blessed, Terre Gastée and Balyn's Dolorous Stroke, Arawn, King of

Hades, Caer Pedryvan, where Pwyll's Cauldron was found by the heathen Arthur, the Mwys of Gwydno-Garanhir, without which Kulhwch might never have Olwen to his bed—all these would have sunk down into the sluices of nothingness, into the weirs of oblivion, if the fair girl had known the bitter truth!

So the exhausted and intently smiling brown-skinned mask listened to her friend's voice, but beneath it the girl's unsatisfied soul wandered off far into the darkness. Over the head of Mr. Barter it wandered, as he weighed his whiskey against his ale, over the house of Dr. Fell, it wandered, where the word murder had been so lately breathed, over the Mayor's bedroom it wandered, where Mr. Geard could still derive amorous pleasure from embracing Megan, over the sleeping head of Sam in his Vicarage room, over the tossing, sleepless head of Sam's begetter, in *his* room, out, far out, away from all these people, away from all these roofs, covering desire and torment and rapture and lechery and despair and paradisiac peace, it wandered free,—free of them all, free even of the body of its own possessor, but still unsatisfied, still wanting something that no flesh and blood could fulfil,—something "that might not be in the world at all," or at least so hidden that none could find it.

Just one word, Mr. Mayor," said Dr. Fell as he stood with his hand on the window of Solly Lew's taxi. "I must have it completely understood that, as this woman's medical adviser, I refuse to give my consent to your taking her."

"Quite right, Doctor," replied Mr. Geard from inside the vehicle, where he was supporting the groaning Tittie, "I receive your protest. Mr. Crow here and my daughter are your witnesses. I take full responsibility." He raised his voice. "You want to come, don't you, Mrs. Petherton?"

"Yes, yes! Oh, Lord! Anything. Oh, Lord! For to make thee stop; for to make thee stop even for a little while, Lord! Yes, yes. Oh, there thee be again!"

The tortured woman had come recently to talk to her cancer as if it were a living person. She called it "Lord"; for it represented the nearest and most wilful power she knew. It was this peculiarity that had begun to get on the nerves of the worthy Nurse Robinson and was one of the chief reasons why she had asked to be relieved from her task. " 'Twill be better for hevery one concerned, for 'er to 'ave a change," she had said when Mat Dekker who had made himself responsible for the nurse's salary protested at this decision. "She'd be far better horf in the 'orspital," she said. And it was this word, overheard by the patient a week ago, that had now made it essential that there *should* be a change, for, after this, the woman's feeling towards the nurse was like what a heretic would feel towards an Inquisition official. The frightened Tittie would not let her come near her without screaming.

"I'll bring house down if yer moves a step!" she threatened; and once she *had* begun shrieking and struggling so terribly that the neighbours had run in and made a scene.

"Drive on, Solly!" commanded Mr. Geard.

Crummie and John, sitting opposite the two principals in this strange event, kept up together—under cover of the unhappy creature's groans—a rapid exchange of comments.

"She's too far gone," said John. "That's what I'm afraid of. If she weren't so far gone she might help him by her faith in him. But she's beyond that!"

"He doesn't care what she thinks, if only he can get her there!" gasped Crummie, wincing with sympathy at every movement the woman made.

"I can't make him out," said John. "He doesn't seem worked up over it. You saw what a good dinner he ate . . . all that Yorkshire pudding! I'd feel happier about it if he were more stirred up. Could you imagine a worse hour of the day for such an experiment? There's St. John's church striking half-past two now."

"What's he going to do with her?" asked the girl. "Has he told *you*?" she went on. "He can't be going to dip her *in* that water! I won't let him, we *mustn't* let him, if he tries anything like that."

"Oh, he'll be sensible," said John, "as far as *that's* concerned. He's got a head on his shoulders. Better leave him alone."

It would have been easy to talk like this before Mr. Geard's face, even if the woman had not been groaning and twitching as she was, for he had a peculiar power of being at once *there* and *not* there, at the same time, under certain conditions.

"Careful!" he shouted out loudly now to the driver. "Don't go through the Square! Go by Bove Town, and down Silver, into Chilkwell."

"Right ho, Sir! As your Worship wishes," replied Mr. Lew. Mr. Geard was certainly at that moment deliberately engaged in breaking a good many natural laws, or at least refuting a good many conventional notions of such laws. With his great belly stuffed with Yorkshire pudding, with the weather around him, hot, moist, muggy and windless, with the sceptical John watching him with the scrutiny of a detached lynx, with the clocks striking that time of day, of all others the most material and when human souls are most drowsy and uninspired, with Crummie full of that particular kind of tender, practical, feminine solicitude, which is of all things most antipathetic to the drastic urge of creative energy, with the subject of his proposed cure so distraught with pain as to be almost out of her mind, it might

indeed have seemed that he could not have been more handicapped in his amazing project, unless perhaps if Dr. Fell, still
vehemently and professionally in opposition, had accompanied
them.

Conditions were worse for their purpose when they finally arrived at the spot, than even John or Crummie had anticipated;
for they found the place occupied by a gang of callous working-
men from the slums of Paradise, still lingering, though their
dinner-hour had been over a long time, at their jests and boisterous fooling.

Solly Lew stopped his taxi just opposite these men and John,
opening the door, gave Crummie his hand. His consciousness of
the moment—of the accumulation of impressions that made up
what the moment brought—had never been more alive. He was
surprised—and ashamed too, so that the blood rushed to his face
—when he found that the grasp of Crummie's warm, electric
fingers had given him a disturbing pleasure. "She's a plump
young baggage," he said to himself, in order to destroy this feeling. "Her legs aren't like a boy's, as Mary's are!" But the truth
was—although he hated to acknowledge it—that his sensual happiness with Mary had made him much less impervious to feminine charm than he had ever been in his life. "There's no de-
pending on my wicked feelings," he said to himself. "I seem to
be just exactly what that Austrian says *all babies* are—polymorphous perverts!"

John had had nothing for lunch himself except a cup of tea
and two mouthfuls of a bath-bun; so that although it was only
thirty-five minutes past two, his nerves were as alert as if it had
been four or even five o'clock. He had had his breakfast early
too, so that he felt like a priest who had fasted in preparation for
some especial function.

While Solly Lew was helping Mr. Geard get Tittie out of the
car John glanced through the great torn gap in the hedge to
where the workmen were engaged. They were beginning to work
again now, with many suppressed glances and whispers and
nudges directed towards the Mayor.

Behind where they were working at this moment, digging a
ditch for further foundations, there already might be seen several

quite substantial rows of walls—the beginning of Mr. Geard's Byzantine rotunda and Saxon arch. These walls, now risen to nearly seven feet high, totally concealed from where the men were working all sight of Chalice Well; for the Mayor's London architect, an expert, it turned out, in the mystical intention of compass-points, had got the entrance arch facing due east, so that vistors to the Well, following in the footsteps of the great Joseph—Agathos-Dikaios, as St. John calls him,—might approach its waters, moving, if they were religious, on their knees, and tapping the ground with their foreheads, in a westerly direction.

"Come!" said Mr. Geard now, in a husky, authoritative voice, addressing his daughter and John.

Helped by Solly Lew he half-carried the suffering woman, still keeping up, heedless of where she was, her hysterical dialogue with her tormentor, over the littered hedge-gap and straight among the workmen.

Most of the men touched their caps, some went on working, all glanced at the Mayor of Glastonbury with that mingled familiarity and respect which he always aroused in the populace. He had come so often to watch them work, and had brought with him so many curious companions, that none of them seemed particularly astonished at the sight of Tittie's contorted figure.

He directed Solly to prop Mrs. Petherton up for a minute against an overturned wheelbarrow; and then drew the man aside, beckoning John and Crummie to join them.

"What I want you three," he said emphatically, but speaking in a quite unexcited, natural voice, "to do for me now, if you will, is to stand in line between here and the Well, and not let a soul go up there! No one will probably want to. But if anyone *does* try they must be stopped. *That's all!* If I want *you*, Crummie, I'll shout. But I probably shan't want anyone. I won't be long. Bless us and keep us!"

Without any further words he moved over to the prostrate woman and lifted her up in his arms, holding her pressed against his chest.

"He be going to christen she, looks so!" said Solly Lew. "Well, Missy, I reckon us had best do what 'a said; but it's sore in me

heart to wish poor Bet were wi' I! Thik poor 'ooman would
give the eyes out of she's head to see these grand doings!"

John was the only one of Mr. Geard's three singular disciples
who had the gall to cast a furtive glance over his shoulder to
watch the Mayor's sturdy, cautious steps, as he carried his distracted burden out of sight behind the newly erected masonry.
When the twain had vanished from view, however, he also turned
round and took up his sentinel's post. Thus John was standing
on the extreme west, Solly on the extreme east, and Crummie in
a position that might be called east by south. Here they all three
settled themselves to wait, as calmly as they could under the
circumstances.

It was remarkable how little notice the labouring men, preoccupied with their digging, and anxious to show the Mayor's
daughter that they were earning their pay, took of their employer's proceedings. John himself, as he watched the motions
of their mattocks and spades, felt a queer trance-like feeling
steal over his restless mind. His gaze, travelling over the stooping backs of the men on the level ground and over the heads
and swinging picks of those working in the ditches, noted, in
this curious dreamlike numbness of his senses—so alert a few
minutes ago—that a flock of sheep was being driven up the road.
These woolly creatures packed close together, but raising in the
damp windless air no cloud of dust and much less than usual of
their accustomed bleating, were moving *en masse*, like a river
of grey, curly wool, eastward, away from the town.

Three figures, a man, a boy, and a sheep-dog, as grey and
woolly as the flock itself, walked patiently and somnolently behind them. As he watched these figures and that moving river of
grey backs in front of them his mind was carried away upon a
long vista of memories. Various roads where he had encountered
such sights, some of them in Norfolk, some of them in France,
came drifting through his mind and with these memories came
a queer feeling that the whole of his life was but a series of
such dream-pictures and that the whole series of these pictures
was something from which, if he made a strong enough effort,
he could awake, and feel them all dispersing, like wisps of
vapour. Pain was real—that woman crying out upon her cancer

and calling it "Lord! Lord!"—but even pain, and all the other indescribable horrors of life seemed, as he stared at the backs of those moving sheep, to be made of a "stuff," as Shakespeare calls it, that could be compelled to yield, to loosen, to melt, to fade, under the right pressure.

Gone were the sheep now; and a second later, following them in that same dreamlike movement, gone was the man, and the boy, and the dog. John's mood changed then with an abrupt jerk. Something in his mind seemed to fall with a machine-like click into its normal groove.

Slyly he turned round and glanced at Crummie. The girl had slipped off her cloak, spread it on the ground, and was sitting with part of it wrapped round her knees. She waved to him as he caught her attention and he waved back. None of these workmen had the least desire to spy upon the master. Bloody Johnny was at liberty to perform any crazy ritual he liked behind those walls. "I might just as well be sitting by Crummie's side," he thought. He peered round the other way to see what the taximan was doing. Solly Lew also was sitting down—on a stone or a log or something—calmly smoking his pipe and contemplating the workmen. But John's imagination was at work now. What on earth was Geard doing to that woman? Most repulsively— for John's mind had a Goya-like twist for the monstrous—he saw his employer dipping that poor creature in his precious chalybeate water! He saw the scene with hideous and telescopic minuteness. He saw the filthy underwear of the poor wretch, unchanged for a week no doubt while she beat the nurse away, and all stained with ordure. He saw vermin, frightened by the water, leaving her clothes and scurrying away across the slabs of the fountain where they would undoubtedly perish miserably. He saw the loathsome image of the cancer itself. Geard was bathing it in that reddish water and muttering his grotesque invocations, while the woman—John could see her face—was terrified into forgetting her pain by the cold shock of the water. No doubt it had come into her simple mind that the Mayor had decided to rid Glastonbury of her. John's imagination after being so dazed by the sheep was now seized with a terrifying clairvoyance. He followed one of Tittie's vermin in its flight from

Bloody Johnny's vigorous ablutions. And he saw it encountering a lusty wood louse which had had to turn itself into a leaden-coloured ball to avoid Mr. Geard's feet but which, appearing now in the other's path like an immense Brontosaurus, had un-curled itself to the view of the human louse.

"All is strange to me," said the human louse to the wood louse. He spoke the lice language with its beautiful vowel sounds to perfection.

"On the contrary," said the wood louse, speaking the same ancient tongue but with a rude rural intonation, "*you* are the only strange thing here to me."

"Could you direct me ——" the human louse enquired, giving its words a classical resonance, indicative of the fact that its ancestors had lived with the Romans, "to any human skin in this vicinity?"

The wood louse rudely disabused this dainty traveller of his high hope; and reported that the only skin except the bark of trees available in that quarter was the skin of a rabbit that had been caught in a trap a year ago.

"Nothing can save you from dying of starvation that *I* can see," said the wood louse, "except to be discovered by some bird small enough to snap you up. If you like I will pass the word round that you are in such mental anguish that ——"

Here the story John had told himself broke off; but he continued thinking about the monstrous arrogance of the human race in lumping together in one clumsy and ridiculous word—"instinct, instinct, instinct"—all the turbulent drama, full of criss-cross psychic currents and convoluted struggles and desperations of the subhuman world.

The thought of the luckless fate of this miserable vermin in the unchanged clothes of this rebel against Nurse Robinson brought into John's mind just then, under that heavy sky, the real ghastliness of the word relative. "It's relatively important that those vermin should escape starvation," he thought. "It's relatively important that Geard should have his miracle. It's relatively important that this wretched woman should be eased of her pain. It's relatively important that my life with Mary should be exquisitely happy. It's relatively important that this grave ass Philip should get the town council's leave to make his road over the marshes. God! What a mix-up it all is. I don't care! I didn't make the world. I'm not responsible. There could not be a sweeter creature than Mary—no! not from Glastonbury to Jerusalem!"

While these thoughts were passing through John's mind, Mr. Geard, stark naked in the Grail Fountain, the water of which came up beyond his waist, and watched by the petrified astonishment of Tittie, who reclined with her back against the base of the Saxon arch, was extending his arms in some sort of command. John was utterly wrong in his imagination. Not once did Mr. Geard call upon the Blood of Christ. Not once did he sprinkle with the blood-red water the woman with cancer. Mr. Geard's clothes lay in a neat heap at Tittie's side; and the woman, in stupefied amazement, was watching his uplifted fingers as they kept mechanically opening and closing in the tempest of his mental struggle.

Mr. Geard was not praying. That was the difference between this occasion and the other occasions when his therapeutic powers had been used. He was not praying. He was commanding.

If the question were asked, what precisely was Mr. Geard thinking and feeling as he lifted his arms from the Red Fountain, the answer would have to be that he was assuming to himself the rôle of a supernatural being! As a matter of literal fact— such were the childish limitations of this singular man's nature —Mr. Geard *had*, for one second, visualised to himself a picture in the Sunday School at Montacute, representing Our Lord in the process of being baptised in the Jordan! There was no conscious blasphemy in this flickering thought, and it had not lasted. Now he was neither thinking nor feeling. Now his whole body and soul were absorbed in an *act*. This act was the act of *commanding* the cancer to come out of the woman; commanding it on his own authority; so that the growth in Tittie's side should wither up!

The truth is that this chalybeate fountain on this particular hillside had been the scene of such a continuous series of mystic rites, going back to the neolithic men of the Lake Village, if not to the still more mysterious race that preceded them, that there had come to hang about it a thick aura of magical vibrations. That rabbit's skin in the trap, referred to by John's wood louse, might lose its virtue owing to rain and frost and bleaching sun; but this psychic aura, charged with the desperate human struggles of five thousand years to break into the arcana of Life, no rains could wash away, no suns could dry up, no frosts could kill.

Immersed to the waist in this ruddy spring which had been the scene for five thousand years of so much passionate credulity, it is not strange that Mr. Geard, whose animal magnetism was double or treble that of an ordinary person, should find himself able to tap a reservoir of miraculous power.

No sacred pool, in Rome, or Jerusalem, or Mecca, or Thibet, has gathered such an historic continuum of psycho-chemical force about it as this spot contained then, and contains still. But Mr. Geard did not confine his reservoir of healing power to what this locality had stored up. He wrestled at that moment with the First Cause Itself. Now it can be understood why he chose a day so damp and dark and windless, so brown, so neutral, so apathetic, so heavy with drowsy mists, for his grand experiment. It was because—led by an instinct which he himself could never have explained—he wanted to get into touch with the First Cause Itself uninterrupted by the dynamic energy of the Sun or Earth or any subordinate Power. The man was now like an athlete of some kind as he stretched out his arms and concentrated his massive and mountainous energy.

The curious thing was that his mind remained perfectly calm, clear and quiet. It was always rare for Mr. Geard to lose his *sangfroid*, even at the most culminating crisis; and he was now quite coolly saying to himself—"If I do it, I do it. If I don't do it, I don't do it—and the woman must die. But I *shall* do it. I feel it in me. I feel it in me."

What Mr. Geard kept his mind steadily upon, all this while, was that crack, that cranny, that slit in Time through which the Timeless—known in those parts for five thousand years as a cauldron, a horn, a krater, a mwys, a well, a kernos, a platter, a cup, and even a nameless stone—had broken the laws of Nature! What Mr. Geard really did—being more practical and less scrupulous than Sam Dekker—was to associate this immemorial *Fetish* with the Absolute, with Its creative as distinct from Its destructive energy. Sam, in his passion for the crucified, opposed himself to the First Cause, as Something so evil in Its cruelty that a man ought to resist It, curse It, defy It, and have no dealings with It. Thus in his loathing of the evil in God, Sam, the Saint, refused to make any use of the beneficence in God; and this refusal was constantly handicapping him in his present "all-or-nothing" existence. Mr. Geard on the other hand was prepared to make use of this ambiguous Emperor of the Cosmos without the slightest scruple.

Mr. Geard now happened to catch the sound of a peewit's cry, a sound that was one of his favourite bird calls, for he associated it with certain particular fields on the road from Montacute to Yeovil, and he regarded it, reaching his ears at this crisis, as a most blessed omen. Simultaneously with this cry, which was not repeated, he noticed, to his intense satisfaction, that Tittie Petherton was yawning! *"I've done it,"* he said to himself, and straining every nerve of his nature, body and soul together, he forced himself to envisage that cancer as something towards which he was directing arrow after arrow of blighting, withering, deadly force. "The great thing is to *see* it," he said to himself, while his black eyes now alight with their most burning fury, stripped the poor woman of every stitch of clothing.

His arrows of thought now became a spear—the Bleeding Lance of the oldest legends of Carbonek—and with an actual tremor of his upraised, naked arms, he felt himself to be plunging this formidable weapon into that worst enemy of all women! "I've done it," he repeated, for the second time, as he saw Tittie's eyes begin slowly to close.

And then Mr. Geard shivered and his teeth began to chatter. Perhaps he wouldn't have succeeded after all if there hadn't come into his head at that moment an actual vision of one tiny living tendril of that murderous octopus under the sleeping woman's flesh. With one terrific upheaval of the whole of his massive frame, its gastric, its pulmonary, its spinal, its phallic force, and even lifting himself up on tiptoe from the gravel at the bottom of the fount, he plunged that Bleeding Lance of his mind into the half-dead cancer.

Then he bowed himself forward, like the trunk of a tree in a great storm, till his forehead touched the surface of the water. From that surface he proceeded to gulp down, in long, panting, gurgling gasps, enough water to satisfy the thirst of the Questing Beast. "Blood of Christ!" he spluttered; and it was the first time during this great struggle that his favourite expression had crossed his lips.

And then his former utterance escaped once more from the depths of his throat, like a veritable grunt of that Questing Beast; and almost inarticulately the words rose from the chalybeate water. "I've done it!" sighed Mr. Geard for the third time.

He now scrambled out upon the new stone slabs, took one quick complacent glance at the foundations of the Saxon arch, and began hurriedly drying himself. For this purpose he used, not his grey flannel shirt, as anyone would have expected, but a new black woollen waistcoat which Megan had just finished knitting for him.

When he had got all his clothes on, including his thin black overcoat and a sort of Low Church parson's hat, which was his favourite headgear and which he now squeezed low down over his forehead, he lifted up the sleeping woman very carefully in his arms and carried her out between the pedestals of his arch. It was Crummie who had dressed Mrs. Petherton for this great excursion—certainly the most important she would ever make, till "the young men," as the Scriptures would put it, "carried her out for her burial"—and Crummie had found an old purple bonnet in a cardboard box which she had placed on her head, tying the strings round her neck.

From Mr. Geard's fingers, spread out now under the woman's back, this hat now dangled by one of its purple strings, flapping against his knees as he carried her down the hillside.

Bloody Johnny's three attendants hurried anxiously to meet him and great was their relief—shared to the full by Mr. Lew—at the cheerful tone in which he greeted them.

While this momentous event was occurring upon Chalice Hill, a certain young man, who was a newcomer in the town and had only recently opened a lawyer's office in High Street, was talking to Merry the curator and to Mr. Sheperd the policeman on a bench in the little gravelly court-yard outside the Museum.

This young man's name was Paul Trent, and the impression he produced upon sensitive people was that he ought to have been endowed with a less brief and less masterful name than this. He was indeed as silky and soft as a moth; and like a moth were his gentle movements. Brown were his eyes, with long lashes; very dark brown was his hair; while his skin was of a delicate ivory-yellow tint with a faint brownish tinge in the cheeks and chin. His lips were red and full, the under lip a good deal larger than the upper; and his mouth, usually a little open, showed beautiful teeth.

Taking him all in all, there was something warm, feline, and caressing about this man, and a certain air, too, for all his gentleness and quietness, of being a tartar, as they say, to meddle with or provoke.

He gave the impression—which was not entirely erroneous—of coming from some region bathed in constant sunshine. He had been called once by an antiquarian friend "Phoenician-looking"; but there seemed to be more of the sun in his composition than of the sea; and an ordinary person would have thought rather of Persia in connection with him than of anything Punic.

Trent was a nephew of old Mr. Merry and it was in consequence of what the curator had been telling him for the last six months in regard to all the new movements in the place that he had decided to come and practise in Glastonbury. He had already made friends with John Crow and Tom Barter and by their means had won for himself an entrance into the Geard household where his original personality had pleased Bloody Johnny so well that he had introduced him to Mr. Bishop, the town clerk. "The Council ought to have its own lawyer," the Mayor had remarked to Mr. Bishop. "Besides Beere is much too conservative."

The Mayor of Glastonbury in the depths of his South-Somerset heart, nourished a profound suspicion of all lawyers; but he had too many definite reasons for distrusting Mr. Beere to allow a few indefinite ones to prejudice him against Paul Trent.

"What I haven't yet been able to find in your town, Mr. Sheperd," the sallow-faced young man was now saying, "is a good vegetarian restaurant."

The Glastonbury policeman opened his left eye wide and half-closed his right eye. This was not a wink, for Mr. Sheperd would have regarded that historic gesture as a confession of confederacy in roguery. Besides he had the peculiarity of being able to retain this particular mask for as long as the precise tone of the conversation required it; namely the narration of something wonderful to the speaker but not wonderful to the hearer. "They eat raw turnips and such-like in them places, don't 'un?" Mr. Sheperd said. "I reckon us country folk see so much o' they things in daily life that us don't want to see 'un when us be enjoying ourselves at public house. Us likes to see a bit o' good meat then; such as a labouring man when *my* father were young, never saw all the year round 'cept Squire gave a parish dinner at Christmas."

It had for so long been a recurrent refrain in Mr. Merry's conversation—"When my nephew Paul comes to practise here"—that when he did come, and even persuaded Grandmother Cole to give up to him her famous front bedroom, looking out on the High Street, everyone was frantic with curiosity. Old Mrs. Cole had retained for twenty years a neat little notice at the door of her High Street house, which contained the words "Front Bedroom To Let for a Single Gentleman" but the old seamstress was so fastidious in her Single Gentlemen that this pleasant sunny retreat had become for years a sort of unused state-parlour. Mr. Barter had visited it on his first arrival; but the presence of Sis and Bert in the back room, for Barter had no love of children, would have prejudiced him against the place even if the austere morality of the old lady had not been so apparent. But "my nephew from the Scilly Isles" as Mr. Merry always called Paul Trent, seemed to have no fear of either children or morality! and something about the long-nosed young man, perhaps his mania for elaborate ablutions in absolutely cold water, perhaps his passion for seedlings in window-boxes, perhaps the unbounded respect in which the whole town held his uncle, had induced Mrs. Cole, not only to give him her front room on trial, "till I sees where we stands and how we feels," but to let him retain it indefinitely.

But if the old Glastonbury policeman had opened his left eye when he was questioned about the vegetarian restaurant, he positively gasped at the next remark of "my nephew from the Scilly Isles."

"Are there any philosophical anarchists, Uncle, in this town of yours?"

"Bless me! Tut! Tut! You don't mean to say you have *those* notions in your head still, Paul? No, I should say not! I should think *not*! Wouldn't you, Mr. Sheperd?"

But the old policeman was too dumbfounded to do more than open his right eye as wide as his left.

"Of course I'm the same as I always was, Uncle. You ought to know that! I wouldn't have come here if you hadn't told me so much about the new Mayor and his municipal factory."

"But Mr. Geard isn't an anarchist, Paul; is he, Mr. Sheperd?"

The policeman spat on the gravel at his feet. His expression seemed to say—"I can't answer for these harum-scarum officials of recent date; but I know that when I first joined the force young men would not dare to talk so wildly."

"Haven't you ever seen an anarchist before?" Paul Trent enquired point-blank of the horrified officer.

"I heard Dickery Cantle say," replied Mr. Sheperd, "that his grandfather served drink to a Chartist once, and were mentioned by name for such doings, in a sermon at St. John's."

"I met John Beere in the square this morning, Paul," interrupted Mr. Merry, in order to change the topic, "and he asked me about you. I thought he would be crusty about your being made the Council's legal advisor; but he spoke quite nicely about you. He told me that Mr. Spear from Bristol was in town again and staying at Cantle's, though not in the same room as his wife. Angela, he told me, has made great friends with Mrs. Spear."

The old policeman looked up sharply. "Thik Spear be a Rooshian spy," he murmured, "leastways that's what they tell I down at Michael's Bar; but I can't vouch for't, ye understands."

"Talk of the devil ——" cried Curator Merry, for at that moment Dave Spear, accompanied by Red Robinson, entered the

courtyard of the museum. "Ah, Mr. Spear!" cried the old
Curator, "We were just talking about you. How do you do, Mr.
Robinson! Mr. Robinson here was one of the first to discover
this vein of tin in Wookey, Paul, about which the Western
Gazette is talking so much. This is my nephew from the Scilly
Isles, gentlemen, Mr. Paul Trent."

"Well, Mr. Merry, I think I'll be taking a step round they
Ruins," threw in the old policeman at this point, feeling unequal
to cope with such an invasion of revolutionary persons.

"Don't get up, Mr. Sheperd," said Dave kindly. "I don't want
to disturb you—or you either, Mr. Merry! We were looking for
your nephew at Mr. Bishop's office; and he told us we'd probably find him here."

"I'll come, I'll come," murmured the moth-like young man,
smoothing down his silky hair with a sun-burnt hand and picking up his felt hat from the gravel. As he went off with them his
uncle could not help noticing how well his loose-fitting brown
clothes suited his general personality.

"We wanted to see you, Mr. Trent, please," began Red Robinson, "on a very important High Deer of Mr. Spear's, an High
Deer which kime to 'im in Bristol."

Dave Spear gave a nervous little laugh. It was part of his
training as a good Communist to restrain his personal feelings
in the furtherance of the cause; but he had never in his life met
with an ally, or a tool, or a confederate, more alien to his spirit
than Red Robinson. The man's vitriolic Jacobinism—reducing
everything to a personal hatred of Philip—got on Dave's nerves.
He had small reason himself on *any* account, to be indulgent to
Philip, but there was that in Red's tone whenever he referred to
him—a feverish murderous ferocity—which shocked and repelled
his whole nature.

"If you two people don't mind," said Dave, "I'd like to get a
little exercise. It's lighter than it was. The sun may come out
presently. But even if it doesn't, I'm sure it's not going to rain.
Let's go to Chalice Hill and see how Geard's buildings and diggings are getting on? I've not seen that new inscription up there,
either, that everyone's talking about."

Spear's two companions agreed at once to this suggestion and they set out along Silver Street, past the Vicarage gate, past Miss Drew's gate, past the ancient Tithe Barn, till they arrived at Chilkwell Street. They did not delay very long contemplating Mr. Geard's improvements. As they peered between the rudimentary columns of the Saxon arch at the disturbed waters of the well, Red Robinson announced that in his opinion the labourers down there had been "bithing" in the fountain. Dave protested strongly against any such idea. "It's not the weather for bathing," he said. "Besides," he added, "they're all Glastonbury men; and everyone here respects this place."

"High'd bithe 'ere if I 'ad the mind," muttered Red.

When they reached the top of Chalice Hill they hunted about for the newly discovered inscription but without success.

"It's either a fike or a bloody superstition," said Red. "If I 'ad my way I'd clear out the whole bilin' 'eap of these bloomin' relics."

"Let's sit down," said Dave, "and then we can tell Mr. Trent what we've thought of."

They all three sat down on the already brown and fast-withering bracken and leaned their backs against a hillock of green moss. Red Robinson became silent now, leaving it to Mr. Spear to explain to Paul Trent what their idea was. Although he would never have confessed it and indeed would have been handicapped by his manner of speech in the expression of it, Red felt at that moment, as the sun began to show signs of breaking through the clouds, a vague feeling of sensuous well-being very unusual to him. The personality of Sally Jones presented itself vividly to his mind. He had been seeing a lot of Sally lately and had come to the conclusion that he would ask her to marry him. He knew it was his mother's notion that he was Sally's social superior, she being the Geard's maid-of-all-work and he being foreman of a factory, but he had grown to be so fond of the girl that he was inclined to risk his mother's social disappointment.

It had been a good deal of a strain upon him, his former aspiration for the hand of Miss Crummie; and it had been worse than a strain the rebuff he had suffered from Blackie Morgan. With Sally he felt, for the first time in his relations with any woman, completely at ease.

Thus as he sat between these two gentlemen, conscious enough that they neither of them liked him, conscious enough that he had offended them by his word about "bithing" in Chalice Well, the effect of that faint flicker of sunshine upon the hillside was to throw around the sturdy figure of Sally a consolatory and comfortable warmth, like and yet unlike, what he used to feel for his mother when he was laughed at at his East-London Board-school.

"It's nice on this hill," said Paul Trent.

"Yes," agreed Dave, "and look at the way that shaft of sun— like a Rubens landscape, isn't it?—falls on Tor Field! It's peculiar to this place, a day like this, with the sun breaking through in spots, and those golden patches on the side of the Tor, and those workmen's figures in the haze. How do *you* feel about Glastonbury, Mr. Robinson? Have you come to get fond of it?"

"High hain't one for these hart and nighture feelin's," said Red bluntly; but so paradoxical is human psychology, that the moment after he had made that remark he felt an overpowering longing to have Sally Jones by his side up here, giggling when he tickled her; and crying out, "Oh, Mister Robinson, how cynical you be!" when he denounced "all this fike and 'umbug!" He didn't think of Rubens and he didn't know purple from gold in the diffusion of all these drifting vapours; but by giving himself up to this melting tenderness towards Sally Jones as associated with what he was now looking at, there took place within him a certain blending of the man's flesh and blood with the chemistry of the elements, such as made that misty October scene really more memorable to him than to either of his companions.

"It's strange to think," said Dave, "that when the Mayor has his grand opening ceremony for this new shrine, this whole hillside may be covered with a surging crowd of people from all over Europe."

"Yes," said Paul Trent. "But you won't get a crowd like that unless there's a miracle; and the time of miracles is past. What I'd like to see in Glastonbury is something very different from any of this miracle-mongering. I'd like to see—but you had something to ask me, hadn't you? We'd better come to business now—and talk later."

Paul Trent sat upright upon his rather womanish haunches, with his arms curved tightly round his knees in their soft brown covering, and his delicate hands clasped together. His figure blent harmoniously with the bracken on which he sat, and the misty sunshine seemed to caress his silky brown head as if it were thankful to find some object more amenable to its wooing than the stubbly cranium of Dave or the carrotty poll of the cockney.

He looked, sitting there, like a figure brought to that spot by the far-journeying sun itself, so that it should be sure of at least one whole-hearted devotee in that land of green shadows.

"Well, gentlemen? What did you want to see me for?" repeated this visitor from the Scilly Isles.

Dave looked at Red; and Red looked at Dave. They both were conscious of that curious nervousness which so often descends on people who have an important communication to make. It is at such times as if the piece of news itself stands with its bearers at the closed door of the unwitting recipient's mind and appears suddenly, to these very attendants, like a bride they have chosen by lamplight and that they feel a little abashed by in the light of full day.

But Dave plunged in boldly and explained how his Bristol organisation, which was the largest in Wessex, had come to the conclusion that with a little skilful local handling a real commune might be established in Glastonbury. Dave confessed that the original idea of this commune had not come from the organisation but from his wife Persephone.

"She's probably forgotten now what she said," he explained. "But she *has* these inspirations sometimes; and when I enlarged on her idea to the leaders of the Party in Bristol they were at once struck by it. You see, Mr. Trent, we all feel that Glastonbury may never again have the luck to have a Mayor like Mr. Geard and that we ought to exploit such a great chance."

The eyes of this moth-like figure grew suddenly lambent with excitement. "Did I . . . hear . . . you . . . correctly?" he cried. "Did I hear you say that your friends thought of starting a *commune* here?"

"*They* didn't think of it—nor did *I* think of it—it was my ——"

But Paul Trent had leapt up from the ground and with his

arms behind him was surveying the autumnal contest that was going on between the fitful sun-bursts and the swallowing clouds. He seemed to be staring at this scene in order to associate it forever with the idea of a Glastonbury commune.

"Goodness gracious!" he cried, "what a place this is for mists! A commune . . . Yes! I would damned well like to see a commune!"

It was quaint to hear the mild feminine expletive of "goodness gracious!" followed by so revolutionary an aspiration.

"Mr. Trent," cried Dave, his cheeks red with nervousness and his blue eyes blinking, "you're not by any chance a Communist, are you?"

The voluptuous mouth, with its heavy underlip, broke into an amused smile. He shook his head vigorously and, as he did so, resumed his seat on the bracken.

"No, Mr. Spear," he cried, laughing lightly, "I'm an anarchist! *My* commune is just the opposite of yours! It's a voluntary association altogether. But part of its natural habit would be to pool its resources for the common benefit; voluntarily of course; not by compulsion; but it would pool them, Mr. Spear!"

The flush upon Dave's cheeks died away; and the gleam faded from his blue eyes. He gave vent to the familiar little sigh which everyone who knew him was so used to, the sigh of an honest man forced by the logic of action in a world of expediency to act against his nature.

"Well," he said, repeating this sigh, "we can work together over *this*, anyway. In the Paris Commune there were Communists and Anarchists; so why not in the Glastonbury one?"

"I won't be 'arf glad to see a guillotine set up in this 'ere bloody 'ole," threw in Red Robinson pensively.

"You're confusing your dates, my good man," chuckled the Phoenician-looking stranger.

"What price dites if I 'ave the bloody 'ead of P. Crow hesquire?"

"You're vindictive, Mr. Robinson," said Paul Trent, turning his warm brown eyes upon this savage Jacobin.

"Hif you'd 'ad the hinsults high've 'ad, you'd be the sime, Mister," rejoined the Cockney touchily.

"I take the liberty to doubt it, Sir," laughed the other. "Goodness gracious! What's the point of getting spiteful? Besides personally I don't like the knife and I don't like to see blood." He gave a little shudder and made a grimace.

"You prefers bombs, I suppose," said Red sulkily. "If I hain't smart with me dites, and if I *be* 'spiteful,' as you call it, high'd never lower myself by throwing them dirty things!"

"Have you never heard of a philosophical anarchist, Mr. Robinson, or of Kropotkin or Tolstoy or Thoreau or Walt Whitman?"

"High'm a workin' man, high ham," said Red bitterly. "They don't teach hus them 'igh-class continental writers in the Old Kent Road!"

"Come, come, you two," cried Dave Spear. "This is far too important a meeting to be wasted in discussion. We've got to establish our Glastonbury commune, before we begin quarrelling how to govern it! Shall I tell Mr. Paul Trent all we've thought of, Red?"

"Has you please, Mister; but I won't 'ave none of that dirty foreign bomb-throwing where high be. 'It the bewger 'ard is what high says; but don't go blowin' up a lot of gals and kiddies!"

And once more, under what he felt to be the contemptuous hostility of both these men, Red recoiled with a delicious slide of his imagination into the soft admiring arms of Sally Jones. He too looked at the sun-smitten vapours on Gwyn-ap-Nud's hill, and allowed his body—the body of an unwearied, neatly dressed foreman—to mix with the elements; registering a vow that the very next afternoon he had a chance he would coax Sally to come up here with him.

"Well, Mr. Trent," said Dave, "it's like this. It appears that the whole of the land on which Glastonbury's built belongs to Lord P. And it appears that on the first of January all the leases of it come to an end. For the last twenty years, as far as I can make out, old Mr. Beere has collected these rents and renewed these leases; but *this* year, Persephone tells me, the old man is getting very shaky and peculiar. Angela tells Persephone that he thinks of nothing nowadays but his meals. Lord P. of course has no idea of what's happening. But the truth is his agent is in his dotage."

While Dave was speaking, Paul Trent's whole nature was leaping for joy. He was one of those people whose souls do not extend, as some souls do, outside the limits of the body. The soul of this man from the Scilly Islands penetrated his resilient, sensitive flesh and blood as the eddying water in a rock-pool might penetrate a sea-sponge.

He thought to himself, "Can it be true that I'm not in a dream? Can it be true that there's a real chance here—if it's only one in a thousand—of trying the great experiment?" His mind whirled back to this and that good omen which had come to him on his journey to Glastonbury. To feel free of all compulsion . . . to feel the physical caress of air and water and earth upon his life, as he earned his living, a free man among free men, the stupidity of society broken up . . . if he could only know it for one year! Through every vein in his warm body rushed wave after wave of excited thought. He remembered a hideous phallic scrawl which he had seen on his way to Glastonbury in a public lavatory at Exeter, the sight of which had given him a sudden loathing for the human race. "It's restraint," he thought, "that makes people like that. Free them, free them! Free life from every compulsion and people will be naturally kind and gentle and decent."

Red Robinson, while Dave was speaking, had got quite deep into a dialogue with Sally Jones, as they lay side by side on this patch of bracken. Sally was now beginning to express not only admiration for his mental qualities but in her own sweet roundabout way a wish that their position on the hillside were not so exposed. "Let's go to Bulwarks Lane," Sally was just saying with a delicious gleam in her eyes.

"The Party's idea was," said Dave Spear, "I mean *my* idea was, or to be absolutely correct Persephone's idea was, that we should get the town council to offer a bigger rent for the ground where Crow's new factory is than Crow has ever paid. But it won't be only *that* land that we'll offer to take! We'll get the town council ———"

At this point Paul Trent's excitement at the chance of realising a dream about which he had thought night and day since he lost the fifth form essay on Freedom at Penzance by advocating free love, became so intense that he remembered the name of his first nurse; a name he'd forgotten for twenty years and had tried again and again to recall. The woman was called "Brocklehurst"; and he now repeated to himself this harmless name, several times over, the name of a thirty-year-old corpse buried near Ashbury Camp in Cornwall and now serving as a Eureka of anarchistic joy upon the top of Chalice Hill.

"We'll get the town council," went on Dave Spear, "and that really means we'll get Geard, for he does just what he likes with them, to rent from Lord P. the whole of his Glastonbury property; and we'll bribe Lord P. into this by giving him a much larger rent than he's been getting from the tradesmen. Why, all High Street belongs to him, except the Abbot's Tribunal, which goes with the Ruins! Once in the position of lease-landlord for the whole of the town, the council could get rid of all opposition and start a co-operative commune. It would have its factories. It would have its own retail shops. Though the Ruins belong to the Nation, or to the Church—I forget which—Chalice Hill, Glastonbury Tor, Wirral Hill, all belong to Lord P.'s estate; and though of course Geard couldn't *buy* the land, if the council got a long lease it would come to the same thing. He'd have the right, that is the council would have the right, to admit visitors, or not to admit them, as it pleased. The Ruins would remain, of course— but they'd remain as church property or national property, whichever they are, in the midst of our commune. They'd be a little island of mediævalism in the most modern city-state in the world!"

Paul Trent sat straight once more upon the extreme tips of his buttocks. He rubbed back his brown hair with both his hands. "Uncle hinted to me that I'd find things pretty interesting down here," he said, "and goodness gracious! I certainly have. Mercy me! What good luck that he told me to come!"

"Of course," said Dave, "I have not had time to get any definite word from Geard yet. It all depends on Geard. He may have to help the council with money on January first, if they can't offer Lord P. enough out of their local taxes. Yes! It all

depends on Geard; but when I talked to him about it a few days
ago he seemed interested. At least I *thought* he was. But I always
feel awkward and uneasy with Geard. I don't know why. I feel as
if I were looking down a precipice where ferns and roots and
grasses protrude but where you can't see the bottom. Do you
have any feeling of that sort, Red?"

The man from the Scilly Isles took this question addressed to
their companion as a deliberate piece of irony; but he was
totally wrong.

Red Robinson's opinion of Crummie's father, uttered in the
attentive ears of his two fellow-conspirators, showed that to him
at all events there was no guile in the question.

"Geard's a 'oly old 'umbug. That's what Geard is. But he's
a harss hover money. No more high-deer of money 'as Bloody
Johnny got than my boot-sole 'as. 'Ees strugglin' to ruin 'isself
as 'ard as you or high are tryin' to better ourselves; and that's
sayin' a lot!" And the foreman leered at Dave, as much as to
say: "We know what a good thing *you* mike of being a
Communist!"

Did any one of these three conspirators to establish a Glastonbury commune realize their deep psychic luck in having let their
idea escape upon the air, *for the first time,* on the summit of
Chalice Hill?

Not one of them! And yet to the invisible naturalists of Glastonbury, commenting curiously upon the strange history of the
place, it must have been apparent that they were led to select this
spot for the inauguration of their wild scheme by some kind of
instinct.

It was at any rate in a voice full of solemn intensity that Paul
Trent now enquired point-blank of his two companions whether
they wanted him to be their intermediary with the great Glastonbury landowner, and Dave and Mr. Robinson delayed not to
make it clear to him that this was precisely what they *did* want
him to do.

"As a lawyer," Dave said to him, "you'll realise better than
we do what arguments to use. But everyone knows how badly
Lord P. is in need of money these days; and of course the council has the power to raise the local taxes; and of course the

Mayor—in so important a matter—would be prepared to advance a good big sum on the Council's security. We ought to be able to offer him at least half as much again as Philip Crow can afford. The man *must* agree. He can't help agreeing when it's a question of so much money! It may just tide him over these difficult days."

"It mikes a pretty enough tile, Misters," said Red sarcastically, "but *high* think, if you harsts *me*, that when Christmas comes we shall be sitting 'ere on our bloody harses just the sime has now, and that blasted Crow—you must excuse a workingman's feelin's, Mr. Spear—siling 'is airplines just the sime! 'Tain't as heasy, as you misters seem to think, to 'umble these 'ere capitalists. They wants lead put in 'em—that's what *they* want—a few hounces of lead in their tin-digging bellies. *That's* what would settle 'em! Set 'em up against a wall and pump some good lead into 'em!"

"Still feeling spiteful, Mr. Robinson?" said the man from the Scilly Isles. "Well! I'll do my best, Mr. Spear, with this landowner of yours. When do you want me to see him? Does he live about here? When will you have a definite offer, ready in writing, for me to show him? And when had I better talk to Geard? Shall I go round to his house after dinner tonight?"

Dave nodded eagerly, his blue eyes radiant. "Yes, yes!" he whispered, as if they were already in the ante-room of Lord P., "by all means go round to Geard's tonight. I don't think I'll go myself. He doesn't like a lot of people fussing about him. Better be quite frank with him about your being an anarchist and so on, and about the Comrades in Bristol being so keen. Better tell him, though, that it wasn't *their* idea. Tell him it was my wife's. He's a great feminist, Geard is!" And Dave grinned like a schoolboy.

While this conspiracy against him was going on on the summit of Chalice Hill Philip Crow, with the Taunton road-contractor and a land-surveyor from Evercreech at his side, was standing between Lake Village Field and the rain-swollen river.

The childish robber band from Red's alley and from Paul Trent's back room had left their friend Number One's gardenfence and had advanced in loose formation, across the big airplane meadow, to see what was going on. While the Evercreech surveyor made his measurements and while the Taunton contractor with notebook and pencil, lost himself in his calculations Philip was left alone with his own thoughts. He was leaning upon one of those many walking-sticks of The Elms' umbrella-stand that lived under the matriarchal rule of Tilly's umbrella. He was following with his eyes the building of the bridge—at present more imaginary than the Eel Bridge or the Sword Bridge of the legend, which was to take his tin across the Brue.

From where he stood he could see dimly through the sun-smitten mists the vague outlines of Pomparlès Bridge on the road to Street, where John had had his vision of the falling sword of the British king. The mist-enveloped sun was luminous enough to cover all the meadows around him with a rich glow. This glow became pure yellow light when Philip, hearing the voices of the children approaching him, turned away from the two men and looked westward. A small lombardy poplar stood up, darkly outlined in the midst of yellow luminousness, and Philip could see a dark bird of some kind—it was really a six months' old rook—perched on a swaying twig on the top of this little tree. The rook was heavy and the twig kept bending under its weight; so that in order to retain its balance it was compelled to flutter with its great wings every now and then. It was Philip's long motionlessness that alone had allowed it to settle so near a human being.

It was at the moment when Philip saw the rook fly off with a terrific flapping of its wings and with an angry caw, that he observed three children, a little boy, and a little girl holding a small child by the hand, standing about three hundred yards away and watching intently the curious movements of another little girl who was apparently approaching him by the furtive method of running from tree to tree.

The child had now reached the poplar from which the rook had just flown and Philip was able to detect her tumbled brown hair and rough grey skirt peeping out from the poplar's trunk. He took a cautious step or two in the direction of the tree. "It's all right, child," he called out. "What is it? Is it a game you're playing? Come here and tell me. I won't hurt you!" Thus spoke the instinctive father in Philip; for he had been quick to recognise the little daughter of Blackie Morgan.

The effect of his call was twofold. It sent the three other children scampering off at top-speed towards the safety of Number One's fence, while it caused Morgan Nelly, in order to prevent herself from yielding to a similar panic, to cling tightly to the poplar trunk with both her thin arms.

It was thus that Philip found his only child when he reached the tree. Her forehead was pressed against it and her fingers were frantically clutching its bark. He began to speak caressingly the moment he approached her, for he was touched by the look of those thin arms; and when he reached the tree he did what was perhaps the wisest thing he could have done, he sat down with his shoulders against it, so that the back of his cap almost touched her clasped hands.

Morgan Nelly could have escaped now if she'd wanted to and run straight off to Number One's fence, from behind which Jackie and Sis and Bert, under the protection of Number One himself, were watching with intense interest the development of this exciting drama; but when her father calmly lighted a cigarette and began to talk to her without trying to pull her arms away from the tree she felt at once reassured.

"I know who you are, child," said Philip. "I knew when I saw your friends. For I know the children you go about with."

There was no reply; but he caught a faint sound over his head which indicated that she'd unclasped her fingers.

"If you'll come and sit down here for a minute and talk to me, I'll give you a penny."

There was no reply to this either; but the surface of the poplar tree served so well as a whispering gallery that he could hear her talking in a low murmur to herself. This was an old psychological device of Morgan Nelly's; and it was a way to exchange thoughts without the overt shock to one's shyness of officially addressing a stranger or being addressed. The stranger listened— indeed if he was wise he listened in silence—and Nelly acted as chorus for both.

"Jackie is just the same as Sis and Bert," she rambled on. "He dared me to do it and said he'd follow me and come close when I were talking to Mr. Crow; but he ain't following me. He's talking to Number One. But they're all looking to see if Mr.

Crow takes me up and sends me to jail for running arter he. If *he* did do that, I'd be glad! I'd be glad to go anywhere that isn't *here*—even if 'twere jail."

Philip puffed on at his cigarette, keeping a sharp eye upon the contractor and upon the surveyor who were now engaged in an earnest colloquy and an alert eye upon the three children and the old man. The only observer of his dialogue with his daughter upon whom Philip cast a relaxed, carefree and devil-may-care eye, the eye of a true begetter of bastards, was Betsy, Number One's brown and white cow, whose neck was stretched beyond all decency and restraint between the rails of her master's fence so as to crop the less familiar grass of Philip's field.

"Perhaps—I say *perhaps*—I might pay for a little girl I know, going to the seaside or to some very *nice* place."

This was a bribe beyond the power of resistance in Philip's daughter. She slipped round the tree and stood in front of him, her hands behind her back.

"Mummy wouldn't let me take no money, for *nothing*," she said emphatically, looking down upon her progenitor with knitted brows. "That is, Mummy wouldn't, unless she were a little squiffy but not too squiffy. When she's *too* squiffy, Mummy do cry for Dad."

"Was your Dad's name . . . Morgan?" enquired Philip with intent to discover how much the child knew.

Morgan Nelly nodded vigorously. "But you," she added, "be me godfather . . . and a wicked, miser one; what'll never do me no good if I wait till Judgment Day."

This revelation of the manner in which his name was passed about between mother and daughter was very significant to Philip.

"I mustn't set fire to the grass, must I?" he remarked amiably, extinguishing his cigarette by pressing it into the side of a mole-hill. He hitched himself up, after this, and fearing dampness in the grass thrust his cap beneath him.

"Your hair baint *very* grey!" exclaimed Morgan Nelly.

Philip smiled and instinctively smoothed his hair down with both his hands under this feminine scrutiny.

"Who said it was?" he enquired casually.

"Red said you was a grey-haired bewger," said the child. "What *be* a bewger, Mister?"

"Red? Oh, you mean that chap Robinson, that I dismissed for cheek. Is *he* a friend of your mother's?"

"He baint now," responded Nelly confidentially. "Mummy do loathe the sight of his ugly mug."

"I'm glad to hear that," said Philip grimly. "Your mother and I are in agreement *there*, anyway."

"Number One says that they wold funny men do walk about when 'tis dark in this here girt field."

"You mean old Abel over there?" said Philip. "What funny men is he talking about?"

"Them as lived where they moundies be . . . them as had King Arthur for their king."

"Your friend's shaky in his history, Nelly," said Philip, and he was conscious of an agreeable warmth under his ribs as he called his daughter by her name.

"Weren't King Arthur king in them days?" she asked.

"Not till much later, Nelly, according to most accounts."

"Who *were* king in they times when folks lived on hurdles in water?"

"Heavens, child! I don't know," groaned her father. A sharp pang at that moment shook some nerve within him. It would be nice to come home of an evening from the office and listen to this child's chatter. "I wonder if Tilly *would* ——" he thought.

But the little girl had become very pensive. She too found it extremely nice to have someone in addition to Number One with whom she could talk on the subjects that filled her mind. Jackie always wanted to *be* the hero of every conversation! What *she* liked was to enjoy prolonged speculation with someone clever enough to know when King Arthur lived but too grown-up to want to *be* King Arthur.

" 'Tis queer," she remarked, "to think of they old funny men rowing in their boats where you be sitting now!"

But though Philip had no desire to be King Arthur, or to be any unknown neolithic hero, he resembled Jackie in his inability to brood for more than a minute over the mystery of the passing of time.

"Have you seen that boat in the museum, Nelly?" he enquired now, bringing the subject down to something concrete.

"No, Mister, I ain't seen 'un; and don't want to see 'un if Mr. Merry be there. He scolded me turble once when us played in museum-yard. He took Jackie's ball away and never gived it back. He kept Jackie's ball, he did, for his own self. 'Tweren't right of 'ee. Jackie said he'd tell policeman. But policeman be his friend. Policeman be allus in thik yard talking to he."

Philip was silent. His daughter's attitude to these local magnates was so different from his own that he felt at a loss for a suitable comment.

"If you was one of they Lake Village men, Mister, and I were talking to 'ee, would you have a girt stick with a sharp flint on 'un and thee-self all naked like, or maybe a few big dock-leaves round thee's waist?"

Annoyed with himself for not being able to deal better with her rambling talk, which had now become so easy and natural, and was thus very agreeable to him, Philip actually felt his cheeks beginning to burn.

"You'd be glad enough I had a spear with a flint top," he remarked, "if that cow over there were a sabre-toothed tiger or a mammoth."

The little girl's eyes shone. "Would 'ee go after it now with thik spear and rip its belly open for it?" she enquired with panting eagerness.

Philip began to experience a definite fear that the child would soon want him to play a game with her, and rush off across the field with his stick, pretending that the harmless Betsy were a mammoth.

"Do you learn history at school, Nelly?" he enquired.

"Would you spear 'un under his ugly tail or would you spear 'un in his girt mouth?" said Nelly, disregarding his reference to school and to the study of history.

Philip liked it when she called him "you" instead of "Mister." He stared at the ground beyond his daughter's grey skirt. Yes, it was certainly a queer thing that this grass should have been covered with a brackish expanse of water in those old days; but it was not a thing he cared to think about. In some subtle way it seemed to make his present activities less important. She certainly had a mind, this child; but it was more like her mother's than his! He remembered that it was just this sort of vague and to him rather desolate brooding that the big-eyed char-girl used to indulge in when he talked to her in Mrs. Legge's "other house."

"I'm going to make a new road into Street and a bridge over the Brue," he suddenly announced to her. He had not intended to say these words. He had not intended to refer to his present undertakings at all. It must have been a subconscious desire to boast of *some* great deed before his offspring, so as to make up to her for not going on with that story about mammoth-spearing.

"I don't like roads," said Morgan Nelly. "I likes tow-paths and cattle-droves best. Jackie and me's going to play Indians in Wick Wood when the leaves are all down!"

"What will the gamekeeper say?" said Philip, whose idea of woods was associated with the sporting activities of his friend Zoyland.

"Oh, Jackie do know a gap into they woods! Sis can't get Bert through thik gap, but *I* can. I lifts he and pushes he till he be over. Us get bluebells there—bunches on 'em! And Jackie found a Muggie's nest wi' five eggs when us were there. Do 'ee hold wi' taking more'n two eggs, Mister? Sis says 'tisn't right to take 'em all. She did cry, Sis did, when Jackie took 'em; and I made him put 'em back; all but two. Sis said the mother bird was wailing something pitiful, but Sis be soft over such things."

"I'm going to make a bridge over there," repeated Philip. He seemed driven by an impulse he could not resist to try at all costs to impress the child's mind. "If you don't like roads, Nelly, you surely like bridges?"

"That's Pomparlès over there," she said in an awed whisper, "where King Arthur threw away his sword."

"I'm going to build a new bridge, another bridge, much bigger than Pomparlès."

The child looked at him with a look of horror. She was evidently deeply shocked.

"Not anywhere *near* Pomparlès, are you?" she asked; while an expression of aversion and distaste came into her eyes.

"But, Nelly——" he pleaded with her, as if she were a grown-up person, "my bridge will be ever so much bigger and broader; and a great many lorries will pass over it. Pomparlès is a shaky old erection. Probably it'll have to be taken down. Progress can't stop because people are sentimental about a heap of old stones. That's narrowness, Nelly; that's prejudice, that's being soft and silly—like you said your friend Sis was!"

But he had shocked the little girl through and through by what he had said; and no special pleading, no references to Sis, could undo the harm he had done.

"Pomparlès taken down? King Arthur's Bridge taken down? I don't like you, Mister! I hate you!"

Philip was astonished at the contortion of fury into which her face was convulsed.

"Come, come, come," he said, "don't let's quarrel the moment we've begun to make friends." He jumped up lightly to his feet and made as if he would lay his hands on her shoulders.

"They won't *let* you pull Pomparlès Bridge down!" she cried, skipping back out of his reach. "Mr. Geard won't *let* you!"

"Mr. Geard couldn't stop me if I decided to do it," cried Philip rapidly growing as angry as the child was. It was not a sign of Philip's littleness but of his greatness that he could get so vehement in a dispute with a little girl. Napoleon would have done so; so would Alexander the Great; so would Nelson, so would Achilles. Most modern rulers would have laughed at her and retorted with some quip too ironical for her to understand.

"He could! He could! He could!" cried the little girl and putting out her tongue she shook her small fist violently at him and scampered off at a wild rush towards Number One's cottage.

Philip put on his cap very carefully and gravely, picked up his stick, and walked with leisurely steps towards the two men. "I shall say I scolded her for her bad behavior," he thought. "She got impatient, like a spoilt child, in a minute, and answered rudely and ran away." Thus would he explain to anyone who had seen their quarrel what it was that had happened.

"You've taken all the steps, I presume, Sir," said the contractor to him a little later, "about getting leave from the county, and so on, to have this new road and this new bridge made?"

"Certainly. Of course!" replied Philip. "I've been to the government offices in London about it, as well as to the county offices in Taunton. The only thing that could possibly delay it would be some of these small proprietors—like that old man over there—making difficulties and asking too much. From what you two gentlemen tell me it would really be most advisable to purchase his permission." He raised his voice at this point so as to include the Evercreech surveyor in his audience. "I was saying that I think it *will* be necessary to pay whatever compensation that old Mr. Twig demands. If we brought it through Lake Village Field there *might* be some red-tape difficulties with the National Office and those things always delay matters so."

"They do, Sir," said the surveyor.

"That's what I always says myself, Sir," said the contractor.

It was at this point that Philip's eye caught sight of two figures advancing along the tow-path on the high bank of the Brue. They were coming from the direction of Street and following the river in its northwesterly windings. Philip had no difficulty in recognising these figures—for he was as long-sighted as an Isle-of-Ely heron watching for fish—as those of Lady Rachel and Ned Athling.

Ned Athling was making his plans to leave his parents at Middlezoy and take a job which Geard had offered him in the town, the alluring job of editing an official Glastonbury newspaper—to come out every week. Ned was to have a completely free hand as editor of this paper, which was to deal with every aspect, political, economical, social, poetical, mystical, of the life of the town.

Lady Rachel's feminine relatives, especially the old Lady in Bath, had been pressing her father with every kind of importunity to bring to an end her stay in Glastonbury. Day by day however she had assiduously been drinking those chalybeate waters, several springs of which could be reached in various places in the town much nearer than the hillside where they originated, and her health was obviously making such improvement that Dr. Fell had had little difficulty in persuading Lord P. to disregard his family's clamourings.

It was a question, however, how far this attitude of his would change—Lady Rachel had now passed her nineteenth birthday—when it reached his ears that Ned Athling was in town and that the girl was assisting him, as she fully intended to do, in his editorial labours. It was about this peril to their exciting project that they were now talking, with their heads close together, as they came drifting along that tow-path, far too engrossed in each other to notice the man and the little girl under the poplar tree or the child's wild escape across the field.

The first number of the Glastonbury paper was to come out in a month from now. The printing presses, the type-setting materials, the machinery and the office furniture were already in working order in a very old building in the outskirts of Paradise, one of the oldest buildings in that neighborhood and one much easier to adapt to their purpose than anything they could have found in the centre of Glastonbury. The only point where the Mayor had not given his editor a free hand was in the matter of the name of the paper. Mr. Geard wished it to be called *The Wayfarer*.

Philip had no desire just then to encounter "Lady Rachel and her young man," as everyone in Glastonbury called tnem; but his searching fen-man's eyes, unconsciously combing the landscape on every side for signs of living creatures, was arrested now by the figures of two men advancing along the same tow-path from the opposite direction. Philip recognised one of these men at once as Sam Dekker; but the other puzzled him for a time. At last he decided, and decided correctly, that it was young Jimmy Rake, a subordinate of Mr. Stilly's in the Glastonbury bank.

Sam had begun to make it a custom of his to befriend the friendless in Glastonbury, of which there were, he very quickly discovered, more and queerer specimens than he had ever surmised existed in the days before he was caught in his Vita Nuova. Jimmy Rake was one of the loneliest of all these friendless ones. The other lads persecuted him at the bank. Mr. Stilly found him incompetent. His landlady in George Street regarded him as "not all there."

The truth was that James Rake, an orphan from the little town of Ilchester, was a youth paralysed by shyness. His miserable shyness was indeed his only claim to his landlady's view of him and the principal cause of Mr. Stilly's contempt for him. In other respects his character was simple, colourless and commonplace. If what is called "distinction" by virtuosos in human qualities was the chief hope of the lad's salvation, Jimmy Rake was undoubtedly damned. "Rake is a Fool" was what one of the little boys at the Sherborne Preparatory had scrawled in chalk one morning on the headmaster's blackboard; and even that indulgent gentleman, as he wiped these marks away with the duster kept on his desk, made no denial of this popular verdict.

Rake *was* a fool. He was a fool at cricket, a fool at football, a fool at examinations, and the worst fool of all with women and girls. There was an old canal in the marshes some six miles from Glastonbury on the borders of Huntspill Moor and because of a rare kind of water-mint that grew there this was a place where Sam and his father had for two or three seasons, and as late as October too, found specimens of the Large Copper butterfly. James Rake was interested in butterflies. He was not stirred over them to the passionate intensity of the two Dekkers; but he *was* interested; and he had made a gallant effort to overcome his shyness when Sam invited him to this walk on early-closing day.

They had gone by way of Meare, and Westhay Level, and Catcott Burtle, and the northern fringe of Edington Heath; and they were now returning by way of Meare Heath and Stileway.

Sam had quickly discovered that there was a solid, compact mass of what might be described as "honest wood" in Jimmy Rake's nature. The lad had the power of walking steadily on, for miles and miles, without uttering a syllable; nor were his remarks, when he did speak, of any very vivid or original character. The most striking observation he had made today in the whole of their ten-mile walk was what he remarked as they were crossing some fallen branches in a spinney near Edington Junction, on the Burnham and Evercreech Railway, "The white ones" —he was speaking of toadstools—"seem to grow on the dead wood; and the black ones on the living wood." Sam had taken advantage of this remark to expatiate at some length on the toadstools of the neighbourhood, in which he and his father had specialised together for one whole autumn a couple of years ago;

but his discourse seemed only to prove that the abundant "woodi-
ness" in the nature of Rake the Fool was not the kind upon which
either black or white fungi spontaneously flourished.

At the moment when Philip's long-sighted vision was concentrated upon the man and the woman approaching from the south
and the two men approaching from the west, Sam himself realised to what an encounter he was leading his shy friend and he
looked about him, wondering how to avoid this couple who were
directly in their path. Ned Athling too became just then aware of
a group of three men standing in the field to the north of them
and a couple of men advancing from the northwest. There was
a small unimportant bridge over the Brue just at that place,
called Cold Harbour Bridge, and it was quite close to this spot
that Philip was now standing. A little tributary of the river left
the main stream at this point and flowed southeast to Northload
Bridge, and thence lost itself among the orchards of the town.
This Cold Harbour Bridge formed, in fact, the centre of an imaginary circle on the circumference of which these three groups of
human beings were now arrested in a threefold consciousness of
one another's presence.

To the surveyor from Evercreech there was nothing in the least
remarkable about the fact that two men should be approaching
Cold Harbour Bridge from the west, and a man and woman from
the south, following the same tow-path. The contractor was wondering whether he would be permitted to bring his own workmen
from Taunton for the construction of the new road or whether
the town council of Glastonbury would insist on his employing
local labourers upon the job. The surveyor from Evercreech was
wondering if his wife's father, now suffering from an attack of
pleurisy, would leave them his small dairy farm of four Jersey
cows, when he came to die.

But there was, as a matter of fact, no geographic section of
the environs of Glastonbury that had not been so often the stage
of portentous human encounters that chance itself seemed, in the
weariness of her long experience, to have found it easier to slide
events through the smooth grooves of fate than to shake them
into her favourite surprises; for from under Cold Harbour Bridge

which was the precise centre of the equilateral triangle formed by these now quite stationary groups of people, all wondering how they should avoid contact with one another, arose the tall lean shape of Mother Legge's aged doorkeeper, Young Tewsy, holding in one hand a large blood-stained fish which he had just killed and in the other a long fishing-rod.

"I've a caught he! I've a caught he!" he kept repeating and gazed round him with the frantic gestures of one demanding an audience.

Philip looked from the surveyor to the contractor with the air of a monarch who asks his courtiers to rid him of an intrusive churl.

"He's a tramp," said the Taunton man.

"He's one of the town's idiots," said the gentleman from Ever-creech who was hoping for the death of his father-in-law in order to inherit four Jersey cows.

But Young Tewsy was so anxious to tell the whole world of his successful kill that he climbed up upon Cold Harbour Bridge and held his catch in the air; waving it first in the direction of Sam and Jimmy and then in the direction of Lady Rachel. It was enough for Lady Rachel that an old dilapidated beggar was appealing to her in some way. She ran forward at top-speed to the bridge, followed at a slow and indeed at a sulky pace by Mr. Athling who began to feel extremely uneasy at the presence of so many people. People seemed to be appearing from every quarter of the horizon. Mr. Athling could see Sam and Jimmy in one direction, Philip and his two companions in another, while in addition to these he could perceive in the distance, on the other side of the big field, a group of children, an old man, and a cow with its head outstretched between wooden railings.

The sun was breaking through the clouds in so irregular a manner that one stream of light fell upon the tall beggar waving the fishing-rod and another upon the children and the cow.

If Rachel Zoyland followed her hereditary instinct by rushing to the spot where a flag of appeal or of disturbance had been raised, Sam Dekker followed *his* hereditary instinct by running at top-speed to where so excited a fisherman was brandishing a great fish. Poor Jim Rake, however, though not from pique or sulkiness like Athling, but from a paralysing spasm of nervousness followed Sam at a snail's pace. *He* looked neither to the right or to the left, for fear of being summoned to shake hands with someone, but kept his eyes fixed on the blood-stained fish, whose own eyes, which five minutes before had been searching the vistas of flowing water through the weed stalks of the Brue, had already taken upon them that glazed lidless stare of a dead creature upon a marble slab.

"You *have* caught a *wonderful* fish!" panted Rachel, when she reached Young Tewsy's side upon the narrow bridge.

"Ain't I, your ladyship,"—for he knew her well by sight— "ain't I?" gasped the old man. " 'Tis the girt chub of Lydford Mill come upstream for they autumn flies. I've a-dipped for he every mornin' since September and every noon when Missus could spare I to come out—and now I've a-hooked 'un. There 'un be, your ladyship—there 'un be, Mr. Dekker"—for Sam, bowing awkwardly to Rachel, was now on the bridge too—"and 'twere I what hooked 'un! Ain't he summat to see? Looksee what a girt mouth!"

"You've killed it too roughly, Tewsy," said Sam. "You shouldn't have bloodied it so." He took the fish in his hands. "Yes, he's right," he remarked to Rachel. "I've seen you myself, haven't I?" he added, this time addressing the fish, as he lifted up its dorsal fin with his forefinger. "I've seen you, down at Lydford in your own Mill Pool; but I never thought to hold you in my hands on Cold Harbour Bridge."

Philip, Jimmy Rake, and Ned Athling were all standing on the tow-path now, while Young Tewsy, supported by Lady Rachel and Sam, remained above them on the bridge. Philip took off his hat to Lord P.'s daughter and made some laconic remark about the nourishing quality of Brue mud.

"Look, Jimmy!" cried Sam, holding up the fish for his friend's inspection.

"It won't be nourishing much longer, Mr. Crow, if your chemicals begin to get into it," said Ned unkindly, venting his vexation upon the manufacturer.

"*My* chemicals!" murmured Philip, "I assure you, Athling, that nothing from my ——"

"This is Mr. James Rake, Lady Rachel," said Sam, handing back the fish to Young Tewsy.

Mr. Rake tried to remember that it was best to take his cap off by the front rather than to clutch it by the top. The lad's cheeks got very red when Rachel remarked that she had seen him in the bank.

The man from Evercreech, forgetting about the four Jersey cows, now approached the group, while the contractor in order to retain his self-respect began writing in his notebook. His West-Country awareness of the presence of Lord P.'s daughter, however, made him feel so self-conscious that all he could write down were the words "Saunders Brothers, Builders and Contractors, Taunton."

So deep however were the centuries-old grooves, into which fate had moulded the historic atmosphere round Lake Village Field, that chance now, playing at being fate, brought to the lips of Young Tewsy a significant retort, as if to compel some-one among these people to take note of what was going on. The contractor from Taunton had just added to the words "Saunders Brothers" the words "Due from Mr. Philip Crow," when Philip, putting his hand into one of his trouser pockets and bringing out a lot of loose silver, said to Young Tewsy, who was endeavouring to take his rod to pieces—"I'll give you ten shillings for that chub, my good fellow!" Philip had been hesitating between men-tioning five shillings or ten; but he had decided on this enormous sum, because of the presence of Lady Rachel, to whom, as soon as he had obtained it, he intended to offer the fish as a chival-rous gift.

It was then that Young Tewsy had uttered the following remark.

" 'Tis for Missus, Sir. Tain't for sale, Sir. Missus 'ave been hinterested, Sir,"—Tewsy in his excitement was reverting to his North London accent—"hever since I began fishing for the fish. The fish 'ave been on Missus' mind, Sir. She 'ave dreamed of the fish, Sir. She wants to heat the fish, Sir. She says—yes, my Lidy, 'tis Mrs. Legge I be speaking of—she says, Sir, when she was little, Sir, they 'ad a sighing in town about the fish. She said they used to sigh:

> 'When Chub of Lydford do speak like human
> On grass where Joseph has broken bread,
> Be it a man or be it a woman,
> In the Isle of Glaston they'll raise the Dead.'

And this 'ere fish"—he had laid the chub down upon the grass while he pulled his rod apart and wound up the line—"this 'ere fish cried 'Whew! Whew! Whew!' just like a dying Christian, when I 'it its 'ead to stop its floppin' on grass. Missus 'as been all wrought-up, Sir, in a manner of speaking, by thinking on this 'ere fish. If I were to sell 'ee the fish, thanking 'ee kindly, Sir, all the sime; or sell it to your Lidyship, thanking *you* kindly all the sime, Missus 'ud be terrible fretted. She do yearn to put 'er 'ands on this 'ere fish's tile and to scratch 'erself with this 'ere fish's fins, and to thrust 'er thumb down this 'ere fish's throat. 'Tis meat and marrow to Missus to 'old this 'ere fish to 'er bosom. So thankin' you, Sir, all the sime and thankin' *you*, my Lidy, it 'ud never do for me to let a living soul 'ave this 'ere ancient fish, save only Missus."

Having uttered this diplomatic ultimatum, the old man, leaving behind him in Lady Rachel's nostrils a mingled odour of sweat and fish-slime, shuffled down the bridge steps muttering: "God-den, gentles, god-den, Lidy!"

Philip could not help following him with a wistful glance as he went off towards Mr. Twig's hut; for he thought to himself—"*She* will like to see that fish!"

The group of persons at Cold Harbour Bridge now began hurriedly to escape from one another; Sam and Jimmy Rake following in the track of Young Tewsy towards the Godney Road, Lady Rachel and Ned turning to their right and pursuing the tributary of the Brue that led to Northload Bridge and the centre of the town.

The great goddess chance, still finding her line of least resistance in the smooth fate-grooves of Glastonbury, now decreed that, as the two lovers passed Number Two's shop they should catch sight of Mr. Evans and old Bartholomew Jones talking in its interior with the door wide open.

Mr. Jones had left the hospital; but finding that his business had increased considerably, owing to the town's curiosity—especially the town's feminine curiosity—with regard to the eccentric Welshman, he had begun to negotiate with Mr. Evans, a slow and infinitely cautious proceeding on the old man's part, on the subject of some sort of partnership. Rachel caught Mr. Evans' eye as they passed and the lovers drifted into the shop.

Ned Athling, his temper now quite recovered, had been discussing with Rachel as they came along the possibility of making this capture of the famous chub of Lydford the subject of his first article for *The Wayfarer*.

Old Jones bowed himself off on the appearance of the two young people; for he said in his sly old heart, "Me pardner will be sprightlier in coaxin' they to buy summat if I baint there."

Athling therefore lost no time in narrating to Mr. Evans the whole adventure of the fish; while Rachel, tired after their long stroll by the river, sank down to rest in one of the big Louis Quatorze chairs. The girl had noticed before that some of her happiest moments came to her when she was feeling exhausted like this. She had noticed it especially since she had come to Glastonbury. She had even spoken of it to Ned. "It's a delicious feeling," she had told him. "It's just as if I sank down through some yielding element, into a world like this one; yes! in every particular like this one, only with all the annoying things left out."

She took off her hat now and let it lie in her lap while she pushed back her brown curls from her forehead, glancing as she did so at one of Old Jones' gilt mirrors. "How white I am," she thought, "and how hot and untidy and funny-looking! I wish I could get the smell of that old man's clothes out of my nose. How some smells do cling to anyone. And there's fish-blood on my hands too." She lay back in the big gilt chair and crossed her legs, clutching the rim of her hat. Yes! It was coming, it was coming, that lovely sensation. It was like sinking through deep water, water of a pale glaucous colour, and seeing everything through water.

"Is that because Glastonbury was an island once?" she thought. But how perfect it was to sit here, with the sounds of the

street and the air-waves of misty sunshine coming in together
through the open door! How handsome Ned looked talking to
this man; and what passionate interest the man was taking in
what he was telling him! But everything was so lovely and
tender and wavering to her as she let her head sink back. "There's
something heavenly," she thought, "about this feeling. It's just
like being dead and yet intensely happy. I've had it before, I
think, in this shop. Certainly I had it the other day in the souvenir shop. It's something about this place. I don't know what it is.
I'll tell Father I *won't* go to London, whatever Aunt Betsy says!"

The girl was right about Mr. Evans looking passionately interested. He looked as if he were plunged into some interior vision
that rendered him totally unaware of what he was doing with his
hands, or with his feet, or with his body. For instance, the moment Ned Athling had finished his narration Mr. Evans sank
down on a small chair opposite Lady Rachel and stretched out
his long legs with their great square-toed boots and grey socks
and allowed his long arms to hang down on each side of the
chair. His shirt, as well as his coat, was so much too short for
him that not only were his bony wrists but perceptible portions
of his lean arms nakedly visible to view, as his hands swung
there with the long fingers dangling.

Lady Rachel was unable to resist a slight flicker of retreat
from the presence of these great boots and rumpled grey socks
thus protruded towards her; but being the well-bred girl she
was, she restrained this movement at once and did not even draw
in her own slender legs. Thus between the boot-soles of Rachel
and the boot-soles of Mr. Evans there was not space to drop a
feather.

Athling approached the back of his lady's chair and leaned
both his elbows upon it so that his knuckles almost touched her
head. Thus as Mr. Evans began his commentary upon what he
had just heard there was no more distance between the lovers
than there was between Mr. Evans and Lady Rachel and the magnetism that accompanied the Welshman's words linked them all
three for a space together.

The extraordinary thing about Mr. Evans' face this afternoon,
as the lovers watched it, was the rapidity of its changes from a

mask of hollow, expressionless desolation into lineaments of prophetic and inspired passion.

"I never thought I would be here . . . in this Death-Island of my people . . . for Glastonbury is the Gwlad-yr-Hav, the Elysian Death-Fields of the Cymric tribes . . . on the day when that fish was killed. Of course I knew about it. Friends of mine, when I was at Jesus, went down to Lydford to see it. They never *did* see it themselves; but they talked to old men and old women who had. It must be fabulously old, that fish! Tewsy ought never to have done it; but if anyone was to do it he was the one. Of course he won't live the year out. But he'll have the happiest year he's ever had in his life; and he'll probably die in his sleep. What I am now telling you two . . . and you can believe I would not tell everyone these things . . . is mostly from the Book of Taliessin and from the Triads and from David ap Gwilym and from Lady Charlotte's Mabinogion and from Sir John Rhys, and from the Red Book of Hergest, and from the Vita Gildae and from the Black Book of Carmarthen, but in my own Vita Merlini I've gone further than any of them into these things. Few Glastonbury people realise that they are actually living in *yr Echwyd*, the land of Annwn, the land of twilight and death, where the shores are of Mortuorum Mare, the Sea of the Departed. This place has always been set apart . . . from the earliest times . . . Urien the Mysterious, Avallach the Unknown, were Fisher Kings here . . . and for what did they fish? The Triads only dare to hint at these things . . . the Englynion only to glance at them . . . Taliessin himself . . . did you know that? . . . was netted with the fish in the weir, by Elphin the son of Gwydno Garanhir . . . And for what . . . and for what did this Fisher King . . ."

Mr. Evans' voice now rose to a tremulous pitch of excitement. Ned Athling's hands crossing the back of Lady Rachel's gilded throne were now actually in contact with the girl's neck, nor did she move her head away. A mutual impulse made it seem desirable that they should touch each other at *some* point while Mr. Evans was talking about "yr Echwyd."

"For what did these mystical Figures . . . rulers in Ynis-Witrin in the time of my people . . . seek . . . when they fished?" The curious thing was that Mr. Evans' body seemed at that moment, while his two young hearers watched him, to grow more and more corpse-like. Those bare hanging wrists, those outstretched feet in their great boots remained absolutely motionless. It was as if his physical form had already sunk into the waters of that Cimmerian sunset-realm which he called "yr Echwyd," while some power from outside of him was making his lips move in his corpse-like face!

"They sought for more than a fish, for more than any great chub of Lydford . . . they sought for the knot of the opposites, for the clasping of the Two Twilights, for the mingling-place of the waters, for the fusion of the metals, for the bride-bed of the contradictions, for the copulation-cry of the Yes and No, for the amalgam of the Is and Is Not! What they sought . . . what the Fisher Kings of my people sought, and no other priests of no other race on earth have ever sought it . . . was not only the Cauldron and the Spear . . . not only the sheath and the knife, not only the Mwys of Gwyddno and the Sword of Arthur, but that which exists in the moment of timeless time when these two are one! What they sought was creation with-out-generation. What they sought was Parthenogenesis and the Self-Birth of Psyche. What they sought was the Stone without Lichen which the people before my people worshipped, when they set up ———" The voice proceeding from the lips of the corpse-face of Mr. Evans became so hoarse and broken at this point that it hardly seemed like a human voice. Lady Rachel could clearly hear the footsteps on the pavement outside, through the street door which they had left ajar; and these steps sounded to her like the steps of all the generations of men treading down the stammerings of the Inanimate Bottom of the World.

Dᴜʀɪɴɢ ᴛʜᴇ ꜰɪʀsᴛ ᴡᴇᴇᴋ ɪɴ Dᴇᴄᴇᴍʙᴇʀ ᴛʜʀᴇᴇ ɴᴇᴡ sᴜʙᴊᴇᴄᴛs ᴏꜰ the King of England entered this world in the little maternity annex of the Glastonbury Hospital. Nell Zoyland was delivered of a boy, while Tossie Stickles—to her immense pride and satis- faction—was delivered of a pair of lusty girl twins. It was con- ducive of certain curious encounters that these two young women and their children should be lying simultaneously in private rooms opening from the same passage. Tom Barter coming to visit Tossie found himself confronted in that passage one day by Will Zoyland and another day by Sam Dekker, while Miss Eliza- beth Crow, who was devoted in her watchfulness over Toss and her twins, met on one and the same evening, Persephone Spear and Dave Spear coming to see Nell, but coming separately on this errand.

Something certainly seemed—at least up to this present date which was now the tenth of December—to be favouring the com- mune conspirators. Dave and Red and their new ally Paul Trent had evidently been well advised in their choice of a locale that day, wherein to broach their daring plot. Philip Crow, like many another Napoleonic tactician, was weakest in the cautious con- sideration of all probable and improbable contingencies. Like the impetuous Corsican and like Oliver Cromwell he swept ahead upon his main idea, allowing sleeping dogs to sleep and open stable doors to remain open. Never for one second did it cross his active brain, any more than it crossed the brain of Tilly, ab- sorbed in making her domestic arrangements for the winter, or the brain of Mr. Tankerville, growing more and more energetic in his commercial flights about Europe, that there was the least chance of any difficulty over his factory leases, the rents of which remained still only paid up to the beginning of the New Year. The construction of his new road and his new bridge was for the moment held up by the flat refusal of Mr. Twig to sell any por- tion of his small patrimony, but the Evercreech man, more anx- ious than ever to serve this rich employer, since his father-in-law

—as obstinate about dying as Number One was about selling—
still persisted in milking his four Jersey cows with his own hand,
was already in correspondence with the county officials over the
possibility of exploiting a section of Lake Village Field. But
though handicapped over his road and his bridge, Philip had
begun his tin mining under the most promising conditions and
already the sound of picks and mattocks and of cranes and engines could be heard proceeding from a big clearing in the hillside under which many unvisited subterranean passages led into
the heart of the hill. Half a dozen truckloads of the precious
metal had already been despatched from the railway station at
Glastonbury; for although this station was further off than the
one at Wells it was easier to make use of and Philip had a much
stronger "pull" with the railroad officials there. It had been just
a month ago, in the middle of November, when the first tin had
begun to emerge, nor would Philip ever forget his feelings when
he beheld the lorry containing it roll off towards the Great
Western station, ready to be taken to Cardiff through the Severn
Tunnel. For the last month the tin had been pouring forth with
such a steady flow that Philip's spirits had mounted up to a pitch
of excitement that was like a kind of diurnal drunkenness. He
dreamed of tin every night. The metal in all its stages began to
obsess him. He collected specimens of it, of every degree of
weight, integrity, purity. He carried bits of it about with him in
his pocket. All manner of quaint fancies—not so much imaginative ones as purely childish ones—connected with tin, kept entering and leaving his mind, and he began to feel as if a portion
of his innermost being were the actual magnet that drew this
long-neglected element out of abysses of prehistoric darkness into
the light of day.

Philip got into the habit of walking every day up the steep
overgrown hillside above Wookey and posting himself in the
heart of a small grove of Scotch firs from which he could observe, without anyone detecting his presence, the lively transactions at the mouth of the big orifice in the earth, where the trees
had been cut away and where the cranes and pulleys stood out
in such startling relief against the ancient sepia-coloured clumps
of hazel and sycamore, still growing around them upon the leafy

slopes. Here he would devour the spectacle of all this activity he had set in motion, until he longed to share the physical exertions of every one of his labourers, diggers, machinists, truckmen, carters, stokers, miners, and haulers. He yearned to be himself boring, dynamiting, shovelling, lifting, carrying, driving; and so intensely had he fixed his eyes on every bodily movement these men had made, that by this time—by the tenth of December—he really could have hired himself out, and won commendation from his foreman in the job, at almost everyone of these several labours. It must not be supposed that he neglected his office-work or his dye works extensions and increasing European sales during these exciting weeks. He worked steadily at the office from nine to one every day, and always looked in there again about five before he went home to tea. After his tea he had recently acquired the custom of retiring to a room which Emma called the study, Tilly the north room and he himself the play-room. Shut up in this room he used to ponder long and deeply over his affairs, plunging into various mathematical and commercial calculations and making rapid notes in a big, foolscap-size notebook with a white vellum binding. This notebook had been given to him by Persephone when she was quite a little girl. Illuminated upon its front page was his name and hers united by a gilt border within which were lilac-coloured hearts, strung upon a green string.

On this tenth of December Philip returned to the north room after Tilly had gone to bed, and gave himself up to an orgy of concentrated thought. He had already brought so many new labourers and working people into Glastonbury that it had begun to be difficult to house them, and Philip—little dreaming what a deadly blow was preparing for him from that quarter—had entered into negotiations with the town council relative to his housing these newcomers in some of the newly built "council houses." The fact that there were so many unemployed among the old-established Glastonbury people, who now saw these lively upstarts from Bristol and Cardiff occupying houses provided by their own socialistic government and built out of local taxes, was a fact that did not redound to Philip's popularity with the populace. Glastonbury's populace was—as they proved in their mobbing of Lord P.—not at all inclined to remain passive and patient when they once got a particular grievance lodged in their brain; and Philip had been surprised by the sullen looks with which he was greeted whenever he had occasion to pass through the poorer portions of the town. He had even heard derisive jeering when he recently crossed, in his little open car, one of the outskirts of Paradise. This extreme unpopularity into which he had fallen was another of these possible causes of catastrophe which Philip neglected. It was part of that element of sheer recklessness in him, to which reference has already been made, to hold public opinion in infinite contempt. Humane enough towards those immediately dependent upon him, Philip was absolutely devoid of imagination when it came to be a question of people he had never seen.

His small, hard, oblong head, very protruding at the back, and rather flat at the sides where the ears clung so closely, had that particular look about it that old-fashioned military men's skulls have. As he pulled his chair round now in front of the fire, leaving the vellum-bound notebook open on the table and sprinkled with cigarette ashes which he had not bothered to blow away, he thought to himself quite calmly: "It would be a good thing if the Glastonbury people would simply die off; die off and leave their houses empty to make room for me to fill the town with a different type altogether! But they seem able to live on forever, feeding on mud and mist! Die! Die! Die! Die quickly and have done with it!" It was at this moment that he saw in the red coals of the fire, a heap of dead people, dead heads and arms and legs and feet. It was a totally unreal illustration of the French Revolution, that set him upon conjuring up this romantic spectacle. It was a picture that he had seen in some silly illustration of some cheap story; and the queer thing about it was that these dead people were not disfigured in any way. They were just dead. "How these Christs and Buddhas," he thought to himself, "ever reached the point of feeling that it was worth their while to save the human race is more than I can understand. I don't want to torture anyone"—here Philip's judgment of himself was absolutely correct, for there was less sadism in him than there was in Mr. Stilly or in Jimmy Rake or in Elphin Cantle—"but it's impossible for me to understand this 'value of human life' that some people make so much of." Once more he stared at the coals; and once more he saw in those red recesses that curious, sentimental assembly of neatly dressed corpses with sad, peaceful, composed features, laid out in that artistic morgue. And then there flickered over his hollow eye-sockets and over his hollow cheeks, as he stared at that fire and stretched out his hands to it, a grim smile, for he thought of what Tilly would say if she could read his thoughts at this moment.

Tilly—good housekeeper as she was in her orderings of well-killed meat—could not bring herself to trap the smallest mouse. If kittens had been born in her house by the dozens, it would only have been by the craftiest deception that Emma could have got her to get rid of one of them. "What actually *would* Tilly say," he wondered, "if she knew that if I could cut off the heads of all the poor of Glastonbury and fill their houses with a picked set of men and women who could really work I'd do it tomorrow? As a matter of fact, if by lifting up my hand now I could destroy those people and get this new population here *tonight*, I'd do it! Yes, and sleep quite soundly afterwards!"

One of the most interesting things about Philip, when he indulged in mental contemplations as he was doing now was the guileless un-maliciousness of his inhumanity. Though it never occurred to him to ask himself by what right could he condemn to death, in his thoughts, a whole section of his fellow-townsmen, he derived no wicked pleasure from the idea of their death. His grey-black, closely cropped skull was as devoid of such notions as one of the mattocks of his workmen at Wookey. He experienced now, in his silent house, with his open figuring-book on the table behind him and these glowing coals in front of him, a delicious sense of soundness, compactness, integrity in solitude. "I am I," his whole being seemed to say, "and the world is my clay and my mortar." Leaving these ill-nourished Glastonbury incompetents safe in their neat and artistic death-pile, his thoughts now turned to what he regarded as the superstitions of the place. Yes, he would willingly, if he could, obliterate all these Gothic Ruins, lay a good solid expanse of lead-piping to drain Chalice Well, pull down that old Tower from the Tor and build a water-tank up there, dig out every twig, sprig, root and branch of this corrupting thorn bush and really set to work to have the best tin centre in this spot that existed anywhere in the world! Here again, in the matter of superstition, Philip's destructive desires were astonishingly un-malicious.

John Crow would have derived a most convoluted vandal-thrill, the wanton excitement of a run-down atheistical adventurer, in obliterating all traces of the Great Legend. Red would have gratified incredible levels of " 'ate" by so doing. Barter would have done it with the grim unction of a sullen executioner, especially if he could have shogged off afterwards with Tossie and the twins to Norfolk! Even Dave would have done it with a certain self-righteous doctrinaire-austerity. But Philip would have done it absolutely without a single *arrière pensée.* He would have done it by the pure necessity of his nature, as a dog twines himself round on a mat before lying down, or a cat scratches the dust over its excrement. He would have wiped the place clean, both of its under-nourished rebellious populace and of its morbid relics, and then set to work, as inevitably as a beaver returns to its job after a flood, to build up an industrial centre out of the richest tin mine and out of the most scientific dye works anywhere on earth!

It was with his head full of these thoughts—thoughts that sprouted from his hard skull like scaly lichen from a gatepost on Brandon Heath—that Philip finally switched off the electric light in the play-room and went up—carrying his patent-leather shoes in hand—to his stuffy bedroom, his cold hot-water bottle, and the invisible wraith of his well-satisfied grandmother.

All the enemies of the Great Legend happened, that night of December the tenth, to be going to sleep about the same time. Glastonbury indeed, under its windy, moonless winter sky, was like many another town that night in the turbulent history of our earth: it was subject to the psychic tearing down and building up of the most violently diverse energies. But all these Legend-Destroyers were of the same sex! *That* was the interesting and significant thing to note. Not one single feminine wish, from Tossie in the hospital to Mother Legge in what she called her nursery, was lifted up from the bed of sleep in hostility to the

immemorial Tradition. But from the bed of Red, and the bed of
Dave, and the bed of Paul Trent, and the bed of Mr. Barter, and
the bed of Lawyer Beere, and the beds of bank-cashier Stilly,
gardener Weatherwax and Will Zoyland and finally from the
bed in Northload Street of John Crow, there rose up, along with
the destructive will-power of Philip, a cumulative malediction
against the Legend. There *had* been a time when Mary would
have joined this gang of iconoclasts—she alone among all the
feminine shapes in the town—but, since her marriage, Mary had
relapsed into a veritable undersea of infinite peace so delicate in
its muted dreaming that she would have no more wished to break
up any of its dream-scenery, any of its deep-sea arches, its deep-
sea columns, its leagues of translucent emerald-coloured floors,
than she would have wished to break the heart of Euphemia
Drew.

The history of any ancient town is as much the history of its
inhabitants' nightly pillows as of any practical activity that they
perform by day. Floating on its softly upheaving sea-surface of
feminine breasts the island-city of mystery gathered itself together to resist this wedge of rational invasion. Backward and
forward, for five thousand years, the great psychic pendulum has
swung between belief in the Glastonbury Legend and disbelief.
It is curious to think of the pertinacity of the attacks upon this
thing and how, like a vapour dispersed by a wind that re-fashions
itself again the moment the wind departs, the moss-grown towers
and moonlit ramparts of its imperishable enchantment survive
and again survive. When the king murdered the last Abbot of this
place he was only doing what Philip and Barter and Red and
Dave and Paul Trent and John would have liked to do to the
indestructible mystery today. In the most ancient times the same
fury of the forces of "reason," must have swept across Glastonbury, only to be followed by the same eternal reaction when the
forces of mystery returned. The psychic history of a place like
Glastonbury is not an easy thing to write down in set terms, for
not only does chance play an enormous part in it, but there are
many forces at work for which human language has at present
no fit terms.

This particular night of the tenth of December was in reality one of the great turning points in the life of Glastonbury, but the issue of the struggle that went on tonight between the Enemies of the Legend and its Lovers would evade all but supernatural narration, however one might struggle to body it forth. Out of John Crow's head, after he had relaxed to sleep that night from his lascivious claspings of Mary's marbly limbs, there leapt up into the darkness the spiritual form of all the suppressed maliciousness from which he had been suffering in his service of Bloody Johnny. This spiritual form was a shape, a presence, an entity. It was, in fact, the essential soul of John Crow, for the vital consciousness of his sleeping body was but a vague, weak diffusion of electric force. What else could the soul of John Crow do when released in sleep from his life of psychic slavery, but join, with an exultant rebound, all those other wandering spirits who were engaged in *killing the Grail*. It was not necessary for any palpable shape to fly out of that window in Northload Street in order to join, in a sort of Warlock's Sabbath, the ill-assorted spirits of Philip Crow and Red Robinson. When I write down the word join, I mean a motion of John's soul that it would be impossible for any scientist to refute, a motion of his whole essential being, now his body was asleep and his diplomacy relaxed, to *kill the Grail*. By joining with Philip, on this night of the tenth of December, to strike this blow at a fragment of the Absolute, the essential soul of John Crow took a considerable risk. For one thing, it was a risk to leave his sly, cautious, saurian neutrality and join his grand enemy. That he did so at all is only one more proof of how deep John's maliciousness went. In his service of Geard, in connexion with the Grail and in connexion with Chalice Well, John was steadily outraging the evasive, trampish, irresponsible essence of his nature. He was taking sides. He was siding with the Grail against its enemies, when all the while, in his heart, he longed to *kill* it! The "something" in Philip and John and Barter that loathed the Grail so deeply was not just simply their Norfolk blood. This fragment of the Absolute was too ticklish a thing not to divide human souls in a disturbing and disconcerting manner, setting brother against brother and friend against friend. All the way down the centuries it had done this, breaking up ordinary normal human relations and exerting whenever it appeared, a startling, shocking, troubling effect.

It was really a monstrous thing now that John and Philip should dislike one another so heartily during the daylight hours but at night rush off together to join in *killing the Grail*. The Grail could not actually be "killed," for the Thing is a morsel of the Absolute and a broken-off fragment of the First Cause. It could not of course be killed literally; not in the sense of being annihilated. But it *could* be struck at and outraged in a way that was a real injury; real enough, anyhow, to stir up a very ambiguous feeling in the tramp-nerves of John Crow! After all, though there was an unknown "element" in the composition of this broken-off piece of its own substance, that the First Cause had flung down upon this spot, there was also something of the "thought-stuff" of the same ultimate Being in the personality of all its living creatures. Thus, in the psychic war that was going on above the three hills of Glastonbury, the Absolute was, in a manner of speaking, pitted against the Absolute.

On this tenth of December the wind blew directly from the west. Over Mark Moor it blew from the marshes of Highbridge and, beyond that, from the brackish mud-flats of Burnham. The tide had been so high indeed in the Burnham estuaries that many of the more pessimistic fishermen there, whose flat-bottomed boats—as they had done since the Vikings came—explored those muddy reaches, prophesied that the dams were going to burst again, as they had burst in November, five years before, flooding the whole country. Over Bridgewater Bay it blew, and over the Bristol Channel, from the mountains of South Wales. A scattered army of little ragged clouds followed each other eastward all that night, blotting out from the vision of nocturnal wanderers, or from such as kept vigil at lonely windows, first one constellation and then another. Thus the nature of the night of that tenth of December was peculiar and unusual, for no fixed star and no planet was free from sudden, quick, hurried and erratic obscurings by these rags and tatters of flying vapour. Endlessly they blew across the welkin, those tattered wisps of clouds, changing their shapes as they blew into the fitful forms of men and beasts and birds and tossing vessels and whirling hulks and flying promontories, and obscuring first one great zodiacal sign in the heavens and then another. The wind that shepherded these wild flocks was full of the scent of channel seaweed and of channel mud, and as it voyaged eastward its speed kept increasing, so that these cloud-shapes, thus broken into smaller and smaller wefts, now began to fly like gigantic leaves across the Glastonbury hills.

Two human beings, one a woman and one a boy, found themselves too restless to sleep that night in this city of sorceries. These were Nancy Stickles in her attic room on the High Street and Elphin Cantle in his father's hostelry, the Old Tavern, which stood on the edge of the Cattle Market. Both these persons, this young married woman and this boy, left their beds between one and two that December night and pulling chairs to their windows, looked out upon those flying clouds. Elphin's room, which was far away from both Persephone's and Dave's, in the rambling, faded, old public house, looked out from a sort of stucco tower, added to the main building in the reign of William the Fourth. His window was a large one composed of many small panes and when Elphin in the dead of night threw this open and sat leaning his elbows upon the window-sill he could not only see a high garden wall covered with mossy coping-stones, but he could see a bare larch tree swaying mournfully in the wind, and, beyond this a little tributary of the Brue, irrigating a piece of municipal ground that had been parcelled out into allotment-gardens, and crossed, although its waters were not deep, by several plank bridges. There was a clump of dead stone-crop upon this mossy wall, and near the stone-crop a single faded wall-flower which bowed and swayed in the wind and seemed to emit, as it swayed, at least so Elphin Cantle fancied, a faint dirge-like sighing. The boy spread out his arms upon his window-sill and stared at the pallid waters of the Brue tributary and at the tossing larch-tree top and at the sighing flower-stalks on the wall. His window was unusually large, as often happens with that particular sort of stucco tower, so that there was a dizzy sensation as well as a very chilly one as he looked out upon the night. But Elphin was much more *in the night*, much more mingled with its vague scents and its morbidly distinct sounds than he would have been in any other room in Glastonbury. His mother had decided to let him sleep in the tower room "till a guest asked for it." Now, as it was unlikely that a guest would even know of the existence of the tower room, Elphin was pretty safe.

He thrust his right arm out of the great window and stroked the stucco wall with his fingers. Something about a stucco wall always fascinated Elphin, and now with this wind wailing in his ears, whistling through the larch tree, moaning across the plank bridges of this Brue ditch, the touch of this material helped him to think. But he was in a blasphemous and a wicked mood that night, for his idol Sam had broken his promise to take him out there, beyond Charlton Mackrell, to the weir at Cary Fitzpaine, on the River Cary, where several tench had been caught this autumn, that queer fish gifted with the gift of healing! Sam had given him no better excuse for the breaking of this promise than that Mrs. Zoyland was all alone, that afternoon, up at the hospital, a state of affairs that by no means seemed to justify such treatment of a friend. Elphin's restless excitement, therefore, in that wet-blowing wind and his queer pleasure in rubbing his hand against that old weather-stained tower wall were mingled with a bitter anger against both women and religion. He associated them together, which was unfair with that particular kind of philosophical unfairness, touched with perverted eroticism, that many famous writers have indulged in. Women were, it is true, now at this very moment, all over this silent city, nourishing the Grail in their sleep, but the great religions of the world were not founded by women. The soul of Elphin Cantle, nevertheless, as, on this tenth of December he leaned out upon the night air, rushed forth to join the souls of Philip and John in their murderous night hunt of the Grail, just as if on this night of the west wind's wild rush through the sky, there really had been a sort of Wizard's Sabbath.

This joining of Philip and John in their orgy of Grail-killing meant no more than that if anyone could have looked down that night upon the mental arena of Glastonbury he would have seen a powerful group of masculine consciousnesses bent upon completing the work of the bestial King Henry, and destroying, once and for all, all traces of this Cymric superstition.

Elphin's heart yearned for Sam, and his nerves throbbed for Sam. His feverish pillow, left over there alone in the darkness now, as he sat at this huge window, could have told a pretty tale of nightly desperations, as the lad tossed and turned and quivered in his perverted passion, while week followed week, and there seemed no satisfaction for him in sight. And so his fury turned upon Sam's religion, and this the boy mixed up, wildly and blindly, in his crazy unfairness, with the existence of all the feminine persons that Sam was in the habit of meeting these days, but especially with Mrs. Zoyland. "May the curse be on her!" cried Elphin now to the flying clouds. "May the curse be on her!" he cried to the tossing wall-flower, to the bending larch, to the rippled streamlet, and to all the wet, hollow, dark spaces, like the wind-swept corridors of a madhouse, that extended between Chalice Hill and Tor Hill, and between Tor Hill and Wirral Hill. "May the curse be on her, and may she be sorry to death that she ever met him!"

This malediction was a much more singular and significant one than poor Nell would have understood. It was in reality—if the full secret purport of Elphin's thoughts had been revealed—directed quite as much against the Grail as against Nell. For the curious thing was that when presently he began again—whispering the words aloud with intense solemnity—to curse the woman whom his hero was so constantly visiting in the hospital, he extended his curse, as his outstretched fingers fumbled at the chilly stucco wall beneath his tower window, to that consecrated Cup in the hands of his friend's father from which Sam was always receiving the Sacrament. His boy's thoughts were all confused, and not having been yet confirmed by the Bishop of Wells he had only the vaguest notion of the meaning of the Mass. The Cup containing the Wine at those "early services," which, like a faithful dog watching his master, he was wont to gaze upon from the back of St. Patrick's Chapel, was the same to him as this mystic Grail, lost or buried in Chalice Hill, of which he heard his parents talk. Elphin's love for Sam was too passionate to be vicious, but it was also far too intense to be innocent, and with a lover's clairvoyant instinct he was fully aware that Sam's worship of Christ absorbed many feelings in the man which if released would turn to human love. What Elphin did not realise was that it was this very love of Christ coming between Sam and his mistress that had given him his place, such as it was, in Sam's life. Had this accursed Grail, or this sacramental Cup that the boy confused with the Grail, become nothing to Sam it would certainly not have been to the love of Elphin Cantle that he would have turned! Thus, as so often happens in the coil of human drama, the very power against which, in his blind passion, the unhappy lad was now pouring out his imprecations, was the one thing that kept him in his idol's life! Sam's pity for this lonely child was part of the grand *tour de force* of his life of a saint. To be interested in boys at all was totally against the grain with him.

While Elphin was at the tower window of the Old Tavern, Nancy, having slipped from the unconscious arms of the heavily breathing Harry Stickles, was at her attic window looking on the back gardens of High Street. This west wind, blowing from the Bristol Channel, blowing from the hills of Pembrokeshire, blowing from that Isle of Gresholm off the western shores, where round the Head of Bran the Blessed fluttered that song of the Birds of Rhiannon which brought death to the living and life to the dead, this west wind was more than an ordinary wind that night to Nancy Stickles. It was her sense of this west wind that had drawn her out of her bed. The feeling of it had reached her in her dreams before she awoke. Sitting on her hard bedroom chair at the window which she had managed to open wide without disturbing Harry, she now gave herself up to the power and the rush of it as it swept past her house. In the other houses everyone was asleep. Not a sound reached her from the street in front. There she was, exposed to the far-stretching sky with its whistling cloud-leaves, to the wide, wet hollows of darkness that covered the earth, and above all to that rushing wind! About a quarter of a mile separated her from Elphin at *his* open window. The boy had put on his overcoat which had been covering him in his bed. The girl wore her rough, thick dressing-gown and also a black woollen shawl. Neither of them had the remotest notion of the presence of the other, although the identity of each, the son of Mr. Cantle of the Old Tavern, and the wife of Mr. Stickles, the chemist, was well-known to each. It was a palpable example of the way in which the desperate wishes of living creatures flung out at random upon the air counter and cancel each other's magnetic force! The boy cursed the religion of Glastonbury and the girl blessed it. Yes, she blessed it, as she gave herself to this wild wind that had been calling to her through her dreams for the last five hours.

Oh, how delicious it was to give herself up to it . . . to feel it take her completely, as she crouched there, with her strong, firm working-girl's fingers clasped together on the window-sill! "I wish," thought Nancy, "that it was the wind and not men who took girls!" And she fell into a fantastic reverie in which she told herself a story about a bride who gave herself rapturously to an enamoured wind-spirit. "Oh, I am so glad I am alive!" thought Nancy, and the brave, optimistic girl, as she let the wind seek out her responsive breasts under her black shawl, began adding up in her mind all the good aspects of her life. She was always doing this. She found it an excellent antidote to all that she suffered from in her husband—that plump, placid baby with eyes of insane avarice—and it always came back to the same thing, to the one grand privilege she had, that of having been born in Glastonbury! Her employment at Miss Crow's, where she was now aided by another distant relative of Tossie's, a certain Daisy Stickles, was a constant delight to her. The walk alone, through the heart of the town and past St. Benignus' churchyard, was a solid pleasure; and there were times, especially after her work was done and she was returning in the evening, that she could have started skipping down the narrow Benedict Street pavement. She could even have snatched up a certain ragged little boy she was always meeting down there and hugged him to her heart and danced him up and down and made him cry with surprise and offended dignity, and all from a delight in life that, as it poured through her sometimes, seemed to know no bounds. Certain ways of her husband's—certain mean little physical peculiarities, and Nancy was not by nature at all fastidious —made her feel sometimes as if she could not go on living with him. But she had devised all manner of devices to deal with these nasty ways and she never felt hopelessly caught, because she was always telling herself stories of running away from him.

Harry Stickles certainly did possess quite a number of peculiarities which would have been nerve-racking to any less well-constituted girl. These nasty little ways were made worse by the man's preposterous and incredible conceit. But Nancy had been given by Nature one supreme gift—wherein only one other person in Glastonbury rivalled her, and that was John Crow— the gift of forgetting. Harry could do something at one minute that offended her to the quick, something that so scraped, jarred, and raked her nerves that she could have rushed to the window and flung into the road one of those big coloured receptacles, red and green, that mark a chemist's shop; and yet, three minutes later, as she sat sewing in her parlour window, what she called her "fancies" would begin as deliciously as ever! Nancy's fancies were simply her sudden recollection of certain moments of intense realisation of life as they had occurred several years ago. They were nothing more than the look of a particular wall, of a particular tract of hedge, of a particular piece of road, of a certain hay-wagon on a certain hillside, of a particular pond with ducks swimming on it and a red cow stepping very slowly through the mud, of a load of seaweed being pulled up from the beach by struggling horses, of the stone bridge crossing the Yeo at Ilchester, of a little toll-pike at Lodmore that seemed to be made up, as she had seen it from the top of a bus beyond Weymouth once, of nothing but whitewashed stones and tarred planks and tall brackish grasses and clouds of white dust. Nancy could never tell which of her fancies would rise up next like a fish, making a circle of delicious ripples round it, from the depths of her mind, nor did she know whether these mental pictures stored up in her brain were limited in number, and whether, at a certain point, they would begin recurring all over again, or whether they were inexhaustible and need never repeat themselves.

But while Nancy and Elphin kept their vigil, what dreams there were in Glastonbury! Dreams without any beginning, as they were without any end. For who ever *began* a dream? People always find themselves immersed *in the middle* of some dream or other. The essence of sleep does not lie in dreaming; it lies in a certain dying to the surface life and sinking down into the life under the surface, where the *other life*—healing and refreshing—exists like an immortal tide of fresh water flowing beneath the salt water of a turbid sea. It is sufficient to remember the lovely and mysterious feeling of falling asleep compared with the crude, raw, iron spikes of the unpleasant things that happen in dreams to realise the difference. Between the process of going to sleep and the process of dreaming exists a great gulf. They seem to belong to different categories of being. But, however this may be, the fact remains that upon certain nights in the year—when the tide at Burnham begins to rise with a weird persistence—the sleep of Glastonbury is a troubled one. The sturdy northeastern invaders—the ancestors of Philip and John—beat back more than Mr. Evans' people when they swept the Celts into South Wales. They beat back with them their thaumaturgic demigods, the Living Corpse, for instance, of Uther Pendragon, the mysterious Urien, King of yr Echwyd, the Land of Glamour and Illusion, the Land whose vapours are always livid blue, that mystic colour named by the bards *gorlassar*, and Arawn, King of Annwn, they beat back, together with those weird protectors of the heathen Grail, the Fisher King Petchere and the Maimed King Pelles. All these Beings, so many of whom seem to recede and vanish away even as they are named among us, like creatures of a blundered incantation, had the ancestors of Philip and John and the ancestors of Dave driven back westward. And along with Mr. Evans' people, and their dark chthonian gods, these healthy-minded invaders had driven back the very *dreams* of these Cymric and Brythonic tribes.

For today it was Mr. Evans and Mrs. Geard and Blackie Morgan, together with that impoverished and mutinous population in the slums, whose holocaust Philip had seen that night in the "artistic" pictures of his red coals, who were the true aboriginals, and the larger part of *their* blood, like that of the old Lake Village dwellers, was both pre-Celtic and prehistoric. So that on this night of all nights, this night of the tenth of December, a date that always, every year—only none but the witch-wives of

Bove Town and Paradise knew about this—was a significant
date for Glastonbury, what really came back upon this terrific
wind, blowing up out of the western sea and the western isles,
were the *dreams* of the conquered, those disordered, extravagant
law-breaking dreams, out of which the Shrines of Glastonbury
had originally been built. Nancy Stickles was perfectly right
when she whispered to the darkness, as her white breasts expanded under her black shawl in response to that wind, "What
a thing sleep is—to be in the world!"

It was only upon those happy heads that did not dream,
however, that the true mystery of sleep, carrying those carefree
foreheads deep down under the sacred waters of yr Echwyd,
really descended. Such was the privilege, that night, of both
Lady Rachel and Miss Elizabeth Crow. Such was the privilege
of Mr. Wollop and of Bert Cole. Such was the privilege of
Young Tewsy, of Tittie Petherton and Tilly Crow, of Penny
Pitches and of old Abel Twig. Among the others the eternal contest went on, as it had gone on for at least five thousand years,
between the friends of the Grail—that fragment of Beyond-Time
fallen through a crack in the world-ceiling upon the Time-Floor
—and its deadly enemies.

The Grail had come to be the magnet-gatherer of all the
religions that had ever come near Glastonbury. A piece of the
Absolute, it attracted these various cults to itself with an indifference as to their divergency from one another that was almost
cruel. Thus the instinct in Philip and John that drove their souls
forth tonight to go Grail-killing was as blind and overpowering
as that which drove Pellenore to pursue his Questing Beast.

Neither Nancy nor Elphin, these watchers at windows, at the
back of High Street and Cattle Market, were aware of this great
mêlée of warring dreams, tossing and heaving, with the gonfalon of the Grail on one side, and on the other the oriflamme
of Reason. Whirled about in that rushing wind, which kept
eddying and ricocheting among the three Glastonbury hills,
drifted those opposed dream-hosts. Every dreamer under those
diverse roofs—from the slate-tiled Elms where Philip lay in
his stuffy room to the draughty stable loft at St. Michael's where

Solly Lew slept his tipsy sleep—was forced, that tenth of December, to mingle his own private dream with this great nocturnal tourney.

John Crow dreamed that they found the Grail on Chalice Hill, found it in the earth about six feet north of the Well; but when it was found all the people present turned into a flock of starlings and flew away, leaving only himself and that philosophic wood louse he had imagined encountering the human louse of the woman with cancer. And he himself was now seized with a frantic necessity to make water and yet he knew that if he made water on the earth that wood louse would be drowned. So John Crow made water into the Holy Grail. When he had finished this blasphemous sacrilege he observed that the wood louse had crawled to the rim of the Vessel. "What are you going to do?" John cried in terror. "Drown myself," replied the louse.

But if that wild wind out of the west disturbed the dreams of men it did not prove less disturbing to the dreams of women. Persephone dreamed that green leaves were growing out of her feet and out of her shoulders and that she was standing stark naked in the centre of a group of silver-barked birch trees who were all, like herself, slim, naked girls with green leaves growing out of their heads and green leaves growing out of their feet. Near this group, where Persephone was standing, there grew that nameless tree from the top of Wirral Hill which Mary had called by one name, Mr. Evans by another, and Mad Bet by another. And Persephone suddenly saw all the girls turn towards this tree and lifting up their hands begin chanting something to it. What they chanted was pure gibberish, but Persephone, when she awoke, remembered this gibberish which was as follows:

"Dominus-Glominus, sow your seed!
Sow your seed, sow your seed!
Glominus-Dominus, rain and dew!
Rain and dew, rain and dew!
We your servants will make your bed!
Make your bed, make your bed!
Some at the foot, and some at the head,
But which of us lies beside you?"

This gibberish was doubtless recalled from some ancient child-ish jingle, repeated in one of those immemorial games that little girls love to play together, during which they take one another's hands and advance and retreat in dancing movements that are as mysterious to any casual onlooker as the fantastic words that accompany them. But though recalled to the mind of Persephone from some half-forgotten game of her childhood, there doubt-less were words added to it in her dream that could hardly have been present in the original version, and which were cer-tainly more suitable to the nature of this wild night of brackish-smelling Wessex wind than to any harmless ring-of-roses dance upon a Norfolk lawn. The curious thing was that in Persephone's own mind, as she dreamed this dream, there occurred one of those confused metamorphoses which so often make dreams so bewildering and misleading—the confusion, namely, of this am-biguous tree with a Cross.

The Mayor of Glastonbury's dreams on that tenth of December were full for instance of a nightmarish mingling of his daughter Crummie with Merlin's fatal Nineue, and both Nineue and Crum-mie with Lady Rachel Zoyland.

Nor were the dreams of the Vicar of Glastonbury less dis-turbing. Mat Dekker dreamed that he was visiting Nell Zoyland at the hospital, where he had, as a matter of fact, visited her already three times, and that he was giving her the Blessed Sacrament, a thing he had often longed to do, but had never dared to suggest doing. He was on the point of raising the Cup to her lips when it grew so heavy in his hands that he could scarcely lift it. The Cup, in fact, transformed itself into Mother Legge's silver bowl—or rather Kitty Camel's silver bowl—with which of course Mat Dekker had been familiar before it passed into its present owner's possession. Whiter and whiter grew this sacramental Cup as the priest struggled with it in his dream. "I must hold it tight," he thought, "I must press it against me." And then there happened a metamorphosis similar to the one that had occurred in Percy's dream, only in the reverse order; for while, with Percy, the tree turned into the Cross, with Mat Dekker the Grail turned into Nell Zoyland. So deep had been the wrestling of this man's majestic character with his passion for this girl, that until tonight, even in his dreams, he had resisted temptation. But tonight there happened to him one of those occasions when great creative Nature manages to outwit the strongest self-control. Nature achieved her end by lodging in Mat Dekker's mind the feeling that at all costs he must hold this white bowl firm and tight against him, so that it should not spill a drop of Christ's blood. But as he held it in his dream, and as it became the body of the girl he so terribly desired, Nature managed to so numb, drug, dull, confuse, cloud, hypnotise, paralyse and otherwise "metagrabolise" Mat Dekker's implacable conscience, that it allowed him to give way with good heart to a spasm of such exquisite love-making that it was, to the poor ascetic priest, like the opening of the gates of heaven!

Little did Elphin Cantle know, as he clutched his father's old stable coat—now his own bed-cover—tighter and tighter round him at his turret window, that the psychic current of his wrath against the Glastonbury superstition was aided by the austere dream-gestures of Dave Spear from another quarter of the Old Tavern. Dave's thoughts before he had gone to sleep that night had been calm and peaceful. He had dined with his wife at Dickery Cantle's old-fashioned ordinary in the tavern parlour, and Percy had listened so sweetly to his stories about their Bristol comrades that he had been tempted to reveal to her the great scheme he had now on foot. Where communism was concerned, however, Dave was a man of iron; and in spite of the fact that their whole plan was originally her own inspiration, he had thought it wiser—as it certainly was!—to hold his tongue over all that. But to all that he *did* allow to pass, in that expressive Homeric phrase, "the barrier of his teeth," Percy had listened with much more than her usual attention. Something in the rising wind had roused her feelings to a pitch of impersonal tenderness, and her husband happened, by good luck, to be the beneficiary of this soft mood. But once asleep Dave's mind reverted at once to his great conspiracy, and the crying of the wind in his chimney and the flapping of the blind in his window worked into his dreams and made them as disturbed as Percy's own, but to a different issue. For the walls of a real commune rose up in Dave's dream as that wild wind, blowing out of Wales, made the historic house about him creak and groan through all its ancient beams and rafters. Thus had it groaned when the emissaries of Henry hunted out of its seclusion the last faithful servants of the Abbey. Thus had it groaned when the spies of James dragged forth the unhappy preachers who had supported Monmouth. The whole conflicting tenor of Dave Spear's life-struggle with himself would have been revealed had his dream been written down. "For the sake of the future," he kept muttering, when, as dictator of his commune, he gave orders for the Abbey Ruins to be destroyed and the Mayor's new buildings to be levelled with the ground. Clean and fresh rose, in his dream, the new Ynis-Witrin, founded, this time, not on the tricks of kings and priests, but on the equal labours and rewards of workingmen. "For the sake of the future!" he cried in his sleep as he watched the destruction of shrine after shrine.

But if Dave's dreams that night were drastic, the *conduct* of his fellow-conspirator, Red Robinson, who was awake and drinking and making love, in complete imperviousness to this mystical procession of bodiless shapes, was neither very drastic nor very brave. Red had persuaded Sally Jones to sit up with him after closing hours in the back parlour of St. Michael's Inn. This was a proceeding that would have got the good-natured landlord into trouble had it been discovered, but Red had grown so tired of his miserably hurried interviews with the girl, in her mother's home and *his* mother's home, after her day's work at the Geards', that he had broken away from his usual caution. Sally, who had a latch-key of her own, would just have to tell her mother that Miss Cordelia had kept her late that day to help with the preparations for her wedding. They had decided that it was best that Sally when she left St. Michael's near midnight, should walk home alone and should even make a short detour so as to approach her home from the direction of the Geards. "Neighbours be such ones for noticing things," she had said, "and 'tis no good to start a lot of talk when there be no cause for talk." To this sentiment Mr. Robinson had given a cordial assent. He found himself, as a matter of fact, extremely comfortable in the little, seldom-used inn-parlour with half a bottle of gin unfinished on the table and a good fire in the grate.

The old lady of the house—Mad Bet's aunt—had been friendly to the Robinsons ever since, owing to Mrs. Robinson's employment in the Palace at Wells, they had first settled in Glastonbury. This friendliness—such is the importance of small matters in small towns—was due to the fact that Mad Bet's aunt had a sister who had married a man "down Richmond way." The man was long dead and so was the sister, but the accent of the Robinsons pleased the landlady. "The way you folks talks," she said, "do mind me of sister's husband."

It would never have done for Red to bring Blackie to this inn, because they knew his mother. Crummie, of course, too could never have come. But he now began to enjoy the full benefit of having found a girl at once so respectable and so simple-minded as Sally Jones. When Sally was going and they stood talking in the hallway, the landlady pointed upstairs and spoke in a whispering voice. " 'Er been a sore trial today, 'er been! John had to lock she up in back room. 'Er were so noisy, you understand, in front. 'Er be asleep now, John thinks, and 'a holds tis best to let she bide where 'a be. She don't, as general rule, settle down to sleep in back room. Back room ain't what you might call the room anyone would *choose* to sleep in, but Bet ain't as pertikkler as some folks be, owing to her *being as she is*." Destiny or chance, whichever it was, now decreed that Red Robinson, having supped full of the sweets of love, was to be deprived of the pleasant half hour of luxurious rumination which he had planned for himself. The old landlord went himself "a step of the way" down Chilkwell Street with Sally. "The wind can't hurt a pretty girl," he said, "but it can ruffle and rumple her worse nor *we* would ever be allowed for to do."

There was a stir and a confusion now in the little passage that led from the back of the bar-room to the old cobbled yard. Solly Lew suddenly appeared in sight from these back premises dragging after him into the lamplight an extraordinary figure. "Missus! Missus!" the stableman was crying. "You . . . must . . . pardon . . . me . . . if ——" Mr. Lew was quite out of breath. He was panting "like a hound in summer" as he struggled to hold back the person who emerged with him now. "I've a told Finn Toller that 'a be too boozed to speak to any Christian man, least of all to any friend of the family, but 'a says 'a must speak in private to Mr. Robinson."

"In . . . private . . . so I said," repeated the drunken dere- lict, staggering to an erect position but keeping his hand on Solly Lew's shoulder. "In . . . private it must be, lookee! And old Finn do know what's in's mind to say to 'un, though 'a *have* had a tidy drop in out-house . . . but old Finn do know . . . old Finn do know!"

The lamplight by which the landlady of St. Michael's now watched with an indignant eye this invasion of her premises hung over the back door of the inn. It swayed to and fro in the wind, and through the open door, behind the two lurching men, Red Robinson could catch a glimpse of faintly gleaming cobblestones and dimly illuminated woodpiles and empty beer- bottles. A large rain-filled water-butt showed too in that gusty door frame, while along with the howling wind there came a strong odour of rank straw and sour human urine.

"Yer ain't fit to talk to the Missus nor to her friends!" re- iterated Solly, "Yer ain't fit for naught but workus, and to workus ye'll come, yer old rum-drinker, yer old deck-swabbler!"

"Stand straight and answer me at once, Finn Toller," ex- claimed the angry landlady. "What were you doing in our yard? Come, come, now. No nonsense! I say, what were you doing there, Finn Toller? Speak up! Can't you understand plain English?"

"I dunno what to say to 'ee, Missus," muttered the helpless ruffian, "but I do know well in me mind that 'tis Mr. Robinson here what I've 'a come for to see . . . for . . . to see . . . for . . . to . . ." At this point, so potent was the Bristol rum to which Solly Lew had been rashly treating this fish from the bottom of the Glastonbury Pond, that, disregarding the land- lady's indignation the wretch actually began murmuring a lewd catch that had been formerly popular in Bove Town and Beckery.

" 'I've a whisper for you, in your mare's-tail-ear';
　　Pillicock crowed to Kate,
'I've a whisper for you, me Coney dear,
　　Your man be away over Hornblotton Mere
And I be at your gate.' "

Mr. Finn Toller in his natural condition was no engaging sight. In his present state he was a revolting object. He was a sandy-haired individual with a loose, straggly, pale-coloured beard. He gave the impression of being completely devoid of both eyebrows and eyelashes, so bleached and whitish in his case were these normal appendages to the human countenance. His mouth was always open and always slobbering, but although his whole expression was furtive and dodging, his teeth were large and strong and wolfish. Mr. Toller looked, in fact, like a man weak to the verge of imbecility who had been ironically endowed with the teeth of a strong beast of prey.

Red Robinson did not at all relish the look of things as this repulsive hang-dog creature shuffled now towards him and fixed upon him a look of revolting confederacy, a look that seemed to say: "Here I am, Mr. Robinson! You've called me up and here I am!" The truth was that at the end of one of his most eloquent revolutionary speeches to the Glastonbury Comrades, Mr. Toller had sneaked up to Red and compelled him to write his name down, in the book they kept, as available for any activities required—"and the dirtier the better!" Mr. Toller had added, as he slobbered over the table. Red had got into trouble with the other Comrades for allowing the man to write his name down in their book. They told him that it was enough for him if the filthiest beggar swore he would spit in the road when Mr. Crow passed by! "That's enough to haul him into the party, eh?" they said. Nor was their sarcasm unjustified. Red took no interest at all in keeping up the quality or integrity of the Comrades. What he was after, as Finn Toller with his wolfish instinct had very quickly detected, were recruits, not to Marxianism, but to 'ate.

"My husband will be back in a minute," said the landlady sternly, "and you remember how he got rid of you the other night when you were hanging about so late!"

"What I've got . . . to say, Missus, be for Mr. Robinson's ear alone. Please allow me, Missus, for all that us poor folks have got left"—he stopped and threw a very sinister leer at Red— "be what be put in our minds by they as be book-larned and glib of tongue, like this clever Mister here, who is foreman of his Worship's. Us poor dogs hasn't got anything left in the world, us hasn't, except they nice, little thoughties, they pretty thoughties, what clever ones, like Mister here, do put into we." It was clear that the threat of the landlord's return had sobered "Codfin," as his neighbors called him, quite a good deal. He seemed able to walk by himself now, for he shook away Solly Lew's supporting arm. His pale, lidless, blue eyes began peering about, like the eyes of a maggot dislodged from its native habitation and seeking a refuge. "If Mr. Robinson will come in here with me," he said now, moving towards the pleasant parlour where Red and Sally had been enjoying themselves, "I won't make no trouble for no one; but if Mister here, what be so clever and so book-larned, won't let I speak to he, I'll raise such a trouble that you'll have to call for the police."

"What impudence is this?" cried the landlady. "You wait till my husband comes back. He'll show you whether he has to call for the police to give you the ——" But to the good woman's complete amazement Red himself intervened at this point.

"High'd better 'ear what 'ee 'as to sigh," he said. " 'Tis no good disturbing the plice when 'ee says 'ee'll go quiet as a lamb of 'is own self, if I tike 'im in there for a jiffy. That's so, ain't it, Codfin?"

Mr. Toller, apparently completely sobered now, bowed to the landlady, made a grimace at Solly Lew, and followed his "clever one" into the parlour where Red shut the door. It would be difficult to explain the subtle cause of Mr. Robinson's submission to this demand of Mr. Toller to speak with him, but undoubtedly, mingled with other things, there had sprung up, the very second these two men met, that curious psychic *fear*, of which mention has already been made in regard to Lord P.'s attitude to his bastard. Glastonbury was, if the real truth were revealed, just as every small town is, crowded with queer, morbid and even humorous instances of this irrational terror of one personality for another. These fear-links can be grotesquely joined up in a spiritual mathematical and nervous pattern of psychic subordination.

Philip Crow himself had been afraid—in this particular way —of Tom Barter. Indeed these mysterious fear-links brought together—in an ascending and descending scale of fear—the great Lord P. and the gentleman called Codfin. For Lord P. was afraid of Zoyland. Zoyland was afraid of Philip. Philip—though this latter did not know it—was afraid of Barter. Barter was afraid of Red. While Red—and here we reach the convoluted secret as to why he was at this very moment so carefully closing the parlour door—was afraid of Mr. Toller.

They were an interesting and curious pair as they stood facing each other now by that parlour fireplace. Red was determined not to offer Codfin a drink or to ask him to sit down. Mr. Toller's watery blue eyes, blotched, freckly face and tow-coloured beard kept turning, with a sort of feeble insistence, like that of a great, dazed, malignant cockchafer, towards the half-empty bottle.

"What is it?" said Red. "What do you want? Tell me quickly, for he'll be back in a minute. He's only taking Miss Jones a bit of the way home." There was no earthly reason why Red should have informed Codfin that the landlord of St. Michael's was taking Miss Jones anywhere! This excessive, hurried, eager confidence, expressed in a cross and peevish tone, was a beautiful example of psychic link-fear, working in accordance with its nature.

After shutting the door Red walked to the fireplace, leaving Finn Toller standing in the middle of the room. Red glanced at the man hurriedly and then, quite as hurriedly, turned his face away. From the straggly beard, the watery eyes, the ragged clothes, there emanated something that Red found extremely per-turbing. It was one of those moments when the pre-birth stirrings of a ghastly idea are huddled and swaddled in an ominous silence. Certain thoughts, that have been long nurtured in deep half-conscious brooding, manifest themselves, when they finally emerge into the light, with a horrid tangibility that is like the impact of something physically shocking. And into this warm, firelit room, full of the aura of a young feminine body that has been so assiduously courted and caressed that its sweet essence pervades the air, there now projected itself a presence that was monstrous, revolting, intolerable.

From each particular hair of Mr. Toller's beard this presence emanated. From the adam's apple in his bare, dirty neck, from the blood-stained rims of his watery eyes, from the yellowish fluff, growing like fungus on cheese from the back of his hands, from a certain beyond-the-pale look of his naked, shirtless wrist-bones, this presence grew and grew and grew in that closed room. It sprang from Toller; but it was distinct from Toller. It seemed to find in the fragrance of the courted body of Sally Jones an air favourable to its monstrous expansion.

Red could not reasonably, normally, have divined the nature of this horrid thought, of this newly born abortion from the broodings of Mr. Toller's brain. There must have been within him some protoplasmic response to it, created by the germinating poisons of his 'ate, of which he himself was unconscious. Violence must have called to violence, like deep calling to deep, between what was unconscious in the one and conscious in the other. Once more he glanced furtively, quickly, at the man standing by the table, and this time their eyes met.

" 'Twas your cleverness what put it first into me head." Had Mr. Toller uttered those words or had he *thought* those words himself? Red felt a peculiar and ghastly unreality stealing over him. The gin-bottle looked unreal. The carpet looked unreal. The low wicker-chair with its flowered cushions where he had so recently held Sally on his lap looked most unreal of all. "What's that you're sighing?" His own words seemed unreal now as soon as they left his mouth.

"A bloated capitalist, like 'im, what do hexploit us poor dawgs, ought to lickidated." It was Mr. Toller undoubtedly who was saying *that*; and Red recognized his own oratorical expression, "liquidated," the meaning of which, for the word had reached him from Bristol, had always puzzled him—though this had not prevented him from using it in his orations.

"A hairy-stow-crat like *he* be oughter be lickidated!" repeated Mr. Toller; and Red's discomfort was augmented by the manner in which the man's mouth dribbled as the words left his throat.

"You're drunk . . . that's what you are . . . too drunk to know your own nime . . . and if I weren't hunwillin' to disturb this quiet 'ouse ——"

"Lickidated be to tap on's bloody head, I tell 'ee . . . tap on's head, till's bloody brains be out!"

It was not the words alone, it was a certain galvanic twitch that accompanied them in Mr. Toller's *hands*, that made Red begin now to feel sick in the pit of his stomach. He suddenly found himself becoming fascinated by Mr. Toller's hands. As he looked at these hands he noticed that they were not only short and stubby hands, but—and this was quite unlike most stubby hands—they were hands that tapered at the fingertips and could bend backwards. How patient, harmless, reassuring, most human hands are! But Red realised now that Mr. Toller's hands were much more disturbing than any expression in the features of his face.

In all minds there are abominable thoughts. We are all potential murderers. But something—some feeling, some motion of the will, some scruple, some principle—intervenes, and we cannot act what we think! But there was a look about Mr. Toller's hands that seemed like the cry of murder in the night, like the underside of bridges, like shrubberies in public parks, like tin-roofed sheds near madhouses, like gasworks beside foul canals, something that *unravelled the skein*, that broke up the fundamental necessity and substituted a monstrous terrifying chaos . . . deep, black holes . . . dangling ropes . . . the desperate dilemma of the indestructible corpse . . . the horror of the secret held by one alone . . .

Red now began to see those hands of Codfin at the throat of life, at the throat of that life which meant the sweet body of Sally Jones, the carved bishop's chair in his mother's kitchen, the liver-and-bacon in his mother's frying-pan not to speak of his nice, new foreman's clothes! It was part of life that there should be persons like Codfin going harmlessly about . . . persons that a workingman foreman could pass by, but that the gentry—like that John Crow who had the office in the station yard—were bound in honour to treat to drinks. And those hands were now to be raised against life . . . the life of a living man! Those hands were tools of "liquidation." No more liver-and-bacon, no more bottles of gin, no more girls on laps, when those hands were lifted up. Unreal! That's what this moment was, and unreal in the way that makes a person feel sick. That straggly beard and slobbering mouth were talking of "lickidation"; but they were thinking of *murder*. The blood began to leave Red's cheeks. Poor people might be hungry, sick people might be sick, weak people might have to carry burdens—but they were all *alive*! And even death, when it came in the natural course of things, had a secret inevitable comfortableness about it! You could talk of such death with a girl on your lap. But *murder*— that was a different thing . . .

"I couldn't do it with a knife, Mister." The words sank down into the fireplace at which Red was now staring. Red allowed them to sink, like eight black marbles thrown by a wicked child into a particularly red hole.

"I don't know what you're talking about, Toller," he whispered in a low voice.

But the other went on: "Nor with a bullet, Mister, for I be feared o' they little pop-guns." Sharply, after the other eight marbles, went these thirteen simple words, all of them into the same red hole. "One of they iron bars 'ud do to do't with, what his workmen do leave about, up alongside o' Wookey." As he spoke, the man made a feeble and fluctuating movement of his whole person towards the table, on which stood the half-empty bottle of gin, a decanter of water, and a plate of gingerbreads.

Red, as his eyes followed him, remembered with miserable vividness how Sally and he had played a merry London board-school game with those gingerbreads, having a racing match together to see how many they could swallow while the little minute hand of his watch went round the circle.

"Toller!" he rapped out. "What, in 'oly 'ell, are you talking about?"

The individual known as Codfin patted the stopper of the bottle with the palm of one of his hands. Then he threw a long, silent, sidelong glance at Red out of his lidless and lachrymose blue eyes. He said slowly: "Don't 'ee go and get crusty wi' I, Mister. I baint a clever one like you be, but I can look up wondrous long words in dick-shone-ary, I can. They do know I well in public library. A person don't have to write no slip o' paper for to take dick-shone-ary down from shelf!"

"Toller!" snapped Red again. "What in 'old 'arry's name are yer mumbling about?"

"Tirry-aniseed be the word you spoke up, so free and strong, when you made thik girt speech about lickidation, Mister. And 'twere wondrous to I, when I did see thik same girt word writ down in dick-shone-ary! Tirry-aniseed were thik long word, and it do mean a sweet and savoury killing of he that lives on poor men's sweat."

"Toller!" gasped Red in horrified alarm. "You stove that, strite and now! You stove it, I say! Shut yer bleedin' mouth and go to 'ell with your hidiocies! People in speeches may curse these bleedin' capitalists, but people what tike to iron bars are *murderers,* that's what they are, pline, downright *murderers*; and people who even 'ear such things be complexes of murderers; and I tell yer, Toller, I won't so much as 'ear one word more o' this from yer bleedin' mouth. I'll call the Missus strite now, and see what *she* says to your blitherin' hidiocies! Yes, I will. I'll call her strite now!" He moved, as he spoke, towards the door, but instead of displaying the least alarm at his threat, Mr. Toller, with ghastly *sangfroid*, began deliberately to pull the cork from the bottle and pour himself out a glass of raw gin.

Red's hand was actually on the handle of the door when he turned round and contemplated this outrageous spectacle. His face worked convulsively, as he stood there; the mixture of fear and fury in his heart almost choking him.

"Put—that stuff—down!" he spluttered; but instead of opening the door he found himself holding it tight shut with a sort of guilty violence. In a flash he beheld himself in the dock at Taunton, accused of plotting Philip Crow's murder at the hands of this slobbering devil. But Finn Toller coolly and quietly replaced the cork in the bottle.

"Thik iron bar be the best thing, then," he repeated. "I thought a man like you be, Mister, would say nothing less! I couldn't do it wi' a knife, nor yet wi' a bullet. One o' they girt iron bars be the very thing for anyone what feels on his mind, as thee and me does, the sweet savour of tirry-aniseed!"

Red glanced past that pock-marked, freckled face, wherein the weak blue eyes were suffused with a watery rheum, and stared miserably at the gingerbread on the table. How foolish people were, he thought, not to enjoy, with a gratitude to fate beyond expression, every minute of respectable, innocent happiness that was not in danger of the jail or the rope!

His moment of supreme misery was brought to an end by the heavenly sound of the front door opening and the voice of the landlord of St. Michael's Inn, raised in genial badinage. Never was a tiresome old gentleman's voice more welcome.

As Red opened the door, so vivid had been his plunge into crime, condemnation, convict's clothes, picking oakum, warders, jailers, chaplains, executioners, black-caps, drops, and burning lime, that he vowed that never again in his whole life would he introduce into a speech the word "tyrannicide." As Finn Toller sneaked off now, under cover of the lively eulogies of "Miss Jones" that poured from the lips of the blustering old man, Red felt that never again, either, would he boast of heroic bloodshed to his admiring Sally. He had got such a glimpse into the *monstrous*, as he watched the adam's apple in Mr. Toller's throat jerk up and down while he drank that gin, that he thought, as he submitted to the old gentleman's jokes, "Better listen to such old-time stuff to the end of me dyes, rather than 'ave the 'orrible tighst in me mouth what I 'ad just then!"

"Well, if ye baint ashamed of yourself, ye ought to be!" pronounced Solly Lew emphatically as he dismissed his late protégé through the back of the old stables and new garage.

"Us haven't done no harm to they, nor they done no harm to we," protested Toller in a wheedling voice. "That were wondrous fine rum you gived I, Mr. Lew, and if the Lord wills I'll pay the good deed back to 'ee, come Christmas. Good night, Mr. Lew,—don't 'ee trouble to come no further. 'Tis a wild night for wind, looks so, but no token o' rain! I never likes these windy nights, Mr. Lew. They disturbs a person's mind. Yes, I knows me way, thank 'ee kindly, god-den to 'ee."

But when Solly Lew had gone back into the house, Mr. Toller made no hurried departure from the scene. He had long been practising in Glastonbury certain patient, quiet, humble little methods of burglary; of burglary so unassuming, so unpretentious, so easily satisfied, that he had only once been caught

at it, and since it was Bloody Johnny who caught him, eating un-
cooked sausages in his larder one November night, Codfin escaped even on that occasion with an eccentric reprimand.

He now set himself to survey the back premises of St. Michael's
Inn. He had long been anxious to find out exactly how the land
lay in this establishment, and tonight he felt in very good spirits,
having found out all he wanted, and at the same time, by a stroke
of what in his own mind he regarded as pure personal superiority,
reduced the Mayor's foreman—and how he had done it he himself hardly knew!—to a position of nervous subordination.

He now planted himself under the protection of a big plum-
tree that grew against the old stable roof and proceeded with uplifted beard to contemplate pensively the rear of the house. It
must not be supposed that all the excited outpourings of human
feeling that were whirling off on that west wind from so many
dreaming heads—not to mention the two watchers at the open
windows—were without their effect upon the nervous organisation of the watery-eyed Mr. Toller. Had Solly Lew, or any other
boon-companion, enquired of him how he felt just then, Codfin
would have doubtless replied—"I never have liked these here
windy nights. These here nights be turble hummy and drummy
to me pore head."

As his weak eyes slowly swept over the ramshackle roofs and
walls and chimneys before him, Toller's figure suddenly stiffened,
like a nocturnal animal conscious of danger. He became aware
that one of the back windows of the main structure of the house
was wide open and that a human face was intently scrutinising
him; and not only scrutinising him, but making signals to attract
his attention.

Now Mr. Toller, who had no scruple about using iron bars
and who had not the slightest fear of Mr. Sheperd, the old Glastonbury policeman, had from his childhood been awed into humble respect by the personality of Mad Bet. He recognised now
that there was nothing for it but that he must do this creature's
bidding. He recognised, in fact, with the same instinctive knowledge which Red had shown in his own case, that when in the
presence of Mad Bet he was in the presence of a nature born
to dominate him.

The woman was beckoning to him to climb up upon the stable-roof and come to her window; an exploit which, for a person with any agility at all, was not a very difficult task. Mr. Toller accordingly made an obeisance with his head and a sort of salaam with his hands, such as Sinbad the Sailor might have made in the presence of some Grandmother of the Djinn, and set himself to climb. The wind was his chief trouble in this ascent; for the plum tree afforded him a ladder at the beginning; and once on the roof, as far as the actual climbing went, all was easy. But the wind made it difficult for the man to keep his balance; made it very difficult for him to advance. He crawled forward upon his knees as best he could; but many times he was forced to lie prone on his stomach and remain absolutely still while the wind-gust whirled over him.

What did Codfin think about during these moments when he lay on the cold slate tiles, in considerable peril of being toppled over and rolled down? To translate his thoughts into ordinary speech would cause their tang, their salt, their fine edge, to be lost; but the drift of them was doubtless something like this: "I'll be glad when Mad Bet lets me go. Mad Bet's got a message for me. Mad Bet's message is to some man she's taken with. I wouldn't mind, same as some would, if Mad Bet were taken wi' I! A 'ooman be a 'ooman; and when a 'ooman do smile at I, it do wrinkle up her face, all soft and sweet, even if she be as ugly as sin."

Such, in rough clumsy short-hand, were some of Codfin's thoughts as he advanced slowly over the stable roof, lying flat when the gusts were worst, and crawling forward when they subsided.

According to the wise, if somewhat tragic philosophy of Dr. Fell, the thoughts of this scum-beetle from the Beckery stews were just as important, in the total sum of things, that night of the tenth of December, as the dreams of Parson Dekker or of the Mayor himself. But it must be remembered too that according to Dr. Fell's philosophy there was a deep importance, perhaps only a *little* less deep, in the feelings of a bewildered flea that Mr. Toller had carried away in his vest with him from his Beckery lodging.

" 'Twere sweet as rum and sugar to make that cockney sod take notice!" Such might be a rough translation of yet another of Mr. Toller's thoughts as he cowered in the wind under the racing clouds and tore his finger-nails in the interstices of the slate tiles. Those old slate tiles, on St. Michael's stable roof, came from the same part of South Wales as did this great west wind and neither they nor it seemed prepared to lend themselves easily to the proceedings of Codfin thus struggling to obey the commands of Mad Bet.

But he reached her window at last and to his dismay found that she intended to descend to the ground in his company! Finn Toller was not the man to shirk; but it must be confessed that if there had been any trace of tipsiness left in him, this command of the madwoman's—and it was given with the calmest certainty of its being obeyed—would have made him deadly sober.

The woman was warmly dressed and warmly shawled for the adventure when he finally reached her. That was one good thing. Another good thing was that her bonnet was tied with very strong tight strings under her chin. He could never have got her down in this wind, though he probably would have tried, if she hadn't herself, with the supernatural cunning of the insane, told him exactly what to do. She told him exactly where he could find a ladder and she told him how he could fix the end of this ladder in the projecting leaden rain-pipe and lay it flat along the roof, thus affording a support for her knees in the wind, and, when they finally reached the gutter, an easy way of getting down.

It took so long to make all these moves, especially when he had the woman out upon the roof with him, that by the time he had got the ladder safe down from the leaden gutter and had it firmly fixed in the earth for her final descent, it was about three o'clock.

"Her be a master-sprite, her be!" he thought to himself, as he looked up at the wind-blown shawl and flapping bonnet huddled at the edge of the water-spout; though where he had picked up the phrase "master-sprite" he could not for the life of him have remembered.

She made him take the ladder back when she was once on the ground, to the place where he had found it. Then, for the first time, she told him what she wanted him to do.

An hour later—but still a long way from the approach of the winter's dawn—Finn Toller found himself seated inside St. Michael's Tower on the top of Glastonbury Tor, facing Mad Bet. Mr. Geard's London architect had lately been making a few necessary repairs in the interior of the structure and it was only for this reason that these two had been able to enter. It would have been totally dark within this stone fortress of Mat Dekker's God had not Betsy—who had made, during the long half hour when her liberator was fighting the wind on that stable roof, the cunning preparations of a crazy one with a fixed idea— brought with her two or three candle-ends, extracted from candle-sticks left by chance in her place of temporary captivity.

Finn Toller produced matches from his pocket and proceeded to light one of these candle-ends, setting it up, by the help of its own grease, upon a piece of boarding. The flickering little flame soon illuminated—but there were no living eyes except their own to envisage the scene—not only Bet's old-fashioned bonnet and quilted shawl, but the straggly beard, freckled face and watery eyes of the derelict who sat opposite her, and who now filled the blackened stub of a clay pipe and set himself to smoke, as he leaned his back against the eastern wall of their square stone refuge.

The howling and shrieking of the wind, as these two sat there, made about their ears a deafening tumult, so that it was neces-sary for them to raise their voices to an unnatural pitch if they were to make their meaning audible. So innocently heathen was Finn Toller that when Bet shouted at him: "Archangel's walls be strong 'gainst they Devils!" he had the notion under his tow-coloured poll that Bet was referring to her familiar spirit by some particular pet name.

But Bet was quite right. Gwyn-ap-Nud's Powers of the Air were surely abroad in full force that night; and Michael's great wings needed to be strong indeed to ward off from Glastonbury these rushing hosts.

"Why don't Mayor Geard build up Archangel's Church?"

shouted the woman, "instead of dipping folk's bodies in thik wold Well?"

Mad Bet had put an unanswerable conundrum this time before her rescuer. Mat Dekker would have altogether entered into the spirit of this question. Over and over again had he remarked to Sam—"There can't be more than a dozen real Christians in this place, me boy; or instead of these fantastical Pageants I'd be celebrating Mass up there in a great new church!"

But Finn Toller puffed away at his clay pipe in silence. His awe in the presence of his companion was so great that he had actually done what he had never in his life done before; asked a woman's permission to light this pipe of his! And Mad Bet's permission had been given in true hieratic fashion. But it was a different thing when she talked to him of rebuilding churches to St. Michael. A patient, though not a sulky silence fell on him then.

Finn Toller took off his cap and leaned back his head against the stone wall. He couldn't see the stars at the top of the great funnel in which they sat, because of certain cross-beams which the Mayor's architect had put across that dark hollow space. He experienced at that moment, however, one of the nearest approaches to religious exultation that he had known since as a child he had been taken to see General Booth pass through town. To be alone with Mad Bet on the top of Glastonbury Tor was something to remember. Burglaries and iron bars were trifles in comparison. But to be alone with a holy 'ooman, as he mentally named his companion, was not destined to be without its penalties. It was with some perturbation that he saw her now bending down over their solitary candle-flame.

"What be doing, Mad Bet?" he enquired nervously, using the epithet mad much as Tossie would have used the word Ladyship in addressing Rachel.

The woman was melting one of her other candle-ends at the lighted candle. Having reduced the wax thereof to the desired softness she rapidly proceeded to mould it into the rough likeness of a human figure.

"Thik be *her*!" she now remarked, holding up this distorted inch of wax.

Then, hurriedly rising, she muttered some devilish incantation, quite inaudible to the dumbfounded Codfin, and proceeded to stamp upon the image she had made, grinding the wax into a shapeless mass of candle-grease and mud and saw-dust, under her heavy heel. As she trod, she began muttering again; but this time her words *were* audible to the astonished waif from the Beckery slum:

"Dirt ye was and dirt ye shall be!" screamed the madwoman ferociously. "I've a done for 'ee now, ye bitch! Dirt ye be now, I tell 'ee! Dirt ye be; as ye were afore he picked 'ee up! Dirt! Dirt! Dirt!" and the grinding heel finished its savage job so completely that there was soon nothing left of that fragment of obliterated wax. Then with several long-drawn panting breaths Mad Bet resumed her seat.

"Can 'ee keep a secret, man?" she shouted at the agitated Mr. Toller whose watery eyes were now staring anxiously at the tower door.

It was in Codfin's mind that her familiar spirit, whom he had heard invoked as "Archangel," might at any second take a palpable shape. This was the only moment in that long eventful night when Mr. Toller experienced a real shock of agitation, save for his first sight of the woman at the window.

"I be a grave for they secrets, Mad Bet," he now remarked, in a resigned voice, puffing furiously at his pipe as if with the intent to evoke a screen of wholesome smoke between himself and the supernatural.

"'Twere *her* what you seed I stamp into nothing," went on the madwoman. "In Archangel's Tower I stamped on she. Looksee!—how candle do splutter and spit! Now 'tis done. 'Twere *her* I stampit out. Hist! How thik wind do blow! 'Twere me wone heel what stampit she into dirt. Her be dirt now; and her'll stay dirt till Judgment!"

Mr. Toller's eyes became more watery than ever owing to the acrid smoke which he sucked out and blew forth. To his companion's tirade he thought best to make no reply. He had almost as strong a desire to disassociate himself from these proceedings as poor Red had recently had to disassociate himself from "tirry-aniseed" and iron bars.

"If I speak her name, Finn Toller, will ye hold 'un mute and mum in thee's deep soul?"

Mr. Toller's lower lip hung down; and two thin streams of saliva, stained with tobacco-juice, dripped upon his filthy shirt and upon his still filthier vest. The flea which he had brought with him from his Beckery shanty snuggled up to his breastbone, deriving much comfort from the pale-coloured hairs, smelling like those of a dead stoat, which grew on the man's chest.

But he answered, as Homer would say, "from his steadfast heart": "What you do tell to I, Mad Bet, be more hid than they hanging-stones in Wookey. Folk can see they stones for sixpence; but not for twenty pound would I betray thee, 'ooman . . . no, not for twenty times twenty!"

Thus reassured, Mad Bet spoke her mind freely.

"Her be thik baggage, thik hell's broth piece o' harlotry, what lives wi' wold Miss Drew. Some do say she be married to 'un; others do say she be his light-o'-love. But whether or no for that, she do go to's bed in Northload, every night, weekday and Sunday. She do bless herself for living soft and cosy wi' thik old 'ooman by day, and she do mightily cherish being colled and clipped in's bed, when night do come! Heigh! but she do like being naked to thik man's dear hand, night by night, and all so daffadown-dilly in pretty bed-clothes! I do know she's feelin's by me wone feelin's, Mr. Toller, and I do thinky and thinky, when night do come, how she do lie so snug and warm wi' he."

Mr. Toller's masculine brain began to be totally confused. Mad Bet was talking of her enemy as sympathetically and understandingly as if it were her daughter. Codfin could understand bringing down an iron bar on the head of a rich mine-owner; but this sympathising with the feelings of someone you were reducing to dirt under your heel was a subtlety of vengeance beyond his grasp.

"I do know thik lass," he contented himself with saying. "I've a-been inside Missy Drew's fine house wi' Bob Rendle from Ditchett Underleaze. Us never took nothin', for Bob were frightened when Lily Rogers talked in she's sleep; but I've a-been upstairs and downstairs in thik fine house."

Mad Bet pushed back her Sunday bonnet, with its forget-me-not border, till Toller could see the gleaming whiteness of her bare skull by the guttering candle-dip. He fidgetted uneasily under the glance she now fixed upon him.

"I've a-never killed a gal yet, Mad Bet, and I be ——" It is probable that no effort of any human will, made in all Glastonbury that night, was more heroic than the effort required from Mr. Toller as he completed this speech—"and I be too old to begin now!"

Having made his stand, Mr. Toller must have felt an overpowering desire to soothe what he supposed would be the madwoman's fury. He had known from the beginning that her present obsession was about Mary; for since Mother Legge's Easter party Bet's mania for John was one of the chief tavern topics. If Finn Toller had in his nervous organisation anything resembling what in popular parlance is called a "complex," such a "complex" consisted in the idea—almost, although not quite, a complete illusion—that people were continually wanting to bribe him to commit some murder.

Was Mr. Toller a homicidal maniac? Any glib answer to this question would be a misleading one. Human character is far more complicated than is suggested by these popular scientific catchwords. Exact and very circumstantial detail would be required just here. Mr. Toller would, as a matter of fact, have found it much harder than Penny Pitches or than Emma Sly to kill a chicken. Cruelty to a child would have been more difficult to Mr. Toller than to anyone in Glastonbury, except perhaps Harry Stickles' wife, or Abel Twig of Backwear Hut. On the other hand, to hide in the bushes with that iron bar; to steal up softly behind Mr. Crow; to crack, with one sweeping horizontal swing of his under-nourished arms, Philip's Norman skull; to beat that unconscious skull into a pulp by hammering it afterwards with the iron bar; these proceedings would undoubtedly have been accompanied by a voluptuous glow of intense sensuality.

Perhaps the strictly correct view of Mr. Toller's nature was that he was a "homicidal maniac" only with regard to the killing of the most powerful personage in his immediate environment. But it is doubtful whether the definitions of tyrannicide, given in the public library dictionary, included the element of voluptuous sensuality in the killing of tyrants. To catch the vibration of *this* element Mr. Toller would have to have looked up other, more modern words; words which, it is quite certain, would have been to him totally unintelligible.

"Six o'clock Solly Lew do open up," remarked Betsy now, pulling down her bonnet into a respectable position. "I reckon it be near five, Mr. Toller. Us better be moving!"

She rose to her feet as she spoke and extinguished the guttering candle, leaving them with no light at all but that which descended from the wind-shaken, cloud-bespattered firmament. This extinguishing of that little yellow pyramid of fire took on a grandiose significance from the austere and deliberate manner in which she did it. It was just as if she were washing her sorceress-hands in that small flame; washing them clean of all further association with such a chicken-hearted "tyrannicide" as Finn Toller.

Thus, when they emerged from St. Michael's Tower, and began to descend the Tor, without having spoken one single definite word, Mad Bet allowed Finn Toller to feel himself to be a cowardly, effeminate, unreliable, untrustworthy traitor!

It was a melancholy proof of how remorseless a tyrant Eros is, that Mad Bet should have descended Tor Hill without one grateful word to her devoted servant! The invisible Watchers of that Glastonbury Divine Comedy must have recognised something curiously unfair in the fact that while the madwoman had this devouring passion for John, Finn Toller had no blinding, drugging, heart-hardening obsession wherewith to armour himself against misfortune. His pale freckled face and straggly beard drooped together under those windy stars, and his arms and legs moved like those of an automaton, as he wearily followed that forget-me-not bonnet and fluttering shawl.

He resembled a scarecrow that this crazy love-bewitched creature had compelled by her incantations to follow her, up that hill. He did not pity himself; he did not say to himself: "Women's ingratitude is like the ingratitude of the Arch-Fiend!" He only thought to himself again and again: "Her wants me to kill that gal what lives wi' old Miss Drew; but I never yet have killed no gal; and I baint going to begin killing gals—no! not even for Mad Bet!"

The most materialistic of human beings must allow that at certain epochs in the life of any history-charged spot there whirls up an abnormal stir and fume and frenzy among the invisible elements or forces that emanate from the soil.

Such a stir, such an invisible air-dance was at its height as this man and this woman descended the hill, between five o'clock and six o'clock, on that dawn of the eleventh of December.

From the poor bones in the town cemetery on the Wells Road —out beyond The Elms—rose up certain faintly stirred and barely perceptible responses to this thaumaturgic wind; but if from *these* bones a dim tremour came, much more did a turmoil of subconscious reciprocity—to use the Wessex poet's great word —gather about Gwyn-ap-Nud's Hill from the royal and sac-rosanct bone-dust buried beneath the Abbey Ruins. The wind arrived at Glastonbury carrying feathers and straws and husks and ditch-vapours with it that it had picked up from Meare Heath and Westhay Level, from Chilton-upon-Polden and Baw-drip, from the banks of the River Parrett, from Combwich and Stogursey Brook, from Chantry Kilve and Quantock's Head. But from Glastonbury it could only carry away, along with other wisps and husks and straws and ditch-vapours, such dreams as were the lighter emanations of the place. It could carry away the dreams of Jimmy Rake and Mr. Stilly, of Bartholomew Jones and Jackie Cole, of Mr. Merry and of Emma Sly, of Solly Lew and of his son Steve; but not of the Town's Mayor or of the Town's Vicar.

But even with these the west wind's burden, as it left Glas-tonbury, was too heavy. For it must needs enter the open win-dows of the hospital and burden itself with the dreams of Nell Zoyland's son—a child with the very lineaments of Sam Dekker, even to his curious chin—and also with the dreams of Tossie's girl twins which were of such incredible lustihood as to resem-ble the sturdy dreams of the winter grass, growing in those low meads where the Evercreech man's father-in-law kept his Jersey cattle.

Crude and coarse and wholesale are our psychic judgments

about newborn children, compared with the careful discrimina-
tions we use in *physical* chemistry. To any scrupulous eye among
the supernatural watchers of Glastonbury it would have been
clear that the soul of Nell's little boy was already avid with by
far the most intense, clutching, insatiable life-greed that existed
in the whole town—a greed that made Philip's egoism seem like
courteous absent-mindedness and Red's inbred hate like the itching of a nettle-sting. It would also have been clear that Tossie's
twins were so easy-going, so sweet-natured, so unselfish, that it
was as if all the humour of Tossie herself had been mingled with
the wisdom of Tossie's mistress and with the piety of cousin
Nance.

By burdening itself with the greedy dreams of Nell's little boy,
who actually cried in his sleep because the nurse refused to wake
his mother so that he might be suckled, and with the vegetative
feelings of Tossie's little girls, who seemed perfectly prepared
to let off *their* mother and enjoy any alien nourishment at any
moment, the wind seemed to need a greater momentum to carry
it away northeast, towards its resting-place on Salisbury Plain,
than it possessed. It flagged a little by the time it reached West
Pennard. It dropped some of its tiny moss-spores, its infinitesimal lichen-scales, its fungus-odours, its oak-apple dust, its sterile
bracken-pollen, its wisps of fluff from the bellies of Sedgemoor
wild-fowl, its feathery husks from the rushes of Mark Moor, its
salt-weed pungencies from the Bay of Bridgewater.

It dropped fragments and morsels of its burden now, all along
the path of its eastern flight. It dropped some at Pylle, some at
Evercreech, some at Wanstrow and Witham Friary, some at
Great Bradley Wood, some at Long Leat Park. Wisps of what it
carried floated down at all those little villages called by the
name of Deverill. At Kingston Deverill, at Monkton Deverill, at
Hill Deverill and at Longbridge Deverill little fragments were
wafted to the ground.

The wind gathered more strength as it reached Old Willoughby
Hedge and Chapel Field Barn. But it dropped some more of its
burden at Two Mile Down and yet more of it among the ancient
British villages and the high hill-tumuli that surround Great
Ridge and Stonehill Copse.

At last it arrived at Salisbury Plain; and it was natural enough that then, in those darkest hours of that long December night, it should sink down and fail.

But for Mr. Evans, at any rate, there would have been something significant that it should thus sink down and fail and find the end of its journey on the very spot where those "foreign stones" were deposited that must have followed, on their mysterious conveyance out of Wales, the self-same path across the heart of Somerset.

It would certainly have been Mr. Evans' opinion that whatever happened to the seaweed smells, and the dyke-mists, and the wild-fowl feathers, and the oak-apple dust, and the brackish marsh-vapours, the more psychic portion of this wind's aërial cargo would have been deposited at one place only—at the actual spot where the two great "Sarsen" monoliths have bowed down, during the centuries, and fallen prostrate, across the stone of "foreign origin" that is still the Altar Stone of Stonehenge.

The Marriage of Mr. Owen Evans and Miss Cordelia Geard had already taken place; and it was in one of the little new town council houses in Old Wells Road that they had settled down, immediately after this event—Cordelia not being one to press Mr. Evans to spend his savings on a holiday just at the moment when Old Jones was coming to terms over the partnership in the shop.

So it was against a background of roadside hedges and garden bushes, stripping themselves, or being stripped, by wind and rain of their perilous-smelling, morbid umbrageousness that these two singular persons went through the experience of being initiated into each other's withheld identity.

Nowhere in all the fertile and leafy regions of Somerset, so heavy in vegetation, does Winter set in with more definite emphasis than in the regions around Glastonbury. The thicker the foliage, the richer the earth odours, the bluer the apple-scented vapours, the more stark and desolate is the contrast. Then begins a wet, chilly, lamentable nakedness; and the three Glastonbury hills weep together like three titanic mourners over Arthur and Merlin and Lancelot and Gwenevere.

Mr. Evans felt that to the end of his days he would be compelled to associate the approach of Winter with the intense nervous reactions through which he was passing in this first intimacy he had ever had with a woman. All through November, as the man went to and fro from his small house in Wells Old Road, a street that lay northwest of Bove Town, to his shop in the High Street, the gradual unleafing of so many twigs and stalks and branches and trunks coincided with his closer and closer intimacy with Cordelia.

To his surprise he found himself completely spared those shocks of physical disgust and sick aversion which he had been expecting and which indeed—in his fantastic self-punishment— he had assumed as the essence of this new adventure. The situation was indeed a very curious one; for until the time of his living with Cordelia every vestige of sensuality in his nature had been absorbed in his weird and monstrous vice.

Now there occurred a reversion of this; and his sadistic tendency fell into the background for a period. It did not leave him. His own belief that it could, by some contact with the miraculous element in Glastonbury, be *compelled* to leave him still remained; but the moment for that had not yet come. His ghastly and nearly tragic experience at the Midsummer Pageant had not, and he never pretended to himself that it had, worked that healing spell. But it slowly began to present itself to his mind as a strange and unexpected phenomenon, that in his new relations with Cordelia there arose in the essential nature of the case, a situation that lent itself to what might be called a harmless and legitimate sadism, a sadism that was so mitigated and diffused that it was difficult to disassociate it from a delicate and tender attraction.

It was a growing astonishment to Mr. Evans to discover what a world of exquisite and thrilling possibilities the mere difference between the sexes creates. It was a surprise to him to find out what subtleties of receptivity exist in the nerves of a girl who is in love for the first time in her life!

And just here the presence of his suppressed perversion stood him in good stead; for it annihilated totally any possibility of that crude and unimaginative craving for novelty which had led Tom Barter such a dance.

Accustomed, just as was his friend John Crow, to derive his wickedest thrills from his imagination, Mr. Evans found that this strange, dim undersea of feminine self-consciousness, whose ebbings and flowings now receded and advanced around him, was a world so full of dark unexpected storms and of mysterious halcyon calms, caused apparently by a word, a look, a gesture, that in association with it, it was impossible to suffer from that withering ennui and horrible life-weariness which hitherto had been—to take a leaf out of Tom Chinnock's book—the particular Terre Gastée of his destiny. The trend of his mind too—as imaginative in his "unpardonable sin" as it was in his antiquarian fantasies—did both him and Cordelia the unspeakably good turn, of rendering what is usually known as beauty in a woman totally unimportant.

Nature was in a position to supply the place of beauty by her basic insistence upon the fact that this awkward and unbeguiling creature was, after all, endowed with both the form and the susceptibilities of a normal feminine being.

The wise irony of those tutelary spirits which do not desert in our need even the worst of us, destined Mr. Evans to find *his* Glastonbury miracle where he least looked for it; for the presence of the Grail in that spot has the effect of digging deep channels for the amorous life of those who touch its soil.

All lovers who have ever visited the place will know at once what is meant by this. None approach these three Glastonbury hills without an intensification of whatever erotic excitement they are capable of and whatever deepening of the grooves of their sublimated desire falls within the scope of their fate.

Cordelia was a true daughter of Glastonbury; and the magic of the place, as Mr. Evans in his first manner was always explaining, had the power of acting as an aphrodisiac of far more potent force than the famous "sea-holly" of Chesil Beach.

The Grail of Glastonbury—and this is why Mr. Geard was entirely justified in making it the centre of his new religious cult—just because of its timeless association with the First Cause had the peculiarity of exciting human souls to concentrate their eroticism upon one single ideal object, as Sam for instance had done in becoming a mediæval lover of his tortured God-Man; while it excited others, among whom was John Crow, to concentrate upon one real human being.

As for Cordelia, she had been living, all that windy November, in a state of such wild and wanton excitement that it is doubtful if there was any woman in Somersetshire through the whole Autumn, as drunken as she was with the lavish ichor of Eros.

Mr. Evans was so ignorant of the ways of women and so confused by his new experience that he did not realise the emotional extremity which his caresses were stirring up in Cordelia, nor the frantic tumultuousness of the feelings which his love-making aroused. The girl was passion-drunk. She never missed taking Mr. Evans to the shop. She never missed calling for him at the shop.

On all possible occasions when he had a day off, or when the shops were officially closed, she would make him take her for long walks in every direction; but principally to the east which meant beginning with Chalice Hill.

On these walks she would cling to his arm and pour into his ear abrupt, excited, and very often hardly coherent rhapsodies. Love in general was the subject of these spasmodic outbursts, rather than any elaborations of her own feeling; nor was Mr. Evans one to miss their poetic quality. Her words flowed and tossed; and then wavered and sank. They drifted and wilted, only to rise up again, mounting, gathering, rushing forward, to a new climax, to be followed in its turn by a new sinking down to exhausted silence.

One particular walk Mr. Evans never forgot. It was when they were following a little field-track between Havyatt Gap and West Pennard that the girl's eloquence mounted to the climax which so especially impressed him. It was a wild, gusty, rainy day; though the rain was discontinuous and the gusts intermittent; but when it neither rained nor blew there fell upon that stripped landscape a cold paralysed interim of shivering stillness, in the midst of which Mr. Evans felt that he could hear the beat of the wings of the Birds of Rhiannon.

On this particular walk to Pennard, Mr. Evans realised that there were moments when his strange companion gathered up into her uncomely face a spiritual grandeur that was astonishing. Cordelia's face lent itself to windy and rainy weather. She had been herself a little shocked, as well as startled by the manner in which, in that twilight escape by herself, seven months before, to the Two Oaks, she had been obsessed by a feeling of dominating power.

It was about four o'clock on this early-darkening December day when their field-path—a very small unfrequented cattle-drove on the way to West Pennard—led them past a solitary Scotch fir. The rough, reddish-brown trunk of this great tree was soaked with rain on its western side; and showers of rain-drops fell on their heads from a big branch above them which stretched towards the west like a gigantic extended arm.

Cordelia wore an old cloth cap of Mr. Evans'; and he himself had come out bare-headed, fearful of not being able to keep on his head, that gusty afternoon, his familiar bowler hat.

Thus as they paused beneath the tree whose upper branches groaned and creaked to greet them, the man found he could kiss the wet cheeks and cold mouth of his woman without the teasing interruption of either of their hats being knocked off, a thing that was always happening with these two clumsy ones.

"I never knew what it was like to kiss," said Mr. Evans, "before I had you! I like kissing you at the end of a dark day and under this Scotch fir."

Their wet cold faces, her shapeless nose and his grotesque hooked nose like the caricature-mask of a Roman soldier, their large, contorted, abnormal mouths, made, it might seem, more for anguished curses against God than for the sweet usage of lovers, were now pressed savagely against each other and, as they kissed, queer sounds came from both their throats, that were answered by the groanings of the tree and by the raindrops as the wind shook it.

A series of long-drawn cawings reached them now, as four black rooks with a faint grinding and grating of their huge wings passed over the tree, aiming for the rookery above Mark Moor Court.

Down somewhere in the southern hedge of the field where this Scotch fir grew, an old holly tree was creaking lamentably in the wind. Uninitiated travellers in that lonely spot would have casually remarked: "What's that creaking over there in that hedge?"—but each of these two ugly skulls with the anguished distinction of the ancient house of Rhys upon their lineaments thought within themselves: "How lucky I am to be happy when God delights to make even trees suffer!"

As a matter of fact, although neither of these human lovers were aware of this, between that Scotch fir and that ancient holly there had existed for a hundred years a strange attraction. Night by night, since the days when the author of Faust lay dying in Weimar and those two embryo trees were in danger of being eaten by grubs, they had loved each other. The magnetic disturbance of the atmosphere at that spot, while the distorted mouth of Mr. Evans was pressed against the distorted mouth of

Cordelia, was an agitation to the old tree in the hedge, so that in its creaking there arose that plaintive yearning of the vegetable world which comes to us more starkly in the winter than in the summer.

In the summer when the wind stirs the trees, there is that rushing, swelling sound of masses of heavy foliage, a sound that drowns, in its full-bosomed, undulating, ocean-like murmur, the individual sorrows of trees. But across this leafless unfrequented field these two evergreens could lift to each other their sub-human voices and cry their ancient vegetation-cry, clear and strong; that cry which always seems to come from some under-world of Being, where tragedy is mitigated by a strange undying acceptance beyond the comprehension of the troubled hearts of men and women.

It is on such gusty, early December afternoons, when darkness falls before people prepare for tea, that the symbolic essence of rain is most deeply felt. And that they should be realised in their essential quiddity, these whirling gusts of grey rain tossed obliquely across the darkening hills, they must not come in a steady, tropic downpour. *Floods* of rain destroy the quality and the significance of rain. Drops they must be, many, many drops; an infinity of drops if you will; but still numberless separate drops, grey or brown or whitish-grey, in order that they may retain that rain-smell, rain-taste, rain-secret, which separates rain from ordinary water.

They were both silent for a space after this embrace, standing under the Scotch fir, and Mr. Evans thought to himself that the look he now caught upon her profile was one of the strangest and most arresting he had ever seen on a human face. And it was no wonder he felt like this; for her face had caught that mysterious secret of the rain which very few faces and very few imaginations are able to catch. But Cordelia's face had caught it today, and held it there now in all its wild far-horizoned meanings.

There are faces made for moonlight. There are faces created to respond to the wind. There are faces for sandy deserts, for lonely seashores, for solitary headlands, for misty dawns, for frosty midnights. Cordelia's face was *made* for rain. It had

nothing in it that was normally beautiful; and yet it became at
this moment the living incarnation of all those long hours when
rain had mingled with her secretest hopes. Her face was charged
with the rain that had streamed down the window-panes at
Cardiff Villa, twilight after twilight, while her thoughts had
been flying far away; far over dripping forests, far over swollen
rivers to green-black castle walls of which she fancied herself
the mistress or the captive.

The path they were following now approached a steep incline
which led between bare muddy banks and along deeply indented
cart-ruts to a small clump of spruce firs at the top of a considerably high hill. They were both familiar with this hill and
with this clump of spruce firs. There was indeed for Mr. Evans
a special interest in this place, which was some distance out of
Glastonbury. He had himself found a deserted sheepfold up
there, in a clearing in the centre of this little fir wood, a rough
building made entirely of ancient blocks of mossy stone, but
quite roofless and windowless.

Pottering about evening after evening, in the environs of
Glastonbury, Mr. Evans and Cordelia had made more than one
interesting find; but with regard to these old stones, that had
been thrown so crudely together here to form a shelter for sheep,
our Welshman had a theory that made them the most interesting
of all his discoveries. He held very strongly to the opinion—
and he had even persuaded Mr. Merry to come round to his
view—that these stones originally belonged to the little chantry
or hermitage to which Launcelot du Lac retired to die, after the
vanishing of Arthur and after Gwenevere's retreat to the nun-
nery at Amesbury.

It was a long tedious ascent up to this little fir clump; nor
had the place any striking aspect or any particular beauty
save this ruined sheepfold in the centre of it. And yet as they
struggled up the bare slope in the rain, Mr. Evans remarked
to his bride:

"Haven't you noticed, Cordy, that it's often some small insignificant place like this that comes back to your mind with a
sudden significance, rather than the more famous spots?"

She was not yet so used to being called "Cordy" by Mr. Evans that it did not strike her as queer to hear it now as they made their way up this nameless and rainswept little eminence. Names are like clothes to girls. The name Cordelia, especially when uttered by her father, always made her feel as if she were wearing her old, weather-worn tailor-made costume, and beneath it, her winter underwear against her skin; whereas when she heard Mr. Evans call her "Cordy" she felt as if she were wearing her thinnest cotton drawers. Since she had been married she had been "Cordy" almost constantly in spite of the fact that she was now wearing her winter clothes.

Like a tree that had begun to gather moss and lichen before it was old, there was so much untouched soil in the rich levels of this girl's nature that the green sprouts of passion grew more lavish and luxuriant every day.

Between the Glastonbury trees stripping themselves bare and this Glastonbury native, stripping herself day by day of new maidenly reserves for the enchantment of her lover there was a similar parallel. It was to the west wind that the Glastonbury foliage yielded and fell; and it was to the gusty intermittent motions of Mr. Evans' erratic desires that Cordy's innate chastity sank away. Not one aspect of her life under those new brick tiles of her little house, fresh from the local brickyard to the north of Bove Town, where the council had bought them, but became associated with her gradual seduction.

The fact that the Welshman cared little for womanly beauty, the fact that behind the concentration of his desire was nothing but the diffused sublimation of his suppressed vice, rendered this girl's initiation into the nervous excitements of Eros an arena of hidden rapture such as, at that epoch, contained no equal within the purlieus of the whole town.

The two descendants of the House of Rhys were now halfway up the ascent of their hill, their boots and stockings already thoroughly soaked by the wet stalks of the dead bracken. The slope they were ascending was to the northward of West Pennard, whose outskirts in following their winding cattle-path they had already passed. Between the summit of this hill topped by the clump of dwarf spruce firs and by the ruined sheepfold, and the banks of Whitelake River there was nothing but the rough tract of untilled country known as Hearty Moor.

It was thus as unfrequented a spot as could well be found within a few miles of Glastonbury; and had a circle been drawn about that town no point upon its circumference save perhaps Crannel Moor to the west of Godney, would have been securer against human invasion. Save for an occasional shepherd-boy, guarding a flock of black-faced ewes from Norwood Farm, no one, even in summer, ever came to this place.

Thus when Mr. Evans suddenly cried out:

"There's a light in the sheepfold, Cordy!" his voice was as startled as if he had informed her of the presence of a gibbet up there with a figure swinging from it! A steadily burning light, when you are convinced of being several miles from any human habitation, is a thing that naturally makes a person's pulses beat.

"Is it the Norwood shepherd?" panted Cordelia, trying to keep pace with her companion's long strides.

"Hush!" was Mr. Evans' reply as he quickened his pace still more.

She followed him in silence; and together they pressed forward, ascending the hill. The wind struck them with such force as they climbed and the darkness had gathered about them there so suddenly that Cordelia began to experience that natural human nervousness which the approach to a flickering light in a lonely spot can induce even in one not usually subject to common timidities.

She whispered something in her companion's ear that the wind rendered inaudible.

"Hush!" replied Mr. Evans again.

It now became apparent that the light they had seen was brighter than any conceivable shepherd's lantern from Norwood Farm. Cordelia could not resist disobeying him; and for the third time during their approach she spoke.

"Someone's lighted a fire," she whispered. "The ghost of Lancelot!" she added with a wild laugh. Her words and her unrestrained laugh seized upon one portion of Mr. Evans' consciousness and carried it, like a wild goose with ruffled, helpless

feathers, to a certain imaginary tract in an ancient dream-land-
scape of his, where he always placed this ruined chantry from
the old legend, surrounding it with the melancholy horses—their
long uncut manes full of dead leaves and their burdock-tangled
tails sweeping the wet grass—growing older and feebler year
after year, as their masters prayed, hoping against hope, the
armourless penitents within those stone walls and the armourless
steeds without, for the return of the lost King.

It was fortunate for the silence of their approach, as they
now, having reached the summit of the little hill, stealthily
pushed their way through the spruce clump, that the wind, blowing obliquely across their profiles, carried that hysteric laugh of
Cordelia's over the darkened valley towards Laverly and Pilton
and Folly Wood.

Mr. Evans possessed himself now of the girl's cold hand and
as he drew her after him between the firs, led by that flickering
firelight and by a smell of burning fir-cones that now accompanied it, he began to feel, rising up within him, a childish delight in adventure such as he thought his terrible obsession had
destroyed forever.

They now heard voices within the walls of the stone sheepfold;
and as step by step they cautiously advanced, anxious to get a
glimpse of the speakers while they themselves remained unseen,
they both recognised the harsh uplifted voice of Mad Bet. The
other voice Mr. Evans did not know, though he could tell it was
a man's; but Cordelia, being a native of the town, recognised
quickly enough who was the madwoman's companion. It was the
disreputable Finn Toller; and later, when in bed that same night
she told Mr. Evans who it was, she received an obscure shock,
like a premonitory warning, when her husband showed an unexpected interest in this sinister figure.

It was through a gap in the stone wall that they saw these two
persons now, sitting beside that fire of sticks and dry ferns. They
dared not move close enough to catch any definite words of what
these two were saying; but the psychic aura of their discussion
reached them; and it must have been this, though Cordelia did
not suspect it then, that accounted for Mr. Evans' subsequent desire to make Codfin's acquaintance. Just as the gods are said to

know one another under any mask so are those whose peculiar vice or perversion separates them from the rest of the world endowed with a sixth sense of recognition.

Retaining his bride's hand in his own, and growing conscious of some appeal to his perilous nerve in what was going on, Mr. Evans compelled her to remain concealed. Concealment was as unsuitable to Mr. Geard's elder daughter as any rôle he could have chosen for her; but she was too happy to be anything but docile; and with their faces brushed by a tall undergrowth of elders they contemplated through its broken wall that ruined sheepfold, whose masonry, at any rate, although not in its present form, had witnessed the death of the noblest of Glastonbury penitents.

The dialogue of which they caught only the psychic vibrations, for the two were speaking in low tones, was as follows: "If so be as thee can't do it to *she*, may-be thee could do it to *he*?"

These words of Mad Bet were a startling surprise to Mr. Toller, for he sat up straight on his log, close to the fire they were feeding, and stretched out his arms to the blaze, clasping and unclasping his fingers in its glowing heat so nervously as to make it obvious he was thinking of something very different from the physical pleasure of warmth. The man's straggly yellow beard wagged in the smoke of the crackling sticks as he turned his watery blue eyes towards his companion. He blinked miserably with his white eyelids beneath his hairless eyebrows and there came a look of panic and even horror into his face.

"But he be your true-love, baint he?" he said, with shocked emphasis and speaking very gravely. "Ye doesn't want me to likidate, as thik Mr. Robinson do call it, your wone true-love, Mad Bet?"

The woman was silent; and what the feelings were that seethed and fermented in her heart it would be hard to put down in words; but after a minute or two she spoke again.

"If he were dead, never would *she* sleep with he again in a pretty night-dress bought for a fairing from Tim Wollop."

But the philosophy of the Glastonbury underworld could not let this idealism pass unchecked.

"But neither would *you* ever sleep long-side of he, Mad Bet. He would be lying in churchyard mould and ye would be yaller-ing in top-room of old John Chinnock's."

There was a long pause at this point during which Finn Toller pensively stirred the fiery embers with one hand while he flung upon their exposed red heart a handful of dry wood with the other.

"Listen, Finn Toller!"

The smooth and freckled face of the workhouse waif composed itself to receive a painful shock of some kind. Never did Mad Bet open her lips, but she caused her devotee some kind of nervous agitation. But so far from decreasing her servitude this constant state of psychic fear in which she kept him accentu-ated his devotion. Fear of her kept him in a perpetual ferment of nervous idolatry.

"Listen, Finn Toller; and answer me careful, for I want to have the truth of this from thee. Will thik iron bar, what you knows of, make my young man *feel* afore he dies? I don't want 'un to feel. I'd be feeling it me wone self, if he had any anguish. I don't want 'un to be able to say as much as his patter-nost, as they papists call it. I want he to be alive, and thinking about his bitchy; and the next tick of the clock I want he to be all blackness; blackness and holy bubbles and dear soul gone!"

Mad Bet was wearing a dark shawl over her poor bald pate; and, as she spoke, she pulled it down over her eyes, as if sym-bolising this final extinction of her "young man's" consciousness.

"And when 'tis all over," she added from beneath this veil, "and he be safe buried in earth, hour by hour I'll go and sit on's sweet grave! *She* won't be there; for 'twill be in thik graveyard out in Wells New Road that they'll lay 'un; and that will be too far for *she* to wend—'cept on Sundays and Holy Days! But old Bet will take her meals there; and day and night keep guard; and that's because it's necessary for someone to drive the devils away; and that's because the devils always love a sweet corpse; and that's because sweet corpses same as his'n, always do smell as sweet as new-mown hay!"

Had Mr. Evans been near enough to see Finn Toller's face in that firelight he would have been reminded of a famous folklore professor, whose lectures at one time he used to attend. When some pupil would propound to him a question that was more audacious than behooved the subject, this good man would frown in blank, bewildered confusion and would open his mouth to its utmost stretch.

Thus did Finn Toller look when Mad Bet asked him whether her "young man" would "feel" anything when that iron bar crushed his skull.

"If he *did* feel it *I* should feel it, Finn Toller," repeated that crouching figure, pulling her shawl so far down over her face that the syllables she emitted issued forth in a muffled tone.

Mr. Toller continued to survey this enveloped head. It was hard for him to tell whether the woman's eyes were scrutinising him closely from beneath it or whether they were blinded by the folds of the shawl. But he watched her intently; as a tame wolf might watch its robber master ere they rose to attack a caravan-serai of travellers.

From Cordelia's post of observation the madwoman's head, illuminated by those red flames, resembled an old Bible picture of the Witch of Endor. Squatting there on the floor of that ruined chantry she might have been an image of Despair confronted by an image of Murder; the former being conscious of every implication of the deed they discussed, the latter wrapped in a dull, stupid, besotted daze of animal uneasiness.

Resting with their heads pressed against their protecting elder bush, both Mr. Evans and Cordelia experienced many queer sensations as the acrid-smelling smoke from this fire hit their nostrils. Beating down his darker feelings, Mr. Evans set himself to recall a certain melancholy passage in Malory, the words of which, from constant perusal, he could reproduce in their precise lilt. These, as the damp twigs flapped against his head, and the wind through the ruined walls made a dull moaning in his ears, he repeated under his breath:

" 'Then Sir Launcelot never after ate but little meat, ne drank, till he was dead. For then he sickened more and more, and dried and dwined away. For the Bishop nor none of his fellows might not make him to eat, and little he drank, that he was waxen by a cubit shorter than he was, that the people could not know him.

For evermore, day and night he prayed; but sometime he slumbered a broken sleep; ever he was grovelling on the tomb of King Arthur and Queen Guenever. So he fell sick and lay in his bed; and then he sent for the Bishop that there was hermit and all his true fellows. . . . "My fair lords," said Sir Launcelot, "wit you well my careful body will into the earth, I have warning more than now I will say; therefore give me my rites" . . . Then there was weeping and wringing of hands; and the greatest dole they made that ever made men.' "

But all the while he was repeating these rhythmical words with one portion of his mind and in this task using all the power of his memory, there flitted through the unrecording portion of his consciousness a vague awareness of something going on over that fire that stirred up his suppressed vice. Mr. Evans was clairvoyant in these things and though he did not hear those murderous words spoken, the impression produced on the surrounding air by the mention of Finn Toller's iron bar was so strong that it roused emotions in him that he had not felt since the Pageant. And while Mr. Evans was struggling to drive back his devil by recalling the death of Lancelot, his bride's attention was hypnotised by the extraordinary figure of Mad Bet; and she kept saying to herself:

"If it wasn't for Owen having come, I'd have soon gone mad just like her!"

There was something so portentous about that head muffled in the black shawl—as if the woman had arrayed herself for some tragic event and were uttering words that could only be spoken from a shrouded face—that the girl found the shocking rags of Finn Toller a relief to look at in comparison.

But what *were* they talking about? These two queer ones had not met in that ruined place for the mere pleasure of meeting! Not from their murmuring voices, not from their dramatic gestures, but from a vibration in the whole atmosphere around them did Cordelia, as well as Mr. Evans, catch, without witting what it was, the revolting smell of a crime against human life.

But now came an interruption. A great fluffy barn-door owl, a galvanised bundle of soft feathers and precipitate alarm, roused by the heat of the fire, suddenly flung itself out of its day-long retreat in one of these old walls, and whirled off with a scream over the elder bush where the two onlookers were hidden. Catching sight of them there, it flew sideways with a sound so unusual that it caused Mad Bet to snatch the shawl from her head. Hurriedly, Mr. Evans pulled Cordelia back, and following an instinct, the childishness of which was natural to both of them, they retreated at a wild rush through the spruces and at a still faster pace down the slope of the hill!

It was not indeed until they reached their Scotch fir that he let her pause to take breath; and then, when between his laboured gasps he tried to kiss her as he had kissed her before, the same wild, horse-like, hysterical laugh broke from her lips. The sound was disquieting but it had the effect of soothing the nerves of her who uttered it. This queer couple resembled each other in the irrelevant and motiveless way they both were accustomed to burst out laughing. "Those two were up to some mischief, Owen," murmured the girl. But Mr. Evans hurriedly veered from this grim topic.

"Where the guide books make their great mistake," he said, as they now turned homeward, "is in treating Glastonbury as a fragment of history, instead of something that's *making* history. Your father's absolutely right. It's the future that's important."

Cordelia made no reply. It was always in relation to her father's ideas that she came nearest to losing her respect for Mr. Evans. As she felt this cool night wind blow against her face, and heard her leather boots creak with their familiar little creakings, and thought of the cake she had made yesterday for their tea today, and fumbled with the handle of Mr. Evans' stick as the next best thing to holding his hand, it seemed to her that this masculine desire to create some "important" future was one of the dreariest mockeries of human values that existed in the world.

"Keep us alive. Give us food. Give us love. Give us children. But take your 'important' Communisms and Capitalisms from around our waists and from about our necks!"

Thus would Cordelia have liked to have expressed herself if she could have found the right words. It would have been a satisfaction to scream out once in her life at the top of her lungs to her father, to her husband, to Dave Spear: "You are all a lot

of babies with your curst politics!" She would have liked John
Crow to have been there too; and, if the moment had permitted
it, she would have liked that odious wretch to have fallen in love
with her, beyond measure, beyond restraint, and tried to kiss
her, so that she could have slapped his face!

"Our good John said something yesterday that was very true,"
Mr. Evans continued, stirred by an unconscious telepathy. "He
said that a great many material things had certain little tricks
of arranging themselves at certain times, as if they all shared in
the process of some secret ritual to which we have lost the clue."

"Do you know what I'd like to do, Owen, when I hear that
man talk in that sort of way?"

There was a tone in her voice that Mr. Evans had come to
know too well and he had the wit to remain silent.

"I've annoyed her," he said to himself, "by dragging her so
fast away from Mad Bet. She doesn't know that I've lost interest
in Mad Bet, now that she's stopped torturing herself and is just
indulging herself. I'm not sure, after all, that she *is* the Grail
Messenger. Cordy is more like the Grail Messenger than *she* is,
but there's a tone in their voices that is *very* similar."

He was totally oblivious of the fact that seriously to compare
his wife with this lamentable creature had something monstrous
about it. But in Mr. Evans' attitude to women there was an obtuseness that was almost ghastly. Certain human souls suffer
from the psychic atrophy of a particular sympathy in regard to
the opposite sex. Persephone Spear had a similar peculiarity,
only in the inverse way. To Persephone no *man* was worthy of
the least subtle consideration. Men to Percy were like fish, whose
gills, though they could open and shut, had no feeling in them.

The spirits of both Cordelia and Mr. Evans sank to a low ebb
when they reached their row of red-tiled roofs, above Bove Town.
This depression had something to do with a straggling line of
little labouringmen's houses, newer even than their own—indeed
not quite finished—which the town council was just now erecting
for the workers in its souvenir factory.

Few things are more desolating to certain human moods than
new uninhabited houses. In addition to this cause of gloom Mr.
and Mrs. Evans were exhausted with their walk and longing for

their tea; a refreshment that could not—in the nature of things —be ready for at least half an hour. But deep down below the surface it was not the new houses nor their craving for tea that made them depressed. It was the emanation reaching out towards them from that ruined sheepfold.

Parlour and kitchen were the only rooms on the ground floor of Five, Old Wells Road; and when he had unlocked the front door and entered the house, Mr. Evans went straight into the parlour and sank down in a big, ugly, purple arm-chair which stood there. Cordelia meanwhile hurried into the kitchen and began her preparations for tea before even taking off her hat. It was not indeed till she had laid the table, cut the bread for toast, and got out the butter—they ate all their meals in the kitchen—that she ran upstairs to wash her hands.

The troubled mood which had descended upon them both did not immediately lift, even after they had been within their walls for a quarter of an hour; and this was the first time in their brief experience of Old Wells Road that such a thing had occurred. Never before had Mr. Evans gone into the parlour in this way and plunged into the arm-chair Mr. Geard had given them without offering to help his wife get the meal! The arm-chair was the biggest that Mr. Wollop had had on sale, and it contrasted oddly with the rest of the furniture of their small house, which was certainly more picturesque than it was comfortable, being in fact almost all the unsalable things in Number Two's shop which had been lent to Mr. Evans by his partner.

The arm-chair was a purple one and a proud-looking one; and it had a lavender-coloured fringe round the bottom of it. It was with the tassels of this fringe that the long nervous fingers of Mr. Evans were now uneasily fumbling. He had lit the gas-jet on entering this room which was only separated from the kitchen by the narrowest of little passages, and he could now see through the open door Cordelia's shadow, thrown by the kitchen-lamp behind her, flickering about upon the floor of this passage.

Mr. Evans' legs were stretched straight out on the new carpet; his muddy boots were resting on their extended heels; while the skin of his ankles exposed above his ruffled black socks looked curiously white and helpless in the glaring gas-light. His great aquiline nose drooped motionless above his chest and his arms hung down at his sides. His face was pale and he kept sucking at his cheeks in some queer manner which emphasised the prominence of his cheek-bones. His thoughts hovered around the forlorn happenings in the olden times that had left Launcelot du Lac to perish so miserably in that little chantry, but these thoughts were affected and the man was not unaware of it, by what he felt, beyond any definite explanation, about that dialogue in the sheepfold.

"Launcelot's death," he said to himself, "was one of the saddest things that have ever happened in this unhappy world." As he went on pondering upon this tall heroic lover's decline and how he lost a cubit of his stature among those flesh-scourging monks, his eyes began to close, and that particular kind of drowsiness that comes to human beings when the pitiableness of all human affairs presses wearily upon them, weighed down his eyelids.

All human minds, as they move about over the face of the earth, are in touch with a dark reservoir of our race's psychic garbage. Just as all the thrilling and vibrating thoughts that have animated human organisms survive the deaths of these organisms, so all the heavy, cloddish, murderous, desolate thoughts, in which free will and faith and happiness perish like asphyxiated gnats, roll themselves in a foul torrent into a great invisible planetary Malebolge. This Malebolge is always present and near, a little way below the surface, for all our human minds; and it only needs certain occurrences, or certain arrangements of matter, to cause an odious and devastating effluvia from its surface-scum to invade the arteries of our consciousness.

Although their ignorance of what that sheepfold talk had been about forbade any discussion of it between them, yet some residue of it floated there above the purple arm-chair and hovered in that little kitchen above the stove, acting as an invoker of those blighting waters of Malebolge, and saturating Number Five, Old Wells Road with that sick and sour undersea of abhorrence which human thoughts in their malice and their weakness have created for their own torment.

By the middle of their tea, however, they both felt more cheer-

ful. The self-protective will to forget licked up with its sorceress
tongue all these poisonous emanations squirted forth from this
underworld Malebolge. Up and down, like a beautiful coral-
tinted tongue, that will to forget moved—as the magic fumes
of the tea mounted to their heads—and very soon it had licked
up every trace of those waters of hell!

Their conversation became excited, emotional, imaginative, as
it usually was at tea-time; and it was with regret that they suddenly heard the sharp tinkle above their heads of the door-bell.

They both got up and moved simultaneously into the little
passage. It fell to Cordelia to open the door and she let in, one
by one, Dave Spear, Paul Trent, and Red Robinson. All the visitors professed roundly that they had had tea in the town.
They even named the tea-shop, which was neither the worst nor
the best available, being the little place kept by Mrs. Jones, the
mother of Sally and Jackie and the sister of Mr. Evans' partner.

Cordelia did her best to find seats in the parlour for them all.
She got Red safely disposed of in the purple chair, with Paul
Trent balanced on its arm; and while she and her husband
propped themselves up, as well as they could, on Number Two's
ricketty antiques, Dave sat squarely down on a kitchen chair
which he himself had carried in. This little touch of officious-
ness on Dave's part—she didn't want any of them in the kitchen
with the tea-things all about—had an instantaneous effect upon
Cordelia's nerves which affected her whole attitude to the business on which the three men came. To the end of his days Dave
would never learn the delicacy and charity of not meddling.

"Women ought not," he would have said, "to be fussy about
how their rooms look! Rooms are for human beings to sit in,
when—protected from wind and darkness—they discuss how to
improve the world."

The three conspirators, whose plot, devised originally by
Persephone, had become now a quite momentous and possibly
even an historic affair, had been visiting so many Glastonbury
houses in the last couple of weeks that they had come to use a
sort of stage-method in dealing with people. This method had
been invented by Paul Trent with a full understanding of the
characters of Dave and Red; and what it really amounted to was

that while he himself explained the statistics of the plan, he left Red to interject the revolutionary dynamite, and Dave the prophetic austerity. He was the lean Cassius of the plot; Dave the incorruptible Brutus; Red the vindictive Casca.

But of course this method was hardly required on this occasion, because rumours and murmurs and maledictions of the great plan had been rumbling and humming at every meal Cordy and Mr. Evans had recently shared at Cardiff Villa.

But such was the notorious absent-mindedness of Mr. Evans that Paul Trent felt justified in being as explicit with him as if he had never heard the subject discussed.

"We came in really," he said, "only to tell you two that everything is moving according to our scheme."

"Has Father decided to lend the council some money?" enquired Cordelia.

Paul Trent was too much of a diplomatist not to sense far-off the electric flicker of opposition. He made a feline movement on the arm of Red's big chair, as if he were a cat preparing to do battle.

"Nothing is decided yet," he said. "We have only been discussing things."

"What does Mother say?"

For a second this question nonplussed the man from the Scilly Isles; for it pushed him out of his legal world into his philosophical world.

"I quite agree with you that a wife's wishes ought to be carefully considered when it comes to any big investment but . . . I'm afraid . . . in this case ——"

"You mean she *doesn't* agree?" said Cordelia, "and I don't wonder either," the girl went on, "she hasn't got the least benefit out of Canon Crow's money so far—and now it's all going to be thrown away!"

Paul Trent leant forward with a flush upon his swarthy cheek and a contraction of his arched eyebrows.

"Not thrown away, lady!" he murmured softly, "not thrown away! He'll still be by far the richest man in Glastonbury."

Cordelia uttered a spasmodic little laugh, a laugh which caused Mr. Evans to give her a grave and anxious glance.

"Your father," interjected Dave, "—and your mother knows *that* perfectly well—would never touch a penny of his fortune for anything but the good of ——"

" 'Ee'll be the biggest stock-'older in our commune, Miss Cordy," remarked Red Robinson, "and 'is will be the only nime what'll be in all the pipers."

"He never got back half what he spent on the Pageant," said Cordelia.

At the word Pageant, Mr. Evans gave an involuntary shiver. He thought to himself: "With Cordy as my Grail Messenger, I'm on a better path now!"

"Miss Crummie told me 'erself," protested Red, "that 'twere only the two and a 'arf hinterest 'ee got from the bank, 'ee spent on *that* silliness!"

"That *is* really true, Miss Cor—I mean Mrs. Evans," murmured Dave, staring at her with puzzled wonder. (Why have women, he thought, so much stronger possessive instincts than men?) "And everybody knows," he went on, fixing his blue eyes steadily upon her, "that he's always regarded Canon Crow's money as a trust for the common good."

"Damn the common good!" cried Cordelia impatiently, "I don't see what you people have got to do with our money! The Rector of Northwold left it to Father without the least restriction. He left it to him because he was his best friend. All his own family had deserted him. Father made those last ten years of his life the happiest he ever had."

"Are you really going to Mark Court today?" enquired Mr. Evans. "I've never seen Lord P. Does he appreciate that amazing old house of his?"

"What we came for officially, Evans," said Paul Trent, thinking to himself, I'll make this commune the first real anarchist experiment that's ever been made; and if this moralizing ass Spear is as stupid with men as he seems to be with women, I'll not have much difficulty with *him*!—"was to tell you that if Lord P. *does* sign over to us the leases of his property, your shop, together with nearly all the shops in High Street, will have to deal with *us* and do your business co-operatively in future. This will mean," he went on hurriedly, noticing an impatient movement from Cordelia, "that Glastonbury tradesmen will pool their profits. Not *all* their profits, of course," here he gave a sidelong, cat-like glance at Dave, "for the whole idea will be to have as much complete personal liberty as possible; but enough to enable the commune to deal as a unit with the outside world."

Mr. Evans' attention had been wandering for some while and his face had grown animated with a child-like excitement.

"Glastonbury," he now cried, rising to his feet and beginning to walk up and down the little parlour with long strides, "Glastonbury will be like she was before that Tudor Devil, and all Welshmen know what the Tudors were, ruined her independence! Glastonbury will be a living Entity again. She will draw a magnetic life from her Three Hills strong enough to attract all the world to her side. She will take her place ――――" he paused and stared gloweringly at Red who was smoking his pipe in the purple chair with a wry, malicious smile. "This pooling of profits is nothing," he went on with a wave of his hand. "We must all earn our living, of course; but *that's* not it. We must free ourselves from Teutonic vandals like this Lord P., of course; but that's not it. We must employ our workers, of course, better than Philip Crow does; but that's not it. The great thing is to revive the old life of Glastonbury Herself—the great thing is to revive the old faith in Glastonbury Herself as an Urbs Beata to which all the . . . all those who are . . . all those who have been . . . all those, I mean, who've put themselves *outside the pale* may be . . . may be . . . purged in their minds!"

His voice had risen so vehemently that when he suddenly stopped and plumped down on one of Number Two's shakiest chairs so that its gilded back cracked, everyone stared at him in embarrassment.

There was a nervous silence in the room. Dave thought to himself: "It's the capitalistic system that breeds these eccentrics. When all able-bodied men in Glastonbury work in our municipal dye works no one will have time to think whether they've purged their minds or not! These nervous maniacs are the result of parasitism. We shall see to it that this fellow works with his hands till he's too tired to think about his manias!"

Red Robinson looked round for something to spit into, but seeing nothing except the fireplace, which was too far away, he swallowed his saliva with a gulp and crossed his legs in the purple chair.

"The pint, Mr. Heavens," he remarked grimly, "hain't whether Glastonbury waters can cure the pox, but whether hus working chaps can get 'old of the bewger's factories."

"Father tells me you're an anarchist, Mr. Trent," said Cordelia, attacking with feminine penetration the weak spot in this ambiguous conspiracy.

The old, weary film of cultivated patience descended upon Dave's blue eyes.

Red Robinson struggled to his feet, approached the small coal fire—the parlour of Number Five, Old Wells Road, was decidedly chilly—spat angrily into it and came back to his chair.

" 'Ee doesn't know nothin' of hanarchy 'cept the nime," he jerked out, "nor nobody helse neither! 'Tis a bleedin' fancy of such as 'as never done a stroke of bleedin' work in their bleedin' lives!"

"Mr. Trent's our lawyer, Red," said Dave quietly. "If he's clever enough to make Lord P. sell those leases, we at least must compromise a little when it comes to our commune."

But Paul Trent had turned to Cordelia and was waiting for an opportunity to speak.

"Real anarchy," he began, in the most caressing and beguiling voice, as if he had been a young Bagdad silk merchant displaying his wares in a luxurious harem, "has never yet been put into practice. Mr. Robinson thinks it a mere fairy-tale, but if your town council leases the shops in High Street and takes over the dye works and gives me a chance to make the few laws which——"

"Laws?" cried Red derisively, " 'Ee's been sighing that we'll all henjoy ourselves and do just what we like; and now 'ee's talking about laws!"

Cordelia, who had begun to gloat over the effect of her apple of discord, surveyed with astonishment the movement of self-control with which the man from the Scilly Isles patted Red's shoulder and joined in the laugh against himself.

"If he can do *that*," she thought, "he'll be a match for Lord P. and reduce old Beere to nothing."

"I cannot . . . think," said Mr. Evans gravely, speaking slowly and emphatically and evidently weighing his words, "that an anarchist commune in Glastonbury is a . . . practical possibility."

"Pardon me, Mr. Evans," said Paul Trent, "but perhaps you spoke just then . . . without . . . altogether . . . realising . . . how dangerous it is to . . . to clash with a man from the Scillies."

Mr. Evans' corrugated countenance broke into a deeply indented smile and he rose up from his creaking chair and crossed the room and shook hands vigorously with the anarchist.

"So you read the authors too?" he cried. "I never knew it! I never knew it! Think of that! And I never knew it!"

When Mr. Evans spoke of "the authors" he always meant one set of authors, those, namely, that dealt with Cymric mythology and Cymric superstition. He dropped the young lawyer's hand now and turned to his wife.

"Cordelia," he said, "you may mark my words that Lord P. will sell them his land! Mr. Trent reads the authors. Mr. Trent knows that it was in the Scillies that the oldest of the gods— Cronos himself—was kept in prison! Mr. Trent knows that since that day it's dangerous to interfere with a man from the Scillies who's set his heart on anything."

" 'Ee don't believe one word, Mister, 'ee don't," put in Red, "of they tiles and fibles what yer pins yer bleedin' fithe on! 'Ee thinks they be all my eye!"

Red looked maliciously at Mr. Evans. His reference was obviously to Paul Trent, who once more astonished Cordelia by his self-control.

"Well!" he said, "if our host can't believe my philosophy, and I can't follow *his* poetry, we can agree at any rate in enjoying your humour, Mr. Robinson!"

"I don't know whether you realise, Mrs. Evans," said Dave Spear, "that your father has decided to put off the opening of his Chalice Hill arch until the end of January; when we hope to have a ceremonious proclamation of the Glastonbury commune."

But in his heart, as he spoke, Dave thought to himself: "Since the only aspect of this affair of the least historic importance will be its move towards England becoming communist, I must see to it that the Gazette says nothing of Trent's absurd anarchism." He sighed heavily. It would have been far easier for him to drill and march and keep step and practise rifle-shooting than to do all this plotting! But the cause demanded it. His dislike of it was part of that bourgeois mentality in him which must be overcome.

"You see, Mrs. Evans," broke in Paul Trent in a soft, caressing voice, "this commune of ours will be a very harmless adventure. We have no intention of bringing the government down on us; and the fact that your father will naturally be the leading spirit in it all will keep politics in the background. His interest in it is entirely . . . *religious* . . . if I can use the word! Our friend Spear, here, thinks of it as an advertisement for communism. I am even more modest. I regard it as a quiet little experiment in philosophical anarchy. Mr. Robinson, whose influence with the labouring element in our town is so great, is less doctrinaire in his notions. He will be content if ——"

"If it makes that bewger Crow sit up and take notice! I 'ate the bloke's bleedin' phyz!"

Red added this last remark almost pensively, puffing out such a quantity of smoke that what Cordelia beheld in her purple chair was an artisan's torso, with a head covered in a cloud.

"It is true as he says," remarked Spear—and it was noticeable that all three conspirators, Dave-Brutus, Trent-Cassius and Robinson-Casca, addressed their remarks to Mr. Geard's daughter rather than to her husband—"our commune will be a very tentative movement and with many facets. I wish," here he gave another of his weary sighs, and his blue eyes took on that hopeless film of disillusionment which had such a curious pathos of its own—"I wish your father wasn't *quite* so absorbed in his religious ideas. He would be such a power, if only ——"

Cordelia pulled down her muddy skirt hem over her ungainly

ankles and let her eyes embrace all the four men in one sweeping and rather contemptuous glance.

"Why don't you make him dismiss that man John Crow?" she threw out harshly. "It's that idiot who urges him on. Father's just putty in his hands. And he doesn't believe in anything himself. He plays with us all. *I* know him, through and through!"

The founders of the Glastonbury commune surveyed their hostess much as a board of directors might have surveyed their office-stenographer if she had suddenly told them that their window-cleaner was the real danger to the firm.

But Mr. Evans, who had returned quietly to his antique chair after his discovery that the lawyer from the Scillies read "the authors," broke in at this point.

"My wife has got fond of John," he said gravely. "And so she always punishes him and holds him up to scorn."

"Owen!" Cordelia's astonishment at this unexpected attack was so great that her big mouth became as round as the letter O in the "Ora pro nobis" of a missal.

" 'Tis Miss Crummie—not Miss Cordy—what's got fond of Crow's cousin!" interjected Red. "She 'as divided 'er 'eart between Crow's cousin and young Mr. Dekker. Hain't I right, Mrs. Heavens? 'Tis 'er and not you what 'ave got soft on Crow's cousin?"

The insanity of Red's obsession against Philip was so extreme that it extended itself to every member of Philip's family. To Red's mind, Miss Crow of Benedict Street as well as Mr. and Mrs. Crow of Northload Street and even Persephone Spear, at present domiciled at Dickery Cantle's, had no individuality of their own. They were the bewger's cousins; and that fact damned them.

"What's *your* opinion, Evans," said Dave Spear, anxious to turn the conversation away from these dangerous personalities, "as to what form our commune should take, if we really do get it started in January?"

" 'Twas yer hone Missus, weren't it," interrupted the incorrigible cockney, addressing Dave, "what first thought of upsetting the bewger by this 'ere commoon?"

Mr. Evans rubbed the side of his great hooked nose with his

left thumb. Everybody in the room except Red, who now, as he reverted to his pipe, found his thoughts leaving the Crow family and summoning up the more soothing image of Sally Jones, fixed their eyes upon the Welshman.

The little parlour had become as stuffy as it was chilly. The gusty wind, beginning to shake the not very solid architecture of Five, Old Wells Road, seemed to join with the bizarre furniture of that small room in calling upon Merlin's biographer to utter some oracular word. At any rate there occurred just then that kind of pregnant silence to which groups of human beings are liable when their private thoughts differ so completely as to evoke a sort of negative equilibrium.

"I think it won't matter very much," Mr. Evans said gravely, "what form your commune takes. You yourself," and he stared at Dave with a mouth from which a small dribble of saliva was descending, "you yourself will oppose our good friend here," and he nodded at Paul Trent, "and that opposition will bring the whole thing to nothing."

His words were the first words, all this long while, that brought Paul Trent, who had been half-concealed in the smoke of Red's pipe, down from his seat on the arm of the chair. The feminine-complexioned, soft-fleshed anarchist, in his beautifully fitting clothes, now moved to the fireplace where he stood upon the rug and contemplated Mr. Evans with a tender indulgence.

The woman and the other men—for even Red seemed conscious of something unusual in the air—watched these two Celts with a faint uneasiness. For it seemed as if these strangely different aboriginals of the Western Isles stared at one another, as though something was passing between them totally obscure to the other persons in the room.

"I've only read," murmured Paul Trent, in a much softer voice than that in which he discoursed on the commune, "books *upon* the authors."

Then, without a moment's pause, as if it were a fragment of some immemorial ritual of which they both held the mystic clue, Paul Trent began to recite, in a sort of grave sing-song, words that seemed to Cordelia to be madness, to Dave to be devilry, and to Red to be pure gibberish.

" 'Complete was the captivity of Gwair in Caer Sidi,
  Lured thither through the emissary of Pwyll and Pryderi.
  Before him no one entered into it,
  Into the heavy dark chain that held ——' "

Here Paul Trent stopped; but only to give place to Mr. Evans
who caught up the refrain; answering him with a sort of antiph-
ony that seemed to their hearers still worse insanity.

" 'The Head of Annwn's Cauldron, what is it like?
  A rim of pearls, it has around the edge;
  It boils not the food of a coward or perjurer.
  The bright sword of Llwch was lifted to it,
  And in the hand of Lleminawc it was left,
  And before the door of Hell's gate lamps were burning;
  Seven alone did we return from the fortress of the Perfect
  Ones.' "

"Did you compose all that, Owen?" enquired Cordelia.

"Certainly not!" answered Paul Trent, speaking for Mr.
Evans. "It's all in the books about the authors. Neither of us
invented it. Rhys, Loomis,—they *all* quote it. It's from a very
ancient Welsh poem called 'The Harryings of Annwn' and it
appears to refer ——"

But Mr. Evans interrupted him.

"It obviously *does* refer," he shouted, "to that ancient heathen
Grail, far older than Christianity, which redeemed . . . and always will redeem . . . everyone who understands it . . . from
. . . from . . . from . . . from the captivity of Gwair in Caer
Sidi!"

He suddenly burst into a spasm of suppressed laughter which
had an extremely disconcerting effect upon the ears of his hearers. Mr. Evans was evidently on the edge of a shameless and
vociferous laughing-fit caused by some interior vision which
struck his mind as a monstrous Rabelaisian jest.

It always has an unpleasant effect when a person of a very
dominant physical personality falls into uncontrollable laughter. There is something indecent in the spectacle of it. This inde-

cency seems to be mysteriously increased when there is an ignorance in the hearers—as in this case there certainly was profound ignorance—as to the cause of the explosion.

Swinging his head and his shoulders backward and forward,
making the most extraordinary chucklings, growing at the same
time very red in the face, he allowed these laughter-tears to run
down his cheeks and to fall upon his waistcoat without attempting the least concealment of his emotion. It was as if he had
suddenly been permitted by a special dispensation of Providence
to catch a glimpse of the monstrous cosmic joke, abominable,
heroic, megalomaniacal, into which the whole creation resolved
itself!

Cordelia rose from her seat and moving to his side laid her
hand on his shoulder. She felt as if her strange mate had suddenly turned into a medium for some huge, earth-cracking supernatural ribaldry, that to her was inscrutable. She looked anxiously at the others to see how this exhibition struck *them*. But
under her touch Mr. Evans quickly recovered himself and what
had so agitated her womanly nerves seemed quite a natural occurrence to the other men.

Their host's laughing-fit evidently partook of that extra-mun-
dane humour to which all men are subject and which remains a
mystery of childishness to their wives and daughters.

Cordelia, surveying the diminishing convulsions of her partner's gaunt frame with an irritable concern, became a symbol
of immemorial feminine annoyance in the presence of such a
masculine outburst when to a man—quite suddenly—the whole
cosmos appears in the light of a monstrous joke. Women never
laugh in this sort of way. Their laughter is pure naughtiness and
unadulterated mischief, or it springs from physical well-being
and is the airy happiness of the innocent earth-bubbles of matter
or, finally, it is hysterical, as when Cordelia laughed like the
neighing of a horse.

But she went quietly back to her seat now and Mr. Evans remarked gravely: "In this affair of yours, gentlemen, I confess
I'm no politician, what I was going to say was . . . when a person touches"—he rolled his eyes towards Mr. Merry's nephew—
"this basic Secret of Life, that our Bards expressed in poems like

The Harrying of Annwn, these external arrangements of Society —capitalism or communism—seem unimportant."

Dave Spear rose to his feet, stretched himself, sighed heavily, squared his shoulders and with his hands clasped behind his back broke into a low, intense appeal, addressed to Mr. Evans alone.

"If you could see human beings *digging*, as I have lately . . . up there at Wookey . . . straining their muscles and going on and on . . . and if you could realise that this same manual labour is required, all the while, to keep the machinery of our industrial system working . . . and that the people who do it . . . upon whose labour we all live . . . the people who *make* the machines and who *feed* the machines . . . are robbed by us nonworkers of all but their bare living, you would not, my dear Mr. Evans, you *could* not, talk of communism as unimportant. You and I, with our bourgeois mentality, shrink from it as we shrink from slavery! But surely it's more righteous that we should all, quite openly, be slaves of the State, than that by an evil and crafty trick, and by our hypocritical talk of mental labour being 'harder' than manual labour, we should prolong this crime . . . this unpardonable sin?"

At the words "unpardonable sin," Mr. Evans, who had been hearing him gravely, gave a guilty start, and automatically looked sideways to the floor, to the place where, if he'd been in the shop, the staircase to the cellar would have been.

"You can't have either communism or anarchism in one little town," he said. "It's the whole country that must go in for it, or it must be let alone. And even if you *were* dictator of all England, Spear, I tell you it isn't money or position in life that makes the difference between happiness and unhappiness. It's something else . . . and when I think of how unimportant all these questions are in comparison with . . . I could . . . I could . . ."

His face which at this moment was a mixture of Don Quixote, the Devil, and Dean Swift, broke into certain deep wrinkles, evidences of another laughing-fit, which contorted it considerably, while he controlled and prevented the outburst.

Paul Trent now looked at his watch.

"Well! gentlemen," he said, "I've decided that I want you two, after all, to come out with me to Mark Moor Court tonight. I only pray we shan't find Will Zoyland closeted with his father! I'm afraid if Will got on our track at this juncture he'd ruin the whole thing. What a blessing he's out at Wookey!"

As soon as the visitors were gone, Cordelia said hurriedly to her husband: "Better take your stroll now, hadn't you, while I do the things?"

"What did you say?" murmured Mr. Evans, giving the back of the purple chair a push to move it towards the fire.

"Better go out and get your evening stroll over, while I wash up," repeated Cordelia.

Mr. Evans stared blankly at her. The natural movement of any couple, in their own house, when a group of visitors have departed, is to draw up to the hearth with an ebullition of relief, and begin a critical analysis of the evening. This was clearly what Mr. Evans expected; and he was a little nonplussed. He had not much to say to Cordelia about communes and commune-makers; but he had a great deal to say to her about The Harrying of Annwn.

The girl had already left him, however, and crossed the little passage into the kitchen; so he snatched up his long black overcoat from its peg and let himself out without a word.

"She's cross," he said to himself, "because I laughed like that. She thinks I made a fool of myself."

He followed the Old Wells Road till he reached a turn to his left, called Edmund Hill Lane, which led to the clay pits and the tile works of Edmund Hill Pottery. This pottery had played an important part in the modern life of Glastonbury, supplying the town council with those fine large brick tiles of a beautiful orange-red colour with which it had roofed all its new workmen's houses not only in Old Wells Road and Bove Town but also in Benedict Street. It was from under these bright red tiles, made of rich Somersetshire clay, that the hopes and despairs of many generations of Glastonbury people were destined to mount up and follow in its gusts, night by night, this dream-burdened westerly wind.

Mr. Evans got glimpses of a tormented half-moon in the sky,

as he walked along, tossed, tumbled, rolled, buffeted by piled-up cloud racks, driven, themselves, across the rain-swept spaces, by this same wind. Edmund Hill Lane was at that hour a lonely place to walk in, as it stretched upward towards those isolated clay pits. Its ruts were clay; its banks were clay; it had been cut out of clay; and it led to the richest clay pit in the West Country. And all this clay, which in time would be moulded and hardened into roofs for the dreams of Glastonbury people; dreams that would be—so Mr. Evans told himself now as he strode along— *much the same*, whether under Dave Spear's commune or Philip Crow's capitalism!—called out to Mr. Evans and tugged softly at him, with wet, mute, rainy, dumbly murmuring mouths, and straining, coldly heavy, corpse-like fingers.

The glimpses he got of that wildly tossed half-moon stirred the imagination of this man in the tight-waisted black coat and bowler hat. The wet clay stuck more and more clingingly to his boots as he advanced up the windy hill, leaving Glastonbury and its conspirators far behind him, and his mind followed those weird, old, chthonian deities of his race, whose dim personalities, veiled under these Cymric syllables, "Pwyll, Pryderi, Llwch, Lleminawc," called to him out of the wet earth. The very dreams of the people behind him, mounting up alongside of him from under the tiled roofs of the town, fell away from him now and sank down like a flutter of autumn leaves. That iron bar in the brain of Finn Toller, of which he had heard without hearing, sank down. The great lorries, full of hermetic tin—diabolus metallorum—of which Philip, in his house in the New Wells Road, was thinking, fell away and sank down. The Harrying of Annwn! How much more there was of the essential sorrow of things and of the essential exultation of things in that queer phrase than in all this absurd business of buying legal parchments from the Marquis of P.!

As he walked along under the sickly moon and the feverish clouds, Mr. Evans thought to himself how much more real the world of consciousness was than the world of matter.

"In any given spot on the earth's surface," he thought, "the consciousnesses of men are flowing and floating just below the blind material surface! They have the same sun, the same moon, the same stars; but it is with the souls of these things, with their under-essences that the consciousnesses of men have dealings!"

He came to a heap of clumsily thatched turnips, by a wayside barn, that the owner had covered up for winter feed for his cattle, and upon this heap he sat down, pressing the tails of his black coat under his thin flanks against the damp of this dark mound. And sitting there alone under that turbulent sky it came over him that the lives of men upon earth were all subject to the captivity of Gwair in Caer Sidi, lured by the emissary of Pwyll and Pryderi; in other words that they were all held in bond by something alien, by something external to their true, free essence. But he got the feeling that his own deeper nature could take hold of his body, yes! and take hold of all this bodily world around him, and drive them both, as this wind was driving these clouds, upon strange, occult purposes of its own.

Mr. Evans rested upon this thought for a second, holding himself aloof with an austere effort and grasping fate itself, as a man grasps the handle of a plough. But even while he was experiencing this masterful sensation there slid into his erotic nerve the quivering forked tongue of his unpardonable sin.

Something about what he had seen that afternoon in the sheepfold had broken a barrier in the fortress of his sensual concentration; and through this hole there now slid, or threatened to slide, the electric-tingling body of the undying worm.

"I must make use," he said to himself, "of what Geard is doing with that Grail Spring. The Pageant didn't kill it . . . but perhaps this water . . . these crowds . . . this white magic of old Geard . . . may kill it!"

So he spoke; but as if in mockery of "old Geard," and all he could do, there moved, there stirred, there awoke, in the remote circles of Being beyond this wild sky, the appalling perilous stuff in the double-natured First Cause. In its primordial Evil, as with its wavering searchlight it fathomed the numberless worlds of its living victims, the First Cause struck straight down now at the responsive nerve of Mr. Evans' vice, and as it stirred that poison it gave itself up to an orgasm of egocentric contemplation. As for Mr. Evans, he saw himself returning to his house with this madness and with this horror upon him; he saw himself mounting the narrow stairs; he saw himself embracing Cordelia . . . and he felt he could not do it . . . he felt he could not . . . go home . . . just then . . . with this reptile lifting up its head.

"Complete was the captivity," he muttered to himself, "of Gwair in Caer Sidi!"

Without realising what he was doing he pressed his left hand under the wet thatch of the turnip heap and pulled out a turnip. This, all muddy as it was, he pressed to his face, smelling at it with his hooked nose, and finally biting it with his strong wolfish front teeth.

While the Welshman sat on that damp heap of turnips and bit, with ferocious and yet hardly conscious impulse, into the flesh of one of the rankest and most astringent turnips in the heap, spitting out each mouthful after he had chewed it and once more plunging his teeth into the sharp-smelling substance, it happened that a microscopic creature—all mouth and yet all belly—was enjoying, or suffering from precisely the same twinge of egocentric mania, as were Mr. Evans and the First Cause, as it lay coiled up upon the surface of this same vegetable.

Thus it was fated for this particular turnip heap in Edmund Hill Lane, halfway between Old Wells Road and the Brick-tile Works to be the occasion of the bringing together, at exactly three minutes to nine o'clock on the night of the twelfth of December, of three identical psychic aberrations, that of the infinitesimal, microscopic parasite, that of Mr. Owen Evans, and that of the ultimate First Cause.

Human beings are however more sensitive to interruptions from chance than are gods or insects; and it was Mr. Evans who was the first to be distracted from this obsession of vicious contemplation. He became aware of the approach of voices coming down Edmund Hill Lane from the direction of the brick works.

They were the voices of a man and a boy; and they were amusing themselves by hooting like screech-owls. Apparently some real nocturnal bird of the species they were imitating was following them in the darkness; for Mr. Evans could hear at intervals a cry that was like an echo of the noises that these pedestrians were making, following them at no considerable distance.

He got up hurriedly from his damp seat and threw the turnip away. In its fall the insect feeding upon its surface was brushed off; which meant the death that very night of that microscopic parasite. The First Cause alone continued its unspeakable contemplation; that motion of evil in the ultimate abyss, against which all the good that is in mankind is forever struggling.

Mr. Evans advanced up the lane to meet the newcomers. This he did because he had the peculiarity of always having a nervous dread of people overtaking him in the dark; and yet he felt reluctant to hurry off home! He found himself even now possessed of a morbid fear of their stumbling upon him unwarned; so,—although with something of an effort—he forced himself to cry out "Hullo there!" in an almost menacing voice.

"Good evening, Mr. Evans!" came the reply out of the darkness; and he found himself shaking hands with Sam Dekker.

"Do you know Elphin Cantle?" said Sam.

And the boy, coming sulkily forward, shook hands too.

"I had an idea we'd meet someone we knew if we came back this way," Sam went on. "Elphin and I have been putting up wild ducks at Decoy Pool and Meare Pool; and we came back by Crannel Moor instead of by the Godney Road. We had our supper at Upper Godney. They gave us half a small pike that Mr. Merry had caught yesterday, when he was over there; in that pond at Lower Crannel. It tasted good, didn't it, Elphin, served with fried parsnips and parsley?"

Mr. Evans peered through the darkness into the boy's face. The name Elphin made him think of Gwydion-Garanhir and of Taliessin.

"I'd have liked to ask you in," he remarked, "but Mrs. Evans may be in bed. What do you make the time, Mr. Dekker?"

Sam looked at his watch and announced that it was after nine.

"You brought back that Saint Augustine I lent you in the spring so faithfully, that you're always welcome to any books you want to take from the shop."

Sam thanked him and then became silent. The two men stood awkwardly side by side; while Elphin, moving to the edge of the fence, set up his owl cry again.

"I'll walk back with you, if I may, as far as my house," said Mr. Evans.

But for some reason—perhaps because the boy Elphin was so occupied with the owls—they neither of them made any move to start forward.

"Your voice sounded just now as if it were bothered by something, Mr. Evans," said Sam at last after an embarrassing pause.

It was in his instinctive recognition of all animals' moods that this patient naturalist, transformed now into the latest Glastonbury saint, exploited his shrewdest wisdom.

"Have you a cigarette, Dekker?" asked Mr. Evans.

Sam gave him one and struck a match. This ancient Promethean act brought the two men together as nothing else could have done just then. On a dark, rainy night even the flicker of a match-flame has a magical power; and the little circle of light extending outward from Sam's concave fingers illuminated not only Mr. Evans' hooked nose, as he bent towards it, not only Sam's own retreating chin, but the frayed edges of a small duodecimo that the latter carried in his rough tweed-smelling jacket pocket.

"What's your book?" enquired the antiquary with professional curiosity.

"Only a St. John's Gospel," answered Sam nervously, shoving the volume down further into its place, and pulling his pocket-flap over it, to hide it.

"The Mayor's favourite book," remarked Mr. Evans. "He says it's the whole Bible of his new religion."

"Too-whit! Too-who! Too-whit! Too-who!" cried Elphin Cantle from the fence.

"Listen, Evans!"

Sam blurted out the words hurriedly; and it was with a trembling hand that he lit a cigarette for himself now from the one which the other was smoking.

"I've been thinking lately, Evans, that our Glastonbury Christ is like Osiris. They've cut him into fragments; and out of each fragment they've made a different Person. I don't care much for this Fourth Gospel. That's why I read it."

Mr. Evans nodded his complete and entire understanding of such a motive.

"My Christ's utterly different from Geard's," Sam said, "and different from my father's. My Christ's like Lucifer—only he's not evil . . . at least not what I call evil. But He's the enemy of God. That is, He's the enemy of Creation! He's always struggling against Life, as we know it . . . this curst, cruel self-assertion . . . this pricking up of fins, this prodding with horns . . . this opening of mouths . . . this clutching, this ravishing, this snatching, this *possessing*."

"Too-whit! Too-who! Too-whit! Too-who!" came Elphin's voice. The lad was on the other side of the fence now.

Mr. Evans cast his eyes round him. The half-moon was dipping, diving, rearing, tumbling, toppling, under that strong, wet, westerly wind. Some of the clouds closest to it took on every now and then, a momentary yellowness, sickly and unearthly, but most of them were of the colour of cold steel. Mr. Evans snuffed the air like one of the seals of Proteus. He thought he could detect the smell of seaweed on the wind.

"The tide must be high tonight at the Burnham mud-flats," he thought to himself. "They must be afraid of the sluices breaking over there."

"Too-whit! Too-who! Too-whit! Too-who!" Elphin and his attendant owl were already across the sloping pasture in the direction of Maidencroft Lane.

Mr. Evans took off his bowler hat, and bending forward tapped Sam on the shoulder with it.

"Canst thou not minister to a mind diseased?" he said. "You're the son of a priest, aren't you? Can't you say to the Demon: 'Come out of him?' "

There was a moment's pause; only broken by the little monotonous taps—like a man knocking off water-drops against a doorpost—of Mr. Evans' hat upon Sam's shoulder.

"There! I was only joking!" cried the Welshman at last. "I expect you don't believe in miracles, any more than you believe in the Fourth Gospel. You're listening to that boy . . . that's all you're doing! You're thinking of owls, as those rascals that came to my house just now were thinking of leases and communes! It makes me laugh, the way you all go on . . . while all the time . . . the Harrying of Annwn . . .''

Here the man's face distorted itself, not with the coming on of that queer, planetary laughing-fit, which had seized him in the room, but with a similar feeling of isolation.

"You don't even know what Annwn is!" he murmured.

Then with a deep sigh, he replaced his hat on his head.

"Complete is the captivity of Gwair in Caer Sidi!" he groaned inarticulately, buttoning a loosened button of his tight-fitting overcoat.

"Elphin! Hullo, Elphin! I'm going on!" Sam's voice rang out across the fields in the direction of Maidencroft Lane.

"No, I don't believe in miracles," he said gravely, "any more than Christ did. What He did was simply to use His will to *kill* His will."

"Too-whit! Too-who!" Elphin was at the fence again now and his attendant bird of the darkness had apparently left him.

Mr. Evans muttered something in Welsh. The thought that came into his heart was a thought of sick terror.

"This man's Christ is a madman like I am. His will holds the rod over His will. He's all strain and torment. It's with torment He drives out torment! I ought never to have spoken to this man."

Elphin joined them now and they all three moved down Edmund's Hill Lane. Not a word did any of them speak till they turned into Wells Old Road; but all the while, just eluding his conscious mind, there hovered about Mr. Evans' soul the sinister impact of that dialogue he had not heard.

"Will thik iron bar what you knows of make my young man feel before he dies?"

Even before they reached Number Five of Wells Old Road, or Old Wells Road—for both designations are in local use—Mr. Evans could see a light in Cordelia's bedroom. At his gate he hesitated whether to bid his companions good-bye or to accompany them a step further. An instinct in him difficult to analyse—perhaps a desire to test to the dregs the spiritual magic of this disciple of a non-miraculous Christ—made him decide to go on with them for a little way.

"I'll turn back in Bove Town," he said to himself. Sam seemed surprised, and Elphin seemed definitely cross, that they had not been able to get rid of this disturbing intruder even when they passed his own gate.

Once again a dead silence fell upon all three as they turned into Bove Town and walked along the well-worn flagstones of the raised path under the stone wall leading to High Street.

Sam, it turned out, had to go into St. John's Church to make the necessary preparations, which his father usually made for himself, for the morning's Mass.

Elphin Cantle hoped against hope—indeed he actually prayed in his heart—that Mr. Evans would see fit to say good-bye to them at the entrance to the churchyard. The boy repeated under his breath, as they approached the great church tower, a sort of ritualistic incantation:

"This bloke ought to go home! Ought to go home; ought to go home! This bloke ought to go home; when St. John's clock strikes the hour!"

What was Elphin's consternation when this prayer of his was not only *not* answered, but the extreme opposite of it was brought to pass!

"Good-night, Elphin!" said Sam when they reached the lamp, swinging from the arch above the entrance. "We mustn't take you any further out of your way."

The boy stared aghast, his feelings smitten through and through as if by a catapult.

"But Sir!" he gasped, "but Sir . . . but Mr. Dekker! I allus helps 'ee with they rinsings and rubbings. I be especial good at it; ye said yer wone self, I were!"

"Shake hands with Mr. Evans, Elphin, and run off, there's a good lad. We've had a nice day together; and we'll have some more; but I'm busy now. Run off home to bed, there's a good kid!"

Not a motion did Elphin Cantle make to shake hands with Mr. Evans or indeed to shake hands with Sam. He turned round without a word, without a sign, and taking to his heels ran off at top speed. He dodged between the people on the pavement. He dodged between the vehicles in the street, and making for his room in his stucco tower, as a wounded animal makes for his lair, he never shed a single tear till he threw himself down— coat, cap, muddy boots, just as he was—prone upon his bed and cried like an unhappy girl.

But Mr. Evans, egocentric though he had grown to be, was not one to view a child's tragic discomfiture with equanimity. He felt angry with Sam. Did the fellow think that he couldn't have talked to him before that boy? Well, he certainly wasn't going to talk to him now! The fellow was a prig, a fool, an ass, to send that lad away . . . a lad called Elphin too; and he had a curious expression under that lamplight . . . a funny face . . . an interesting face!

Such were Mr. Evans' thoughts as he followed Sam into the church.

"I know you'll be pleased to see," said Sam, "what Father has done to St. Joseph's tomb!"

He led him to the famous, empty sarcophagus—one of the most moving, if not one of the most authentic ossuaries of our planet's history—where the bones of the man who gave up his own tomb to Jesus are reported to have been laid.

Mr. Evans could not see very clearly in the dim lamplight that radiated down the isle what Sam's father *had* done; but it evidently was no great matter, for the tomb looked exactly as it had looked to him when he had visited it in the early Spring with the man who was now his father-in-law. But if Mr. Evans thought of his father-in-law as he stood tonight by that great scooped-out concavity, his companion had a much more poignant thought; for the image of Nell, as he had talked to her and quarrelled with her here, before the begetting of their child, came with cruel vividness upon him.

"I may never," Sam forced himself now to say, "have such a good chance to . . . to tell you, Evans, what I really feel about . . . all these things."

He leant forward wearily as he spoke, for he was tired and drowsy after his long walk, and he had never felt less clear-headed and less inspired.

"What I feel is this," he went on, pressing both his hands against the rim of the tomb and bowing his head forward above its dusky emptiness. "I feel that the whole Creation is on the wrong track . . . all scrambling for happiness and the satisfaction of the senses. I feel that the only thing to do is to follow Christ in making the will *kill* the will."

He lifted his ill-moulded beast-like lineaments and darted a quick nervous glance at the tall, black-coated figure standing aloof with his hands behind his back.

"How like *the shirt of Nessus* is this curst vice of mine!" thought Mr. Evans, when, to his loathing, he found that the mere distress of this will-killing Christ-lover had begun to cause him a lively mental shiver of a dark sort of pleasure. "The poor devil, the poor devil!" he said to himself. "I must not *let* myself feel like this!"

Tightly he clasped his long fingers behind his back, squeezing them angrily together so as to suppress his wicked feeling by their discomfort.

"If I let myself feel like this now," he thought, "I'll be creating an atrocious thought-imp that'll drive him from worse to worse. Down with you! Down with you, you living leprosy! I *will* wash you off—if it's in my own blood!"

"Don't 'ee see, Evans," Sam was now murmuring hoarsely, "it's the whole stream of life that's got this possessive instinct, this snatching, scrabbling, scraping, ravishing instinct. What Christ has to do is to deny the whole thing, root and branch! And it's no use saying it's for 'fuller life,' or 'more life,' that He has to do it. It's all poison. It's all one glittering, shining, seething tide of poisonous selfishness! We are all scales, scurf, scab, on the same twisting, cresting dragon of the slime. The tide of *life itself* is evil. That's the great secret of Christ. And what He's aiming at now—the tortured Anti-God that he is!—is the freezing up of the life stream! Christ doesn't give a damn for morality, Evans! *That's* not the point with Him. He's out for something far greater and deeper. He's out for the Beyond-Life! Do you remember what I said to you on Tor Hill, Evans, about His redeeming Matter? I didn't realise then how He redeems Matter. He does it by freezing the life force in it. He knows what the life force is; and he can track it down. He can find it bubbling and seething and horning and pricking and taking and tormenting and triumphing in every direction. And then he touches it with his cross and freezes it up!"

Mr. Evans became aware that old Mrs. Robinson, who had been waiting for Sam's late appearance before going home, had now crept up with her broom and duster till she was within hearing. The ex-servant of the Bishop must have caught some word of their discourse—one of those tragic clue-words of our human Tournament such as old women rejoice to lap up, as cats lap milk—and she probably thought of this scene at the Arimathean's tomb as a sort of moving-picture close-up, which, if she could get a good seat, " 'ud be the sime as the theayter."

"I can't help thinking, Mr. Dekker," said the Welshman now, "that your ideas have changed a good deal since you talked to us that spring day on the Tor. It seems to me that *then* your ideas were more orthodox. I seem to remember your quoting the words of the Mass, *Verbum caro factum est*, but from what you say now ——"

"Yes, yes, yes,—I *have* changed, Mr. Evans, and everything about me's changed; and the whole world has changed! The world can't go on devouring itself, as it's doing now, snatching, biting, stinging, poisoning, ravishing its flesh, and pressing itself with *its beautiful breasts*"—he threw a very queer expression into these last words, the reason of which was obscure to his chief hearer, but from the way her little rat's eyes glittered in the dusky aisle, not so obscure to Mrs. Robinson!—"against reality!"

Mr. Evans found it very difficult to look at this agitated figure on the other side of the tomb of the great tomb-lender without a stir in the coils of the nerve-snake within him that fed upon such food.

"You are lucky in one thing, Mr. Dekker," he said. "I mean in your quiet life at the Vicarage with your father."

"I'm afraid Elphin's feelings were hurt," said Sam, looking up and turning his head towards the door.

His eyes fell upon Mrs. Robinson who was dusting the seat of a perfectly spotless oaken pew and edging nearer and nearer.

"Hullo, Mrs. Robinson!" he called out; and his mouth worked

convulsively before he could say another word in the irritation
of her presence and his desire to get rid of her.

"Will yer be wantin' me henny more, Mister?" the old woman
responded. "Because, if not, I'll be miking me way 'ome."

"Nothing, nothing, thank you!" he replied, impatiently and
added in the same tone, "You can go now, Mrs. Robinson."

(" 'Twas a shime to 'ear the way they two were talking," the
old lady said to her son when she got home that night. "Ondecent
'eathen talk 'twere such as never ought to be 'eard hinside of a
'orspital, least still of a church. Mr. Sammy, 'ee 'urried me hout
of door as if I'd catch a palsy by stighin' a minute in their
company!")

"Boys are very sensitive creatures, Dekker," announced Mr.
Evans sententiously. "When I was young there was an old man
in the Pembrokeshire hills, where we lived, that I used to watch
milking his goats. I used to catch them for him sometimes. He
used to get angry with them and I used to be glad when he got
angry with them. But one day he sent me away for throwing
stones at them. And—do you know, Dekker, I wouldn't go home!
I stayed out on the hills for a whole summer's night. I slept in
a gully on a heap of heather, and all that night when I thought
of the goats ——" He stopped abruptly; for he saw that Sam
was no longer listening. Sam indeed had only heard a small portion of this speech and that portion not very distinctly. He was
keeping his eyes fixed on the retreating form of old Mrs. Robinson; but the eyes of his heart were fixed upon Nell Zoyland.

The girl was back again now from the hospital, and established—with Mrs. Pippard as a nurse for the child—once more
at Whitelake Cottage.

Mr. Evans had done more than blush as he told about the
goats. A deep swarthiness had actually mounted to his cheeks,
his forehead, his neck. For this story was a sacred story. Led on
by the hour and by the place he had told one of the important
stories of his youth.

But Sam Dekker wasn't interested enough even to know
whether he had been speaking of goats or of rabbits or sheep.
Mr. Evans' black-coated figure had begun to grow misty and
faint for Sam; and Mrs. Robinson, issuing forth from the church

door, had become for Sam like some fantastical curlicue on the lettering of a tragic volume. Even a saint cannot bear up always; and at that moment, so great was his physical exhaustion that something in him nearly broke down.

Mr. Evans little knew how near this student of the Fourth Gospel, standing over the tomb of the man who had buried Jesus, had come to crying out a wild curse upon the divine Lover.

"She's my girl! She's my girl!" Sam moaned in his heart. "What hast Thou given me; what canst Thou *ever* give me, in exchange for my girl?"

When they were all at last out of the church and got home— Sam asleep; Mr. Evans asleep; Mrs. Robinson asleep; but Elphin Cantle still sitting at the window of his stucco tower—there ensued a singular *dialogue without words* between the red light of the Reserved Sacrament and the empty sarcophagus of St. Joseph. This was one of those dialogues which it is never fantastical to interpret in human language, because no one can deny that in some language they must be perpetually occurring.

"Aren't you tired, red light, of shining so long without a pause in front of this Miracle of the faith?"

Thus, in a cold, flat, toneless voice, enquired the empty Sarcophagus.

"Yes," answered the red light, "I am very tired."

"If you could get anyone to move you," said the Sarcophagus, "you could rest here, within me; for *I* am tired of being empty!"

And the echo of the clock in St. John's Tower, coming down through the belfry into the church, repeated in a voice faint as an old man's last whisper:

"*Tired . . . tired . . . tired . . . tired . . . tired . . . tired . . . tired . . . tired . . . tired . . . tired . . .*" as it echoed the striking of the hour of ten over the roofs of Glastonbury.

T OSSIE STICKLES' LUSTY TWIN GIRLS WERE CHRISTENED BY THE Vicar of Glastonbury—bastards though they were!—with all due ceremony and at the regular hour for that ritual, after the children's service, on the day following the Evans' visit to the ruined sheepfold. Immediately after this ceremony the young mother and her small daughters were established once again under Miss Elizabeth's roof in Benedict Street. Nancy Stickles still continued to come each day "to help out"; so that Toss was enabled to divide her time between looking after her infants and cooking for the family, which still included—after several battles royal with my Lord's sister in Bath—the independent Lady Rachel, who now went regularly to work with Ned Athling in the little office of the weekly *Wayfarer.*

Deep in Miss Elizabeth's heart was lodged the fixed idea that eventually Mr. Barter would marry Tossie; and with a view to this natural and ethical contingency, she now had begun encouraging the manager of the municipal factory to pay constant visits to his illegitimate family under her roof, going so far as even to give up her drawing-room, whenever that gentleman came, to his conversations with Tossie.

It was one of those fantastic and incredible arrangements that in real life are always occurring; situations which, in premonition, seem absurdly impossible, but which are the very ones that Nature, moulding the prejudices of men to her own views, takes a humorous pleasure in bringing about.

The christening of Nell Zoyland's child was something much less easily dealt with; just as the fate of its mother was in the hands of more eccentric and wayward persons than either Tom Barter or Miss Crow. Will Zoyland had made up his mind that his father, the Marquis, should stand godfather to the little boy, who was to be called Henry after the great man. But the Marquis had a nervous dislike of appearing in public in Glastonbury— a place which he had come heartily to distrust and dislike since he had been mobbed by the rabble on that eventful Pageant-day

—and so after long discussions and procrastinations it had been worked out that Nell's child was to be baptised at Whitelake Cottage by Mat Dekker on the fifteenth of December.

Hearing that Lord P. was coming for this occasion, as well as Dave and Persephone who were the little Harry's other god-parents, what must the good Mrs. Pippard do—who was related to half Glastonbury—but beg from her mistress the privilege of giving a little christening party of her own to celebrate this aus-picious day. Thus the fifteenth of December that year was to be a lively occasion out at Whitelake; and it was a fortunate occur-rence, and a good omen too, for babe Harry, that this day, after so much rain, was one of cloudy and intermittent but still of quite perceptible sunshine. Harry was a tragic little boy in cer-tain ways. He clung desperately to his mother; and it was always touching to see the struggle in his small heart between his intense greediness and his hatred of being fed by any other "Mwys," as Mr. Evans would have called it, than his mother's lovely breasts.

The proletarian contingent of Master Henry's party was to include Mother Legge and her now quite convalescent niece, Tittie Petherton, Nancy Stickles, who was also a relative, Sally Jones who had once been in service along with Doxy Pippard, the old woman's daughter, and last, but not least, our old acquaint-ance Mr. Abel Twig, who was Mrs. Pippard's cousin.

All these persons were to have their tea in Nell's kitchen, while Lord P., together with Mr. and Mrs. Spear and the Vicar, re-freshed themselves in her small parlour.

The present dwellers of Whitelake Cottage included not only Mrs. Pippard herself, but her daughter, Eudoxia, a girl who was now acting as the Zoyland's housemaid. Both mother and daugh-ter slept in the ante-room of Will's private retreat at the back of the cottage, while Nell and her child slept in the front bedroom.

Since the show season at Wookey had come to an end Will Zoyland had been employed by Philip in the much more impor-tant rôle of assistant-overseer of the new tin-mining works. The head overseer—an industrious and clever technician—was not good at keeping his subordinates up to the scratch; nor had he much initiative with regard to tracking out new veins of metal-deposit. Thus Zoyland's job at the tin mine was partly a dis-

ciplinary one and partly a geological one, neither of which occupations exactly suited his peculiar gifts. But he did not demand
much salary; ten times less, in fact, than Philip would have had
to give to anyone else; and all the labourers on the works held him
in respect because of his name.

Lord P. had announced that he would drive over in his dog-
cart from Mark Moor Court, picking up Lady Rachel on his way
through Glastonbury. The christening was roughly timed for
between four and five; and Mat Dekker had told Nell that he
would try to come over himself soon after three, so as to enjoy
a little talk with her alone before her other guests arrived.

Will Zoyland had come to the secret conclusion, after first
setting eyes on his wife's infant, that this was none of his; but he
had concealed this certainty so successfully that Nell had not the
least suspicion that he had divined the truth; and this secret
knowledge of his gave him a great and unfair advantage in the
daily struggle for the mastery between them; for he found that
to have such a weapon, and *not* to use it, was the strongest
weapon he could possibly have; and he took full advantage of
this. His position, just then, was in many respects a singular and
crucial one. The fact that Nell was suckling the child herself,
though old Mrs. Pippard helped her washing and dressing him,
made it psychologically difficult for Will to start making love
to her again. He had a curious penchant for babies, amounting
almost to a mania for these odd little poppets, whose angers are
so nerve-racking and whose philosophical calm is so soothing; so
that he won Nell's maternal gratitude willy-nilly by his tenderness to her offspring, especially as he consented to sleep on the
couch in the parlour and to leave her and child the uninterrupted
use of their bedroom. It had given Nell a queer kind of shock
when she saw Mrs. Pippard making up that particular couch for
the master of the house; that couch which had not been used as
a bed by anyone since that day in March!

But Will's passionate devotion to the child disarmed her completely because it was more than she had dreamed would happen, and she took it to imply that he had not the least suspicion
that the little Harry was not his.

The baby, on its side, seemed to take to Will with a degree of awareness and attraction unusual at that age. He was a child of colossal egoism and of an immense power of love. He loved Nell with a piquant zest that was delicious to behold; but his love for her was a hot, feverish, violent thing; while his response to Zoyland was a sort of rapturous calm. In his furious fits of temper, which were of a tragic intensity and prophetic of a future that made the girl tremble to think of, Zoyland alone could handle him, quell him, console him. Time and again, old Mrs. Pippard, who could do nothing with him, would say to Nell—"If it weren't for the mëaster, thik mommet 'ud fling 'isself into convoolsions."

"He *can't* not think it his own child!" Nell would say to herself; but how he could have been so deceived, when its pathetic little chin was so exactly like Sam's, she never considered. She was very grateful, too, at being let off all love-making; and this she attributed to Will's passion for the child; and it made her uneasy, with a sort of shamefaced discomfort, to think that she owed her escape from his amorous advances to this deception. But in this matter, too, as much as over the child, the girl, for all her feminine insight, had been completely outwitted by the crafty huntsman. It was really the sly old Zookey Pippard who engineered this treachery. Perhaps, being a relative of Mother Legge, she had it in her blood to play procuress. But it was she who had persuaded her daughter to come up to Whitelake Cottage from a very good place at a farm near Witham Friary, and her arguments must have been very subtle ones; for the wench received, in return for her work, probably the lowest wage that has ever been paid to a maid, at any rate in a gentlefolk's house, from Westbury Beacon on the north to Huish Episcopi on the south. But Zookey was—as Mr. Weatherwax, who knew her "up hill and down dale" said to Penny, when those old gossips first "larn'd who 'twere were looking 'arter Missy Zoyland"—"the cunningest bitch-badger this side o' Tarnton."

Eudoxia Pippard, when she finally appeared in response to her crafty parent's beguiling hints, completely turned Will Zoyland's head.

Having lived a chaste life for nearly half a year and having recognised the fact that he had been made the bread-winner for another man's child, Zoyland found nothing in his passion for Nell's baby to prevent him from committing delicious adultery with Doxy Pippard. Eudoxia was indeed dedicated, it seemed, to give immoral delight to Lord P.'s bastard.

She was not at all what you would call a pretty girl. Her lips were much too thin, her nose was a little twisted to one side and her neck was decidedly too long; but she had one peculiarity which, as soon as he discovered it, set Zoyland's Varangian senses on fire, and that was the most satiny skin that ever a Glastonbury amorist had clipped, as Malory would say, since the days of the damosel Linet, of the Castle Perilous! It may be easily that, in the category of feminine desirability, such polished flanks, such slippery knees, such satiny hips, and all such other sinuous slendernesses, do not by any means constitute what is called "classical beauty" or even romantic charm; but whatever they constitute, as they slide in or out of a seducer's arms they evoke a ravishing and transporting satisfaction.

Now there was an outside wooden staircase at the back of the house, leading into the ante-room of the "smoking-room"; so that when Nell and Sam's child were fast asleep, in the front of the house, Eudoxia could easily come in through the kitchen door. This door, if Zookey remembered to leave it ajar, had well-oiled hinges; so that when Doxy found herself—at first with agitated surprise, but later with entrancing coquetry—clothed only in her night-gown and in the presence of the master of the house, lying upon his couch bed, there was no danger of surprisal if they spoke in low whispers.

Now Nell, although Zoyland had loved her dearly and had got great enjoyment from her, had never been really responsive to his embraces. Her body had responded faintly, her heart a little, but her inmost imaginative nerve, the crucial chord to the essential quiver of a girl's stirred senses, not at all. The full-blooded bastard, as may well be believed, had had many loves before he became infatuated with Nell Spear, but none of these had been adepts at the art of provocation, none of these had been viciously exciting.

Now Doxy Pippard possessed, among other original characteristics, a curious mania for retaining her virginity. Vicious and

inflammable as she was with the feverish, reckless, almost swooning intensity of the pseudo-consumptive type, she had lavished
her nervous provocations on all her men and yet had managed
matters so skilfully as to be a maiden still. The mere idea of
lying in the arms of the son of the Marquis of P. was intoxicating
to the romantic yearning in her snake-smooth, leaf-cool body;
while the herculean proportions of Zoyland as a human being
fulfilled all her secretest girlhood's dreams as to what a real
masculine bedfellow should be.

On the eve of the day of the christening Eudoxia had come
down to him soon after midnight, entering the kitchen by the
door left unlatched by Zookey; and it was after a couple of
hours of paradisiac dalliance, wherein her protection of herself
from "mortal sin" prolonged her companion's tantalised delight
beyond what he would have dreamed possible, that the couple sat
up suddenly on that single-pillowed couch-bed under the heavily
curtained window and started to listen with all their ears. What
had disturbed them was an outburst of crying from the child,
followed by Nell's voice calling Will's name. It is probable that
no possible re-arrangements of society—not even that most ideal
commune pictured by Paul Trent—will ever bring it about that
the fear of discovery in erotic infidelities will be abolished. Such
"alarums and excursions," such panic-stricken beatings of the
heart, seem as deeply implicit in the fatality of human relations
as is the indestructibleness of jealousy itself.

Zoyland had already thrown one of his herculean limbs out of
bed; and with his heel on the floor was clutching the bed-clothes,
preparatory to obeying his wife's summons, when Eudoxia, who
had curled up her supple slenderness like a frightened grass-
snake, close under the window-sill, heard Zookey's voice reassur-
ring both mother and child.

"There's Mother!" she whispered. She was right. For once, it
seemed, the old woman's influence had succeeded with the headstrong baby; for they heard its shrill cries die down now; and
soon after they could catch the creaking of the heavy shoes she
wore and the drag of her lame foot—for Zookey suffered from
eczema and the chief ornament on her extemporised toilet-table,
which was a big black trunk with Nell's maiden initials on it,

was a great china pot of zinc ointment—as she returned into the ante-room.

Even his herculean capacity for amorous play being exhausted, and this alarm having roused them both to extreme wakefulness, Zoyland and Miss Pippard fell to talking in low whispers.

A luminous half-moon, disencumbered tonight of those eternally eastward-travelling clouds, threw a silvery stream between the brown curtains of their window; a stream which fell on the man's bushy beard and on the girl's old-fashioned night-gown and on her slippers tossed down upon the floor. In his rough eagerness, Zoyland had torn away the top button from the front of this gown, and the girl's long thin neck protruded wantonly and weirdly; sometimes entering that ray of moonlight and sometimes receding from it, like a slender birch-trunk surrounded by swaying bracken. Close beside Miss Pippard's faded blue slippers Zoyland had thrown down his own muddy boots, one of which lay on its side, contented and at ease, in that little pool of moonlight, while the other, left in the outer darkness, stared sadly at the ceiling.

They were both sitting up in the bed, their backs against the western wall of the cottage, while the stream of moonlight entering on their right hand and illuminating the girl's neck and the fringe of his beard, left their upraised knees, over which the rumpled bed-clothes extended in confusion, partly in light and partly in shadow. One of his arms was hanging loosely over the edge of the couch while the other, flung round her waist and against her bare side was teasing his tired senses with an aftermath of delicate tantalisation. As he rested there, Will Zoyland felt extremely grateful to Miss Pippard for the pleasure she had given him and for the pleasure she was still suffusing through every nerve of his deliciously lethargic frame. Sexual gratitude is an emotion much less frequent in modern days than in mediæval times, owing to the fact that industrialism has cheapened the value of the sex-thrill by lowering the ritual-walls surrounding it. In modern times it needs a profoundly magnanimous and even quixotic nature to feel this emotion to any extreme degree. It is doubtless this absence of sexual gratitude that accounts for the cold-blooded and savage hatred that so many separated couples feel for each other today; and the furious vindictiveness of their disputes over money. But it is a sign of meanness in a man or a woman, and of a certain thinness of character, when such gratitude is so quickly forgotten. A large nature may find it necessary to hit fiercely back; may find it necessary to escape altogether; but even in its retorts, even in its avoidance, it retains a certain fundamental tenderness and indulgence, based upon physical gratitude for the thrilling sensations of the past.

It was largely his over-brimming gratitude to Nell for the thrills which he had got from the touch of her body that had made Zoyland so indulgent in the matter of Sam. Men that sail the sea are as a rule, by reason of their isolation from women, more grateful to them for their favours than landsmen are. A jealous peasant, a jealous tradesman is much more common than a jealous sailor; and though Lord P.'s bastard had never sailed the sea, his Norse ancestors had, and that manner of life lay deep in his blood.

Miss Pippard was a complete stranger to Will Zoyland; and, for this very reason, the fact that the shuffling of life's cards—or as some would say, the machinations of Zookey—had given him the thrilling privilege of enjoying the satiny texture, cool and slippery as the leaves of waterlilies, of the girl's limbs, endowed their moonlit whispers with a piquancy as delicate and exalted as a bird's song or a butterfly's flight in a monastic cloister.

"I'm glad your mother's asked Mother Legge tomorrow," whispered Will, "for I've always had a fancy for that old lady. She's a classic figure, if you know what I mean, my dear. My father used to say she made him think of a whore-mistress in Rome."

"Is it true, Mr. Zoyland," came a faint response from the white figure at his side, "that the Mayor of Glaston cured poor Tittie of a killing cancer?"

"God! my dear, *I* don't know! I've been out at Wookey all the autumn. Perhaps it wasn't cancer at all. You'd better ask her tomorrow and see what she says. *I* wouldn't go to that pious old humbug, if I had the worst cancer ever known. I'd shoot myself first."

"They say there'll be rare doings," went on Miss Pippard, offering as she spoke just the kind of resistance to his caresses that enhanced their value while it did not waylay their direction, "when Mr. Geard opens his new arch on Chalice Hill. They say they foreigners be due to come in trainloads to see 'um. I were out at Moorleaze, by Witham Friary, on Pageant Day. Missus went to it, and so did the childer; but Master kept I by 'un, to ——" She interrupted herself with a little click of her tongue against her teeth. This sound usually denotes some gentle disaster when uttered by a young girl. In the case of Miss Pippard it denoted an indulgent awareness of amorous advances.

"To play in the hayloft with him?" whispered Zoyland.

"There were a lot o' new goslings," Eudoxia continued gravely, "out there by Croft Pond; and I were the only maid in Dairy what he trusted wi' they. Old Madge Dill was too rheumatic to cross barton. She be the one I told 'ee about, Mr. Zoyland, what got the rheumatiz, from picking watercress."

"I remember, sweetheart," whispered Zoyland. "She was the one who stinted you in butter till you scared her by that tale of the corpse candles."

"So she was," sighed Eudoxia, "and arter that tale I were the richest-nourished woman in Mid-Somerset. I wish often—and sweet Jesus do know I wish it now!—that Mother had never made me leave that good place. Master often would say I were the deftest maid for smelling out mushrooms that he'd ever seen. He often said that when I married he'd give me a solid gold bracelet wi' filgree lacework on 'en." Thus whispered Eudoxia and sighed heavily.

She gave her bed-fellow plenty of time to meditate on the lavish liberality of Moorleaze and upon ways and means of rivalling it. Then she sighed again.

"I'd like Mother to try if the Mayor's Miracle Spring on Chalice Hill could cure her eczema." This pious wish was breathed into the moonlight with intense gravity. And then, even at the very moment when her resistance to her seducer's one-handed caresses perceptibly slackened, she added in a still graver whisper:

"It makes her toes itch terrible—poor Mother! I'd give half a year's wages to ease her of thiccy devil's smart!"

Zoyland's lechery was of a very subdued kind just now, so he

could afford to moralise at this moment to any extent. "Sometimes," he said to himself, "these girls seem to have no nervous
system at all. They can respond without responding, and think
of God knows what! If anyone asked me what I valued most in
a woman I'd say attention! It's like dealing with a creature that's
half an animal and half an angel. The larger part of your talk,
of your love-making, of your ideas, of your thoughts, pass over
them like water off a duck's back!" He had arrived at this finale
in his meditations when the girl suddenly stiffened herself like
a galvanic wire and shrank against the brown curtain, pulling
the bed-clothes over her head. Zoyland had time to catch one
faint rustle on the staircase leading to the bedroom above, and
one slight creaking of the bannister; but he had no sooner leapt
out of bed and stumbled over the girl's slippers, than the door at
the foot of the staircase was flung open, and Nell—in her blue
dressing-gown and with a flat silver candlestick in her hand—
stepped into the room.

To the end of his days Zoyland remembered the expression of
Nell's face. Her eyes were gleaming with a fierce, hard, bright
lustre when she first came in; but as she raised her candle one
side of her features was blotted out in shadow.

"Aren't you ashamed of yourselves?" she cried in a clear ringing voice, and with a hand that he could see was neither trembling nor shaking she carried the candle into the middle of the
room and laid it on the little green card-table, pushing a vase
of small-flowering chrysanthemums that stood there out of the
way with the candlestick rim.

The bearded man, looking very tall and formidable in the
candlelight, held his ground and remained with his massive legs
firmly planted on the rug, his bare feet widely apart, his flannel
shirt hanging loose over his bare thighs. But Nell came right up
to him and with an imperious gesture with her hand made as if
she would push him out of the way as she went to the couch to
confront Miss Pippard. Not being able to do this and apparently
surprised at the man's imperturbable sangfroid, Nell made a step
sideways toward the wall on her left and called out to the huddled figure on the couch.

"Aren't you ashamed of yourself, Eudoxia? Aren't you

ashamed to treat me like this and your mother upstairs too; and
me with little Harry? I can't understand you, Eudoxia. I can't
understand how you *could* do such a thing!"

While Nell was thus expressing her indignation to the form on
the couch, Zoyland's mind was rapidly considering two alternative lines of action. Should he pick up his clothes, which lay
there, piled up on a wicker chair, near the bookcase—that bookcase that contained the massive volumes of Arabia Deserta—and
retire with them to his "smoking-room," leaving Eudoxia to the
mercy of Nell? Or should he, by hook or by crook, compel
his wife to go back to her bedroom and her child? Huntsman
as he was, Will had only to decide on the line to take, and he
would follow it up recklessly and defiantly. Up to this point,
Nell, in her righteous anger, had had the whiphand over both of
them. But Zoyland's one clear instinct now was to save Miss Pippard from further humiliation. Lovely though Nell looked in
her blue dressing-gown, the banked-up righteousness of her indignation seemed to have changed her personality in a very
subtle way. Zoyland could not help experiencing a queer shock
when he saw how this gross incursion had dragged the beautiful
girl into the rôle of jealous, sport-spoiling domesticity, wherein
it is hard for any woman to play an attractive part.

The man's sensations followed one another, like straws on
a splashing water-fall, during the few seconds of Nell's words to
that tumbled couch from which his own burly form now warded
off the candleflame.

"Come on upstairs, Nell," he said, moving toward her. "We'll
talk this out better upstairs. It's not Eudoxia's fault."

"Don't come near me—don't touch me!" cried his wife, with
scarlet cheeks and flashing eyes.

"Come on upstairs, Nell!" he repeated in a quiet voice that was
full nevertheless of a formidable resolution. Those invisible
naturalists—belonging to regions of Being more powerful, I will
not say "higher" than ours—who take a peculiar and doubtless
sometimes a decisive interest, as Mat Dekker did with his
aquarium, in human dramas as tense as this—must have been
impressed by Zoyland's calm and masterful handling of this
situation. They would have seen that all his real tenderness was

for his wife—they would have seen that he regarded his affair with Miss Pippard as of no more consequence than if he'd been caught stealing cherries. But they would also have noted that he had the rare gift of *using violence in cold blood*. For instead of being in the remotest degree intimidated by Nell's electric fury—and in her fit of blind sex-reaction the gentle girl struggled like a pantheress in his arms—he lifted her up, as Zookey might have lifted little Master Henry, and carried her bodily up the stairs into the room above, when he laid her—Zookey Pippard having discreetly closed the door of the ante-room—upon the bed, by the side of her sleeping first-born.

The aforementioned celestial naturalists would not have been deceived, as certainly the terrified Eudoxia was, into regarding Nell's furious anger as a deep and tragic feeling. They would have commented to one another—over this Whitelake aquarium of anthropoid minnows—to the effect that had Nell been really tragically hurt she would have hugged her baby to her heart where she was, and never come down those stairs so deliberately, so softly, and so bent on righteous retribution!

What Eudoxia beheld when she removed the bedclothes from her head was the wide-open door of the staircase, the flickering candle on the table, the twisted blue girdle of Nell's dressing gown lying in the same pool of moonlight as her own slippers and her paramour's boot, and the untouched heap of the master's clothes piled up in the wicker chair over by the bookcase.

Sitting up in bed with beating heart, the girl surveyed these objects for a second or two. Then, under her breath, deeply, passionately, concisely—and it must be confessed with no little justification—she cursed "the womb that bore her and the paps that had given her suck."

"It's all your fault, Mother!" she wailed in her heart. "This is the last time I'll listen to 'ee! I'll go back to Moorleaze tomorrow, so help me God!" . . .

The first of the guests to arrive on the following afternoon, which turned out to be a neutral day, as days go, neither wet nor fine, neither windless nor gusty, neither warm nor particularly chill, was the Marquis of P. and the Lady Rachel.

Lord P. arrived in a thoroughly nervous and crusty humour. Zoyland and Nell had barely finished their late lunch, cooked by Zookey in sulky silence—her daughter having gone off to catch the nine o'clock bus to Frome, intending to quit the bus at Wanstrow, and make the best of her way, without even risking a telegram, safe back to her deserted goslings of Croft Pond.

The Marquis went at once for a stroll by the river with his son, leaving Sergeant Blimp to dispose of the green-wheeled dog-cart and the black horse, as best he might.

"I've got a piece of news for you, Will," he declared with an assumed eagerness, as soon as they were out of hearing. The bastard shrugged his great shoulders. He knew his father too well. The long-winded dissimulation of the House of Lords pulled no wool over *his* eyes.

"The Governor's been making an ass of himself," he thought grimly. "This is his regular beginning!"

The old man's profile, as he watched it moving by his side with the scrubby vandyke beard and prominent nose, seemed to have grown perceptibly sharper since he saw it last. The aged nobleman had a pinched, frustrated, tired look on his old warrior's face, as if he'd been wearing his suit of chain-armour too many years, and would be glad enough to make his will and lie down with his forefathers in Wells Cathedral.

"I shan't have to sell Mark Court," said Lord P., "that's one good thing. I did a good stroke of business last night, me boy. I wish you could have seen how I led 'em on and hustled 'em and rustled 'em and tussled 'em."

"Christ, Dad!" cried the other, in great alarm, snatching at his father's sleeve and bringing him to a halt, while he swung round to face him. "What have you gone and done now?"

"They came last night," said the old gentleman. "Three of the devils came! One was your wife's brother, the Bolshevist—an honest chap, by the way, that fellow is,—and an agitator of some sort—an impossible individual; and the third bloke was a clever lawyer from the Scilly Isles—called Trent. He very soon realised with whom he had to deal. The other two had seemed inclined to sermonise me. They took the tone that if I didn't let 'em have their way this time now, I'd be far worse caught later on. But I soon let 'em see I wasn't the sort of person they could rush like that! But this fellow Trent seems to have made a pretty close study of all the Glastonbury leases and properties; and he helped me to make your Bolshevist relative see my points when I explained the situation."

"For God's sake what *have* you done, Sir?" cried the bastard, mightily alarmed.

The old man straightened his shoulders and leaned forward a little, bowing stiffly from his waist, like a soldier and a courtier, but digging his cane deeply into the tow-path mud.

"Well, I'll tell you, lad," he said, leaning on the handle of his stick. "I've fixed things now so that I shan't have to worry any more about my income, for years to come. I've been looking up the entail and those brothers of yours—damn their souls! A lot *they* care for my troubles!—have no word to speak in this. The Zoyland entail doesn't touch Glastonbury."

"You've gone and sold——" cried the bastard.

"No, I haven't, lad. Don't get excited too soon. All I've *sold* to 'em, and for a good round sum too, I can assure you, is that section of the dye works properties that are on my land. That's the newest section, you know. That Crow fellow will look yellow in the gizzard when I clear him out; and a good thing too. He's been taking things too much for granted, the snappy close-mouthed rogue! But for the rest; for the High Street shops and for the Bove Town and Paradise property; I've let 'em have *those* on a fifty years' lease, and at a thousand pounds higher rent, too, than I got from the tradesmen and the slum-tenants. It's a first-rate piece of business, lad! Old Beere is furious, of course. But that's because I did it over his head. But a lot he's done for me these last years—except eat my pheasants and tell me indecent yarns about his daughter and your wife's sister-in-law, who everybody told *me* was soft on Crow! He's in his dotage, old Beere is. He thinks it's a great glory and a mark of gentility in him that he's got a daughter who don't run after the boys! I told the old fool that *his* sort of gal would murder him for his cash if he wasn't careful."

William Zoyland jerked himself uncivilly away from his father and took a hurried step along the tow-path.

So this was what that slippery lawyer from Cornwall had been up to all these weeks in that new office of his! Had he got round old Beere? No!—impossible. But brother Dave was certainly behind it! Who would have supposed that that funny little man would have had the gumption —— But of course the fellow at the back of the whole thing was that wily old humbug, Geard. He was the one! "I must run off and tell Philip," he thought, "this afternoon; as soon as the christening is over. The newest section of the dye works sold!—Why it's a serious blow! Of course he has the others . . . but it's serious, it's *terribly* serious. How on earth will Philip take it?"

He came striding back to his father.

"Well . . . you *have* gone and done it!" he rapped out brutally. "But let's see if I've got it clear what you've done. You've sold that *newest* piece of factory-land to them? The one north of Manor House Road and southeast of the Burnham and Evercreech Railway? That *other* one, east of the cemetery, doesn't belong to you? Philip Crow is still safe there? But listen—are you sure that the *buildings* on that newest section are yours to sell? I mean the whole plant? Didn't that man—what's-his-name, that Crow bought out—sell him all those buildings with the good-will?"

The Marquis stroked the point of his grey beard.

"Couldn't sell what wasn't his, lad! No, no! That newest section of buildings near the Burnham Railway, was built by the business man of our family, your great-uncle, Lord Edward. That was before the days when you were a baby in petticoats, out there at Limoges. I took your mother to see 'em . . . had a pretty narrow shave too, that day, of being nabbed . . . she had the devil's own spirit, that woman, . . . when it came to skating on thin ice . . . just like you, me boy!"

While this conversation was going on, Lady Rachel was being introduced to little Master Henry.

Zookey Pippard recovered her temper a little in the excitement of dressing the babe in its christening-robe; and for some reason only known to its own passionate and highly strung spirit the infant took a violent fancy to Rachel, clinging to the finger she gave it and smiling and slobbering in rapture when she received it in her lap.

The next to arrive among the expected guests was none other than Mat Dekker. The tall massive form of the priest was arrayed in his long black Sunday coat, and he had taken a lot of trouble to wipe his thick boots with swathes of grass before presenting himself at the door of Whitelake Cottage. He had forgotten, however, to change his week-day trousers, and these looked more faded and shabby than usual. The man was obviously strung-up and full of seething emotions; but he kept himself well in control, and begged quite naturally for a little tête-à-tête with the mother of this newly enrolled soldier of Christ.

It was a strange moment for both of them when the mother and the grandfather of Henry Sangamore Rollo Zoyland sat opposite each other in that low-ceilinged bedroom, at the top of those stairs down which the girl had carried her candle to such drastic purpose the night before.

She lay now at full length on the bed, propped up on two pillows, while her child, though fast asleep in its cradle between them, did not separate her very far from the priest.

Fortunately or unfortunately, as it may chance to be, the amorous clairvoyance of a woman is lulled, drugged, drowsed, deliciously stupefied, by the magical sensation of giving suck. Although her child was fast asleep now, the feeling of its exacting lips, of its masterful thirst for the fount of her life, was still clinging to her responsive body, and rendering it dull, tranced, entoiled, preoccupied, to all other sensitised awareness! Thus as she allowed Mat Dekker to retain her cold schoolgirl fingers across the counterpane of the sleeping child, resting her hand with his, in fact, upon the wicker edge of the cradle, it never entered her head that this man—her dear love's father—had anything in his heart toward her except a deep priestly sympathy. She knew she felt no shyness of him; she knew she felt a lovely and relaxed security in his presence; she knew she was deriving from the touch of his rough fingers an inrush of spiritual strength; but beyond this she experienced, or, was conscious of experiencing, no intimate link between them.

There was *one* restraint, however, that did come over her, and that puzzled her a little as she struggled in her mind to overcome it—a singular difficulty in mentioning his son's name to him. She longed to call out to this silent, rugged, friendly supporter: "And now tell me everything about my Sam!" But some inexplicable force always held back the words, just as they slid, like drops of recurrent rain from the smooth stalk of her happy peace, to the tip of her tongue.

"Why can't I ask him how Sam is?" she thought to herself. "It must be because of his religion. He's come to baptise Sam's child—but he doesn't want to think of us together."

With this explanation in her mind, she let herself relax again on her pillows and close her eyes, pressing the hand that held her own in a confiding and trusting clasp. It was Mat himself who broke this silence, at last.

"I've been thinking a great deal lately, Nell," he said, "about this grand consecration day of the Mayor's. It's to be in January they tell me now; and I hear the wildest tales, as I go about among my people, as to what the man is planning." He sighed heavily, as he spoke, and Nell took the opportunity of repossessing herself of her right hand which she promptly made use of to pull her blue robe more tightly about her.

Deeply had Mat Dekker sighed when he spoke of the Mayor of Glastonbury; and the girl, in her maternal atrophy of the sex nerve, had put the sigh down entirely to the delicate professional problem of how to deal with Mr. Geard's wild and fantastic schemes. But, of course, in reality, not more than a thousandth part of this heavy sigh had anything to do with Mr. Geard's activities.

They were interrupted by the appearance of Zookey Pippard who came to tell them that all the other guests had duly arrived and that his Lordship was growing impatient for the ceremony to begin.

Zookey approached the cradle and Mat Dekker stood up.

"I hope this isn't the first time, Zookey," said the priest with a kindly chuckle—he was always a transformed man when he dealt with the native-born, a touch of the old Quantocks' accent entering, so to speak, his very manner as well as his intonation—

"that you'll have heard me say a prayer, since—but us won't let the Missus know how well we know each other, shall us?"

Under normal conditions this indulgent indiscretion, referring to an occasion when the worthy man had rescued this tricky old baggage from the clutches of Mr. Sheperd, would have met with a roguish retort. But the naughty old woman was still smarting from Nell's anger over Eudoxia.

"His Lordship said to her Ladyship just now," Mrs. Pippard retorted, humming and murmuring over the baby and giving its tiny red cheek a fillip with her finger-nail. "What be Dr. Dekker doing upstairs? Be he a-baptising of *she*?"

"Nonsense, Zookey!" cried Nell, "aren't you ashamed to tell such fibs? But you *had* better go and get ready, Mr. Dekker. Tell them Zookey and I will bring Henry down in less than five minutes. . . ."

"And so she said her must go; and Doxy said Mister would be best pleased for *she* to go, her wone self." These exciting words echoed through the kitchen of Whitelake Cottage half an hour later, when the christening was well over and the upper-class portion of its audience was having their tea in the parlour.

"She shouldn't a-spoke up like that," said Nancy Stickles reproachfully, putting down a great piece of new bread and blackcurrant jam, for they were all squarely seated round the kitchen table, and looking with a straight open gaze into the equivocal face of Zookey—"After all it weren't nice for Mr. Zoyland to be talking to she on sofa in parlour, like you says he were, and she in bed with Master Henry, and house all hushed and still."

"Will you have another piece of sponge cake, Auntie Legge?" threw in the hospitable Zookey. "Us all do know how 'spectable and proper *you* be, Nance Stickles, when all the town know of how Red Robinson was turned out of house by your Harry because of the fuss you made of 'ee and the clipping and colling that went on when your Harry was to bed. I do know for sure how 'twere, because Mr. Robinson told me of it, his wone self."

It was at this point that Abel Twig broke in, interrupting this altercation among the women with such a quavering faint voice that it seemed like the voice of Philosophy itself come forth from those old Lake Village mounds.

"Thik Red Robinson were zour, no doubt, when Mistress Nance didn't let 'un do what 'a wanted to do . . . and so 'a went and cast up this tale agin' her, same as thik dirty Potiphar-scrub did agin' King Joseph in History."

There was an uncomfortable silence round the kitchen table, during which the more peacefully inclined among the guests turned to Mother Legge for protection. That great provider of Cyprian pleasures had so far hardly uttered a word. She had kept her eyes fixed upon the door which led into the parlour; a door which had been carried bodily to the cottage from Mark Court and was of excessively thick oak.

"Don't let them get quarrellin', Auntie," pleaded Tittie Petherton with her mouth full of buttered scone.

Sally Jones added her voice to that of Tittie, from whose appearance no one certainly would ever have supposed that a few months ago she was screaming so pitiably for morphia.

"Mrs. Legge!" cried Sally, as if the old procuress were very deaf. "Didn't 'ee hear, Mrs. Legge, what Zookey Pippard said to Nance Stickles?"

The mother of Eudoxia was not slow in defending herself.

"Auntie be hard of hearing," she threw in spitefully, "when her eats her tea with poor volk in kitchen, 'stead of with gentry in parlour."

These words hit Mother Legge straight to the heart. For the truth was that the old lady *had* half-thought when she received the invitation to attend the Zoyland christening, that her place would have been with the gentry rather than with her humble relatives. It was indeed in pensive consideration of this unhappy nuance that the portly lady, though they had given her the only chair that had arms and the only tea-cup that wasn't a kitchen-cup and had taken care to help her first to every dainty on the table, now stared gravely at this great oaken door through which the one voice of the people within that was at all articulate— and that only now and again—was the voice of William Zoyland. The other voices were lost in a vague indistinguishable murmur.

Zookey Pippard was among the few women in Glastonbury who ever stood up to the present tenant of Camelot and of "my other house." But there was a majestic dignity in the rebuke that the old lady administered now and an incredible daring too. She actually got up from her chair, walked to the oaken door, opened it wide enough for her person to fill the whole space and said with perfect sangfroid to Nell: "Your servant here, Ma'am, is unwilling to leave us to look after ourselves; but you *must*, please, tell us *the moment* you need her; for we can get on perfectly well without her."

"Oh, thank you, Mrs. Legge; thank you very much!" cried Nell, half-rising from her chair in that particular flurry of perturbation that young hostesses feel when there are signs of a mutiny below deck. It was the Marquis who saved the situation.

"Why, if that isn't my old friend from Paradise! They never told me they'd got *you* here! Where have they been hiding you? Come over here—is that all right, Nell?—and sit by me." He gave the arm-chair in which Persephone was seated a little jerk with his finger and thumb—he behaved exactly as if he had been Theodoric the Ostrogoth, patronising some harem at Algiers and indicating by the slightest tap upon his Gothic sword-hilt that he would be more amused by the aged story-teller of the tents than by the cleverest young houri.

Persephone as she languidly rose, smiling very sweetly upon Mrs. Legge and extending one of her long arms toward her, gave Lord P. one single quick, flashing, steel-piercing glance that not only succeeded in making the old despot feel uncomfortable, but in making him heartily wish her back; so lovely did she look in her anger.

"She could have stabbed me, the little minx," he thought. "And I must see her again," he thought.

Once settled in this capacious chair, with all her black satin flounces and her voluminous black laces deposited about her, Mother Legge gazed round her with impenetrable aplomb. Under the protection of my Lord she felt ready to be indulgent to her enemies and more than bountiful to her friends. She even felt she owed something to Zookey Pippard for having been the one to give her the final prod that had led to this public recognition of her true status in Glastonbury society.

"He be fast asleep, the pretty babe," she remarked now, glancing upwards at the ceiling. "You splashed 'un well with the holy water, Passon! It put me in mind of me wone Baptism to see how they drops did trickle over 'un."

There arose at this moment a pressing necessity for more hot water in Nell's best silver tea-pot, which had been a present from her communist brother. To that brother the young mother looked now, for she noticed that Persephone, in her reaction from the rebuff she had received from my Lord, was flirting outrageously with Will.

Dave got up with alacrity, opened the thick oak door and entered the kitchen, allowing a clatter of excited women's voices, mingled with the husky bass tones of Number One, to pour into the parlour.

He returned with the kettle and filled up the tea-pot, which his sister carefully held out to him across the sun-burnt wrists and clean Sunday shirt-cuffs of the Vicar. The door between the two rooms remained open while this transaction went on; and that curious tension that comes over two confronted groups of people, between whom yawns the social gulf, reduced Whitelake Cottage to one complete self-conscious silence. It was through the middle of this silence that Dave, like a young doctor walking down a ward of expectant patients, took the kettle back to the kitchen and returned to his place, closing the oak door behind him.

"I can't think how we people," he said, "can be content to go on with this sort of thing. I suppose there isn't one of us here who casts a thought on all those picks and shovels that are working now, over at Wookey, getting out that tin which Nature put into the Mendips for the benefit of everybody."

Will Zoyland rolled his amorous blue eyes lazily round from his contemplation of Percy's supple figure and stared at the speaker, who now took his seat by Lady Rachel.

A splutter of bullying raillery burst from him before his brain had the wit to think of a good retort.

> "What is your name?
> Elacampaine!
> If you ask me again
> I'll tell you the same,"

he chanted in an aggravating manner; and then he added:

"You and I and the Vicar, Dave, my friend, are the only ones here who could use those shovels for five minutes; and *we* couldn't use them—at least *I* couldn't—for half an hour without getting exhausted. What are you going to do about *that*, eh? There *must* be division of labour in this world."

"But *we're* not labouring at all!" cried Lady Rachel, making room for Dave to take his seat by her side.

"Not labouring, Rachel? That's a nice thing to say," cried Zoyland in a great voice, "when I've given up my one single holiday for months to entertain all you people and have Henry christened! You should see how I work out there, my good child. Why, I'm often in that draughty little office, hours after Spear's precious shovellers have gone home to their suppers."

He shouted all this so loudly that Dave's answer was made the more effective by its extreme quietness.

"We all can't dig, Will. That's true enough; but we'd all dodge it *if we could*. I'd be content if those who did the dirty work got more pay than the rest of us—instead of much less; and being looked down upon by us as well."

Zoyland must have been conscious of the advantage that Spear's quietness gave him. He must have been nourishing a bitter grievance too about Eudoxia and a still deeper one over what his father had just told him with regard to the sale; for he now cried out quite uncivilly:

"Bosh! Rats! All these theories are the merest clap-trap! It's the same all over the world! Wherever you go you see men ordering and men obeying. Would you yourself be found with a pick and shovel, I'd like to know, if you could drill us all into your precious commune tomorrow?"

A humorous smile flickered across Dave's face at the mention of the word commune. "They little guess," he thought to himself, "how near they are to a commune in Glastonbury!"

But before he could reply, Lady Rachel had leaped into the breach.

"The point you entirely slur over, Will," cried the young girl, quoting with a touching faithfulness to her lover, a paragraph in next Saturday's *Wayfarer* "is whether these labourers would prefer working for a single individual like Philip Crow, or *working for themselves*—that's to say for the community."

"Well said, Lady Rachel!" murmured Mr. Spear.

There were actually tears in his eyes as he looked at her, so delighted was he to find how far she had travelled along the path, since he had last talked with her.

"Well said, little traitor!" mimicked Zoyland.

"If you'd think a little more and shout a little less, Will, it would be a good thing," retorted his half-sister with a red flush on her cheeks.

"What she said is unanswerable," remarked Dave Spear sternly.

The Marquis of P. rose to his feet ——

"Will," he said in a slow drawling voice, "I wish you'd be so good as to tell the Sergeant to put my horse in and bring him round." He then turned politely to Nell, fumbling for a minute in the pockets of his coat, and finally producing an object tied up in tissue paper.

"I picked up Rachel at the curiosity shop in Glastonbury," he said, "and she helped me to choose this little trifle for the child. That man . . . that extraordinary individual . . . who's always there now . . . took a long time hunting it up . . . but it's genuine . . . *he* said it was rather valuable . . . it's got our arms on it anyway . . . which I thought was a rather happy coincidence."

However long Mr. Evans may have taken in finding the object referred to, he certainly hadn't taken very long in tying it up; for, as Lord P. brought it out of his pocket, the tissue paper was already in tatters. It was a tiny little cup, but it was apparently made of gold; and there was a general rush of the company to look at it.

Nell made a very pretty, hesitating, upward tilt of her face; and the bastard's father didn't hesitate to take advantage of this. He held her upraised chin gently between his finger and thumb for a second as he brushed her full lips with his grey mustache.

"Bless you, my dear," whispered the old man softly. "After all it's you mothers who are the real workers."

The fuss over the golden cup, which Nell presently, to prevent the portly lady having to struggle to her feet, placed in Mother Legge's lap, occupied the company sufficiently and laid—like the council's water-cart—the cloud of controversial dust, until Sergeant Blimp appeared at the back door with the green-wheeled dog-cart.

The Marquis and his daughter had to pass through the kitchen to reach the vehicle, and Zookey Pippard wisely placed a block of wood against the oak door to keep it open.

The Sergeant and his big horse were soon surrounded by a mingled company from both the two rooms; for a horse is still the one thing in England that obliterates all social embarrassment.

"How be, Sergeant?" said Abel Twig familiarly to the solemn-faced coachman.

"Pretty tidy, Mr. Twig, thank'ee—I'd like it well enough down here and be glad enough—I would—to stay down here, if 'tweren't for they Bellamys. Those two old warlocks, Mr. Twig, were made by Satan, to bother a man's life out of him."

"I can believe it, Sergeant, I can believe it. I only once set eyes on thik wold couple; and that were at Somerton girt Fair; but I seed 'un haggling wi' they gippoos in a manner onbefitting decent Christian volk. I were sorry for they gippoos . . . and that's the truth, Sergeant . . . when I heerd how thik pair were carryin' on."

Sally Jones now hurried forward to stroke the mane of the black horse.

"How does yer uncle Bart enjoy 'is-sell, Sal, now he be back in shop?"

"He ain't doing only half what he were, Mr. Twig," replied Sal, "and 'ee have gived up his place over shop too. He have taken a room at Dickery Cantle's where he can see the cattle market from his windy. He says, 'Them as has had a zysty as bad as my zysty do like to see a bit of the girt world, afore they caves in.'"

When the Marquis and his daughter appeared upon the scene, and were helped into the dog-cart there was quite a little crowd around them.

Though most of these friendly adherents were only women,

Lord P. received an old-fashioned feudal ovation as he drove off
by Blimp's side with Lady Rachel perched upon the back seat.

" 'Tis fine to smell a whiff of good horse's dung again," said
Abel Twig to Zookey, as they turned back into the house, "in
place of this here gasoline."

"That's what my darter Doxy said, only this very marnin', as
her went off to get the Frome bus. 'Mother,' my darter said, 'I
reckon I'll go back where people aren't so finicky and so per-
tickler, and where they girt cart-horses have silver bells on
their necks.' "

Indeed with the departure of the head of the Zoyland family
a strange and uncanny irritation seized that whole group of
people, an irritation that seemed to flow like an evil electricity
from kitchen to parlour, and from parlour back again to kitchen.
The little golden christening cup, with the Zoyland falcon on it,
which the Marquis had brought, became now the innocent cause
of a violent quarrel between Zookey and Sally Jones.

Nell had brought the cup in to show them, as soon as the dog-
cart had driven off, and Sally had said that Uncle Bart had told
her long ago about that gold cup and that Miss Crummie had
wanted to see it, but Miss Cordy, what's now Mrs. Evans—had
said 'tweren't right "to show things to people unless people were
thinking of buying things."

It was then that Zookey had rudely remarked:

"Thik wold Number Two do blurt out lies as fast as his lungs
do pant. I reckon he thought thik cup were common silver-plate
till Mr. Evans told 'un 'twere gold."

To this insult Sally had replied in an incoherent rush of
words, the drift of which was that she had heard Mr. Geard tell
Mrs. Geard that if he were blessed by Providence to find his dear
Lord's cup, there'd be something in Glaston that would divide
lies from truth forevermore. "And that," Sally had added
fiercely, "that would be the last of *thee*, and of *thee's* devil's
tongue!"

"Ye'll be saying next that his Lordship's gold cup," retorted
Zookey, "with his Lordship's wone trade-mark on it, be the
Mayor's cup. *That* comes of letting Red Robinson take 'ee, where
no decent woman *should* be took! I've a seed ye two, sneaking

whöam at night down Chilkwell Street and if thee don't mind thee's manners, I'll let the Mayor know thee do go round town, telling tales of what he says to his Missus, when none be by!"

Nell had gone upsairs by this time to suckle little Henry; Zookey was clearing away the tea-things in the parlour; Zoyland and Percy were standing together by the nearest pollard willow in the direction of that deep weir, into the waters of which, on the occasion of Mat Dekker's first appearance here last March, Sam had been so strongly tempted to fling his bearded rival.

Dave Spear, using Percy's little motor car for this purpose, was occupying himself by patiently driving, in two successive trips, first one party and then another of the proletarian guests to their various homes in the town. He took Mother Legge and Tittie first. Then, on his return, he took Abel Twig, Nancy Stickles and Sally Jones, Sally sitting on Nancy's lap. This occupied him altogether, with the inevitable lingering conversations in doorways, nearly a whole hour; and thus it was getting on for seven o'clock when he finally found himself turning out the lights of his machine on that gravel patch at the back door, upon which lay the wholesome-smelling droppings of the black horse from Mark's Court.

Entering the kitchen by that well-oiled outer door that Doxy Pippard had found so serviceable, he discovered Doxy's mother laboriously coping with an enormous pile of dirty dishes. Will had purchased at the last moment, in the china department at Wollop's, a number of cheap tea-cups and plates that Nell had cordially disliked, but that Zookey, hearing the altercation about them, cast an envious eye upon, regarding them as a possible perquisite. These new cups and plates, although not to be compared for intrinsic beauty with Nell's own collection, possessed for Zookey a far greater value than these, just because there hung over them this vague premonitory glamour of future ownership. Without doing it deliberately Zookey broke two of Nell's nicest cups, treasured relics of the quiet Spear family, objects that bore no predatory falcon upon their gilt-bordered whiteness; but not one of these new "Wollop things" did she so much as crack, partly because of their sturdier substance, but also because in her acquisitive mind, they were destined for her own dresser in Bove

Town. After standing to chat for a few minutes with Mrs. Pippard, a friendly gesture that was rewarded by several wickedly barbed pieces of information ("Parson can't hang over Missus long enough, when she have child at breast," being one of these, and "Thee's preety lady and the Master do seem to like thik dark river-bank" being another and " 'Twere wondrous to see how Auntie Legge's eyes did shine when gold cup were on lap" being a third) Dave Spear pushed open the door and went into the parlour. Here he found an aura of such forlorn emptiness and hushed sterility that even his vigorous and phlegmatic nerves were affected by it.

Nell—or Mat Dekker when he went up to Nell—had blown out all the candles save one and the first thing Dave did was to light two more. All three at his elbow on the table, he sat down to read and to smoke, taking both book and pipe from his own capacious pocket. A treatise upon the Lost Atlantis it was that Dave produced and it interested him as an imaginative picture of an ancient communistic state.

A certain interior feeling, however, of quite another order than any emotional reaction to wife or sister, refused to be stilled by his reading. This feeling was that of extreme hunger. Dave had had no lunch; and the thin bread and butter and scotch scones of their tea had been devoured so quickly by Zoyland and Mr. Dekker that before their economic dispute began he had had only a nibble at them; and once launched into his argument he had naturally forgotten such a personal thing as a craving for food.

Most of the pathetic scenes in almost everybody's life are scenes unnoted by anyone and totally disregarded by the person in question. Such was this moment in Dave's life; when, with his head full of the signing of those documents at Mark Court, he was pondering on these legends and rumours of Atlantis in connexion with his historic experiment in Glastonbury, and all the time wondering against his will whether Zookey intended to cook them any supper.

He was successful in rigidly keeping out of his mind every image of Dekker bending over Nell in the room above, and of Zoyland bending over Percy in the darkness outside; but as his three candles flickered upon these legends of the drowned continent, he could not prevent his thoughts from running upon baked potatoes and gravy.

Twice, while Dave had been reading his book on Atlantis, and thinking against his will about potatoes and gravy, Percy came straight up to the window outside where those brown curtains were, and peeped in upon him. Being the man's wife, and yet with no essential kindness for him, the girl when she saw him there did not feel the least sense of the pathos of that short flaxen-haired figure, with its schoolboy earnestness, turning the pages of "Atlantis" and every now and then making a pencil-note in the margin of the book. Thinking himself completely alone in that candlelit room Dave gave way to a childish trick, that his dead mother had long ago tried to cure him of—a trick of sucking his upper lip, and pulling it as far as it would go, into his mouth, while he licked it with the tip of his tongue. But Percy, while she had grown so familiar with his ways as to take them all for granted and while she had come to value his opinions so as to accept them for her own, felt toward him not one single kindly human feeling.

"There he is—reading that book!" she had said to herself the first time she peeped in. "How his ears *do* stick out!" And the second time she peeped in, it was much the same.

"There he is—still reading!" she thought. "How insensitive his hands are!"

Will Zoyland had not yet forgiven Nell for his humiliation of last night. He had agreed to the precipitate departure of Eudoxia; but there had been no reconciliation between himself and Nell . . . in fact very few words of any kind had passed between them since he had carried her bodily up the attic stairs to spare the feelings of Miss Pippard.

Aggravated rather than appeased by his protracted dalliance with Doxy, Zoyland's senses were irritably on edge after his long summer of celibate virtue.

The electric response of Persephone to his careless courtship— for, as we have discovered, to excite a man's desire to the point of desperation was a recurrent aspect of this singular girl's perversity—very quickly heightened this rebellious wantonness into a leaping flame of desire. Nell's unforgivingness over the trifling incident of Eudoxia rankled in the bastard's mind as something extraordinarily unfair. Here was he playing the wittol for Nell's sake and what was she doing in return? He couldn't blame her for being absorbed in her maternity; but she might at least have been indulgent to his natural and pardonable lapse.

As he pulled Percy away from the parlour window after her second spying upon her husband, he glanced up at the window of the attic and noted by the faint light there that she had only lit one of her bedroom candles. He could hear no sound of the Vicar's deep voice either; and he thought to himself, "The Padre is holding her hand and rocking the cradle—a pretty family picture! But where do I come in?"

Will's complaisance over the child was, if he had troubled to analyse it, more for the baby's sake than its mother's. His rich animal nature—the lavish temperament of a born outlaw—responded exuberantly to the helplessness of babyhood. He found Henry sweet to his taste; but if a wandering gipsy-woman had left a foundling on his doorstep he would have made the same kind of pet of it.

The little golden christening-cup, having been handed here and there between parlour and kitchen, and now reposing in peace at the foot of Henry's cradle, had been an added cause of annoyance between Zoyland and Nell. The girl had expressed a desire to have the baby's name engraved on the cup, but this had seemed to William a paltry, middle-class addition. Did not the cup already carry the proud falcon of his race? Thus there had been yet more bitter words between them on this head, which added still further to the rankling score of grievance.

"Come on, sweet one," he now whispered, dragging Persephone away, from the house towards the tow-path and this time in an easterly direction. "They don't want us in there. He's plotting revolution, and they're plotting sentiment! We're out of it tonight, you and I; and we'd better make the best of being out of it!"

Percy had always enjoyed flirting with Zoyland, but they were both in a completely different mood tonight. . . . They were both in the same mood too, by some fatality; which always means a vibration between men and women full of delicious danger.

"Is it *possible*," her incorrigible spirit pondered, "that this man is going to do what Phil and Dave couldn't do? This is a glorious moment anyway. I wish it could last forever!"

The half-moon, looking water-logged and labouring, like a rudderless ship, in the mottled sky, poured down a stream of ambiguous influence upon the swollen river. Too many feminine nerves, of every level of organic life, were draining just then that strange Being's vitality, so that the magic touch that fell upon Percy's relaxed limbs as Zoyland dragged her along by the hand, was a mere accidental overflow; casual, uncalculated. It gave enough light however to guide their steps as they followed the tow-path; and the whole nature of that night was such that nothing emphatic or arresting in the elements distracted their attention from each other.

"He willing and she willing," as Homer says, they speedily receded out of all sight of the cottage.

The truth is that women like Nell, absorbed in their motherhood, and men like Dave, absorbed in their politics, will to the end of time throw into each other's arms reckless, restless, irresponsible, wandering stars, like Percy and Zoyland. It is upon these strangely *neutral* nights, such as was this fifteenth of December, that the real power of darkness as opposed to daylight gathers itself together to assert its essential identity. Complete darkness is usually so empty of all discrimination as to be practically a negation; but darkness faintly touched by a sickly moon has a certain positive character. The absence of high wind or pouring rain, too, enables the mind to receive, in uninterrupted concentration, those simpler emanations of earth-life, such as the leap of a fish, the rustling of a rabbit, the cry of a nocturnal bird, the bark of a farm-dog, the lowing of a cow in an isolated barton, the faint soughing of reeds, the creaking of a bough, the fall of a twig into a silent pond, the shy stirrings of aimless little night-winds amid the dead bracken, which are destroyed and obliterated by the more startling play of the elements.

Zoyland paused only once in his predatory stride and that was to make the girl lean on his arm in place of holding his hand.

She was indeed following him so gallantly and with such an easy swing over the muddy ground that he felt proud of her as a companion. The truth was that in a rough-and-tumble country walk, Percy, for all her sophistication, would have beaten any woman in Glastonbury except her cousin Mary. It was perhaps the vigorous Norfolk strain in their blood. But whatever it was, no Glastonbury-born girl could have rivalled these two in this. Further and further eastward he led her; for he knew well by this time what he had in his mind.

What he was aiming at, and he found it without any trouble, was a spot that had always made him think of just this very contingency though not necessarily with his present lady! About half a mile from Whitelake Cottage there was a reed-thatched shed where the farmer of those fields kept his dry hay. The fields on both sides of the stream belonged to this man just there; and in order to convey his hay across to his cattle on the opposite bank he kept a flat-bottomed boat tied by a rope to an iron stake, beneath this hayshed. Zoyland had made use of this boat many a time before, and without leave asked either, for the purpose of shooting wild fowl; and it now entered his mind that nothing could be more congruous with the hour and the girl than to embrace his present delicious companion where the waters of the river would be flowing within an inch of their bodies.

Percy laughed aloud—a low, merry, young-girl's laugh of pure mischief—when she found herself laid upon a mattress of hay in this floating bed. Her mind flew to that grey strip of subterranean shingle under the Witch of Wookey. Her only desire now—and even that was a languid one—was to put off her final yielding to the bearded man until she had enjoyed to the extreme limit the excited tension of his craving.

"How queer it is, in my life," she thought to herself, "the way the same situation keeps repeating itself! Is it possible that that Bristol Wharf"—she was thinking of her early encounters with Dave—"and Wookey Hole, and Saint Mary's Ruin,"—she was thinking of one particular meeting with Angela Beere—"and that room in the hospital"—she was thinking of the last of her morbid visits to Mr. Evans—"were all rehearsals of this breaking of the ice with Will? When a person's life repeats itself—

from that shore of Phil's to this boat of Will's!—there's a doom of some sort in it. He *may* be able to do it. He *may*! Will! *Can't* you do it? *Can't* you show poor Percy where her heart is? Oh, find it, oh, find it, darling Will! Touch it, hurt it, bruise it, *break* it! So long as you show her where it is—poor Percy's lost treacherous heart—that she can never, never, never find!''

It may well be believed, with a piratical amorist like Zoyland, that it was not long before Persephone's body, whatever happened to her heart, belonged, as far as it could belong to anyone, to this herculean ravisher.

In the matter of pure lust, Will did not get half the satisfaction from his taking of Percy that he got from his dallying with Eudoxia. But in every other respect—aye! how he did enjoy the unequalled circumstances of these violent embraces!

The gurgling of the water beneath this keel-less vessel, the rubbing of the rope against the bark of a little bush, the drooping down as if in sympathy with his heathen satisfaction, of the whole cloudy heaven, the smell of the river-mud, the glittering slide from the high zenith of a falling star in the direction of North Wooton and Croscombe, and most wonderful of all and actually simultaneous with the apogee of his delight, the sudden rising of a great, broad-winged heron and its heavy retreat over the moonlit marshes towards Westholme and Hearne House— all these things gave to the bastard's sensuality that sort of romantic elemental margin, which was the thing of all things that he relished most in the world. Thus, it may be imagined in what a mood of tender gratitude he took Percy back, holding her hand tight, very tight, and repeatedly kissing it.

As they moved along, he thought to himself—"Girls really ought to be allowed everything they want in this world, when they can give a person such entrancing pleasure!"

He felt in a delicious mood now; at peace with Man and at peace with God; and he would have got home in this mood, if it had not been, as he approached the house, that he caught sight of a particular branch of a particular tree which he had noted— it was blasted by lightning—while the Marquis was telling him of the sale of the factories and of the leasing of the shops.

Quite irrelevantly, and not very discreetly, he burst out, upon catching sight of this branch—"The old man brought bad news, tonight, kid . . . devilish news. He's selling I don't know what of his Glastonbury property to I don't know who; and leasing, for an ordinary person's life-term, what he can't sell! It's old Geard, of course, who's at the bottom of it; but it'll be terribly, *terribly* serious for Philip. I ought really to let Philip know tonight, so that he can take measures, if there *are* any measures to take! He says distinctly that he's sold at least a third of the Crow dye works. They are only the newest ones—but still! I was perfectly flabbergasted. I knew he owned the land, of course; but I somehow thought Philip had *built* all the dye works. But of course he didn't! He only improved the old ones out by the cemetery. And it now appears he's only had these new ones on a lease; and this lease is now up. If these people—Geard and the rest—don't choose to lease 'em to him again, they can kick him out. And they *will* kick him out! There's no doubt about it. They all hate him like the devil; and nothing would give 'em more pleasure than to bring him down a few pegs."

Persephone herself was a little surprised and shocked by what she felt in response to this. For many dark and complicated reasons she actually felt a spasm of pleasure at hearing of this disaster to Philip. She had been deeply piqued, for one thing, by his obvious ability to get on perfectly well without her. For another thing, she had accepted, for good and all, her husband's views as to the injustice of the capitalist system. But there was a much subtler reason than either of these for Percy's throb of uncousinly pleasure at hearing this startling news. Philip's chief hold upon her imagination had been her idea of him as a swift raptorial man of action, competent, unscrupulous, deadly. But this news showed him as outwitted and something of a fool; and this development left the fortress of her heart free for Zoyland. She was in her queer fashion watching with an intense inner interest her feelings about Zoyland. She felt that she was still, though they were far from the boat, under the spell of his portentous magnetism, of his overpowering physique. After Wookey Hole, when Philip had loosened his hold upon her, she had very quickly become mistress of herself. She had shaken off her contact with him as if it had been no more than a kiss. But

something surely . . . deeper than that . . . *had* been touched
by Zoyland's possession of her in the hay-boat. Furtively in the
darkness she allowed herself to fondle the man's muscular wrist;
and then from his wrist her long slim hand slipped down to his
great swaying hips. Here, as her fingers strayed, she found one of
the leather straps of his braces hanging loose; for when he had
been buying that set of heavy tea-cups at Wollop's, he had been
persuaded to purchase a new pair of braces for himself by the
youth who read Nietzsche and these articles his powerful fingers
found it very difficult to button. When he felt her knuckles
against his side the spontaneous intimacy of the gesture tickled
his fancy as much as her actual touch tickled his ribs; and with
a deep-drawn chuckle he stopped dead.

"Do it up, if you can, kid!" he laughed. "It's beaten *me*, that
bit of leather!"

She put both her hands to it and finally—though not without
an effort—she got it fastened. This was the first time in Persephone's whole life that she had buttoned a man's button.

It was a quaint little incident, but in its particular kind of
intimacy it affected some nerve in her wild, perverse nature that
sent a delicious shiver through her whole frame. She felt like
some elemental creature of the night, some wandering elfish
thing, that was taking care of a primeval earth-giant. No woman
in all Glastonbury had less of the maternal in her composition
than this erratic boy-girl; but by thinking of herself as an elf-
waif and of her paramour as a fairy-tale giant, she made of this
trifling incident, as they stood there in the river-scented darkness, something that was significant and even symbolical.

To their surprise—for human beings are very like animals in
their expectation of finding what they have left exactly as it was
when they left it—they found, on their re-entrance into the
parlour, Nell and Dave and Mat Dekker seated round a small cold
supper. Dave rose quickly to get them chairs, for their places
at the table had been prepared for them; and while they sat
down, they could hear Zookey Pippard crooning and murmuring
to the baby in the room above. In the centre of the table, side by
side with the vase of small bronze-coloured chrysanthemums, Nell

had placed the little golden cup; and this small object at once became again the topic of general conversation.

Although Mat Dekker had made a stubborn struggle with his religious conscience not to allow his overwhelming feeling for his son's mistress to betray itself in any overt manner, his whole being had been so stirred by these long, sweet, lonely hours, in semi-darkness, with her and her child, that he flooded her, saturated her, drowned her in the heady worship of his suppressed passion. It was therefore from an atmosphere of limitless and enfolding idolatry that Nell found herself faced, at first by the bodily absence, and then by the absence of mind, of her husband and her sister-in-law. She had kept Mat Dekker and Dave waiting half an hour for their supper; but then, when the absent ones had not returned, she had told Zookey to bring in "all there was in the house."

Mat Dekker was too excited to eat very much; but half his normal appetite was enough, with the aid of Dave, who was ravenous for food, to dispose of the more substantial viands that Zookey had been able to find, and there was little left for Zoyland and Percy except sponge cake and black-currant jam.

Now, although suppressed desire is destructive of appetite, satisfied desire is creative of extreme hunger, and happy as Zoyland and Percy were in their secret union they both felt a very sharp craving for some kind of solid and substantial nourishment.

Below the surface of the most civilised human beings, the hunger-lust darts and snaps like a fish, snatches and rends like a bird, growls like a wolf, snarls like a panther, buzzes like a hornet, bleats like a sheep and stamps like a bull; and there is nothing so aggravating to hungry stomachs as the sight of dirty plates pushed away from satisfied rival stomachs. Mrs. Pippard was so tired and cross after her party that Nell had not liked to demur at anything she did; and indeed when cold ham, tinned sardines, and scrambled eggs appeared, she knew well enough that the resources of her larder were exhausted.

Unfortunately, nothing looks more tantalizing to hungry eyes than bits of cold toast upon which scrambled eggs have been served, or more offensive to the aesthetic sense of hunger—for hunger *has* its aesthetic sense—than the scales and tails of sardines upon oily plates.

Thus, however happy the two adulterers were in each other's society, and whatever secrets of this curious neutral night they brought into Whitelake Cottage with them, when they found themselves confronted by the sponge cake, it was very difficult to retain their high spirits.

"Percy would like a couple of boiled eggs and a cup of tea," cried Zoyland in a casual, airy, jaunty manner.

"I'm sorry," said Nell, "but the kettle is cold and there are no more eggs."

"Well . . . anyway . . . let's have some cheese," Zoyland's voice had become a good deal less airy. But Mat Dekker broke in:

"I'm so sorry—I told you how it might be ——" he muttered, looking anxiously at Nell, for he had finished every bit of her excellent cheddar cheese before he proceeded to light his pipe.

"I'm—afraid—I ate—more than my fair share of the sardines," said Dave anxiously, "but I expect there is ——" and he looked at Nell with a pathetic masculine faith in the unlimited resources of feminine providing—"I expect there is *something*."

"Well, I know what I *can* get for Percy, anyway," cried Zoyland angrily, leaping up and rushing into the kitchen.

"Take off your boots, if you go up to your room," warned Nell. "He'll be sure to hear; and Zookey has only just this minute got him off to sleep."

But Zoyland took not the slightest notice of this request; and sure enough in a short time they could all hear the creaking sound of his heavy steps as he walked through the attic anteroom into his smoking-room. Nell rose indignantly to her feet, listening intently.

Persephone helped herself to a piece of thin bread and butter, a piece that had already acquired a certain dry consistency, which indicated that it had been left over from tea. From somewhere outside, away to the back of the house, where there was a clump of naked larches, came the barking of a fox; but for once Mat Dekker was oblivious to this exciting sound.

His eyes were fixed with a furious sympathy upon Nell's white face; his long fingers were clenching themselves under the table, their nails pressing into the palms of his hands. As for Dave *he* was occupied in a vain attempt to open a ginger-beer bottle.

"You'd like some of this, *wouldn't you*?" he whispered across the table to his wife. Then he added in a still lower voice, "It won't open though."

In the silence that ensued everybody could catch the audible lifting up of an angry infant's moan, a moan full of a self-pity that amounted to anguish.

"He's woke up," cried Nell, biting her lip, and casting a wild look of blind appeal upon Mat Dekker.

"Hush . . . listen!" whispered Persephone.

And while in the further distance the heavy tramp of Zoyland's boots was audible, they all caught the lilt of an esoteric jumble of West-country rhymes, chanted over the cradle.

> "Oon, two, dree, vour . . .
> Bells of Girt Sedgemoor!
> Who can mëake pancëake
> 'Thout fat or vlour?
>
> Zee-Zaw, Harry's mother,
> Sold her bed and laid in clover,
> Wadden she a dirty slut
> Da zell her bed and lay in dirt?
>
> 'Pon my life an' honner!
> Gwine to Mark's Tower,
> Who should I see,
> But Zookey's Babee?
> 'Pon my life an' honner!"

In the interior of Whitelake Cottage this singular lullaby was very audible and not devoid of significance. But its effect upon the infant was the reverse of soothing. Something in the sound of the child's crying, when it burst out again now, made Mat Dekker think of a small vivisected dog he had heard howling once and that he could never get out of his head. Nell's face became distorted with anger. She felt as if each step Zoyland took, upon those creaking boards up there, was taken upon the outstretched nerves of Sam's child! She could see the way its funny chin, the very replica of Sam's, was wrinkling itself up in its blind suffering!

But she clutched the back of her chair and tried to force herself to remain where she was. "If I go up," she thought, "I'll say something to Will which he'll never forgive—and which I never shall *want* him to forgive!"

But Will had got what he wanted now; and the creaking up there ceased, as he came down the outside steps and entered the kitchen.

"I'll have something really decent for you to drink in a minute, Percy!" he shouted through the oak door, pushing it open for a second with his hand.

Nell sank down mechanically into her chair; but some new thought had entered her head—some desperate thought—and she sat staring into vacancy, disregarding them all.

The child's crying grew louder and louder in the room above —Zookey was scolding it now; but that was even less effective than her "oon, two, dree, vour." Dave had recommenced his attempts to loosen the ginger-beer stopper; and Persephone was swallowing her second piece of dry bread and butter.

"I can't think how ——" began Mat Dekker, half-rising from his chair. There were beads of sweat on his forehead and his whole face had darkened to a dusky red. Zoyland came rushing in now from the kitchen, opening the oak door with a heavy kick and letting it close behind him. In one hand he held the bottle; in the other three tumblers.

"Here's something that'll make you forget whether we've starved you in this house or not!" he shouted, pouring out a stiff glass of the stuff for Percy. It was of Percy and Percy alone he thought. Everybody else was non-existent. It was as though he and Percy were still by themselves on the bottom of the hay-boat.

"I can't think why ——" stammered Mat Dekker, staring at Nell in helpless, pitiful expectancy.

If Zoyland saw only Persephone just then, Mat Dekker all that evening had seen nothing but Nell!

Dave relinquished the ginger-beer stopper as hopeless. He stared at the smoke which continued to rise from Mat Dekker's lips, in big convulsive puffs, floating away above the candle-flames. Persephone gulped down the whiskey and held out her glass for more.

"It's good, Will," she murmured gratefully. "It's better than food." They exchanged a long, entranced look. He filled her glass again; and again she emptied it in a few quick gulps. Her brown eyes had a dazed, ensorcerised film over them as she sank back in her chair. "I do love him. He cares nothing about anything," she thought. "He's just like me." The drink kept mounting and mounting to her brain.

Zoyland drank out of her glass and then refilled it for her for the third time. He made an automatic motion of passing the bottle to Dave, who shook his head. He had ignored Mat Dekker completely all that evening, since they had first entered, and he continued to ignore him. His eyes were as luminous with excitement now as Percy's were languid with enchantment. They sat opposite each other, and as they drank they stared at each other; and more and more it seemed to both of them that they were each other's true love. They kept drinking out of the same glass, which might have been drugged for them by that same Dame Brisen, who, in the days when love was all, brought Launcelot du Lac to the bed of young Elaine.

Dave as he looked now from one to another of this distracted company, said to himself in his heart—"And this sort of thing is what they call a personal life! These people are thinking of nothing else but their own personal emotions; and they are proud of it. And while they are wasting their time like this, the men from Crow's Dye Works, the men in Bove Town, in Edmund's Hill Road, in Benedict Street, in Paradise, are sleeping soundly and freely, without any fuss.

"If I can keep Trent from spoiling it all with his anarchism, I'll teach these good friends of mine how to be impersonal! These people think that their feelings are the only serious thing in the world. *Their feelings!* When, at this very moment in China, in India, in New York, in Berlin, in Vienna—Good God! . . . *their feelings!* When, at this moment, if all the pain in the world caused by this accursed personal life, by this accursed individual life were to rise up in one terrific cry . . . it would ——" The little Henry's crying—as if to round off Dave's thoughts—rose to a pitch that was distressing to hear. And yet Nell did not move to go to the child. Her forehead was knitted into an intense frown and her eyes continued to stare straight in front of her.

"Damn that child!" cried Zoyland, jumping suddenly to his feet. "Here! I'll give him his cup. *That* will stop him!" He snatched the little cup of gold from the centre of the table, and flinging open the staircase door, rushed upstairs.

Nell instinctively sprang to her feet too; but sat down again immediately, her head remaining turned towards the staircase and a queer, distorted, rather unnatural smile on her face.

Whatever Zoyland may have done when he reached the top of the stairs, he was evidently completely successful in soothing the child; for the listeners at that candlelit table—and none of them spoke a word—were aware of the baby's cries suddenly dying down. Little gurgling whimperings followed; and then a profound hush; a hush that was broken finally by the voice of Zookey, uttering the words: "God be on us!"—which was the woman's favorite commentary upon the ways of Providence, when thoroughly surprised by any curious occurrence.

Apparently satisfied that the personal manias of his troublesome relatives had reached some kind of temporary surcease, and made aware by the look of their countenances that objective conversation was for the moment suspended, Dave Spear slipped his hand into his side pocket and brought out his book on Atlantis. He was too polite to read in company, but the sight of the volume, laid on the table by the side of his plate, gave him a sort of reassurance that speculative thought upon serious matters was not wholly impossible, even in Whitelake Cottage!

Thud . . . Thud . . . Thud . . . "What on earth," thought Dave, "is this bearded drunkard doing now? "Stop! stop, Master Zoyland!" the agitated voice of Mrs. Pippard and her shuffling scramble in pursuit revealed the nature of the bastard's action. He was carrying the baby downstairs! His appearance with the child in his arms was a signal for them all, except Dave, to rise from their seats. Nell rushed straight up to him, and without a word spoken, snatched the infant from his hands and set herself smoothing its rumpled clothes.

She took it to the couch under the brown curtains by the window and began rocking it on her lap, swaying her body backward and forward, as she did so, and murmuring to the child apologetic whisperings.

"She'd forgotten him . . . she had! She'd forgotten her baby in her bad, bad thoughts! There . . . there . . . there . . . go to sleep my precious . . . go to sleep . . . there . . . there . . . there . . ." Both Zoyland and Persephone were already under the power of what they had drunk; but he now filled their glasses again from the oblong flat-sided bottle he had brought down from his room, and once more they resumed their seats opposite each other. With each drink she took, the tall girl's entrancement increased. Her dark eyes were swimming now with a newly awakened desire for the man's embraces.

She watched every movement he made; and her whole body as she lay back in her chair cried out to him in wordless yearning: "We are yours!" her child-breasts cried. "We are yours!" her long relaxed limbs answered. "We are yours!" whispered her warm neck and her glowing curls. "We are yours!" echoed her sinuous waist and her boy-hips. Meanwhile, Mrs. Pippard had begun to clear away the supper things.

Each time she took anything from the table she threw a disapproving, disgusted glance at the state Persephone was in, and did her best to catch the deep-set sombre eyes of the Vicar of Glastonbury. But Mat Dekker had no eyes for anyone but Nell. The man's inmost nature was seething, fermenting, heaving, upheaving, beyond restraint. Of the bastard and Percy he noticed nothing. They made part of a hateful burden of enemies, all of whom, including even poor Dave with his Atlantis book, the pages of which the indignant revolutionary was now permitting himself to turn, were to his mind persecuting, outraging, tormenting his divinely enduring lady and her sweet child!

When the table was clear of everything except the small golden cup, Zookey Pippard stretched out her hand to seize upon this, so that she might fold up and carry away the tablecloth. But Zoyland intervened.

"Christen little Harry's christening-mug!" he cried in a thick drunken voice; and rising to his feet he snatched the thing up and began pouring raw whiskey into it, out of the bottle. Having achieved this much of sacrilege with his shaky hand, what must the bearded rogue do but forget his first intention—whatever that may have been—and hand the shining mug to Percy, who, without a second's hesitation, raised it in the air, preparatory to pressing it to her lips.

This sight was more than Nell could stand. "Zookey!" she called out in a voice that rang through the room. The old woman, who had been standing like a glaring Phorkyad of secular Judgment in the doorway, hurried to her side.

"Here, take him! Hold him!"

She transferred the child to Mrs. Pippard's arms and came forward towards the table. "Mr. Dekker!" she murmured, from a mouth that looked like a sword-cut in a linen sheet spread over a scarlet counterpane, "Mr. Dekker!"

It may be believed that the passionate Quantocks nature was uppermost at *that* appeal and that the priest was forgotten.

"Yes, my dear?" he murmured huskily . . . and then, under his breath, "Oh, my darling!"

But whatever the impulse had been that made her call out to him, it died away now when she saw the fatal devotion burning beneath his bushy eyebrows, and she sank down at the end of the table and covered her face with her hands.

Persephone, who had only just touched the liquor in the golden cup with her lips, pushed the thing impatiently away from her at the sight of Nell covering her face like that. But Mat Dekker had reached the end of his tether. The point had come, as he stood there, while Zoyland, pushing hurriedly past him, began talking wild nonsense to the child in Zookey's arms, when he must either tear the priest's mask from him and cover that bowed head with more than a religious consolation, or get away from her . . . leave her . . . get home to his son . . . to his aquarium . . . to his dead wife—to his God . . . The heavily built man stood there panting, like a great dog whose mistress has gone down one path and his master down another. His greenish-black trousers remained so still above his square-toed

muddy boots that to a whimsical eye—only there was no whimsical eye just then in Whitelake Cottage—they became objects
quite distinct from his head and shoulders; objects that hung,
like a drowned man's trousers, on a post by the wharf.

It was the way her knuckles looked, half-buried in her wavy
hair, that he couldn't endure another second. If only she would
speak to him he could choke down this feeling! He shut his
eyes and pressed his clenched hands against the flapping coat-
tails which hung down on each side of those baggy trousers.

"If I don't get out of here at once," he thought, "I shall forget myself completely."

Behind his closed eyes he forced himself into a mood in which
his feeling for Nell turned into anger against her enemies:
"Damn that drunken whore! She drank out of the christening
cup!" It was finally by the aid of a self-tyrannous auto-flagel-
lation which it now becomes only too clear his son had inherited
from him that he decided to leave Whitelake Cottage at once.
"Damn that tipsy bitch!" he said to himself before he made any
move; hitting out at poor Percy just as a child, suffering from
a nettle-sting, might have beaten the grass.

"Good-night, my dear Nell!"

His words sounded curiously irrelevant in that disturbed room.
Indeed, to Nell's ears they sounded as if he had uttered them
in an earthquake or a shipwreck. She could not take their meaning seriously.

"You . . . are . . . not . . . *going?*" she said, raising her
head and fixing upon his face her large, tear-wet, reproachful
eyes. It seemed impossible to her at that moment that she was
going to be deserted by her only real friend in that whole house.

"Yes, I *am*, Nell dear," he answered, looking vaguely around
for his coat and hat and stick.

Dave Spear closed his book and jumped up. "I'll drive you
in a jiffy!" he said. "I've driven twice into town already tonight
. . . in Percy's car you know . . . I like driving . . . I like it
very much."

His words aroused Persephone from the semi-comatose state
into which she had fallen and she fixed upon him a tipsy stare.

"Good Dave!" she murmured—just as if he had been a dog

—"good, kind, thoughtful Dave! Yes, you fellows, yes it's true —he *can* drive. He's quite right in saying that. He drives very nicely. *I* didn't teach him. The Comrades in Bristol taught him. They said he *must* learn. He didn't like it when he first heard that! But he obeyed them—he always obeys them. He'd obey them if they told him to kill Philip!"

There was no reason why she should have brought in Philip; but something very deep in her nature was drowsily comparing the various people to whom she had given herself up to be enjoyed.

"I'll never . . . know . . . what love is!" she thought to herself. This thought came to her with such a strong feeling of having made a momentous discovery, that she fancied she had spoken it out loud; and she looked round the room, in a kind of shamefaced challenge, to justify herself for so doing.

Mat Dekker waved his hand for Dave to sit down.

He disregarded Persephone with studied discourtesy. Nell looked at him aghast.

"You don't have to *go*, Mr. Dekker?" she cried, beginning to see that he actually was collecting his things. He spoke in a quiet voice now, but a voice that was resolute and final. "Yes, I've got to be getting home. But I love the walk . . . *you* know that—don't you, Nell? But I've got to be getting home; or Penny and Sam will be coming out to look for me, among the rhynes of Splott's Moor."

This allusion to Sam was a wise and crafty one, worthy of any old Quantock shepherd. It brought their two dwellings near each other and it softened his departure by involving her in his consideration for Sam and Sam's anxiety about him. Nell rose to her feet.

"Well, if you must, you must," she said. "I shall never forget your goodness to me today and . . . and always!"

Zoyland made a mock bow to the priest as the man passed him, carrying his surplice bag in one hand and his stick and hat in the other.

Nell opened the door to let him out.

"Good-night, little girl!" he murmured. "God bless you. God protect you!" he added huskily as he strode off towards the river.

She closed the door on his retreating figure and drew a miserable sigh.

Percy still sat on in a tipsy daze. As for Will Zoyland, he seemed unable to stop talking nonsense to the sleepy, but thoroughly placated infant. Little Harry's long-robed body lay contentedly now in Zookey's arms. She swung him to and fro as she leaned against the wall.

"Harry says his christening-cup hasn't been christened yet," cried Zoyland suddenly. With one of those impulsive, irrational angers that sometimes seize on drunkards, he turned fiercely upon Nell. "It's my cup. It's my father's cup," he gabbled. "And *I* say the cup hasn't been christened yet, Harry's little cup. Harry says it *must* be christened!" He moved with unsteady steps to the table. Here he picked up the cup and raising it to his mouth, tossed off its contents.

"That's . . . not . . . christening . . . Will . . . that's only . . . that's only . . ." mumbled Persephone in a drowsy voice.

"You're right . . . my girl . . . you're always right! It's wonderful how she's always right, isn't it, little Hal? It's my cup; it's my father's cup. It's got our falcon on it. By God! I'll christen it in river water!" He ran to the door carrying the cup in his hand.

Nell clung frantically to him, calling out repeatedly: "Are you mad, Will? What are you doing, Will? It's not yours . . . it's Harry's. It's Harry's, I tell you, Will! It's Harry's cup!"

But he wrenched himself loose from her and managed to get the door open. She followed him into the garden; and a breath of cold night air floated into that whiskey-smelling room.

Dave stood there motionless, hesitating whether to follow them or not. How calm and impersonal looked that little book about Atlantis lying on the table face-down and open!

"Let 'un alone, Mr. Spear," cried Zookey. " 'Twill only vex 'un worse for thee to meddle. Her can quiet him. Him won't hurt his Lordship's golden mug."

Percy looked dreamily at her husband while her eyelids sank down . . . opened again . . . and sank down again.

Her lulled and drugged senses had drifted back to the hayboat. Never had she felt like that before! Never had she given herself up like that before! She had not known the least little thing about "love." No wonder people made so much of it, and priests called it "mortal sin!" "I'm sleepy," she thought—"I'd like to go to sleep in his arms. How strong he is! I'd like to melt away in his arms; and sleep . . . and sleep . . . and sleep . . ."

Meanwhile Nell was following Zoyland down the sloping lawn towards the river.

She was wearing a tight-fitting lavender-coloured dress with loose, beautifully cut sleeves. This particular dress she had seen in Wollop's window and Mr. Wollop's head-seamstress had worked hard to alter it for her, against the day when she came out of the hospital.

She overtook him long before he reached the river bank and clung to him desperately and they struggled together, trampling upon her wild-flower bed and the last of her marjoram plants that were sinking down into the wet winter mould.

In the struggle between them, for he kept holding the little cup high up in the air and she kept dragging at his arm to reach it, it happened that one of her sleeves got caught in some way as they swayed together and was badly ripped, evoking as the fabric tore, that particular sound which is, of all others, the most agitating to a woman, when she is struggling—whether in love or in hate—with a man. The tearing of her dress and the ease with which Zoyland—even in his drunkenness—held the cup out of her reach caused Nell to lose her self-control completely.

She struck at his face again and again with her clenched hand; a proceeding which astonished him so much that he could only murmur, without attempting to defend himself, "Do it again, darling! Do it again, Nell!"

It is a memorable epoch in a man's life, the first time a woman strikes him in anger. In most cases a certain subtle link is broken between them that can never be mended. But there are exceptions to this.

In the relations between men and women the taking of virginity is undeniably the symbolic as well as the psychic root of all complications. This act causes pleasure to the one and suffering to the other—therefore, when a woman strikes a man, a deeply hidden, basic relation is broken; and broken in a manner that, as a rule, is dangerous for both.

The Reverend Dr. Sodbury, Rector of St. Benignus', who was Megan Geard's favourite among "God's Ministers" as the lady put it, "in all Glaston," in an eloquent sermon preached on the occasion when Mrs. Legge of Camelot, then in the prime of her life, was summoned for violently striking the father of Mr. Wollop, spoke of there being something in a woman's striking a man that was monstrous, perverted, unnatural, forbidden, impious, shocking, obscene and—the worthy Doctor in his original manuscript had added the word "bestial"; but in a later version he had modified this into:—"More proper to the insect world than to the world of humanity."

"Do it again, darling! Do it again, Nell!"

Zoyland was debarred from making any serious attempt to defend himself from these blows not only by gallantry but also by his obstinate efforts—natural to the gravity of drunkenness— to keep the cup far out of her reach.

Into her blows Nell threw all the mounting tide of her feelings; feelings that had been gathering and gathering against Zoyland ever since Sam gave up making love to her, ever since her child's conception began. To the end of her life she remembered what she felt as she hit him. It was the sight of his beard in the moonlight, more than anything else, that made her repeat her blows so often. And each blow—as she felt the flesh she struck at yield under her knuckles—seemed to avenge her, and liberate her, and heal some deep hurt in her, and fulfil some profound necessity of her nature.

It was as if she were striking something more than Zoyland. It was as if she was striking at that whole procession of rank, hirsute, brutal, abominable men that she had seen that day, when in the first recognition of her maternity she had burnt up her brother's pamphlet—it was as if she were striking with her schoolgirl hand, all that unfair advantage that men possessed over women in this world; their easy escapes, their light-hearted irresponsibility, their shifting of burdens, their abysmal conceit. How she had hated that "thud . . . thud . . . thud

. . ." of her husband's heavy steps coming down those stairs! Well! It was with another "thud . . . thud . . . thud," of her woman's knuckles against his bearded face, that she had countered that!

It was not, of course that the girl had time to feel all this in *sequence*; but she did feel the overpowering impetus of all this as she struck her blows.

The tearing of her dress was the raising of the sluice and the flood simply followed. The truth seems to be that the attraction between men and women lets down a drawbridge across a fretting current of hopeless differences that has only to be exposed to lead at once to these wild outbursts.

As long as she had not met Sam, or known that there was a Sam in the world, there was enough sensuality in her to make Zoyland a tolerable partner. But when Sam and Sam's child came between them, Zoyland was thrust at once into that category of unilluminated maleness towards which it takes a born courtesan to be indulgent.

It was the appearance of Dave Spear's figure now—for the impersonalist had decided to disobey Zookey—that drove the tipsy giant to his next move.

"I said I'd christen 'ee, little cup," he roared, "and so I will! How do 'ee like *that?*"

So speaking he ran down the slope of the moonlit lawn, treading carelessly on her rain-beaten patch of rosemary, and flung the golden cup clear into the middle of the misty stream.

There was a shriek of astounded dismay from Nell and a cry:—"What on earth——" from the bewildered Communist; and with a much smaller splash than anyone would have expected —in fact with hardly any splash at all—the "Doll's House Grail" as Mr. Evans had called it when he sold it to Lord P., sank down to the bottom of Whitelake River!

The spasm of her anger all spent now, only a sick disgust at his folly remained in Nell's mind. But this was enough to give her the final push to what she had been gathering up her courage to do all that agitated evening. She had not missed— no woman *could* have missed, not even one who loved another! —the vibrant aura of infatuation between Zoyland and Percy.

It had been her vision of their two faces as they drank that whiskey that had tipped the scale.

"Will," she said very quietly when the two men, the one approaching her from the house and the other from the river, met at her side, "Will—listen!"

"I *am* listening; and so's brother Dave listening!" jeered Zoyland.

But she went on in a steady ice-cold voice.

"I . . . am . . . going . . . to . . . *leave* . . . you," she said. "I'm going to leave you . . . now . . . tonight. Dave is going to drive baby and me to—where I tell him—but that's not for you—and yet it *is* for you—yes—I'm going to the Vicarage. Mr. Dekker will take me in. I've had enough of this sort of thing, Will. But . . . but—" she hesitated for a second—"but . . . I'm sorry I hit you. I oughtn't to have done that. I don't know what came over me."

Lord P.'s bastard drew a deep breath. The light from the drifting half-moon made his great bushy beard look twice as big as it did by day and his figure twice as formidable.

What passed through his mind like a falling star was the thought of Percy's naked body, alone with him in that little silent house.

"Very well, Nell," he said, as quiet and composed as a man could be. "Very well, Nell."

"I shall leave Mrs. Pippard here," she went on, "you can keep her or let her go, just as you like ——"

"I'm listening, Nell," he repeated. "Very well, Nell."

But she turned to her brother now. "Dave," she said humbly and gently, "Dear Dave, I'm sorry to drag you into all this . . . . besides I know how you . . . I know what we both . . ."

"Oh, it's all right, Nelly," Dave cried hurriedly, anxious, above everything, to stop her from referring to Percy before Zoyland. "We'll get off at once. Don't 'ee fret! We'll get off at once. Dekker's a fast walker. He'll be home before we're there. Don't 'ee fret, Nelly. The Vicarage won't hurt you for one night anyway . . . and we can see later . . . we can all talk . . . reasonably and quietly . . . later . . . and try and see things . . . later . . . *outside our own skin!*"

This expression "outside our own skin" came suddenly into Dave's head. It was his personal reaction from all this long day spent in stroking the electric skins of so many personalised animals!

"Don't 'ee fret, little Nell!" How many times in her earlier life had this absent-minded half-brother uttered these words! They brought more comfort to her now, in her distress and her shame, than she would have thought possible if she could have foreseen how this day was going to end. Dave put his arm shyly and stiffly round her waist. There were no directions in the Marxian philosophy—nor indeed in his Atlantis book—telling a reformer of society how to comfort a woman. But between his sister's soft waist under her torn sleeve and his own arm, just then, there seemed to be something spontaneously generated which was outside the sphere of reason.

Not more than an hour later Mrs. William Zoyland and Master Henry Sangamore Rollo Zoyland were safely deposited, together with a modicum of luggage, on the steps of the Vicarage front door.

It was the Vicar himself who opened the door to let them in.

The child, disturbed by the ceasing of the movement of the car, began to cry loudly; and in spite of her agitation his mother could not help recalling how, when they left Whitelake Cottage to the tune of Zookey Pippard's "oon, two, dree, vour," her husband had said: "I know one person who'll miss me, Nell, in that monastery of yours!"—and how tenderly he had brushed the baby's face with his great yellow beard.

As for Dave Spear, he was free that night to read his Atlantis book till the candle in Dickery Cantle's third back bedroom burnt to the socket. But he read only three pages. It is hard to be impersonal in a cosmos that runs to personality.

CHRISTMAS CAME AND WENT IN THE USUAL IMPERCEPTIBLE Somersetshire manner.

Mild, open weather prevailed, so that Jackie and his robber band, exploring the Wick Woods for trapped rabbits, used frequently to drag the exhausted, but still enquiring Bert, home to his grandmother, with two or three untimely primrose buds clutched tight in his hot little palm.

But with the appearance of the New Year the barometer fell, and a series of sharp black frosts followed one another, constricting the damp Avalon clay and killing off these premature buddings. The lease of the bulk of his Glastonbury property to the reorganised town council realised for Lord P. so large a sum of ready money that he was able to establish his heavily taxed finances on a new and more satisfactory basis, and Will Zoyland, with his new companion at Whitelake Cottage, got the benefit of this change in several substantial presents of money. The Marquis had never liked his son's wife and his sympathies were entirely with the bastard in the estrangement from Nell. Persephone on the contrary proved to be an adept at cajoling the great man. As to Bloody Johnny's fortune, the inroads upon it by these new transactions, were, thanks to the council's power of borrowing, much less than the Mayor had anticipated; and as the visitors from abroad, attracted by John's advertisements, poured into the town all that winter in increasing numbers, the new Glastonbury commune, under the dictatorship of the Mayor's assessors, showed signs of being more than able to keep its proletariat satisfied and its tradesmen active and content.

The business done in Mr. Wollop's shop alone surpassed all the holiday seasons the ex-Mayor could remember, so that although his establishment did not officially come under the new régime, he was willing enough to hand over to the communal purse, sooner than break with the authorities, all the percentage they demanded of these increasing profits. The bank, the railway, Philip's *older* dye works, and his Wookey Hole tin mine, were

therefore, as the early weeks of January passed, the only strong-
holds of individualism left untouched by the new order.

The official opening of Geard's Saxon arch and of a curious building near it which was really a sort of Platonic Academia
for his new religion, but which, for want of a better name, was
hitherto styled the Rotunda, was to take place on January the
twentieth of this new year. So widely had John's clever circulars
advertised this event, that by the morning of the great day every
available lodging in the place was crowded, and those incorrigible capitalistic railways were running their loaded excursion
trains into the town soon after daylight began.

"Are you really off to Wookey now?" enquired Mrs. Crow of
her husband at an unusually late breakfast at The Elms. "Emma
says there won't be a stroke of work done anywhere in the neighbourhood today."

Tilly was not a little disturbed, for reasons of her own, at
the lateness of the hour; but the master of the house had slept
heavily that morning.

Philip looked across the table at her with his indulgent smile.
How dear she was to him, after all, this quaint little lady for
whom he felt no more erotic attraction than if she had been his
aunt, like that Aunt Maria who had lived for the last thirty years
at Aix-les-Bains! "You wouldn't want me to sit twiddling my
thumbs at home, would you," he said, "while Geard has his
grand glorification?"

"Emma says she thinks *you ought to be there!*" In all the last
decade of their relations Philip's wife had never dared to speak
so decisively; but her private nervousness made things leap out
that she had not meant to say. But her words troubled him. Had
even she, then, joined the increasing circle of their neighbors
who were drifting away from his side towards that of the Mayor?
He glanced down frowningly at his plate. He began biting his
underlip beneath its grey mustache. He felt hedged round by
enemies, cornered, run to earth, like a hunted fox.

Paul Trent's *coup d'état* in the matter of Lord P.'s property,
his own eviction from his new dye works, a sudden deplorable
diminishing of the expected tin ore from his Wookey Hole vein,

all these blows, coming together, had driven this grandson of "the Devereux woman" fairly to the wall.

"Ought to be there," he thought bitterly, "ought to be *there*, to help hoist this crazy charlatan, who's ruining me with Grandfather's money, upon the final pinnacle of his folly."

His tin was running out before either his new road or his new bridge was ready to transport it. The *old* dye works which was all that was left him of his special industry, taken over thirty years ago, was devoid of a manager.

Bob Tankerville, entangled with one of those servants of Miss Drew's, was not half the adventurous air-pilot he used to be. The airplane itself had become an impossible expense in the present state of his finances. He had come down finally in the last few days to endure some very humiliating discussions about his bankloans with the Glastonbury bank-manager. Even the bank itself, flooded with communal money from the huge inrush of visitors, was beginning to turn against him! He had seen too with his own eyes a row of trucks full of his tin ore shunted on a siding to make room for the loads of clay which the council was bringing in as material for their preposterous figurines. And only a year ago, with Barter as his manager, he was in the full flush of his success! Yes, it was the treachery of that accursed Didlington cad that was at the bottom of his trouble! He had thought he was going to do better without him and he *had* done better without him at first. But that was before old Beere fell into his dotage and let this smart rascal Trent outwit him at every point.

"Emma thinks"—began the irrepressible Tilly again, and never had the Perfect Servant been consigned to so deep a pit as her master consigned her to now—"that you ought to stand up to that crowd at the opening and tell them what you feel about these fol-de-lols."

He lifted up his face and tried to smile at his wife with his old tender, humorous, superior smile.

"They'd howl me down," he muttered.

"Oh, no they wouldn't, Philip—Oh, no they wouldn't! Not one of them, as Emma says, can speak as well as you do. Not one of them can ——"

But there was a look upon Philip's face that she had never

seen before, a dangerous, reckless, desperate look; and she began suddenly to feel that it was wiser, with a man who could
look like that, not to *dare* him to do hard things.

Tilly subsided into silence; and stretching out her arm, with
the tea-pot in her hand, re-filled her husband's cup, which he had
mechanically held out to her. She was worried by a little conspiracy of her own at that moment, for the success of which she
wanted Philip out of the way that morning. Completely unknown
to him, she and Emma had been visiting Jenny Morgan, or
Blackie, as Red Robinson called her.

This had been Tilly's own immediate reaction to the disclosure
Emma had at last consented to make to her, pushed on by the
chattering tongues of the servants from the Abbey House. Even
Emma—who thought she knew her mistress well—was surprised
by the spirit which the little lady showed under this communication; and thus it was proved—to the astonished interest of the
Invisible Naturalists—that the human minnow of the species
"Housewife" is liable to act heroically at a great emotional
crisis.

Tilly had indeed, in several trying and disconcerting interviews with her husband's ex-mistress, tried to persuade Blackie
to give up the child and allow her formally to adopt it. But so
far these attempts had proved fruitless.

Though Nelly Morgan went about during all her playtime,
with Jackie and Sis and Bert, her mother seemed obstinately unwilling to part with a daughter she hardly ever saw. Since this
particular morning however was, by reason of the opening of the
arch, a general Glastonbury holiday, Tilly had induced the child
to come up to The Elms after breakfast and pay her a formal
visit. She had done this on the strength of an assurance from
Philip that he would be away all day at Wookey; but she herself
was begging him not to go to Wookey!

Tilly's interior nervousness grew so great at last that she felt
she must get Philip off her hands, at least as far as that nondescript out-of-the-way room where he kept his geological specimens. But Philip had got up now from the table. He moved over
to the fireplace and sat down in one of his grandfather's chairs
and proceeded deliberately to light his pipe. Tilly pondered.

How could she say to him, "I want to get rid of you so that I can welcome your girl's child!" It was one of those ironic private contingencies that some especially dedicated troop of imps seems to delight to contrive on occasions devoted to important public events.

Tilly thought to herself: "He's bound to hear the child's voice if he stays here. How crazy I was to let her come this morning!"

She began piling the breakfast things on a tray, a task which she delighted in—for if Tilly hadn't been a mistress she would have been a flawless parlour-maid—when there was a bold, loud ring at the front-door, a ring twice repeated, the ring of a child, who enjoys pulling the bell-iron out to its furthest reach! Well! there was nothing to be done. The fat was in the fire and the cat out of the bag.

She went herself to the door and opened it; and Philip, quick to catch something unusual in her manner, followed her into the hall. The worthy Emma, primary cause of this embarrassing contretemps, issued at the same second from the kitchen and advanced firmly, quietly, discreetly down the passage.

"Mummy were dead-asleep," declared Nelly in her shrill child's voice. "So I thought I'd come in me week-day clothes. Mummy were turble sick last night."

"Do you mean *drunk*?" growled Philip grossly, while Emma carefully shut the front door and began dusting with her apron the brass lion upon the hall-table; this last gesture being a symbol of the occasion's dramatic importance.

"Drunk-sick," responded the child with a wicked gleam in her dark eyes. "Be you wanting to have me live here," she added, turning to her sulky and disturbed father.

"*Live* here, child? I didn't know——" But he turned sharp round upon Emma, venting his discomfort upon the onlooker. "Don't stand there like that, woman!" he snapped. "We don't want any help with this child."

"You can clear away, Emma," said Tilly apologetically, making a move to take the child into the drawing-room. But Emma, hurt to the quick, was already retreating towards the kitchen door, when she heard by the sounds behind her (for her ears were like the ears of a mouse in her own domain) exactly where her mistress was going. This knowledge brought her professional tact into play with an automatic force that overcame her injured feelings, for the new house-maid was cleaning the drawing-room and it would not do for her to notice things.

"Ethel is in there'm cleaning'm," she said, indicating that the dining-room was the place for this domestic tragi-comedy.

"You shouldn't have spoken like that to Emma, Philip," said Tilly, as soon as the faithful servant had withdrawn again.

"*Damn* Emma! Come in here, both of you," and he pushed his wife and his child before him into the dining-room. "What I want to know first of all *is* this," he began, when they were all inside; and he actually turned the lock of the door to make sure of no further invasion; "how long have you two been seeing each other?"

Tilly who had taken her usual place at the table was beginning to reply when the child cut her short. "Her's been seeing Mummy and me since Christmas. Her brought Mummy and me some crystal-ginger, didn't you, Marm? and some Reading biscuits, and some French sardines, and some Spanish olives, and some Turkish delight, and some tangerine oranges and some ——"

"Here! hold up, kid!" cried Philip, unable to help smiling at this long enumeration of dainties. It crossed his mind how extraordinarily characteristic it was of Tilly to woo his mistress and his mistress' child with objects from the grocer's.

"I went once *before* Christmas," said Tilly, who through this whole episode had preserved her equanimity perfectly except when Philip called Emma "woman." "You've forgotten to tell him *that*, Nelly!"

"I always knowed," cried the child in a shrill voice, when she interrupted herself by staring frantically at the little blue flame under Tilly's polished hot-water urn, and finally by stretching out a long thin arm towards this strange object, feeling with extended forefinger, to see if that queer flame was hot, "that father weren't me próper father, by mother pushing me away when her cried for he. Be *he* my proper father?" and she sidled up close to Tilly in the most coaxing and ingratiating way, and pointed with her finger at Philip, who now stood with

his back to the fire regarding the pair with a bemused scowl.
Tilly put one hand round Nelly's waist and with the other began smoothing down the creases of her frock. "Yes, child," she
said hurriedly, "I'm afraid he is; though he hasn't been a very
good father to you, not telling me about you long before this."
She kept her eyes on the child's dress and even began putting
both hands to a place in the waistband that was held by a safety
pin that had got loose.

"How could we know, kid, how could we know," said Philip,
addressing the child, "that she would have liked little girls who
belong to robber bands and who trespass in Wick Woods and
let rabbits out of snares?"

"She likes me!" said Nelly with decision and with one of
her sudden impetuous movements she imprinted a quick, hot,
excited kiss on Tilly's shoulder.

Tilly bent low down in her efforts to close the safety pin. She
was extremely unwilling that Philip should detect that her eyes
were swimming with tears. "She likes us both," she said sharply
and emphatically, "and she likes Emma too—don't you, Nelly?"

But Nelly had burst away from her hold and had rushed to
the window. "There's a bicycle!" she cried, "and he's thrown a
paper down! Oh, *may* I see if it's the Gazette? Mummy always
lets me see the Gazette. It told about *him* and Mummy once!
Mummy said that wicked Red put it in." Without waiting for
permission she ran out and brought the paper into the room.
While she was gone Tilly and Philip exchanged a long, wordless look, that contained an exhaustive and conclusive commentary upon the whole episode.

He thought, "How ironical that both she and I were visiting
Jenny in that house. Suppose we had met one day at the door!"

"May I open it?" asked Morgan Nelly when she was back
again.

"It'll be all over town that she's here now," thought Philip.
"That paper-boy will tell everyone."

The Gazette contained prominent headlines about the opening
of the arch. "Mayor's Speech Eagerly Awaited," Philip could
read, from where he stood by the fire. "Jackie's Sally be going
to marry Red," announced Morgan Nelly, finding no sign of

the pictures she had hoped for in this number and offering her own quota of Glastonbury news. "Mummy says 'tis more than he deserves."

She remained silent for a second, her brows puckered. "What do bewger mean?" she suddenly enquired gravely of the man by the fire. She evidently felt that The Elms' dining-room was a source of supply for certain gaps in her knowledge of the world. "Do bewger mean the Devil?"

But there was heard now a discreet little tap at the locked door, and Tilly sprang to her feet. "I've got to order lunch," she said. "Shall we keep her here for the day?"

Philip nodded without speaking; and then as Tilly's hand was on the door handle, "I think perhaps I *will* go up there presently," he said.

"To the opening?"

"Yes. That's what you said, wasn't it?" This appealing to *her* for advice on so momentous an occasion, on the question of his confronting in public his grand enemy, took the little lady's breath away.

He seemed *different* in some way as she looked at him now, standing over there; and for their mates to look different is extremely disconcerting to women. They prefer the most familiar tempers to anything inexplicable.

"I . . . wouldn't . . . care . . . to . . . interfere . . . with your . . . plans, Phil," she stammered nervously. "But if you *do* go I must tell Emma lunch won't be till after two. The opening is announced to begin at eleven, you know; but it won't be over till after one, I'm sure."

While this memorable encounter was taking place in The Elms' dining-room, for it was already long past ten, an enormous crowd had assembled at the foot of Chalice Hill, where, as the Western Gazette had justly remarked, the Mayor's speech was being "eagerly waited by all Wessex."

It was not only the opening of the Saxon arch and of the Rotunda, but the inauguration of the new Glastonbury commune that this twentieth of January was to see; and the possibility of all manner of exciting clashes between those friendly to the

Mayor and those hostile to him, gave the sort of spice to the occasion that always attracts a crowd.

Tom Barter had come across to Northload Street, puzzled as to what he and Tossie were to do that day with the twins, for Toss had left Benedict Street and had taken a furnished room of her own. Mary had made him stay and have a second breakfast with her; for she wanted to talk to him about Tossie and the children.

This other Mr. and Mrs. Crow were indeed as late that morning as the pair at The Elms. John lay in bed still, propped up on his pillows. He had had a feverish night; he felt sick now in his stomach; he was unable to eat a morsel; he declined to smoke a cigarette; he was insatiable only for endless cups of strong tea.

Mary was boldly sounding Tom on the delicate topic of his marrying Tossie; and she was telling him that if they *did* marry, there was an unfurnished room to be let on the floor beneath their own in this same house.

"It would be so nice, Tom," she said, "for us all four to be together; and I could look after the children sometimes, while you and Toss get away for an afternoon."

"You . . . don't . . . think," muttered the cautious Tom who was on his knees by the fire with the toasting-fork, as he glanced furtively round at Mary, afraid of being rushed by a conjunction of feminine influence out of some precious bachelor freedom whose benefits he might be forgetting at this time. "You . . . don't . . . think . . . that . . . being married would spoil it all?"

"Spoil it for you, or for *her*, do you mean?" asked Mary, wondering a little, in her own mind, exactly why she was pressing their old friend so hard. "But he used to live so miserably," she thought, "so squalidly and miserably."

"For both of us!" murmured Tom. "You don't want any *more* toast, do you, if *he's* not going to have any? For both of us! I might feel caught; and she might get—oh, I don't know— heavy and domestic, and stop laughing and all that!"

"She isn't so *very* thin, now, Tom, is she?"

"Shut up, Mary! You know what I mean—you know how girls

are when they've got settled—I couldn't bear it for Toss to change a single bit!"

"She won't change, Tom. She won't change. I'd be ready to bear all your reproaches, old friend, if she did; so well do I know that she *won't*. And I don't think . . . very much . . . that you will, either," she added archly; smiling down at him with her hand on the toast she was buttering.

John turned his face away from this scene at the fire between his wife and their friend. He was not at all sure, at the bottom of his mind, that he wanted Tossie and Tom established in the same house.

"What a demon I am," he thought. "I love old Tom when I've got him to myself; but these mixings up—good Lord!"

"How do you feel now?" enquired Mary, turning to him when she and Tom were seated at the table. He refused to meet her eyes. "I'm a devil, I'm a devil, I'm a devil!" he muttered, without a thought of Barnaby Rudge's raven.

"Don't keep bothering, Mary," he groaned peevishly. "You know what's the matter with me and so does Tom."

"You're not getting jealous, are you, old chap, because I've got your place?" chuckled Barter.

Mary thought to herself: "How dangerously these men fool each other! Doesn't he *know* that when he says a thing like that, he makes John hate him so much that he could strike him dead?"

"I hope you realise, John," she said, "that nothing will induce me to let you go to *that thing* this morning? You've got nervous prostration—that's what's the matter with you; and you're going to stay in bed."

"So that Tom can take you to the Hill, I suppose? I thought something like that was in your mind."

Mary said to herself, "I must be more careful. Oh, these men, these men! Our jealousies are serious or nothing. But with them——" She had already come to the conclusion that under a certain "cannikin-clink" brusqueness, like that of Iago, her husband concealed black holes of malice that went down to the nether pit.

This judgment was not *quite* accurate. John's fits of "miching-mallecho" came and went, like the weather. Often when she thought he was most affectionate, his heart had turned as cold as ice; and again, when she fancied she detected abysses of malicious aloofness, he was merely worrying because he was afraid he was going to have dyspepsia.

"If you can't go," she said emphatically, "*I* shan't go. Tom can take Tossie and leave the babies with us here. Why don't you *do* that, Tom? Toss would love to see the crowds and hear the speeches."

Barter admitted that so far they had been unable to find anyone to leave the twins with. All Glastonbury seemed resolved to be at Chalice Hill this morning.

They finished their meal in silence, John's feverish querulousness exercising a discouraging effect upon them.

"Do you want me to come over with you, Tom, and get the twins?" she asked, as soon as they were done. "It's after ten, and you and Tossie should be starting if you want to get good places."

As soon as Barter and Mary had departed on this errand, John Crow struggled up from his bed and somewhat stiffly and weakly stood erect upon the floor—Yes, he felt pretty wretched; but it tickled his vagabond fancy to trick the two people he loved best in the world; and he set himself obstinately to put on his clothes. When he was dressed, and had his overcoat on, he went to the sink and sponged his face with cold water. This made him feel a little better; and moving to the table, he filled Mary's tea-cup with milk and poured it down his throat.

"Nervous prostration," he said to himself, "what a phrase that is! Well, I certainly have done something for old Geard and his Saxon arch; and I'm damned if they're going to keep me from seeing the sport."

Half an hour later he had succeeded by the exercise of both blandishments and violence in pushing his way through the surging crowd, which already filled the road and spread up the slope of the hill, till he was standing right against the new arch itself.

It was a fine piece of work, this Saxon arch, now it rose uncovered to the watery sunshine of that January day, but little as John knew about architecture he felt sure that the great architect had fooled Mr. Geard, and that this massive stone edifice was a completely new and original work, no more Saxon than Cardiff Villa was Saxon. But it was a noble erection; and John had an inkling that in some very subtle way the architect had actually caught something of the spirit of Mr. Geard's new religion!

It was not easy to define to himself what he felt; but he did feel that if he, John Crow, had had to express in solid stone what he had come to understand of the Mayor's strange notions, it would have been almost exactly in this way that he would have done it. How queer that crowd of human heads looked, as it swayed and undulated beneath him! A line from Homer's description of the pallid ghosts, flocking up from Erebus, came into his mind—"The powerless heads of the dead."

He still felt curiously dizzy and feverish; so much so that between himself and that vast undulating crowd—and how silent and patient they were! They only swayed and moved and eddied and drifted. They really *were* like ghosts from Erebus! Why were they all so spellbound?—Yes, between him and them there seemed to be a cold, grey, clammy, Cimmerian mist.

On the opposite side of the arch from where he was standing, and he was himself inside some sort of rope-barrier—how had he crossed that barrier? He could remember nothing just now—was a broad, empty platform, covered entirely with a heavy black cloth, "God! it looks like a place of execution," he thought; and then it came over him that it was towards this draped platform, though there was no one there, that this vast concourse of people were lifting their hushed, awe-struck, hypnotised heads—the "powerless heads of the dead."

And John began to receive a most uncanny feeling—the feeling namely that Mr. Geard really was standing on that platform now. Either his own brain was too dizzy to see him there, when everybody else saw him, or there was an actual invisible presence up there which everybody in the crowd felt without seeing anything.

But it certainly was, for John, the most extraordinary experience he had ever had, that swaying, shifting, drifting, *undulating* crowd—men, women, and children, young men and young maids, foreigners and natives—all lifting up strained, tense, hushed, white faces, as they surged slowly about, while their vast mass moved, like a sea-flood stirred by tides that could not be seen, here and there about the ribs of the hill.

Feeling too dizzy to stand much longer upon his feet, and yet unwilling to sink down upon the grass, John began examining the great unhewn rock-boulders out of which the architect had constructed this singular monument. While he did this he began to experience the feeling that he was really entirely alone on this hillside, and at any moment this illusion, the mirage of these faces, might melt away. He was aroused from this sensation by a sudden spasm of recognition. Where had he seen this particular type of stone before? The stone was inserted between two blocks of Portland stone—for among the architect's original effects in the Saxon arch was the use of several varieties of material—and as John now leaned his forehead against it, for it was on a level with his face and he had come hatless from Northload Street, he knew well where he had seen its like before. It resembled one of those strange "foreign stones," which Mr. Evans assured him came from South Wales, which he had seen at Stonehenge.

The contact of his skull with this stone—and it is likely enough it would have happened with any stone of a similar texture—put new strength into him and cleared the mists from his brain. He now discovered that he was not by any means alone in this roped-off enclosure. There was in fact quite a large group of people assembled here, though in his dizziness, and his preoccupation with the vast array of faces upraised from the slope below, he had felt as if he were the only person close to the arch.

"It's like the ones at Stonehenge," he remarked to his nearest neighbour, who turned out to be the beautiful wife of Harry Stickles, the chemist. Nancy had indeed traded shamelessly on her unusual good looks to get inside this privileged barrier, and it was only because all the officials were local people that she had attained her desire.

"Where is he now?" she responded to John's remark about the stone.

"Where is who?"

"He; Mr. Geard."

"I don't know," said John. "To tell you the truth, Mrs.

Stickles, I feel as if he were standing on that platform now! I seem to *feel* him there . . . but of course it's empty." He ran his fingers over the stone that interested him so much. "It's like the ones at Stonehenge," he repeated aloud.

"There must be more sacred stones," said Nancy, "in Glastonbury than anywhere else in England. I heard people talking just now about a stone with funny marks on it that's been found quite lately on this Hill."

"So they've got it, have they?" he said. "It must be the one that this new antiquary was after, not the King Edgar Chapel man, but this new fellow who's been about here—but Mr. Geard never told me about this stone."

"That's just what they were saying about the other one with the marks on it," said Nancy. "They were saying he hides these stones where no one can find them."

"Only when he thinks they've got something to do with Merlin!" said John. "He knows nothing really about the Legend. He's never read a word of Malory. It's old Evans who's put all this Merlin business into his head."

"He's a very great man," said Nancy gravely.

"I never said he wasn't!" responded John. "They'll be making a legend out of *him* soon. Geard of Glastonbury—it sounds like history already!"

They both were silent; and John, with his fingers still pressed against that South Wales stone, began to feel again the strange sensation of being quite alone up here under Geard's arch and by the side of Geard's black-draped platform. The touch of this foreign stone seemed to isolate him, along with all the Glastonbury stones. It gave him the power to feel the life of Glastonbury with all its long historic centuries as if it were the mere motions of beetles and earth-worms across the surface of a platform of primordial rock, the rock of the Island of Avalon. That vast crowd of white upturned faces, that were like ghosts from Erebus, seemed to become real ghosts, the ghosts of all the men and women whose little, turbulent earth-lives had disturbed the planetary repose of this rock island in the tide-swept marshes. Yes! He felt them rise up multitudinously about him, *kluta ethnea nekrōn*, "the glorious tribes of the dead," and he, the wornout

Danish adventurer, privileged by a strange fate to be the one to feel them there, with Geard's arch above him and Geard's platform beside him.

He glanced up from that sea of pallid faces to the coping-stone of the arch which had been rudely carved into a rough resemblance of Dunstan of Baltonsborough. Baltonsborough itself was over there, hidden by the Tor, an abode of living people still, and nearer him, beyond Edgarley, was Havyatt Gap, where his own unsuperstitious Danes had been stopped by these mad monks. Mad they were then; mad they were still; and old Geard was the maddest of them all!

This stone, all these stones, how much nobler was their long-enduring life than the follies and fevers of men! Surrounded by the great waters had they once been, by the tossing salt waves of that free sea, over which the Viking ships had swept. Would that some strong new flood might come up from its ocean-bed, and sweep over all these morbid-legended fields! How he hated them, these lies, these frauds, these illusions, which he had been paid to propagate! And yet there was something about old Geard, that seemed as much on *his* side as on the side of these mad monks. Was Geard himself, secretly in his deep heart, as heathen as he was? Was that black-draped empty platform only waiting even now, for the lifting of some huge gonfalon of defiance to all this? Was this opening of the man's Saxon arch into these Latin-Celtic mysteries of Glastonbury, in reality a reversal of that stopping of the Danes at Havyatt?

How well he remembered his own first entrance into the town, more than ten months ago, in Mr. Evans' little motor car. Well! Evans and he were both married men now; married and settled, and far away from Stonehenge!

"I can't *think* where he is!" It was the beautiful Nancy addressing him again.

"How do *I* know," John replied peevishly. "He's probably asleep in Wookey Hole, like he was last time, when Cousin Philip shoved himself into his place. Why! Talk of the devil—if there's not Philip himself, coming over here now!"

Nancy turned round and sure enough there was Philip Crow,

pushing through the crowd that gave way before him, and making straight for the platform.

Behind him, as he came, rose a low angry murmur from the natives present. They were evidently already expectant of a second grand anti-climax.

Philip skirted the platform steps, evidently surprised to see no sign of Geard, and passing—a thing no one else had dared to do—right *under* the arch, came up to Nancy and John.

John held out his hand. They had not met many times since that day at Northwold Rectory.

"Come to address us in place of the Mayor?" said John, his cheek twitching with the family twitch and his eyelids blinking under the grip that Philip gave his fingers.

"Perhaps . . . it will . . . fall on me," responded Philip with an air of contemptuous nonchalance. "I'm ready for the job . . . if Lord P. and our good Vicar are dodging it! Has the Mayor got no one to introduce him? How oddly all these things are arranged!"

"Do you know Mrs. Nancy Stickles, Philip?"

Philip took off his hat and bowed. "It's just like the scamp," he thought, "to saddle me with some pretty pick-up at a moment like this."

But before Nancy could do more than return an embarrassed smile to his exaggerated deference, none other than Mr. Geard himself appeared quietly among them, as if materialising out of the air. The Mayor nodded kindly at Nancy, winked at John, and offered his plump hand to Philip. His appearance was so sudden that it was like the appearance of Teiresias at that Cimmerian scene which John had already called up.

John stepped back a little and regarded with concentrated attention the Protagonist and Antagonist of this memorable occasion. Never had the contrast between the two men been more marked.

Philip was dressed in a fawn-coloured overcoat and light soft grey hat. He wore spats beneath his blue-serge trousers and in his hand he carried a cane with a round jasper knob that Persephone had given him. He had a red camellia in his buttonhole and his whole demeanour was composed, debonair, alert.

Bloody Johnny, on the contrary, was really scandalously attired. He had dodged, as his custom was, on public occasions, all attempts of his family to groom him. He was not even picturesquely untidy. He looked like a deboshed verger who had turned billiard-marker in some fifth-rate club.

"He's been drinking," thought John, "and that's why he's so late."

John was not in error. From a very early hour that morning, Mr. Geard, on this supreme occasion of his life, had been sipping brandy with that old crony and convertite of his, the ostler at the Pilgrims'.

John now approached a step nearer to these two Glastonbury magnates. He forgot all about his dizziness, in his anxiety to hear what they could possibly be saying to each other on this day of all days. But as often happens when two formidable personalities meet, they each seemed desirous of avoiding any real contact with the other.

Nancy also moved up close to Mr. Geard's side. She seemed to have an obscure feminine instinct that it would be fatal for her Prophet to have a serious encounter with this enemy at this juncture.

The murmurs that rose from the crowd at Philip's appearance now changed into shouts and yells when the two men were clearly observed talking together.

"Begin! Begin! Begin! Leave your chattering and begin!"

Such was the burden of a storm of confused cries, not only in English but in every European tongue, that now rose like a howl of demons from the crowded slope of Chalice Hill.

"We are being chaffed by the populace," said Philip with a bitter smile. "The chap's half-seas-over," he thought. "Tilly was right to tell me to come. He's going to make an absolute zany of himself. This is my chance, if I can keep cool. I wonder if my voice can carry as far as the road. I'll let these foreigners know that this sham commune and this mountebank Mayor are not the only representatives of Glastonbury."

Thus did Philip Crow gather his wits together; but what were Mr. Geard's thoughts at this crisis? *He had none at all;* none, that is to say, beyond a lively interest in the camellia in Philip's buttonhole! He was as empty of abstract considerations or even rational considerations as ex-Mayor Wollop himself. But let no one suppose that this physical placidity meant that Mr. Geard was *hors-de-combat*. It only meant that he was in such peace with himself that his whole being moved in harmony to the least stray thought that came into his head. It is true he was drunk. But Philip was a fool to regard that condition as a handicap to Geard of Glastonbury. Not even John—who knew him so much better than Philip—realised the power that resided in the man's complete freedom from self-consciousness.

All that his tipsiness did was to make him five times more his natural self than in normal times. And Mr. Geard's natural self was a thing of mountainous potency. It is likely enough that Nancy's Prophet of the Lord had quite deliberately repaired to the ostler's bar at the Pilgrims', so as to leave no shred of fussy vain human self-thought between his intellect and his world-deep sensations.

"Do you know where the steps are to that platform?" said Mr. Geard. "They'll be quiet enough presently. Do you mind if I sit down for a moment?"

"My chance is coming," thought Philip, "my chance is coming."

Mr. Geard now deliberately sat down on the grass. This performance was almost as disconcerting to John as it was to Nancy; and it was a good deal worse than disconcerting to the officials of the commune in the crowd below. John began to feel it imperative that someone should intervene; for Mr. Geard seemed to have fallen into a trance of imperturbable quiescence.

As he sat there cross-legged, with his plump fingers extended on the grass at either side of him, he looked like some neolithic beast-god, paramour perhaps of the Witch of Wookey!

But quick as lightning Philip accepted this grand chance offered him by the fates and stepping lightly past John and Nancy mounted the steps of the platform and presented himself before the audience.

"You have all come here," he began, and out of mere curiosity they let him get as far as that, "to show your interest in our great historic town and to learn what we are trying to do to make it not only a beautiful place, worthy of its old traditions,

but also a place where the noblest achievements of Progress can
be carried——"

But "Progress" was the last word that was audible; for at that
point he was simply shouted down. Yes, there was nothing for
Philip to do but to descend those platform steps as proudly
and contemptuously as he had mounted them. This he accomplished with self-control, dignity and grace. Once on the ground,
however, he gave a swift malicious glance at the grotesque person squatting on the grass, over whom Nancy and John were
bending, shrugged his shoulders, replaced his hat upon his
head, waved his cane, and made his way down the hill.

But with John pulling at one arm and Nancy pulling at the
other, Bloody Johnny *was* now raised to his feet. This achievement, every detail of which the crowd watched from below, was
grossly and humourously cheered, the "*hoch, hochs*" of the Ger-
manic element and the "*vivas*" of the Italians being especially
vehement.

Once on his feet, Mr. Geard smilingly dispensed with Nancy's
help; but permitted John to assist him to mount the platform;
and John himself, amid the tumult of applause that greeted the
Mayor, slipped down again and took his seat on the lowest stair
of the steps, side by side with Bob Sheperd, the old policeman,
and Mr. Merry, the old museum curator.

It was at that moment of the proceedings that Miss Barbara
Fell was overheard to say that it was a pity dear Mr. Crow should
have been shouted down; while Dr. Fell was heard explaining
to his neighbors in philosophic language that Mr. Geard was
probably not *very* drunk and had probably *staged* the whole
episode, with the view of arousing in his audience "that particular psychological mood of sympathetic nervous hilarity which
can be so quickly changed by a crafty orator into passionate
receptivity."

Certainly in its whole long and turbulent history no man in
the county of Somerset has ever received an ovation comparable
with the ovation that Bloody Johnny received at this moment
before he began to speak. And when he did begin, a silence like
the silence of fishes in the sea, or of birds at midnight, fell upon
that crowd, so that angry heads were turned round when anyone

coughed or sneezed or shuffled or struck a match or even turned up his coat collar.

From the point of view of oratory, there was nothing at all remarkable in the way the Mayor's speech began. Many of his later discourses, as they were taken down in the next two months, were far more eloquent. He thanked his hearers for allowing him to speak at all—"under the circumstances." He said that he was sure people would come from all parts of the world to drink of the Grail Spring. He emphasised the historical interest of the new experiment in government that Glastonbury was making. He begged "those who were strange to our system of a just and equitable division of those benefits which human brains and human labour, working in harmony with Nature, give to humanity, to suspend their judgment till they see the thing in working order."

He rambled off at that point into quite a childishly grave recital of early Glastonbury history. He referred to the Lake Village neolithic race. He spoke of the Ancient Britons. He alluded to the importance of the work of the great Saxon king, Edgar.

As John watched the faces of the audience from his position by Bob Sheperd's side he was struck by one very curious phenomenon. The fact that the Mayor was blundering along in a quite commonplace way, uttering brief and cursory remarks that were really platitudes, made no difference at all to the extraordinary impression he produced. John found it amusing afterward to notice the various ways in which the great London newspapers handled this striking difference; this discrepancy between the substance of the man's speech and the spellbound *awe* —there was no other word for it—with which his uninspired remarks were received. Once more John began (or was it his dizziness returning upon him?) to feel as if all those upturned faces were thousands and thousands of ghosts, all the *nekuōn ameneena kareena*, "the powerless heads of the dead," of the long Glastonbury history, listening to Mr. Geard.

It was not long, however, before John's ears heard the phrase: "I therefore declare this arch to the Grail Spring of our dear town, *open*, free of charge, to all persons who, who, who care to come!" and he became aware that, in the same droning and uninspired manner, Mr. Geard had begun to allude to various familiar aspects of the Grail story; aspects such as the simplest schoolchild in the place had been acquainted with since infancy.

This preposterous narrating and countenancing, in solemn seriousness, of what John felt to be a mass of fantastic and gruesome fairy-tales, made something stark and dangerous rise up within his East-Anglian soul. He turned his eyes away from these hypnotised ghosts and fixed them upon that stone in the new arch which had made him think of Stonehenge. And it was borne in upon his mind with a frozen certitude that however phantasmal *matter* might be in its interior essence there was something about it *when it hardened into stone* that reduced all organic flesh into the transient, the impermanent, the perishable. He saw the birth and the death of the generations—men and beasts and birds and fishes—their tremulous loves, their wretched tribulations, their vain hopes, their importunate passions, and all swept away by wind and water from the enduring majesty of these stones, that themselves changed not, save by cosmic catastrophe.

"If I could destroy," he thought, "in one overwhelming stroke all this whole maze of delusion; if I could bring the free sea in upon it, and the north wind down upon it, if I could burn it with fire and cleanse it with water, if I could purify the air of it and purge the earth of it, how calm and clean the world-floor would be!"

"And thus," boomed on above him the monotonous voice of Bloody Johnny, "the Grail-worship at Glastonbury has become——"

An impulse of anger too great to be resisted took hold upon John Crow. Leaping to his feet he turned his back to the crowd and looking up at Mr. Geard who was near enough now to the edge of the platform to see his convulsed face, he uttered in a low hissing tone and so that Mr. Geard alone could hear him, the words:—"Lies! Lies! Lies!"

His effort had been so great that his dizziness came back upon him with a rush. So blindingly it came, that everything swam before his eyes and he began swaying to and fro at the foot of the platform, groping at the air with his hands and gurgling in his throat. As he swayed like this, all began to grow dark before him, and he had just time to think to himself, "What have I done? Have I ruined his speech?" when he fell prone on the ground in a dead faint.

The speaker had drawn back a little towards the centre of the platform, so that when old Bob Sheperd and Mr. Merry, with the help of two other younger men, lifted John up and carried him towards the Rotunda, all that crossed Geard's mind was, "Someone has fainted," and it never occurred to him to associate this incident with that convulsed face and the word, "Lies!"

One of the officials produced the key of the Rotunda and here they laid John; but it was not till the Mayor's speech was over and the crowd had dispersed that he really awoke to full consciousness.

"People say these things are lies," shouted Mr. Geard, after a pause, in a voice that rolled away over that hypnotised assembly with such thunderous force that it reached the ears of Mad Bet, as kneeling at her window on the other side of the road she thought of Codfin's iron bar. "People say we must have the naked Truth in place of these lies. Now what the Spirit and the Blood command me to tell you is this ——"

An inspiration was reaching him at last from the dark recesses of his being. It seemed to tear itself through him and force its way out, like a dragon escaping from a thunder-split cavern. And Mr. Geard felt himself in full command of this inspiration. Unlike Faust, with his earth-spirit, Mr. Geard held the bridle of this demonic winged creature. This was proved by the dramatic pause he made at this point, quietly taking his breath and, as he did so, glancing towards the Rotunda where they had taken that person who had fainted.

Then, as if he were releasing, in absolute aplomb, this wind-dragon of the abyss, he lifted up his voice again:—"*Any lie,*" he shouted, "I tell you, *any lie* as long as a multitude of souls believes it and presses that belief to the cracking point, *creates new life*, while the slavery of what is called truth drags us down to death and to the dead! Lies, magic, illusion—these are names we give to the ripples on the water of our experience when the Spirit of Life blows upon it. I have myself"—here he made another of his dramatic pauses—"I have myself cured a woman of cancer in that spring." He stretched out his arm towards the Grail Fount. "Miracles are lies; and yet they are happening. Immortality is a lie; and yet we are attaining it. Christ is a lie; and yet I am living in Him. It . . . is . . . given . . . unto . . . me . . . to tell you that if any man brought a dead body before me . . . in the power of what people call a 'lie' I would, even now, here and before you all, restore that dead one to life!"

His voice died away in a silence so profound that Nancy Stickles, whose face was distorted with emotion, told Tossie later that she could hear the tinkle of the far-away sheep-bell, on the throat of Tupper, the old fence-breaking ram, in the Edgarley Great Field.

Heavily and awkwardly and all hunched up, his broad back stooping as if a weight beyond what he could bear had been laid upon it, Mr. Geard now began shambling down from the platform. Having reached the ground he stood for a time with his whole massive body bent forward, and his eyes tightly shut. At last, waving his hand every now and then to keep away anyone who approached him, he moved slowly down the slope towards the road.

There were so many conflicting accounts of what now happened, that a compilation of them all, and a comparison of them with one another, would leave upon the mind a feeling that certain great human events do not occur in a direct, clear-cut absolute manner; but include a wavering margin of actuality which changes in accordance with the human medium through which it passes.

As he came down the hill, the bulk of the people remained perfectly motionless, save for an attempt to pursue him with their eyes. He seemed protected, isolated, defended from intrusion by some interior power.

It was not long, however, before a little group of devotees who were now pushing their way towards him made a kind of half-circle round him; but even these did not dare to speak to him or approach him closely. There had been a great many references in European newspapers of late, to the Mayor's desire to make of Glastonbury a sort of English Lourdes, where an atmosphere of miraculous healing is charged with the electricity of Faith, and everyone present felt that something momentous was in the air. But it was not only sick people who were now awaiting this man in the road below.

There always had lingered among the natives of Glastonbury, an obstinate notion that their Grail Spring possessed healing qualities; and no doubt Ned Athling's writings in the *Wayfarer* had played upon this obscure belief and stirred it up. At any rate it is certain that there had spread through Paradise and Bove Town a rumour that the Mayor wanted all the Glastonbury sick people, who could possibly be moved, to come to the Grail Fount that day; and along with these sick people Something Else had been carried to the foot of Chalice Hill, Something that now awaited him there.

Moving straight towards this small dead form, carried upon a stretcher, while the sick people—none of whom was seriously ill —forgot their own condition as they watched him, Mr. Geard followed the example of the prophet in the Old Testament and stretched himself upon the wooden bier, covering the dead child's body with his own. The man's disciples while he did this kept the child's relatives from approaching, all except the mother, whose hands as she knelt pressed the child's feet to her breast . . .

What sceptics said afterwards was that no doctor had seen the child since he died; and what the parents had mistaken for death was in reality a death-like trance, from which the exceptional animal-magnetism of the Mayor's heavy form naturally aroused him. This was the view taken of the incident by Dr. Fell, who came upon the scene soon after the child revived. Meanwhile— inside the Rotunda—John Crow was coming to his senses. When he did so he found his friend Tom bending over him, and Tom's overcoat spread out across his legs.

"You're shivering, Tom!" he whispered.

Barter made a wry face at him. "You haven't seen what *I've* just seen, or you wouldn't be surprised if my teeth were chattering."

John sighed. He made a weak motion with his hand. "What's up? What's he doing now?"

Barter realised that he was talking about Geard; and without delay he poured out his extraordinary story.

"It's that little boy who died this morning. They brought him on a stretcher. I saw the kid once myself. His mother's a drunken bitch, who lived in my house. I knew who it was the moment I heard the woman's voice. Two terrible old trots, Betsy Burt and Mrs. Carey, were with her when I saw the child *then*; and they were with her just now. They all lived in my house. I fetched the doctor once for this child myself. Dr. Fell said it was a sort of epilepsy."

"Did he know they'd brought him, before he made his speech?"

Barter cast a hurried glance round the edifice in which they were holding this intense and strange conversation. In his mind there was the dim thought that there is something monstrous and horrible about bringing the dead to life; something that interferes with Nature and has an obscure and shocking profanity in it. He stared at what was around them in this queer building. It was crowded with litter and scaffolding, for it was but half finished; but there was a peculiar personal quality in the workmanship and in the materials, that separated it from all the newly erected buildings that he had ever seen.

"It might be something erected *to* Geard," he thought, "rather than *by* Geard!"

"Did he *know* they'd brought him, Tom?"

"How do *I* know what he knew? You know him better than I."

"I don't believe he knew," whispered John.

They were both silent then and something very peculiar passed between them. There are certain topics which resemble certain *substances* in the world, such as blood and semen and the liquefaction of decomposition, in that they trouble some unique nerve in human mortality and produce, even in the naming, a peculiar *frisson*. Such a *frisson* they experienced now, and as they gazed in each other's faces in this dim, littered, empty place, these two cynical East-Anglians felt like dogs who had met an absolutely new smell; dogs, let us say, who are sniffing at a new-fallen meteorite!

"Dead? White and stiff and with *that look*, was he? And did old Geard ——"

Barter nodded like a China-mandarin. "Yes, old cock, yes, my sweet cod, Geard did it——"

"Brought it to life?"

"Yes, old top-knot! To life, old white-face!"

"Where's Tossie?"

"She's with Miss Crow and Lady Rachel."

They were both silent then for a while; and during their silence the uttermost mystery of the world, that unspeakable coldness, stiffness, stillness of an organism that has lived and breathed, and now has been *changed into something else* held them by the throat.

"This child," they both thought, "has been *behind life,* and if it could only remember what that Something Else——"

"Where are those two who were here?"

"Sheperd and Mr. Merry?"

"Were *they* here?"

"They've gone to look at the child."

"They'll kill it again, crowding round it."

"Do you know what *I* think, John? I think the whole thing has been——"

Barter was going to say "planned," but once more that shivering took him; and in his mind he saw that ghastly rigor mortis which holds the secret of the universe.

John made a desperate struggle to get up. "I'd like to see that child," he murmured, rising on his elbow, "I'd like to see someone who has really been dead."

"Dead, old cock; but not *buried*! Cataleptic, old man!"

"I can't breathe properly," groaned John. "I feel as weak as a baby. I wish you'd get him to come to *me*."

"Shut up, you fool! *You'll* be all right in a jiffy."

"Water," moaned John. "If I don't have a drop of water, I'll go off again."

"The child was sitting up on the stretcher. They were feeding it!"

"Water," moaned John, "water."

Barter gave one more hurried glance at the strange interior around them. Then he went out quickly into the air. Hurrying under the Saxon arch—the irony of fate thus brought it about that the first two persons to use that new entrance were Philip and his ex-manager—he filled one of the little cups that were kept there and brought it to his friend.

"Chalybeate," he said with a leer, as John satisfied his craving and showed signs of recovery, "or Christ's Precious Blood; you can toss up which it is!"

The prostrate man jerked himself up on his elbow, and stared at the Rotunda door which Tom had left open.

"I'd like to know," he muttered, "what dreams that child had!"

Barter gave vent to a quick welcoming shout and ran again to the door.

"What's up now?" sighed John, subsiding into his former position. "Is he coming?"

"He? He's in the town by now. It's Toss, I tell you. Hullo! Hullo! Here he is! Here we are!"

But John Crow was not the only unbeliever in Glastonbury to be confronted with the inexplicable that eventful twentieth of January. The Marquis of P., making his way to the snug little lodging above the offices of the *Wayfarer*, where Ned Athling had his rooms, wondered to himself as he went along whether after all he *was* well advised to pay a surprise visit, at ten o'clock at night, to his daughter's lover. He had dined at the Pilgrims', where Sergeant Blimp had put up as usual the famous green-wheeled dog-cart, and warmed by a bottle of first-rate port, sipped in company with his old servant in the quiet room he always occupied, he had resolved to make a frontal attack upon this troubler of the Zoyland pride.

"If they're not married, I don't care," he said to himself. "Sister will have to swallow it. I'm not going to quarrel with the girl for Betsy's sake."

It was easier to find the place at that hour of the night than to discover how to get into Athling's room when he *had* found it. What a shabby down-and-out location for the Mayor's official newspaper!

But one of the battered doors opened easily to his hand, though there was no bell or knocker. Groping about inside a dark passage Lord P. began to feel more like a nervous burglar than like an indignant peer of the realm pursuing his daughter's seducer.

"Athling! Athling!" he called out in a voice a good deal less authoritative and formidable than he would have liked it to be.

There was no response; and, since he had shut the street door, there was not even light enough to see whether he had to ascend a staircase, or rap at some chamber, in this musty passage.

"Damn the young idiot!" muttered the Marquis. "Why the devil don't he keep a light in this place?"

Annoyance increased the power of his voice.

"Athling! Athling!"

A door did open now, at the top of a straight flight of broad, bare, old-fashioned steps. A bright ray of light, from inside a warm, mellow, glowing room, streamed down the staircase. A girlish figure, obviously in a night-dress and dressing-gown, stood in the entrance of the room.

"Why it's Dad!" cried Lady Rachel in a low, soft, rich voice. "It's Dad, Ned!" she repeated, turning half-round as the amazed peer with an indrawn gasp of his breath and a muttered, "Well, I'll be damned!" gravely ascended the staircase.

"How *sweet* of you to come and see us!" she cried, in the same low, rich-laughing, self-composed manner.

The Marquis bowed to the young man who in a rough tweed suit had clearly just risen up from beside a table covered with sheets of manuscript. The room was lighted by a dim rose-shaded lamp. A pleasant fire burned in the grate; and an open door, leading out of the back of the room, revealed a double-bed, with the white sheets turned down, and a second cheerful fire, in a sort of alcove.

"Sit down, Dad," said Lady Rachel, offering her speechless parent a low wicker chair close to the hearth.

"Get some of that cherry brandy for my father, Ned."

Athling, whose hands were trembling with nervousness, lifted down from a shelf a beautiful little decanter made of fine cut-glass of a greenish tint. He spilled quite a lot of the gleaming cordial as he poured it and it was running down the edge of the tiny glass over his own fingers as he handed it to the Marquis.

Lord P. declined it with a wave of his hand. "Just had a bottle of wine," he said. "Blimp ferreted it out for me. I'll have a cigarette though, if you've got one anywhere."

As he spoke he allowed his eyes to roam over the walls of
the room. They were adorned with nothing but a great number
of striking water-colour sketches, all of them painted in a very
peculiar and extremely unusual manner.

Lord P. was something of a virtuoso in this kind; and in
spite of the dumbfounded condition of his nerves he mechanically
got up and approached some of the more remarkable of these
pictures.

"Damned good!" he muttered. "Which of you children did
these things?"

"They're all Ned's!" cried the girl eagerly. "They're lovely,
aren't they?"

"I should . . . say . . . they are." He went solemnly round
the room, carefully examining each one of these singular pro-
ductions. As he did so, turning his back to both of them, he
thought to himself: "Betsy needn't know anything about it.
They're not married. She's sure to get tired of him after a bit.
I suppose they understand about contraception."

And he found himself slipping into an imaginary conversation with his friend Godfrey Bent at his club.

"My daughter's picked up with an artist-chap, you know the
sort of thing, down there in the country. An old family, they
tell me, one of the oldest in the county, but not a brass farthing.
Can't you get him a show of some sort, Godfrey, next season?
They're damned good, his things. They really might make a hit
if they had half a chance!"

When he turned round and took his place again at the fire
he regarded the young man with a very much more sympathetic
eye. Lord P. was totally devoid of any poetical taste; but he
really was a competent connoisseur in painting, and it pleased
him to think that in all his encounters with this lad, the boy
had kept this astonishing talent in the background.

Rachel sat down on the arm of her father's chair enveloping
him in the warm sweetness of her glowing happiness.

"Well, Dad?" she said. "So you're not going to scold, after
all?"

He looked whimsically at the fingers she had placed in his.
No! There was no sign of a wedding ring.

"You've not gone and got married by any chance?" he asked.

She shook her head. "I'm not thinking of marrying for years and years. Ned would like to. But he never teases me about it. Do you, Ned?"

"Wiser not—to tease 'em about anything; eh, lad?" chuckled her father, glancing slyly at the young man. "You understand how to keep—you mustn't be cross at an old man's grossness —from getting—into trouble, as the servants say?"

Rachel nodded mischievously, and then smiled gravely and quietly straight into his eyes.

"And what lie do you tell to our worthy Miss Crow, Rachel? I presume you still ostensibly live with her?"

This time the girl blushed scarlet. He had touched the sore spot—the one spot that rankled—in her romantic adventure.

"I tell her I have to work all night in the office," she whispered. "She sends me to bed for hours!" she added ruefully, and without a smile.

He changed the conversation then, asking Ned some very searching technical questions about his methods of painting. The talk between the three of them flagged and wilted a little after that and he soon rose to go.

"Did you hear old Johnny's speech today?" he asked, as he picked up his coat and hat and gloves.

"Haven't you seen our special edition, Dad?" cried Lady Rachel, placing in the hands of the grey, elderly man, whose figure in that warmly lighted room—a room so full of a radiant atmosphere of youthful happiness—seemed to dwindle at that moment and become old and pinched and rather forlorn, a copy of the *Wayfarer* with the most startling headlines that any human chronicle could conceivably carry, short of the announcement of an approaching Deluge.

"*What's* this, eh? *What's* this? Gad! but he couldn't have been really *dead*! Come now, come now, this is getting a bit *too* thick. But . . . of course . . . if you wild children . . . are going . . . to turn this place . . . into . . . into . . . this *will*, I suppose . . . be the kind of thing—but, good God, Rachel, *you* don't really think . . . *yourself* . . . that my old Johnny Geard could ——"

The Marquis stood there in that rosy light, between the girl in her soft night-attire looking like some enamoured nymph out of a Welsh fairy-tale, and the sturdy young poet-painter in his Norfolk jacket, frowning and bewildered. He kept folding up the paper he held, as if to conceal that troublesome word "Miracle" in those big black letters, and then unfolding it again. What *was* the world coming to?

"Good-night, little one," he murmured at last, kissing her tenderly. "You might send over a few of those sketches before I leave Mark Court," he added gravely. "I'll take 'em up to town with me."

He turned to her once more as she held the door open to light him down the staircase.

"Don't 'ee do this too often, girlie," he said. "The good Miss Crow is no fool. Besides, we don't want any confounded scandal."

He was at the bottom of the stairs now.

"Remember what long ears your Aunt Betsy has!" he called back, as he turned to go to the street door.

Once in the dark street, buttoning his coat to face a frosty wind, and pulling on his grey gloves, an emotion of miserable depression took hold of him.

His little Rachel, his *little* Rachel! And yet how radiant the wench had looked. But, oh, what a man had to see, and bear, and endure, if, in these days he meant to keep a child's love and not make her hate him!

"But they're not out for marrying," he thought, "that's one good thing. And she's playing safe with the Crow woman, I can see *that*, though she hates it like the devil! Well, who can blame her? She'll never be young again. And the lad's a decent lad . . . nothing caddish or tricky about the lad."

He was moving along now beside a dark row of wretched houses. The pavement was uneven. The wind had got up and had become icy cold. It moaned and whistled over the slate roofs of this poorer portion of the town. Very old and very desolate did Henry Zoyland, Marquis of P., feel as he walked along! Those enchanting, unconventional retreats with his little Rachel at Mark Court all, all over! She had been restless and *distrait*, the last time he had had her with him up there; and those

Bellamys! Their quarrels with poor Blimp were becoming intolerable. Yet he hadn't the heart to turn them out.

"The place is nothing without her," he thought, and he saw
himself sitting by that big, lonely hearth with the ancient staircase leading up and up; and then *her* room, and then that stone
causeway, and the Merlin room—was it during his night in
that place that old Johnny had learnt these devil's tricks of putting
life into dead babies?

The man's desolation grew apace as he approached the outskirts of Paradise. "Old; I'm getting old," he thought. "And no
Merlin cantrips, learnt by any modern Messire Bleheris, could
make *me* stir when once I was knocked on the head. No, damn
it! I won't put *anything* in the child's way. Let her have her
fling. Zoyland women always begin with a passionate romance
in their teens; and then settle down into savage harridans at
forty! Betsy did it; and never married at all! The child's not
half as wild as Betsy was. To hell with middle-class pruderies!
The Zoylands always *did what they wanted*; and, by gad, my
little girl shall."

Thus the old diplomatist swaggered in his mood, doing his
best to rationalise, as they call it, his doting partiality for that
glowing child in her soft night-dress. But the ice-cold wind went
shrieking over the roofs and wailing down the cobbled alley-
ways, and a feeling of bitter desolation chilled the man to the
very bone.

The touch of her warmth as she sat just now on the arm of his
chair had insinuated into his veins a craving for young blood
and feminine softness. It was for her sake he had given up
that French woman in Soho, the successor of Will's German
mother. For years he had lived like a monk for the child's
sake and this was his reward! And these curst communists turning Glastonbury into a bedlam of follies, while old Johnny was
working miracles!

He'd better get back to town at once, get hold of a good
lawyer—Beere was no use any more—and make sure that those
ungrateful sons of his couldn't touch a stiver of what he'd left
to Rachel and to Will, of all this new cash.

He was passing Mother Legge's ambiguous domain now and

as he glanced at that familiar "other house," which in younger days he had so often entered, he saw the door furtively opened and a man and a woman came out. He stepped into the shadow of a wall-buttress to let them pass and he could not help recognising them. One was Clarissa Smith, the pretty head-waitress at the Pilgrims', and the other was a man he'd seen in the stables there—none other in fact than the converted ostler with whom the miracle-worker had been drinking that very morning.

"What does the old woman make people like that fork out?" he wondered. "She must be hard pressed these days if *those* are her clients!"

But when he emerged from his retreat he actually found himself hesitating for the fraction of a second and imagining himself ringing that Cyprian door-bell!

"I suppose Young Tewsy's there still," he thought. "Who *was* it told me these communists were going to give the old boy a job at the Grail Spring? From Camelot to Chalice Hill! Well . . . that's how this world wags!"

He could still see the two figures moving along in front of him, Clarissa clinging tenderly to her ostler's arm.

"I hope *he* feels the same," he said to himself. "That sort of thing leaves the girl more loving, but the man—not always! By gad, if that boy of Rachel's plays any games ——"

But the sight of that waitress and ostler clinging together so happily troubled the senses of this elderly gentleman as he walked behind them. The girl had the sort of plump figure he used to like; he could see *that* well enough even in this dark street! Garment by garment he undressed the unconscious Clarissa in that ice-cold wind. He was traversing the very pavement that Red Robinson had traversed, that night of the party at Mother Legge's, and precisely the same sort of soul-sick craving for a warm fire and a warm feminine body came over him as had devastated the angry proletarian. Had the ambitious Clarissa only known!

But that young lady continued to cling to her ostler's arm, whispering amid her endearments, if the truth must be confessed, certain wickedly intimate strictures upon the character of Mr. Thomas Barter. Strange that the guileless warmth of

Rachel's romance should be driving her father on now to undress Clarissa Smith!

Rachel . . . Clarissa . . . oh, how cold the wind blew, and how harsh and desolate and comfortless the world was! In the warmth of the bodies of women, in their ways, in their laughter, in their clinging, yes! even in their anger and their mockery there is the only real refuge, he thought.

"Let 'em scold and rave. However cruel their words, their limbs are still satiny to our touch, their souls still free of our curst laws and labours and fuss and fume."

He slackened his pace, for Clarissa's arm was now round her companion's neck. He actually stopped again while his heart, as he imagined himself returning on his steps and ringing that door-bell, began to beat within him in the way it used to do, twenty, thirty years ago! But the Sergeant would be sitting up for him. Besides, what was he thinking of? That "other house" wasn't a brothel. Young Tewsy would expect—damn it! He was just a fool. The figures in front of him had turned the corner now; and he walked rapidly on.

Tommy Chinnock's "I'd like to, Clarissa," ebbed quickly from the life-weary pulses of the Marquis of P. When he reached the lighted lamps of the High Street, a bare-footed boy came rushing past him calling out a late edition of a Yeovil paper.

"*Mir-acle at Glaston-bury!*" the boy shouted. Lord P. smiled a bitter, man-of-the-world's smile.

"There's only one miracle in this world," he muttered aloud, "that can make old men young and that's not for old men who've outlived their time!"

As may be easily imagined the situation in Glastonbury Vicarage as the winter passed, with Nell and her child under the same roof as her former lover, although it was not strained to the limit of human endurance, was sufficiently uncomfortable to all the three persons concerned. It was obvious, too, that the little boy, though his expressions of it were obscure, missed the rollicking caresses of his mother's husband.

Mrs. Pippard who took upon herself all through December the rôle of ambassador—though hardly of peacemaker—between Nell's new sanctuary and her old home, kept them pretty closely informed of what was going on in Whitelake Cottage.

The trend of events seemed to be that Will Zoyland and Persephone were living out there in an irresponsible trance of amorous happiness, completely self-absorbed and self-contained, and prepared to await any deluge that fate might send, with the reckless defiance of their new-found delight in each other.

It struck Nell that it was totally unlike all she had ever known of Will, this ensorcerised interim of moonstruck quiescence. As week followed week at the Vicarage—each week bringing new agitations between the father and the son, and between herself and each of the two men,—she was constantly expecting Zoyland to appear in person, having quarrelled with Percy, and full of angry and despotic demands that his wife and her child should return home. But the New Year came and nothing of the kind happened!

In the end the cantankerous Mrs. Pippard, having played the part of eavesdropper to the infatuated pair at Whitelake till Zoyland nearly threw her out, and having clung desperately to the little Master Henry in the Vicarage, till Penny Pitches actually did throw her out, retired from domestic labours altogether and took up her abode with the mother of Red Robinson's bride, as a partner-assistant in the tea-shop business.

Hearing that Sally was leaving Cardiff Villa in order to be married to Red, Mrs. Pippard offered herself as the girl's suc-

cessor in the Mayor's household; but Mrs. Geard, glad enough
to return to her old freedom from any servants, very brusquely
declined this honour; and thus it was left for the patient visitors
to the town to endure the ministrations and be subjected to the
all-seeing eye of Eudoxia's diplomatic parent.

The astounding nature of the scandals which many of these
innocent pilgrims carried home, along with Mr. Barter's and
Lady Rachel's Arthurian figurines, concerning the more intimate
life of Glastonbury, can thus be accounted for; but it is hardly
necessary in this modest chronicle to state that Zoyland did *not*
beat his wife black and blue, and that Nell did *not* live with
three men at the same time.

But although the wild tales related by Mrs. Pippard were far
from the truth, the two weeks that followed the arrival of Nell
under the roof of her child's father and her child's grandfather
were charged with explosive electricity.

Sam's attitude was the same as it had always been, since he
had decided to trample down and to kill all natural sex pleasure.
He didn't avoid her. On the contrary he snatched every moment
he could, when his father was out of sight, to enjoy her society.
He helped her with the child, though not proving as skilful as
Zoyland in quieting him and distracting him. He kept Penny
from intruding into the spare-room, for they had given Nell the
William-of-Orange bed to sleep in. He tried to coax her to give
up her awkward and timid habit of retreating into the never-used
drawing-room, a room that smelt, not of dust and mustiness for
it was the only room in the house where Penny was allowed to
scrub and tidy up without let or hindrance, but of the Dead Time
itself, like a palpable ghost brooding there inside that locked
door, brooding over the heavy, magenta coloured tassels that hung
down above the front of the mantelpiece, brooding over the green
plush sofa, brooding over the massive marble clock that never
ticked, brooding over the footstool, trimmed with tarnished gold
thread, brooding over the upstanding wool basket of Sam's
mother that had never been touched since that young woman
died.

It was a shock to Sam when one morning, a few days after
the opening of the arch, he found Nell sitting in this drawing-

room with her sewing—which he knew she was shy of his catching her with—on that gold-threaded footstool, over a wretched newly lit fire.

"Good Lord!" he cried, "does Father know you're in the drawing-room? *One* second—I'll be back in *one* second!"

Nell smiled and bending her head down drew her needle rapidly and nervously through the small, white garment she was making for her son. There was already descending upon her that resigned, effortless passivity, patient, docile, unresisting in which, because of some hereditary pliability in her ancestors, or at any rate in the women among her ancestors, though Dave had something of it too, it was easy for her to sink. She was surprised herself at the drowsy weight of this curious passivity. It had come over her the very first morning she had awaked in William-of-Orange's bed. She had cried herself passionately to sleep the night before; but that had been rather because, in a briefly snatched talk she had had alone with Sam, he had nervously disengaged her warm arms from his neck, than because of any culminating wave of self-pity. Yes! not a tear of all those tears of that first night could Zoyland claim to have evoked, nor the treacherous Percy either! It was Sam alone; Sam not pressing her to his heart, Sam not treating her as his love, Sam not crying out, "Let's take our child and go away from here, away from all of them!" that had broken her down. But she had experienced when she woke up at dawn, a feeling towards Sam that was like the feeling which those sweet persecuted lemans in the old ballads, kept, through weal and woe, for their cruel lords!

Yes, she had been astonished herself, as day followed day and it became clearer and clearer that Sam's whole nature was set upon this inexorable quest of his, at the apathy with which she accepted it. She came near to accusing herself of having allowed her heart to die within her, so numb, so paralysed, so atrophied did her emotions—after that first night of wild sobbing—seem to have grown. Even a strangely detached amusement had in these last weeks been rising up in her heart; an amusement that was rather schoolgirlish mischief than a ma-

ternal humor, at the thought of all these great hulking, blundering men following so crudely the prickings of their desire.

Under the pressure of this mood she had even begun to feel
friendly again to Zoyland. Persephone was a totally different
matter; and she kept telling herself several malevolent stories
of imaginary encounters with Persephone, during which she
brought down that young woman very wholesomely to her knees!
But to her yellow-bearded Will she *did* begin to feel indulgent
again; especially when she noted the contorted tricks and arbitrary devices which religion compels its votaries to undergo,
if they are to love and to refrain from loving, as the two Dekkers were now trying to do at one and the same time!

Yes, she was wondering to herself now at this very minute,
as she glanced up at the marble clock which had stopped at
twenty minutes past two—perhaps the very hour in the night at
which Sam's mother had died!—what her Sam, and her Sam's
father, in their preposterous attempts not to quarrel savagely
over her, would feel if they could read this queer humorous
turn that her thoughts had taken of late! What had begun to
strike her as specially quaint was the way they seemed to
assume that whatever treaty or truce or peace they patched up
between themselves about her, she would accede to without
any question!

She was like a sack of exciting oats placed in a manger
between two champing steeds. Well! she wasn't so sure that she
would submit to being a sack of oats! As this thought came
upon her once again this morning, the corners of her mouth
quivered in the second silent smile in which she had indulged
since Sam told her to "wait a second"; and her eyes moved
from the marble clock to the green plush sofa.

"What's come over me?" she said to herself. "Am I growing
cynical? Am I getting like Percy?"

A slight puckering of her forehead followed this mental question; and as if in proof that her new detachment was a girlish,
rather than a maternal emotion, she found herself hoping that
her little son—it was about eleven o'clock in the morning—
would sleep sound till noon, and allow her to leave him alone
for another hour, in his cradle by the big bed.

Mercy! but she did miss her own house! *That* at least was certain. It teased her to think of Percy messing about with her cups and saucers, and forgetting to put the bread in the cake-box and the rolls in the biscuit-tin.

"I'm sure she doesn't wash out the sugar-basin," she thought to herself, "and I *know* she doesn't keep the cheese on a shelf by itself!"

And as she stared at the green plush sofa the incorrigible immorality of her woman's mind sighed just a little for the free, careless swing of the Zoyland attitude to life, compared with the impassioned pieties of this monastic establishment.

"What I really am now," she thought, "in place of being the mistress of a wicked baron, is the petted bone of contention in a hermitage!"

The door which had been left ajar was now kicked open and Sam came in with a coal-scuttle full of coal in one hand and a pile of large bits of wood in the other.

"I've told Penny to make you up a good fire," he said, "next time you want to sit in here; but why you don't stay in the museum, where Father likes to see you sewing in that chair while he's writing his sermon, I can't think!"

He spoke irritably; but he knew in his heart it was because of his own bad humour, when he found her ensconced with his father, that she had invaded this closed-up shrine of the past.

"Sit down, Sam, my dear," she said, when he had made the fire blaze, "I want to talk to you."

He obeyed her. But it was not at her side, but upon the plush sofa that he took his seat.

"You know, my dearest one," she said gravely, folding up her son's night-shirt upon her lap, "that if *you* can stand the way we're living, *I* can't! Now stop, my dear; stop! Don't interrupt, till you've heard what I'm going to say! I'm not going to beg you to do anything you don't want to; so you needn't glower at me as if I were a wicked girl trying to tempt you. It's only this, dear. I was talking to Dave last week and he says that Percy refuses to take a penny of his money. He says that he can't *make* her take it; but nothing will induce him to keep it himself. He says if I won't take it he'll just throw it into the town council fund. I've been thinking about this, Sam dear; and I've decided that I *will* take it. Even if Philip chucks Will out because of Percy they'll be all right. Lord P. won't let them come to grief. He's always been offering to help Will; and with all this money he's getting for this great sale—No! *They'll* be all right. I'm not going to bother my head about *them*."

Sam turned and stretched out his heavy hands over his knees, extending all his fingers. It was as if his hands were yawning with an amorous relaxation unpermitted to the rest of his frame. His shirt-sleeves disappeared under the frayed edges of his coat-cuffs and his wrists showed hairy and red.

"But Nell? What then?" he murmured. "You're not going to leave Father and me, are you?"

She rubbed one of her ankles automatically with the warm, shapeless, schoolgirl palms of her soft hands. Then she turned her head and surveyed Sam upon the sofa. She surveyed, too, an ironwork stand behind Sam's head, containing several hart's tongue ferns, kept alive for years by Penny, for whom this room represented an everlasting Seventh Day of drowsy and futile piety. A big wastepaper basket with ornamented handles stood at the end of the sofa, into which nothing had been put—except Penny's broom—for twenty-five years. By the side of this basket, resting upon the faded green carpet, lay a large, oblong pebble-stone from Chesil Beach, upon which the short-lived Mrs. Dekker had painted, during her confinement, a brightly coloured picture of her native Swiss lake.

From all these things Nell's nostrils inhaled the same curious smell, the smell of inanimate objects left *in status quo* for a quarter of a century. Why, if she were in such an old ballad mood of patient docility, had she ever started this disturbing conversation, worrying Sam about Dave's money, and protesting that she, for her part, *could not* go on as they were? The truth was she happened to be under the moon that particular day, and if another woman had asked her why she was behaving like this, she would have replied that she was "nervous."

As a matter of fact—though what did the simpleton on the sofa, with the hairy red wrists, know about such things?—the blind creative energy within her was in the vein for troubling, for disturbing, for agitating, for darkening all the unruffled waters it could approach.

"You don't suppose, Sam, do you, that any girl with any spirit could go on like this?"

Sam pulled in his outstretched arms and thrust them deep into his pockets.

"I don't see why not, Nell. I don't see why not!"

Her eyes, that had dark shadows beneath them, narrowed suddenly into little gentian-blue shuttles of darting anger.

"No, I suppose you *don't* see!" she cried. "I suppose you and your father could go on with your precious aquarium and your precious Holy Grail, till the crack of doom, while a girl ate her heart out in a place like this!"

"Nell—little Nell!" he murmured reproachfully. The gentleness of his tone disconcerted her.

At that moment what her nerves would have liked above everything else was for him to have risen to his feet and roundly scolded her; told her that she was *his*, that she was his chattel, his possession, his slave, his whore, that her child was his child, her body *his* body, her will *his* will.

"Oh, I don't know!" she breathed wearily, expanding her breasts and clasping her hands behind the back of her head. "I don't know what I'm saying, Sam. But I know everything is all wrong."

But his forehead was corrugated now in a heavy frown and his freckled chin was wrinkling itself downwards into his neck.

"Your Holy Grail?" he thought to himself, "O Christ, my Christ, if you would but once, just once, for one minute, give me a sign, only the smallest faintest sign that you are really *there*, behind it all; then I could go on, without aching to have her, to hold her, night and day!"

Because of his heavy unimaginative nature, because of his preference for minnows and stickle-backs and loach over mythical abstractions, Sam had never given much thought to the legend of the Grail. The Christ whose deadly, cruel imperative had come between him and his love had been as much of a Person as Nell herself. Was He a Person still?

How different was Sam's Christ from Mr. Geard's! Mr. Geard's

Christ was a Power to be exploited. In his weird gnostic dialogues with *his* Master, the Mayor of Glastonbury addressed Him like a friend, almost like an equal. He was the Mayor's great magician, his super-Merlin, by whose strength and support he became strong. Never once had it crossed the threshold of Mr. Geard's consciousness that it was his duty to live a life of self-sacrifice.

"I live *as I like to live*," he would have retorted to any ascetic protest, "and my Master lives as He likes to live. His Blood is the Water of Life!"

"Christ in His Grail," repeated Sam to himself, "and Father in his aquarium and Nell in my mother's room!"

She had turned her face away from him now. She was bending over the fire, prodding it pensively with the poker. As he watched her doing this, the feeling came over him that just behind the physical drama that was going on at the minute, another, a corresponding drama, was going on in the Invisible.

"Aquarium-Grail . . . Grail-aquarium," he muttered; and his ichthyological mind visioned a Fish that was a real fish and yet something more than a fish shedding a mystic light out of an enchanted vessel.

Sam lowered his eyes and let his head sink deeper and deeper into his chest, while his hands, that were in his pockets, clenched their fists. He thought of a particular spot on the banks of the Brue where he had often fished with his father as a boy. It was at a turn of the river and it was several fields westward from the wooden bridge where Young Tewsy had caught his recent surprising catch, to the delight of Mother Legge.

"Aquarium-Grail," he repeated, in the dark trans-lunar cave of his consciousness, "Grail-aquarium"; and it came over him, just as if his tormented and tormenting God had whispered it into his ear, that the sacrifice which was laid upon him now was to leave the Vicarage himself.

"If she can't stand Father and me together," he thought, "and I expect we *have* made it too much for her, it's not she that must go . . . that's unthinkable . . . how would she get on alone . . . alone with our child? . . . it's myself that must go . . . it's you, Sam, that must go."

He had reached a point in his asceticism when he often felt his imperative soul to be standing over against his reluctant body like an austere slave-driver. Indeed he had come to think of his soul as in some way *external* to his body. There was not much pleasure about this; but there was just the faintest flicker of a strange satisfaction in it. At any rate it gave him a sense that his soul was totally independent of his body and was the proud master of his body. He pulled up his legs with a jerk and removed his hands from his pockets.

"It's you, Sam, that must go!" he repeated grimly in his heart.

Thus what had begun as a pure wanton troubling of the waters, because Nell felt nervous, had become another tragic turning point in the girl's life. Something in her was vaguely aware of this as Sam rose up from the green sofa.

Impulsively, with a movement that was entirely self-forgetful, she leapt to her feet and ran towards him; while he—just because he *had* given his body its implacable orders and because this was perhaps a moment that would never come back again—pressed her so tightly to his heart that she could hardly breathe. She had just time to think: "This is how I'd like to die . . . crushed to death by Sam," when the door opened and Mat Dekker came in. They were so tightly clasped that they were like two trees that have grown together, each with its bark eroded by the pressure of the other, each with the same ivy or vine imprisoning its limbs, and when they broke apart and turned to the man at the door it was as if each of them, as they swung into independent life, carried away something of the living texture of the other.

"I thought . . . I understood . . ." began Mat Dekker, and he turned with a portentous and passionate solemnity to the door by which he had entered, opening it, looking out into the passage, closing it again, and finally locking it. He seemed prepared to behave towards this door, the drawing-room door of Glastonbury Vicarage, as Diogenes behaved to his tub, venting upon its unfeeling wood emotions excited by the aberrations of human passion.

The truth was that Mat Dekker was seized at that moment with a murderous fury against his son; and it was only by concen-

trating on the door—was it locked? was Penny listening behind
it?—that his better nature was able to steal a moment's breathing space wherein to gather up its self-control.

The door carried above its handle a decorative panel of prettily
flowered porcelain, to protect it from sticky fingers, and over
this cool china surface Mat Dekker now passed his thumb as if
to see whether those hundred-years-old roses would come off.
All this took a very brief time, but it was long enough to restore
to him a modicum of his self-control; and turning now towards
the two of them, he addressed Nell with a slightly forward-
moving inclination of his massive grey head.

"I've been hearing the child crying for quite a few minutes,"
he remarked. "I came to tell you."

His own words gave him an opportunity to return once more
to the redoubtable door, and he tugged at the handle to open
it—for he assumed she would rush upstairs at once—forgetting
that in his agitation he had turned its key. He unlocked it and
held the door open.

The voice of an extremely impatient infant was now quite
audible from upstairs. But Nell at first drew back.

"It isn't good for him to be taken up the first minute he cries,"
she said.

She knew by instinct that Mat Dekker was anxious to avenge
himself upon his son for what he had just seen. But the glare of
concentrated command that shot out at her from under those
bushy eyebrows, as she lingered, was too formidable to be dis-
obeyed. She flung a hurried, tender, guilty, accomplice's look at
her ambiguous lover; but Sam seemed to be lost in some deep
thought of his own, for he was staring fixedly at the marble clock
with its hands pointing to twenty minutes after two.

"You'll make me spoil him," she cried. "You are all on his
side, however naughty he is."

With these words and giving Mat Dekker a smile that had
something supplicating about it, she passed by him and went
out. Evidently a sense that she had been treated more like a little
girl than a grown woman irritated her as soon as she was in the
hall, for she called back, in quite a defiant voice, "Will was just
the same! You'd all spoil him if you could!" But she ran upstairs

now, and with the closing of the door behind her the child's angry cries were shut out.

Mat Dekker walked over to where his son stood.

"This sort of thing must stop, my boy."

It was with a palpable effort to restrain his feelings that he added the two syllables, "my boy."

"As I've been telling you all the time," he went on, "there are only two things a *gentleman*"—he emphasised the word—"could do in your situation. He could either make her get a divorce from her husband and marry her, or . . . or . . . or he could ——"

Sam interrupted his father, looking him straight in the eyes: "Or he could clear off himself? Is that what you were going to say?"

The blood had rushed to Sam's head as he uttered this retort; but in a second he had recovered his equanimity.

"Come along, Father," he said quietly, "let's go into the museum. It seems unnatural to talk here. I *can't* talk here."

It was Sam's turn now to open the door with the rose-painted china panel. It was Sam's turn, too, by the very power of his calmness, to compel the grizzled, ruddy-faced man with the quivering upper lip to go out into the hall. Down the passage they walked together and together they entered the museum. Here in the presence of the familiar aquarium, the familiar iron candlesticks, the familiar daguerreotypes, the father and son faced each other. Neither of them sat down, and there was indeed little attraction about the few fading coals in the grate—Mat Dekker had evidently been too absorbed in his thoughts to keep his fire up—to lure them to sit down, but the father on the right of the fireplace with his hand on the mantelpiece, and the son on the left with *his* hand on the mantelpiece, confronted each other like two duellists.

"Grail-aquarium . . . aquarium-Grail," ran like a refrain through Sam's head; and he began suddenly to feel again that queer sensation he had felt in the drawing-room, a sensation like that of the presence of a *double world*, every motion and gesture in the first being a symbol of something that was taking place in the second. The sensation was accompanied by an absolute conviction of the boundless importance of every thought that a human being had.

It was also accompanied—strange though it may seem at this tragic moment—by a faint thrill of mysterious happiness—the first authentic leap of spontaneous happiness in him that poor Sam had known for many a month.

He glanced round at the aquarium, as his father began speaking, and Nell's sarcastic cry "your precious aquarium" transmuted itself into a spasm of sweetness that was like a prolongation of what he had felt just now when he pressed her to his heart.

"It's against all I've believed—this damned business of divorce," burst out Mat Dekker fiercely, "but the church has always retained the right to deal with special conditions in special ways; and with that brute, over there, behaving as he is ——"

The man's formidable upper lip began quivering again, and Sam noticed that there was a blood-stain upon the white clerical tie that in the old-fashioned evangelical manner this eccentric high-churchman wore round his muscular neck.

"His hand must have shaken when he was shaving," thought Sam. "Jesus give me strength not to get angry!"

"With that brute like he is, and doing it openly—turning her out in fact—I can make short work of him. I shall go and see John Beere this afternoon. It's not a thing"—he made an automatic humorous grimace of disgust—"that I like doing. All lawyers are rogues. But it's what I'm going to do; and I'm going to do it willy-nilly as far as *she's* concerned. *She* shan't be worried with it till I've got the thing well under way!"

He looked so pathetically proud of himself in this display of worldly sagacity before his simple and blundering son, that Sam felt a stab of remorse at having broken up their life and brought all these things down on that grey head.

"I wouldn't do that, Father," he cried. "I wouldn't tell Beere, or anyone else, a word about it unless she asks you to. How do you know that she *wants* to divorce him? Women are funny in these things. Oh, I know, I *know* she wouldn't like it for you to do that, without telling her! Besides, Father, I don't believe that Mr. Beere would even discuss it unless she came herself. They always have to go themselves. That's how it is in the newspapers. They have to go to court. That's why they hate it. They can't bear to go to court."

Mr. Dekker began striding up and down the floor of the museum. He seemed irritated by his clerical dress at this crisis in his life. What he would really have liked to do was to go out to Whitelake and challenge Zoyland to a bout of fisticuffs, then have it out with his son—he could not quite have explained what form this scene would have taken—*and then* —— And it was this "and then" that was the whole crux of the situation.

In his passion and in his professional and religious restrictions, this sturdy son of the Quantocks looked like a caged wild animal as he paced back and forth. His feelings were expressed in the way he hitched up his long broadcloth coat-tails so as to thrust his hands into his pockets and the way he let these tails hang, one over each wrist, as he walked up and down.

To ruffle his priest's attire was a small gesture; but it belonged to the same category of gestures as his ordering the girl to go up to her baby and his telling Sam about his resolve to visit Lawyer Beere.

"The best thing *you* can do then," he brought out now, standing still by the edge of the aquarium, into which even as he spoke he could not help giving a sidelong glance, "the best thing *you* can do is to take her to see Beere yourself. You'll have to be— what's their word—co-respondent, of course; that is, if he brings a counter-suit on his side, as I have no doubt the beggar will."

Once more Sam was aware of a pathetic note of self-complacency in his father's tone.

"The old man," he thought to himself, "is proud of his worldly knowledge. He thinks I've never heard the words co-respondent or counter-suit. Christ, don't let me get angry with him!"

The moment had come when he had to tell his father what was in his mind; but it was a fearful wrench to utter the words and it would be a worse thing for his father when he heard them. Aye! he had come to it. He never thought he would; but he had. He had to tell his father that he was going to leave him. Sam knew much better than did this grey-haired man, hunching up

his coat-tails, what it would mean to both of them, this separation. "Of course," he thought, "I shall be still in Glastonbury.
But it'll be the end of our real life together. It'll be the end of
our long evenings in this room. It'll be the end of our mornings
in the potato garden."

"You know more about the law than I do, Father," he remarked. But he said it only to gain time. "And I certainly should
not draw back from helping her in any way I could."

His father's hands came out of his pockets now and one of
them was thrust into the aquarium! He had caught sight of
something there that Sam, at any rate, had never seen in the
aquarium; no! not since as a small child, he had watched his
father changing its water and its weeds.

There were now three kinds of weeds in the aquarium, two of
them river-weeds, and one of them a pond-weed; and it was in
an entanglement of this pond-weed that Mat Dekker had found
what was such a shock to him and what, at any other time, would
have been an event of the first importance in Glastonbury Vicarage. He had found a dead fish.

"Dead! One of the Meare-Rhyne ones!" muttered Mat Dekker
now, holding out the tiny little corpse for Sam to see.

It looked very small indeed in the priest's great brown palm—
very small and silvery—like an "animula, vagula, blandula" in
the hand of God.

"That's what it is—one of the Meare-Rhyne ones!" echoed
Sam.

"We didn't change the water yesterday," said his father.

"Nor the green weed last week," added Sam.

"And we left that duck-week," said his father, "when we *knew*
it ought to come out."

"And we never got that fresh gravel from Keinton Mande-
ville," sighed Sam.

"Or a trowel-full of that sand we saw at Athelney," groaned
his father.

"It's our own fault that this minnow's dead," said Sam.

"We've killed it," echoed the Vicar of Glastonbury, "as surely
and certainly as if we'd fished it out and thrown it into the fire."

"Put it here," said Sam, hurriedly bringing from the chimney-piece a little copper plaque with the head of St. Dunstan engraved on it.

Mr. Dekker tipped the little fish from his hand into the centre of this plate where it lay across the sullen brow of the despotic ecclesiastic.

"Let's see what happens to it *now*," murmured Sam, tossing some drops of water out of a tumbler and covering up the fish.

"What'll happen to all of us, my boy!" sighed his father, sinking into one of the creaking wicker chairs, while Sam took possession of the other.

They surveyed each other in silence; and a moment passed during which they knew—those two heavily breathing, staring men—that it would take more than the maddening breasts of that sweet creature upstairs, suckling her child, really to separate them, the one from the other.

But Sam pulled himself together. It was not for the sake of peace with his father that he had to go. It was not even because Nell had said:—"If *you* can stand the way we're living, *I* can't!" It was because, without question, or doubt, or any compromise, his "external soul" had commanded him to leave this house.

He drew in his breath several times before he spoke, inhaling with it that old familiar smell of his father's workroom that seemed as much composed of some wholesome emanation from the priest's massive animal-frame as from the fumes of his pipe and the musty odour of the leather bindings of Dr. Simeon's Sermons.

"I've got something to tell you, Father," he said.

"Eh, boy—speak up; out with it!"

The tone was identical with the tone which Sam had heard from him when, on leaving Cambridge, he had announced that he could not be ordained; but somehow, hearing it now, it put him back into the Eton collar of his first term of the Sherborne Prep.

"Don't interrupt me then, Father, please, and I'll tell you."

Oh, these deadly pauses, these creakings of chairs, these swallowings of saliva, when the outer coat of the human stomach seems to be inflating and deflating itself like the belly of a frog!

"I've decided to leave this house, Father, and take lodgings for myself in the—" His words came pattering out . . . *tit-tot* . . . *tit-tat* . . . *tit-tut* . . . like the tread of the Sherborne Cadet Corps when commanded to advance at quick time—"in the town, somewhere, and earn my own living. I want to earn it as a working-man, and I'm pretty sure I can get a job that wouldn't take me much time to learn at this new municipal factory. I understand that—no! don't interrupt me, Father!—that there are several places unfilled there, because they can't find enough people to take such poor wages. This won't mean my becoming a Socialist, or anything like that! They're ready to take anyone; and they know I'm not interested in politics. I'm going round to the Tribunal this afternoon to talk to this new lawyer they've got, this nephew of old Merry's, and when I've got my job, can 'ee guess where I'm going to live, Father? No! Stop! Let me tell you! I'm going to live in the attic of that old warehouse, with the Gothic door, that we've so often noticed when we've started on our walks towards Meare. You spoke of it yourself . . . don't you remember? . . . that day we took our lunch and got as far as Bawdrip?"

He stopped breathlessly. Well! it was done now! He had crossed his Rubicon. He had severed that animal-male link, stronger in some ways even than the umbilical cord itself, which had bound him so long, hirsute flesh against hirsute flesh, to his begetter. He didn't dare to look at his father now. He raised his head and stared at the aquarium. It was Nell's chance-word that had suddenly made his path so clear; just as it had been Crummie's chance-word, reported to him by Red Robinson, that had started the whole thing.

"Girls' words, tossed out without thought—they've changed my whole life," he said to himself. "I said good-bye to *her* in Mother's room and now——"

He jumped to his feet, lurched forward and clutching his father's forehead in both his hands, bent down over it and kissed it. "And now," he added, in his deepest heart, "I've said good-bye to *him* in our room."

After kissing his father's bent head—for Mat Dekker, as if under the blinding glare of his enemy the sun, had lowered his

face and closed his eyes—Sam walked to the door. As he put out
his hand to its handle he seemed to see the whole of his life as
nothing but doors—study doors, drawing-room doors, church
doors, privy doors, kitchen doors, bedroom doors . . .

"Sam!" His father was on his feet, straightening his shoulders, tightening his lips, fumbling blindly with his heavy gold
watch-chain.

The priest's thoughts and feelings at that moment were incoherent to a point of physical distress. They were like a whirl-
pool, tossing up opposite things, drowned bodies, ravening
sharks, shimmering mother-of-pearl, cowry shells, dogfish, from
the bottom of the mind's deep sea.

"Alone in the house with her . . . going past her bedroom
. . . alone with her . . . Sam leaving me . . . Sam going out
of my house . . . Sam's place empty . . ." Being the man he
was, it was natural enough that the distress caused to him by
the conflicting nature of his thoughts vented itself in irrational
anger.

"Sam!"

"Yes, Father?"

"You shan't sneak off like this! Do you hear me? I say you
shan't! Leaving your wench . . . and your child . . . and everything. Have you no natural feeling at all? You promised me
you'd let her alone until she was properly divorced and you
were properly married to her . . . and what do I find? I find
you turning your mother's room into a place to ——" The trick
had worked. The man's upper lip was once more protruding and
trembling with injury and grievance—"into a place to forni-
cate in!"

The ugly word belched itself forth from the priest's contorted
mouth like the dark wine and the gobbets of human flesh from
the guts of the drunken Polyphemus. How could Sam know that
the secret urge of this anger was a wild, heathen delight at being
left alone, alone without a rival, with those suckling breasts
upstairs? How could Sam know that it was the man's own *"I'd
like to, Susie! I'd like to, Dolly! I'd like to, Nelly!"* of the
stone-throwing Tommy Chinnock, that was being lambasted and
foul-named by this bewildered priest? Mother Legge would have

been the person to have set Sam right upon this riddle of his
father's wrath; though doubtless Mr. Evans, who had seen the
contents of the Camel Bowl touch Nell's lips before all the rest,
might have been able to instruct even the wise Mother Legge
about the maddening power of this girl's fatal passivity. A
bundle she was—that was it! an aphrodisiac bundle of cloves,
cinnamon and aniseed—a fever-raising, fever-allaying *bundle of
catnip* for one, two, three, and how many more? prowling, feral
carnivores!

And there was, after all,—for Sam was his father's son—a
similar introversion of righteous anger on Sam's side. Why else
should the word used by his father, and associated by his father
with that room of the dumb clock, have made his chin work so,
and a spurt of black anger almost choke him? If he *hadn't*
forgot everything—even that it was "the last time"—when he
hugged Nell so furiously in the drawing-room this word of his
father's would doubtless have gone over his head like badly
aimed duck-shot.

It was certainly the word "fornication" that led Sam now, for
after all he was a very young saint, to close *this* door, of all
doors, with so resounding a repercussion throughout the whole
house, that Nell, doing up the front of her dress after nursing
her baby, ran quickly to the door of William-of-Orange's room,
opened it, and listened in frightened concern.

It was in this manner that Sam Dekker was heard leaving the
house of his birth which he had entered, through the body of the
servant from Geneva, some twenty-five years ago. And what was
the first thing that Mat Dekker did when he heard his son cross
the hall, open the front door, and go out?

He moved slowly to the mantelpiece, removed the tumbler that
Sam had placed over the little fish from Meare-Rhyne, picked it
up from its place upon the surly countenance of St. Dunstan,
and, raising it to his nostrils, snuffed at it with inquisitive
interest!

Meanwhile Sam himself, arrived in the presence of Paul Trent
in the Abbot's Tribunal, soon found that he was completely right
about there being no lack of communal jobs as long as he was
content with the barest living wage. And since such a wage—just

enough to keep body and soul together—was exactly what suited his life-illusion just then, both parties in this transaction were speedily rendered content.

And so before that day was over both Mr. Dekker and Nell received brief notes from this quixotic young man, notes that were delivered in person, for he had no desire that Penny and Mr. Weatherwax should sauce their favorite "gorlas" with his emotional confidences, telling them of his success.

The two devoted boys, Elphin Cantle and Steve Lew, were Sam's messengers. Steve's hero-worship for Elphin had begun during the last few months to reproduce almost exactly Elphin's for Sam, and a mission of this sort being meat and drink to such romantic lads, the recipients of these missives received them privately, separately, faithfully, and in all due secrecy before night fell.

Mat Dekker's note ran:

Dearest Father,

You can always find me in case of necessity at the top of that house I spoke of. They call it the Old Malt House and it is in the middle of Manor House Lane. I'll see you, of course, before long; but for a week or two I want to collect my thoughts.

Give my love to Penny.

Your affectionate son,

Sam.

P.S. I've got a good job so I am in no need of money.
P.P.S. Would you mind telling Penny to give the bearer my big sponge.

The note to Nell, which it was Steve's task to deliver—Sam had tact enough to make this quite clear—ran as follows:

Nell, my little Nell,

You must forgive me if I hide away from both you and Father for a week or two. I am all right. I am not unhappy. If I've made *you* unhappy, please, please try and forgive me. I needn't tell you any more about my religion and my new life; but I *have* to tell you this, once and for all, that I love you more than I ever did! *Now* you may smile, in the way you do; but what I say is true; and we both realised it this morning. Father knows where I am living.

Your Sam, spite of all, for ever and always.
P.S. Give Henry a lot of kisses from me.

Sam's job at the municipal factory proved the simplest, as it was the heaviest that the whole business offered. The new types of legendary figurines were largely constructed of a certain kind of clay that was brought in trucks from the neighbourhood and Sam's job, which was shared by some of the roughest labouring-men in the town, consisted in emptying trucks of this clay into hand-carts, and these carts again into receptacles outside the factory.

Thus he was kept very busy, and felt, during the first week or so, extremely tired; but his day ended at five o'clock, when he was free to do what he pleased, and these first free evenings in spite of his extreme exhaustion were times of more peace and quiet than he had known for a long while. The heavy physical labour saved him from morbid broodings and made each night an orgy of delicious dreamless sleep; while as his muscles began slowly to adapt themselves to his work—and it must be remembered that Sam was endowed with super-vigorous health—this nightly weariness grew less and less. What *was* a torture to him was the treatment he received, though only at first, from his fellow-labourers. Intrinsically they were men of no exceptional brutality. Among themselves they were friendly enough. But everything about Sam, the fact that he was an educated man, the fact that his father was a priest, and above all the fact that he was trying to live like a saint, excited their bitter hostility. If Sam had not come to this job of clay-hauling and truck-emptying with the direct purpose of sharing the sufferings of his perse-cuted god he would have been reduced to abject and sullen misery by these men.

"Holy Sam" became his nickname almost at once; and the pleasure with which they tormented him was abominable. It would be erroneous to say that all good and valuable things spring from the individual, and all evil things from the crowd; for everyone is aware on various occasions of a crude and raw warmth, a radiating glow, a lively enthusiasm, that emanates from any group or mass of people. And there springs up from the crowd, too, under certain conditions, a formidable power of magnetic faith. But this faith which is the most striking thing the crowd engenders cannot for one second be compared with the creative faith of the individual. It is by the faith of the individual upon which the crowd feeds like an oil-devouring flame that the latter is able to move mountains, to tear down Bastilles, to destroy inquisitions, to inaugurate revolutions.

Among his fellow-workmen in this clay-hauling job Sam was an individual pitted against a crowd. *He* was not against *them*. *They* were against him. He was no Coriolanus. He was no aristocrat, answering hate with contempt. It was enough that he lacked their humour, that he did not chew their tobacco, that he could not fling back their particular kind of badinage. In a situation of this kind an upper middle-class recluse like Sam was at a much worse disadvantage than Will Zoyland would have been. Zoyland's dog-and-gun slang, his Rabelaisian obscenities and roaring guffaws would have won these people's respect. He would have browbeaten the more aggressive and cajoled the others. He would have speedily become a sort of bandit chief among them.

But Sam they totally despised. They regarded him as a softy, as a preacher, as a spy, as a blackleg, as a dark horse up to some tricky game, as a ne'er-do-well with a screw loose, as the idiot son of a canting parson. They amused themselves with him. They mimicked his mannerisms, they hustled him, they put the heaviest work upon him. He was their sport, their quarry, their lawful prey. The fact that he was no weakling gave an added spice to their bullying. It was like bear-baiting; and all day long they worried him, like dogs worrying a great patient beast.

But all this was only for a time. It did not last. Little by little the clumsy sweetness of Sam's nature won its way with them. What actually was at first, it may be, a tinge of priggishness in his attitude towards them, wore off. He came to forget that he was Sam Dekker, the son of Mat Dekker. He became a labouring-man among other labouring-men. And the psychic awareness that he really was ceasing to separate himself from them affected them without their realising it. The manner in which he received their derision changed insensibly too. He began to cease regarding it as directed especially and maliciously towards himself, and he ceased to encourage it and stir it up for his own masochistic satisfaction. Thus the telepathic message from his subconscious self to their self-conscious selves which had formerly called out, "I am different from you. It hurts here. Hit me harder here!" began to sing another tune and to call out, "We're all in the same mill. To hell with differences! All souls at the bottom are equal."

And this new mood in Sam was no conscious part of his struggle after a holy life. It arose from the innate heathen goodness of his nature, emitting its sweet odour like thyme or mint that has been heavily trodden upon. And so by degrees it came about that the heathen virtue in Holy Sam was responded to by the heathen virtue in these other Glastonbury aboriginals, and the feeling:—"We are all of one blood"—gave to the clay-hauling upon which Mr. Barter's business depended a certain autochthonous solidity.

For Tom Barter with Red Robinson as his foreman and Lady Rachel as his adviser, was beginning to display his mettle as a manager; and the figurines, statuettes, plaster-of-paris busts, hand-painted vases, plates, crocks and jars, which they were now manufacturing showed signs of spreading Glastonbury wares— with the help of the visitors and pilgrims—all over Europe. Both in the designing and executing portions of his business Barter's personal limitations in matters of art were an advantage to him. He came upon one young person after another, girls as well as men, who possessed unusual artistic feeling; and encouraged by Lady Rachel, he left these young Glastonbury natives a completely free hand.

The result of this was that there began to spring up—out of the void as it almost seemed—a very exciting and most original school of Glastonbury design, genuinely indigenous and wherein the roughnesses and crudities of drawing, colouring and perspective, and their variations too under so many different hands, possessed the imaginative freshness and childlike appeal of an authentically primitive art, an art which the whole western world seemed especially to thirst for, an art which embodied in it not only the communal spirit of the town's socialistic rulers but something—a nuance, a tinge, a suspicion—of the new religion of Glastonbury's Mayor! Their earliest output had been confined to toys and souvenirs; but as soon as Lady Rachel became intimate with Barter—and she had an active ally in Tossie

—the little clay figurines of the legendary personages of the town's history, from Morgan-le-Fay to St. Joseph, ousted everything else; and the council's timely contract with certain clay-haulers of the neighbourhood changed the whole trend of the business, so that toys were forgotten and a real movement of imaginative art, at once modern and mystical, swept everything before it.

At the end of a week Sam paid a hurried visit to his father and Nell; but so distressing and agitating to all three of them did this visit prove that he did not attempt to repeat it, but henceforth gave himself up completely to the raptures and torments of his *Imitatio Christi*.

It would have been a different story altogether if his labours had been *inside* the municipal factory. There he would have been under Barter's eye, there he would have met Lady Rachel. But except for the first afternoon of his hiring he saw nothing of the art-work of the place. All he saw, all he handled, was truck-loads of this particular clay.

Sam's nature, always rather earthbound and earthdrawn, sank into this clay as into the tomb of his Christ. He washed away his thoughts about Nell and her child in this clay. In this clay he soaked up the subterranean sorrow, scarcely less hurting than what he felt for Nell, of his separation from his father. He was at once bruised along with his God, by his wrestlings with his fellow-workmen, and buried along with his God, in this heavy Somersetshire clay.

What made the task of winning over his companions so slow was the fact that the men around him were always changing. Their pay was so poor and their work so heavy that few of them could stand it for more than a brief time. Then others came— all of them out of the poorest districts of Bove Town and Paradise—and in their turn were tempted to make sport of Sam. None of them had the toughness or the stamina that he had. They were lean and lanky men, descendants by centuries of inbreeding of those heathen aboriginals of the Isle of Glastonbury who resisted St. Joseph, St. David, St. Indractus, St. Gildas, St. Patrick, St. Dunstan, St. Benignus and St. Bridget, in their attempts to spiritualise them, who were forever revolting against both church and state, who seemed inspired in their rebellions by the old chtho-nian divinities of Tor Hill, whose re-awakened malignity on the day of the Pageant nearly destroyed Lord P. and whom no-body but Bloody Johnny seemed able to manage.

What *did* give Sam a real thrill of natural pleasure was the scrubbing and the whitewashing of his loft floor at the top of the Old Malt House. He had no furniture here at all except a small camp-bed, a kitchen chair, a three-legged table and a white thick water-jug and basin. When he had whitewashed the walls and ceiling, he scrubbed the big bare beams of the oak floor till they were as clean as the cleanest floor-expanse in the town, that is to say, Emma Sly's kitchen at The Elms.

As day followed day in Sam's new life, finding him working from seven to five at clay-hauling and then associating, when his work was over, with the most destitute of his neighbours, the full implication of his abandonment of the normal human desires began to unfold. He was so strong, and his health was so sound, that he very quickly found his day's labour no more exhausting to him than if he had spent the time walking about the fields.

This growing freedom from physical weariness made it pos-sible for him, after he had washed himself and changed his clothes and had his tea, to explore many of the poorer districts of the town of which he already knew a little. He would leave Manor House Road about half-past six and make his way through a small alley, by the side of the house where John and Mary lived, into a section of Paradise that abutted upon the Burnham and Evercreech Railway and stretched as far to the north as the four crossways, where the roads to Meare and Godney met North-load Street and Dye House Lane.

That Holy Sam, as even the children of this quarter already began to call him, had an equanimity of temper beyond what many holy men have had, was proved by the way he let himself be interrupted upon at least three week-days out of his six, as he sat down to his well-earned tea in his white-washed attic loft. This interruption came from Jimmy Bagge, a semi-imbecile beg-gar, a little older than Sam, who lived with his father and mother in a one-storied stone house, black with age and smoke, that leaned against the bank of the Evercreech Railway. Sam had

found Jimmy scraping and groping in a filthy refuse-heap behind the Northload houses and he had brought him home with
him to Manor House Lane and given him a supper of hot tea and
bread and treacle. After this Jimmy Bagge soon found out how
long Sam worked and the exact hour of his return home; and he
used to sit in the malt-yard, hidden behind a row of ancient
barrels between which he constantly peeped out.

He was too wise to present himself ere Sam had washed,
changed his clothes and made tea; but he had timed these proceedings to such a nicety that it was pretty well almost always
just as Sam was lifting his first cup to his lips that Jimmy
knocked at his door. Sam accepted the situation as if it were his
destiny to spend his life with Jimmy, as indeed perhaps it was,
but he displayed one small weakness on all these occasions,
which betrayed the difference between an Anglo-Saxon "holy
man" and one of Latin or Oriental blood; for he gave up his
one chair to his visitor, and himself sat down on his camp-bed;
not, it must be confessed out of politeness, but with an irrepressible awareness of the verminous condition of the beggar's filthy
clothes.

It was on the occasion of the fifth visit of Jimmy Bagge to the
Malt House loft floor that the obstinate imbecile suggested, after
many wavering circumlocutions, that Sam should accompany him
to his home beneath the Evercreech railway bank. It was a lovely
evening when the two men set out together with this purpose in
view, and Sam could not help thinking, as he walked along by
his new friend's side, of a certain curious change that had taken
place in his recent responses to the visible world.

The back gardens of Northload Street sloped down into a
region of desolate and forlorn litter where those warm and mellow brick tiles for which Glastonbury is famous gave place to
an older style of roofing, of dull grey, moss-patched slate. As he
glanced about him he felt a slight touch again of this new sensation he had been receiving lately. What he felt was a strange
and singular reciprocity between his soul and every little fragment of masonry, of stony ground, of mossy ground, of woodwork, of trodden mud, of clumps of last year's dusty nettles, of
withered dock leaves or of mildewed palings.

It is true that to the intellectual eyes of oriental spirituality, or of Latin devotion, Sam's attempts at living the ideal life would have seemed like those of an ascetic schoolmaster or a priggish boy scout, childish, and lacking in maturity, dignity, subtlety, and intellectual passion. Sam's whole system of moral values—his puritanical stress upon sexual restraint, his fidgetty preoccupation with isolated acts of benevolence—would have seemed to a Celtic or Latin nature a form of tiresome and Pharisaic fussiness, more akin to the pragmatic virtue of some modern lay-brother than to the sublime heroism of real mediæval sanctity. Nevertheless, to the Invisible Observers of the magic-charged atmosphere of Glastonbury this resolute and sturdy descendant of Somersetshire yeomen displayed a certain humble simplicity and a certain stolid good-humoured piety that rendered many more picturesque struggles to live the saintly life appear trickily theatrical and even self-deceiving in comparison!

And certainly on this particular evening as he adapted his pace to the shuffling and shambling gait of Jimmy Bagge, Sam began to be aware that some subtle barrier between his inmost being and certain particular objects in Nature had begun to give way. The truth was that without being in the least conscious of the importance for humanity of the psychic law he had blundered upon or of its rarity in the world, Sam had found out that when a person is liberated from possessiveness, from ambition, from the exigencies of desire, from domestic claims, from every sort of authority over others, he can enjoy sideways and incidentally, as he follows any sort of labour or quest the most exquisite trances of absorption into the mysterious essence of any patch of earth-mould, or any fragment of gravel, or any slab of paving-stone, or any tangle of weeds, or any lump of turf that he may come upon as he goes along.

There is always a peculiar pleasure in arriving suddenly through a narrow aperture between masses of masonry at some wide-open expanse; and this is especially the case in the evening twilight and when such an expanse opens out towards the west. The misty glow, filtering through the smouldering ditch-vapours of this open ground, as Sam saw it tonight, lifted into a grandiose and dusky importance every pigsty, every stickhouse, every pigeon-tower, every hovel-roof; and under a stone arch where the muddy path they followed dived beneath the railway Sam could see, as they approached the dwelling of Jimmy's aged parents, a great red semi-cirque, like a huge blood-stained mushroom, which was the setting sun!

His father's arch-enemy was too close upon his own dissolution over the rim of the planet to throw out any magnetic power, whether good or bad; but to see him like this at all, as Sam descending from the ramparted greyness of that gap in Northload Street saw that crimson half-circle, was as if a person saw the sinking head of some titanic invader retreating from a threatened city.

Such is the human mind—or at least such is the mind of a son of Somersetshire clay fumbling towards a holy life—that Sam's consciousness gave a momentary harbourage to the unsanctified thought that he was glad that his present companion's rags had not touched his camp-bed; but, like a black fly that lodges for a second upon the shaft of a moving wagon, this thought was quickly lost in the outstretched solemnity of that evening scene.

"Fayther be a turble stark man for a bed-rid," remarked Jimmy Bagge, " 'a do eat and drink, Fayther do, all there be, when there be any! Mum be a thinned-out ghosty compared wi' he."

The imbecile paused for a moment and looked at the crimson half-sun as it went down under the moss-wet stone arch, the walls of which seemed to drip with a moisture that was neither rain nor dew, but rather some malady-sweat of its own private enduring.

"Mum do sarve he for nothink and it be a pity to see such sarvice. He do lie and eat; and her do wear 'erself to bone feeding he! I be afeared of he just as Mum be; but Finn Toller, what be Mum's nephy, baint afeared of he. Mum do send I to fetch Finn Toller and when Fayther do zee 'un cooming oop path through chink o' windy, 'a do beller and holler, awful vor to hear. 'A do zay, 'thik Codfin be come to murder I,' and 'a do hide 'isself under blanket."

"Does your mother let Mr. Toller come in?" asked Sam.

Jimmy's countenance, which was as a rule as empty of intelligence as a washed-out signboard, emitted at that point a pallid ray of cunning, as if the wind-blown reflection of a streak of moonlight, caught in a rain tub, had been tossed upward upon that board.

"Mum do allus zay the sëame. She do zay:—'Thee's pore uncle be starvin', Codfin. Have 'ee got a bite o' summat for'n today?"

"And what does Mr. Toller do then?"

"'A do empty his wallet on Fayther's bed and sometimes there be a girt hunk o' sweet Cheddar in 'un; but 'a never sits down for more'n a minute. 'I must be movin' on, Auntie,' 'a zays, and then 'a zays to Mum, lookin' at Fayther, wot's head be hid under blanket—'I've 'a jest coom from settlin' woon account an' I be ponderin' in me mind about settlin' another. I be a grand settler of accounts, Auntie,' he says, and 'a looks, wi' 'is weepy eyes, at Fayther's blanket, till bed do creak, Fayther do shake so."

Once seated in that forlorn stone edifice, built long ago under the railway bank, it came over Sam with a weight like that of the first shovelful of earth thrown into an open grave, what kind of mental aura is projected in a given locality by experience of sheer physical want. Preparations had evidently been made for what in the Bagge ménage passed for supper, for every object in that miserable room—the walls of bare stone, where patches of soot and grease and indecipherable and nameless stains alternated with greenish mould and oozing damp, the small smoky wood-fire under a great iron pot where steamed the most watery concoction ever wrung from the twice-boiled bones of a skinny rabbit, bare wooden chairs with their seats full of holes, a broken water-jug on the smoke-darkened chimney-piece,—seemed to group themselves round a piece of newspaper laid flat upon the table on which rested the half of a loaf and two small salted herrings.

A strong, bony face, angular as the face of a half-starved, overworked horse, did Mrs. Bagge turn towards the visitor while she settled herself on a wooden stool by the hearth and watched his movements as a hungry fieldfare, that bird of wintry bane, might sit with ruffled feathers watching an absent-minded tramp in the road-hedge. Her identity too, like that of the damp walls and the ricketty chairs and the innutritious liquid in the black pot, and the broken jug on the chimney-piece, seemed, even while she gazed at Sam, to yearn towards the half loaf and the two small fishes upon the outstretched newspaper.

And as for the figure in the bed under a patched blanket—the figure of the bed-ridden Thomas Bagge—*its* woebegone rapacious eyes seemed to point at these objects with the irreversible necessity of a compass needle pointing to the north.

Sam couldn't bear to think he was keeping them from this wretched meal, such as it was, but he, too, seemed to succumb to the hypnotic influence of that half loaf on the table. For nearly a quarter of an hour he murmured various broken comments upon the new Glastonbury government and the chances it offered of monetary advantage to the destitute.

The woman's interruptions were however entirely irrelevant to what he was saying. They seemed more like the feeble echoes of the mechanical chatter of a gipsy at a fair, and they kept referring to him as "the sweet lovely gentleman what be minded to make our Jimmy's fortune." Once she jumped up from her stool and with a billet of wood snatched from the floor killed a large bug upon the sooty wall. But the piece of wood as she threw it down, and her stool as she took her seat again, and another bug observed by Sam that had escaped her gesture, all these things seemed to his mind to be focussed upon that half loaf and those wretched herrings.

Gazing at Mrs. Bagge's hollow cheeks, scoriated neck, cavernous eye-sockets, Sam began to feel as if his attempts to understand the sufferings of a Promethean demi-god had hardly scratched the surface of the sufferings of his own human race; and he seemed to hear his "exterior soul" whispering in his ears that his tortured God was nothing less than a tortured humanity.

As he contemplated the damp stones so sooty and greasy and stained with nameless stains, above the woman's head, and as he looked at the bread upon the table, the two fundamental concepts—bread and stone—seemed to associate themselves with the concept *suffering*, as forming a sort of ultimate Trinity of Experience towards which he was being conducted. Thankless labour, eternal hunger, the deadening throb of a pain that refused to cease, if these things lived on and on in this room under the Evercreech Railway bank, why should he have been permitted to eat sweet treacle and to look out of his window from the top of the Old Malt House?

From the hollow eye-sockets of this woman his mind reverted to similar eye-sockets, and far worse ones than hers, that were at this very second in other parts of the world opening and contracting under the pressure of the cruelty of the First Cause.

Why didn't suffering carried to a certain point, why didn't pain carried to a certain point, simply kill their victims? And since they didn't, to what point must a person go, in sympathy for these things, who had, by pure accident, been spared their worst scrapings and scoopings?

As he went on mumbling about what the Glastonbury council would soon be doing for its poor, Sam's under-mind came to the conclusion that the most serious question of all questions was *at what point*, if life was to go on with any degree of endurance, is it necessary to harden our hearts and cease to think of the pain of others? Mathematicians talked of invisible "points," of formal "points," that were the pivots of all the vast spirals of reality. Here, in this question—how far must we share suffering? —had he touched the "point of points" round which all sensitised consciences revolved?

The vital common sense in Sam stirred up an interior honesty that told him he must draw back somewhere or the natural selfishness in him would rise like Enceladus and throw off all restraint. Did St. Francis stop in the midst of composing his Hymn to the Sun, to ponder on the problem of how far he ought, in place of giving himself up to such magical ecstasy, to visualise the fate of the tortured in that neighbouring stone tower and to ponder on what man *at that point of time*, was doing to man, in Algiers, in London, in Seville, in Trebizond, in Paris, and even in Assisi?

Sam's sluggish nature had been receiving so many jolts of late and he had been reducing his physical nourishment to so meagre a point of late that his nerves were much more sensitised these days than was usual with him. That is perhaps why he stared so fixedly on that bug on the wall.

"Every locality," he thought, "has its own midges, its own gnats, its own beetles, its own lice, its own bugs. They may resemble the others of their tribe; but they must be affected—few will dispute this—by the particular climatic conditions which exist around them. This bug was a Glastonbury bug. Had it any message for him, a Glastonbury man? Can't *you* throw light on this?" he thought, addressing the bug on the wall. But the bug was so extreme an individualist that it regarded the gibberish which reached it from this man's brain as the same sort of telepathic nonsense that it was accustomed to hear when in her heart Mrs. Bagge cried out:—"How long, O Lordy, O Lordy, how long, how long?" and it proceeded upon its tortuous way with less curiosity—not to speak of sympathy—than even ex-Mayor Wollop would have felt.

Sam, however, while he exchanged a few words now with his friend Jimmy who continued to stand at the foot of his father's bed,—Mr. Bagge himself seemed to be awaiting events in gloomy taciturnity—wrestled stubbornly in the depths of his mind with this problem.

"A limit there must be," thought Sam, "to the sympathy one soul can give to other souls—or all would perish. Absolute sympathy with suffering would mean death. If Christ had sympathised *to the limit* with the pain of the world it would have been hard for him to have lived until the day of his Crucifixion. But what does that mean? Does it mean drawing back from the hell we stare at? Does it mean that every soul has a right to forget if it *can* forget? Sympathy with pain kills happiness. There comes a point when to live at all we *must* forget!"

His conclusion left him with a feeling of unutterable weakness, cowardice, contemptibleness. Submerged in sickening humility he groaned aloud. He had taken the precaution before starting, in anticipation of the penury of his friend's domicile, to put in his pocket several thick slices of bread and treacle and these, wrapped up in paper, he now took out and handed to his hostess. It was then that the truth of Jimmy's words about his parents became most painfully apparent; for his mother, after swallowing two or three hasty bites of one of these sandwiches, presented the rest of them just as they were to the silent man in the bed, who when once they were in his hands neither spoke nor looked up until there was not one crumb left upon the sticky paper in which they had been wrapped.

He was not an ill-looking man either, Sam thought, as those sallow jaws masticated the food and his Adam's apple rose and fell as he swallowed it; but there was something repulsive to the mind—and even a vague sense of something tragic and ghastly—in the way the sunken black eyes of Mrs. Bagge followed every morsel as it disappeared.

"Town council do see us don't starve," said the woman presently, "but they gives us no food, only money; and Mr. Bagge feels money be too precious to be throwed away on victuals; so he puts it where't be safe."

Mr. Bagge's puffy white face—not an unhandsome face—rising out of his filthy open shirt, lit up complacently on hearing this and his expression struck Sam as being the meanest human expression he had ever seen.

"Too precious to be throwed away," he repeated with unctuous satisfaction, "on wittles . . . so us puts it where't be safe."

Sam was still wondering at the back of his mind what could be done to a bedridden miser who was starving his wife, when Mrs. Bagge, who looked positively transparent from lack of nutrition, though she was a large-framed bony woman, lifted up her voice from where she sat on the stool by the fire, with her discoloured skirts hanging so loosely between her gaunt knees that it looked as though they had been thrown across the handles of a plough, and remarked to Jimmy:

"Did yer arst yer friend, the sweet lovely gen'l'man, whether he could bless this house with half of a silver shilling?"

The wheedling gipsy-like tone of her voice—which yet was not the voice of a real gipsy—grated unpleasantly upon Sam's ears. He felt inclined to cry out, "I'll give you a *whole* shilling if you'll turn it into food and let me see you eat it!" He mentally decided that he would come here on the following day with some pork-pies that he had seen in the window of a little shop in Manor House Lane and give one to each member of the Bagge family and insist upon their eating them before his face.

But the voice of the master of the house became audible now

Mr. Bagge was apparently addressing the smoke-darkened, greasy ceiling.

"When I over'ears folk mention shillinses I zays to meself— 'put 'un where 'un be safe. Too precious be they shillinses to be squandered on wittles!' "

Sam rose to his feet. "I've got no money on me," he said; and then, after a pause, "Well, I'll say good-night now, and go down to the river for a bit, to get a breath of air. I always sleep better after a breath of air. Don't get up, Mrs. Bagge."

Jimmy followed him wistfully with his eyes as he moved to the door. The imbecile's face had a certain blank handsomeness, like the puffy good looks of the man under the blanket, but his expression was submissive and docile, like his mother's. Sam was alarmed lest his own conscience, that merciless and authoritative voice that nowadays always stood by his side, would insist on his allowing Jimmy to accompany him. It was therefore with a certain relief—for which he blamed himself as soon as he was out of the house—that he heard Mrs. Bagge say:—

"Ye'll get some wood for I, Jim, won't 'ee, afore 'ee do go to Pilgrims' to arst for coppers? Jim be a good lad, Mister," the woman called after Sam as he went out. "If it 'tweren't for Jim, Mr. Bagge and me would be separated from each other and put in thik Wells wukkus."

"If you're not separated from Mr. Bagge," thought Sam, "you'll certainly get into the Wells Road Cemetery."

But standing in the doorway he threw back a warm and enthusiastic commendation of Jimmy.

"I knew he was a good son," he said, "as soon as he began talking about you both. Well! I hope he'll have good luck tonight at the Pilgrims'."

"Not for to squander!" shouted the handsome, puffy-faced man from his bed, "but for being kept where't be safe!"

And as he went off Sam couldn't help giving vent to a wicked wish that nephew Codfin would discover this "safe" hiding-place!

It was nearly dark when having threaded his way past many scattered hovels and desolate out-houses he finally reached the bank of the Brue. He was in an excited frame of mind, to which his anger at the behaviour of the man in the bed contributed not a little.

As he stood staring at the dark flow of the water he could see that Adam's apple moving up and down as Mr. Bagge swallowed. But Sam nodded his head like one making a resolution that must wait its fulfillment, and began following the bank of the river in a southerly direction. He was now about midway between the wooden Northload Bridge and the stone Pomparlès Bridge and in the obscurity of the twilight he could see rising out of the mud the scaffolding of Philip Crow's unfinished iron bridge.

As has been hinted, for several weeks Sam had begun to notice with a puzzled wonder that certain unpromising and unlikely objects gave him, as he glanced casually at them, thrilling spasms of a quivering happiness. It was only as these sudden seizures or shocks of unaccountable ecstasy increased upon him that he came to give them any particular attention. He was not of an analytic turn of mind; nor was he in any sense what is called "psychic." It might even be maintained that Sam's temperament was rather below than above the normal level of what the world has agreed to name "spiritual." Mystical he certainly was not. There was more mysticism in John Crow's little finger—for all his sceptical perversity—than in Sam's whole body. But he would have been worse than unimaginative; he would have been "duller than the fat weed on Lethe's wharf" not to have noted these recurrences of unaccountable transport in which his whole being seemed caught up and transfigured. What made this phenomenon harder to understand was the fact that the objects that served to evoke this ecstasy were so varied and in themselves so insignificant. Not one of them was important enough to afford any satisfactory clue to the nature of the meaning of these thrilling sensations. It was almost as if some mysterious centre of magnetic force had been actually moving for some while through the thick darkness of the chemical constitution of that Glastonbury mud and those Glastonbury stones towards Sam's sluggish receptivity; seeking in that receptivity a pre-ordained objective.

He came suddenly at this moment, as he stumbled along the river bank under the moonless and cloudy sky, upon yet another of these chance-sent mediums of unaccountable feeling. This was

an aged post, with an iron ring attached to it, used formerly for
the purpose of mooring the small barges that in old days brought
corn up the Brue. The post was but an obscure landmark by the
flow of that dark tide; but Sam knew its exact position and he
knew every detail of the landscape from this particular spot. He
couldn't really see the iron ring upon the post; but he knew so
well that it was there that he saw it without seeing it. But for
some reason the mere sight of this post filled him with the most
releasing, liberating and exultant of all his recent transports.
His mind was so occupied with the idea of pain that he quite
consciously began opposing this thrilling sensation with the
opacity of pain. It was as if he took up great spadefuls of pain
and flung them into the pathway of the delicious current that
flowed through him; and in proportion as the current increased,
so he threw more spadefuls of pain in front of it. But it swept
them away as it flowed on, drank them up, swallowed them all
into itself! And yet it would not be true to say that they became
identical with the rushing flood of this ecstatic feeling. They were
not absorbed as a natural sustenance. They nourished this flood;
but the flood existed independently of them and did not depend
upon them for its origin or its issue.

Sam found himself on his knees by this old post, so thrilled
was he by the transport that poured through him; and, in his
exultation, he pressed his forehead against it and ran his fingers
up and down its damp sides. And he did begin, quite desperately
now, to solve the mystery of all these experiences. He began to
realise that the soul of the inanimate, the indwelling breath of
life in all these ancient lifeless things, whereof the town was so
full, was really moving towards him.

The emotion he experienced now was a good deal stronger
than what had been produced in him until tonight by stones, and
gates, and paving slabs, and patches of moss, and fragments of
old walls, and carved mouldings and dead tree stumps, and
ploughed-up furrows, and wayside puddles and gutters; but it
was the same kind of mood.

Something in the atomic nature of the inorganic substance of
these things must have answered to an inarticulate craving of
Sam's, until Matter itself, the old obstinate Protean mystery,

moved and stirred to meet him. He could actually feel a magnetic power pouring forth into his fingers from this post against which he leaned.

Sam had been born in Glastonbury. Glastonbury sights and sounds and smells, the psychic *eidola* that radiate forth from the surface of ancient inanimate substances, had surrounded him from his birth. Having concentrated his sluggish, earthy nature so steadily and so long upon birds and beasts and fishes, he must have accumulated an enormous mass of casually imprinted memories concerning his contact with the inorganic surroundings of these living creatures. By day and by night he must have touched —going up and down the fields, lanes, hillsides, valleys, fenlands, tow-paths, spinneys, rhynes—innumerable gates, weirs, walls, marsh tussocks, mole hills, pond rails, heaps of stones, fallen trees, moss-grown ruins, and all these touches and casual contacts must have established between his inmost being and the mystery of matter in these things, deep correspondencies which were ready to rush forth at any summons.

Where lay the difference between the curious feeling he got as his fingers ran up and down the surface of this old barge post and the other recent sensation of the same nature? The difference was that the feeling he had now associated itself suddenly and strangely with that little dead fish that his father had taken out of the aquarium! The secret of matter had suddenly assumed a definite shape; and this shape was of a living kind—no longer inanimate but electric with animation. "Ichthus, the World-Fish,"—where had he picked up this singular expression? Not from any book he could think of in his father's shelves; not from the Sermons of Mr. Simeon! That the mystery of matter which had of late shivered through him in so many accidental contacts, should resolve itself in its primal leap, in its slippery quiver, in its up-rising from the pools of silence, into the actual form of a fish would have been an insane fancy for anyone else, but for Sam, with his up-bringing and environment, it bore an organic naturalness. Did he actually see in his mind's eye, then, the red fins, the greenish markings, the black stripes, the silvery tail, of any *real* fish? No! it was more subtle than this. But he *did* feel as if the solid matter all round him had become porous, so that some essence of life could move swiftly through it. In the mute balancing of this finny life-essence, passing through the primeval watery element that existed in all things, lay the inexplicable clue.

As he knelt in the damp mud of the tow-path beside this post, while the darkness deepened over him and the river flowed beneath him, he was driven forward once more by the honesty of his soul to face the ultimate dilemma. He became vividly conscious of himself as one entity among all the rest, carried along upon the night journey of the voyaging planet, and he seemed able to catch upon the breathing wind, mingled with the gurglings and suckings of the water, the cries of pain which at that second, all over the world, were rising up. There must be a limit to pity or the life-stream would stop; all would grow stagnant, and "Ichthus, the World-Fish," would float dead upon its back!

The first motive of every living creature must be to realise its own identity—to fight for itself against the cruelty of life, while the second motive of all conscious souls turned about towards the others.

One-two . . . One-two . . . went the heartbeat of the world! Was there a third pulse there that no one could yet hear? Why was it that Sam suddenly leapt up in great excitement to his feet? His fingers had encountered in the darkness at the foot of the post, an iron chain! This chain was not fastened to the ring, else he would have detected it before. It was fastened round the bottom of the post, so that it lay hidden in the grass. Sam crawled forward on his hands and knees following the course of the chain and he soon became aware of something floating on the water to which it was attached. From what he could discern, down there in the dark flow, it was a small black coal-barge. This accounted for the constant gurglings and suckings that he had been aware of for some time, and by which his ear, trained to the river sounds as it was, had been obscurely fretted.

Hastily he rose to his feet and scrambling down the bank stepped into the barge. Yes! It still had some coal in it; and Sam could detect from the sharp turpentine smell that it had been newly tarred. There was a half-empty coal sack at one end; and groping with his fingers he turned this over on its side and sat down upon it, with his back against the barge's stern. The tarry smell was overpowered as he rested here by the smell of the river, and soon the flapping-up of some biggish bird—it wasn't a moor-hen, he knew *that*, but it wasn't large enough for a heron—gave him a desire to think out in his mind exactly what his geographical position was; for this would be a help to establishing the identity of that bird.

It was a habit natural to Sam and strengthened by long association with his father to take his bearings, as he called it; but at this juncture it did not seem as easy as usual to grasp the lay of the land as he sat in this barge. But he got it at last to his satisfaction. He was about half a mile northeast of Cradle Bridge Farm and about half a mile southwest of Cold Harbour Bridge where Young Tewsy had showed him that fish. If that bird, which *may* have been a stray wild duck, had flown due west from where he sat, it would have passed over the roofs of the villages of Catcott and Chilton-upon-Polden, and hit the swampy estuaries of the Parrett, somewhere about the centre of Horsey Level where the great Sedgemoor Drain flows into them.

All these places lay behind him as he sat in that barge on the Brue, for his face was turned directly towards the three eminences of the Isle of Glastonbury, Wirral Hill, Chalice Hill, and the Tor. Thus rested Sam Dekker; and then—without a second's warning—the earth and the water and the darkness *cracked*. . . . Whence it came, whether it came of its own volition and whether it was that same transformation of matter, which had been affecting him so of late, carried one degree further, Sam never knew; but he knew what was happening to him, and he knew it without the least doubt or question.

What he saw was at first accompanied by a crashing pain. That was the word Sam himself thought of to express it—the word *crashing*. But as the vision clarified before him and grew distinct this pain died away. But it was dazzling, hurting, blinding, at first, and it was associated in his mind with the sense of a sharp, long-shaped thing piercing his guts. His sensation was indeed strangely definite. The pain was so overwhelming that it was as if the whole of Sam's consciousness became the hidden darkness of his inmost organism; and when this darkness was split, and the whole atmosphere split, and the earth and the air split, what he felt to be a gigantic spear was struck into his bowels and struck *from below.*

He had ceased to be a man sitting on a coal sack at the stern of a barge. He had become a bleeding mass of darkness. His consciousness was a dark surface of water; and up through this water, tearing it, rending it, dividing it, turning it into blood, shivered this crashing stroke, this stroke that was delivered from abysses of the earth, far deeper than the bottom of the Brue.

Whatever this "spear" was that struck him, to his whole animal nature quivering under it, it was as much the shock of something totally unknown, something new to human experience, outrageous in its strangeness, that tore so at his vitals, as the crashing pain that it brought with it.

But when the vision appeared, and it came sailing into the midst of this bleeding darkness that was Sam's consciousness, healing everything, changing everything, each detail of what he saw he saw with a clearness that branded it forever upon his brain. He saw a globular chalice that had two circular handles. The substance it was made of was clearer than crystal; and within it there was dark water streaked with blood, and within the water was a shining fish.

Sam's first thought was: "This is the Grail! This is the Grail! It has come back to Glastonbury!" His second thought was: "I must tell Father and Nell about this." His third thought was more realistic; and it was one so congruous with his deepest being that the mere fact that he had had it—when he remembered the whole thing—put the seal of authenticity upon his vision. He thought in his heart: "What *is* that fish? It is a Tench. Surely it is a Tench!"

So anxious did he become to ascertain, before it vanished away, that this *Ichthus* out of the Absolute was what he thought it was, that Sam actually struggled up to his feet and cried the question aloud—"Christ!" he groaned in a harsh, queer voice that resembled the voice of a priest speaking from a scaffold. "Is it a Tench?"

He had been deriving such transports of late from rubble and mud and stones, that to see Christ in the form of a Tench seemed at that moment perfectly natural. He had read nothing of the Grail legends; so that it was no half-consciousness that all the successful Grail-seers cried out some crucial question, that tore from him these words.

Whole-hearted was Sam's groan to the Mystery, carried southward against the flowing waters of the Brue and westward across its mud-banks, towards Cradle Bridge Farm. It rose from his pity; it rose from his new insight into pain; it rose from that blood-stained umbel-cord across the gulf between his own ecstasies and the anguish he had glimpsed. It rose from the quick of his being, where life itself was strangling pity lest pity strangle life in the ultimate contest. It was the final desperate cry of humanity to the crushing, torturing universe that had given it birth.

Is it a Tench? Is there a fish of healing, one chance against all chances, at the bottom of the world-tank? *Is it a Tench?* Is cruelty always triumphant, or is there a hope beyond hope, a Something somewhere hid perhaps in the twisted heart of the cruel First Cause itself and able to break in *from outside* and smash to atoms this torturing chain of Cause and Effect?

The crystal goblet with the two curved handles was quite close to him now. He could see the darkness in the throat of the shining fish balanced motionless in its centre, but because of its position he could not see the Creature's eyes.

"Is it a Tench?" And then all at once it began to fade away. He felt sure afterwards that it was not his leaping to his feet or his raising his voice as he did, that made it vanish and he stood there in crushed humility like a man who says to himself: "It cannot be I who have seen this! It is a mistake; it was surely meant for another!"

But after he had remained, pondering upon what he had seen, for the space of five or six minutes, he clambered up out of the barge and with one final glance backward at the waters of the Brue, which looked exactly as they had looked before, he made his way slowly back to Manor House Road and to his room at the top of the Old Malt House.

It was a Saturday when Sam had his vision of the Grail and his first instinct was to take what he had seen and to plunge back

with it into the ordinary routine of his new life. He must, however, tell his father and Nell about it. "I'll go to the Vicarage,"
he thought, "tomorrow night, when Father's mind will be free
from his work and ready to listen." And then he thought: "I
must tell everyone about it. It was a pure chance that it appeared
to me. It has come back to Glastonbury. Many will see it now!"

He remembered that he had promised to go to Backwear Hut
in the course of the next day and help old Abel Twig doctor himself. He had been over there several times of late and had found
the old man so grievously afflicted with constipation that he
wanted help with an enema. "I'll do that first," he thought, "and
then we'll see! It's lucky tomorrow's Sunday."

Too excited to go to bed he spent half that night washing and
scrubbing; and completely exhausted, when the work was over,
sank down on his camp-bed under the window and slept till the
bells of St. John's roused him in the morning. His window
opened due west, and over the roofs of several barns and pigsties
he could see the willows of the Brue bordering upon Lake Village Field. He could also see the telegraph posts of the Burnham
and Evercreech Railway, and the white, winding road leading
to Meare.

He noticed as soon as he was awake by the way St. John's bells
were answered by St. Benignus' bells, and these again by many
chapel bells from outlying districts, that it was for the regular
morning service that they were ringing. It was half-past ten
then! He had indeed slept long and deep. He gathered his pillow
into a tight lump and sat propped up in bed, staring out of the
window into a windless atmosphere of delicate haze, where a
vague diffusion of sunlight floated upon the undispersed ditch-
vapours and a sweet, rather sickly smell of mud came up from
the meadows.

It was the sort of Sunday morning he had known so well all
his life—the typical Glastonbury Sunday. He could hear the
shuffling of the feet of the passers-by, some of them going to
church, some of them strolling out to enjoy themselves, many
of them just drifting round to some favourite bridge, or low stone
wall, or tavern-side bench, where they might meet a crony or
two and discuss life.

The absence of the ordinary sounds of week-day work was something much more than a negation. It was a positive essence. It wrapt itself around Sam, soothing, drowsing, lulling him. One after another as he lay there, came memory pictures out of his past.

But full as he was of quite other intentions than the recalling of mere memory pictures, he soon broke the spell and jumped out of bed. Washing himself on his knees by his basin (for he had no washing stand) he made his preparations for breakfast. Over his tea package, his half loaf, his sugar, his butter, his tin of golden syrup, Sam had placed upside-down, a large earthenware bowl. Milk, though he had previously always drunk it with his tea, he had decided to give up altogether; and this resolution simplified his housekeeping a great deal. A small tin receptacle he now placed over a tiny methylated stove and filling it with water from his jug, for he had no water-bottle, he lit the flame beneath it. Then rising from his knees he spread out bread, butter, sugar, tea upon the three-legged table, picking up these objects from the scrubbed floor where they had been covered by the earthenware bowl. From the broad window-sill he now took his knife, his spoon, his cup, his saucer, and his plate, and arranged them with the utmost nicety upon the three-legged table.

No prayer did Sam utter, whether ecclesiastical or traditional, but having made his tea he sat down on his kitchen chair and began pulling his loaf to pieces, crust and crumb, in great untidy lumps, and with a hungry and simple satisfaction; dabbing the butter upon these pieces with his knife and the treacle with his teaspoon.

As he ate, Sam's thoughts concentrated themselves upon what he had resolved to do now that he had seen the Grail. He had resolved to obey that "externalised soul" of his in every least detail, and just see where it led him! If it led him to more and more suffering, well and good. If it led him to some secret revelation of blinding happiness, all the better! But for weal or for woe it was the command of his soul that he intended to follow.

As he went on chewing the sticky, buttery morsels and licking the tips of his fingers, and obscurely wishing that methylated stoves held a little more hot water, he thought about the change that had come over his conception of his tortured God since he had begun his new life on that day he took Mad Bet home from Wirral Hill.

"In those days," he thought, "He was a tangible Person, a Person living in Space and Time, a Person conscious of my identity. But now He is different. I don't quite know what He is now. But I have seen the Grail and I shall find out what He is!"

Rising impatiently from the table, feeling still thirsty, and anxious to wash the sweetness of treacle out of his gullet, he filled his minute tin kettle with cold water from his jug and poured it down his throat. Then he opened a fresh packet of Player's Navy Cut cigarettes—for he was troubled with no ascetic scruples about smoking—and striking a match, which he was careful to throw out of the window rather than upon his newly scrubbed floor, he flung himself down upon his ricketty little couch and continued his meditations.

"I've got to face it," he said to himself. "I've seen the Grail, and I've got to face it. He's been dead and buried for two thousand years."

Two thousand years? But even as he shaped this thought there rose up and stood in the frame of his closed door, as if it were open, the Figure of the personality he denied. Piercing the ice-cold, frozen darkness of more death-levels than a universe of dead suns, this Figure—harder to visualise than Time or Eternity for it contains the essence of both—gazed upon the man on the bed.

"Have it as thou wilt, my child!"

Sam listened to the bells for a moment. "But of course that's not putting it right," he thought. "What He has become is a power in ourselves that sets itself up *contra mundum crudelem,* against the whole bloody world! Everybody feels it, and now that I've seen the Grail, it's got me by the throat! Man buried Him and Man has brought Him out of his Tomb. That's what the Grail means!"

He stared out at the vague, misty, translucent landscape, shot with fluctuating sun-streaks and sun-patches. His thoughts kept contradicting each other. "Christ is in the Stones and in the Water; it is Jesus who is dead and buried. There's something in Nature that has turned against Nature and is escaping from

Nature. There's a Christ in matter that is nearer the Grail than the Christ of the Church."

He heaved up from the creaking little bed, his body alert and at attention. His arbitrary soul, standing over his body, told it that it had been enjoying itself long enough at that pleasant window.

"You know perfectly well what you've got to do this morning, Monsieur!" his soul said to his body. "You've got to go over to Backwear Hut and give old Twig his enema."

His body agreed at once to obey this mandate but it craftily intimated that since it was already so late it would be better to start at once upon this excursion rather than make the bed and tidy the room and wash up the breakfast things. But Sam Dekker, although a very youthful "holy man" had not been a priest's assistant so long without knowing something about the cunning devices of what St. Francis calls "my brother the ass."

Chuckling to himself at his desire to escape doing his housework, he was soon re-lighting his methylated lamp and running downstairs to refill his jug at the pump in the yard. Even with this delay he was so fast a walker that he reached Backwear Hut not long after Number One had put his pot of onions, potatoes and chicken bones upon his kitchen-stove.

Poor old Abel had been suffering of late from two most vexing physical maladies, either of which would have rendered him miserable, but which together broke down his spirit. One was his villainous constipation, and the other a still worse attack of piles. With the utmost difficulty, under the encouragement of his faithful crony Number Two, the old man had been persuaded to go to the hospital clinic; but the slap-dash methods of the internes, and an interview, in an ether-smelling corridor, with the competent Aunt Laura, had sent him home trembling with nervous indignation, and resolute to confine himself henceforward to his own private remedies—Beecham's Pills for the first trouble and copious vaseline for the second.

When he reached Backwear Hut, Old Twig ("and small blame for him," thought Sam) was all for putting off the enema for a few minutes. There, however, it was—the kind where you have to pinch an India-rubber ball in order to squirt the water—reposing, unused, in its cardboard box, just as Number One had bought it at the establishment of Harry Stickles.

Mr. Twig, with the proper delicacy of an elderly gentleman buying medical aid, had peeped through the window of the little chemist's shop, till he made sure that the beautiful Nancy was safe upstairs; and it may be taken for granted that the avaricious husband of Nancy made him pay heavily for this engaging shyness! But at this moment the good old man, with the enema lying safe in its box on the table, cajoled his visitor into sitting down for a few minutes in his front room. It was mild enough to have the door open; and as Sam stretched out his Penny-patched knickerbockers and his Penny-darned stockings by the side of the old man's Sunday trousers, and listened to his talk as the fowls clucked and scratched on the threshold, a delicious sensation of calm flowed through him.

Motor cars were few at that hour upon the Godney Road; and from the distant town there came uninterrupted a murmur, a rumour of drowsy life, of a life that was not the life of man or of beast, but of Glastonbury herself, murmuring softly in her long historic trance of the past, of the present and of the future.

Sam thought to himself: "This Christ that is hidden in matter and contradicts all cruelty, can He possibly come from Nature?"

"What I'd-ur-zay consarnin' this here commoon," Mr. Twig was now observing, "is that it be a play-acting of the eddicated. For such as understands them things, 'tis no doubt a very good commoon. But I baint a book-larned man. Conservative be a plain word to I and so be Liberal, in a manner of speaking, though not *so* plain; but I reckon a man must be pretty far along wi' his book-larnin' afore he gets the hang of a commoon."

"Well, Mr. Twig," said Sam sententiously, "my father's got a lot of books in his study; but I remember quite well when the first number of the *Wayfarer* came out and there was a long article about Communism in it by Mr. Athling, he said very much what you're saying now."

"Me wold pard, Bart Jones, do zay," went on Mr. Twig, "that it be they noises what he heered in orspital, they rumblings and blearings from they ruings, what have brought such things to pass. But if 'ee 'arst me, Mister, what have called down these

wonders to earth, I'd-ud-zay 'tis thik young man from they Silly
Isles."

"How are your nieces at Miss Drew's?" enquired Sam.

The old man leaned forward, his hands on his knees and his
finger on his lips.

"Lily did tell I, last time they was here, that Louie be keepin'
company with young Tankerville, what be Mr. Crow's new pilot.
Lily says it be tender-'eartedness in dear Louie, seein' Mr. Tankerville be a lone man with a wife in cemetery."

Sam was not enough of a psychologist to catch the full flavour
of this "wife in cemetery," in relation to Lily's interest in her
sister's good fortune, although there did rise up on the utmost
verge of his consciousness like a beautiful apparition at a
séance, the pure cold melancholy of the parlour-maid's face.

"And what about Lily herself? Hasn't *she* got a young man
yet?"

Number One gave him the queerest look of mischievous gravity, a look that seemed to say: "Lily of course is our Lily—but
if any outsider considered her wilfulnesses from the point of
view of real common sense, he would be flabbergasted."

"Lily hasn't no young man," Abey Twig replied. "Louie thinks
she've aspired, in her tender 'eart, higher than the state of life
to which it has pleased God to call her. Louie thinks she be
anglin' for Mr. Barter."

The old man leaned back in his chair and surveyed Sam with
quizzical gravity.

"What they gals can say of one another to a wold relative
passes comprehension."

"What do you say to them, Mr. Twig?"

"I listens. I chucks 'em under chin. I tells 'em how pretty their
ribbings be. I waggles my head."

Sam could hear the great pot boiling on the kitchen stove and
the kettle lid rising and falling beside it.

"Well, Mr. Twig," he said, "we'd better be getting to business.
If I thought that you could hold yourself in, between your bedroom and the end of your garden, I'd say—but I don't believe
you could! Which being so, I fancy it would be wiser to use your
chamber-pot."

Poor Uncle Abel was on his feet now, his knees knocking together, his face pale.

"When . . . operation . . . be over," he stammered, "do 'ee mean that 'ee be going to leave I, alone with me burstin' backside?"

Sam hesitated. In his anticipations of this scene he had visualised every detail of the giving of the enema; but once given, he had imagined himself saying good-bye. To learn that he had to wait upon the old man's subsequent discomfort—a process which might easily take half an hour—was a shock of some magnitude. But his soul, like a stern corporal, rose up tall and metallic and commanded his body to obey orders.

"All right," he said aloud. "Don't you be afraid, Mr. Twig. I'll see you through to the bitter end."

Having uttered these words Sam picked up the cardboard box from the table and surveyed its contents.

"I shall want some hot water and some soap," he said.

The melting of the soap, the conveyance of the hot and cold water upstairs, took a few more minutes; but the wheels of time, as with people condemned to die, moved remorselessly on, and the moment arrived when Sam was following the old man upstairs to get the thing done.

As he went up behind Abel Twig he thought to himself, "It would be a much easier thing if it wasn't for the piles." These piles, as he entered the bedroom and glanced at all his careful preparations, presented themselves to his mind as a shocking obstacle.

"Those people would probably hurt you much less in the hospital," his body weakly murmured.

Poor old Abel with his teeth chattering and his braces and shirt hanging loose, turned upon his man-nurse eyes of such wild terror, eyes so much like that of a bullock before a slaughterer, that Sam hurriedly apologised for mentioning the word hospital. But his cowardly body was still trying to escape. There was a double-edged treachery in the words he uttered now.

"It's how you take the whole thing," he said, "that makes the difference. Well, I don't know what to think, Mr. Twig. It can't be good to feel—perhaps it might, after all, be better to get the doc ——"

But at the merest suggestion of that unlucky word, Mr. Twig looked as if he would willingly let Sam cut off his leg.

"Go ahead, Sir," he said. "If I hollers you must be patient wi' I. I be a dodderin' old man, nigh four-score years old. I baint as strong as I were once and they pains do make I call out. They bloody piles be a worse tribulation than any girt zisty. . . . Oh, me humpty, me humpty! But I be fearful bad. Be 'ee tender of I, Mister; be 'ee tender of I! A man's backside be a turble squeamy plëace."

Sam was not, it must be confessed, a born nurse; but he was a born naturalist and an unfastidious countryman. As he struggled with his task, bending over the old gentleman's rear, the tension of his spirit brought back with a rush the miraculous power of the vision he had seen. The two extremes of his experience, the anus of an aged man and the wavering shaft of an Absolute, piercing his own earthly body, mingled and fused together in his consciousness. Holy Sam felt, as he went on with the business, a strange second sight, an inkling, as to some incredible secret, whereby the whole massed weight of the world's tormented flesh was labouring towards some release.

As he kept pinching that rubber tube, for which Number One had been so scurvily cheated by the unworthy Mr. Stickles, there came over him a singular clairvoyance about the whole nature of the world. In the silence around him, unbroken save when the old man cried out his queer expletive: "Me humpty! Me humpty!" he seemed conscious of their two figures, cowering there beneath eternity, towards whom he felt directed, in magnetic waves, the influence of the sun, and the influence of the great mysterious ether beyond the sun! He felt as if they were surrounded, there in Backwear Hut, by hosts upon hosts of conscious personalities, some greater, some less, than themselves. A sharp pang took him when—in this extremity of clairvoyance—he realised that his living tortured Christ was now changed to something else. But whatever Sam's priggishness may have been, it was mercilessly honest, and he said to himself: "If Christ be dead, I still have seen the Grail."

The anguish he was compelled to give the old man because of the piles, made the process a delicate and difficult one. Beads of perspiration stood out on Sam's forehead before it was over. When it *was* over—and, as he had foreseen, it took more than half an hour—poor Number One was completely prostrate. Pallid and groaning, when at last Sam helped him up from his seat of purgation, he lay helplessly on his bed. It was all Sam could do to persuade him to get under the bed-clothes.

"Four-score years old I be, four-score years, come Whitsun," he groaned, "and I be a wambly carcass; not fit for a gentleman to op'rate on. I be a burden to king and country, turble weak in me stummick and turble sore in me backside."

Through the open window, there came now a shrill chattering of sparrows.

"Them birds be different nor us be," murmured Abel Twig. "Them birds can scatter, even as them do fly, and all be sweet as clover."

In his weakness and helplessness and in the physical relief he was then experiencing two or three big tears rolled down his cheeks. In some mysterious way the idea of the droppings of sparrows being so clean a thing filled Number One just then with a melting tenderness.

"I'll carry this away," said Sam, "and then I'll bring you up a glass of something hot. I suppose you're not quite equal to your pipe yet?"

"Oh, you prig! Oh, you asinine prig!" Nell's husband would have roared at this point. "Equal to it? No, not quite equal to it yet! Not quite equal! But presently perhaps——"

"I be all right without 'un for a bit, Mister," replied the old man. "I be . . . thinking . . . of me chicks and me wold cow; and how glad I'll be to see all they again, after me operation."

Sam said no more, but taking up the chamber-pot he opened the door and carried it downstairs. Stepping gingerly along the stone slabs across the little garden he emptied the thing in the privy, and carrying it back to the house rinsed it out at Number One's out-door tap. Then he went into the kitchen and surveyed the polished sauce-pan wherein the old man had prepared his Sunday stew.

It appeared to him that the contents of this capacious receptacle, judging by the steam which emerged from under its lid,
was cooked enough to provide at least a fairly savoury soup; so
he took it off the fire, and finding a strainer among Uncle Abel's
utensils he filled a small bowl with the onion-smelling liquid
and carried it upstairs.

He found Number One nearly asleep, and instead of being
pleased at the sight of this refreshment the old gentleman seemed
vexed with him for meddling with his culinary arrangements.

"Do you want me to pour this back again, then?" said Sam.
Abel Twig nodded faintly and closed his eyes.

"Me pipe and me baccy be best for I," he murmured.

Sam once more assumed the tone that Zoyland would have
howled with contempt to hear.

"A man likes his own tobacco," he said, "or I'd offer you a
pipe of my father's. This is what he smokes."

And he displayed before the eyes of the somnolent invalid a
tobacco-pouch which he had been keeping in his pocket since
he left the Vicarage.

"I be minded to have a wink o' sleep," was Abel Twig's sole
comment upon this proceeding.

To Sam's astonishment, when having descended the stairs and
having poured back the half-cooked stew into the sauce-pan he
returned to the front room of the house, he found himself confronted by a little girl in the doorway, panting and sobbing.
Floods of tears were streaming down her cheeks and her voice
was hardly audible. Sam knew who she was, though he had had
little to do with her.

"What *is* the matter . . . Nelly? You *are* Nelly, aren't you?"

It gave him a very odd feeling to say the word Nelly at this
hour and in this place.

"I . . . knows . . . who *you* . . . be!" gasped the child,
struggling for breath and wiping her wet cheeks with the back
of her hand, "You be Holy Sam!"

"I see we know each other, Nelly," he said; "but what's the
matter? Has Jackie Jones been hitting you again?"

Her tears had not yet ceased pouring down, but, at this word, her eyes flashed so fiercely that it was as if a dark lantern had suddenly been turned upon him out of a torrent of rain.

"I hit Jackie. I hit he into ditch! 'A said 'twas sport to see thik   poor . . . dog . . . stand   on . . . hind-legs . . . when that wicked . . . wicked . . . *wicked* man beat at he with . . . beat . . . at he . . ."

Her tears fell so desperately, as the image of what she had beheld came over her, that it seemed to Sam as if her thin little form would melt away before him. He had never seen a human countenance so dissolved, so literally *melted* in pitiful crying.

"Where? What? Who?" he cried. "Tell me, Nelly, tell me quick!"

"Will 'ee come and knock that wicked, wicked ——"

Again the floods of tears broke her utterance. Sam pulled the child into the house and set her down upon a chair.

"Now stop crying, Nelly, and tell me quick *where* this man is who's hurting this dog."

"Will 'ee . . . come wi' I . . . Holy Sam . . . and kill thik wicked . . . wicked . . . *wicked* ——"

"*Where* is he? *Where* is it?" cried Sam again.

And then the child explained to him, clearly enough now, through her streaming tears, that it was in that portion of the town between Paradise and the river—a district known as Beckery—that this was going on. As far as Sam could gather from what she said the owner of the dog belonged to a group of small circus people who had been running a solitary merry-go-round in one of those outlying Beckery fields that are called "brides," a name that reverts to the vanished chapel of Mary Magdalene founded by St. Bridget. The child kept referring to Beckery Mill; and Sam knew that there was a sort of common with a right of way through it near that place. Beckery Mill in fact gave him the clue; and he visualised with instantaneous vividness the spot she referred to; and this time it was quite unnecessary for his despotic soul to issue any categorical commands.

"I'll go at once, Nelly," he cried excitedly, "only listen, child! I'll only go on one condition; and it's a fair exchange! *You* stay here to look after Mr. Twig; and I'll go to Beckery.

Yes, he's ill, upstairs! I've had to put him to bed; but he's asleep now. I wouldn't go upstairs if I were you till you hear him stirring, or till you hear him calling. Do you understand, Nelly dear? He's ill in bed; but he's not *very* ill; only a *little* ill."

A few minutes later Sam was making his way with resolute haste towards the quarter of the town the child had indicated. Yes! Nelly Morgan was right. Near Beckery Mill he soon found the crowd of nondescript loiterers; and there was the dog, a little black cocker spaniel, in the midst of them! When Sam came up to the outskirts of the crowd he could catch at once by the peculiar *timbre* of these young ruffians' voices that they were still engaged in their cruel sport.

The dog was evidently beginning now to refuse to perform any further tricks and to turn on his tormentors; nor was there any sign of the circus people. They must have gone to their dinner leaving the animal to the mercy of these lads.

"Let that dog alone! What are you doing to him? Who does he belong to?"

His interference was greeted with howls of derision and mocking cries of "Holy Sam! Holy Sam!"

Some of them were throwing stones at the dog who kept running from side to side within their circle seeking refuge but finding none.

"Who does it belong to?" shouted Sam. "Where is its master?"

"He've a-gived he to I," cried one of the boys, whom Sam recognised at once as the stone-thrower of Terre Gastée, the originator of the phrase "I'd like to ———"

"He did bite he bad and 'a did give 'un to I," repeated young Chinnock, making a clutch at the dog's collar which was received with a frightened snarl.

"Tom be feared o' touching he," cried one of the other lads.

"Tom did try to pick he up," explained a third, "but 'a bit his hand. He be a nasty varmint, thik black dog, . . . he be a biting dog!"

All this while the wretched little creature, which had a coal-black glossy coat, long flapping ears, feathery legs and a clipped tail held tightly in its frantic fear against its rump, kept making desperate and insane rushes here and there. It seemed to have been hunted and harried quite beyond the stage of barking, and had grown beside itself with terror.

Sam strode forward into the middle of this circle of young demons and uttering various assuaging murmurs endeavoured to catch the black dog. Tom Chinnock who was nearly as tall as Sam barged against him with his shoulders as if in a game of football.

"His master gave 'un to I," he cried. "You ain't got no right to 'un!"

"Holy Sam! Holy Sam!" shrieked the excited crowd.

"Don't 'ee let 'un have 'un, lads," cried an evil-looking man who now appeared from the back of the circle.

"Tony Quart gave 'un to Tom Chinnock! 'Tis Tony Quart's dog. 'Tisn't your'n!"

"Holy Sam! Holy Sam!"

"Take *that*, ye biting cur!" shouted young Chinnock.

These last words were accompanied by a vicious kick. Sam threw the lad aside and pursuing the dog, till it crouched snarling on the ground, bent down and picked it up, clutching its growling form from which emanated a hot, sweet, dog-flesh odour, against his chest. Blindly the panic-stricken spaniel fixed its teeth in one of Sam's wrists as he strove to prevent its jumping down. Impeded though he was by the struggling creature whose feathery paws scraped furiously against his body as it tried to free itself, Sam managed to fling Tom Chinnock back when he tried to drag the dog away. But the lad came at him again, and this time in such a fury that he hit Sam a nasty blow on the chin.

Sam's right hand, which was quite free at that minute, instinctively clenched itself to strike back; and he was within an ace of giving the boy a blow that would have bowled him over. But that portion of his consciousness which had come to feel to him like an "external soul" issued, in a flash, one of its most imperative mandates.

"Don't be a bloody fool!" he said sternly, dropping his arm.

Chinnock gave him one glance of wide-eyed wonder and cringed away.

"Hit 'un with stones!" he shouted as soon as he was safe back amongst the rest. "Hit 'un with stones! Stones 'ull make he give up thik dog! Did yer see the girt clip I give 'un?"

His advice was seconded by the grown man in the rear of the boys; but having encouraged them to go on with the fray, this individual now began to shog off, evidently feeling that Sam was a ticklish customer and that there are moments in life when the satisfaction of cruelty must yield to the dictates of prudence.

Sam looked about him, his mind moving sluggishly as he hugged the black dog against his stomach. He was surrounded now by a half-circle of stone-throwers.

"It's silly to stay here and make an Aunt Sally of myself," he thought. "The best thing I can do is to break through them and clear off."

He had scarcely formulated this thought when a stone hit the spaniel in his arms, causing it to utter a shrill yelp of pain. This decided him and he made a fierce rush forward, heading straight for young Chinnock. Although so energetic a collector of sharp stones, the nephew of Mad Bet had not been endowed by Providence with the gift of fortitude. At the sight of Sam clutching the growling dog against his ribs and running straight towards him, he took ignominiously to his heels.

"You know where to find me," shouted Sam after him.

The flight of Tom Chinnock quelled the belligerency of the whole crowd and not a single stone was thrown after Sam and his struggling captive.

Now Beckery Mill lies on the outskirts of a certain municipal enclosure known as Wirral Park which borders on the lower slope of Wirral Hill. Sam sank exhausted upon the first public seat he came to in Wirral Park. Placing the black spaniel on the ground but retaining his hold upon it, he began searching his pockets for his handkerchief, till he remembered that he had left it in Number One's bedroom. After a second's hesitation he then took off his necktie, and using this as an extemporary leash he tied it to the dog's collar.

By some curious psychological process no sooner was the dog secured by Sam's tie than it accepted Sam as the liege-lord of its destiny; *and* in quite a symbolic manner, like a feudal servant of some cruel baron transferring his allegiance to a cockle-shell pilgrim, he rose up on his hind legs and licked Sam's bleeding wrist. Having tasted his new master's blood, so desperately shed by himself, nothing could exceed the animal's intense contentment.

He stretched himself out on the ground at Sam's feet, not lying as most dogs do, but with his feathery legs stretched straight out behind him.

Sam had not been long seated on his bench, when a tremulously vibrant feeling, that could only be described as a shiver of exultant ecstasy, flowed through him. "I have seen it! I have seen it!" the heart within him cried; and in a vague, delicious, dreamy reverie he became aware of an important psychic change in his inmost self-consciousness. This change was nothing less than a coming together of his body and soul. Although his soul still felt independent of his body, and free of his body, it no longer felt contemptuous of his body. It had ceased to utter its mandates in the tone of a slave-driver. Its mere presence within his body at this moment seemed to make Sam's flesh feel porous and transparent, as if large, cool, undulating waves were sweeping through it.

Presently, towards the seat where he rested, came a solitary girlish figure; which, as it approached him, assumed the unmistakable form of Miss Angela Beere. What this strange girl was doing in that place, on the edge of Wirral Park, at half-past two on Sunday afternoon, Sam was not inquisitive enough to ask her; but it was clear that even Angela's virginal placidity was a little startled and ruffled by seeing a dishevelled man rise up from the side of a black dog, a dog whom he held fast by means of a bright blue necktie!

"What a beautiful little dog!" was however this imperturbable young lady's greeting, as if it were the most natural thing in the world to encounter the son of Mat Dekker between Wirral Hill and Beckery Mill on a quiet Sunday. "Oh, what a darling little spaniel!"

Sam felt so abysmally happy at that moment that in his confused rapture he raised the small gloved fingers she held out to him to his lips and made way for her to sit down by his side.

The little black dog who had already shown signs of intense nervousness at the approach of this composed figure in her costume of fastidious delicacy, and had even uttered three short barks, became panic-striken at this. He tugged frantically at the blue tie, lowering his belly almost to the ground and extending his four feathery paws in a wide-straddled flurry of panic. Finding that the blue tie did not yield, and hearing from the tone of the human invader that she was not at present ill-using his new master or belabouring him with sticks and stones, the dog rose to a natural standing position and remained there stationary. But, although his body was motionless, his short tail pressed down in quivering terror over the round black rump, uttered the words, as clear as language could utter them: "Nothing, I say *nothing* could persuade me to look round at the terrifying transactions that are now taking place behind me."

"I'm *so* glad I've met you," Angela Beere observed, rubbing nonchalantly at a tiny red stain that had appeared on her white glove, and glancing coyly round at the stiff back of the little dog, "for I wanted to ask you whether Mrs. Zoyland would like me to call upon her at the Vicarage. Do you think she would? I keep hearing"—here her pale lips displayed her white teeth in a proud smile—"*such* silly gossip about you all! But Father always says, 'Believe *nothing* that you hear, and only *half* of what you see!'"

Sam turned his face full upon her. "If I," he said, "believed only half of what *I've* just seen, I'd be the happiest person ever born in Glastonbury!"

The girl's arched eyebrows lifted a little upon her smooth white forehead.

"Did what you saw hurt your wrist?" she said; and then, in a really charming access of compunction, that brought a rose-petal flush to her white cheeks, "Let me tie it up for you, Mr. Dekker!"

She produced a little lace-edged handkerchief; and as she bandaged his hurt, the softening influence of medical tenderness that had made Number One weep to think of the innocuousness of sparrow dung, brought tears to Sam's eyes.

"Will he let me pat him, do you think?" she said, and leaning across Sam's knees she gave a jerk at the straining blue tie. This movement had the result of causing the dog to sink down

instantly on his belly, straddle his legs wide apart to gain the
necessary purchase, and then tug at his leash with the energy
of a frightened alligator.

"All right—don't 'ee mind!" cried Sam to his new pet.

But the girl drew back with flushed cheeks, evidently a little
hurt.

"Don't *you* mind!" he repeated, turning from the dog, who
now stood erect, although still shivering with terror, to his disappointed companion, "he's a rather nervous little beast."

"*Rather* nervous!" laughed Angela Beere. "He's like I'd feel
if I came to see your Nell and she didn't want to see me!"

This "your Nell" ought to have given the stupid Sam an inkling as to how he was regarded by the richer gossips of the town.
He very clearly was anything but Holy Sam in the upper circles
of Glastonbury! But he answered guilelessly:

"Nell would be overjoyed to see you, I *know*."

"You'd better go home, Mr. Dekker," she said, "and get that
Penny of yours to attend to your wrist."

But when he took not the slightest notice of this, "What,"
she enquired, "did you say just now that you saw?"

The man was far too happy to be squeamish about telling
her everything. He would have liked to have stopped every soul
in the streets of the town and told them everything. He was in
the mood to shout everything to everyone from the top of the
Tor.

"But how *can* you go on saying, Mr. Dekker," protested Angela
after an interval of silence, when he had talked about it to her
for nearly a quarter of an hour, "as you did just now, that
there's no God, and no life after death, and no Personal Christ.
You *couldn't* have seen the Grail if there wasn't a God; certainly
not if there wasn't a Christ. Come now, Mr. Dekker! You *know*
you couldn't! I'm afraid it's a man's pride in you that makes
you talk like this."

"Listen, Angela Beere! Until a few months ago, though I didn't
believe in God or in Immortality, I believed in Christ. I believed
in Him as the tortured Enemy of God, as the friend of all the
oppressed in the world! And I *still* believe in Him—but not in

the same way—do you understand? No! I suppose you don't!—
not in the same way, but far *more* than before!"

He stopped and stared at her; and there was a wild light in
his little, greenish-coloured, animal eyes that made the calm young
lady say to herself: "I must talk to Dr. Fell about him. I believe
he's had some terrible mental shock."

"Do you think, Angela Beere," he went on, while the muscles
of his chin worked frantically, and without knowing what he did
he tugged so hard at the blue tie that he made the dog rear up
like a rearing horse, "do you think a person could give up the
sweetest happiness in his life—not just *one* great thing, but *the*
thing, the *only* thing, if he weren't drawn on by some Reality?"

"You poor darling!" thought Angela to herself. "Don't you
know that people have been driven on by the *Unreal*—by lies,
and illusions, and fables, and pure madness—to the point of
killing the only thing they've ever loved!"

"I can see you think I've gone dotty, my dear," he added with
an indulgent smile, laying his bare hand on her gloved ones as
they lay clasped in her lap. "And I've no doubt you and your
friends think I've been a devil incarnate to leave Nell. Well,
never mind that! What I'd like to know, if you wouldn't mind
telling me—for I know what a friend you are of Percy's and
that——"

His voice broke when he marked the flood of colour that rushed
to Angela's pale cheeks. Never had Sam beheld such a scarlet
blush. It literally flooded her under her black hat. It flowed
down her white neck. Her very ears seemed to yield themselves
to it. Up went both her gloved hands to her face and the fact
that she had to make this gesture increased her shyness. She
looked to Sam as if she might be going to rise from the bench
and run away.

"I didn't mean——" stammered Sam.

The girl struggled with herself and dropped her hands, staring at him with round blue eyes, while her underlip quivered.
Slowly her colour receded, and her face became paler even than
its wont.

"You seem to know all about us—about our friendship—
Mr. Dekker, or you wouldn't ask me. So . . . so I may as well

. . . *tell* you. All Glastonbury will know in a day or two. . . . Yes, I've heard from her. I haven't seen her . . . but I've heard from her. *She's gone to Russia!*"

Sam was flabbergasted. He knew so little of the great world outside Glastonbury that there sounded to him a shock of startling finality in this. It was a second before he realised the import of this news in his own life. Zoyland was alone again then!

He looked at the girl by his side. Angela was searching in the same little handbag from which had come the handkerchief that now bound his wrist. She brought out a letter in an envelope now, and snapping the clasp of her bag with an impatient jerk, threw the letter upon Sam's knee.

"You can read what she says if you like!" she cried.

There was a French stamp upon the envelope and Sam commented upon this.

"Read it! Read it!" she murmured.

The letter was certainly not difficult to read. Written in Persephone's bold boy-like hand it was brief and to the point.

"Darling Angel," it ran, "long before you get this I shall be in Paris, waiting to catch the express to Warsaw, en route for Russia. I couldn't stand it a day longer. I couldn't stand *anything* in our damned country. I must have a complete change or kill myself. I've gone back to politics, my dear, now that I've found love a fizzle. I believe Russia will suit me to a T. When I'm settled I may send for you to join me! if you like me still, that's to say! Tell Mr. Beere that the meals on French trains are adorable. Don't be cross now, for it *had* to be . . . your hopeless Percy."

Sam handed the letter back to her while the words "He's alone at Whitelake again," formed themselves in his mind.

"I'm sorry you've lost your friend, Miss Beere," he said gravely. "But, as she says, perhaps one day you'll go too—to Russia."

He uttered these last words as if they referred to some region so remote—as indeed they did—from his present world, that it was as if he'd said: "To the Isles of the Blest."

The girl lowered her fair head, in its black hat, over her handbag and replaced the letter with slow deliberation. She seemed

to be pondering deeply; for she remained motionless for a minute, her fingers on the envelope within the little silk-lined receptacle. Then she rose slowly to her feet and shook the front of
her skirt and passed her fingers quickly over the back of it.

"Well," she said, holding out her hand with a smile, "I've got
to prepare my school lesson now, so I won't ask you which way
you're going. But if I were you, Mr. Dekker, I'd go and see your
Penny at once about your wrist!"

Two hours later, in fact just as St. John's clock was chiming
half-past four, Sam left his loft chamber, with the black dog
comfortably asleep under his camp-bed, and sallied forth into
the street. His face was washed and clean. His step was light.
Angela's handkerchief was still round his wrist just as she had
tied it. He came out that afternoon impatient to tell all the
world what he had seen.

"I'll go to Nell and Father tonight," he thought, "but not till
after the evening service."

He was so dazed with his new happiness that he gave no
heed at all to the direction in which he was walking. He moved
along like a somnambulist. Now and again he talked to himself
in low mutterings. For normal persons to talk to themselves is
either a sign of great happiness or of great unhappiness or a
sign that they know themselves to be surrounded by absolute
physical loneliness.

"Is it a Tench?" he kept muttering quite audibly. What he
was always reverting to in his thoughts was the necessity he was
under to tell everybody in Glastonbury that he had seen the
Grail; and several times he stopped various errand boys and
tradesmen's wives, whom he knew by sight, and began to tell
them, or began to gather himself up to tell them, but by some
queer psychological law they seemed inevitably to slip away
from him before he had forced them to listen to him. He came by
degrees to have that queer sensation that we have sometimes in
dreams, that everything we touch eludes us and slides away. He
even got the feeling that the pavements were soft under his feet
and that the people he passed were like ghosts who moved *without moving their legs.*

At last he found himself walking in the immediate rear of ex-

Mayor Wollop whose corporeality did seem to strike him as more emphatic, and Sam, hurrying to overtake him, entered into conversation as they walked side by side. It seemed much easier to tell Mr. Wollop about his Vision than in these other cases. This was no doubt due to the fact that it was something *seen*; and not something felt, or thought, or imagined, or supposed, that Sam had to relate.

The great haberdasher took him in tow at once, even going so far as to rest two of his plump fingers upon the visionary's arm. Sam's heart so warmed to the man's kind tone that as he talked to him he felt for the second time that day the sensation of tears mounting to his eyes.

Mr. Wollop told him that it was his father's birthday and that in honour of this anniversary he was on his way to take tea with Mrs. Legge.

"You know the house," he said, "it is called Camelot," and he invited Sam to follow him to this auspicious domicile.

"She'll be overjoyed to see you, Sir," he asseverated again and again. "Overjoyed she'll be! And there'll be nobody there but we two. 'Three's company', you know, Sir, 'and two's immorality,' as my old Dad used to say. She'll be ravaged with what you saw, Sir, . . . just as I am . . . ravaged."

By degrees, under the redoubtable companionship of the friendly draper, Sam's wits began to grow a little less ensorcerised, and by the time they reached the aged procuress' house his pulses were beating to a rhythm that was nearly normal.

Behold him now, therefore, this girl-betrayer and child-deserter, this—to quote Zoyland's subsequent comments upon Sam's behaviour—"this double-dyed idiot and arch-prig," seated at Mother Legge's mahogany table, under the staring eyes of the smug Recorders, drinking tea—with a touch of Bridgewater punch super-added—and eating buttered scones! He was ravenously hungry; for the black spaniel, refusing to touch the only raw meat he could procure for it, had swallowed with gusto every scrap of bread and treacle he had prepared for himself.

And as he ate and drank, and as the strong and delicately doctored tea warmed his blood, his tongue became unloosened as it had rarely been unloosened in his life before. The rapturous happiness that thrilled him was not, at least not all of it, directly due to his sight of the Holy Grail. It was undoubtedly partly due —but this itself was an indirect result of the vision—to some new adjustment of his soul and his body. For his soul was no longer an "external" soul! Yes! It no longer stood apart, by the side of his flesh, issuing categorical mandates; and indeed he felt now as if Mother Legge's very tea—Bridgewater punch and all —was nourishing both his soul and his body.

As his words flowed on—describing every detail of his great experience—he was surprised to find himself using words and phrases that he had made use of on that occasion on the top of the Tor, when he had defended the Incarnation against the Manichæan doctrines of Mr. Evans. He could even feel under his fingers the grass roots that he had plucked up that morning, nearly a year ago, in that sudden outburst of inspiration. His conception of the thing was very different now—for his Personal Christ had vanished—but with that curious pride in consistency that even "holy men" feel, he began glossing over this difference; as if a gardener, when a viola cornutus came up, where he had planted pansies, were to insist, "It is the same"; and use his ancient rigmarole on the beauty of pansies for this totally new growth!

But there may have entered into his eloquence at this point some slight stammering and hesitation which gave the aged procuress her cue.

"What worrits a simple old bitch like me," protested Mother Legge, "is how an atheist, like you say you are, Holy Sam, could see the Blood o' the Blessed One, when there ain't, and never 'as been, no Blessed One to bleed!"

Mr. Wollop glanced cautiously round the big apartment and looked with some nervousness at the heavy black curtains.

"What a man do see," he remarked sententiously, "be one thing. What a man do *think* he sees be another. But what a man do say he sees be a proper knock-out! The mistress 'ere 'ave seed me poor old Dad—rest his merry soul!—raised up and a-wisiting 'er for no good purpose in 'er beauty sleep. But that don't mean that the old gent really comes out from's grave; do it, Marm?"

He kept his eyes on those black curtains of the late Kitty

Camel's reception-room, as if he greatly preferred that the elder Mr. Wollop should remain quiescent where he had been laid in the Wells Road graveyard.

"Were it like my silver bowl when 'ee seed it, Holy Sam?" enquired the old lady, settling her portentous frame more comfortably in her tall straight-backed chair and raising her tea-cup to her lips.

Sam's little green eyes shone radiantly. "It wasn't like anything on earth," he cried. "And the moment I saw it I knew what it was. Everything will be different from now on, with the Grail come back to Glastonbury! It was a pure accident that I was the one who saw it first; but I'm going all round town today, telling everybody about it; and I expect hundreds of people will see it. I expect even the visitors will see it."

"Will that 'andsome young man in me shop what I 'as such trouble with; the one what reads Neetsky to 'arden 'is 'eart when he gets the gals into trouble, see the 'Oly Grail?"

It would be difficult to believe that Mr. Wollop was not being facetious, unless you were seated opposite him and saw the guileless stare in his round eyes. The old procuress was much less guileless. Indeed she was positively clairvoyant in the subtle penetration of her next question.

"Have the Vision what you've been privileged with, Holy Sam, made 'ee forget they torments what the Saviour did bear for we pore sinners?"

This question of the aged woman—and it may well be that in the course of her long life as the purveyor of the sweets of sin she had acquired a diabolical insight—did assuredly hit Sam between the joints of his armour. But the cresting wave of excitement on which he rode was so great that he answered without a second's hesitation.

"If you, or our friend here," he said, "had gone through unspeakable pains for anyone you loved, and these pains had been turned into heavenly wine and heavenly bread, wouldn't you feel it ungrateful in that person not to take and eat, not to take and drink and be filled with gratitude to you?"

It was natural enough, when Sam left the hospitable domain of Mother Legge, that he should find himself inevitably drifting towards the Vicarage. But he restrained himself from entering; and, in place of that, went on a sudden impulse up the drive of the Abbey House. It can be imagined what a shock it was to him when, having rung at the front door, he was informed by Lily that Miss Drew was "not at home."

"But—Lily, my good girl! Where *is* she, if she *isn't* at home? She's *always* at home on Sunday afternoons! She's been at home on Sunday afternoons, reading the *Guardian* before tea and looking at the *Illustrated London News* after tea, from days before you and I were born! Come now, Lily, what is it? What's up? Is she sick? Is she lying down? I've got something to tell her—something very important—something that would interest you and Louie too!"

Pestered in this way by a gentleman she had familiarly known as "Mr. Sam" since the days when she wore even shorter frocks than were the present fashion, Lily broke down, and with tears in her eyes confessed the sorrowful truth; the truth namely that Miss Drew had decided in the interests of public virtue never to have him in her home again.

"She's been to see Mr. Dekker too," Lily went on, after a glance over her shoulder to make certain that the drawing-room door was closed, "and Mr. Weatherwax says he heard her, through the study window, storming at your Dad, Mr. Sam, like she was St. Dunstan scolding Satan. Mr. Weatherwax says he heard her tell your Dad that she'd write to the Lord Bishop, in his Palace at Wells, and tell him that Glastonbury Vicarage were become an Asylum for Fallen Women."

Sam hardly listened to the latter part of this revelation. He was thinking to himself: "Such news as I've got for the people of Glastonbury oughtn't to be confined to masters and mistresses. Lily is a good girl, a romantic girl, and she'll be thrilled to hear my news. I've always thought there was a dreamy expression in her eyes that showed she was ——"

"I've had a great experience, Lily," he began, "and that was what I came to talk to Miss Drew about. It was yesterday it happened. I may as well tell *you* if Miss Drew won't see me. I was down by the river, Lily, and I saw distinctly ——"

But Lily interrupted him.

"Another time, Mr. Sam, another time, if you *please*! I'm sure you saw something very nice—but I've *got* to shut the door now. Louie wants to go to the Methodist Chapel tonight and she's going to dress now and I've got to lay the supper. Missus have asked Miss Crummie to supper—so *please* excuse me."

She gave him one of her most dim, beguiling, and tender smiles; a smile that seemed to say, "Life is more full of romance than a simple gentleman like you can possibly know! Even Louie, when she goes to the Methodist Chapel with Bob Tankerville ——" but at this point she firmly closed the door.

Although Sam was quite in the dark about Miss Drew's new interest in Crummie, the truth was that as Mary slipped away from her, the lonely woman had begun to find not a little consolation in the spell that the beauty of Mr. Geard's daughter had already cast over her. Sam couldn't help smiling as he mentally envisaged the beautiful Crummie seated opposite her entertainer and listening sweetly to her well-chosen words across the silver candlesticks; but this piece of news set him off in Crummie's direction.

"I'll be with Nell and Father tonight," he thought, "but I'll go to the Geards' now. I'll catch her easily before she starts, if I hurry up."

He retraced his steps down Silver Street and soon reached the High Street near St. John's Church. A small group of people were just coming out from an afternoon's christening, and the first person Sam encountered was Mrs. Philip Crow, who, under the advice of Emma, who assured her that "Mr. Dekker be more 'isself when he be preaching to godfathers and godmothers than when 'tis the common crowd," had attended this brief and pleasant service.

Tilly shook hands with him cordially; for the gossip retailed by Emma was of a much more detailed and much more authentic kind than that conveyed to Miss Drew's ears by Mr. Weatherwax; and it excited Tilly's particular type of sympathy to think of this quiet young man living by himself in the Old Malt House.

"He's made a mistake and he's sorry for it," she thought, and vaguely in her mind she dreamed that it would be nice one day if she and Emma could clean up that top floor for this well-meaning youth who had no wife and no servant.

"You must have heard good news, Mr. Dekker," Tilly said, "for your eyes are shining. They shone like that when you were a boy and Philip and I were giving our first party at The Elms. I recall it clearly, because it was when Emma had just come to us, and I thought she did so well when the dog we had then—we've never had a dog since, Mr. Dekker; but I was weak then and silly about Philip, and Philip was fond of dogs and what was I saying?—made a sad mess in the dining-room."

"Mrs. Crow," said Sam, staring at the lavender fringe of the book-marker which dangled from the large prayer book she carried, and then letting his gaze move to their two shadows, which the declining sun caused to extend clean across the street and which resembled a child's drawing of two fantastic dolls, "Mrs. Crow, I have something to tell you that will interest you."

"Oh dear!" she cried, "don't look so wild! And don't tell *me* any of your secrets. I've never said one word to anyone about you and Mrs. Zoyland, and I'd rather not hear anything."

There came over Sam just then a desire to laugh aloud. That no one in this town could be brought even to listen to what he had seen seemed like a crazy dream. He felt as if he were living in two worlds at the same time, and one of them, by far the less real and by far the more absurd, was trying to convince him that the other was a fantasy.

"Mrs. Crow," he repeated with a certain irritation in his voice, "what has happened to me has nothing to do with Mrs. Zoyland. It's a vision—yes! it's the *great* vision we've *all* been waiting for! I've . . . seen . . . the Holy Grail . . . Mrs. Crow."

Sam felt so light-headed just then that he longed to laugh, or cry, or shout. It would have seemed perfectly natural to him if Tilly Crow had fallen on her knees, there and then, upon the pavement, and offered thanks to God. But the little lady only gave vent to a deep sigh.

"Emma always said," she remarked, looking at him with grave concern, "that if *that woman* didn't manage better for you and your dear father there would be no telling ——"

She had said enough. Sam quickly saw that she regarded him as a well-meaning victim of protracted undernourishment. He lifted his hat to take his leave; and as he did so his chin twitched a little and there was a pucker on his brow. His eyes began to roam up and down the street as if he sought for someone whose shadow was less doll-like than Tilly's.

Tilly saw that she had hurt his feelings in some way and she held out her hand to him. When he took it she detained him, as she often detained Philip when she had misunderstood him.

"I'm sure with so good a father," she murmured hurriedly, "you could see anything, even angels, Mr. Dekker," and when Sam smiled at this, she added eagerly, giving to him of her best, "Your floors up there are all oak, aren't they? Aunt Tappity, you know, who was Euphemia Drew's great-aunt, used to have them beeswaxed. Euphemia never likes to talk of that branch of our family, because of the malt business. But we all have a drop of bad blood somewhere, haven't we? But Euphemia can remember sliding on those floors when she was little, so slippery they were!"

When Sam had left her and was wandering down the High Street he felt his spirits a little dashed. "I thought," he said to himself, "that they'd all cry: 'It's impossible! It's too good to be true!' Instead of which they seemed ready to accept it as perfectly true, but in some way—unimportant!"

He had not got very far down High Street, for it was in his mind to reach Street Road, where Cardiff Villa was, by way of Magdalene Street, when he overtook old Bartholomew Jones shuffling slowly along with the aid of a stick. In spite of its being Sunday, Number Two was all agog to attend to something in his shop, probably to attend to his accounts, for he was a great miser, and the financial problems of his partnership with Mr. Evans seemed, sometimes, well-nigh insoluble.

The old man greeted Sam with effusiveness. He had known him from his childhood, and Sam had sold to him many of his Cambridge books. He now took the opportunity of informing Number Two of the feeble state in which he had left Number One that morning.

"I've a-allus told he," said Mr. Jones, "that the 'orspital was the place for we old folk when our innards turn foul on us. Look at my girt zisty! If it weren't for that clever head-doctor, who studied me case with all them European engines, where would I be now? Abe Twig, he be a fool when it comes to taking care of 'isself. He do say trust nature; whereas I do say, 'tis nature what did the damage. Us must go farther afield for the cure of thik damage. Us must go to Science."

While he was thus speaking, Mr. Jones was staring in sorrowful wonder at his interlocutor's bound-up wrist.

"Seems to me, Sir," he remarked, "*you'd* do no harm to go to 'orspital, your own self. That wrist o' your'n be bleedin' into bandage."

Sam instinctively touched Angela's handkerchief with the tip of one of his fingers.

"I'm too excited today to think of hospitals, Mr. Jones," he said. "Do you know what's happened to me, my friend?"

He lowered his voice to an intense and concentrated whisper.

"You ain't gone and murdered Mr. Zoyland, have 'ee?" cried Number Two, retreating a pace or so from the proximity of this excited adulterer.

"No, no, my good man, Mr. Zoyland and I have never even had a fight and certainly are not likely to now."

As Sam spoke, the thought came into his head—"Alone at Whitelake; alone at Whitelake——"

But Mr. Jones looked up the street and down the street. Then he remarked: "I've still got that grand edition of Saint Augustine. I suppose you don't feel inclined to ——"

But Sam interrupted him. "Do you know what my fellow-workers call me these days, Mr. Jones?"

"A darned ninny!" was what leapt up in Number Two's mind; but he responded soothingly, as if addressing a candidate for the county asylum: "I've a-heered, Sir, that down in Paradise they name 'ee Holy Sam."

Sam nodded his head, and then began working the muscles of his chin so violently that the old man longed, as he afterwards explained to Mr. Evans, "to catch hold of that monkey-face and quiet 'un."

"I want to tell everyone in the town," cried Sam, "what has

happened. For the most important thing has happened that *could* happen; *and I have seen it.*"

The tone in which he said this and the gleaming light in his eyes alarmed Mr. Jones but it occurred to him that it was just in states of mind of this kind that young gentlemen were liable to buy expensive theological books.

"It's the best Saint Augustine on the market," he said.

"I saw Eternity this morning," remarked Sam. Whether in the long history of Glastonbury, anyone had uttered these simple words before, no one knows, but if anyone *had* done so, the chances are that the remark was received in the same manner then as now.

"It's a Baskerville edition," insisted Bartholomew Jones.

Sam bade him good afternoon, and strode off quicker than the old man could follow. He had fully expected to be ridiculed or scoffed at for his revelation; but it had never entered his head that his great difficulty would be to arouse any interest in it. He began to wonder if he were, after all, the only person who had seen the Grail since the ancient days. Perhaps the Grail had appeared to a great many people and not one of these people had been able to persuade anyone even to attend to what they had to say about it! Perhaps life in Glastonbury was full of such miracles; and yet those who reported them always found their excitement falling on deaf ears.

He soon reached the curiosity shop itself. At the door he met Red Robinson, who was about to attend a meeting of the Comrades in their old meeting-place at the top of the house. Mr. Robinson looked a good deal sprucer and more neatly dressed than when he had accosted Sam last Spring at the gate of St. John's churchyard. He had a white collar on now; but he still wore the same old, brown cloth cap, pulled down rather rakishly over his forehead and tilted a little to one side. This cap, whatever else he wore, brought into the Glastonbury High Street an indescribable air of Whitechapel and the Old Kent Road.

It came over Sam with a rush of emotion how it had been Robinson's speech, reporting Crummie's words, that had started him upon this whole new psychic pilgrimage.

" 'Ee 'as the fice of a sightn," had been the man's rendering of Crummie's fatal sentence; and it all came back to Sam now, together with Nell's words across the empty tomb of St. Joseph, breaking the news of her return to Zoyland's bed.

"Hullo, Robinson! Are you speaking up there tonight?" said Sam with the affable though rather forced geniality of the parson's son addressing a working-man.

Red gave him a furtive, challenging look, and yet a quizzical look—the sort of look that a terrier caught in the mouth of a rabbit hole would give a setter, as it passed gravely by, on the trail of a covey of partridges.

"We'll be doing something better than speak soon," retorted the man. "There'll be a fine stir in Glastonbury soon—and *some* that I knows on—some bewgers what doesn't know what's coming to 'em will 'ave to tike notice!'"

"I hear that you and young Trent and Mr. Spear have been appointed our new aldermen," said Sam politely.

"Aldermen, do yer call it?" snorted Red contemptuously. "We'll be more than aldermen shortly, Mister; just as Bloody Johnny's more than a Mayor to-die!'"

"Yes, I've heard something about this," said Sam. "It's a kind of independent Commune, they tell me, that you're setting up. Well, I wish you good luck, Robinson! I've nothing against any arrangement that brings more meat into the larders of our poor people."

But in his inevitable desire to take exception to anything that a Vicar's son might say, Red now veered round.

"But it's a bleedin' farce, hall the sime! That's what I'm going to tell 'em in a minute. Commune? 'Ell! This 'ere stunt 'as its pint, in miking some bewgers we know cough up a bit, but there'll be no Commune in this 'ere bleedin' 'ole till we've got 'old of the bank and the rileway."

"Well," repeated Sam, "I'm for you, Robinson. But I wish you could persuade some of the labouring men of this town to be a little less savage when a person works along side of them."

Red eyed him with malevolent glee.

"So yer finds it haint all 'unny, does yer, doing the jobs you blighters have put on us for hall these years? You're beginning to know, are yer, what it tighsts like to eat 'umble pie?"

"But if the working-man has been ill-used, as no doubt he has, why should he take it out on those who wish him well?"

"Tike it out, do yer sigh?" cried Red Robinson indignantly. "That's just like you virtuous gentlemen. What's got on our nerves is that very sime tone of yours. It's your why of tiking things! Is a man a foot-stool, Mister? Is a man a piece of bleedin' junk, that a bloke should sigh to you: ' 'ow kind yer are, Mr. Dekker, Hesquire' "—Red's whole frame quivered with sarcasm —" ' 'ow kind yer are to work side by side with us and to use yer own fine 'ands along of us!' "

He paused for a second and then spoke with such a rush of formidable emotion that Sam, with all his preoccupied excitement, was considerably impressed.

"Don't yer see . . . will you hupper-classes *never* see . . . that you've been just sitting, 'eavy and sife, on the top of us workers? When a man's been lying on 'is fice, hunder the harse of a great bewger all 'is life long, 'tisn't heasy when he's thrown the bewger off to talk sweet to 'im. 'Tisn't heasy to sigh, 'Poor rich man, did I 'urt yer when I threw yer bleedin' harse off of my fice?' "

Sam was silent. For the first time that day he felt that he couldn't bring himself to speak of his Vision. And yet what a thing that he couldn't. Had human beings maltreated one another to such a tune that it was a sort of mockery even to mention that the Holy Grail had come back to earth?

Without breathing a word of what he had seen to this man, he could hear him say: "It's because you've 'ad your leisure from our sweat that you've got any spunk left to fuss with the 'Oly Grile. We be too dog-gone done-in of a Sunday morning to do anything but sleep in our bleedin' beds!"

Thus it happened that in spite of his having declared to Mother Legge and Mr. Wollop that he was going to tell everyone he met, he found, when he went on down Magdalene Street, along the southern wall of the Abbey meadow, that not only had he *not* told Robinson, but that when he met Harry Stickles, the chemist, bustling home to his tea and his beautiful Nancy, he made no attempt, although he had bought his Windsor soap of him a day

or two ago, to interrupt a busy citizen of his kidney, with news
of such a bagatelle!

While Sam was approaching the turn to Street Road, Crummie, left quite alone in Cardiff Villa to prepare for her supper
with Miss Drew, for the Mayor and the Mayoress had gone for
the evening to the city of Wells, was sitting, as she often was
these days, by herself in her childhood's bedroom, where all
the pictures on the wall, the little childish sketch entitled "Crummie by Crummie," and the eloquent, if not artistic, Series of the
Seasons, jabbered and gibbered at her, languished and lisped at
her, with memories of the married Cordelia.

As usual the younger daughter of Geard of Glastonbury sat
on the edge of her maiden bed admiring her legs. If it had not
been that Crummie's heart, independently of her legs altogether,
had fallen in love with Sam, the chances are that from sheer
good-nature she would long ago have married one of her innumerable admirers in the town. But if the truth about the girl
must be told, Crummie, in reality, was not attracted to men. This
is a paradox which poor Cordelia—who *was* strongly attracted
to men and was now living a life of intoxicated eroticism with
Mr. Evans—would have laughed at, considering how the sight of
Crummie's admirers had troubled her. But such was the exact
truth! What Crummie was attracted to, was not her men—their
personalities, their looks, their ways—but the reflection of herself, and particularly of her incomparable legs, in the mirror of
her men's eyes.

It is the greatest mistake in the world to assume that the sort
of narcissism in which Crummie indulged was selfish or ungen-
erous. It is true she derived an exquisite and indescribably voluptuous pleasure from admiring herself, from caressing herself,
as she was doing at this moment; but it was a pleasure she longed
to share with as many people as possible—women quite as much
as men! Nor was she fastidious. Naturally not, considering that
what primarily stirred her was not these alien personalities in
their intrinsic qualities but the degree of their excitement in the
presence of her own charms.

On the other hand the girl was so essentially humble and so
free from malice or spitefulness, that a very small measure of

this excitement was enough to satisfy her. But in Sam's case everything was different. Her feeling for Sam was a most delicate, vibrant and totally self-forgetful feeling. Nor would she have
been at all anxious for Sam to enter at this moment and see
her beautiful bare legs. Sam was the only person in the world
before whom Crummie was bashful, shamefaced, super-modest.
She would have felt like sinking into the ground with shame—
that is how she would have expressed it to herself—if Sam had
burst in now and beheld the satiny whiteness of her limbs; soft
and tantalising and of maddening loveliness. What she wanted
Sam to admire in her was her intellect, her searching intelligence,
her ideal sentiment, her religious soul; and the pathetic thing
was that Providence had not only refrained from endowing
Crummie with these gifts but had not even given her a limited
success in the art of pretending to possess them.

Crummie's unique gift from Nature, the most exquisite thighs
that had been seen in Glastonbury since those of Merlin's perfidi-
ous Nineue, and which to herself, in her orgies of narcissism,
were so pleasure-yielding, were, as far as Sam was concerned,
something almost to be ashamed of. She would have preferred
to appear before Sam in a heavy nun's garment descending to
the ground and with her fair hair covered up by a black hood.
How could she have possibly known that it *was* Sam before
whom she was now destined to appear, when, hearing the door-
bell ring, she hurriedly put on her skirt, wrapt herself in an
old woolen dressing-gown, and with her fair hair loose and her
bare feet in little tattered slippers ran downstairs.

Her feelings when she saw him standing there were so overwhelming that for a second she swayed in the doorway and
nearly fainted away. Had she done so it would have been precisely in the manner of those tender impossible heroines in the
only works of art she had ever honestly enjoyed! What she felt
was something that no consecutive human language, trying to
convey a clear-edged impression, could possibly express. Sam's
figure suddenly appearing before her at her own doorstep evoked
that bewildering, staggering sense of the very nature of things
shifting, altering, transforming, which the Magdalene must have

had when the apparent gardener at the Arimathean tomb murmured the magic word "Mary!"

It was not so much a living man she saw, as her whole secret
life, all the gathered up and accumulated longings, reserves,
broodings, dreams of the last twelve months. He was not a thing
of palpable outline at all, of definite contour or of solid substance. He was a cloud of filmy essences, vague yearnings, precious dreams, dear hopes, wild idolatries. It was a shivering anguish as well as a wild ecstasy to see him embodied there, in an
ordinary human form, familiar and natural.

So un-selfconscious did this adorer of her own sweet flesh
become in her rapture of seeing him, hearing him, touching him,
that when she had taken his coat and hat and brought him into
the musty drawing-room and put him in her father's chair with
the bear rug at his feet, she sank down before the fire without a
thought of stirring its dying embers, or of lighting more than
one solitary candle with a spill thrust deep into those flickering
coals. Across her bare feet, before she realised the necessity of
hiding them under her robe, fluttered the rosy fire gleams. Down
upon her loosened hair fell the yellow rays of that solitary candle,
while from the un-shuttered window, open at the top as her
mother had left it, the cool evening air circled round them
both, full of the dewy smells of the damp meadows at the road's
end.

Even our poor vision-wrought Holy Sam was not so dehumanised as not to feel that there was something about this moment that was charged with portentous issues, something fatal,
something totally unforeseen, something that held the future in
its quivering crucible.

Crummie was in such a mood of unutterable awe and pent-up
ecstasy at having her idol, her more than earthly lover, alone in
the house with her, that she found difficulty in uttering a word,
and when she did speak it was in a solemn, breathless whisper.
So potent however is the concentrated love of the feminine heart,
that although this man, sitting there above her, had just beheld
—actually in the flesh—that elusive Mystery which was the cause
of Glastonbury's being Glastonbury, it was the girl and not the

man who dominated that moment, *her* exultation, and not his, that held the thunder-flash of that charged air.

"I never . . . thought," she whispered with intense emotion, not presuming to raise her eyes above the muddy soles of Sam's boots, "that I'd ever . . . have you . . . here alone."

"*Dear* Crummie!" and he made a timid movement of his hand towards her head, but quelled by the intensity of her feeling let his wrist fall back on his knee, where it lay limp, with Angela's handkerchief round it.

"I've got . . . so much . . . to say to you . . . that it's . . . hard to begin."

She made an effort to lift up her face and smile at him; but down her fair head sank again, as if she had been rehearsing once more her Pageant-part of the Lady of Shalott.

"*Dear* Crummie!" he repeated in a scarcely more audible voice than her own.

But then, gathering up the happiness within him as if it were a crystal cup that he stretched out to her, "I've had an experience today, Crummie," he said, "that has unsettled all my ideas; that's made me feel as if I'd never lived till today. I told Nell once, Crummie, that I thought I had a dead nerve in me. Well! Well! You don't want to hear about that . . . but it was true . . . but——"

"I can understand you," the girl murmured. "You needn't stop telling me for any reason—no! Not for any reason!"

"It wasn't a fancy; it wasn't a madness," he went on, "Crummie dear, I *saw* it! Yes, I saw the Grail Itself."

Now that he had told her, instead of his happiness being less, it became greater. Her long, slow, grave, childish look of absolute faith made him feel that this was the first time he had spoken of it to anyone. To those other people he must have been speaking of something else!

"And the effect it's had on me, Crummie, is to make me feel that I've seen Eternity. So that now I needn't worry myself any more about so many things! Behind the tortured Christ, behind that *other* Christ, behind the people we love and the people we've hurt . . . behind everything that's sacred to us . . . is Eternity. Do you know what I mean, little Crummie? I feel now"—there was a poignant tenderness, not so much an affectionate or even human tenderness, as it was something resembling the feeling her father would have shown for a wounded loach, about the tone in which he spoke to her; and it seemed in a sense to be a grotesque tone for that superbly beautiful creature crouching between the candle flame and the dying coals—"I feel now that my life has really finished itself, accomplished itself somehow; and what I want to do now is just to take it as it is and to give it to anyone, to anything, to whatever comes along, following chance and accident, and not bothering very much—do you see what I mean, Crummie?—taking everything as it happens—since I've seen Eternity!"

He needn't have asked her if she understood him. She had been following every word with the absorbed attention with which a prisoner hears his sentence or a gambler watches his throw of the dice. When he had finished she moved away from him a little, and bending down before the high bronze fender pressed her forehead against its top bar, while with her hands she clutched its shining knobs.

It was clear, even to the bemused and bewildered Sam that she was struggling with herself and making some momentous decision. Her decision, whatever it was, was made very quickly. She lifted her head from the fender and rose to her feet, clutching her robe tightly round her and gazing down upon him, where he still lay back at ease in her father's big arm-chair.

"I've got something to tell you, Mr. Sam," she said. All his father's parishioners called him Mr. Sam. Never in her life had she called him Sam.

He gave her at once his full attention. He sat straight up on the extreme edge of the arm-chair; his hands on his elbows, his heels beneath it, his head raised. He looked like a boy whose pockets are full of apples and pears giving polite attention to the conversation of an elder sister.

"There are very few men," she began, "who can live alone as you do, Mr. Sam. But I know you are doing wrong in doing it. Mrs. Zoyland belongs to you; she has given herself completely to you; she has had a child; and I know that I am telling you what's right when I tell you that you two ought not to live separated any more. There are things that a girl knows more about than any man and this is ——"

She stopped abruptly. From a portion of her powerful nature—for after all she was Mr. Geard's daughter—that had never been roused by Sam, she suddenly felt a wave of irrational anger against him. Once when she was a little girl and had been caressing a rag doll, for which she nourished, just as she did for Sam, a devoted, idealising love, she caught a look on its face that seemed so unresponsive that, filled with wrath against it, she snatched it up and dashed it upon the floor.

In the midst of her present speech—it was when she reached the words "she has had a child"—she gesticulated with her hands, forgetting to hold the folds of her long dressing-gown. Released from her fingers her robe fell apart, revealing the fact that beneath her skirt her legs and feet were bare.

It was then that she imagined she beheld, mingling with the dazed, indulgent, stupid courtesy of Sam's attention to her that particular look upon his face that women are so quick to catch; the look, namely, of displeasure rather than pleasure at some intimate and revealing gesture they have made. That such a look should have appeared on her idolised Sam's face, on this night of all nights, hurt her to the quick.

It was a swift blinking of the eyelids, a scarcely perceptible twitch of the chin; but she received the impression that the sight of her bare ankles had affected him as something disconcerting. She knew well that normal men have two distinct reactions to a girl's bare legs—the first one of provoked desire, with all its glamour and mystery, and the second, one of fastidious shrinking; and although towards her idealised love she was humble as a child about her beauty, she was also as shy and touchy as a child about any personal exposure.

The fact, therefore, that she had caught, or fancied she had caught, for in reality Sam was not thinking of her legs at all, that particular look upon his face, made her anger leap up furiously against them both; against herself for forgetting to conceal her ankles, and against him for that unconscious flicker of cold-blooded awareness that caused her to feel conscious of them. Her anger with Holy Sam, like her anger against her old idealised doll, made her totally forget that this dazed well-meaning man sitting up in such an absurd posture of forced attention, with his heels under the chair and his head raised, was her romantic idol, and in one swift ungovernable impulse she seized him by the hair of his head, and shook his skull with all her force backward and forward repeating those interrupted words: "More about than any man . . . more about than any man . . ." over and over again.

Sam in his unimaginative simplicity thought the girl was doing this for fun, or at least in amiable irritation. He was so full of her startling words about Nell that to have his hair seized upon and his skull shaken was an interlude of small moment. But when she let him go and flung herself down sobbing upon the bear rug, he realised that it was anything but fun. He realised then that he knew no more about the ways of women than he knew about the philosophy of "Neetsky" in dealing with them. He crouched down by her side on the bear rug and did his best to console her, not daring to snatch her arm away from her eyes, but petting and coaxing her in every way he could think of, and talking endearingly and tenderly to her. But she seemed to come to herself quite independently of his blundering consolation. All at once she scrambled swiftly to her feet. A curious notion had suddenly come into her head.

"Get me your coat," she said. "I want to put on your coat."

He obeyed her. He fetched his great coat. He held it for her, while she slipped into it. Very gently, as he stood behind her, he extricated her curls and let them hang free over the collar. She took him by the hand and led him to the sofa. It satisfied something very deep in her to feel that old overcoat she knew so well wrapped about her. It was like covering herself with the finer essence of her love. She was completely mistress of herself now, and of Holy Sam too, as this latter felt in the very marrow of his bones!

Every woman—the most abject as well as the most beautiful—has certain moments in her life when the whole feminine principle in the universe seems to pour through her, and when men, when every man obeys her in helpless enthrallment as if she held the wand of Circe. This was the great hour of Crummie's life, nor was she ignorant of the nature of the magic that now flowed through her veins.

"Mr. Sam," she said when they were seated side by side upon the sofa, "you *must* go back to Mrs. Zoyland; back to her and to your child—no, stop! I've not finished—I don't mean go back to the Vicarage! You're perfectly right in leaving your father. You couldn't live out your new ideas freely without being independent. And, as I say, those are some things women know more about than men; and one is that people who love each other ought to live alone together—*never* with a third one! When you left your Nell, you did it because you thought kissing her and loving her *in that way* was wrong. *She* never thought it was wrong! And now, Mr. Sam, you must live with her again; for I tell you those things are *not* wrong. But not at the Vicarage. She ought never to have gone there! That's the one thing I cannot understand in Mrs. Zoyland, that she ever agreed to stay under the same roof with two men like you and your father." She paused upon this, giving Sam a flash of something more dangerous from her soft grey-blue eyes than he had ever received. She looked so incredibly lovely in the dim light of that solitary candle, with her bright loose curls flowing over his own coat collar that Sam stared at her in humble admiration.

He was not in a mood to take exception to anything she said; and once having broken the ice and having got control of herself, she seemed prepared to say a great deal.

"You are both . . . very good men," she went on gravely, "but Mr. Dekker cares nothing what people think. He doesn't seem to realise what scandal-makers that old man and that old woman are! You ought at once to take Mrs. Zoyland away. *Then* you and she will be the ones to get into trouble—if there *is* any trouble, and not your father. We're in the middle of great changes here in Glastonbury. Mrs. Zoyland and you, if you're brave enough to despise the Miss Drews and Miss Fells of the town, will have the support of her brother Mr. Spear, and of course of my father and Mr. Trent. I don't know what furniture you've got in your attic in that Old Malt House—you see I know all about you, Mr. Sam!—but if you haven't got enough up there to make a woman and child comfortable you ought to take furnished rooms.

Why don't you go to Dickery Cantle's, Mr. Sam? They're not fussy or squeamish there. Besides Mr. Spear lives there now, and he's her brother. He'd help you with your expenses. He gets a good salary since my father's made him one of the big men in Glastonbury."

Sam's whole nature was in a turmoil. As the girl's rapid, practical words followed one another, they carried a shameful conviction with them. Yes, he had been unforgivably selfish in all he had done! Little thought had he given to the passionate torment of his father, tantalized by Nell's sweet presence, and bearing the whole weight of that ambiguous situation. Little had he thought of what Nell might be enduring. He had thought solely of himself, solely of his own soul in relation to his martyred God; and meanwhile he had been cruel to his girl, and if not cruel to his father, at least completely irresponsible, completely careless of his peace of mind. With a lover's instinct combined with the instinct of a son he knew exactly what his father would suffer if he took Nell away; but he knew also—who better?—the deep relief with which the older man left to himself, and free from this daily tantalisation of his darker mood, would revert to his simple, traditional, unquestioning faith. Besides, Nell would go and see him. She could go often and see him. He wouldn't be separating those two. By removing her from the Vicarage he wouldn't be taking her out of his father's life.

Thus as he watched that white face in the dimness, framed in its wavy curls, he gave himself reason upon reason for obeying the competent advice which came so impressively from its lips. But, as he listened, the image of his sweet love's form, the caressing sound of her voice, the whole aura of her personality, rose up in the very heart of his being. It was perhaps an ironic thing, but the truth was that the mood he had been thrown into by his vision of the great Glastonbury Mystery had abolished all his ascetic scruples about making love to Nell. Such scruples seemed to him now like a tight, irrelevant, self-inflicted contrariety!

There is no doubt that if ever Sam came to talk of the secret things of his life—which was not very likely—with Mr. Evans, that incorrigible biographer of Merlin would have found this particular effect of the Grail Vision a proof that the thing was a thing of magic, and not of religion; and likely enough—like the Mwys of Gwydion-Garanhir—was an actual symbol of fertility!

"Well, Mr. Sam, I've got to have supper with Miss Drew tonight; and it's now five minutes to the hour she expects me!"

Even as she spoke he was making his great decision.

"I'll take you to her door, little Crummie," he said. "You've been more than a crumb of the loaf to me tonight; and if I do manage to establish myself at Dickery Cantle's, I'll pray to you every day as if you were a god."

So he spoke, recalling a passage in one of the old poignant Homeric scenes, which he had had to read when he was in the sixth form at Sherborne School.

"Will you?" she exclaimed, leaping to her feet and rushing to the chimney-piece where their only candle was guttering down. "Will you?" she repeated, occupied with the struggle to light a second flame from the one that was drowning in its own melted wax.

And then he became aware from the heaving of her shoulders under his heavy coat that Crummie was crying—not audibly, as she had done after shaking him, but silently. Having lit that second candle, she seemed to be seized with a mania for lighting candles, and went round the room doing it everywhere, but keeping her face hid from him. She might just as well have spared herself this illumination of her tragedy, for the tears were still running down her cheeks when she turned round.

"I don't know why I'm doing this," she said. "It must be thankfulness because you're going to do what I've told you to do." As she spoke she made an heroic effort to smile. For the beat of a swallow's wing she could not compass it. Then she did; and the smile which wavered up, lovely and tender, from the very bottom of her soul, made her face, under the up-mounting flames of all her candles, more beautiful than any face that Holy Sam had ever seen.

On their way to Miss Drew's—and they traversed Magdalene Street to its end and then followed Bere Lane to the Tithe Barn, thus avoiding the town—Crummie talked to him unreservedly about her father. "He is fonder of me," she said in a low voice,

when they reached the great mediæval barn and paused confronting it, "than Mother thinks he ought to be. Mother never
has liked it. But I think nothing of it! I think it's silly to have
those ideas about it. I suppose I'm queer in things like that;
and so is Father, except when it worries Mother. I don't mind—
why should I mind?—his loving me so."

"The last time I talked to him," said Sam, "I thought he
was rather restless; but that may have been these communistic
ways of running the town."

"I've never told this to a living soul," said Crummie, "but
sometimes Father frightens me. Not with his petting and so on:
for I don't care tuppence about that. But once or twice lately
he's talked of death with such an extraordinary look on his
face! Almost always he talks of death when he's been petting
me, or has seemed especially fond of me, but not unhappily,
mind you! It's rather as if—it's so hard to put it, Mr. Sam!—as
if there were another me, someone *like* me, only of course much
more exciting, down there in Hades. I've seen his eyes, Mr. Sam
—and you know how dark they are!—shine like funnels of black
fire when he's been talking of death and holding me on his knee."

"Were you surprised that I should see the Holy Grail?" asked
Sam irrelevantly.

"I've thought you were seeing it all the time!" said Crummie
quickly.

He was looking at the strange apocalyptic creatures on the
barn now, and he thought to himself that there was something
about them that reminded him of Mr. Geard. In fact it was easy
for him to imagine that Mr. Geard's architect, after the Mayor
was dead, might carve a fifth evangelistic symbol for this new
Gospel. Sam even began to think of his own "Ichthus—the World-
Fish."

He left Crummie at Miss Drew's drive gate, and waited there
till he heard, by the sound of the opening and closing door, that
she was safely in the house. In the confused waves of the exultant happiness which she, the "Crumb of the Loaf," as he had
called her, had given him, soaking up for him and interpreting
in practical terms the meaning of his Vision, Holy Sam had blun-

dered again more grossly, more unpardonably, than he had ever done in his life. He had made a clumsy and awkward attempt to kiss Crummie. The girl had turned her head away and he had only brushed her cheek, but the contact of her flesh, at the entrance to that damp and dark shrubbery of the Abbey House, chilled him to the bone, as if he had touched that other, that Cimmerian Crummie, in the realms of Death, of whom her father was so enamoured!

As he turned away and crossed the road to enter his father's drive gate Sam had the wit to realize that he had acted grossly in trying to kiss her. He had made the gesture in simple and spontaneous gratitude. She knew *that* as well as he did. Why then had she turned her head away? She turned it away so that the great Love of her life, the secret Ideal of her girlhood, should not kiss her on the lips before he went in to her rival. Would she then have let him kiss her if there had been no question of Nell; but only the fact between them that he did not love her? Oh, still less so, Oh, far less so! For it might easily have been that this matter of rivalry would have led her to snatch fiercely, wickedly, maliciously, at his proferred kiss; but nothing would have induced her to let him kiss her on the lips—she loving him and he not loving her—if that malice of rivalry hadn't entered. Crummie being what she was, it had *not* entered, and her lips remained virginal. And yet she had been kissed full upon the mouth, again and again, by many of the men who had been wont to caress her.

Oh, deep beyond understanding is this curious secret! The whole Being of the coldest, plainest, ugliest girl in the world resembles a sensitive plant whereof her reluctant lips are the leaves. Organised for receptivity by the whole structure, substance and nerve-responses of her identity, the electric yieldingness of a girl's body vibrates to the least pressure upon her mouth. Only the craftiest and subtlest of lovers know the preciousness, the tragic, unique, perilous preciousness, of that moment when, under the pressure of a kiss, her lips are parted.

The two greatest Realists that have ever lived, those super-human delvers into the crook of a knee, or the dimple of a cheek, or the furrow of a brow, or the hollow of an eye-socket, Dante and Leonardo da Vinci, were at one in finding in women's lips the *entelecheia* of all Nature's secretest designs. A man's laugh—what a simple, nondescript "haw! haw! ho! ho!" *that* sound is, half a lion's roar and half an ass's bray, compared with the subtle waxing or waning, the broken ripple of the moon's reflection upon flowing water, of a woman's smile! To Dante a maid's smile meant the latitude of the least little span of a thin eyelash between inexorable Acheron and the mystical circles of the Empyrean; and to Leonardo the wavering beginning of a girl's smile carried, folded within its calyx, the blue veins of her thighs, the wild-rose tips of her nipples, the arch of her instep, the silkiness of her flanks, the unfathomable recessions of her final yielding to the pressure of desire.

Some shamefaced and scattered inkling of all this hovered about Holy Sam's mind as he entered the familiar driveway of his father's home. Oh, he had been brutally selfish in all this whole business of his relations with the people of his life! But he would change it all now. He would take this new happiness of his and lavish it among them!

Sam hurriedly opened the front door of the Vicarage and plunged at once, as a dog into the odour of a familiar kennel, into the well-known smell of his birthplace. He heard the voices of Penny and Mr. Weatherwax raised loudly in the kitchen and he felt glad that some lively interest of their own had prevented them from hearing his entrance. For a second he stood listening and hesitating, "this way and that dividing the swift mind," unable to decide whether to go in to his father first, or run up to Nell.

But it was to his girl and his child that he must betake himself now; *now* and for the rest of his days! That was the mandate of the Grail. That was the dictate of her, whose word, " 'ee 'as the fice of a sighnt," had started him on his quest. As lightly as he could—but he was a heavy man and the stairs creaked woefully—he rushed to the upper landing. He found himself actually forming upon his lips his cry to his Love, "I have come back to you; back to you forever!" and, as people do, outside a door that will reveal, in a second, a dear and familiar form, he hugged her to his heart in his mind with the very cling of reality. He knocked lightly twice—two little sharp, excited raps with his knuckles—and then without waiting for a reply flung open the door.

All was darkness. Faintly between the dark undrawn curtains he could see the dim shapes of the trees outside, outlined against a few pale stars. Empty was the great four-posted bed of the Prince of Orange; cold and desolate in the deserted room.

"Nell, little Nell!" His voice came back to him like the voice of someone who speaks in a place of the dead. With the first sickening catch of his heart he thought to himself: "She's taken him down to supper with Father!" Leaving the door of the big empty room wide open, he rushed out upon the landing and ran down the stairs. He opened the dining-room door. Pallid in the darkness shone the white tablecloth, laid for their evening meal. It made him think of a cloth upon an altar when they have put out the candles.

Instinctively delaying—because of something ice-cold gathering about his heart—his plunge into the museum, he opened the drawing-room door. Doors, doors, *doors*, always doors—and only emptiness within! With the musty smell of the fireless drawing-room—that room where he had held Nell to his heart on the morning he'd decided to go away—there smote upon his strung-up consciousness a sharp quick death-odour, the sense of the dying woman's body from which Dr. Fell had torn him into this bitter life, twenty-six years ago!

Well! He must make the plunge. Hearing still the voices of Penny and the gardener from the rear of the house and the noise of chairs being pushed violently about—"They're *both* drunk," he thought—he opened the museum door and went in. The lamp was untrimmed and smoking. The place seemed foul with lamp-soot; but this room at any rate was not empty! In his accustomed wicker chair sat his father. But to the son's surprise, for Sam had never known him do such a thing before, Mat Dekker had pulled his chair close up to the fire; and he was in the act, apparently, of making the brightest blaze he could; for his big hands were fumbling at the grate, and the flames were rising high from the wood he had been piling on, and it looked as if, now that his great solar enemy had done his worst to him, he were making a lonely, sullen, Promethean gesture in defiance of all these cruel gods.

Sam closed the door behind him. For the first time in his life he did *not* give even a glance at the aquarium. "What is it, Father? Where is she? What has happened?" But even while he was asking these questions his heart knew perfectly well; for he remembered what Angela had told him and he recalled that letter with the foreign stamp.

Mat Dekker raised his head from the flames which were throwing all the indents and wrinkles and corrugations of his ruddy face into startling prominence. He spoke no word however. All he did was to make a gesture with his hand towards the table.

Sam went to the table and turned down the smoking lamp. There, between the lamp and the aquarium, lay a folded scrap of paper, with "For Sam" written on it in pencil. He read it, standing by the lamp, while his father went on selecting the most inflammable bits of wood from the wood-box, at each increase in the heat of the blaze giving his chair a jerk still nearer. The pencilled scrawl was of some length, but it was evidently traced in a great hurry. Nell's hand, however, was so schoolgirlish that Sam had no difficulty in making out the words:

Sam, my darling Sam, I shall always love you best of all. Whatever happens to me, whatever anyone says or does, you'll always be my one *Great Love*. But he came and made me go back with him. She's been gone a long time—gone to Russia, he says. He doesn't like her any more. Will and I spoke freely of everything before I would let him take me away. He says he always knew the child was yours, but he says he loves it for my sake and always will. This is true, Sam; and I think baby loves *him* more than either his father or mother! Will has no anger against *you* and I've forgiven him about *her*. Oh, Sam, never, never, never will I forget you. Later [she had crossed out the word "later" and written "soon"] we must see each other again. We've got used to seeing each other in your way, haven't we? But Will was *so unhappy*, Sam. He said he'd go to Africa if I didn't come back. I was sad and your father was making himself miserable about us; so I *know* it's the best thing. You'll come back now, Sam, won't you, *now that I'm gone,* and live with him again? My arms are tight round my Sam's neck and always will be.

Your Nell.

P.S. I hadn't time to tidy up my room. Oh, Sam I can't help it. But I love you, I love you!

He folded the letter up and stood motionless for a while, staring at the aquarium, but seeing nothing except Nell's face. Then he moved across to his father and laid his hand on his shoulder.

The older man turned round fiercely upon him, and Sam never forgot the gleam of anger—blind, bewildered, tragic anger—in his deep-set grey eyes. "Go!" he cried hoarsely. "Get out of here! Go back to your clay-hauling. When I want your pity, I'll send for you!" It was clear that the man's whole mind was completely obsessed at present by his own frustrated passion. His emotions had smouldered and smouldered till they had become like a lump of darkly burning peat, self-scorched, self-fed, self-consumed.

Sam sighed heavily and went to the door. He still held Nell's letter tightly crumpled up in his hand. "Don't set the chimney on fire, Father!" he called back as he went out. He walked down the long dark passage and went into the kitchen. Here there were many signs of some recent riotous scene but the two old cronies were at peace again, facing each other by the stove, each with a bowl of the famous "gorlas" on their knees. They were too fuddled to rise from their chairs at Sam's entrance.

"Why, Penny," he said, "I thought you never drank with Mr. Weatherwax."

"Her baint drinking wi' I. Her be hearing I zing me zongs," and the enormous countenance of the gardener, radiant with tipsy contentment, burst into his favorite ditty:

> "The Miller, the Malster, the Devil and I
> Had a heifer, had a filly, had a Ding-Dong,
> But now in a grassy green glade she do lie.
> Pass along, boys! Pass along!"

But Penny Pitches looked dreamily from one to the other. "Best for 'un to zing," she muttered brokenly. "Let 'un zing, Master Sam, let us all zing and ding! I'd 'a never drunk wi' he if thik bare-faced baggage hadn't called I names to me veäce when I gave she a piece o' me mind. Yes, you may work your chin at me as much as thee likes, me lad! Her've gone back where her hasn't to sleep single no more. They baggages be all the seäme! Master Zoyland had only to ring bell and call 'Nell,' and up she picks her baby, and pop goes the weasel! I did me best for to hold she for 'ee, Mr. Sam; but her only called I names, and Master Zoyland curst I for a wold bitch."

Seeing that there was nothing better than this to be got tonight out of his foster-mother; and too sick at the heart to be able to endure another stave of "Ding-Dong," Sam wearily went on his way. Slowly, very slowly, as he returned through the crowded Sunday-night streets to Manor House Road, past the calm, familiar tower of St. John's, the influence of his Vision came back a little; and he had regained enough acquiescence in the decree of destiny by the time he reached his top floor, to receive a certain homely comfort from the wild extravagant pleasure with which the black spaniel, emerging from beneath his bed, leaped up to lick his hands.

His conscious mind was sad, even to the verge of a sort of inert despair, from this loss of Nell at the very moment when he was ready to live with her; but, below his conscious mind, stirring still in the depths of his being, was the feeling: "I can endure whatever fate can do to me, for I have seen the Grail!"

IT WAS NOW THE END OF FEBRUARY. THE NEWSPAPERS ALL OVER England had contained startling headlines for the last week about the Glastonbury commune, most of them calling upon the government to put a stop—by some drastic action—to this scandalous interference with the rights of private property. Nothing, however, was done except what was done by Philip Crow to protect the building of his new cement road leading down from Wookey Hole and his new steel bridge over the Brue on the south side of Lake Village Field; and Philip's action was confined to the introduction of police protection.

There had been so many disputes that year all over the country between town councils and local land-owners that it was difficult for Philip to make the authorities realise that this sudden transforming of Glastonbury into one single co-operative polity was anything more than what the chief of the Taunton police called "another of them sky-larking council tricks."

The government probably would have interfered all the same —for unemployment in all the big neighbouring towns, such as Bristol and Cardiff, was acute just then, and there was a dangerous restlessness throughout the country—if it had not been that the really important fortress of private property, namely the Glastonbury bank, remained untouched by this socialistic experiment.

On the twenty-third of February Mr. Evans came down to his shop in the High Street, in exceptional good spirits. The day was one of unusually delicate atmospheric effects. Grey upon grey abounded, with occasional fragments of what looked almost like mother-of-pearl as the ditch-mists were blown here and there over walled courts and mossy lawns while the sun struggled with the clouds.

"I have got an exciting bit of news for you when you come back, Owen," Cordelia had said to him at the door of their little house as he set off, "but I'll keep it for tea! Only be sure and don't be later than five, will you?"

"No, no, I'll be back by five, *si fractus inlabatur orbis*! I'll be back, Cordy, I swear it," he had replied.

As he hurried down the long, sloping road, flanked by workmen's houses, the black tails of his tight-waisted overcoat flapping like the feathers of an excited jackdaw heading against the wind, he wondered to himself what Cordy's news was. "Something to do with her father," he thought to himself. "Perhaps he's found he's richer than he supposed, after counting up his expenses." When he got to the town he met Finn Toller slouching into Dickery Cantle's tavern. Several encounters of late had Mr. Evans had with Codfin since a certain momentous meeting, a few days after the sheepfold incident, when he had actually challenged the man about his singular encounter with Mad Bet.

Codfin from the start had detected with that extraordinary clairvoyance which imbeciles share with children, that Mr. Evans had a morbid interest in physical violence; not even excluding murder. He felt too that he was absolutely free from any danger that the "curiosity man"—as he called him to his colleagues— would ever betray him to the authorities. "He be a funny one, his wone self," he would say to his friends in the tap-room at Cantle's where all the poorest and shabbiest of Glastonbury's derelicts were wont to gather.

"I . . . be . . . going . . . to do it . . . tonight . . . Mister," Codfin whispered to him now, with his hand on the tavern door-handle. The blinds of the place were down. By the law of England it was closed. By the connivance of the Mayor of Glastonbury people could enter and be served all the morning from the best cellar in Wessex.

"I can't hear you, man. I'm deaf this morning, deaf as an iron bar," said Mr. Evans, giving him a look like that of a malevolent executioner. "If you do anything—anything *really*, you know, I'll come and stop it! You understand *that* I suppose? I'll come, wherever you are, for I can always find you, *and put a stop to it.*"

He spoke in a threatening tone and laid his hand with a vicious grip upon Finn Toller's left arm just above the elbow. Codfin, whose right hand was still on the handle of the tap-room, showed not the slightest sign of nervousness.

"Tonight will be the time, Mister, then," he said slowly, "for thee to come and put a stop to it; and I'll be here all morning, 'sknow, if thee wants to come and hear *where* thee'd best come to stop it; and maybe hear too *when* thee'd best come to stop it. There's nothink like being in the know, pard; for then a fellow can please his own self. If so be as thee *does* drop in ere the mornin's over, maybe thee'll have a sip of beer wi' I, to christen this pretty day, 'sknow? afore thee comes up hill to *see* what must be stopped."

The man's straw-coloured beard wagged as he spoke and his pale eyes swam with an unholy amusement. Every word he uttered seemed to carry a double meaning, seemed loaded with hints that his leering eyes completed and confirmed. His weak subhuman intelligence seemed to wriggle into the interstices of Mr. Evans' wickedest and secretest thoughts and snuggle and nuzzle and nestle there, as if Mr. Evans' thoughts were the nipples of the many-breasted Diana of the Ephesians.

This encounter between the two men was indeed the culmination of several furtive meetings, in all of which there had been, below the surface of what audibly passed between them, a wordless conspiracy of understanding, mounting higher and higher; just as if their under-consciousness—the worm-snakes within them —had learned the art of an obscene intertwining. Codfin had quickly discovered that his own homicidal instinct, in which the mental image of the iron bar played so lively a part, was responded to by something darker and far more evil, as it was far less simple, in Mr. Evans' nature.

Once he had touched the fringe of this dark knowledge, the tramp was led on—for all his imbecility—to play most subtly upon this obscure chord, recognising that the accident of the sheepfold had helped him to acquire a definite power over this queer "curiosity gent" who took such an interest in talking to him. A potential murderer, going about among supposedly normal people, acts as a perambulating magnet, drawing to himself a cloud of curious tokens; such an one's recklessness in regard to the upshot—the police, the jail, the judge, the gibbet—endows him with the same sort of power over less desperate minds that an Alpine guide, immune to dizziness, acquires over the would-be summit climbers whose faltering steps he supports with his rope.

Codfin had already tasted—in his crafty imbecile manner—this sharp, delicious arctic breath of unexpected power, in his talk with Red Robinson in Mrs. Chinnock's parlor. Robinson, however, had escaped him completely; thereby indicating that emotional 'ate as an urge to crime, cannot compete with the worm-snake of the sexual nerve.

"Well! I've got to get on now," said Mr. Evans. "Good-day to 'ee, Toller! We mustn't carry our joking too far."

"Joking?" thought the tramp as he went in. "That's just the way you *would* talk, my fine gent!" He sighed heavily as he shambled up to the bar counter behind which young Elphin was standing. "If you'd a-heard Mad Bet tell I last night what she'd do to I, if I didn't kill her beau quick, you wouldna' talk about joking!"

As soon as Mr. Evans turned the corner by the Cattle Market, he saw before him, about three hundred yards away, the familiar figure of Miss Elizabeth Crow, seated on a wooden bench just outside a seldom-used cattlepen.

Over the empty enclosures behind her, where the animals formerly were tethered, over the wooden posts and the asphalt paving, over bits of stray nondescript paper blown in there between the iron railings of the bench where she was sitting, the flickering misty sunlight fell with the same caressing benediction as it would have carried had it fallen upon the dancing waves of Weymouth Bay or upon the mossy stones of Mark Court.

Miss Crow was holding a closed umbrella in her hand, with the ferule of which she was scrawling vague meaningless marks in the trodden mud at her feet. She was pondering upon an interview she had had that morning, as soon as his clinic opened, with Dr. Fell, and wondering why it was that doctors never come right out with what they know of their patient's case. "Why didn't he say in plain words," she thought, " 'your heart is dangerously affected? Those symptoms you have are an indelible sign that you might go off at any moment. The best thing you can do will be to go to bed as soon as you get home and stay there.' " She had indeed known herself for the last three months that her heart was getting worse and this morning's interview, though Fell had been so cautious, was the convincing blow. She had read the good man's conclusions, shrewd old woman as she was, like a book; and if he had said to her, "You've only three weeks more to live," she could not have received her sentence more definitely than she did from his evasive humming and hawing.

The chief effect upon Elizabeth's mind was to render her enjoyment of the air and the wind of this day more vivid and intense than she could have believed possible. It was as if this verdict condemning her to death had taken away a thin screen between herself and life.

There was a little leafless poplar tree not far from her bench with the bark rubbed off its northern side, the side facing the cattlepens and some dried dogs' excrement fouling its roots on the side facing the street. In the bare branches of this tree chattered and wrangled half a dozen sparrows and upon its trunk, out of reach of cattle or dogs, some tall wastrel had cut with a knife the initials of himself and his girl.

The way the broken misty light fell upon this little tree gave it that special quality of magic that familiar objects often receive, whether there is any human eye to see it or not, under certain effects of the atmosphere.

Elizabeth Crow's feelings were ebbing and flowing just then between a faint, cold, shuddering recoil from the shock of death —it was when she felt this recoil that she made those meaningless marks in the mud with her umbrella—and an intense, lingering, melting, weeping delight in the smallest familiar earth-objects. It was the sight of this poplar tree with its rubbed and disfigured bark and with certain enchanting and almost mystical shadows on some of its branches, as they wavered in the light breeze, which transported her then and thrilled her through and through with a tearful rapture at being still alive.

Mr. Evans took only about two minutes to reach her from the moment when he first came round the corner; but during those two minutes Miss Crow had experienced the eternal alternations, the great antipodal feelings of human experience, the shudder of death and "the pleasure which there is in life itself!" And she was a woman to miss little, though she kept her own counsel of these experiences!

She thought to herself: "There's that man Evans coming! I'll get him to send me that St. Augustine Sam talked about; and I'll give it to Mat. I can afford that now!" How fast the mind moves from margin to margin of these opposite feelings! Mr. Evans was rapidly coming to a point within hearing; and if she wanted to speak to him about St. Augustine she would have to stop him; and yet behind Mr. Evans' approaching figure and behind the image of that expensive book, and even behind the image of Mat Dekker's pleasure in the book, that cold, shuddering recoil still possessed her, and that magical light flickering on the poplar tree still possessed her.

The invisible watchers—those scientific collectors of interesting human experiences in this ancient town—communicated to one another the conclusion that certain essences and revelations are caught and appropriated by an old maiden lady, like Miss Crow, which are never touched by turbulent, tormented lives like those of Mr. Evans and Codfin.

How could Mr. Evans, now lifting his hat to greet this dignified figure of voluminous skirts and flounced bosom, become a medium for these calm platonic essences? What could Codfin, who was risking the hangman's rope for the sake of the mania of a madwoman, know of the deep natural shrinking of a normal heart in the presence of death, or of its rapturous awareness of the enchantment of what it is leaving?

Miss Crow had arranged to meet Lady Rachel and Athling for lunch at the Pilgrims' that day. She was a little nervous in her heart of hearts about this encounter, because in her growing disapproval—shared it may well be imagined by the girl's father— of the intimacy in which the lovers now seemed to be living, she had of late avoided seeing Ned Athling. Rachel still officially lived with her; but there had been whole nights when the girl had remained working, so she declared, in the offices of the *Wayfarer*; and gossip had already begun to speak on the prolonged visits she paid to the bachelor attic which the young editor had furnished for himself above these offices.

Lord P. had had recently several grave and diplomatic talks

with Miss Crow as to what measures they could take to stop the outbreak of a serious scandal; but neither she nor he had yet dared to risk any drastic ultimatum to the wilful girl for fear of precipitating the very disaster they dreaded.

"I shan't stay long after lunch," Miss Crow thought, as she responded to the salute of Mr. Evans, "and I won't go to their printing-place with them today. I'll get them to leave me free for the afternoon; and I'll go to Wirral Hill, if I'm not too exhausted, and sit on that seat where Mat and I used to sit thirty years ago."

She beckoned now to Mr. Evans and he came up to where she was and stood in front of her. There was something about Miss Crow—her Devereux mother perhaps—that commanded more respect from the Glastonbury tradesmen than any other person in the town.

Mr. Evans, though certainly not a tradesman, was not insensible to this quality, and he stood awkwardly now, but quite deferentially, waiting what she had to say.

"You've got rather an expensive edition of St. Augustine among your books, haven't you, Mr. Evans?" she said quietly.

"Yes, Mam," admitted Number Two's partner, "the best on the market."

It is an old and bitter experience of the human race that when once a gulf-stream of a particular evil has got started, it is always being whipped forward by some new little breeze, or enlarged by some new little stream emptying itself into it. A magnetic power, it seems, in such a gulf-stream of evil, attracts these casual and accidental encouragements.

Why, of all things, should Mr. Evans have been reminded of their collection of books at that juncture, and why, of all their books, of the particular one that was neighbour to "The Unpardonable Sin"?

"I think, if your partner has not sold it yet," said Miss Crow, "I'd like to have that book."

"I'll put it aside for you, Mam," murmured Mr. Evans. "It *is* expensive, I'm afraid, but if ——"

"I'll be extravagant for once," cried the lady with a smile. "So

I think you can send it today if you've got anyone to send. You know my number in Benedict Street?"

Mr. Evans bowed. Everyone knew Miss Crow's number. Hadn't it been the chief topic of the town when she left her nephew's establishment and went to live in a workman's cottage?

"I hope Mrs. Evans is well?" enquired the lady.

This simple question caused the brain of the hook-nosed man, bending towards her, to whirl up in an angry revolt against the smoothed-out pigeonhole of public propriety in which a married tradesman lived. It rose to the tip of his tongue, in his nervous state, to ask this quiet embodiment of conventional dignity some outrageous question in return; such as "How does your Tossie feel, married to Mr. Barter?" or "How will you manage about the way Lady Rachel is carrying on with young Athling?"

"*Very* well, Mam, thank you," he replied. And then he even took upon himself to add, "We've got a house that's quite easy for her to look after."

Miss Crow smiled. "I'm glad to hear *that*. It's a mistake for young married women to be overworked." She made a little movement then with the handle of her umbrella to signify that she had no further need for Mr. Evans' society.

The Welshman straightened his back, bowed to her in a manner that even Mrs. Geard could not have felt disgraced the House of Rhys, and went off, settling his hat upon his head as he went in little angry jerks and vowing that he would not remove it again till he reached his destination.

He was hardly gone—for Miss Crow had selected a very public place for her matutinal rest—than Comrade Trent, as the populace in their mocking rustic humour always called him, came softly and airily by. Miss Elizabeth only just knew Paul Trent "to speak to," as they say, and she was cordially prejudiced against the man. She had long ago put down, in her heart, this whole wretched business of the new régime to this alien from the Scilly Isles.

It was clearly he who had devised the scheme of buying the leases and the ground-rents from the lord of the manor and doling out, in this pauperising manner, all that the visitors brought in among the town's poor. Neither honest Dave, nor that hot-headed agitator Robinson, and certainly not Mr. Geard with his fancies, would have had the wit to plot such a daring move. Miss Elizabeth had scant admiration for her nephew Philip, but she felt sorry for him and even sympathetic with him, when she beheld this affected, sly, young lawyer prancing about the town as if he were the master of all. In the relations between human beings it is always natural to attribute the grossest selfish motives to the people we instinctively dislike.

Of the real Paul Trent, who inherited from his mother an idealism passionate as that of the poet Shelley, and who would have perished willingly on a barricade if he could have started an anarchistic revolution, Miss Crow knew absolutely nothing.

"Good morning, Miss Crow," said Paul Trent, "enjoying this beautiful weather?"

"*Au contraire*, Mr. Trent, I'm doing my accounts! Before plunging into Wollop's, you know, a woman has to think out what she can afford without ruining herself. I always slip off, in the middle of my shopping day, to do a little solitary thinking."

This allusion to Wollop's was a covert feminine taunt at this arrogant young man; for it was well known in the town that Mr. Wollop owned his shop and the ground it stood on in fee simple. Wollop's, like the Glastonbury bank, remained an obstinate island of capitalism in a socialistic lake.

"What a treasure your Mr. Wollop is!" murmured Paul Trent; and taking advantage of this faint crack in the ice—like a cat rubbing itself against the knees of someone who hates cats—he proceeded to slip down into the seat at her side. "How do *you* like our new Glastonbury constitution?" he asked her in an airy tone.

"I don't meddle with politics, Sir," she replied; and the way she moved away from him as she spoke seemed to add: "And I can't abide politicians!"

"I agree with you entirely," he said; and then, to Miss Crow's horror, he pulled up one of his soft neatly socked legs upon the seat between them and slipped his arm along the back of the bench.

"I'll get up the minute my heart stops thumping," the lady

thought. "What *does* this objectionable young man want with me?"

"A woman like you, Miss Crow," he went on, with what she thought was pure impertinence, "can understand better what I am doing in Glastonbury than the most intelligent man could."

Miss Crow tapped the ground with her umbrella. Then she produced a clicking noise between her tongue and her teeth; and having expressed with these physical movements her disapproval of Paul Trent, she made her mock-modest retort to his ambiguous compliment by uttering the syllables "Tut-tut-tut!" But her insidious invader only pulled his rounded feminine knee and his neatly trousered calf a little further along the seat of the bench and slid his delicately moulded hand an inch nearer along its back, till the scrupulously clean nail of his little finger was within the length of a sparrow's beak of Miss Crow's jacket collar. These outward gestures, which gave his companion a tickling sensation down her spine, were methods of approach inherited from his father, a Cornishman who had the suavity of some old Phoenician trader; but below all this there stirred in Paul Trent an intense idealistic longing, inherited from his mother, to convert Miss Crow to his revolutionary ideas.

"I'm very serious, lady," he said. "You mustn't get cross with me. There really aren't so many women one can talk to in Glastonbury. Most of my thoughts are entirely wasted on these people."

"This nice, unusual day seems to make you moralise, Mr. Trent, just as it makes me sit in the sun and wonder about my bills."

"What I've found out is," he went on eagerly, quite oblivious of this snub, "that none of these people, that you quite properly call politicians, Miss Crow, know what liberty is. The capitalists take liberty away from us in the name of liberty, which, under *them*, means liberty to work like a slave, or, to starve. But your relative Mr. Spear isn't much better! He takes liberty away from the individual in the name of the community. So there you are, you see! I am probably the only *man* in Glastonbury who fights for real liberty—which means, of course, a voluntary association of free spirits to enjoy the ideal life—but women understand these things much better. It was my mother who ——"

Miss Crow looked at him with surprise. There had stolen into his affectedly genteel intonation a vibration of such authentic emotion that it startled her. She didn't repeat that clicking of her tongue. She allowed her umbrella to lie still, its handle between her knees. She forgot the sinister palpitations of her heart.

"Your mother who?"

"Who taught me what liberty really meant. Who made me an anarchist, lady!"

"But you don't mean to say ——"

"Stop, Miss Crow! I know what's coming! You're going to talk about throwing bombs and killing innocent people. No, no. My mother didn't teach me how to throw bombs. What she taught me was—what *every* woman knows in her heart!—that all these man-made institutions only get in the way of real life and have nothing to do with it. It's the policeman in our minds, Miss Crow, that stops us all from being ourselves and letting other people be themselves."

He stopped to take breath and found that he was gesticulating furiously with his free hand right in front of Miss Crow's face, and that Miss Crow had shut her eyes tight, as if she were in the process of being shampooed, and that in his eagerness he actually *had* emitted a small globule of white sputum which now adhered to the black frill of Miss Crow's maternal but maidenly bosom.

Around this anarchistic spittle, a minute yellowish fly, attracted by the smell of humanity and dreaming perhaps that one of the old-fashioned Glastonbury markets was about to commence, hovered with pulsing and heaving desire.

Paul Trent drew out his elegant pocket-handkerchief from his breast-pocket, and therewith wiped his forehead. Then he hesitated for a minute. He would dearly have liked to have wiped away that little bubble from his too voluble mouth which still adhered in annoying prominence to the lady's bosom, but he simply had not the courage to attempt such a deed. It is easier to defy society than to outrage a small propriety; and the man from what Malory calls the country of the Surluse, and what Sir John Rhys calls the Sorlingues, or Les Isles Lointaines, replaced his dainty handkerchief in his breast-pocket and sank back in his place, with an inward sigh and an outward smile. "No good!" he thought to himself, and a wave of bitter futility swept over him.

During the last four or five weeks he had come to feel as hostile to Glastonbury as any one of the Crows had ever felt. He would have hated the town as much as Tom Barter did, if it had not been for this unique chance of giving an anarchical twist to the policies of the tiny commune. But he had encountered disillusionment after disillusionment.

Simple and direct as Dave Spear's methods were compared with his, the young Communist defeated him every time their ideas clashed. The cause of this was obvious. Dave had a clear-cut set of adamantine principles, which he combined with a practical and even unscrupulous opportunism that was a perpetual surprise to everyone.

Thus when the dictators of this microscopic state came to loggerheads, it was always the Anarchist whose principles were vague and his practice unbending, who was forced to yield; while the Communist, whose principles were crystal-clear and his practice malleable and flexible, carried the point. Had Paul Trent been more sympathetic to the Mayor's mysticism he might have won Mr. Geard over to his view. Had he been more personal in his destructiveness, he might have propitiated the emotional Red and plotted with his help some catastrophic blow to Philip's dye works, or tin mine, or bridge, or road, these wedges of capitalism in this co-operative community; but the truth was that Paul Trent, like the poet Shelley, was far too ideal in his instincts for his instincts to prevail; and in a world where liberty and independence and sweet reasonableness are forced to yield to fanaticism and dominating faith, his curious double nature, wherein his mother's masculine soul concealed in his father's effeminate body, divided his energy and confused his purpose, it was easier for him to outwit the Marquis of P. than to turn Glastonbury into a voluntary association of free philosophers. As he now jumped up from Miss Crow's side, made his courtly Carthaginian obeisance and cleared off, directing his steps towards the central offices of the commune, which were in the upper floors of

the Abbot's Tribunal, he said to himself that his real difficulty
was with the wayward and emotional nature of the Glastonbury
natives themselves. "And it's the same," he thought, "with Spear
and old Geard; yes! and even with the double-dyed fool
Robinson.

"Our little society can deal easily enough with these pilgrims
and visitors. We can grow rich upon *them*; and we can make
them obey our rules or keep them out by our requisitions. It's the
natives who'll break this thing up, when it *is* broken up; and
I don't give it more than a couple of years, at the best! Yes, it's
the natives who'll ruin the whole thing!"

Thus he pondered; and to the same tune and to the same moan
had Avallach and Arthur, Alfred and Edmund, Dunstan and
Edgar, Whiting and Monmouth, yes, and Mr. Recorder King! all
pondered in their day and in their hour.

He paused for a moment at the gate of the Tribunal, just as
Mary Crow had once done and gazed with a sad, disenchanted
eye upon that beautiful late-gothic façade.

"Does it need a brute like Judge Jeffreys," he thought, "or does
it need a saint like St. Joseph, or like this crazy Sam Dekker,
to deal with these Glastonbury autochthones? Old Geard can
handle them when he wants to; but he never seems to want to.
God knows where that old charlatan's mind is carrying him now.
Not to the building up of any possible community that *I* can
visualise!"

His hand was upon the handle of the Tribunal's main entrance
when two little girls—one of them carrying a sturdy child in her
arms—passed close by him.

"Bert can say 'Glastonbury be a commune,' Bert can; just like
teacher tells we to," said the little girl who was carrying the
child.

"C...O...M...*com*—U...N...E...*oon*...
commoon!" murmured Bert proudly, from the arms of a still
prouder Sis.

But Morgan Nelly, as usual, dashed this simple glory into a
thousand melancholy pieces, to be carried away on an obscure
wind. "Glaston baint no such thing," she cried in her shrill,
mocking elf-voice. "Glaston be a person, like I be, and persons

can't be spelt by no teacher, nor taught by no teacher. 'Twere Mad Bet who told I that Glaston were a person and I arst Holy Sam if such 'un were, and 'a said, 'Sure-*lie*, girlie, sure-*lie*. Glaston be the 'Ooman of Sorrows what holds Christ in lap!' " The children passed on, out of the gloomy triumvir's hearing; but, though anything save superstitious, the young lawyer from Les Isles Lointaines found it hard not to regard Morgan Nelly's curious remark as a significant omen. He gazed down the street at the massive, pinnacled tower of St. John's. It was certainly a peculiar day for lights and shadows! A soft, elusive, fluctuating radiance that seemed *contained* within a delicate sub-aqueous vapour, at once faintly rose-tinged and faintly greenish, hovered like the submerged lamp of a drowned ship, over the roofs and masonry of the ancient town.

Glastonbury a person? Well, perhaps, after all, that *was* the solution of their troubles! These old, obstinate, irrational indigenes of the place understood this wayward and mysterious Personality better than any philosophical triumvirate could do, and had expressed their feeling through the mouth of this wild-eyed child!

But if this was the solution, was not he, the man from Malory's Surluse, nearer to the secret than the rest? Or was it, after all, a mistake to make even the wilfulness and the irrationality of Persons into a principle and a doctrine? Was old Geard, in the long run, the one who was the wisest of them all; he for whom all these exciting events were only half-real, the dreams of an absent-minded Wayfarer, "drunk upon the milk" of an unseen Paradise?

The young Anarchist found it difficult to break up this indefinable spell into which Morgan Nelly's casual words had flung him.

He knew so well the trim, prim, fussily orderly look of the communal offices above his head where the depersonalised mind of his colleague Dave dominated the very typing machines and the very postage stamps; making everything seem like those scissored patterns in paper, from which patient seamstresses cut their garments! Why was it that the *real reality* of life always struck a person sideways and incidentally, and seemed just the very thing that no one allowed for?

What Paul Trent felt just then was a dim suspicion that if everybody in Glastonbury—these difficult natives as well as these easy visitors—were only to stop doing anything at all, just stop and listen, just stop and grow porous, something far more important than a "Voluntary Association of Free Spirits" would reveal itself!

A feeling stole over him as if all the way down its long history Glastonbury, the Feminine Person, like Mary at the feet of the Master, had been waiting for the fuss to cease, for the voices to subside, for the dust to sink down.

As when a boy catches upon the face of a girl, as when a man catches upon the face of a woman, that unique feminine look which forever is waiting, watching, listening, dreaming, in a trance of mindless passivity for something that never quite comes, so Paul Trent felt himself now to be watching the Glastonbury atmosphere, on this day of such strange lights and shadows.

Could it be possible that the secret of ecstatic human happiness only arrived, when all outward machinery of life was suspended, all practical activity held in abeyance? Man must live, of course, and children must be born of women; but was there not something else, something more important than any conceivable organisation for these great necessary ends?

A doubt came into Paul Trent's mind, different from any he had ever felt, as to whether his inmost ideal—this thing that corresponded to the word liberty—was enough to live by. Wasn't it only the gap, the space, the vacuum, the hollow and empty no-man's land, into which the fleeting nameless essence could flow and abide? He felt as if he were on the edge of some thrilling secret, as this thought, this doubt, touched him with its breath. It was as if all the moments of dark, cool, lovely, quiet emptiness that had come to the generations of men living in Glastonbury, had incarnated themselves in this Feminine Emanation of the place, which now seemed brushing him with its overshadowing wings.

Comrade Spear wanted to "liquidate" the Grail Quest on behalf of Communism, Red Robinson wanted to destroy it because of the treacheries and oppressions it had condoned. He himself had wanted to shake it off, as a morbid, mediæval superstition, hurtful to free spirits, like a clammy miasma! And all this while Old Geard was working his miracles by its aid; but casually, carelessly, almost indifferently; as if he had discovered that the whole Grail Quest were a mere by-product of some vast planetary reservoir of an unknown force.

Oh, dear! His thoughts had become too analytical, too concrete; and his good moment was gone. With a shrug of his shoulders he turned the handle, entered the Tribunal, and ran upstairs to the orderly rooms from which Glastonbury was now ruled.

When Mr. Evans arrived at his shop after his interview with Miss Crow by the railings of the Cattle Market he found his partner, Mr. Jones, extremely excited by the quantity of foreigners there were that day in the town, and bent upon devoting the whole day to a lively concentration upon their business.

"I know better than thee can know what these Continentals require, seeing as I've lived in Glaston afore thee was born," persisted the old man, "and the best thing thee can do is to bring up a pile of they books out of basement and put 'em in windy. Them Germans and Rooshians be more for books than they be for bricky-brack."

Mr. Evans struggled out of his tight overcoat, making portentous grimaces as he pulled at its sleeves, hung it up on a nail at the back of the shop and rubbing his face with both his hands, prepared to do what his partner bade him. He had taken good care since his marriage to avoid that descent into his Avernus but the human mind is so constructed that when he received this point-blank push from his business confederate, a hundred reasons sprang up like a hundred sly lawyers, each of them full of subtle arguments why he should do what the old man bade him to do. This was the third little breeze that had helped forward that day his gulf-stream of evil!

His high spirits that morning had been largely due to the fact that he had just arrived, in his Life of Merlin, at the beginning of the final scene where the Magician passes into that state of Being hinted at in the mysterious word Esplumeoir.

Mr. Evans had been writing, of late, every evening in their small sitting-room in the Edmund's Hill district above Bove Town. He would sit on a little chair that creaked under his bony figure in front of a flimsy table, covered with publications of various antiquarian and folklore societies, and as he stared at a cheap coloured print in a variegated frame, of a river and a boat and a woman reading—a print that took the heart out of all rivers and all boats and all women!—he would give himself up to the exquisite and sweet pain of weighing every word he was writing, changing it, re-setting it, substituting another, replacing the first, till the particular sort of rhythm he aimed at had at last been caught.

A boat . . . a river . . . a woman reading . . . this incredibly feeble production, in which the blotchy frame and the sentimental picture seemed to melt into each other till they became a weak blur of meaningless twists and curves, had grown to be so dear, so sweet, so familiar to Mr. Evans, whose æsthetic taste was nil, that it not only reminded him of a picture in his parents' farm but it also associated itself with the word Esplumeoir. It was under the spell of this entirely worthless, but to him almost sacred object that Mr. Evans was now considering and weighing in his mind two simple sentences: "And so in the wet vapour that hung in woeful water-drops upon his beard he bowed himself down and stooped right low over the rain-soaked earth where yesterday had been the drawbridge of Caer Sidi. The Dolorous Blow had fallen: the Spear of Longinus had done its work; where was he now to hide his forehead and cover his eyelids, who knew too well the causes of all these happenings; their echoes, their ripples, their waxing and waning moons?"

Pleased with the way these paragraphs sounded in his mind and finding in his broodings over the word Esplumeoir a strange vibration of peace, Mr. Evans had emerged from his threshold that morning,—but now all was different. As he traversed that little dark staircase from shop to cellar and from cellar to shop, carrying many enormous armfuls of books, he found his mood of dreamy self-satisfaction changed into something else. Number

Two was scrupulously honest in his handling of their diurnal gains, which, with the increase of foreign visitors, began to grow very considerably. He kept two large collecting-boxes, one of them with the letters "G.C."—Glastonbury Commune—written in pencil on it, and he divided all their increment into two portions and then sub-divided their own share.

During the time that Mr. Evans was bringing up these books, the shop was crowded with people; and old Jones had all he could do to deal with the pushing and jostling that was taking place.

But he was right about the books. Not a German, not a Russian entered, but he began turning over the pages of these books; while not a Frenchman came in, but he wanted to see all the china ornaments that the establishment boasted.

This learned interest in their stock of books—most of which were old parchment folios—kept Mr. Evans at his job; but his mood had completely changed. And in a most subtle way it had changed; for while his broodings were still upon his mystical interpretation of the word Esplumeoir there slipped into his thoughts certain episodes in the earlier life of his magician which led insensibly to his subterranean temptation.

He recalled, for instance, that occasion when Merlin came rushing down in a howling storm from the forest hills driving before him a herd of stags, himself riding upon the back of the hindmost, and rending off one of its great horns, flung this wild weapon at the daring chieftain who was stealing the magician's wife.

The dark and bloody violence of this scene disturbed the current of Mr. Evans' mind. Something in the sinister action of tearing out that branched horn by its roots reminded him of a deadly, a most perilous passage in "The Unpardonable Sin." The evil tide was indeed full upon him now. With trembling knees he put down his candle—for little daylight could enter that cellar—and snatching the book from its place by St. Augustine, he began feverishly turning its pages till he found that abominable and terrible passage.

His hands shook so much and his knees knocked together so violently, as he gloated over this dreadful scene, that anyone beholding him would have supposed him to be the victim of St. Vitus' dance. The man's bones seemed to melt within him as he read on and on now, passing from this passage to another and from that to another, till all sense of place or time was completely lost. The long winter months in which he had lived so happily with Cordelia fell away from him like a cinematograph picture passing across an artificial screen.

Nothing in the world seemed to matter, nothing in the world seemed of the least importance, compared with the overpowering mania that re-possessed him now. It returned upon him with all the more irresistible power because of his long suppression of it. Had anyone been down there watching his face they would have seen that he was biting his lower lip so violently—sucking it indeed into his mouth as well as biting it—that his whole countenance was transfigured. His nostrils kept twitching, opening and shutting like those of a savage stallion, and his eyes burned with so insane a light that one could fancy that they would actually cause the paper upon which these atrocious things were written to smoulder and shrivel like leaves held into a consuming flame.

The man's absorption in his frenzied vice was so horribly complete that when the door at the top of the staircase opened and Number Two's voice called upon him to come up into the shop it was no more than if he had heard a moth beating against the wall. But a moment came—for even in the throes of a cerebral excitement driven to a pitch like this a human being grows aware of that calling horizon that we name the future, those beckoning fluctuating cross-roads, those bridges—Perilous, Pomparlès Bridge, Eel Bridge, Sword Bridge, Water Bridge, that make a person feel that wicked thoughts are not enough—a moment came when Mr. Evans resolved to *do* something. It was no vague thing that he resolved to do; for his imaginative projection was as concrete and palpable as the worst of these silhouettes of horror engraved in the holy excess of sadistic satisfaction, by Dante's rationalized dementia.

He now closed the leaves of the book, letting the page that had overpowered him fall down upon its neighbour as delicately as a person might cover up a wound with its own eroded skin.

He rose to his full height and possessed himself of the candle. His knees ceased to knock together, his pulses ceased their frantic tattoo, the beads of sweat on his forehead began to dry. It was the curious phase in the pitiful evolution of temptation when the insane desire sinks down and sinks in, and the practical resolution of what we are going to do hardens and crystallises in all the veins and fibres.

There is no longer now any localised sensual stir in the person's being. All is diffused, all is spread out through body, soul and spirit. The man does not only want to do this abominable thing with his wrought-up sex-nerve, he wants to do it with his whole nature. That sex-nerve is still at the bottom of it. But that nerve of imaginative evil, now so quietly coiled up—only its little radium-burning eye, of glacier-livid tint, crossed by flickering red levin, remaining alert, only its forked tongue quivering like a compass needle—has projected its dynamic energy through the whole organism, has converted the whole organism into its obedient slave, so that its *immediate* functioning can lie latent.

And the most dangerous aspect of this diffused energy, which now fills the man's whole nature, so that his intellect is inspired by it and his soul is inspired by it and his spirit is inspired by it, is its deadly cunning.

That little coiled-up nerve-snake, now suddenly grown so innocently quiescent that if Mr. Evans were to strip himself naked there would have been nothing indecent in the exposure, gathered the dynamic energy which it spread through his whole being directly from the First Cause.

In the nature of the First Cause there are two windows of manifestation corresponding most precisely to the eyes of such creatures as have no more than two eyes. From one of these slits into the Infinite pours forth good; from the other evil.

When Spinoza taught that the will of God was limited by the nature of God, he was not deducing such doctrine from his intimate experience but from his mathematical reason. Intimate experience of reality—whether it be the experience of the First Cause or of any one of its innumerable creatures—is always reporting "magic, mystery, and miracle" and, along with these, an unbounded faith in the power of the will to *change the nature of the organism.* The whole stream of what is called Evolution depends on this autocreativeness of living things. Nor is there any creature that does not share with the First Cause the power of being good or being evil at its own intrinsic will.

It is the created, not the creator, who so constantly produce good out of evil; and this they do of their absolute free-will. Certain created souls have indeed willed the good rather than the evil so habitually—and these souls are not confined to the human race—that they have rendered themselves impervious to the evil Eye of the First Cause and porous only to the Eye of infinite compassion. The Mr. Evans who now issued forth from Number Two's basement and blew out his candle at the top of those narrow stairs was a Mr. Evans whose will, for that crisis in his life, was entirely evil and whose cunning craftiness in the achievement of his outrageous intention, was supernatural in its flexibility.

"I forget if I told you, Mr. Jones," he said, pulling on his tight black overcoat with twenty times the ease with which he had pulled it off, for no overcoats, no fur-tipped jackets either, slip on so quickly as the ones that are destined for a wicked quest, "that I've got an appointment this morning with Father Paleologue?"

"Aye? What's that? Do you mean you're going, Sir?"

"Father Paleologue. You will remember him if you think a little! He brought a collection of icons to sell for his monastery. A Greek monk he is. Catholic monks are discouraged from coming here—their authorities know, by a secret tradition of scholastic warning, what the Twilight, 'Yr Echwyd,' really means, to which the Grail leads."

Number Two stared at him. "Pardon me, Marm," he murmured to the lady he was waiting upon.

"I've had very few o' they High Cones in me shop," he went on speaking quietly and earnestly to Mr. Evans. "Do 'ee think there'll be a big enough demand for such things as they, to make it worth our ——"

But Mr. Evans was already taking down his bowler hat from the peg where it always rested.

"I'll bring you back a couple in my pocket to show you, Mr. Jones, and I'm sure you'll agree——"

The truth was that Number Two, although no bad judge of a portrait of John Locke, when he saw one, had never seen an icon and had not the faintest notion what such a thing looked like.

But Mr. Evans had opened the street door and was gone; while Old Jones, turning to his customer with an air of confiding all the eccentricities of his partner to her intelligent ear, said something about the study of High Cones being one of those branches of his profession that he'd never aspired to. "Do *you* happen to have picked up a few on 'em, in your travels, Marm?"

While the lady stared at this curious purveyor of rarities, Number Two's partner was some distance down the street, walking very fast towards the Cattle Market. When he reached the entrance to Dickery Cantle's tavern, he opened the door marked "Tap" a little way and peeped in. The tap-room was full of beer drinkers and the air was thick with smoke.

Mrs. Cantle, a pale, worn-out woman, was serving at the bar, assisted by her son Elphin.

Mr. Evans opened the door a little further and remained hesitating.

The small place was so crowded, for it was a favourite resort among those of the Glastonbury unemployed who could lay hands on a penny or two, that neither Mrs. Cantle nor Elphin —nor indeed anyone in the room—noticed that hooked nose, and those gleaming eyes under the bowler hat, snuffing and peering in the entrance like the Devil at Auerbach's Cellar.

Backward and forward went the thin white arm of Mrs. Cantle above the counter; to and fro went the thin, frail figure of Elphin among the little tables in front of the wooden seats. It must have been a scene that with certain trifling differences in cut of costume and tone of voice went back to the time when Glastonbury was a mediæval town of no small importance.

There was not a man here this morning among those drinking who had not come to *forget his troubles* and there was not a man among all these men who had not already realised that purpose in the thick smoke-filled air with its strong smell of beer and cheese and masculine sweat.

The present dictators of Glastonbury—that is to say, Dave Spear, Paul Trent and Red Robinson—would of a surety never have dared officially to interfere with the national regulations about the closing hours of public houses, but when once the local police-force, represented in this case by Bob Sheperd, had received a hint in favour of greater laxity from the mayor of the town, it became easy for the smaller taverns, like St. Michael's on Chilkwell Street, and Dickery's at the Cattle Market, to admit a group of habitual customers, while keeping their blinds down and their shutters closed. Such a group this morning then, at a time when the public bar at the Pilgrims' was authentically shut, was enjoying itself after the fashion of their ancestors and talking loudly about the new commune. No one took the least notice of the gaunt bowler-hatted individual hesitating in the doorway and searching the room with an eye of wild expectancy. Apparently he found what he wanted for he gave vent to a sudden sound between a laugh and a groan. His hesitation came at once to an end now. Closing the door very softly behind him he moved through the smoke and the noisy crowd, past the little tables and the wooden benches, till he reached the counter. Here he stood in complete silence till he caught the landlady's eye.

"Good morning, Mr. Heavings," said Mrs. Cantle in a faint voice. "Have 'ee come about what Dickery do owe Old Jones, for thik second-'and bed and they 'arf a dozen bedroom chairs?"

"Certainly not, Mam," muttered Mr. Evans. "I've come . . . I've come for . . . I've come to . . . have a drink and look round a bit."

"What are ye taking, Mr. Heavings? Straight Scotch, or a peg of Our Special?"

Since neither she nor her husband ever touched a drop of what they sold this latter alternative was understood by everyone in the room to refer to a brand of liquour, more potent even than Mother Legge's Bridgewater punch, which had mellowed for generations in a great butt in the famous Cantle cellar.

The truth was that Our Special was a species of old sack that the years had converted into a liquid gold that was heady and heartening to a degree unparalleled save perhaps by the contents of one of the great historic casks at Bremen. Only the boldest visitors paid their half-a-crowns for a sip of this ancestral fire-water; and a spot of colour came into the hollow cheeks of the thin lady when Mr. Evans, ignorant of the formality of this offer, murmured his preference for the select beverage.

"Us can't afford to treat 'ee to 'un, Mr. Heavings. Thee dost know that, don't 'ee?"

As a reply to this the tall Welshman put his hand into his pocket and produced a big handful of loose silver. "Will that pay for a *double* glass, Mam?" he enquired.

She gave him one of those quick nervous looks that women of all classes are in the habit of giving when in the presence of some striking evidence of masculine extravagance. " 'Twould pay for a three times over," she said.

"Give me just that, please, Mrs. Cantle—a 'three times over.' "

"I baint responsible, Mr. Heavings, if a three times of Our Special sends thee's stumick into thee's head!"

The smile, if it could be called a smile, with which the unfortunate man replied to this warning, awed the woman into obedience. " 'Twill cost 'ee the best of ten shillingses," she said solemnly as she turned to give the order to Elphin. Elphin had been gazing in mute wonder for some while at this unusual customer.

" 'Twill be a full tumbler, Mother," he whispered. "Will Dad be angry?"

"Do as I'm telling 'ee, Elph! The gentleman knows what it be. 'Tisn't for we to say naught if he pours a sovereign's worth down's throat!"

While Elphin was away on this mission and his mother was once more serving her more normal customers with beer, Mr. Evans moved slowly to a wooden bench at the back of the room where the person was seated for whose presence in that place he had been hoping against hope. This person was none other than Finn Toller. The sandy-haired Codfin was sitting alone with an empty flagon in front of him, gazing vacantly into the smoke-filled atmosphere. Watery as usual were his staring, blue eyes within their red circles, and the pale hairs of his eyelashes showed round those rims like the white bristles of a young pig; while his underlip hung down like the lobe of a monstrous purple snapdragon.

"A grey day, Codfin!" remarked Mr. Evans.

"So it be, Mister, I were just thinking there might be rain afore night; but I hopes not. I've a deal to do today one way and the other."

"Do you feel when you have anything to do, Codfin, that everything's unreal, the people and everything, till you've got it done?"

The man gave him a sudden quick look; for the tone of his voice was queer.

"Some people be afraid to sit by I, Mister, but you baint skeered o' little old Coddie, be 'ee?"

"Perhaps you've given them reason to be afraid of you."

Again the queer tone! Mr. Toller experienced the uncomfortable sensation that he got sometimes when he woke up at two o'clock in the night. "Red Robinson be death-sick with fear when he do see I coming. Tother day 'a turned clean round and showed 'is bleedin' arse sooner than for we to meet."

"How do you account for his doing that, Codfin?" said Mr. Evans with burning eyes.

"Dunno. I've done nothink to 'un!"

"Oh, yes, you have, Codfin—Oh, yes, you have. As I was telling you in this place before, you and I are linked together in the movements of the stars and when you come to do what you want to do I'll do what *I* want to do!"

Toller's gaze drew itself away from vacancy and became the expression of a rabbit contemplating a weasel.

"What do *you* know about I, Mister?"

"A great deal, Codfin, more than you guess! And that's because we're in the same boat."

"You be laughing at a poor working-man, Mr. Evans."

"Not at all, Codfin. Do you want my hand on it? There . . . there . . . good luck to you. In the same boat . . . that's where we are, Finn Toller, my friend!"

Elph Cantle's eyes nearly started out of his head, when approaching the little table in front of the two men, with the tumbler of pallid gold in his hand, he saw them shaking hands.

"Mother sez 'tis ten shillingses, Sir, if you please," he whispered, as he put Our Special down. It was Mr. Toller's turn to look surprised when he saw the great handful of silver emerge from his companion's trouser-pocket.

"Bring us another glass, my lad," said Owen Evans gravely.

Young Cantle went off with the money and returned with the glass. He was too hypnotised by what he saw to turn away till Mr. Evans had poured half the drink into this empty receptacle and pushed it towards the tramp.

"Off with you, lad! This isn't ginger pop, or I'd treat you to some too."

When Elphin's figure was swallowed up in the smoke-obscured crowd of labourers, Mr. Evans lifted his glass and nodded to his companion to do the same. It was not often that what he quaffed made Mr. Codfin choke; but the man gasped and spluttered like a woman in his attempt to despatch Our Special at one gulp. As for Mr. Evans he kept murmuring some queer Welsh syllables of carnal approval as he sipped and sipped and sipped at this ancient sack.

"In . . . the same . . . boat . . . Codfin," he repeated, allowing his eyes, with a terrible gleam in them, to rest upon the other's, over the rim of his glass.

There is a danger-instinct in trampish murderers, imbecile thieves, and rural degenerates, which holds out antennæ of warning more responsive than the petal-edges of sensitive plants. Had there been the faintest smell of the official, of the normal-respectable, of the moralistic, of the legal, about Mr. Evans, Codfin would have drawn in his horns and been dumb as a deep-sea fish. There was the devil's own luck too about this encounter in that the noisy buzz of talk around them and the fact that their fellow-topers were all the simplest and roughest type of labouring-men rendered their intercourse as safe and private as if it had been held inside Gwyn-ap-Nud's Stone Tower, on the top of the Tor. It was of this tower that the tramp began soon to murmur, as his wits seethed up into savage confidence under the fumes of the Drink Perilous.

Mr. Evans had already spoken of the iron bar; and the drunken man seemed to have got it lodged in his imbecile brain that this hook-nosed personage with the blazing eyes had been his confederate from the start.

"Her had been better pleased if it had been she rayther nor he, that I were to hit with me bar. But I never struck a 'ooman in me life and never will . . . no! not for Mad Bet herself."

Mr. Evans listened to his words with the blood boiling in his veins and his wrist-pulses beating so hard that he felt he must press them against the cold hard edge of the table. The passage in the book that had driven him forth that day had to do with an iron bar; and as often happens with the symbolic images of crime, this eidolon of violence, which had been floating in the back of his mind ever since that evening at the sheep-fold, drew to itself like a magnet all the other mental pictures in the book and absorbed them into itself.

"You're certain, Codfin—absolutely certain—that they're going up the hill today?"

"Sartin, Mister! In the twilight. That's what Frenchy Crow—us working-chaps calls he Frenchy—said himself when I were listening. Tossie—that's the maidie Boss Barter's gone and married, since her kids were born—have never been up Tor Hill of a night-time. And as they all jabbered there and I listed to un, they said as they was minded—the whole three on 'em—to meet up there 'in the twilight' so's to show thik gal what a dark night be when it do fall on Hill. "Only, us must *see* it fall!" Frenchy Crow kept saying. 'Tisn't naught unless us *sees* it fall."

"Could . . . I . . . be . . . hid . . . inside . . . the tower . . . with you, and watch while you . . . while you . . . do it?"

"Sartinly you can be inside tower. There be a chink in thik door; for I've used it many a times to watch for Mad Bet coming and going; and you can see me bring iron bar down on him, snug and pretty—I'se warrant—from inside thik little pussy-crack!"

Mr. Evans in his agitation now began humming a mid-Victorian sentimental catch, that contained the words "In the gloaming, oh, my darling, ere the night begins to fall," and Mr. Toller with Our Special mounting to his head, caught the spirit of this, just as though some ghastly phosphorescence of unholy glee in the contemplation of murder had bubbled up from both their brains, and began to troll a similar stave: "Once I . . . loved . . . a-maiden-fair . . . *and* . . . she did . . . de-*ceive* me!"

A few labourers glanced towards that sequestered bench, when amid the general confusion of voices these cracked tunes rose up, like the wind in a couple of broken potsherds, and Elph Cantle pulled at his mother's sleeve; but the outburst was followed by a lowering and pregnant silence.

"To see, to see, to see—through that crack—up-down, up-down, the iron bar, up-down, up-down, the iron bar, and the man, up, up, and then down, the iron bar *down*."

From the livid evil Eye of the First Cause, that evil eye that crieth throughout eternity, "Up-down, up-down, the iron bar and the man!" there shivered through Mr. Evans' frame a concentrated essence of all the knee-shaking and pulse-beating passages in his Book of Books.

His hooked nose hung low over his empty glass, low over his two clenched hands upon the wooden table; his bowler hat—for he had not removed it—was pushed far back upon his head; and behold! along the rim of it walked, upon its own purpose bent, a small black fly.

As Mr. Evans' thoughts drove him on, this hat-walker, like a complacent acrobat upon a dizzy ledge, paused in his performance and proceeded to clean his front legs by meticulously rubbing them together.

It has long since been noted how Mr. Evans possessed, in addition to his deeper vision, a furiously precise vein of foreground pedantry.

He now envisaged with infernal exactitude the minutest details of the scene to which his whole body and soul—magnetised by that coiled-up snake-nerve—were rushing forward. And he envisaged too—for instead of being dulled or drugged, his intelligence was quickened and heightened—the issue, the issue of it all.

He felt in advance the sucked-out, scooped-out, blood-rusted hollowness of the gap—the eye-tooth of the world wrenched from its nether-place—that would sink down, that rusty-brown gaping hole that was himself, his very life, down to the deepest abyss. This deadly clear envisaging of the issue of today's business—would it were done and over with now!—drained up every drop of pleasure from the doing of it.

What drove him on to it then? What drove him on to this pleasure-divested horror? The coiled snake-nerve of sex! And the strange thing is that the *insane will to the satisfaction* of this terrible sex-nerve does not demand pleasure. Pleasure? Little do the moralists know! A perverted criminal is called a pleasure-seeker. Great Horns of God! Why, one little tiny drop of the deadly nightshade Mr. Evans was now draining—let it follow the burning path of Our Special down his Cymric gullet!—laid on the tongue of those who talk of pleasure would teach them how feel the sucking lips of the undying Wriggler. No, no, *that* was the curious thing. Mr. Evans was compelled to contemplate with cold-blooded precision the state of being to which this up-and-down iron bar—whatever it did to its victim—would conduct himself.

Pity of Jesus! he was there, even now, as he stared at the tiny golden bubbles in the bottom of his tumbler. He was there and looking *back* at the iron bar, at the blood, at the murdered man. It is a strange fact and a pretty proof of how deep the double nature of the First Cause sinks, that a person could go marching on like this towards the iron bar, and derive not one single half drop of pleasure out of it. Or of satisfaction either!—though it is the will to satisfaction that drives it forward.

If Mr. Evans' thoughts, in spite of Our Special, were far from being frolicsome, the thoughts of Codfin were no less accurst and no less full of "minute particulars."

"I'll *have* to let this gent see it done," he thought, "for he's so crazy-bent on't that, if I dunna let 'un he'll go and give I up to Tarntan Jail. That's where I'll end anyway; and 'twould be Gibbet Hill, only they hangs 'em behind walls now, so us pore buggers can't wave to our aunties. I wouldna' mind Gibbet Hill one 'arf what I minds behind walls. Behind walls makes a person feel like a damned abortion, the kind of nothing-no-more what Dr. Fell sticks in back garden between pig-house and privy. I never *have* liked behind walls and I never will." What force was it that drove Codfin on to the iron bar; that object which he had already so carefully concealed inside Gwyn-ap-Nud's Tower? It was certainly not any sex-nerve. It was purely and solely his sense of honour. Codfin was honourably committed to do the bidding of Mad Bet, and it had never, for one second, since their talk in the sheepfold, presented itself to his mind as a possibility that he could get out of doing it. All this expectation of ending "behind walls" had been accepted by Codfin at the very start as a Jesuit accepts his superior's command or a revolutionary assassin his sealed orders.

While the two heads of these bewitched slaves of the iron bar drooped thus low over their empty glasses, there was a sudden disturbance in that smoke-filled room to which they both remained totally oblivious. This disturbance was caused by the sudden entrance from the interior of the tavern of Dave Spear.

Dave had quite perceptibly changed since he had become one of the dictators of Glastonbury. His youthful bloom had faded. His pleasant good nature had dried up. His out-going impulsive spontaneity had been replaced by a certain strained reserve, and his honest simplicity had given place to a worried, self-conscious caution. The many-sided struggles he was now engaged upon, his attempt to outwit the incorrigible anarchism of one of his fellow-dictators, to give a rational Marxist turn to the destructive Jacobinism of the other, his constant effort to guide into orthodox Communist channels, the mystic religiosity of their erratic chief, caused a stiff, troubled, harassed look to descend upon his boyish countenance, hardening its disarming contours into something anxious, wistful, and at the same time austere.

His appearance was greeted by a clamour of voices and a rush towards him of a group of puzzled, excited, acquisitive labouring-men, who were all dissatisfied with the arrangements of the new Glastonbury exchequer.

" 'Tisn't the money what worries I, Mister," explained a cadaverous shoemaker from Butts Close, " 'tis seeing these chaps what wouldn't work, if they had the chanst, getting the same as I, who've worked meself into a bloody consumpty."

"What I wants to know," cried a burly street-cleaner, pushing himself forward, "is why a man with seven children, same as I've got, only gets five bob more than them as has got two!"

"Listen here, Mister," cried a chimney sweep from the Beckery district, "Didn't us read in Johnny Geard's paper last week that Glaston belong to Glaston folk and none else i' the world? What I'd like to know, and there's many of us working-chaps who want to know the same, who 'twere that elected these 'ere Trents and Robinsons to be bosses over we and who 'twere that gave these 'ere bosses their girt pay? I've got a wife in the family way, four big-grown hungry kids; whereas this Robinson has got only his Sall; and I dunno what Trent's got; no one I reckon! And Trent's not even a Zoomerset man. They tell I 'ee do come from the Scilly Isles. I wish to hell 'ee'd stayed in the Scilly Isles." ("Hear! Hear!" cried a lot of excited voices.)

"Zoomerset money," went on the chimney sweep, "ought to go into Zoomerset pockets; and so 'twould if Bloody Johnny had his zay. Who made this here Trent from Scilly Isles and this here Robinson from London bosses over we Glaston folk? Us selected Johnny Geard, 'cause us knows he; and he be a good drinking man and a good praying man. But us knows naught of this 'ere Trent and this 'ere Robinson. They may be Rooshians, for all us do know!"

Dave Spear was so hustled by all these people that he was driven backward across the room till he was standing close to the table at which Mr. Evans and Finn Toller were seated. He opened his mouth with a gasp of astonishment at seeing Mr. Evans and was on the point of addressing him when a plumber who lived in a little house by the edge of the river and suffered from asthma seized him roughly by the wrist.

"Us be going to keep 'ee wi' us, now us has got 'ee, Mr. Spear," muttered this man, in a hoarse, unpleasant voice—he had evidently been drinking heavily and had reached the quarrelsome stage.

"Let me go! What do you mean by touching me?" cried the indignant Dave. "You don't know what you are talking about. None of you do. No, no; none of you do. You are all thinking only of yourselves. You're all thinking only of getting more money for yourselves—you're all just as bad as Philip Crow."

Things began to look nasty after this bold defiance.

"Knock him on the head!" cried one voice. "Tie 'im up and gie 'em summat to remember us by!" cried a second. "Where be you come from, thee wone self?" yelled a voice from the back of the room, "that's what us wants to know! You baint a Glastonbury man, and us 'ud like to know what you *be*!" So it had come at last. He who had no thought in his mind but to lift up humanity, now saw humanity as it is and was hated, spurned, rejected by it.

He was standing close to the round table by the wall where Evans and Codfin were drowsing over their empty glasses. Here he swung round with his hands deep in his pockets.

"Comrades!" he began in a clear voice.

The uproar stopped, as such turbulence will sometimes, under the spell of a professional speech.

"I don't think you realise, Comrades, how difficult it is to give you back what your bourgeois slave-drivers have stolen from you. You can't get it back for yourselves, because *you* are disorganised and *they* are organised, because you are without leaders and *they* have trained leaders. The only way things can be changed from top to bottom is by a dictatorship that represents you. Mr. Geard your Mayor ——" he was interrupted by shouts at this point: "He's all right. Bloody Johnny's no bleedin' politician. Three cheers for good old Johnny Geard!"—but he went steadily and quietly on: "Mr. Geard, your Mayor—and I'm glad you do justice to him—was elected by your town council; and it is Mr. Geard who has appointed Comrade Robinson and Comrade Trent and myself to act with him in obtaining for you by legal means—for the council has bought up the leases that belong to Lord P.—what Mr. Crow and his shareholders have been keeping from ——" here again he was interrupted. Loud shouts arose, "We know all about Lord P. Lord P. be feared to show his ugly phyz in Glast'n! Lord P. can't sell what isn't his'n to sell! Go back to Lord P. thee own self, and tell the old blighter we'll knock his bleedin' head off and thee's too!"—but once more Dave struggled to go on quietly with his speech.

"By legal means it is, Comrades, that we, your representatives in this town, are now trying, with your assistance and by your help, to start an experiment that has never yet been ——"

"Shut yer bleedin' jaw! Who be you, we'd like to know, that you should rule over us?"

Violent hands were now laid upon him and clenched hands were raised to strike him. The uproar rose again from every part of the room. Something leapt up within Dave then and he lost all his calm self-possession. His ruddy cheeks went white. He struggled with the men. He flung off the hands that had begun clutching at him in the midst of that smoke-obscured confusion.

Like a normal waking-sound caught through the anguish of an insane dream he heard the feeble voice of Mrs. Cantle calling for her husband. "Dickery! Dickery!" Like a sardonic drum the refrain beat upon his ears:

> *"Dickery, dickery, dock—!*
> *The mouse ran up the clock!"*

He pulled out an empty chair from under the little round table at which Mr. Evans and Mr. Toller sat and scrambled up upon it. From this position he cried aloud in a tone so vibrant and so commanding that it brought the room once more to a dead hush.

"Silence!"

"Dickery! Dickery!" echoed the voice of Mrs. Cantle, now reaching that room from some remote place in the rear of the house.

"Oh, brothers, my brothers, you *must* hear me, even though you kill me afterward. You ask *who* I am? I'll tell you who I am! I am the voice of the Future. I am the voice of what is to come when we are all dead. You talk of your rights; the rights of Glastonbury? Brothers, my brothers! In that Future there'll be no more rights. In that Future there'll be no more Glastonburys against Rome, or English against Russia, or West against East. In that Future there'll be only the human race, sprung from the earth, returning to the earth, loving the earth. In the Future none of us, none, I say none, will want to possess this or possess that! We shall struggle then for one thing alone, fight for one advantage alone, the right to labour for a victory of life over want, over disease, over cruelty, over malice, over wicked,

stupid ignorance. Brothers, brothers! Don't let these Christians
say that we who break up their altars and close their churches
only do it for greed. We do it for the Future. We *are* killing God,
the old God, we *are* turning from magic and miracles, those old,
outworn, selfish things, but it is for more Life we're doing it.
Oh, can't you feel it, brothers? We all have the same heart, below
our greeds and our angers and our envies; the same heart, the
same heart. We're all equal before the great spirit of life. Oh,
look into your deep hearts, brothers, and feel it. It is the Truth!
At this moment, here in this place, we are all one. I am you and
you are me! We're all the same, old and young, men and women,
it's one heart we have in us. Here! you can take me. I'll come
down in a minute and you can tear me to bits; but you'll be only
tearing yourselves! There's something in us that's the same, that
belongs to us all; and I'll tell you what it is. It's the Future
being born in us—It's the Future tearing us, breaking us, bruis-
ing us so that it may be born. Brothers, brothers! Even while you
kill me I'll be the same as you are; no different! The same heart
I'll be. For I am Life and you are Life. Life is our child, our
precious child, that we're all perishing for, that we are being torn
to bits for. But in the Future it will know what we did. In the
Future it will say: 'They took their happiness and tore it to bits
for me. They were the tortured Creators; and I,—I am their
offspring.' The same heart in us all, brothers, and this heart cries,
'Drop all this furious fighting for your own hands! Slip aside
from it, escape from it, give it up, let it go, melt into the calm,
cool, universal air!' Brothers! Don't 'ee go on with this eternal,
'I . . . I . . . I . . . I!' Let the heart in you speak, let it be
felt; for *it is always there*! Slip out of this hard, tight knot, this
old evil knot, this old grasping, greedy knot, slip out of it and
be free.

"The Life in us, in them, in Glastonbury, in Rome, in Jerusalem, in India, in America, in China, is the same heart! Brothers!
Can't you feel it? Let it melt that stone, that old, hard, wicked
stone, that stone which is Christ's grave. Let it melt it, be it
Arthur's or Cæsar's, so that we can all flow into one, one Sea,
one Flood, one great calm . . . and quiet . . . and peace.
Brothers, you can take me now and tear me to pieces. You cannot

kill this heart in me, this heart that they have buried in Glastonbury, in Rome, in Jerusalem. You cannot kill it because it's in the killer as well as in the killed. It needs nothing, it wants nothing, it asks nothing. It always gives. It never takes. What can it take, when it is Life, God, the universe, the future? Brothers, my brothers, don't 'ee feel it? It is melting in me to you now, and in you to me! It isn't the self any more. It isn't the Stone against other stones anymore. You ask me who I am. You say I'm not a Glastonbury man. I say to you, 'None of *ye* are Glastonbury men!' I say to you, 'Ye are the passing of the present into the future, ye are the motion of life into fuller life—the heart in you melts in tears, in tears, in tears towards me and mine . . . melts . . . in . . . tears . . . towards you. Who am I, brothers? I am the voice of the Future out of the heart of the present; and that is why . . . that is . . . why . . . I must be . . . why I am . . . a trouble to you . . . a thing that you would like . . . would like . . .' "

He did really burst now into a flood of weeping. The tears— big, child's tears—poured down his face. They poured down his face while his face under their stream remained unmoved, the mouth quiet and stern, the features fixed and rigid, the weeping eyes fixed upon some remote spot in space.

For a moment, while he stood there like that, crying in dead silence, crying as if his round boy's head were made of marble and were a figure in a fountain, Mr. Evans slowly lifted up his bowed forehead, with its great hooked nose, and stared at Dave's muddy trouser-bottoms. What Mr. Evans felt now was, "I must go through with this, though I get no pleasure from it." The curious thing, in the mind of this slave of the iron bar, was that it was *the iron bar itself* that now excited in him this relentless, pleasureless necessity to go on. What it was that sank down under the iron bar, a man, an ox, a sheep, a pig, mattered little to Mr. Evans. That it was his old acquaintance John, picked up at Stonehenge, who was the destined victim, hardly reached his intelligence. Nor did he think of the victim as even destined to be killed. It was not *that* at all! Oh, it was something very different from that. It was an anonymous action too. That was the whole point! "The Unpardonable Sin," like all other extreme forms of vice, was totally impersonal. It was motiveless—except for its own single urge—and it was surrounded by a vacuum of anonymity.

If these were Mr. Evans' thoughts as the young Communist closed his appeal by this fit of passionate tears, the thoughts of the crowd who had listened to him were totally submerged in a spellbound fit of stupefied bewilderment. The room remained absolutely hushed, no one lifted a finger to meddle with what he chose to do now.

He stepped down slowly from the chair to the floor. He was in a trance. That is how it felt to himself and that is how it looked to the crowd in the room—a trance and a complete forgetfulness of where he was.

Vaguely and with short shuffling steps, more like those of a convalescent than a somnambulist, he went to the street door, opened it, and just as he was, with an overcoat on, but without hat or stick, walked off towards Street Road. He felt at that moment a strong desire to look into the sympathetic and yet non-human eyes of the head of the Glastonbury commune. He felt purged, relaxed, reduced to an almost feminine softness, and he longed for the sympathy of Mr. Geard as a young girl might have done.

When Mr. Evans awoke from the drowsiness caused by Our Special he no longer perceived in front of him, mounted upon a chair, a pair of grey, ready-made trousers, and in his sudden awakening he leaned towards his nodding companion.

"When had I better meet you up there?" he said.

Finn Toller only let his straggling beard sink still lower over the table. Mr. Evans grew irritable and shook him violently, gripping the lean man's shambly shoulder unnecessarily hard with his bony fingers. Not so very many people in Glastonbury had fallen gently upon sleep that forenoon,—upon sleep softer than the mosses of Maidencroft Lane, tenderer than the blue vapours of Wick Wood—but among these fortunate ones there were certainly only two, Mr. Toller and Owen Evans, whose thoughts, as they gave way to slumber, had run upon murder.

"When . . . had I . . . better . . . meet you . . . up there?" It was not Mr. Evans who spoke these words. It was a little forked-tongued worm-snake. This worm-snake was jerking and curving and cresting and lifting a head that kept changing colour like a salamander; and it was doing all this inside a human automaton—dead as a corpse—the carcass of what used to be Mr. Evans! Whatever this worm-snake—which kept emitting a poisonous froth, like a snail that has been wounded—ordered this corpse-man, this *homo mortuus*, to do, the corpse-man obeyed. To the excited worm-snake it was a swooning, gasping, fainting ecstasy to think of that iron bar. There was a quivering, dissolving melting sweetness connected with it. The iron bar and the life it was going to blot out were altogether detached from ordinary experience. It was not John Crow who was going to perish. It was simply the man under the bar. The corpselike executioner who obeyed the worm was the galvanized body of the pedantic and highly strung Mr. Evans, who, under normal conditions, could not hurt a daddy-long-legs. Once, when he was very young and seized by a sadistic frenzy—and it is quite possible that the whole thing started from his father's forcing his mother to let him enjoy her long after the child's conception had begun—he had killed something with a piece of iron. After that the little Owen would frantically turn over the pages of all his children's books to find pictures of creatures being killed, especially killed by heavily crushing instruments. It *had* to be a thing of iron and it had to come crashing down, smashing everything, smashing skull and vertebrae together, or the performance, demanded with such a swooning, trembling, fainting orgasm by the worm-snake, would not be a master one! Mr. Evans' tone as he said, "Meet you up there" was like the tone of some Asmodeus whispering to some Baphomet.

"Meet you up there," echoed the sticky surface of their table. "Meet you up there," echoed the dregs of Our Special. "Meet you up there," echoed a little bit of dried-up dog's dung which had been detached from one of the thick-soled boots of Dave Spear and left behind on the chair.

To the worm-snake inside what was once Mr. Evans this harmless sentence "Meet you up there" partook of the nature of an overpowering sexual temptation. The actual sound of the brief syllables . . . "meet . . . up . . . there" was like an erotic provocation of a kind that none could bear and not yield. The fangs of the worm-snake dripped with a frothy milk. In mounted and erected expectancy, in blunt-nosed expectancy, in forked-tongued expectancy, it danced a lust-dance of delirious joy when it found that it could make this slave-corpse, this dead soul, this *rex mortuus*, that *had* been a human being, utter these simple words!

And to what end? To the end of observing how an iron bar, if given a modicum of propulsion from the thin arms of Codfin, would obey the law of gravitation!

The pale blue eyes of Codfin opened now just a little. They were blinking and confused and a moisture trickled from their lids. "Eh? what's that, pard? Meet ye, did ye say?"

"Yes, yes, yes, yes," cried the cresting worm through the lips of Mr. Evans. "When shall I meet you up there?"

About five hours later, Mr. Evans was seated on one of the iron seats on the slope of Wirral Hill, watching the little boys play rounders. Now rounders might be defined as the innocent childhood of baseball, of which it is obviously the original source, and it is a game of the simplest and most primitive hit-and-run nature. And Mr. Evans became extremely interested in rounders that afternoon.

Every time one of the boys hit the ball, Mr. Evans could see the lean stooping figure; not of the John he knew, but of an abstract victim whose name was called John, and of a victim so completely dehumanised and depersonalised that all question of "saving" him disappeared. The only thing to do was to stop the horror. As Mad Bet had screamed to Mr. Evans at Mother Legge's party on Easter Monday, the only thing to do was to "stop" and then to wash the sand clean in the mind's fatal Colosseum.

But Mr. Evans could not "stop." He watched this hit-and-run game with peculiar and special interest because it was exactly what he was going to do himself. *He* was going to hit and run or rather to watch, but Christ would say it was the same thing, someone else hit and run.

Was Mr. Evans mad? Not unless all sexual desire, from the satisfaction of which other sentiencies suffer unnecessary suffering, is mad.

If any stranger had approached Mr. Evans on that afternoon, as he sat watching this game of rounders on Wirral Hill, and induced him to enter into conversation, it is extremely unlikely that the faintest notion of the man's being mad would have crossed such a stranger's intelligence. He had, it is true, been totally unable to eat a morsel of anything since breakfast. But he had been drinking again. He had gone into a little nameless beer-house on the way to Wirral Hill and had drunk glass after glass of beer. "I must drink," he had thought grimly to himself as he tossed off the heel-taps of each separate glass. "I must drink to 'render myself stupid'; as Pascal said about believing the Christian faith." But he had not rendered himself stupid. He had, on the contrary, given himself a racking headache; but otherwise nothing could be clearer than Mr. Evans' mind. He was to "go up there" at sunset and wait inside the tower to see—actually in his flesh to see—what he had been telling himself stories about all his life long.

Let no one think that the obedient *rex mortuus* or *deus mortuus* that was Mr. Evans' soul, did not weigh the possible consequences, down to every smallest detail of what he was going to do, making himself, by thus knowing about it beforehand and doing nothing to stop it, an accomplice in a murder. "Undoubtedly, I shall land in jail," he thought. "It's possible enough that it will be worse than that. Why in God's name then, don't I walk straight back to the shop, or home to Cordy, and shake off this monstrous weight? The police? To go to the police? No, no, no, no! The thing to do is"—at this point the invisible worm itself began whispering a subtle self-deception, a cunning compromise—"go up there and get hold of the iron bar myself— yes! yes! yes! That's the thing to do, from every point of view— to go up there *presently*—it's too early yet—and, as soon as Toller appears, just take the thing from him and pack him off; and then tell Crow, or not tell Crow, as I consider best at the time—get hold of that thing from Toller first anyway, and pack *him* off and perhaps it would be better never to tell Crow, or any other living soul, about it— yes, yes, never tell anyone about it— but would Toller try it again? It's some madness of that bald-headed woman—the Grail Messenger—I couldn't follow it when he was telling me—madness of some kind—*damn!*"

His mind called up the image of Mad Bet as she had seemed to him that night when she had made him kiss her naked skull. A wry smile twisted his lips as he thought of that night and he clutched the iron bar—another and a different one—that made the elbow of his present resting place!

A sardonic and tormented chuckle, a veritable damned soul's chuckle, broke from his twisted mouth.

"Hee! Hee! Hee! *My* Grail Messenger! It's all mixed up with Crow. It was Crow who asked me, that night, if I could embrace a woman who was perfectly hideous, and I told him then about the Grail Messenger. Hee! Hee! Malory, you old devil! There's life still in your Norman book! Yes, yes! you understand these little things. Life's not changed. It all comes round—round and back again." What had happened now, as the man sat there clutching the iron elbow of that cold seat, while the little boys kept hitting and running in front of him, was that his first nature—the antiquarian one—was all stirred up into a writhing weft of self-protective fantasy. And this had come about in a very subtle manner; for by saying to himself that what he must do anyway was *to go up there*, even if he snatched the iron bar from the bewitched assassin and confessed everything to John Crow, he had covered with a sort of adhesive plaster the gaping hole of his tormented conscience; and this covering up of the dark, sweet, irresistible twitching of the snake-worm, left his normal upper-consciousness free to deceive him to the limit with accumulated plausibilities; while all the time the worm licked its devouring fangs in the darkness below!

What the worm said to itself was: "Let us only once *go up there*, and the swooning, drowning, dissolving ecstasy of the Dolorous Blow will soon sweep away all these conscientious hesitations!" Calmed and eased a great deal by this crafty compromise with his conscience which rendered his rendezvous with the iron bar a necessity if he were to save John Crow as well as a possibility of playing the ecstatic voyeur at a murder orgy if he decided *against* saving John Crow, his eyes now fell upon the figure of an elderly woman walking heavily and stumblingly up.

the slope of the hill below the level where he was sitting and the boys were playing.

There was an iron seat, like the one he himself was occupying, a little below the boys and a little above the woman; and it was towards this seat that she was evidently advancing.

She was well dressed and she was using her umbrella as a stick to lean upon; and as he followed her with his eyes, stumbling and exhausted, moving up the slope of the hill, he decided that he knew who she was, and that she was none other than Miss Crow. Miss Crow indeed it was, and a Miss Crow on the verge of a fainting-fit from her bad heart. There were several people passing both ways, both to the north and to the south, along the gravel path below the place where the lady with the umbrella was tottering; but it was a group of complete strangers—strangers to her as well as to him, for they were visitors to Glastonbury from the northeast of Germany—who, when she fell, as he saw her do now, rushed up the slope to her aid. There certainly was a peculiar atmospheric effect abroad, this February day. A soft, light mist, filmy and gossamery as a wet sea-vapour, hung over the town; while the sun, shining between heavy banks of clouds, touched with a curious opalescence, pearly and tender, the portion of the hill upon which he was now seated.

The boys ceased at once playing their game, when they observed the disturbance made by the lady's fall, and calling to each other in shrill, excited cries scrambled down the slope and huddled, as children will, pushing, whispering, jostling to get the clearest view between the burly figures of the Germans. These latter were now talking in vociferous and guttural tones across the body of the prostrate woman. One of them was actually on his knees beside her, loosening the throat of her dress and trying to pull off her gloves.

When Mr. Evans joined the group he was accepted at once as a native of the place and everyone appealed to him as an authority upon what ought to be done with a lady of distinction and refinement who apparently had had a fit.

He was aghast at the spectacle of the poor lady's face as he bent over it. In unqualified concern and pity he surveyed the unnatural redness of her skin, the drops of white froth issuing from her open mouth, and the family twitch, palpitating still, though she was quite unconscious, in her flaccid cheeks. She had been acting recklessly and unwisely all that day after her morning visit to the doctor. She had stopped at Wollop's longer than she should; she had kept her appointment to lunch at the Pilgrims' with Rachel and Athling; and as soon as she could escape from these young people she had made her way, slowly but obstinately, to Wirral Hill, being seized with a passionate desire to rest upon the particular iron seat where, thirty years before, she was accustomed to meet Mat Dekker. As Mr. Evans now surveyed her unconscious form he found that he was not so devoid of natural philosophy as not to be grimly aware of the irony of the fact that he, the insane pervert, was now contemplating with lively concern the blow which heart trouble, that gentlest of all wielders of iron bars, had brought down on this warm mass of corpulent femininity.

It was clear that the players at rounders, as they inserted their small perspiring bodies between the anxious foreigners, thought that Miss Crow was dead: and the words "She has it got, my God!" and "Death her has taken, God in Heaven!" in the thick intonation of the great Mid-European plain, showed that the foreigners laboured under the same delusion. "The woman something to say wishes!" cried the man suddenly who was bending over her on his knees. "To fetch the Herr Doctor it better were!" replied another; and a third—an extremely sturdy little man, planted upon his heels so firmly, as if nothing could ever bowl *him* out—uttered the expressive, the impenetrable, the massively undying word, consonant to all occasions, reassuring under all invasions of disorder, the word "Police"! How fast the mind works and how self-centred the human ego is!

Even as he came forward and knelt down by Miss Crow's side, even as he lowered his ears to Miss Crow's murmuring lips, the Welshman was thinking to himself: "Who's to know—if Codfin doesn't speak when they arrest him—that I wasn't in the tower by chance? No . . . no . . . no! I shall never in all my life have another chance of seeing, of drinking up with my very eyes, what I've been telling my pillow about night after night since I first knew what . . . *what I was!*"

She was murmuring intelligible words now. She was taking Mr. Evans for someone else, for a different tall bony man. But, as he listened to her and smelt upon her grey hair, from which the hat had been torn, a faint scent of eau de cologne, he remembered how more than once he had dressed up that pillow of his in his own vest and shirt and had pounded it with the poker from the fender while an orgasm of terrible ecstasy dissolved his very soul.

"I can't let this chance go . . . no! not if I'm hanged for it . . . I can't . . . I can't!" But nothing seemed able to keep away from him—as he heard the sturdy little man, whose feet were so firm in the grass and so wide apart, repeat the word "Police"—a thin ice-cold bodkin-point of ice-cold terror—the police . . . the police . . . the police . . . the police . . . This is a crime I'm going up there to see . . . different from any secret vice, however shameful . . . this is a crime . . . the worst of crimes . . . and when I've had *that ecstasy* . . . to the end of my days all will be exposed . . . Owen Evans the pervert . . . Owen Evans the malefactor . . . Owen Evans the murderer. They'll have me in Madame Tussaud's moulded in wax . . . my nose, that everyone laughs at so . . . in wax . . . "Have you been down to the Chamber of Horrors yet, and seen Owen Evans? Anyone would know from his face what *he* was . . . the human carnivore!"

Meanwhile from the contorted mouth of the unconscious woman, whose eyelids kept flickering but did not open, the breathing grew louder and less human, and between the great animal gasps, like the flapping of a bellows, broken, incoherent words forced out their way.

The German upon his knees by her side seemed to be dimly acquainted with the sort of attack she was suffering from, for he lifted up her head and began pouring down her throat something from a small flask that he produced. But instead of recovering her from her fit this treatment only had the effect of stopping her attempts at speech and of throwing her back again into complete immobility.

For a moment Mr. Evans thought she was really dead now; but

the German with his hand on her heart muttered emphatically:
"Life she still has, the poor woman! Life she still has!"

"Has anybody sent for the—police?" Mr. Evans whispered to
the German with the flask. He had meant to say—"for the
doctor."

The kneeling man rose to his feet now, shrugged his shoulders
and addressed some question to his companions. It appeared
from what they said that nobody had gone for anybody. The soul
of the obsessed Welshman now made a hurried rush down the
corridors of his consciousness, closing the door to the iron bar
chamber down there, and opening more normal vestibules of
awareness. "I . . . go . . . get . . . Herr Doctor!" he announced, surveying these simple guardians of the unconscious
lady. Thus speaking, he raised his bowler hat with a grandiose
gesture, both to the woman on the ground and to the strangers
round her, and made off at a great pace down the gravel path
that led to the town.

In the confusion of his wits, however, it was not to Dr. Fell's
house but to his own house that he directed his way; a secret
urge within him driving him now, as in all practical crises, to
go at once to Cordelia. But if a beneficent chance moved him
to this self-preservative action, a malefic chance willed it that
when at last, panting and breathless, he entered his little house
in Old Wells Road he found Cordelia deep in conversation in
her parlour with her mother, Mrs. Geard.

Mrs. Geard had been confiding to Cordelia her growing worry
about the girl's father; how he persisted in spending the bulk
of his time over at Chalice Hill, and how he had been several
times of late upon some mysterious errands to the Glastonbury
bank. " 'Tisn't that he be changed, Cordy, you understand. 'Tis
that he be more his own self than I've a ever known him. Crum
sees it too. 'Tis as if this commune silliness has wrought on him
to let himself go. He talks more about the Blood and the Master
and the Water of Life than I've ever known him. He talks every
night, Cordy, on and on, after us have put out the gas. I wish
he would tell me what he goes to the bank for! Mr. Trent brings
him his pay for being Mayor regular enough. There's no reason
why he should go to the bank. I don't like, nor I never *have*

liked, that young man Robert Stilly. What do you think he goes to the bank for, Cordy?"

If Mr. Evans had caught a glimpse of Mrs. Geard through the window he would have shot off again, but fortunately the two women were seated out of sight of the window, so that it wasn't till he opened the parlour door that he knew she was there. Cordelia recognised at once that something was very wrong with him; for he stood in the doorway muttering about Dr. Fell, Bob Sheperd, Germans, rounders, Miss Elizabeth Crow fainting on Wirral Hill, and his having an appointment at sunset that night . . . a very important appointment . . . at sunset . . . with Father Paleologue . . . at sunset . . . about some icons.

The mother and daughter were both of them on their feet, looking at him with an uneasy stare, Cordy with a passionate and frightened stare, Mrs. Geard with a worried and anxious stare. "I hope *he* has not been going to the bank," the latter thought to herself; and in her heart she began wondering whether icons were some species of familiar spirits, like her own Pembrokeshire fairies, that this Mr. Paleologue claimed he could conjure up.

"I only came in to tell you, Cordelia," said Mr. Evans now in a clearer, more intelligible manner, "that I've got to send Dr. Fell to Wirral Hill, where Miss Crow lies unconscious. After I've been *there*, I've got this engagement at . . . at sunset. Did I say sunset? Yes, at sunset. I hope you are feeling very well, Cousin Megan?"

At this actual moment, towards this man in a disordered state of mind—an iron bar tapping on the inside door of his locked-up intention—and towards two women staring at this man in bewildered uneasiness, the First Cause poured forth its double magnetic streams of white and black vibrations. Out of Nothing, out of pre-existing vortices of energy that themselves issued from Nothing by the creative will of this Being, Mr. Evans, his wife, and his wife's mother had been created. In them the First Cause reproduced itself, the Macrocosm in these three microcosms; and, like the First Cause, these three persons, Mr. Evans standing in the doorway, Cordelia standing by her husband's writing desk, and Mrs. Geard standing by the purple chair, had the power of giving themselves up to the good in their nature or to the evil.

For Mr. Evans *could* at that very moment, even as he gazed at that picture of the river, the woman and the boat, which he associated with the word Esplumeoir, have transformed himself into a saint as devoted, as spiritual, as tenderly considerate as Sam Dekker, who in his normal state was a good deal less like a saint than Mr. Evans was! This he *might* have done, even as he stood there, after telling these plain-faced women, while the mother-of-pearl sunlight flickered into the room, those lies about Father Paleologue; and in doing so have rendered himself morally superior to the First Cause, if it had not been that from the word Esplumeoir his mind reverted to Merlin's early life and to that incident of the horn of the stag. "So good-bye, Cordy. So good-bye, Cousin Megan. I *must* get hold of Dr. Fell and I *must* meet Father Paleologue."

This moment was a moment of such a fatal parting of the ways, that the Invisible Watchers who were standing at the brink of the deep Glastonbury Aquarium, watching the motions of its obsessed animalculae, had never crowded more eagerly around their microscope to learn what the issue would be. It all depended upon which of the two vibrations proceeding from the First Cause Cordelia would welcome and which she would reject. The destructive vibration, at this important crisis, willed her to be cold, chaste, inert, irresponsible, absorbed in her own personal condition, which had never been more interesting to her!

The creative vibration, on the contrary, willed her to be warm, alluring, unchaste, and self-forgetful, thinking only of her love for the unhappy man before her! In her earlier relations with Mr. Evans, Cordy had frequently been stupid and remiss; but the "sweet usage" to which her ungainly form had been subjected, and the caresses by which her cold nerves had been quickened, had changed all this. It was not that she had come to understand the nature of his perversion; but she had come to understand, to a nicety, the place in his consciousness where that closed chamber was, and to be an adept in the art of keeping it closed. She had discovered that by certain devices—devices into which it is not necessary just now to follow her—it was possible to give Mr. Evans so much erotic excitement, of an abnormal, but perfectly harmless kind, that his soul could go up and down past that locked-up chamber without a thought of the temptations it contained.

It was lucky for Mr. Evans that at this crisis Cordelia was fully aware that to be inert and irresponsible would have been a devilish sin. The vibration of eternal creative energy which poured down into her nerves from that remote double-natured Force at the root of all life was now deliberately welcomed by the spirited girl and the opposite vibration heroically rejected. She moved up hurriedly to Mr. Evans, got behind him, drew him forward by the sleeve till she got him to the hearth; and then, linking her arm in his, turned emphatically and imperatively to Mrs. Geard.

"Mother!"

"Yes, Cordy."

"I want you to call at Dr. Fell's. It won't take you so very far out of your way if you go by the allotment gardens and that alley I showed you the other day. And just tell him, or Miss Barbara, if he's out, what Owen has said about Miss Crow having fainted—by those seats, wasn't it, Owen?—on Wirral Hill, and those Germans looking after her. I expect she's all right by this time; or someone else has gone for the doctor; but in any case do go quick, Mother, please, because I can see Owen's very worried about it."

There were no doubt some quick private glances between mother and daughter after this, in which the mother said: "What's up, my dear? Has he been drinking?" and the daughter said: "Don't ask me now, but just go! I'll tell you everything another time"—but the upshot was that Mrs. Geard hurried off.

The good lady's lilac-coloured bonnet rose up like a flag of onset from her grey head as she walked down Wells Old Road, and her old-fashioned velvet-sided boots delivered short quick taps to the brick pavement under the railings of those red-tiled houses, and every now and then she automatically unclicked and clicked-up the metal fastening of her purse, as if she were rejecting all assistance from Mr. Robert Stilly in the management of her affairs. "I cannot *think* why John keeps going to the bank," she kept saying to herself as she crossed the allotments.

Mr. Evans was now alone with Cordelia; and the first thing the girl did was something that at once provoked a faint flicker of natural erotic excitement in the man's perverted nerves. She began pulling down the parlour's brown blinds upon that sunset period of the day. Woman-like, she had absolutely no notion of the explosives she was handling, of the volcano-fires under the crater-surface she was stirring up. But woman-like, too, she, who had been virgin so long, was a cunninger adept than a thousand Thaïses in the primeval arts of provocation. Daughter of Bloody Johnny as she was, her own erotic nature, now that it had been once excited was inexhaustible in its amorous devices; and since her moods and her lures were forever changing, Mr. Evans was in the position of the fortunate possessor of a whole harem of ardent play-fellows. In none of her Cyprian disguises could poor Cordy be called pretty; but wanton and freshly blooming she certainly *could* be called; such is the magical power of Eros.

She had a surprise for her man now. Pulling down the blinds of their tiny parlour on the general principle announced so often by Mother Legge, that she "could not abide onlookers," and throwing her hat and cloak on their big arm-chair she went up to the fireplace where a newly lit flame was making the wood crackle, and leaning against the edge of the mantelpiece, she began a rapid flow of excited words. She was going, she told him, without any doubt, to have a child. She had already gone two months with it. She had been yesterday to see Dr. Fell about it. It would be born sometime in September.

Mr. Evans dropped his bowler hat on the floor and sank down exhausted in his black overcoat on the big purple chair. Half of her jacket and the rim of *her* hat were squeezed under him as he sank down, for she had just come in when her mother arrived; but he did not make the least move to extricate them. Nor indeed did she! Watching him with swimming eyes she waited in silence for what she hoped and prayed would prove to be a rush of natural emotion at what she had told him. And drawn towards them by the intensity of their feeling, drawn towards this embryo grandchild of Geard of Glastonbury, there came floating into that room through the pulled-down blinds a flock of obscure, half-material presences, the sort of etherealised thought-projections that are liable to hover over certain crises in human lives. Like invisible birds these presences gathered, sweeping into the room out of the aqueous mists of that unusual day, gibbering and chittering to one another and circling about Cordelia.

Neither the man nor the woman, he in the purple chair whose tasselled valances swept the floor, and she leaning against the flimsy mantelpiece, could have been conscious at that moment that this embryo in the room with them was beginning to assert itself as an entity with its own contact with the life-mysteries. What they both felt just then as these thought-elementals fluttered round the new life in Cordelia's womb, as blow-flies are attracted to carrion, or as humming-bird moths to the hearts of carnations, was something very different from these ethereal visitors. What they were aware of was the dumb, numb, cold, heavy downward drag of the vast undersea forces that are sub-human; chemical forces, that belong to that formless world of the half-created and the half-organic whereof bodies of lower dimensions than ours are composed and which has a mysterious weight that draws down, a pull, a tug, a centripetal gravitation, against which the soul within us struggles and upon the surface of which it swims, and over which, when the process of decomposition commences, it spreads its contemptuous wings.

This down-dragging sensation in their nerves neutralized and counter-balanced these half-embodied air-presences, the elemental projections of old magical minds upon that sensitised Glastonbury air, floating like a cloud of disturbed river gnats through those lowered brownish-coloured afternoon blinds, out again into that subaqueous mist, out again into the wide water-meadows.

No philosopher has yet appeared who has realised as it should be realised, the creative power of the human mind. Behind these brownish-coloured, pulled-down blinds on the way to St. Edmund's pottery, where all those little town-council houses carried their red-tiled roofs so trim, there emerged from Cordelia's mind as she stood with her staring, swimming, dazed eyes fixed on her mate and her awkward elbow propped on that ridiculous mantelpiece, such an intensity of feeling that it had the power to draw out of the air, although she knew it not, these wandering half-lives. Any clairvoyant sense could have seen them there hovering about her body, and making their weak, chittering signals to the subhuman progeny of her womb, whose embryo consciousness must have been on a level with their own half-created fumblings. But why did this thick, dumb, numb, down-dragging pull of cosmic entropy, this dark gravitation-weight, sinking into decomposition and dissolution, tug at those two just then, at the man in the purple chair, with the tasselled valances trailing upon the floor, and at the woman who had just told him he was a begetter? Was it because—with that iron bar hammering to get out from its locked-up prison—Mr. Evans' fungus-grown mind groped amid after-births and abortions and corpses dead in their travail?

Whatever the cause may have been of what happened to those two behind those drawn blinds, both visitations came and went in no more than a hundred tickings of the watch in the man's pocket. Phenomena that pass so quickly—thought-elementals floating in and floating out, and this death-cold touch of the draught of decomposition—surely they are beneath notice, beneath analysis, beneath explanation? On the contrary, the very essence of life is revealed in such fleeting impressions; and in experiences such as these Eternity itself can be heard moaning and weeping, as its Cimmerian waters advance and recede around the lamplit promontories of Time.

"What shall we call him if he's a boy, Owen?" Her voice just then was more than he could bear. Nothing makes human nerves dance with such blind fury as a voice piercing the hollow of the ear at the moment when the will is stretched out like a piece of India rubber on the rack of indecision.

"Torture!" he shouted, sitting up in the purple chair and clutching its elbows furiously, while the rim of her hat was now completely crushed beneath him. "We'll call him Torture; and if she's a girl we'll call her Finis, the End. For she'll *be* the end. And all is the end."

Cordy's face went white, white as the surface of the little

china pussy-cat which Crummie had given her, and which now fell over sideways as she jerked her arm from the mantelpiece. But she wasn't the daughter of Geard of Glastonbury for nothing. Incontinently she rushed straight to his side.

"You're unhappy, Owen; you're ill; you're hurt. Something horrible's troubling you."

He pushed her arms away. He lurched to his feet. He bent down and picked up his bowler hat which was lying on its smooth crown, its dirty interior uppermost. "It's nearly sunset," he muttered. "If I don't go now I'll never go."

"Where are you going, Owen?"

He looked at her wildly. "Well! he must be *stopped*, mustn't he? It's one thing or the other, isn't it?"

"What *are* you talking about, Owen? Are you crazy?"

"Oh, nothing . . . nothing . . . nothing . . . nothing!" he muttered. "You don't want to see me in the dock, do you? In the dock, woman!" These last words came from him with a wild shout.

Cordy glanced at the brown blinds which were bulging a little. There was a wind blowing up. She went to the door leading into the passage, locked it, and placed her back against it. "You don't leave this room, Owen," she gasped.

He was now buttoning up his black overcoat. His hat was on his head, pressed down so low over his eyes that his eyebrows were invisible. This produced a most curious effect as he glared at her from under its shadow. But an unexpected change of mood came upon him. He began wheedling and coaxing and imploring.

"It's only a little way . . . just up the hill . . . it's necessary too . . . necessary . . . very necessary . . . *Please* move, Cordy, and let me go. . . . You'll be sorry if you don't. . . . You won't forgive yourself afterwards . . . if you don't." He almost wept as he beseeched her. In his own mind just then to stop a murder and to taste an appalling sweetness were motives both lost in the wild *necessity* he was in to get out of this room!

But she kept her eyes upon him all the time and she now noticed that he had begun casting a furtive, hurried, crafty look at the window. Nothing indeed would have been easier for him than to lift up that bulging blind and get out of that window!

"I must do something to keep him here," she thought, "and I mustn't struggle with him . . . because of the child. Besides, he'd hit me. He'd hit me savagely." A wild strange thought came to her then; came to her from seeing the look of that lowered blind. Very often in the evening she had undressed for his pleasure, with the blind pulled down like that, and the door locked.

She began feverishly stripping off her clothes. He followed every movement of her hands with those burning eyes, under the shadow of that bowler. His coat was buttoned up tight under his chin. He looked like a man ready to rush out upon pikes or bayonets. Crossing her arms over her chest she pulled her dress over her head and then her slip. Then she unloosed her petticoat and drawers. Stamping with her feet she extricated herself from these objects, letting her stockings and shoes remain. Backing against the door, she bent down and pulled off her vest, dragging it over her head. This final movement, when her head was bent low, and when her face was hidden, and when the garment, dragged forward by her eager hands was caught for a second on one of her hairpins, did stir some deep chord of excited desire in the man with the burning eyes.

He snatched off his hat and flung it in the purple chair. But she rose up to her full height now, her back still to the door, her long arms hanging limp by her sides, her chin lifted high, her head thrown back. Mr. Evans came slowly towards her. Poor Cordy's figure was anything but classical. She resembled a nude of Cranach. But there was such an heroic abandonment about her pose, and her eyes shone with such a lustrous appeal, that something happened within that other locked room, the room containing the iron bar. Not for nothing was this brave girl the child of Geard of Glastonbury. Roused to the uttermost her soul suddenly became a psychic force, a magnet of destruction, an annihilating ray, and the murderous instrument, summoning up page seventy-seven of that fatal book, crumbled into a pinch of dust.

Grotesque and Cranach-like though poor Cordy's naked body was, it was the body of a woman still, it was the ultimate symbol, the uttermost "Gleichnis," of life's wild experiment. Grotesque it might be, as nakedness went, but combined with the look she managed to fling, like a passion of immortal wine over the dark flame of his obsession, it overcame, it triumphed. . . .

One hour later Mr. Evans and Cordelia might both have been seen jumping with frantic haste out of Solly Lew's taxi, and to the astonishment of that not easily surprised conveyor of mortal men, racing with desperate impatience up the slope of Gwyn-ap-Nud's hill. "They're there, Cordy! They're there! I see them!" panted Mr. Evans, trying in vain to out-distance Mr. Geard's daughter.

It had been with some reluctance that Tossie Stickles—now for some heavenly months Tossie Barter—had been persuaded to leave her babies and accompany her husband and John Crow on this fanciful excursion to see the night fall upon Glastonbury from the summit of the Tor. Barter himself had been followed by one good piece of luck after another ever since they had been married. He had hired spacious and airy rooms in the same house in Northload Street where John and Mary lived, and between the two ménages there had been unruffled and uninterrupted harmony. With the establishment of the new régime in Glastonbury he had been entirely freed from the annoying presence of Red Robinson at the Factory. Robinson had now become what might be called the third triumvir among the magnates who, under Mr. Geard, dictatorially administered the affairs of the small community; and Barter was at liberty to manage the making of souvenirs entirely at his own discretion.

The one topic of conversation in these days that Barter indulged in and upon which he expatiated at inordinate length to Mary when they were alone was, what had been the psychological reason for the miserable way in which he had lived before he met Tossie. Into Mary's private thoughts—and they were subtle and ironical enough—as she listened to these discourses, it is not necessary to go; but what she *said* to Barter was, that all unattached men are curiously ignorant of "what things a girl can do"—such was Mary's expression—to make life pleasant.

Meanwhile, so happy was Tom Barter these days, that in a brief two months his whole expression changed and the whole cast of his countenance was altered. He positively looked fatter, too; and his manner of speech was different. He spoke in a

tone much more easy, much more assured. It was their Rabelaisian sense of humour that was one of the greatest links between Tom and Tossie; and morning and night—with the twins
sometimes included and sometimes not—their fits of giggling and
chuckling and unrestrained laughter, going on and on and on,
made the second storey of that gloomy old house sound as if a
party of hilarious schoolboys was staying the night with a party
of hilarious schoolgirls.

The mention of school is relevant enough in this connection;
for what this *vita nuova* of Tom Barter really meant was that
Tossie had picked up what might be called the man's lost flesh-
and-blood pride just where he had dropped it in his youth under
his unlucky experiences at Gladman's House at Sherborne. Something in him, some psychic organ full of a delicious, animal
gusto for simple things, and an invincible desire to giggle at
everything in existence, had been restored to him by his contact
with Tossie and not only this: for it soon became apparent, even
to John and Mary, that Barter was no longer afraid to "stand
up," as Toss would put it, to "they bloomin' gentry." This aspect
of what the girl had done for him had been brought especially
into evidence of late by reason of his association with Lady
Rachel, who—still unmarried to young Athling but still constantly at his side—found herself asking Barter, in place of anybody else, to meet her father whenever he came to the Pilgrims'.

Lord P. was constantly coming to the Pilgrims' now; not because he loved a communistic Glastonbury, for he was still
excessively nervous of the mob that had attacked him; but because he had become seriously worried about Rachel's relations
with her Ned; and the queer thing was that with his Norfolk
youthfulness restored to him, and the Gladman House years
erased from his life, by these perpetual giggling fits with Tossie,
Barter proved much more a match for the elderly nobleman and
a much more agreeable table-companion to him than anyone
else that Rachel could have picked up.

Lady Rachel's own genius, too, for these little souvenir figures
that his factory was now turning out by the thousands and sending all over the world, had by this time really got Barter interested in his job. The souvenir factory was doing by far the

most flourishing business in Glastonbury. More money was being made by it than either by the new dye works that the municipality had communized or by the old dye works that Philip was still running, and far more than by the Crow tin mine at Wookey, which now began to show signs of having exhausted its vein of the precious metal; and Barter's professional pride, as the head of so flourishing a business, being mingled with his new psychological self-respect and his new freedom from the wearisome hunt for erotic novelty, made him just now the happiest and best-balanced *male* animal in the town; although in the intoxication of a pure zest for life in its essence he was probably surpassed not only by his own radiant Tossie but also by Tossie's relative by marriage, the beautiful and mystical Nancy.

" 'Tis a shame," Tossie remarked to Mary as she poured out tea for her and John while awaiting Barter's return from the factory, " 'tis a shame for you to stay and look after the kids. They'd really stay asleep just as they be and no one would disturb 'em if I just locked up the place."

"I wouldn't think of it, Toss dear," said Mary emphatically, "so don't speak of it again. Tom'll be back soon, John; so don't finish the tea-cakes!"

"I wasn't thinking of finishing them," protested John indignantly, "but to make sure, I'll put 'em on the stove, if I may, Toss?" He rose, as he spoke, and replaced the dish in question near the big smoking tea-kettle. As he surveyed the scene at the table, Mary's dark head and Tossie's fair one, both bent towards the cradle at its side, and a bowl of snowdrops, their stems protruding from green moss, resting near its edge with a baby's milk-bottle propped against it, John got a sudden delicious feeling of the continuity of these *domestic vignettes*, as they gather themselves together and take varied patterns all the way down the centuries! He paused for a second, his hand on the dresser shelf above the stove where Tossie kept her pepper-pot and salt-bowl, and the fanciful idea seized him that groups of this sort—the two girls' heads, the cottage-loaf on the rough linen tablecloth, the two babies' heads in the cradle on the floor —were all answering and responding as they reappeared down the ages, from the dawn of time, to some invisible pattern of pre-ordained harmony which was forever being struggled after by Nature and forever being just missed, or lost as soon as it came together.

As he stood there watching those four feminine heads, the grown ones and the others, grouped about that cottage-loaf and that bowl of snowdrops, the scene wavered and fluctuated before him, melted, dissolved and changed. Through that Glastonbury room, as he gave himself up to his waking-trance, flowed the big river at Northwold, rose the span of Foulden Bridge, whitish and narrow, deepened and darkened the dim pools of Dye's Hole, under their ancient willow roots! Why should he wait for old Tom's return, why should he wait till he and Mary were alone together, to tell her the thrilling news with which his mind was brimming over that afternoon? He had come to this tea-party at Tossie's to find Mary already there; and except for what his wife could read in his excited face—and he knew she had read something already!—he had had no chance even to whisper to her by herself. Where had John come from on this twenty-fifth of February, this day of such unusual atmospheric effects?

He had found a little note from the Mayor when he reached his office-shanty down by the railway after lunching with Mary at his favourite Othery Dairy in Street Road; and back again to Street Road he had immediately dragged himself, not a little peevish at having to retrace his steps across the whole width of the town. But once inside Cardiff Villa, once ensconced in Mrs. Geard's chair, with the well-known knitted antimacassar of bright coloured wools behind his head, and old Geard nodding his great white face opposite him, he had known, by one of his swift vagabond instincts, that, as far as he was concerned, this day of strange under-water lights was a bringer of incredible, undreamed-of luck. To the end of his days would John Crow remember that interview with his master. The first thing he had noticed—for he had seen little of Mr. Geard since the man had become so much more than the Mayor of Glastonbury—was that Bloody Johnny had got older. Yes, his hair was greyer, his face was whiter, his plump hands were more wrinkled and the stomach over which they were folded was more capacious.

"And that's why, lad," Mr. Geard said, "I can talk to 'ee about things I can't speak of to anyone else. 'Twould make Crummie unhappy, and the sweet lass is unhappy enough over Holy Sam, and 'twould make Cordy nervous; and as for my dear wife —— The truth is, lad, I've been telling He, ever since our opening of the arch, that His work for me here be about done. At first He wouldn't give ear to what I said. He thought 'twas laziness, or the Devil in me bosom. But when I went on telling He how 'twere, He came little by little to give heed. 'Tweren't that He were deaf, even afore, ye must understand, sonny; but 'twere that I be such a queer one, and that I had summat in me—yes, laddie, that's the solemn truth—what He couldn't get the hang of!"

John looked at the diabolical black eyes—now gleaming like two fuliginous mine shafts out of some Tartarean tin mine— and he thought to himself: "I don't wonder that Christ finds it hard to understand him. The truth is the old chap's never been more than half a Christian."

"You are not easy to understand, Mr. Geard," he murmured aloud.

The remark seemed to displease the Mayor of Glastonbury. "That's because I'm too simple for 'ee. I be too simple for anything in this clever town. I be a Montagu man, I be."

"I don't call you simple, Mr. Geard!" John was growing excessively bold in this interview with his master. Was it that his drifting tramp's mind had gathered up an inkling that this was the very last time, upon this earth, that he would talk to Mr. Geard face to face?. It is not often given to human beings to be able to treat a fragment of time that can never return again with the intense and ritualistic concentration appropriate to a moment irretrievably slipping away into an everlasting impossibility of repetition.

But on this February afternoon John Crow did touch exactly and precisely such an intense concentration. He attained it—and again and again, after it was all over, he thanked his stars he *had* attained it—partly because of his childish and greedy high spirits under the pressure of his instinct about some incredible good fortune and partly because, beneath the semi-hypnotism that

Geard's black eyes exercised over him, there was a direct transference of thought between them.

But was it really possible that Christ Himself found it hard
to understand in this singular Servant of His, what he, John
Crow, the eternal heathen, the Stone-worshipper, the forehead-
tapper upon Stones, understood quite easily? What he *did* see
was, or at least, what he imagined he saw was that Geard of
Glastonbury, having built his Saxon arch, having worked his
Miracle, having inaugurated his new, mystical, Johannine and
anti-Pauline cult, had decided that it was an appropriate time—
although there was no hurry about it and it was necessary to
avoid any unpleasant shocks—to leave this misty, rainy, sub-
aqueous atmosphere of Glastonbury and pay an exploring visit to
the Isles of the Dead.

"I believe you are so little of a simple person, Sir," John had
the gall to say to him now, "that you are meditating what many
people would bluntly call *suicide*, although there might be, I
am ready to admit, other and prettier names for it."

Bloody Johnny lifted his left eyebrow at this, a sign with him
that he acknowledged the receipt of a palpable hit. He shuffled
in his chair, leaned forward a little and smiled. "But I've hardly
begun my talks to these foreigners," he said.

"If you'll excuse my saying so, Sir," said John, who now
seemed driven on by some demon within him to try and frighten
away his good luck even at the moment when it was on the
point of falling into his lap, "I think you express your ideas
more effectively by just being what you are and talking casually
to your friends. Leave it to Athling and Lady Rachel, in your
Wayfarer, Sir, to make your thoughts reasonable and logical.
Christ, if I may be allowed to refer to Him, left it to His followers to round off His ideas."

Mr. Geard leaned back again in his chair. With half-shut eyes
and with the tips of his fingers held together in the way old
family lawyers hold them, he looked dreamily and a little quizzically at John.

"I . . . *would* . . . rather like . . . to ask you a question,
young man," he said slowly.

"Say on, dear my Lord," quoth John.

"Could you conceive anyone, could you, in fact, for there's no need to beat about the bush, conceive *me*, committing suicide out of love of life, instead of out of weariness of it or out of hatred for it?"

"Love of life?" questioned John.

He pulled up his legs under him in Megan's chair and leaning forward with his hands on its elbows allowed his lank frame to relax with a certain voluptuousness and then grow rigid with an eager, intense, magnetic curiosity. "Death and what's beyond death," went on Mr. Geard, "are only what ye might call the unknown aspects of life. What I want to ask you is, do you suppose anyone's ever committed suicide out of an *excess of life*, simply to enjoy the last experience in full consciousness?" John's eyes were now shining with lively curiosity. He had forgotten all about his premonition of his master's benevolence. His whole being quivered with a hyena-like lust for spiritual blood. Curiously enough, it was exactly at that same hour, in this afternoon of sub-aquatic lights and shadows, that Paul Trent pulled up *his* legs, on to the bench by the Cattle Market railings, to reveal his secret feelings to the death-doomed Miss Elizabeth.

It was the privilege of that stricken lady to listen to the confession of a feline idealist. It was the privilege—or the trial—of Mr. Geard to be inquisitioned by a prowling sceptic. In a town of so many "heavy-weather" somnambulists, these light-footed jungle cats and jackals seemed lured, by a necessity in their nature, to rub themselves with excited tails or with panting nostrils against the most formidable characters in their vicinity.

"But, Sir," John protested now. "Don't you think that whatever the minds or spirits of people want to do, their bodies, or the central vital nerve in their bodies must always hold them back at the last? Don't you think, Sir, that though our minds can desire death for many reasons it's a different story when we come actually to try killing ourselves? Don't you think that something automatically leaps up then, that loathes death, and must fight against death, do what you can, until the bitter end?"

Hearing these words from the figure in his wife's chair, Mr. Geard emitted a sound that might be rendered by the syllables "rumti-dum-ti-dum."

"But if this quick-spring-nerve or this jumping-jack-nerve in us, boy," he said, "gets in the way of what we yearn for, can't we pinch its throat, or give its fretful pulse a little tap?"

John sighed and the light died out of his face. He uncurled his long legs and straightened them out. He ceased to be the eager intellectual jackal, and became the helpless, slouching, sunshine-loving tramp. There had suddenly come over him as he looked into the eyes of this man a chilly sense of something so monstrously different from anything he had ever met, that it frightened him. The tone in which Mr. Geard had said "pinch its throat" sounded like the shuddering heave of all the ground underneath all the things that were warm, familiar, natural. What *were* the huge antennae of Bloody Johnny's soul fumbling towards, out of the depths in which it stirred and moved?

"I shouldn't wonder," thought John, "if the old man's not got bored to extinction by all this Grail business and miracle business and new religion business. I shouldn't wonder if what he really wants is that delicious death-to-boredom that I get when I make love to Mary. The old girl upstairs couldn't give him any thrill of *that* kind and he's been snubbing Rachel lately. I *know* that; for I've seen 'em together; and he cares nothing for boys. I believe he's turned against the whole caboodle of this Glastonbury stunt. Sick to death of it he is; and I don't blame him, the poor old beggar! What he wants is a plump little Abishag to cuddle. He's a warm-blooded old rogue and he's gone cold i' the vitals."

Thus did John struggle, by the use of the most cynical considerations from his heathen Stone-worshipping nature, to cover up the primordial ice-crack, the glacier-crevasse among his sunlit earth-rocks, which the problem of Mr. Geard perhaps quite erroneously—had uncovered before his pessimistic imagination. To an earth-loving vicious East-Anglian it was impossible even to conceive the idea that Geard of Glastonbury might deliberately kill himself in order to gain more life. He could do it to escape from life; *that* was easily imaginable; but not this other.

"No, no," thought John. "There never has been, and there never will be, among all the millions and millions and millions of suicides, since the beginning of the world, one single one like this. It's as impossible as for a man to get out of his own skin. Life itself would fight against it with tooth and nail. The old chap is just fooling himself. What he really wants is a sweet young doxy to his bed . . . but, heigh-ho! The fellow would never hurt his old woman to *that* tune . . . so there we are . . . I wonder if he *is* going to pension me off?"

It was at this point in this memorable interview—the last that John was ever destined to have with his grandfather's friend—that Mr. Geard did turn to practical matters.

He laid before his secretary the whole array of the startling things he had already—though strongly against the advice of Mr. Robert Stilly—arranged with the bank to have done.

It was a sad witness to the difficulty of starting a real independent commune in the midst of an old kingdom like England that the Glastonbury bank remained absolutely untouched by the new régime, save in so far as the large sums of money piled up by the town passed into its hands.

Mr. Geard had bought small annuities for his wife, for Cordelia, and for Crummie. He had also—John was perfectly right in his instinct there—purchased for John himself an annuity of one hundred and fifty pounds a year.

He had, in these arrangements, entirely exhausted the whole forty thousand pounds' legacy left by Canon Crow.

And so John was wondering as he stood by Tossie's dresser watching those four feminine heads, whether to wait till tonight to tell Mary, or whether to tell her at once, and obtain her reaction—and Tossie's too—to the exciting news before Tom came in. He recalled exactly how Mr. Geard had looked, as he let him out of his front door only an hour ago, and how the man had abruptly cut short his almost tearful gratitude by the curious words: " 'Tis His Blood-money, lad. 'Tis His Blood-money. And ye must never forget that, none o' ye, when Easter comes round and ye eat and drink the Life in the Death!"

John found himself, when later in that spring twilight they were walking past the Vicarage gate together, sorry he had *not* waited till he got Mary alone to tell her about it, instead of blurting it all out as he had done, and making her jump up from the table with her grey eyes big as saucers.

It was the way Tom had taken it, when he came in, that troubled him now. They hadn't been very considerate of Tom's feelings, chattering together, he and Mary, about how they would clear off to Northwold at once and hunt for a cottage on the Didlington Road.

It was Toss, of course, who had been the one—not he or Mary at all—to notice how Tom was hit. The girl had begun hurriedly talking at once about how Tom and she would have to save up and come and join them in a few years when the twins were bigger.

"But Toss," Mary had murmured at that point, *"you'd* never bear to leave Glastonbury, would you?" and the words had hung suspended in the air, full of subtle reproach for them both. It was then that he had for the first time caught the grim bitterness of what Tom was feeling and his aching longing for his native soil and his craving to show Tossie the wide waters of Didlington Lake full of pike and perch and waterlilies.

They caught sight of the shirtsleeves of Mr. Weatherwax as they passed the Vicarage gate. The old rogue was pulling up weeds underneath some rhododendron bushes at the edge of the shrubbery; and as he laboured he sang: "The Brewer, the Miller, the Malster and I lost a heifer, lost a filly, lost a Ding-Dong; When Daffadowndillies look up at the sky; Pass along boys! Pass along! The Brewer, the Miller, the Malster and I Left a heifer, left a filly, left a Ding-Dong; Down in a grassy green grave for to lie; Pass along boys! Pass along!"

The gardener's back was turned to them and he did not rise from his stooping position as they passed. Something, however, about the sound of his thick bass voice, muffled and muted by his bending position, was so gross, so earthy, so suggestive of rank-smelling roots, tossed up lob-worms, slug-slime on a pronged fork, and bitter-sweet human sweat, that when Barter, who always relished talking in Rabelaisian fashion to Tossie in front of the fastidious though not exactly squeamish John, made some coarse joke about the fellow's enormous rump, John got a sudden, quick, spontaneous revulsion from his old friend, which was not lessened when Tossie started off on one of her ringing peals of Benedict Street laughter.

"Oh, how glad I'll be," he thought to himself, "when I'm safe back in that boat on the Wissey! By God! I know what I'll do. I'll hire that boat in Alder Dyke from that fellow, so that we'll have it when we want it."

It suddenly occurred to him that it was in connection with the smell of alders and with the look of their dark sturdy foliage that he had thought of Tom that day he was with Mary and he set himself to recall the boyish figure of his childish memories.

As they debouched into Chilkwell Street and were passing the old Tithe Barn, John heard Tossie, Glastonbury girl as she was, say something about one of the evangelistic creatures. It must have been a remark of more surprising lewdness and more amusing originality than John could quite follow, and it did not win much favour in his ears.

"The truth is," he thought, "I'm not suited for a sociable life, or to make merry with my friends. When once I've got Mary to myself in Northwold, I swear I won't see a single soul; and I won't invite a single soul. We'll live absolutely alone, Mary and I; absolutely alone and to ourselves! This girl's a decent girl, and her kids are nice kids; but I couldn't have stood living in the same house and having everything *à quatre* much longer. This hundred and fifty from the old man is a heavenly escape. It's a windfall out of the air; it's a benediction. *Tonnerre de Dieu!* It's as much one of his miracles as his curing any of those people. Christ! I'd soon be converted to the worship of Geard the Saviour if the old chap *did* kick the bucket. I hope he saw how grateful I was. I *did* kiss his hand. I'm damned glad I did *that*; for I think it pleased him. Perhaps in his whole life, the life I daresay of one of the greatest men who've ever lived, I'm the only person who's ever kissed his hand! And think of the number of ridiculous society-whores whose hands are kissed every day. Oh, damn and blast this human breed!"

They were passing all Mr. Geard's improvements on Chalice Hill now. In the green twilight, in spite of the litter and the presence of many unsightly shanties, the Mayor's Saxon arch stood out nobly and impressively. Beyond the Grail Fount, too, they could see the newly erected Rotunda and this also had a dignity of its own at this hour. It was indeed a sort of heretical temple that Bloody Johnny's architect was building. John surveyed it with infinite disgust.

"The dear old chap," he thought, "ought never to be betrayed into playing the mountebank. If he's anything, he's the founder, not the expounder. He'll spoil it all if he goes on trying to explain."

"Who *were* them Saxons, Tom?" enquired Tossie as they passed these various erections. "Were 'un savages, them Early Christians? Did 'un worship King Arthur?"

Her question seemed to tickle Barter hugely and he at once began chaffing her about her ignorance of history. But John thought to himself, "Evans would say that the real cause of old Geard's getting on the rocks and talking of suicide is his disregard of Arthur and his Welsh Demons. I wonder if it's possible that ——" and his mind went back to that inexplicable event that had happened to himself at Pomparlès Bridge. John's hatred of Glastonbury and its traditions was betrayed to the end by his incorrigible interest in psychic problems. Mr. Geard's mysticism had always influenced him more than he was willing to admit; and in any case he was a temperamental heathen rather than a materialist. He was quite as sceptical of materialistic explanations as he was of the occult occurrences that gave rise to them.

The fancy came into his head now that in his daily visits to Chalice Hill and his constant disturbance of that dangerous earth Mr. Geard might have come under some deliberately evil spell prepared long ago by these old Celtic magicians.

"Evans ought to have stopped him," he said to himself as they passed St. Michael's Inn, "from fooling those Welsh fairies by resuscitating a great thundering Saint like Dunstan!"

"Mad Bet's window be shut," said Tossie, "and she's curtain drawn. I be afeared thik means her's peeping out at we and making faces at we."

"Bosh!" muttered Barter crossly.

For some reason this particular fuss that all the Glastonbury girls made about Mad Bet irritated the man's Norfolk stolidity.

"Bosh, Toss! What a baby you are! The window's shut because it's a chilly night. The woman's probably in bed."

"No more in bed than thee be, Tom!" replied his wife with spirit. "Tom don't like I talking about Mad Bet," she added, "He be more afraid of she than I be!"

"I tell you," grumbled Barter, more vehemently than the occasion seemed to demand, "that woman is in bed; or else she's strolling harmlessly up Tor Hill, just as we are, in the cool of the evening. You Somerset people make too much of an old trot's eccentricity. Your Betsy, or whatever you call her, wouldn't excite any attention at all if she lived in Norfolk. You've pampered her down here and petted her till she thinks she's a regular Mother Shipton."

So spoke Tom Barter; and his temper about such a trifle might be considered as a premonitory sign that he was not completely impervious to the distant hum of the catastrophic avalanche.

At that very moment as the three of them reached the gate into Tor Field, the obedient and respectful Codfin was helping Betsy Chinnock to ascend a complicated system of precipitous workmen's ladders which now connected the interior floor of St. Michael's Tower with its ruined belfry, and this again with its airy summit. Here, once more, the Mayor's tireless architect from London had been at work; for the communal council had decided that if a light circular wooden staircase were erected inside from bottom to top, it would be possible to charge a shilling's admission to this magnificent watch-tower, which would greatly increase their weekly revenue. Alone among the council's recent expenditures this invasion of St. Michael's Tower interested the Vicar of Glastonbury, who regarded it as the beginning of that rebuilding of the old church of which he had been talking so long.

Mr. Dekker had indeed several times of late, before even Penny Pitches was down in her kitchen, slipped out of his lonely house and ascended the hill and climbed all these ladders in order to challenge the sunrise and to think about Nell and about his son. They were not difficult ladders to climb; and being inside so narrow a space, a climber was not so liable to dizziness as would have been the case if they had been propped up on the outside.

Not a soul in Glastonbury, if we rule out the infuriated spirit of Gwyn-ap-Nud as too insubstantial a presence to be called a soul—had beheld the Quantocks man's dark figure, standing erect up there at dawn, defying his ancient enemy as it rose like an enormous red balloon out of Bridgewater Bay, and praying there for his son and for his son's lost girl.

It was not the first time that Codfin had attended Mr. Evans' Grail Messenger upon a climbing adventure, and if overpowering sexual passion had not made the woman's knees shake, very much as Mr. Evans' own knees did when he opened "The Unpardonable Sin," Codfin would have got her to the top very easily.

To the top he did eventually get her, after a long rest at the black worm-eaten Jacobean oak-beams that were all that was left of the ancient belfry; and if Gwyn-ap-Nud *had* been more than an insubstantial presence he would surely have taken these two for a real witch being helped to her pulpit of far-flung curses by her attendant demon. Once at the top and leaning over the edge like two mediæval gargoyles, Codfin snuffed the pure twilight with aesthetic rapture. The fact that he was, in less than half an hour, going to commit murder, rather enhanced than otherwise this natural ecstasy. How could Codfin contemplate so calmly, as he surveyed this aerial landscape, the idea of putting to death a person who had never done him any harm, simply because he was moved to this maniacal issue by this crazy woman? How could Codfin, when he himself enjoyed in so intense a fashion the physical thrill of breathing this fragrant twilight, deliberately condemn another man to eternal unconsciousness, and himself to an almost certain death in a prison courtyard?

The feelings of hired assassins, and such really was Codfin—though what hired him was religious awe for his witch-queen—must be of a different nature from those of all other murderers.

Completely devoid of any previous personal attitude to their allotted victim they take upon themselves to establish between them the most personal of all attitudes. But how could Codfin risk the gallows for the sake of the frenzy of Mad Bet? Ask the fanatic devotee of some outraged idol how he can risk death to avenge his deity!

Mad Bet had become Codfin's deity. To obey Mad Bet had become Codfin's religion. Between two unpleasant experiences— the hangman's rope which he had never felt, and the look of reproach in Mad Bet's eyes which he *had* felt—he selected, without giving the alternative so much as a second thought, the one that shocked his imagination the less. Compared with the problem of Codfin, however, how easy, how natural, was that of Mad Bet! Mad Bet was actuated, just as Mr. Evans had been, till the nakedness of Mr. Geard's daughter exorcised it, by the nerve-worm of sex.

To be middle-aged, to be of a personal hideousness that was revolting, to be threatened by the county asylum, to be the laughing-stock of the children of several streets, to have a skull under your hat bald as an egg, all these things weigh in the balances as nothing when that little nerve-worm begins to heave and froth and spit.

"There 'un be! Do 'ee see 'un, Missus?" cried Codfin suddenly, lowering his head below the level of the battlements and pressing his companion's shoulder to force her to crouch down.

"Thee be sure 'twon't make 'un suffer, Finn Toller?" she said, as their four eyes watched the three figures entering Tor Field.

Codfin emitted a faint chuckle at this. "Didn't 'ee see thik bar?" he whispered. "Thik bar did make me poor arm ache wi' carrying 'un. Thik bar be enough to stunny a elaphint."

"Oh, me king, oh, me love, oh, me sweet marrow!" cried the madwoman from the bottom of her worm-driven heart.

"Don't 'ee let they see thee's head over edge of Tower," remarked the other calmly. "I be going down now. And don't 'ee scream nor cry out anythink when I do it, and don't 'ee holler if thik Barter catches hold of I. Just 'ee stay where 'ee be till all be quiet; and don't 'ee say nothink either to no one when tomorrow be come and they've a put poor Coddy in canary-cage!"

As Finn Toller scrambled quickly down the long ladders to the belfry and then down the others to the floor, he said to himself: "I knewed Mr. Curiosity wouldn't come after all his talk. They scholards what reads of fornications wouldn't fuggle a fly, nor them as reads of stiff 'uns wouldn't drown a cat. But 'a won't tell tales of Coddy neither, for fear of 's own skin!"

With these sagacious comments upon human psychology Mr. Toller went calmly to the place where he had propped up his murderous weapon. Chance or fate—or the air-squadrons of Gwyn-ap-Nud—seemed resolved to make Mr. Toller's task as easy as possible that night.

When the three friends reached the top they turned round and stood panting and out of breath on a ledge of grass a yard or so below the threshold stone of the tower.

Tossie quickly turned their attention to the vast, sad, greenish-coloured plain stretched out before them; and even before they had got their breath she entangled them in the absorbing and piquant subject as to exactly at what spot in this airy map their own Northload house was situated. This was where Chance—or the spirit of Gwyn-ap-Nud—was so favourable to Codfin; for unless the girl had started some especially beguiling topic the second they paused, John would, almost certainly, have gone straight to the tower, following the natural human instinct of attaining an objective, and also obeying a personal fondness for touching cold stones with his hand, and thus made it impossible for the assassin to steal forth from that door with the monstrous piece of iron on his shoulder.

This is however exactly what the murderer was permitted now to do. Step by step, as the girl pointed towards one spot and John pointed towards another and Barter protested that both were too far to the south, Finn Toller came softly and quietly, down the slope behind them, with the iron bar now lifted up in both his hands.

Nature the great healer is also the great destroyer; and the tendency to giggle at the same things and at the same second which had wiped out all memories of Gladman's House for Barter now wiped out for him all memories of every kind. For a remark that John now made started off the pair of them uttering such ungovernable peals of laughter that Barter was forced to shift his position a little.

In that shifting of his position he saw in a flash the figure of Codfin standing behind John and he realised in the twinkling of an eyelid that the hideous instrument in the tramp's hands was already trembling in the air.

The inevitable material laws of balance, of rhythm, of gravitation, of dynamics, had already decided that the iron bar was going to descend on John's head. What they had not counted on, or taken into their mechanical consideration, was the automatic swiftness, swifter than the descent of death itself, with which the instinct of a Norfolk gentleman could express itself in action at a deadly crisis.

To ward off this blow, to arrest this descent of the iron bar, Barter now plunged forward, with the natural result that, in place of the thing descending on his friend's head, it descended on his own, cracking his skull full above the forehead and killing him instantaneously.

Just as twenty-five years ago the young Tom had come so often to John's rescue when their boat got entangled in the weeds of the Wissey, so the grown-up Tom, father of twins, and husband of Tossie Stickles, now gave up his life for the same friend on this Somersetshire hill. He was killed instantaneously, the front of his skull being bashed in so completely, that bits of bone covered with bloody hair surrounded the deep dent which the iron made. His consciousness, the "I am I" of Tom Barter, shot up into the ether above them like a released fountain-jet and quivering there pulsed forth a spasm of feeling, in which outrage, ecstasy, indignation, recognition, pride, touched a dimension of Being more quick with cosmic life than Tom had ever reached before in his thirty-seven years of conscious existence. This heightened—nay! this quadrupled—awareness dissolved in a few seconds, after its escape from the broken cranium, but whether it passed, with its personal identity intact, into that invisible envelope of rarefied matter which surrounds our astronomic sphere or whether it perished irrecoverably, the present chronicler knows not.

Tossie flung herself on Barter's body with a piercing scream that rang out over the whole valley. Scream after scream tore itself from that soft mass of clinging female loss till her fair hair was dabbled with Tom's blood and actually entangled with broken bits of hair-covered bone that had been Tom's hard skull.

Some said they heard her screams as far down the valley as Tithe Barn. Lily Rogers maintained she heard them as she picked parsley for Miss Drew's dinner in the Abbey House garden.

John made an ·instinctive movement to pursue the murderer; but the tramp, hearing wild cries from the slope of the hill, and seeing Mr. Evans and Cordelia rushing up the ascent towards him, dashed back into the tower and clambered, swift as a monkey, up the tall ladders inside. For quite the space of a couple of minutes, after his first motion of pursuit, John stood stock-still, his face so contorted with horror that it assumed the appearance of a wooden puppet, listening in spellbound, frozen apathy to the girl's heart-rending screams.

A semi-cirque of flying rooks, just seven in number, flapped with creaking wings across the top of the tower, making their way northwest towards Mark Moor. Little did *they* reck of the cracking of the skull of a man upon a patch of grass! As for a tiny earth beetle that was foraging for its insect prey just there, it scurried away from Tom's blood as if it had been a lake of brimstone.

In addition to this, a panic-stricken hare, fleeing in wild terror from the man and woman who were rushing up the hill, came with its long desperate leaps almost up to John's feet, and then, remaining motionless there for a second, rushed past the tower and away down the slope towards Havyatt Gap. The appearance of this hare aroused John from his paralysis. He ran to the door of the tower and pulled it wide open. The couple of minutes' delay, however, had enabled Finn Toller to ascend, for he climbed like an animal rather than a man, to the top of the last ladder; but here he was met by Mad Bet, in a cold paroxysm of frenzied remorse. Without giving her unfortunate devotee time to reach the stone platform where she knelt to receive him, the woman seized the thin bare wrists that Codfin extended towards her and flung him off the ladder. Finn Toller fell backwards, head downwards; and John, stepping hurriedly from the door at the man's death cry, saw his body crash to the

ground in a cloud of dust and heard the ghastly thud upon the
ground with which his neck was broken.

Like a great bald-headed vulture that has been shot through
the wing, Mad Bet, on the stone summit of the tower, crouched
with convulsive shudderings against the parapet. Here she lay,
without thought or purpose, moaning in a low voice to herself,
and covering the cold slab against which she pressed her face
with piteous tears and murmuring endearments, as though it
were the mangled body of the man who had roused that terrible
nerve-worm that devours hearts. Mad Bet had not seen what
had really occurred down there. To her disturbed and tragic consciousness, it was John who lay dead at the foot of the tower
with his skull smashed in.

There is that about an uttermost sorrow which levels all
distinctions; and not Deianeira for Heracles, not Iseult for Tristram, moaned and murmured to her lost love with more absoluteness of pitiful grief than did this bald-headed creature on
the top of the tower to her supposedly dead idol. Round about
her crouching form a couple of great swifts, those pointed-
winged demons of the high air, flew in narrowing circles, uttering
their short shrill cries, and these sharp sounds were answered
by the melancholy and more familiar wailings of the peewits
in the lower levels of Tor Field, disturbed by Tossie's screams
and calling out warnings to one another.

Broken under that bar, Mad Bet envisaged the sweet head of
her dear love; while the wild screams of Tossie over Tom's body
joined the age-old chorus: *"Quis desiderio sit pudor aut modus
tam cari capitis?"*

The green twilight was being sucked down now by undulations of the green earth. The invisible dews were falling. A gusty
night-wind was rising up from beyond Queen's Sedgemoor. The
first cold stars were coming out over the three horizons. Where
the sun had gone down in the west, there lingered only a faint
dying trace of the livid before-night whiteness. At this actual
moment of the earth revolution, although under very different
atmospheric conditions, in China, in India, on the banks of the
Danube, by the Black Sea and in the tents of the Sahara, in

battle, murder, pestilence and shipwreck, in bolted doom sudden death was rushing on the hairy scalps of men.

Did Tossie feel her grief worse than any of those who mourned? Or were the moans of some old Chinese wife on the banks of the Yellow River yet more heart-broken, the terrible silence of some despairing Malay in a Singapore hovel yet more crushing?

As for John, the worst moment of the whole unspeakable nightmare was when he lifted that plump bundle of wild hysteria from off the body of his friend and laying her on the grass dabbed with his handkerchief at her brow and cheeks and actually removed with his finger and thumb a fragment of Tom's smashed skull from her sticky hair. She rolled over—and he was glad she did, for her face was shocking to him—and began smothering her convulsions in the green grass, her fingers plucking and clutching at its cold earthy roots.

It was then, just before Evans and Cordelia reached them, that he snatched off his overcoat and covered Tom's head and shoulders with it.

"Oh, what has happened? What *has* happened?" panted Cordelia, "Has that man gone? Has he hurt you? *Who* is hurt? Is Mr. Barter hurt? Has he *killed* Mr. Barter? Where is he? Have you let him go?"

Mr. Evans spoke not a single word. He did two things. And these he did with the punctual, mechanical precision of a consummate actor performing a long-ago perfectly rehearsed part. He stared round him till he caught sight of the iron bar lying on the ground; and stooping down he lifted up the bloodied end from the earth and deliberately wiped it with a handful of grass. Then he went over to where the body was lying. Hesitating for the flicker of a second, he fell on his knees and removing John's coat from Barter's crushed head, gazed at what was revealed.

The sight had an immediate physical effect upon him. He replaced the coat calmly enough; but rising to his feet and turning his back to the corpse, he began vomiting with cataclysmic heavings of his tall frame. Was the sexual nerve in Mr. Evans, that sadism-drunk Worm of the Pit, stirred to abominable excitement as he went through these motions? Mercy of Jesus forbid! That nerve-worm lay, stretched out in the man's vitals as he vomited there, cold and constricted, limp as the sloughed off skin of a summer snake.

Cordelia, who had showed signs of being more concerned over Mr. Evans as he swayed and retched, and retched and swayed, than over the murder itself, now sat down on the grass by Tossie's side and took her head in her lap. The first time she did this the distracted girl beat her off with her hands and tried to get up and rush over to Barter's body; but the sight of that coat hiding the crushed head brought so sickening a sense of her loss that she hid her face between Cordelia's knees and broke into piteous wailings. These wailings carried no longer, however, that terrifying note in them that her first shrill screams had had, and by degrees they sank down from sheer exhaustion into low moans; till at last the unhappy girl lay quite silent and still.

Mr. Evans, whose paroxysm of vomiting had ceased now, obeyed John with humble docility, as the latter demanded his help in dragging forth the body of the murderer from the tower. This quiet but by no means stupid docility became a fixed habit with Mr. Evans from now on. It was not that the man's sanity was affected by the accumulating shocks of this day. What it seemed to be was a substitution of a definite sense of guilt over Barter's death for the less tangible but far more deadly remorse over his sadistic dreams and fantasies. This new guilt of his the man took calmly, and in a certain sense sanely; but it had a much more disastrous effect upon him from an external and practical point of view than the other. When the twenty-sixth of February dawned poor Cordy was startled to discover that her Owen's hair had turned white. He had indeed become visibly and palpably and in every physical respect, if not an old man, certainly an elderly man.

It was lucky for Cordelia that the tiny annuity, so carefully purchased for her by Mr. Geard, was enough for their bare needs in that little house above Bove Town, on the hill leading up to St. Edmund's Brick Yard; for after this crisis in his days, Mr. Evans found himself quite incapable of going on with his work in Number Two's shop. That *really* elderly and indeed extremely aged gentleman did not feel it incumbent upon him to regard his now sleeping partner as in any way entitled to share the ensuing increment from their more than ever lucrative business; nor, in spite of Cordelia's indignation, could she induce Mr. Evans to make any claims.

Slowly and laboriously—sometimes writing no more than a few pages a day—did Mr. Evans continue working at his life's task, the monumental "Vitus Merlini Ambrosiani"; but luckily for him Cordelia did not extend to the intellectual interests of her husband that impatient contempt which she always felt for her father's religious doctrines.

That culminating scene when she had exorcised, by her heroic gesture behind the brown blinds, the nerve-devil in Mr. Evans, had endeared the man to her in the way mothers are endeared to a deformed or an idiot child; and when her real child perished later after a premature birth she lavished upon its helpless parent all the savage maternal protectiveness that the infant would have claimed if it had lived.

Visitors to Glastonbury can still see, when a little weary perhaps of romantic antiquities they wander up Wells Old Road towards Edmund Hill Lane, with a view of inspecting those famous tile works that have given the town its mellow roofs, a slow-moving, absent-minded, white-haired gentleman, reading a blue-covered book as he walks along or as he leans upon the fence that leads into those suburban fields between Wells Old Road and Maidencroft Lane.

This book, if any passer-by were bold enough to peruse its title, would turn out to be Malory's "Morte D'Arthur," but such a stranger would not be able to guess that what Mr. Evans is searching for there is something not to be found in Malory at all—nor indeed in any Grail Book, since the time of the great Welshman Bleheris—namely the real meaning of the mystical word Esplumeoir.

It was not, as the devoted Codfin had warned her it had best not be, till all was dark and deserted upon Glastonbury Tor that Mad Bet climbed down those long ladders and made her way home to St. Michael's Inn. So great was the hubbub of voices, all relating various and contradictory versions of that evening's tragedy, and so crowded were bar-room, parlour and kitchen, that it was easy for the demented woman to slip back into her unlit room unobserved by old John Chinnock or by his wife. It was indeed Tom Chinnock, her nephew, who found her outstretched on her bed when he came long after closing-time to bring her her supper. She was still alive and perfectly conscious; but she had hurt her heart in some way in climbing alone down those steep ladders, and she never left her bed again.

Not a word did she breathe as to her share in Barter's death. Not a sign did she make that she wanted to see her "Dilly darling gent," her "sweet moon's marrow" again before she died; but Tommy Chinnock reported later (for the Terre Gastée stone-thrower was her best friend at the last, though Solly Lew used to come up and sit by her bed of an evening) that the day before she died, which happened on the first of March, she had asked him to go for Mr. Geard.

No one, save Tommy, till his aunt was safe in the Wells Road Cemetery knew that the woman herself had sent for the Mayor; though they all knew that the Mayor had gone up to her room— after having a stiff glass of ale with old John—and had stayed there for nearly half an hour; but no one at all ever learned from the Mayor what passed between them.

Dr. Fell had been summoned to hurry to Wirral Hill long before Mrs. Geard reached Manor House Road, and he had found Miss Crow already in full possession of her consciousness. He thanked the Germans heartily, especially the one with the flask; and then in spite of her weak state, he took the opportunity of scolding Miss Crow very earnestly and roundly for her fool-hardy behavior that day.

"A woman like you," he said as he carried her home in Solly Lew's taxi, "ought to know better than to act like this! What you've really done, Miss Crow, is to try and commit suicide."

Elizabeth was too weak to defend herself. It did strike her as ironical however, that this doctor, who she knew was in the habit of defending the right of self-killing, and whose death by his own hand Tossie's Mr. Barter was always predicting, should lapse into this mode of speech.

Dr. Fell had the wit to read what lay behind the smile she gave him.

"The wrong of it lies," he said, growing rather red in the face and displaying signs of peevishness at being caught by his old friend in so conventional a vein, "the wrong of it lies in the example that a happy person like you, with so lucky a temperament ought to give to us poor dogs."

She was clever enough to take this chance, when she had disturbed his professional aplomb, of asking him point-blank how long he supposed she had to live.

"Five would astonish me," he said. "Three would surprise me. From my personal experience, such as it is, I'd give you about two."

"Years, Dr. Fell?"

"Years, years, years!" he answered querulously. "What else do you think I meant? Love-affairs?"

She peered out of the taxi window at the tower of St. Benignus'. She thought of the thousands of times she had looked up at that solid mass of masonry that shared with St. John's and the high Tor the distinction of giving its visual character to the town of Glastonbury from all the quarters.

"Is that a shock to you?" he said in a more kindly tone. "I oughtn't to have told you that, I expect."

She still continued to look out of the window without replying. Miss Crow's thoughts, just then, were indeed those wordless thoughts of the Vital Principle itself, when the days of the years of its brief life have had their term set by constituted authority.

"You're not upset, I hope?"

The simplicity of this question, addressed to her when she might easily, it was clear, have been lying dead on Wirral Hill, tickled Miss Crow's fancy.

"So upset, Doctor dear," she replied, "that I hereby invite you to have tea with me in Benedict Street this day *three* years hence! The twenty-fourth, isn't it?"

Dr. Fell corrected her. "The twenty-fifth," he said.

"Well? Will you come? And if I'm dead you must come to my grave in the cemetery. Is that a promise, Doctor?"

He lifted her hand courteously to his lips. Both of them turned after that to the dirty windows of Solly Lew's taxi; but not to the same window.

The problem that arose immediately after Barter's death, that arose in both John's and Mary's minds before his body was taken to the police station, was the problem of Tossie and her twins. It was Mary—as she and John lay awake in their room on the floor above, after Dr. Fell had given the stricken girl a sleeping-draught, and Nancy Stickles had been called in to spend the night with her—who first broached the startling suggestion.

"Why don't we take Toss and the children with us to North-wold? Toss could easily get charwork, or laundry-work, or something like that, to do; and I could look after the babies while she was out. Old Tom will be happy in his grave if he knows his children are back again in Norfolk. Nothing would please him more than the thought of our taking them with us on the big river."

"The thought of *your* taking them!" said John.

"Hush! How can you? You know perfectly well," she retorted, "which of us it was that he really cared for."

"I *do* know," he doggedly repeated. "It was you."

"John!" she cried indignantly, pulling her arm from under his head and sitting up in bed. "You've no right to say such a thing. It's you, first and last, that Tom loved! He came to me when he was in trouble and sad; just as I went to him when I was unhappy; but in his heart of hearts it was always you."

So she spoke; but neither of them realised how that ill-fated prayer from the boat on the Wissey had been neutralised by Tom, any more than they thought of those silvery fish and those green weeds as things that the dead man would never see again.

"What I cannot for the life of me understand," said John, for he was too cautious and selfish to commit himself in a hurry to her plan of taking Tossie, "is what motive that man had for murdering him. Old Sheperd said he'd had his eye on him for a long time, and that he suspected him of several burglaries; but what possible grudge could he have against Tom?"

"Why, didn't you hear what Toss was talking about in her hysterics, when Fell gave her that drug?"

"No, I can't say I did. I wasn't listening. I was talking to the

policeman and to Mr. Bishop. I didn't come in till you got her
quiet again."

Mary stretched out her hand to the little table which was
upon John's side of their bed. She stretched it out above John's
face, and he caught at it with his hand and playfully, and yet
not without malice, bit it sharply.

"What are you doing? You hurt me!" she cried with asperity.
He chuckled to himself as the taste of her flesh, that taste he
loved so well, hung about him, while she busied herself with
matchbox and candle.

When the little yellow flame was mounting up and her red rug
and red curtains were coming by leaps and starts into view,
she drew back and resumed her own place. But she balanced
both her pillows between her shoulders and the head of the
bed and sat straight up.

"I've been meaning to tell you this ever since we came upstairs," she said, "but I kept putting it off." As she spoke she
remembered another occasion when she had kept putting off—
an agitating topic; and that was when she had had to tell him
about her friendship with Tom, in that boat on the Wissey.

"To tell me what? Something that Toss cried in her fever?
God, Mary! She might have cried out practically anything. You
saw what a state she was in? But let's have it. Let's hear the
great revelation!"

"Toss spoke as if she'd seen that tramp aiming his iron thing
at *you*; and Tom rushing in to take the blow."

John certainly got a queer sensation as he heard this. The
odd thing was, however, that while he accepted what Tossie had
said without questioning it, he did *not* feel a rush of tender,
melting gratitude to his dead friend! The truth was he had so
long played the feminine rôle with Barter, so long leaned upon
him, and relied upon his strength that he only felt now as if
they had been in some desperate mêlée together, where Tom as
he always did, had taken the lead; and for that reason had got
hurt . . . had . . . got . . . in fact . . . killed; but when it
came to making Tom's tragic death a sublime act of sacrifice
and of sacrifice for him, John dodged that tremendous conclusion
with shamefully blinking eyelids.

"But what on earth could the fellow have got against *me*?" said John, "Or do you suppose he meant to kill us both and ravish Tossie?"

He had such a very quaint expression, at once cringing and quizzical, panicky and humorous, as he sat up in bed, his flannel pyjamas, with their pierrot-like black-and-white stripes, showing so fantastical in the candlelight, that Mary could not suppress a smile. She thought, in her heart: "How queer men are! Here he is with his best friend—his boyhood friend—dead to save him; and all he can do is to try and scare himself like a child!" She sighed heavily when her smile died away. "It is in these matters of life and death," she thought, "that men and women are especially different. Women want to suck up to the last dregs every drop of the awful things that happen. They want to soak themselves in their feelings, to swim in them, to float on them, to drown in them, whereas John is squeezing all the love he really feels for Tom into a tight little juggler's ball and throwing it from hand to hand!"

She turned her head towards him from its white pillows. From each side of her cold clear forehead the brown hair was drawn smoothly back; and she had pulled the coil of it from off the nape of her neck and allowed it to fall over her left shoulder in a long single plait. She did not know that John had thought to himself, as in his heart-felt bewilderment he had done what he had never done before in his life, put on his pyjama-trousers over his drawers: "How queer girls are! Mary is looking in the mirror to see whether she has plaited her hair properly. I suppose she'll loosen it with her fingers, over her ears, just in that same careful way, when I'm lying in my coffin as cold as poor Tom!"

"Give me a cigarette, will you?" was what she had apparently turned her head towards him to say. It was his turn now to fumble among the objects on the little table at his side; but they were soon, both of them, smoking in pensive peace.

"What's the time, John dearest?"

He pulled out his watch from under his pillow. "A quarter past three," he told her.

"You don't think that drug's stopped acting, and she's awake again, do you?"

John was silent; trying to catch every least sound in Number Fifteen, Northload Street.

"*Could* you bear it, dearest, to have Toss and the children with us out there?"

It would have been as impossible for John to have said "no" to this speech as it would have been for him to have got up and gone down to the room below.

"Of course, if *you* could!" he said.

Mary sighed. "Well, that's settled then. And the sooner we get away, the better for Toss. We could all stay in that North-wold Inn, couldn't we, till we get our place and get these things out there?"

"Tom must have left . . . a fair sum . . . in the . . . bank," murmured John in a ruminating voice.

"Now, you stop that!" cried Mary. "Tom's money must be kept for those little girls. These people here . . . Spear and Trent and Robinson . . . will have to get us all out there! It's the least they can do, with all Tom has done for their factory."

John relapsed into silence again. It was impossible for him to refrain from thinking how his delectable plan for being left absolutely alone with Mary out there was now smashed to bits.

"Do you hate Glastonbury as much as you ever did?"

Mary was surprised at herself for asking this question. It seemed to have come into her head and rushed to her lips inde-pendently of her conscious will.

"No," said John laconically.

"Why not?" pressed the girl.

"Oh, damn it all!" cried John. "A person never knows *why* he feels these things. It's old Geard, I think! I've got fond of that old rascal in some odd sort of way." He bent over the little table and extinguished his cigarette.

"I'll miss Geard like the devil!" he muttered hoarsely.

Mary was conscious of a funny sensation, like the impact of a piece of ice against her bare bosom. Had this queer being to whom she now belonged, body and soul, transferred his dis-turbing and perverse sexuality from Tom to the Mayor of Glastonbury? To conceal what she felt, "It's Geard, then," she said, "not his Grail or his new religion, that interests you?"

"I don't know, Mary, and that's the truth," sighed John. And then, as if continuing some line of thought that he had not revealed, "I wish, my dear, we could all stop on our way at Salisbury and see Stonehenge."

"Well, we can't do that, John, dearest, so it's no use your talking about it. We've got to take Tom with us, you know!"

John turned round upon her with a startled swing of his pierrot-like white-and-black figure ———

"Take Tom?" he echoed.

"Of course! you don't think Toss is going to leave Tom in Glastonbury, do you? If she did, *I* wouldn't."

"No, I suppose not," he murmured; and it was his turn to feel a funny sensation go shivering through him. He had always been careful to avoid any probing of his feeling about the relations between his wife and his friend.

"Bury him in the Northwold churchyard, eh? Where Grandfather is, and *his* people? Yes, I suppose that *is* the thing to do!"

They both were silent for a while after that; and into that rosy-coloured room, where their two shadows hovered so waveringly and ambiguously over Mr. Wollop's simple furniture, there came the etherealised essence of that road across Brandon Heath where they had met nearly a year ago; came the phantom-faint image of Harrod's mill-pool, of the spacious drawing-room with its low windows opening upon that grey twilit lawn, of their boat carried so fast on the glittering tide above the weeds and the darting fish of the Wissey, and of the great ash tree in that open field, where they said their farewells to their native pastures. Well! they were going back to those pastures again; going back to them to live the life they had dreamed of then but had not dared to hope for, going back to bury her friend and his friend, where that old man lay—his curly hair still fresh and white as the Head in the Apocalypse—who had been the friend of Geard of Glastonbury! Why was it then, that they both felt a curious and irresistible sadness as they thought of their return? Had they been captured in spite of themselves, by the terrible magic of this spot? Was John's clinging to his strange master a sign that something would be gone forever from each of their lives, when they went away, something that their dearest love for each other could only replace in a measure, in a fluctuating substitution? Did Mary recall the dawn of St. John's Day?

"Come back to us, Tom! Come back to us!" the big river and the little river were both calling; and it *was* with Tom that they were going back to the place where they would be; but they were carrying a corpse with them; not only the corpse of Tom Barter but the corpse of their stillborn never-returning opportunity of touching the Eternal in the enchanted soil where the Eternal once sank down into time!

The great waves of the far Atlantic, rising from the surface of unusual spring tides, were drawn, during the first two weeks of that particular March, by a moon more magnetic and potent as she approached her luminous rondure than any moon that had been seen on that coast for many a long year. Up the sands and shoals and mudflats, up the inlets and estuaries and backwaters of that channel-shore raced steadily, higher and higher as day followed day, these irresistible hosts of invading waters. Across the far-stretching flats of Bridgewater Bay these moon-drawn death-bringers gathered, stealing, shoaling, rippling, tossing, waves and ground-swells together, cresting billows and unruffled curves of slippery water, rolling in with a volume that increased its momentum with every tide that advanced, till it covered sand-wastes and sand-dunes, grassy shelves and sea-banks, that had not felt the sea for centuries. Out of the misty western horizon they came, rocking, heaving, rising, sinking, and beneath them were shoals of unusual fish and above them were flocks of unusual gulls. There was a strange colour upon them, too, these far-travelled deep-sea waves, and a strange smell rose up from them, a smell that came from the far-off mid-Atlantic for many days. They were like the death mounds of some huge wasteful battlefield carried along by an earthquake and tossed up into millions of hill summits and dragged down into millions of valley hollows as the whole earth heaved. They were not churned into flying spray, these swelling spring tides; they were not lashed into tossing spindrift. Each one of them rolled forward, over the sand and the mud, converting these expanses from a familiar tract of yellow-grey silence into a vast plain of hummings and murmurings that went on all night. Wide, wet reaches of sand, over which for years fishermen had walked in the dawn with wavering lanterns and whispering voices, and where decrepit posts, eaten by centuries of sea-worms and hung with festoons of grass-green seaweed, leaned to the left or leaned to the right, as chance willed it, were now changed into a waste of grey water. Ancient sand-sunk boat skeletons, their very names forgotten, that had caught for years the blood-reflections of sunset in the pools of dead memories and lost disasters, were now totally submerged. Many of these incoming deep-sea waves had curving crest-heads that were smooth and slippery as the purest marble, heads that seemed to grow steadily darker and darker, as they gathered towards the land, till they added something menacing to every dawn and to every twilight.

And as these tides came in, over the brown desolate mudflats, they awoke strange legends and wild half-forgotten memories along that coast. Ancient prophecies seemed to awake and flicker again, prophecies that had perished long ago, like blown-out candles in gusty windows, cold as the torch-flames by which they were chanted and the extinct fires by which they were conceived.

Between the imaginations of men, especially such as are stirred up and made tense by wrestlings with the Unknown, and the geographical pattern of the earth's surface, are subtle correspondencies that may survive many sunken torch flares and many lost harp notes once heard across the capes and promontories. And the western coast that Spring seemed almost to welcome this sea invasion. Liberated from the frost and ice of winter, a thousand unfrequented backwaters, bordered by dead, wind-swept rushes, clammy with salt-smelling marsh-lichens and thick-stalked glaucous-grey weeds, seemed actually calling out to the sea to come and cover their brackish pools. Salt amphibious growths, weeds of the terraqueous marshes, they seemed to be yearning, these neutral children of the margin, for the real salt sea to rush over them and ravish them. Little did they dream how soon this ravishment would take place, how soon they would be drowned and with how deep a drowning!

Amid the forlorn and untraversed mudflats in that singular region various patches of cultivated ground appear and inhabited buildings, some of stone, some of wattles and lath-and-plaster cement. It is about these outlying farms and hamlets—in this strange region of sluices and weirs and dams and rhynes—that so many curious Celtic syllables still cling, like the appellative *Gore*, for instance, syllables full of old mythological associations.

It was from these isolated farm-houses, situated among sandy reaches where such old magical names lingered intact, that the first rumours began to spread of a serious sea invasion. These rumours, once started among these outposts of human habitation, excited anxious alarm; and well they might, for that whole district is a very peculiar one. On one side of it lies the great Western Channel of those moon-drawn tides, and on the other so many brackish ditches and inland meres that the dams and dykes, if they once yield to the mounting-up of the waters, are liable to give way in vast numbers. In the memory of the older dwellers in those regions—a queer amphibious race, descended from Norse invaders and from Celticised aboriginals—was a vivid image of the last time the sea-banks had broken and the land had been flooded, an image of drowned cattle and ruined pastures and hurried and tumultuous human flights and escapes. On *that* occasion the waters of the sea had swept so far inland, mingling with the waters of the land, that the configuration of the country had completely changed. Overtopping the banks, breaking the sluices, turning rivers into huge floods and tiny streams into rushing rivers, the sea had come so far that the land—in many cases always lower than sea-level—had reverted to the sea and become part of the sea. With the waning of the moon, on that occasion, the waters retreated, but not before they had left their tribute. Many infinitesimal sea creatures, tiny sea animalculæ and microscopic salt-water beings must have been carried over the land where these unnatural tides pushed their way, and it is likely enough that many of these marine invaders, when the waters receded, were deposited in the rich loam of the Isle of Glastonbury. An island indeed did Glastonbury become in those strange days! Mr. Sheperd, the Glastonbury policeman, and Mr. Merry, the Glastonbury curator, would frequently speak of that epoch with bated breath.

Well! if some of the rumours that ran along those sandy flats and leapt, like living messengers of disaster, from bog-tussock to bog-tussock, were not without cause, there was likely to be this year, ere March ended, an inundation even more serious than that land had known since very ancient days. For these dark-green waves, smooth and slippery, without spray, without spin-

drift, and smelling so strangely of the mid-Atlantic, brought
memories of far-off mysterious disasters. Intimations, they
brought, of lost islands and submerged sea-reefs, where, if
Plutarch is to be trusted, Demetrius the Traveller, a hundred
years before Christ heard tales of superhuman personalities
living remote and sea-encircled.

Yes, even before the fifteenth of March these terrific ocean
waves had disturbed the cormorants at St. Audrie's Bay and
scattered the gulls at Black Rock, at Blue Ben, and at Quantock's
Head. The dwellers at Kilve Chantry had grown uneasy; and
from Benhole to Wick Moor, and from Stert Flats to the mouth
of the River Parrett, and over Bridgewater Bar to Gore Sand
there were wild gusts of ragged wings and shrieking sea cries
and vague sobbings and lappings and murmurs in the night; and
all this under a moon that continued growing larger and larger,
until it reached a size that seemed pregnant with terrifying
events. The mouths of the Parrett and the Brue are not far from
each other, opposite Stert Island, and the whole seven miles from
Otterhampton to Mark's Causeway, across Pawlett Level and
Huntspill Level, inland from Highbridge and Burnham, are in-
tersected with dams and sluices and weirs, holding back the sea
floods. From Huntspill Level to Glastonbury cannot be much
more than eight miles' distance, as the crow flies, and it is across
these eight miles that the waters of the Channel would flow—for
it is all beneath sea-level—if those dykes, as they had done at
least once in the memory of living men, should yield to the
rising of the tides.

Of all mortal senses the sense of smell carries the human soul
back the farthest in its long psychic pilgrimage; and by these
far-drawn channel airs and remote sea odours the inmost souls of
many dwellers in northwest Somerset must have been roused, during those weeks of March. It is the old recurrent struggle with
the elements, as the sense of these things reaches the spirit by the
sharp sudden poignance of smell, that brings one age of human
life into contact with another. There is a comfort in these con-
tinuities and a feeling of mysterious elation, but strange forebod-
ings, too, and uneasy warnings. That hidden wanderer, incarnated
in our temporary flesh and blood, that so many times before—

centuries and æons before—has smelt deep-sea seaweed and sun-bleached driftwood and the ice-cold chills of Arctic seas, sinks down upon such far-off memories, as upon the stern of a voyaging ship, and sees, as if in a dream, the harbours and the islands of its old experience.

Thus as these unnatural tides under this unusual moon gathered and rose out of the Western Channel, feelings that had not come to the population of those places for many a long year caught them unawares, as they went to and fro about their business, and disturbed them with thoughts "beyond the reaches of their souls."

But the people of Glastonbury that year—especially the ones with whom the reader has most to do in this present narration—were so preoccupied with the exciting public events of that epoch that they gave little heed to these "airy syllables." The humbler people, especially, continued to buy and sell, as the new fashion dictated, much as their fathers had done before in *their* fashion, without paying any attention to these fleeting intimations drawn forth from the recesses of their beings by these ocean smells, smells so soul-piercing and so mysterious, following the waxing of this portentous moon.

Meanwhile the strangely constituted Glastonbury commune—a little microcosmic state within the historic kingdom of England—continued to function in its own queer, unprecedented manner. The London newspapers had grown recently a little weary of this nine days' wonder and the various protracted lawsuits, evoked by the small commune's interferences with private property, excited much less attention than they had done a couple of months before, when the thing began.

Philip Crow no longer required the protection of the Taunton police for his non-union labourers, brought into Wookey from Bristol and Birmingham; and all the various legal actions that he had initiated against this new tiny state—this microscopic *imperium in imperio*—were dragging on in the London courts without doing anything to change the curious *status quo* at Glastonbury. Both his new road, however, proudly skirting Mr. Twig's fields, and his great new bridge, proudly disregarding the ancient Bridge Perilous, were growing towards completion. Of solid cement the new road was, and the new bridge was of solid steel, and the chief troubles that still spasmodically arose were wordy battles—mounting sometimes to fisticuffs and the throwing of stones—between the Glastonbury mob and the men hired by Philip's Taunton contractor.

The surveyor from Shepton Mallet—whose father-in-law, with demonic longevity, still continued to milk his Jersey cattle—appeared and disappeared at intervals in that debatable ground, replacing his stakes and strings along the edge of the Lake Village Mounds, tokens of private possession which, although watched imperturbably by Number One's inquisitive Betsy, were always being carried off by invaders from Bove Town and Paradise, invaders not unaided, you may be sure, by a familiar robber band.

It was surprising how the new co-operative or collective system of retail trade introduced among the various shops that had been included in the new lease from the lord of the manor, proceeded, running much more smoothly than anyone would have supposed possible. This, however, was largely due to a somewhat extraneous cause, namely the overwhelming influx of religious pilgrims into the little commune from every portion of the inhabited globe.

Not quite three months had passed since the Mayor's notorious opening of his Saxon arch and doubtless there were places in Africa, India and China where pilgrims were only then just setting out for Glastonbury; but the world was so unsettled and there was such a spirit of restlessness abroad, that this new outburst of magic and miracle in a spot so easy of access, had been responded to in a wave of excitement from every country upon the earth. And as all these pilgrims had to be fed, and as all these visitors wanted souvenirs to carry back to their homes, the town began to grow rich. Thus when the Glastonbury councilmen—now promoted to be bureaucrats in an independent community—came to divide, as they did on the first day of each week, the profits of the new commune, these profits were found to be so considerable and so far beyond anything that the worthy tradesmen had ever earned for themselves under normal conditions, that their tendency was to make hay while the sun shone and allow the methods and sources of this new increment to pass unquestioned.

They were of course unaware, these good men, for Providence had not endowed many of them with the acquisitive wit of Harry Stickles, how large a portion of what came to the town from the feeding of pilgrims and from the selling of curiosities, both to the religious and to the profane, was divided among the real proletariat of the place; but since this proletariat, in *its* turn not accustomed to such wealth, hurried to spend it in these very shops, there was—as can easily be believed—a sort of revival of those fortunate mediæval times, when the whole of Glastonbury throve and grew fat upon the Saint Joseph's Pence of religious Christendom.

Mr. Geard himself, in these lucky days, grew more and more indifferent to the practical and economic aspects of his great design. Having, as we have seen, taken measures to get rid of every penny of Canon Crow's large fortune, the Mayor accepted whatever salary, as head of the commune, was set apart for him each week by the energetic assessors and bothered his brains no more about the matter. Had he been "Head of Hades," or Lord of that "Annwn" of which Mr. Evans had so obstinately murmured; had he been a reincarnation of that old Celtic divinity mentioned in the Mabinogi as *Bendigeitvran*, or Brân the Blessed, he could not have worried less about these mundane affairs.

What he was now doing all this time was receiving religious disciples, or, if it is too early in the history of the new Glastonbury Religion to call them by that name, followers, learners, pupils, neophytes. These he received, not in Cardiff Villa—indeed he was seldom to be found in Cardiff Villa now; and Megan had required all her dignified Rhys blood to be reserved and patient over this—but in that solid erection, something between a farm-barn and a collegiate chapel, which his London architect had built for him near his Saxon arch within sound of the trickling of his Fountain of Life and that had come to be called "The Rotunda."

It was with a positive genius for what might be named the *psychic nuances* of building, that this great adept in stone had constructed out of timber, bought in the same woodyard of the worthy

Mr. Johnson where Mr. Evans' Cross had been purchased, a sort of Platonic lecture hall. Like the Saxon arch which now rose triumphantly over the Grail Fount, this wooden erection, when Geard first spoke of it, sounded as if it would be something in unbelievably bad taste. But the very reverse of this was what developed. By an extensive use of carving—for many of the heavy cross-beams of this edifice were terminated by massive heads of the old Saxon Kings, while a colossal image of Saint Dunstan looked down from above the entrance—this secular hall was made to correspond with the mystical arch which covered the path to the Grail Spring.

The ritual, or, if the reader prefers it, "the procedure," that came to establish itself in this singular hall, originated in so spontaneous and natural a manner as to excite in the architect —who refused to leave the place till he had satisfied himself with what he did—a desire to supply an organic *outward form* for such a repetition of spontaneous religious gestures.

Mr. Geard—growing more and more obsessed by his ideas as he was given a fuller chance to express them—had caused a mysterious altar to be constructed and placed in the centre of this wooden building, an altar dedicated to the worship of his heretical Christ. The bulk of this altar was made of oak, in harmony with the finely chiselled wainscotting that the architect had designed for the lower portion of the walls, but on the top of this wooden base—placed there suddenly in the night, none but Mr. Geard himself knowing its origin—appeared a square slab of about five inches thick, of a substance, colour, texture and polish completely different from any stone that had, until that day, been found in Glastonbury.

Mr. Merry the curator shook his head very knowingly, after he had spent some time examining this stone, which he declared was much older than the one in St. Patrick's chapel, and in private conversations with his nephew, Paul Trent, he maintained the daring opinion that it was an altar stone of the Bronze Age, "probably used in the invocation of some god of fertility." How Mr. Merry deduced this opinion, or what evidence he found for it in his examination of the stone has not become common knowledge; for the curator held the view that there were enough mischief-makers already in the town; and far too much talk about subjects which, in wiser times, were restricted to the learned alone. Our architect from London, however, by no means confined himself to the erection of this altar upon which Bloody Johnny's younger daughter had placed in little vases of clear glass the season's earliest primroses. He also caused to be constructed, in the same solid oak, a hieratic seat for the founder of the new western religion. Few things about this "Hall of Marvels," as John Crow called it, interested the Mayor less than this pontifical throne. Its extreme discomfort was, nevertheless, modified by Megan Geard, as soon as she saw it. She unceremoniously threw over it the familiar threadbare bearskin snatched up from the floor on the Cardiff Villa drawing-room. The architect did make a somewhat wry face when he saw what she had done; but he uttered no overt protest; and from his place in this singular chair of office Mr. Geard continued to expound, day by day—it seemed to be the dominant purpose of his life now, and he pursued it with massive concentration—the doctrines of his new mystical faith.

The strange man never lacked an audience for these uninterrupted discourses. Sometimes indeed that circular hall was packed tightly with people. But whether there were many there, or the merest handful, the Mayor would always be ready to carry further and further his mystical doctrines about the Blood of his Glastonbury Christ. Megan and Crummie brought him his meals once or twice out there; but this soon became unnecessary, because Mrs. Jones, Sally's mother, who through Red Robinson, her son-in-law, possessed an advantage over the other tea-shops of the town, started a refreshment booth just inside the entrance to Chalice Hall.

This ramshackle edifice, run up over-night by some artisan-relative of Mrs. Jones, ruined entirely, from a purely æsthetic point of view, the whole beauty of what the architect had done. But the architect only laughed when this was pointed out to him, declaring that the reason why the gaudy tinsel ornaments in a Roman Church were less irreligious than the collegiate dignity of a London church, was that they were the expression of the inherent barbarism and crudity of rank human nature with

which any genuine Religion—to be really organic—must keep
in close touch. "Our communal refreshment-booth," he said to
Paul Trent, whose taste was offended by this circus-looking
shanty, "is like the crowds of beggars outside St. Peter's, or the
guides outside the Mosque of Omar. If Glastonbury is destined
to become—as with all these foreigners it looks as if she were—
a mystical rival to Rome and Jerusalem, you must expect worse
things than a few catch-penny cook-shops!"

And indeed with this concession of the architect—for the man
had come to exercise the dominant influence over what was going on in Chalice Hill—Mrs. Jones' initiative was followed by a
rush of enterprising pedlars who set up far more unsightly stalls
than hers. They had to turn over their gains to the assessors every
evening, but as their bookkeeping was very casual and as private
property, in spite of Dave Spear, still existed in Glastonbury, it
was an extremely *approximate* sum that was thus poured daily
into the community's exchequer.

But the heart of Glastonbury was still the Fountain on Chalice
Hill. To this Fountain, passing to and fro under the Saxon arch,
came a constant influx of visitors. Mr. Geard had insisted upon
one restriction alone, namely, that there should be no sacer-
dotalism. Women were allowed to come bareheaded. Men were
allowed to bring their hats and sticks. Children were allowed to
drift in and out at will. At the Fountain itself, dressed in cordu-
roys like a gamekeeper, stood, in the morning, none other than
our friend, Young Tewsy, while in the afternoon, when the
crowds were much greater, a strapping youth from the upper
Mendips who had been "converted" by Bloody Johnny in his
street-preaching days and who was too simple in his wits to
notice the difference between what the man taught now and what
he had taught then, kept the crowd in order. This powerfully
built lad had been dismissed for poaching by one of Lord P.'s
tenant-farmers, and he had turned up in Glastonbury in his old-
fashioned shepherd's smock with an eye to communal flocks and
herds. It had been Paul Trent—the only one of the town's rulers
who had the faintest artistic feeling—who had advised Geard to
let the lad wear this primitive garment when he was about the
business of guarding the Grail Spring; and the Mayor, who re-

membered a highly-coloured picture in his native national school of Our Lord Himself, clothed in a costume resembling that of old Bill Chant, Farmer Manley's head-shepherd, had jumped at this proposal.

Curiously enough it was the eastern-European visitors—or pilgrims, if you will—and indeed there were many of both types, who seemed most impressed by these discourses of the head of the new commune; and among these none were more affected than certain monastic wayfarers from the slopes of Mount Athos. There was no lack of scribes taking serious and copious notes of all the man said; and although the London papers had grown weary of him, "Geard of Glastonbury" was already a legendary figure in Bulgaria, in Bessarabia, and in many a remote religious retreat upon the Black Sea. The main drift of Geard's singular Gospel was that an actual new Revelation had been made in Glastonbury.

The crucial thing for Western humanity at this moment was to concentrate a magnetic flood of desperate faith upon this magic casement, now pushed a little open. "Scientists," explained Mr. Geard, only he used homelier and less abstract language, "are continually finding new cosmic vibrations, totally unknown or only suspected before; and why should not a new element belonging to the Unknown Dimension in which our present dream-life floats, be discovered by *psychic*, in place of physiological experiment? It is all a matter of experience. The miraculous is as much a portion of the experience of our race as is the most thoroughly accepted scientific law. The human soul"—so Mr. Geard in his sublime ignorance of modern phraseology hesitated not to declare—"possesses levels of power and possibilities of experience that have hitherto been tapped only at rare epochs in the world's history. These powers we who live in Glastonbury must now claim as our own; and not only enjoy them for ourselves, but fling them abroad throughout the whole earth."

It was on the fifteenth of March that Mr. Geard's morning discourse—for he was often found in his Heathen Pantheon, as Miss Drew called it, as early as eight o'clock—was interrupted in the startling and dramatic manner that has now become part of Glastonbury's history. There had been disturbing news for the past

three days from Burnham and Highbridge. On the twelfth of
the month information had come to the town of the flooding of
the Parrett Valley as far as Bridgewater and of the complete sub-
merging of such low-lying districts as Horsey Level, Puriton
Level, and Pawlett Hams. On the thirteenth the long-stretching
clay banks that defended the month of the Brue were reported
to be down and the Burnham and Evercreech line under water.
By the afternoon of the fourteenth there was definite news that
a great flood was advancing rapidly, hour by hour, between
Tadham Moor and Catcott Burtle; and that the flats from Moore
Pool to Decoy Rhyne, and from Decoy Rhyne to Mudgley, were
already one unbroken lake. On the night before the fifteenth
many old residents of Glastonbury who realised the danger much
better than the younger generation refused to go to bed. In several of the workmen's cottages down by the river on the way to
Street and in others in the district called Beckery people carried
their more precious belongings into their upper rooms before
they dared to sleep; and in not a few of the smaller beer-houses
certain among the habitual topers refused to go home that night.

It was not only the pusillanimous among the dwellers along
the banks of the Brue and along its tributaries who trembled a little as they pulled up their blinds on that morning of March
the fifteenth. The more weather-wise among the inhabitants of
these cottages were too restless to await that delayed dawn.
For the night seemed as if it would never come to an end; and
seldom above the Glastonbury hills had so grey a twilight prolonged itself to so late an hour. Cold and steel-like, when it did
come at last, was that dawn; livid and menacing as the stricken
light that falls upon a lost battlefield. There were many indica-
tions that a heavy rain would shortly add a new burden of
waters to the already accumulated volume; but until eight
o'clock, the hour when Mr. Geard, with the tattered bear rug
pulled over his knees for warmth, usually began his prophetic
monologue, no actual rain had fallen.

From the windows of Cardiff Villa itself no view was available
of the surrounding country extensive enough to enable the family to get any idea of what was occurring; so that at four o'clock,
which was the hour when the last of the neighbouring dams broke

and the flood of waters began sweeping through the streets of the town, the Geards were as ignorant of the extent of the disaster as was Red Robinson in his little new house in Bove Town. This ignorance of the authorities of the new commune as to the extent of the flood in the early hours of the fifteenth was brought against them afterwards in the general public criticism of these events; but as a matter of fact both Dave Spear and Paul Trent were up and out of their rooms by half-past four that morning. It was about six o'clock that the railway lines became impassable; but before that hour the early luggage trains that left the town brought news of the coming disaster to Taunton, to Bristol, to Yeovil, to Wareham, to Bournemouth, to Sherborne, to Dorchester.

Dave Spear and Paul Trent were doing their utmost to convey warnings to the threatened houses and to get the people out of them; but when officials from Taunton began interfering with them they relinquished their authority and handed over the whole management of affairs to Lord Brent, a cousin of Lord P., who at that time was the High Sheriff of Somersetshire. This energetic gentleman who had a house not far from Middlezoy, had been rendered sleepless by the fact that his own dwelling was on low-lying ground. Lord Brent had kept in close touch with both police and military all through that agitating night and was on the spot at a very early hour. It was he who, before the little commune's authorities had thought it necessary to make such an appeal, had stirred up the local air-force commanders and caused military aircraft carrying tents and provisions to land at Wirral Hill and establish an emergency camp up there. Thus before the Mayor of Glastonbury had the least idea that the water was pouring down the High Street and standing at least a foot deep amid the Abbey Ruins, airmen with searchlights and soldiers with lanterns and spades were already established upon the summit of Wirral Hill.

It was from this point of observation, while he rested from his labours of directing rescue-parties, that Dave Spear surveyed the ghastly dawn of that fifteenth of March. By his side as he stood up there was none other than Philip Crow. Philip, like Lord Brent, and for the same reason, had kept his clothes on all that night. The water was already three feet deep in Wells Road, and drowning deep in the Lake Village Great Field. He had soon realised that there was no chance of using *his* airplane, and indeed he felt he would be very lucky if it were not utterly ruined. But what worried him, as he stood by Dave's side now, was not his airplane. It was not his wife, either. Hours ago Tilly and Emma had been driven away by Bob Tankerville, safe to Wells. No; what was worrying Philip as he surveyed through his field-glass that rising expanse of waters was the peril to his half-constructed steel bridge over the river. He felt nervous, too, about his new cement road, leading down from Wookey Hole, though he kept telling himself that a few days' labour would clear away the mud and the silt when the flood sank down. But the half-finished bridge? He had already felt some qualms as he turned his glass upon those cement bases, those wooden scaffolds, those jagged steel uprights; and now, as he gazed at them, it seemed to him that part of the scaffolding had been already washed away.

In his anxiety he handed his glasses to Dave. "Doesn't it seem to you that some of my bridge supports are gone?" he said.

Dave obediently surveyed the objects in question. "The whole thing, Cousin Philip, I'm afraid," murmured the Communist grimly as he returned the glasses. "The whole business will go in a minute or two. The tide's terrifically strong just there!"

"Damn it, man. But it *can't* wash those things away! I saw them put in; and they were ——"

"You'd better come over to *us*, Cousin Phil, before you're ruined! We'd give you the biggest salary of all; and you'd have no more worry or fuss over anything, for the rest of your life!"

But Philip was in no mood even to chuckle over this. "If my bridge goes," he said, "it's more money washed away than I would dare to tell anyone! It'll knock me out. It'll mean bankruptcy."

"Haven't you paid for it then?"

"Paid for it!" The contempt with which the manufacturer rebuked Spear's ignorance of high finance was an edifying spectacle.

"Well, you'd better say your prayers, Cousin, and prepare for a quiet life; for there won't be much of your bridge left in a few minutes." Dave spoke without bitterness, for he felt none. He had been thinking several times that morning: "I hope those people at Whitelake haven't slept too long and too sound. But probably they're safe in Wells by now. They'd never try to get across Splott's Moor."

"Well, Cousin Phil, I must be off to the boats again. I wish you'd tell that Colonel What's-his-name, up there, to stop those women from shrieking so. They'll start a panic, if he's not careful. Good-bye! Looks to me as if old Pomparlès was standing up to it pretty well."

Philip bit his lip. It was hard to believe that the innocent Dave hadn't meant that remark, at least, as a nasty dig at the modern bridge-builder. Damn! It *would* be just like the devilish irony of things for that old stone bridge to survive, while his new steel bridge was washed away! He lifted his glasses again. What a sight it was!

The sun had risen now, and though its red orb was hidden by lowering grey clouds, the ghastly expanse of water spread away before him under a light that displayed the full extent of this overwhelming "Act of God," which had reduced the difference between Capitalism and Communism to such a tragic neutrality. By the aid of his glasses Philip could see some very curious details of this appalling panorama of a drowned world. He could see certain birds, for instance, that were obviously blackbirds or thrushes, collected in sheer panic-terror upon a line of telegraph wires that followed the railway and that had not yet been swamped. He could see the bodies of several drowned animals—he could not make out whether they were cows or horses—floating rapidly along the tide of the river, which was differentiated from the mass of waters both by the colour of its waves and the speed of their flow. He could see huddled human figures on the roofs of several houses in the Paradise slums and still more of them along the outlying quarter of the town known as Beckery. He could see the boats of the rescuers moving about among the semi-detached houses and villas in Wells Road, and, as far as he could make out, there was a large crowd of people on the roof of Dickery Cantle's tavern near the Cattle Market.

But it was the livid tint of the waters where there were no streets that was so particularly ghastly.

Philip, as we know, was the extreme reverse of an imaginative person; but even he was struck by the lurid effect produced by certain isolated houses, near the sinister rush of the main current of the Brue. The water positively foamed, as it swirled and eddied about these luckless edifices, which hardly looked like houses at all now, but rather resembled ugly and shapeless islands of dark rock, against which the tops of the wretched garden trees were swaying and tossing, as if they were masses of green seaweed. One especial thing that struck his pragmatic and literal mind was the extraordinary difference between this murderous-looking flood-water and all other bodies of water he had ever seen or known. The brownish-grey expanse before him was not like the sea; nor was it like a lake. It was a thing different from every other natural phenomenon. A breath of abominable and shivering chilliness rose up from this moving plain of waters, a chilliness that was more than material, a chilliness that carried with it a wafture of mental horror. It was as if some ultimate cosmogonic catastrophe implying the final extinction of all planetary life had commenced. A wind of death rose from that mounting flood that carried a feeling of water-soaked disfigured corpses!

Philip knew that the actual victims could only at the worst amount to a few score; but that *death-look* upon those livid waters suggested a disaster that could not be estimated in physical numbers. That hard, narrow cranium beneath its grey cloth cap was not stunned or numbed, was not distracted or crazed, was not even bewildered by what it confronted. This might prove the final Waterloo to this furious strategist; but it left his limited, concentrated, fighting intelligence quite unclouded, indeed strung-up and abnormally alert. As far as his emotional response to it was concerned, it was the response of the most average and thick-skinned person; and for that very reason it caught the spectacle of what lay before it in what might be called its primeval *animal-skin* shiver. "Glastonbury is in peril," is what Ned Athling would have felt; but apart from the fate of his bridge and his road, what Philip was aware of was simply the threat of a down-swallowing, in-sucking enemy.

Let it be noted, here and now, that no living human being who passed through the appalling hours of that fifteenth of March was less *frightened*—in the ordinary sense of that word—than was Philip Crow. It had always been—secretly, exultantly, proudly—with the natural elements, rather than with men and women, that Philip had felt himself contending. Such a skin-to-skin, belly-to-belly contest with Nature was his notion of the whole meaning of existence; so that unlike other minds, who had to see torn away an elaborate psychic complication of social feelings, before they came down to the bedrock issue, he was confused by no marginal qualms.

Its eccentric Mayor was not the only magnate of the little Glastonbury commune who awoke that day to a somewhat belated knowledge of the approaching catastrophe. Red Robinson and his easy-natured bride were so enamoured of each other and so busy in preparing breakfast in their small dwelling on the slope above Bove Town, that they discounted for quite a long while the agitated bustlings to and fro of their less self-centred neighbors.

"There go the people from the end house!" Sally cried out as she left their table and rushed to the little window. "There go them others, Reddy, and they be carrying their pots and pans! Flood be come, me darlin'. But us baint going to run away, carrying no sauce-pans nor no teapots, be us?"

Red put down his knife and fork and joined his wife at the window, pushing aside the muslin curtains and leaning across the girl's big sewing machine. There certainly was an unusual stir abroad and startling shouts and cries upon the wind! And yet Red could see the three yellow crocuses and the two purple crocuses in their patch of garden that had been there yesterday and the green paint that he had put on their little gate in the afternoon.

"High'd give ten pounds for this 'ere bloomin' flood to 'it the bewger's bloody bridge and soak the cligh till the bewger's bleedin' new road falls in! But it'll be pore men what'll suffer, girlie; not rich ones like 'im, if these 'ere waters rise hup and hover."

Sally put her plump arm affectionately round his neck. "You

never loved Miss Crummie like you love me, did you, Red?" she whispered coaxingly.

"Garn!" cried Red.

They were both silent then, Sally thinking to herself, "Shall I ever dare to ask him about Jenny Morgan? And what should I do if Jenny Morgan came to see Mother?" and Red thinking to himself, "High wouldn't care a wriggle what 'appened to this bastard commune, has long has the bewger got it in 'is bleedin' neck!"

This passive trance of Red and Sally at their window was interrupted by the inrush through Red's green gate of a couple of excited neighbours: "Jenny Morgan be drowned in flood," they cried, "and little Nelly be clinging, fit to perish, to her mother's corpsy."

Sally Robinson turned quickly to her husband. "We must go down there, Red," she said.

Red sighed heavily, but he did not gainsay her words.

Long before the flood had reached the point at which Red and Sally were called upon to confront it, the Mayor of Glastonbury was making his way dry-shod to his morning lecture at Chalice Hill. Before his wife and Crummie were out of bed and before any sign of the incoming water had reached the end of Street Road, Bloody Johnny was hurrying in blind excitement, with his head bent and his hands clasped behind his back, to his beloved Rotunda. His own word for all the buildings on Chalice Hill was simply Town's End—an old Montacute name which helped to make him feel at home there. "I'm off to Town's End, my precious," he would say to Mrs. Geard; or "I'll be back from Town's End, my sweet, by tea-time today, never fear!"

On this historical morning the Mayor's head was so full of a new inspiration which he had received, or dreamed he had received, from his Master that night, that he had not even paused in his kitchen to make himself a cup of tea before setting out. It would be a mistake to assume, as some afterwards did, that Bloody Johnny was oblivious of the perils of the waters that just then threatened Glastonbury. The man was like some desperate mediæval artist, some frantically inspired craftsman who, even though the enemy is at the gates of his city, *must*, by an urge that endures no withstanding, complete his unfinished statue, his picture, his fresco, his molten cast. To enter into the real heart of what he had been feeling during the last forty-eight hours it would be necessary to remember that the man had for weeks, nay, for a couple of months, dropped all active connexion with the administration of that tiny dictatorship of which he was the technical head. What he felt in his mind now was only an intensified awareness of what he had been vaguely feeling ever since that momentous opening of his Saxon Arch. "The Lord's going to let me take my life," he kept saying to himself, "and I must finish my work before I go." What he thought of as his "work" was the rounding off and completion of his *Fifth Gospel*, delivered to all and sundry at Town's End.

Had the flood been accompanied by a fire, had the flood and the fire been accompanied by a murderous uprising of the mob, and that again by signs and portents, by thunderings and lightnings, in air and sky, Bloody Johnny would still have hurried off to his heathen Academia. He had hardly slept at all that night; and now quite heedless of the rumours of the broken dams, heedless of the overcrowded state of the threatened town, heedless of any danger that might be threatening his wife and menacing his daughter, thinking always in his heart: "My end is near and I *must* finish my work before I go"—Mr. Geard arrived at Chalice Hill. He found himself, before he knew what he was doing, helplessly fumbling at the closed door of Mrs. Jones' tea-booth, which stood not far from his Saxon arch. Mrs. Jones, however, like most of the Glastonbury people, was far from sharing the Mayor's indifference to the overwhelming catastrophe that was imminent that fatal day. It began to look as if Bloody Johnny's craving for tea—which his sleepless and rather feverish night had rendered extreme—was not destined to be satisfied. By good luck, however, young Elphin Cantle and his friend Steve Lew had slept together that night in Solly's loft above the St. Michael's Garage. Mat Dekker had shaken his head of late very gravely over what he called "that young degenerate's seduction of such a wholesome lad," but without avail. Elphin was a more slippery customer than Tommy Chinnock! Young Cantle at this moment had the key to his father's little booth among this assemblage of acquisitive wooden shanties and the two boys had already got their kettle boiling in this little shelter, and were just beginning to enjoy their bread and jam when they heard the Mayor thumping at the door of Mrs. Jones' ramshackle storehouse.

Elphin peeped out. "It's Master Geard!" he whispered excitedly to his friend. "And he be all white and shivery. He've a heerd summat. He've a heered the girt flood. He be come to tell Mother Jones she best climb up Tor-top wi' he!"

Steve Lew stood up with wide-open eyes. His mouth was full of bread and jam, but he was too agitated to masticate or even to swallow. The wild and extravagant thought rushed through his head that perhaps Mr. Geard would condescend to share their amateur repast. "It would . . . be fine, Elph, wouldn't 'un," he blurted out, "if Mayor drank a cup o' tea along wi' we?"

Elphin sighed. He had anticipated the pleasure of uninterrupted colloquy with his young friend when he had strengthened his heart with raspberry jam. He wished the Mayor of Glastonbury at the devil! Why was fate always snatching the few hours of romance which he had in life away from him? It had been like this when he was with Mr. Sam. Someone was always interrupting!

Elphin stood hesitating in the doorway now, one agitated eye upon the obese, bare-headed man, who was now muttering to himself and gazing hopelessly around, and one upon his stuttering and excited friend. But the Mayor of Glastonbury had caught sight of him.

"Do 'ee know where a man could get a sip of hot tea, me boy?" he enquired humbly, almost in the tone of a thirsty tramp.

Elphin scowled savagely; but his sense of honour compelled him to report the great man's request to the boy in the hut. "He be asking for summat hot," he whispered.

Steve swallowed his mouthful so hurriedly that it almost choked him, and rushed to the door. "Please come in here, Sir!" he cried, pushing his friend unceremoniously out of the way, "Me and Elph be having a bite, us be, and us 'ud be proud to give 'ee all!"

Bloody Johnny responded to this invitation with alacrity and his gratitude and good temper when he had eaten and drunk were so winning that even the jealous heart of Elphin Cantle was beguiled. Sounds of such lively merriment soon began to emerge from the Cantle beer-shop that the little crowd of early visitors who had already assembled in front of the Saxon arch got the impression that the master—rumour soon told them where he was—had been drinking all night in that shanty. This story, that on the morning of the fifteenth, the day above all others when the man's wits should have been clearest, he was found hopelessly drunk "in company with two degenerate slum-boys" spread all over Somerset before the end of the week and was mixed up in the most hopeless manner with the official accounts of the Glastonbury flood. But Bloody Johnny thanked his young entertainers with a pure heart and a clear head and made his way into his Rotunda. He paused for a moment, however, to speak with Young Tewsy whose cadaverous grin above his neat corduroy suit suggested a death's head in the attire of an operatic forester.

"Mother Legge 'ad 'er breakfast upstairs, and her bided upstairs," the old man reported.

It was astonishing how full of people the Rotunda was when Bloody Johnny finally pushed his way to his uncomfortable throne and took up his mystical discourse where he had left it the day before. It was a relief to him on this occasion, when he was obsessed by the idea that he had had a special Revelation, to notice that there were a couple of young men from his own *Wayfarer* in the corner of the Rotunda armed with the most professional-looking notebooks. "He knows his business," he thought, "that Middlezoy lad. I'd 'a never have supposed he'd send 'em to Town's End when flood be rising."

Slowly he let his formidable black eyes glance over his audience. There seemed to be a predominance of Welsh people there this morning, judging from the rising inflexion of the excited murmurs that he caught from many parts of the crowded circle. "I expect being mountaineers they know nothing of floods!" he thought. "I hope they'll all get safe home." And then he became aware of Young Tewsy standing at his elbow.

"Flood be rushing down 'igh Street, your Wash'p! Town council be meetin' in Church so as to be near tower in case of accidents. Town-crier 'ave been sent round to tell the foreigners to take to the 'ills; and they've a-commanded every boat there be on river, and Mr. Trent and Mr. Spear and Mr. Dekker and the fire-brigade men and the Boy Scout lads be taking folk from their 'ouse-windies and carrying of they to the foot of Wirral. Old Bob Sheperd be waiting outside, your Wash'p, for to take 'ee to where town council be."

"Tell Sheperd not to wait for me, Tewsy," whispered the Mayor. "Tell him to tell them I'll come later, when I've finished what I have got to do here. Tell him to tell them to telegraph for boats to Taunton and Bridgewater and every town with a river; and do it quickly—before the wires are down. Tell them to *tele-phone* to Bristol if the wires *aren't* down and make 'em send a dozen airplanes with bread and wine and milk straight to Wirral Hill; and tell 'em that they *can* make a landing beyond those trees up there, though it's rather difficult. But I *know* it's possi-ble—tell 'em—because I've seen poor Barter do it when he pi-loted Crow." He paused for a moment while the whispering in the audience rose to an agitated pitch. "Are the trains running still, Tewsy?" he enquired.

"They wasn't when I left 'un, your Wash'p, and these here waters be mountin' up hour by hour. No trains 'ull leave Glaston today, your Wash'p. If I were the council, meeself, I'd send town-crier round to say that all foreigners what has cars of any kind *leave this town at onst* on pain of being shot."

The Mayor chuckled at this; and the audience looked at each other and smiled. They were evidently thinking to themselves: "He must have heard that the floods are going down, or he *couldn't* take things so easy."

Young Tewsy went off to convey his message, or what he could remember of his message, to Bob Sheperd.

Bloody Johnny pulled himself up upon his feet by the carved oaken arms of his great chair. He felt languid, indolent, weighed down by a "whoreson lethargy." In the manner of a lazy monk, in some perfunctory office that he has repeated so often that his mind can think of other things while his lips utter the sacred incantations, he turned his back to the audience and faced the altar. Candles were burning on the altar, by the side of Crummie's primroses, and in the chilly light which floated in beneath the majestic, drowsy, heavy-jowled Saxon Kings and Saints—for Geard of Glastonbury had kept his word and it was the Saxon element that predominated in the Rotunda—he shut his eyes tight and repeated the formula: "Christ give strength to our souls, so that we may drink up Life and defy evil. Blood of Christ give us peace. Blood of Christ give us rest. Blood of Christ give us joy forever!" These words Mr. Geard uttered in the mechanical tone of one who has so much faith in the magic of the syllables that he has no need to intellectualise them or to emotionalise them. Some of the audience remained seated while this invocation took place; others stood up, a very few fell upon their knees. But Mr. Geard swung round now and sat down, pulling the bearskin over his thighs for he suddenly felt cold.

It was the man's extraordinary *sangfroid*, his heavy, languid aplomb that many people found to be so effective. To the Welsh element in this particular audience, itself so highstrung and excitable, this unruffled phlegm of the prophet was profoundly impressive.

"The point I had reached in my argument, my dears," he began, "had to do with the souls of microscopic insects." This personal appeal to his hearers as "my dears" always had a very queer effect when people heard it for the first time. The sturdy, virile, moralistic hearers were often so shocked and felt such deep resentment and distaste that the man lost them completely. They became enemies for life, from the moment when the word "dears" left his mouth; but others felt exactly the opposite, felt, in fact, a responsive tenderness towards Mr. Geard. "You often hear people say," he went, "that insects have no souls. Now what Christ came and told me this very night is that *every insect,* down to the smallest mite, microbe or bacillus, has an immortal soul. It must have been about half-past two last night that the Master told me about insects having souls. I know it was about then, because I'd heard the Church clock strike two. And I asked him if worms, and such things as slugs and snails had souls. 'Every Jack one o' them, Sonny,' he said, 'every Jack one o' them.' All these souls, my dears, the Master explained to me, though perishable in relation to the visible, are imperishable in relation to the invisible. They do not . . . as the heathen poet says . . . *die all*. Something in them sinks down and escapes into the under-sea of undying Being. Bodies are only one expression of souls; and when the bodies of worms and gnats and zoophytes, yea! of the smallest amœbæ that exist, perish in *this* dimension, some-thing, perduring and indestructible, that has been the living identity of these tiny creatures, escapes into the dream-world whose margins overlap ours. This other world, this invisible di-mension, is as much a dream-world as our own. Into this se-quence of dream-worlds our souls drive us forward, drinking up Life and struggling with evil; seeking rest and peace. To ask where can there be space, where room, for all the myriads of consciousnesses, spawned by the life-stream since our planet began, is to ask a babyish question! Space and time, such as we know them, have no meaning in this other dream-world into which the undying souls of all dead organisms pass. Christ's Blood, my dears, is the life-sap that pours forth when any or-ganism, pierced by the thorns of this troublesome dream, passes into the one that surrounds it. Out of this deeper dream there fell of old upon our Glastonbury Something that bewilders and troubles us unto this day. To approach it gives us a shock, a per-turbation, a spasm, a shudder of the life-nerves. None can touch it without a fit of travail-throes, an ecstasy of sweet insanity. None can take it up wholly into themselves and live. To touch this Thing at all is to drink up Life at its source. Such a draught renders us strong as lions. *Fortis imaginatio generat causas*, as the old Schoolman says; and with wills thus fortified we can drink up day and night from all things in the world—from the winds and the rains, from earth and fire and water and air—the Blood of the Eternal! And the Master told me more than this, my dears. Be we men or women, He said, our souls can embrace the sweet bodies of one another till flesh and blood yield up their essences. Only good can come, my dears, from every embrace. It matters not at all from what cups, or from what goblets, we drink, so long as without being cruel, we drink up Life. The sole meaning, purpose, intention, and secret of Christ, my dears, is not to understand Life, or mould it, or change it, or even to love it, but to drink of its undying essence! Drinking up Life in this manner, we become more and more identified with that in us which death cannot kill, with that in us which sinks down, through dream after dream of what passes away, into . . . into . . . into something, my dears, that is . . . something that is . . . is . . . the Blood and the Water and the . . ."

Geard of Glastonbury stopped without finishing his sentence. The two young reporters from the *Wayfarer* received the impression that he might have finished with: "and the mud and the sand, and the sea and the land," or any other indolent and sleepy gibberish. Stretching out his legs, however, he allowed the tattered bearskin to fall away from his knees. Shamelessly then, in front of them all, he lifted himself up a little in his chair and broke wind. Then, with unabashed aplomb and scarcely covering his mouth with his hand he yawned portentously.

"Any question for me, my dears?" he muttered in a voice still half-strangled by his yawning.

An unemployed Welsh miner—tall, lean, starved, tragic—who had worked his passage to Bristol from Fishguard and then had tramped to Glastonbury from Bristol, and who was now subsisting on a special fund that Dave Spear had placed aside for working-class visitors, rose up on his feet at the back of the Rotunda, under the great, placid, comfortable head of King Edgar, the Peacemaker, and said in a low, troubled tone that rang through that assembly like a broken harp-string: "I'd like to know, Mr. Mayor, now that you've finished telling us to enjoy ourselves like the beasts . . . *when you think King Arthur is going to come back!*"

Instead of waiting for any reply to this question, which was uttered in a voice trembling with indignation, the tall miner, with a contemptuous jerk of his shoulders that expressed deep loathing for the Rotunda and everything in it, pushed his way through the crowd at the back and left the place.

But the bolt he had flung down created a violent disturbance among the audience. High words arose. The Welsh people in the hall began arguing fiercely among themselves, some of them sympathising with the man, some of them denouncing his uncivil outburst.

"Hush! Hush! Let Mr. Geard answer!" These words came

from the lips of Nancy Stickles, who from the very beginning of
what she called "the Mayor's Ministry" had left her house day
after day, the moment she had got her Harry's breakfast, and
slipped off to Chalice Hill.

The two young neophytes from Athling's office, who had been
nudging each other nervously as they noted how ruffled and disturbed the great man in the big chair seemed to be by what had
just transpired, looked at each other excitedly when they heard
Nancy's voice. "Quite right, Mrs. Stickles!" one of them could
not help crying. "Quite right!" It was these two young men who
when their prophet was dead maintained steadily that he committed suicide from pure disappointment over the fiasco of this
final discourse. It certainly did seem that the reference to Rex
Arturus, just at the climax of what had been revealed that day,
hit Bloody Johnny some sort of incalculable blow. The interruption seemed, however, to cause huge delight to his Welsh
audience.

The curiously airy and upward-tilting intonation of the Welsh
accent began to echo through the Rotunda, drowning everything
else. It seemed as if nothing but the inexhaustible complacency
of King Edgar and the two King Edmunds kept the Rotunda
from complete domination by these excited Celts. Geard of Glastonbury surveyed his disturbed flock, like a bewildered shepherd
whose woolly subjects have plunged into a forbidden field. In
vain he stared at the calm lineaments of King Edgar. In vain he
turned his gaze upon the majestic gravity of Edmund Ironsides.
The best he seemed able to do, just then, was to look with a
pitiful and wistful appeal into the intent, grey eyes of Nancy
Stickles. "What . . . do . . . *you* think . . . Missis," he stammered, "about what our brother has . . ."

It was a supreme moment in the life of Nancy. If the truth
were known, this mystic-minded girl was playing now the historic
rôle of the devoted disciple who, at an unexpected crisis, supports the Master's weakness with a faith greater than his own.
Nancy got up upon her feet. All the heads in that circular room
were turned upon her; for all could see that the man in the
carved chair was waiting anxiously for her to speak.

The Welsh controversy died down; the angry disputants were

silent. A few puzzled Germans, not having caught the miner's words about King Arthur, cried, "Hush, hush!" in their own tongue.

"Mr. Geard," began Nancy Stickles. The girl was in her morning print dress with an old faded jacket hanging loose from her shoulders. She was bare-headed. Wet or fine she never stopped to put on a hat for this morning excursion. Her big umbrella with a black curved handle, the only one of her wedding presents that Harry hadn't put away as "too good to use," was propped up against a chair by her side. "Mr. Geard . . . and kind friends . . ." She was so sweet-looking, as she stood there, with her back to the oak panelling of the Rotunda, that a low sigh of appreciation rustled, like a faint breath over reed-tops, across the whole audience.

Bloody Johnny's discourses had often closed with questions; and Nancy's modest "kind friends" was a familiar opening at many an Adult School meeting in Pembroke and Glamorgan: "The brother from Wales, who asked your opinion, Sir, about King Arthur's return, seems to me like the Jews who are still waiting for a Messiah. Most of us in Glastonbury feel that God has been kind enough to us already, in sending us a man like you; a man from whose mouth, as we have just heard, the Living Water of Life flows!"

The girl stopped and searched about in her mind for something else she was obscurely anxious to say. "This terrible flood," she went on in a low voice, "that we must all face in a few minutes when we go back to the town, must have been sent as a Sign." She paused again and then went on in a louder voice. "A Sign that all this tin-mining and road-making and bridge-building is contrary to God's purpose." She sat down blushing deeply and staring at her lap.

Bloody Johnny was displeased rather than pleased by the girl's reference to his enemy's activities. He sighed heavily, and, sinking back in his carved seat, closed his eyes. He felt weary, disappointed, dispirited. All night long he had been telling himself of the incredible impression that his divine Revelation—for so he felt it to be—would make upon these people; stirred up, excited, panic-stricken as they already were by the rising waters.

But in place of one great final outpouring of the Spirit, obliter-ating all divisions, all quarrels, all maliciousness, and setting him free, they were back again in the old wrangling human arena, Celt against Saxon, Capitalist against Communist, and every Philip against every John! Mr. Geard had come to Town's End that day in the mood of Elijah when he was transported to Heaven in a chariot of fire. But now he began to feel that his Lord had forsaken him and left him alone with the false prophets.

"I cannot quite see," an interested watchmaker from Lland-overy was explaining to the meeting, "why the perfectly sensible question of the departed brother from Fishguard should have met with the disapproval it seems to have met with in our hon-oured chairman. It is natural enough to mix altogether"—his voice now took on that irritating intonation which self-sufficient ma-terialists assume when they indicate their mental superiority to their hearers—"to mix together Arthur's Return and Geard's Water of Life. Both are myths. Both are imaginary. Both belong to that world of fantastic unrealities which ——"

"They both are true!" cried one of Athling's reporters. "We've got one of them with us here now," cried the other, "and Arthur will yet come!"

A deplorable hubbub now arose. People argued with one an-other in every part of the room, some siding with the Llandovery atheist, some repeating the words of Nancy, others putting for-ward long-winded compromises of their own. Mr. Geard re-mained quiescent in the midst of all this. He lay back in his carved chair with his eyes half-closed. As upon that occasion when he had been locked into Wookey Hole, he felt that sleep was his only refuge. In this tendency to fall asleep when things were crucial, Bloody Johnny resembled Mat Dekker; the only difference being that Dekker's sleep was lighter and more easily disturbed. There was undoubtedly something in the chemical composition of that climate, in the languorous blue vapour that hovered over Glastonbury most of the year, and that seemed to emanate from all those drooping, heavy-lichen'd apple boughs and from all that green moss, which conduced to sleep, as the grand panacea for the strong characters of the place. What happened now was that in proportion as his crowd of Welsh theologians got more and more absorbed in their complicated arguments the Mayor got more and more sleepy.

Nancy could hardly bear to see him nodding so awkwardly there, with his big head drooping, first on one side and then on the other, while every now and then the sheer weight of that massive skull would wake him up with an unpleasant start. But there was nothing the girl could do; and she had already stayed away from the shop as long as she possibly dared. "God knows," she thought, "what I shall find when I get back." She pushed her way between the chairs to the entrance of the Rotunda and hurried out of the door. The majestic and self-satisfied head of St. Dunstan did not give her a glance. With abysmal and unctuous contentment it continued to gaze into space, while it seemed to murmur to itself—"What matter if Arthur never *does* return. *I* am here." St. Dunstan would have been much more horrified than Nancy herself was, and she was a *little* shocked, at the nature of the thought that just then the devil put into her head; the thought, namely, what a relief it would be, if, when she got back, she found that her husband, Harry the chemist, had been painlessly and peacefully *drowned*!

Young Tewsy had hardly turned away from following Mrs. Stickles' departure with the eye of a veteran connoisseur of ladies, when a yet more beautiful apparition met his gaze, entering the Rotunda. This was none other than the Mayor of Glastonbury's younger daughter. Crummie was not altogether surprised to find the place in a state of noisy commotion and her father fast asleep in his chair. "Poor darling!" she said to herself, "I expect he didn't sleep at all last night. But he *must* come. He *must* come straight home now." She went up to him and shook him by the shoulder. "It's me, Father . . . it's all right . . . it's only me! But Mother says you *must* come home. The water's quite deep in Magdalene Street, and oh, they've got boats there, Father. And it's coming up Street Road now from both ends! Mother's afraid she'll be caught in the upper rooms if she goes upstairs. I told her not to wait for us if anyone came by with a boat!"

"How hot and panting you are, my pretty. There, there, get

your breath! I'll come, I'll come." He pulled himself up from his chair and stood by Crummie's side for a second, regarding the quarrelsome mystics from the principality with an amused stare. He was still only half awake. His face was puffy with sleep, his eyes blurred and filmy. "Let's go, let's go, my treasure," he murmured, dragging her to the door by the arm.

As they left the Rotunda Crummie saw him turn sideways in a very quaint and casual way and automatically make a hurried inclination of his head towards the altar. Nothing would have induced Crummie to imitate him in this, for Sam's influence was still strong, and he had said: "God knows what sort of a Deity your father's got down there," but it did strike her as a curious thing that Mr. Geard should have already grown so used to this place that he could treat his devil-worship, or whatever it was, in that self-forgetful, careless, *mechanical* fashion. They had hardly reached the road than they met Paul Trent, calm and feline as ever, though he was drenched to the skin from the waist down, and his teeth were chattering.

"Five deaths already, Comrades," he announced grimly, drawing his beautifully curved womanish lips away from his white chattering teeth, in a grin worthy of Young Tewsy. "Two children out in Beckery, and a mother and two children in Dye House Lane. But there are probably lots of others by now; for the water keeps rising every moment! It's sea-water, Mr. Geard; that's what it is; and till this moon wanes the tides will go on keeping at this height."

"Have any boats come? Have we got enough boats?"

"I should think they *have* come! From every direction they've been arriving. A motor-boat, if you please, has come in from Bridgewater. But there aren't half enough yet. It's been rowing and wading, rowing and punting, rowing and hauling people out of top-windows, and pulling people off roofs, since six o'clock this morning! My hands are blistered with rowing. We've missed you sorely, Sir. I can tell you that. All the poor people in Paradise ——" Here Crummie pushed herself between her father and the man from the Scilly Islands and pinched his arm as hard as she could. But Paul Trent was not to be stopped. "All the poor people in Paradise are saying that the Mayor deserted the town

and that he left last night by the last train that ran . . . for
Yeovil or somewhere."

"Did you really hear that said?" Bloody Johnny's voice was
so menacing that Crummie thrust her hand into his, and then
turning to Paul Trent cried in vibrant tones: "Stop that now!
You only say that to torment him. You *knew* where he was. You
could have got him any moment! You've always hated Father,
Mr. Trent; and now you've got your chance, you're happy to hit
him! Yes, you are . . . you've always hated him."

But Mr. Geard stopped dead in the middle of the road and
caught the young lawyer by the sleeve. *"Did you really hear that
said?"* His voice was like the rumble of underground thunder.

Paul Trent shrugged his shoulders and looked at Crummie.
Under normal conditions the Mayor's intensity of emotion would
have overawed him; but he had seen such sights and had had
such experiences in the last few hours that he was in a mood to
face anything. "Of course. And not only in Paradise. I was in
Butts Close and Beckery and Manor Road and Dye House Lane;
and wherever I was I heard the same thing. They don't care much
for our commune, and I don't blame 'em. That confounded little
ass, Spear, has ruined everything with his absurd assessors and
his meddling and fumbling with people's lives. But if our commune ain't popular, our Mayor—no! I'm *not* going to stop, Miss
Geard! Why *should* I stop? I owe nothing to Glastonbury. I'm a
Cornishman; and I give you all to the devil, and your drowned
town too!—our Mayor is *despised*! Yes, your poorer fellow-
comrades, Mr. Geard, say on all sides, as the police from Bridgewater and the soldiers from Taunton come in to help—it's eleven
o'clock now and they say the whole Cadet-Corps from Sherborne
School will be here by noon!—that the only person no one has
seen near the water is the Mayor! I've been telling 'em that the
Mayor was praying for 'em; but they say the Reverend Dekker
and the Reverend Dr. Sodbury are hard at work in the boats,
and it seems funny that ——" The man's ungovernable spitefulness was brought to a pause at this point by the chattering of his
teeth and by a fit of violent shivering that took possession of his
whole body.

These physical manifestations were not lost upon Mr. Geard,

and, as if an actual hand had smitten the scales from his eyes, his awareness of these things transformed in a second the whole cast of his feelings. "Yes, I ought to have got up earlier, much earlier!" he said. "You are right, Trent. You are quite right. No, no, my precious," he went on, addressing Crummie now and speaking calmly and sadly. "We do what we can, but we are all weak . . . all blind and weak. Well! come . . . come . . . come . . . Let us go on and save all we can. One minute, though, *my dears*!" With the familiar expression "my dears" the old dark fire resumed its accustomed glow in Bloody Johnny's eyes. He dropped Crummie's hand and began searching in his pockets. Presently he brought out a brandy flask and quickly untwisted its glass stopper. "Here, sonny," he cried, in a tone he might have used to Elphin Cantle or Steve Lew, "take a swig of this and finish it if you can. You'll be feverish soon."

Abashed and uneasy, Paul Trent, instead of putting out his hand to take the proffered liquour, addressed himself nervously to Crummie. "You'd better not come any further, Miss Geard," he said. "They'll have taken your mother off by this time. You'd better make straight for Wirral. Depend on it you'll find her there now. That's just how people come to grief, wading madly through the water to get to their homes."

But Crummie tossed these words aside. "Drink what he gives you, when you have the chance," she said, "and don't be silly."

Under the weight of the combined authority of father and daughter Paul Trent received the brandy from the Mayor and put it to his lips. Deep and long did he drink; and when he returned the flask his voice had a very different tone. "Avanti!" he cried. "Let's get into any boat that can carry us, and do some more roof-climbing!"

The last few hours in the life of Paul Trent had been more stirring and exciting than any he had ever known; and there came now to both father and daughter one of the queerest sensations *they* had ever known when from the raised footpath under the great Tithe Barn they actually encountered those rushing waters. The first sight of that brownish flood, flecked with foam that had ceased to be foam, foam that had become a whitish scum entangled with every sort of floating refuse, was something that no one who saw it could forget until the day of his death. More dramatic sights, more tragic sights might follow, and *did* follow for both Bloody Johnny and his daughter that day, but it was that first impression *of the power of the waters* that sank into the girl's mind and returned to her afterward, again and again, to the last hour of her consciousness. The things that she saw floating upon that turbid flood were what lodged themselves most in Crummie's mind. Dead puppies, dead kittens, dead chickens, children's dolls, children's toys, bits of broken furniture, pieces of furniture that were not broken but were upside down and horribly disfigured—such were some of the objects she caught sight of, as they stood on that stone-flagged curb with the flood swirling at their feet. She saw towel-horses and laundry baskets. She saw wicker cradles, and pitiful wooden chairs with their legs in the air. And these were only a few of the intimate utensils of human life that were exposed in that primeval indecency to the eye of the onlooker as the eddying torrent whirled them forward. Fire is the great devourer; but it is so swift and deadly with its blinding flames and suffocating smoke, that it spreads a kind of vacuum round it, a psychic vacuum, created by the annihilating suction of that Heraclitean force which is the beginning and the end of all life. Water, on the other hand, except in the wildest tempests at sea, kills more calmly, paralyses more slowly; and the terror that it creates does not shrivel up the normal nerves of our human awareness. For this very reason the slow ghastliness of death by water seems more natural to humanity than the swift horror of death by fire.

It was a quaint example of the obstinate self-assertion of human beings that now, as they were waiting there, Paul Trent took upon himself to point out that a flood was the sort of occasion when governments and states showed what frauds they were. "There'll be a boat this way in a minute," he said, "but it'll be rowed by private people, not the soldiers!" The lawyer's teeth-chatterings and shiverings had ceased after that deep drink from the Mayor's flask. "It's like Venice. It's like waiting for a gondola," he chuckled with a leer.

Bloody Johnny's bare head was bent forward a little as he fronted the rushing, swirling torrent at his feet, but his eyes were turned westward in their deep sockets, and were staring intently at the corner of Silver Street, round which the expected boat seemed most likely to appear. Crummie stooped down and turned up several times the bottoms of her father's black trousers, revealing his loose, bedraggled bootlaces. "There's a boat! There's two of 'em!" cried Mr. Geard. Two boats did indeed now appear, shooting round the corner of Silver Street with a great deal of splashing and shouting. Both were rowed, in spite of the anarchist's prediction, by a soldier; but in one of them was a large and huddled group of sobbing children, while in the other, a much bigger boat, save for the figures of Lily and Louie Rogers clinging tightly to each other in the stern, there was nobody at all.

The young soldier who was rowing the large boat was evidently totally unused to handling oars and it was his clumsiness, angrily rebuked by the older man in the crowded boat, that produced the splashing and confusion. Every time his oar slipped, or got caught between the rushing water and the wooden rowlock, Lily would turn an appealing glance, like the gaze of a Christian Martyr in an early Victorian print, towards the older soldier whom the helpless oarsman seemed to be addressing as corporal.

"Tike the lidy aboard, Bill!" now commanded the corporal. "Tike the two gents as well. Blime me! Do 'ee think yer goin' to do nothink but row young lidies? Do 'ee think yer in Wyemouth Bye, of a Satur-die arternoon? Tike the three on 'em aboard at once! Pull with yer other oar, ye bleedin' bibe! The other one, yer prize fool, the other one. Gawd damn yer! Yer'll brike that oar to bits in a jiffy. Stand up, yer fool! Stand up, and pull it out o' the bloody water! Gawd, Almighty! was there ever such a ninny born of man's 'oly seed!"

The martyrised glances of Lily, lovely in her pallor, seemed to increase the bewilderment of the hapless young soldier even more than the abuse of his corporal. Three times the big canalboat from Bridgewater was carried by the flood past the place where the three stood. At the fourth attempt, when it looked as if the corporal, purple with rage, would soon be upsetting his own load of now screaming children, Paul Trent, wading up to his knees in the brown flood, clambered into the boat. "What have you done with your mistress?" he threw out hurriedly to the sisters Rogers as he regained his balance.

"Miss Drew couldn't leave her things, Sir," murmured Lily faintly. Once inside the unwieldy craft—for there were other oars under its seats—the lawyer had no difficulty in bringing it so close to their vantage ground that both father and daughter could clamber in without entering the water. Both Mr. Geard and Crummie were staggered at the sight that awaited them when the keel of their boat grounded at last in the trodden mud at the foot of Wirral Hill.

All Glastonbury seemed to have taken refuge on this eminence and there were terrific hummings and dronings from the air and frantic screams from the hillside, and wild contradictory cries from both above and below, as several private airplanes and a couple of capacious military aircraft landed and re-started again in a roped-off enclosure. In fact the whole of the southern portion of Wirral Hill had been by that time taken over by the authorities and it was perhaps the best distraction that the terrified children of Glastonbury could possibly have had, the thrill of watching these constant landings and departures and seeing so many soldiers. Army tents had already been put up and sackcloth shelters; and the whole hillside was a tumultuous scene of confusion. Parents with convulsed faces and distracted wits were rushing about looking for children they had lost, and a wildly struggling crowd kept fighting to get to the flood's edge at the arrival of every boatload that reached the hill from the submerged portions of the town. It was the aged town clerk, struggling among the crowd at the water's edge, who was the messenger sent by Mrs. Geard to bring them to the tent the officials had set apart for her, and Crummie was so caught up out of herself by the wild scene before her, that she kissed the old gentleman when he turned to her from some altercation that he was having with a small boy. "What's that?" she asked, noticing in Mr. Bishop's hands a curiously bound book that looked as if it had been floating in the flood for several hours. "A boy here picked it up out of the water," replied the old man gravely. "It's about pardoning sin; but I've lost my glasses."

As Bloody Johnny stepped from the boat upon the slope of

Wirral Hill he first glanced back at the level expanse of brown water and then turned and surveyed the singular scene of shocking disorder and scrambling confusion which that familiar grassy eminence offered to his view. It was indeed a unique spectacle. Its movement and agitation carried an aura completely different from anything he had ever seen. It was not like a fair at Yeovil. It was not like a military field day at Dorchester. It was not like a scene on Weymouth Beach. On the other hand it was not like a refuge camp in war, famine, or pestilence. A certain minority of the younger people there—especially lads between seventeen and twenty whose relatives were in no danger—were evidently hugely enjoying the excitement. But the queer thing was that everyone seemed to carry some flood-mark about them. Their clothes were wet or they were mud-stained, or some particular article of attire was missing. They would have resembled the inhabitants of a town escaping from a bombardment save that *the fear of water*, the flood-panic, evokes an utterly different atmosphere from the fear of bursting shells or exploding bombs. A flood-panic is a steady and continuous presence lacking in the expectancy of anything crashing or deafening. A flood-panic is essentially a silent thing; and in this respect has nothing of the wild distraction of a shipwreck, or of an ocean-storm, or of a mob-riot.

"Out of the way there, please!" Two men were lifting a woman's body from a boat to the land. The Mayor recognized Dr. Fell as one of them and he laid his hand on his arm. The doctor greeted him; and addressed by name the man at the dead woman's feet. "Stop a bit, Dickery, it's Mr. Geard!"

No one knew better than Dickery Cantle who it was, but he was so dazed and stupefied that all he could do was to tighten his hold upon the ankles of his burden, as if Mr. Geard were a body-snatcher.

"I've been trying to revive her for an hour, Geard," went on Dr. Fell, "but it's no use. She's out of it. God! I wish *I* were!"

But Bloody Johnny did not hear him. If he had said "I've decided to take those tablets tonight and end the whole thing," the Mayor would not have heard him. The Mayor's attention was rivetted upon the body in their arms which was of extraordinary beauty, though a bloody scar from a recent fall crossed her forehead.

"Who is she," asked Mr. Geard. "I don't know her. She has a lovely face. Who is she?"

"She's Jenny Morgan. She's the mother of that little girl Nelly. She's the woman Red Robinson wrote about in the Gazette till you stopped him. She was Mr. Crow's girl at one time."

"Is the child drowned too?"

The doctor shook his head. "This poor creature wouldn't have been drowned if she hadn't been practically dead-drunk. She was fishing things out of the water at the end of Dye House Lane. Her little girl was with her."

"Where's the child now?" As he asked this question Mr. Geard noticed that some small insect, a minute beetle or fly it was, with tiny yellow stripes, was moving gingerly across the dead girl's face just as it would have done over a leaf or a stone. He flicked it off with his finger-nail. That she couldn't feel that small tickling seemed stranger than that she couldn't open her big eyes.

"The child's with Comrade Robinson and his wife," replied the doctor. "Nelly knows those two very well; better than she ever knew this beautiful creature, I expect. Well! you died the easiest death, my dear, that anyone *could* die, just as easy as ——" Dr. Fell's mind wandered off from the calm face where the dark-fringed eyelids were covering those eyes that had always seemed *too* wide, as if they were forever seeing the things that normal people dodge, and he was thinking in his heart: "It's funny . . . but I believe I've got a real idea while I've been holding this girl. Why don't I just simply *leave* Bibby in the house and take lodgings with this chap Dickery? Dave Spear lives there; and why shouldn't I? I could keep my clinic."

As he thought of this, and imagined the triumphant way in which he would lock up his consulting room in Manor House Road every time he left it, he suddenly caught upon Mr. Geard's face the most extraordinary expression he had ever seen on the countenance of any human being. Bloody Johnny had raised his hand again to the dead woman, this time to re-arrange a fold of her dress which her rescuers in their attempts to save her had disarranged. But no sooner had his hand encountered that ice-cold exposed bosom than he left it there, lying like a heavy horse-mushroom on the girl's breast. And with his hand resting there his face took upon itself the very expression of this dead woman. His eyes closed. His jaw fell open. His nostrils grew pinched and thin. Certain lines disappeared from his face altogether and certain completely new ones showed themselves.

"Are you faint? Are you ill, Mr. Geard?" The doctor could not let go his hold upon Jenny Morgan, but the sound of his quick, anxious voice seemed enough without anything else to deliver the other from this curious sort of fit. His eyes flickered and opened, his nostrils quivered and expanded, his mouth closed tightly.

The doctor and Dickery Cantle moved off now with their burden and Mr. Geard was left standing by the water watching the manœuvres of Paul Trent. But Crummie, who had carried Mr. Bishop off to ask him about her mother and had learned that Lord Brent had put aside one of the officers' tents for the Mayoress, now returned and asked who that woman was and whether she was dead. Her father dodged her questions about the dead girl and told her to thank Paul Trent and say good-bye to him. Paul Trent was still engaged in a struggle to be allowed to keep the big Bridgewater boat, but Crummie noticed that after he'd deposited Lily and Louie safely on the muddy grass he turned out the young soldier too. "Take these young ladies to the top of the hill, my lad," he commanded, "and give them something hot to drink. Hi there! *You* look as if you could row! Come on in here and let's push off!"

His words were addressed to none other than Tommy Chinnock. "Sure I can row, Mister Trent! Sure I can! I larned it down to Bridport when I were wi' uncle. I can row with two oars if I be wanted to!"

Paul Trent was considerate enough, however, to wait for the arrival of the young soldier's superior officer before finally dismissing him.

"Please yourself, Sir," conceded this authority. "Please yourself; and tike them lidies to their famblies, stright now, Thompson; this ain't no bloomin' esplanade."

When they reached the tent that had been allotted to Mrs.

Geard, she certainly embraced her husband and daughter with more emotion than she was accustomed to display. Did she feel any premonition of what was coming? There can be no doubt that some curious electric telepathy does sometimes link together the present and the future. Not always, however! That mysterious act of the human will, that resembles creation out of nothing and that every living soul shares with its begetter, the First Cause, has the power of breaking up and completely altering any fatal series in the mysterious streams of causative energy. But so powerful, in Bloody Johnny's case, was his desire to die, so strong was his conviction that his Master had resolved that he *should* die, that this arbitrary wilful power in his nature could naturally be discounted in advance. This being the case, while for Mrs. Geard and for Fred Thompson, the soldier who could not row, and for Nancy Stickles and for Young Tewsy, the future might be malleable, for Mr. Geard the future was decided—and decided entirely by himself.

"Well, my chicks," he now remarked with an easy sigh. "I can't stay all day with you up here in this elegant tent. Bugger me black, but these officer-lads know how to make themselves comfortable! Is this the sleeping quarters they've given us? 'Tisn't like whoäm, ha? . . . but it's all shipshape. Well! I'm off, my pretties. There'll only be need for one night for 'ee up here. I know *that*. So tomorrow you'll be back in the old bed, Megan."

He looked queerly at his wife as he said this, weighing to himself what she would feel tomorrow night without her John. The man's detachment just then was so abysmal that he could even conjure up the way she would go about the house without him, and how in the midst of her bewildered grief she would get comfort in thinking out every detail of his funeral, including the very smallest matters, such as whether to bury him in one of his old flannel shirts, or to use one of her best linen counterpanes. She would wonder, too, he felt sure, whether to let Crummie wear her new black hat, which *was* black, but not mourning-black, or whether to buy her a real funeral one at Wollop's!

"Well, I'm off," he repeated, but, instead of departing, he took his seat on a shaky camp-stool and pulled Crummie down upon his knees. " 'Tisn't every man o' my age," he murmured, using, as he always did when he was upset, the old Montacute accent, "has a darter as pretty as you be and unmarried, too, and a comfort to thee's wold parents."

"Well, if you be going to go, John, ye best go now," said Megan crossly. She never liked it when Crummie sat on her father's lap and she was afraid now that the soldiers could see into the tent. She was unpacking her old black vanity-bag at that moment, into which she had stuffed all manner of alien objects, and the way she did this, trying to make herself at home under these weird conditions, and glancing at herself in the little mirror she took out, and pushing back her grey hairs with both her hands under her lilac bonnet, struck Bloody Johnny with a sudden rush of overpowering tenderness.

"Don't 'ee forget, my precious," he blurted out, addressing his wife from behind Crummie's white neck, which filled his nostrils with a faint, sweet smell, as of new-mown hay, "don't 'ee forget to go every month now, and draw that monthly annuity I've arranged for Bob Stilly to pay 'ee. I be liable, 'tis a great sin, but so it is with me, to get so lost in me work at Town's End that my memory baint what it used to be."

"What are you talking about, John? There be no need for us to go to bank, as long as these councilmen bring your salary in a chamois-leather case like they've always done. What are you thinking about? You ain't going to try rescuing folk, be 'ee, in one of them tipply boats?"

"No, no. That's all right, my angel. I only meant—I only mentioned—I'm not going to get into any boat—don't 'ee think it!—only I've got things to see to. After all, I *be* Mayor, my treasure; and mayors be like captains of ships; they don't sit in cabins. They go on deck."

Crummie slipped off his knee and faced him. "I won't have you going anywhere, Dad!" she cried with flashing eyes. "Mother's quite right. Your place is with *us* when things be as terrible as they be today."

Bloody Johnny got up slowly and stiffly. His expression was such that Crummie yielded at once. The voices that reached their ears through that tent door were of a kind that he had never thought to hear in Glastonbury. Some woman was now screaming pitifully, someone was dragging her away. "Good-bye till to-night, my chicks," he said in a low voice. "I suppose," he added to Crummie, "your mother and I are to sleep in *there* . . . and you are to sleep *here*? Is that how they've fixed it up? Well—the same earth will be under all our beds, I reckon, wherever we sleep. Don't 'ee be afeared! I won't be long."

He moved aside the flap of the tent and went out. There was no sign of the woman he had heard screaming; but he noticed, as he emerged, that some kind of orderly had been placed at the entrance, with the idea, evidently, of keeping less privileged homeless persons from encroaching upon the Mayor's privacy.

"A bad business, Sir," said the man, peering past Bloody Johnny into the interior of the tent. The psychology of refuge camps had already begun to work, and the beauty of Crummie's person had not been missed by this guardian of her retreat.

"All life's a funny business, lad," replied Mr. Geard; and then, fumbling in his pocket, he produced one of the council's half-pound notes. "Put this in your pocket, boy," he said, "and don't let anyone frighten the ladies. I'll be back soon."

"Oh, Mother, Mother, what *shall* we do?" cried the girl, when the tent-flap swung back and the two were left alone, "I don't believe we'll ever see him again!"

Megan Geard hugged the agitated young woman to her heart, a thing she had not done—not in this solemn way—since Crummie was a small child. "We must pray for him, my pet. Don't 'ee take on so; don't 'ee, Crum! The good Lord be above all still."

No one took the least notice of the burly bare-headed man in his old greenish-black coat and his turned-up shiny black trousers, as he hurried off down the hillside towards the surging crowd at the flood's edge. There happened to be a very small boat emptying itself of a lanky young labourer from Paradise who was carrying an infant child.

"It's *my* boat," growled the youth sulkily, as Mr. Geard, pushing impetuously through the crowd, snatched up the oars.

"It *was* your boat," replied the Mayor; but he added more kindly, a second after, as he pushed one of the oarblades deep into the grass to steady the little craft while he stepped into it. "If you can't find anyone to take your child, sonny, ask for the Mayor's tent and tell Mrs. Geard that Mr. Geard said——"

His voice was lost in the arrival of a big flat barge, punted by Sam and his father, each armed with an enormous pole. It was a hay-barge from the Brue; and the Dekkers, after having been twice upset out of less solid craft, had at last found a vessel suited to both their weight and their strength. Water dripped from their drenched clothes. Sweat poured from their tired faces. But the impression that Mr. Geard received from them both was that of an exultant happiness.

It is a recurrent phenomenon in the affairs of men that certain emotional conflicts, which no normal events can affect nor any spontaneous efforts alter, are brought to an end, reconciled, harmonised, blotted out, by some startling elemental catastrophe. It was not until they both had been working desperately for some hours at rescuing marooned people that the father and son met, but when once they had met—without a word having been spoken between them of a personal character—it was taken for granted by both of them that they should remain together. Once in possession of this huge hay-barge they began picking up the terrified and stranded people from their flooded houses in far larger numbers than any other rescuers, except, perhaps, those who used the motor-boat from Bridgewater.

It gave Mr. Geard, in the midst of all the conflicting emotions that were surging through him, a feeling of puzzled satisfaction to confront this glowing emanation of primeval life-zest. He looked at the two big men in amused wonder. They seemed drunk with delight at simply being together. Strong and deep love between a father and a son is not rare. But the maudlin, doting, inebriated rapture of these two as they helped their tottering cargo to disembark, for it had been people from the old men's almshouse they had been rescuing, seemed the most extreme example of such a feeling that Mr. Geard had ever encountered.

The Dekkers were both completely exhausted. It was easy to see that. But the passionate surge of life-joy which they revealed, hauling, dragging, heaving, lifting, balancing and wading, was something that carried a curious and special elation to Bloody

Johnny's mind. It was no easy task to get their cargo of aged and feeble almshousemen out of their barge and on to the land; and some of the old people looked quite dazed and at the end of their tether. But Mr. Geard, taking hold of one of his own oars with both hands, was able to give the stern of the big barge a most timely propulsion, for which Sam, who was nearest to him, gave him a grateful nod.

"Thank you, Sir! That's *just* right. One more shove and you'll get us in."

Mr. Geard repeated his effort, but being not much more skilful at these manœuvres than young Private Thompson, there was no small danger of his falling headfront into the water between the boat and the barge. Sam, however, caught at his oar-blade and flung him back. He collapsed across the seat of his tiny skiff, but the little tub righted itself, and all was well.

"Look 'ee here, Mr. Mayor, what my father insisted on putting in!" Taking advantage of Mat Dekker's lifting one of the old men out and wading with him through the water, Sam stooped down in the stern of the barge and lifted up a rabbit-hutch. "Three lop-ears and one little black one!" he shouted above the uproar. "The Vicarage, you know, is high and dry; and I *think* Miss Drew's all right, though her servants got panicky. I saw them perched on their drive gate calling to every boat that passed. But I'll have to hang on to this hutch till Father goes home. We found it in the water near Backwear Hut, where Abel Twig lives. We couldn't see anything of the old man. We punted far out of our way till we were quite close to his place. But nothing except the chimneys could we see. It's so near the river. The water's terribly deep there. All you can see are a few mounds— the Ancient British mounds." All these remarks Sam shouted to Mr. Geard as the current of the flood swept between them and carried the latter's little boat away.

Bloody Johnny nodded farewell to him as he took his oars firmly in his hands and set himself to row in the direction of those Ancient British mounds. He rowed directly towards the river which he realised he could easily follow by reason of its swifter current, and which he knew, after it had skirted Beckery and Paradise, would lead him near Lake Village Field. What

Sam had said about Abel Twig's rabbit-hutch and about the old man's chimneys being all that was visible had been accepted by Bloody Johnny as an omen sent by his Master. "Rescue Abel Twig," he muttered to himself, "Rescue Abel Twig ———"

He was now resolutely set upon dying, set upon dying before night fell. He did not think of this as suicide. The thought of suicide never once crossed even that nimbus of feeling which connects the double horns of the mind, like the old moon within the crescent of the new moon. Mr. Geard had the peculiarity of believing absolutely and without question in the existence of the next world. He also knew for certain, by the evidence of personal experience, that a living Being, who might, or might not, be the Christ the churches worshipped, awaited his presence in what he called "the next dream." Mr. Geard had been made to understand by the mediumship of this Being, that conditions of life after the death of the body were immeasurably superior to those now existing. He had also been promised that this Being would meet him face to face and would satisfy to the full the accumulated erotic desires, at once mystical and sensual, which were the master-craving of his nature.

Not long after Mr. Geard's death, not long after the sifting out of all these dramatic events, one of the cleverest women psychologists of our time brought forward an interpretation of the man's mood on this fatal day that deserves to be recorded. According to this view of his feelings during these last hours of his life, the stress ought to be laid upon the curious pathological necessity, under which he was known to labour, of actually sharing with all his bodily nerves the physical suffering of those around him. This authority hesitated not to point out that in the case of Tittie, and in the case of the idiot-boy outside the Pilgrims', and in the case of Owen Evans in the hospital, the man had been seen to display actual physical signs of suffering exactly parallel to those endured by Mrs. Petherton, and by the boy, and by Mr. Evans as he told his stupendous story. The amazing—but surely not impossible explanation—offered by this penetrating woman is that a violent psychic radiation from all the minds of the twenty-seven people, including children, who were actually drowned during those twelve ghastly hours riddled

Mr. Geard's hyper-sensitised and super-porous sympathy with what might be called the *drowning-spasm*, and produced in him a craving for death by drowning that really amounted to a kind of drowning-hypnosis. This brilliant writer points out further, in regard to the mystery of the death of Geard of Glastonbury, that his growing preoccupation with the Grail Fount on Chalice Hill was itself a hydro-philiastic obsession. While many pathological subjects, this writer maintains, seek a pre-natal peace in death, what Mr. Geard in his planetary consciousness desired was a return to that remote and primal element of Water, which was literally the great maternal womb of all organic earth-life. It was this woman's far-fetched pamphlet that with its use of pathological technical terms had such a large share in turning the attention of intellectual people away from the religious aspects of the problem.

What Bloody Johnny was really struggling with, however, as he splashed along in his frail tub, past the outskirts of Beckery and of Paradise till he reached the swirling current of the flood-swamped river, was his love for Megan and Crummie. Of Cordelia he hardly thought at all; though it must be confessed that a faint and clinging sweetness, like a fragrance within a fragrance, drew his mind now and then towards the figure of Lady Rachel.

It *was* painful to him to condemn his wife and daughter—left up there on Wirral Hill in that strange camp tent—to what he knew well enough would be a pitiful if not a rending shock. Over and over again he placed the alternatives before himself—to go on with his life and spare them this blow, or to follow the devouring death-lust which had gathered upon him and ruthlessly plunge them into this human loss.

He was in the river current now, flowing westward in furious angry eddies which the incoming sea tide forced back upon themselves. In spite of the roll of the great flood eastward, as soon as he reached the centre of the river the current swept him westward, rocking his tiny skiff in the most threatening manner and rendering it totally unnecessary for a while even to attempt to use his oars. So he just pulled them in and let them lie across the little boat in front of his big stomach.

Mr. Geard's character will never be understood—or the monstrous inhumanity of his departure from the visible world condoned—until it is realised that the unruffled amiability and the unfailing indulgence of his attitude to those near and dear to him concealed a hidden detachment from them that had always been an unbridged gulf.

The mass and volume of his being was composed of a weight of cold phlegmatic substance that was always sinking down, by a weird gravitational pull, to a species of preorganic cosmic inertia. His great moments came when this heavy inertness, pulling him down into the silt and slime of the chemical basis of life, was roused to activity by his erotic mysticism. For the truth is that the psychic-sensual life-lust in Mr. Geard was always being lulled to dormant quiescence under the weight of his sluggish physical nature. The spirit within him needed to be roused and stirred up, before it could feel really alive, by some super-formidable and super-dramatic Quest. Such a Quest had been his passion for the Grail Fount; till that Welshman's question about Arthur had confused his mind.

But he was weary of all that now; and if his nature was not to sink back into its heavier elements of sluggish neutral indifference, he must get into closer contact with his invisible Master than was possible in this "muddy vesture" of earth-life!

He was muttering to himself now as his little boat began whirling round and round in one of these dangerous confluences where the salt flood met the river's current. Ha! The ocean smell was in his nostrils, and there in the water, whirling round with his cockle-shell boat, was an authentic piece of *white seaweed*! He stretched out one of his plump hands—his left hand it was—to clutch this bit of seaweed, his mind racing back to old childish days on Weymouth Beach. This would have been the end of him; for the water was very deep here, and Mr. Geard had never learnt to swim; but at the moment he began this stretching gesture, which—carried an inch further would have upset his boat—the river current defeated the sea flood, and swept him on, out of the dangerous circle of that vortex, and carried him forward with increasing rapidity towards Lake Village Great Field. He had lost the white seaweed; but he had escaped being drowned *by an accident.* But what was this? Something vast and glittering swept into view in the very midst of the river.

A portion of Philip's new bridge! Torn from its shaft holes in the mud banks, and dragged, steel and scaffolding and crossbeams and all, into the centre of the torrent, this towering symbol of the power of Capital, of the power of Science, was now the sport of what looked like a mocking, mischievous, taunting cuckoo-spit out of Chaos itself!

Mr. Geard neither smiled, nor chuckled, nor congratulated himself at this surprising sight. He just surveyed it with a lively, objective, inquisitive interest, an interest worthy of Bert Cole or of Timothy Wollop.

But the apparition of this costly piece of wreckage served to divert the drifting of the boat that carried him, sweeping it, as the two objects collided, across the submerged northern bank of the Brue towards the middle of Lake Village Field.

Here the water was a little shallower; but still quite deep enough to drown a man whose height was not over six feet, and in special hollows on the edges of the mounds much deeper than that.

Mr. Geard now re-claimed possession of his oars, thrusting them into the row-locks and pulling energetically towards all he could see of the dwelling of Abel Twig.

Yes, Sam Dekker was right. There was not much else than the chimney of Backwear Hut, together with a small fragment of its roof, visible across the surface of a mud-coloured lake, above which its brickwork showed almost black. But several of the bigger mounds of the old Lake Village were still visible, their round tops protruding from the waste of waters like diseased excrescences on the wrinkled surface of a vast brown leaf.

But Mr. Geard found himself confronted now by several objects more exciting to a human brain, lodged in a wooden tub on a brown flood, than mere chimney-tops. He became aware that upon the largest of these Lake Village mounds there were living figures, consisting, as far as he could make out, of a man, a child, and an animal, among whom the man and the child were desperately summoning him to their aid. There was something

floating in the water too, with a dark object clinging to it that
was also waving to him.

So detached was the man's mind at this juncture, with his own
life and death held in the balance, that he found himself in the
coolest and calmest fashion comparing the scene before him with
an old Bible picture of the Flood which used to obsess his mind
as a little boy at Town's End in Montacute. Here, again, the difference between water and fire rose up and manifested itself!
Had the element that threatened the lives of all these living
creatures been *fire*, there would have been such an automatic beat
of panic fear in his pulses that such mental detachment as he now
felt would have been impossible.

Living spirits they were—he and these two gesticulating figures—each one of them with a whole world of clear-cut feelings,
images, memories. And now, against them, this swirling brown
mass of water, this enormous entity without consciousness, or
purpose, or feeling, or pity, was gathering itself up to obliterate
in one swallowing gulp of drowning suction, everything, everyone—until blackness alone remained.

Blackness? But what was he thinking? It was not to gain
blackness that he was choosing to die rather than to live this day!
Or *was* it? Was what he fancied to be his superhuman mania for
heightened life in reality a secret longing to plunge into the dark
abyss of non-existence?

Mr. Geard now allowed his oars to rest on the water, which
was comparatively calm just here, and hoisting himself up on
the palms of his big hands endeavoured to get a clear sense of
what confronted him, before he took any action. "Why didn't
the Dekkers see those two?" he thought. "That barge of theirs
must have come from the other side of the Hut and unless they
were so occupied with their rabbit-hutch ——"

He could now observe that the ground beyond the Hut, on the
further side of Godney Road rose up well out of the water; and
it occurred to him that a strong swimmer, from any of these
mound-islands, could reach dry land without much difficulty.

"Bugger me black!" he muttered to himself, "if there isn't a
man on that floating thing over there!"

With distended eyes he surveyed this man astride of the outstretched wing of what he now recognized as the Crow airplane. Yes, it was Philip himself! Drawn by an irresistible instinct towards his steel flying machine and his steel bridge, the manufacturer had done exactly what Mr. Geard had been thinking a spirited man *might* do, he had swum from the high ground above Godney Road—which he had managed somehow to reach on foot—and had got hold of the airplane. The unlucky thing was that when he got there he found himself seized with such an evil cramp in both his legs as rendered him totally *hors-de-combat*.

Seeing the man clinging so helplessly to the wing of his submerged machine, Mr. Geard naturally supposed that, like himself, Philip was no swimmer. Without thinking very much about it he vaguely took it for granted that the manufacturer had tried to land from the air in the darkness of last night, and had found water where he had expected to find grass.

"He must have been hours in the water, poor devil!" thought Mr. Geard. "I'll deal with *him* first and let the ones on the mound go for a while." He began—after his curious fashion—to shiver and shake just as he imagined the man in the water must be doing, after so long an immersion! Why it was that he began to experience, as he gazed at him, an extremely unpleasant feeling in his legs, was more than he could explain.

He now proceeded to row straight up to the floating airplane; a movement which evoked cries of disappointment and then a miserable silence from the man and the boy on the mound. But Philip received him with a smile of intense gratitude. The rival kings of Avalon met thus at last on what was certainly a spot— though it could scarcely be called a ground—of undeniable neutrality.

"I don't think she's seriously injured," was Philip's characteristic remark as Mr. Geard clutched at the edge of the great protruding wing and steadied his cockle-shell craft.

"Legs hurt?" panted Mr. Geard, thinking of the man rather than of his machine.

"The bridge is down," went on Philip, his face giving a convulsive, involuntary twinge as he dragged himself a little further out of the water. Being a Crow, this twinge, which was repeated every time he made this least movement, took the form of the twitching nerve in John's face. Mr. Geard thought of John as he saw this twitching face above the water-line.

"I'm glad *he's* safe out of this anyway, the poor lad," he said to himself.

"Legs hurt?" he repeated, refusing to join this builder of bridges in his present straining effort to get a glimpse of that steel wreck.

"I've got a devilish cramp," murmured Philip.

"You swam out here?"

The manufacturer nodded. "Only from just over there," he said. "From just beyond the road. *I've got cramp*," he repeated.

"We'll deal with it," said Mr. Geard, "presently. Only first we must change places. It's only your legs, eh? Your arms are all right?"

Philip re-assured him about his arms with a feeble smile.

"There are people on those mounds," went on Mr. Geard. "When we've got you safe to land, we'll cope with *that* trouble. But one thing at a time is my motto—and I daresay it's yours too. We're agreed anyway *there*. And I think we're agreed too, Mr. Crow, whatever folk may say, on one other thing."

"What's that, Mr. Mayor?" enquired the twitching white face above the airplane's wing.

Bloody Johnny noticed that the water had been washing so long in the same place—for the man's legs hurt him at the slightest move—that it had deposited a sort of windrow of minute bits of scum and weed across Philip's neck. A bit of green dyke-scum clung, too, to one corner of the man's mustache, producing an effect that was unpleasantly grotesque. But Mr. Geard's mind had already forgotten what it was; this second point upon which their characters agreed!

"What we've got to do now, Mister," announced Bloody Johnny from his seat in his coracle—and the jostling in the water of these two vessels, the boat and the aircraft, were like the coming together of two æons of time—"is to change places! *You've* got to get into my boat . . . and *I've* got to get into your airplane!"

Philip smiled a rather sickly and tantalised smile.

"You've come to mock me, Mr. Mayor! When I first saw you coming I thought, here's someone who'll pick me up, but I see now that your little tub couldn't possibly hold —— Well, off with you! And if——"

"That's just what *I* say," remarked Geard of Glastonbury, and without more ado, he began divesting himself of his coat, his trousers and his drawers.

Philip, with the green weed hanging from his mustache and his neck surrounded by a windrow of scum, contemplated these movements with astonishment. There was even a faint glint of class-conscious physical distaste in his white flood-dirtied face as he beheld, so shamelessly displayed before him, the private parts of the tenant of Cardiff Villa.

But Mr. Geard now pulled himself close to the wing of the airplane and peered down into the water where the other man's cramped legs were twisted between him.

"Are you standing on anything?" he asked.

Philip did not seem to hear this question. The wrinkles of his forehead as he hoisted himself a little out of the water showed a swift, violent, interior conflict.

"If I take his offer," he thought, "I'll get into the town and have him picked up much quicker than he could do it for me. The fellow's no more good at rowing a boat than he is at spending a fortune! Damn! I suppose the noble thing to do would be to refuse his help. *But what if I get cramp in my belly?* My plane's ruined. My bridge is down. My road is sunk. Not an ounce of tin in Wookey for the last three weeks. That Birmingham man thought the whole vein's exhausted. The new dye works —all that these demons have left me—a foot deep in water! What have I got to live for?"

But the hard, narrow, invincible back portion of his skull visualised the new start of his career as if it were a steam-tug in this brown littered water!

"Begin again," he thought to himself; "and to Hell with mock-heroism! Geard and I are two beasts fighting for our lives. *I know it*. He doesn't know it! His soft, crazy idealisms, his I-am-the-one-to-give-my-life-for-my-enemy, is simply his handicap in our struggle. If the man *does* drown before I get back, it'll only prove that he preferred his ideal gestures to life. I prefer *nothing* to life. Oh, to the devil with these haverings!" In Philip's secret heart was a blind confidence in the airplane as equal to this crisis. He had so closely identified himself with this potent, yet pliable structure, that below all practical reasoning he had a superstitious faith in the spirit of his machine to outmatch the elements.

If any of those invisible Watchers of human psychology in Glastonbury had been overlooking these two just now—the man in the coracle and the man in the water—a lively discussion might have risen among them as to which of the two was the stronger lover of life.

"Begin over again!" This was the cry of the man in the water, with the yellowish scum adhering to his neck and a weft of dead seaweed—the kind that has on it those slippery blown-out pustules that children love to pinch between their fingers—caught in his hair, and the wisp of green sea-gluten twisted into his mustache. And this "Begin again!" was the out-jetting of the inmost essence of his nature. As he formulated this "Begin again!" the image of a steam-tug crossing this swirling flood, with a resolute *tick . . . tick . . . tick . . .* of its engines, became the image of his recovery in spite of all opposition.

But Bloody Johnny's exultation as he peered into the water to see what was beneath his rival's cramped legs was of a very different sort.

"So *this* is how I shall do it!" he said to himself, with a convulsive chuckle, a chuckle that caused the pit of his stomach to flutter up and down like sail-cloth on a beach that is held in its place by pebble-stones. "What . . . could . . . be . . . better?"

A huge dark wave of indescribable emotion rose up from a psychic reservoir within him that seemed to reduce all this business of drowning to a mere splash of rain.

"Megan . . . Crummie . . . forgive me . . . my treasures! . . . I won't be divided from you . . . I'll be nearer you . . . but I *must* drink it . . . the Water . . . the Water of . . ."

"Standing on anything under there?" he repeated; but again the muddied hawk-face above that brown tide only twitched with the intensity of its thinking and with the pain of its cramped legs.

The eyes of the man in the coracle lifted themselves away from the eyes of the man in the water. Bloody Johnny was always a person of punctilious scrupulousness when it came to eaves-dropping; and to watch this face before him just now was eaves-dropping of the worst sort.

"He'll change with me," Geard thought. "But he don't *altogether* relish the situation!"

By the mere mental motion of having chosen death of his own free will the Mayor fancied he had acquired easily, naturally, inevitably, an advantage so great over this desperate life-clinger that he could afford to treat him like a child. Whether in the eyes of those mysterious Watchers, this fancied advantage of the death-lust over the life-lust could really establish itself as a maturer, wiser, superior mood, was a very different question! What is certain is that Bloody Johnny felt himself just then to be like a grown person dealing with a child. And this was something that would have certainly astonished Philip had he realised it.

"Are you standing on anything?"

"I'm astride of her wing," said the other. "I expect I *could* find more of her if I cared to, only I don't want to press her down any further than she is."

"You think of your machine as if she had a soul," whispered Mr. Geard, slipping down over the side of his little craft into the water.

It may be believed how the coracle of this heavily built magician leapt up out of the flood when relieved of his weight! It soon sank again, however, though not as before, to within a few inches of the row-locks, when Philip, actuated now as much by a fear lest their combined weights should sink the plane as by a desire to save himself from drowning, scrambled, groaning and cursing, for his cramp was cruel, into the empty skiff.

"Don't let go!" he cried as he rowed off. "If you'll only hang on to her she'll hold up till I send someone. If I can get that motor-boat ——"

As he turned the boat round a shrill cry from the child on the half-submerged hillock arrested his attention. The sight of this small figure made him think of his little daughter whose whereabouts in this disaster had been constantly in his mind during these agitating hours. "This thing would hold a child all right," he thought. But the cramp that contracted his legs was so intense that the idea of any delay seemed more than he could bear. "They're in no danger," he said to himself. "It's Geard who's got to be thought of." He glanced towards the Mayor's large face and black staring eyes which were a good deal lower in the water than his own had ever been. But those black eyes had evidently not missed this moment of indecision; for they flung a look at him that was like a command. "Best take 'un while 'ee have the chance!" came his thick voice out of the water. Philip's cramp was agonising. His face was contorted with what he endured. Most men would have crumpled up, moaning and helpless. But the Norman will in the man—that will that had ruled England since the Conquest—compelled his arms, though his legs were doubled up under him, to perform the motion of rowing, and of rowing with smooth, powerful, calculated strokes. It only needed a little adroit steering to avoid the mounds that were almost submerged and that might have struck the keel of his craft, and a little hard pulling against a wind that was beginning to ruffle the water, to reach the big tumulus upon which were collected these living creatures. They were barely known to Philip Crow; but to many Glastonbury people they would have been absurdly well known; for they were Number One's cow, Betsy, Jackie Jones, and Number One himself.

It was certainly an exciting experience for Jackie Jones when with his slender figure reposing between the cramped feet of Mr. Crow he saw himself being rowed rapidly toward the town. "I'll come back for you," Philip had explained hurriedly to Abel Twig.

"One of they girt barges, Mister, be the thing I wants," had been the reply of Number One, "what'll take me wold cow in 'un!"

"Have you seen Nelly Morgan, Jackie?" enquired that young lady's father with a hesitating shyness as well as an acute anxiety, when they were approaching safety.

"Her were out with her Mummy, Mister, picking up Treasure from where it be washed up."

"Treasure?"

"They things what be washed up, Mister! Us calls 'un Treasure by reason of us being Pirates and Smugglers."

Mr. Geard, low down in the water now, observed his late coracle flying over the flood propelled by Philip's vigorous strokes. Between two sheds in the outskirts of Paradise it was just possible for the submerged man to catch sight of the top of Glastonbury Tor. He had very quickly found that the body of the airplane kept sinking deeper and deeper in the water under his heavy weight. He could just rest on it now with his feet, and that was all. Clenching his teeth he gave it a violent kick. It sank immediately out of his reach. He was now propped up solely upon the wing of the machine; but since he was floating in the water and divested of coat and trousers, a very little support was enough to keep him up. "Well," he said to himself, "I be the same Johnny Geard as used to see West Drive and Drive Gates and Batemoor and Scotch Firs and Yeovil Road. I can see 'em now as clear as I can see this machine wing in this water! And I be the same what used to follow Father up Park Cover and over to Pitt, and back by Woodhouse Lane. I be the same what Mother used to take to Zunday School, longside o' King's Arms." He fumbled with his hands along the surface of the wing that supported him.

"Thee be a-drowning, thee be, Johnny Geard, and airplane be a-drowning, s'know! Thee's rung Montacute Bells in thee's time, and airplane have been up so high as a'seed Glaston no bigger nor a waspy's nest."

The plane's wing that supported him now began to sink still lower in the flood. It sank so low that Mr. Geard's chin was on a level with the water. He gulped down a mouthful; and this mouthful tasted like the cold salt sweat of a corpse. This mouthful gave him the first pang of physical shrinking from what he was doing that he had yet known. This mouthful struck him as not only a forerunner of choking suffocation, but as carrying with it a sensation of atrocious strangeness, of ghastly unnaturalness, of perfidy, of *the unallowed-for*! He gulped down his second mouthful now; and with the outrage to his whole body that this gulping of salt death brought, the spasm of strangeness shivered through him and hummed in his ears and drummed at his heart. Yes, this was the end.

Bloody Johnny lost. All dark. The bed is deep . . . Where is
Megan's head? *Gulp—gulp—gulp*—— He was drinking it fast
now; and it was going up his nose too. Yes, it was getting into
some cavity between his nose and his mouth and doing something
there that had the effect of making him gurgle and gargle and
choke and spit. If only this deadly coldness hadn't smelt so vilely!
It smelt of vinegar. And this vinegar was getting into his lungs.
Not to breathe—when you had to breathe! Not to breathe, but to
sink gurgling down; and to see and to touch and to smell and to
taste and to become something that gurgled and gargled and
gulped!

Sinking, that was what he was doing now, gulping and sinking.
That wing had yielded. He had leaned on it with his full weight
and it had gone clear down. Nothing to lean upon. Nothing but
brown darkness that sank under him and sucked and sucked. He
came up to the top now and gasped at the air with heaving in-
drawing spasms. Physical necessity had him by the throat like
the dripping mouth of a dog, of an enormous brown dog. It was
the turn for *his* face to carry now those blotches of scum and
tidal slime upon it! His black eyes were opened preternaturally
wide, staring across the water. What he stared at now was Glastonbury Tor; and on the top of the Tor was the tower; and the
tower was like the handle of an enormous cloudy goblet that
grew larger and larger and larger——

But down he went again—Geard of Glastonbury—dying his
chosen death by drowning. Yes, it was all at his own volition;
but when the final beating and lashing and threshing with the
arms began, and the final gurgling and gulping in the throat
began, it seemed as if the man's condemned body ran amok and
revolted. Bloody Johnny's body danced, in fact, its own private
death-dance, in brute defiance of the spirit that had brought it to
this pass.

For the last time he came up to the surface. Again his black
eyes opened; opened so wide that anyone would have thought
their sockets must crack. He was staring frantically at Glastonbury Tor, but what he was seeing up there now will never be
known.

The books say that Arthur saw the Grail in five different

shapes; and that what the fifth shape was has never been revealed. Perhaps it was this fifth shape now that caused the black demonic eyes of Bloody Johnny to start out of his head. The feet treading water where there was now nothing for them to rest upon; the big white cheeks sinking down, while the water lapped around them, in the same way as it would have lapped round a log that was sinking; the sensual mouth opening wide, using just the same muscles as it did when he was preaching or yawning; the thick lips with the same abandoned relaxation dividing them, as it did when he used to kiss Crummie; the heavy shoulders, the great belly under its soaked flannel shirt, all engulfed, all going down, all *with nothing to rest upon.*

The little bubbles of brown water that swam so persistently round that open mouth and round those staring eyes, behaved just as they would have done if it had been a waterlogged chamber-pot rather than a living man full of thoughts "that wandered through eternity." They were in such a hurry, those bubbles, to float over the empty space *where his head had been.* They could not wait to float freely over that particular space on the surface of the water. There! They had their will now. Nothing remained now but broken brown bubbles going slowly round and round in reduced circles; and in an incredible silence!

But great creative Nature, working her vast death-magic, beyond the magic of any Merlin, brought it about, in her fathomless inhuman compassion, that all suffering, all struggling, all beating with the arms, all frog-action with the legs, subsided, collapsed, ceased, fell upon an unbelievably delicious calm. Nor was Bloody Johnny's mind clouded any more. His body had made its automatic protest. It was now docile. It was now obedient. Geard of Glastonbury's will to die enjoyed at last its premeditated satisfaction.

In calm, inviolable peace Mr. Geard saw his life, saw his death, and saw also that nameless Object, that fragment of the Absolute, about which all his days he had been murmuring. He was now totally free from remorse about Megan and Crummie. The ruthless element in his leaving them, purely for his own satisfaction, seemed to him justified in these last moments. He was at peace, too, about what should happen in the future to his new Religion. It was as if he had ceased to belong to our world of looking-glass pantomime wherein we are driven to worship we know not what; and had slipped down among the gods and taken his place among those who cast their own mysterious reflections in the Glastonbury of our bewilderment.

The brown flood that drowned him—bitter and cold from the Arctic tides of the far Atlantic—stirred up in his consciousness at the last all those buried layers in his nature that were so much greater than his speech, than his theories, than his achievements. In his dying moments, Geard of Glastonbury did actually pass, consciously and peacefully, into those natural elements that he had always treated with a certain careless and unæsthetic aplomb.

He had never been an artistic man. He had never been a fastidious man. He had got pleasure from smelling at dung-hills, from making water in his wife's garden, from snuffing up the sweet sweat of those he loved. He had no cruelty, no culture, no ambition, no breeding, no refinement, no curiosity, no conceit. He believed that there was a borderland of the miraculous round everything that existed and that "everything that lived was holy." Such was the Mr. Geard who was now drowning in the exact space of water that covered the spot where the ancient Lake Villagers had their temple to the neolithic goddess of fertility. He would be dead and past reviving by any charm—charmed they never so wisely—in a few minutes.

For an eternity of time there had been no Mr. Geard of Glastonbury. For an eternity of time there *would* be no Mr. Geard of Glastonbury, though there might well be some mysterious conscious Being in the orbit of whose vast memory that particular Avatar was concealed. This moment, however, along with many infinitesimal animalculæ, the Mayor of Glastonbury lived still, though he did not breathe, above Philip's airplane, below those revolving air-bubbles.

What was he thinking about now? Not of Glastonbury; nor of Death. He was lying in the green spring grass of the Park at Montacute; and an incarnate Sweetness that was his daughter and yet not his daughter was running to meet him with outstretched arms.

That it was in his power to rise up and meet this figure and feel as he embraced her that he was embracing the very Life of Life was doubtless the result of what he had seen—the Grail under its fifth shape—upon the top of Gwyn-ap-Nud's hill.

Unlike the experience of his patron and friend, the Rector of Northwold, the consciousness of Bloody Johnny's soul suffered a complete suspension after his body was dead. Whether this suspension outlasted his burial in the Wells Road Cemetery, which happened immediately after the flood, and whether it will outlast the life of this planet, and of all other such bubbles of material substance that the torrent of Life throws up, is unknown to the writer of this book.

It is certain however that Mr. Geard was not mistaken when he decided that to plunge into the bitterness of death in order to gain more life was an action that at least would destroy what he had found so hampering to his spirit in the infirmities of his flesh. Gone now forever, gone like his own breath, were the bubbles that had floated rejoicing across the place where he had sunk.

Over the fragments of Philip's bridge, over that old Lake Village Mound, with the figures of the crouching old man and the frightened animal, over the great mass of swirling waters, drifted, floated, faded, dissolved, the dying visions of the drowned man.

Above the mounting flood rose still the broken tower arch of the ruined Abbey, rose still the tower of the Baptist, rose still the tower of the Archangel. These remain; enduring this deluge, as they had endured others; but the doomsday of these also must finally come. Towers are they, like those of Rome and Jerusalem, built to storm the Infinite, to besiege the Absolute, but subject like those others to the shocks of time and of chance.

For the great goddess Cybele, whose forehead is crowned with the Turrets of the Impossible, moves through the generations from one twilight to another; and of her long journeying from cult to cult, from shrine to shrine, from revelation to revelation, there is no end. Mountains have rolled down upon many of her temples. The depths of the Atlantic and Pacific have gathered others into their dim silt and monstrous slime at the bottom of the world. The obliterating sand storms of the desert have buried not a few. Some are lost in the untraversed forests of the new hemisphere. The days of the years of men's lives are like leaves upon the wind and like ripples upon the water; but wherever the Tower-bearing Goddess moves, journeying from one madness of Faith to another, these pinnacles of desperation mount up again.

The builders of Stonehenge have perished; but there are those who worship its stones still. The builders of Glastonbury have perished; but there are people, yet living among us, whose eyes have seen the Grail. The ribs of our ancient earth are riddled with desperate pieties; her hollow caves are scooped out with frantic asseverations; and the end is not yet.

The Towers of Cybele still move in the darkness from cult to cult, from revelation to revelation. Made of a stuff more lasting than granite, older than basalt, harder than marble, and yet as insubstantial as the airiest mystery of thought, these Towers of the journeying Mother still trouble the dreams of men with their tremulous up-rising. Bowed beneath the desolation of futility, eaten by the worm of despair, these tragic Towers still rise from our planet's surface, still sway disconsolately in the wind of its orbit, still gleam cold and white under its recurrent moons.

The Philip Crows of this world build their new roads and their new bridges; but She, the ancient Tower-Bearer, neither follows the one, nor crosses the other. By different paths she moves than those made for the engines of traffic. The ships of the air turn aside as they approach her. The inventions of men touch her not. About her turreted head blows the breath of what is beyond life and beyond death; and none, but such as are covenanted and sealed as her own, discern her goings and her comings.

The powers of reason and science gather in the strong light of the Sun to beat her down. But evermore she rises again, moving from the mists of dawn to the mists of twilight, passing through the noon-day like the shadow of an eclipse and through the mid-night like an unblown trumpet, until she finds the land that has called her and the people whose heart she alone can fill.

For the turrets upon the head of Cybele are made of those strange second thoughts of all the twice-born in the world; the liberated thoughts of men as they return from their labour and the brooding thoughts of women as they pause in the midst of their work. The powers of reason may number the Stones of Stonehenge and guess at the origin of the Grail of Glastonbury; but they cannot explain the mystery of the one, nor ask the required magic question of the other.

No man has seen Our Lady of the Turrets as She moves over the land, from twilight to twilight; but those "topless towers" of hers are the birth-cries of occult generation, raised up in defiance of Matter, in defiance of Fate, and in defiance of cruel knowledge and despairing wisdom.

Men may deride them, deny them, tear them down. They may drive their engines through the ruins of Glastonbury and their airplanes over the Stones of Stonehenge.

Still in the strength of the Unknown Dimension the secret of these places is carried forward to the unborn, their oracles to our children's children.

For She whom the ancients named Cybele is in reality that beautiful and terrible Force by which the Lies of great creative Nature give birth to Truth that is to be.

Out of the Timeless she came down into time. Out of the Un-named she came down into our human symbols.

Through all the stammerings of strange tongues and murmurings of obscure invocations she still upholds her cause; the cause of the unseen against the seen, of the weak against the strong, of that which is not, and yet is, against that which is, and yet is not.

Thus she abides; her Towers forever rising, forever vanishing. Never or Always.

THE END